William
Shakespeare
Comedies

William Shakespeare Comedies

Word Cloud Classics

San Diego

Canterbury Classics
An imprint of Printers Row Publishing Group
10350 Barnes Canyon Road, Suite 100, San Diego, CA 92121
www.canterburyclassicsbooks.com • mail@canterburyclassicsbooks.com

© 2019 Canterbury Classics

Printers Row Publishing Group is a division of Readerlink Distribution Services, LLC. Canterbury Classics and Word Cloud Classics are registered trademarks of Readerlink Distribution Services, LLC.

Correspondence concerning the content of this book should be addressed to Canterbury Classics, Editorial Department, at the above address.

Publisher: Peter Norton • Associate Publisher: Ana Parker
Senior Developmental Editor: April Graham Farr
Editor: Dan Mansfield • Editorial Team: Traci Douglas
Senior Product Manager: Kathryn C. Dalby
Production Team: Jonathan Lopes, Rusty von Dyl

Cover designers: Tina Vaughan and Rusty von Dyl

Library of Congress Cataloging-in-Publication Data

Names: Shakespeare, William, 1564-1616, author.
Title: William Shakespeare comedies.
Description: San Diego : Word Cloud Classics, [2019] | Summary: "The comedies of William Shakespeare-including The Tempest, The Comedy of Errors, A Midsummer Night's Dream, and As You Like It-have entertained readers and theatergoers for centuries. This elegant Word Cloud edition of Shakespeare's Comedies includes all fourteen of the Bard's comedies in a single volume so readers can revisit their favorite plays and passages with ease"-- Provided by publisher.
Identifiers: LCCN 2019027216 (print) | LCCN 2019027217 (ebook) | ISBN 9781645171546 (paperback) | ISBN 9781645171843 (ebook)
Subjects: LCSH: English drama (Comedy)
Classification: LCC PR2761 2019 (print) | LCC PR2761 (ebook) | DDC 822.3/3--dc23
LC record available at https://lccn.loc.gov/2019027216
LC ebook record available at https://lccn.loc.gov/2019027217

Printed in China
23 22 21 20 19 1 2 3 4 5

Editor's Note: These works have been published in their original form to preserve the author's intent and style.

CONTENTS

The Tempest

DRAMATIS PERSONAE

ALONSO, *King of Naples*
SEBASTIAN, *his brother*
PROSPERO, *the right Duke of Milan*
ANTONIO, *his brother, the usurping Duke of Milan*
FERDINAND, *son to the King of Naples*
GONZALO, *an honest old counsellor*
ADRIAN, *a lord*
FRANCISCO, *a lord*
CALIBAN, *a savage and deformed slave*
TRINCULO, *a jester*
STEPHANO, *a drunken butler*
SHIPMASTER
BOATSWAIN

MARINERS
MIRANDA, *daughter to Prospero*
ARIEL, *an airy spirit*
IRIS, *presented by spirits*
CERES, *presented by spirits*
JUNO, *presented by spirits*
NYMPHS, *presented by spirits*
REAPERS, *presented by spirits*
Other SPIRITS *attending on Prospero*

SCENE: *The sea, with a ship; afterwards an island.*

ACT I
SCENE I

On a ship at sea; a tempestuous noise of thunder and lightning heard.
[*Enter a* SHIPMASTER *and a* BOATSWAIN.]
SHIPMASTER.
Boatswain!
BOATSWAIN.
Here, master: what cheer?
SHIPMASTER.
Good! Speak to the mariners: fall to't yarely, or we run ourselves aground: bestir, bestir.
[*Exit.*]
[*Enter* MARINERS.]
BOATSWAIN.
Heigh, my hearts! cheerly, cheerly, my hearts! yare, yare! Take in the topsail. Tend to th' master's whistle. Blow till thou burst thy wind, if room enough.

[*Enter* ALONSO, SEBASTIAN, ANTONIO, FERDINAND, GONZALO, *and* OTHERS.]
ALONSO.
Good boatswain, have care. Where's the master?
Play the men.

BOATSWAIN.
I pray now, keep below.
ANTONIO.
Where is the master, boatswain?
BOATSWAIN.
Do you not hear him? You mar our labour: keep your cabins: you do assist the storm.
GONZALO.
Nay, good, be patient.
BOATSWAIN.
When the sea is. Hence! What cares these roarers for the name of king? To cabin! silence! Trouble us not.
GONZALO.
Good, yet remember whom thou hast aboard.
BOATSWAIN.
None that I more love than myself. You are counsellor: if you can command these elements to silence, and work the peace of the present, we will not hand a rope more. Use your authority: if you cannot, give thanks you have lived so long, and make yourself ready in your cabin for the mischance of the hour, if it so hap.—

Cheerly, good hearts!—Out of our way, I say.

[Exit.]

GONZALO.

I have great comfort from this fellow. Methinks he hath no drowning mark upon him: his complexion is perfect gallows. Stand fast, good Fate, to his hanging! make the rope of his destiny our cable, for our own doth little advantage! If he be not born to be hang'd, our case is miserable.

[Exeunt.]

[Re-enter BOATSWAIN.]

BOATSWAIN.

Down with the topmast! yare! lower, lower! Bring her to try wi' th' maincourse. *[A cry within.]* A plague upon this howling! They are louder than the weather or our office. *[Re-enter* SEBASTIAN, ANTONIO, *and* GONZALO.] Yet again! What do you here? Shall we give o'er, and drown? Have you a mind to sink?

SEBASTIAN.

A pox o' your throat, you bawling, blasphemous, incharitable dog!

BOATSWAIN.

Work you, then.

ANTONIO.

Hang, cur, hang! you whoreson, insolent noisemaker, we are less afraid to be drowned than thou art.

GONZALO.

I'll warrant him for drowning, though the ship were no stronger than a nutshell, and as leaky as an unstanched wench.

BOATSWAIN.

Lay her a-hold, a-hold! set her two courses: off to sea again: lay her off.

[Enter MARINERS, wet.]

MARINERS.

All lost! to prayers, to prayers! all lost!

[Exeunt.]

BOATSWAIN.

What, must our mouths be cold?

GONZALO.

The king and prince at prayers! let us assist them,
For our case is as theirs.

SEBASTIAN.

I am out of patience.

ANTONIO.

We are merely cheated of our lives by drunkards:
This wide-chapp'd rascal—would thou might'st lie drowning
The washing of ten tides!

GONZALO.

He'll be hang'd yet,
Though every drop of water swear against it,
And gape at wid'st to glut him.
[A confused noise within: "Mercy on us!"—
"We split, we split!"—"Farewell, my wife and children!"—"Farewell, brother!"—
"We split, we split, we split!"]

ANTONIO.

Let's all sink wi' the king.
[Exit.]

SEBASTIAN.

Let's take leave of him.
[Exit.]

GONZALO.

Now would I give a thousand furlongs of sea for an acre of barren ground; long heath, brown furze, any thing. The wills above be done! but I would fain die dry death.
[Exit.]

SCENE II

The island. Before the cell of Prospero.
[Enter PROSPERO and MIRANDA.]

MIRANDA.

If by your art, my dearest father, you have
Put the wild waters in this roar, allay them.
The sky, it seems, would pour down stinking pitch,
But that the sea, mounting to th' welkin's cheek,
Dashes the fire out. O! I have suffered
With those that I saw suffer: a brave vessel,
Who had, no doubt, some noble creatures in her,
Dash'd all to pieces. O! the cry did knock
Against my very heart. Poor souls, they perish'd.

Had I been any god of power, I would
Have sunk the sea within the earth, or e'er
It should the good ship so have swallow'd
   and
The fraughting souls within her.

PROSPERO.
                    Be collected:
No more amazement: tell your piteous
   heart
There's no harm done.

MIRANDA.
               O! woe the day!

PROSPERO.
                  No harm.
I have done nothing but in care of thee,
Of thee, my dear one, thee, my daughter,
   who
Art ignorant of what thou art, nought
   knowing
Of whence I am: nor that I am more
   better
Than Prospero, master of a full poor cell,
And thy no greater father.

MIRANDA.
               More to know
Did never meddle with my thoughts.

PROSPERO.
               'Tis time
I should inform thee farther. Lend thy
   hand,
And pluck my magic garment from
   me.—So:
       [*Lays down his mantle.*]
Lie there my art. Wipe thou thine eyes; have
   comfort.
The direful spectacle of the wrack, which
   touch'd
The very virtue of compassion in thee,
I have with such provision in mine art
So safely ordered that there is no soul—
No, not so much perdition as an hair
Betid to any creature in the vessel
Which thou heard'st cry, which thou
   saw'st sink. Sit down;
For thou must now know farther.

MIRANDA.
             You have often
Begun to tell me what I am: but stopp'd,

And left me to a bootless inquisition,
Concluding, "Stay; not yet."

PROSPERO.
            The hour's now come,
The very minute bids thee ope thine ear;
Obey, and be attentive. Canst thou
   remember
A time before we came unto this cell?
I do not think thou canst: for then thou
   wast not
Out three years old.

MIRANDA.
            Certainly, sir, I can.

PROSPERO.
By what? By any other house, or person?
Of any thing the image, tell me, that
Hath kept with thy remembrance.

MIRANDA.
               'Tis far off,
And rather like a dream than an assurance
That my remembrance warrants. Had I not
Four, or five, women once, that tended me?

PROSPERO.
Thou hadst, and more, Miranda. But how
   is it
That this lives in thy mind? What seest
   thou else
In the dark backward and abysm of time?
If thou rememb'rest aught ere thou cam'st
   here,
How thou cam'st here, thou mayst.

MIRANDA.
           But that I do not.

PROSPERO.
Twelve year since, Miranda, twelve year
   since,
Thy father was the Duke of Milan, and
A prince of power.

MIRANDA.
           Sir, are not you my father?

PROSPERO.
Thy mother was a piece of virtue, and
She said thou wast my daughter: and thy
   father
Was Duke of Milan, and his only heir
And princess,—no worse issued.

MIRANDA.
             O, the heavens!

What foul play had we that we came from
    thence?
Or blessed was't we did?

PROSPERO.

                Both, both, my girl.
By foul play, as thou say'st, were we heav'd
    thence;
But blessedly holp hither.

MIRANDA.

              O! my heart bleeds
To think o' th' teen that I have turn'd you to,
Which is from my remembrance. Please
    you, further.

PROSPERO.

My brother and thy uncle, call'd Antonio—
I pray thee, mark me,—that a brother
    should
Be so perfidious!—he, whom next thyself,
Of all the world I lov'd, and to him put
The manage of my state; as at that time
Through all the signories it was the first,
And Prospero the prime duke, being so
    reputed
In dignity, and for the liberal arts,
Without a parallel: those being all my
    study,
The government I cast upon my brother,
And to my state grew stranger, being
    transported
And rapt in secret studies. Thy false
    uncle—
Dost thou attend me?

MIRANDA.

             Sir, most heedfully.

PROSPERO.

Being once perfected how to grant suits,
How to deny them, who t' advance, and
    who
To trash for over-topping; new created
The creatures that were mine, I say, or
    chang'd 'em,
Or else new form'd 'em: having both the
    key
Of officer and office, set all hearts i' th'
    state
To what tune pleas'd his ear: that now he
    was
The ivy which had hid my princely trunk,

And suck'd my verdure out on't. Thou
    attend'st not.

MIRANDA.

O, good sir! I do.

PROSPERO.

            I pray thee, mark me.
I thus neglecting worldly ends, all
    dedicated
To closeness and the bettering of my mind
With that, which, but by being so retir'd,
O'er-priz'd all popular rate, in my false
    brother
Awak'd an evil nature; and my trust,
Like a good parent, did beget of him
A falsehood, in its contrary as great
As my trust was; which had indeed no
    limit,
A confidence sans bound. He being thus
    lorded,
Not only with what my revenue yielded,
But what my power might else exact,—
    like one
Who having, into truth, by telling of it,
Made such a sinner of his memory,
To credit his own lie,—he did believe
He was indeed the duke; out o' the
    substitution,
And executing th' outward face of royalty,
With all prerogative. Hence his ambition
    growing:
Dost thou hear?

MIRANDA.

        Your tale, sir, would cure deafness.

PROSPERO.

To have no screen between this part he
    play'd
And him he play'd it for, he needs will be
Absolute Milan. Me, poor man—my
    library
Was dukedom large enough: of temporal
    royalties
He thinks me now incapable;
    confederates,—
So dry he was for sway,—wi' th' King of
    Naples
To give him annual tribute, do him
    homage;
Subject his coronet to his crown, and bend

The dukedom, yet unbow'd—alas, poor
    Milan!—
To most ignoble stooping.

MIRANDA.

O the heavens!

PROSPERO.

Mark his condition, and the event; then
    tell me
If this might be a brother.

MIRANDA.

I should sin
To think but nobly of my grandmother:
Good wombs have borne bad sons.

PROSPERO.

Now the condition.
This King of Naples, being an enemy
To me inveterate, hearkens my brother's
    suit;
Which was, that he, in lieu o' the premises
Of homage and I know not how much
    tribute,
Should presently extirpate me and mine
Out of the dukedom, and confer fair
    Milan,
With all the honours on my brother:
    whereon,
A treacherous army levied, one midnight
Fated to the purpose, did Antonio open
The gates of Milan; and, i' th' dead of
    darkness,
The ministers for th' purpose hurried
    thence
Me and thy crying self.

MIRANDA.

Alack, for pity!
I, not rememb'ring how I cried out then,
Will cry it o'er again: it is a hint
That wrings mine eyes to't.

PROSPERO.

Hear a little further,
And then I'll bring thee to the present
    business
Which now's upon us; without the which
    this story
Were most impertinent.

MIRANDA.

Wherefore did they not
That hour destroy us?

PROSPERO.

Well demanded, wench:
My tale provokes that question. Dear, they
    durst not,
So dear the love my people bore me, nor
    set
A mark so bloody on the business; but
With colours fairer painted their foul ends.
In few, they hurried us aboard a bark,
Bore us some leagues to sea, where they
    prepared
A rotten carcass of a boat, not rigg'd,
Nor tackle, sail, nor mast: the very rats
Instinctively have quit it. There they hoist
    us,
To cry to th' sea, that roar'd to us: to sigh
To th' winds, whose pity, sighing back
    again,
Did us but loving wrong.

MIRANDA.

Alack! what trouble
Was I then to you!

PROSPERO.

O, a cherubin
Thou wast that did preserve me! Thou
    didst smile,
Infused with a fortitude from heaven,
When I have deck'd the sea with drops
    full salt,
Under my burden groan'd: which rais'd
    in me
An undergoing stomach, to bear up
Against what should ensue.

MIRANDA.

How came we ashore?

PROSPERO.

By Providence divine.
Some food we had and some fresh water
    that
A noble Neapolitan, Gonzalo,
Out of his charity,—who being then
    appointed
Master of this design,—did give us, with
Rich garments, linens, stuffs, and
    necessaries,
Which since have steaded much: so, of his
    gentleness,
Knowing I lov'd my books, he furnish'd me,

From mine own library with volumes that
I prize above my dukedom.
Miranda.
                    Would I might
But ever see that man!
Prospero.
          Now I arise. [*Resumes his mantle.*]
Sit still, and hear the last of our sea-sorrow.
Here in this island we arriv'd: and here
Have I, thy schoolmaster, made thee more
    profit
Than other princes can, that have more
    time
For vainer hours, and tutors not so careful.
Miranda.
Heavens thank you for't! And now, I pray
    you, sir,
For still 'tis beating in my mind,—your
    reason
For raising this sea-storm?
Prospero.
                    Know thus far forth.
By accident most strange, bountiful
    Fortune,
Now my dear lady, hath mine enemies
Brought to this shore; and by my
    prescience
I find my zenith doth depend upon
A most auspicious star, whose influence
If now I court not but omit, my fortunes
Will ever after droop. Here cease more
    questions;
Thou art inclin'd to sleep; 'tis a good
    dulness,
And give it way; I know thou canst not
    choose.—
              [Miranda *sleeps.*]
Come away, servant, come! I am ready
    now.
Approach, my Ariel; come!
              [*Enter* Ariel.]
Ariel.
All hail, great master! grave sir, hail! I come
To answer thy best pleasure; be't to fly,
To swim, to dive into the fire, to ride
On the curl'd clouds; to thy strong bidding
    task
Ariel and all his quality.

Prospero.
                    Hast thou, spirit,
Perform'd to point the tempest that I bade
    thee?
Ariel.
To every article.
I boarded the king's ship; now on the beak,
Now in the waist, the deck, in every cabin,
I flam'd amazement; sometime I'd divide,
And burn in many places; on the topmast,
The yards, and boresprit, would I flame
    distinctly,
Then meet and join: Jove's lightning, the
    precursors
O' th' dreadful thunder-claps, more
    momentary
And sight-outrunning were not: the fire
    and cracks
Of sulphurous roaring the most mighty
    Neptune
Seem to besiege and make his bold waves
    tremble,
Yea, his dread trident shake.
Prospero.
                         My brave spirit!
Who was so firm, so constant, that this coil
Would not infect his reason?
Ariel.
                         Not a soul
But felt a fever of the mad, and play'd
Some tricks of desperation. All but
    mariners
Plunged in the foaming brine and quit
    the vessel,
Then all afire with me: the king's son,
    Ferdinand,
With hair up-staring—then like reeds,
    not hair—
Was the first man that leapt; cried, "Hell
    is empty,
And all the devils are here."
Prospero.
                    Why, that's my spirit!
But was not this nigh shore?
Ariel.
                    Close by, my master.
Prospero.
But are they, Ariel, safe?

ARIEL.

Not a hair perish'd;
On their sustaining garments not a
   blemish,
But fresher than before: and, as thou bad'st
   me,
In troops I have dispers'd them 'bout the
   isle.
The king's son have I landed by himself,
Whom I left cooling of the air with sighs
In an odd angle of the isle, and sitting,
His arms in this sad knot.

PROSPERO.

Of the king's ship
The mariners, say how thou hast dispos'd,
And all the rest o' th' fleet?

ARIEL.

Safely in harbour
Is the king's ship; in the deep nook, where
   once
Thou call'dst me up at midnight to fetch
   dew
From the still-vex'd Bermoothes; there
   she's hid:
The mariners all under hatches stowed;
Who, with a charm join'd to their suff'red
   labour,
I have left asleep: and for the rest o' th'
   fleet
Which I dispers'd, they all have met again,
And are upon the Mediterranean flote
Bound sadly home for Naples,
Supposing that they saw the king's ship
   wrack'd,
And his great person perish.

PROSPERO.

Ariel, thy charge
Exactly is perform'd; but there's more work:
What is the time o' th' day?

ARIEL.

Past the mid season.

PROSPERO.

At least two glasses. The time 'twixt six
   and now
Must by us both be spent most preciously.

ARIEL.

Is there more toil? Since thou dost give
   me pains,

Let me remember thee what thou hast
   promis'd,
Which is not yet perform'd me.

PROSPERO.

How now! moody?
What is't thou canst demand?

ARIEL.

My liberty.

PROSPERO.

Before the time be out! No more!

ARIEL.

I prithee,
Remember I have done thee worthy service;
Told thee no lies, made no mistakings,
   serv'd
Without or grudge or grumblings: thou didst
   promise
To bate me a full year.

PROSPERO.

Dost thou forget
From what a torment I did free thee?

ARIEL.

No.

PROSPERO.

Thou dost; and think'st it much to tread
   the ooze
Of the salt deep,
To run upon the sharp wind of the north,
To do me business in the veins o' th' earth
When it is bak'd with frost.

ARIEL.

I do not, sir.

PROSPERO.

Thou liest, malignant thing! Hast thou
   forgot
The foul witch Sycorax, who with age and
   envy
Was grown into a hoop? Hast thou forgot
   her?

ARIEL.

No, sir.

PROSPERO.

Thou hast. Where was she born?
Speak; tell me.

ARIEL.

Sir, in Argier.

PROSPERO.

O! was she so? I must

Once in a month recount what thou hast
    been,
Which thou forget'st. This damn'd witch
    Sycorax,
For mischiefs manifold, and sorceries
    terrible
To enter human hearing, from Argier,
Thou know'st, was banish'd: for one thing
    she did
They would not take her life. Is not this
    true?

ARIEL.

Ay, sir.

PROSPERO.

This blue-ey'd hag was hither brought
    with child,
And here was left by the sailors. Thou, my
    slave,
As thou report'st thyself, wast then her
    servant:
And, for thou wast a spirit too delicate
To act her earthy and abhorr'd commands,
Refusing her grand hests, she did confine
    thee,
By help of her more potent ministers,
And in her most unmitigable rage,
Into a cloven pine; within which rift
Imprison'd, thou didst painfully remain
A dozen years; within which space she
    died,
And left thee there, where thou didst vent
    thy groans
As fast as mill-wheels strike. Then was this
    island—
Save for the son that she did litter here,
A freckl'd whelp, hag-born—not honour'd
    with
A human shape.

ARIEL.

                    Yes; Caliban her son.

PROSPERO.

Dull thing, I say so; he, that Caliban,
Whom now I keep in service. Thou best
    know'st
What torment I did find thee in; thy
    groans
Did make wolves howl, and penetrate the
    breasts

Of ever-angry bears: it was a torment
To lay upon the damn'd, which Sycorax
Could not again undo; it was mine art,
When I arriv'd and heard thee, that made
    gape
The pine, and let thee out.

ARIEL.

                    I thank thee, master.

PROSPERO.

If thou more murmur'st, I will rend an oak
And peg thee in his knotty entrails till
Thou hast howl'd away twelve winters.

ARIEL.

                    Pardon, master:
I will be correspondent to command,
And do my spriting gently.

PROSPERO.

                    Do so; and after two days
I will discharge thee.

ARIEL.

                    That's my noble master!
What shall I do? Say what? What shall
    I do?

PROSPERO.

Go make thyself like a nymph o' th' sea:
    be subject
To no sight but thine and mine; invisible
To every eyeball else. Go, take this shape,
And hither come in 't: go, hence with
    diligence!
                    [Exit ARIEL.]
Awake, dear heart, awake! thou hast slept
    well;
Awake!

MIRANDA. [Waking.]
                    The strangeness of your story put
Heaviness in me.

PROSPERO.

                    Shake it off. Come on;
We'll visit Caliban my slave, who never
Yields us kind answer.

MIRANDA.

                    'Tis a villain, sir,
I do not love to look on.

PROSPERO.

                    But as 'tis,
We cannot miss him: he does make our
    fire,

Fetch in our wood; and serves in offices
That profit us.—What ho! slave! Caliban!
Thou earth, thou! Speak.
CALIBAN. [*Within.*]
        There's wood enough within.
PROSPERO.
Come forth, I say; there's other business
  for thee:
Come, thou tortoise! when?
    [*Re-enter* ARIEL *like a water-nymph.*]
Fine apparition! My quaint Ariel,
Hark in thine ear.
ARIEL.
        My lord, it shall be done.
        [*Exit.*]
PROSPERO.
Thou poisonous slave, got by the devil
  himself
Upon thy wicked dam, come forth!
    [*Enter* CALIBAN.]
CALIBAN.
As wicked dew as e'er my mother brush'd
With raven's feather from unwholesome
  fen
Drop on you both! A south-west blow
  on ye,
And blister you all o'er!
PROSPERO.
For this, be sure, to-night thou shalt have
  cramps,
Side-stitches that shall pen thy breath up;
  urchins
Shall forth at vast of night that they may
  work
All exercise on thee: thou shalt be pinch'd
As thick as honeycomb, each pinch more
  stinging
Than bees that made them.
CALIBAN.
        I must eat my dinner.
This island's mine, by Sycorax my mother,
Which thou tak'st from me. When thou
  cam'st first,
Thou strok'st me and made much of me;
  wouldst give me
Water with berries in't; and teach me how
To name the bigger light, and how the
  less,

That burn by day and night: and then I
  lov'd thee,
And show'd thee all the qualities o' th' isle,
The fresh springs, brine-pits, barren place,
  and fertile.
Curs'd be I that did so! All the charms
Of Sycorax, toads, beetles, bats, light on
  you!
For I am all the subjects that you have,
Which first was mine own king; and here
  you sty me
In this hard rock, whiles you do keep from
  me
The rest o' th' island.
PROSPERO.
        Thou most lying slave,
Whom stripes may move, not kindness! I
  have us'd thee,
Filth as thou art, with human care, and
  lodg'd thee
In mine own cell, till thou didst seek to
  violate
The honour of my child.
CALIBAN.
Oh ho! Oh ho! Would it had been done!
Thou didst prevent me; I had peopl'd else
This isle with Calibans.
PROSPERO.
        Abhorred slave,
Which any print of goodness wilt not take,
Being capable of all ill! I pitied thee,
Took pains to make thee speak, taught
  thee each hour
One thing or other: when thou didst not,
  savage,
Know thine own meaning, but wouldst
  gabble like
A thing most brutish, I endow'd thy
  purposes
With words that made them known: but thy
  vile race,
Though thou didst learn, had that in't
  which good natures
Could not abide to be with; therefore wast
  thou
Deservedly confin'd into this rock, who
  hadst
Deserv'd more than a prison.

CALIBAN.

You taught me language, and my profit on't
Is, I know how to curse: the red plague
 rid you,
For learning me your language!

PROSPERO.

                    Hag-seed, hence!
Fetch us in fuel; and be quick, thou'rt best,
To answer other business. Shrug'st thou,
 malice?
If thou neglect'st, or dost unwillingly
What I command, I'll rack thee with old
 cramps,
Fill all thy bones with aches; make thee
 roar,
That beasts shall tremble at thy din.

CALIBAN.

                    No, pray thee.
[*Aside.*] I must obey. His art is of such
 power,
It would control my dam's god, Setebos,
And make a vassal of him.

PROSPERO.

                    So, slave: hence!
        [*Exit* CALIBAN.]
    [*Re-enter* ARIEL *invisible, playing and
        singing;* FERDINAND *following.*]

ARIEL. [*Sings.*]

  Come unto these yellow sands,
    And then take hands:
  Curtsied when you have, and kiss'd,—
    The wild waves whist,—
  Foot it featly here and there;
  And, sweet sprites, the burden bear.
    Hark, hark!
  [*Burden, dispersedly, within:* "Bow-wow."]
    The watch-dogs bark:
  [*Burden, dispersedly, within:* "Bow-wow."]
    Hark, hark! I hear
    The strain of strutting chanticleer.
        [*Cry:* "Cock-a-diddle-dow."]

FERDINAND.

Where should this music be? i' th' air or
 th' earth?
It sounds no more;—and sure it waits upon
Some god o' th' island. Sitting on a bank,
Weeping again the king my father's wrack,
This music crept by me upon the waters,

Allaying both their fury and my passion,
With its sweet air: thence I have follow'd
 it,—
Or it hath drawn me rather,—but 'tis gone.
No, it begins again.

ARIEL. [*Sings.*]

  Full fathom five thy father lies;
    Of his bones are coral made;
  Those are pearls that were his eyes;
    Nothing of him that doth fade
  But doth suffer a sea-change
  Into something rich and strange.
  Sea-nymphs hourly ring his knell:
    [*Burden, within:* "Ding-dong."]
  Hark! now I hear them—ding-dong, bell.

FERDINAND.

The ditty does remember my drown'd
 father.
This is no mortal business, nor no sound
That the earth owes:—I hear it now above
 me.

PROSPERO.

The fringed curtains of thine eye advance,
And say what thou seest yond.

MIRANDA.

                    What is 't? a spirit?
Lord, how it looks about! Believe me, sir,
It carries a brave form:—but 'tis a spirit.

PROSPERO.

No, wench; it eats and sleeps, and hath
 such senses
As we have, such; this gallant which thou
 see'st
Was in the wrack; and but he's something
 stain'd
With grief,—that beauty's canker,—thou
 mightst call him
A goodly person: he hath lost his fellows
And strays about to find 'em.

MIRANDA.

                    I might call him
A thing divine; for nothing natural
I ever saw so noble.

PROSPERO. [*Aside.*]

                    It goes on, I see,
As my soul prompts it. Spirit, fine spirit! I'll
 free thee
Within two days for this.

FERDINAND.

Most sure, the goddess
On whom these airs attend! Vouchsafe,
    my prayer
May know if you remain upon this island;
And that you will some good instruction
    give
How I may bear me here: my prime
    request,
Which I do last pronounce, is,—O you
    wonder!—
If you be maid or no?

MIRANDA.

No wonder, sir;
But certainly a maid.

FERDINAND.

My language! Heavens!—
I am the best of them that speak this
    speech,
Were I but where 'tis spoken.

PROSPERO.

How! the best?
What wert thou, if the King of Naples
    heard thee?

FERDINAND.

A single thing, as I am now, that wonders
To hear thee speak of Naples. He does
    hear me;
And, that he does, I weep: myself am
    Naples,
Who with mine eyes,—never since at
    ebb,—beheld
The king my father wrack'd.

MIRANDA.

Alack, for mercy!

FERDINAND.

Yes, faith, and all his lords, the Duke of
    Milan,
And his brave son being twain.

PROSPERO. [*Aside.*]

The Duke of Milan,
And his more braver daughter could
    control thee,
If now 'twere fit to do't.—At the first sight
[*Aside.*] They have changed eyes;—delicate
    Ariel,
I'll set thee free for this! [*To* FERDINAND.]
    A word, good sir:

I fear you have done yourself some wrong:
    a word.

MIRANDA. [*Aside.*]

Why speaks my father so ungently? This
Is the third man that e'er I saw; the first
That e'er I sigh'd for: pity move my father
To be inclin'd my way!

FERDINAND. [*Aside.*]

O! if a virgin,
And your affection not gone forth, I'll
    make you
The Queen of Naples.

PROSPERO.

Soft, sir; one word more—
[*Aside.*] They are both in either's powers:
    but this swift business
I must uneasy make, lest too light winning
Make the prize light. [*To* FERDINAND.]
    One word more: I charge thee
That thou attend me. Thou dost here usurp
The name thou ow'st not; and hast put
    thyself
Upon this island as a spy, to win it
From me, the lord on't.

FERDINAND.

No, as I am a man.

MIRANDA.

There's nothing ill can dwell in such a
    temple:
If the ill spirit have so fair a house,
Good things will strive to dwell with't.

PROSPERO.

[*To* FERDINAND.] Follow me.—
[*To* MIRANDA.] Speak not you for him;
    he's a traitor. [*To* FERDINAND.] Come;
I'll manacle thy neck and feet together:
Sea-water shalt thou drink; thy food shall
    be
The fresh-brook mussels, wither'd roots,
    and husks
Wherein the acorn cradled. Follow.

FERDINAND.

No;
I will resist such entertainment till
Mine enemy has more power.
    [*He draws, and is charmed from moving.*]

MIRANDA.

O dear father!

Make not too rash a trial of him, for
He's gentle, and not fearful.

PROSPERO.

                What! I say,
My foot my tutor? Put thy sword up,
    traitor;
Who mak'st a show, but dar'st not strike,
    thy conscience
Is so possess'd with guilt: come from thy
    ward,
For I can here disarm thee with this stick
And make thy weapon drop.

MIRANDA.

               Beseech you, father!

PROSPERO.

Hence! Hang not on my garments.

MIRANDA.

                 Sir, have pity;
I'll be his surety.

PROSPERO.

           Silence! One word more
Shall make me chide thee, if not hate thee.
    What!
An advocate for an impostor? hush!
Thou think'st there is no more such shapes
    as he,
Having seen but him and Caliban: foolish
    wench!
To the most of men this is a Caliban,
And they to him are angels.

MIRANDA.

              My affections
Are then most humble; I have no ambition
To see a goodlier man.

PROSPERO. [*To* FERDINAND.]

             Come on; obey:
Thy nerves are in their infancy again,
And have no vigour in them.

FERDINAND.

              So they are:
My spirits, as in a dream, are all bound up.
My father's loss, the weakness which I feel,
The wrack of all my friends, nor this man's
    threats,
To whom I am subdued, are but light to me,
Might I but through my prison once a day
Behold this maid: all corners else o' th'
    earth

Let liberty make use of; space enough
Have I in such a prison.

PROSPERO. [*Aside.*]

           It works.—Come on.
[*To* ARIEL.] Thou hast done well, fine
    Ariel! [*To* FERDINAND.] Follow me.
[*To* ARIEL.] Hark what thou else shalt
    do me.

MIRANDA.

              Be of comfort;
My father's of a better nature, sir,
Than he appears by speech: this is
    unwonted,
Which now came from him.

PROSPERO.

            Thou shalt be as free
As mountain winds; but then exactly do
All points of my command.

ARIEL.

              To the syllable.

PROSPERO. [*To* FERDINAND.]
Come, follow.—Speak not for him.
           [*Exeunt.*]

ACT II
SCENE I

Another part of the island.
[*Enter* ALONSO, SEBASTIAN, ANTONIO,
GONZALO, ADRIAN, FRANCISCO, *and*
OTHERS.]

GONZALO.

Beseech you, sir, be merry; you have
    cause,
So have we all, of joy; for our escape
Is much beyond our loss. Our hint of
    woe
Is common: every day, some sailor's
    wife,
The masters of some merchant and the
    merchant,
Have just our theme of woe; but for the
    miracle,
I mean our preservation, few in millions
Can speak like us: then wisely, good sir,
    weigh
Our sorrow with our comfort.

ALONSO.

             Prithee, peace.

Sebastian.
He receives comfort like cold porridge.
Antonio.
The visitor will not give him o'er so.
Sebastian.
Look, he's winding up the watch of his wit;
by and by it will strike.
Gonzalo.
Sir,—
Sebastian.
One: tell.
Gonzalo.
When every grief is entertain'd that's
    offer'd,
Comes to the entertainer—
Sebastian.
A dollar.
Gonzalo.
Dolour comes to him, indeed: you have
spoken truer than you purposed.
Sebastian.
You have taken it wiselier than I meant you
should.
Gonzalo.
Therefore, my lord,—
Antonio.
Fie, what a spendthrift is he of his tongue!
Alonso.
I prithee, spare.
Gonzalo.
Well, I have done: but yet—
Sebastian.
He will be talking.
Antonio.
Which, of he or Adrian, for a good wager,
first begins to crow?
Sebastian.
The old cock.
Antonio.
The cockerel.
Sebastian.
Done. The wager?
Antonio.
A laughter.
Sebastian.
A match!
Adrian.
Though this island seem to be desert,—

Sebastian.
Ha, ha, ha! So, you're paid.
Adrian.
Uninhabitable, and almost inaccessible,—
Sebastian.
Yet—
Adrian.
Yet—
Antonio.
He could not miss it.
Adrian.
It must needs be of subtle, tender, and
delicate temperance.
Antonio.
Temperance was a delicate wench.
Sebastian.
Ay, and a subtle; as he most learnedly
delivered.
Adrian.
The air breathes upon us here most sweetly.
Sebastian.
As if it had lungs, and rotten ones.
Antonio.
Or, as 'twere perfum'd by a fen.
Gonzalo.
Here is everything advantageous to life.
Antonio.
True; save means to live.
Sebastian.
Of that there's none, or little.
Gonzalo.
How lush and lusty the grass looks! how
green!
Antonio.
The ground indeed is tawny.
Sebastian.
With an eye of green in't.
Antonio.
He misses not much.
Sebastian.
No; he doth but mistake the truth totally.
Gonzalo.
But the rarity of it is,—which is indeed
almost beyond credit,—
Sebastian.
As many vouch'd rarities are.
Gonzalo.
That our garments, being, as they were,

drenched in the sea, hold notwithstanding their freshness and glosses, being rather new-dyed than stain'd with salt water.

ANTONIO.
If but one of his pockets could speak, would it not say he lies?

SEBASTIAN.
Ay, or very falsely pocket up his report.

GONZALO.
Methinks, our garments are now as fresh as when we put them on first in Afric, at the marriage of the king's fair daughter Claribel to the King of Tunis.

SEBASTIAN.
'Twas a sweet marriage, and we prosper well in our return.

ADRIAN.
Tunis was never graced before with such a paragon to their queen.

GONZALO.
Not since widow Dido's time.

ANTONIO.
Widow! a pox o' that! How came that widow in? Widow Dido!

SEBASTIAN.
What if he had said, widower Aeneas too? Good Lord, how you take it!

ADRIAN.
Widow Dido said you? You make me study of that; she was of Carthage, not of Tunis.

GONZALO.
This Tunis, sir, was Carthage.

ADRIAN.
Carthage?

GONZALO.
I assure you, Carthage.

ANTONIO.
His word is more than the miraculous harp.

SEBASTIAN.
He hath rais'd the wall, and houses too.

ANTONIO.
What impossible matter will he make easy next?

SEBASTIAN.
I think he will carry this island home in his pocket, and give it his son for an apple.

ANTONIO.
And, sowing the kernels of it in the sea, bring forth more islands.

ALONSO.
Ay.

ANTONIO.
Why, in good time.

GONZALO. [*To* ALONSO.]
Sir, we were talking that our garments seem now as fresh as when we were at Tunis at the marriage of your daughter, who is now queen.

ANTONIO.
And the rarest that e'er came there.

SEBASTIAN.
Bate, I beseech you, widow Dido.

ANTONIO.
O! widow Dido; ay, widow Dido.

GONZALO.
Is not, sir, my doublet as fresh as the first day I wore it? I mean, in a sort.

ANTONIO.
That sort was well fish'd for.

GONZALO.
When I wore it at your daughter's
    marriage?

ALONSO.
You cram these words into mine ears
    against
The stomach of my sense. Would I had
    never
Married my daughter there! for, coming
    thence,
My son is lost; and, in my rate, she too,
Who is so far from Italy remov'd,
I ne'er again shall see her. O thou, mine
    heir
Of Naples and of Milan! what strange fish
Hath made his meal on thee?

FRANCISCO.
                    Sir, he may live:
I saw him beat the surges under him,
And ride upon their backs: he trod the
    water,
Whose enmity he flung aside, and
    breasted
The surge most swoln that met him: his
    bold head

'Bove the contentious waves he kept, and
    oar'd
Himself with his good arms in lusty stroke
To th' shore, that o'er his wave-worn basis
    bowed,
As stooping to relieve him. I not doubt
He came alive to land.

Alonso.
                No, no; he's gone.

Sebastian.
Sir, you may thank yourself for this great
    loss,
That would not bless our Europe with your
    daughter,
But rather lose her to an African;
Where she, at least, is banish'd from your
    eye,
Who hath cause to wet the grief on't.

Alonso.
                Prithee, peace.

Sebastian.
You were kneel'd to, and importun'd
    otherwise
By all of us; and the fair soul herself
Weigh'd between loathness and obedience
    at
Which end o' th' beam should bow. We
    have lost your son,
I fear, for ever: Milan and Naples have
More widows in them of this business'
    making,
Than we bring men to comfort them;
The fault's your own.

Alonso.
           So is the dearest of the loss.

Gonzalo.
My lord Sebastian,
The truth you speak doth lack some
    gentleness
And time to speak it in; you rub the sore,
When you should bring the plaster.

Sebastian.
                Very well.

Antonio.
And most chirurgeonly.

Gonzalo.
It is foul weather in us all, good sir,
When you are cloudy.

Sebastian.
              Foul weather?

Antonio.
                  Very foul.

Gonzalo.
Had I plantation of this isle, my lord,—

Antonio.
He'd sow 't with nettle-seed.

Sebastian.
              Or docks, or mallows.

Gonzalo.
And were the king on't, what would I do?

Sebastian.
'Scape being drunk for want of wine.

Gonzalo.
I' the commonwealth I would by contraries
Execute all things; for no kind of traffic
Would I admit; no name of magistrate;
Letters should not be known; riches,
    poverty,
And use of service, none; contract,
    succession,
Bourn, bound of land, tilth, vineyard,
    none;
No use of metal, corn, or wine, or oil;
No occupation; all men idle, all:
And women too, but innocent and pure;
No sovereignty,—

Sebastian.
            Yet he would be king on't.

Antonio.
The latter end of his commonwealth forgets
the beginning.

Gonzalo.
All things in common nature should
    produce
Without sweat or endeavour; treason,
    felony,
Sword, pike, knife, gun, or need of any
    engine,
Would I not have; but nature should bring
    forth,
Of it own kind, all foison, all abundance,
To feed my innocent people.

Sebastian.
No marrying 'mong his subjects?

Antonio.
None, man: all idle; whores and knaves.

GONZALO.
I would with such perfection govern, sir,
To excel the golden age.
SEBASTIAN.
               Save his Majesty!
ANTONIO.
Long live Gonzalo!
GONZALO.
          And,—do you mark me, sir?
ALONSO.
Prithee, no more: thou dost talk nothing
    to me.
GONZALO.
I do well believe your highness; and did it
to minister occasion to these gentlemen,
who are of such sensible and nimble lungs
that they always use to laugh at nothing.
ANTONIO.
'Twas you we laugh'd at.
GONZALO.
Who in this kind of merry fooling am
nothing to you; so you may continue, and
laugh at nothing still.
ANTONIO.
What a blow was there given!
SEBASTIAN.
An it had not fallen flat-long.
GONZALO.
You are gentlemen of brave mettle: you
would lift the moon out of her sphere, if
she would continue in it five weeks without
changing.
    [*Enter* ARIEL, *invisible, playing solemn*
                         music.]
SEBASTIAN.
We would so, and then go a-bat-fowling.
ANTONIO.
Nay, good my lord, be not angry.
GONZALO.
No, I warrant you; I will not adventure my
discretion so weakly. Will you laugh me
asleep, for I am very heavy?
ANTONIO.
Go sleep, and hear us.
    [*All sleep but* ALONSO, SEBASTIAN, *and*
                  ANTONIO.]
ALONSO.
What! all so soon asleep! I wish mine eyes

Would, with themselves, shut up my
    thoughts: I find
They are inclin'd to do so.
SEBASTIAN.
                Please you, sir,
Do not omit the heavy offer of it:
It seldom visits sorrow; when it doth,
It is a comforter.
ANTONIO.
            We two, my lord,
Will guard your person while you take
    your rest,
And watch your safety.
ALONSO.
          Thank you. Wondrous heavy!
    [ALONSO *sleeps. Exit* ARIEL.]
SEBASTIAN.
What a strange drowsiness possesses
    them!
ANTONIO.
It is the quality o' th' climate.
SEBASTIAN.
                    Why
Doth it not then our eyelids sink? I find
    not
Myself dispos'd to sleep.
ANTONIO.
           Nor I: my spirits are nimble.
They fell together all, as by consent;
They dropp'd, as by a thunder-stroke.
    What might,
Worthy Sebastian? O! what might?—No
    more:—
And yet methinks I see it in thy face,
What thou should'st be: The occasion
    speaks thee; and
My strong imagination sees a crown
Dropping upon thy head.
SEBASTIAN.
          What! art thou waking?
ANTONIO.
Do you not hear me speak?
SEBASTIAN.
                 I do: and surely
It is a sleepy language, and thou speak'st
Out of thy sleep. What is it thou didst
    say?
This is a strange repose, to be asleep

With eyes wide open; standing, speaking,
    moving,
And yet so fast asleep.
Antonio.
                    Noble Sebastian,
Thou let'st thy fortune sleep—die rather; wink'st
Whiles thou art waking.
Sebastian.
                    Thou dost snore distinctly:
There's meaning in thy snores.
Antonio.
I am more serious than my custom; you
Must be so too, if heed me: which to do
Trebles thee o'er.
Sebastian.
                    Well, I am standing water.
Antonio.
I'll teach you how to flow.
Sebastian.
                    Do so: to ebb,
Hereditary sloth instructs me.
Antonio.
                                    O!
If you but knew how you the purpose
    cherish
Whiles thus you mock it! how, in stripping
    it,
You more invest it! Ebbing men indeed,
Most often, do so near the bottom run
By their own fear or sloth.
Sebastian.
                    Prithee, say on:
The setting of thine eye and cheek proclaim
A matter from thee, and a birth, indeed
Which throes thee much to yield.
Antonio.
                            Thus, sir:
Although this lord of weak remembrance,
    this
Who shall be of as little memory
When he is earth'd, hath here almost
    persuaded,—
For he's a spirit of persuasion, only
Professes to persuade,—the king his son's
    alive,
'Tis as impossible that he's undrown'd
As he that sleeps here swims.

Sebastian.
                    I have no hope
That he's undrown'd.
Antonio.
                    O! out of that "no hope"
What great hope have you! No hope that
    way is
Another way so high a hope, that even
Ambition cannot pierce a wink beyond,
But doubts discovery there. Will you grant
    with me
That Ferdinand is drown'd?
Sebastian.
                    He's gone.
Antonio.
                    Then tell me,
Who's the next heir of Naples?
Sebastian.
                    Claribel.
Antonio.
She that is Queen of Tunis; she that
    dwells
Ten leagues beyond man's life; she that
    from Naples
Can have no note, unless the sun were
    post—
The Man i' th' Moon's too slow—till
    newborn chins
Be rough and razorable: she that from
    whom
We all were sea-swallow'd, though some
    cast again,
And by that destiny, to perform an act
Whereof what's past is prologue, what to
    come
In yours and my discharge.
Sebastian.
            What stuff is this! How say you?
'Tis true, my brother's daughter's Queen
    of Tunis;
So is she heir of Naples; 'twixt which
    regions
There is some space.
Antonio.
                A space whose every cubit
Seems to cry out, "How shall that Claribel
Measure us back to Naples?—Keep in
    Tunis,

And let Sebastian wake."—Say this were
   death
That now hath seiz'd them; why, they were
   no worse
Than now they are. There be that can rule
   Naples
As well as he that sleeps; lords that can
   prate
As amply and unnecessarily
As this Gonzalo: I myself could make
A chough of as deep chat. O, that you bore
The mind that I do! What a sleep were this
For your advancement! Do you understand
   me?

SEBASTIAN.
Methinks I do.

ANTONIO.
               And how does your content
Tender your own good fortune?

SEBASTIAN.
                     I remember
You did supplant your brother Prospero.

ANTONIO.
                         True.
And look how well my garments sit upon
   me;
Much feater than before; my brother's
   servants
Were then my fellows; now they are my
   men.

SEBASTIAN.
But, for your conscience,—

ANTONIO.
Ay, sir; where lies that? If 'twere a kibe,
'Twould put me to my slipper: but I feel
   not
This deity in my bosom: twenty consciences
That stand 'twixt me and Milan, candied
   be they
And melt ere they molest! Here lies your
   brother,
No better than the earth he lies upon,
If he were that which now he's like, that's
   dead:
Whom I, with this obedient steel, three
   inches of it,
Can lay to bed for ever; whiles you, doing
   thus,

To the perpetual wink for aye might put
This ancient morsel, this Sir Prudence,
   who
Should not upbraid our course. For all
   the rest,
They'll take suggestion as a cat laps milk:
They'll tell the clock to any business that
We say befits the hour.

SEBASTIAN.
                Thy case, dear friend,
Shall be my precedent: as thou got'st
   Milan,
I'll come by Naples. Draw thy sword: one
   stroke
Shall free thee from the tribute which
   thou pay'st,
And I the king shall love thee.

ANTONIO.
                   Draw together:
And when I rear my hand, do you the like,
To fall it on Gonzalo.

SEBASTIAN.
                O! but one word.
            [*They converse apart.*]
   [*Music. Re-enter* ARIEL, *invisible.*]

ARIEL.
My master through his art foresees the
   danger
That you, his friend, are in; and sends me
   forth—
For else his project dies—to keep thee
   living.
        [*Sings in* GONZALO's *ear.*]
     While you here do snoring lie,
     Open-ey'd Conspiracy
       His time doth take.
     If of life you keep a care,
     Shake off slumber, and beware.
       Awake! awake!

ANTONIO.
Then let us both be sudden.

GONZALO. [*Waking.*]
                Now, good angels
Preserve the king!

ALONSO. [*Waking.*]
Why, how now! Ho, awake! Why are you
   drawn?
Wherefore this ghastly looking?

GONZALO.

What's the matter?

SEBASTIAN.

Whiles we stood here securing your
repose,

Even now, we heard a hollow burst of
bellowing

Like bulls, or rather lions; did't not wake
you?

It struck mine ear most terribly.

ALONSO.

I heard nothing.

ANTONIO.

O! 'twas a din to fright a monster's ear,

To make an earthquake: sure it was the
roar

Of a whole herd of lions.

ALONSO.

Heard you this, Gonzalo?

GONZALO.

Upon mine honour, sir, I heard a
humming,

And that a strange one too, which did
awake me.

I shak'd you, sir, and cried; as mine eyes
open'd,

I saw their weapons drawn:—there was
a noise,

That's verily. 'Tis best we stand upon our
guard,

Or that we quit this place: let's draw our
weapons.

ALONSO.

Lead off this ground: and let's make
further search

For my poor son.

GONZALO.

Heavens keep him from these beasts!

For he is, sure, i' th' island.

ALONSO.

Lead away.

[*Exit with the* OTHERS.]

ARIEL.

Prospero my lord shall know what I have
done:

So, king, go safely on to seek thy son.

[*Exit.*]

SCENE II

Another part of the island.

[*Enter* CALIBAN, *with a burden of wood.*
A noise of thunder heard.]

CALIBAN.

All the infections that the sun sucks up

From bogs, fens, flats, on Prosper fall, and
make him

By inch-meal a disease! His spirits hear
me,

And yet I needs must curse. But they'll
nor pinch,

Fright me with urchin-shows, pitch me i'
the mire,

Nor lead me, like a firebrand, in the dark

Out of my way, unless he bid 'em; but

For every trifle are they set upon me:

Sometime like apes that mow and chatter
at me,

And after bite me; then like hedge-hogs
which

Lie tumbling in my bare-foot way, and
mount

Their pricks at my foot-fall; sometime
am I

All wound with adders, who with cloven
tongues

Do hiss me into madness.—Lo, now, lo!

Here comes a spirit of his, and to torment
me

For bringing wood in slowly. I'll fall flat;

Perchance he will not mind me.

[*Enter* TRINCULO.]

TRINCULO.

Here's neither bush nor shrub to bear
off any weather at all, and another storm
brewing; I hear it sing i' th' wind; yond
same black cloud, yond huge one, looks
like a foul bombard that would shed
his liquor. If it should thunder as it did
before, I know not where to hide my head:
yond same cloud cannot choose but fall
by pailfuls.—What have we here? a man
or a fish? dead or alive? A fish: he smells
like a fish: a very ancient and fish-like
smell; a kind of not of the newest Poor-
John. A strange fish! Were I in England
now,—as once I was, and had but this

fish painted, not a holiday fool there but would give a piece of silver: there would this monster make a man; any strange beast there makes a man. When they will not give a doit to relieve a lame beggar, they will lay out ten to see a dead Indian. Legg'd like a man, and his fins like arms! Warm, o' my troth! I do now let loose my opinion: hold it no longer; this is no fish, but an islander, that hath lately suffered by thunderbolt. [*Thunder.*] Alas, the storm is come again! My best way is to creep under his gaberdine; there is no other shelter hereabout: misery acquaints a man with strange bed-fellows. I will here shroud till the dregs of the storm be past.

[*Enter* STEPHANO *singing; a bottle in his hand.*]

STEPHANO.

    I shall no more to sea, to sea,
        Here shall I die a-shore:—
This is a very scurvy tune to sing at a man's funeral: Well, here's my comfort.

[*Drinks.*]

    The master, the swabber, the boatswain,
        and I,
        The gunner, and his mate,
    Lov'd Mall, Meg, and Marian, and
    Margery,
        But none of us car'd for Kate:
        For she had a tongue with a tang,
        Would cry to a sailor "Go hang!"
    She lov'd not the savour of tar nor of
        pitch,
    Yet a tailor might scratch her wher-e'er
        she did itch.
    Then to sea, boys, and let her go hang!
This is a scurvy tune too: but here's my comfort.

[*Drinks.*]

CALIBAN.

Do not torment me: O!

STEPHANO.

What's the matter? Have we devils here? Do you put tricks upon us with savages and men of Ind? Ha! I have not 'scaped drowning, to be afeard now of your four legs; for it hath been said, As proper a man

as ever went on four legs cannot make him give ground: and it shall be said so again, while Stephano breathes at nostrils.

CALIBAN.

The spirit torments me: O!

STEPHANO.

This is some monster of the isle with four legs, who hath got, as I take it, an ague. Where the devil should he learn our language? I will give him some relief, if it be but for that; if I can recover him and keep him tame and get to Naples with him, he's a present for any emperor that ever trod on neat's-leather.

CALIBAN.

Do not torment me, prithee; I'll bring my wood home faster.

STEPHANO.

He's in his fit now and does not talk after the wisest. He shall taste of my bottle: if he have never drunk wine afore, it will go near to remove his fit. If I can recover him, and keep him tame, I will not take too much for him: he shall pay for him that hath him, and that soundly.

CALIBAN.

Thou dost me yet but little hurt; thou wilt anon, I know it by thy trembling: now Prosper works upon thee.

STEPHANO.

Come on your ways: open your mouth; here is that which will give language to you, cat. Open your mouth: this will shake your shaking, I can tell you, and that soundly: [*Gives* CALIBAN *a drink.*] you cannot tell who's your friend: open your chaps again.

TRINCULO.

I should know that voice: it should be— but he is drowned; and these are devils. O! defend me.

STEPHANO.

Four legs and two voices; a most delicate monster! His forward voice now is to speak well of his friend; his backward voice is to utter foul speeches, and to detract. If all the wine in my bottle will recover him, I will help his ague. Come. Amen! I will pour some in thy other mouth.

TRINCULO.
Stephano!

STEPHANO.
Doth thy other mouth call me? Mercy! mercy! This is a devil, and no monster: I will leave him: I have no long spoon.

TRINCULO.
Stephano!—If thou be'st Stephano, touch me, and speak to me; for I am Trinculo:— be not afeared—thy good friend Trinculo.

STEPHANO.
If thou be'st Trinculo, come forth. I'll pull thee by the lesser legs: if any be Trinculo's legs, these are they. Thou art very Trinculo indeed! How cam'st thou to be the siege of this moon-calf? Can he vent Trinculos?

TRINCULO.
I took him to be kill'd with a thunderstroke. But art thou not drown'd, Stephano? I hope now thou are not drown'd. Is the storm overblown? I hid me under the dead moon-calf's gaberdine for fear of the storm. And art thou living, Stephano? O Stephano, two Neapolitans 'scaped!

STEPHANO.
Prithee, do not turn me about: my stomach is not constant.

CALIBAN. [*Aside.*]
These are fine things, an if they be not
    sprites.
That's a brave god, and bears celestial
    liquor;
I will kneel to him.

STEPHANO.
How didst thou 'scape? How cam'st thou hither? swear by this bottle how thou cam'st hither—I escaped upon a butt of sack, which the sailors heaved overboard, by this bottle! which I made of the bark of a tree, with mine own hands, since I was cast ashore.

CALIBAN.
I'll swear upon that bottle to be thy true subject, for the liquor is not earthly.

STEPHANO.
Here: swear then how thou escapedst.

TRINCULO.
Swum ashore, man, like a duck: I can swim like a duck, I'll be sworn.

STEPHANO. [*Passing the bottle.*]
Here, kiss the book. [*Gives* TRINCULO *a drink.*] Though thou canst swim like a duck, thou art made like a goose.

TRINCULO.
O Stephano! hast any more of this?

STEPHANO.
The whole butt, man: my cellar is in a rock by the seaside, where my wine is hid. How now, moon-calf! How does thine ague?

CALIBAN.
Hast thou not dropped from heaven?

STEPHANO.
Out o' the moon, I do assure thee: I was the Man in the Moon, when time was.

CALIBAN.
I have seen thee in her, and I do adore thee, my mistress showed me thee, and thy dog and thy bush.

STEPHANO.
Come, swear to that; kiss the book; I will furnish it anon with new contents; swear.

TRINCULO.
By this good light, this is a very shallow monster.—I afeard of him!—A very weak monster.—The Man i' the Moon! A most poor credulous monster!—Well drawn, monster, in good sooth!

CALIBAN.
I'll show thee every fertile inch o' the island; and I will kiss thy foot. I prithee, be my god.

TRINCULO.
By this light, a most perfidious and drunken monster: when his god's asleep, he'll rob his bottle.

CALIBAN.
I'll kiss thy foot: I'll swear myself thy subject.

STEPHANO.
Come on, then; down, and swear.

TRINCULO.
I shall laugh myself to death at this puppy-headed monster. A most scurvy monster! I could find in my heart to beat him,—

STEPHANO.
Come, kiss.

TRINCULO.
But that the poor monster's in drink: an abominable monster!

CALIBAN.
I'll show thee the best springs; I'll pluck
    thee berries;
I'll fish for thee, and get thee wood
    enough.
A plague upon the tyrant that I serve!
I'll bear him no more sticks, but follow
    thee,
Thou wondrous man.
TRINCULO.
A most ridiculous monster, to make a
wonder of a poor drunkard!
CALIBAN.
I prithee, let me bring thee where crabs
    grow;
And I with my long nails will dig thee
    pig-nuts;
Show thee a jay's nest, and instruct thee
    how
To snare the nimble marmozet; I'll bring
    thee
To clust'ring filberts, and sometimes I'll
    get thee
Young scamels from the rock. Wilt thou go
    with me?
STEPHANO.
I prithee now, lead the way without any
more talking—Trinculo, the king and all
our company else being drowned, we will
inherit here.—Here, bear my bottle.—
Fellow Trinculo, we'll fill him by and by
again.
CALIBAN. [*Sings drunkenly.*]
    Farewell, master; farewell, farewell!
TRINCULO.
A howling monster, a drunken monster.
CALIBAN. [*Sings.*]
    No more dams I'll make for fish;
      Nor fetch in firing
        At requiring,
    Nor scrape trenchering, nor wash dish;
      'Ban 'Ban, Ca—Caliban,
      Has a new master: get a new man.
Freedom, high-day! high-day, freedom!
freedom, high-day, freedom!
STEPHANO.
O brave monster! lead the way.
                [*Exeunt.*]

ACT III
SCENE I
Before Prospero's cell.
[*Enter* FERDINAND, *bearing a log.*]
FERDINAND.
There be some sports are painful, and their
    labour
Delight in them sets off: some kinds of
    baseness
Are nobly undergone, and most poor
    matters
Point to rich ends. This my mean task
Would be as heavy to me as odious; but
The mistress which I serve quickens what's
    dead,
And makes my labours pleasures: O! she is
Ten times more gentle than her father's
    crabbed,
And he's compos'd of harshness. I must
    remove
Some thousands of these logs, and pile
    them up,
Upon a sore injunction: my sweet mistress
Weeps when she sees me work, and says
    such baseness
Had never like executor. I forget:
But these sweet thoughts do even refresh
    my labours,
Most busy, least when I do it.
[*Enter* MIRANDA; *and* PROSPERO *behind.*]
MIRANDA.
                Alas! now pray you,
Work not so hard: I would the lightning
    had
Burnt up those logs that you are enjoin'd
    to pile!
Pray, set it down and rest you: when this
    burns,
'Twill weep for having wearied you. My
    father
Is hard at study; pray, now, rest yourself:
He's safe for these three hours.
FERDINAND.
              O most dear mistress,
The sun will set, before I shall discharge
What I must strive to do.
MIRANDA.
                If you'll sit down,

I'll bear your logs the while. Pray give me
    that;
I'll carry it to the pile.
FERDINAND.
                        No, precious creature:
I had rather crack my sinews, break my
    back,
Than you should such dishonour undergo,
While I sit lazy by.
MIRANDA.
                        It would become me
As well as it does you: and I should do it
With much more ease; for my good will
    is to it,
And yours it is against.
PROSPERO. [*Aside.*]
                        Poor worm! thou art infected!
This visitation shows it.
MIRANDA.
                        You look wearily.
FERDINAND.
No, noble mistress; 'tis fresh morning with
    me
When you are by at night. I do beseech
    you—
Chiefly that I might set it in my prayers—
What is your name?
MIRANDA.
                        Miranda—O my father!
I have broke your hest to say so.
FERDINAND.
                        Admir'd Miranda!
Indeed, the top of admiration; worth
What's dearest to the world! Full many
    a lady
I have ey'd with best regard, and many a
    time
The harmony of their tongues hath into
    bondage
Brought my too diligent ear: for several
    virtues
Have I lik'd several women; never any
With so full soul but some defect in her
Did quarrel with the noblest grace she
    ow'd,
And put it to the foil: but you, O you!
So perfect and so peerless, are created
Of every creature's best.

MIRANDA.
                        I do not know
One of my sex; no woman's face
    remember,
Save, from my glass, mine own; nor have
    I seen
More that I may call men than you, good
    friend,
And my dear father: how features are
    abroad,
I am skill-less of; but, by my modesty,—
The jewel in my dower,—I would not wish
Any companion in the world but you;
Nor can imagination form a shape,
Besides yourself, to like of. But I prattle
Something too wildly, and my father's
    precepts
I therein do forget.
FERDINAND.
                        I am, in my condition,
A prince, Miranda; I do think, a king;—
I would not so!—and would no more
    endure
This wooden slavery than to suffer
The flesh-fly blow my mouth. Hear my
    soul speak:
The very instant that I saw you, did
My heart fly to your service; there resides,
To make me slave to it; and for your sake
Am I this patient log-man.
MIRANDA.
                        Do you love me?
FERDINAND.
O heaven! O earth! bear witness to this
    sound,
And crown what I profess with kind event,
If I speak true: if hollowly, invert
What best is boded me to mischief! I,
Beyond all limit of what else i' the world,
Do love, prize, honour you.
MIRANDA.
                        I am a fool
To weep at what I am glad of.
PROSPERO. [*Aside.*]
                        Fair encounter
Of two most rare affections! Heavens rain
    grace
On that which breeds between them!

FERDINAND.

Wherefore weep you?

MIRANDA.

At mine unworthiness, that dare not offer
What I desire to give; and much less take
What I shall die to want. But this is
    trifling;
And all the more it seeks to hide itself,
The bigger bulk it shows. Hence, bashful
    cunning!
And prompt me, plain and holy
    innocence!
I am your wife, if you will marry me;
If not, I'll die your maid: to be your fellow
You may deny me; but I'll be your servant,
Whether you will or no.

FERDINAND.

My mistress, dearest;
And I thus humble ever.

MIRANDA.

My husband, then?

FERDINAND.

Ay, with a heart as willing
As bondage e'er of freedom: here's my
    hand.

MIRANDA.

And mine, with my heart in't: and now
    farewell
Till half an hour hence.

FERDINAND.

A thousand thousand!

[*Exeunt* FERDINAND *and* MIRANDA
severally.]

PROSPERO.

So glad of this as they, I cannot be,
Who are surpris'd withal; but my rejoicing
At nothing can be more. I'll to my book;
For yet, ere supper time, must I perform
Much business appertaining.

[*Exit.*]

SCENE II

Another part of the island.
[*Enter* CALIBAN, *with a bottle,* STEPHANO,
and TRINCULO.]

STEPHANO.

Tell not me:—when the butt is out we will
drink water; not a drop before: therefore
bear up, and board 'em.—Servant-monster,
drink to me.

TRINCULO.

Servant-monster! The folly of this island!
They say there's but five upon this isle;
we are three of them; if th' other two be
brained like us, the state totters.

STEPHANO.

Drink, servant-monster, when I bid thee:
thy eyes are almost set in thy head.

TRINCULO.

Where should they be set else? He were a
brave monster indeed, if they were set in
his tail.

STEPHANO.

My man-monster hath drown'd his tongue
in sack: for my part, the sea cannot drown
me; I swam, ere I could recover the shore,
five-and-thirty leagues, off and on, by this
light. Thou shalt be my lieutenant, monster,
or my standard.

TRINCULO.

Your lieutenant, if you list; he's no standard.

STEPHANO.

We'll not run, Monsieur monster.

TRINCULO.

Nor go neither: but you'll lie like dogs, and
yet say nothing neither.

STEPHANO.

Moon-calf, speak once in thy life, if thou
beest a good moon-calf.

CALIBAN.

How does thy honour? Let me lick thy
    shoe.
I'll not serve him: he is not valiant.

TRINCULO.

Thou liest, most ignorant monster: I am
in case to justle a constable. Why, thou
deboshed fish thou, was there ever man a
coward that hath drunk so much sack as
I to-day? Wilt thou tell a monstrous lie,
being but half fish and half a monster?

CALIBAN.

Lo, how he mocks me! wilt thou let him,
my lord?

TRINCULO.

"Lord" quoth he!—That a monster should
be such a natural!

CALIBAN.
Lo, lo again! bite him to death, I prithee.
STEPHANO.
Trinculo, keep a good tongue in your head:
if you prove a mutineer, the next tree! The
poor monster's my subject, and he shall not
suffer indignity.
CALIBAN.
I thank my noble lord. Wilt thou be pleas'd
to hearken once again to the suit I made
to thee?
STEPHANO.
Marry will I; kneel, and repeat it: I will
stand, and so shall Trinculo.

[Enter ARIEL, invisible.]
CALIBAN.
As I told thee before, I am subject to a
tyrant, sorcerer, that by his cunning hath
cheated me of the island.
ARIEL.
Thou liest.
CALIBAN.
Thou liest, thou jesting monkey, thou;
I would my valiant master would destroy
    thee;
I do not lie.
STEPHANO.
Trinculo, if you trouble him any more in his
tale, by this hand, I will supplant some of
your teeth.
TRINCULO.
Why, I said nothing.
STEPHANO.
Mum, then, and no more. *[To* CALIBAN.*]*
Proceed.
CALIBAN.
I say, by sorcery he got this isle;
From me he got it: if thy greatness will,
Revenge it on him,—for I know, thou
    dar'st;
But this thing dare not,—
STEPHANO.
That's most certain.
CALIBAN.
Thou shalt be lord of it and I'll serve thee.
STEPHANO.
How now shall this be compassed? Canst
thou bring me to the party?

CALIBAN.
Yea, yea, my lord: I'll yield him thee asleep,
Where thou may'st knock a nail into his
    head.
ARIEL.
Thou liest: thou canst not.
CALIBAN.
What a pied ninny's this! Thou scurvy
    patch!—
I do beseech thy greatness, give him blows,
And take his bottle from him: when that's
    gone
He shall drink nought but brine; for I'll
    not show him
Where the quick freshes are.
STEPHANO.
Trinculo, run into no further danger:
interrupt the monster one word further
and, by this hand, I'll turn my mercy out o'
doors, and make a stock-fish of thee.
TRINCULO.
Why, what did I? I did nothing. I'll go
    farther off.
STEPHANO.
Didst thou not say he lied?
ARIEL.
Thou liest.
STEPHANO.
Do I so? Take thou that. *[Strikes* TRINCULO.*]*
As you like this, give me the lie another
time.
TRINCULO.
I did not give the lie:—out o' your wits and
hearing too?—A pox o' your bottle! this can
sack and drinking do.—A murrain on your
monster, and the devil take your fingers!
CALIBAN.
Ha, ha, ha!
STEPHANO.
Now, forward with your tale.—Prithee
stand further off.
CALIBAN.
Beat him enough: after a little time,
I'll beat him too.
STEPHANO.
                    Stand farther.—Come, proceed.
CALIBAN.
Why, as I told thee, 'tis a custom with him

I' th' afternoon to sleep: there thou may'st
   brain him,
Having first seiz'd his books; or with a log
Batter his skull, or paunch him with a
   stake,
Or cut his wezand with thy knife. Remember
   Remember
First to possess his books; for without
   them
He's but a sot, as I am, nor hath not
One spirit to command: they all do hate
   him
As rootedly as I. Burn but his books;
He has brave utensils,—for so he calls
   them,—
Which, when he has a house, he'll deck
   withal:
And that most deeply to consider is
The beauty of his daughter; he himself
Calls her a nonpareil: I never saw a
   woman
But only Sycorax my dam and she;
But she as far surpasseth Sycorax
As great'st does least.

Stephano.
                  Is it so brave a lass?

Caliban.
Ay, lord: she will become thy bed, I
   warrant,
And bring thee forth brave brood.

Stephano.
Monster, I will kill this man; his daughter
and I will be king and queen,—save our
graces!—and Trinculo and thyself shall be
viceroys. Dost thou like the plot, Trinculo?

Trinculo.
Excellent.

Stephano.
Give me thy hand: I am sorry I beat thee;
but while thou livest, keep a good tongue
in thy head.

Caliban.
Within this half hour will he be asleep;
Wilt thou destroy him then?

Stephano.
                  Ay, on mine honour.

Ariel.
This will I tell my master.

Caliban.
Thou mak'st me merry: I am full of
   pleasure.
Let us be jocund: will you troll the catch
You taught me but while-ere?

Stephano.
At thy request, monster, I will do reason,
any reason. Come on, Trinculo, let us sing.
                 [*Sings.*]
   Flout 'em and scout 'em; and scout 'em
      and flout 'em:
   Thought is free.

Caliban.
That's not the tune.
   [Ariel *plays the tune on a tabor and pipe.*]

Stephano.
What is this same?

Trinculo.
This is the tune of our catch, played by the
picture of Nobody.

Stephano.
If thou beest a man, show thyself in thy
likeness: if thou beest a devil, take't as thou
list.

Trinculo.
O, forgive me my sins!

Stephano.
He that dies pays all debts: I defy thee.—
Mercy upon us!

Caliban.
Art thou afeard?

Stephano.
No, monster, not I.

Caliban.
Be not afeard: the isle is full of noises,
Sounds, and sweet airs, that give delight,
   and hurt not.
Sometimes a thousand twangling
   instruments
Will hum about mine ears; and sometimes
   voices,
That, if I then had wak'd after long sleep,
Will make me sleep again: and then, in
   dreaming,
The clouds methought would open and
   show riches
Ready to drop upon me; that, when I wak'd,
I cried to dream again.

Stephano.
This will prove a brave kingdom to me,
where I shall have my music for nothing.
Caliban.
When Prospero is destroyed.
Stephano.
That shall be by and by: I remember the
story.
Trinculo.
The sound is going away: let's follow it, and
after do our work.
Stephano.
Lead, monster: we'll follow.—I would I
could see this taborer! he lays it on. Wilt
come?
Trinculo.
I'll follow, Stephano.
                    [*Exeunt.*]

SCENE III

Another part of the island.
[*Enter* Alonso, Sebastian, Antonio,
Gonzalo, Adrian, Francisco, *and*
Others.]
Gonzalo.
By'r lakin, I can go no further, sir;
My old bones ache: here's a maze trod,
indeed,
Through forth-rights and meanders! By
your patience,
I needs must rest me.
Alonso.
                    Old lord, I cannot blame thee,
Who am myself attach'd with weariness
To th' dulling of my spirits: sit down, and
rest.
Even here I will put off my hope, and
keep it
No longer for my flatterer: he is drown'd
Whom thus we stray to find; and the sea
mocks
Our frustrate search on land. Well, let
him go.
Antonio. [*Aside to* Sebastian.]
I am right glad that he's so out of hope.
Do not, for one repulse, forgo the
purpose
That you resolv'd to effect.

Sebastian. [*Aside to* Antonio.]
                    The next advantage
Will we take throughly.
Antonio. [*Aside to* Sebastian.]
                    Let it be to-night;
For, now they are oppress'd with travel,
they
Will not, nor cannot, use such vigilance
As when they are fresh.
Sebastian. [*Aside to* Antonio.]
                    I say, to-night: no more.
[*Solemn and strange music: and* Prospero
above, invisible. Enter several strange
Shapes, *bringing in a banquet: they dance
about it with gentle actions of salutation; and
inviting the* King &c., *to eat, they depart.*]
Alonso.
What harmony is this? my good friends,
hark!
Gonzalo.
Marvellous sweet music!
Alonso.
Give us kind keepers, heavens! What were
these?
Sebastian.
A living drollery. Now I will believe
That there are unicorns; that in Arabia
There is one tree, the phoenix' throne; one
phoenix
At this hour reigning there.
Antonio.
                    I'll believe both;
And what does else want credit, come to
me,
And I'll be sworn 'tis true: travellers ne'er
did lie,
Though fools at home condemn them.
Gonzalo.
                    If in Naples
I should report this now, would they
believe me?
If I should say, I saw such islanders,—
For, certes, these are people of the
island,—
Who, though, they are of monstrous shape,
yet, note,
Their manners are more gentle-kind than
of

Our human generation you shall find
Many, nay, almost any.
PROSPERO. [*Aside.*]
                              Honest lord,
Thou hast said well; for some of you there
    present
Are worse than devils.
ALONSO.
                    I cannot too much muse
Such shapes, such gesture, and such sound,
    expressing,—
Although they want the use of tongue,—a
    kind
Of excellent dumb discourse.
PROSPERO. [*Aside.*]
                              Praise in departing.
FRANCISCO.
They vanish'd strangely.
SEBASTIAN.
                          No matter, since
They have left their viands behind; for we
    have stomachs.—
Will't please you taste of what is here?
ALONSO.
                                        Not I.
GONZALO.
Faith, sir, you need not fear. When we
    were boys,
Who would believe that there were
    mountaineers
Dewlapp'd like bulls, whose throats had
    hanging at them
Wallets of flesh? or that there were such
    men
Whose heads stood in their breasts? which
    now we find
Each putter-out of five for one will bring
    us
Good warrant of.
ALONSO.
                    I will stand to, and feed,
Although my last; no matter, since I feel
The best is past.—Brother, my lord the
    duke,
Stand to and do as we.
    [*Thunder and lightning. Enter* ARIEL, *like
    a harpy; claps his wings upon the table; and,
    with a quaint device, the banquet vanishes.*]

ARIEL.
You are three men of sin, whom Destiny,
That hath to instrument this lower world
And what is in't,—the never-surfeited sea
Hath caused to belch up you; and on this
    island
Where man doth not inhabit; you 'mongst
    men
Being most unfit to live. I have made you
    mad:
    [*Seeing* ALONSO, SEBASTIAN, &C., *draw
                            their swords.*]
And even with such-like valour men hang
    and drown
Their proper selves. You fools! I and my
    fellows
Are ministers of fate: the elements
Of whom your swords are temper'd may
    as well
Wound the loud winds, or with bemock'd-
    at stabs
Kill the still-closing waters, as diminish
One dowle that's in my plume; my fellow-
    ministers
Are like invulnerable. If you could hurt,
Your swords are now too massy for your
    strengths,
And will not be uplifted. But, remember—
For that's my business to you,—that you
    three
From Milan did supplant good Prospero;
Expos'd unto the sea, which hath requit it,
Him, and his innocent child: for which
    foul deed
The powers, delaying, not forgetting, have
Incens'd the seas and shores, yea, all the
    creatures,
Against your peace. Thee of thy son,
    Alonso,
They have bereft; and do pronounce, by
    me
Lingering perdition,—worse than any
    death
Can be at once,—shall step by step attend
You and your ways; whose wraths to guard
    you from—
Which here, in this most desolate isle,
    else falls

Upon your heads,—is nothing but heart-
sorrow,
And a clear life ensuing.
[*He vanishes in thunder: then, to soft music,
enter the* SHAPES *again, and dance, with
mocks and mows, and carry out the table.*]
PROSPERO. [*Aside.*]
Bravely the figure of this harpy hast thou
Perform'd, my Ariel; a grace it had,
devouring;
Of my instruction hast thou nothing
bated
In what thou hadst to say: so, with good
life
And observation strange, my meaner
ministers
Their several kinds have done. My high
charms work,
And these mine enemies are all knit up
In their distractions; they now are in my
power;
And in these fits I leave them, while I visit
Young Ferdinand, whom they suppose is
drown'd,
And his and mine lov'd darling.
                    [*Exit above.*]
GONZALO.
I' the name of something holy, sir, why
stand you
In this strange stare?
ALONSO.
                    O, it is monstrous! monstrous!
Methought the billows spoke, and told
me of it;
The winds did sing it to me; and the
thunder,
That deep and dreadful organ-pipe,
pronounc'd
The name of Prosper: it did bass my
trespass.
Therefore my son i' th' ooze is bedded; and
I'll seek him deeper than e'er plummet
sounded,
And with him there lie mudded.
                    [*Exit.*]
SEBASTIAN.
                    But one fiend at a time,
I'll fight their legions o'er.

ANTONIO.
                    I'll be thy second.
[*Exeunt* SEBASTIAN *and* ANTONIO.]
GONZALO.
All three of them are desperate: their great
guilt,
Like poison given to work a great time
after,
Now 'gins to bite the spirits. I do beseech
you
That are of suppler joints, follow them
swiftly
And hinder them from what this ecstasy
May now provoke them to.
ADRIAN.
                    Follow, I pray you.
                    [*Exeunt.*]

ACT IV
SCENE I
Before Prospero's cell.
[*Enter* PROSPERO, FERDINAND, *and*
MIRANDA.]
PROSPERO.
If I have too austerely punish'd you,
Your compensation makes amends: for I
Have given you here a third of mine own
life,
Or that for which I live; who once again
I tender to thy hand: all thy vexations
Were but my trials of thy love, and thou
Hast strangely stood the test: here, afore
Heaven,
I ratify this my rich gift. O Ferdinand!
Do not smile at me that I boast her off,
For thou shalt find she will outstrip all
praise,
And make it halt behind her.
FERDINAND.
                    I do believe it
Against an oracle.
PROSPERO.
Then, as my gift and thine own acquisition
Worthily purchas'd, take my daughter: but
If thou dost break her virgin knot before
All sanctimonious ceremonies may
With full and holy rite be minister'd,
No sweet aspersion shall the heavens let fall

To make this contract grow; but barren hate,
Sour-ey'd disdain, and discord, shall bestrew
The union of your bed with weeds so loathly
That you shall hate it both: therefore take heed,
As Hymen's lamps shall light you.

FERDINAND.
                  As I hope
For quiet days, fair issue, and long life,
With such love as 'tis now, the murkiest den,
The most opportune place, the strong'st suggestion
Our worser genius can, shall never melt
Mine honour into lust, to take away
The edge of that day's celebration,
When I shall think, or Phoebus' steeds are founder'd,
Or Night kept chain'd below.

PROSPERO.
                  Fairly spoke:
Sit, then, and talk with her, she is thine own.
What, Ariel! my industrious servant, Ariel!

[Enter ARIEL.]

ARIEL.
What would my potent master? here I am.

PROSPERO.
Thou and thy meaner fellows your last service
Did worthily perform; and I must use you
In such another trick. Go bring the rabble,
O'er whom I give thee power, here to this place;
Incite them to quick motion; for I must
Bestow upon the eyes of this young couple
Some vanity of mine art: it is my promise,
And they expect it from me.

ARIEL.
                  Presently?

PROSPERO.
Ay, with a twink.

ARIEL.
Before you can say "Come" and "Go,"

And breathe twice; and cry "So, so,"
Each one, tripping on his toe,
Will be here with mop and mow.
Do you love me, master? no?

PROSPERO.
Dearly, my delicate Ariel. Do not approach
Till thou dost hear me call.

ARIEL.
                  Well, I conceive.
[Exit.]

PROSPERO.
Look, thou be true; do not give dalliance
Too much the rein: the strongest oaths are straw
To th' fire i' the blood: be more abstemious,
Or else good night your vow!

FERDINAND.
                  I warrant you, sir;
The white-cold virgin snow upon my heart
Abates the ardour of my liver.

PROSPERO.
                  Well.—
Now come, my Ariel! bring a corollary,
Rather than want a spirit: appear, and pertly.
No tongue! all eyes! be silent.
[Soft music.]
[A masque. Enter IRIS.]

IRIS.
Ceres, most bounteous lady, thy rich leas
Of wheat, rye, barley, vetches, oats, and peas;
Thy turfy mountains, where live nibbling sheep,
And flat meads thatch'd with stover, them to keep;
Thy banks with pioned and twilled brims,
Which spongy April at thy hest betrims,
To make cold nymphs chaste crowns; and thy broom groves,
Whose shadow the dismissed bachelor loves,
Being lass-lorn: thy pole-clipt vineyard;
And thy sea-marge, sterile and rocky-hard,
Where thou thyself dost air: the queen o' the sky,
Whose watery arch and messenger am I,

Bids thee leave these; and with her
    sovereign grace,
Here on this grass-plot, in this very place,
To come and sport; her peacocks fly
    amain:
Approach, rich Ceres, her to entertain.
               [*Enter* CERES.]

CERES.
Hail, many-colour'd messenger, that ne'er
Dost disobey the wife of Jupiter;
Who with thy saffron wings upon my
    flowers
Diffusest honey drops, refreshing showers:
And with each end of thy blue bow dost
    crown
My bosky acres and my unshrubb'd down,
Rich scarf to my proud earth; why hath
    thy queen
Summon'd me hither to this short-grass'd
    green?

IRIS.
A contract of true love to celebrate,
And some donation freely to estate
On the blest lovers.

CERES.
             Tell me, heavenly bow,
If Venus or her son, as thou dost know,
Do now attend the queen? Since they did
    plot
The means that dusky Dis my daughter
    got,
Her and her blind boy's scandal'd company
I have forsworn.

IRIS.
             Of her society
Be not afraid. I met her deity
Cutting the clouds towards Paphos and
    her son
Dove-drawn with her. Here thought they
    to have done
Some wanton charm upon this man and
    maid,
Whose vows are, that no bed-rite shall
    be paid
Till Hymen's torch be lighted; but in vain.
Mars's hot minion is return'd again;
Her waspish-headed son has broke his
    arrows,

Swears he will shoot no more, but play with
    sparrows,
And be a boy right out.

CERES.
             Highest queen of state,
Great Juno comes; I know her by her gait.
               [*Enter* JUNO.]

JUNO.
How does my bounteous sister? Go with
    me
To bless this twain, that they may
    prosperous be,
And honour'd in their issue.
                  [*Song.*]

JUNO.
    Honour, riches, marriage-blessing,
    Long continuance, and increasing,
    Hourly joys be still upon you!
    Juno sings her blessings on you.

CERES.
    Earth's increase, foison plenty,
    Barns and gamers never empty;
    Vines with clust'ring bunches growing;
    Plants with goodly burden bowing;
    Spring come to you at the farthest,
    In the very end of harvest!
    Scarcity and want shall shun you;
    Ceres' blessing so is on you.

FERDINAND.
This is a most majestic vision, and
Harmonious charmingly; may I be bold
To think these spirits?

PROSPERO.
             Spirits, which by mine art
I have from their confines call'd to enact
My present fancies.

FERDINAND.
             Let me live here ever:
So rare a wonder'd father and a wise,
Makes this place Paradise.
[JUNO *and* CERES *whisper, and send* IRIS *on*
                 employment.]

PROSPERO.
             Sweet now, silence!
Juno and Ceres whisper seriously,
There's something else to do: hush, and
    be mute,
Or else our spell is marr'd.

Iris.

You nymphs, call'd Naiads, of the windring
    brooks,
With your sedg'd crowns and ever-
    harmless looks,
Leave your crisp channels, and on this
    green land
Answer your summons: Juno does
    command.
Come, temperate nymphs, and help to
    celebrate
A contract of true love: be not too late.
                    [*Enter certain* Nymphs.]
You sun-burn'd sicklemen, of August weary,
Come hither from the furrow, and be
    merry:
Make holiday: your rye-straw hats put on,
And these fresh nymphs encounter every
    one
In country footing.
    [*Enter certain* Reapers, *properly habited:*
    they join with the Nymphs *in a graceful*
    dance; towards the end whereof Prospero
    starts suddenly, and speaks; after which, to
    a strange, hollow, and confused noise, they
    heavily vanish.]

Prospero. [*Aside.*]

I had forgot that foul conspiracy
Of the beast Caliban and his confederates
Against my life: the minute of their plot
Is almost come. [*To the* Spirits.] Well
    done! avoid no more!

Ferdinand.

This is strange: your father's in some
    passion
That works him strongly.

Miranda.

                        Never till this day
Saw I him touch'd with anger so
    distemper'd.

Prospero.

You do look, my son, in a mov'd sort,
As if you were dismay'd: be cheerful, sir:
Our revels now are ended. These our
    actors,
As I foretold you, were all spirits and
Are melted into air, into thin air:
And, like the baseless fabric of this vision,

The cloud-capp'd towers, the gorgeous
    palaces,
The solemn temples, the great globe itself,
Yea, all which it inherit, shall dissolve
And, like this insubstantial pageant faded,
Leave not a rack behind. We are such stuff
As dreams are made on, and our little life
Is rounded with a sleep.—Sir, I am vex'd:
Bear with my weakness; my old brain is
    troubled.
Be not disturb'd with my infirmity.
If you be pleas'd, retire into my cell
And there repose: a turn or two I'll walk,
To still my beating mind.

Ferdinand and Miranda.

                        We wish your peace.
                            [*Exeunt.*]

Prospero.

Come, with a thought. [*To them.*] I thank
    thee: Ariel, come!
                    [*Enter* Ariel.]

Ariel.

Thy thoughts I cleave to. What's thy
    pleasure?

Prospero.

                                Spirit,
We must prepare to meet with Caliban.

Ariel.

Ay, my commander; when I presented
    Ceres,
I thought to have told thee of it: but I
    fear'd
Lest I might anger thee.

Prospero.

Say again, where didst thou leave these
    varlets?

Ariel.

I told you, sir, they were red-hot with
    drinking;
So full of valour that they smote the air
For breathing in their faces; beat the
    ground
For kissing of their feet; yet always
    bending
Towards their project. Then I beat my
    tabor;
At which, like unback'd colts, they prick'd
    their ears,

Advanc'd their eyelids, lifted up their noses
As they smelt music: so I charm'd their
    ears,
That calf-like they my lowing follow'd
    through
Tooth'd briers, sharp furzes, pricking goss
    and thorns,
Which enter'd their frail shins: at last I
    left them
I' the filthy-mantled pool beyond your cell,
There dancing up to the chins, that the
    foul lake
O'erstunk their feet.

PROSPERO.

This was well done, my bird.
Thy shape invisible retain thou still:
The trumpery in my house, go bring it
    hither
For stale to catch these thieves.

ARIEL.

I go, I go.

[*Exit.*]

PROSPERO.

A devil, a born devil, on whose nature
Nurture can never stick; on whom my
    pains,
Humanely taken, all, all lost, quite lost;
And as with age his body uglier grows,
So his mind cankers. I will plague them
    all,
Even to roaring.

[*Re-enter* ARIEL, *loaden with glistering
    apparel, etc.*]

Come, hang them on this line.

[PROSPERO *and* ARIEL *remain invisible.
    Enter* CALIBAN, STEPHANO, *and*
    TRINCULO, *all wet.*]

CALIBAN.

Pray you, tread softly, that the blind mole
    may not
Hear a foot fall: we now are near his cell.

STEPHANO.

Monster, your fairy, which you say is a
harmless fairy, has done little better than
played the Jack with us.

TRINCULO.

Monster, I do smell all horse-piss; at which
my nose is in great indignation.

STEPHANO.

So is mine.—Do you hear, monster? If I
should take a displeasure against you, look
you,—

TRINCULO.

Thou wert but a lost monster.

CALIBAN.

Good my lord, give me thy favour still:
Be patient, for the prize I'll bring thee to
Shall hoodwink this mischance: therefore
    speak softly;
All's hush'd as midnight yet.

TRINCULO.

Ay, but to lose our bottles in the pool!—

STEPHANO.

There is not only disgrace and dishonour in
that, monster, but an infinite loss.

TRINCULO.

That's more to me than my wetting: yet this
is your harmless fairy, monster.

STEPHANO.

I will fetch off my bottle, though I be o'er
ears for my labour.

CALIBAN.

Prithee, my king, be quiet. Seest thou here,
This is the mouth o' the cell: no noise, and
    enter.
Do that good mischief which may make
    this island
Thine own for ever, and I, thy Caliban,
For aye thy foot-licker.

STEPHANO.

Give me thy hand: I do begin to have
bloody thoughts.

TRINCULO.

O King Stephano! O peer! O worthy
Stephano! Look what a wardrobe here is
for thee!

CALIBAN.

Let it alone, thou fool; it is but trash.

TRINCULO.

O, ho, monster! we know what belongs to a
frippery. O King Stephano!

STEPHANO.

Put off that gown, Trinculo; by this hand,
I'll have that gown.

TRINCULO.

Thy Grace shall have it.

CALIBAN.

The dropsy drown this fool! What do
   you mean
To dote thus on such luggage? Let's
   along,
And do the murder first. If he awake,
From toe to crown he'll fill our skins
   with pinches;
Make us strange stuff.

STEPHANO.

Be you quiet, monster.—Mistress line, is
not this my jerkin? Now is the jerkin under
the line: now, jerkin, you are like to lose
your hair, and prove a bald jerkin.

TRINCULO.

Do, do: we steal by line and level, an't like
your Grace.

STEPHANO.

I thank thee for that jest: here's a garment
for't: wit shall not go unrewarded while I
am king of this country: "Steal by line and
level," is an excellent pass of pate: there's
another garment for't.

TRINCULO.

Monster, come, put some lime upon your
fingers, and away with the rest.

CALIBAN.

I will have none on't. We shall lose our
   time,
And all be turn'd to barnacles, or to apes
With foreheads villainous low.

STEPHANO.

Monster, lay-to your fingers: help to bear
this away where my hogshead of wine is,
or I'll turn you out of my kingdom. Go to;
carry this.

TRINCULO.

And this.

STEPHANO.

Ay, and this.

[*A noise of hunters heard. Enter divers*
SPIRITS, *in shape of hounds, and hunt
them about;* PROSPERO *and* ARIEL
setting them on.]

PROSPERO.

Hey, Mountain, hey!

ARIEL.

Silver! there it goes, Silver!

PROSPERO.

Fury, Fury! There, Tyrant, there! hark, hark!
[CALIBAN, STEPHANO, *and* TRINCULO
are driven out.]
Go, charge my goblins that they grind
   their joints
With dry convulsions; shorten up their
   sinews
With aged cramps, and more pinch-
   spotted make them
Than pard, or cat o' mountain.

ARIEL.

                              Hark, they roar!

PROSPERO.

Let them be hunted soundly. At this hour
Lies at my mercy all mine enemies;
Shortly shall all my labours end, and thou
Shalt have the air at freedom; for a little
Follow, and do me service.
                          [*Exeunt.*]

ACT V
SCENE I
Before the cell of Prospero.
[*Enter* PROSPERO *in his magic robes; and*
ARIEL.]

PROSPERO.

Now does my project gather to a head:
My charms crack not; my spirits obey, and
   time
Goes upright with his carriage. How's the
   day?

ARIEL.

On the sixth hour; at which time, my lord,
You said our work should cease.

PROSPERO.

                              I did say so,
When first I rais'd the tempest. Say, my
   spirit,
How fares the king and's followers?

ARIEL.

                          Confin'd together
In the same fashion as you gave in charge;
Just as you left them: all prisoners, sir,
In the line-grove which weather-fends
   your cell;
They cannot budge till your release. The
   king,

His brother, and yours, abide all three
   distracted,
And the remainder mourning over them,
Brim full of sorrow and dismay; but
   chiefly
Him you term'd, sir, "the good old lord,
   Gonzalo":
His tears run down his beard, like winter's
   drops
From eaves of reeds; your charm so
   strongly works them,
That if you now beheld them, your
   affections
Would become tender.

PROSPERO.
                  Dost thou think so, spirit?

ARIEL.
Mine would, sir, were I human.

PROSPERO.
                  And mine shall.
Hast thou, which art but air, a touch, a
   feeling
Of their afflictions, and shall not myself,
One of their kind, that relish all as sharply,
Passion as they, be kindlier mov'd than
   thou art?
Though with their high wrongs I am
   struck to the quick,
Yet with my nobler reason 'gainst my fury
Do I take part: the rarer action is
In virtue than in vengeance: they being
   penitent,
The sole drift of my purpose doth extend
Not a frown further. Go release them,
   Ariel.
My charms I'll break, their senses I'll
   restore,
And they shall be themselves.

ARIEL.
                I'll fetch them, sir.
                  [Exit.]

PROSPERO.
Ye elves of hills, brooks, standing lakes,
   and groves;
And ye that on the sands with printless
   foot
Do chase the ebbing Neptune, and do fly
   him

When he comes back; you demi-puppets
   that
By moonshine do the green sour ringlets
   make,
Whereof the ewe not bites; and you whose
   pastime
Is to make midnight mushrooms, that
   rejoice
To hear the solemn curfew; by whose
   aid,—
Weak masters though ye be,—I have
   bedimm'd
The noontide sun, call'd forth the
   mutinous winds,
And 'twixt the green sea and the azur'd
   vault
Set roaring war: to the dread rattling
   thunder
Have I given fire, and rifted Jove's stout
   oak
With his own bolt: the strong-bas'd
   promontory
Have I made shake; and by the spurs
   pluck'd up
The pine and cedar: graves at my command
Have wak'd their sleepers, op'd, and let
   them forth
By my so potent art. But this rough magic
I here abjure; and, when I have requir'd
Some heavenly music,—which even now
   I do,—
To work mine end upon their senses that
This airy charm is for, I'll break my staff,
Bury it certain fathoms in the earth,
And deeper than did ever plummet sound
I'll drown my book.
            [Solemn music.]
[Re-enter ARIEL: *after him,* ALONSO, *with
   frantic gesture, attended by* GONZALO;
SEBASTIAN *and* ANTONIO *in like manner,
   attended by* ADRIAN *and* FRANCISCO:
   they all enter the circle which* PROSPERO
   had made, and there stand charmed: which
          PROSPERO observing, speaks.]
A solemn air, and the best comforter
To an unsettled fancy, cure thy brains,
Now useless, boil'd within thy skull! There
   stand,

For you are spell-stopp'd.
Holy Gonzalo, honourable man,
Mine eyes, even sociable to the show of
    thine,
Fall fellowly drops. The charm dissolves
    apace;
And as the morning steals upon the night,
Melting the darkness, so their rising
    senses
Begin to chase the ignorant fumes that
    mantle
Their clearer reason.—O good Gonzalo!
My true preserver, and a loyal sir
To him thou follow'st, I will pay thy
    graces
Home, both in word and deed.—Most
    cruelly
Didst thou, Alonso, use me and my
    daughter:
Thy brother was a furtherer in the act;—
Thou'rt pinch'd for't now, Sebastian. Flesh
    and blood,
You, brother mine, that entertain'd
    ambition,
Expell'd remorse and nature, who, with
    Sebastian,
Whose inward pinches therefore are most
    strong,
Would here have kill'd your king; I do
    forgive thee,
Unnatural though thou art! Their
    understanding
Begins to swell, and the approaching tide
Will shortly fill the reasonable shores
That now lie foul and muddy. Not one of
    them
That yet looks on me, or would know
    me.—Ariel,
Fetch me the hat and rapier in my cell:—
           [*Exit* Ariel.]
I will discase me, and myself present,
As I was sometime Milan.—Quickly,
    spirit;
Thou shalt ere long be free.
[Ariel *re-enters, singing, and helps to attire*
           Prospero.]
Ariel.
    Where the bee sucks, there suck I:

In a cowslip's bell I lie;
There I couch when owls do cry.
    On the bat's back I do fly
    After summer merrily:
Merrily, merrily shall I live now
Under the blossom that hangs on the
    bough.
Prospero.
Why, that's my dainty Ariel! I shall miss
    thee;
But yet thou shalt have freedom;—so, so,
    so.—
To the king's ship, invisible as thou art:
There shalt thou find the mariners asleep
Under the hatches; the master and the
    boatswain
Being awake, enforce them to this place,
And presently, I prithee.
Ariel.
I drink the air before me, and return
Or ere your pulse twice beat.
               [*Exit.*]
Gonzalo.
All torment, trouble, wonder and
    amazement
Inhabits here. Some heavenly power guide
    us
Out of this fearful country!
Prospero.
               Behold, sir king,
The wronged Duke of Milan, Prospero.
For more assurance that a living prince
Does now speak to thee, I embrace thy
    body;
And to thee and thy company I bid
A hearty welcome.
Alonso.
           Whe'er thou be'st he or no,
Or some enchanted trifle to abuse me,
As late I have been, I not know: thy pulse
Beats, as of flesh and blood; and, since I
    saw thee,
Th' affliction of my mind amends, with
    which,
I fear, a madness held me: this must
    crave,—
An if this be at all—a most strange story.
Thy dukedom I resign, and do entreat

Thou pardon me my wrongs.—But how
    should Prospero
Be living and be here?
PROSPERO.
                        First, noble friend,
Let me embrace thine age; whose honour
    cannot
Be measur'd or confin'd.
GONZALO.
                        Whether this be
Or be not, I'll not swear.
PROSPERO.
                       You do yet taste
Some subtleties o' the isle, that will not
    let you
Believe things certain.—Welcome, my
    friends all:
    [*Aside to* SEBASTIAN *and* ANTONIO.]
But you, my brace of lords, were I so
    minded,
I here could pluck his Highness' frown
    upon you,
And justify you traitors: at this time
I will tell no tales.
SEBASTIAN. [*Aside.*]
             The devil speaks in him.
PROSPERO.
                             No.—
For you, most wicked sir, whom to call
    brother
Would even infect my mouth, I do
    forgive
Thy rankest fault; all of them; and require
My dukedom of thee, which, perforce, I
    know
Thou must restore.
ALONSO.
               If thou beest Prospero,
Give us particulars of thy preservation;
How thou hast met us here, whom three
    hours since
Were wrack'd upon this shore; where I
    have lost,—
How sharp the point of this remembrance
    is!—
My dear son Ferdinand.
PROSPERO.
                  I am woe for't, sir.

ALONSO.
Irreparable is the loss, and patience
Says it is past her cure.
PROSPERO.
                    I rather think
You have not sought her help; of whose
    soft grace,
For the like loss I have her sovereign aid,
And rest myself content.
ALONSO.
                   You the like loss!
PROSPERO.
As great to me, as late; and, supportable
To make the dear loss, have I means much
    weaker
Than you may call to comfort you, for I
Have lost my daughter.
ALONSO.
                    A daughter?
O heavens! that they were living both in
    Naples,
The king and queen there! That they were,
    I wish
Myself were mudded in that oozy bed
Where my son lies. When did you lose
    your daughter?
PROSPERO.
In this last tempest. I perceive, these lords
At this encounter do so much admire
That they devour their reason, and scarce
    think
Their eyes do offices of truth, their words
Are natural breath; but, howsoe'er you have
Been justled from your senses, know for
    certain
That I am Prospero, and that very duke
Which was thrust forth of Milan; who most
    strangely
Upon this shore, where you were wrack'd,
    was landed
To be the lord on't. No more yet of this;
For 'tis a chronicle of day by day,
Not a relation for a breakfast nor
Befitting this first meeting. Welcome, sir:
This cell's my court: here have I few
    attendants
And subjects none abroad: pray you, look
    in.

My dukedom since you have given me
   again,
I will requite you with as good a thing;
At least bring forth a wonder, to content
   ye
As much as me my dukedom.
   [*The entrance of the cell opens, and discovers*
      FERDINAND *and* MIRANDA *playing at*
         chess.]
MIRANDA.
Sweet lord, you play me false.
FERDINAND.
                     No, my dearest love,
I would not for the world.
MIRANDA.
Yes, for a score of kingdoms you should
   wrangle,
And I would call it fair play.
ALONSO.
                        If this prove
A vision of the island, one dear son
Shall I twice lose.
SEBASTIAN.
                  A most high miracle!
FERDINAND.
Though the seas threaten, they are
   merciful:
I have curs'd them without cause.
            [*Kneels to* ALONSO.]
ALONSO.
                  Now all the blessings
Of a glad father compass thee about!
Arise, and say how thou cam'st here.
MIRANDA.
                        O, wonder!
How many goodly creatures are there here!
How beauteous mankind is! O brave new
   world
That has such people in't!
PROSPERO.
                  'Tis new to thee.
ALONSO.
What is this maid, with whom thou wast
   at play?
Your eld'st acquaintance cannot be three
   hours:
Is she the goddess that hath sever'd us,
And brought us thus together?

FERDINAND.
                     Sir, she is mortal;
But by immortal Providence she's mine.
I chose her when I could not ask my father
For his advice, nor thought I had one. She
Is daughter to this famous Duke of Milan,
Of whom so often I have heard renown,
But never saw before; of whom I have
Receiv'd a second life: and second father
This lady makes him to me.
ALONSO.
                     I am hers:
But, O! how oddly will it sound that I
Must ask my child forgiveness!
PROSPERO.
                        There, sir, stop:
Let us not burden our remembrances with
A heaviness that's gone.
GONZALO.
                  I have inly wept,
Or should have spoke ere this. Look down,
   you gods,
And on this couple drop a blessed crown;
For it is you that have chalk'd forth the way
Which brought us hither.
ALONSO.
                  I say, Amen, Gonzalo!
GONZALO.
Was Milan thrust from Milan, that his
   issue
Should become kings of Naples? O, rejoice
Beyond a common joy, and set it down
With gold on lasting pillars. In one voyage
Did Claribel her husband find at Tunis,
And Ferdinand, her brother, found a wife
Where he himself was lost; Prospero his
   dukedom
In a poor isle; and all of us ourselves,
When no man was his own.
ALONSO. [*To* FERDINAND *and* MIRANDA.]
                  Give me your hands:
Let grief and sorrow still embrace his heart
That doth not wish you joy!
GONZALO.
                     Be it so. Amen!
   [*Re-enter* ARIEL, *with the* MASTER *and*
      BOATSWAIN *amazedly following.*]
O look, sir! look, sir! Here are more of us.

I prophesied, if a gallows were on land,
This fellow could not drown.—Now, blasphemy,
That swear'st grace o'erboard, not an oath
    on shore?
Hast thou no mouth by land? What is the
    news?

BOATSWAIN.

The best news is that we have safely found
Our king and company: the next, our
    ship,—
Which but three glasses since we gave out
    split,—
Is tight and yare, and bravely rigg'd as when
We first put out to sea.

ARIEL. [*Aside to* PROSPERO.]

             Sir, all this service
Have I done since I went.

PROSPERO. [*Aside to* ARIEL.]

              My tricksy spirit!

ALONSO.

These are not natural events; they
    strengthen
From strange to stranger. Say, how came
    you hither?

BOATSWAIN.

If I did think, sir, I were well awake,
I'd strive to tell you. We were dead of sleep,
And,—how, we know not,—all clapp'd
    under hatches,
Where, but even now, with strange and
    several noises
Of roaring, shrieking, howling, jingling
    chains,
And mo diversity of sounds, all horrible,
We were awak'd; straightway, at liberty:
Where we, in all her trim, freshly beheld
Our royal, good, and gallant ship; our
    master
Cap'ring to eye her: on a trice, so please
    you,
Even in a dream, were we divided from
    them,
And were brought moping hither.

ARIEL. [*Aside to* PROSPERO.]

             Was't well done?

PROSPERO. [*Aside to* ARIEL.]

Bravely, my diligence. Thou shalt be free.

ALONSO.

This is as strange a maze as e'er men trod;
And there is in this business more than
    nature
Was ever conduct of: some oracle
Must rectify our knowledge.

PROSPERO.

              Sir, my liege,
Do not infest your mind with beating on
The strangeness of this business: at pick'd
    leisure,
Which shall be shortly, single I'll resolve
    you,—
Which to you shall seem probable—of
    every
These happen'd accidents; till when, be
    cheerful
And think of each thing well. [*Aside to*
    ARIEL.] Come hither, spirit;
Set Caliban and his companions free;
Untie the spell. [*Exit* ARIEL.] How fares
    my gracious sir?
There are yet missing of your company
Some few odd lads that you remember not.

[*Re-enter* ARIEL, *driving in* CALIBAN,
    STEPHANO, *and* TRINCULO, *in their
    stolen apparel.*]

STEPHANO.

Every man shift for all the rest, and let
no man take care for himself, for all is but
fortune.—Coragio! bully-monster, Coragio!

TRINCULO.

If these be true spies which I wear in my
head, here's a goodly sight.

CALIBAN.

O Setebos, these be brave spirits indeed.
How fine my master is! I am afraid
He will chastise me.

SEBASTIAN.

             Ha, ha!
What things are these, my lord Antonio?
Will money buy them?

ANTONIO.

            Very like; one of them
Is a plain fish, and, no doubt, marketable.

PROSPERO.

Mark but the badges of these men, my
    lords,

Then say if they be true. This mis-shapen
   knave—
His mother was a witch; and one so
   strong
That could control the moon, make flows
   and ebbs,
And deal in her command without her
   power.
These three have robb'd me; and this
   demi-devil,—
For he's a bastard one,—had plotted
   with them
To take my life: two of these fellows
   you
Must know and own; this thing of
   darkness I
Acknowledge mine.

Caliban.
                     I shall be pinch'd to death.

Alonso.
Is not this Stephano, my drunken butler?

Sebastian.
He is drunk now: where had he wine?

Alonso.
And Trinculo is reeling-ripe: where should
   they
Find this grand liquor that hath gilded
   them?
How cam'st thou in this pickle?

Trinculo.
I have been in such a pickle since I saw you
last that, I fear me, will never out of my
bones. I shall not fear fly-blowing.

Sebastian.
Why, how now, Stephano!

Stephano.
O! touch me not: I am not Stephano, but
   a cramp.

Prospero.
You'd be king o' the isle, sirrah?

Stephano.
I should have been a sore one, then.

Alonso.
This is as strange a thing as e'er I look'd on.
             [*Pointing to* Caliban.]

Prospero.
He is as disproportioned in his manners
As in his shape.—Go, sirrah, to my cell;

Take with you your companions: as you look
To have my pardon, trim it handsomely.

Caliban.
Ay, that I will; and I'll be wise hereafter,
And seek for grace. What a thrice-double
   ass
Was I, to take this drunkard for a god,
And worship this dull fool!

Prospero.
                            Go to; away!

Alonso.
Hence, and bestow your luggage where you
   found it.

Sebastian.
Or stole it, rather.
             [*Exeunt* Caliban, Stephano, *and*
                          Trinculo.]

Prospero.
Sir, I invite your Highness and your train
To my poor cell, where you shall take your
   rest
For this one night; which—part of it—I'll
   waste
With such discourse as, I not doubt, shall
   make it
Go quick away; the story of my life
And the particular accidents gone by
Since I came to this isle: and in the morn
I'll bring you to your ship, and so to Naples,
Where I have hope to see the nuptial
Of these our dear-belov'd solemnized;
And thence retire me to my Milan, where
Every third thought shall be my grave.

Alonso.
                                      I long
To hear the story of your life, which must
Take the ear strangely.

Prospero.
                        I'll deliver all;
And promise you calm seas, auspicious
   gales,
And sail so expeditious that shall catch
Your royal fleet far off. [*Aside to* Ariel.]
   My Ariel, chick,
That is thy charge: then to the elements
Be free, and fare thou well! Please you,
   draw near.
                        [*Exeunt.*]

EPILOGUE
[*Spoken by* PROSPERO.]

Now my charms are all o'erthrown,
And what strength I have's mine own;
Which is most faint; now 'tis true,
I must be here confin'd by you,
Or sent to Naples. Let me not,
Since I have my dukedom got,
And pardon'd the deceiver, dwell
In this bare island by your spell:
But release me from my bands
With the help of your good hands.
Gentle breath of yours my sails
Must fill, or else my project fails,
Which was to please. Now I want
Spirits to enforce, art to enchant;
And my ending is despair,
Unless I be reliev'd by prayer,
Which pierces so that it assaults
Mercy itself, and frees all faults.
As you from crimes would pardon'd be,
Let your indulgence set me free.

The Two Gentlemen of Verona

DRAMATIS PERSONAE

DUKE OF MILAN, *father to Silvia*
VALENTINE, *one of the two gentlemen*
PROTEUS, *one of the two gentlemen*
ANTONIO, *father to Proteus*
THURIO, *a foolish rival to Valentine*
EGLAMOUR, *agent for Silvia in her escape*
SPEED, *a clownish servant to Valentine*
LAUNCE, *the like to Proteus*
PANTHINO, *servant to Antonio*
HOST, *where Julia lodges in Milan*

OUTLAWS, *with Valentine*
JULIA, *a lady of Verona, beloved of Proteus*
SILVIA, *beloved of Valentine*
LUCETTA, *waiting-woman to Julia*
SERVANTS and MUSICIANS

SCENE: *Verona; Milan; the frontiers of Mantua.*

ACT I
SCENE I
Verona. An open place.
[*Enter* VALENTINE *and* PROTEUS.]

VALENTINE.
Cease to persuade, my loving Proteus:
Home-keeping youth have ever homely wits.
Were't not affection chains thy tender days
To the sweet glances of thy honour'd love,
I rather would entreat thy company
To see the wonders of the world abroad,
Than, living dully sluggardiz'd at home,
Wear out thy youth with shapeless idleness.
But since thou lov'st, love still, and thrive therein,
Even as I would, when I to love begin.

PROTEUS.
Wilt thou be gone? Sweet Valentine, adieu!
Think on thy Proteus, when thou haply seest
Some rare noteworthy object in thy travel:
Wish me partaker in thy happiness
When thou dost meet good hap; and in thy danger,

If ever danger do environ thee,
Commend thy grievance to my holy prayers,
For I will be thy headsman, Valentine.

VALENTINE.
And on a love-book pray for my success?

PROTEUS.
Upon some book I love I'll pray for thee.

VALENTINE.
That's on some shallow story of deep love,
How young Leander cross'd the Hellespont.

PROTEUS.
That's a deep story of a deeper love;
For he was more than over shoes in love.

VALENTINE.
'Tis true; for you are over boots in love,
And yet you never swum the Hellespont.

PROTEUS.
Over the boots? Nay, give me not the boots.

VALENTINE.
No, I will not, for it boots thee not.

PROTEUS.
                              What?

VALENTINE.
To be in love, where scorn is bought with
    groans;
Coy looks with heart-sore sighs; one
    fading moment's mirth
With twenty watchful, weary, tedious
    nights:
If haply won, perhaps a hapless gain;
If lost, why then a grievous labour won:
However, but a folly bought with wit,
Or else a wit by folly vanquished.

PROTEUS.
So, by your circumstance, you call me fool.

VALENTINE.
So, by your circumstance, I fear you'll
    prove.

PROTEUS.
'Tis love you cavil at: I am not Love.

VALENTINE.
Love is your master, for he masters you;
And he that is so yoked by a fool,
Methinks, should not be chronicled for
    wise.

PROTEUS.
Yet writers say, as in the sweetest bud
The eating canker dwells, so eating love
Inhabits in the finest wits of all.

VALENTINE.
And writers say, as the most forward bud
Is eaten by the canker ere it blow,
Even so by love the young and tender wit
Is turned to folly; blasting in the bud,
Losing his verdure even in the prime,
And all the fair effects of future hopes.
But wherefore waste I time to counsel thee
That art a votary to fond desire?
Once more adieu! my father at the road
Expects my coming, there to see me
    shipp'd.

PROTEUS.
And thither will I bring thee, Valentine.

VALENTINE.
Sweet Proteus, no; now let us take our
    leave.
To Milan let me hear from thee by letters
Of thy success in love, and what news else
Betideth here in absence of thy friend;
And I likewise will visit thee with mine.

PROTEUS.
All happiness bechance to thee in Milan!

VALENTINE.
As much to you at home! and so farewell!
                                    [Exit.]

PROTEUS.
He after honour hunts, I after love;
He leaves his friends to dignify them
    more:
I leave myself, my friends, and all for love.
Thou, Julia, thou hast metamorphos'd
    me;—
Made me neglect my studies, lose my
    time,
War with good counsel, set the world at
    nought;
Made wit with musing weak, heart sick
    with thought.
                        [Enter SPEED.]

SPEED.
Sir Proteus, save you! Saw you my master?

PROTEUS.
But now he parted hence to embark for
    Milan.

SPEED.
Twenty to one then he is shipp'd already,
And I have play'd the sheep in losing him.

PROTEUS.
Indeed a sheep doth very often stray,
An if the shepherd be a while away.

SPEED.
You conclude that my master is a shepherd
    then, and I a sheep?

PROTEUS.
I do.

SPEED.
Why then, my horns are his horns,
    whether I wake or sleep.

PROTEUS.
A silly answer, and fitting well a sheep.

SPEED.
This proves me still a sheep.

PROTEUS.
True; and thy master a shepherd.

SPEED.
Nay, that I can deny by a circumstance.

PROTEUS.
It shall go hard but I'll prove it by another.

Speed.
The shepherd seeks the sheep, and not the sheep the shepherd; but I seek my master, and my master seeks not me; therefore, I am no sheep.

Proteus.
The sheep for fodder follow the shepherd; the shepherd for food follows not the sheep: thou for wages followest thy master; thy master for wages follows not thee. Therefore, thou art a sheep.

Speed.
Such another proof will make me cry "baa."

Proteus.
But, dost thou hear? gavest thou my letter to Julia?

Speed.
Ay, sir; I, a lost mutton, gave your letter to her, a laced mutton; and she, a laced mutton, gave me, a lost mutton, nothing for my labour.

Proteus.
Here's too small a pasture for such store of muttons.

Speed.
If the ground be overcharged, you were best stick her.

Proteus.
Nay, in that you are astray: 'twere best pound you.

Speed.
Nay, sir, less than a pound shall serve me for carrying your letter.

Proteus.
You mistake; I mean the pound,—a pinfold.

Speed.
From a pound to a pin? fold it over and over,
'Tis threefold too little for carrying a letter to your lover.

Proteus.
But what said she? [Speed *nods.*] Did she nod?

Speed.
Ay.

Proteus.
Nod, ay? Why, that's noddy.

Speed.
You mistook, sir; I say she did nod; and you ask me if she did nod; and I say, Ay.

Proteus.
And that set together is—noddy.

Speed.
Now you have taken the pains to set it together, take it for your pains.

Proteus.
No, no; you shall have it for bearing the letter.

Speed.
Well, I perceive I must be fain to bear with you.

Proteus.
Why, sir, how do you bear with me?

Speed.
Marry, sir, the letter, very orderly; having nothing but the word "noddy" for my pains.

Proteus.
Beshrew me, but you have a quick wit.

Speed.
And yet it cannot overtake your slow purse.

Proteus.
Come, come; open the matter; in brief: what said she?

Speed.
Open your purse, that the money and the matter may be both at once delivered.

Proteus.
Well, sir, here is for your pains. [*Giving him money.*] What said she?

Speed.
Truly, sir, I think you'll hardly win her.

Proteus.
Why, couldst thou perceive so much from her?

Speed.
Sir, I could perceive nothing at all from her; no, not so much as a ducat for delivering your letter; and being so hard to me that brought your mind, I fear she'll prove as hard to you in telling your mind. Give her no token but stones, for she's as hard as steel.

Proteus.
What! said she nothing?

SPEED.

No, not so much as "Take this for thy pains." To testify your bounty, I thank you, you have testerned me; in requital whereof, henceforth carry your letters yourself; and so, sir, I'll commend you to my master.

PROTEUS.

Go, go, be gone, to save your ship from wrack;

Which cannot perish, having thee aboard,

Being destin'd to a drier death on shore.—

[*Exit* SPEED.]

I must go send some better messenger.

I fear my Julia would not deign my lines,

Receiving them from such a worthless post.

[*Exit.*]

SCENE II

The same. The garden of Julia's house.
[*Enter* JULIA *and* LUCETTA.]

JULIA.

But say, Lucetta, now we are alone,

Wouldst thou then counsel me to fall in love?

LUCETTA.

Ay, madam; so you stumble not unheedfully.

JULIA.

Of all the fair resort of gentlemen

That every day with parle encounter me,

In thy opinion which is worthiest love?

LUCETTA.

Please you, repeat their names; I'll show my mind

According to my shallow simple skill.

JULIA.

What think'st thou of the fair Sir Eglamour?

LUCETTA.

As of a knight well-spoken, neat, and fine;

But, were I you, he never should be mine.

JULIA.

What think'st thou of the rich Mercatio?

LUCETTA.

Well of his wealth; but of himself, so so.

JULIA.

What think'st thou of the gentle Proteus?

LUCETTA.

Lord, Lord! to see what folly reigns in us!

JULIA.

How now! what means this passion at his name?

LUCETTA.

Pardon, dear madam; 'tis a passing shame

That I, unworthy body as I am,

Should censure thus on lovely gentlemen.

JULIA.

Why not on Proteus, as of all the rest?

LUCETTA.

Then thus,—of many good I think him best.

JULIA.

Your reason?

LUCETTA.

I have no other but a woman's reason:

I think him so, because I think him so.

JULIA.

And wouldst thou have me cast my love on him?

LUCETTA.

Ay, if you thought your love not cast away.

JULIA.

Why, he, of all the rest, hath never moved me.

LUCETTA.

Yet he, of all the rest, I think, best loves ye.

JULIA.

His little speaking shows his love but small.

LUCETTA.

Fire that's closest kept burns most of all.

JULIA.

They do not love that do not show their love.

LUCETTA.

O! they love least that let men know their love.

JULIA.

I would I knew his mind.

LUCETTA.

Peruse this paper, madam. [*Gives a letter.*]

JULIA.

"To Julia"—Say, from whom?

LUCETTA.

That the contents will show.

JULIA.

Say, say, who gave it thee?

Lucetta.
Sir Valentine's page, and sent, I think,
    from Proteus.
He would have given it you; but I, being
    in the way,
Did in your name receive it; pardon the
    fault, I pray.
Julia.
Now, by my modesty, a goodly broker!
Dare you presume to harbour wanton
    lines?
To whisper and conspire against my youth?
Now, trust me, 'tis an office of great worth,
And you an officer fit for the place.
There, take the paper; see it be return'd;
Or else return no more into my sight.
Lucetta.
To plead for love deserves more fee than
    hate.
Julia.
Will ye be gone?
Lucetta.
           That you may ruminate.
               [*Exit.*]
Julia.
And yet, I would I had o'erlook'd the letter.
It were a shame to call her back again,
And pray her to a fault for which I chid
    her.
What fool is she, that knows I am a maid
And would not force the letter to my view!
Since maids, in modesty, say "No" to that
Which they would have the profferer
    construe "Ay."
Fie, fie, how wayward is this foolish love,
That like a testy babe will scratch the
    nurse,
And presently, all humbled, kiss the rod!
How churlishly I chid Lucetta hence,
When willingly I would have had her
    here:
How angerly I taught my brow to frown,
When inward joy enforc'd my heart to
    smile.
My penance is, to call Lucetta back
And ask remission for my folly past.
What ho! Lucetta!
         [*Re-enter* Lucetta.]

Lucetta.
           What would your ladyship?
Julia.
Is it near dinner time?
Lucetta.
                I would it were;
That you might kill your stomach on your
    meat
And not upon your maid.
Julia.
What is't that you took up so gingerly?
Lucetta.
Nothing.
Julia.
Why didst thou stoop, then?
Lucetta.
To take a paper up that I let fall.
Julia.
And is that paper nothing?
Lucetta.
Nothing concerning me.
Julia.
Then let it lie for those that it concerns.
Lucetta.
Madam, it will not lie where it concerns,
Unless it have a false interpreter.
Julia.
Some love of yours hath writ to you in rime.
Lucetta.
That I might sing it, madam, to a tune:
Give me a note: your ladyship can set.
Julia.
As little by such toys as may be possible;
Best sing it to the tune of "Light o' Love."
Lucetta.
It is too heavy for so light a tune.
Julia.
Heavy! belike it hath some burden then?
Lucetta.
Ay; and melodious were it, would you
    sing it.
Julia.
And why not you?
Lucetta.
I cannot reach so high.
Julia.
Let's see your song. [*Taking the letter.*]
    How now, minion!

LUCETTA.
Keep tune there still, so you will sing it
   out:
And yet methinks, I do not like this tune.
JULIA.
You do not?
LUCETTA.
No, madam; it is too sharp.
JULIA.
You, minion, are too saucy.
LUCETTA.
Nay, now you are too flat
And mar the concord with too harsh a
   descant;
There wanteth but a mean to fill your song.
JULIA.
The mean is drown'd with your unruly
   bass.
LUCETTA.
Indeed, I bid the base for Proteus.
JULIA.
This babble shall not henceforth trouble
   me.
Here is a coil with protestation!—[*Tears
   the letter.*]
Go, get you gone; and let the papers lie:
You would be fingering them, to anger me.
LUCETTA.
She makes it strange; but she would be
   best pleas'd
To be so anger'd with another letter.
            [*Exit.*]
JULIA.
Nay, would I were so anger'd with the
   same!
O hateful hands, to tear such loving
   words!
Injurious wasps, to feed on such sweet
   honey
And kill the bees that yield it with your
   stings!
I'll kiss each several paper for amends.
Look, here is writ "kind Julia." Unkind
   Julia!
As in revenge of thy ingratitude,
I throw thy name against the bruising
   stones,
Trampling contemptuously on thy disdain.

And here is writ "love-wounded Proteus":
Poor wounded name! my bosom, as a bed,
Shall lodge thee till thy wound be
   throughly heal'd;
And thus I search it with a sovereign kiss.
But twice or thrice was "Proteus" written
   down:
Be calm, good wind, blow not a word away
Till I have found each letter in the letter
Except mine own name; that some
   whirlwind bear
Unto a ragged, fearful-hanging rock,
And throw it thence into the raging sea!
Lo, here in one line is his name twice writ:
"Poor forlorn Proteus, passionate Proteus,
To the sweet Julia":—that I'll tear away;
And yet I will not, sith so prettily
He couples it to his complaining names:
Thus will I fold them one upon another:
Now kiss, embrace, contend, do what you
   will.
        [*Re-enter* LUCETTA.]
LUCETTA.
Madam,
Dinner is ready, and your father stays.
JULIA.
Well, let us go.
LUCETTA.
What! shall these papers lie like tell-tales
   here?
JULIA.
If you respect them, best to take them up.
LUCETTA.
Nay, I was taken up for laying them down;
Yet here they shall not lie, for catching
   cold.
JULIA.
I see you have a month's mind to them.
LUCETTA.
Ay, madam, you may say what sights you
   see;
I see things too, although you judge I
   wink.
JULIA.
Come, come; will't please you go?
           [*Exeunt.*]

SCENE III

The same. A room in Antonio's house.
[*Enter* ANTONIO *and* PANTHINO.]

ANTONIO.
Tell me, Panthino, what sad talk was that
Wherewith my brother held you in the
   cloister?

PANTHINO.
'Twas of his nephew Proteus, your son.

ANTONIO.
Why, what of him?

PANTHINO.
       He wonder'd that your lordship
Would suffer him to spend his youth at
   home,
While other men, of slender reputation,
Put forth their sons to seek preferment
   out:
Some to the wars, to try their fortune
   there;
Some to discover islands far away;
Some to the studious universities.
For any, or for all these exercises,
He said that Proteus, your son, was meet;
And did request me to importune you
To let him spend his time no more at
   home,
Which would be great impeachment to
   his age,
In having known no travel in his youth.

ANTONIO.
Nor need'st thou much importune me to
   that
Whereon this month I have been
   hammering.
I have consider'd well his loss of time,
And how he cannot be a perfect man,
Not being tried and tutor'd in the world:
Experience is by industry achiev'd,
And perfected by the swift course of time.
Then tell me whither were I best to send
   him?

PANTHINO.
I think your lordship is not ignorant
How his companion, youthful Valentine,
Attends the emperor in his royal court.

ANTONIO.
I know it well.

PANTHINO.
'Twere good, I think, your lordship sent
   him thither:
There shall he practise tilts and
   tournaments,
Hear sweet discourse, converse with
   noblemen,
And be in eye of every exercise
Worthy his youth and nobleness of birth.

ANTONIO.
I like thy counsel; well hast thou advis'd;
And that thou mayst perceive how well I
   like it,
The execution of it shall make known:
Even with the speediest expedition
I will dispatch him to the emperor's
   court.

PANTHINO.
To-morrow, may it please you, Don
   Alphonso
With other gentlemen of good esteem
Are journeying to salute the emperor
And to commend their service to his will.

ANTONIO.
Good company; with them shall Proteus
   go.
And in good time:—now will we break
   with him.
           [*Enter* PROTEUS.]

PROTEUS.
Sweet love! sweet lines! sweet life!
Here is her hand, the agent of her heart;
Here is her oath for love, her honour's
   pawn.
O! that our fathers would applaud our
   loves,
To seal our happiness with their consents!
O heavenly Julia!

ANTONIO.
How now! What letter are you reading
   there?

PROTEUS.
May't please your lordship, 'tis a word or
   two
Of commendations sent from Valentine,
Deliver'd by a friend that came from him.

ANTONIO.
Lend me the letter; let me see what news.

PROTEUS.
There is no news, my lord; but that he
    writes
How happily he lives, how well belov'd
And daily graced by the emperor;
Wishing me with him, partner of his
    fortune.
ANTONIO.
And how stand you affected to his wish?
PROTEUS.
As one relying on your lordship's will,
And not depending on his friendly wish.
ANTONIO.
My will is something sorted with his wish.
Muse not that I thus suddenly proceed;
For what I will, I will, and there an end.
I am resolv'd that thou shalt spend some
    time
With Valentinus in the emperor's court:
What maintenance he from his friends
    receives,
Like exhibition thou shalt have from me.
To-morrow be in readiness to go:
Excuse it not, for I am peremptory.
PROTEUS.
My lord, I cannot be so soon provided;
Please you, deliberate a day or two.
ANTONIO.
Look, what thou want'st shall be sent after
    thee:
No more of stay; to-morrow thou must go.
Come on, Panthino: you shall be employ'd
To hasten on his expedition.
        [*Exeunt* ANTONIO *and* PANTHINO.]
PROTEUS.
Thus have I shunn'd the fire for fear of
    burning,
And drench'd me in the sea, where I am
    drown'd.
I fear'd to show my father Julia's letter,
Lest he should take exceptions to my love;
And with the vantage of mine own excuse
Hath he excepted most against my love.
O! how this spring of love resembleth
The uncertain glory of an April day,
Which now shows all the beauty of the sun,
And by an by a cloud takes all away!
        [*Re-enter* PANTHINO.]

PANTHINO.
Sir Proteus, your father calls for you;
He is in haste; therefore, I pray you, go.
PROTEUS.
Why, this it is: my heart accords thereto,
And yet a thousand times it answers "no."
        [*Exeunt.*]

ACT II
SCENE I
Milan. A room in the duke's palace.
[*Enter* VALENTINE *and* SPEED.]
SPEED.
Sir, your glove. [*Offering a glove.*]
VALENTINE.
                Not mine; my gloves are
    on.
SPEED.
Why, then, this may be yours; for this is
    but one.
VALENTINE.
Ha! let me see; ay, give it me, it's mine;
Sweet ornament that decks a thing divine!
Ah, Silvia! Silvia!
SPEED. [*Calling.*]
Madam Silvia! Madam Silvia!
VALENTINE.
How now, sirrah?
SPEED.
She is not within hearing, sir.
VALENTINE.
Why, sir, who bade you call her?
SPEED.
Your worship, sir; or else I mistook.
VALENTINE.
Well, you'll still be too forward.
SPEED.
And yet I was last chidden for being too
slow.
VALENTINE.
Go to, sir. tell me, do you know Madam
    Silvia?
SPEED.
She that your worship loves?
VALENTINE.
Why, how know you that I am in love?
SPEED.
Marry, by these special marks: first, you

have learned, like Sir Proteus, to wreath your arms like a malcontent; to relish a love-song, like a robin redbreast; to walk alone, like one that had the pestilence; to sigh, like a school-boy that had lost his A B C; to weep, like a young wench that had buried her grandam; to fast, like one that takes diet; to watch, like one that fears robbing; to speak puling, like a beggar at Hallowmas. You were wont, when you laughed, to crow like a cock; when you walked, to walk like one of the lions; when you fasted, it was presently after dinner; when you looked sadly, it was for want of money. And now you are metamorphosed with a mistress, that, when I look on you, I can hardly think you my master.

Valentine.
Are all these things perceived in me?

Speed.
They are all perceived without ye.

Valentine.
Without me? They cannot.

Speed.
Without you? Nay, that's certain; for, without you were so simple, none else would; but you are so without these follies that these follies are within you, and shine through you like the water in an urinal, that not an eye that sees you but is a physician to comment on your malady.

Valentine.
But tell me, dost thou know my lady Silvia?

Speed.
She that you gaze on so as she sits at supper?

Valentine.
Hast thou observed that? Even she, I mean.

Speed.
Why, sir, I know her not.

Valentine.
Dost thou know her by my gazing on her, and yet know'st her not?

Speed.
Is she not hard-favoured, sir?

Valentine.
Not so fair, boy, as well-favoured.

Speed.
Sir, I know that well enough.

Valentine.
What dost thou know?

Speed.
That she is not so fair as, of you, well-favoured.

Valentine.
I mean that her beauty is exquisite, but her favour infinite.

Speed.
That's because the one is painted, and the other out of all count.

Valentine.
How painted? and how out of count?

Speed.
Marry, sir, so painted to make her fair, that no man counts of her beauty.

Valentine.
How esteem'st thou me? I account of her beauty.

Speed.
You never saw her since she was deformed.

Valentine.
How long hath she been deformed?

Speed.
Ever since you loved her.

Valentine.
I have loved her ever since I saw her, and still I see her beautiful.

Speed.
If you love her, you cannot see her.

Valentine.
Why?

Speed.
Because Love is blind. O! that you had mine eyes; or your own eyes had the lights they were wont to have when you chid at Sir Proteus for going ungartered!

Valentine.
What should I see then?

Speed.
Your own present folly and her passing deformity; for he, being in love, could not see to garter his hose; and you, being in love, cannot see to put on your hose.

Valentine.
Belike, boy, then you are in love; for last

morning you could not see to wipe my shoes.

SPEED.
True, sir; I was in love with my bed. I thank you, you swinged me for my love, which makes me the bolder to chide you for yours.

VALENTINE.
In conclusion, I stand affected to her.

SPEED.
I would you were set, so your affection would cease.

VALENTINE.
Last night she enjoined me to write some lines to one she loves.

SPEED.
And have you?

VALENTINE.
I have.

SPEED.
Are they not lamely writ?

VALENTINE.
No, boy, but as well as I can do them. Peace! here she comes.

[*Enter* SILVIA.]

SPEED. [*Aside.*]
O excellent motion! O exceeding puppet! Now will he interpret to her.

VALENTINE.
Madam and mistress, a thousand good morrows.

SPEED. [*Aside.*]
O, give ye good even: here's a million of manners.

SILVIA.
Sir Valentine and servant, to you two thousand.

SPEED. [*Aside.*]
He should give her interest, and she gives it him.

VALENTINE.
As you enjoin'd me, I have writ your letter Unto the secret nameless friend of yours; Which I was much unwilling to proceed in, But for my duty to your ladyship.

[*Gives a letter.*]

SILVIA.
I thank you, gentle servant. 'Tis very clerkly done.

VALENTINE.
Now trust me, madam, it came hardly off; For, being ignorant to whom it goes, I writ at random, very doubtfully.

SILVIA.
Perchance you think too much of so much pains?

VALENTINE.
No, madam; so it stead you, I will write, Please you command, a thousand times as much; And yet—

SILVIA.
A pretty period! Well, I guess the sequel; And yet I will not name it; and yet I care not. And yet take this again; and yet I thank you, Meaning henceforth to trouble you no more.

SPEED. [*Aside.*]
And yet you will; and yet another yet.

VALENTINE.
What means your ladyship? Do you not like it?

SILVIA.
Yes, yes; the lines are very quaintly writ; But, since unwillingly, take them again: Nay, take them.

[*Gives back the letter.*]

VALENTINE.
Madam, they are for you.

SILVIA.
Ay, ay, you writ them, sir, at my request; But I will none of them; they are for you. I would have had them writ more movingly.

VALENTINE.
Please you, I'll write your ladyship another.

SILVIA.
And when it's writ, for my sake read it over; And if it please you, so; if not, why, so.

VALENTINE.
If it please me, madam, what then?

SILVIA.
Why, if it please you, take it for your labour. And so good morrow, servant.

[*Exit.*]

Speed.
O jest unseen, inscrutable, invisible,
As a nose on a man's face, or a
    weathercock on a steeple!
My master sues to her; and she hath
    taught her suitor,
He being her pupil, to become her
    tutor.
O excellent device! Was there ever
    heard a better,
That my master, being scribe, to himself
    should write the letter?

Valentine.
How now, sir! What are you reasoning
    with yourself?

Speed.
Nay, I was rhyming: 'tis you that have
    the reason.

Valentine.
To do what?

Speed.
To be a spokesman from Madam Silvia.

Valentine.
To whom?

Speed.
To yourself; why, she woos you by a
    figure.

Valentine.
What figure?

Speed.
By a letter, I should say.

Valentine.
Why, she hath not writ to me?

Speed.
What need she, when she hath made you
    write to yourself?
Why, do you not perceive the jest?

Valentine.
No, believe me.

Speed.
No believing you indeed, sir. But did you
    perceive her earnest?

Valentine.
She gave me none except an angry word.

Speed.
Why, she hath given you a letter.

Valentine.
That's the letter I writ to her friend.

Speed.
And that letter hath she delivered, and
    there an end.

Valentine.
I would it were no worse.

Speed.
I'll warrant you 'tis as well.
For often have you writ to her; and she,
    in modesty,
Or else for want of idle time, could not
    again reply;
Or fearing else some messenger that
    might her mind discover,
Herself hath taught her love himself to
    write unto her lover.
All this I speak in print, for in print I
    found it.
Why muse you, sir? 'Tis dinner time.

Valentine.
I have dined.

Speed.
Ay, but hearken, sir; though the chameleon
Love can feed on the air, I am one that am
nourished by my victuals, and would fain
have meat. O! be not like your mistress! Be
moved, be moved.
                              [*Exeunt.*]

SCENE II
Verona. A room in Julia's house.
[*Enter* Proteus *and* Julia.]

Proteus.
Have patience, gentle Julia.

Julia.
I must, where is no remedy.

Proteus.
When possibly I can, I will return.

Julia.
If you turn not, you will return the sooner.
Keep this remembrance for thy Julia's
    sake.
                    [*Gives him a ring.*]

Proteus.
Why, then, we'll make exchange. Here,
    take you this.
                    [*Gives her another.*]

Julia.
And seal the bargain with a holy kiss.

PROTEUS.
Here is my hand for my true constancy;
And when that hour o'erslips me in the
    day
Wherein I sigh not, Julia, for thy sake,
The next ensuing hour some foul
    mischance
Torment me for my love's forgetfulness!
My father stays my coming; answer not;
The tide is now: nay, not thy tide of tears:
That tide will stay me longer than I
    should.
Julia, farewell!
                [*Exit* JULIA.]
            What, gone without a word?
Ay, so true love should do: it cannot speak;
For truth hath better deeds than words to
    grace it.
                [*Enter* PANTHINO.]
PANTHINO.
Sir Proteus, you are stay'd for.
PROTEUS.
Go; I come, I come.
Alas! this parting strikes poor lovers dumb.
                [*Exeunt.*]

SCENE III
The same. A street.
[*Enter* LAUNCE, *leading a dog.*]
LAUNCE.
Nay, 'twill be this hour ere I have done
weeping; all the kind of the Launces
have this very fault. I have received my
proportion, like the prodigious son, and
am going with Sir Proteus to the imperial's
court. I think Crab my dog be the sourest-
natured dog that lives: my mother weeping,
my father wailing, my sister crying, our
maid howling, our cat wringing her hands,
and all our house in a great perplexity; yet
did not this cruel-hearted cur shed one
tear. He is a stone, a very pebble stone,
and has no more pity in him than a dog;
a Jew would have wept to have seen our
parting; why, my grandam having no eyes,
look you, wept herself blind at my parting.
Nay, I'll show you the manner of it. This
shoe is my father; no, this left shoe is my

father; no, no, left shoe is my mother; nay,
that cannot be so neither; yes, it is so, it is
so, it hath the worser sole. This shoe with
the hole in it is my mother, and this my
father. A vengeance on 't! There 'tis: now, sir,
this staff is my sister, for, look you, she is
as white as a lily and as small as a wand;
this hat is Nan our maid; I am the dog; no,
the dog is himself, and I am the dog—O!
the dog is me, and I am myself; ay, so, so.
Now come I to my father: "Father, your
blessing." Now should not the shoe speak
a word for weeping; now should I kiss my
father; well, he weeps on. Now come I to
my mother;—O, that she could speak now
like a wood woman! Well, I kiss her; why
there 'tis; here's my mother's breath up
and down. Now come I to my sister; mark
the moan she makes. Now the dog all this
while sheds not a tear, nor speaks a word;
but see how I lay the dust with my tears.
                [*Enter* PANTHINO.]
PANTHINO.
Launce, away, away, aboard! Thy master is
shipped, and thou art to post after with
oars. What's the matter? Why weep'st thou,
man? Away, ass! You'll lose the tide if you
tarry any longer.
LAUNCE.
It is no matter if the tied were lost; for it is
the unkindest tied that ever any man tied.
PANTHINO.
What's the unkindest tide?
LAUNCE.
Why, he that's tied here, Crab, my dog.
PANTHINO.
Tut, man, I mean thou'lt lose the flood, and,
in losing the flood, lose thy voyage, and, in
losing thy voyage, lose thy master, and, in
losing thy master, lose thy service, and, in
losing thy service,—Why dost thou stop
my mouth?
LAUNCE.
For fear thou shouldst lose thy tongue.
PANTHINO.
Where should I lose my tongue?
LAUNCE.
In thy tale.

PANTHINO.
In thy tail!

LAUNCE.
Lose the tide, and the voyage, and the master, and the service, and the tied! Why, man, if the river were dry, I am able to fill it with my tears; if the wind were down, I could drive the boat with my sighs.

PANTHINO.
Come, come away, man; I was sent to call thee.

LAUNCE.
Sir, call me what thou darest.

PANTHINO.
Will thou go?

LAUNCE.
Well, I will go.

[Exeunt.]

SCENE IV

Milan. A room in the duke's palace.
[Enter SILVIA, VALENTINE, THURIO, and SPEED.]

SILVIA.
Servant!

VALENTINE.
Mistress?

SPEED.
Master, Sir Thurio frowns on you.

VALENTINE.
Ay, boy, it's for love.

SPEED.
Not of you.

VALENTINE.
Of my mistress, then.

SPEED.
'Twere good you knock'd him.

SILVIA.
Servant, you are sad.

VALENTINE.
Indeed, madam, I seem so.

THURIO.
Seem you that you are not?

VALENTINE.
Haply I do.

THURIO.
So do counterfeits.

VALENTINE.
So do you.

THURIO.
What seem I that I am not?

VALENTINE.
Wise.

THURIO.
What instance of the contrary?

VALENTINE.
Your folly.

THURIO.
And how quote you my folly?

VALENTINE.
I quote it in your jerkin.

THURIO.
My jerkin is a doublet.

VALENTINE.
Well, then, I'll double your folly.

THURIO.
How?

SILVIA.
What, angry, Sir Thurio! Do you change colour?

VALENTINE.
Give him leave, madam; he is a kind of chameleon.

THURIO.
That hath more mind to feed on your blood than live in your air.

VALENTINE.
You have said, sir.

THURIO.
Ay, sir, and done too, for this time.

VALENTINE.
I know it well, sir; you always end ere you begin.

SILVIA.
A fine volley of words, gentlemen, and quickly shot off.

VALENTINE.
'Tis indeed, madam; we thank the giver.

SILVIA.
Who is that, servant?

VALENTINE.
Yourself, sweet lady; for you gave the fire. Sir Thurio borrows his wit from your ladyship's looks, and spends what he borrows kindly in your company.

THURIO.
Sir, if you spend word for word with me, I
shall make your wit bankrupt.

VALENTINE.
I know it well, sir; you have an exchequer
of words, and, I think, no other treasure to
give your followers; for it appears by their
bare liveries that they live by your bare
words.

SILVIA.
No more, gentlemen, no more. Here comes
my father.

[*Enter the* DUKE.]

DUKE.
Now, daughter Silvia, you are hard beset.
Sir Valentine, your father is in good health.
What say you to a letter from your friends
Of much good news?

VALENTINE.
            My lord, I will be thankful
To any happy messenger from thence.

DUKE.
Know ye Don Antonio, your countryman?

VALENTINE.
Ay, my good lord, I know the gentleman
To be of worth and worthy estimation,
And not without desert so well reputed.

DUKE.
Hath he not a son?

VALENTINE.
Ay, my good lord; a son that well deserves
The honour and regard of such a father.

DUKE.
You know him well?

VALENTINE.
I knew him as myself; for from our infancy
We have convers'd and spent our hours
together;
And though myself have been an idle
truant,
Omitting the sweet benefit of time
To clothe mine age with angel-like
perfection,
Yet hath Sir Proteus,—for that's his
name,—
Made use and fair advantage of his days:
His years but young, but his experience
old;

His head unmellowed, but his judgment
ripe;
And, in a word,—for far behind his worth
Comes all the praises that I now bestow,—
He is complete in feature and in mind,
With all good grace to grace a gentleman.

DUKE.
Beshrew me, sir, but if he make this good,
He is as worthy for an empress' love
As meet to be an emperor's counsellor.
Well, sir, this gentleman is come to me
With commendation from great
potentates,
And here he means to spend his time
awhile.
I think 'tis no unwelcome news to you.

VALENTINE.
Should I have wish'd a thing, it had been
he.

DUKE.
Welcome him, then, according to his
worth.
Silvia, I speak to you, and you, Sir
Thurio:—
For Valentine, I need not cite him to it.
I will send him hither to you presently.
[*Exit.*]

VALENTINE.
This is the gentleman I told your ladyship
Had come along with me but that his
mistress
Did hold his eyes lock'd in her crystal
looks.

SILVIA.
Belike that now she hath enfranchis'd
them
Upon some other pawn for fealty.

VALENTINE.
Nay, sure, I think she holds them prisoners
still.

SILVIA.
Nay, then, he should be blind; and, being
blind,
How could he see his way to seek out you?

VALENTINE.
Why, lady, Love hath twenty pair of eyes.

THURIO.
They say that Love hath not an eye at all.

Valentine.
To see such lovers, Thurio, as yourself:
Upon a homely object Love can wink.
Silvia.
Have done, have done; here comes the
    gentleman.
            [*Enter* Proteus.]
Valentine.
Welcome, dear Proteus! Mistress, I
    beseech you
Confirm his welcome with some special
    favour.
Silvia.
His worth is warrant for his welcome
    hither,
If this be he you oft have wish'd to hear
    from.
Valentine.
Mistress, it is; sweet lady, entertain him
To be my fellow-servant to your ladyship.
Silvia.
Too low a mistress for so high a servant.
Proteus.
Not so, sweet lady; but too mean a servant
To have a look of such a worthy mistress.
Valentine.
Leave off discourse of disability;
Sweet lady, entertain him for your servant.
Proteus.
My duty will I boast of, nothing else.
Silvia.
And duty never yet did want his meed.
Servant, you are welcome to a worthless
    mistress.
Proteus.
I'll die on him that says so but yourself.
Silvia.
That you are welcome?
Proteus.
            That you are worthless.
            [*Enter a* Servant.]
Servant.
Madam, my lord your father would speak
    with you.
Silvia.
I wait upon his pleasure.
            [*Exit* Servant.]
            Come, Sir Thurio,

Go with me. Once more, new servant,
    welcome.
I'll leave you to confer of home affairs;
When you have done we look to hear
    from you.
Proteus.
We'll both attend upon your ladyship.
            [*Exeunt* Silvia, Thurio, *and* Speed.]
Valentine.
Now, tell me, how do all from whence you
    came?
Proteus.
Your friends are well, and have them much
    commended.
Valentine.
And how do yours?
Proteus.
I left them all in health.
Valentine.
How does your lady, and how thrives your
    love?
Proteus.
My tales of love were wont to weary you; I
    know you joy not in a love-discourse.
Valentine.
Ay, Proteus, but that life is alter'd now;
I have done penance for contemning Love;
Whose high imperious thoughts have
    punish'd me
With bitter fasts, with penitential groans,
With nightly tears, and daily heart-sore
    sighs;
For, in revenge of my contempt of love,
Love hath chas'd sleep from my enthralled
    eyes
And made them watchers of mine own
    heart's sorrow.
O, gentle Proteus! Love's a mighty lord,
And hath so humbled me as I confess,
There is no woe to his correction,
Nor to his service no such joy on earth.
Now no discourse, except it be of love;
Now can I break my fast, dine, sup, and
    sleep,
Upon the very naked name of love.
Proteus.
Enough; I read your fortune in your eye.
Was this the idol that you worship so?

Valentine.
Even she; and is she not a heavenly saint?
Proteus.
No; but she is an earthly paragon.
Valentine.
Call her divine.
Proteus.
     I will not flatter her.
Valentine.
O! flatter me; for love delights in praises.
Proteus.
When I was sick you gave me bitter pills,
And I must minister the like to you.
Valentine.
Then speak the truth by her; if not divine,
Yet let her be a principality,
Sovereign to all the creatures on the earth.
Proteus.
Except my mistress.
Valentine.
     Sweet, except not any,
Except thou wilt except against my love.
Proteus.
Have I not reason to prefer mine own?
Valentine.
And I will help thee to prefer her too:
She shall be dignified with this high
  honour,—
To bear my lady's train, lest the base earth
Should from her vesture chance to steal
  a kiss,
And, of so great a favour growing proud,
Disdain to root the summer-swelling
  flower
And make rough winter everlastingly.
Proteus.
Why, Valentine, what braggardism is this?
Valentine.
Pardon me, Proteus; all I can is nothing
To her, whose worth makes other worthies
  nothing;
She is alone.
Proteus.
    Then, let her alone.
Valentine.
Not for the world: why, man, she is mine
  own;
And I as rich in having such a jewel

As twenty seas, if all their sand were pearl,
The water nectar, and the rocks pure gold.
Forgive me that I do not dream on thee,
Because thou see'st me dote upon my love.
My foolish rival, that her father likes
Only for his possessions are so huge,
Is gone with her along; and I must after,
For love, thou know'st, is full of jealousy.
Proteus.
But she loves you?
Valentine.
Ay, and we are betroth'd; nay more, our
  marriage-hour,
With all the cunning manner of our flight,
Determin'd of: how I must climb her
  window,
The ladder made of cords, and all the
  means
Plotted and 'greed on for my happiness.
Good Proteus, go with me to my chamber,
In these affairs to aid me with thy counsel.
Proteus.
Go on before; I shall enquire you forth:
I must unto the road to disembark
Some necessaries that I needs must use;
And then I'll presently attend you.
Valentine.
Will you make haste?
Proteus.
I will.
    [*Exit* Valentine *and* Speed.]
Even as one heat another heat expels
Or as one nail by strength drives out
  another,
So the remembrance of my former love
Is by a newer object quite forgotten.
Is it my mind, or Valentinus' praise,
Her true perfection, or my false
  transgression,
That makes me reasonless to reason thus?
She is fair; and so is Julia that I love,—
That I did love, for now my love is thaw'd;
Which like a waxen image 'gainst a fire
Bears no impression of the thing it was.
Methinks my zeal to Valentine is cold,
And that I love him not as I was wont.
O! but I love his lady too-too much,
And that's the reason I love him so little.

How shall I dote on her with more advice
That thus without advice begin to love
    her?
'Tis but her picture I have yet beheld,
And that hath dazzled my reason's light;
But when I look on her perfections,
There is no reason but I shall be blind.
If I can check my erring love, I will;
If not, to compass her I'll use my skill.
    [*Exit.*]

SCENE V
The same. A street.
[*Enter* SPEED *and* LAUNCE.]

SPEED.
Launce! by mine honesty, welcome to
Milan!

LAUNCE.
Forswear not thyself, sweet youth, for I am
not welcome. I reckon this always, that a
man is never undone till he be hanged,
nor never welcome to a place till some
certain shot be paid, and the hostess say
"Welcome!"

SPEED.
Come on, you madcap; I'll to the alehouse
with you presently; where, for one shot of
five pence, thou shalt have five thousand
welcomes. But, sirrah, how did thy master
part with Madam Julia?

LAUNCE.
Marry, after they clos'd in earnest, they
parted very fairly in jest.

SPEED.
But shall she marry him?

LAUNCE.
No.

SPEED.
How then? Shall he marry her?

LAUNCE.
No, neither.

SPEED.
What, are they broken?

LAUNCE.
No, they are both as whole as a fish.

SPEED.
Why then, how stands the matter with
them?

LAUNCE.
Marry, thus: when it stands well with him,
it stands well with her.

SPEED.
What an ass art thou! I understand thee
not.

LAUNCE.
What a block art thou that thou canst not!
My staff understands me.

SPEED.
What thou sayest?

LAUNCE.
Ay, and what I do too; look thee, I'll but
lean, and my staff understands me.

SPEED.
It stands under thee, indeed.

LAUNCE.
Why, stand-under and under-stand is all
one.

SPEED.
But tell me true, will't be a match?

LAUNCE.
Ask my dog. If he say ay, it will; if he say no,
it will; if he shake his tail and say nothing,
it will.

SPEED.
The conclusion is, then, that it will.

LAUNCE.
Thou shalt never get such a secret from me
but by a parable.

SPEED.
'Tis well that I get it so. But, Launce, how
sayest thou that my master is become a
notable lover?

LAUNCE.
I never knew him otherwise.

SPEED.
Than how?

LAUNCE.
A notable lubber, as thou reportest him to
be.

SPEED.
Why, thou whoreson ass, thou mistak'st me.

LAUNCE.
Why, fool, I meant not thee, I meant thy
master.

SPEED.
I tell thee my master is become a hot lover.

Launce.

Why, I tell thee I care not though he burn
himself in love. If thou wilt, go with me to
the alehouse; if not, thou art an Hebrew, a
Jew, and not worth the name of a Christian.

Speed.

Why?

Launce.

Because thou hast not so much charity in
thee as to go to the ale with a Christian.
Wilt thou go?

Speed.

At thy service.

[*Exeunt.*]

SCENE VI

The same. The duke's palace.
[*Enter* Proteus.]

Proteus.

To leave my Julia, shall I be forsworn;
To love fair Silvia, shall I be forsworn;
To wrong my friend, I shall be much
    forsworn;
And even that power which gave me first
    my oath
Provokes me to this threefold perjury:
Love bade me swear, and Love bids me
    forswear.
O sweet-suggesting Love! if thou hast
    sinn'd,
Teach me, thy tempted subject, to excuse
    it.
At first I did adore a twinkling star,
But now I worship a celestial sun.
Unheedful vows may heedfully be broken;
And he wants wit that wants resolved will
To learn his wit t' exchange the bad for
    better.
Fie, fie, unreverend tongue, to call her bad,
Whose sovereignty so oft thou hast
    preferr'd
With twenty thousand soul-confirming
    oaths.
I cannot leave to love, and yet I do;
But there I leave to love where I should
    love.
Julia I lose, and Valentine I lose;
If I keep them, I needs must lose myself;

If I lose them, thus find I by their loss,
For Valentine, myself; for Julia, Silvia.
I to myself am dearer than a friend,
For love is still most precious in itself;
And Silvia—witness heaven, that made
    her fair!—
Shows Julia but a swarthy Ethiope.
I will forget that Julia is alive,
Remembering that my love to her is dead;
And Valentine I'll hold an enemy,
Aiming at Silvia as a sweeter friend.
I cannot now prove constant to myself
Without some treachery us'd to Valentine.
This night he meaneth with a corded
    ladder
To climb celestial Silvia's chamber window,
Myself in counsel, his competitor.
Now presently I'll give her father notice
Of their disguising and pretended flight;
Who, all enrag'd, will banish Valentine;
For Thurio, he intends, shall wed his
    daughter;
But, Valentine being gone, I'll quickly
    cross,
By some sly trick blunt Thurio's dull
    proceeding.
Love, lend me wings to make my purpose
    swift,
As thou hast lent me wit to plot this drift!
[*Exit.*]

SCENE VII

Verona. A room in Julia's house.
[*Enter* Julia *and* Lucetta.]

Julia.

Counsel, Lucetta; gentle girl, assist me:
And, ev'n in kind love, I do conjure thee,
Who art the table wherein all my thoughts
Are visibly character'd and engrav'd,
To lesson me and tell me some good mean
How, with my honour, I may undertake
A journey to my loving Proteus.

Lucetta.

Alas, the way is wearisome and long.

Julia.

A true-devoted pilgrim is not weary
To measure kingdoms with his feeble
    steps;

Much less shall she that hath Love's wings
   to fly,
And when the flight is made to one so
   dear,
Of such divine perfection, as Sir Proteus.
LUCETTA.
Better forbear till Proteus make return.
JULIA.
O! know'st thou not his looks are my soul's
   food?
Pity the dearth that I have pined in
By longing for that food so long a time.
Didst thou but know the inly touch of
   love.
Thou wouldst as soon go kindle fire with
   snow
As seek to quench the fire of love with
   words.
LUCETTA.
I do not seek to quench your love's hot fire,
But qualify the fire's extreme rage,
Lest it should burn above the bounds of
   reason.
JULIA.
The more thou damm'st it up, the more it
   burns.
The current that with gentle murmur
   glides,
Thou know'st, being stopp'd, impatiently
   doth rage;
But when his fair course is not hindered,
He makes sweet music with th' enamell'd
   stones,
Giving a gentle kiss to every sedge
He overtaketh in his pilgrimage;
And so by many winding nooks he strays,
With willing sport, to the wild ocean.
Then let me go, and hinder not my course.
I'll be as patient as a gentle stream,
And make a pastime of each weary step,
Till the last step have brought me to my
   love;
And there I'll rest as, after much turmoil,
A blessed soul doth in Elysium.
LUCETTA.
But in what habit will you go along?
JULIA.
Not like a woman, for I would prevent

The loose encounters of lascivious men.
Gentle Lucetta, fit me with such weeds
As may beseem some well-reputed page.
LUCETTA.
Why then, your ladyship must cut your
   hair.
JULIA.
No, girl; I'll knit it up in silken strings
With twenty odd-conceited true-love
   knots:
To be fantastic may become a youth
Of greater time than I shall show to be.
LUCETTA.
What fashion, madam, shall I make your
   breeches?
JULIA.
That fits as well as "Tell me, good my lord,
What compass will you wear your
   farthingale?"
Why even what fashion thou best likes,
   Lucetta.
LUCETTA.
You must needs have them with a
   codpiece, madam.
JULIA.
Out, out, Lucetta, that will be ill-favour'd.
LUCETTA.
A round hose, madam, now's not worth
   a pin,
Unless you have a codpiece to stick pins
   on.
JULIA.
Lucetta, as thou lov'st me, let me have
What thou think'st meet, and is most
   mannerly.
But tell me, wench, how will the world
   repute me
For undertaking so unstaid a journey?
I fear me it will make me scandaliz'd.
LUCETTA.
If you think so, then stay at home and go
   not.
JULIA.
Nay, that I will not.
LUCETTA.
Then never dream on infamy, but go.
If Proteus like your journey when you
   come,

No matter who's displeas'd when you are
    gone.
I fear me he will scarce be pleas'd withal.
Julia.
That is the least, Lucetta, of my fear:
A thousand oaths, an ocean of his tears,
And instances of infinite of love,
Warrant me welcome to my Proteus.
Lucetta.
All these are servants to deceitful men.
Julia.
Base men that use them to so base effect!
But truer stars did govern Proteus' birth;
His words are bonds, his oaths are
    oracles,
His love sincere, his thoughts immaculate,
His tears pure messengers sent from his
    heart,
His heart as far from fraud as heaven from
    earth.
Lucetta.
Pray heav'n he prove so when you come
    to him.
Julia.
Now, as thou lov'st me, do him not that
    wrong
To bear a hard opinion of his truth;
Only deserve my love by loving him.
And presently go with me to my chamber,
To take a note of what I stand in need of
To furnish me upon my longing journey.
All that is mine I leave at thy dispose,
My goods, my lands, my reputation;
Only, in lieu thereof, dispatch me hence.
Come, answer not, but to it presently!
I am impatient of my tarriance.
    [*Exeunt.*]

ACT III
SCENE I

Milan. An anteroom in the duke's palace.
[*Enter* Duke, Thurio, *and* Proteus.]
Duke.
Sir Thurio, give us leave, I pray, awhile;
We have some secrets to confer about.
    [*Exit* Thurio.]
Now tell me, Proteus, what's your will
    with me?

Proteus.
My gracious lord, that which I would
    discover
The law of friendship bids me to conceal;
But, when I call to mind your gracious
    favours
Done to me, undeserving as I am,
My duty pricks me on to utter that
Which else no worldly good should draw
    from me.
Know, worthy prince, Sir Valentine, my
    friend,
This night intends to steal away your
    daughter;
Myself am one made privy to the plot.
I know you have determin'd to bestow her
On Thurio, whom your gentle daughter
    hates;
And should she thus be stol'n away from
    you,
It would be much vexation to your age.
Thus, for my duty's sake, I rather chose
To cross my friend in his intended drift
Than, by concealing it, heap on your head
A pack of sorrows which would press you
    down,
Being unprevented, to your timeless grave.
Duke.
Proteus, I thank thee for thine honest care,
Which to requite, command me while I
    live.
This love of theirs myself have often seen,
Haply when they have judg'd me fast asleep,
And oftentimes have purpos'd to forbid
Sir Valentine her company and my court;
But, fearing lest my jealous aim might err
And so, unworthily, disgrace the man,—
A rashness that I ever yet have shunn'd,—
I gave him gentle looks, thereby to find
That which thyself hast now disclos'd to
    me.
And, that thou mayst perceive my fear of
    this,
Knowing that tender youth is soon
    suggested,
I nightly lodge her in an upper tower,
The key whereof myself have ever kept;
And thence she cannot be convey'd away.

Proteus.

Know, noble lord, they have devis'd a mean
How he her chamber window will ascend
And with a corded ladder fetch her down;
For which the youthful lover now is gone,
And this way comes he with it presently;
Where, if it please you, you may intercept
    him.
But, good my lord, do it so cunningly
That my discovery be not aimed at;
For love of you, not hate unto my friend,
Hath made me publisher of this pretence.

Duke.

Upon mine honour, he shall never know
That I had any light from thee of this.

Proteus.

Adieu, my lord; Sir Valentine is coming.
                [*Exit.*]
            [*Enter* Valentine.]

Duke.

Sir Valentine, whither away so fast?

Valentine.

Please it your Grace, there is a messenger
That stays to bear my letters to my friends,
And I am going to deliver them.

Duke.

Be they of much import?

Valentine.

The tenour of them doth but signify
My health and happy being at your court.

Duke.

Nay then, no matter; stay with me awhile;
I am to break with thee of some affairs
That touch me near, wherein thou must
    be secret.
'Tis not unknown to thee that I have
    sought
To match my friend Sir Thurio to my
    daughter.

Valentine.

I know it well, my lord; and, sure, the match
Were rich and honourable; besides, the
    gentleman
Is full of virtue, bounty, worth, and
    qualities
Beseeming such a wife as your fair
    daughter.
Cannot your grace win her to fancy him?

Duke.

No, trust me; she is peevish, sullen,
    froward,
Proud, disobedient, stubborn, lacking duty;
Neither regarding that she is my child
Nor fearing me as if I were her father;
And, may I say to thee, this pride of hers,
Upon advice, hath drawn my love from
    her;
And, where I thought the remnant of
    mine age
Should have been cherish'd by her
    childlike duty,
I now am full resolv'd to take a wife
And turn her out to who will take her in.
Then let her beauty be her wedding-
    dower;
For me and my possessions she esteems
    not.

Valentine.

What would your Grace have me to do
    in this?

Duke.

There is a lady of Verona here,
Whom I affect; but she is nice, and coy,
And nought esteems my aged eloquence.
Now, therefore, would I have thee to my
    tutor,
For long agone I have forgot to court;
Besides, the fashion of the time is chang'd,
How and which way I may bestow myself
To be regarded in her sun-bright eye.

Valentine.

Win her with gifts, if she respect not
    words:
Dumb jewels often in their silent kind
More than quick words do move a
    woman's mind.

Duke.

But she did scorn a present that I sent her.

Valentine.

A woman sometime scorns what best
    contents her.
Send her another; never give her o'er,
For scorn at first makes after-love the
    more.
If she do frown, 'tis not in hate of you,
But rather to beget more love in you;

If she do chide, 'tis not to have you gone;
For why, the fools are mad if left alone.
Take no repulse, whatever she doth say;
For "Get you gone" she doth not mean
    "Away!"
Flatter and praise, commend, extol their
    graces;
Though ne'er so black, say they have
    angels' faces.
That man that hath a tongue, I say, is no
    man,
If with his tongue he cannot win a woman.

DUKE.
But she I mean is promis'd by her friends
Unto a youthful gentleman of worth;
And kept severely from resort of men,
That no man hath access by day to her.

VALENTINE.
Why then I would resort to her by night.

DUKE.
Ay, but the doors be lock'd and keys kept
    safe,
That no man hath recourse to her by night.

VALENTINE.
What lets but one may enter at her
    window?

DUKE.
Her chamber is aloft, far from the ground,
And built so shelving that one cannot
    climb it
Without apparent hazard of his life.

VALENTINE.
Why then a ladder, quaintly made of cords,
To cast up with a pair of anchoring hooks,
Would serve to scale another Hero's tow'r,
So bold Leander would adventure it.

DUKE.
Now, as thou art a gentleman of blood,
Advise me where I may have such a ladder.

VALENTINE.
When would you use it? Pray, sir, tell me
    that.

DUKE.
This very night; for Love is like a child,
That longs for everything that he can
    come by.

VALENTINE.
By seven o'clock I'll get you such a ladder.

DUKE.
But, hark thee; I will go to her alone;
How shall I best convey the ladder
    thither?

VALENTINE.
It will be light, my lord, that you may
    bear it
Under a cloak that is of any length.

DUKE.
A cloak as long as thine will serve the
    turn?

VALENTINE.
Ay, my good lord.

DUKE.
              Then let me see thy cloak.
I'll get me one of such another length.

VALENTINE.
Why, any cloak will serve the turn, my
    lord.

DUKE.
How shall I fashion me to wear a cloak?
I pray thee, let me feel thy cloak upon me.
    [*Pulls open* VALENTINE's *cloak.*]
What letter is this same? What's
    here?—"To Silvia"!
And here an engine fit for my proceeding!
I'll be so bold to break the seal for once.
    [*Reads.*] "My thoughts do harbour with
    my Silvia nightly,
And slaves they are to me, that send them
    flying.
O! could their master come and go as
    lightly,
Himself would lodge where, senseless, they
    are lying!
My herald thoughts in thy pure bosom
    rest them,
While I, their king, that thither them
    importune,
Do curse the grace that with such grace
    hath blest them,
Because myself do want my servants'
    fortune.
I curse myself, for they are sent by me,
That they should harbour where their lord
    should be."
What's here?
"Silvia, this night I will enfranchise thee."

'Tis so; and here's the ladder for the
    purpose.
Why, Phaethon—for thou art Merops'
    son—
Wilt thou aspire to guide the heavenly car,
And with thy daring folly burn the world?
Wilt thou reach stars because they shine
    on thee?
Go, base intruder! over-weening slave!
Bestow thy fawning smiles on equal mates,
And think my patience, more than thy
    desert,
Is privilege for thy departure hence.
Thank me for this more than for all the
    favours
Which, all too much, I have bestow'd on
    thee.
But if thou linger in my territories
Longer than swiftest expedition
Will give thee time to leave our royal court,
By heaven! my wrath shall far exceed the
    love
I ever bore my daughter or thyself.
Be gone! I will not hear thy vain excuse;
But, as thou lov'st thy life, make speed
    from hence.
        [Exit.]
VALENTINE.
And why not death rather than living
    torment?
To die is to be banish'd from myself,
And Silvia is myself; banish'd from her
Is self from self,—a deadly banishment!
What light is light, if Silvia be not seen?
What joy is joy, if Silvia be not by?
Unless it be to think that she is by,
And feed upon the shadow of perfection.
Except I be by Silvia in the night,
There is no music in the nightingale;
Unless I look on Silvia in the day,
There is no day for me to look upon.
She is my essence, and I leave to be
If I be not by her fair influence
Foster'd, illumin'd, cherish'd, kept alive.
I fly not death, to fly his deadly doom:
Tarry I here, I but attend on death;
But fly I hence, I fly away from life.
    [Enter PROTEUS and LAUNCE.]

PROTEUS.
Run, boy; run, run, seek him out.
LAUNCE.
Soho! soho!
PROTEUS.
What seest thou?
LAUNCE.
Him we go to find: there's not a hair on 's
head but 'tis a Valentine.
PROTEUS.
Valentine?
VALENTINE.
No.
PROTEUS.
Who then? his spirit?
VALENTINE.
Neither.
PROTEUS.
What then?
VALENTINE.
Nothing.
LAUNCE.
Can nothing speak? Master, shall I strike?
PROTEUS.
Who wouldst thou strike?
LAUNCE.
Nothing.
PROTEUS.
Villain, forbear.
LAUNCE.
Why, sir, I'll strike nothing. I pray you,—
PROTEUS.
Sirrah, I say, forbear.—Friend Valentine,
    a word.
VALENTINE.
My ears are stopp'd and cannot hear good
    news,
So much of bad already hath possess'd them.
PROTEUS.
Then in dumb silence will I bury mine,
For they are harsh, untuneable, and bad.
VALENTINE.
Is Silvia dead?
PROTEUS.
No, Valentine.
VALENTINE.
No Valentine, indeed, for sacred Silvia.
Hath she forsworn me?

Proteus.
No, Valentine.
Valentine.
No Valentine, if Silvia have forsworn me.
What is your news?
Launce.
Sir, there is a proclamation that you are
    vanished.
Proteus.
That thou art banished, O, that's the news,
From hence, from Silvia, and from me thy
    friend.
Valentine.
O, I have fed upon this woe already,
And now excess of it will make me surfeit.
Doth Silvia know that I am banished?
Proteus.
Ay, ay; and she hath offer'd to the doom—
Which, unrevers'd, stands in effectual
    force—
A sea of melting pearl, which some call
    tears;
Those at her father's churlish feet she
    tender'd;
With them, upon her knees, her humble
    self,
Wringing her hands, whose whiteness so
    became them
As if but now they waxed pale for woe:
But neither bended knees, pure hands
    held up,
Sad sighs, deep groans, nor silver-shedding
    tears,
Could penetrate her uncompassionate sire;
But Valentine, if he be ta'en, must die.
Besides, her intercession chaf'd him so,
When she for thy repeal was suppliant,
That to close prison he commanded her,
With many bitter threats of biding there.
Valentine.
No more; unless the next word that thou
    speak'st
Have some malignant power upon my life:
If so, I pray thee breathe it in mine ear,
As ending anthem of my endless dolour.
Proteus.
Cease to lament for that thou canst not
    help,

And study help for that which thou
    lament'st.
Time is the nurse and breeder of all good.
Here if thou stay thou canst not see thy
    love;
Besides, thy staying will abridge thy life.
Hope is a lover's staff; walk hence with
    that
And manage it against despairing
    thoughts.
Thy letters may be here, though thou art
    hence,
Which, being writ to me, shall be deliver'd
Even in the milk-white bosom of thy love.
The time now serves not to expostulate:
Come, I'll convey thee through the city-
    gate;
And, ere I part with thee, confer at large
Of all that may concern thy love-affairs.
As thou lov'st Silvia, though not for
    thyself,
Regard thy danger, and along with me!
Valentine.
I pray thee, Launce, an if thou seest my
    boy,
Bid him make haste and meet me at the
    North-gate.
Proteus.
Go, sirrah, find him out. Come, Valentine.
Valentine.
O my dear Silvia! Hapless Valentine!
    [*Exeunt* Valentine *and* Proteus.]
Launce.
I am but a fool, look you, and yet I have the
wit to think my master is a kind of a knave;
but that's all one if he be but one knave. He
lives not now that knows me to be in love;
yet I am in love; but a team of horse shall
not pluck that from me; nor who 'tis I love;
and yet 'tis a woman; but what woman I will
not tell myself; and yet 'tis a milkmaid; yet
'tis not a maid, for she hath had gossips; yet
'tis a maid, for she is her master's maid and
serves for wages. She hath more qualities
than a water-spaniel—which is much in a
bare Christian. [*Pulling out a paper.*] Here
is the catelog of her condition. [*Reads.*]
"*Imprimis*: She can fetch and carry." Why,

a horse can do no more: nay, a horse cannot fetch, but only carry; therefore is she better than a jade. "*Item*: She can milk." Look you, a sweet virtue in a maid with clean hands.

[*Enter* Speed.]

Speed.

How now, Signior Launce! What news with your mastership?

Launce.

With my master's ship? Why, it is at sea.

Speed.

Well, your old vice still: mistake the word. What news, then, in your paper?

Launce.

The blackest news that ever thou heardest.

Speed.

Why, man? how black?

Launce.

Why, as black as ink.

Speed.

Let me read them.

Launce.

Fie on thee, jolthead! thou canst not read.

Speed.

Thou liest; I can.

Launce.

I will try thee. Tell me this: who begot thee?

Speed.

Marry, the son of my grandfather.

Launce.

O, illiterate loiterer! It was the son of thy grandmother. This proves that thou canst not read.

Speed.

Come, fool, come; try me in thy paper.

Launce.

There; and Saint Nicholas be thy speed!

Speed.

"*Imprimis*, She can milk."

Launce.

Ay, that she can.

Speed.

"*Item*, She brews good ale."

Launce.

And thereof comes the proverb, "Blessing of your heart, you brew good ale."

Speed.

"*Item*, She can sew."

Launce.

That's as much as to say "Can she so?"

Speed.

"*Item*, She can knit."

Launce.

What need a man care for a stock with a wench, when she can knit him a stock?

Speed.

"*Item*, She can wash and scour."

Launce.

A special virtue; for then she need not be washed and scoured.

Speed.

"*Item*, She can spin."

Launce.

Then may I set the world on wheels, when she can spin for her living.

Speed.

"*Item*, She hath many nameless virtues."

Launce.

That's as much as to say, bastard virtues; that indeed know not their fathers, and therefore have no names.

Speed.

"Here follow her vices."

Launce.

Close at the heels of her virtues.

Speed.

"*Item*, She is not to be kissed fasting, in respect of her breath."

Launce.

Well, that fault may be mended with a breakfast. Read on.

Speed.

"*Item*, She hath a sweet mouth."

Launce.

That makes amends for her sour breath.

Speed.

"*Item*, She doth talk in her sleep."

Launce.

It's no matter for that, so she sleep not in her talk.

Speed.

"*Item*, She is slow in words."

Launce.

O villain, that set this down among her vices! To be slow in words is a woman's only virtue. I pray thee, out with't; and place it for her chief virtue.

SPEED.
"*Item*, She is proud."

LAUNCE.
Out with that too: it was Eve's legacy, and cannot be ta'en from her.

SPEED.
"*Item*, She hath no teeth."

LAUNCE.
I care not for that neither, because I love crusts.

SPEED.
"*Item*, She is curst."

LAUNCE.
Well; the best is, she hath no teeth to bite.

SPEED.
"*Item*, She will often praise her liquor."

LAUNCE.
If her liquor be good, she shall: if she will not, I will; for good things should be praised.

SPEED.
"*Item*, She is too liberal."

LAUNCE.
Of her tongue she cannot, for that's writ down she is slow of; of her purse she shall not, for that I'll keep shut. Now of another thing she may, and that cannot I help. Well, proceed.

SPEED.
"*Item*, She hath more hair than wit, and more faults than hairs, and more wealth than faults."

LAUNCE.
Stop there; I'll have her; she was mine, and not mine, twice or thrice in that last article. Rehearse that once more.

SPEED.
"*Item*, She hath more hair than wit"—

LAUNCE.
More hair than wit it may be; I'll prove it: the cover of the salt hides the salt, and therefore it is more than the salt; the hair that covers the wit is more than the wit, for the greater hides the less. What's next?

SPEED.
"And more faults than hairs."—

LAUNCE.
That's monstrous! O, that that were out!

SPEED.
"And more wealth than faults."

LAUNCE.
Why, that word makes the faults gracious. Well, I'll have her; an if it be a match, as nothing is impossible,—

SPEED.
What then?

LAUNCE.
Why, then will I tell thee,—that thy master stays for thee at the North-gate.

SPEED.
For me?

LAUNCE.
For thee! ay, who art thou? He hath stay'd for a better man than thee.

SPEED.
And must I go to him?

LAUNCE.
Thou must run to him, for thou hast stayed so long that going will scarce serve the turn.

SPEED.
Why didst not tell me sooner? Pox of your love letters!
[*Exit.*]

LAUNCE.
Now will he be swing'd for reading my letter. An unmannerly slave that will thrust himself into secrets! I'll after, to rejoice in the boy's correction.
[*Exit.*]

SCENE II

The same. A room in the duke's palace.
[*Enter* DUKE *and* THURIO.]

DUKE.
Sir Thurio, fear not but that she will love you
Now Valentine is banish'd from her sight.

THURIO.
Since his exile she hath despis'd me most,
Forsworn my company and rail'd at me,
That I am desperate of obtaining her.

DUKE.
This weak impress of love is as a figure
Trenched in ice, which with an hour's heat

Dissolves to water and doth lose his form.
A little time will melt her frozen thoughts,
And worthless Valentine shall be forgot.
            [*Enter* PROTEUS.]
How now, Sir Proteus! Is your
    countryman,
According to our proclamation, gone?
PROTEUS.
Gone, my good lord.
DUKE.
My daughter takes his going grievously.
PROTEUS.
A little time, my lord, will kill that grief.
DUKE.
So I believe; but Thurio thinks not so.
Proteus, the good conceit I hold of thee,—
For thou hast shown some sign of good
    desert,—
Makes me the better to confer with thee.
PROTEUS.
Longer than I prove loyal to your Grace
Let me not live to look upon your Grace.
DUKE.
Thou know'st how willingly I would
    effect
The match between Sir Thurio and my
    daughter.
PROTEUS.
I do, my lord.
DUKE.
And also, I think, thou art not ignorant
How she opposes her against my will.
PROTEUS.
She did, my lord, when Valentine was here.
DUKE.
Ay, and perversely she persevers so.
What might we do to make the girl forget
The love of Valentine, and love Sir Thurio?
PROTEUS.
The best way is to slander Valentine
With falsehood, cowardice, and poor
    descent,
Three things that women highly hold in
    hate.
DUKE.
Ay, but she'll think that it is spoke in hate.
PROTEUS.
Ay, if his enemy deliver it;

Therefore it must with circumstance be
    spoken
By one whom she esteemeth as his friend.
DUKE.
Then you must undertake to slander him.
PROTEUS.
And that, my lord, I shall be loath to do:
'Tis an ill office for a gentleman,
Especially against his very friend.
DUKE.
Where your good word cannot advantage
    him,
Your slander never can endamage him;
Therefore the office is indifferent,
Being entreated to it by your friend.
PROTEUS.
You have prevail'd, my lord; if I can do it
By aught that I can speak in his dispraise,
She shall not long continue love to him.
But say this weed her love from Valentine,
It follows not that she will love Sir Thurio.
THURIO.
Therefore, as you unwind her love from
    him,
Lest it should ravel and be good to none,
You must provide to bottom it on me;
Which must be done by praising me as
    much
As you in worth dispraise Sir Valentine.
DUKE.
And, Proteus, we dare trust you in this
    kind,
Because we know, on Valentine's report,
You are already Love's firm votary
And cannot soon revolt and change your
    mind.
Upon this warrant shall you have access
Where you with Silvia may confer at large;
For she is lumpish, heavy, melancholy,
And, for your friend's sake, will be glad
    of you;
Where you may temper her by your
    persuasion
To hate young Valentine and love my
    friend.
PROTEUS.
As much as I can do I will effect.
But you, Sir Thurio, are not sharp enough;

You must lay lime to tangle her desires
By wailful sonnets, whose composed rhymes
Should be full-fraught with serviceable vows.

Duke.
Ay,
Much is the force of heaven-bred poesy.

Proteus.
Say that upon the altar of her beauty
You sacrifice your tears, your sighs, your heart.
Write till your ink be dry, and with your tears
Moist it again, and frame some feeling line
That may discover such integrity:
For Orpheus' lute was strung with poets' sinews,
Whose golden touch could soften steel and stones,
Make tigers tame, and huge leviathans
Forsake unsounded deeps to dance on sands.
After your dire-lamenting elegies,
Visit by night your lady's chamber-window
With some sweet consort: to their instruments
Tune a deploring dump; the night's dead silence
Will well become such sweet-complaining grievance.
This, or else nothing, will inherit her.

Duke.
This discipline shows thou hast been in love.

Thurio.
And thy advice this night I'll put in practice.
Therefore, sweet Proteus, my direction-giver,
Let us into the city presently
To sort some gentlemen well skill'd in music.
I have a sonnet that will serve the turn
To give the onset to thy good advice.

Duke.
About it, gentlemen!

Proteus.
We'll wait upon your Grace till after-supper,
And afterward determine our proceedings.

Duke.
Even now about it! I will pardon you.
[*Exeunt.*]

ACT IV
SCENE I

A forest between Milan and Verona.
[*Enter certain* Outlaws.]

First Outlaw.
Fellows, stand fast; I see a passenger.

Second Outlaw.
If there be ten, shrink not, but down with 'em.
[*Enter* Valentine *and* Speed.]

Third Outlaw.
Stand, sir, and throw us that you have about ye;
If not, we'll make you sit, and rifle you.

Speed.
Sir, we are undone: these are the villains
That all the travellers do fear so much.

Valentine.
My friends,—

First Outlaw.
That's not so, sir; we are your enemies.

Second Outlaw.
Peace! we'll hear him.

Third Outlaw.
Ay, by my beard, will we, for he is a proper man.

Valentine.
Then know that I have little wealth to lose;
A man I am cross'd with adversity;
My riches are these poor habiliments,
Of which if you should here disfurnish me,
You take the sum and substance that I have.

Second Outlaw.
Whither travel you?

Valentine.
To Verona.

First Outlaw.
Whence came you?

Valentine.
From Milan.

Third Outlaw.
Have you long sojourn'd there?
Valentine.
Some sixteen months, and longer might
    have stay'd,
If crooked fortune had not thwarted me.
First Outlaw.
What! were you banish'd thence?
Valentine.
I was.
Second Outlaw.
For what offence?
Valentine.
For that which now torments me to
    rehearse:
I kill'd a man, whose death I much repent;
But yet I slew him manfully in fight,
Without false vantage or base treachery.
First Outlaw.
Why, ne'er repent it, if it were done so.
But were you banish'd for so small a fault?
Valentine.
I was, and held me glad of such a doom.
Second Outlaw.
Have you the tongues?
Valentine.
My youthful travel therein made me
    happy,
Or else I often had been miserable.
Third Outlaw.
By the bare scalp of Robin Hood's fat friar,
This fellow were a king for our wild
    faction!
First Outlaw.
We'll have him: Sirs, a word.
Speed.
Master, be one of them; it's an honourable
kind of thievery.
Valentine.
Peace, villain!
Second Outlaw.
Tell us this: have you anything to take to?
Valentine.
Nothing but my fortune.
Third Outlaw.
Know, then, that some of us are
    gentlemen,
Such as the fury of ungovern'd youth

Thrust from the company of awful men:
Myself was from Verona banished
For practising to steal away a lady,
An heir, and near allied unto the duke.
Second Outlaw.
And I from Mantua, for a gentleman
Who, in my mood, I stabb'd unto the
    heart.
First Outlaw.
And I for such-like petty crimes as these.
But to the purpose; for we cite our faults,
That they may hold excus'd our lawless
    lives;
And, partly, seeing you are beautified
With goodly shape, and by your own
    report
A linguist, and a man of such perfection
As we do in our quality much want—
Second Outlaw.
Indeed, because you are a banish'd man,
Therefore, above the rest, we parley to you.
Are you content to be our general?
To make a virtue of necessity
And live as we do in this wilderness?
Third Outlaw.
What say'st thou? Wilt thou be of our
    consort?
Say "ay" and be the captain of us all:
We'll do thee homage, and be rul'd by thee,
Love thee as our commander and our king.
First Outlaw.
But if thou scorn our courtesy thou diest.
Second Outlaw.
Thou shalt not live to brag what we have
    offer'd.
Valentine.
I take your offer, and will live with you,
Provided that you do no outrages
On silly women or poor passengers.
Third Outlaw.
No, we detest such vile base practices.
Come, go with us; we'll bring thee to our
    crews,
And show thee all the treasure we have
    got;
Which, with ourselves, all rest at thy
    dispose.
                              [*Exeunt.*]

SCENE II

Milan. The court of the duke's palace.
[*Enter* PROTEUS.]

PROTEUS.
Already have I been false to Valentine,
And now I must be as unjust to Thurio.
Under the colour of commending him,
I have access my own love to prefer:
But Silvia is too fair, too true, too holy,
To be corrupted with my worthless gifts.
When I protest true loyalty to her,
She twits me with my falsehood to my
    friend;
When to her beauty I commend my
    vows,
She bids me think how I have been
    forsworn
In breaking faith with Julia whom I
    lov'd;
And notwithstanding all her sudden
    quips,
The least whereof would quell a lover's
    hope,
Yet, spaniel-like, the more she spurns my
    love
The more it grows and fawneth on her
    still.
But here comes Thurio. Now must we to
    her window,
And give some evening music to her ear.
[*Enter* THURIO *and* MUSICIANS.]

THURIO.
How now, Sir Proteus! are you crept
    before us?

PROTEUS.
Ay, gentle Thurio; for you know that love
Will creep in service where it cannot go.

THURIO.
Ay, but I hope, sir, that you love not here.

PROTEUS.
Sir, but I do; or else I would be hence.

THURIO.
Who? Silvia?

PROTEUS.
                Ay, Silvia, for your sake.

THURIO.
I thank you for your own. Now, gentlemen,
Let's tune, and to it lustily awhile.

[*Enter* HOST, *and* JULIA *in boy's clothes.*]

HOST.
Now, my young guest, methinks you're
allicholly; I pray you, why is it?

JULIA.
Marry, mine host, because I cannot be
    merry.

HOST.
Come, we'll have you merry; I'll bring you
where you shall hear music, and see the
gentleman that you asked for.

JULIA.
But shall I hear him speak?

HOST.
Ay, that you shall.

JULIA.
That will be music.
                    [*Music plays.*]

HOST.
Hark! hark!

JULIA.
Is he among these?

HOST.
Ay; but peace! let's hear 'em.
                    [*Song.*]
    Who is Silvia? What is she,
        That all our swains commend her?
    Holy, fair, and wise is she;
        The heaven such grace did lend her,
        That she might admired be.
    Is she kind as she is fair?
    For beauty lives with kindness.
        Love doth to her eyes repair,
    To help him of his blindness;
        And, being help'd, inhabits there.
    Then to Silvia let us sing
        That Silvia is excelling;
    She excels each mortal thing
        Upon the dull earth dwelling.
    To her let us garlands bring.

HOST.
How now, are you sadder than you were
before? How do you, man? The music likes
you not.

JULIA.
You mistake; the musician likes me not.

HOST.
Why, my pretty youth?

JULIA.
He plays false, father.
HOST.
How? out of tune on the strings?
JULIA.
Not so; but yet so false that he grieves my
very heart-strings.
HOST.
You have a quick ear.
JULIA.
Ay, I would I were deaf; it makes me have
a slow heart.
HOST.
I perceive you delight not in music.
JULIA.
Not a whit,—when it jars so.
HOST.
Hark! what fine change is in the music!
JULIA.
Ay, that change is the spite.
HOST.
You would have them always play but one
    thing?
JULIA.
I would always have one play but one
    thing.
But, Host, doth this Sir Proteus, that we
    talk on,
Often resort unto this gentlewoman?
HOST.
I tell you what Launce, his man, told me: he
lov'd her out of all nick.
JULIA.
Where is Launce?
HOST.
Gone to seek his dog, which to-morrow, by
his master's command, he must carry for a
present to his lady.
JULIA.
Peace! stand aside: the company parts.
PROTEUS.
Sir Thurio, fear not you; I will so plead
That you shall say my cunning drift
    excels.
THURIO.
Where meet we?
PROTEUS.
At Saint Gregory's well.

THURIO.
Farewell.
        [*Exeunt* THURIO *and* MUSICIANS.]
        [*Enter* SILVIA *above, at her window.*]
PROTEUS.
Madam, good even to your ladyship.
SILVIA.
I thank you for your music, gentlemen.
Who is that that spake?
PROTEUS.
One, lady, if you knew his pure heart's
    truth,
You would quickly learn to know him by
    his voice.
SILVIA.
Sir Proteus, as I take it.
PROTEUS.
Sir Proteus, gentle lady, and your servant.
SILVIA.
What's your will?
PROTEUS.
That I may compass yours.
SILVIA.
You have your wish; my will is even this,
That presently you hie you home to bed.
Thou subtle, perjur'd, false, disloyal man!
Think'st thou I am so shallow, so
    conceitless,
To be seduced by thy flattery,
That hast deceiv'd so many with thy vows?
Return, return, and make thy love amends.
For me, by this pale queen of night I swear,
I am so far from granting thy request
That I despise thee for thy wrongful suit,
And by and by intend to chide myself
Even for this time I spend in talking to
    thee.
PROTEUS.
I grant, sweet love, that I did love a lady;
But she is dead.
JULIA. [*Aside.*]
'Twere false, if I should speak it;
For I am sure she is not buried.
SILVIA.
Say that she be; yet Valentine, thy friend,
Survives, to whom, thyself art witness,
I am betroth'd; and art thou not asham'd
To wrong him with thy importunacy?

Proteus.
I likewise hear that Valentine is dead.
Silvia.
And so suppose am I; for in his grave,
Assure thyself my love is buried.
Proteus.
Sweet lady, let me rake it from the earth.
Silvia.
Go to thy lady's grave, and call hers thence;
Or, at the least, in hers sepulchre thine.
Julia. [*Aside.*]
He heard not that.
Proteus.
Madam, if your heart be so obdurate,
Vouchsafe me yet your picture for my love,
The picture that is hanging in your
    chamber;
To that I'll speak, to that I'll sigh and
    weep;
For, since the substance of your perfect self
Is else devoted, I am but a shadow;
And to your shadow will I make true love.
Julia. [*Aside.*]
If 'twere a substance, you would, sure,
    deceive it
And make it but a shadow, as I am.
Silvia.
I am very loath to be your idol, sir;
But since your falsehood shall become
    you well
To worship shadows and adore false
    shapes,
Send to me in the morning, and I'll send
    it;
And so, good rest.
Proteus.
As wretches have o'ernight
That wait for execution in the morn.
    [*Exeunt Proteus and Silvia, above.*]
Julia.
Host, will you go?
Host.
By my halidom, I was fast asleep.
Julia.
Pray you, where lies Sir Proteus?
Host.
Marry, at my house. Trust me, I think 'tis
    almost day.

Julia.
Not so; but it hath been the longest night
That e'er I watch'd, and the most heaviest.
    [*Exeunt.*]

SCENE III

The same.
[*Enter Eglamour.*]
Eglamour.
This is the hour that Madam Silvia
Entreated me to call and know her mind:
There's some great matter she'd employ
    me in.
Madam, madam!
    [*Enter Silvia above, at her window.*]
Silvia.
Who calls?
Eglamour.
Your servant and your friend;
One that attends your ladyship's
    command.
Silvia.
Sir Eglamour, a thousand times good
    morrow.
Eglamour.
As many, worthy lady, to yourself.
According to your ladyship's impose,
I am thus early come to know what service
It is your pleasure to command me in.
Silvia.
O Eglamour, thou art a gentleman—
Think not I flatter, for I swear I do not—
Valiant, wise, remorseful, well
    accomplish'd.
Thou art not ignorant what dear good will
I bear unto the banish'd Valentine;
Nor how my father would enforce me
    marry
Vain Thurio, whom my very soul abhors.
Thyself hast lov'd; and I have heard thee
    say
No grief did ever come so near thy heart
As when thy lady and thy true love died,
Upon whose grave thou vow'dst pure
    chastity.
Sir Eglamour, I would to Valentine,
To Mantua, where I hear he makes abode;
And, for the ways are dangerous to pass,

I do desire thy worthy company,
Upon whose faith and honour I repose.
Urge not my father's anger, Eglamour,
But think upon my grief, a lady's grief,
And on the justice of my flying hence,
To keep me from a most unholy match,
Which heaven and fortune still rewards
    with plagues.
I do desire thee, even from a heart
As full of sorrows as the sea of sands,
To bear me company and go with me;
If not, to hide what I have said to thee,
That I may venture to depart alone.

EGLAMOUR.
Madam, I pity much your grievances;
Which since I know they virtuously are
    plac'd,
I give consent to go along with you,
Recking as little what betideth me
As much I wish all good befortune you.
When will you go?

SILVIA.
                    This evening coming.

EGLAMOUR.
Where shall I meet you?

SILVIA.
                    At Friar Patrick's cell,
Where I intend holy confession.

EGLAMOUR.
I will not fail your ladyship. Good morrow,
    gentle lady.

SILVIA.
Good morrow, kind Sir Eglamour.
            [*Exeunt severally.*]

SCENE IV
The same.
[*Enter* LAUNCE *with his dog.*]

LAUNCE.
When a man's servant shall play the cur
with him, look you, it goes hard; one that
I brought up of a puppy; one that I saved
from drowning, when three or four of his
blind brothers and sisters went to it. I have
taught him, even as one would say precisely
"Thus I would teach a dog." I was sent to
deliver him as a present to Mistress Silvia
from my master; and I came no sooner
into the dining-chamber, but he steps me
to her trencher and steals her capon's leg.
O! 'tis a foul thing when a cur cannot keep
himself in all companies! I would have, as
one should say, one that takes upon him to
be a dog indeed, to be, as it were, a dog at all
things. If I had not had more wit than he,
to take a fault upon me that he did, I think
verily he had been hang'd for't; sure as I
live, he had suffer'd for't; you shall judge.
He thrusts me himself into the company
of three or four gentleman-like dogs under
the duke's table; he had not been there—
bless the mark, a pissing-while, but all the
chamber smelt him. "Out with the dog!"
says one; "What cur is that?" says another;
"Whip him out" says the third; "Hang him
up" says the duke. I, having been acquainted
with the smell before, knew it was Crab,
and goes me to the fellow that whips the
dogs: "Friend," quoth I "you mean to whip
the dog?" "Ay, marry do I," quoth he. "You
do him the more wrong," quoth I; "'twas I
did the thing you wot of." He makes me
no more ado, but whips me out of the
chamber. How many masters would do
this for his servant? Nay, I'll be sworn, I
have sat in the stock for puddings he hath
stolen, otherwise he had been executed; I
have stood on the pillory for geese he hath
killed, otherwise he had suffered for't. Thou
think'st not of this now. Nay, I remember
the trick you serv'd me when I took my
leave of Madam Silvia: did not I bid thee
still mark me and do as I do? When didst
thou see me heave up my leg and make
water against a gentlewoman's farthingale?
Didst thou ever see me do such a trick?
[*Enter* PROTEUS, *and* JULIA *in boy's clothes.*]

PROTEUS.
Sebastian is thy name? I like thee well,
And will employ thee in some service
    presently.

JULIA.
In what you please; I'll do what I can.

PROTEUS.
I hope thou wilt. [*To* LAUNCE.] How now,
    you whoreson peasant!

Where have you been these two days
   loitering?

LAUNCE.

Marry, sir, I carried Mistress Silvia the dog
you bade me.

PROTEUS.

And what says she to my little jewel?

LAUNCE.

Marry, she says your dog was a cur, and tells
you currish thanks is good enough for such
a present.

PROTEUS.

But she received my dog?

LAUNCE.

No, indeed, did she not: here have I brought
him back again.

PROTEUS.

What! didst thou offer her this from me?

LAUNCE.

Ay, sir; the other squirrel was stolen from
me by the hangman boys in the market-
place; and then I offered her mine own,
who is a dog as big as ten of yours, and
therefore the gift the greater.

PROTEUS.

Go, get thee hence and find my dog again,
Or ne'er return again into my sight.
Away, I say. Stayest thou to vex me here?
A slave that still an end turns me to shame!
       [*Exit* LAUNCE.]
Sebastian, I have entertained thee
Partly that I have need of such a youth
That can with some discretion do my
   business,
For 'tis no trusting to yond foolish lout;
But chiefly for thy face and thy behaviour,
Which, if my augury deceive me not,
Witness good bringing up, fortune, and
   truth:
Therefore, know thou, for this I entertain
   thee.
Go presently, and take this ring with thee,
Deliver it to Madam Silvia:
She lov'd me well deliver'd it to me.

JULIA.

It seems you lov'd not her, to leave her
   token.
She's dead, belike?

PROTEUS.

           Not so: I think she lives.

JULIA.

Alas!

PROTEUS.

Why dost thou cry "Alas"?

JULIA.

              I cannot choose
But pity her.

PROTEUS.

      Wherefore shouldst thou pity her?

JULIA.

Because methinks that she lov'd you as
   well
As you do love your lady Silvia.
She dreams on him that has forgot her
   love:
You dote on her that cares not for your
   love.
'Tis pity love should be so contrary;
And thinking on it makes me cry "alas!"

PROTEUS.

Well, give her that ring, and therewithal
This letter: that's her chamber. Tell my lady
I claim the promise for her heavenly
   picture.
Your message done, hie home unto my
   chamber,
Where thou shalt find me sad and solitary.
          [*Exit.*]

JULIA.

How many women would do such a
   message?
Alas, poor Proteus! thou hast entertain'd
A fox to be the shepherd of thy lambs.
Alas, poor fool! why do I pity him
That with his very heart despiseth me?
Because he loves her, he despiseth me;
Because I love him, I must pity him.
This ring I gave him, when he parted from
   me,
To bind him to remember my good will;
And now am I—unhappy messenger—
To plead for that which I would not
   obtain,
To carry that which I would have refus'd,
To praise his faith, which I would have
   disprais'd.

I am my master's true-confirmed love,
But cannot be true servant to my master
Unless I prove false traitor to myself.
Yet will I woo for him, but yet so coldly
As, heaven it knows, I would not have him
    speed.
        [*Enter* Silvia, *attended.*]
Gentlewoman, good day! I pray you be
    my mean
To bring me where to speak with Madam
    Silvia.

Silvia.
What would you with her, if that I be she?

Julia.
If you be she, I do entreat your patience
To hear me speak the message I am sent on.

Silvia.
From whom?

Julia.
From my master, Sir Proteus, madam.

Silvia.
O! he sends you for a picture?

Julia.
Ay, madam.

Silvia.
Ursula, bring my picture there.
        [*A picture brought.*]
Go, give your master this. Tell him from me,
One Julia, that his changing thoughts
    forget,
Would better fit his chamber than this
    shadow.

Julia.
Madam, please you peruse this letter.—
Pardon me, madam; I have unadvis'd
Deliver'd you a paper that I should not:
This is the letter to your ladyship.

Silvia.
I pray thee, let me look on that again.

Julia.
It may not be: good madam, pardon me.

Silvia.
There, hold. I will not look upon your
    master's lines:
I know they are stuff'd with protestations
And full of new-found oaths, which he
    will break
As easily as I do tear his paper.

Julia.
Madam, he sends your ladyship this ring.

Silvia.
The more shame for him that he sends
    it me;
For I have heard him say a thousand times
His Julia gave it him at his departure.
Though his false finger have profan'd the
    ring,
Mine shall not do his Julia so much wrong.

Julia.
She thanks you.

Silvia.
What say'st thou?

Julia.
I thank you, madam, that you tender her.
Poor gentlewoman, my master wrongs her
    much.

Silvia.
Dost thou know her?

Julia.
Almost as well as I do know myself:
To think upon her woes, I do protest
That I have wept a hundred several times.

Silvia.
Belike she thinks, that Proteus hath
    forsook her.

Julia.
I think she doth, and that's her cause of
    sorrow.

Silvia.
Is she not passing fair?

Julia.
She hath been fairer, madam, than she is.
When she did think my master lov'd her
    well,
She, in my judgment, was as fair as you;
But since she did neglect her looking-glass
And threw her sun-expelling mask away,
The air hath starv'd the roses in her cheeks
And pinch'd the lily-tincture of her face,
That now she is become as black as I.

Silvia.
How tall was she?

Julia.
About my stature; for at Pentecost,
When all our pageants of delight were
    play'd,

Our youth got me to play the woman's
    part,
And I was trimm'd in Madam Julia's gown,
Which served me as fit, by all men's
    judgments,
As if the garment had been made for me:
Therefore I know she is about my height.
And at that time I made her weep agood;
For I did play a lamentable part.
Madam, 'twas Ariadne passioning
For Theseus' perjury and unjust flight;
Which I so lively acted with my tears
That my poor mistress, mov'd therewithal,
Wept bitterly; and would I might be dead
If I in thought felt not her very sorrow!

SILVIA.
She is beholding to thee, gentle youth.—
Alas, poor lady, desolate and left!
I weep myself, to think upon thy words.
Here, youth, there is my purse; I give thee
    this
For thy sweet mistress' sake, because thou
    lov'st her.
Farewell.

JULIA.
And she shall thank you for't, if e'er you
    know her.—
    [*Exit* SILVIA *with* ATTENDANTS.]
A virtuous gentlewoman, mild and
    beautiful!
I hope my master's suit will be but cold,
Since she respects my mistress' love so
    much.
Alas, how love can trifle with itself!
Here is her picture; let me see. I think,
If I had such a tire, this face of mine
Were full as lovely as is this of hers;
And yet the painter flatter'd her a little,
Unless I flatter with myself too much.
Her hair is auburn, mine is perfect yellow:
If that be all the difference in his love,
I'll get me such a colour'd periwig.
Her eyes are grey as glass, and so are mine;
Ay, but her forehead's low, and mine's as
    high.
What should it be that he respects in her
But I can make respective in myself,
If this fond Love were not a blinded god?

Come, shadow, come, and take this
    shadow up,
For 'tis thy rival. O thou senseless form!
Thou shalt be worshipp'd, kiss'd, lov'd, and
    ador'd,
And, were there sense in his idolatry,
My substance should be statue in thy
    stead.
I'll use thee kindly for thy mistress' sake,
That us'd me so; or else, by Jove I vow,
I should have scratch'd out your unseeing
    eyes,
To make my master out of love with thee.
    [*Exit.*]

ACT V
SCENE I
Milan. An abbey.
[*Enter* EGLAMOUR.]

EGLAMOUR.
The sun begins to gild the western sky,
And now it is about the very hour
That Silvia at Friar Patrick's cell should
    meet me.
She will not fail; for lovers break not hours
Unless it be to come before their time,
So much they spur their expedition.
See, where she comes.
    [*Enter* SILVIA.]
                    Lady, a happy evening!

SILVIA.
Amen, amen! Go on, good Eglamour,
Out at the postern by the abbey wall.
I fear I am attended by some spies.

EGLAMOUR.
Fear not: the forest is not three leagues off;
If we recover that, we are sure enough.
    [*Exeunt.*]

SCENE II
The same. A room in the duke's palace.
[*Enter* THURIO, PROTEUS, *and* JULIA.]

THURIO.
Sir Proteus, what says Silvia to my suit?

PROTEUS.
O, sir, I find her milder than she was;
And yet she takes exceptions at your
    person.

THURIO.
What! that my leg is too long?
PROTEUS.
No; that it is too little.
THURIO.
I'll wear a boot to make it somewhat
    rounder.
JULIA. [*Aside.*]
But love will not be spurr'd to what it
    loathes.
THURIO.
What says she to my face?
PROTEUS.
She says it is a fair one.
THURIO.
Nay, then, the wanton lies; my face is
    black.
PROTEUS.
But pearls are fair; and the old saying is:
"Black men are pearls in beauteous ladies'
    eyes."
JULIA. [*Aside.*]
'Tis true, such pearls as put out ladies'
    eyes;
For I had rather wink than look on them.
THURIO.
How likes she my discourse?
PROTEUS.
Ill, when you talk of war.
THURIO.
But well when I discourse of love and
    peace?
JULIA. [*Aside.*]
But better, indeed, when you hold your
    peace.
THURIO.
What says she to my valour?
PROTEUS.
O, sir, she makes no doubt of that.
JULIA. [*Aside.*]
She needs not, when she knows it
    cowardice.
THURIO.
What says she to my birth?
PROTEUS.
That you are well deriv'd.
JULIA. [*Aside.*]
True; from a gentleman to a fool.

THURIO.
Considers she my possessions?
PROTEUS.
O, ay; and pities them.
THURIO.
Wherefore?
JULIA. [*Aside.*]
That such an ass should owe them.
PROTEUS.
That they are out by lease.
JULIA.
                    Here comes the duke.
                [*Enter* DUKE.]
DUKE.
How now, Sir Proteus! how now, Thurio!
Which of you saw Sir Eglamour of late?
THURIO.
Not I.
PROTEUS.
      Nor I.
DUKE.
          Saw you my daughter?
PROTEUS.
                        Neither.
DUKE.
Why then,
She's fled unto that peasant Valentine;
And Eglamour is in her company.
'Tis true; for Friar Lawrence met them
    both
As he in penance wander'd through the
    forest;
Him he knew well, and guess'd that it was
    she,
But, being mask'd, he was not sure of it;
Besides, she did intend confession
At Patrick's cell this even; and there she
    was not.
These likelihoods confirm her flight from
    hence.
Therefore, I pray you, stand not to
    discourse,
But mount you presently, and meet with me
Upon the rising of the mountain-foot
That leads toward Mantua, whither they
    are fled.
Dispatch, sweet gentlemen, and follow me.
                [*Exit.*]

Thurio.

Why, this it is to be a peevish girl
That flies her fortune when it follows her.
I'll after, more to be reveng'd on Eglamour
Than for the love of reckless Silvia.

[*Exit.*]

Proteus.

And I will follow, more for Silvia's love
Than hate of Eglamour, that goes with her.

[*Exit.*]

Julia.

And I will follow, more to cross that love
Than hate for Silvia, that is gone for love.

[*Exit.*]

SCENE III

Frontiers of Mantua. The forest.
[*Enter* Outlaws *with* Silvia.]

First Outlaw.

Come, come.
Be patient; we must bring you to our
    captain.

Silvia.

A thousand more mischances than this one
Have learn'd me how to brook this
    patiently.

Second Outlaw.

Come, bring her away.

First Outlaw.

Where is the gentleman that was with her?

Second Outlaw.

Being nimble-footed, he hath outrun us;
But Moyses and Valerius follow him.
Go thou with her to the west end of the
    wood;
There is our captain; we'll follow him
    that's fled.
The thicket is beset; he cannot 'scape.

[*Exeunt all except the* First Outlaw
    and Silvia.]

First Outlaw.

Come, I must bring you to our captain's
    cave.
Fear not; he bears an honourable mind,
And will not use a woman lawlessly.

Silvia.

O Valentine, this I endure for thee!

[*Exeunt.*]

SCENE IV

Another part of the forest.
[*Enter* Valentine.]

Valentine.

How use doth breed a habit in a man!
This shadowy desert, unfrequented
    woods,
I better brook than flourishing peopled
    towns.
Here can I sit alone, unseen of any,
And to the nightingale's complaining
    notes
Tune my distresses and record my woes.
O thou that dost inhabit in my breast,
Leave not the mansion so long tenantless,
Lest, growing ruinous, the building fall
And leave no memory of what it was!
Repair me with thy presence, Silvia!
Thou gentle nymph, cherish thy forlorn
    swain.

[*Noise within.*] What halloing and what
    stir is this to-day?
These are my mates, that make their wills
    their law,
Have some unhappy passenger in chase.
They love me well; yet I have much to do
To keep them from uncivil outrages.
Withdraw thee, Valentine: who's this
    comes here?

[*Steps aside.*]

[*Enter* Proteus, Silvia, *and* Julia.]

Proteus.

Madam, this service I have done for you—
Though you respect not aught your servant
    doth—
To hazard life, and rescue you from him
That would have forc'd your honour and
    your love.
Vouchsafe me, for my meed, but one fair
    look;
A smaller boon than this I cannot beg,
And less than this, I am sure, you cannot
    give.

Valentine. [*Aside.*]

How like a dream is this I see and hear!
Love, lend me patience to forbear awhile.

Silvia.

O miserable, unhappy that I am!

Proteus.
Unhappy were you, madam, ere I came;
But by my coming I have made you happy.
Silvia.
By thy approach thou mak'st me most
    unhappy.
Julia. [*Aside.*]
And me, when he approacheth to your
    presence.
Silvia.
Had I been seized by a hungry lion,
I would have been a breakfast to the beast,
Rather than have false Proteus rescue me.
O! heaven be judge how I love Valentine,
Whose life's as tender to me as my soul,
And full as much—for more there cannot
    be—
I do detest false, perjur'd Proteus.
Therefore be gone; solicit me no more.
Proteus.
What dangerous action, stood it next to
    death,
Would I not undergo for one calm look!
O, 'tis the curse in love, and still approv'd,
When women cannot love where they're
    belov'd!
Silvia.
When Proteus cannot love where he's
    belov'd!
Read over Julia's heart, thy first best love,
For whose dear sake thou didst then rend
    thy faith
Into a thousand oaths; and all those oaths
Descended into perjury, to love me.
Thou hast no faith left now, unless thou'dst
    two,
And that's far worse than none: better
    have none
Than plural faith, which is too much by
    one.
Thou counterfeit to thy true friend!
Proteus.
                                    In love,
Who respects friend?
Silvia.
                        All men but Proteus.
Proteus.
Nay, if the gentle spirit of moving words

Can no way change you to a milder form,
I'll woo you like a soldier, at arms' end,
And love you 'gainst the nature of love,—
    force ye.
Silvia.
O heaven!
Proteus.
                    I'll force thee yield to my desire.
Valentine. [*Coming forward.*]
Ruffian! let go that rude uncivil touch;
Thou friend of an ill fashion!
Proteus.
                                    Valentine!
Valentine.
Thou common friend, that's without faith
    or love—
For such is a friend now—treacherous
    man,
Thou hast beguil'd my hopes; nought but
    mine eye
Could have persuaded me. Now I dare
    not say
I have one friend alive: thou wouldst
    disprove me.
Who should be trusted, when one's own
    right hand
Is perjur'd to the bosom? Proteus,
I am sorry I must never trust thee more,
But count the world a stranger for thy
    sake.
The private wound is deep'st. O time most
    curst!
'Mongst all foes that a friend should be
    the worst!
Proteus.
My shame and guilt confounds me.
Forgive me, Valentine; if hearty sorrow
Be a sufficient ransom for offence,
I tender 't here; I do as truly suffer
As e'er I did commit.
Valentine.
                            Then I am paid;
And once again I do receive thee honest.
Who by repentance is not satisfied
Is nor of heaven nor earth, for these are
    pleas'd.
By penitence the Eternal's wrath's
    appeas'd:

And, that my love may appear plain and
    free,
All that was mine in Silvia I give thee.

JULIA.
O me unhappy! [*Swoons.*]

PROTEUS.
        Look to the boy.

VALENTINE.
              Why, boy!
Why, wag! how now! What's the matter?
Look up; speak.

JULIA.
      O good sir, my master charg'd me
To deliver a ring to Madam Silvia,
Which, out of my neglect, was never done.

PROTEUS.
Where is that ring, boy?

JULIA.
          Here 'tis; this is it.
    [*Gives a ring.*]

PROTEUS.
How! let me see.
Why, this is the ring I gave to Julia.

JULIA.
O, cry you mercy, sir, I have mistook;
This is the ring you sent to Silvia.
    [*Shows another ring.*]

PROTEUS.
But how cam'st thou by this ring?
At my depart I gave this unto Julia.

JULIA.
And Julia herself did give it me;
And Julia herself have brought it hither.

PROTEUS.
How! Julia!

JULIA.
Behold her that gave aim to all thy oaths,
And entertain'd them deeply in her heart:
How oft hast thou with perjury cleft the
    root!
O Proteus! let this habit make thee blush.
Be thou asham'd that I have took upon
    me
Such an immodest raiment; if shame live
In a disguise of love. It is the lesser blot,
    modesty finds,
Women to change their shapes than men
    their minds.

PROTEUS.
Than men their minds! 'tis true. O heaven!
    were man
But constant, he were perfect: that one
    error
Fills him with faults; makes him run
    through all the sins:
Inconstancy falls off ere it begins.
What is in Silvia's face, but I may spy
More fresh in Julia's with a constant eye?

VALENTINE.
Come, come, a hand from either.
Let me be blest to make this happy close;
'Twere pity two such friends should be
    long foes.

PROTEUS.
Bear witness, heaven, I have my wish for
    ever.

JULIA.
And I mine.
    [*Enter* OUTLAWS, *with* DUKE *and*
           THURIO.]

OUTLAW.
A prize, a prize, a prize!

VALENTINE.
Forbear, forbear, I say; it is my lord the
    duke.
Your Grace is welcome to a man disgrac'd,
Banished Valentine.

DUKE.
Sir Valentine!

THURIO.
Yonder is Silvia; and Silvia's mine.

VALENTINE.
Thurio, give back, or else embrace thy
    death;
Come not within the measure of my
    wrath;
Do not name Silvia thine; if once again,
Verona shall not hold thee. Here she
    stands:
Take but possession of her with a touch;
I dare thee but to breathe upon my love.

THURIO.
Sir Valentine, I care not for her, I;
I hold him but a fool that will endanger
His body for a girl that loves him not:
I claim her not, and therefore she is thine.

Duke.
The more degenerate and base art thou
To make such means for her as thou hast
    done,
And leave her on such slight conditions.
Now, by the honour of my ancestry,
I do applaud thy spirit, Valentine,
And think thee worthy of an empress'
    love.
Know then, I here forget all former griefs,
Cancel all grudge, repeal thee home again,
Plead a new state in thy unrivall'd merit,
To which I thus subscribe: Sir Valentine,
Thou art a gentleman, and well deriv'd;
Take thou thy Silvia, for thou hast deserv'd
    her.

Valentine.
I thank your Grace; the gift hath made
    me happy.
I now beseech you, for your daughter's
    sake,
To grant one boon that I shall ask of you.

Duke.
I grant it for thine own, whate'er it be.

Valentine.
These banish'd men, that I have kept withal,
Are men endu'd with worthy qualities:
Forgive them what they have committed
    here,
And let them be recall'd from their exile:
They are reformed, civil, full of good,
And fit for great employment, worthy lord.

Duke.
Thou hast prevail'd; I pardon them, and
    thee;
Dispose of them as thou know'st their
    deserts.
Come, let us go; we will include all jars
With triumphs, mirth, and rare solemnity.

Valentine.
And, as we walk along, I dare be bold
With our discourse to make your Grace
    to smile.
What think you of this page, my lord?

Duke.
I think the boy hath grace in him; he
    blushes.

Valentine.
I warrant you, my lord, more grace than
    boy.

Duke.
What mean you by that saying?

Valentine.
Please you, I'll tell you as we pass along,
That you will wonder what hath fortuned.
Come, Proteus; 'tis your penance but to
    hear
The story of your loves discovered:
That done, our day of marriage shall be
    yours;
One feast, one house, one mutual
    happiness.

                              [*Exeunt.*]

The Merry Wives of Windsor

DRAMATIS PERSONAE

SIR JOHN FALSTAFF
FENTON, *a young gentleman*
SHALLOW, *a country justice*
SLENDER, *cousin to Shallow*
FORD, *a gentleman dwelling at Windsor*
PAGE, *a gentleman dwelling at Windsor*
WILLIAM PAGE, *a boy, son to Page*
SIR HUGH EVANS, *a Welsh parson*
DOCTOR CAIUS, *a French physician*
HOST *of the Garter Inn*
BARDOLPH, PISTOL, NYM, *followers of Falstaff*

ROBIN, *page to Falstaff*
SIMPLE, *servant to Slender*
RUGBY, *servant to Doctor Caius*
MISTRESS FORD
MISTRESS PAGE
MISTRESS ANNE PAGE, *her daughter, in love with Fenton*
MISTRESS QUICKLY, *servant to Doctor Caius*
SERVANTS *to Page, Ford, &c.*

SCENE: *Windsor and the neighbourhood.*

ACT I
SCENE I

Windsor. Before Page's house.
[*Enter* JUSTICE SHALLOW, SLENDER, *and* SIR HUGH EVANS.]

SHALLOW.
Sir Hugh, persuade me not; I will make a Star Chamber matter of it; if he were twenty Sir John Falstaffs, he shall not abuse Robert Shallow, esquire.

SLENDER.
In the county of Gloucester, Justice of Peace, and *coram*.

SHALLOW.
Ay, cousin Slender, and *cust-alorum*.

SLENDER.
Ay, and *rato-lorum* too; and a gentleman born, Master Parson, who writes himself *armigero* in any bill, warrant, quittance, or obligation—*armigero*.

SHALLOW.
Ay, that I do; and have done any time these three hundred years.

SLENDER.
All his successors, gone before him, hath done't; and all his ancestors, that come after him, may: they may give the dozen white luces in their coat.

SHALLOW.
It is an old coat.

EVANS.
The dozen white louses do become an old coat well; it agrees well, passant; it is a familiar beast to man, and signifies love.

SHALLOW.
The luce is the fresh fish; the salt fish is an old coat.

SLENDER.
I may quarter, coz?

SHALLOW.
You may, by marrying.

EVANS.
It is marring indeed, if he quarter it.

SHALLOW.
Not a whit.

EVANS.
Yes, py'r lady! If he has a quarter of your

coat, there is but three skirts for yourself, in my simple conjectures; but that is all one. If Sir John Falstaff have committed disparagements unto you, I am of the church, and will be glad to do my benevolence to make atonements and compremises between you.

Shallow.
The council shall hear it; it is a riot.

Evans.
It is not meet the council hear a riot; there is no fear of Got in a riot; the council, look you, shall desire to hear the fear of Got, and not to hear a riot; take your vizaments in that.

Shallow.
Ha! o' my life, if I were young again, the sword should end it.

Evans.
It is petter that friends is the sword and end it; and there is also another device in my prain, which peradventure prings goot discretions with it. There is Anne Page, which is daughter to Master George Page, which is pretty virginity.

Slender.
Mistress Anne Page? She has brown hair, and speaks small like a woman.

Evans.
It is that fery person for all the orld, as just as you will desire; and seven hundred pounds of moneys, and gold, and silver, is her grandsire upon his death's-bed—Got deliver to a joyful resurrections!—give, when she is able to overtake seventeen years old. It were a goot motion if we leave our pribbles and prabbles, and desire a marriage between Master Abraham and Mistress Anne Page.

Shallow.
Did her grandsire leave her seven hundred pound?

Evans.
Ay, and her father is make her a petter penny.

Shallow.
I know the young gentlewoman; she has good gifts.

Evans.
Seven hundred pounds, and possibilities, is goot gifts.

Shallow.
Well, let us see honest Master Page. Is Falstaff there?

Evans.
Shall I tell you a lie? I do despise a liar as I do despise one that is false; or as I despise one that is not true. The knight Sir John is there; and, I beseech you, be ruled by your well-willers. I will peat the door for Master Page. [*Knocks.*] What, hoa! Got pless your house here!

Page. [*Within.*]
Who's there?

Evans.
Here is Got's plessing, and your friend, and Justice Shallow; and here young Master Slender, that peradventures shall tell you another tale, if matters grow to your likings.
[*Enter* Page.]

Page.
I am glad to see your worships well. I thank you for my venison, Master Shallow.

Shallow.
Master Page, I am glad to see you; much good do it your good heart! I wished your venison better; it was ill killed. How doth good Mistress Page?—and I thank you always with my heart, la! with my heart.

Page.
Sir, I thank you.

Shallow.
Sir, I thank you; by yea and no, I do.

Page.
I am glad to see you, good Master Slender.

Slender.
How does your fallow greyhound, sir? I heard say he was outrun on Cotsall.

Page.
It could not be judged, sir.

Slender.
You'll not confess, you'll not confess.

Shallow.
That he will not: 'tis your fault; 'tis your fault. 'Tis a good dog.

Page.
A cur, sir.
Shallow.
Sir, he's a good dog, and a fair dog; can there be more said? he is good, and fair. Is Sir John Falstaff here?
Page.
Sir, he is within; and I would I could do a good office between you.
Evans.
It is spoke as a Christians ought to speak.
Shallow.
He hath wronged me, Master Page.
Page.
Sir, he doth in some sort confess it.
Shallow.
If it be confessed, it is not redressed: is not that so, Master Page? He hath wronged me; indeed he hath;—at a word, he hath,—believe me; Robert Shallow, esquire, saith he is wronged.
Page.
Here comes Sir John.
[*Enter* Sir John Falstaff, Bardolph, Nym, *and* Pistol.]
Falstaff.
Now, Master Shallow, you'll complain of me to the king?
Shallow.
Knight, you have beaten my men, killed my deer, and broke open my lodge.
Falstaff.
But not kiss'd your keeper's daughter?
Shallow.
Tut, a pin! this shall be answered.
Falstaff.
I will answer it straight: I have done all this. That is now answered.
Shallow.
The council shall know this.
Falstaff.
'Twere better for you if it were known in counsel: you'll be laughed at.
Evans.
Pauca verba, Sir John; goot worts.
Falstaff.
Good worts! good cabbage! Slender, I broke your head; what matter have you against me?

Slender.
Marry, sir, I have matter in my head against you; and against your cony-catching rascals, Bardolph, Nym, and Pistol. They carried me to the tavern, and made me drunk, and afterwards picked my pocket.
Bardolph.
You Banbury cheese!
Slender.
Ay, it is no matter.
Pistol.
How now, Mephostophilus!
Slender.
Ay, it is no matter.
Nym.
Slice, I say! *pauca, pauca*; slice! That's my humour.
Slender.
Where's Simple, my man? Can you tell, cousin?
Evans.
Peace, I pray you. Now let us understand. There is three umpires in this matter, as I understand: that is—Master Page, *fidelicet* Master Page; and there is myself, *fidelicet* myself; and the three party is, lastly and finally, mine host of the Garter.
Page.
We three to hear it and end it between them.
Evans.
Fery goot: I will make a prief of it in my note-book; and we will afterwards ork upon the cause with as great discreetly as we can.
Falstaff.
Pistol!
Pistol.
He hears with ears.
Evans.
The tevil and his tam! what phrase is this, "He hears with ear"? Why, it is affectations.
Falstaff.
Pistol, did you pick Master Slender's purse?
Slender.
Ay, by these gloves, did he—or I would I might never come in mine own great

chamber again else!—of seven groats in mill-sixpences, and two Edward shovel-boards that cost me two shilling and two pence a-piece of Yead Miller, by these gloves.

FALSTAFF.

Is this true, Pistol?

EVANS.

No, it is false, if it is a pick-purse.

PISTOL.

Ha, thou mountain-foreigner!—Sir John and master mine,
I combat challenge of this latten bilbo.
Word of denial in thy labras here!
Word of denial! Froth and scum, thou liest.

SLENDER.

By these gloves, then, 'twas he.

NYM.

Be avised, sir, and pass good humours; I will say "marry trap" with you, if you run the nuthook's humour on me; that is the very note of it.

SLENDER.

By this hat, then, he in the red face had it; for though I cannot remember what I did when you made me drunk, yet I am not altogether an ass.

FALSTAFF.

What say you, Scarlet and John?

BARDOLPH.

Why, sir, for my part, I say the gentleman had drunk himself out of his five sentences.

EVANS.

It is his "five senses"; fie, what the ignorance is!

BARDOLPH.

And being fap, sir, was, as they say, cashier'd; and so conclusions passed the careires.

SLENDER.

Ay, you spake in Latin then too; but 'tis no matter; I'll ne'er be drunk whilst I live again, but in honest, civil, godly company, for this trick; if I be drunk, I'll be drunk with those that have the fear of God, and not with drunken knaves.

EVANS.

So Got udge me, that is a virtuous mind.

FALSTAFF.

You hear all these matters denied, gentlemen; you hear it.

[*Enter* ANNE PAGE *with wine;* MISTRESS FORD *and* MISTRESS PAGE, *following.*]

PAGE.

Nay, daughter, carry the wine in; we'll drink within.

[*Exit* ANNE PAGE.]

SLENDER.

O heaven! this is Mistress Anne Page.

PAGE.

How now, Mistress Ford!

FALSTAFF.

Mistress Ford, by my troth, you are very well met; by your leave, good mistress. [*Kissing her.*]

PAGE.

Wife, bid these gentlemen welcome. Come, we have a hot venison pasty to dinner; come, gentlemen, I hope we shall drink down all unkindness.

[*Exeunt all but* SHALLOW, SLENDER, *and* EVANS.]

SLENDER.

I had rather than forty shillings I had my Book of Songs and Sonnets here. [*Enter* SIMPLE.] How, Simple! Where have you been? I must wait on myself, must I? You have not the Book of Riddles about you, have you?

SIMPLE.

Book of Riddles! why, did you not lend it to Alice Shortcake upon Allhallowmas last, a fortnight afore Michaelmas?

SHALLOW.

Come, coz; come, coz; we stay for you. A word with you, coz; marry, this, coz: there is, as 'twere, a tender, a kind of tender, made afar off by Sir Hugh here: do you understand me?

SLENDER.

Ay, sir, you shall find me reasonable; if it be so, I shall do that that is reason.

SHALLOW.

Nay, but understand me.

SLENDER.

So I do, sir.

Evans.
Give ear to his motions, Master Slender: I will description the matter to you, if you be capacity of it.

Slender.
Nay, I will do as my cousin Shallow says; I pray you pardon me; he's a justice of peace in his country, simple though I stand here.

Evans.
But that is not the question; the question is concerning your marriage.

Shallow.
Ay, there's the point, sir.

Evans.
Marry is it; the very point of it; to Mistress Anne Page.

Slender.
Why, if it be so, I will marry her upon any reasonable demands.

Evans.
But can you affection the 'oman? Let us command to know that of your mouth or of your lips; for divers philosophers hold that the lips is parcel of the mouth: therefore, precisely, can you carry your good will to the maid?

Shallow.
Cousin Abraham Slender, can you love her?

Slender.
I hope, sir, I will do as it shall become one that would do reason.

Evans.
Nay, Got's lords and his ladies! you must speak possitable, if you can carry her your desires towards her.

Shallow.
That you must. Will you, upon good dowry, marry her?

Slender.
I will do a greater thing than that upon your request, cousin, in any reason.

Shallow.
Nay, conceive me, conceive me, sweet coz; what I do is to pleasure you, coz. Can you love the maid?

Slender.
I will marry her, sir, at your request; but if there be no great love in the beginning,

yet heaven may decrease it upon better acquaintance, when we are married and have more occasion to know one another; I hope upon familiarity will grow more contempt. But if you say "Marry her," I will marry her; that I am freely dissolved, and dissolutely.

Evans.
It is a fery discretion answer; save, the fall is in the ort "dissolutely": the ort is, according to our meaning, "resolutely." His meaning is good.

Shallow.
Ay, I think my cousin meant well.

Slender.
Ay, or else I would I might be hanged, la!

Shallow.
Here comes fair Mistress Anne. [*Re-enter* ANNE PAGE.] Would I were young for your sake, Mistress Anne!

Anne.
The dinner is on the table; my father desires your worships' company.

Shallow.
I will wait on him, fair Mistress Anne!

Evans.
Od's plessed will! I will not be absence at the grace.
[*Exeunt* SHALLOW *and* EVANS.]

Anne.
Will't please your worship to come in, sir?

Slender.
No, I thank you, forsooth, heartily; I am very well.

Anne.
The dinner attends you, sir.

Slender.
I am not a-hungry, I thank you, forsooth. Go, sirrah, for all you are my man, go wait upon my cousin Shallow. [*Exit* SIMPLE.] A justice of peace sometime may be beholding to his friend for a man. I keep but three men and a boy yet, till my mother be dead. But what though? Yet I live like a poor gentleman born.

Anne.
I may not go in without your worship: they will not sit till you come.

SLENDER.
I' faith, I'll eat nothing; I thank you as much as though I did.

ANNE.
I pray you, sir, walk in.

SLENDER.
I had rather walk here, I thank you. I bruised my shin th' other day with playing at sword and dagger with a master of fence; three veneys for a dish of stewed prunes—and, by my troth, I cannot abide the smell of hot meat since. Why do your dogs bark so? Be there bears i' the town?

ANNE.
I think there are, sir; I heard them talked of.

SLENDER.
I love the sport well; but I shall as soon quarrel at it as any man in England. You are afraid, if you see the bear loose, are you not?

ANNE.
Ay, indeed, sir.

SLENDER.
That's meat and drink to me now. I have seen Sackerson loose twenty times, and have taken him by the chain; but I warrant you, the women have so cried and shrieked at it that it passed; but women, indeed, cannot abide 'em; they are very ill-favoured rough things.

[Re-enter PAGE.]

PAGE.
Come, gentle Master Slender, come; we stay for you.

SLENDER.
I'll eat nothing, I thank you, sir.

PAGE.
By cock and pie, you shall not choose, sir! come, come.

SLENDER.
Nay, pray you lead the way.

PAGE.
Come on, sir.

SLENDER.
Mistress Anne, yourself shall go first.

ANNE.
Not I, sir; pray you keep on.

SLENDER.
Truly, I will not go first; truly, la! I will not do you that wrong.

ANNE.
I pray you, sir.

SLENDER.
I'll rather be unmannerly than troublesome. You do yourself wrong indeed, la!

[Exeunt.]

SCENE II
The same.
[Enter SIR HUGH EVANS and SIMPLE.]

EVANS.
Go your ways, and ask of Doctor Caius' house which is the way; and there dwells one Mistress Quickly, which is in the manner of his nurse, or his dry nurse, or his cook, or his laundry, his washer, and his wringer.

SIMPLE.
Well, sir.

EVANS.
Nay, it is petter yet. Give her this letter; for it is a 'oman that altogether's acquaintance with Mistress Anne Page; and the letter is to desire and require her to solicit your master's desires to Mistress Anne Page. I pray you be gone: I will make an end of my dinner; there's pippins and cheese to come.

[Exeunt.]

SCENE III
A room in the Garter Inn.
[Enter FALSTAFF, HOST, BARDOLPH, NYM, PISTOL, and ROBIN.]

FALSTAFF.
Mine host of the Garter!

HOST.
What says my bully rook? Speak scholarly and wisely.

FALSTAFF.
Truly, mine host, I must turn away some of my followers.

HOST.
Discard, bully Hercules; cashier; let them wag; trot, trot.

Falstaff.
I sit at ten pounds a week.

Host.
Thou'rt an emperor, Caesar, Keiser, and Pheazar. I will entertain Bardolph; he shall draw, he shall tap; said I well, bully Hector?

Falstaff.
Do so, good mine host.

Host.
I have spoke; let him follow. [*To* Bardolph.] Let me see thee froth and lime. I am at a word; follow.

[Exit Host.]

Falstaff.
Bardolph, follow him. A tapster is a good trade; an old cloak makes a new jerkin; a withered serving-man a fresh tapster. Go; adieu.

Bardolph.
It is a life that I have desired; I will thrive.

Pistol.
O base Hungarian wight! Wilt thou the spigot wield?

[Exit Bardolph.]

Nym.
He was gotten in drink. Is not the humour conceited?

Falstaff.
I am glad I am so acquit of this tinder-box: his thefts were too open; his filching was like an unskilful singer—he kept not time.

Nym.
The good humour is to steal at a minim's rest.

Pistol.
"Convey" the wise it call. "Steal!" foh! A fico for the phrase!

Falstaff.
Well, sirs, I am almost out at heels.

Pistol.
Why, then, let kibes ensue.

Falstaff.
There is no remedy; I must cony-catch; I must shift.

Pistol.
Young ravens must have food.

Falstaff.
Which of you know Ford of this town?

Pistol.
I ken the wight; he is of substance good.

Falstaff.
My honest lads, I will tell you what I am about.

Pistol.
Two yards, and more.

Falstaff.
No quips now, Pistol. Indeed, I am in the waist two yards about; but I am now about no waste; I am about thrift. Briefly, I do mean to make love to Ford's wife; I spy entertainment in her; she discourses, she carves, she gives the leer of invitation; I can construe the action of her familiar style; and the hardest voice of her behaviour, to be Englished rightly, is "I am Sir John Falstaff's."

Pistol.
He hath studied her will, and translated her will out of honesty into English.

Nym.
The anchor is deep; will that humour pass?

Falstaff.
Now, the report goes she has all the rule of her husband's purse; he hath a legion of angels.

Pistol.
As many devils entertain; and "To her, boy," say I.

Nym.
The humour rises; it is good; humour me the angels.

Falstaff.
I have writ me here a letter to her; and here another to Page's wife, who even now gave me good eyes too, examined my parts with most judicious oeillades; sometimes the beam of her view gilded my foot, sometimes my portly belly.

Pistol.
Then did the sun on dunghill shine.

Nym.
I thank thee for that humour.

Falstaff.
O! she did so course o'er my exteriors with such a greedy intention that the appetite of her eye did seem to scorch me up like

a burning-glass. Here's another letter to her: she bears the purse too; she is a region in Guiana, all gold and bounty. I will be cheator to them both, and they shall be exchequers to me; they shall be my East and West Indies, and I will trade to them both. Go, bear thou this letter to Mistress Page; and thou this to Mistress Ford. We will thrive, lads, we will thrive.

Pistol.

Shall I Sir Pandarus of Troy become,

And by my side wear steel? then Lucifer
    take all!

Nym.

I will run no base humour. Here, take the humour-letter; I will keep the haviour of reputation.

Falstaff. [*To* Robin.]

Hold, sirrah; bear you these letters tightly;

Sail like my pinnace to these golden shores.

Rogues, hence, avaunt! vanish like
    hailstones, go;

Trudge, plod away o' hoof; seek shelter, pack!

Falstaff will learn the humour of this age;

French thrift, you rogues; myself, and
    skirted page.

    [*Exeunt* Falstaff *and* Robin.]

Pistol.

Let vultures gripe thy guts! for gourd and
    fullam holds,

And high and low beguile the rich and
    poor;

Tester I'll have in pouch when thou shalt
    lack,

Base Phrygian Turk!

Nym.

I have operations in my head which be humours of revenge.

Pistol.

Wilt thou revenge?

Nym.

By welkin and her star!

Pistol.

With wit or steel?

Nym.

With both the humours, I:

I will discuss the humour of this love to
    Page.

Pistol.

And I to Ford shall eke unfold

How Falstaff, varlet vile,

His dove will prove, his gold will hold,

And his soft couch defile.

Nym.

My humour shall not cool: I will incense Page to deal with poison; I will possess him with yellowness, for the revolt of mine is dangerous: that is my true humour.

Pistol.

Thou art the Mars of malcontents; I second thee; troop on.

    [*Exeunt.*]

SCENE IV

A room in Doctor Caius's house.
[*Enter* Mistress Quickly *and*
Simple.]

Quickly.

What, John Rugby! [*Enter* Rugby.] I pray thee go to the casement, and see if you can see my master, Master Doctor Caius, coming: if he do, i' faith, and find anybody in the house, here will be an old abusing of God's patience and the king's English.

Rugby.

I'll go watch.

Quickly.

Go; and we'll have a posset for't soon at night, in faith, at the latter end of a sea-coal fire. [*Exit* Rugby.] An honest, willing, kind fellow, as ever servant shall come in house withal; and, I warrant you, no tell-tale nor no breed-bate; his worst fault is that he is given to prayer; he is something peevish that way; but nobody but has his fault; but let that pass. Peter Simple you say your name is?

Simple.

Ay, for fault of a better.

Quickly.

And Master Slender's your master?

Simple.

Ay, forsooth.

Quickly.

Does he not wear a great round beard, like a glover's paring-knife?

SIMPLE.
No, forsooth; he hath but a little whey face, with a little yellow beard—a cane-coloured beard.
QUICKLY.
A softly-sprighted man, is he not?
SIMPLE.
Ay, forsooth; but he is as tall a man of his hands as any is between this and his head; he hath fought with a warrener.
QUICKLY.
How say you?—O! I should remember him. Does he not hold up his head, as it were, and strut in his gait?
SIMPLE.
Yes, indeed, does he.
QUICKLY.
Well, heaven send Anne Page no worse fortune! Tell Master Parson Evans I will do what I can for your master: Anne is a good girl, and I wish—
            [Re-enter RUGBY.]
RUGBY.
Out, alas! here comes my master.
QUICKLY.
We shall all be shent. Run in here, good young man; go into this closet. [Shuts SIMPLE in the closet.] He will not stay long. What, John Rugby! John! what, John, I say! Go, John, go inquire for my master; I doubt he be not well that he comes not home.
            [Exit RUGBY.]
[Sings.] And down, down, adown-a, etc.
            [Enter DOCTOR CAIUS.]
CAIUS.
Vat is you sing? I do not like des toys. Pray you, go and vetch me in my closet une boitine verde—a box, a green-a box: do intend vat I speak? a green-a box.
QUICKLY.
Ay, forsooth, I'll fetch it you. [Aside.] I am glad he went not in himself: if he had found the young man, he would have been horn-mad.
CAIUS.
Fe, fe, fe fe! ma foi, il fait fort chaud. Je m'en vais à la cour—la grande affaire.

QUICKLY.
Is it this, sir?
CAIUS.
Oui; mettez le au mon pocket: dépêchez, quickly—Vere is dat knave, Rugby?
QUICKLY.
What, John Rugby? John!
            [Re-enter RUGBY.]
RUGBY.
Here, sir.
CAIUS.
You are John Rugby, and you are Jack Rugby: come, take-a your rapier, and come after my heel to de court.
RUGBY.
'Tis ready, sir, here in the porch.
CAIUS.
By my trot, I tarry too long—Od's me! Qu'ay j'oublié? Dere is some simples in my closet dat I vill not for the varld I shall leave behind.
QUICKLY. [Aside.]
Ay me, he'll find the young man there, and be mad!
CAIUS.
O diable, diable! vat is in my closet?— Villainy! larron! [Pulling SIMPLE out.] Rugby, my rapier!
QUICKLY.
Good master, be content.
CAIUS.
Verefore shall I be content-a?
QUICKLY.
The young man is an honest man.
CAIUS.
What shall de honest man do in my closet? dere is no honest man dat shall come in my closet.
QUICKLY.
I beseech you, be not so phlegmatic. Hear the truth of it: he came of an errand to me from Parson Hugh.
CAIUS.
Vell.
SIMPLE.
Ay, forsooth, to desire her to—
QUICKLY.
Peace, I pray you.

Caius.
Peace-a your tongue!—Speak-a your tale.
Simple.
To desire this honest gentlewoman, your maid, to speak a good word to Mistress Anne Page for my master, in the way of marriage.
Quickly.
This is all, indeed, la! but I'll ne'er put my finger in the fire, and need not.
Caius.
Sir Hugh send-a you?—Rugby, *baillez* me some paper: tarry you a little-a while. [*Writes.*]
Quickly.
I am glad he is so quiet: if he had been throughly moved, you should have heard him so loud and so melancholy. But notwithstanding, man, I'll do you your master what good I can; and the very yea and the no is, the French doctor, my master—I may call him my master, look you, for I keep his house; and I wash, wring, brew, bake, scour, dress meat and drink, make the beds, and do all myself—
Simple.
'Tis a great charge to come under one body's hand.
Quickly.
Are you avis'd o' that? You shall find it a great charge; and to be up early and down late; but notwithstanding,—to tell you in your ear,—I would have no words of it— my master himself is in love with Mistress Anne Page; but notwithstanding that, I know Anne's mind, that's neither here nor there.
Caius.
You jack'nape; give-a dis letter to Sir Hugh; by gar, it is a shallenge: I will cut his troat in de Park; and I will teach a scurvy jack-a-nape priest to meddle or make. You may be gone; it is not good you tarry here: by gar, I will cut all his two stones; by gar, he shall not have a stone to throw at his dog.
[*Exit* Simple.]
Quickly.
Alas, he speaks but for his friend.

Caius.
It is no matter-a ver dat:—do not you tell-a me dat I shall have Anne Page for myself? By gar, I vill kill de Jack priest; and I have appointed mine host of de Jartiere to measure our weapon. By gar, I vill myself have Anne Page.
Quickly.
Sir, the maid loves you, and all shall be well. We must give folks leave to prate: what, the good-jer!
Caius.
Rugby, come to the court vit me. By gar, if I have not Anne Page, I shall turn your head out of my door. Follow my heels, Rugby.
[*Exeunt* Caius *and* Rugby.]
Quickly.
You shall have An fool's-head of your own. No, I know Anne's mind for that: never a woman in Windsor knows more of Anne's mind than I do; nor can do more than I do with her, I thank heaven.
Fenton. [*Within.*]
Who's within there? ho!
Quickly.
Who's there, I trow? Come near the house, I pray you.
[*Enter* Fenton.]
Fenton.
How now, good woman! how dost thou?
Quickly.
The better, that it pleases your good worship to ask.
Fenton.
What news? how does pretty Mistress Anne?
Quickly.
In truth, sir, and she is pretty, and honest, and gentle; and one that is your friend, I can tell you that by the way; I praise heaven for it.
Fenton.
Shall I do any good, thinkest thou? Shall I not lose my suit?
Quickly.
Troth, sir, all is in His hands above; but notwithstanding, Master Fenton, I'll be

sworn on a book she loves you. Have not your worship a wart above your eye?

FENTON.

Yes, marry, have I; what of that?

QUICKLY.

Well, thereby hangs a tale; good faith, it is such another Nan; but, I detest, an honest maid as ever broke bread. We had an hour's talk of that wart; I shall never laugh but in that maid's company;—but, indeed, she is given too much to allicholy and musing. But for you—well, go to.

FENTON.

Well, I shall see her to-day. Hold, there's money for thee; let me have thy voice in my behalf: if thou seest her before me, commend me.

QUICKLY.

Will I? i' faith, that we will; and I will tell your worship more of the wart the next time we have confidence; and of other wooers.

FENTON.

Well, farewell; I am in great haste now.

QUICKLY.

Farewell to your worship.—

[*Exit* FENTON.]

Truly, an honest gentleman; but Anne loves him not; for I know Anne's mind as well as another does. Out upon 't, what have I forgot?

[*Exit.*]

ACT II
SCENE I

Before Page's house.

[*Enter* MISTRESS PAGE, *with a letter.*]

MISTRESS PAGE.

What! have I scaped love-letters in the holiday-time of my beauty, and am I now a subject for them? Let me see. [*Reads.*]
"Ask me no reason why I love you; for though Love use Reason for his precisian, he admits him not for his counsellor. You are not young, no more am I; go to, then, there's sympathy: you are merry, so am I; ha! ha! then there's more sympathy; you love sack, and so do I; would you desire better

sympathy? Let it suffice thee, Mistress Page, at the least, if the love of soldier can suffice, that I love thee. I will not say, pity me: 'tis not a soldier-like phrase; but I say, Love me. By me,

> Thine own true knight,
> By day or night,
> Or any kind of light,
> With all his might,
> For thee to fight,
>   John Falstaff."

What a Herod of Jewry is this! O wicked, wicked world! One that is well-nigh worn to pieces with age to show himself a young gallant. What an unweighed behaviour hath this Flemish drunkard picked, with the devil's name! out of my conversation, that he dares in this manner assay me? Why, he hath not been thrice in my company! What should I say to him? I was then frugal of my mirth:—Heaven forgive me! Why, I'll exhibit a bill in the parliament for the putting down of men. How shall I be revenged on him? for revenged I will be, as sure as his guts are made of puddings.

[*Enter* MISTRESS FORD.]

MISTRESS FORD.

Mistress Page! trust me, I was going to your house.

MISTRESS PAGE.

And, trust me, I was coming to you. You look very ill.

MISTRESS FORD.

Nay, I'll ne'er believe that; I have to show to the contrary.

MISTRESS PAGE.

Faith, but you do, in my mind.

MISTRESS FORD.

Well, I do, then; yet, I say, I could show you to the contrary. O, Mistress Page! give me some counsel.

MISTRESS PAGE.

What's the matter, woman?

MISTRESS FORD.

O woman, if it were not for one trifling respect, I could come to such honour!

MISTRESS PAGE.

Hang the trifle, woman; take the honour.

What is it?—Dispense with trifles;—what is it?

Mistress Ford.

If I would but go to hell for an eternal moment or so, I could be knighted.

Mistress Page.

What? thou liest. Sir Alice Ford! These knights will hack; and so thou shouldst not alter the article of thy gentry.

Mistress Ford.

We burn daylight: here, read, read; perceive how I might be knighted. I shall think the worse of fat men as long as I have an eye to make difference of men's liking: and yet he would not swear; praised women's modesty; and gave such orderly and well-behaved reproof to all uncomeliness that I would have sworn his disposition would have gone to the truth of his words; but they do no more adhere and keep place together than the Hundredth Psalm to the tune of "Greensleeves." What tempest, I trow, threw this whale, with so many tuns of oil in his belly, ashore at Windsor? How shall I be revenged on him? I think the best way were to entertain him with hope, till the wicked fire of lust have melted him in his own grease. Did you ever hear the like?

Mistress Page.

Letter for letter, but that the name of Page and Ford differs. To thy great comfort in this mystery of ill opinions, here's the twin-brother of thy letter; but let thine inherit first, for, I protest, mine never shall. I warrant he hath a thousand of these letters, writ with blank space for different names, sure, more, and these are of the second edition. He will print them, out of doubt; for he cares not what he puts into the press, when he would put us two: I had rather be a giantess and lie under Mount Pelion. Well, I will find you twenty lascivious turtles ere one chaste man.

Mistress Ford.

Why, this is the very same; the very hand, the very words. What doth he think of us?

Mistress Page.

Nay, I know not; it makes me almost ready to wrangle with mine own honesty. I'll entertain myself like one that I am not acquainted withal; for, sure, unless he know some strain in me that I know not myself, he would never have boarded me in this fury.

Mistress Ford.

"Boarding" call you it? I'll be sure to keep him above deck.

Mistress Page.

So will I; if he come under my hatches, I'll never to sea again. Let's be revenged on him; let's appoint him a meeting, give him a show of comfort in his suit, and lead him on with a fine-baited delay, till he hath pawned his horses to mine host of the Garter.

Mistress Ford.

Nay, I will consent to act any villainy against him that may not sully the chariness of our honesty. O, that my husband saw this letter! It would give eternal food to his jealousy.

Mistress Page.

Why, look where he comes; and my good man too: he's as far from jealousy as I am from giving him cause; and that, I hope, is an unmeasurable distance.

Mistress Ford.

You are the happier woman.

Mistress Page.

Let's consult together against this greasy knight. Come hither. [*They retire.*]

[*Enter* Ford, Pistol, *and* Page *and* Nym.]

Ford.

Well, I hope it be not so.

Pistol.

Hope is a curtal dog in some affairs:
Sir John affects thy wife.

Ford.

Why, sir, my wife is not young.

Pistol.

He woos both high and low, both rich
    and poor,
Both young and old, one with another,
    Ford;
He loves the gallimaufry. Ford, perpend.

Ford.

Love my wife!

PISTOL.

With liver burning hot: prevent, or go
  thou,

Like Sir Actaeon he, with Ringwood at
  thy heels.—

O! odious is the name!

FORD.

What name, sir?

PISTOL.

The horn, I say. Farewell:

Take heed; have open eye, for thieves do
  foot by night;

Take heed, ere summer comes, or cuckoo
  birds do sing.

Away, Sir Corporal Nym.

Believe it, Page; he speaks sense.

  [*Exit* PISTOL.]

FORD. [*Aside.*]

I will be patient: I will find out this.

NYM. [*To* PAGE.]

And this is true; I like not the humour
of lying. He hath wronged me in some
humours: I should have borne the
humoured letter to her; but I have a sword,
and it shall bite upon my necessity. He
loves your wife; there's the short and the
long. My name is Corporal Nym; I speak,
and I avouch 'tis true. My name is Nym,
and Falstaff loves your wife. Adieu. I love
not the humour of bread and cheese; and
there's the humour of it. Adieu.

  [*Exit* NYM.]

PAGE. [*Aside.*]

"The humour of it," quoth a'! Here's a
fellow frights English out of his wits.

FORD.

I will seek out Falstaff.

PAGE.

I never heard such a drawling, affecting
rogue.

FORD.

If I do find it: well.

PAGE.

I will not believe such a Cataian, though
the priest o' the town commended him for
a true man.

FORD.

'Twas a good sensible fellow: well.

PAGE.

How now, Meg!

  [MISTRESS PAGE *and* MISTRESS FORD
    come forward.]

MISTRESS PAGE.

Whither go you, George?—Hark you.

MISTRESS FORD.

How now, sweet Frank! why art thou
melancholy?

FORD.

I melancholy! I am not melancholy. Get
you home, go.

MISTRESS FORD.

Faith, thou hast some crotchets in thy head
now. Will you go, Mistress Page?

MISTRESS PAGE.

Have with you. You'll come to dinner,
George? [*Aside to* MISTRESS FORD.]
Look who comes yonder: she shall be our
messenger to this paltry knight.

MISTRESS FORD. [*Aside to* MISTRESS
  PAGE.]

Trust me, I thought on her: she'll fit it.

  [*Enter* MISTRESS QUICKLY.]

MISTRESS PAGE.

You are come to see my daughter Anne?

QUICKLY.

Ay, forsooth; and, I pray, how does good
Mistress Anne?

MISTRESS PAGE.

Go in with us and see; we'd have an hour's
talk with you.

  [*Exeunt* MISTRESS PAGE, MISTRESS FORD,
    and MISTRESS QUICKLY.]

PAGE.

How now, Master Ford!

FORD.

You heard what this knave told me, did you
not?

PAGE.

Yes; and you heard what the other told
me?

FORD.

Do you think there is truth in them?

PAGE.

Hang 'em, slaves! I do not think the knight
would offer it; but these that accuse him in
his intent towards our wives are a yoke of

his discarded men; very rogues, now they be out of service.

FORD.

Were they his men?

PAGE.

Marry, were they.

FORD.

I like it never the better for that. Does he lie at the Garter?

PAGE.

Ay, marry, does he. If he should intend this voyage toward my wife, I would turn her loose to him; and what he gets more of her than sharp words, let it lie on my head.

FORD.

I do not misdoubt my wife; but I would be loath to turn them together. A man may be too confident. I would have nothing "lie on my head": I cannot be thus satisfied.

PAGE.

Look where my ranting host of the Garter comes. There is either liquor in his pate or money in his purse when he looks so merrily. [*Enter* HOST *and* SHALLOW.] How now, mine host!

HOST.

How now, bully-rook! Thou'rt a gentleman. Cavaliero-justice, I say!

SHALLOW.

I follow, mine host, I follow. Good even and twenty, good Master Page! Master Page, will you go with us? We have sport in hand.

HOST.

Tell him, cavaliero-justice; tell him, bully-rook.

SHALLOW.

Sir, there is a fray to be fought between Sir Hugh the Welsh priest and Caius the French doctor.

FORD.

Good mine host o' the Garter, a word with you.

HOST.

What say'st thou, my bully-rook?

[*They go aside.*]

SHALLOW. [*To* PAGE.]

Will you go with us to behold it? My

merry host hath had the measuring of their weapons; and, I think, hath appointed them contrary places; for, believe me, I hear the parson is no jester. Hark, I will tell you what our sport shall be.

[*They converse apart.*]

HOST.

Hast thou no suit against my knight, my guest-cavaliero?

FORD.

None, I protest: but I'll give you a pottle of burnt sack to give me recourse to him, and tell him my name is Brook, only for a jest.

HOST.

My hand, bully; thou shalt have egress and regress; said I well? and thy name shall be Brook. It is a merry knight. Will you go, mynheers?

SHALLOW.

Have with you, mine host.

PAGE.

I have heard the Frenchman hath good skill in his rapier.

SHALLOW.

Tut, sir! I could have told you more. In these times you stand on distance, your passes, stoccadoes, and I know not what: 'tis the heart, Master Page; 'tis here, 'tis here. I have seen the time with my long sword I would have made you four tall fellows skip like rats.

HOST.

Here, boys, here, here! Shall we wag?

PAGE.

Have with you. I had rather hear them scold than fight.

[*Exeunt* HOST, SHALLOW, *and* PAGE.]

FORD.

Though Page be a secure fool, and stands so firmly on his wife's frailty, yet I cannot put off my opinion so easily. She was in his company at Page's house, and what they made there I know not. Well, I will look further into 't; and I have a disguise to sound Falstaff. If I find her honest, I lose not my labour; if she be otherwise, 'tis labour well bestowed.

[*Exit.*]

SCENE II

A room in the Garter Inn.

[*Enter* FALSTAFF *and* PISTOL.]

FALSTAFF.

I will not lend thee a penny.

PISTOL.

Why then, the world's mine oyster,
Which I with sword will open.
I will retort the sum in equipage.

FALSTAFF.

Not a penny. I have been content, sir, you
should lay my countenance to pawn; I have
grated upon my good friends for three
reprieves for you and your coach-fellow,
Nym; or else you had looked through
the grate, like a geminy of baboons. I am
damned in hell for swearing to gentlemen
my friends you were good soldiers and tall
fellows; and when Mistress Bridget lost
the handle of her fan, I took 't upon mine
honour thou hadst it not.

PISTOL.

Didst not thou share? Hadst thou not
    fifteen pence?

FALSTAFF.

Reason, you rogue, reason. Thinkest thou I'll
endanger my soul gratis? At a word, hang
no more about me, I am no gibbet for you:
go: a short knife and a throng!—to your
manor of Picht-hatch! go. You'll not bear
a letter for me, you rogue!—you stand upon
your honour!—Why, thou unconfinable
baseness, it is as much as I can do to keep
the terms of my honour precise. I, I, I myself
sometimes, leaving the fear of God on the
left hand, and hiding mine honour in my
necessity, am fain to shuffle, to hedge, and
to lurch; and yet you, rogue, will ensconce
your rags, your cat-a-mountain looks, your
red-lattice phrases, and your bold-beating
oaths, under the shelter of your honour!
You will not do it, you!

PISTOL.

I do relent; what wouldst thou more of
    man?

[*Enter* ROBIN.]

ROBIN.

Sir, here's a woman would speak with you.

FALSTAFF.

Let her approach.

[*Enter* MISTRESS QUICKLY.]

QUICKLY.

Give your worship good morrow.

FALSTAFF.

Good morrow, good wife.

QUICKLY.

Not so, an't please your worship.

FALSTAFF.

Good maid, then.

QUICKLY.

I'll be sworn;
As my mother was, the first hour I was
    born.

FALSTAFF.

I do believe the swearer. What with me?

QUICKLY.

Shall I vouchsafe your worship a word or
    two?

FALSTAFF.

Two thousand, fair woman; and I'll
vouchsafe thee the hearing.

QUICKLY.

There is one Mistress Ford, sir,—I pray,
come a little nearer this ways:—I myself
dwell with Master Doctor Caius.

FALSTAFF.

Well, on: Mistress Ford, you say,—

QUICKLY.

Your worship says very true;—I pray your
worship come a little nearer this ways.

FALSTAFF.

I warrant thee nobody hears—mine own
people, mine own people.

QUICKLY.

Are they so? God bless them, and make
them His servants!

FALSTAFF.

Well: Mistress Ford, what of her?

QUICKLY.

Why, sir, she's a good creature. Lord, Lord!
your worship's a wanton! Well, heaven
forgive you, and all of us, I pray.

FALSTAFF.

Mistress Ford; come, Mistress Ford—

QUICKLY.

Marry, this is the short and the long of it.

You have brought her into such a canaries as 'tis wonderful: the best courtier of them all, when the court lay at Windsor, could never have brought her to such a canary; yet there has been knights, and lords, and gentlemen, with their coaches; I warrant you, coach after coach, letter after letter, gift after gift; smelling so sweetly,—all musk, and so rushling, I warrant you, in silk and gold; and in such alligant terms; and in such wine and sugar of the best and the fairest, that would have won any woman's heart; and I warrant you, they could never get an eye-wink of her. I had myself twenty angels given me this morning; but I defy all angels, in any such sort, as they say, but in the way of honesty: and, I warrant you, they could never get her so much as sip on a cup with the proudest of them all; and yet there has been earls, nay, which is more, pensioners; but, I warrant you, all is one with her.

Falstaff.

But what says she to me? be brief, my good she-Mercury.

Quickly.

Marry, she hath received your letter; for the which she thanks you a thousand times; and she gives you to notify that her husband will be absence from his house between ten and eleven.

Falstaff.

Ten and eleven?

Quickly.

Ay, forsooth; and then you may come and see the picture, she says, that you wot of: Master Ford, her husband, will be from home. Alas! the sweet woman leads an ill life with him; he's a very jealousy man; she leads a very frampold life with him, good heart.

Falstaff.

Ten and eleven. Woman, commend me to her; I will not fail her.

Quickly.

Why, you say well. But I have another messenger to your worship: Mistress Page hath her hearty commendations to you too; and let me tell you in your ear, she's as fartuous a civil modest wife, and one, I tell you, that will not miss you morning nor evening prayer, as any is in Windsor, whoe'er be the other; and she bade me tell your worship that her husband is seldom from home, but she hopes there will come a time. I never knew a woman so dote upon a man: surely I think you have charms, la! yes, in truth.

Falstaff.

Not I, I assure thee; setting the attraction of my good parts aside, I have no other charms.

Quickly.

Blessing on your heart for 't!

Falstaff.

But, I pray thee, tell me this: has Ford's wife and Page's wife acquainted each other how they love me?

Quickly.

That were a jest indeed! They have not so little grace, I hope: that were a trick indeed! But Mistress Page would desire you to send her your little page, of all loves: her husband has a marvellous infection to the little page; and, truly, Master Page is an honest man. Never a wife in Windsor leads a better life than she does; do what she will, say what she will, take all, pay all, go to bed when she list, rise when she list, all is as she will; and truly she deserves it; for if there be a kind woman in Windsor, she is one. You must send her your page; no remedy.

Falstaff.

Why, I will.

Quickly.

Nay, but do so then; and, look you, he may come and go between you both; and in any case have a nay-word, that you may know one another's mind, and the boy never need to understand any thing; for 'tis not good that children should know any wickedness: old folks, you know, have discretion, as they say, and know the world.

Falstaff.

Fare thee well; commend me to them

both. There's my purse; I am yet thy debtor. Boy, go along with this woman. [*Exeunt* MISTRESS QUICKLY *and* ROBIN.] This news distracts me.

PISTOL.
This punk is one of Cupid's carriers;
Clap on more sails; pursue; up with your fights;
Give fire; she is my prize, or ocean whelm them all!
[*Exit* PISTOL.]

FALSTAFF.
Say'st thou so, old Jack? go thy ways; I'll make more of thy old body than I have done. Will they yet look after thee? Wilt thou, after the expense of so much money, be now a gainer? Good body, I thank thee. Let them say 'tis grossly done; so it be fairly done, no matter.
[*Enter* BARDOLPH, *with a cup of sack.*]

BARDOLPH.
Sir John, there's one Master Brook below would fain speak with you and be acquainted with you: and hath sent your worship a morning's draught of sack.

FALSTAFF.
Brook is his name?

BARDOLPH.
Ay, sir.

FALSTAFF.
Call him in. [*Exit* BARDOLPH.] Such Brooks are welcome to me, that o'erflow such liquor. Ah, ha! Mistress Ford and Mistress Page, have I encompassed you? Go to; via!
[*Re-enter* BARDOLPH, *with* FORD *disguised.*]

FORD.
Bless you, sir!

FALSTAFF.
And you, sir; would you speak with me?

FORD.
I make bold to press with so little preparation upon you.

FALSTAFF.
You're welcome. What's your will?—Give us leave, drawer.
[*Exit* BARDOLPH.]

FORD.
Sir, I am a gentleman that have spent much: my name is Brook.

FALSTAFF.
Good Master Brook, I desire more acquaintance of you.

FORD.
Good Sir John, I sue for yours: not to charge you; for I must let you understand I think myself in better plight for a lender than you are: the which hath something embold'ned me to this unseasoned intrusion; for they say, if money go before, all ways do lie open.

FALSTAFF.
Money is a good soldier, sir, and will on.

FORD.
Troth, and I have a bag of money here troubles me; if you will help to bear it, Sir John, take all, or half, for easing me of the carriage.

FALSTAFF.
Sir, I know not how I may deserve to be your porter.

FORD.
I will tell you, sir, if you will give me the hearing.

FALSTAFF.
Speak, good Master Brook; I shall be glad to be your servant.

FORD.
Sir, I hear you are a scholar,—I will be brief with you, and you have been a man long known to me, though I had never so good means, as desire, to make myself acquainted with you. I shall discover a thing to you, wherein I must very much lay open mine own imperfection; but, good Sir John, as you have one eye upon my follies, as you hear them unfolded, turn another into the register of your own, that I may pass with a reproof the easier, sith you yourself know how easy is it to be such an offender.

FALSTAFF.
Very well, sir; proceed.

FORD.
There is a gentlewoman in this town, her husband's name is Ford.

FALSTAFF.

Well, sir.

FORD.

I have long loved her, and, I protest to you, bestowed much on her; followed her with a doting observance; engrossed opportunities to meet her; fee'd every slight occasion that could but niggardly give me sight of her; not only bought many presents to give her, but have given largely to many to know what she would have given; briefly, I have pursued her as love hath pursued me; which hath been on the wing of all occasions. But whatsoever I have merited, either in my mind or in my means, meed, I am sure, I have received none, unless experience be a jewel that I have purchased at an infinite rate, and that hath taught me to say this:

Love like a shadow flies when substance love pursues;

Pursuing that that flies, and flying what pursues.

FALSTAFF.

Have you received no promise of satisfaction at her hands?

FORD.

Never.

FALSTAFF.

Have you importuned her to such a purpose?

FORD.

Never.

FALSTAFF.

Of what quality was your love, then?

FORD.

Like a fair house built on another man's ground; so that I have lost my edifice by mistaking the place where I erected it.

FALSTAFF.

To what purpose have you unfolded this to me?

FORD.

When I have told you that, I have told you all. Some say that though she appear honest to me, yet in other places she enlargeth her mirth so far that there is shrewd construction made of her. Now, Sir John, here is the heart of my purpose: you are a gentleman of excellent breeding, admirable discourse, of great admittance, authentic in your place and person, generally allowed for your many war-like, court-like, and learned preparations.

FALSTAFF.

O, sir!

FORD.

Believe it, for you know it. There is money; spend it, spend it; spend more; spend all I have; only give me so much of your time in exchange of it as to lay an amiable siege to the honesty of this Ford's wife: use your art of wooing, win her to consent to you; if any man may, you may as soon as any.

FALSTAFF.

Would it apply well to the vehemency of your affection, that I should win what you would enjoy? Methinks you prescribe to yourself very preposterously.

FORD.

O, understand my drift. She dwells so securely on the excellency of her honour that the folly of my soul dares not present itself; she is too bright to be looked against. Now, could I come to her with any detection in my hand, my desires had instance and argument to commend themselves; I could drive her then from the ward of her purity, her reputation, her marriage-vow, and a thousand other her defences, which now are too too strongly embattled against me. What say you to't, Sir John?

FALSTAFF.

Master Brook, I will first make bold with your money; next, give me your hand; and last, as I am a gentleman, you shall, if you will, enjoy Ford's wife.

FORD.

O good sir!

FALSTAFF.

I say you shall.

FORD.

Want no money, Sir John; you shall want none.

FALSTAFF.

Want no Mistress Ford, Master Brook; you shall want none. I shall be with her,

I may tell you, by her own appointment; even as you came in to me her assistant or go-between parted from me: I say I shall be with her between ten and eleven; for at that time the jealous rascally knave, her husband, will be forth. Come you to me at night; you shall know how I speed.

FORD.

I am blest in your acquaintance. Do you know Ford, sir?

FALSTAFF.

Hang him, poor cuckoldly knave! I know him not; yet I wrong him to call him poor; they say the jealous wittolly knave hath masses of money; for the which his wife seems to me well-favoured. I will use her as the key of the cuckoldly rogue's coffer; and there's my harvest-home.

FORD.

I would you knew Ford, sir, that you might avoid him if you saw him.

FALSTAFF.

Hang him, mechanical salt-butter rogue! I will stare him out of his wits; I will awe him with my cudgel; it shall hang like a meteor o'er the cuckold's horns. Master Brook, thou shalt know I will predominate over the peasant, and thou shalt lie with his wife. Come to me soon at night. Ford's a knave, and I will aggravate his style; thou, Master Brook, shalt know him for knave and cuckold. Come to me soon at night.

[*Exit* FALSTAFF.]

FORD.

What a damned Epicurean rascal is this! My heart is ready to crack with impatience. Who says this is improvident jealousy? My wife hath sent to him; the hour is fixed; the match is made. Would any man have thought this? See the hell of having a false woman! My bed shall be abused, my coffers ransacked, my reputation gnawn at; and I shall not only receive this villanous wrong, but stand under the adoption of abominable terms, and by him that does me this wrong. Terms! names! Amaimon sounds well; Lucifer, well; Barbason, well; yet they are devils' additions, the names of

fiends. But Cuckold! Wittol!—Cuckold! the devil himself hath not such a name. Page is an ass, a secure ass; he will trust his wife; he will not be jealous; I will rather trust a Fleming with my butter, Parson Hugh the Welshman with my cheese, an Irishman with my aqua-vitae bottle, or a thief to walk my ambling gelding, than my wife with herself; then she plots, then she ruminates, then she devises; and what they think in their hearts they may effect, they will break their hearts but they will effect. God be praised for my jealousy! Eleven o'clock the hour. I will prevent this, detect my wife, be revenged on Falstaff, and laugh at Page. I will about it; better three hours too soon than a minute too late. Fie, fie, fie! cuckold! cuckold! cuckold!

[*Exit.*]

SCENE III
A field near Windsor.
[*Enter* CAIUS *and* RUGBY.]

CAIUS.

Jack Rugby!

RUGBY.

Sir?

CAIUS.

Vat is de clock, Jack?

RUGBY.

'Tis past the hour, sir, that Sir Hugh promised to meet.

CAIUS.

By gar, he has save his soul, dat he is no come; he has pray his Pible vell dat he is no come: by gar, Jack Rugby, he is dead already, if he be come.

RUGBY.

He is wise, sir; he knew your worship would kill him if he came.

CAIUS.

By gar, de herring is no dead so as I vill kill him. Take your rapier, Jack; I vill tell you how I vill kill him.

RUGBY.

Alas, sir, I cannot fence!

CAIUS.

Villany, take your rapier.

Rugby.

Forbear; here's company.

[*Enter* Host, Shallow, Slender, *and* Page.]

Host.

Bless thee, bully doctor!

Shallow.

Save you, Master Doctor Caius!

Page.

Now, good Master Doctor!

Slender.

Give you good morrow, sir.

Caius.

Vat be all you, one, two, tree, four, come for?

Host.

To see thee fight, to see thee foin, to see thee traverse; to see thee here, to see thee there; to see thee pass thy punto, thy stock, thy reverse, thy distance, thy montant. Is he dead, my Ethiopian? Is he dead, my Francisco? Ha, bully! What says my Aesculapius? my Galen? my heart of elder? Ha! is he dead, bully stale? Is he dead?

Caius.

By gar, he is de coward Jack priest of de world; he is not show his face.

Host.

Thou art a Castalion King Urinal! Hector of Greece, my boy!

Caius.

I pray you, bear witness that me have stay six or seven, two, tree hours for him, and he is no come.

Shallow.

He is the wiser man, Master Doctor: he is a curer of souls, and you a curer of bodies; if you should fight, you go against the hair of your professions. Is it not true, Master Page?

Page.

Master Shallow, you have yourself been a great fighter, though now a man of peace.

Shallow.

Bodykins, Master Page, though I now be old, and of the peace, if I see a sword out, my finger itches to make one. Though we are justices, and doctors, and churchmen,

Master Page, we have some salt of our youth in us; we are the sons of women, Master Page.

Page.

'Tis true, Master Shallow.

Shallow.

It will be found so, Master Page. Master Doctor Caius, I come to fetch you home. I am sworn of the peace; you have showed yourself a wise physician, and Sir Hugh hath shown himself a wise and patient churchman. You must go with me, Master Doctor.

Host.

Pardon, guest-justice. A word, Monsieur Mockwater.

Caius.

Mock-vater! Vat is dat?

Host.

Mockwater, in our English tongue, is valour, bully.

Caius.

By gar, then I have as much mockvater as de Englishman.—Scurvy jack-dog priest! By gar, me vill cut his ears.

Host.

He will clapper-claw thee tightly, bully.

Caius.

Clapper-de-claw! Vat is dat?

Host.

That is, he will make thee amends.

Caius.

By gar, me do look he shall clapper-de-claw me; for, by gar, me vill have it.

Host.

And I will provoke him to't, or let him wag.

Caius.

Me tank you for dat.

Host.

And, moreover, bully—but first: Master guest, and Master Page, and eke Cavaliero Slender, go you through the town to Frogmore.

[*Aside to them.*]

Page.

Sir Hugh is there, is he?

Host.

He is there: see what humour he is in; and

I will bring the doctor about by the fields.
Will it do well?

SHALLOW.
We will do it.

PAGE, SHALLOW, AND SLENDER.
Adieu, good Master Doctor.

[*Exeunt* PAGE, SHALLOW, *and*
SLENDER.]

CAIUS.
By gar, me vill kill de priest; for he speak for
a jack-an-ape to Anne Page.

HOST.
Let him die. Sheathe thy impatience;
throw cold water on thy choler; go about
the fields with me through Frogmore; I will
bring thee where Mistress Anne Page is, at
a farm-house a-feasting; and thou shalt
woo her. Cried I aim! Said I well?

CAIUS.
By gar, me tank you for dat: by gar, I love
you; and I shall procure-a you de good
guest, de earl, de knight, de lords, de
gentlemen, my patients.

HOST.
For the which I will be thy adversary
toward Anne Page: said I well?

CAIUS.
By gar, 'tis good; vell said.

HOST.
Let us wag, then.

CAIUS.
Come at my heels, Jack Rugby.

[*Exeunt.*]

ACT III
SCENE I
A field near Frogmore.
[*Enter* SIR HUGH EVANS *and* SIMPLE.]

EVANS.
I pray you now, good Master Slender's
serving-man, and friend Simple by your
name, which way have you looked for
Master Caius, that calls himself doctor of
physic?

SIMPLE.
Marry, sir, the pittie-ward, the park-ward,
every way; old Windsor way, and every way
but the town way.

EVANS.
I most fehemently desire you you will also
look that way.

SIMPLE.
I will, Sir.

[*Exit* SIMPLE.]

EVANS.
Pless my soul, how full of chollors I am,
and trempling of mind! I shall be glad if
he have deceived me. How melancholies I
am! I will knog his urinals about his knave's
costard when I have goot opportunities for
the ork: pless my soul!

[*Sings.*]
To shallow rivers, to whose falls
Melodious birds sings madrigals;
There will we make our peds of roses,
And a thousand fragrant posies.
To shallow—

Mercy on me! I have a great dispositions
to cry.

[*Sings.*]
Melodious birds sing madrigals,—
Whenas I sat in Pabylon,—
And a thousand vagram posies.
To shallow,—

[*Re-enter* SIMPLE.]

SIMPLE.
Yonder he is, coming this way, Sir Hugh.

EVANS.
He's welcome.

[*Sings.*]
To shallow rivers, to whose falls—
Heaven prosper the right!—What
weapons is he?

SIMPLE
No weapons, sir. There comes my master,
Master Shallow, and another gentleman,
from Frogmore, over the stile, this way.

EVANS.
Pray you give me my gown; or else keep it
in your arms. [*Reads in a book.*]

[*Enter* PAGE, SHALLOW, *and* SLENDER.]

SHALLOW.
How now, Master Parson! Good morrow,
good Sir Hugh. Keep a gamester from the
dice, and a good student from his book, and
it is wonderful.

SLENDER. [*Aside.*]

Ah, sweet Anne Page!

PAGE.

Save you, good Sir Hugh!

EVANS.

Pless you from his mercy sake, all of you!

SHALLOW.

What, the sword and the word! Do you study them both, Master Parson?

PAGE.

And youthful still, in your doublet and hose, this raw rheumatic day!

EVANS.

There is reasons and causes for it.

PAGE.

We are come to you to do a good office, Master Parson.

EVANS.

Fery well; what is it?

PAGE.

Yonder is a most reverend gentleman, who, belike having received wrong by some person, is at most odds with his own gravity and patience that ever you saw.

SHALLOW.

I have lived fourscore years and upward; I never heard a man of his place, gravity, and learning, so wide of his own respect.

EVANS.

What is he?

PAGE.

I think you know him: Master Doctor Caius, the renowned French physician.

EVANS.

Got's will and His passion of my heart! I had as lief you would tell me of a mess of porridge.

PAGE.

Why?

EVANS.

He has no more knowledge in Hibbocrates and Galen,—and he is a knave besides; a cowardly knave as you would desires to be acquainted withal.

PAGE.

I warrant you, he's the man should fight with him.

SLENDER. [*Aside.*]

O, sweet Anne Page!

SHALLOW.

It appears so, by his weapons. Keep them asunder; here comes Doctor Caius.

[*Enter* HOST, CAIUS, *and* RUGBY.]

PAGE.

Nay, good Master Parson, keep in your weapon.

SHALLOW.

So do you, good Master Doctor.

HOST.

Disarm them, and let them question; let them keep their limbs whole and hack our English.

CAIUS.

I pray you, let-a me speak a word with your ear: verefore will you not meet-a me?

EVANS. [*Aside to* CAIUS.]

Pray you use your patience; in good time.

CAIUS.

By gar, you are de coward, de Jack dog, John ape.

EVANS. [*Aside to* CAIUS.]

Pray you, let us not be laughing-stogs to other men's humours; I desire you in friendship, and I will one way or other make you amends. [*Aloud.*] I will knog your urinals about your knave's cogscomb for missing your meetings and appointments.

CAIUS.

Diable!—Jack Rugby,—mine Host de Jarretiere,—have I not stay for him to kill him? Have I not, at de place I did appoint?

EVANS.

As I am a Christians soul, now, look you, this is the place appointed. I'll be judgment by mine host of the Garter.

HOST.

Peace, I say, Gallia and Gaullia; French and Welsh, soul-curer and body-curer!

CAIUS.

Ay, dat is very good; excellent!

HOST.

Peace, I say! Hear mine host of the Garter. Am I politic? am I subtle? am I a Machiavel? Shall I lose my doctor? No; he gives me the potions and the motions. Shall I lose my parson, my priest, my Sir Hugh? No; he gives me the proverbs and the no-

verbs. Give me thy hand, terrestrial; so;—
give me thy hand, celestial; so. Boys of art,
I have deceived you both; I have directed
you to wrong places; your hearts are mighty,
your skins are whole, and let burnt sack be
the issue. Come, lay their swords to pawn.
Follow me, lads of peace; follow, follow,
follow.

SHALLOW.
Trust me, a mad host!—Follow, gentlemen,
follow.

SLENDER. [*Aside.*]
O, sweet Anne Page!

[*Exeunt* SHALLOW, SLENDER, PAGE, *and*
HOST.]

CAIUS.
Ha, do I perceive dat? Have you make-a de
sot of us, ha, ha?

EVANS.
This is well; he has made us his vlouting-
stog. I desire you that we may be friends;
and let us knog our prains together to be
revenge on this same scall, scurvy, cogging
companion, the host of the Garter.

CAIUS.
By gar, with all my heart. He promise to
bring me where is Anne Page; by gar, he
deceive me too.

EVANS.
Well, I will smite his noddles. Pray you
follow.

[*Exeunt.*]

SCENE II
A street in Windsor.
[*Enter* MISTRESS PAGE *and* ROBIN.]

MISTRESS PAGE.
Nay, keep your way, little gallant: you were
wont to be a follower, but now you are a
leader. Whether had you rather lead mine
eyes, or eye your master's heels?

ROBIN.
I had rather, forsooth, go before you like a
man than follow him like a dwarf.

MISTRESS PAGE.
O! you are a flattering boy: now I see you'll
be a courtier.

[*Enter* FORD.]

FORD.
Well met, Mistress Page. Whither go you?

MISTRESS PAGE.
Truly, sir, to see your wife. Is she at home?

FORD.
Ay; and as idle as she may hang together,
for want of company. I think, if your
husbands were dead, you two would marry.

MISTRESS PAGE.
Be sure of that—two other husbands.

FORD.
Where had you this pretty weathercock?

MISTRESS PAGE.
I cannot tell what the dickens his name is
my husband had him of. What do you call
your knight's name, sirrah?

ROBIN.
Sir John Falstaff.

FORD.
Sir John Falstaff!

MISTRESS PAGE.
He, he; I can never hit on's name. There is
such a league between my good man and
he! Is your wife at home indeed?

FORD.
Indeed she is.

MISTRESS PAGE.
By your leave, sir: I am sick till I see her.

[*Exeunt* MISTRESS PAGE *and* ROBIN.]

FORD.
Has Page any brains? Hath he any eyes?
Hath he any thinking? Sure, they sleep; he
hath no use of them. Why, this boy will carry
a letter twenty mile as easy as a cannon will
shoot point-blank twelve score. He pieces
out his wife's inclination; he gives her folly
motion and advantage; and now she's going
to my wife, and Falstaff's boy with her. A
man may hear this shower sing in the wind:
and Falstaff's boy with her! Good plots!
They are laid; and our revolted wives share
damnation together. Well; I will take him,
then torture my wife, pluck the borrowed
veil of modesty from the so seeming
Mistress Page, divulge Page himself for
a secure and wilful Actaeon; and to these
violent proceedings all my neighbours shall
cry aim. [*Clock strikes.*] The clock gives me

my cue, and my assurance bids me search; there I shall find Falstaff. I shall be rather praised for this than mocked; for it is as positive as the earth is firm that Falstaff is there. I will go.

[*Enter* PAGE, SHALLOW, SLENDER, HOST, SIR HUGH EVANS, CAIUS, *and* RUGBY.]

SHALLOW, PAGE, &C.
Well met, Master Ford.

FORD.
Trust me, a good knot; I have good cheer at home, and I pray you all go with me.

SHALLOW.
I must excuse myself, Master Ford.

SLENDER.
And so must I, sir; we have appointed to dine with Mistress Anne, and I would not break with her for more money than I'll speak of.

SHALLOW.
We have lingered about a match between Anne Page and my cousin Slender, and this day we shall have our answer.

SLENDER.
I hope I have your good will, father Page.

PAGE.
You have, Master Slender; I stand wholly for you. But my wife, Master Doctor, is for you altogether.

CAIUS.
Ay, be-gar; and de maid is love-a me: my nursh-a Quickly tell me so mush.

HOST.
What say you to young Master Fenton? He capers, he dances, he has eyes of youth, he writes verses, he speaks holiday, he smells April and May; he will carry 't, he will carry 't; 'tis in his buttons; he will carry 't.

PAGE.
Not by my consent, I promise you. The gentleman is of no having: he kept company with the wild prince and Pointz; he is of too high a region, he knows too much. No, he shall not knit a knot in his fortunes with the finger of my substance; if he take her, let him take her simply; the wealth I have waits on my consent, and my consent goes not that way.

FORD.
I beseech you, heartily, some of you go home with me to dinner: besides your cheer, you shall have sport; I will show you a monster. Master Doctor, you shall go; so shall you, Master Page; and you, Sir Hugh.

SHALLOW.
Well, fare you well; we shall have the freer wooing at Master Page's.

[*Exeunt* SHALLOW *and* SLENDER.]

CAIUS.
Go home, John Rugby; I come anon.

[*Exit* RUGBY.]

HOST.
Farewell, my hearts; I will to my honest knight Falstaff, and drink canary with him.

[*Exit* HOST.]

FORD. [*Aside.*]
I think I shall drink in pipe-wine first with him. I'll make him dance. Will you go, gentles?

ALL.
Have with you to see this monster.

[*Exeunt.*]

SCENE III
A room in Ford's house.

[*Enter* MISTRESS FORD *and* MISTRESS PAGE.]

MISTRESS FORD.
What, John! what, Robert!

MISTRESS PAGE.
Quickly, quickly:—Is the buck-basket—

MISTRESS FORD.
I warrant. What, Robin, I say!

[*Enter* SERVANTS *with a basket.*]

MISTRESS PAGE.
Come, come, come.

MISTRESS FORD.
Here, set it down.

MISTRESS PAGE.
Give your men the charge; we must be brief.

MISTRESS FORD.
Marry, as I told you before, John and Robert, be ready here hard by in the brew-house; and when I suddenly call you, come forth, and, without any pause or staggering,

take this basket on your shoulders: that done, trudge with it in all haste, and carry it among the whitsters in Datchet-Mead, and there empty it in the muddy ditch close by the Thames side.

MISTRESS PAGE.
You will do it?

MISTRESS FORD.
I have told them over and over; they lack no direction. Be gone, and come when you are called.

[Exeunt SERVANTS.]

MISTRESS PAGE.
Here comes little Robin.

[Enter ROBIN.]

MISTRESS FORD.
How now, my eyas-musket! what news with you?

ROBIN.
My Master Sir John is come in at your back-door, Mistress Ford, and requests your company.

MISTRESS PAGE.
You little Jack-a-Lent, have you been true to us?

ROBIN.
Ay, I'll be sworn. My master knows not of your being here, and hath threatened to put me into everlasting liberty, if I tell you of it; for he swears he'll turn me away.

MISTRESS PAGE.
Thou'rt a good boy; this secrecy of thine shall be a tailor to thee, and shall make thee a new doublet and hose. I'll go hide me.

MISTRESS FORD.
Do so. Go tell thy master I am alone. *[Exit ROBIN.]* Mistress Page, remember you your cue.

MISTRESS PAGE.
I warrant thee; if I do not act it, hiss me.

[Exit MISTRESS PAGE.]

MISTRESS FORD.
Go to, then; we'll use this unwholesome humidity, this gross watery pumpion; we'll teach him to know turtles from jays.

[Enter FALSTAFF.]

FALSTAFF.
"Have I caught thee, my heavenly jewel?"

Why, now let me die, for I have lived long enough: this is the period of my ambition: O this blessed hour!

MISTRESS FORD.
O, sweet Sir John!

FALSTAFF.
Mistress Ford, I cannot cog, I cannot prate, Mistress Ford. Now shall I sin in my wish; I would thy husband were dead. I'll speak it before the best lord, I would make thee my lady.

MISTRESS FORD.
I your lady, Sir John! Alas, I should be a pitiful lady.

FALSTAFF.
Let the court of France show me such another. I see how thine eye would emulate the diamond; thou hast the right arched beauty of the brow that becomes the ship-tire, the tire-valiant, or any tire of Venetian admittance.

MISTRESS FORD.
A plain kerchief, Sir John; my brows become nothing else; nor that well neither.

FALSTAFF.
By the Lord, thou art a traitor to say so: thou wouldst make an absolute courtier; and the firm fixture of thy foot would give an excellent motion to thy gait in a semi-circled farthingale. I see what thou wert, if Fortune thy foe were not, Nature thy friend. Come, thou canst not hide it.

MISTRESS FORD.
Believe me, there's no such thing in me.

FALSTAFF.
What made me love thee? Let that persuade thee there's something extraordinary in thee. Come, I cannot cog and say thou art this and that, like a many of these lisping hawthorn-buds that come like women in men's apparel, and smell like Bucklersbury in simple-time; I cannot; but I love thee, none but thee; and thou deservest it.

MISTRESS FORD.
Do not betray me, sir; I fear you love Mistress Page.

FALSTAFF.
Thou mightst as well say I love to walk by

the Counter-gate, which is as hateful to me as the reek of a lime-kiln.

MISTRESS FORD.
Well, heaven knows how I love you; and you shall one day find it.

FALSTAFF.
Keep in that mind; I'll deserve it.

MISTRESS FORD.
Nay, I must tell you, so you do; or else I could not be in that mind.

ROBIN. [*Within.*]
Mistress Ford! Mistress Ford! here's Mistress Page at the door, sweating and blowing and looking wildly, and would needs speak with you presently.

FALSTAFF.
She shall not see me; I will ensconce me behind the arras.

MISTRESS FORD.
Pray you, do so; she's a very tattling woman.
[*FALSTAFF hides himself.*]
[*Re-enter* MISTRESS PAGE *and* ROBIN.]
What's the matter? How now!

MISTRESS PAGE.
O Mistress Ford, what have you done? You're shamed, you are overthrown, you are undone for ever!

MISTRESS FORD.
What's the matter, good Mistress Page?

MISTRESS PAGE.
O well-a-day, Mistress Ford! having an honest man to your husband, to give him such cause of suspicion!

MISTRESS FORD.
What cause of suspicion?

MISTRESS PAGE.
What cause of suspicion? Out upon you! how am I mistook in you!

MISTRESS FORD.
Why, alas, what's the matter?

MISTRESS PAGE.
Your husband's coming hither, woman, with all the officers in Windsor, to search for a gentleman that he says is here now in the house, by your consent, to take an ill advantage of his absence: you are undone.

MISTRESS FORD. [*Aside.*]
'Tis not so, I hope.

MISTRESS PAGE.
Pray heaven it be not so that you have such a man here! but 'tis most certain your husband's coming, with half Windsor at his heels, to search for such a one. I come before to tell you. If you know yourself clear, why, I am glad of it; but if you have a friend here, convey, convey him out. Be not amazed; call all your senses to you; defend your reputation, or bid farewell to your good life for ever.

MISTRESS FORD.
What shall I do?—There is a gentleman, my dear friend; and I fear not mine own shame as much as his peril: I had rather than a thousand pound he were out of the house.

MISTRESS PAGE.
For shame! never stand "you had rather" and "you had rather": your husband's here at hand; bethink you of some conveyance; in the house you cannot hide him. O, how have you deceived me! Look, here is a basket; if he be of any reasonable stature, he may creep in here; and throw foul linen upon him, as if it were going to bucking: or—it is whiting-time—send him by your two men to Datchet-Mead.

MISTRESS FORD.
He's too big to go in there. What shall I do?

FALSTAFF. [*Coming forward.*]
Let me see 't, let me see 't. O, let me see 't! I'll in, I'll in; follow your friend's counsel; I'll in.

MISTRESS PAGE.
What, Sir John Falstaff! Are these your letters, knight?

FALSTAFF.
I love thee and none but thee; help me away: let me creep in here. I'll never—
[*He gets into the basket; they cover him with foul linen.*]

MISTRESS PAGE.
Help to cover your master, boy. Call your men, Mistress Ford. You dissembling knight!

MISTRESS FORD.
What, John! Robert! John!

[*Exit* Robin.]

[*Re-enter* Servants.]

Go, take up these clothes here, quickly; where's the cowl-staff? Look how you drumble! Carry them to the laundress in Datchet-Mead; quickly, come.

[*Enter* Ford, Page, Caius, *and* Sir Hugh Evans.]

Ford.

Pray you come near. If I suspect without cause, why then make sport at me, then let me be your jest; I deserve it. How now, whither bear you this?

Servant.

To the laundress, forsooth.

Mistress Ford.

Why, what have you to do whither they bear it? You were best meddle with buck-washing.

Ford.

Buck! I would I could wash myself of the buck! Buck, buck, buck! ay, buck; I warrant you, buck; and of the season too, it shall appear. [*Exeunt* Servants *with the basket.*] Gentlemen, I have dreamed to-night; I'll tell you my dream. Here, here, here be my keys: ascend my chambers; search, seek, find out. I'll warrant we'll unkennel the fox. Let me stop this way first. [*Locking the door.*] So, now uncape.

Page.

Good Master Ford, be contented: you wrong yourself too much.

Ford.

True, Master Page. Up, gentlemen, you shall see sport anon; follow me, gentlemen.

[*Exit* Ford.]

Evans.

This is fery fantastical humours and jealousies.

Caius.

By gar, 'tis no the fashion of France; it is not jealous in France.

Page.

Nay, follow him, gentlemen; see the issue of his search.

[*Exeunt* Evans, Page, *and* Caius.]

Mistress Page.

Is there not a double excellency in this?

Mistress Ford.

I know not which pleases me better, that my husband is deceived, or Sir John.

Mistress Page.

What a taking was he in when your husband asked who was in the basket!

Mistress Ford.

I am half afraid he will have need of washing; so throwing him into the water will do him a benefit.

Mistress Page.

Hang him, dishonest rascal! I would all of the same strain were in the same distress.

Mistress Ford.

I think my husband hath some special suspicion of Falstaff's being here, for I never saw him so gross in his jealousy till now.

Mistress Page.

I will lay a plot to try that, and we will yet have more tricks with Falstaff: his dissolute disease will scarce obey this medicine.

Mistress Ford.

Shall we send that foolish carrion, Mistress Quickly, to him, and excuse his throwing into the water, and give him another hope, to betray him to another punishment?

Mistress Page.

We will do it; let him be sent for to-morrow eight o'clock, to have amends.

[*Re-enter* Ford, Page, Caius, *and* Sir Hugh Evans.]

Ford.

I cannot find him: may be the knave bragged of that he could not compass.

Mistress Page. [*Aside to* Mistress Ford.]

Heard you that?

Mistress Ford. [*Aside to* Mistress Page.]

Ay, ay, peace.—You use me well, Master Ford, do you?

Ford.

Ay, I do so.

Mistress Ford.

Heaven make you better than your thoughts!

Ford.
Amen!
Mistress Page.
You do yourself mighty wrong, Master Ford.
Ford.
Ay, ay; I must bear it.
Evans.
If there be any pody in the house, and in the chambers, and in the coffers, and in the presses, heaven forgive my sins at the day of judgment!
Caius.
Be gar, nor I too; there is no bodies.
Page.
Fie, fie, Master Ford, are you not ashamed? What spirit, what devil suggests this imagination? I would not ha' your distemper in this kind for the wealth of Windsor Castle.
Ford.
'Tis my fault, Master Page: I suffer for it.
Evans.
You suffer for a pad conscience. Your wife is as honest a 'omans as I will desires among five thousand, and five hundred too.
Caius.
By gar, I see 'tis an honest woman.
Ford.
Well, I promised you a dinner. Come, come, walk in the park: I pray you pardon me; I will hereafter make known to you why I have done this. Come, wife, come, Mistress Page; I pray you pardon me; pray heartily, pardon me.
Page.
Let's go in, gentlemen; but, trust me, we'll mock him. I do invite you to-morrow morning to my house to breakfast; after, we'll a-birding together; I have a fine hawk for the bush. Shall it be so?
Ford.
Any thing.
Evans.
If there is one, I shall make two in the company.
Caius.
If there be one or two, I shall make-a the turd.

Ford.
Pray you go, Master Page.
Evans.
I pray you now, remembrance to-morrow on the lousy knave, mine host.
Caius.
Dat is good; by gar, with all my heart.
Evans.
A lousy knave! to have his gibes and his mockeries!

[*Exeunt.*]

SCENE IV

A room in Page's house.
[*Enter* Fenton, Anne Page, *and* Mistress Quickly. Mistress Quickly *stands apart.*]

Fenton.
I see I cannot get thy father's love;
Therefore no more turn me to him, sweet
   Nan.
Anne.
Alas! how then?
Fenton.
Why, thou must be thyself.
He doth object, I am too great of birth;
And that my state being gall'd with my
   expense,
I seek to heal it only by his wealth.
Besides these, other bars he lays before
   me,
My riots past, my wild societies;
And tells me 'tis a thing impossible
I should love thee but as a property.
Anne.
May be he tells you true.
Fenton.
No, heaven so speed me in my time to
   come!
Albeit I will confess thy father's wealth
Was the first motive that I wooed thee,
   Anne:
Yet, wooing thee, I found thee of more
   value
Than stamps in gold, or sums in sealed
   bags;
And 'tis the very riches of thyself
That now I aim at.

ANNE.

                Gentle Master Fenton,
Yet seek my father's love; still seek it, sir.
If opportunity and humblest suit
Cannot attain it, why then,—hark you
   hither.
       [*They converse apart.*]
    [*Enter* SHALLOW, SLENDER, *and*
      MISTRESS QUICKLY.]

SHALLOW.

Break their talk, Mistress Quickly: my
kinsman shall speak for himself.

SLENDER.

I'll make a shaft or a bolt on 't. 'Slid, 'tis but
venturing.

SHALLOW.

Be not dismayed.

SLENDER.

No, she shall not dismay me. I care not for
that, but that I am afeard.

QUICKLY.

Hark ye; Master Slender would speak a
word with you.

ANNE.

I come to him. [*Aside.*] This is my father's
   choice.
O, what a world of vile ill-favour'd faults
Looks handsome in three hundred pounds
   a year!

QUICKLY.

And how does good Master Fenton? Pray
you, a word with you.

SHALLOW.

She's coming; to her, coz. O boy, thou hadst
a father!

SLENDER.

I had a father, Mistress Anne; my uncle
can tell you good jests of him. Pray you,
uncle, tell Mistress Anne the jest how my
father stole two geese out of a pen, good
uncle.

SHALLOW.

Mistress Anne, my cousin loves you.

SLENDER.

Ay, that I do; as well as I love any woman in
Gloucestershire.

SHALLOW.

He will maintain you like a gentlewoman.

SLENDER.

Ay, that I will come cut and long-tail, under
the degree of a squire.

SHALLOW.

He will make you a hundred and fifty
pounds jointure.

ANNE.

Good Master Shallow, let him woo for
himself.

SHALLOW.

Marry, I thank you for it; I thank you for
that good comfort. She calls you, coz; I'll
leave you.

ANNE.

Now, Master Slender.

SLENDER.

Now, good Mistress Anne.—

ANNE.

What is your will?

SLENDER.

My will! 'od's heartlings, that's a pretty jest
indeed! I ne'er made my will yet, I thank
heaven; I am not such a sickly creature, I
give heaven praise.

ANNE.

I mean, Master Slender, what would you
with me?

SLENDER.

Truly, for mine own part I would little or
nothing with you. Your father and my uncle
hath made motions; if it be my luck, so; if
not, happy man be his dole! They can tell
you how things go better than I can. You
may ask your father; here he comes.
    [*Enter* PAGE *and* MISTRESS PAGE.]

PAGE.

Now, Master Slender: love him, daughter
   Anne.
Why, how now! what does Master Fenton
   here?
You wrong me, sir, thus still to haunt my
   house:
I told you, sir, my daughter is dispos'd of.

FENTON.

Nay, Master Page, be not impatient.

MISTRESS PAGE.

Good Master Fenton, come not to my
   child.

PAGE.
She is no match for you.
FENTON.
Sir, will you hear me?
PAGE.
                    No, good Master Fenton.
Come, Master Shallow; come, son Slender,
    in.
Knowing my mind, you wrong me, Master
    Fenton.
[*Exeunt* PAGE, SHALLOW, *and* SLENDER.]
QUICKLY.
Speak to Mistress Page.
FENTON.
Good Mistress Page, for that I love your
    daughter
In such a righteous fashion as I do,
Perforce, against all checks, rebukes, and
    manners,
I must advance the colours of my love
And not retire: let me have your good will.
ANNE.
Good mother, do not marry me to yond
    fool.
MISTRESS PAGE.
I mean it not; I seek you a better husband.
QUICKLY.
That's my master, Master Doctor.
ANNE.
Alas! I had rather be set quick i' the
    earth.
And bowl'd to death with turnips.
MISTRESS PAGE.
Come, trouble not yourself. Good Master
    Fenton,
I will not be your friend, nor enemy;
My daughter will I question how she
    loves you,
And as I find her, so am I affected.
Till then, farewell, sir: she must needs
    go in;
Her father will be angry.
FENTON.
Farewell, gentle mistress. Farewell, Nan.
    [*Exeunt* MISTRESS PAGE *and* ANNE.]
QUICKLY.
This is my doing now: "Nay," said I, "will
you cast away your child on a fool, and a

physician? Look on Master Fenton." This
is my doing.
FENTON.
I thank thee; and I pray thee, once to-
    night
Give my sweet Nan this ring. There's for
    thy pains.
QUICKLY.
Now Heaven send thee good fortune! [*Exit*
FENTON.] A kind heart he hath; a woman
would run through fire and water for such a
kind heart. But yet I would my master had
Mistress Anne; or I would Master Slender
had her; or, in sooth, I would Master
Fenton had her; I will do what I can for
them all three, for so I have promised, and
I'll be as good as my word; but speciously
for Master Fenton. Well, I must of another
errand to Sir John Falstaff from my two
mistresses: what a beast am I to slack it!
    [*Exit.*]

SCENE V
A room in the Garter Inn.
[*Enter* FALSTAFF *and* BARDOLPH.]
FALSTAFF.
Bardolph, I say,—
BARDOLPH.
Here, sir.
FALSTAFF.
Go fetch me a quart of sack; put a toast
in 't. [*Exit* BARDOLPH.] Have I lived to be
carried in a basket, and to be thrown in the
Thames like a barrow of butcher's offal?
Well, if I be served such another trick, I'll
have my brains ta'en out and buttered, and
give them to a dog for a new year's gift. The
rogues slighted me into the river with as
little remorse as they would have drowned
a blind bitch's puppies, fifteen i' the litter;
and you may know by my size that I have
a kind of alacrity in sinking; if the bottom
were as deep as hell I should down. I had
been drowned but that the shore was
shelvy and shallow; a death that I abhor, for
the water swells a man; and what a thing
should I have been when had been swelled!
I should have been a mountain of mummy.

[*Re-enter* BARDOLPH, *with the sack.*]

BARDOLPH.

Here's Mistress Quickly, sir, to speak with you.

FALSTAFF.

Come, let me pour in some sack to the Thames water; for my belly's as cold as if I had swallowed snowballs for pills to cool the reins. Call her in.

BARDOLPH.

Come in, woman.

[*Enter* MISTRESS QUICKLY.]

QUICKLY.

By your leave. I cry you mercy. Give your worship good morrow.

FALSTAFF.

Take away these chalices. Go, brew me a pottle of sack finely.

BARDOLPH.

With eggs, sir?

FALSTAFF.

Simple of itself; I'll no pullet-sperm in my brewage. [*Exit* BARDOLPH.] How now!

QUICKLY.

Marry, sir, I come to your worship from Mistress Ford.

FALSTAFF.

Mistress Ford! I have had ford enough; I was thrown into the ford; I have my belly full of ford.

QUICKLY.

Alas the day! good heart, that was not her fault: she does so take on with her men; they mistook their erection.

FALSTAFF.

So did I mine, to build upon a foolish woman's promise.

QUICKLY.

Well, she laments, sir, for it, that it would yearn your heart to see it. Her husband goes this morning a-birding; she desires you once more to come to her between eight and nine; I must carry her word quickly. She'll make you amends, I warrant you.

FALSTAFF.

Well, I will visit her. Tell her so; and bid her think what a man is; let her consider his frailty, and then judge of my merit.

QUICKLY.

I will tell her.

FALSTAFF.

Do so. Between nine and ten, sayest thou?

QUICKLY.

Eight and nine, sir.

FALSTAFF.

Well, be gone; I will not miss her.

QUICKLY.

Peace be with you, sir.

[*Exit* MISTRESS QUICKLY.]

FALSTAFF.

I marvel I hear not of Master Brook; he sent me word to stay within. I like his money well. O! here he comes.

[*Enter* FORD *disguised.*]

FORD.

Bless you, sir!

FALSTAFF.

Now, Master Brook, you come to know what hath passed between me and Ford's wife?

FORD.

That, indeed, Sir John, is my business.

FALSTAFF.

Master Brook, I will not lie to you: I was at her house the hour she appointed me.

FORD.

And how sped you, sir?

FALSTAFF.

Very ill-favouredly, Master Brook.

FORD.

How so, sir? did she change her determination?

FALSTAFF.

No. Master Brook; but the peaking cornuto her husband, Master Brook, dwelling in a continual 'larum of jealousy, comes me in the instant of our encounter, after we had embraced, kissed, protested, and, as it were, spoke the prologue of our comedy; and at his heels a rabble of his companions, thither provoked and instigated by his distemper, and, forsooth, to search his house for his wife's love.

FORD.

What! while you were there?

FALSTAFF.

While I was there.

Ford.
And did he search for you, and could not find you?

Falstaff.
You shall hear. As good luck would have it, comes in one Mistress Page; gives intelligence of Ford's approach; and, in her invention and Ford's wife's distraction, they conveyed me into a buck-basket.

Ford.
A buck-basket!

Falstaff.
By the Lord, a buck-basket! rammed me in with foul shirts and smocks, socks, foul stockings, greasy napkins, that, Master Brook, there was the rankest compound of villainous smell that ever offended nostril.

Ford.
And how long lay you there?

Falstaff.
Nay, you shall hear, Master Brook, what I have suffered to bring this woman to evil for your good. Being thus crammed in the basket, a couple of Ford's knaves, his hinds, were called forth by their mistress to carry me in the name of foul clothes to Datchet-lane; they took me on their shoulders; met the jealous knave their master in the door; who asked them once or twice what they had in their basket. I quaked for fear lest the lunatic knave would have searched it; but Fate, ordaining he should be a cuckold, held his hand. Well, on went he for a search, and away went I for foul clothes. But mark the sequel, Master Brook: I suffered the pangs of three several deaths: first, an intolerable fright to be detected with a jealous rotten bell-wether; next, to be compassed like a good bilbo in the circumference of a peck, hilt to point, heel to head; and then, to be stopped in, like a strong distillation, with stinking clothes that fretted in their own grease: think of that; a man of my kidney, think of that, that am as subject to heat as butter; a man of continual dissolution and thaw: it was a miracle to 'scape suffocation. And in the height of this bath, when I was more than half stewed in grease, like a Dutch dish, to be thrown into the Thames, and cooled, glowing hot, in that surge, like a horse-shoe; think of that, hissing hot, think of that, Master Brook!

Ford.
In good sadness, sir, I am sorry that for my sake you have suffered all this. My suit, then, is desperate; you'll undertake her no more.

Falstaff.
Master Brook, I will be thrown into Etna, as I have been into Thames, ere I will leave her thus. Her husband is this morning gone a-birding; I have received from her another embassy of meeting; 'twixt eight and nine is the hour, Master Brook.

Ford.
'Tis past eight already, sir.

Falstaff.
Is it? I will then address me to my appointment. Come to me at your convenient leisure, and you shall know how I speed, and the conclusion shall be crowned with your enjoying her: adieu. You shall have her, Master Brook; Master Brook, you shall cuckold Ford.

[*Exit* Falstaff.]

Ford.
Hum! ha! Is this a vision? Is this a dream? Do I sleep? Master Ford, awake; awake, Master Ford. There's a hole made in your best coat, Master Ford. This 'tis to be married; this 'tis to have linen and buck-baskets! Well, I will proclaim myself what I am; I will now take the lecher; he is at my house. He cannot 'scape me; 'tis impossible he should; he cannot creep into a half-penny purse, nor into a pepper box; but, lest the devil that guides him should aid him, I will search impossible places. Though what I am I cannot avoid, yet to be what I would not, shall not make me tame; if I have horns to make one mad, let the proverb go with me; I'll be horn-mad.

[*Exit.*]

ACT IV
SCENE I
The street.

[*Enter* MISTRESS PAGE, MISTRESS
QUICKLY, *and* WILLIAM.]

MISTRESS PAGE.
Is he at Master Ford's already, think'st thou?

QUICKLY.
Sure he is by this; or will be presently; but
truly he is very courageous mad about his
throwing into the water. Mistress Ford
desires you to come suddenly.

MISTRESS PAGE.
I'll be with her by and by; I'll but bring my
young man here to school. Look where his
master comes; 'tis a playing day, I see.

[*Enter* SIR HUGH EVANS.]

How now, Sir Hugh, no school to-day?

EVANS.
No; Master Slender is let the boys leave to
play.

QUICKLY.
Blessing of his heart!

MISTRESS PAGE.
Sir Hugh, my husband says my son profits
nothing in the world at his book; I pray you
ask him some questions in his accidence.

EVANS.
Come hither, William; hold up your head;
come.

MISTRESS PAGE.
Come on, sirrah; hold up your head; answer
your master; be not afraid.

EVANS.
William, how many numbers is in nouns?

WILLIAM.
Two.

QUICKLY.
Truly, I thought there had been one
number more, because they say "Od's
nouns."

EVANS.
Peace your tattlings! What is fair, William?

WILLIAM.
Pulcher.

QUICKLY.
Polecats! There are fairer things than
polecats, sure.

EVANS.
You are a very simplicity 'oman; I pray you,
peace. What is *lapis*, William?

WILLIAM.
A stone.

EVANS.
And what is a stone, William?

WILLIAM.
A pebble.

EVANS.
No, it is *lapis*; I pray you remember in your
prain.

WILLIAM.
Lapis.

EVANS.
That is a good William. What is he,
William, that does lend articles?

WILLIAM.
Articles are borrowed of the pronoun, and
be thus declined: *Singulariter, nominativo;
hic, haec, hoc.*

EVANS.
Nominativo, hig, hag, hog; pray you, mark:
genitivo, hujus. Well, what is your accusative
case?

WILLIAM.
Accusativo, hinc.

EVANS.
I pray you, have your remembrance, child.
Accusativo, hung, hang, hog.

QUICKLY.
"Hang-hog" is Latin for bacon, I warrant
you.

EVANS.
Leave your prabbles, 'oman. What is the
focative case, William?

WILLIAM.
O vocativo, O.

EVANS.
Remember, William: focative is *caret.*

QUICKLY.
And that's a good root.

EVANS.
'Oman, forbear.

MISTRESS PAGE.
Peace!

EVANS.
What is your genitive case plural, William?

William.
Genitive case?

Evans.
Ay.

William.
Genitivo: horum, harum, horum.

Quickly.
Vengeance of Jenny's case; fie on her! Never name her, child, if she be a whore.

Evans.
For shame, 'oman.

Quickly.
You do ill to teach the child such words. He teaches him to hick and to hack, which they'll do fast enough of themselves; and to call *horum*; fie upon you!

Evans.
'Oman, art thou lunatics? Hast thou no understandings for thy cases, and the numbers of the genders? Thou art as foolish Christian creatures as I would desires.

Mistress Page.
Prithee, hold thy peace.

Evans.
Show me now, William, some declensions of your pronouns.

William.
Forsooth, I have forgot.

Evans.
It is *qui, quae, quod*; if you forget your *quis*, your *quaes*, and your *quods*, you must be preeches. Go your ways and play; go.

Mistress Page.
He is a better scholar than I thought he was.

Evans.
He is a good sprag memory. Farewell, Mistress Page.

Mistress Page.
Adieu, good Sir Hugh. [*Exit* Sir Hugh.] Get you home, boy. Come, we stay too long.
                    [*Exeunt.*]

SCENE II

A room in Ford's house.

[*Enter* Falstaff *and* Mistress Ford.]

Falstaff.
Mistress Ford, your sorrow hath eaten up my sufferance. I see you are obsequious in your love, and I profess requital to a hair's breadth; not only, Mistress Ford, in the simple office of love, but in all the accoutrement, complement, and ceremony of it. But are you sure of your husband now?

Mistress Ford.
He's a-birding, sweet Sir John.

Mistress Page. [*Within.*]
What ho! gossip Ford, what ho!

Mistress Ford.
Step into the chamber, Sir John.
                    [*Exit* Falstaff.]
              [*Enter* Mistress Page.]

Mistress Page.
How now, sweetheart! who's at home besides yourself?

Mistress Ford.
Why, none but mine own people.

Mistress Page.
Indeed!

Mistress Ford.
No, certainly. [*Aside to her.*] Speak louder.

Mistress Page.
Truly, I am so glad you have nobody here.

Mistress Ford.
Why?

Mistress Page.
Why, woman, your husband is in his old lunes again. He so takes on yonder with my husband; so rails against all married mankind; so curses all Eve's daughters, of what complexion soever; and so buffets himself on the forehead, crying "Peer out, peer out!" that any madness I ever yet beheld seemed but tameness, civility, and patience, to this his distemper he is in now. I am glad the fat knight is not here.

Mistress Ford.
Why, does he talk of him?

Mistress Page.
Of none but him; and swears he was carried out, the last time he searched for him, in a basket; protests to my husband he is now here; and hath drawn him and the rest of their company from their sport, to make another experiment of his suspicion. But I am glad the knight is not here; now he shall see his own foolery.

Mistress Ford.
How near is he, Mistress Page?

Mistress Page.
Hard by, at street end; he will be here anon.

Mistress Ford.
I am undone! the knight is here.

Mistress Page.
Why, then, you are utterly shamed, and he's but a dead man. What a woman are you! Away with him, away with him! better shame than murder.

Mistress Ford.
Which way should he go? How should I bestow him? Shall I put him into the basket again?

[*Re-enter* Falstaff.]

Falstaff.
No, I'll come no more i' the basket. May I not go out ere he come?

Mistress Page.
Alas! three of Master Ford's brothers watch the door with pistols, that none shall issue out; otherwise you might slip away ere he came. But what make you here?

Falstaff.
What shall I do? I'll creep up into the chimney.

Mistress Ford.
There they always use to discharge their birding-pieces.

Mistress Page.
Creep into the kiln-hole.

Falstaff.
Where is it?

Mistress Ford.
He will seek there, on my word. Neither press, coffer, chest, trunk, well, vault, but he hath an abstract for the remembrance of such places, and goes to them by his note: there is no hiding you in the house.

Falstaff.
I'll go out then.

Mistress Page.
If you go out in your own semblance, you die, Sir John. Unless you go out disguised,—

Mistress Ford.
How might we disguise him?

Mistress Page.
Alas the day! I know not! There is no woman's gown big enough for him; otherwise he might put on a hat, a muffler, and a kerchief, and so escape.

Falstaff.
Good hearts, devise something: any extremity rather than a mischief.

Mistress Ford.
My maid's aunt, the fat woman of Brainford, has a gown above.

Mistress Page.
On my word, it will serve him; she's as big as he is; and there's her thrummed hat, and her muffler too. Run up, Sir John.

Mistress Ford.
Go, go, sweet Sir John. Mistress Page and I will look some linen for your head.

Mistress Page.
Quick, quick! we'll come dress you straight; put on the gown the while.

[*Exit* Falstaff.]

Mistress Ford.
I would my husband would meet him in this shape; he cannot abide the old woman of Brainford; he swears she's a witch, forbade her my house, and hath threatened to beat her.

Mistress Page.
Heaven guide him to thy husband's cudgel; and the devil guide his cudgel afterwards!

Mistress Ford.
But is my husband coming?

Mistress Page.
Ay, in good sadness is he; and talks of the basket too, howsoever he hath had intelligence.

Mistress Ford.
We'll try that; for I'll appoint my men to carry the basket again, to meet him at the door with it as they did last time.

Mistress Page.
Nay, but he'll be here presently; let's go dress him like the witch of Brainford.

Mistress Ford.
I'll first direct my men what they shall do with the basket. Go up; I'll bring linen for him straight.

[*Exit* Mistress Ford.]

Mistress Page.

Hang him, dishonest varlet! we cannot misuse him enough.

We'll leave a proof, by that which we will do,

Wives may be merry and yet honest too.

We do not act that often jest and laugh;

'Tis old but true: "Still swine eats all the draff."

[*Exit.*]

[*Re-enter* Mistress Ford, *with two* Servants.]

Mistress Ford.

Go, sirs, take the basket again on your shoulders; your master is hard at door; if he bid you set it down, obey him. Quickly, dispatch.

[*Exit* Mistress Ford.]

First Servant.

Come, come, take it up.

Second Servant.

Pray heaven, it be not full of knight again.

First Servant.

I hope not; I had lief as bear so much lead.

[*Enter* Ford, Page, Shallow, Caius, *and* Sir Hugh Evans.]

Ford.

Ay, but if it prove true, Master Page, have you any way then to unfool me again? Set down the basket, villain! Somebody call my wife. Youth in a basket! O you panderly rascals! there's a knot, a ging, a pack, a conspiracy against me. Now shall the devil be shamed. What, wife, I say! Come, come forth! behold what honest clothes you send forth to bleaching!

Page.

Why, this passes, Master Ford! you are not to go loose any longer; you must be pinioned.

Evans.

Why, this is lunatics! this is mad as a mad dog.

Shallow.

Indeed, Master Ford, this is not well, indeed.

Ford.

So say I too, sir. [*Re-enter* Mistress

Ford.] Come hither, Mistress Ford, the honest woman, the modest wife, the virtuous creature, that hath the jealous fool to her husband! I suspect without cause, Mistress, do I?

Mistress Ford.

Heaven be my witness, you do, if you suspect me in any dishonesty.

Ford.

Well said, brazen-face! hold it out. Come forth, sirrah. [*Pulling clothes out of the basket.*]

Page.

This passes!

Mistress Ford.

Are you not ashamed? Let the clothes alone.

Ford.

I shall find you anon.

Evans.

'Tis unreasonable. Will you take up your wife's clothes? Come away.

Ford.

Empty the basket, I say!

Mistress Ford.

Why, man, why?

Ford.

Master Page, as I am a man, there was one conveyed out of my house yesterday in this basket: why may not he be there again? In my house I am sure he is; my intelligence is true; my jealousy is reasonable. Pluck me out all the linen.

Mistress Ford.

If you find a man there, he shall die a flea's death.

Page.

Here's no man.

Shallow.

By my fidelity, this is not well, Master Ford; this wrongs you.

Evans.

Master Ford, you must pray, and not follow the imaginations of your own heart; this is jealousies.

Ford.

Well, he's not here I seek for.

Page.

No, nor nowhere else but in your brain.

[Servants *carry away the basket.*]

FORD.
Help to search my house this one time. If
I find not what I seek, show no colour for
my extremity; let me for ever be your table-
sport; let them say of me "As jealous as
Ford, that searched a hollow walnut for his
wife's leman." Satisfy me once more; once
more search with me.

MISTRESS FORD.
What, hoa, Mistress Page! Come you and
the old woman down; my husband will
come into the chamber.

FORD.
Old woman? what old woman's that?

MISTRESS FORD.
Why, it is my maid's aunt of Brainford.

FORD.
A witch, a quean, an old cozening quean!
Have I not forbid her my house? She comes
of errands, does she? We are simple men;
we do not know what's brought to pass
under the profession of fortune-telling. She
works by charms, by spells, by the figure,
and such daubery as this is, beyond our
element. We know nothing. Come down,
you witch, you hag you; come down, I say!

MISTRESS FORD.
Nay, good sweet husband! Good gentlemen,
let him not strike the old woman.

[*Re-enter* FALSTAFF *in woman's clothes, led
by* MISTRESS PAGE.]

MISTRESS PAGE.
Come, Mother Prat; come, give me your
hand.

FORD.
I'll prat her. [*Beats him.*] Out of my door,
you witch, you rag, you baggage, you
polecat, you ronyon! Out, out! I'll conjure
you, I'll fortune-tell you.

[*Exit* FALSTAFF.]

MISTRESS PAGE.
Are you not ashamed? I think you have
killed the poor woman.

MISTRESS FORD.
Nay, he will do it. 'Tis a goodly credit for
you.

FORD.
Hang her, witch!

EVANS.
By yea and no, I think the 'oman is a witch
indeed; I like not when a 'oman has a
great peard; I spy a great peard under her
muffler.

FORD.
Will you follow, gentlemen? I beseech you
follow; see but the issue of my jealousy; if
I cry out thus upon no trail, never trust me
when I open again.

PAGE.
Let's obey his humour a little further.
Come, gentlemen.

[*Exeunt* FORD, PAGE, SHALLOW, CAIUS,
and EVANS.]

MISTRESS PAGE.
Trust me, he beat him most pitifully.

MISTRESS FORD.
Nay, by the mass, that he did not; he beat
him most unpitifully methought.

MISTRESS PAGE.
I'll have the cudgel hallowed and hung o'er
the altar; it hath done meritorious service.

MISTRESS FORD.
What think you? May we, with the warrant
of womanhood and the witness of a good
conscience, pursue him with any further
revenge?

MISTRESS PAGE.
The spirit of wantonness is sure scared
out of him; if the devil have him not in
fee-simple, with fine and recovery, he will
never, I think, in the way of waste, attempt
us again.

MISTRESS FORD.
Shall we tell our husbands how we have
served him?

MISTRESS PAGE.
Yes, by all means; if it be but to scrape the
figures out of your husband's brains. If they
can find in their hearts the poor unvirtuous
fat knight shall be any further afflicted, we
two will still be the ministers.

MISTRESS FORD.
I'll warrant they'll have him publicly
shamed; and methinks there would be no
period to the jest, should he not be publicly
shamed.

Mistress Page.
Come, to the forge with it then; shape it. I would not have things cool.
[*Exeunt.*]

SCENE III
A room in the Garter Inn.
[*Enter* Host *and* Bardolph.]
Bardolph.
Sir, the Germans desire to have three of your horses; the duke himself will be to-morrow at court, and they are going to meet him.

Host.
What duke should that be comes so secretly? I hear not of him in the court. Let me speak with the gentlemen; they speak English?

Bardolph.
Ay, sir; I'll call them to you.

Host.
They shall have my horses, but I'll make them pay; I'll sauce them; they have had my house a week at command; I have turned away my other guests. They must come off; I'll sauce them. Come.
[*Exeunt.*]

SCENE IV
A room in Ford's house.
[*Enter* Page, Ford, Mistress Page, Mistress Ford, *and* Sir Hugh Evans.]
Evans.
'Tis one of the best discretions of a 'oman as ever I did look upon.

Page.
And did he send you both these letters at an instant?

Mistress Page.
Within a quarter of an hour.

Ford.
Pardon me, wife. Henceforth, do what thou wilt;
I rather will suspect the sun with cold
Than thee with wantonness: now doth thy honour stand,
In him that was of late an heretic,
As firm as faith.

Page.
                'Tis well, 'tis well; no more.
Be not as extreme in submission
As in offence;
But let our plot go forward: let our wives
Yet once again, to make us public sport,
Appoint a meeting with this old fat fellow,
Where we may take him and disgrace him
    for it.

Ford.
There is no better way than that they
    spoke of.

Page.
How? To send him word they'll meet him in the park at midnight? Fie, fie! he'll never come!

Evans.
You say he has been thrown in the rivers; and has been grievously peaten as an old 'oman; methinks there should be terrors in him, that he should not come; methinks his flesh is punished; he shall have no desires.

Page.
So think I too.

Mistress Ford.
Devise but how you'll use him when he
    comes,
And let us two devise to bring him thither.

Mistress Page.
There is an old tale goes that Herne the
    hunter,
Sometime a keeper here in Windsor
    Forest,
Doth all the winter-time, at still midnight,
Walk round about an oak, with great
    ragg'd horns;
And there he blasts the tree, and takes the
    cattle,
And makes milch-kine yield blood, and
    shakes a chain
In a most hideous and dreadful manner:
You have heard of such a spirit, and well
    you know
The superstitious idle-headed eld
Received, and did deliver to our age,
This tale of Herne the hunter for a truth.

Page
Why, yet there want not many that do fear

In deep of night to walk by this Herne's
   oak.
But what of this?
MISTRESS FORD.
            Marry, this is our device;
That Falstaff at that oak shall meet with
   us,
Disguis'd, like Herne, with huge horns on
   his head.
PAGE.
Well, let it not be doubted but he'll come,
And in this shape. When you have
   brought him thither,
What shall be done with him? What is
   your plot?
MISTRESS PAGE.
That likewise have we thought upon, and
   thus:
Nan Page my daughter, and my little son,
And three or four more of their growth,
   we'll dress
Like urchins, ouphs, and fairies, green and
   white,
With rounds of waxen tapers on their
   heads,
And rattles in their hands. Upon a sudden,
As Falstaff, she, and I, are newly met,
Let them from forth a sawpit rush at once
With some diffused song; upon their sight
We two in great amazedness will fly:
Then let them all encircle him about,
And fairy-like, to pinch the unclean
   knight;
And ask him why, that hour of fairy revel,
In their so sacred paths he dares to tread
In shape profane.
MISTRESS FORD.
          And till he tell the truth,
Let the supposed fairies pinch him sound,
And burn him with their tapers.
MISTRESS PAGE.
          The truth being known,
We'll all present ourselves; dis-horn the
   spirit,
And mock him home to Windsor.
FORD.
          The children must
Be practis'd well to this or they'll ne'er do 't.

EVANS.
I will teach the children their behaviours;
and I will be like a jack-an-apes also, to
burn the knight with my taber.
FORD.
That will be excellent. I'll go buy them
   vizards.
MISTRESS PAGE.
My Nan shall be the Queen of all the
   Fairies,
Finely attired in a robe of white.
PAGE.
That silk will I go buy. [*Aside.*] And in
   that time
Shall Master Slender steal my Nan away,
And marry her at Eton. Go, send to
   Falstaff straight.
FORD.
Nay, I'll to him again, in name of
   Brook;
He'll tell me all his purpose. Sure,
   he'll come.
MISTRESS PAGE.
Fear not you that. Go, get us properties
And tricking for our fairies.
EVANS.
Let us about it. It is admirable pleasures,
and fery honest knaveries.
      [*Exeunt* PAGE, FORD, *and* EVANS.]
MISTRESS PAGE.
Go, Mistress Ford.
Send Quickly to Sir John to know his
   mind.
          [*Exit* MISTRESS FORD.]
I'll to the doctor; he hath my good will,
And none but he, to marry with Nan
   Page.
That Slender, though well landed, is an
   idiot;
And he my husband best of all affects:
The doctor is well money'd, and his
   friends
Potent at court: he, none but he, shall
   have her,
Though twenty thousand worthier come
   to crave her.
          [*Exit.*]

SCENE V

A room in the Garter Inn.
[*Enter* HOST *and* SIMPLE.]

HOST.
What wouldst thou have, boor? What, thick-skin? Speak, breathe, discuss; brief, short, quick, snap.

SIMPLE.
Marry, sir, I come to speak with Sir John Falstaff from Master Slender.

HOST.
There's his chamber, his house, his castle, his standing-bed and truckle-bed; 'tis painted about with the story of the Prodigal, fresh and new. Go knock and call; he'll speak like an Anthropophaginian unto thee; knock, I say.

SIMPLE.
There's an old woman, a fat woman, gone up into his chamber; I'll be so bold as stay, sir, till she come down; I come to speak with her, indeed.

HOST.
Ha! a fat woman? The knight may be robbed. I'll call. Bully knight! Bully Sir John! Speak from thy lungs military. Art thou there? It is thine host, thine Ephesian, calls.

FALSTAFF. [*Above.*]
How now, mine host?

HOST.
Here's a Bohemian-Tartar tarries the coming down of thy fat woman. Let her descend, bully, let her descend; my chambers are honourable. Fie! privacy? fie!
[*Enter* FALSTAFF.]

FALSTAFF.
There was, mine host, an old fat woman even now with, me; but she's gone.

SIMPLE.
Pray you, sir, was't not the wise woman of Brainford?

FALSTAFF.
Ay, marry was it, mussel-shell: what would you with her?

SIMPLE.
My master, sir, my Master Slender, sent to her, seeing her go thorough the streets, to know, sir, whether one Nym, sir, that beguiled him of a chain, had the chain or no.

FALSTAFF.
I spake with the old woman about it.

SIMPLE.
And what says she, I pray, sir?

FALSTAFF.
Marry, she says that the very same man that beguiled Master Slender of his chain cozened him of it.

SIMPLE.
I would I could have spoken with the woman herself; I had other things to have spoken with her too, from him.

FALSTAFF.
What are they? Let us know.

HOST
Ay, come; quick.

SIMPLE.
I may not conceal them, sir.

FALSTAFF.
Conceal them, or thou diest.

SIMPLE.
Why, sir, they were nothing but about Mistress Anne Page: to know if it were my master's fortune to have her or no.

FALSTAFF.
'Tis, 'tis his fortune.

SIMPLE.
What sir?

FALSTAFF.
To have her, or no. Go; say the woman told me so.

SIMPLE.
May I be bold to say so, sir?

FALSTAFF.
Ay, Sir Tike; like who more bold?

SIMPLE.
I thank your worship; I shall make my master glad with these tidings.
[*Exit* SIMPLE.]

HOST.
Thou art clerkly, thou art clerkly, Sir John. Was there a wise woman with thee?

FALSTAFF.
Ay, that there was, mine host; one that hath taught me more wit than ever I learned

before in my life; and I paid nothing for it neither, but was paid for my learning.

[Enter BARDOLPH.*]*

BARDOLPH.
Out, alas, sir! cozenage, mere cozenage!

HOST.
Where be my horses? Speak well of them, varletto.

BARDOLPH.
Run away, with the cozeners; for so soon as I came beyond Eton, they threw me off, from behind one of them, in a slough of mire; and set spurs and away, like three German devils, three Doctor Faustuses.

HOST.
They are gone but to meet the duke, villain; do not say they be fled; Germans are honest men.

[Enter SIR HUGH EVANS.*]*

EVANS.
Where is mine host?

HOST.
What is the matter, sir?

EVANS.
Have a care of your entertainments: there is a friend of mine come to town tells me there is three cozen-germans that has cozened all the hosts of Readins, of Maidenhead, of Colebrook, of horses and money. I tell you for good will, look you; you are wise, and full of gibes and vlouting-stogs, and 'tis not convenient you should be cozened. Fare you well.

[Exit EVANS.*]*

[Enter DOCTOR CAIUS.*]*

CAIUS.
Vere is mine host de Jarteer?

HOST.
Here, Master Doctor, in perplexity and doubtful dilemma.

CAIUS.
I cannot tell vat is dat; but it is tell-a me dat you make grand preparation for a Duke de Jamany. By my trot, dere is no duke that the court is know to come; I tell you for good will: Adieu.

[Exit DOCTOR CAIUS.*]*

HOST.
Hue and cry, villain, go! Assist me, knight; I am undone. Fly, run, hue and cry, villain; I am undone!

[Exeunt HOST *and* BARDOLPH.*]*

FALSTAFF.
I would all the world might be cozened, for I have been cozened and beaten too. If it should come to the ear of the court how I have been transformed, and how my transformation hath been washed and cudgelled, they would melt me out of my fat, drop by drop, and liquor fishermen's boots with me; I warrant they would whip me with their fine wits till I were as crest-fallen as a dried pear. I never prospered since I forswore myself at primero. Well, if my wind were but long enough to say my prayers, I would repent. *[Enter* MISTRESS QUICKLY.*]* Now! whence come you?

QUICKLY.
From the two parties, forsooth.

FALSTAFF.
The devil take one party and his dam the other! And so they shall be both bestowed. I have suffered more for their sakes, more than the villainous inconstancy of man's disposition is able to bear.

QUICKLY.
And have not they suffered? Yes, I warrant; speciously one of them; Mistress Ford, good heart, is beaten black and blue, that you cannot see a white spot about her.

FALSTAFF.
What tellest thou me of black and blue? I was beaten myself into all the colours of the rainbow; and was like to be apprehended for the witch of Brainford. But that my admirable dexterity of wit, my counterfeiting the action of an old woman, delivered me, the knave constable had set me i' the stocks, i' the common stocks, for a witch.

QUICKLY.
Sir, let me speak with you in your chamber; you shall hear how things go, and, I warrant, to your content. Here is a letter will say somewhat. Good hearts, what ado

here is to bring you together! Sure, one of
you does not serve heaven well, that you are
so crossed.

FALSTAFF.

Come up into my chamber.

[*Exeunt.*]

SCENE VI

Another room in the Garter Inn.
[*Enter* FENTON *and* HOST.]

HOST.

Master Fenton, talk not to me; my mind is
heavy; I will give over all.

FENTON.

Yet hear me speak. Assist me in my
    purpose,
And, as I am a gentleman, I'll give thee
A hundred pound in gold more than your
    loss.

HOST.

I will hear you, Master Fenton; and I will,
at the least, keep your counsel.

FENTON.

From time to time I have acquainted you
With the dear love I bear to fair Anne
    Page,
Who, mutually, hath answered my
    affection,
So far forth as herself might be her
    chooser,
Even to my wish. I have a letter from her
Of such contents as you will wonder at;
The mirth whereof so larded with my
    matter
That neither, singly, can be manifested
Without the show of both; wherein fat
    Falstaff
Hath a great scare: the image of the jest
I'll show you here at large. Hark, good
    mine host:
To-night at Herne's oak, just 'twixt twelve
    and one,
Must my sweet Nan present the Fairy
    Queen;
The purpose why is here: in which
    disguise,
While other jests are something rank on
    foot,

Her father hath commanded her to slip
Away with Slender, and with him at Eton
Immediately to marry; she hath consented:
Now, sir,
Her mother, even strong against that
    match
And firm for Doctor Caius, hath
    appointed
That he shall likewise shuffle her away,
While other sports are tasking of their
    minds;
And at the deanery, where a priest
    attends,
Straight marry her: to this her mother's
    plot
She seemingly obedient likewise hath
Made promise to the doctor. Now thus
    it rests:
Her father means she shall be all in white;
And in that habit, when Slender sees his
    time
To take her by the hand and bid her go,
She shall go with him: her mother hath
    intended
The better to denote her to the doctor,—
For they must all be mask'd and
    vizarded—
That quaint in green she shall be loose
    enrob'd,
With ribands pendent, flaring 'bout her
    head;
And when the doctor spies his vantage
    ripe,
To pinch her by the hand: and, on that
    token,
The maid hath given consent to go with
    him.

HOST.

Which means she to deceive, father or
    mother?

FENTON.

Both, my good host, to go along with me:
And here it rests, that you'll procure the
    vicar
To stay for me at church, 'twixt twelve
    and one,
And in the lawful name of marrying,
To give our hearts united ceremony.

HOST.

Well, husband your device; I'll to the vicar. Bring you the maid, you shall not lack a priest.

FENTON.

So shall I evermore be bound to thee; Besides, I'll make a present recompense.

[*Exeunt.*]

ACT V
SCENE I

A room in the Garter Inn.

[*Enter* FALSTAFF *and* MISTRESS QUICKLY.]

FALSTAFF.

Prithee, no more prattling; go: I'll hold. This is the third time; I hope good luck lies in odd numbers. Away! go. They say there is divinity in odd numbers, either in nativity, chance, or death. Away!

QUICKLY.

I'll provide you a chain, and I'll do what I can to get you a pair of horns.

FALSTAFF.

Away, I say; time wears; hold up your head, and mince.

[*Exit* MISTRESS QUICKLY.]

[*Enter* FORD, *disguised.*]

How now, Master Brook! Master Brook, the matter will be known tonight, or never. Be you in the park about midnight, at Herne's oak, and you shall see wonders.

FORD.

Went you not to her yesterday, sir, as you told me you had appointed?

FALSTAFF.

I went to her, Master Brook, as you see, like a poor old man; but I came from her, Master Brook, like a poor old woman. That same knave Ford, her husband, hath the finest mad devil of jealousy in him, Master Brook, that ever governed frenzy. I will tell you: he beat me grievously in the shape of a woman; for in the shape of man, Master Brook, I fear not Goliath with a weaver's beam, because I know also life is a shuttle. I am in haste; go along with me; I'll tell you all, Master Brook. Since I plucked geese, played truant, and whipped top, I knew not

what 'twas to be beaten till lately. Follow me: I'll tell you strange things of this knave Ford, on whom to-night I will be revenged, and I will deliver his wife into your hand. Follow. Strange things in hand, Master Brook! Follow.

[*Exeunt.*]

SCENE II

Windsor Park.

[*Enter* PAGE, SHALLOW, *and* SLENDER.]

PAGE.

Come, come; we'll couch i' the castle-ditch till we see the light of our fairies. Remember, son Slender, my daughter.

SLENDER.

Ay, forsooth; I have spoke with her, and we have a nay-word how to know one another. I come to her in white and cry "mum"; she cries "budget," and by that we know one another.

SHALLOW.

That's good too; but what needs either your "mum" or her "budget"? The white will decipher her well enough. It hath struck ten o'clock.

PAGE.

The night is dark; light and spirits will become it well. Heaven prosper our sport! No man means evil but the devil, and we shall know him by his horns. Let's away; follow me.

[*Exeunt.*]

SCENE III

The street in Windsor.

[*Enter* MISTRESS PAGE, MISTRESS FORD, *and* DOCTOR CAIUS.]

MISTRESS PAGE.

Master Doctor, my daughter is in green; when you see your time, take her by the hand, away with her to the deanery, and dispatch it quickly. Go before into the park; we two must go together.

CAIUS.

I know vat I have to do; adieu.

MISTRESS PAGE.

Fare you well, sir. [*Exit* CAIUS.] My

husband will not rejoice so much at the abuse of Falstaff as he will chafe at the doctor's marrying my daughter; but 'tis no matter; better a little chiding than a great deal of heart break.

MISTRESS FORD.
Where is Nan now, and her troop of fairies, and the Welsh devil, Hugh?

MISTRESS PAGE.
They are all couched in a pit hard by Herne's oak, with obscured lights; which, at the very instant of Falstaff's and our meeting, they will at once display to the night.

MISTRESS FORD.
That cannot choose but amaze him.

MISTRESS PAGE.
If he be not amazed, he will be mocked; if he be amazed, he will every way be mocked.

MISTRESS FORD.
We'll betray him finely.

MISTRESS PAGE.
Against such lewdsters and their lechery, Those that betray them do no treachery.

MISTRESS FORD.
The hour draws on: to the oak, to the oak!
[*Exeunt.*]

SCENE IV
Windsor Park.
[*Enter* SIR HUGH EVANS, *disguised, with* OTHERS *as fairies.*]

EVANS.
Trib, trib, fairies; come; and remember your parts. Be pold, I pray you; follow me into the pit; and when I give the watch-ords, do as I pid you. Come, come; trib, trib.
[*Exeunt.*]

SCENE V
Another part of the park.
[*Enter* FALSTAFF *disguised as Herne with a buck's head on.*]

FALSTAFF.
The Windsor bell hath struck twelve; the minute draws on. Now the hot-blooded gods assist me! Remember, Jove, thou wast a bull for thy Europa; love set on thy horns. O powerful love! that in some respects,

makes a beast a man; in some other a man a beast. You were also, Jupiter, a swan, for the love of Leda. O omnipotent love! how near the god drew to the complexion of a goose! A fault done first in the form of a beast; O Jove, a beastly fault! and then another fault in the semblance of a fowl: think on't, Jove, a foul fault! When gods have hot backs what shall poor men do? For me, I am here a Windsor stag; and the fattest, I think, i' the forest. Send me a cool rut-time, Jove, or who can blame me to piss my tallow? Who comes here? my doe?
[*Enter* MISTRESS FORD *and* MISTRESS PAGE.]

MISTRESS FORD.
Sir John! Art thou there, my deer? my male deer?

FALSTAFF.
My doe with the black scut! Let the sky rain potatoes; let it thunder to the tune of "Greensleeves"; hail kissing-comfits and snow eringoes; let there come a tempest of provocation, I will shelter me here.
[*Embracing her.*]

MISTRESS FORD.
Mistress Page is come with me, sweetheart.

FALSTAFF.
Divide me like a brib'd buck, each a haunch; I will keep my sides to myself, my shoulders for the fellow of this walk, and my horns I bequeath your husbands. Am I a woodman, ha? Speak I like Herne the hunter? Why, now is Cupid a child of conscience; he makes restitution. As I am a true spirit, welcome!
[*Noise within.*]

MISTRESS PAGE.
Alas! what noise?

MISTRESS FORD.
Heaven forgive our sins!

FALSTAFF.
What should this be?

MISTRESS FORD.
Away, away!

MISTRESS PAGE.
Away, away!
[*They run off.*]

FALSTAFF.
I think the devil will not have me damned,
lest the oil that's in me should set hell on
fire; he would never else cross me thus.
[*Enter* SIR HUGH EVANS *like a satyr,*
PISTOL *as a hobgoblin,* ANNE PAGE *as the*
fairy queen, attended by her BROTHERS *and*
OTHERS, *as fairies, with waxen tapers on*
their heads.]

ANNE.
Fairies, black, grey, green, and white,
You moonshine revellers, and shades of
night,
You orphan heirs of fix'd destiny,
Attend your office and your quality.
Crier Hobgoblin, make the fairy oyes.

PISTOL.
Elves, list your names: silence, you airy toys!
Cricket, to Windsor chimneys shalt thou
leap:
Where fires thou find'st unrak'd, and
hearths unswept,
There pinch the maids as blue as bilberry:
Our radiant Queen hates sluts and
sluttery.

FALSTAFF.
They are fairies; he that speaks to them
shall die:
I'll wink and couch: no man their works
must eye.
[*Lies down upon his face.*]

EVANS.
Where's Bede? Go you, and where you
find a maid
That, ere she sleep, has thrice her prayers
said,
Rein up the organs of her fantasy,
Sleep she as sound as careless infancy;
But those as sleep and think not on their
sins,
Pinch them, arms, legs, backs, shoulders,
sides, and shins.

ANNE.
About, about!
Search Windsor castle, elves, within and
out:
Strew good luck, ouphes, on every sacred
room,

That it may stand till the perpetual doom,
In state as wholesome as in state 'tis fit,
Worthy the owner and the owner it.
The several chairs of order look you scour
With juice of balm and every precious
flower:
Each fair instalment, coat, and several
crest,
With loyal blazon, evermore be blest!
And nightly, meadow-fairies, look you
sing,
Like to the Garter's compass, in a ring:
The expressure that it bears, green let it be,
More fertile-fresh than all the field to see;
And *Honi soit qui mal y pense* write
In emerald tufts, flowers purple, blue and
white;
Like sapphire, pearl, and rich embroidery,
Buckled below fair knighthood's bending
knee.
Fairies use flowers for their charactery.
Away! disperse! But, till 'tis one o'clock,
Our dance of custom round about the oak
Of Herne the hunter let us not forget.

EVANS.
Pray you, lock hand in hand; yourselves in
order set;
And twenty glow-worms shall our
lanterns be,
To guide our measure round about the
tree.
But, stay; I smell a man of middle-earth.

FALSTAFF.
Heavens defend me from that Welsh fairy,
lest he transform me to a piece of cheese!

PISTOL.
Vile worm, thou wast o'erlook'd even in
thy birth.

ANNE.
With trial-fire touch me his finger-end:
If he be chaste, the flame will back descend
And turn him to no pain; but if he start,
It is the flesh of a corrupted heart.

PISTOL.
A trial! come.

EVANS.
                    Come, will this wood take fire?
[*They burn him with their tapers.*]

FALSTAFF.
Oh, oh, oh!

ANNE.
Corrupt, corrupt, and tainted in desire!
About him, fairies; sing a scornful rhyme;
And, as you trip, still pinch him to your
  time.
                    [*Song.*]
Fie on sinful fantasy!
Fie on lust and luxury!
Lust is but a bloody fire,
Kindled with unchaste desire,
Fed in heart, whose flames aspire,
As thoughts do blow them, higher and
  higher.
Pinch him, fairies, mutually;
Pinch him for his villany;
Pinch him and burn him and turn him
  about,
Till candles and star-light and moonshine
  be out.
[*During this song the fairies pinch* FALSTAFF.
  DOCTOR CAIUS *comes one way, and steals
  away a fairy in green;* SLENDER *another
  way, and takes off a fairy in white; and*
  FENTON *comes, and steals away* ANNE
PAGE. *A noise of hunting is heard within. All
  the fairies run away.* FALSTAFF *pulls off his
  buck's head, and rises.*]
[*Enter* PAGE, FORD, MISTRESS PAGE,
  MISTRESS FORD. *They lay hold on*
  FALSTAFF.]

PAGE.
Nay, do not fly; I think we have watch'd
  you now:
Will none but Herne the hunter serve
  your turn?

MISTRESS PAGE.
I pray you, come, hold up the jest no
  higher.
Now, good Sir John, how like you
  Windsor wives?
See you these, husband? do not these fair
  yokes
Become the forest better than the town?

FORD.
Now, sir, who's a cuckold now? Master
Brook, Falstaff's a knave, a cuckoldly knave;

here are his horns, Master Brook; and,
Master Brook, he hath enjoyed nothing
of Ford's but his buck-basket, his cudgel,
and twenty pounds of money, which must
be paid to Master Brook; his horses are
arrested for it, Master Brook.

MISTRESS FORD.
Sir John, we have had ill luck; we could
never meet. I will never take you for my
love again; but I will always count you my
deer.

FALSTAFF.
I do begin to perceive that I am made an
ass.

FORD.
Ay, and an ox too; both the proofs are
extant.

FALSTAFF.
And these are not fairies? I was three or
four times in the thought they were not
fairies; and yet the guiltiness of my mind,
the sudden surprise of my powers, drove
the grossness of the foppery into a received
belief, in despite of the teeth of all rhyme
and reason, that they were fairies. See now
how wit may be made a Jack-a-Lent when
'tis upon ill employment!

EVANS.
Sir John Falstaff, serve Got, and leave your
desires, and fairies will not pinse you.

FORD.
Well said, fairy Hugh.

EVANS.
And leave you your jealousies too, I pray
  you.

FORD.
I will never mistrust my wife again, till thou
art able to woo her in good English.

FALSTAFF.
Have I laid my brain in the sun, and dried
it, that it wants matter to prevent so gross
o'er-reaching as this? Am I ridden with a
Welsh goat too? Shall I have a cox-comb of
frieze? 'Tis time I were choked with a piece
of toasted cheese.

EVANS.
Seese is not good to give putter: your belly
is all putter.

FALSTAFF.
"Seese" and "putter"! Have I lived to stand at the taunt of one that makes fritters of English? This is enough to be the decay of lust and late-walking through the realm.

MISTRESS PAGE.
Why, Sir John, do you think, though we would have thrust virtue out of our hearts by the head and shoulders, and have given ourselves without scruple to hell, that ever the devil could have made you our delight?

FORD.
What, a hodge-pudding? a bag of flax?

MISTRESS PAGE.
A puffed man?

PAGE.
Old, cold, withered, and of intolerable entrails?

FORD.
And one that is as slanderous as Satan?

PAGE.
And as poor as Job?

FORD.
And as wicked as his wife?

EVANS.
And given to fornications, and to taverns, and sack and wine, and metheglins, and to drinkings and swearings and starings, pribbles and prabbles?

FALSTAFF.
Well, I am your theme; you have the start of me; I am dejected; I am not able to answer the Welsh flannel. Ignorance itself is a plummet o'er me; use me as you will.

FORD.
Marry, sir, we'll bring you to Windsor, to one Master Brook, that you have cozened of money, to whom you should have been a pander: over and above that you have suffered, I think to repay that money will be a biting affliction.

MISTRESS FORD.
Nay, husband, let that go to make amends; Forget that sum, so we'll all be friends.

FORD.
Well, here's my hand: all is forgiven at last.

PAGE.
Yet be cheerful, knight; thou shalt eat a posset tonight at my house; where I will desire thee to laugh at my wife, that now laughs at thee. Tell her, Master Slender hath married her daughter.

MISTRESS PAGE. [*Aside.*]
Doctors doubt that; if Anne Page be my daughter, she is, by this, Doctor Caius' wife.
[*Enter* SLENDER.]

SLENDER.
Whoa, ho! ho! father Page!

PAGE.
Son, how now! how now, son! have you dispatched?

SLENDER.
Dispatched! I'll make the best in Gloucestershire know on't; would I were hanged, la, else!

PAGE.
Of what, son?

SLENDER.
I came yonder at Eton to marry Mistress Anne Page, and she's a great lubberly boy: if it had not been i' the church, I would have swinged him, or he should have swinged me. If I did not think it had been Anne Page, would I might never stir! and 'tis a postmaster's boy.

PAGE.
Upon my life, then, you took the wrong.

SLENDER.
What need you tell me that? I think so, when I took a boy for a girl. If I had been married to him, for all he was in woman's apparel, I would not have had him.

PAGE.
Why, this is your own folly. Did not I tell you how you should know my daughter by her garments?

SLENDER.
I went to her in white and cried "mum" and she cried "budget" as Anne and I had appointed; and yet it was not Anne, but a postmaster's boy.

EVANS.
Jeshu! Master Slender, cannot you see but marry boys?

PAGE.
O I am vexed at heart: what shall I do?

Mistress Page.

Good George, be not angry: I knew of your purpose; turned my daughter into green; and, indeed, she is now with the doctor at the deanery, and there married.

[*Enter* Doctor Caius.]

Caius.

Vere is Mistress Page? By gar, I am cozened; I ha' married *un garçon*, a boy; *un paysan*, by gar, a boy; it is not Anne Page; by gar, I am cozened.

Mistress Page.

Why, did you take her in green?

Caius.

Ay, by gar, and 'tis a boy: by gar, I'll raise all Windsor.

[*Exit* Doctor Caius.]

Ford.

This is strange. Who hath got the right Anne?

Page.

My heart misgives me; here comes Master Fenton.

[*Enter* Fenton *and* Anne Page.]

How now, Master Fenton!

Anne.

Pardon, good father! good my mother, pardon!

Page.

Now, Mistress, how chance you went not with Master Slender?

Mistress Page.

Why went you not with Master Doctor, maid?

Fenton.

You do amaze her: hear the truth of it. You would have married her most shamefully, Where there was no proportion held in love. The truth is, she and I, long since contracted,

Are now so sure that nothing can dissolve us. The offence is holy that she hath committed, And this deceit loses the name of craft, Of disobedience, or unduteous title, Since therein she doth evitate and shun A thousand irreligious cursed hours, Which forced marriage would have brought upon her.

Ford.

Stand not amaz'd: here is no remedy: In love, the heavens themselves do guide the state: Money buys lands, and wives are sold by fate.

Falstaff.

I am glad, though you have ta'en a special stand to strike at me, that your arrow hath glanced.

Page.

Well, what remedy?—Fenton, heaven give thee joy! What cannot be eschew'd must be embrac'd.

Falstaff.

When night-dogs run, all sorts of deer are chas'd.

Mistress Page.

Well, I will muse no further. Master Fenton, Heaven give you many, many merry days! Good husband, let us every one go home, And laugh this sport o'er by a country fire; Sir John and all.

Ford.

           Let it be so. Sir John, To Master Brook you yet shall hold your word; For he, to-night, shall lie with Mistress Ford.

[*Exeunt.*]

Measure for Measure

Dramatis Personae

VICENTIO, *Duke of Vienna*
ANGELO, *lord deputy in the duke's absence*
ESCALUS, *an ancient lord, joined with Angelo in the deputation*
CLAUDIO, *a young gentleman*
LUCIO, *a fantastic*
Two other like GENTLEMEN
VARRIUS, *a gentleman, servant to the duke*
PROVOST
THOMAS, *friar*
PETER, *friar*
A JUSTICE
ELBOW, *a simple constable*
FROTH, *a foolish gentleman*

CLOWN, *servant to Mistress Overdone*
ABHORSON, *an executioner*
BARNARDINE, *a dissolute prisoner*
ISABELLA, *sister to Claudio*
MARIANA, *betrothed to Angelo*
JULIET, *beloved by Claudio*
FRANCISCA, *a nun*
MISTRESS OVERDONE, *a bawd*
LORDS, GENTLEMEN,
 GUARDS, OFFICERS, *and other*
 ATTENDANTS

SCENE: *Vienna.*

ACT I
SCENE I

An apartment in the duke's palace.
[*Enter* DUKE, ESCALUS, LORDS, *and* ATTENDANTS.]

DUKE.
Escalus,—

ESCALUS.
My lord.

DUKE.
Of government the properties to unfold,
Would seem in me to affect speech and
 discourse;
Since I am put to know that your own
 science
Exceeds, in that, the lists of all advice
My strength can give you: then no more
 remains
But that to your sufficiency, as your worth
 is able,
And let them work. The nature of our
 people,
Our city's institutions, and the terms
For common justice, you are as pregnant in
As art and practice hath enriched any

That we remember. There is our
 commission,
From which we would not have you
 warp.—Call hither,
I say, bid come before us, Angelo.—
 [*Exit an* ATTENDANT.]
What figure of us think you he will bear?
For you must know we have with special
 soul
Elected him our absence to supply;
Lent him our terror, drest him with our
 love,
And given his deputation all the organs
Of our own power: what think you of it?

ESCALUS.
If any in Vienna be of worth
To undergo such ample grace and honour,
It is Lord Angelo.
 [*Enter* ANGELO.]

DUKE.
 Look where he comes.

ANGELO.
Always obedient to your grace's will,
I come to know your pleasure.

DUKE.
                                        Angelo,
There is a kind of character in thy life
That to th' observer doth thy history
Fully unfold. Thyself and thy belongings
Are not thine own so proper as to waste
Thyself upon thy virtues, they on thee.
Heaven doth with us as we with torches
    do,
Not light them for themselves: for if our
    virtues
Did not go forth of us, 'twere all alike
As if we had them not. Spirits are not
    finely touch'd
But to fine issues: nor nature never lends
The smallest scruple of her excellence
But, like a thrifty goddess, she determines
Herself the glory of a creditor,
Both thanks and use. But I do bend my
    speech
To one that can my part in him advertise;
Hold, therefore, Angelo;
In our remove be thou at full ourself:
Mortality and mercy in Vienna
Live in thy tongue and heart! Old Escalus,
Though first in question, is thy secondary:
Take thy commission.
ANGELO.
                            Now, good my lord,
Let there be some more test made of my
    metal,
Before so noble and so great a figure
Be stamped upon it.
DUKE.
                        No more evasion:
We have with a leaven'd and prepared
    choice
Proceeded to you; therefore take your
    honours.
Our haste from hence is of so quick
    condition
That it prefers itself, and leaves
    unquestion'd
Matters of needful value. We shall write
    to you
As time and our concernings shall
    importune,
How it goes with us; and do look to know

What doth befall you here. So, fare you
    well:
To the hopeful execution do I leave you
Of your commissions.
ANGELO.
                            Yet give leave, my lord,
That we may bring you something on the
    way.
DUKE.
My haste may not admit it;
Nor need you, on mine honour, have to do
With any scruple: your scope is as mine
    own:
So to enforce or qualify the laws
As to your soul seems good. Give me your
    hand;
I'll privily away: I love the people,
But do not like to stage me to their eyes:
Though it do well, I do not relish well
Their loud applause and "Aves" vehement:
Nor do I think the man of safe discretion
That does affect it. Once more, fare you
    well.
ANGELO.
The heavens give safety to your purposes!
ESCALUS.
Lead forth and bring you back in
    happiness.
DUKE.
I thank you. Fare you well.
                            [*Exit.*]
ESCALUS.
I shall desire you, sir, to give me leave
To have free speech with you; and it
    concerns me
To look into the bottom of my place:
A pow'r I have, but of what strength and
    nature
I am not yet instructed.
ANGELO.
'Tis so with me.—Let us withdraw
    together,
And we may soon our satisfaction have
Touching that point.
ESCALUS.
                            I'll wait upon your honour.
                            [*Exeunt.*]

SCENE II
A street.
[*Enter* LUCIO *and two* GENTLEMEN.]
LUCIO.
If the duke, with the other dukes, come not to composition with the King of Hungary, why then all the dukes fall upon the king.
FIRST GENTLEMAN.
Heaven grant us its peace, but not the King of Hungary's!
SECOND GENTLEMAN.
Amen.
LUCIO.
Thou concludest like the sanctimonious pirate that went to sea with the Ten Commandments, but scraped one out of the table.
SECOND GENTLEMAN.
Thou shalt not steal?
LUCIO.
Ay, that he razed.
FIRST GENTLEMAN.
Why, 'twas a commandment to command the captain and all the rest from their functions; they put forth to steal. There's not a soldier of us all that, in the thanksgiving before meat, do relish the petition well that prays for peace.
SECOND GENTLEMAN.
I never heard any soldier dislike it.
LUCIO.
I believe thee; for I think thou never wast where grace was said.
SECOND GENTLEMAN.
No? A dozen times at least.
FIRST GENTLEMAN.
What? in metre?
LUCIO.
In any proportion or in any language.
FIRST GENTLEMAN.
I think, or in any religion.
LUCIO.
Ay! why not? Grace is grace, despite of all controversy. As, for example;—thou thyself art a wicked villain, despite of all grace.
FIRST GENTLEMAN.
Well, there went but a pair of shears between us.

LUCIO.
I grant; as there may between the lists and the velvet. Thou art the list.
FIRST GENTLEMAN.
And thou the velvet: thou art good velvet; thou'rt a three-piled piece, I warrant thee: I had as lief be a list of an English kersey as be piled, as thou art piled, for a French velvet. Do I speak feelingly now?
LUCIO.
I think thou dost; and, indeed, with most painful feeling of thy speech. I will, out of thine own confession, learn to begin thy health; but, whilst I live, forget to drink after thee.
FIRST GENTLEMAN.
I think I have done myself wrong; have I not?
SECOND GENTLEMAN.
Yes, that thou hast, whether thou art tainted or free.
LUCIO.
Behold, behold, where Madam Mitigation comes! I have purchased as many diseases under her roof as come to—
SECOND GENTLEMAN.
To what, I pray?
FIRST GENTLEMAN.
Judge.
SECOND GENTLEMAN.
To three thousand dollars a year.
FIRST GENTLEMAN.
Ay, and more.
LUCIO.
A French crown more.
FIRST GENTLEMAN.
Thou art always figuring diseases in me, but thou art full of error; I am sound.
LUCIO.
Nay, not, as one would say, healthy; but so sound as things that are hollow: thy bones are hollow: impiety has made a feast of thee.
[*Enter* MISTRESS OVERDONE.]
FIRST GENTLEMAN.
How now! which of your hips has the most profound sciatica?
MISTRESS OVERDONE.
Well, well; there's one yonder arrested and

carried to prison was worth five thousand of you all.

FIRST GENTLEMAN.
Who's that, I pray thee?

MISTRESS OVERDONE.
Marry, sir, that's Claudio, Signior Claudio.

FIRST GENTLEMAN.
Claudio to prison! 'tis not so.

MISTRESS OVERDONE.
Nay, but I know 'tis so: I saw him arrested; saw him carried away; and, which is more, within these three days his head to be chopped off.

LUCIO.
But, after all this fooling, I would not have it so. Art thou sure of this?

MISTRESS OVERDONE.
I am too sure of it: and it is for getting Madam Julietta with child.

LUCIO.
Believe me, this may be: he promised to meet me two hours since, and he was ever precise in promise-keeping.

SECOND GENTLEMAN.
Besides, you know, it draws something near to the speech we had to such a purpose.

FIRST GENTLEMAN.
But most of all agreeing with the proclamation.

LUCIO.
Away; let's go learn the truth of it.
[*Exeunt* LUCIO *and* GENTLEMEN.]

MISTRESS OVERDONE.
Thus, what with the war, what with the sweat, what with the gallows, and what with poverty, I am custom-shrunk. How now! what's the news with you?
[*Enter* CLOWN.]

CLOWN.
Yonder man is carried to prison.

MISTRESS OVERDONE.
Well: what has he done?

CLOWN.
A woman.

MISTRESS OVERDONE.
But what's his offence?

CLOWN.
Groping for trouts in a peculiar river.

MISTRESS OVERDONE.
What! is there a maid with child by him?

CLOWN.
No; but there's a woman with maid by him. You have not heard of the proclamation, have you?

MISTRESS OVERDONE.
What proclamation, man?

CLOWN.
All houses in the suburbs of Vienna must be plucked down.

MISTRESS OVERDONE.
And what shall become of those in the city?

CLOWN.
They shall stand for seed: they had gone down too, but that a wise burgher put in for them.

MISTRESS OVERDONE.
But shall all our houses of resort in the suburbs be pulled down?

CLOWN.
To the ground, mistress.

MISTRESS OVERDONE.
Why, here's a change indeed in the commonwealth! What shall become of me?

CLOWN.
Come, fear not you; good counsellors lack no clients: though you change your place you need not change your trade; I'll be your tapster still. Courage; there will be pity taken on you: you that have worn your eyes almost out in the service, you will be considered.

MISTRESS OVERDONE.
What's to do here, Thomas Tapster? Let's withdraw.

CLOWN.
Here comes Signior Claudio, led by the provost to prison: and there's Madam Juliet.
[*Exeunt.*]
[*Enter* PROVOST, CLAUDIO, JULIET, *and* OFFICERS.]

CLAUDIO.
Fellow, why dost thou show me thus to
   the world?
Bear me to prison, where I am committed.

PROVOST.
I do it not in evil disposition,
But from Lord Angelo by special charge.

CLAUDIO.
Thus can the demi-god Authority
Make us pay down for our offence by
 weight.—
The words of heaven;—on whom it will,
 it will;
On whom it will not, so; yet still 'tis just.
 [*Enter* LUCIO *and two* GENTLEMEN.]

LUCIO.
Why, how now, Claudio, whence comes
 this restraint?

CLAUDIO.
From too much liberty, my Lucio,
 liberty:
As surfeit is the father of much fast,
So every scope by the immoderate use
Turns to restraint. Our natures do
 pursue,—
Like rats that ravin down their proper
 bane,—
A thirsty evil; and when we drink we
 die.

LUCIO.
If I could speak so wisely under an arrest,
I would send for certain of my creditors;
and yet, to say the truth, I had as lief have
the foppery of freedom as the morality
of imprisonment.—What's thy offence,
Claudio?

CLAUDIO.
What but to speak of would offend again.

LUCIO.
What, is't murder?

CLAUDIO.
No.

LUCIO.
Lechery?

CLAUDIO.
Call it so.

PROVOST.
Away, sir; you must go.

CLAUDIO.
One word, good friend.—Lucio, a word
 with you.
 [*Takes him aside.*]

LUCIO.
A hundred, if they'll do you any good.
Is lechery so look'd after?

CLAUDIO.
Thus stands it with me:—Upon a true
 contract
I got possession of Julietta's bed:
You know the lady; she is fast my wife,
Save that we do the denunciation lack
Of outward order; this we came not to
Only for propagation of a dower
Remaining in the coffer of her friends;
From whom we thought it meet to hide
 our love
Till time had made them for us. But it
 chances
The stealth of our most mutual
 entertainment,
With character too gross, is writ on Juliet.

LUCIO.
With child, perhaps?

CLAUDIO.
                    Unhappily, even so.
And the new deputy now for the duke,—
Whether it be the fault and glimpse of
 newness,
Or whether that the body public be
A horse whereon the governor doth ride,
Who, newly in the seat, that it may know
He can command, lets it straight feel the
 spur:
Whether the tyranny be in his place,
Or in his eminence that fills it up,
I stagger in.—But this new governor
Awakes me all the enrolled penalties
Which have, like unscour'd armour, hung
 by the wall
So long that nineteen zodiacs have gone
 round
And none of them been worn; and, for a
 name,
Now puts the drowsy and neglected act
Freshly on me; 'tis surely for a name.

LUCIO.
I warrant it is: and thy head stands so tickle
on thy shoulders that a milkmaid, if she be
in love, may sigh it off. Send after the duke,
and appeal to him.

CLAUDIO.
I have done so, but he's not to be found.
I pr'ythee, Lucio, do me this kind service:

This day my sister should the cloister enter,
And there receive her approbation:
Acquaint her with the danger of my state;
Implore her, in my voice, that she make
    friends
To the strict deputy; bid herself assay him;
I have great hope in that: for in her youth
There is a prone and speechless dialect
Such as moves men; beside, she hath
    prosperous art
When she will play with reason and
    discourse,
And well she can persuade.

Lucio.

I pray she may; as well for the
encouragement of the like, which else
would stand under grievous imposition, as
for the enjoying of thy life, who I would be
sorry should be thus foolishly lost at a game
of tick-tack. I'll to her.

Claudio.

I thank you, good friend Lucio.

Lucio.

Within two hours,—

Claudio.

             Come, officer, away.
    [*Exeunt.*]

SCENE III

A monastery.
[*Enter* Duke *and* Friar Thomas.]

Duke.

No; holy father; throw away that thought;
Believe not that the dribbling dart of love
Can pierce a complete bosom: why I desire
    thee
To give me secret harbour hath a purpose
More grave and wrinkled than the aims
    and ends
Of burning youth.

Friar.

           May your grace speak of it?

Duke.

My holy sir, none better knows than you
How I have ever lov'd the life remov'd,
And held in idle price to haunt assemblies
Where youth, and cost, a witless bravery
    keeps.

I have deliver'd to Lord Angelo,—
A man of stricture and firm abstinence,—
My absolute power and place here in
    Vienna,
And he supposes me travell'd to Poland;
For so I have strew'd it in the common ear,
And so it is received. Now, pious sir,
You will demand of me why I do this?

Friar.

Gladly, my lord.

Duke.

We have strict statutes and most biting
    laws,—
The needful bits and curbs to headstrong
    steeds,—
Which for this fourteen years we have let
    sleep,
Even like an o'ergrown lion in a cave,
That goes not out to prey. Now, as fond
    fathers,
Having bound up the threat'ning twigs
    of birch,
Only to stick it in their children's sight
For terror, not to use, in time the rod
Becomes more mock'd than fear'd; so our
    decrees,
Dead to infliction, to themselves are dead;
And liberty plucks justice by the nose;
The baby beats the nurse, and quite
    athwart
Goes all decorum.

Friar.

             It rested in your grace
To unloose this tied-up justice when you
    pleas'd;
And it in you more dreadful would have
    seem'd
Than in Lord Angelo.

Duke.

             I do fear, too dreadful:
Sith 'twas my fault to give the people
    scope,
'Twould be my tyranny to strike and gall
    them
For what I bid them do: for we bid this
    be done
When evil deeds have their permissive
    pass

And not the punishment. Therefore,
    indeed, my father,
I have on Angelo impos'd the office;
Who may, in the ambush of my name,
    strike home,
And yet my nature never in the fight
To do in slander. And to behold his sway,
I will, as 'twere a brother of your order,
Visit both prince and people: therefore, I
    pr'ythee,
Supply me with the habit, and instruct me
How I may formally in person bear me
Like a true friar. Moe reasons for this action
At our more leisure shall I render you;
Only, this one:—Lord Angelo is precise;
Stands at a guard with envy; scarce
    confesses
That his blood flows, or that his appetite
Is more to bread than stone: hence shall
    we see,
If power change purpose, what our
    seemers be.
                    [*Exeunt.*]

SCENE IV

A nunnery.
[*Enter* Isabella *and* Francisca.]
Isabella.
And have you nuns no further privileges?
Francisca.
Are not these large enough?
Isabella.
Yes, truly; I speak not as desiring more,
But rather wishing a more strict restraint
Upon the sisterhood, the votarists of Saint
    Clare.
Lucio. [*Within.*]
Ho! Peace be in this place!
Isabella.
                    Who's that which calls?
Francisca.
It is a man's voice. Gentle Isabella,
Turn you the key, and know his business
    of him;
You may, I may not; you are yet unsworn:
When you have vow'd, you must not speak
    with men
But in the presence of the prioress;

Then, if you speak, you must not show
    your face;
Or, if you show your face, you must not
    speak.
He calls again; I pray you answer him.
                    [*Exit* Francisca.]
Isabella.
Peace and prosperity! Who is't that calls?
                    [*Enter* Lucio.]
Lucio.
Hail, virgin, if you be; as those cheek-roses
Proclaim you are no less! Can you so stead
    me
As bring me to the sight of Isabella,
A novice of this place, and the fair sister
To her unhappy brother Claudio?
Isabella.
Why her unhappy brother? let me ask;
The rather, for I now must make you know
I am that Isabella, and his sister.
Lucio.
Gentle and fair, your brother kindly greets
    you:
Not to be weary with you, he's in prison.
Isabella.
Woe me! For what?
Lucio.
For that which, if myself might be his
    judge,
He should receive his punishment in
    thanks:
He hath got his friend with child.
Isabella.
Sir, make me not your story.
Lucio.
                    'Tis true.
I would not—though 'tis my familiar sin
With maids to seem the lapwing, and to
    jest,
Tongue far from heart—play with all
    virgins so:
I hold you as a thing ensky'd and sainted;
By your renouncement an immortal spirit;
And to be talk'd with in sincerity,
As with a saint.
Isabella.
You do blaspheme the good in mocking
    me.

Lucio.
Do not believe it. Fewness and truth, 'tis
  thus:
Your brother and his lover have embraced:
As those that feed grow full: as blossoming
  time,
That from the seedness the bare fallow
  brings
To teeming foison; even so her plenteous
  womb
Expresseth his full tilth and husbandry.
Isabella.
Some one with child by him?—My cousin
  Juliet?
Lucio.
Is she your cousin?
Isabella.
Adoptedly, as school-maids change their
  names
By vain though apt affection.
Lucio.
                    She it is.
Isabella.
O, let him marry her!
Lucio.
                  This is the point.
The duke is very strangely gone from hence;
Bore many gentlemen, myself being one,
In hand, and hope of action: but we do
  learn
By those that know the very nerves of
  state,
His givings out were of an infinite distance
From his true-meant design. Upon his
  place,
And with full line of his authority,
Governs Lord Angelo: a man whose blood
Is very snow-broth; one who never feels
The wanton stings and motions of the
  sense.
But doth rebate and blunt his natural edge
With profits of the mind, study, and fast.
He,—to give fear to use and liberty,
Which have for long run by the hideous
  law,
As mice by lions,—hath pick'd out an act,
Under whose heavy sense your brother's
  life

Falls into forfeit: he arrests him on it;
And follows close the rigour of the statute
To make him an example; all hope is gone.
Unless you have the grace by your fair
  prayer
To soften Angelo: and that's my pith
Of business 'twixt you and your poor
  brother.
Isabella.
Doth he so seek his life?
Lucio.
                    Has censur'd him
Already; and, as I hear, the provost hath
A warrant for his execution.
Isabella.
Alas! what poor ability's in me
To do him good.
Lucio.
                Assay the power you have.
Isabella.
My power! alas, I doubt,—
Lucio.
                Our doubts are traitors,
And make us lose the good we oft might
  win
By fearing to attempt. Go to Lord Angelo,
And let him learn to know, when maidens
  sue,
Men give like gods; but when they weep
  and kneel,
All their petitions are as freely theirs
As they themselves would owe them.
Isabella.
I'll see what I can do.
Lucio.
                But speedily.
Isabella.
I will about it straight;
No longer staying but to give the Mother
Notice of my affair. I humbly thank you:
Commend me to my brother: soon at
  night
I'll send him certain word of my success.
Lucio.
I take my leave of you.
Isabella.
                Good sir, adieu.
                [Exeunt.]

ACT II
SCENE I

A hall in Angelo's house.
[*Enter* ANGELO, ESCALUS, *a*
JUSTICE, PROVOST, OFFICERS, *and*
other ATTENDANTS.]

ANGELO.
We must not make a scarecrow of the law,
Setting it up to fear the birds of prey,
And let it keep one shape till custom
    make it
Their perch, and not their terror.
ESCALUS.
                              Ay, but yet
Let us be keen, and rather cut a little
Than fall and bruise to death. Alas! this
    gentleman,
Whom I would save, had a most noble
    father.
Let but your honour know,—
Whom I believe to be most strait in
    virtue,—
That, in the working of your own
    affections,
Had time coher'd with place, or place with
    wishing,
Or that the resolute acting of your blood
Could have attain'd the effect of your own
    purpose,
Whether you had not sometime in your
    life
Err'd in this point which now you censure
    him,
And pull'd the law upon you.
ANGELO.
'Tis one thing to be tempted, Escalus,
Another thing to fall. I not deny
The jury, passing on the prisoner's life,
May, in the sworn twelve, have a thief or
    two
Guiltier than him they try. What's open
    made to justice,
That justice seizes. What knows the laws
That thieves do pass on thieves? 'Tis very
    pregnant,
The jewel that we find, we stoop and take
    it,
Because we see it; but what we do not see

We tread upon, and never think of it.
You may not so extenuate his offence
For I have had such faults; but rather tell
    me,
When I, that censure him, do so offend,
Let mine own judgment pattern out my
    death,
And nothing come in partial. Sir, he must
    die.
ESCALUS.
Be it as your wisdom will.
ANGELO.
                              Where is the provost?
PROVOST.
Here, if it like your honour.
ANGELO.
                              See that Claudio
Be executed by nine to-morrow morning:
Bring him his confessor; let him be
    prepar'd;
For that's the utmost of his pilgrimage.
                    [*Exit* PROVOST.]
ESCALUS.
Well, heaven forgive him! and forgive us
    all!
Some rise by sin, and some by virtue fall:
Some run from brakes of vice, and answer
    none,
And some condemned for a fault alone.
        [*Enter* ELBOW, FROTH, CLOWN,
                    OFFICERS, &c.]
ELBOW.
Come, bring them away: if these be good
people in a commonweal that do nothing
but use their abuses in common houses, I
know no law; bring them away.
ANGELO.
How now, sir! What's your name? and
what's the matter?
ELBOW.
If it please your honour, I am the poor
duke's constable, and my name is Elbow;
I do lean upon justice, sir, and do bring
in here before your good honour two
notorious benefactors.
ANGELO.
Benefactors! Well; what benefactors are
they? are they not malefactors?

Elbow.
If it please your honour, I know not well what they are; but precise villains they are, that I am sure of; and void of all profanation in the world that good Christians ought to have.

Escalus.
This comes off well; here's a wise officer.

Angelo.
Go to;—what quality are they of? Elbow is your name? Why dost thou not speak, Elbow?

Clown.
He cannot, sir; he's out at elbow.

Angelo.
What are you, sir?

Elbow.
He, sir? a tapster, sir; parcel-bawd; one that serves a bad woman; whose house, sir, was, as they say, plucked down in the suburbs; and now she professes a hot-house, which, I think, is a very ill house too.

Escalus.
How know you that?

Elbow.
My wife, sir, whom I detest before heaven and your honour,—

Escalus.
How! thy wife!

Elbow.
Ay, sir; who, I thank heaven, is an honest woman,—

Escalus.
Dost thou detest her therefore?

Elbow.
I say, sir, I will detest myself also, as well as she, that this house, if it be not a bawd's house, it is pity of her life, for it is a naughty house.

Escalus.
How dost thou know that, constable?

Elbow.
Marry, sir, by my wife; who, if she had been a woman cardinally given, might have been accused in fornication, adultery, and all uncleanliness there.

Escalus.
By the woman's means?

Elbow.
Ay, sir, by Mistress Overdone's means: but as she spit in his face, so she defied him.

Clown.
Sir, if it please your honour, this is not so.

Elbow.
Prove it before these varlets here, thou honourable man, prove it.

Escalus. [*To* Angelo.]
Do you hear how he misplaces?

Clown.
Sir, she came in great with child; and longing,—saving your honour's reverence—for stew'd prunes; sir, we had but two in the house, which at that very distant time stood, as it were, in a fruit dish, a dish of some threepence; your honours have seen such dishes; they are not China dishes, but very good dishes.

Escalus.
Go to, go to; no matter for the dish, sir.

Clown.
No, indeed, sir, not of a pin; you are therein in the right; but to the point. As I say, this Mistress Elbow, being, as I say, with child, and being great-bellied, and longing, as I said, for prunes; and having but two in the dish, as I said, Master Froth here, this very man, having eaten the rest, as I said, and, as I say, paying for them very honestly;—for, as you know, Master Froth, I could not give you threepence again,—

Froth.
No, indeed.

Clown.
Very well; you being then, if you be remember'd, cracking the stones of the foresaid prunes,—

Froth.
Ay, so I did indeed.

Clown.
Why, very well: I telling you then, if you be remember'd, that such a one and such a one were past cure of the thing you wot of, unless they kept very good diet, as I told you,—

Froth.
All this is true.

Clown.

Why, very well then.

Escalus.

Come, you are a tedious fool: to the purpose. What was done to Elbow's wife that he hath cause to complain of? Come me to what was done to her.

Clown.

Sir, your honour cannot come to that yet.

Escalus.

No, sir, nor I mean it not.

Clown.

Sir, but you shall come to it, by your honour's leave. And, I beseech you, look into Master Froth here, sir, a man of fourscore pound a-year; whose father died at Hallowmas:—was't not at Hallowmas, Master Froth?

Froth.

All-hallond eve.

Clown.

Why, very well; I hope here be truths: He, sir, sitting, as I say, in a lower chair, sir;—'twas in the "Bunch of Grapes," where, indeed, you have a delight to sit, have you not?—

Froth.

I have so; because it is an open room, and good for winter.

Clown.

Why, very well then;—I hope here be truths.

Angelo.

This will last out a night in Russia,
When nights are longest there: I'll take my leave,
And leave you to the hearing of the cause;
Hoping you'll find good cause to whip them all.

Escalus.

I think no less. Good morrow to your lordship. [*Exit* Angelo.] Now, sir, come on; what was done to Elbow's wife, once more?

Clown.

Once, sir? there was nothing done to her once.

Elbow.

I beseech you, sir, ask him what this man did to my wife.

Clown.

I beseech your honour, ask me.

Escalus.

Well, sir: what did this gentleman to her?

Clown.

I beseech you, sir, look in this gentleman's face.—Good Master Froth, look upon his honour; 'tis for a good purpose.—Doth your honour mark his face?

Escalus.

Ay, sir, very well.

Clown.

Nay, I beseech you, mark it well.

Escalus.

Well, I do so.

Clown.

Doth your honour see any harm in his face?

Escalus.

Why, no.

Clown.

I'll be supposed upon a book his face is the worst thing about him. Good then; if his face be the worst thing about him, how could Master Froth do the constable's wife any harm? I would know that of your honour.

Escalus.

He's in the right. Constable, what say you to it?

Elbow.

First, an it like you, the house is a respected house; next, this is a respected fellow; and his mistress is a respected woman.

Clown.

By this hand, sir, his wife is a more respected person than any of us all.

Elbow.

Varlet, thou liest; thou liest, wicked varlet: the time is yet to come that she was ever respected with man, woman, or child.

Clown.

Sir, she was respected with him before he married with her.

Escalus.

Which is the wiser here, Justice or Iniquity?—is this true?

Elbow.

O thou caitiff! O thou varlet! O thou

wicked Hannibal! I respected with her before I was married to her? If ever I was respected with her, or she with me, let not your worship think me the poor duke's officer.—Prove this, thou wicked Hannibal, or I'll have mine action of battery on thee.

ESCALUS.
If he took you a box o' th' ear, you might have your action of slander too.

ELBOW.
Marry, I thank your good worship for it. What is't your worship's pleasure I should do with this wicked caitiff?

ESCALUS.
Truly, officer, because he hath some offences in him that thou wouldst discover if thou couldst, let him continue in his courses till thou knowest what they are.

ELBOW.
Marry, I thank your worship for it.—Thou seest, thou wicked varlet, now, what's come upon thee; thou art to continue now, thou varlet; thou art to continue.

ESCALUS. [*To* FROTH.]
Where were you born, friend?

FROTH.
Here in Vienna, sir.

ESCALUS.
Are you of fourscore pounds a-year?

FROTH.
Yes, an't please you, sir.

ESCALUS.
So. [*To the* CLOWN.] What trade are you of, sir?

CLOWN.
A tapster; a poor widow's tapster.

ESCALUS.
Your mistress' name?

CLOWN.
Mistress Overdone.

ESCALUS.
Hath she had any more than one husband?

CLOWN.
Nine, sir; Overdone by the last.

ESCALUS.
Nine!—Come hither to me, Master Froth. Master Froth, I would not have you acquainted with tapsters: they will draw you, Master Froth, and you will hang them. Get you gone, and let me hear no more of you.

FROTH.
I thank your worship. For mine own part, I never come into any room in a taphouse but I am drawn in.

ESCALUS.
Well, no more of it, Master Froth: farewell. [*Exit* FROTH.] Come you hither to me, master tapster; what's your name, master tapster?

CLOWN.
Pompey.

ESCALUS.
What else?

CLOWN.
Bum, sir.

ESCALUS.
'Troth, and your bum is the greatest thing about you; so that, in the beastliest sense, you are Pompey the great. Pompey, you are partly a bawd, Pompey, howsoever you colour it in being a tapster. Are you not? come, tell me true; it shall be the better for you.

CLOWN.
Truly, sir, I am a poor fellow that would live.

ESCALUS.
How would you live, Pompey? by being a bawd? What do you think of the trade, Pompey? is it a lawful trade?

CLOWN.
If the law would allow it, sir.

ESCALUS.
But the law will not allow it, Pompey: nor it shall not be allowed in Vienna.

CLOWN.
Does your worship mean to geld and splay all the youth of the city?

ESCALUS.
No, Pompey.

CLOWN.
Truly, sir, in my poor opinion, they will to't then. If your worship will take order for the drabs and the knaves, you need not to fear the bawds.

ESCALUS.
There is pretty orders beginning, I can tell
you. It is but heading and hanging.
CLOWN.
If you head and hang all that offend that
way but for ten year together, you'll be glad
to give out a commission for more heads.
If this law hold in Vienna ten year, I'll rent
the fairest house in it, after threepence a
bay. If you live to see this come to pass, say
Pompey told you so.
ESCALUS.
Thank you, good Pompey; and, in requital
of your prophecy, hark you,—I advise you,
let me not find you before me again upon
any complaint whatsoever, no, not for
dwelling where you do; if I do, Pompey,
I shall beat you to your tent, and prove a
shrewd Caesar to you; in plain dealing,
Pompey, I shall have you whipt: so for this
time, Pompey, fare you well.
CLOWN.
I thank your worship for your good
    counsel—
[*Aside.*] But I shall follow it as the flesh and
fortune shall better determine.
Whip me? No, no; let carman whip his
    jade;—
The valiant heart's not whipt out of his
    trade.
            [*Exit.*]
ESCALUS.
Come hither to me, Master Elbow; come
hither, Master Constable. How long have
you been in this place of constable?
ELBOW.
Seven year and a half, sir.
ESCALUS.
I thought, by the readiness in the office,
you had continued in it some time. You say
seven years together?
ELBOW.
And a half, sir.
ESCALUS.
Alas, it hath been great pains to you!—They
do you wrong to put you so oft upon't. Are
there not men in your ward sufficient to
serve it?

ELBOW.
Faith, sir, few of any wit in such matters: as
they are chosen, they are glad to choose me
for them; I do it for some piece of money,
and go through with all.
ESCALUS.
Look you, bring me in the names of some
six or seven, the most sufficient of your
parish.
ELBOW.
To your worship's house, sir?
ESCALUS.
To my house. Fare you well. [*Exit* ELBOW.]
What's o'clock, think you?
JUSTICE.
Eleven, sir.
ESCALUS.
I pray you home to dinner with me.
JUSTICE.
I humbly thank you.
ESCALUS.
It grieves me for the death of Claudio;
But there's no remedy.
JUSTICE.
Lord Angelo is severe.
ESCALUS.
                  It is but needful:
Mercy is not itself that oft looks so;
Pardon is still the nurse of second woe:
But yet,—Poor Claudio!—There's no
    remedy.
Come, sir.
           [*Exeunt.*]

SCENE II
Another room in the same.
[*Enter* PROVOST *and a* SERVANT.]
SERVANT.
He's hearing of a cause; he will come
    straight.
I'll tell him of you.
PROVOST.
Pray you do. [*Exit* SERVANT.] I'll know
His pleasure; may be he will relent. Alas,
He hath but as offended in a dream!
All sects, all ages, smack of this vice; and he
To die for it!
          [*Enter* ANGELO.]

Angelo.

            Now, what's the matter, provost?

Provost.

Is it your will Claudio shall die to-morrow?

Angelo.

Did not I tell thee yea? hadst thou not
    order?

Why dost thou ask again?

Provost.

            Lest I might be too rash:

Under your good correction, I have seen

When, after execution, judgment hath

Repented o'er his doom.

Angelo.

            Go to; let that be mine:

Do you your office, or give up your place,

And you shall well be spared.

Provost.

I crave your honour's pardon:

What shall be done, sir, with the groaning
    Juliet?

She's very near her hour.

Angelo.

               Dispose of her

To some more fitter place; and that with
    speed.

        [Re-enter Servant.]

Servant.

Here is the sister of the man condemned

Desires access to you.

Angelo.

            Hath he a sister?

Provost.

Ay, my good lord; a very virtuous maid,

And to be shortly of a sisterhood,

If not already.

Angelo.

         Well, let her be admitted.

            [Exit Servant.]

See you the fornicatress be remov'd;

Let her have needful but not lavish means;

There shall be order for it.

     [Enter Lucio *and* Isabella.]

Provost. [*Offering to retire.*]

              Save your honour!

Angelo.

Stay a little while. [*To* Isabella.] You are
    welcome. What's your will?

Isabella.

I am a woeful suitor to your honour,

Please but your honour hear me.

Angelo.

            Well; what's your suit?

Isabella.

There is a vice that most I do abhor,

And most desire should meet the blow of
    justice;

For which I would not plead, but that I
    must;

For which I must not plead, but that I am

At war 'twixt will and will not.

Angelo.

              Well; the matter?

Isabella.

I have a brother is condemn'd to die;

I do beseech you, let it be his fault,

And not my brother.

Provost.

       Heaven give thee moving graces.

Angelo.

Condemn the fault and not the actor of it!

Why, every fault's condemn'd ere it be
    done;

Mine were the very cipher of a function,

To find the faults whose fine stands in
    record,

And let go by the actor.

Isabella.

           O just but severe law!

I had a brother, then.—Heaven keep your
    honour!

            [Retiring.]

Lucio. [*To* Isabella.]

Give't not o'er so: to him again, entreat him;

Kneel down before him, hang upon his
    gown;

You are too cold: if you should need a pin,

You could not with more tame a tongue
    desire it:

To him, I say.

Isabella.

Must he needs die?

Angelo.

           Maiden, no remedy.

Isabella.

Yes; I do think that you might pardon him,

And neither heaven nor man grieve at the
    mercy.

ANGELO.

I will not do't.

ISABELLA.
                But can you, if you would?

ANGELO.

Look, what I will not, that I cannot do.

ISABELLA.

But might you do't, and do the world no
    wrong,
If so your heart were touch'd with that
    remorse
As mine is to him?

ANGELO.
            He's sentenc'd; 'tis too late.

LUCIO. [*To* ISABELLA.]

You are too cold.

ISABELLA.

Too late? Why, no; I, that do speak a word,
May call it back again. Well, believe this,
No ceremony that to great ones 'longs,
Not the king's crown nor the deputed
    sword,
The marshal's truncheon nor the judge's
    robe,
Become them with one half so good a
    grace
As mercy does.
If he had been as you, and you as he,
You would have slipp'd like him; but he,
    like you,
Would not have been so stern.

ANGELO.
               Pray you, be gone.

ISABELLA.

I would to heaven I had your potency,
And you were Isabel! should it then be
    thus?
No; I would tell what 'twere to be a judge
And what a prisoner.

LUCIO. [*Aside.*]

Ay, touch him; there's the vein.

ANGELO.

Your brother is a forfeit of the law,
And you but waste your words.

ISABELLA.
                Alas! alas!

Why, all the souls that were were forfeit
    once;
And He that might the vantage best have
    took
Found out the remedy. How would you be
If He, which is the top of judgment,
    should
But judge you as you are? O, think on that;
And mercy then will breathe within your
    lips,
Like man new made.

ANGELO.
            Be you content, fair maid:
It is the law, not I, condemns your brother:
Were he my kinsman, brother, or my son,
It should be thus with him; he must die
    to-morrow.

ISABELLA.

To-morrow! O, that's sudden! Spare him,
    spare him!
He's not prepared for death. Even for our
    kitchens
We kill the fowl of season: shall we serve
    heaven
With less respect than we do minister
To our gross selves? Good, good my lord,
    bethink you:
Who is it that hath died for this offence?
There's many have committed it.

LUCIO.
                  Ay, well said.

ANGELO.

The law hath not been dead, though it
    hath slept:
Those many had not dared to do that evil
If the first that did the edict infringe
Had answer'd for his deed: now 'tis awake;
Takes note of what is done; and, like a
    prophet,
Looks in a glass that shows what future
    evils,—
Either now, or by remissness new conceiv'd,
And so in progress to be hatch'd and
    born,—
Are now to have no successive degrees,
But, where they live, to end.

ISABELLA.
              Yet show some pity.

Angelo.
I show it most of all when I show justice;
For then I pity those I do not know,
Which a dismiss'd offence would after gall,
And do him right that, answering one foul wrong,
Lives not to act another. Be satisfied;
Your brother dies to-morrow; be content.
Isabella.
So you must be the first that gives this sentence;
And he that suffers. O, it is excellent
To have a giant's strength; but it is tyrannous
To use it like a giant.
Lucio.
                        That's well said.
Isabella.
Could great men thunder
As Jove himself does, Jove would ne'er be quiet,
For every pelting petty officer
Would use his heaven for thunder: nothing but thunder.—
Merciful Heaven!
Thou rather, with thy sharp and sulphurous bolt,
Splits the unwedgeable and gnarled oak
Than the soft myrtle; but man, proud man!
Dress'd in a little brief authority,—
Most ignorant of what he's most assured,
His glassy essence,—like an angry ape,
Plays such fantastic tricks before high heaven
As makes the angels weep; who, with our spleens,
Would all themselves laugh mortal.
Lucio.
O, to him, to him, wench: he will relent;
He's coming; I perceive 't.
Provost.
                        Pray heaven she win him!
Isabella.
We cannot weigh our brother with ourself:
Great men may jest with saints: 'tis wit in them;
But, in the less, foul profanation.

Lucio.
Thou'rt i' the right, girl; more o' that.
Isabella.
That in the captain's but a choleric word
Which in the soldier is flat blasphemy.
Lucio.
Art advised o' that? more on't.
Angelo.
Why do you put these sayings upon me?
Isabella.
Because authority, though it err like others,
Hath yet a kind of medicine in itself
That skins the vice o' the top. Go to your bosom;
Knock there; and ask your heart what it doth know
That's like my brother's fault: if it confess
A natural guiltiness such as is his,
Let it not sound a thought upon your tongue
Against my brother's life.
Angelo.
                        She speaks, and 'tis
Such sense that my sense breeds with it.—
Fare you well.
Isabella.
Gentle my lord, turn back.
Angelo.
I will bethink me:—Come again to-morrow.
Isabella.
Hark how I'll bribe you. Good my lord, turn back.
Angelo.
How! bribe me?
Isabella.
Ay, with such gifts that heaven shall share with you.
Lucio.
You had marr'd all else.
Isabella.
Not with fond shekels of the tested gold,
Or stones, whose rates are either rich or poor
As fancy values them: but with true prayers,
That shall be up at heaven, and enter there,

Ere sunrise: prayers from preserved souls,
From fasting maids, whose minds are
    dedicate
To nothing temporal.
Angelo.
          Well; come to me to-morrow.
Lucio. [*Aside to* Isabella.]
Go to; 'tis well; away.
Isabella.
Heaven keep your honour safe!
Angelo. [*Aside.*]
                Amen: for I
Am that way going to temptation,
Where prayers cross.
Isabella.
          At what hour to-morrow
Shall I attend your lordship?
Angelo.
           At any time 'fore noon.
Isabella.
Save your honour!
[*Exeunt* Lucio, Isabella, *and* Provost.]
Angelo.
       From thee; even from thy virtue!—
What's this, what's this? Is this her fault
    or mine?
The tempter or the tempted, who sins
    most? Ha!
Not she; nor doth she tempt; but it is I
That, lying by the violet, in the sun
Do, as the carrion does, not as the flower,
Corrupt with virtuous season. Can it be
That modesty may more betray our sense
Than woman's lightness? Having waste
    ground enough,
Shall we desire to raze the sanctuary,
And pitch our evils there? O, fie, fie, fie!
What dost thou? or what art thou,
    Angelo?
Dost thou desire her foully for those things
That make her good? O, let her brother
    live;
Thieves for their robbery have authority
When judges steal themselves. What! do
    I love her,
That I desire to hear her speak again
And feast upon her eyes? What is't I
    dream on?

O cunning enemy, that, to catch a saint,
With saints dost bait thy hook! Most
    dangerous
Is that temptation that doth goad us on
To sin in loving virtue: never could the
    strumpet,
With all her double vigour, art, and nature,
Once stir my temper; but this virtuous
    maid
Subdues me quite.—Ever till now,
When men were fond, I smil'd and
    wonder'd how.
             [*Exit.*]

SCENE III

A room in a prison.
[*Enter* Duke, *habited like a friar, and*
             Provost.]

Duke.
Hail to you, provost! so I think you are.
Provost.
I am the provost. What's your will, good
    friar?
Duke.
Bound by my charity and my bless'd order,
I come to visit the afflicted spirits
Here in the prison: do me the common
    right
To let me see them, and to make me know
The nature of their crimes, that I may
    minister
To them accordingly.
Provost.
I would do more than that, if more were
    needful.
           [*Enter* Juliet.]
Look, here comes one; a gentlewoman of
    mine,
Who, falling in the flaws of her own
    youth,
Hath blister'd her report. She is with child;
And he that got it, sentenc'd: a young man
More fit to do another such offence
Than die for this.
Duke.
When must he die?
Provost.
          As I do think, to-morrow.

[*To* Juliet.] I have provided for you; stay
    awhile
And you shall be conducted.

Duke.
Repent you, fair one, of the sin you carry?

Juliet.
I do; and bear the shame most patiently.

Duke.
I'll teach you how you shall arraign your
    conscience,
And try your penitence, if it be sound
Or hollowly put on.

Juliet.
              I'll gladly learn.

Duke.
Love you the man that wrong'd you?

Juliet.
Yes, as I love the woman that wrong'd him.

Duke.
So then, it seems, your most offenceful act
Was mutually committed.

Juliet.
              Mutually.

Duke.
Then was your sin of heavier kind than his.

Juliet.
I do confess it, and repent it, father.

Duke.
'Tis meet so, daughter: but lest you do
    repent
As that the sin hath brought you to this
    shame,—
Which sorrow is always toward ourselves,
    not heaven,
Showing we would not spare heaven as
    we love it,
But as we stand in fear,—

Juliet.
I do repent me as it is an evil,
And take the shame with joy.

Duke.
              There rest.
Your partner, as I hear, must die to-
    morrow,
And I am going with instruction to
    him.—
Grace go with you! *Benedicite!*
           [*Exit.*]

Juliet.
Must die to-morrow! O, injurious law,
That respites me a life whose very comfort
Is still a dying horror!

Provost.
            'Tis pity of him.
           [*Exeunt.*]

SCENE IV
A room in Angelo's house.
    [*Enter* Angelo.]

Angelo.
When I would pray and think, I think
    and pray
To several subjects. Heaven hath my
    empty words;
Whilst my invention, hearing not my
    tongue,
Anchors on Isabel: Heaven in my mouth,
As if I did but only chew his name;
And in my heart the strong and swelling
    evil
Of my conception. The state whereon I
    studied
Is, like a good thing, being often read,
Grown sear'd and tedious; yea, my gravity,
Wherein—let no man hear me—I take
    pride,
Could I with boot change for an idle
    plume,
Which the air beats for vain. O place! O
    form!
How often dost thou with thy case, thy
    habit,
Wrench awe from fools, and tie the wiser
    souls
To thy false seeming! Blood, thou art
    blood:
Let's write good angel on the devil's horn,
'Tis not the devil's crest.
           [*Enter* Servant.]
How now, who's there?

Servant.
            One Isabel, a sister,
Desires access to you.

Angelo.
            Teach her the way.
           [*Exit* Servant.]

O heavens!
Why does my blood thus muster to my
    heart,
Making both it unable for itself
And dispossessing all the other parts
Of necessary fitness?
So play the foolish throngs with one that
    swoons;
Come all to help him, and so stop the air
By which he should revive: and even so
The general, subject to a well-wished king
Quit their own part, and in obsequious
    fondness
Crowd to his presence, where their
    untaught love
Must needs appear offence.
                    [*Enter* ISABELLA.]
How now, fair maid?

ISABELLA.
            I am come to know your pleasure.

ANGELO.
That you might know it, would much
    better please me
Than to demand what 'tis. Your brother
    cannot live.

ISABELLA.
Even so?—Heaven keep your honour!
                    [*Retiring.*]

ANGELO.
Yet may he live awhile: and, it may be,
As long as you or I: yet he must die.

ISABELLA.
Under your sentence?

ANGELO.
Yea.

ISABELLA.
When? I beseech you? that in his reprieve,
Longer or shorter, he may be so fitted
That his soul sicken not.

ANGELO.
Ha! Fie, these filthy vices! It were as good
To pardon him that hath from nature
    stolen
A man already made, as to remit
Their saucy sweetness that do coin
    heaven's image
In stamps that are forbid; 'tis all as easy
Falsely to take away a life true made

As to put metal in restrained means
To make a false one.

ISABELLA.
'Tis set down so in heaven, but not in earth.

ANGELO.
Say you so? then I shall pose you quickly.
Which had you rather,—that the most
        just law
Now took your brother's life; or, to redeem
        him,
Give up your body to such sweet
        uncleanness
As she that he hath stain'd?

ISABELLA.
                        Sir, believe this,
I had rather give my body than my soul.

ANGELO.
I talk not of your soul; our compell'd sins
Stand more for number than accompt.

ISABELLA.
                        How say you?

ANGELO.
Nay, I'll not warrant that; for I can speak
Against the thing I say. Answer to this;—
I, now the voice of the recorded law,
Pronounce a sentence on your brother's
        life:
Might there not be a charity in sin,
To save this brother's life?

ISABELLA.
                        Please you to do't,
I'll take it as a peril to my soul
It is no sin at all, but charity.

ANGELO.
Pleas'd you to do't at peril of your soul,
Were equal poise of sin and charity.

ISABELLA.
That I do beg his life, if it be sin,
Heaven let me bear it! You granting of
        my suit,
If that be sin, I'll make it my morn prayer
To have it added to the faults of mine,
And nothing of your answer.

ANGELO.
                        Nay, but hear me:
Your sense pursues not mine: either you
        are ignorant
Or seem so, craftily; and that's not good.

Isabella.
Let me be ignorant, and in nothing good
But graciously to know I am no better.
Angelo.
Thus wisdom wishes to appear most bright
When it doth tax itself: as these black
    masks
Proclaim an enshielded beauty ten times
    louder
Than beauty could, displayed.—But mark
    me;
To be received plain, I'll speak more
    gross:
Your brother is to die.
Isabella.
So.
Angelo.
And his offence is so, as it appears,
Accountant to the law upon that pain.
Isabella.
True.
Angelo.
Admit no other way to save his life,—
As I subscribe not that, nor any other,
But, in the loss of question,—that you,
    his sister,
Finding yourself desir'd of such a person,
Whose credit with the judge, or own great
    place,
Could fetch your brother from the
    manacles
Of the all-binding law; and that there
    were
No earthly mean to save him but that
    either
You must lay down the treasures of your
    body
To this suppos'd, or else to let him suffer;
What would you do?
Isabella.
As much for my poor brother as myself:
That is, were I under the terms of death,
The impression of keen whips I'd wear as
    rubies,
And strip myself to death, as to a bed
That longing have been sick for, ere I'd
    yield
My body up to shame.

Angelo.
                    Then must
Your brother die.
Isabella.
                    And 'twere the cheaper way:
Better it were a brother died at once
Than that a sister, by redeeming him,
Should die for ever.
Angelo.
Were not you, then, as cruel as the sentence
That you have slandered so?
Isabella.
Ignominy in ransom and free pardon
Are of two houses; lawful mercy
Is nothing kin to foul redemption.
Angelo.
You seem'd of late to make the law a
    tyrant;
And rather prov'd the sliding of your
    brother
A merriment than a vice.
Isabella.
O, pardon me, my lord! It oft falls out,
To have what we would have, we speak not
    what we mean:
I something do excuse the thing I hate
For his advantage that I dearly love.
Angelo.
We are all frail.
Isabella.
                    Else let my brother die,
If not a feodary, but only he,
Owe, and succeed by weakness.
Angelo.
                    Nay, women are frail too.
Isabella.
Ay, as the glasses where they view
    themselves;
Which are as easy broke as they make
    forms.
Women! Help heaven! men their creation
    mar
In profiting by them. Nay, call us ten times
    frail;
For we are soft as our complexions are,
And credulous to false prints.
Angelo.
                    I think it well:

And from this testimony of your own
   sex,—
Since, I suppose, we are made to be no
   stronger
Than faults may shake our frames,—let me
   be bold;—
I do arrest your words. Be that you are,
That is, a woman; if you be more, you're
   none;
If you be one,—as you are well express'd
By all external warrants,—show it now
By putting on the destin'd livery.

ISABELLA.
I have no tongue but one: gentle, my
   lord,
Let me intreat you, speak the former
   language.

ANGELO.
Plainly conceive, I love you.

ISABELLA.
My brother did love Juliet; and you tell me
That he shall die for it.

ANGELO.
He shall not, Isabel, if you give me love.

ISABELLA.
I know your virtue hath a license in't,
Which seems a little fouler than it is,
To pluck on others.

ANGELO.
          Believe me, on mine honour,
My words express my purpose.

ISABELLA.
Ha! little honour to be much believed,
And most pernicious purpose!—Seeming,
   seeming!—
I will proclaim thee, Angelo; look for't:
Sign me a present pardon for my brother
Or, with an outstretch'd throat, I'll tell the
   world
Aloud what man thou art.

ANGELO.
          Who will believe thee, Isabel?
My unsoil'd name, th' austereness of my
   life,
My vouch against you, and my place i' the
   state,
Will so your accusation overweigh
That you shall stifle in your own report,

And smell of calumny. I have begun,
And now I give my sensual race the
   rein:
Fit thy consent to my sharp appetite;
Lay by all nicety and prolixious blushes
That banish what they sue for: redeem
   thy brother
By yielding up thy body to my will;
Or else he must not only die the death,
But thy unkindness shall his death draw
   out
To lingering sufferance: answer me to-
   morrow,
Or, by the affection that now guides me
   most,
I'll prove a tyrant to him. As for you,
Say what you can, my false o'erweighs
   your true.
                 [Exit.]

ISABELLA.
To whom should I complain? Did tell
   this,
Who would believe me? O perilous
   mouths
That bear in them one and the self-same
   tongue
Either of condemnation or approof!
Bidding the law make court'sy to their
   will;
Hooking both right and wrong to the
   appetite,
To follow as it draws! I'll to my brother:
Though he hath fallen by prompture of
   the blood,
Yet hath he in him such a mind of
   honour
That, had he twenty heads to tender
   down
On twenty bloody blocks, he'd yield
   them up
Before his sister should her body stoop
To such abhorr'd pollution.
Then, Isabel, live chaste, and, brother, die:
More than our brother is our chastity.
I'll tell him yet of Angelo's request,
And fit his mind to death, for his soul's
   rest.
                 [Exit.]

ACT III
SCENE I

A room in the prison.

[*Enter* DUKE, CLAUDIO, *and* PROVOST.]

DUKE.

So, then you hope of pardon from Lord
   Angelo?

CLAUDIO.

The miserable have no other medicine
But only hope:
I have hope to live, and am prepar'd to die.

DUKE.

Be absolute for death; either death or life
Shall thereby be the sweeter. Reason thus
   with life,—
If I do lose thee, I do lose a thing
That none but fools would keep: a breath
   thou art,
Servile to all the skiey influences,
That dost this habitation, where thou
   keep'st
Hourly afflict; merely, thou art death's
   fool;
For him thou labour'st by thy flight to
   shun,
And yet runn'st toward him still. Thou art
   not noble;
For all the accommodations that thou
   bear'st
Are nurs'd by baseness. Thou art by no
   means valiant;
For thou dost fear the soft and tender fork
Of a poor worm. Thy best of rest is sleep,
And that thou oft provok'st; yet grossly
   fear'st
Thy death, which is no more. Thou art not
   thyself:
For thou exist'st on many a thousand
   grains
That issue out of dust. Happy thou art not;
For what thou hast not, still thou striv'st
   to get;
And what thou hast, forgett'st. Thou art
   not certain;
For thy complexion shifts to strange
   effects,
After the moon. If thou art rich, thou art
   poor;
For, like an ass whose back with ingots
   bows,
Thou bear'st thy heavy riches but a journey,
And death unloads thee. Friend hast thou
   none;
For thine own bowels, which do call thee
   sire,
The mere effusion of thy proper loins,
Do curse the gout, serpigo, and the rheum,
For ending thee no sooner. Thou hast nor
   youth nor age,
But, as it were, an after-dinner's sleep,
Dreaming on both: for all thy blessed
   youth
Becomes as aged, and doth beg the alms
Of palsied eld; and when thou art old and
   rich
Thou hast neither heat, affection, limb, nor
   beauty,
To make thy riches pleasant. What's yet
   in this
That bears the name of life? Yet in this life
Lie hid more thousand deaths: yet death
   we fear,
That makes these odds all even.

CLAUDIO.

                            I humbly thank you.
To sue to live, I find I seek to die;
And, seeking death, find life. Let it come
   on.

ISABELLA. [*Within.*]

What, ho! Peace here; grace and good
   company!

PROVOST.

Who's there? come in: the wish deserves
   a welcome.

DUKE.

Dear sir, ere long I'll visit you again.

CLAUDIO.

Most holy sir, I thank you.

                    [*Enter* ISABELLA.]

ISABELLA.

My business is a word or two with Claudio.

PROVOST.

And very welcome. Look, signior, here's
   your sister.

DUKE.

Provost, a word with you.

PROVOST.

As many as you please.

DUKE.

Bring me to hear them speak, where I may
be conceal'd.

[*Exeunt* DUKE *and* PROVOST.]

CLAUDIO.

Now, sister, what's the comfort?

ISABELLA.

Why,
As all comforts are; most good, most good,
in deed:
Lord Angelo, having affairs to heaven,
Intends you for his swift ambassador,
Where you shall be an everlasting leiger:
Therefore, your best appointment make
with speed;
To-morrow you set on.

CLAUDIO.

Is there no remedy?

ISABELLA.

None, but such remedy as, to save a head,
To cleave a heart in twain.

CLAUDIO.

But is there any?

ISABELLA.

Yes, brother, you may live:
There is a devilish mercy in the judge,
If you'll implore it, that will free your life,
But fetter you till death.

CLAUDIO.

Perpetual durance?

ISABELLA.

Ay, just; perpetual durance; a restraint,
Though all the world's vastidity you had,
To a determin'd scope.

CLAUDIO.

But in what nature?

ISABELLA.

In such a one as, you consenting to't,
Would bark your honour from that trunk
you bear,
And leave you naked.

CLAUDIO.

Let me know the point.

ISABELLA.

O, I do fear thee, Claudio; and I quake,
Lest thou a feverous life shouldst entertain,

And six or seven winters more respect
Than a perpetual honour. Dar'st thou die?
The sense of death is most in
apprehension;
And the poor beetle that we tread upon
In corporal sufferance finds a pang as great
As when a giant dies.

CLAUDIO.

Why give you me this shame?
Think you I can a resolution fetch
From flowery tenderness? If I must die,
I will encounter darkness as a bride
And hug it in mine arms.

ISABELLA.

There spake my brother; there my father's
grave
Did utter forth a voice! Yes, thou must die:
Thou art too noble to conserve a life
In base appliances. This outward-sainted
deputy,—
Whose settled visage and deliberate word
Nips youth i' the head, and follies doth
emmew
As falcon doth the fowl,—is yet a devil;
His filth within being cast, he would
appear
A pond as deep as hell.

CLAUDIO.

The priestly Angelo?

ISABELLA.

O, 'tis the cunning livery of hell
The damned'st body to invest and cover
In precise guards! Dost thou think,
Claudio,
If I would yield him my virginity
Thou mightst be freed?

CLAUDIO.

O heavens! it cannot be.

ISABELLA.

Yes, he would give it thee, from this rank
offence,
So to offend him still. This night's the time
That I should do what I abhor to name,
Or else thou diest to-morrow.

CLAUDIO.

Thou shalt not do't.

ISABELLA.

O, were it but my life,

I'd throw it down for your deliverance
As frankly as a pin.
CLAUDIO.
                    Thanks, dear Isabel.
ISABELLA.
Be ready, Claudio, for your death to-
    morrow.
CLAUDIO.
Yes.—Has he affections in him
That thus can make him bite the law by
    the nose
When he would force it? Sure it is no sin;
Or of the deadly seven it is the least.
ISABELLA.
Which is the least?
CLAUDIO.
If it were damnable, he, being so wise,
Why would he for the momentary trick
Be perdurably fined?—O Isabel!
ISABELLA.
What says my brother?
CLAUDIO.
                    Death is a fearful thing.
ISABELLA.
And shamed life a hateful.
CLAUDIO.
Ay, but to die, and go we know not where;
To lie in cold obstruction, and to rot;
This sensible warm motion to become
A kneaded clod; and the delighted spirit
To bathe in fiery floods or to reside
In thrilling regions of thick-ribbed ice;
To be imprison'd in the viewless winds,
And blown with restless violence round
    about
The pendent world; or to be worse than
    worst
Of those that lawless and incertain
    thought
Imagine howling!—'tis too horrible!
The weariest and most loathed worldly life
That age, ache, penury, and imprisonment
Can lay on nature is a paradise
To what we fear of death.
ISABELLA.
Alas, alas!
CLAUDIO.
                    Sweet sister, let me live:

What sin you do to save a brother's life
Nature dispenses with the deed so far
That it becomes a virtue.
ISABELLA.
                    O you beast!
O faithless coward! O dishonest wretch!
Wilt thou be made a man out of my vice?
Is't not a kind of incest to take life
From thine own sister's shame? What
    should I think?
Heaven shield my mother play'd my father
    fair!
For such a warped slip of wilderness
Ne'er issued from his blood. Take my
    defiance:
Die; perish! might but my bending down
Reprieve thee from thy fate, it should
    proceed:
I'll pray a thousand prayers for thy
    death,—
No word to save thee.
CLAUDIO.
Nay, hear me, Isabel.
ISABELLA.
                    O fie, fie, fie!
Thy sin's not accidental, but a trade:
Mercy to thee would prove itself a bawd:
'Tis best that thou diest quickly.
                    [Going.]
CLAUDIO.
                    O, hear me, Isabella.
                    [Re-enter DUKE.]
DUKE.
Vouchsafe a word, young sister, but one
    word.
ISABELLA.
What is your will?
DUKE.
Might you dispense with your leisure, I
would by and by have some speech with
you: the satisfaction I would require is
likewise your own benefit.
ISABELLA.
I have no superfluous leisure; my stay must
be stolen out of other affairs; but I will
attend you awhile.
DUKE. [Aside to CLAUDIO.]
Son, I have overheard what hath passed

between you and your sister. Angelo had never the purpose to corrupt her; only he hath made an assay of her virtue to practise his judgment with the disposition of natures; she, having the truth of honour in her, hath made him that gracious denial which he is most glad to receive: I am confessor to Angelo, and I know this to be true; therefore prepare yourself to death. Do not satisfy your resolution with hopes that are fallible: to-morrow you must die; go to your knees and make ready.

CLAUDIO.

Let me ask my sister pardon. I am so out of love with life that I will sue to be rid of it.

DUKE.

Hold you there. Farewell.

[*Exit* CLAUDIO.]
[*Re-enter* PROVOST.]

Provost, a word with you.

PROVOST.

What's your will, father?

DUKE.

That, now you are come, you will be gone. Leave me a while with the maid; my mind promises with my habit no loss shall touch her by my company.

PROVOST.

In good time.

[*Exit* PROVOST.]

DUKE.

The hand that hath made you fair hath made you good; the goodness that is cheap in beauty makes beauty brief in goodness; but grace, being the soul of your complexion, shall keep the body of it ever fair. The assault that Angelo hath made to you, fortune hath conveyed to my understanding; and, but that frailty hath examples for his falling, I should wonder at Angelo. How will you do to content this substitute, and to save your brother?

ISABELLA.

I am now going to resolve him; I had rather my brother die by the law than my son should be unlawfully born. But, O, how much is the good duke deceived in Angelo! If ever he return, and I can speak to him,

I will open my lips in vain, or discover his government.

DUKE.

That shall not be much amiss: yet, as the matter now stands, he will avoid your accusation; he made trial of you only.— Therefore fasten your ear on my advisings; to the love I have in doing good a remedy presents itself. I do make myself believe that you may most uprighteously do a poor wronged lady a merited benefit; redeem your brother from the angry law; do no stain to your own gracious person; and much please the absent duke, if peradventure he shall ever return to have hearing of this business.

ISABELLA.

Let me hear you speak further; I have spirit to do anything that appears not foul in the truth of my spirit.

DUKE.

Virtue is bold, and goodness never fearful. Have you not heard speak of Mariana, the sister of Frederick, the great soldier who miscarried at sea?

ISABELLA.

I have heard of the lady, and good words went with her name.

DUKE.

She should this Angelo have married; was affianced to her by oath, and the nuptial appointed: between which time of the contract and limit of the solemnity her brother Frederick was wrecked at sea, having in that perished vessel the dowry of his sister. But mark how heavily this befell to the poor gentlewoman: there she lost a noble and renowned brother, in his love toward her ever most kind and natural; with him the portion and sinew of her fortune, her marriage-dowry; with both, her combinate husband, this well-seeming Angelo.

ISABELLA.

Can this be so? Did Angelo so leave her?

DUKE.

Left her in her tears, and dried not one of them with his comfort; swallowed his vows whole, pretending, in her, discoveries of dishonour; in few, bestow'd her on her own lamentation, which she yet wears for his sake; and he, a marble to her tears, is washed with them, but relents not.

ISABELLA.

What a merit were it in death to take this poor maid from the world! What corruption in this life that it will let this man live!—But how out of this can she avail?

DUKE.

It is a rupture that you may easily heal; and the cure of it not only saves your brother, but keeps you from dishonour in doing it.

ISABELLA.

Show me how, good father.

DUKE.

This forenamed maid hath yet in her the continuance of her first affection; his unjust unkindness, that in all reason should have quenched her love, hath, like an impediment in the current, made it more violent and unruly. Go you to Angelo; answer his requiring with a plausible obedience; agree with his demands to the point: only refer yourself to this advantage,—first, that your stay with him may not be long; that the time may have all shadow and silence in it; and the place answer to convenience: this being granted in course, and now follows all. We shall advise this wronged maid to stead up your appointment, go in your place; if the encounter acknowledge itself hereafter, it may compel him to her recompense: and here, by this, is your brother saved, your honour untainted, the poor Mariana advantaged, and the corrupt deputy scaled. The maid will I frame and make fit for his attempt. If you think well to carry this as you may, the doubleness of the benefit defends the deceit from reproof. What think you of it?

ISABELLA.

The image of it gives me content already; and I trust it will grow to a most prosperous perfection.

DUKE.

It lies much in your holding up. Haste you speedily to Angelo; if for this night he entreat you to his bed, give him promise of satisfaction. I will presently to Saint Luke's; there, at the moated grange, resides this dejected Mariana. At that place call upon me; and despatch with Angelo, that it may be quickly.

ISABELLA.

I thank you for this comfort. Fare you well, good father.

[Exeunt severally.]

SCENE II

The street before the prison.
[*Enter* DUKE, *as a friar; to him,* ELBOW, CLOWN, *and* OFFICERS.]

ELBOW.

Nay, if there be no remedy for it, but that you will needs buy and sell men and women like beasts, we shall have all the world drink brown and white bastard.

DUKE.

O heavens! what stuff is here?

CLOWN.

'Twas never merry world since, of two usuries, the merriest was put down, and the worser allowed by order of law a furred gown to keep him warm; and furred with fox on lamb-skins too, to signify that craft, being richer than innocency, stands for the facing.

ELBOW.

Come your way, sir.—Bless you, good father friar.

DUKE.

And you, good brother father. What offence hath this man made you, sir?

ELBOW.

Marry, sir, he hath offended the law; and, sir, we take him to be a thief too, sir; for we have found upon him, sir, a strange picklock, which we have sent to the deputy.

DUKE.

Fie, sirrah, a bawd, a wicked bawd;
The evil that thou causest to be done,
That is thy means to live. Do thou but think

What 'tis to cram a maw or clothe a back
From such a filthy vice: say to thyself—
From their abominable and beastly touches
I drink, I eat, array myself, and live.
Canst thou believe thy living is a life,
So stinkingly depending? Go mend, go
    mend.

CLOWN.
Indeed, it does stink in some sort, sir; but
yet, sir, I would prove—

DUKE.
Nay, if the devil have given thee proofs
    for sin,
Thou wilt prove his. Take him to prison,
    officer;
Correction and instruction must both
    work
Ere this rude beast will profit.

ELBOW.
He must before the deputy, sir; he has given
him warning: The deputy cannot abide a
whoremaster: if he be a whoremaster, and
comes before him, he were as good go a
mile on his errand.

DUKE.
That we were all, as some would seem to be,
free from our faults, as faults from seeming
free!

ELBOW.
His neck will come to your waist, a cord, sir.

CLOWN.
I spy comfort; I cry bail! Here's a gentleman,
and a friend of mine.

        [Enter LUCIO.*]*

LUCIO.
How now, noble Pompey? What, at the
wheels of Caesar! Art thou led in triumph?
What, is there none of Pygmalion's images,
newly made woman, to be had now,
for putting the hand in the pocket and
extracting it clutched? What reply, ha?
What say'st thou to this tune, matter, and
method? Is't not drowned i' the last rain,
ha? What say'st thou to't? Is the world as it
was, man? Which is the way? Is it sad, and
few words? or how? The trick of it?

DUKE.
Still thus, and thus! still worse!

LUCIO.
How doth my dear morsel, thy mistress?
Procures she still, ha?

CLOWN.
Troth, sir, she hath eaten up all her beef,
and she is herself in the tub.

LUCIO.
Why, 'tis good: it is the right of it: it
must be so: ever your fresh whore and
your powdered bawd—an unshunned
consequence; it must be so. Art going to
prison, Pompey?

CLOWN.
Yes, faith, sir.

LUCIO.
Why, 'tis not amiss, Pompey. Farewell; go,
say I sent thee thither. For debt, Pompey?
or how?

ELBOW.
For being a bawd, for being a bawd.

LUCIO.
Well, then, imprison him: if imprisonment
be the due of a bawd, why, 'tis his right:
bawd is he doubtless, and of antiquity,
too: bawd-born. Farewell, good Pompey.
Commend me to the prison, Pompey. You
will turn good husband now, Pompey; you
will keep the house.

CLOWN.
I hope, sir, your good worship will be my
bail.

LUCIO.
No, indeed, will I not, Pompey; it is not
the wear. I will pray, Pompey, to increase
your bondage: if you take it not patiently,
why, your mettle is the more. Adieu, trusty
Pompey.—Bless you, friar.

DUKE.
And you.

LUCIO.
Does Bridget paint still, Pompey, ha?

ELBOW.
Come your ways, sir; come.

CLOWN.
You will not bail me then, sir?

LUCIO.
Then, Pompey, nor now.—What news
abroad, friar? what news?

ELBOW.
Come your ways, sir; come.
LUCIO.
Go,—to kennel, Pompey, go:
　　　　[*Exeunt* ELBOW, CLOWN, *and*
　　　　　　OFFICERS.]
What news, friar, of the duke?
DUKE.
I know none. Can you tell me of any?
LUCIO.
Some say he is with the Emperor of Russia;
other some, he is in Rome: but where is he,
think you?
DUKE.
I know not where; but wheresoever, I wish
him well.
LUCIO.
It was a mad fantastical trick of him to
steal from the state and usurp the beggary
he was never born to. Lord Angelo dukes
it well in his absence; he puts transgression
to't.
DUKE.
He does well in't.
LUCIO.
A little more lenity to lechery would do no
harm in him: something too crabbed that
way, friar.
DUKE.
It is too general a vice, and severity must
cure it.
LUCIO.
Yes, in good sooth, the vice is of a great
kindred; it is well allied: but it is impossible
to extirp it quite, friar, till eating and
drinking be put down. They say this Angelo
was not made by man and woman after this
downright way of creation: is it true, think
you?
DUKE.
How should he be made, then?
LUCIO.
Some report a sea-maid spawned him;
some, that he was begot between two
stock-fishes.—But it is certain that when
he makes water, his urine is congealed ice;
that I know to be true. And he is a motion
ungenerative; that's infallible.

DUKE.
You are pleasant, sir, and speak apace.
LUCIO.
Why, what a ruthless thing is this in him,
for the rebellion of a codpiece to take away
the life of a man! Would the duke that is
absent have done this? Ere he would have
hanged a man for the getting a hundred
bastards, he would have paid for the
nursing a thousand. He had some feeling
of the sport; he knew the service, and that
instructed him to mercy.
DUKE.
I never heard the absent duke much
detected for women; he was not inclined
that way.
LUCIO.
O, sir, you are deceived.
DUKE.
'Tis not possible.
LUCIO.
Who, not the duke? yes, your beggar of
fifty;—and his use was to put a ducat in
her clack-dish: the duke had crotchets in
him. He would be drunk too: that let me
inform you.
DUKE.
You do him wrong, surely.
LUCIO.
Sir, I was an inward of his. A shy fellow was
the duke: and I believe I know the cause of
his withdrawing.
DUKE.
What, I pr'ythee, might be the cause?
LUCIO.
No,—pardon;—'tis a secret must be locked
within the teeth and the lips: but this I can
let you understand,—the greater file of the
subject held the duke to be wise.
DUKE.
Wise? why, no question but he was.
LUCIO.
A very superficial, ignorant, unweighing
fellow.
DUKE.
Either this is envy in you, folly, or mistaking;
the very stream of his life, and the business
he hath helmed, must, upon a warranted

need, give him a better proclamation. Let him be but testimonied in his own bringings forth, and he shall appear to the envious a scholar, a statesman, and a soldier. Therefore you speak unskilfully; or, if your knowledge be more, it is much darkened in your malice.

LUCIO.
Sir, I know him, and I love him.

DUKE.
Love talks with better knowledge, and knowledge with dearer love.

LUCIO.
Come, sir, I know what I know.

DUKE.
I can hardly believe that, since you know not what you speak. But, if ever the duke return,—as our prayers are he may,—let me desire you to make your answer before him. If it be honest you have spoke, you have courage to maintain it: I am bound to call upon you; and, I pray you, your name?

LUCIO.
Sir, my name is Lucio; well known to the duke.

DUKE.
He shall know you better, sir, if I may live to report you.

LUCIO.
I fear you not.

DUKE.
O, you hope the duke will return no more; or you imagine me too unhurtful an opposite. But, indeed, I can do you little harm: you'll forswear this again.

LUCIO.
I'll be hanged first! thou art deceived in me, friar. But no more of this. Canst thou tell if Claudio die to-morrow or no?

DUKE.
Why should he die, sir?

LUCIO.
Why? for filling a bottle with a tun-dish. I would the duke we talk of were returned again: this ungenitured agent will unpeople the province with continency; sparrows must not build in his house-eaves because they are lecherous. The duke yet would

have dark deeds darkly answered; he would never bring them to light: would he were returned! Marry, this Claudio is condemned for untrussing. Farewell, good friar; I pr'ythee pray for me. The duke, I say to thee again, would eat mutton on Fridays. He's not past it; yet, and, I say to thee, he would mouth with a beggar though she smelt brown bread and garlic. Say that I said so.—Farewell.
                              [*Exit.*]

DUKE.
No might nor greatness in mortality
Can censure 'scape; back-wounding calumny
The whitest virtue strikes. What king so strong
Can tie the gall up in the slanderous tongue?
But who comes here?
    [*Enter* ESCALUS, PROVOST, MISTRESS
        OVERDONE, *and* OFFICERS.]

ESCALUS.
Go, away with her to prison.

MISTRESS OVERDONE.
Good my lord, be good to me; your honour is accounted a merciful man; good my lord.

ESCALUS.
Double and treble admonition, and still forfeit in the same kind? This would make mercy swear and play the tyrant.

PROVOST.
A bawd of eleven years' continuance, may it please your honour.

MISTRESS OVERDONE.
My lord, this is one Lucio's information against me: Mistress Kate Keepdown was with child by him in the duke's time; he promised her marriage: his child is a year and a quarter old come Philip and Jacob; I have kept it myself; and see how he goes about to abuse me.

ESCALUS.
That fellow is a fellow of much license:—let him be called before us.—Away with her to prison. Go to; no more words. [*Exeunt* MISTRESS OVERDONE *and* OFFICERS.] Provost, my brother Angelo will not be

altered, Claudio must die to-morrow: let him be furnished with divines, and have all charitable preparation: if my brother wrought by my pity it should not be so with him.

PROVOST.

So please you, this friar hath been with him, and advised him for the entertainment of death.

ESCALUS.

Good even, good father.

DUKE.

Bliss and goodness on you!

ESCALUS.

Of whence are you?

DUKE.

Not of this country, though my chance is now
To use it for my time: I am a brother
Of gracious order, late come from the see
In special business from his holiness.

ESCALUS.

What news abroad i' the world?

DUKE.

None, but that there is so great a fever on goodness, that the dissolution of it must cure it: novelty is only in request; and as it is as dangerous to be aged in any kind of course as it is virtuous to be constant in any undertaking. There is scarce truth enough alive to make societies secure; but security enough to make fellowships accurst: much upon this riddle runs the wisdom of the world. This news is old enough, yet it is every day's news. I pray you, sir, of what disposition was the duke?

ESCALUS.

One that, above all other strifes, contended especially to know himself.

DUKE.

What pleasure was he given to?

ESCALUS.

Rather rejoicing to see another merry, than merry at anything which professed to make him rejoice: a gentleman of all temperance. But leave we him to his events, with a prayer they may prove prosperous; and let me desire to know how you find Claudio

prepared. I am made to understand that you have lent him visitation.

DUKE.

He professes to have received no sinister measure from his judge, but most willingly humbles himself to the determination of justice: yet had he framed to himself, by the instruction of his frailty, many deceiving promises of life; which I, by my good leisure, have discredited to him, and now he is resolved to die.

ESCALUS.

You have paid the heavens your function, and the prisoner the very debt of your calling. I have laboured for the poor gentleman to the extremest shore of my modesty; but my brother justice have I found so severe that he hath forced me to tell him he is indeed—justice.

DUKE.

If his own life answer the straitness of his proceeding, it shall become him well: wherein if he chance to fail, he hath sentenced himself.

ESCALUS.

I am going to visit the prisoner. Fare you well.

DUKE.

Peace be with you!

[*Exeunt* ESCALUS *and* PROVOST.]

He who the sword of heaven will bear
Should be as holy as severe;
Pattern in himself to know,
Grace to stand, and virtue go;
More nor less to others paying
Than by self-offences weighing.
Shame to him whose cruel striking
Kills for faults of his own liking!
Twice treble shame on Angelo,
To weed my vice and let his grow!
O, what may man within him hide,
Though angel on the outward side!
How may likeness, made in crimes,
Make a practice on the times,
To draw with idle spiders' strings
Most pond'rous and substantial things!
Craft against vice I must apply;
With Angelo to-night shall lie

His old betrothed but despis'd;
So disguise shall, by the disguis'd,
Pay with falsehood false exacting,
And perform an old contracting.
[*Exit.*]

ACT IV
SCENE I
A room in Mariana's house.
[MARIANA *discovered sitting;*
a BOY *singing.*]
[*Song.*]
Take, O, take those lips away,
    That so sweetly were forsworn;
And those eyes, the break of day,
    Lights that do mislead the morn:
But my kisses bring again, bring again
Seals of love, but seal'd in vain, seal'd in
    vain.

MARIANA.
Break off thy song, and haste thee quick
    away;
Here comes a man of comfort, whose
    advice
Hath often still'd my brawling
    discontent.—
[*Exit* BOY.]
[*Enter* DUKE.]
I cry you mercy, sir; and well could wish
You had not found me here so musical:
Let me excuse me, and believe me so,
My mirth it much displeas'd, but pleas'd
    my woe.

DUKE.
'Tis good: though music oft hath such a
    charm
To make bad good and good provoke to
    harm.—
I pray you, tell me hath anybody inquired
for me here to-day? Much upon this time
have I promised here to meet.

MARIANA.
You have not been inquired after: I have sat
here all day.
[*Enter* ISABELLA.]

DUKE.
I do constantly believe you.—The time
is come even now. I shall crave your

forbearance a little: may be I will call upon
you anon, for some advantage to yourself.

MARIANA.
I am always bound to you.
[*Exit.*]

DUKE.
Very well met, and welcome.
What is the news from this good deputy?

ISABELLA.
He hath a garden circummur'd with brick,
Whose western side is with a vineyard
    back'd;
And to that vineyard is a planched gate
That makes his opening with this bigger
    key:
This other doth command a little door
Which from the vineyard to the garden
    leads;
There have I made my promise to call on
    him
Upon the heavy middle of the night.

DUKE.
But shall you on your knowledge find this
    way?

ISABELLA.
I have ta'en a due and wary note upon't;
With whispering and most guilty
    diligence,
In action all of precept, he did show me
The way twice o'er.

DUKE.
                    Are there no other tokens
Between you 'greed concerning her
    observance?

ISABELLA.
No, none, but only a repair i' the dark;
And that I have possess'd him my most
    stay
Can be but brief: for I have made him
    know
I have a servant comes with me along,
That stays upon me; whose persuasion is
I come about my brother.

DUKE.
                    'Tis well borne up.
I have not yet made known to Mariana
A word of this.—What ho, within! come
    forth.

[Re-enter MARIANA.*]*

I pray you be acquainted with this maid;
She comes to do you good.

ISABELLA.

I do desire the like.

DUKE.

Do you persuade yourself that I respect
  you?

MARIANA.

Good friar, I know you do, and have found
  it.

DUKE.

Take, then, this your companion by the
  hand,
Who hath a story ready for your ear:
I shall attend your leisure; but make haste;
The vaporous night approaches.

MARIANA.

Will't please you walk aside?

[Exeunt MARIANA *and* ISABELLA.*]*

DUKE.

O place and greatness, millions of false eyes
Are stuck upon thee! volumes of report
Run with these false, and most contrarious
  quest
Upon thy doings! Thousand 'scapes of wit
Make thee the father of their idle dream,
And rack thee in their fancies!

[Re-enter MARIANA *and* ISABELLA.*]*

Welcome! how agreed?

ISABELLA.

She'll take the enterprise upon her, father,
If you advise it.

DUKE.

It is not my consent,
But my entreaty too.

ISABELLA.

Little have you to say,
When you depart from him, but, soft and
  low,
"Remember now my brother."

MARIANA.

Fear me not.

DUKE.

Nor, gentle daughter, fear you not at all;
He is your husband on a pre-contract:
To bring you thus together 'tis no sin,
Sith that the justice of your title to him

Doth flourish the deceit. Come, let us go;
Our corn's to reap, for yet our tithe's to
  sow.

[Exeunt.]

SCENE II

A room in the prison.

[Enter PROVOST *and* CLOWN.*]*

PROVOST.

Come hither, sirrah. Can you cut off a
man's head?

CLOWN.

If the man be a bachelor, sir, I can: but if he
be a married man, he's his wife's head, and I
can never cut off a woman's head.

PROVOST.

Come, sir, leave me your snatches and yield
me a direct answer. To-morrow morning
are to die Claudio and Barnardine. Here
is in our prison a common executioner,
who in his office lacks a helper; if you will
take it on you to assist him, it shall redeem
you from your gyves; if not, you shall have
your full time of imprisonment, and your
deliverance with an unpitied whipping; for
you have been a notorious bawd.

CLOWN.

Sir, I have been an unlawful bawd time out
of mind; but yet I will be content to be a
lawful hangman. I would be glad to receive
some instruction from my fellow-partner.

PROVOST.

What ho, Abhorson! Where's Abhorson,
there?

[Enter ABHORSON.*]*

ABHORSON.

Do you call, sir?

PROVOST.

Sirrah, here's a fellow will help you to-
morrow in your execution. If you think
it meet, compound with him by the year,
and let him abide here with you; if not, use
him for the present, and dismiss him. He
cannot plead his estimation with you; he
hath been a bawd.

ABHORSON.

A bawd, sir? Fie upon him; he will discredit
our mystery.

PROVOST.
Go to, sir; you weigh equally; a feather will
turn the scale.
                    [*Exit.*]
CLOWN.
Pray, sir, by your good favour,—for, surely,
sir, a good favour you have, but that you
have a hanging look,—do you call, sir, your
occupation a mystery?
ABHORSON.
Ay, sir; a mystery.
CLOWN.
Painting, sir, I have heard say, is a mystery;
and your whores, sir, being members of my
occupation, using painting, do prove my
occupation a mystery: but what mystery
there should be in hanging, if I should be
hanged, I cannot imagine.
ABHORSON.
Sir, it is a mystery.
CLOWN.
Proof.
ABHORSON.
Every true man's apparel fits your thief: if
it be too little for your thief, your true man
thinks it big enough; if it be too big for
your thief, your thief thinks it little enough;
so every true man's apparel fits your thief.
                    [*Re-enter* PROVOST.]
PROVOST.
Are you agreed?
CLOWN.
Sir, I will serve him; for I do find your
hangman is a more penitent trade than
your bawd; he doth oftener ask forgiveness.
PROVOST.
You, sirrah, provide your block and your axe
to-morrow four o'clock.
ABHORSON.
Come on, bawd; I will instruct thee in my
trade; follow.
CLOWN.
I do desire to learn, sir; and I hope, if you
have occasion to use me for your own turn,
you shall find me yare; for truly, sir, for your
kindness I owe you a good turn.
PROVOST.
Call hither Barnardine and Claudio.

                    [*Exeunt* CLOWN *and* ABHORSON.]
One has my pity; not a jot the other,
Being a murderer, though he were my
          brother.
                    [*Enter* CLAUDIO.]
Look, here's the warrant, Claudio, for thy
          death:
'Tis now dead midnight, and by eight
          to-morrow
Thou must be made immortal. Where's
          Barnardine?
CLAUDIO.
As fast lock'd up in sleep as guiltless labour
When it lies starkly in the traveller's bones:
He will not wake.
PROVOST.
                    Who can do good on him?
Well, go, prepare yourself. [*Knocking
          within.*] But hark, what noise?
Heaven give your spirits comfort! [*Exit
          CLAUDIO.*] By and by!—
I hope it is some pardon or reprieve
For the most gentle Claudio.
                    [*Enter* DUKE.]
                    Welcome, father.
DUKE.
The best and wholesom'st spirits of the
          night
Envelop you, good provost! Who call'd
          here of late?
PROVOST.
None, since the curfew rung.
DUKE.
Not Isabel?
PROVOST.
                    No.
DUKE.
                    They will then, ere't be long.
PROVOST.
What comfort is for Claudio?
DUKE.
There's some in hope.
PROVOST.
                    It is a bitter deputy.
DUKE.
Not so, not so: his life is parallel'd
Even with the stroke and line of his great
          justice;

He doth with holy abstinence subdue
That in himself which he spurs on his
    power
To qualify in others: were he meal'd
With that which he corrects, then were he
    tyrannous;
But this being so, he's just.—Now are they
    come.
    [*Knocking within;* Provost *goes out.*]
This is a gentle provost: seldom when
The steeled gaoler is the friend of men.—
How now? what noise? That spirit's
    possess'd with haste
That wounds the unsisting postern with
    these strokes.
    [Provost *returns, speaking to one
        at the door.*]
Provost.
There he must stay until the officer
Arise to let him in; he is call'd up.
Duke.
Have you no countermand for Claudio yet,
But he must die to-morrow?
Provost.
                None, sir, none.
Duke.
As near the dawning, provost, as it is,
You shall hear more ere morning.
Provost.
                Happily
You something know; yet I believe there
    comes
No countermand; no such example have
    we:
Besides, upon the very siege of justice,
Lord Angelo hath to the public ear
Profess'd the contrary.
        [*Enter a* Messenger.]
Duke.
                This is his lordship's man.
Duke.
And here comes Claudio's pardon.
Messenger.
My lord hath sent you this note; and by
me this further charge, that you swerve not
from the smallest article of it, neither in
time, matter, or other circumstance. Good
morrow; for as I take it, it is almost day.

Provost.
I shall obey him.
        [*Exit* Messenger.]
Duke. [*Aside.*]
This is his pardon, purchas'd by such
    sin,
For which the pardoner himself is in:
Hence hath offence his quick celerity,
When it is borne in high authority:
When vice makes mercy, mercy's so
    extended
That for the fault's love is the offender
    friended.—
Now, sir, what news?
Provost.
I told you: Lord Angelo, belike thinking me
remiss in mine office, awakens me with this
unwonted putting-on; methinks strangely,
for he hath not used it before.
Duke.
Pray you, let's hear.
Provost. [*Reads.*]
"Whatsoever you may hear to the contrary,
let Claudio be executed by four of the
clock; and, in the afternoon, Barnardine:
for my better satisfaction, let me have
Claudio's head sent me by five. Let this be
duly performed; with a thought that more
depends on it than we must yet deliver.
Thus fail not to do your office, as you will
answer it at your peril."
What say you to this, sir?
Duke.
What is that Barnardine who is to be
executed in the afternoon?
Provost.
A Bohemian born; but here nursed up and
bred: one that is a prisoner nine years old.
Duke.
How came it that the absent duke had
not either delivered him to his liberty or
executed him? I have heard it was ever his
manner to do so.
Provost.
His friends still wrought reprieves for
him; and, indeed, his fact, till now in the
government of Lord Angelo, came not to
an undoubtful proof.

Duke.

It is now apparent?

Provost.

Most manifest, and not denied by himself.

Duke.

Hath he borne himself penitently in prison? How seems he to be touched?

Provost.

A man that apprehends death no more dreadfully but as a drunken sleep; careless, reckless, and fearless, of what's past, present, or to come; insensible of mortality and desperately mortal.

Duke.

He wants advice.

Provost.

He will hear none; he hath evermore had the liberty of the prison; give him leave to escape hence, he would not: drunk many times a-day, if not many days entirely drunk. We have very oft awaked him, as if to carry him to execution, and showed him a seeming warrant for it: it hath not moved him at all.

Duke.

More of him anon. There is written in your brow, provost, honesty and constancy: if I read it not truly, my ancient skill beguiles me; but in the boldness of my cunning I will lay myself in hazard. Claudio, whom here you have warrant to execute, is no greater forfeit to the law than Angelo who hath sentenced him. To make you understand this in a manifested effect, I crave but four days' respite; for the which you are to do me both a present and a dangerous courtesy.

Provost.

Pray, sir, in what?

Duke.

In the delaying death.

Provost.

Alack! How may I do it? having the hour limited; and an express command, under penalty, to deliver his head in the view of Angelo? I may make my case as Claudio's, to cross this in the smallest.

Duke.

By the vow of mine order, I warrant you, if

my instructions may be your guide. Let this Barnardine be this morning executed, and his head borne to Angelo.

Provost.

Angelo hath seen them both, and will discover the favour.

Duke.

O, death's great disguiser: and you may add to it. Shave the head and tie the beard; and say it was the desire of the penitent to be so bared before his death. You know the course is common. If anything fall to you upon this, more than thanks and good fortune, by the saint whom I profess, I will plead against it with my life.

Provost.

Pardon me, good father; it is against my oath.

Duke.

Were you sworn to the duke, or to the deputy?

Provost.

To him and to his substitutes.

Duke.

You will think you have made no offence if the duke avouch the justice of your dealing?

Provost.

But what likelihood is in that?

Duke.

Not a resemblance, but a certainty. Yet since I see you fearful, that neither my coat, integrity, nor persuasion, can with ease attempt you, I will go further than I meant, to pluck all fears out of you. Look you, sir, here is the hand and seal of the duke. You know the character, I doubt not; and the signet is not strange to you.

Provost.

I know them both.

Duke.

The contents of this is the return of the duke; you shall anon over-read it at your pleasure, where you shall find within these two days he will be here. This is a thing that Angelo knows not: for he this very day receives letters of strange tenour: perchance of the duke's death; perchance entering into some monastery; but, by chance, nothing of what is writ. Look, the unfolding star calls up the shepherd. Put not yourself into amazement how these things should be: all difficulties are but easy when they are known. Call your executioner, and off with Barnardine's head: I will give him a present shrift, and advise him for a better place. Yet you are amazed: but this shall absolutely resolve you. Come away; it is almost clear dawn.

[Exeunt.]

SCENE III
Another room in the same.
[Enter CLOWN.*]*

CLOWN.
I am as well acquainted here as I was in our house of profession: one would think it were Mistress Overdone's own house, for here be many of her old customers. First, here's young Master Rash; he's in for a commodity of brown paper and old ginger, nine score and seventeen pounds; of which he made five marks ready money: marry, then ginger was not much in request, for the old women were all dead. Then is there here one Master Caper, at the suit of Master Threepile the mercer, for some four suits of peach-coloured satin, which now peaches him a beggar. Then have we here young Dizy, and young Master Deepvow, and Master Copperspur, and Master Starvelackey, the rapier and dagger man, and young Dropheir that killed lusty Pudding, and Master Forthlight the tilter, and brave Master Shoetie the great traveller, and wild Halfcan that stabbed Pots, and, I think, forty more; all great doers in our trade, and are now "for the Lord's sake."

[Enter ABHORSON.*]*

ABHORSON.
Sirrah, bring Barnardine hither.

CLOWN.
Master Barnardine! You must rise and be hanged, Master Barnardine!

ABHORSON.
What ho, Barnardine!

BARNARDINE. *[Within.]*
A pox o' your throats! Who makes that noise there? What are you?

CLOWN.
Your friend, sir; the hangman. You must be so good, sir, to rise and be put to death.

BARNARDINE. *[Within.]*
Away, you rogue, away; I am sleepy.

ABHORSON.
Tell him he must awake, and that quickly too.

CLOWN.
Pray, Master Barnardine, awake till you are executed, and sleep afterwards.

ABHORSON.
Go in to him, and fetch him out.

CLOWN.
He is coming, sir, he is coming; I hear his straw rustle.

[Enter BARNARDINE.*]*

ABHORSON.
Is the axe upon the block, sirrah?

CLOWN.
Very ready, sir.

BARNARDINE.
How now, Abhorson? what's the news with you?

ABHORSON.
Truly, sir, I would desire you to clap into your prayers; for, look you, the warrant's come.

BARNARDINE.
You rogue, I have been drinking all night; I am not fitted for't.

CLOWN.
O, the better, sir; for he that drinks all night and is hanged betimes in the morning may sleep the sounder all the next day.

[Enter DUKE.*]*

ABHORSON.
Look you, sir, here comes your ghostly father. Do we jest now, think you?

DUKE.
Sir, induced by my charity, and hearing how hastily you are to depart, I am come to advise you, comfort you, and pray with you.

BARNARDINE.
Friar, not I; I have been drinking hard all

night, and I will have more time to prepare me, or they shall beat out my brains with billets: I will not consent to die this day, that's certain.

Duke.

O, sir, you must; and therefore I beseech you,
Look forward on the journey you shall go.

Barnardine.

I swear I will not die to-day for any man's persuasion.

Duke.

But hear you,—

Barnardine.

Not a word; if you have anything to say to me, come to my ward; for thence will not I to-day.

[*Exit.*]

Duke.

Unfit to live or die. O gravel heart!—
After him, fellows; bring him to the block.

[*Exeunt* Abhorson *and* Clown.]
[*Enter* Provost.]

Provost.

Now, sir, how do you find the prisoner?

Duke.

A creature unprepar'd, unmeet for death;
And to transport him in the mind he is
Were damnable.

Provost.

Here in the prison, father,
There died this morning of a cruel fever
One Ragozine, a most notorious pirate,
A man of Claudio's years; his beard and head
Just of his colour. What if we do omit
This reprobate till he were well inclined;
And satisfy the deputy with the visage
Of Ragozine, more like to Claudio?

Duke.

O, 'tis an accident that Heaven provides!
Despatch it presently; the hour draws on
Prefix'd by Angelo: see this be done,
And sent according to command; whiles I
Persuade this rude wretch willingly to die.

Provost.

This shall be done, good father, presently.
But Barnardine must die this afternoon:

And how shall we continue Claudio,
To save me from the danger that might come
If he were known alive?

Duke.

Let this be done;—put them in secret holds;
Both Barnardine and Claudio.
Ere twice the sun hath made his journal greeting
To the under generation, you shall find
Your safety manifested.

Provost.

I am your free dependant.

Duke.

Quick, dispatch,
And send the head to Angelo.

[*Exit* Provost.]

Now will I write letters to Angelo,—
The provost, he shall bear them,—whose contents
Shall witness to him I am near at home,
And that, by great injunctions, I am bound
To enter publicly: him I'll desire
To meet me at the consecrated fount,
A league below the city; and from thence,
By cold gradation and well-balanced form.
We shall proceed with Angelo.

[*Re-enter* Provost.]

Provost.

Here is the head; I'll carry it myself.

Duke.

Convenient is it. Make a swift return;
For I would commune with you of such things
That want no ear but yours.

Provost.

I'll make all speed.

[*Exit.*]

Isabella. [*Within.*]

Peace, ho, be here!

Duke.

The tongue of Isabel. She's come to know
If yet her brother's pardon be come hither:
But I will keep her ignorant of her good,
To make her heavenly comforts of despair
When it is least expected.

[*Enter* Isabella.]

ISABELLA.

Ho, by your leave!

DUKE.

Good morning to you, fair and gracious
    daughter.

ISABELLA.

The better, given me by so holy a man.
Hath yet the deputy sent my brother's
    pardon?

DUKE.

He hath released him, Isabel, from the
    world:
His head is off and sent to Angelo.

ISABELLA.

Nay, but it is not so.

DUKE.

It is no other: Show your wisdom,
    daughter,
In your close patience.

ISABELLA.

O, I will to him and pluck out his eyes!

DUKE.

You shall not be admitted to his sight.

ISABELLA.

Unhappy Claudio! Wretched Isabel!
Injurious world! Most damned Angelo!

DUKE.

This nor hurts him nor profits you a jot:
Forbear it, therefore; give your cause to
    Heaven.
Mark what I say; which you shall find
By every syllable a faithful verity:
The duke comes home to-morrow;—nay,
    dry your eyes;
One of our convent, and his confessor,
Gives me this instance. Already he hath
    carried
Notice to Escalus and Angelo,
Who do prepare to meet him at the gates,
There to give up their power. If you can,
    pace your wisdom
In that good path that I would wish it go,
And you shall have your bosom on this
    wretch,
Grace of the duke, revenges to your heart,
And general honour.

ISABELLA.

I am directed by you.

DUKE.

This letter, then, to Friar Peter give;
'Tis that he sent me of the duke's
    return.
Say, by this token, I desire his company
At Mariana's house to-night. Her cause
    and yours
I'll perfect him withal; and he shall
    bring you
Before the duke; and to the head of
    Angelo
Accuse him home, and home. For my
    poor self,
I am combined by a sacred vow,
And shall be absent. Wend you with
    this letter:
Command these fretting waters from
    your eyes
With a light heart; trust not my holy
    order,
If I pervert your course.—Who's here?
        [*Enter* LUCIO.]

LUCIO.

Good even. Friar, where is the provost?

DUKE.

Not within, sir.

LUCIO.

O pretty Isabella, I am pale at mine heart to
see thine eyes so red; thou must be patient:
I am fain to dine and sup with water and
bran; I dare not for my head fill my belly;
one fruitful meal would set me to't. But
they say the duke will be here to-morrow.
By my troth, Isabel, I loved thy brother. If
the old fantastical duke of dark corners had
been at home, he had lived.
        [*Exit* ISABELLA.]

DUKE.

Sir, the duke is marvellous little beholding
to your reports; but the best is, he lives not
in them.

LUCIO.

Friar, thou knowest not the duke so well
as I do: he's a better woodman than thou
takest him for.

DUKE.

Well, you'll answer this one day. Fare ye
well.

LUCIO.
Nay, tarry; I'll go along with thee; I can tell thee pretty tales of the duke.

DUKE.
You have told me too many of him already, sir, if they be true: if not true, none were enough.

LUCIO.
I was once before him for getting a wench with child.

DUKE.
Did you such a thing?

LUCIO.
Yes, marry, did I; but I was fain to forswear it: they would else have married me to the rotten medlar.

DUKE.
Sir, your company is fairer than honest. Rest you well.

LUCIO.
By my troth, I'll go with thee to the lane's end. If bawdy talk offend you, we'll have very little of it. Nay, friar, I am a kind of burr; I shall stick.

[*Exeunt.*]

SCENE IV
A room in Angelo's house.
[*Enter* ANGELO *and* ESCALUS.]

ESCALUS.
Every letter he hath writ hath disvouched other.

ANGELO.
In most uneven and distracted manner. His actions show much like to madness; pray heaven his wisdom be not tainted! And why meet him at the gates, and re-deliver our authorities there?

ESCALUS.
I guess not.

ANGELO.
And why should we proclaim it in an hour before his entering that, if any crave redress of injustice, they should exhibit their petitions in the street?

ESCALUS.
He shows his reason for that: to have a dispatch of complaints; and to deliver us

from devices hereafter, which shall then have no power to stand against us.

ANGELO.
Well, I beseech you, let it be proclaim'd:
Betimes i' the morn I'll call you at your house:
Give notice to such men of sort and suit
As are to meet him.

ESCALUS.
            I shall, sir: fare you well.
            [*Exit.*]

ANGELO.
Good night.—
This deed unshapes me quite, makes me unpregnant,
And dull to all proceedings. A deflower'd maid!
And by an eminent body that enforced
The law against it!—But that her tender shame
Will not proclaim against her maiden loss,
How might she tongue me? Yet reason dares her—no:
For my authority bears a so credent bulk,
That no particular scandal once can touch
But it confounds the breather. He should have liv'd,
Save that his riotous youth, with dangerous sense,
Might in the times to come have ta'en revenge,
By so receiving a dishonour'd life
With ransom of such shame. Would yet he had liv'd!
Alack, when once our grace we have forgot,
Nothing goes right; we would, and we would not.
            [*Exit.*]

SCENE V
Fields without the town.
[*Enter* DUKE *in his own habit, and* FRIAR PETER.]

DUKE.
These letters at fit time deliver me. [*Giving letters.*]
The provost knows our purpose and our plot.

The matter being afoot, keep your
  instruction
And hold you ever to our special drift;
Though sometimes you do blench from
  this to that
As cause doth minister. Go, call at
  Flavius' house,
And tell him where I stay: give the like
  notice
To Valentinus, Rowland, and to Crassus,
And bid them bring the trumpets to the
  gate;
But send me Flavius first.

PETER.
                    It shall be speeded well.
            [*Exit* FRIAR.]
            [*Enter* VARRIUS.]

DUKE.
I thank thee, Varrius; thou hast made
  good haste:
Come, we will walk. There's other of our
  friends
Will greet us here anon, my gentle
  Varrius.
                    [*Exeunt.*]

SCENE VI

Street near the city gate.
[*Enter* ISABELLA *and* MARIANA.]

ISABELLA.
To speak so indirectly I am loath;
I would say the truth; but to accuse him
  so,
That is your part: yet I am advis'd to do it;
He says, to vailfull purpose.

MARIANA.
                    Be ruled by him.

ISABELLA.
Besides, he tells me that, if peradventure
He speak against me on the adverse side,
I should not think it strange; for 'tis a
  physic
That's bitter to sweet end.

MARIANA.
I would Friar Peter.—

ISABELLA.
            O, peace! the friar is come.
            [*Enter* FRIAR PETER.]

PETER.
Come, I have found you out a stand most
  fit,
Where you may have such vantage on the
  duke
He shall not pass you. Twice have the
  trumpets sounded;
The generous and gravest citizens
Have hent the gates, and very near upon
The duke is entering; therefore, hence,
  away.
                    [*Exeunt.*]

ACT V
SCENE I

A public place near the city gate.
[MARIANA *veiled,* ISABELLA, *and* PETER,
at a distance. Enter at opposite doors DUKE,
VARRIUS, LORDS; ANGELO, ESCALUS,
LUCIO, PROVOST, OFFICERS, *and*
CITIZENS.]

DUKE.
My very worthy cousin, fairly met;—
Our old and faithful friend, we are glad to
  see you.

ANGELO AND ESCALUS.
Happy return be to your royal grace!

DUKE.
Many and hearty thankings to you both.
We have made inquiry of you; and we hear
Such goodness of your justice that our soul
Cannot but yield you forth to public
  thanks,
Forerunning more requital.

ANGELO.
You make my bonds still greater.

DUKE.
O, your desert speaks loud; and I should
  wrong it
To lock it in the wards of covert bosom,
When it deserves, with characters of brass,
A forted residence 'gainst the tooth of
  time
And rasure of oblivion. Give me your hand,
And let the subject see, to make them
  know
That outward courtesies would fain
  proclaim

Favours that keep within.—Come,
   Escalus;
You must walk by us on our other hand:
And good supporters are you.
   [PETER *and* ISABELLA *come forward.*]
PETER.
Now is your time; speak loud, and kneel
   before him.
ISABELLA.
Justice, O royal duke! Vail your regard
Upon a wrong'd, I'd fain have said, a maid!
O worthy prince, dishonour not your eye
By throwing it on any other object
Till you have heard me in my true
   complaint,
And given me justice, justice, justice,
   justice!
DUKE.
Relate your wrongs. In what? By whom?
   Be brief:
Here is Lord Angelo shall give you justice.
Reveal yourself to him.
ISABELLA.
               O worthy duke,
You bid me seek redemption of the devil:
Hear me yourself; for that which I must
   speak
Must either punish me, not being believ'd,
Or wring redress from you; hear me, O,
   hear me here!
ANGELO.
My lord, her wits, I fear me, are not firm:
She hath been a suitor to me for her
   brother,
Cut off by course of justice.
ISABELLA.
              By course of justice!
ANGELO.
And she will speak most bitterly and
   strange.
ISABELLA.
Most strange, but yet most truly, will I
   speak:
That Angelo's forsworn, is it not strange?
That Angelo's a murderer, is't not strange?
That Angelo is an adulterous thief,
An hypocrite, a virgin-violator,
Is it not strange and strange?

DUKE.
           Nay, it is ten times strange.
ISABELLA.
It is not truer he is Angelo
Than this is all as true as it is strange:
Nay, it is ten times true; for truth is truth
To the end of reckoning.
DUKE.
          Away with her!—Poor soul,
She speaks this in the infirmity of sense.
ISABELLA.
O prince! I conjure thee, as thou believ'st
There is another comfort than this world,
That thou neglect me not with that opinion
That I am touch'd with madness: make not
   impossible
That which but seems unlike; 'tis not
   impossible
But one, the wicked'st caitiff on the
   ground,
May seem as shy, as grave, as just, as
   absolute,
As Angelo; even so may Angelo,
In all his dressings, characts, titles, forms,
Be an arch-villain; believe it, royal prince,
If he be less, he's nothing; but he's more,
Had I more name for badness.
DUKE.
             By mine honesty,
If she be mad, as I believe no other,
Her madness hath the oddest frame of
   sense,
Such a dependency of thing on thing,
As e'er I heard in madness.
ISABELLA.
            O gracious duke,
Harp not on that: nor do not banish
   reason
For inequality; but let your reason serve
To make the truth appear where it seems
   hid
And hide the false seems true.
DUKE.
           Many that are not mad
Have, sure, more lack of reason.—What
   would you say?
ISABELLA.
I am the sister of one Claudio,

171

Condemn'd upon the act of fornication
To lose his head; condemn'd by Angelo:
I, in probation of a sisterhood,
Was sent to by my brother: one Lucio
As then the messenger;—

Lucio.
           That's I, an't like your grace:
I came to her from Claudio, and desir'd her
To try her gracious fortune with Lord
     Angelo
For her poor brother's pardon.

Isabella.
           That's he, indeed.

Duke.
You were not bid to speak.

Lucio.
           No, my good lord;
Nor wish'd to hold my peace.

Duke.
           I wish you now, then;
Pray you take note of it: and when you
     have
A business for yourself, pray Heaven you
     then
Be perfect.

Lucio.
I warrant your honour.

Duke.
The warrant's for yourself; take heed to it.

Isabella.
This gentleman told somewhat of my tale.

Lucio.
Right.

Duke.
It may be right; but you are in the wrong
To speak before your time.—Proceed.

Isabella.
           I went
To this pernicious caitiff deputy.

Duke.
That's somewhat madly spoken.

Isabella.
           Pardon it;
The phrase is to the matter.

Duke.
Mended again. The matter;—proceed.

Isabella.
In brief,—to set the needless process by,

How I persuaded, how I pray'd, and
     kneel'd,
How he refell'd me, and how I replied,—
For this was of much length,—the vile
     conclusion
I now begin with grief and shame to
     utter:
He would not, but by gift of my chaste
     body
To his concupiscible intemperate lust,
Release my brother; and, after much
     debatement,
My sisterly remorse confutes mine honour,
And I did yield to him. But the next morn
     betimes,
His purpose surfeiting, he sends a warrant
For my poor brother's head.

Duke.
           This is most likely!

Isabella.
O, that it were as like as it is true!

Duke.
By heaven, fond wretch, thou know'st not
     what thou speak'st,
Or else thou art suborn'd against his
     honour
In hateful practice. First, his integrity
Stands without blemish:—next, it imports
     no reason
That with such vehemency he should
     pursue
Faults proper to himself: if he had so
     offended,
He would have weigh'd thy brother by
     himself,
And not have cut him off. Some one hath
     set you on;
Confess the truth, and say by whose advice
Thou cam'st here to complain.

Isabella.
           And is this all?
Then, O you blessed ministers above,
Keep me in patience; and, with ripen'd
     time,
Unfold the evil which is here wrapt up
In countenance!—Heaven shield your
     grace from woe,
As I, thus wrong'd, hence unbelieved go!

Duke.
I know you'd fain be gone.—An officer!
To prison with her!—Shall we thus permit
A blasting and a scandalous breath to fall
On him so near us? This needs must be a
   practice.
Who knew of your intent and coming
   hither?

Isabella.
One that I would were here, Friar
   Lodowick.

Duke.
A ghostly father, belike. Who knows that
   Lodowick?

Lucio.
My lord, I know him; 'tis a meddling friar.
I do not like the man: had he been lay,
   my lord,
For certain words he spake against your
   grace
In your retirement, I had swing'd him
   soundly.

Duke.
Words against me? This's a good friar,
   belike!
And to set on this wretched woman here
Against our substitute!—Let this friar be
   found.

Lucio.
But yesternight, my lord, she and that friar,
I saw them at the prison: a saucy friar,
A very scurvy fellow.

Peter.
           Bless'd be your royal grace!
I have stood by, my lord, and I have heard
Your royal ear abus'd. First, hath this
   woman
Most wrongfully accus'd your substitute;
Who is as free from touch or soil with her
As she from one ungot.

Duke.
           We did believe no less.
Know you that Friar Lodowick that she
   speaks of?

Peter.
I know him for a man divine and holy;
Not scurvy, nor a temporary meddler,
As he's reported by this gentleman;

And, on my trust, a man that never yet
Did, as he vouches, misreport your grace.

Lucio.
My lord, most villainously; believe it.

Peter.
Well, he in time may come to clear
   himself;
But at this instant he is sick, my lord,
Of a strange fever. Upon his mere
   request,—
Being come to knowledge that there was
   complaint
Intended 'gainst Lord Angelo,—came I
   hither
To speak, as from his mouth, what he doth
   know
Is true and false; and what he, with his
   oath
And all probation, will make up full clear,
Whensoever he's convented. First, for this
   woman—
To justify this worthy nobleman,
So vulgarly and personally accus'd,—
Her shall you hear disproved to her eyes,
Till she herself confess it.

Duke.
           Good friar, let's hear it.
[Isabella *is carried off, guarded; and*
    Mariana *comes forward.*]
Do you not smile at this, Lord Angelo?—
O heaven! the vanity of wretched fools!
Give us some seats.—Come, cousin
   Angelo;
In this I'll be impartial; be you judge
Of your own cause.—Is this the witness,
   friar?
First let her show her face, and after speak.

Mariana.
Pardon, my lord; I will not show my face
Until my husband bid me.

Duke.
What! are you married?

Mariana.
No, my lord.

Duke.
Are you a maid?

Mariana.
No, my lord.

DUKE.
A widow, then?

MARIANA.
Neither, my lord.

DUKE.
Why, you are nothing then:—neither maid,
widow, nor wife?

LUCIO.
My lord, she may be a punk; for many of
them are neither maid, widow, nor wife.

DUKE.
Silence that fellow: I would he had some
    cause
To prattle for himself.

LUCIO.
Well, my lord.

MARIANA.
My lord, I do confess I ne'er was married,
And I confess, besides, I am no maid:
I have known my husband; yet my
    husband knows not
That ever he knew me.

LUCIO.
He was drunk, then, my lord; it can be no
    better.

DUKE.
For the benefit of silence, would thou wert
    so too!

LUCIO.
Well, my lord.

DUKE.
This is no witness for Lord Angelo.

MARIANA.
Now I come to't, my lord:
She that accuses him of fornication,
In self-same manner doth accuse my
    husband;
And charges him, my lord, with such a time
When I'll depose I had him in mine arms,
With all the effect of love.

ANGELO.
Charges she more than me?

MARIANA.
                                     Not that I know.

DUKE.
No? you say your husband.

MARIANA.
Why, just, my lord, and that is Angelo,

Who thinks he knows that he ne'er knew
    my body,
But knows he thinks that he knows Isabel's.

ANGELO.
This is a strange abuse.—Let's see thy face.

MARIANA.
My husband bids me; now I will unmask.
                          [*Unveiling.*]
This is that face, thou cruel Angelo,
Which once thou swor'st was worth the
    looking on:
This is the hand which, with a vow'd
    contract,
Was fast belock'd in thine; this is the body
That took away the match from Isabel,
And did supply thee at thy garden-house
In her imagin'd person.

DUKE.
                          Know you this woman?

LUCIO.
Carnally, she says.

DUKE.
                          Sirrah, no more!

LUCIO.
Enough, my lord.

ANGELO.
My lord, I must confess I know this
    woman;
And five years since there was some
    speech of marriage
Betwixt myself and her; which was broke
    off,
Partly for that her promis'd proportions
Came short of composition; but in chief
For that her reputation was disvalued
In levity: since which time of five years
I never spake with her, saw her, nor heard
    from her,
Upon my faith and honour.

MARIANA.
                          Noble prince,
As there comes light from heaven and
    words from breath,
As there is sense in truth and truth in
    virtue,
I am affianc'd this man's wife as strongly
As words could make up vows: and, my
    good lord,

But Tuesday night last gone, in his
    garden-house,
He knew me as a wife. As this is true,
Let me in safety raise me from my
    knees,
Or else for ever be confixed here,
A marble monument!
ANGELO.
                I did but smile till now;
Now, good my lord, give me the scope of
    justice;
My patience here is touch'd. I do perceive
These poor informal women are no more
But instruments of some more mightier
    member
That sets them on. Let me have way, my
    lord,
To find this practice out.
DUKE.
                Ay, with my heart;
And punish them to your height of
    pleasure.—
Thou foolish friar, and thou pernicious
    woman,
Compact with her that's gone, thinkst
    thou thy oaths,
Though they would swear down each
    particular saint,
Were testimonies against his worth and
    credit,
That's seal'd in approbation?—You, Lord
    Escalus,
Sit with my cousin; lend him your kind
    pains
To find out this abuse, whence 'tis
    deriv'd.—
There is another friar that set them on;
Let him be sent for.
PETER.
Would he were here, my lord; for he
    indeed
Hath set the women on to this complaint:
Your provost knows the place where he
    abides,
And he may fetch him.
DUKE.
                Go, do it instantly.—
        [*Exit* PROVOST.]

And you, my noble and well-warranted
    cousin,
Whom it concerns to hear this matter
    forth,
Do with your injuries as seems you best
In any chastisement. I for a while
Will leave you: but stir not you till you
    have well
Determined upon these slanderers.
ESCALUS.
                My lord, we'll do it throughly.
        [*Exit* DUKE.]
Signior Lucio, did not you say you knew
that Friar Lodowick to be a dishonest
person?
LUCIO.
Cucullus non facit monachum: honest in
nothing but in his clothes; and one that
hath spoke most villainous speeches of the
duke.
ESCALUS.
We shall entreat you to abide here till he
come and enforce them against him: we
shall find this friar a notable fellow.
LUCIO.
As any in Vienna, on my word.
ESCALUS.
Call that same Isabel here once again.
[*To an* ATTENDANT.] I would speak with
her. Pray you, my lord, give me leave to
question; you shall see how I'll handle her.
LUCIO.
Not better than he, by her own report.
ESCALUS.
Say you?
LUCIO.
Marry, sir, I think, if you handled her
privately, she would sooner confess:
perchance, publicly, she'll be ashamed.
        [*Re-enter* OFFICERS, *with* ISABELLA.]
ESCALUS.
I will go darkly to work with her.
LUCIO.
That's the way; for women are light at
midnight.
ESCALUS. [*To* ISABELLA.]
Come on, mistress. Here's a gentlewoman
denies all that you have said.

Lucio.
My lord, here comes the rascal I spoke of,
here with the provost.
[*Re-enter the* Duke *in his friar's habit,
and* Provost.]
Escalus.
In very good time:—speak not you to him
till we call upon you.
Lucio.
Mum.
Escalus.
Come, sir: did you set these women on to
slander Lord Angelo? they have confessed
you did.
Duke.
'Tis false.
Escalus.
How! Know you where you are?
Duke.
Respect to your great place! and let the
devil
Be sometime honour'd for his burning
throne!—
Where is the duke? 'tis he should hear me
speak.
Escalus.
The duke's in us; and we will hear you
speak:
Look you speak justly.
Duke.
Boldly, at least. But, O, poor souls,
Come you to seek the lamb here of the fox,
Good night to your redress! Is the duke
gone?
Then is your cause gone too. The duke's
unjust
Thus to retort your manifest appeal,
And put your trial in the villain's mouth
Which here you come to accuse.
Lucio.
This is the rascal; this is he I spoke of.
Escalus.
Why, thou unreverend and unhallow'd
friar,
Is't not enough thou hast suborn'd these
women
To accuse this worthy man, but, in foul
mouth,

And in the witness of his proper ear,
To call him villain?
And then to glance from him to the duke
himself,
To tax him with injustice? Take him
hence;
To the rack with him!—We'll touze you
joint by joint,
But we will know his purpose.—
What! unjust?
Duke.
          Be not so hot; the duke
Dare no more stretch this finger of mine
than he
Dare rack his own; his subject am I not,
Nor here provincial. My business in this
state
Made me a looker-on here in Vienna,
Where I have seen corruption boil and
bubble
Till it o'errun the stew: laws for all faults,
But faults so countenanc'd that the strong
statutes
Stand like the forfeits in a barber's shop,
As much in mock as mark.
Escalus.
Slander to the state! Away with him to
prison!
Angelo.
What can you vouch against him, Signior
Lucio?
Is this the man that you did tell us of?
Lucio.
'Tis he, my lord. Come hither, good-man
bald-pate. Do you know me?
Duke.
I remember you, sir, by the sound of your
voice. I met you at the prison, in the
absence of the duke.
Lucio.
O did you so? And do you remember what
you said of the duke?
Duke.
Most notedly, sir.
Lucio.
Do you so, sir? And was the duke a
fleshmonger, a fool, and a coward, as you
then reported him to be?

Duke.
You must, sir, change persons with me ere
you make that my report: you, indeed, spoke
so of him; and much more, much worse.

Lucio.
O thou damnable fellow! Did not I pluck
thee by the nose for thy speeches?

Duke.
I protest I love the duke as I love myself.

Angelo.
Hark how the villain would gloze now,
after his treasonable abuses!

Escalus.
Such a fellow is not to be talked withal.
Away with him to prison!—Where is the
provost?—Away with him to prison! lay
bolts enough upon him: let him speak no
more.—Away with those giglots too, and
with the other confederate companion!

[*The* Provost *lays hands on the* Duke.]

Duke.
Stay, sir; stay awhile.

Angelo.
What! resists he?—Help him, Lucio.

Lucio.
Come, sir; come, sir! come, sir; foh, sir!
Why, you bald-pated lying rascal! you
must be hooded, must you? Show your
knave's visage, with a pox to you! show your
sheep-biting face, and be hanged an hour!
Will't not off? [*Pulls off the friar's hood and
discovers the* Duke.]

Duke.
Thou art the first knave that e'er made a
duke.—
First, provost, let me bail these gentle
three:—
[*To* Lucio.] Sneak not away, sir; for the
friar and you
Must have a word anon:—Lay hold on
him.

Lucio.
This may prove worse than hanging.

Duke. [*To* Escalus.]
What you have spoke I pardon; sit you
down.—
We'll borrow place of him. [*To* Angelo.]
Sir, by your leave.

Hast thou or word, or wit, or impudence,
That yet can do thee office? If thou hast,
Rely upon it till my tale be heard,
And hold no longer out.

Angelo.
                    O my dread lord,
I should be guiltier than my guiltiness,
To think I can be undiscernible,
When I perceive your grace, like power
divine,
Hath look'd upon my passes. Then, good
prince,
No longer session hold upon my shame,
But let my trial be mine own confession:
Immediate sentence then, and sequent
death,
Is all the grace I beg.

Duke.
                    Come hither, Mariana:—
Say, wast thou e'er contracted to this
woman?

Angelo.
I was, my lord.

Duke.
Go, take her hence and marry her
instantly.
Do you the office, friar; which
consummate,
Return him here again.—Go with him,
provost.
[*Exeunt* Angelo, Mariana, Peter, *and*
Provost.]

Escalus.
My lord, I am more amazed at his
dishonour
Than at the strangeness of it.

Duke.
                    Come hither, Isabel:
Your friar is now your prince. As I was
then
Advertising and holy to your business,
Not changing heart with habit, I am still
Attorney'd at your service.

Isabella.
                    O, give me pardon,
That I, your vassal, have employ'd and
pain'd
Your unknown sovereignty.

DUKE.
　　　　　　　　　You are pardon'd, Isabel.
And now, dear maid, be you as free to us.
Your brother's death, I know, sits at your
　　heart;
And you may marvel why I obscur'd
　　myself,
Labouring to save his life, and would not
　　rather
Make rash remonstrance of my hidden
　　power
Than let him so be lost. O most kind maid,
It was the swift celerity of his death,
Which I did think with slower foot came
　　on,
That brain'd my purpose. But peace be
　　with him!
That life is better life, past fearing death,
Than that which lives to fear: make it your
　　comfort,
So happy is your brother.

ISABELLA.
　　　　　　　　　　　　I do, my lord.

[*Re-enter* ANGELO, MARIANA, PETER,
　　　　　and PROVOST.]

DUKE.
For this new-married man approaching
　　here,
Whose salt imagination yet hath wrong'd
Your well-defended honour, you must
　　pardon
For Mariana's sake: but as he adjudg'd your
　　brother,—
Being criminal, in double violation
Of sacred chastity and of promise-breach,
Thereon dependent, for your brother's
　　life,—
The very mercy of the law cries out
Most audible, even from his proper tongue,
"An Angelo for Claudio, death for death."
Haste still pays haste, and leisure answers
　　leisure;
Like doth quit like, and measure still for
　　measure.
Then, Angelo, thy fault's thus
　　manifested,—
Which, though thou wouldst deny, denies
　　thee vantage.—

We do condemn thee to the very block
Where Claudio stoop'd to death, and with
　　like haste.—
Away with him!

MARIANA.
　　　　　　　　　O my most gracious lord,
I hope you will not mock me with a
　　husband!

DUKE.
It is your husband mock'd you with a
　　husband.
Consenting to the safeguard of your
　　honour,
I thought your marriage fit; else
　　imputation,
For that he knew you, might reproach
　　your life,
And choke your good to come: for his
　　possessions,
Although by confiscation they are ours,
We do instate and widow you withal
To buy you a better husband.

MARIANA.
　　　　　　　　　　　O my dear lord,
I crave no other, nor no better man.

DUKE.
Never crave him; we are definitive.

MARIANA.
Gentle my liege,—[*Kneeling.*]

DUKE.
　　　　　　　You do but lose your labour.—
Away with him to death! [*To* LUCIO.]
　　Now, sir, to you.

MARIANA.
O my good lord!—Sweet Isabel, take my
　　part;
Lend me your knees, and all my life to
　　come
I'll lend you all my life to do you service.

DUKE.
Against all sense you do importune her.
Should she kneel down in mercy of this
　　fact,
Her brother's ghost his paved bed would
　　break,
And take her hence in horror.

MARIANA.
　　　　　　　　　　　　Isabel,

Sweet Isabel, do yet but kneel by me;
Hold up your hands, say nothing,—I'll
    speak all.
They say, best men moulded out of faults;
And, for the most, become much more
    the better
For being a little bad: so may my husband.
O Isabel, will you not lend a knee?
Duke.
He dies for Claudio's death.
Isabella. [*Kneeling.*]
                    Most bounteous sir,
Look, if it please you, on this man
    condemn'd,
As if my brother liv'd: I partly think
A due sincerity govern'd his deeds
Till he did look on me; since it is so,
Let him not die. My brother had but
    justice,
In that he did the thing for which he died:
For Angelo,
His act did not o'ertake his bad intent,
And must be buried but as an intent
That perish'd by the way. Thoughts are no
    subjects;
Intents but merely thoughts.
Mariana.
                    Merely, my lord.
Duke.
Your suit's unprofitable; stand up, I say.—
I have bethought me of another fault.—
Provost, how came it Claudio was
    beheaded
At an unusual hour?
Provost.
                    It was commanded so.
Duke.
Had you a special warrant for the deed?
Provost.
No, my good lord; it was by private
    message.
Duke.
For which I do discharge you of your office:
Give up your keys.
Provost.
                    Pardon me, noble lord:
I thought it was a fault, but knew it not;
Yet did repent me, after more advice:

For testimony whereof, one in the prison,
That should by private order else have
    died,
I have reserved alive.
Duke.
                    What's he?
Provost.
                    His name is Barnardine.
Duke.
I would thou hadst done so by Claudio.—
Go fetch him hither; let me look upon
    him.
            [*Exit* Provost.]
Escalus.
I am sorry one so learned and so wise
As you, Lord Angelo, have still appear'd,
Should slip so grossly, both in the heat of
    blood
And lack of temper'd judgment afterward.
Angelo.
I am sorry that such sorrow I procure:
And so deep sticks it in my penitent heart
That I crave death more willingly than
    mercy;
'Tis my deserving, and I do entreat it.
    [*Re-enter* Provost, *with* Barnardine,
        Claudio *muffled, and* Juliet.]
Duke.
Which is that Barnardine?
Provost.
                    This, my lord.
Duke.
There was a friar told me of this man:—
Sirrah, thou art said to have a stubborn
    soul,
That apprehends no further than this
    world,
And squar'st thy life according. Thou'rt
    condemn'd;
But, for those earthly faults, I quit them
    all,
And pray thee take this mercy to provide
For better times to come:—Friar, advise
    him;
I leave him to your hand.—What muffled
    fellow's that?
Provost.
This is another prisoner that I sav'd,

Who should have died when Claudio lost
   his head;
As like almost to Claudio as himself.
       [*Unmuffles* CLAUDIO.]
DUKE. [*To* ISABELLA.]
If he be like your brother, for his sake
Is he pardon'd; and for your lovely sake,
Give me your hand and say you will be
   mine;
He is my brother too: but fitter time for
   that.
By this Lord Angelo perceives he's safe;
Methinks I see a quick'ning in his eye.—
Well, Angelo, your evil quits you well:
Look that you love your wife; her worth
   worth yours.
I find an apt remission in myself;
And yet here's one in place I cannot
   pardon.—
[*To* LUCIO.] You, sirrah, that knew me for
   a fool, a coward,
One all of luxury, an ass, a madman;
Wherein have I so deserved of you
That you extol me thus?
LUCIO.
Faith, my lord, I spoke it but according to
the trick. If you will hang me for it, you
may; but I had rather it would please you I
might be whipped.
DUKE.
Whipp'd first, sir, and hang'd after.—
Proclaim it, provost, round about the city,
If any woman wrong'd by this lewd
   fellow,—
As I have heard him swear himself there's
   one
Whom he begot with child,—let her
   appear,
And he shall marry her: the nuptial
   finish'd,
Let him be whipp'd and hang'd.

LUCIO.
I beseech your highness, do not marry me
to a whore! Your highness said even now
I made you a duke; good my lord, do not
recompense me in making me a cuckold.
DUKE.
Upon mine honour, thou shalt marry her.
Thy slanders I forgive; and therewithal
Remit thy other forfeits.—Take him to
   prison;
And see our pleasure herein executed.
LUCIO.
Marrying a punk, my lord, is pressing to
death, whipping, and hanging.
DUKE.
Slandering a prince deserves it.—
      [*Exeunt* OFFICERS *with* LUCIO.]
She, Claudio, that you wrong'd, look you
   restore.—
Joy to you, Mariana!—Love her, Angelo;
I have confess'd her, and I know her
   virtue.—
Thanks, good friend Escalus, for thy much
   goodness
There's more behind that is more gratulate.
Thanks, provost, for thy care and secrecy;
We shall employ thee in a worthier
   place.—
Forgive him, Angelo, that brought you
   home
The head of Ragozine for Claudio's:
The offence pardons itself.—Dear Isabel,
I have a motion much imports your good;
Whereto if you'll a willing ear incline,
What's mine is yours, and what is yours is
   mine:—
So, bring us to our palace; where we'll
   show
What's yet behind, that's meet you all
   should know.
          [*Exeunt.*]

The Comedy of Errors

Dramatis Personae

SOLINUS, *Duke of Ephesus*
AEGEON, *a merchant of Syracuse*
ANTIPHOLUS OF EPHESUS *and*
ANTIPHOLUS OF SYRACUSE, *twin*
  brothers and sons to Aegeon and Aemilia,
  but unknown to each other
DROMIO OF EPHESUS *and*
DROMIO OF SYRACUSE, *twin*
  brothers, and attendants on the two
  Antipholuses
BALTHAZAR, *a merchant*
ANGELO, *a goldsmith*
A MERCHANT, *friend to Antipholus of*
  Syracuse

PINCH, *a schoolmaster and a conjurer*
AEMILIA, *wife to Aegeon, an abbess at*
  Ephesus
ADRIANA, *wife to Antipholus of Ephesus*
LUCIANA, *her sister*
LUCE, *her servant*
A COURTEZAN
A GAOLER, OFFICERS, *and*
  ATTENDANTS

SCENE: *Ephesus.*

ACT I
SCENE I

A hall in the Duke's palace.
[*Enter the* DUKE, AEGEON, GAOLER,
OFFICERS, *and other* ATTENDANTS.]

AEGEON.
Proceed, Solinus, to procure my fall,
And, by the doom of death, end woes and
  all.

DUKE.
Merchant of Syracuse, plead no more;
I am not partial to infringe our laws:
The enmity and discord which of late
Sprung from the rancorous outrage of
  your Duke
To merchants, our well-dealing
  countrymen,—
Who, wanting guilders to redeem their
  lives,
Have seal'd his rigorous statutes with their
  bloods,—
Excludes all pity from our threat'ning
  looks.
For, since the mortal and intestine jars
'Twixt thy seditious countrymen and us,

It hath in solemn synods been decreed,
Both by the Syracusians and ourselves,
To admit no traffic to our adverse towns;
Nay, more,
If any born at Ephesus be seen
At any Syracusian marts and fairs;—
Again, if any Syracusian born
Come to the bay of Ephesus, he dies,
His goods confiscate to the Duke's
  dispose;
Unless a thousand marks be levied,
To quit the penalty and to ransom him.—
Thy substance, valued at the highest rate,
Cannot amount unto a hundred marks:
Therefore by law thou art condemn'd to
  die.

AEGEON.
Yet this my comfort,—when your words
  are done,
My woes end likewise with the evening
  sun.

DUKE.
Well, Syracusan, say, in brief, the cause
Why thou departedst from thy native
  home,

181

And for what cause thou cam'st to
    Ephesus.

AEGEON.

A heavier task could not have been
    impos'd
Than I to speak my griefs unspeakable!
Yet, that the world may witness that my
    end
Was wrought by nature, not by vile
    offence,
I'll utter what my sorrow gives me leave.
In Syracuse was I born; and wed
Unto a woman, happy but for me,
And by me too, had not our hap been bad.
With her I liv'd in joy; our wealth increas'd
By prosperous voyages I often made
To Epidamnum, till my factor's death,
And he,—great care of goods at random
    left,—
Drew me from kind embracements of my
    spouse:
From whom my absence was not six
    months old,
Before herself,—almost at fainting under
The pleasing punishment that women
    bear,—
Had made provision for her following me,
And soon and safe arrived where I was.
There had she not been long but she
    became
A joyful mother of two goodly sons;
And, which was strange, the one so like
    the other
As could not be distinguish'd but by
    names.
That very hour, and in the self-same inn,
A mean woman was delivered
Of such a burden, male twins, both alike:
Those,—for their parents were exceeding
    poor,—
I bought, and brought up to attend my
    sons.
My wife, not meanly proud of two such
    boys,
Made daily motions for our home return:
Unwilling I agreed; alas! too soon!
We came aboard:
A league from Epidamnum had we sail'd

Before the always-wind-obeying deep
Gave any tragic instance of our harm;
But longer did we not retain much hope:
For what obscured light the heavens did
    grant
Did but convey unto our fearful minds
A doubtful warrant of immediate death;
Which though myself would gladly have
    embrac'd,
Yet the incessant weepings of my wife,
Weeping before for what she saw must
    come,
And piteous plainings of the pretty babes,
That mourn'd for fashion, ignorant what
    to fear,
Forc'd me to seek delays for them and me.
And this it was,—for other means was
    none.—
The sailors sought for safety by our boat,
And left the ship, then sinking-ripe, to us;
My wife, more careful for the latter-born,
Had fast'ned him unto a small spare mast,
Such as sea-faring men provide for storms:
To him one of the other twins was bound,
Whilst I had been like heedful of the
    other.
The children thus dispos'd, my wife and I,
Fixing our eyes on whom our care was
    fix'd,
Fast'ned ourselves at either end the mast,
And, floating straight, obedient to the
    stream,
Were carried towards Corinth, as we
    thought.
At length the sun, gazing upon the earth,
Dispers'd those vapours that offended us;
And, by the benefit of his wish'd light,
The seas wax'd calm, and we discover'd
Two ships from far making amain to us,—
Of Corinth that, of Epidaurus this:
But ere they came—O, let me say no
    more!—
Gather the sequel by that went before.

DUKE.

Nay, forward, old man, do not break off so;
For we may pity, though not pardon thee.

AEGEON.

O, had the gods done so, I had not now

Worthily term'd them merciless to us!
For, ere the ships could meet by twice five
   leagues,
We were encount'red by a mighty rock,
Which being violently borne upon,
Our helpful ship was splitted in the midst;
So that, in this unjust divorce of us,
Fortune had left to both of us alike
What to delight in, what to sorrow for.
Her part, poor soul! seeming as burdened
With lesser weight, but not with lesser
   woe,
Was carried with more speed before the
   wind;
And in our sight they three were taken up
By fishermen of Corinth, as we thought.
At length another ship had seiz'd on us;
And, knowing whom it was their hap to
   save,
Gave healthful welcome to their ship-
   wreck'd guests;
And would have reft the fishers of their
   prey,
Had not their bark been very slow of sail,
And therefore homeward did they bend
   their course.—
Thus have you heard me sever'd from my
   bliss;
That by misfortunes was my life prolong'd,
To tell sad stories of my own mishaps.

DUKE.
And, for the sake of them thou sorrowest
   for,
Do me the favour to dilate at full
What have befall'n of them and thee till
   now.

AEGEON.
My youngest boy, and yet my eldest care,
At eighteen years became inquisitive
After his brother, and importun'd me
That his attendant,—so his case was like,
Reft of his brother, but retain'd his name,—
Might bear him company in the quest of
   him:
Whom whilst I laboured of a love to see,
I hazarded the loss of whom I lov'd.
Five summers have I spent in furthest
   Greece,

Roaming clean through the bounds of
   Asia,
And, coasting homeward, came to
   Ephesus;
Hopeless to find, yet loath to leave
   unsought
Or that or any place that harbours men.
But here must end the story of my life;
And happy were I in my timely death,
Could all my travels warrant me they live.

DUKE.
Hapless Aegeon, whom the fates have
   mark'd
To bear the extremity of dire mishap!
Now, trust me, were it not against our
   laws,
Against my crown, my oath, my dignity,
Which princes, would they, may not
   disannul,
My soul should sue as advocate for thee.
But though thou art adjudged to the
   death,
And passed sentence may not be recall'd
But to our honour's great disparagement,
Yet will I favour thee in what I can:
Therefore, merchant, I'll limit thee this day
To seek thy help by beneficial help:
Try all the friends thou hast in Ephesus:
Beg thou, or borrow, to make up the sum,
And live; if not, then thou art doom'd to
   die.—
Gaoler, take him to thy custody.

GAOLER.
I will, my lord.

AEGEON.
Hopeless and helpless doth Aegeon wend.
But to procrastinate his lifeless end.
               [Exeunt.]

SCENE II
A public place.
[*Enter* ANTIPHOLUS *and* DROMIO OF
SYRACUSE, *and a* MERCHANT.]

MERCHANT.
Therefore, give out you are of Epidamnum,
Lest that your goods too soon be
   confiscate.
This very day a Syracusian merchant

Is apprehended for arrival here;
And, not being able to buy out his life,
According to the statute of the town,
Dies ere the weary sun set in the west.—
There is your money that I had to keep.

Antipholus of Syracuse.
Go bear it to the Centaur, where we host,
And stay there, Dromio, till I come to
   thee.
Within this hour it will be dinner-time;
Till that, I'll view the manners of the
   town,
Peruse the traders, gaze upon the
   buildings,
And then return and sleep within mine
   inn;
For with long travel I am stiff and
   weary.—
Get thee away.

Dromio of Syracuse.
Many a man would take you at your word,
And go indeed, having so good a mean.
     [*Exit* Dromio.]

Antipholus of Syracuse.
A trusty villain, sir, that very oft,
When I am dull with care and melancholy,
Lightens my humour with his merry jests.
What, will you walk with me about the
   town,
And then go to my inn and dine with me?

Merchant.
I am invited, sir, to certain merchants,
Of whom I hope to make much benefit:
I crave your pardon. Soon, at five o'clock,
Please you, I'll meet with you upon the
   mart,
And afterward consort you till bed-time:
My present business calls me from you
   now.

Antipholus of Syracuse.
Farewell till then: I will go lose myself,
And wander up and down to view the city.

Merchant.
Sir, I commend you to your own content.
     [*Exit* Merchant.]

Antipholus of Syracuse.
He that commends me to mine own
   content

Commends me to the thing I cannot get.
I to the world am like a drop of water
That in the ocean seeks another drop;
Who, failing there to find his fellow forth,
Unseen, inquisitive, confounds himself:
So I, to find a mother and a brother,
In quest of them, unhappy, lose myself.
     [*Enter* Dromio of Ephesus.]
Here comes the almanac of my true date.
What now? How chance thou art return'd
   so soon?

Dromio of Ephesus.
Return'd so soon! rather approach'd too
   late.
The capon burns, the pig falls from the
   spit;
The clock hath strucken twelve upon the
   bell—
My mistress made it one upon my cheek:
She is so hot because the meat is cold;
The meat is cold because you come not
   home;
You come not home because you have no
   stomach;
You have no stomach, having broke your
   fast;
But we, that know what 'tis to fast and
   pray,
Are penitent for your default to-day.

Antipholus of Syracuse.
Stop—in your wind, sir; tell me this, I
   pray:
Where have you left the money that I
   gave you?

Dromio of Ephesus.
O,—sixpence that I had o' Wednesday last
To pay the saddler for my mistress'
   crupper;—
The saddler had it, sir, I kept it not.

Antipholus of Syracuse.
I am not in a sportive humour now;
Tell me, and dally not, where is the
   money?
We being strangers here, how dar'st thou
   trust
So great a charge from thine own custody?

Dromio of Ephesus.
I pray you jest, sir, as you sit at dinner:

I from my mistress come to you in post:
If I return, I shall be post indeed;
For she will score your fault upon my pate.
Methinks your maw, like mine, should be
    your clock,
And strike you home without a messenger.

Antipholus of Syracuse.

Come, Dromio, come, these jests are out
    of season;
Reserve them till a merrier hour than this.
Where is the gold I gave in charge to thee?

Dromio of Ephesus.

To me, sir? why, you gave no gold to me!

Antipholus of Syracuse.

Come on, sir knave, have done your
    foolishness,
And tell me how thou hast dispos'd thy
    charge.

Dromio of Ephesus.

My charge was but to fetch you from the
    mart
Home to your house, the Phoenix, sir, to
    dinner:
My mistress and her sister stay for you.

Antipholus of Syracuse.

Now, as I am a Christian, answer me,
In what safe place you have bestow'd my
    money:
Or I shall break that merry sconce of yours,
That stands on tricks when I am
    undispos'd;
Where is the thousand marks thou hadst
    of me?

Dromio of Ephesus.

I have some marks of yours upon my pate,
Some of my mistress' marks upon my
    shoulders,
But not a thousand marks between you
    both.—
If I should pay your worship those again,
Perchance you will not bear them
    patiently.

Antipholus of Syracuse.

Thy mistress' marks! what mistress, slave,
    hast thou?

Dromio of Ephesus.

Your worship's wife, my mistress at the
    Phoenix;

She that doth fast till you come home to
    dinner,
And prays that you will hie you home to
    dinner.

Antipholus of Syracuse.

What, wilt thou flout me thus unto my
    face,
Being forbid? There, take you that, sir
    knave.

Dromio of Ephesus.

What mean you, sir? for God's sake hold
    your hands!
Nay, an you will not, sir, I'll take my heels.
                [*Exit* Dromio.]

Antipholus of Syracuse.

Upon my life, by some device or other,
The villain is o'er-raught of all my money.
They say this town is full of cozenage;
As, nimble jugglers that deceive the eye,
Dark-working sorcerers that change the
    mind,
Soul-killing witches that deform the body,
Disguised cheaters, prating mountebanks,
And many such-like liberties of sin:
If it prove so, I will be gone the sooner.
I'll to the Centaur to go seek this slave:
I greatly fear my money is not safe.
                [*Exit.*]

ACT II
SCENE I
A public place.
[*Enter* Adriana *and* Luciana.]

Adriana.

Neither my husband nor the slave
    return'd
That in such haste I sent to seek his
    master!
Sure, Luciana, it is two o'clock.

Luciana.

Perhaps some merchant hath invited him,
And from the mart he's somewhere gone
    to dinner.
Good sister, let us dine, and never fret:
A man is master of his liberty;
Time is their master; and when they see
    time,
They'll go or come. If so, be patient, sister.

ADRIANA.
Why should their liberty than ours be
    more?
LUCIANA.
Because their business still lies out o' door.
ADRIANA.
Look when I serve him so, he takes it ill.
LUCIANA.
O, know he is the bridle of your will.
ADRIANA.
There's none but asses will be bridled so.
LUCIANA.
Why, headstrong liberty is lash'd with woe.
There's nothing situate under heaven's eye
But hath his bound in earth, in sea, in sky;
The beasts, the fishes, and the winged
    fowls,
Are their males' subjects, and at their
    controls:
Man, more divine, the masters of all these,
Lord of the wide world and wild wat'ry
    seas,
Indued with intellectual sense and souls
Of more pre-eminence than fish and
    fowls,
Are masters to their females, and their
    lords:
Then let your will attend on their accords.
ADRIANA.
This servitude makes you to keep unwed.
LUCIANA.
Not this, but troubles of the marriage-bed.
ADRIANA.
But, were you wedded, you would bear
    some sway.
LUCIANA.
Ere I learn love, I'll practise to obey.
ADRIANA.
How if your husband start some other
    where?
LUCIANA.
Till he come home again, I would forbear.
ADRIANA.
Patience unmov'd, no marvel though she
    pause:
They can be meek that have no other cause.
A wretched soul, bruis'd with adversity,
We bid be quiet when we hear it cry;

But were we burd'ned with like weight
    of pain,
As much, or more, we should ourselves
    complain:
So thou, that hast no unkind mate to
    grieve thee,
With urging helpless patience would
    relieve me:
But if thou live to see like right bereft,
This fool-begg'd patience in thee will be
    left.
LUCIANA.
Well, I will marry one day, but to try:—
Here comes your man, now is your
    husband nigh.
        [*Enter* DROMIO OF EPHESUS.]
ADRIANA.
Say, is your tardy master now at hand?
DROMIO OF EPHESUS.
Nay, he's at two hands with me, and that
my two ears can witness.
ADRIANA.
Say, didst thou speak with him? know'st
    thou his mind?
DROMIO OF EPHESUS.
Ay, ay, he told his mind upon mine ear.
Beshrew his hand, I scarce could
    understand it.
LUCIANA.
Spake he so doubtfully thou could'st not
feel his meaning?
DROMIO OF EPHESUS.
Nay, he struck so plainly I could too well
feel his blows; and withal so doubtfully that
I could scarce understand them.
ADRIANA.
But say, I pr'ythee, is he coming home?
It seems he hath great care to please his
    wife.
DROMIO OF EPHESUS.
Why, mistress, sure my master is horn-mad.
ADRIANA.
Horn-mad, thou villain?
DROMIO OF EPHESUS.
I mean not cuckold-mad; but, sure, he's
    stark mad.
When I desir'd him to come home to
    dinner,

He ask'd me for a thousand marks in gold:
" 'Tis dinner time," quoth I; "My gold,"
  quoth he:
"Your meat doth burn," quoth I; "My gold,"
  quoth he:
"Will you come home?" quoth I; "My gold,"
  quoth he:
"Where is the thousand marks I gave thee,
  villain?"
"The pig," quoth I, "is burn'd"; "My gold,"
  quoth he:
"My mistress, sir," quoth I; "Hang up thy
  mistress;
I know not thy mistress; out on thy
  mistress!"

Luciana.
Quoth who?

Dromio of Ephesus.
Quoth my master:
"I know," quoth he, "no house, no wife, no
  mistress."
So that my errand, due unto my tongue,
I thank him, I bare home upon my
  shoulders;
For, in conclusion, he did beat me there.

Adriana.
Go back again, thou slave, and fetch him
  home.

Dromio of Ephesus.
Go back again! and be new beaten home?
For God's sake, send some other messenger.

Adriana.
Back, slave, or I will break thy pate across.

Dromio of Ephesus.
And he will bless that cross with other
  beating:
Between you I shall have a holy head.

Adriana.
Hence, prating peasant: fetch thy master
  home.

Dromio of Ephesus.
Am I so round with you, as you with me,
That like a football you do spurn me thus?
You spurn me hence, and he will spurn me
  hither:
If I last in this service, you must case me
  in leather.
                    [Exit.]

Luciana.
Fie, how impatience low'reth in your face!

Adriana.
His company must do his minions grace,
Whilst I at home starve for a merry look.
Hath homely age the alluring beauty took
From my poor cheek? then he hath wasted
  it:
Are my discourses dull? barren my wit?
If voluble and sharp discourse be marr'd,
Unkindness blunts it more than marble
  hard:
Do their gay vestments his affections bait?
That's not my fault; he's master of my
  state:
What ruins are in me that can be found
By him not ruin'd? then is he the ground
Of my defeatures: my decayed fair
A sunny look of his would soon repair;
But, too unruly deer, he breaks the pale
And feeds from home; poor I am but his
  stale.

Luciana.
Self-harming jealousy!—fie, beat it hence.

Adriana.
Unfeeling fools can with such wrongs
  dispense.
I know his eye doth homage otherwhere;
Or else what lets it but he would be here?
Sister, you know he promis'd me a
  chain;—
Would that alone, alone he would detain,
So he would keep fair quarter with his
  bed!
I see the jewel best enamelled
Will lose his beauty; yet the gold 'bides
  still
That others touch, yet often touching will
Wear gold; and no man that hath a name
By falsehood and corruption doth it
  shame.
Since that my beauty cannot please his
  eye,
I'll weep what's left away, and weeping
  die.

Luciana.
How many fond fools serve mad jealousy!
                    [Exeunt.]

SCENE II

The same.

[*Enter* ANTIPHOLUS OF SYRACUSE.]

ANTIPHOLUS OF SYRACUSE.

The gold I gave to Dromio is laid up
Safe at the Centaur; and the heedful slave
Is wander'd forth in care to seek me out.
By computation and mine host's report
I could not speak with Dromio since at
    first
I sent him from the mart. See, here he
    comes.

[*Enter* DROMIO OF SYRACUSE.]

How now, sir! is your merry humour
    alter'd?
As you love strokes, so jest with me again.
You know no Centaur? you receiv'd no
    gold?
Your mistress sent to have me home to
    dinner?
My house was at the Phoenix? Wast thou
    mad,
That thus so madly thou didst answer me?

DROMIO OF SYRACUSE.

What answer, sir? when spake I such a
    word?

ANTIPHOLUS OF SYRACUSE.

Even now, even here, not half-an-hour
    since.

DROMIO OF SYRACUSE.

I did not see you since you sent me hence,
Home to the Centaur with the gold you
    gave me.

ANTIPHOLUS OF SYRACUSE.

Villain, thou didst deny the gold's receipt;
And told'st me of a mistress and a dinner;
For which, I hope, thou felt'st I was
    displeas'd.

DROMIO OF SYRACUSE.

I am glad to see you in this merry vein:
What means this jest? I pray you, master,
    tell me.

ANTIPHOLUS OF SYRACUSE.

Yea, dost thou jeer and flout me in the
    teeth?
Think'st thou I jest? Hold, take thou that,
    and that.

[*Beating him.*]

DROMIO OF SYRACUSE.

Hold, sir, for God's sake: now your jest is
    earnest:
Upon what bargain do you give it me?

ANTIPHOLUS OF SYRACUSE.

Because that I familiarly sometimes
Do use you for my fool, and chat with
    you,
Your sauciness will jest upon my love,
And make a common of my serious hours.
When the sun shines let foolish gnats
    make sport,
But creep in crannies when he hides his
    beams.
If you will jest with me, know my aspect,
And fashion your demeanour to my looks,
Or I will beat this method in your sconce.

DROMIO OF SYRACUSE.

Sconce, call you it? so you would leave
battering, I had rather have it a head: an
you use these blows long, I must get a
sconce for my head, and ensconce it too; or
else I shall seek my wit in my shoulders.—
But I pray, sir, why am I beaten?

ANTIPHOLUS OF SYRACUSE.

Dost thou not know?

DROMIO OF SYRACUSE.

Nothing, sir, but that I am beaten.

ANTIPHOLUS OF SYRACUSE.

Shall I tell you why?

DROMIO OF SYRACUSE.

Ay, sir, and wherefore; for, they say, every
    why hath a wherefore.—

ANTIPHOLUS OF SYRACUSE.

Why, first,—for flouting me; and then
    wherefore,
For urging it the second time to me.

DROMIO OF SYRACUSE.

Was there ever any man thus beaten out
    of season,
When in the why and the wherefore is
    neither rhyme nor reason?—
Well, sir, I thank you.

ANTIPHOLUS OF SYRACUSE.

Thank me, sir! for what?

DROMIO OF SYRACUSE.

Marry, sir, for this something that you
    gave me for nothing.

ANTIPHOLUS OF SYRACUSE.
I'll make you amends next, to give you nothing for something.—
But say, sir, is it dinner-time?

DROMIO OF SYRACUSE.
No, sir; I think the meat wants that I have.

ANTIPHOLUS OF SYRACUSE.
In good time, sir, what's that?

DROMIO OF SYRACUSE.
Basting.

ANTIPHOLUS OF SYRACUSE.
Well, sir, then 'twill be dry.

DROMIO OF SYRACUSE.
If it be, sir, I pray you eat none of it.

ANTIPHOLUS OF SYRACUSE.
Your reason?

DROMIO OF SYRACUSE.
Lest it make you choleric, and purchase me another dry basting.

ANTIPHOLUS OF SYRACUSE.
Well, sir, learn to jest in good time:
There's a time for all things.

DROMIO OF SYRACUSE.
I durst have denied that before you were so choleric.

ANTIPHOLUS OF SYRACUSE.
By what rule, sir?

DROMIO OF SYRACUSE.
Marry, sir, by a rule as plain as the plain bald pate of Father Time himself.

ANTIPHOLUS OF SYRACUSE.
Let's hear it.

DROMIO OF SYRACUSE.
There's no time for a man to recover his hair, that grows bald by nature.

ANTIPHOLUS OF SYRACUSE.
May he not do it by fine and recovery?

DROMIO OF SYRACUSE.
Yes, to pay a fine for a periwig, and recover the lost hair of another man.

ANTIPHOLUS OF SYRACUSE.
Why is Time such a niggard of hair, being, as it is, so plentiful an excrement?

DROMIO OF SYRACUSE.
Because it is a blessing that he bestows on beasts: and what he hath scanted men in hair he hath given them in wit.

ANTIPHOLUS OF SYRACUSE.
Why, but there's many a man hath more hair than wit.

DROMIO OF SYRACUSE.
Not a man of those but he hath the wit to lose his hair.

ANTIPHOLUS OF SYRACUSE.
Why, thou didst conclude hairy men plain dealers without wit.

DROMIO OF SYRACUSE.
The plainer dealer, the sooner lost: yet he loseth it in a kind of jollity.

ANTIPHOLUS OF SYRACUSE.
For what reason?

DROMIO OF SYRACUSE.
For two; and sound ones too.

ANTIPHOLUS OF SYRACUSE.
Nay, not sound, I pray you.

DROMIO OF SYRACUSE.
Sure ones, then.

ANTIPHOLUS OF SYRACUSE.
Nay, not sure, in a thing falsing.

DROMIO OF SYRACUSE.
Certain ones, then.

ANTIPHOLUS OF SYRACUSE.
Name them.

DROMIO OF SYRACUSE.
The one, to save the money that he spends in tiring; the other, that at dinner they should not drop in his porridge.

ANTIPHOLUS OF SYRACUSE.
You would all this time have proved there is no time for all things.

DROMIO OF SYRACUSE.
Marry, and did, sir; namely, no time to recover hair lost by nature.

ANTIPHOLUS OF SYRACUSE.
But your reason was not substantial why there is no time to recover.

DROMIO OF SYRACUSE.
Thus I mend it: Time himself is bald, and, therefore, to the world's end will have bald followers.

ANTIPHOLUS OF SYRACUSE.
I knew 'twould be a bald conclusion:
But, soft! who wafts us yonder?

[*Enter* ADRIANA *and* LUCIANA.]

ADRIANA.
Ay, ay, Antipholus, look strange and frown;
Some other mistress hath thy sweet
    aspects:
I am not Adriana, nor thy wife.
The time was, once, when thou unurg'd
    wouldst vow
That never words were music to thine ear,
That never object pleasing in thine eye,
That never touch well welcome to thy
    hand,
That never meat sweet-savour'd in thy
    taste,
Unless I spake, or look'd, or touch'd, or
    carv'd to thee.
How comes it now, my husband, oh, how
    comes it,
That thou art then estranged from thyself?
Thyself I call it, being strange to me,
That, undividable, incorporate,
Am better than thy dear self's better part.
Ah, do not tear away thyself from me;
For know, my love, as easy mayst thou fall
A drop of water in the breaking gulf,
And take unmingled thence that drop
    again,
Without addition or diminishing,
As take from me thyself, and not me too.
How dearly would it touch thee to the
    quick,
Should'st thou but hear I were licentious,
And that this body, consecrate to thee,
By ruffian lust should be contaminate!
Wouldst thou not spit at me and spurn
    at me,
And hurl the name of husband in my face,
And tear the stain'd skin off my harlot
    brow,
And from my false hand cut the wedding-
    ring,
And break it with a deep-divorcing vow?
I know thou canst; and, therefore, see thou
    do it.
I am possess'd with an adulterate blot;
My blood is mingled with the crime of
    lust:
For if we two be one, and thou play false,
I do digest the poison of thy flesh,

Being strumpeted by thy contagion.
Keep then fair league and truce with thy
    true bed;
I live dis-stain'd, thou undishonoured.
ANTIPHOLUS OF SYRACUSE.
Plead you to me, fair dame? I know you
    not:
In Ephesus I am but two hours old,
As strange unto your town as to your talk;
Who, every word by all my wit being
    scann'd,
Want wit in all one word to understand.
LUCIANA.
Fie, brother! how the world is chang'd
    with you:
When were you wont to use my sister
    thus?
She sent for you by Dromio home to
    dinner.
ANTIPHOLUS OF SYRACUSE.
By Dromio?
DROMIO OF SYRACUSE.
By me?
ADRIANA.
By thee; and this thou didst return from
    him,—
That he did buffet thee, and in his blows
Denied my house for his, me for his wife.
ANTIPHOLUS OF SYRACUSE.
Did you converse, sir, with this
    gentlewoman?
What is the course and drift of your
    compact?
DROMIO OF SYRACUSE.
I, sir? I never saw her till this time.
ANTIPHOLUS OF SYRACUSE.
Villain, thou liest; for even her very words
Didst thou deliver to me on the mart.
DROMIO OF SYRACUSE.
I never spake with her in all my life.
ANTIPHOLUS OF SYRACUSE.
How can she thus, then, call us by our
    names,
Unless it be by inspiration?
ADRIANA.
How ill agrees it with your gravity
To counterfeit thus grossly with your slave,
Abetting him to thwart me in my mood!

Be it my wrong, you are from me exempt,
But wrong not that wrong with a more
  contempt.
Come, I will fasten on this sleeve of thine:
Thou art an elm, my husband, I a vine,
Whose weakness, married to thy stronger
  state,
Makes me with thy strength to
  communicate:
If aught possess thee from me, it is dross,
Usurping ivy, brier, or idle moss;
Who all, for want of pruning, with
  intrusion
Infect thy sap, and live on thy confusion.

Antipholus of Syracuse.
To me she speaks; she moves me for her
  theme:
What, was I married to her in my dream?
Or sleep I now, and think I hear all this?
What error drives our eyes and ears amiss?
Until I know this sure uncertainty
I'll entertain the offer'd fallacy.

Luciana.
Dromio, go bid the servants spread for
  dinner.

Dromio of Syracuse.
O, for my beads! I cross me for a sinner.
This is the fairy land;—O spite of spites!
We talk with goblins, owls, and sprites;
If we obey them not, this will ensue,
They'll suck our breath, or pinch us black
  and blue.

Luciana.
Why prat'st thou to thyself, and answer'st
  not?
Dromio, thou drone, thou snail, thou slug,
  thou sot!

Dromio of Syracuse.
I am transformed, master, am not I?

Antipholus of Syracuse.
I think thou art in mind, and so am I.

Dromio of Syracuse.
Nay, master, both in mind and in my
  shape.

Antipholus of Syracuse.
Thou hast thine own form.

Dromio of Syracuse.
                    No, I am an ape.

Luciana.
If thou art chang'd to aught, 'tis to an ass.

Dromio of Syracuse.
'Tis true; she rides me, and I long for
  grass.
'Tis so, I am an ass; else it could never be
But I should know her as well as she
  knows me.

Adriana.
Come, come, no longer will I be a fool,
To put the finger in the eye and weep,
Whilst man and master laughs my woes
  to scorn.—
Come, sir, to dinner;—Dromio, keep the
  gate:—
Husband, I'll dine above with you to-day,
And shrive you of a thousand idle
  pranks:—
Sirrah, if any ask you for your master,
Say he dines forth, and let no creature
  enter.—
Come, sister:—Dromio, play the porter
  well.

Antipholus of Syracuse.
Am I in earth, in heaven, or in hell?
Sleeping or waking, mad, or well-advis'd?
Known unto these, and to myself disguis'd!
I'll say as they say, and persever so,
And in this mist at all adventures go.

Dromio of Syracuse.
Master, shall I be porter at the gate?

Adriana.
Ay; and let none enter, lest I break your
  pate.

Luciana.
Come, come, Antipholus, we dine too late.
                              [*Exeunt.*]

ACT III
SCENE I
The same.

[*Enter* Antipholus of Ephesus, Dromio
of Ephesus, Angelo, *and* Balthazar.]

Antipholus of Ephesus.
Good Signior Angelo, you must excuse
  us all.
My wife is shrewish when I keep not
  hours:

Say that I linger'd with you at your shop
To see the making of her carcanet,
And that to-morrow you will bring it
  home.
But here's a villain that would face me
  down.
He met me on the mart; and that I beat
  him,
And charg'd him with a thousand marks
  in gold;
And that I did deny my wife and house:—
Thou drunkard, thou, what didst thou
  mean by this?

Dromio of Ephesus.
Say what you will, sir, but I know what I
  know:
That you beat me at the mart I have your
  hand to show;
If the skin were parchment, and the blows
  you gave were ink,
Your own handwriting would tell you
  what I think.

Antipholus of Ephesus.
I think thou art an ass.

Dromio of Ephesus.
Marry, so it doth appear
By the wrongs I suffer and the blows I
  bear.
I should kick, being kick'd; and being at
  that pass,
You would keep from my heels, and
  beware of an ass.

Antipholus of Ephesus.
You are sad, Signior Balthazar; pray God
  our cheer
May answer my good will and your good
  welcome here.

Balthazar.
I hold your dainties cheap, sir, and your
  welcome dear.

Antipholus of Ephesus.
O, Signior Balthazar, either at flesh or fish,
A table full of welcome makes scarce one
  dainty dish.

Balthazar.
Good meat, sir, is common; that every
  churl affords.

Antipholus of Ephesus.
And welcome more common; for that's
  nothing but words.

Balthazar.
Small cheer and great welcome makes a
  merry feast.

Antipholus of Ephesus.
Ay, to a niggardly host and more sparing
  guest.
But though my cates be mean, take them
  in good part;
Better cheer may you have, but not with
  better heart.
But, soft; my door is lock'd: go bid them
  let us in.

Dromio of Ephesus.
Maud, Bridget, Marian, Cicely, Gillian, Jen!

Dromio of Syracuse. [*Within.*]
Mome, malt-horse, capon, coxcomb, idiot,
  patch!
Either get thee from the door, or sit down
  at the hatch:
Dost thou conjure for wenches, that thou
  call'st for such store,
When one is one too many? Go, get thee
  from the door.

Dromio of Ephesus.
What patch is made our porter? My
  master stays in the street.

Dromio of Syracuse.
Let him walk from whence he came, lest
  he catch cold on's feet.

Antipholus of Ephesus.
Who talks within there? Ho, open the
  door!

Dromio of Syracuse.
Right, sir; I'll tell you when an you'll tell
  me wherefore.

Antipholus of Ephesus.
Wherefore! For my dinner: I have not
  dined to-day.

Dromio of Syracuse.
Nor to-day here you must not; come again
  when you may.

Antipholus of Ephesus.
What art thou that keep'st me out from
  the house I owe?

DROMIO OF SYRACUSE.
The porter for this time, sir, and my name
   is Dromio.
DROMIO OF EPHESUS.
O villain, thou hast stolen both mine office
   and my name;
The one ne'er got me credit, the other
   mickle blame.
If thou hadst been Dromio to-day in my
   place,
Thou wouldst have chang'd thy face for a
   name, or thy name for an ass.
LUCE. [*Within.*]
What a coil is there! Dromio, who are
   those at the gate?
DROMIO OF EPHESUS.
Let my master in, Luce.
LUCE.
         Faith, no, he comes too late;
And so tell your master.
DROMIO OF EPHESUS.
         O Lord, I must laugh;—
Have at you with a proverb: Shall I set in
   my staff?
LUCE.
Have at you with another, that's: When?
   can you tell?
DROMIO OF SYRACUSE.
If thy name be called Luce,—
Luce, thou hast answer'd him well.
ANTIPHOLUS OF EPHESUS.
Do you hear, you minion? you'll let us in,
   I hope?
LUCE.
I thought to have ask'd you.
DROMIO OF SYRACUSE.
         And you said no.
DROMIO OF EPHESUS.
So, come, help: well struck; there was blow
   for blow.
ANTIPHOLUS OF EPHESUS.
Thou baggage, let me in.
LUCE.
         Can you tell for whose sake?
DROMIO OF EPHESUS.
Master, knock the door hard.

LUCE.
         Let him knock till it ache.
ANTIPHOLUS OF EPHESUS.
You'll cry for this, minion, if I beat the
   door down.
LUCE.
What needs all that, and a pair of stocks
   in the town?
ADRIANA. [*Within.*]
Who is that at the door, that keeps all this
   noise?
DROMIO OF SYRACUSE.
By my troth, your town is troubled with
   unruly boys.
ANTIPHOLUS OF EPHESUS.
Are you there, wife? you might have come
   before.
ADRIANA.
Your wife, sir knave! go, get you from the
   door.
DROMIO OF EPHESUS.
If you went in pain, master, this knave
   would go sore.
ANGELO.
Here is neither cheer, sir, nor welcome: we
   would fain have either.
BALTHAZAR.
In debating which was best, we shall part
   with neither.
DROMIO OF EPHESUS.
They stand at the door, master; bid them
   welcome hither.
ANTIPHOLUS OF EPHESUS.
There is something in the wind, that we
   cannot get in.
DROMIO OF EPHESUS.
You would say so, master, if your garments
   were thin.
Your cake here is warm within; you stand
   here in the cold:
It would make a man mad as a buck, to be
   so bought and sold.
ANTIPHOLUS OF EPHESUS.
Go, fetch me something, I'll break ope
   the gate.
DROMIO OF SYRACUSE.
Break any breaking here, and I'll break
   your knave's pate.

DROMIO OF EPHESUS.
A man may break a word with you, sir;
   and words are but wind;
Ay, and break it in your face, so he break it
   not behind.
DROMIO OF SYRACUSE.
It seems thou want'st breaking; out upon
   thee, hind!
DROMIO OF EPHESUS.
Here's too much out upon thee: I pray
   thee, let me in.
DROMIO OF SYRACUSE.
Ay, when fowls have no feathers and fish
   have no fin.
ANTIPHOLUS OF EPHESUS.
Well, I'll break in; go borrow me a crow.
DROMIO OF EPHESUS.
A crow without feather; master, mean
   you so?
For a fish without a fin, there's a fowl
   without a feather:
If a crow help us in, sirrah, we'll pluck a
   crow together.
ANTIPHOLUS OF EPHESUS.
Go, get thee gone; fetch me an iron crow.
BALTHAZAR.
Have patience, sir: O, let it not be so:
Herein you war against your reputation,
And draw within the compass of suspect
The unviolated honour of your wife.
Once this,—your long experience of her
   wisdom,
Her sober virtue, years, and modesty,
Plead on her part some cause to you
   unknown;
And doubt not, sir, but she will well excuse
Why at this time the doors are made
   against you.
Be rul'd by me; depart in patience,
And let us to the Tiger all to dinner:
And, about evening, come yourself alone,
To know the reason of this strange
   restraint.
If by strong hand you offer to break in,
Now in the stirring passage of the day,
A vulgar comment will be made of it;
And that supposed by the common rout
Against your yet ungalled estimation
That may with foul intrusion enter in,
And dwell upon your grave when you are
   dead:
For slander lives upon succession,
For ever hous'd where it gets possession.
ANTIPHOLUS OF EPHESUS.
You have prevail'd. I will depart in quiet,
And, in despite of mirth, mean to be
   merry.
I know a wench of excellent discourse,—
Pretty and witty; wild, and yet, too,
   gentle;—
There will we dine: this woman that I
   mean,
My wife,—but, I protest, without
   desert,—
Hath oftentimes upbraided me withal;
To her will we to dinner.—Get you home
And fetch the chain: by this I know 'tis
   made:
Bring it, I pray you, to the Porcupine;
For there's the house; that chain will I
   bestow,—
Be it for nothing but to spite my wife,—
Upon mine hostess there: good sir, make
   haste:
Since mine own doors refuse to entertain
   me,
I'll knock elsewhere, to see if they'll
   disdain me.
ANGELO.
I'll meet you at that place some hour
   hence.
ANTIPHOLUS OF EPHESUS.
Do so; this jest shall cost me some
   expense.
                    [*Exeunt.*]

SCENE II
The same.
[*Enter* LUCIANA *with* ANTIPHOLUS OF
SYRACUSE.]
LUCIANA.
And may it be that you have quite forgot
A husband's office? Shall, Antipholus,
Even in the spring of love, thy love-
   springs rot?
Shall love, in building, grow so ruinate?

If you did wed my sister for her wealth,
Then for her wealth's sake use her with
   more kindness;
Or, if you like elsewhere, do it by stealth;
Muffle your false love with some show of
   blindness;
Let not my sister read it in your eye;
Be not thy tongue thy own shame's orator;
Look sweet, speak fair, become disloyalty;
Apparel vice like virtue's harbinger;
Bear a fair presence though your heart be
   tainted;
Teach sin the carriage of a holy saint;
Be secret-false: what need she be
   acquainted?
What simple thief brags of his own
   attaint?
'Tis double wrong, to truant with your bed
And let her read it in thy looks at board:—
Shame hath a bastard fame, well managed;
Ill deeds is doubled with an evil word.
Alas, poor women! make us but believe,
Being compact of credit, that you love us:
Though others have the arm, show us the
   sleeve;
We in your motion turn, and you may
   move us.
Then, gentle brother, get you in again;
Comfort my sister, cheer her, call her wife:
'Tis holy sport to be a little vain
When the sweet breath of flattery
   conquers strife.

Antipholus of Syracuse.

Sweet mistress,—what your name is else,
   I know not,
Nor by what wonder you do hit on
   mine,—
Less, in your knowledge and your grace,
   you show not
Than our earth's wonder: more than earth
   divine.
Teach me, dear creature, how to think and
   speak;
Lay open to my earthy gross conceit,
Smother'd in errors, feeble, shallow, weak,
The folded meaning of your words' deceit.
Against my soul's pure truth why labour
   you

To make it wander in an unknown field?
Are you a god? would you create me new?
Transform me, then, and to your power
   I'll yield.
But if that I am I, then well I know
Your weeping sister is no wife of mine,
Nor to her bed no homage do I owe:
Far more, far more, to you do I decline.
O, train me not, sweet mermaid, with thy
   note,
To drown me in thy sister's flood of tears:
Sing, siren, for thyself, and I will dote;
Spread o'er the silver waves thy golden
   hairs,
And as a bed I'll take thee, and there lie;
And, in that glorious supposition, think
He gains by death that hath such means
   to die:—
Let love, being light, be drowned if she
   sink!

Luciana.

What, are you mad, that you do reason so?

Antipholus of Syracuse.

Not mad, but mated; how, I do not know.

Luciana.

It is a fault that springeth from your eye.

Antipholus of Syracuse.

For gazing on your beams, fair sun, being
   by.

Luciana.

Gaze where you should, and that will clear
   your sight.

Antipholus of Syracuse.

As good to wink, sweet love, as look on
   night.

Luciana.

Why call you me love? call my sister so.

Antipholus of Syracuse.

Thy sister's sister.

Luciana.

That's my sister.

Antipholus of Syracuse.

No;
It is thyself, mine own self's better part;
Mine eye's clear eye, my dear heart's dearer
   heart;
My food, my fortune, and my sweet hope's
   aim,

My sole earth's heaven, and my heaven's
   claim.
LUCIANA.
All this my sister is, or else should be.
ANTIPHOLUS OF SYRACUSE.
Call thyself sister, sweet, for I aim thee;
Thee will I love, and with thee lead my
   life:
Thou hast no husband yet, nor I no wife;
Give me thy hand.
LUCIANA.
                    O, soft, sir, hold you still;
I'll fetch my sister to get her good-will.
            [*Exit* LUCIANA.]
      [*Enter from the house of Antipholus of
      Ephesus*, DROMIO OF SYRACUSE.]
ANTIPHOLUS OF SYRACUSE.
Why, how now, Dromio? where runn'st
thou so fast?
DROMIO OF SYRACUSE.
Do you know me, sir? am I Dromio? am I
your man? am I myself?
ANTIPHOLUS OF SYRACUSE.
Thou art Dromio, thou art my man, thou
art thyself.
DROMIO OF SYRACUSE.
I am an ass, I am a woman's man, and
beside myself.
ANTIPHOLUS OF SYRACUSE.
What woman's man? and how besides
thyself?
DROMIO OF SYRACUSE.
Marry, sir, besides myself, I am due to
a woman; one that claims me, one that
haunts me, one that will have me.
ANTIPHOLUS OF SYRACUSE.
What claim lays she to thee?
DROMIO OF SYRACUSE.
Marry, sir, such claim as you would lay to
your horse: and she would have me as a
beast; not that, I being a beast, she would
have me; but that she, being a very beastly
creature, lays claim to me.
ANTIPHOLUS OF SYRACUSE.
What is she?
DROMIO OF SYRACUSE.
A very reverent body; ay, such a one as
a man may not speak of without he say

sir-reverence. I have but lean luck in
the match, and yet is she a wondrous fat
marriage.
ANTIPHOLUS OF SYRACUSE.
How dost thou mean?—a fat marriage?
DROMIO OF SYRACUSE.
Marry, sir, she's the kitchen-wench, and all
grease; and I know not what use to put her
to, but to make a lamp of her and run from
her by her own light. I warrant, her rags,
and the tallow in them will burn a Poland
winter: if she lives till doomsday, she'll burn
week longer than the whole world.
ANTIPHOLUS OF SYRACUSE.
What complexion is she of?
DROMIO OF SYRACUSE.
Swart, like my shoe; but her face nothing
like so clean kept: for why? she sweats, a
man may go over shoes in the grime of it.
ANTIPHOLUS OF SYRACUSE.
That's a fault that water will mend.
DROMIO OF SYRACUSE.
No, sir, 'tis in grain; Noah's flood could not
do it.
ANTIPHOLUS OF SYRACUSE.
What's her name?
DROMIO OF SYRACUSE.
Nell, sir; but her name and three-quarters,
that is an ell and three quarters, will not
measure her from hip to hip.
ANTIPHOLUS OF SYRACUSE.
Then she bears some breadth?
DROMIO OF SYRACUSE.
No longer from head to foot than from hip
to hip: she is spherical, like a globe: I could
find out countries in her.
ANTIPHOLUS OF SYRACUSE.
In what part of her body stands Ireland?
DROMIO OF SYRACUSE.
Marry, sir, in her buttocks; I found it out
by the bogs.
ANTIPHOLUS OF SYRACUSE.
Where Scotland?
DROMIO OF SYRACUSE.
I found it by the barrenness, hard in the
palm of the hand.
ANTIPHOLUS OF SYRACUSE.
Where France?

DROMIO OF SYRACUSE.
In her forehead; armed and reverted, making war against her hair.
ANTIPHOLUS OF SYRACUSE.
Where England?
DROMIO OF SYRACUSE.
I looked for the chalky cliffs, but I could find no whiteness in them; but I guess it stood in her chin, by the salt rheum that ran between France and it.
ANTIPHOLUS OF SYRACUSE.
Where Spain?
DROMIO OF SYRACUSE.
Faith, I saw it not; but I felt it hot in her breath.
ANTIPHOLUS OF SYRACUSE.
Where America,—the Indies?
DROMIO OF SYRACUSE.
O, sir, upon her nose, an o'er embellished with rubies, carbuncles, sapphires, declining their rich aspect to the hot breath of Spain; who sent whole armadoes of carracks to be ballast at her nose.
ANTIPHOLUS OF SYRACUSE.
Where stood Belgia,—the Netherlands?
DROMIO OF SYRACUSE.
O, sir, I did not look so low.—To conclude: this drudge or diviner laid claim to me; called me Dromio; swore I was assured to her; told me what privy marks I had about me, as the mark of my shoulder, the mole in my neck, the great wart on my left arm, that I, amazed, ran from her as a witch: and, I think, if my breast had not been made of faith and my heart of steel, she had transformed me to a curtail-dog, and made me turn i' the wheel.
ANTIPHOLUS OF SYRACUSE.
Go, hie thee presently post to the road;
An if the wind blow any way from shore,
I will not harbour in this town to-night.
If any bark put forth, come to the mart,
Where I will walk till thou return to me.
If every one knows us, and we know none,
'Tis time, I think, to trudge, pack and be gone.

DROMIO OF SYRACUSE.
As from a bear a man would run for life,
So fly I from her that would be my wife.
[*Exit.*]
ANTIPHOLUS OF SYRACUSE.
There's none but witches do inhabit here;
And therefore 'tis high time that I were hence.
She that doth call me husband, even my soul
Doth for a wife abhor; but her fair sister,
Possess'd with such a gentle sovereign grace,
Of such enchanting presence and discourse,
Hath almost made me traitor to myself:
But, lest myself be guilty to self-wrong,
I'll stop mine ears against the mermaid's song.
[*Enter* ANGELO.]
ANGELO.
Master Antipholus?
ANTIPHOLUS OF SYRACUSE.
Ay, that's my name.
ANGELO.
I know it well, sir. Lo, here is the chain;
I thought to have ta'en you at the Porcupine:
The chain unfinish'd made me stay thus long.
ANTIPHOLUS OF SYRACUSE.
What is your will that I shall do with this?
ANGELO.
What please yourself, sir; I have made it for you.
ANTIPHOLUS OF SYRACUSE.
Made it for me, sir! I bespoke it not.
ANGELO.
Not once nor twice, but twenty times you have:
Go home with it, and please your wife withal;
And soon at supper-time I'll visit you,
And then receive my money for the chain.
ANTIPHOLUS OF SYRACUSE.
I pray you, sir, receive the money now,
For fear you ne'er see chain nor money more.

ANGELO.
You are a merry man, sir; fare you well.
                    [*Exit.*]
ANTIPHOLUS OF SYRACUSE.
What I should think of this I cannot tell:
But this I think, there's no man is so vain
That would refuse so fair an offer'd chain.
I see a man here needs not live by shifts,
When in the streets he meets such golden
    gifts.
I'll to the mart, and there for Dromio stay;
If any ship put out, then straight away.
                    [*Exit.*]

ACT IV
SCENE I
The same.
[*Enter a* MERCHANT, ANGELO, *and an*
OFFICER.]

MERCHANT.
You know, since Pentecost the sum is due,
And since I have not much importun'd
    you;
Nor now I had not, but that I am bound
To Persia, and want guilders for my
    voyage;
Therefore make present satisfaction,
Or I'll attach you by this officer.
ANGELO.
Even just the sum that I do owe to you
Is growing to me by Antipholus;
And in the instant that I met with you
He had of me a chain; at five o'clock
I shall receive the money for the same:
Pleaseth you walk with me down to his
    house,
I will discharge my bond, and thank you
    too.
[*Enter* ANTIPHOLUS OF EPHESUS, *and*
DROMIO OF EPHESUS.]
OFFICER.
That labour may you save: see where he
    comes.
ANTIPHOLUS OF EPHESUS.
While I go to the goldsmith's house, go
    thou
And buy a rope's end; that will I bestow
Among my wife and her confederates,

For locking me out of my doors by day.—
But, soft; I see the goldsmith: get thee
    gone;
Buy thou a rope, and bring it home to me.
DROMIO OF EPHESUS.
I buy a thousand pound a year! I buy a
    rope!
                    [*Exit* DROMIO.]
ANTIPHOLUS OF EPHESUS.
A man is well holp up that trusts to you:
I promised your presence, and the chain;
But neither chain nor goldsmith came
    to me:
Belike you thought our love would last
    too long,
If it were chain'd together; and therefore
    came not.
ANGELO.
Saving your merry humour, here's the
    note,
How much your chain weighs to the
    utmost carat;
The fineness of the gold, and chargeful
    fashion;
Which doth amount to three odd ducats
    more
Than I stand debted to this gentleman:
I pray you, see him presently discharg'd,
For he is bound to sea, and stays but for it.
ANTIPHOLUS OF EPHESUS.
I am not furnished with the present
    money;
Besides I have some business in the town:
Good Signior, take the stranger to my
    house,
And with you take the chain, and bid my
    wife
Disburse the sum on the receipt thereof;
Perchance I will be there as soon as you.
ANGELO.
Then you will bring the chain to her
    yourself?
ANTIPHOLUS OF EPHESUS.
No; bear it with you, lest I come not time
    enough.
ANGELO.
Well, sir, I will: have you the chain about
    you?

ANTIPHOLUS OF EPHESUS.
An if I have not, sir, I hope you have,
Or else you may return without your
    money.
ANGELO.
Nay, come, I pray you, sir, give me the
    chain;
Both wind and tide stays for this
    gentleman,
And I, to blame, have held him here too
    long.
ANTIPHOLUS OF EPHESUS.
Good Lord, you use this dalliance to
    excuse
Your breach of promise to the Porcupine:
I should have chid you for not bringing it,
But, like a shrew, you first begin to brawl.
MERCHANT.
The hour steals on; I pray you, sir,
    despatch.
ANGELO.
You hear how he importunes me: the
    chain,—
ANTIPHOLUS OF EPHESUS.
Why, give it to my wife, and fetch your
    money.
ANGELO.
Come, come, you know I gave it you even
    now;
Either send the chain or send by me some
    token.
ANTIPHOLUS OF EPHESUS.
Fie! now you run this humour out of
    breath:
Come, where's the chain? I pray you, let
    me see it.
MERCHANT.
My business cannot brook this dalliance:
Good sir, say whe'r you'll answer me or no;
If not, I'll leave him to the officer.
ANTIPHOLUS OF EPHESUS.
I answer you! What should I answer you?
ANGELO.
The money that you owe me for the chain.
ANTIPHOLUS OF EPHESUS.
I owe you none till I receive the chain.
ANGELO.
You know I gave it you half-an-hour since.

ANTIPHOLUS OF EPHESUS.
You gave me none: you wrong me much
    to say so.
ANGELO.
You wrong me more, sir, in denying it:
Consider how it stands upon my credit.
MERCHANT.
Well, officer, arrest him at my suit.
OFFICER.
I do; and charge you in the Duke's name
    to obey me.
ANGELO.
This touches me in reputation:
Either consent to pay this sum for me,
Or I attach you by this officer.
ANTIPHOLUS OF EPHESUS.
Consent to pay thee that I never had!
Arrest me, foolish fellow, if thou dar'st.
ANGELO.
Here is thy fee; arrest him, officer:—
I would not spare my brother in this
    case,
If he should scorn me so apparently.
OFFICER.
I do arrest you, sir: you hear the suit.
ANTIPHOLUS OF EPHESUS.
I do obey thee till I give thee bail:—
But, sirrah, you shall buy this sport as dear
As all the metal in your shop will answer.
ANGELO.
Sir, sir, I shall have law in Ephesus,
To your notorious shame, I doubt it not.
    [*Enter* DROMIO OF SYRACUSE.]
DROMIO OF SYRACUSE.
Master, there's a bark of Epidamnum
That stays but till her owner comes aboard,
And then, sir, bears away: our fraughtage,
    sir,
I have convey'd aboard; and I have bought
The oil, the balsamum, and aqua-vitae.
The ship is in her trim; the merry wind
Blows fair from land; they stay for nought
    at all
But for their owner, master, and yourself.
ANTIPHOLUS OF EPHESUS.
How now! a madman? Why, thou peevish
    sheep,
What ship of Epidamnum stays for me?

Dromio of Syracuse.
A ship you sent me to, to hire waftage.
Antipholus of Ephesus.
Thou drunken slave! I sent the for a rope;
And told thee to what purpose and what
    end.
Dromio of Syracuse.
You sent me, sir, for a rope's-end as soon:
You sent me to the bay, sir, for a bark.
Antipholus of Ephesus.
I will debate this matter at more leisure,
And teach your ears to list me with more
    heed.
To Adriana, villain, hie thee straight:
Give her this key, and tell her, in the desk
That's cover'd o'er with Turkish tapestry
There is a purse of ducats; let her send it:
Tell her I am arrested in the street,
And that shall bail me: hie thee, slave; be
    gone.
On, officer, to prison till it come.
    [*Exeunt* Merchant, Angelo, Officer,
       and Antipholus of Ephesus.]
Dromio of Syracuse.
To Adriana! that is where we din'd,
Where Dowsabel did claim me for her
    husband:
She is too big, I hope, for me to compass.
Thither I must, although against my will,
For servants must their masters' minds
    fulfil.
            [*Exit.*]

SCENE II
The same.
[*Enter* Adriana *and* Luciana.]
Adriana.
Ah, Luciana, did he tempt thee so?
Might'st thou perceive austerely in his eye
That he did plead in earnest, yea or no?
Look'd he or red or pale, or sad or merrily?
What observation mad'st thou in this case
Of his heart's meteors tilting in his face?
Luciana.
First he denied you had in him no right.
Adriana.
He meant he did me none; the more my
    spite.

Luciana.
Then swore he that he was a stranger here.
Adriana.
And true he swore, though yet forsworn
    he were.
Luciana.
Then pleaded I for you.
Adriana.
                 And what said he?
Luciana.
That love I begg'd for you he begg'd of me.
Adriana.
With what persuasion did he tempt thy
    love?
Luciana.
With words that in an honest suit might
    move.
First he did praise my beauty, then my
    speech.
Adriana.
Didst speak him fair?
Luciana.
              Have patience, I beseech.
Adriana.
I cannot, nor I will not hold me still;
My tongue, though not my heart, shall
    have his will.
He is deformed, crooked, old, and sere,
Ill-fac'd, worse bodied, shapeless
    everywhere;
Vicious, ungentle, foolish, blunt, unkind;
Stigmatical in making, worse in mind.
Luciana.
Who would be jealous then of such a one?
No evil lost is wail'd when it is gone.
Adriana.
Ah! but I think him better than I say,
And yet would herein others' eyes were
    worse:
Far from her nest the lapwing cries, away;
My heart prays for him, though my
    tongue do curse.
        [*Enter* Dromio of Syracuse.]
Dromio of Syracuse.
Here, go; the desk, the purse: sweet now,
    make haste.
Luciana.
How hast thou lost thy breath?

Dromio of Syracuse.
By running fast.
Adriana.
Where is thy master, Dromio? is he well?
Dromio of Syracuse.
No, he's in Tartar limbo, worse than hell.
A devil in an everlasting garment hath
  him;
One whose hard heart is button'd up with
  steel;
A fiend, a fairy, pitiless and rough;
A wolf—nay worse, a fellow all in buff;
A back-friend, a shoulder-clapper, one
  that countermands
The passages of alleys, creeks, and narrow
  lands;
A hound that runs counter, and yet draws
  dry foot well;
One that, before the judgment, carries
  poor souls to hell.
Adriana.
Why, man, what is the matter?
Dromio of Syracuse.
I do not know the matter: he is 'rested on
  the case.
Adriana.
What, is he arrested? tell me at whose
  suit?
Dromio of Syracuse.
I know not at whose suit he is arrested,
  well;
But he's in a suit of buff which 'rested him,
  that can I tell.
Will you send him, mistress, redemption,
  the money in his desk?
Adriana.
Go fetch it, sister. This I wonder at,
          [*Exit* Luciana.]
Thus he unknown to me should be in
  debt.—
Tell me, was he arrested on a band?
Dromio of Syracuse.
Not on a band, but on a stronger thing;
A chain, a chain: do you not hear it ring?
Adriana.
What, the chain?
Dromio of Syracuse.
No, no, the bell; 'tis time that I were gone.

It was two ere I left him, and now the
  clock strikes one.
Adriana.
The hours come back! that did I never
  hear.
Dromio of Syracuse.
O yes. If any hour meet a sergeant, 'a turns
  back for very fear.
Adriana.
As if time were in debt! how fondly dost
  thou reason!
Dromio of Syracuse.
Time is a very bankrupt, and owes more
  than he's worth to season.
Nay, he's a thief too: have you not heard
  men say
That Time comes stealing on by night
  and day?
If he be in debt and theft, and a sergeant
  in the way,
Hath he not reason to turn back an hour
  in a day?
          [*Enter* Luciana.]
Adriana.
Go, Dromio, there's the money, bear it
  straight;
And bring thy master home
  immediately.—
Come, sister; I am press'd down with
  conceit—
Conceit my comfort and my injury.
          [*Exeunt.*]

SCENE III
The same.
[*Enter* Antipholus of Syracuse.]
Antipholus of Syracuse.
There's not a man I meet but doth salute
  me
As if I were their well-acquainted friend;
And every one doth call me by my name.
Some tender money to me, some invite
  me;
Some other give me thanks for kindnesses;
Some offer me commodities to buy;
Even now a tailor call'd me in his shop,
And show'd me silks that he had bought
  for me,

And therewithal took measure of my body.
Sure, these are but imaginary wiles,
And Lapland sorcerers inhabit here.
   [*Enter* Dromio of Syracuse.]
Dromio of Syracuse.
Master, here's the gold you sent me for.
What, have you got the picture of old
 Adam new apparelled?
Antipholus of Syracuse.
What gold is this? What Adam dost thou
 mean?
Dromio of Syracuse.
Not that Adam that kept the paradise, but
that Adam that keeps the prison; he that
goes in the calf's skin that was killed for
the Prodigal; he that came behind you, sir,
like an evil angel, and bid you forsake your
liberty.
Antipholus of Syracuse.
I understand thee not.
Dromio of Syracuse.
No? Why, 'tis a plain case: he that went like
a bass-viol in a case of leather; the man, sir,
that, when gentlemen are tired, gives them
a sob, and 'rests them; he, sir, that takes pity
on decayed men, and gives them suits of
durance; he that sets up his rest to do more
exploits with his mace than a morris-pike.
Antipholus of Syracuse.
What! thou mean'st an officer?
Dromio of Syracuse.
Ay, sir,—the sergeant of the band: that
brings any man to answer it that breaks his
band; one that thinks a man always going
to bed, and says "God give you good rest!"
Antipholus of Syracuse.
Well, sir, there rest in your foolery. Is there
any ship puts forth to-night? may we be
 gone?
Dromio of Syracuse.
Why, sir, I brought you word an hour since
that the bark Expedition put forth to-
night; and then were you hindered by the
sergeant, to tarry for the hoy, Delay: here
are the angels that you sent for to deliver
you.
Antipholus of Syracuse.
The fellow is distract, and so am I;

And here we wander in illusions:
Some blessed power deliver us from hence!
   [*Enter a* Courtezan.]
Courtezan.
Well met, well met, Master Antipholus.
I see, sir, you have found the goldsmith
 now:
Is that the chain you promis'd me to-day?
Antipholus of Syracuse.
Satan, avoid! I charge thee, tempt me not!
Dromio of Syracuse.
Master, is this Mistress Satan?
Antipholus of Syracuse.
It is the devil.
Dromio of Syracuse.
Nay, she is worse,—she is the devil's dam;
and here she comes in the habit of a light
wench; and thereof comes that the wenches
say "God damn me!" That's as much to say
"God make me a light wench!" It is written
they appear to men like angels of light:
light is an effect of fire, and fire will burn;
ergo, light wenches will burn: come not
near her.
Courtezan.
Your man and you are marvellous merry,
 sir.
Will you go with me? We'll mend our
 dinner here.
Dromio of Syracuse.
Master, if you do; expect spoon-meat, or
bespeak a long spoon.
Antipholus of Syracuse.
Why, Dromio?
Dromio of Syracuse.
Marry, he must have a long spoon that
must eat with the devil.
Antipholus of Syracuse.
Avoid then, fiend! What tell'st thou me of
 supping?
Thou art, as you are all, a sorceress;
I conjure thee to leave me and be gone.
Courtezan.
Give me the ring of mine you had at
 dinner,
Or, for my diamond, the chain you
 promis'd,
And I'll be gone, sir, and not trouble you.

Dromio of Syracuse.
Some devils ask but the paring of one's nail,
A rush, a hair, a drop of blood, a pin,
A nut, a cherry-stone; but she, more
    covetous,
Would have a chain.
Master, be wise; an if you give it her,
The devil will shake her chain, and fright
    us with it.
Courtezan.
I pray you, sir, my ring, or else the chain;
I hope you do not mean to cheat me so.
Antipholus of Syracuse.
Avaunt, thou witch! Come, Dromio, let
    us go.
Dromio of Syracuse.
Fly pride, says the peacock: Mistress, that
    you know.
    [*Exeunt* Antipholus of Syracuse *and*
        Dromio of Syracuse.]
Courtezan.
Now, out of doubt, Antipholus is mad,
Else would he never so demean himself:
A ring he hath of mine worth forty ducats,
And for the same he promis'd me a chain;
Both one and other he denies me now:
The reason that I gather he is mad,—
Besides this present instance of his rage,—
Is a mad tale he told to-day at dinner,
Of his own doors being shut against his
    entrance.
Belike his wife, acquainted with his fits,
On purpose shut the doors against his way.
My way is now to hie home to his house,
And tell his wife, that being lunatic,
He rush'd into my house and took perforce
My ring away: this course I fittest choose,
For forty ducats is too much to lose.
    [*Exit.*]

SCENE IV

The same.
[*Enter* Antipholus of Ephesus
    and an Officer.]
Antipholus of Ephesus.
Fear me not, man; I will not break away:
I'll give thee, ere I leave thee, so much
    money,

To warrant thee, as I am 'rested for.
My wife is in a wayward mood to-day;
And will not lightly trust the messenger
That I should be attach'd in Ephesus;
I tell you, 'twill sound harshly in her ears.
    [*Enter* Dromio of Ephesus, *with
        a rope's end.*]
Here comes my man: I think he brings the
    money.
How now, sir! have you that I sent you for?
Dromio of Ephesus.
Here's that, I warrant you, will pay them
    all.
Antipholus of Ephesus.
But where's the money?
Dromio of Ephesus.
Why, sir, I gave the money for the rope.
Antipholus of Ephesus.
Five hundred ducats, villain, for rope?
Dromio of Ephesus.
I'll serve you, sir, five hundred at the rate.
Antipholus of Ephesus.
To what end did I bid thee hie thee home?
Dromio of Ephesus.
To a rope's end, sir; and to that end am I
    return'd.
Antipholus of Ephesus.
And to that end, sir, I will welcome you.
    [*Beating him.*]
Officer.
Good sir, be patient.
Dromio of Ephesus.
Nay, 'tis for me to be patient; I am in
    adversity.
Officer.
Good now, hold thy tongue.
Dromio of Ephesus.
Nay, rather persuade him to hold his hands.
Antipholus of Ephesus.
Thou whoreson senseless villain!
Dromio of Ephesus.
I would I were senseless, sir, that I might
not feel your blows.
Antipholus of Ephesus.
Thou art sensible in nothing but blows, and
so is an ass.
Dromio of Ephesus.
I am an ass indeed; you may prove it by

my long ears. I have served him from the
hour of my nativity to this instant, and
have nothing at his hands for my service
but blows: when I am cold he heats me
with beating; when I am warm he cools me
with beating. I am waked with it when I
sleep; raised with it when I sit; driven out
of doors with it when I go from home;
welcomed home with it when I return: nay,
I bear it on my shoulders as beggar wont
her brat; and I think, when he hath lamed
me, I shall beg with it from door to door.

Antipholus of Ephesus.

Come, go along; my wife is coming yonder.

[*Enter* Adriana, Luciana, *and the*
Courtezan, *with* Pinch *and* Others.]

Dromio of Ephesus.

Mistress, "respice finem," respect your end;
or rather, the prophesy, like the parrot,
"Beware the rope's-end."

Antipholus of Ephesus.

Wilt thou still talk?

[*Beats him.*]

Courtezan.

How say you now? is not your husband
mad?

Adriana.

His incivility confirms no less.—
Good Doctor Pinch, you are a conjurer;
Establish him in his true sense again,
And I will please you what you will
demand.

Luciana.

Alas, how fiery and how sharp he looks!

Courtezan.

Mark how he trembles in his ecstasy!

Pinch.

Give me your hand, and let me feel your
pulse.

Antipholus of Ephesus.

There is my hand, and let it feel your ear.

Pinch.

I charge thee, Satan, hous'd within this
man,
To yield possession to my holy prayers,
And to thy state of darkness hie thee
straight:
I conjure thee by all the saints in heaven.

Antipholus of Ephesus.

Peace, doting wizard, peace; I am not mad.

Adriana.

O, that thou wert not, poor distressed soul!

Antipholus of Ephesus.

You minion, you, are these your customers?
Did this companion with the saffron face
Revel and feast it at my house to-day,
Whilst upon me the guilty doors were
shut,
And I denied to enter in my house?

Adriana.

O husband, God doth know you din'd at
home,
Where would you had remain'd until this
time,
Free from these slanders and this open
shame!

Antipholus of Ephesus.

I din'd at home! Thou villain, what sayest
thou?

Dromio of Ephesus.

Sir, sooth to say, you did not dine at home.

Antipholus of Ephesus.

Were not my doors lock'd up and I shut
out?

Dromio of Ephesus.

Perdy, your doors were lock'd and you shut
out.

Antipholus of Ephesus.

And did not she herself revile me there?

Dromio of Ephesus.

Sans fable, she herself revil'd you there.

Antipholus of Ephesus.

Did not her kitchen-maid rail, taunt, and
scorn me?

Dromio of Ephesus.

Certes, she did: the kitchen-vestal scorn'd
you.

Antipholus of Ephesus.

And did not I in rage depart from thence?

Dromio of Ephesus.

In verity, you did;—my bones bear witness,
That since have felt the vigour of his rage.

Adriana.

Is't good to soothe him in these contraries?

Pinch.

It is no shame; the fellow finds his vein,

And, yielding to him, humours well his
frenzy.

ANTIPHOLUS OF EPHESUS.

Thou hast suborn'd the goldsmith to arrest
me.

ADRIANA.

Alas! I sent you money to redeem you,
By Dromio here, who came in haste for it.

DROMIO OF EPHESUS.

Money by me! heart and goodwill you
might,
But surely, master, not a rag of money.

ANTIPHOLUS OF EPHESUS.

Went'st not thou to her for purse of
ducats?

ADRIANA.

He came to me, and I deliver'd it.

LUCIANA.

And I am witness with her that she did.

DROMIO OF EPHESUS.

God and the rope-maker, bear me witness
That I was sent for nothing but a rope!

PINCH.

Mistress, both man and master is
possess'd;
I know it by their pale and deadly looks:
They must be bound, and laid in some
dark room.

ANTIPHOLUS OF EPHESUS.

Say, wherefore didst thou lock me forth
to-day?—
And why dost thou deny the bag of gold?

ADRIANA.

I did not, gentle husband, lock thee forth.

DROMIO OF EPHESUS.

And, gentle master, I receiv'd no gold;
But I confess, sir, that we were lock'd out.

ADRIANA.

Dissembling villain, thou speak'st false in
both.

ANTIPHOLUS OF EPHESUS.

Dissembling harlot, thou art false in all;
And art confederate with a damned pack,
To make a loathsome abject scorn of me:
But with these nails I'll pluck out these
false eyes
That would behold in me this shameful
sport.

[PINCH *and* ASSISTANTS *bind*
ANTIPHOLUS OF EPHESUS *and*
DROMIO OF EPHESUS.]

ADRIANA.

O, bind him, bind him; let him not come
near me.

PINCH.

More company;—the fiend is strong
within him.

LUCIANA.

Ah me, poor man! how pale and wan he
looks!

ANTIPHOLUS OF EPHESUS.

What, will you murder me? Thou gaoler,
thou,
I am thy prisoner: wilt thou suffer them
To make a rescue?

OFFICER.

                    Masters, let him go:
He is my prisoner, and you shall not have
him.

PINCH.

Go, bind this man, for he is frantic too.

ADRIANA.

What wilt thou do, thou peevish officer?
Hast thou delight to see a wretched man
Do outrage and displeasure to himself?

OFFICER.

He is my prisoner: if I let him go,
The debt he owes will be requir'd of me.

ADRIANA.

I will discharge thee ere I go from thee;
Bear me forthwith unto his creditor,
And, knowing how the debt grows, I will
pay it.
Good master doctor, see him safe convey'd
Home to my house.—O most unhappy
day!

ANTIPHOLUS OF EPHESUS.

O most unhappy strumpet!

DROMIO OF EPHESUS.

Master, I am here enter'd in bond for you.

ANTIPHOLUS OF EPHESUS.

Out on thee, villian! wherefore dost thou
mad me?

DROMIO OF EPHESUS.

Will you be bound for nothing? be mad,
good master; cry, the devil.—

Luciana.
God help, poor souls, how idly do they talk!
Adriana.
Go bear him hence.—Sister, go you with
   me.—
   [*Exeunt* Pinch *and* Assistants, *with*
      Antipholus *of* Ephesus *and*
        Dromio *of* Ephesus.]
Say now, whose suit is he arrested at?
Officer.
One Angelo, a goldsmith; do you know
   him?
Adriana.
I know the man: what is the sum he owes?
Officer.
Two hundred ducats.
Adriana.
          Say, how grows it due?
Officer.
Due for a chain your husband had of him.
Adriana.
He did bespeak a chain for me, but had
   it not.
Courtezan.
When as your husband, all in rage, to-day
Came to my house, and took away my
   ring,—
The ring I saw upon his finger now,—
Straight after did I meet him with a chain.
Adriana.
It may be so, but I did never see it:
Come, gaoler, bring me where the
   goldsmith is,
I long to know the truth hereof at large.
[*Enter* Antipholus of Syracuse, *with his
rapier drawn, and* Dromio of Syracuse.]
Luciana.
God, for thy mercy! they are loose again.
Adriana.
And come with naked swords: let's call
   more help,
To have them bound again.
Officer.
         Away, they'll kill us.
   [*Exeunt* Officer, Adriana, *and*
        Luciana.]
Antipholus of Syracuse.
I see these witches are afraid of swords.

Dromio of Syracuse.
She that would be your wife now ran from
   you.
Antipholus of Syracuse.
Come to the Centaur; fetch our stuff from
   thence:
I long that we were safe and sound aboard.
Dromio of Syracuse.
Faith, stay here this night; they will surely
do us no harm; you saw they speak us fair,
give us gold; methinks they are such a
gentle nation, that, but for the mountain of
mad flesh that claims marriage of me, could
find in my heart to stay here still and turn
witch.
Antipholus of Syracuse.
I will not stay to-night for all the town;
Therefore away to get our stuff aboard.
        [*Exeunt.*]

ACT V
SCENE I
The same.
[*Enter* Merchant *and* Angelo.]
Angelo.
I am sorry, sir, that I have hinder'd you;
But I protest he had the chain of me,
Though most dishonestly he doth deny it.
Merchant.
How is the man esteem'd here in the city?
Angelo.
Of very reverend reputation, sir;
Of credit infinite, highly belov'd,
Second to none that lives here in the city:
His word might bear my wealth at any
   time.
Merchant.
Speak softly: yonder, as I think, he walks.
   [*Enter* Antipholus of Syracuse *and*
      Dromio of Syracuse.]
Angelo.
'Tis so; and that self chain about his
   neck
Which he forswore most monstrously to
   have.
Good sir, draw near to me, I'll speak to
   him.—
Signior Antipholus, I wonder much

That you would put me to this shame and
    trouble;
And, not without some scandal to yourself,
With circumstance and oaths so to deny
This chain, which now you wear so openly:
Beside the charge, the shame,
    imprisonment,
You have done wrong to this my honest
    friend;
Who, but for staying on our controversy,
Had hoisted sail and put to sea to-day;
This chain you had of me; can you deny it?

ANTIPHOLUS OF SYRACUSE.
I think I had: I never did deny it.

MERCHANT.
Yes, that you did, sir, and forswore it too.

ANTIPHOLUS OF SYRACUSE.
Who heard me to deny it or forswear it?

MERCHANT.
These ears of mine, thou know'st, did hear
    thee.
Fie on thee, wretch! 'tis pity that thou liv'st
To walk where any honest men resort.

ANTIPHOLUS OF SYRACUSE.
Thou art a villain to impeach me thus;
I'll prove mine honour and mine honesty
Against thee presently, if thou dar'st stand.

MERCHANT.
I dare, and do defy thee for a villain.
                    [*They draw.*]
[*Enter* ADRIANA, LUCIANA, COURTEZAN,
        and OTHERS.]

ADRIANA.
Hold, hurt him not, for God's sake; he is
    mad.
Some get within him, take his sword away:
Bind Dromio too, and bear them to my
    house.

DROMIO OF SYRACUSE.
Run, master, run; for God's sake, take a
    house.
This is some priory;—in, or we are spoil'd.
[*Exeunt* ANTIPHOLUS OF SYRACUSE *and*
    DROMIO OF SYRACUSE *to the priory.*]
        [*Enter the* ABBESS.]

ABBESS.
Be quiet, people. Wherefore throng you
    hither?

ADRIANA.
To fetch my poor distracted husband
    hence:
Let us come in, that we may bind him fast,
And bear him home for his recovery.

ANGELO.
I knew he was not in his perfect wits.

MERCHANT.
I am sorry now that I did draw on him.

ABBESS.
How long hath this possession held the
    man?

ADRIANA.
This week he hath been heavy, sour, sad,
And much different from the man he was:
But till this afternoon his passion
Ne'er brake into extremity of rage.

ABBESS.
Hath he not lost much wealth by wreck
    of sea?
Buried some dear friend? Hath not else
    his eye
Stray'd his affection in unlawful love?
A sin prevailing much in youthful men
Who give their eyes the liberty of gazing.
Which of these sorrows is he subject to?

ADRIANA.
To none of these, except it be the last;
Namely, some love that drew him oft from
    home.

ABBESS.
You should for that have reprehended him.

ADRIANA.
Why, so I did.

ABBESS.
                    Ay, but not rough enough.

ADRIANA.
As roughly as my modesty would let me.

ABBESS.
Haply in private.

ADRIANA.
And in assemblies too.

ABBESS.
Ay, but not enough.

ADRIANA.
It was the copy of our conference.
In bed, he slept not for my urging it;
At board, he fed not for my urging it;

Alone, it was the subject of my theme;
In company, I often glanced it;
Still did I tell him it was vile and bad.

ABBESS.
And thereof came it that the man was
    mad:
The venom clamours of a jealous woman
Poisons more deadly than a mad dog's
    tooth.
It seems his sleeps were hindered by thy
    railing:
And thereof comes it that his head is light.
Thou say'st his meat was sauc'd with thy
    upbraidings:
Unquiet meals make ill digestions;
Thereof the raging fire of fever bred;
And what's a fever but a fit of madness?
Thou say'st his sports were hinder'd by thy
    brawls:
Sweet recreation barr'd, what doth ensue
But moody and dull melancholy,—
Kinsman to grim and comfortless
    despair,—
And, at her heels, a huge infectious troop
Of pale distemperatures and foes to life?
In food, in sport, and life-preserving rest,
To be disturb'd would mad or man or
    beast:
The consequence is, then, thy jealous fits
Hath scar'd thy husband from the use of's
    wits.

LUCIANA.
She never reprehended him but mildly,
When he demean'd himself rough, rude,
    and wildly.
Why bear you these rebukes, and answer
    not?

ADRIANA.
She did betray me to my own reproof.—
Good people, enter, and lay hold on him.

ABBESS.
No, not a creature enters in my house.

ADRIANA.
Then let your servants bring my husband
    forth.

ABBESS.
Neither: he took this place for sanctuary,
And it shall privilege him from your hands

Till I have brought him to his wits again,
Or lose my labour in assaying it.

ADRIANA.
I will attend my husband, be his nurse,
Diet his sickness, for it is my office,
And will have no attorney but myself;
And therefore let me have him home with
    me.

ABBESS.
Be patient; for I will not let him stir
Till I have used the approved means I
    have,
With wholesome syrups, drugs, and holy
    prayers,
To make of him a formal man again:
It is a branch and parcel of mine oath,
A charitable duty of my order;
Therefore depart, and leave him here with
    me.

ADRIANA.
I will not hence and leave my husband
    here;
And ill it doth beseem your holiness
To separate the husband and the wife.

ABBESS.
Be quiet, and depart: thou shalt not have
    him.
                [*Exit* ABBESS.]

LUCIANA.
Complain unto the Duke of this indignity.

ADRIANA.
Come, go; I will fall prostrate at his feet,
And never rise until my tears and prayers
Have won his grace to come in person
    hither
And take perforce my husband from the
    abbess.

MERCHANT.
By this, I think, the dial points at five:
Anon, I'm sure, the Duke himself in
    person
Comes this way to the melancholy vale;
The place of death and sorry execution,
Behind the ditches of the abbey here.

ANGELO.
Upon what cause?

MERCHANT.
To see a reverend Syracusian merchant,

Who put unluckily into this bay
Against the laws and statutes of this town,
Beheaded publicly for his offence.

ANGELO.

See where they come: we will behold his
  death.

LUCIANA.

Kneel to the Duke before he pass the
  abbey.

  [*Enter the* DUKE, *attended;* AEGEON,
    bareheaded; with the HEADSMAN
        and other OFFICERS.]

DUKE.

Yet once again proclaim it publicly,
If any friend will pay the sum for him,
He shall not die; so much we tender him.

ADRIANA.

Justice, most sacred Duke, against the
  abbess!

DUKE.

She is a virtuous and a reverend lady;
It cannot be that she hath done thee wrong.

ADRIANA.

May it please your grace, Antipholus, my
  husband,—
Who I made lord of me and all I had,
At your important letters,—this ill day
A most outrageous fit of madness took
  him;
That desp'rately he hurried through the
  street,—
With him his bondman all as mad as
  he,—
Doing displeasure to the citizens
By rushing in their houses, bearing thence
Rings, jewels, anything his rage did like.
Once did I get him bound and sent him
  home,
Whilst to take order for the wrongs I
  went,
That here and there his fury had
  committed.
Anon, I wot not by what strong escape,
He broke from those that had the guard
  of him;
And, with his mad attendant and himself,
Each one with ireful passion, with drawn
  swords,

Met us again, and, madly bent on us,
Chased us away; till, raising of more aid,
We came again to bind them: then they
  fled
Into this abbey, whither we pursued them:
And here the abbess shuts the gates on us,
And will not suffer us to fetch him out,
Nor send him forth that we may bear him
  hence.
Therefore, most gracious Duke, with thy
  command
Let him be brought forth and borne hence
  for help.

DUKE.

Long since thy husband serv'd me in my
  wars;
And I to thee engag'd a prince's word,
When thou didst make him master of
  thy bed,
To do him all the grace and good I
  could.—
Go, some of you, knock at the abbey-gate,
And bid the lady abbess come to me:
I will determine this before I stir.

        [*Enter a* SERVANT.]

SERVANT.

O mistress, mistress, shift and save
  yourself!
My master and his man are both broke
  loose,
Beaten the maids a-row, and bound the
  doctor;
Whose beard they have singed off with
  brands of fire;
And ever as it blazed they threw on him
Great pails of puddled mire to quench
  the hair:
My master preaches patience to him,
  while
His man with scissors nicks him like a
  fool:
And, sure, unless you send some present
  help,
Between them they will kill the conjurer.

ADRIANA.

Peace, fool, thy master and his man are
  here;
And that is false thou dost report to us.

Servant.
Mistress, upon my life, I tell you true:
I have not breath'd almost since I did see
  it.
He cries for you, and vows, if he can take
  you,
To scorch your face, and to disfigure you:
     [*Cry within.*]
Hark, hark, I hear him, mistress; fly, be
  gone!

Duke.
Come, stand by me; fear nothing. Guard
  with halberds.

Adriana.
Ah me, it is my husband! Witness you
That he is borne about invisible.
Even now we hous'd him in the abbey
  here,
And now he's there, past thought of
  human reason.
    [*Enter* Antipholus *and* Dromio of
      Ephesus.]

Antipholus of Ephesus.
Justice, most gracious Duke; oh, grant me
  justice!
Even for the service that long since I did
  thee,
When I bestrid thee in the wars, and took
Deep scars to save thy life; even for the
  blood
That then I lost for thee, now grant me
  justice.

Aegeon.
Unless the fear of death doth make me
  dote,
I see my son Antipholus, and Dromio.

Antipholus of Ephesus.
Justice, sweet prince, against that woman
  there.
She whom thou gav'st to me to be my
  wife;
That hath abused and dishonour'd me
Even in the strength and height of injury!
Beyond imagination is the wrong
That she this day hath shameless thrown
  on me.

Duke.
Discover how, and thou shalt find me just.

Antipholus of Ephesus.
This day, great Duke, she shut the doors
  upon me,
While she with harlots feasted in my
  house.

Duke.
A grievous fault. Say, woman, didst thou
  so?

Adriana.
No, my good lord;—myself, he, and my
  sister,
To-day did dine together. So befall my
  soul
As this is false he burdens me withal!

Luciana.
Ne'er may I look on day nor sleep on night
But she tells to your highness simple
  truth!

Angelo.
O perjur'd woman! they are both forsworn.
In this the madman justly chargeth them.

Antipholus of Ephesus.
My liege, I am advised what I say;
Neither disturb'd with the effect of wine,
Nor, heady-rash, provok'd with raging ire,
Albeit my wrongs might make one wiser
  mad.
This woman lock'd me out this day from
  dinner:
That goldsmith there, were he not pack'd
  with her,
Could witness it, for he was with me then;
Who parted with me to go fetch a chain.
Promising to bring it to the Porcupine,
Where Balthazar and I did dine together.
Our dinner done, and he not coming
  thither,
I went to seek him. In the street I met
  him,
And in his company that gentleman.
There did this perjur'd goldsmith swear
  me down,
That I this day of him receiv'd the chain,
Which, God he knows, I saw not: for the
  which
He did arrest me with an officer.
I did obey, and sent my peasant home
For certain ducats: he with none return'd.

Then fairly I bespoke the officer
To go in person with me to my house.
By the way we met
My wife, her sister, and a rabble more
Of vile confederates: along with them
They brought one Pinch; a hungry lean-
    faced villain,
A mere anatomy, a mountebank,
A threadbare juggler, and a fortune-teller;
A needy, hollow-ey'd, sharp-looking
    wretch;
A living dead man; this pernicious slave,
Forsooth, took on him as a conjurer;
And gazing in mine eyes, feeling my
    pulse,
And with no face, as 'twere, outfacing me,
Cries out, I was possess'd: then altogether
They fell upon me, bound me, bore me
    thence;
And in a dark and dankish vault at home
There left me and my man, both bound
    together;
Till, gnawing with my teeth my bonds in
    sunder,
I gain'd my freedom, and immediately
Ran hither to your grace; whom I beseech
To give me ample satisfaction
For these deep shames and great
    indignities.

ANGELO.
My lord, in truth, thus far I witness with
    him,
That he din'd not at home, but was lock'd
    out.

DUKE.
But had he such a chain of thee, or no?

ANGELO.
He had, my lord: and when he ran in here
These people saw the chain about his neck.

MERCHANT.
Besides, I will be sworn these ears of mine
Heard you confess you had the chain of
    him,
After you first forswore it on the mart,
And thereupon I drew my sword on you;
And then you fled into this abbey here,
From whence, I think, you are come by
    miracle.

ANTIPHOLUS OF EPHESUS.
I never came within these abbey walls,
Nor ever didst thou draw thy sword on
    me:
I never saw the chain, so help me heaven!
And this is false you burden me withal.

DUKE.
What an intricate impeach is this!
I think you all have drunk of Circe's cup.
If here you hous'd him, here he would have
    been:
If he were mad, he would not plead so
    coldly:—
You say he din'd at home: the goldsmith
    here
Denies that saying:—Sirrah, what say you?

DROMIO OF EPHESUS.
Sir, he dined with her there, at the
    Porcupine.

COURTEZAN.
He did; and from my finger snatch'd that
    ring.

ANTIPHOLUS OF EPHESUS.
'Tis true, my liege; this ring I had of her.

DUKE.
Saw'st thou him enter at the abbey here?

COURTEZAN.
As sure, my liege, as I do see your grace.

DUKE.
Why, this is strange:—Go call the abbess
    hither:
I think you are all mated, or stark mad.
            [*Exit an* ATTENDANT.]

AEGEON.
Most mighty Duke, vouchsafe me speak
    a word;
Haply, I see a friend will save my life
And pay the sum that may deliver me.

DUKE.
Speak freely, Syracusian, what thou wilt.

AEGEON.
Is not your name, sir, call'd Antipholus?
And is not that your bondman Dromio?

DROMIO OF EPHESUS.
Within this hour I was his bondman, sir,
But he, I thank him, gnaw'd in two my
    cords:
Now am I Dromio and his man unbound.

AEGEON.
I am sure you both of you remember me.
DROMIO OF EPHESUS.
Ourselves we do remember, sir, by you;
For lately we were bound as you are now.
You are not Pinch's patient, are you, sir?
AEGEON.
Why look you strange on me? you know
me well.
ANTIPHOLUS OF EPHESUS.
I never saw you in my life, till now.
AEGEON.
Oh! grief hath chang'd me since you saw
me last;
And careful hours with Time's deformed
hand,
Have written strange defeatures in my
face:
But tell me yet, dost thou not know my
voice?
ANTIPHOLUS OF EPHESUS.
Neither.
AEGEON.
Dromio, nor thou?
DROMIO OF EPHESUS.
No, trust me, sir, nor I.
AEGEON.
I am sure thou dost.
DROMIO OF EPHESUS.
Ay, sir, but I am sure I do not; and
whatsoever a man denies, you are now
bound to believe him.
AEGEON.
Not know my voice! O time's extremity!
Hast thou so crack'd and splitted my poor
tongue,
In seven short years that here my only son
Knows not my feeble key of untun'd cares?
Though now this grained face of mine
be hid
In sap-consuming winter's drizzled snow,
And all the conduits of my blood froze up,
Yet hath my night of life some memory,
My wasting lamps some fading glimmer
left,
My dull deaf ears a little use to hear:
All these old witnesses,—I cannot err,—
Tell me thou art my son Antipholus.

ANTIPHOLUS OF EPHESUS.
I never saw my father in my life.
AEGEON.
But seven years since, in Syracusa, boy,
Thou know'st we parted; but perhaps, my
son,
Thou sham'st to acknowledge me in
misery.
ANTIPHOLUS OF EPHESUS.
The Duke and all that know me in the city,
Can witness with me that it is not so:
I ne'er saw Syracusa in my life.
DUKE.
I tell thee, Syracusan, twenty years
Have I been patron to Antipholus,
During which time he ne'er saw Syracusa:
I see thy age and dangers make thee dote.
[Enter the ABBESS, with ANTIPHOLUS OF
SYRACUSE and DROMIO OF SYRACUSE.]
ABBESS.
Most mighty Duke, behold a man much
wrong'd.
[All gather to see them.]
ADRIANA.
I see two husbands, or mine eyes deceive
me.
DUKE.
One of these men is genius to the other;
And so of these. Which is the natural
man,
And which the spirit? Who deciphers
them?
DROMIO OF SYRACUSE.
I, sir, am Dromio; command him away.
DROMIO OF EPHESUS.
I, sir, am Dromio; pray let me stay.
ANTIPHOLUS OF SYRACUSE.
Aegeon, art thou not? or else his ghost?
DROMIO OF SYRACUSE.
O, my old master! who hath bound him
here?
ABBESS.
Whoever bound him, I will loose his
bonds,
And gain a husband by his liberty.—
Speak, old Aegeon, if thou be'st the man
That hadst a wife once called Aemilia,
That bore thee at a burden two fair sons:

O, if thou be'st the same Aegeon, speak,
And speak unto the same Aemilia!

AEGEON.

If I dream not, thou art Aemilia:
If thou art she, tell me where is that son
That floated with thee on the fatal raft?

ABBESS.

By men of Epidamnum, he and I,
And the twin Dromio, all were taken up:
But, by and by, rude fishermen of Corinth
By force took Dromio and my son from
    them,
And me they left with those of
    Epidamnum:
What then became of them I cannot tell;
I to this fortune that you see me in.

DUKE.

Why, here begins his morning story right:
These two Antipholus', these two so like,
And these two Dromios, one in
    semblance,—
Besides her urging of her wreck at sea,—
These are the parents to these children,
Which accidentally are met together.
Antipholus, thou cam'st from Corinth
    first?

ANTIPHOLUS OF SYRACUSE.

No, sir, not I; I came from Syracuse.

DUKE.

Stay, stand apart; I know not which is
    which.

ANTIPHOLUS OF EPHESUS.

I came from Corinth, my most gracious
    lord.

DROMIO OF EPHESUS.

And I with him.

ANTIPHOLUS OF EPHESUS.

Brought to this town by that most famous
    warrior,
Duke Menaphon, your most renowned
    uncle.

ADRIANA.

Which of you two did dine with me
    to-day?

ANTIPHOLUS OF SYRACUSE.

I, gentle mistress.

ADRIANA.

And are not you my husband?

ANTIPHOLUS OF EPHESUS.

No; I say nay to that.

ANTIPHOLUS OF SYRACUSE.

And so do I, yet did she call me so;
And this fair gentlewoman, her sister
    here,
Did call me brother.—What I told you
    then,
I hope I shall have leisure to make good;
If this be not a dream I see and hear.

ANGELO.

That is the chain, sir, which you had of me.

ANTIPHOLUS OF SYRACUSE.

I think it be, sir; I deny it not.

ANTIPHOLUS OF EPHESUS.

And you, sir, for this chain arrested me.

ANGELO.

I think I did, sir: I deny it not.

ADRIANA.

I sent you money, sir, to be your bail,
By Dromio; but I think he brought it not.

DROMIO OF EPHESUS.

No, none by me.

ANTIPHOLUS OF SYRACUSE.

This purse of ducats I receiv'd from you,
And Dromio my man did bring them me:
I see we still did meet each other's man,
And I was ta'en for him, and he for me,
And thereupon these errors are arose.

ANTIPHOLUS OF EPHESUS.

These ducats pawn I for my father here.

DUKE.

It shall not need; thy father hath his life.

COURTEZAN.

Sir, I must have that diamond from you.

ANTIPHOLUS OF EPHESUS.

There, take it; and much thanks for my
    good cheer.

ABBESS.

Renowned Duke, vouchsafe to take the
    pains
To go with us into the abbey here,
And hear at large discoursed all our
    fortunes:—
And all that are assembled in this place,
That by this sympathized one day's error
Have suffer'd wrong, go, keep us company,
And we shall make full satisfaction—

Twenty-five years have I but gone in
    travail
Of you, my sons; nor till this present hour
My heavy burdens are delivered:—
The Duke, my husband, and my children
    both,
And you the calendars of their nativity,
Go to a gossips' feast, and go with me;
After so long grief, such nativity!

Duke.

With all my heart, I'll gossip at this feast.
        [*Exeunt* Duke, Abbess, Aegeon,
    Courtezan, Merchant, Angelo, *and*
            Attendants.]

Dromio of Syracuse.

Master, shall I fetch your stuff from
    shipboard?

Antipholus of Ephesus.

Dromio, what stuff of mine hast thou
    embark'd?

Dromio of Syracuse.

Your goods that lay at host, sir, in the
    Centaur.

Antipholus of Syracuse.

He speaks to me; I am your master,
    Dromio:
Come, go with us: we'll look to that anon:
Embrace thy brother there; rejoice with
    him.

        [*Exeunt* Antipholus of Syracuse
            and Antipholus of Ephesus,
            Adriana, *and* Luciana.]

Dromio of Syracuse.

There is a fat friend at your master's
    house,
That kitchen'd me for you to-day at
    dinner:
She now shall be my sister, not my wife.

Dromio of Ephesus.

Methinks you are my glass, and not my
    brother:
I see by you I am a sweet-faced youth.
Will you walk in to see their gossiping?

Dromio of Syracuse.

Not I, sir; you are my elder.

Dromio of Ephesus.

That's a question; how shall we try it?

Dromio of Syracuse.

We'll draw cuts for the senior: till then,
    lead thou first.

Dromio of Ephesus.

Nay, then, thus:—
We came into the world like brother and
    brother:
And now let's go hand in hand, not one
    before another.
            [*Exeunt.*]

Much Ado About Nothing

Dramatis Personae

DON PEDRO, *Prince of Arragon*
DON JOHN, *his bastard brother*
CLAUDIO, *a young lord of Florence*
BENEDICK, *a young lord of Padua*
LEONATO, *governor of Messina*
ANTONIO, *his brother*
BALTHAZAR, *servant to Don Pedro*
BORACHIO, *follower of Don John*
CONRADE, *follower of Don John*
DOGBERRY, *a constable*
VERGES, *a headborough*
FRIAR FRANCIS, *a sexton*

A BOY
HERO, *daughter to Leonato*
BEATRICE, *niece to Leonato*
MARGARET, *waiting-gentlewoman attending on Hero*
URSULA, *waiting-gentlewoman attending on Hero*
MESSENGERS, WATCH, ATTENDANTS, &C.

SCENE: *Messina.*

ACT I
SCENE I

Before Leonato's house.
[*Enter* LEONATO, HERO, *and* BEATRICE, *with a* MESSENGER.]

LEONATO
I learn in this letter that Don Peter of Arragon comes this night to Messina.

MESSENGER
He is very near by this: he was not three leagues off when I left him.

LEONATO
How many gentlemen have you lost in this action?

MESSENGER
But few of any sort, and none of name.

LEONATO
A victory is twice itself when the achiever brings home full numbers. I find here that Don Peter hath bestowed much honour on a young Florentine called Claudio.

MESSENGER.
Much deserved on his part, and equally remembered by Don Pedro. He hath borne himself beyond the promise of his age, doing in the figure of a lamb the feats of a lion: he hath indeed better bettered

expectation than you must expect of me to tell you how.

LEONATO.
He hath an uncle here in Messina will be very much glad of it.

MESSENGER.
I have already delivered him letters, and there appears much joy in him; even so much that joy could not show itself modest enough without a badge of bitterness.

LEONATO.
Did he break out into tears?

MESSENGER.
In great measure.

LEONATO.
A kind overflow of kindness. There are no faces truer than those that are so washed; how much better is it to weep at joy than to joy at weeping!

BEATRICE.
I pray you, is Signior Mountanto returned from the wars or no?

MESSENGER.
I know none of that name, lady: there was none such in the army of any sort.

LEONATO.
What is he that you ask for, niece?

HERO.
My cousin means Signior Benedick of Padua.

MESSENGER.
O! he is returned, and as pleasant as ever he was.

BEATRICE.
He set up his bills here in Messina and challenged Cupid at the flight; and my uncle's fool, reading the challenge, subscribed for Cupid, and challenged him at the bird-bolt. I pray you, how many hath he killed and eaten in these wars? But how many hath he killed? for, indeed, I promised to eat all of his killing.

LEONATO.
Faith, niece, you tax Signior Benedick too much; but he'll be meet with you, I doubt it not.

MESSENGER.
He hath done good service, lady, in these wars.

BEATRICE.
You had musty victual, and he hath holp to eat it; he is a very valiant trencher-man; he hath an excellent stomach.

MESSENGER.
And a good soldier too, lady.

BEATRICE.
And a good soldier to a lady; but what is he to a lord?

MESSENGER.
A lord to a lord, a man to a man; stuffed with all honourable virtues.

BEATRICE.
It is so indeed; he is no less than a stuffed man; but for the stuffing,—well, we are all mortal.

LEONATO.
You must not, sir, mistake my niece. There is a kind of merry war betwixt Signior Benedick and her; they never meet but there's a skirmish of wit between them.

BEATRICE.
Alas! he gets nothing by that. In our last conflict four of his five wits went halting off, and now is the whole man governed with one! so that if he have wit enough to keep himself warm, let him bear it for a difference between himself and his horse; for it is all the wealth that he hath left to be known a reasonable creature. Who is his companion now? He hath every month a new sworn brother.

MESSENGER.
Is't possible?

BEATRICE.
Very easily possible: he wears his faith but as the fashion of his hat; it ever changes with the next block.

MESSENGER.
I see, lady, the gentleman is not in your books.

BEATRICE.
No; an he were, I would burn my study. But, I pray you, who is his companion? Is there no young squarer now that will make a voyage with him to the devil?

MESSENGER.
He is most in the company of the right noble Claudio.

BEATRICE.
O Lord, he will hang upon him like a disease: he is sooner caught than the pestilence, and the taker runs presently mad. God help the noble Claudio! If he have caught the Benedick, it will cost him a thousand pound ere a' be cured.

MESSENGER.
I will hold friends with you, lady.

BEATRICE.
Do, good friend.

LEONATO.
You will never run mad, niece.

BEATRICE.
No, not till a hot January.

MESSENGER.
Don Pedro is approached.

[*Enter* DON PEDRO, DON JOHN, CLAUDIO, BENEDICK, BALTHAZAR, *and* OTHERS.]

DON PEDRO.
Good Signior Leonato, you are come to meet your trouble: the fashion of the world is to avoid cost, and you encounter it.

LEONATO.
Never came trouble to my house in the

likeness of your Grace, for trouble being gone, comfort should remain; but when you depart from me, sorrow abides and happiness takes his leave.

Don Pedro.
You embrace your charge too willingly. I think this is your daughter.

Leonato.
Her mother hath many times told me so.

Benedick.
Were you in doubt, sir, that you asked her?

Leonato.
Signior Benedick, no; for then were you a child.

Don Pedro.
You have it full, Benedick: we may guess by this what you are, being a man. Truly the lady fathers herself. Be happy, lady, for you are like an honourable father.

Benedick.
If Signior Leonato be her father, she would not have his head on her shoulders for all Messina, as like him as she is.

Beatrice.
I wonder that you will still be talking, Signior Benedick: nobody marks you.

Benedick.
What! my dear Lady Disdain, are you yet living?

Beatrice.
Is it possible Disdain should die while she hath such meet food to feed it as Signior Benedick? Courtesy itself must convert to disdain if you come in her presence.

Benedick.
Then is courtesy a turncoat. But it is certain I am loved of all ladies, only you excepted; and I would I could find in my heart that I had not a hard heart; for, truly, I love none.

Beatrice.
A dear happiness to women: they would else have been troubled with a pernicious suitor. I thank God and my cold blood, I am of your humour for that. I had rather hear my dog bark at a crow than a man swear he loves me.

Benedick.
God keep your ladyship still in that mind;

so some gentleman or other shall scape a predestinate scratched face.

Beatrice.
Scratching could not make it worse, an 'twere such a face as yours were.

Benedick.
Well, you are a rare parrot-teacher.

Beatrice.
A bird of my tongue is better than a beast of yours.

Benedick.
I would my horse had the speed of your tongue, and so good a continuer. But keep your way, i' God's name; I have done.

Beatrice.
You always end with a jade's trick: I know you of old.

Don Pedro.
That is the sum of all, Leonato: Signior Claudio, and Signior Benedick, my dear friend Leonato hath invited you all. I tell him we shall stay here at the least a month, and he heartily prays some occasion may detain us longer: I dare swear he is no hypocrite, but prays from his heart.

Leonato.
If you swear, my lord, you shall not be forsworn. [*To* Don John.] Let me bid you welcome, my lord: being reconciled to the prince your brother, I owe you all duty.

Don John.
I thank you: I am not of many words, but I thank you.

Leonato.
Please it your Grace lead on?

Don Pedro.
Your hand, Leonato; we will go together.
        [*Exeunt all but* Benedick
           and Claudio.]

Claudio.
Benedick, didst thou note the daughter of Signior Leonato?

Benedick.
I noted her not; but I looked on her.

Claudio.
Is she not a modest young lady?

Benedick.
Do you question me, as an honest man

should do, for my simple true judgment; or would you have me speak after my custom, as being a professed tyrant to their sex?

CLAUDIO.

No; I pray thee speak in sober judgment.

BENEDICK.

Why, i' faith, methinks she's too low for a high praise, too brown for a fair praise, and too little for a great praise; only this commendation I can afford her, that were she other than she is, she were unhandsome, and being no other but as she is, I do not like her.

CLAUDIO.

Thou thinkest I am in sport: I pray thee tell me truly how thou likest her.

BENEDICK.

Would you buy her, that you enquire after her?

CLAUDIO.

Can the world buy such a jewel?

BENEDICK.

Yea, and a case to put it into. But speak you this with a sad brow, or do you play the flouting Jack, to tell us Cupid is a good hare-finder, and Vulcan a rare carpenter? Come, in what key shall a man take you, to go in the song?

CLAUDIO.

In mine eye she is the sweetest lady that ever I looked on.

BENEDICK.

I can see yet without spectacles and I see no such matter: there's her cousin an she were not possessed with a fury, exceeds her as much in beauty as the first of May doth the last of December. But I hope you have no intent to turn husband, have you?

CLAUDIO.

I would scarce trust myself, though I had sworn to the contrary, if Hero would be my wife.

BENEDICK.

Is't come to this, i' faith? Hath not the world one man but he will wear his cap with suspicion? Shall I never see a bachelor of threescore again? Go to, i' faith; an thou wilt needs thrust thy neck

into a yoke, wear the print of it and sigh away Sundays. Look! Don Pedro is returned to seek you.

[*Re-enter* DON PEDRO.]

DON PEDRO.

What secret hath held you here, that you followed not to Leonato's?

BENEDICK.

I would your Grace would constrain me to tell.

DON PEDRO.

I charge thee on thy allegiance.

BENEDICK.

You hear, Count Claudio: I can be secret as a dumb man; I would have you think so; but on my allegiance mark you this, on my allegiance: he is in love. With who? now that is your Grace's part. Mark how short his answer is: with Hero, Leonato's short daughter.

CLAUDIO.

If this were so, so were it uttered.

BENEDICK.

Like the old tale, my lord: "it is not so, nor 'twas not so; but indeed, God forbid it should be so."

CLAUDIO.

If my passion change not shortly. God forbid it should be otherwise.

DON PEDRO.

Amen, if you love her; for the lady is very well worthy.

CLAUDIO.

You speak this to fetch me in, my lord.

DON PEDRO.

By my troth, I speak my thought.

CLAUDIO.

And in faith, my lord, I spoke mine.

BENEDICK.

And by my two faiths and troths, my lord, I spoke mine.

CLAUDIO.

That I love her, I feel.

DON PEDRO.

That she is worthy, I know.

BENEDICK.

That I neither feel how she should be loved nor know how she should be worthy, is the opinion that fire cannot melt out of me: I will die in it at the stake.

DON PEDRO.
Thou wast ever an obstinate heretic in the despite of beauty.

CLAUDIO.
And never could maintain his part but in the force of his will.

BENEDICK.
That a woman conceived me, I thank her; that she brought me up, I likewise give her most humble thanks; but that I will have a recheat winded in my forehead, or hang my bugle in an invisible baldrick, all women shall pardon me. Because I will not do them the wrong to mistrust any, I will do myself the right to trust none; and the fine is,—for the which I may go the finer,—I will live a bachelor.

DON PEDRO.
I shall see thee, ere I die, look pale with love.

BENEDICK.
With anger, with sickness, or with hunger, my lord; not with love: prove that ever I lose more blood with love than I will get again with drinking, pick out mine eyes with a ballad-maker's pen and hang me up at the door of a brothel-house for the sign of blind Cupid.

DON PEDRO.
Well, if ever thou dost fall from this faith, thou wilt prove a notable argument.

BENEDICK.
If I do, hang me in a bottle like a cat and shoot at me; and he that hits me, let him be clapped on the shoulder and called Adam.

DON PEDRO.
Well, as time shall try: "In time the savage bull doth bear the yoke."

BENEDICK.
The savage bull may; but if ever the sensible Benedick bear it, pluck off the bull's horns and set them in my forehead; and let me be vilely painted, and in such great letters as they write, "Here is good horse to hire," let them signify under my sign "Here you may see Benedick the married man."

CLAUDIO.
If this should ever happen, thou wouldst be horn-mad.

DON PEDRO.
Nay, if Cupid have not spent all his quiver in Venice, thou wilt quake for this shortly.

BENEDICK.
I look for an earthquake too then.

DON PEDRO.
Well, you will temporize with the hours. In the meantime, good Signior Benedick, repair to Leonato's: commend me to him and tell him I will not fail him at supper; for indeed he hath made great preparation.

BENEDICK.
I have almost matter enough in me for such an embassage; and so I commit you—

CLAUDIO.
To the tuition of God: from my house, if I had it,—

DON PEDRO.
The sixth of July: your loving friend, Benedick.

BENEDICK.
Nay, mock not, mock not. The body of your discourse is sometime guarded with fragments, and the guards are but slightly basted on neither: ere you flout old ends any further, examine your conscience: and so I leave you.
                              [*Exit.*]

CLAUDIO.
My liege, your highness now may do me
      good.

DON PEDRO.
My love is thine to teach: teach it but how,
And thou shalt see how apt it is to learn
Any hard lesson that may do thee good.

CLAUDIO.
Hath Leonato any son, my lord?

DON PEDRO.
No child but Hero's; she's his only heir.
Dost thou affect her, Claudio?

CLAUDIO.
                              O! my lord,
When you went onward on this ended
      action,
I looked upon her with a soldier's eye,

That lik'd, but had a rougher task in hand
Than to drive liking to the name of love;
But now I am return'd, and that war-
    thoughts
Have left their places vacant, in their
    rooms
Come thronging soft and delicate desires,
All prompting me how fair young Hero is,
Saying, I lik'd her ere I went to wars.

DON PEDRO.
Thou wilt be like a lover presently,
And tire the hearer with a book of words.
If thou dost love fair Hero, cherish it,
And I will break with her, and with her
    father,
And thou shalt have her. Was't not to this
    end
That thou began'st to twist so fine a story?

CLAUDIO.
How sweetly you do minister to love,
That know love's grief by his complexion!
But lest my liking might too sudden seem,
I would have salv'd it with a longer treatise.

DON PEDRO.
What need the bridge much broader than
    the flood?
The fairest grant is the necessity.
Look, what will serve is fit: 'tis once, thou
    lov'st,
And I will fit thee with the remedy.
I know we shall have revelling to-night:
I will assume thy part in some disguise,
And tell fair Hero I am Claudio;
And in her bosom I'll unclasp my heart,
And take her hearing prisoner with the
    force
And strong encounter of my amorous tale:
Then, after to her father will I break;
And the conclusion is, she shall be thine.
In practice let us put it presently.
           [Exeunt.]

SCENE II
A room in Leonato's house.
[Enter LEONATO and ANTONIO, meeting.]

LEONATO.
How now, brother! Where is my cousin
your son? Hath he provided this music?

ANTONIO.
He is very busy about it. But, brother, I can
tell you strange news that you yet dreamt
not of.

LEONATO.
Are they good?

ANTONIO.
As the event stamps them: but they have
a good cover; they show well outward. The
prince and Count Claudio, walking in a
thick-pleached alley in my orchard, were
thus much overheard by a man of mine:
the prince discovered to Claudio that he
loved my niece your daughter and meant to
acknowledge it this night in a dance; and if
he found her accordant, he meant to take
the present time by the top and instantly
break with you of it.

LEONATO.
Hath the fellow any wit that told you this?

ANTONIO.
A good sharp fellow: I will send for him;
and question him yourself.

LEONATO.
No, no; we will hold it as a dream till
it appear itself: but I will acquaint my
daughter withal, that she may be the better
prepared for an answer, if peradventure this
be true. Go you, and tell her of it. *[Several
persons cross the stage.]* Cousins, you know
what you have to do. O! I cry you mercy,
friend; go you with me, and I will use your
skill. Good cousin, have a care this busy
time.

           [Exeunt.]

SCENE III
Another room in Leonato's house.
[Enter DON JOHN and CONRADE.]

CONRADE.
What the good-year, my lord! why are you
thus out of measure sad?

DON JOHN.
There is no measure in the occasion that
breeds; therefore the sadness is without
limit.

CONRADE.
You should hear reason.

Don John.
And when I have heard it, what blessings brings it?

Conrade.
If not a present remedy, at least a patient sufferance.

Don John.
I wonder that thou, being,—as thou say'st thou art,—born under Saturn, goest about to apply a moral medicine to a mortifying mischief. I cannot hide what I am: I must be sad when I have cause, and smile at no man's jests; eat when I have stomach, and wait for no man's leisure; sleep when I am drowsy, and tend on no man's business; laugh when I am merry, and claw no man in his humour.

Conrade.
Yea; but you must not make the full show of this till you may do it without controlment. You have of late stood out against your brother, and he hath ta'en you newly into his grace; where it is impossible you should take true root but by the fair weather that you make yourself: it is needful that you frame the season for your own harvest.

Don John.
I had rather be a canker in a hedge than a rose in his grace; and it better fits my blood to be disdained of all than to fashion a carriage to rob love from any: in this, though I cannot be said to be a flattering honest man, it must not be denied but I am a plain-dealing villain. I am trusted with a muzzle and enfranchised with a clog; therefore I have decreed not to sing in my cage. If I had my mouth, I would bite; if I had my liberty, I would do my liking: in the meantime, let me be that I am, and seek not to alter me.

Conrade.
Can you make no use of your discontent?

Don John.
I make all use of it, for I use it only. Who comes here?

[*Enter* Borachio.]

What news, Borachio?

Borachio.
I came yonder from a great supper: the prince your brother is royally entertained by Leonato; and I can give you intelligence of an intended marriage.

Don John.
Will it serve for any model to build mischief on? What is he for a fool that betroths himself to unquietness?

Borachio.
Marry, it is your brother's right hand.

Don John.
Who? the most exquisite Claudio?

Borachio.
Even he.

Don John.
A proper squire! And who, and who? which way looks he?

Borachio.
Marry, on Hero, the daughter and heir of Leonato.

Don John.
A very forward March-chick! How came you to this?

Borachio.
Being entertained for a perfumer, as I was smoking a musty room, comes me the prince and Claudio, hand in hand, in sad conference: I whipt me behind the arras, and there heard it agreed upon that the prince should woo Hero for himself, and having obtained her, give her to Count Claudio.

Don John.
Come, come; let us thither: this may prove food to my displeasure. That young start-up hath all the glory of my overthrow: if I can cross him any way, I bless myself every way. You are both sure, and will assist me?

Conrade.
To the death, my lord.

Don John.
Let us to the great supper: their cheer is the greater that I am subdued. Would the cook were of my mind! Shall we go to prove what's to be done?

Borachio.
We'll wait upon your lordship.

[*Exeunt.*]

ACT II
SCENE I
A hall in Leonato's house.
[*Enter* LEONATO, ANTONIO, HERO,
BEATRICE, *and* OTHERS.]

LEONATO.
Was not Count John here at supper?

ANTONIO.
I saw him not.

BEATRICE.
How tartly that gentleman looks! I never can see him but I am heart-burned an hour after.

HERO.
He is of a very melancholy disposition.

BEATRICE.
He were an excellent man that were made just in the mid-way between him and Benedick: the one is too like an image, and says nothing; and the other too like my lady's eldest son, evermore tattling.

LEONATO.
Then half Signior Benedick's tongue in Count John's mouth, and half Count John's melancholy in Signior Benedick's face,—

BEATRICE.
With a good leg and a good foot, uncle, and money enough in his purse, such a man would win any woman in the world if a' could get her good will.

LEONATO.
By my troth, niece, thou wilt never get thee a husband, if thou be so shrewd of thy tongue.

ANTONIO.
In faith, she's too curst.

BEATRICE.
Too curst is more than curst: I shall lessen God's sending that way; for it is said, "God sends a curst cow short horns"; but to a cow too curst he sends none.

LEONATO.
So, by being too curst, God will send you no horns?

BEATRICE.
Just, if he send me no husband; for the which blessing I am at him upon my knees every morning and evening. Lord! I could not endure a husband with a beard on his face: I had rather lie in the woollen.

LEONATO.
You may light on a husband that hath no beard.

BEATRICE.
What should I do with him? dress him in my apparel and make him my waiting-gentlewoman? He that hath a beard is more than a youth, and he that hath no beard is less than a man; and he that is more than a youth is not for me; and he that is less than a man, I am not for him: therefore I will even take sixpence in earnest of the bear-ward, and lead his apes into hell.

LEONATO.
Well then, go you into hell?

BEATRICE.
No; but to the gate; and there will the devil meet me, like an old cuckold, with horns on his head, and say, "Get you to heaven, Beatrice, get you to heaven; here's no place for you maids": so deliver I up my apes, and away to Saint Peter for the heavens; he shows me where the bachelors sit, and there live we as merry as the day is long.

ANTONIO. [*To* HERO.]
Well, niece, I trust you will be ruled by your father.

BEATRICE.
Yes, faith; it is my cousin's duty to make curtsy, and say, "Father, as it please you"—but yet for all that, cousin, let him be a handsome fellow, or else make another curtsy, and say, "Father, as it please me."

LEONATO.
Well, niece, I hope to see you one day fitted with a husband.

BEATRICE.
Not till God make men of some other metal than earth. Would it not grieve a woman to be over-mastered with a piece of valiant dust? to make an account of her life to a clod of wayward marl? No, uncle, I'll none: Adam's sons are my brethren; and truly, I hold it a sin to match in my kindred.

LEONATO.
Daughter, remember what I told you: if the

prince do solicit you in that kind, you know your answer.

BEATRICE.
The fault will be in the music, cousin, if you be not wooed in good time: if the prince be too important, tell him there is measure in everything, and so dance out the answer. For, hear me, Hero: wooing, wedding, and repenting is as a Scotch jig, a measure, and a cinque-pace: the first suit is hot and hasty, like a Scotch jig, and full as fantastical; the wedding, mannerly-modest, as a measure, full of state and ancientry; and then comes Repentance, and with his bad legs, falls into the cinque-pace faster and faster, till he sink into his grave.

LEONATO.
Cousin, you apprehend passing shrewdly.

BEATRICE.
I have a good eye, uncle: I can see a church by daylight.

LEONATO.
The revellers are entering, brother: make good room.

[*Enter,* DON PEDRO, CLAUDIO, BENEDICK, BALTHASAR, DON JOHN, BORACHIO, MARGARET, URSULA, *and* OTHERS, *masked.*]

DON PEDRO.
Lady, will you walk about with your friend?

HERO.
So you walk softly and look sweetly and say nothing, I am yours for the walk; and especially when I walk away.

DON PEDRO.
With me in your company?

HERO.
I may say so, when I please.

DON PEDRO.
And when please you to say so?

HERO.
When I like your favour; for God defend the lute should be like the case!

DON PEDRO.
My visor is Philemon's roof; within the house is Jove.

HERO.
Why, then, your visor should be thatch'd.

DON PEDRO.
Speak low, if you speak love.
                    [*Takes her aside.*]

BALTHAZAR.
Well, I would you did like me.

MARGARET.
So would not I, for your own sake; for I have many ill qualities.

BALTHAZAR.
Which is one?

MARGARET.
I say my prayers aloud.

BALTHAZAR.
I love you the better; the hearers may cry Amen.

MARGARET.
God match me with a good dancer!

BALTHAZAR.
Amen.

MARGARET.
And God keep him out of my sight when the dance is done! Answer, clerk.

BALTHAZAR.
No more words: the clerk is answered.

URSULA.
I know you well enough: you are Signior Antonio.

ANTONIO.
At a word, I am not.

URSULA.
I know you by the waggling of your head.

ANTONIO.
To tell you true, I counterfeit him.

URSULA.
You could never do him so ill-well, unless you were the very man. Here's his dry hand up and down: you are he, you are he.

ANTONIO.
At a word, I am not.

URSULA.
Come, come; do you think I do not know you by your excellent wit? Can virtue hide itself? Go to, mum, you are he: graces will appear, and there's an end.

BEATRICE.
Will you not tell me who told you so?

BENEDICK.
No, you shall pardon me.

BEATRICE.
Nor will you not tell me who you are?
BENEDICK.
Not now.
BEATRICE.
That I was disdainful, and that I had my good wit out of the "Hundred Merry Tales." Well, this was Signior Benedick that said so.
BENEDICK.
What's he?
BEATRICE.
I am sure you know him well enough.
BENEDICK.
Not I, believe me.
BEATRICE.
Did he never make you laugh?
BENEDICK.
I pray you, what is he?
BEATRICE.
Why, he is the prince's jester: a very dull fool; only his gift is in devising impossible slanders: none but libertines delight in him; and the commendation is not in his wit, but in his villany; for he both pleases men and angers them, and then they laugh at him and beat him. I am sure he is in the fleet: I would he had boarded me!
BENEDICK.
When I know the gentleman, I'll tell him what you say.
BEATRICE.
Do, do: he'll but break a comparison or two on me; which, peradventure not marked or not laughed at, strikes him into melancholy; and then there's a partridge wing saved, for the fool will eat no supper that night. [*Music within.*] We must follow the leaders.
BENEDICK.
In every good thing.
BEATRICE.
Nay, if they lead to any ill, I will leave them at the next turning.
    [*Dance. Then exeunt all but* DON JOHN,
        BORACHIO, *and* CLAUDIO.]
DON JOHN.
Sure my brother is amorous on Hero, and

hath withdrawn her father to break with him about it. The ladies follow her and but one visor remains.
BORACHIO.
And that is Claudio: I know him by his bearing.
DON JOHN.
Are you not Signior Benedick?
CLAUDIO.
You know me well; I am he.
DON JOHN.
Signior, you are very near my brother in his love: he is enamoured on Hero; I pray you, dissuade him from her; she is no equal for his birth: you may do the part of an honest man in it.
CLAUDIO.
How know you he loves her?
DON JOHN.
I heard him swear his affection.
BORACHIO.
So did I too; and he swore he would marry her to-night.
DON JOHN.
Come, let us to the banquet.
    [*Exeunt* DON JOHN *and* BORACHIO.]
CLAUDIO.
Thus answer I in name of Benedick,
But hear these ill news with the ears of
    Claudio.
'Tis certain so; the prince wooes for
    himself.
Friendship is constant in all other
    things
Save in the office and affairs of love:
Therefore all hearts in love use their
    own tongues;
Let every eye negotiate for itself
And trust no agent; for beauty is a
    witch
Against whose charms faith melteth
    into blood.
This is an accident of hourly proof,
Which I mistrusted not. Farewell,
    therefore, Hero!
        [*Re-enter* BENEDICK.]
BENEDICK.
Count Claudio?

CLAUDIO.
Yea, the same.

BENEDICK.
Come, will you go with me?

CLAUDIO.
Whither?

BENEDICK.
Even to the next willow, about your own business, count. What fashion will you wear the garland of? About your neck, like a usurer's chain? or under your arm, like a lieutenant's scarf? You must wear it one way, for the prince hath got your Hero.

CLAUDIO.
I wish him joy of her.

BENEDICK.
Why, that's spoken like an honest drovier: so they sell bullocks. But did you think the prince would have served you thus?

CLAUDIO.
I pray you, leave me.

BENEDICK.
Ho! now you strike like the blind man: 'twas the boy that stole your meat, and you'll beat the post.

CLAUDIO.
If it will not be, I'll leave you.

[*Exit.*]

BENEDICK.
Alas! poor hurt fowl. Now will he creep into sedges. But, that my Lady Beatrice should know me, and not know me! The prince's fool! Ha! it may be I go under that title because I am merry. Yea, but so I am apt to do myself wrong; I am not so reputed: it is the base though bitter disposition of Beatrice that puts the world into her person, and so gives me out. Well, I'll be revenged as I may.

[*Re-enter* DON PEDRO.]

DON PEDRO.
Now, signior, where's the count? Did you see him?

BENEDICK.
Troth, my lord, I have played the part of Lady Fame. I found him here as melancholy as a lodge in a warren. I told him, and I think I told him true, that your Grace had got the good will of this young lady; and I offered him my company to a willow tree, either to make him a garland, as being forsaken, or to bind him up a rod, as being worthy to be whipped.

DON PEDRO.
To be whipped! What's his fault?

BENEDICK.
The flat transgression of a school-boy, who, being overjoy'd with finding a bird's nest, shows it his companion, and he steals it.

DON PEDRO.
Wilt thou make a trust a transgression? The transgression is in the stealer.

BENEDICK.
Yet it had not been amiss the rod had been made, and the garland too; for the garland he might have worn himself, and the rod he might have bestowed on you, who, as I take it, have stolen his bird's nest.

DON PEDRO.
I will but teach them to sing, and restore them to the owner.

BENEDICK.
If their singing answer your saying, by my faith, you say honestly.

DON PEDRO.
The Lady Beatrice hath a quarrel to you: the gentleman that danced with her told her she is much wronged by you.

BENEDICK.
O! she misused me past the endurance of a block: an oak but with one green leaf on it, would have answered her: my very visor began to assume life and scold with her. She told me, not thinking I had been myself, that I was the prince's jester, that I was duller than a great thaw; huddling jest upon jest with such impossible conveyance upon me, that I stood like a man at a mark, with a whole army shooting at me. She speaks poniards, and every word stabs: if her breath were as terrible as her terminations, there were no living near her; she would infect to the north star. I would not marry her, though she were endowed with all that Adam had left him before he transgressed: she would have made Hercules have turned

spit, yea, and have cleft his club to make the fire too. Come, talk not of her; you shall find her the infernal Ate in good apparel. I would to God some scholar would conjure her, for certainly, while she is here, a man may live as quiet in hell as in a sanctuary; and people sin upon purpose because they would go thither; so indeed, all disquiet, horror and perturbation follow her.

[*Re-enter* CLAUDIO, BEATRICE, HERO, *and* LEONATO.]

DON PEDRO.
Look! here she comes.

BENEDICK.
Will your Grace command me any service to the world's end? I will go on the slightest errand now to the Antipodes that you can devise to send me on; I will fetch you a toothpicker now from the furthest inch of Asia; bring you the length of Prester John's foot; fetch you a hair off the Great Cham's beard; do you any embassage to the Pygmies, rather than hold three words' conference with this harpy. You have no employment for me?

DON PEDRO.
None, but to desire your good company.

BENEDICK.
O God, sir, here's a dish I love not: I cannot endure my Lady Tongue.
[*Exit.*]

DON PEDRO.
Come, lady, come; you have lost the heart of Signior Benedick.

BEATRICE.
Indeed, my lord, he lent it me awhile; and I gave him use for it, a double heart for a single one: marry, once before he won it of me with false dice, therefore your Grace may well say I have lost it.

DON PEDRO.
You have put him down, lady, you have put him down.

BEATRICE.
So I would not he should do me, my lord, lest I should prove the mother of fools. I have brought Count Claudio, whom you sent me to seek.

DON PEDRO.
Why, how now, count! wherefore are you sad?

CLAUDIO.
Not sad, my lord.

DON PEDRO.
How then? Sick?

CLAUDIO.
Neither, my lord.

BEATRICE.
The count is neither sad, nor sick, nor merry, nor well; but civil count, civil as an orange, and something of that jealous complexion.

DON PEDRO.
I' faith, lady, I think your blazon to be true; though, I'll be sworn, if he be so, his conceit is false. Here, Claudio, I have wooed in thy name, and fair Hero is won; I have broke with her father, and, his good will obtained; name the day of marriage, and God give thee joy!

LEONATO.
Count, take of me my daughter, and with her my fortunes: his Grace hath made the match, and all grace say Amen to it!

BEATRICE.
Speak, Count, 'tis your cue.

CLAUDIO.
Silence is the perfectest herald of joy: I were but little happy, if I could say how much. Lady, as you are mine, I am yours: I give away myself for you and dote upon the exchange.

BEATRICE.
Speak, cousin; or, if you cannot, stop his mouth with a kiss, and let not him speak neither.

DON PEDRO.
In faith, lady, you have a merry heart.

BEATRICE.
Yea, my lord; I thank it, poor fool, it keeps on the windy side of care. My cousin tells him in his ear that he is in her heart.

CLAUDIO.
And so she doth, cousin.

BEATRICE.
Good Lord, for alliance! Thus goes every

one to the world but I, and I am sunburnt. I may sit in a corner and cry heigh-ho for a husband!

Don Pedro.

Lady Beatrice, I will get you one.

Beatrice.

I would rather have one of your father's getting. Hath your Grace ne'er a brother like you? Your father got excellent husbands, if a maid could come by them.

Don Pedro.

Will you have me, lady?

Beatrice.

No, my lord, unless I might have another for working days: your Grace is too costly to wear every day. But, I beseech your Grace, pardon me; I was born to speak all mirth and no matter.

Don Pedro.

Your silence most offends me, and to be merry best becomes you; for out of question, you were born in a merry hour.

Beatrice.

No, sure, my lord, my mother cried; but then there was a star danced, and under that was I born. Cousins, God give you joy!

Leonato.

Niece, will you look to those things I told you of?

Beatrice.

I cry you mercy, uncle. By your Grace's pardon.

[Exit.]

Don Pedro.

By my troth, a pleasant spirited lady.

Leonato.

There's little of the melancholy element in her, my lord: she is never sad but when she sleeps; and not ever sad then, for I have heard my daughter say, she hath often dreamed of unhappiness and waked herself with laughing.

Don Pedro.

She cannot endure to hear tell of a husband.

Leonato.

O! by no means: she mocks all her wooers out of suit.

Don Pedro.

She were an excellent wife for Benedick.

Leonato.

O Lord! my lord, if they were but a week married, they would talk themselves mad.

Don Pedro.

Count Claudio, when mean you to go to church?

Claudio.

To-morrow, my lord. Time goes on crutches till love have all his rites.

Leonato.

Not till Monday, my dear son, which is hence a just seven-night; and a time too brief too, to have all things answer my mind.

Don Pedro.

Come, you shake the head at so long a breathing; but, I warrant thee, Claudio, the time shall not go dully by us. I will in the interim undertake one of Hercules' labours, which is, to bring Signior Benedick and the Lady Beatrice into a mountain of affection the one with the other. I would fain have it a match; and I doubt not but to fashion it, if you three will but minister such assistance as I shall give you direction.

Leonato.

My lord, I am for you, though it cost me ten nights' watchings.

Claudio.

And I, my lord.

Don Pedro.

And you too, gentle Hero?

Hero.

I will do any modest office, my lord, to help my cousin to a good husband.

Don Pedro.

And Benedick is not the unhopefullest husband that I know. Thus far can I praise him; he is of a noble strain, of approved valour, and confirmed honesty. I will teach you how to humour your cousin, that she shall fall in love with Benedick; and I, with your two helps, will so practise on Benedick that, in despite of his quick wit and his queasy stomach, he shall fall in love with Beatrice. If we can do this, Cupid is no longer an archer: his glory shall be ours, for we are the only love-gods. Go in with me, and I will tell you my drift.

[*Exeunt.*]

SCENE II

Another room in Leonato's house.
[*Enter* DON JOHN *and* BORACHIO.]

DON JOHN.
It is so; the Count Claudio shall marry the daughter of Leonato.

BORACHIO.
Yea, my lord; but I can cross it.

DON JOHN.
Any bar, any cross, any impediment will be medicinable to me: I am sick in displeasure to him, and whatsoever comes athwart his affection ranges evenly with mine. How canst thou cross this marriage?

BORACHIO.
Not honestly, my lord; but so covertly that no dishonesty shall appear in me.

DON JOHN.
Show me briefly how.

BORACHIO.
I think I told your lordship, a year since, how much I am in the favour of Margaret, the waiting-gentlewoman to Hero.

DON JOHN.
I remember.

BORACHIO.
I can, at any unseasonable instant of the night, appoint her to look out at her lady's chamber window.

DON JOHN.
What life is in that, to be the death of this marriage?

BORACHIO.
The poison of that lies in you to temper. Go you to the prince your brother; spare not to tell him, that he hath wronged his honour in marrying the renowned Claudio,—whose estimation do you mightily hold up,—to a contaminated stale, such a one as Hero.

DON JOHN.
What proof shall I make of that?

BORACHIO.
Proof enough to misuse the prince, to vex Claudio, to undo Hero, and kill Leonato. Look you for any other issue?

DON JOHN.
Only to despite them, I will endeavour anything.

BORACHIO.
Go then; find me a meet hour to draw Don Pedro and the Count Claudio alone: tell them that you know that Hero loves me; intend a kind of zeal both to the prince and Claudio, as—in love of your brother's honour, who hath made this match, and his friend's reputation, who is thus like to be cozened with the semblance of a maid,—that you have discovered thus. They will scarcely believe this without trial: offer them instances, which shall bear no less likelihood than to see me at her chamber-window, hear me call Margaret Hero, hear Margaret term me Claudio; and bring them to see this the very night before the intended wedding: for in the meantime I will so fashion the matter that Hero shall be absent; and there shall appear such seeming truth of Hero's disloyalty, that jealousy shall be called assurance, and all the preparation overthrown.

DON JOHN.
Grow this to what adverse issue it can, I will put it in practice. Be cunning in the working this, and thy fee is a thousand ducats.

BORACHIO.
Be you constant in the accusation, and my cunning shall not shame me.

DON JOHN.
I will presently go learn their day of marriage.

[*Exeunt.*]

SCENE III

Leonato's garden.
[*Enter* BENEDICK.]

BENEDICK.
Boy!

[*Enter a* BOY.]

BOY.
Signior?

BENEDICK.
In my chamber-window lies a book; bring it hither to me in the orchard.
BOY.
I am here already, sir.
BENEDICK.
I know that; but I would have thee hence, and here again. [*Exit* BOY.] I do much wonder that one man, seeing how much another man is a fool when he dedicates his behaviours to love, will, after he hath laughed at such shallow follies in others, become the argument of his own scorn by falling in love: and such a man is Claudio. I have known, when there was no music with him but the drum and the fife; and now had he rather hear the tabor and the pipe: I have known when he would have walked ten mile afoot to see a good armour; and now will he lie ten nights awake, carving the fashion of a new doublet. He was wont to speak plain and to the purpose, like an honest man and a soldier; and now is he turned orthography; his words are a very fantastical banquet, just so many strange dishes. May I be so converted, and see with these eyes? I cannot tell; I think not: I will not be sworn but love may transform me to an oyster; but I'll take my oath on it, till he have made an oyster of me, he shall never make me such a fool. One woman is fair, yet I am well; another is wise, yet I am well; another virtuous, yet I am well; but till all graces be in one woman, one woman shall not come in my grace. Rich she shall be, that's certain; wise, or I'll none; virtuous, or I'll never cheapen her; fair, or I'll never look on her; mild, or come not near me; noble, or not I for an angel; of good discourse, an excellent musician, and her hair shall be of what colour it please God. Ha! the prince and Monsieur Love! I will hide me in the arbour. [*Withdraws.*]

[*Enter* DON PEDRO, LEONATO, *and* CLAUDIO, *followed by* BALTHAZAR *and* MUSICIANS.]

DON PEDRO.
Come, shall we hear this music?

CLAUDIO.
Yea, my good lord.—How still the evening is,
As hush'd on purpose to grace harmony!
DON PEDRO.
See you where Benedick hath hid himself?
CLAUDIO.
O! very well, my lord: the music ended,
We'll fit the kid-fox with a penny-worth.
DON PEDRO.
Come, Balthazar, we'll hear that song again.
BALTHAZAR.
O! good my lord, tax not so bad a voice
To slander music any more than once.
DON PEDRO.
It is the witness still of excellency,
To put a strange face on his own perfection.
I pray thee, sing, and let me woo no more.
BALTHAZAR.
Because you talk of wooing, I will sing;
Since many a wooer doth commence his suit
To her he thinks not worthy; yet he woos;
Yet will he swear he loves.
DON PEDRO.
               Nay, pray thee come;
Or if thou wilt hold longer argument,
Do it in notes.
BALTHAZAR.
           Note this before my notes;
There's not a note of mine that's worth the noting.
DON PEDRO.
Why these are very crotchets that he speaks;
Notes, notes, forsooth, and nothing!
                    [*Music.*]
BENEDICK.
Now, divine air! now is his soul ravished! Is it not strange that sheep's guts should hale souls out of men's bodies? Well, a horn for my money, when all's done.
BALTHAZAR. [*Sings.*]
    Sigh no more, ladies, sigh no more,
       Men were deceivers ever;
    One foot in sea, and one on shore,
       To one thing constant never.

Then sigh not so,
But let them go,
And be you blithe and bonny,
Converting all your sounds of woe
Into Hey nonny, nonny.

Sing no more ditties, sing no moe
Of dumps so dull and heavy;
The fraud of men was ever so,
Since summer first was leavy.
Then sigh not so,
But let them go,
And be you blithe and bonny,
Converting all your sounds of woe
Into Hey nonny, nonny.

DON PEDRO.
By my troth, a good song.

BALTHAZAR.
And an ill singer, my lord.

DON PEDRO.
Ha, no, no, faith; thou singest well enough
for a shift.

BENEDICK. [*Aside.*]
An he had been a dog that should have
howled thus, they would have hanged
him; and I pray God his bad voice bode no
mischief. I had as lief have heard the night-
raven, come what plague could have come
after it.

DON PEDRO.
Yea, marry; dost thou hear, Balthazar? I
pray thee, get us some excellent music, for
to-morrow night we would have it at the
Lady Hero's chamber-window.

BALTHAZAR.
The best I can, my lord.

DON PEDRO.
Do so: farewell. [*Exeunt* BALTHAZAR *and*
MUSICIANS.] Come hither, Leonato: what
was it you told me of to-day, that your niece
Beatrice was in love with Signior Benedick?

CLAUDIO.
O! ay:—[*Aside to* DON PEDRO] Stalk on,
stalk on; the fowl sits. I did never think that
lady would have loved any man.

LEONATO.
No, nor I neither; but most wonderful that
she should so dote on Signior Benedick,

whom she hath in all outward behaviours
seemed ever to abhor.

BENEDICK. [*Aside.*]
Is't possible? Sits the wind in that corner?

LEONATO.
By my troth, my lord, I cannot tell what to
think of it but that she loves him with an
enraged affection: it is past the infinite of
thought.

DON PEDRO.
May be she doth but counterfeit.

CLAUDIO.
Faith, like enough.

LEONATO.
O God! counterfeit! There was never
counterfeit of passion came so near the life
of passion as she discovers it.

DON PEDRO.
Why, what effects of passion shows she?

CLAUDIO. [*Aside.*]
Bait the hook well: this fish will bite.

LEONATO.
What effects, my lord? She will sit you. [*To*
CLAUDIO.] You heard my daughter tell you
how.

CLAUDIO.
She did, indeed.

DON PEDRO.
How, how, I pray you? You amaze me: I
would have thought her spirit had been
invincible against all assaults of affection.

LEONATO.
I would have sworn it had, my lord;
especially against Benedick.

BENEDICK. [*Aside.*]
I should think this a gull, but that the
white-bearded fellow speaks it: knavery
cannot, sure, hide itself in such reverence.

CLAUDIO. [*Aside.*]
He hath ta'en the infection: hold it up.

DON PEDRO.
Hath she made her affection known to
Benedick?

LEONATO.
No; and swears she never will: that's her
torment.

CLAUDIO.
'Tis true, indeed; so your daughter says:

"Shall I," says she, "that have so oft encountered him with scorn, write to him that I love him?"

Leonato.
This says she now when she is beginning to write to him; for she'll be up twenty times a night, and there will she sit in her smock till she have writ a sheet of paper: my daughter tells us all.

Claudio.
Now you talk of a sheet of paper, I remember a pretty jest your daughter told us of.

Leonato.
O! when she had writ it, and was reading it over, she found Benedick and Beatrice between the sheet?

Claudio.
That.

Leonato.
O! she tore the letter into a thousand halfpence; railed at herself, that she should be so immodest to write to one that she knew would flout her: "I measure him," says she, "by my own spirit; for I should flout him, if he writ to me; yea, though I love him, I should."

Claudio.
Then down upon her knees she falls, weeps, sobs, beats her heart, tears her hair, prays, curses; "O sweet Benedick! God give me patience!"

Leonato.
She doth indeed; my daughter says so; and the ecstasy hath so much overborne her, that my daughter is sometimes afeard she will do a desperate outrage to herself. It is very true.

Don Pedro.
It were good that Benedick knew of it by some other, if she will not discover it.

Claudio.
To what end? he would make but a sport of it and torment the poor lady worse.

Don Pedro.
An he should, it were an alms to hang him. She's an excellent sweet lady, and, out of all suspicion, she is virtuous.

Claudio.
And she is exceeding wise.

Don Pedro.
In everything but in loving Benedick.

Leonato.
O! my lord, wisdom and blood combating in so tender a body, we have ten proofs to one that blood hath the victory. I am sorry for her, as I have just cause, being her uncle and her guardian.

Don Pedro.
I would she had bestowed this dotage on me; I would have daffed all other respects and made her half myself. I pray you, tell Benedick of it, and hear what a' will say.

Leonato.
Were it good, think you?

Claudio.
Hero thinks surely she will die; for she says she will die if he love her not, and she will die ere she make her love known, and she will die if he woo her, rather than she will bate one breath of her accustomed crossness.

Don Pedro.
She doth well: if she should make tender of her love, 'tis very possible he'll scorn it; for the man,—as you know all,—hath a contemptible spirit.

Claudio.
He is a very proper man.

Don Pedro.
He hath indeed a good outward happiness.

Claudio.
Fore God, and in my mind, very wise.

Don Pedro.
He doth indeed show some sparks that are like wit.

Claudio.
And I take him to be valiant.

Don Pedro.
As Hector, I assure you: and in the managing of quarrels you may say he is wise; for either he avoids them with great discretion, or undertakes them with a most Christian-like fear.

Leonato.
If he do fear God, a' must necessarily keep

peace: if he break the peace, he ought to enter into a quarrel with fear and trembling.

Don Pedro.
And so will he do; for the man doth fear God, howsoever it seems not in him by some large jests he will make. Well, I am sorry for your niece. Shall we go seek Benedick and tell him of her love?

Claudio.
Never tell him, my lord: let her wear it out with good counsel.

Leonato.
Nay, that's impossible: she may wear her heart out first.

Don Pedro.
Well, we will hear further of it by your daughter: let it cool the while. I love Benedick well, and I could wish he would modestly examine himself, to see how much he is unworthy so good a lady.

Leonato.
My lord, will you walk? dinner is ready.

Claudio. [*Aside.*]
If he do not dote on her upon this, I will never trust my expectation.

Don Pedro. [*Aside.*]
Let there be the same net spread for her; and that must your daughter and her gentle-woman carry. The sport will be, when they hold one an opinion of another's dotage, and no such matter: that's the scene that I would see, which will be merely a dumb-show. Let us send her to call him in to dinner.

[*Exeunt* Don Pedro, Claudio, *and* Leonato.]

Benedick. [*Advancing from the arbour.*]
This can be no trick: the conference was sadly borne. They have the truth of this from Hero. They seem to pity the lady: it seems her affections have their full bent. Love me! why, it must be requited. I hear how I am censured: they say I will bear myself proudly, if I perceive the love come from her; they say too that she will rather die than give any sign of affection. I did never think to marry: I must not seem proud: happy are they that hear their

detractions, and can put them to mending. They say the lady is fair: 'tis a truth, I can bear them witness; and virtuous: 'tis so, I cannot reprove it; and wise, but for loving me: by my troth, it is no addition to her wit, nor no great argument of her folly, for I will be horribly in love with her. I may chance have some odd quirks and remnants of wit broken on me, because I have railed so long against marriage; but doth not the appetite alter? A man loves the meat in his youth that he cannot endure in his age. Shall quips and sentences and these paper bullets of the brain awe a man from the career of his humour? No; the world must be peopled. When I said I would die a bachelor, I did not think I should live till I were married. Here comes Beatrice. By this day! she's a fair lady: I do spy some marks of love in her.

[*Enter* Beatrice.]

Beatrice.
Against my will I am sent to bid you come in to dinner.

Benedick.
Fair Beatrice, I thank you for your pains.

Beatrice.
I took no more pains for those thanks than you take pains to thank me: if it had been painful, I would not have come.

Benedick.
You take pleasure then in the message?

Beatrice.
Yea, just so much as you may take upon a knife's point, and choke a daw withal. You have no stomach, signior: fare you well.

[*Exit.*]

Benedick.
Ha! "Against my will I am sent to bid you come in to dinner," there's a double meaning in that. "I took no more pains for those thanks than you took pains to thank me," that's as much as to say, Any pains that I take for you is as easy as thanks. If I do not take pity of her, I am a villain; if I do not love her, I am a Jew. I will go get her picture.

[*Exit.*]

ACT III
SCENE I
Leonato's garden.
[*Enter* Hero, Margaret, *and* Ursula.]
Hero.
Good Margaret, run thee to the parlour;
There shalt thou find my cousin Beatrice
Proposing with the prince and Claudio:
Whisper her ear, and tell her, I and Ursula
Walk in the orchard, and our whole
   discourse
Is all of her; say that thou overheard'st us,
And bid her steal into the pleached bower,
Where honey-suckles, ripen'd by the sun,
Forbid the sun to enter; like favourites,
Made proud by princes, that advance their
   pride
Against that power that bred it. There will
   she hide her,
To listen our propose. This is thy office;
Bear thee well in it and leave us alone.
Margaret.
I'll make her come, I warrant you, presently.
   [*Exit.*]
Hero.
Now, Ursula, when Beatrice doth come,
As we do trace this alley up and down,
Our talk must only be of Benedick:
When I do name him, let it be thy part
To praise him more than ever man did
   merit.
My talk to thee must be how Benedick
Is sick in love with Beatrice: of this matter
Is little Cupid's crafty arrow made,
That only wounds by hearsay.
   [*Enter* Beatrice, *behind.*]
Now begin;
For look where Beatrice, like a lapwing,
   runs
Close by the ground, to hear our
   conference.
Ursula.
The pleasant'st angling is to see the fish
Cut with her golden oars the silver stream,
And greedily devour the treacherous bait:
So angle we for Beatrice; who even now
Is couched in the woodbine coverture.
Fear you not my part of the dialogue.
Hero.
Then go we near her, that her ear lose
   nothing
Of the false sweet bait that we lay for it.
   [*They advance to the bower.*]
No, truly, Ursula, she is too disdainful;
I know her spirits are as coy and wild
As haggards of the rock.
Ursula.
             But are you sure
That Benedick loves Beatrice so entirely?
Hero.
So says the prince, and my new-trothed
   lord.
Ursula.
And did they bid you tell her of it, madam?
Hero.
They did entreat me to acquaint her of it;
But I persuaded them, if they lov'd
   Benedick,
To wish him wrestle with affection,
And never to let Beatrice know of it.
Ursula.
Why did you so? Doth not the gentleman
Deserve as full as fortunate a bed
As ever Beatrice shall couch upon?
Hero.
O god of love! I know he doth deserve
As much as may be yielded to a man;
But nature never fram'd a woman's heart
Of prouder stuff than that of Beatrice;
Disdain and scorn ride sparkling in her
   eyes,
Misprising what they look on, and her wit
Values itself so highly, that to her
All matter else seems weak. She cannot
   love,
Nor take no shape nor project of affection,
She is so self-endear'd.
Ursula.
            Sure I think so;
And therefore certainly it were not good
She knew his love, lest she make sport
   at it.
Hero.
Why, you speak truth. I never yet saw man,
How wise, how noble, young, how rarely
   featur'd,

But she would spell him backward: if
    fair-fac'd,
She would swear the gentleman should be
    her sister;
If black, why, Nature, drawing of an antick,
Made a foul blot; if tall, a lance ill-headed;
If low, an agate very vilely cut;
If speaking, why, a vane blown with all
    winds;
If silent, why, a block moved with none.
So turns she every man the wrong side
    out,
And never gives to truth and virtue that
Which simpleness and merit purchaseth.
URSULA.
Sure, sure, such carping is not
    commendable.
HERO.
No; not to be so odd, and from all
    fashions,
As Beatrice is, cannot be commendable.
But who dare tell her so? If I should
    speak,
She would mock me into air: O! she
    would laugh me
Out of myself, press me to death with wit.
Therefore let Benedick, like cover'd fire,
Consume away in sighs, waste inwardly:
It were a better death than die with mocks,
Which is as bad as die with tickling.
URSULA.
Yet tell her of it: hear what she will say.
HERO.
No; rather I will go to Benedick,
And counsel him to fight against his
    passion.
And, truly, I'll devise some honest slanders
To stain my cousin with. One doth not
    know
How much an ill word may empoison
    liking.
URSULA.
O! do not do your cousin such a wrong.
She cannot be so much without true
    judgment,—
Having so swift and excellent a wit
As she is priz'd to have,—as to refuse
So rare a gentleman as Signior Benedick.

HERO.
He is the only man of Italy,
Always excepted my dear Claudio.
URSULA.
I pray you, be not angry with me,
    madam,
Speaking my fancy: Signior Benedick,
For shape, for bearing, argument and
    valour,
Goes foremost in report through Italy.
HERO.
Indeed, he hath an excellent good name.
URSULA.
His excellence did earn it, ere he had it.
When are you married, madam?
HERO.
Why, every day, to-morrow. Come, go in:
I'll show thee some attires, and have thy
    counsel
Which is the best to furnish me to-
    morrow.
URSULA.
She's lim'd, I warrant you: we have caught
    her, madam.
HERO.
If it prove so, then loving goes by haps:
Some Cupid kills with arrows, some with
    traps.
      [*Exeunt* HERO *and* URSULA.]
BEATRICE. [*Advancing.*]
What fire is in mine ears? Can this be
    true?
Stand I condemn'd for pride and scorn
    so much?
Contempt, farewell! and maiden pride,
    adieu!
No glory lives behind the back of such.
And, Benedick, love on; I will requite
    thee,
Taming my wild heart to thy loving hand:
If thou dost love, my kindness shall incite
    thee
To bind our loves up in a holy band;
For others say thou dost deserve, and I
Believe it better than reportingly.
               [*Exit.*]

SCENE II

A room in Leonato's house.

[*Enter* DON PEDRO, CLAUDIO, BENEDICK, *and* LEONATO.]

DON PEDRO.
I do but stay till your marriage be consummate, and then go I toward Arragon.

CLAUDIO.
I'll bring you thither, my lord, if you'll vouchsafe me.

DON PEDRO.
Nay, that would be as great a soil in the new gloss of your marriage, as to show a child his new coat and forbid him to wear it. I will only be bold with Benedick for his company; for, from the crown of his head to the sole of his foot, he is all mirth; he hath twice or thrice cut Cupid's bowstring, and the little hangman dare not shoot at him. He hath a heart as sound as a bell, and his tongue is the clapper; for what his heart thinks his tongue speaks.

BENEDICK.
Gallants, I am not as I have been.

LEONATO.
So say I: methinks you are sadder.

CLAUDIO.
I hope he be in love.

DON PEDRO.
Hang him, truant! there's no true drop of blood in him, to be truly touched with love. If he be sad, he wants money.

BENEDICK.
I have the tooth-ache.

DON PEDRO.
Draw it.

BENEDICK.
Hang it.

CLAUDIO.
You must hang it first, and draw it afterwards.

DON PEDRO.
What! sigh for the tooth-ache?

LEONATO.
Where is but a humour or a worm?

BENEDICK.
Well, every one can master a grief but he that has it.

CLAUDIO.
Yet say I, he is in love.

DON PEDRO.
There is no appearance of fancy in him, unless it be a fancy that he hath to strange disguises; as to be a Dutchman to-day, a Frenchman to-morrow; or in the shape of two countries at once, as a German from the waist downward, all slops, and a Spaniard from the hip upward, no doublet. Unless he have a fancy to this foolery, as it appears he hath, he is no fool for fancy, as you would have it appear he is.

CLAUDIO.
If he be not in love with some woman, there is no believing old signs: a' brushes his hat a mornings; what should that bode?

DON PEDRO.
Hath any man seen him at the barber's?

CLAUDIO.
No, but the barber's man hath been seen with him; and the old ornament of his cheek hath already stuffed tennis-balls.

LEONATO.
Indeed he looks younger than he did, by the loss of a beard.

DON PEDRO.
Nay, a' rubs himself with civet: can you smell him out by that?

CLAUDIO.
That's as much as to say the sweet youth's in love.

DON PEDRO.
The greatest note of it is his melancholy.

CLAUDIO.
And when was he wont to wash his face?

DON PEDRO.
Yea, or to paint himself? for the which, I hear what they say of him.

CLAUDIO.
Nay, but his jesting spirit; which is now crept into a lute-string, and new-governed by stops.

DON PEDRO.
Indeed, that tells a heavy tale for him. Conclude, conclude he is in love.

CLAUDIO.
Nay, but I know who loves him.

Don Pedro.
That would I know too: I warrant, one that knows him not.

Claudio.
Yes, and his ill conditions; and in despite of all, dies for him.

Don Pedro.
She shall be buried with her face upwards.

Benedick.
Yet is this no charm for the tooth-ache. Old signior, walk aside with me: I have studied eight or nine wise words to speak to you, which these hobby-horses must not hear.

[*Exeunt* Benedick *and* Leonato.]

Don Pedro.
For my life, to break with him about Beatrice.

Claudio.
'Tis even so. Hero and Margaret have by this played their parts with Beatrice, and then the two bears will not bite one another when they meet.

[*Enter* Don John.]

Don John.
My lord and brother, God save you!

Don Pedro.
Good den, brother.

Don John.
If your leisure served, I would speak with you.

Don Pedro.
In private?

Don John.
If it please you; yet Count Claudio may hear, for what I would speak of concerns him.

Don Pedro.
What's the matter?

Don John. [*To* Claudio.]
Means your lordship to be married to-morrow?

Don Pedro.
You know he does.

Don John.
I know not that, when he knows what I know.

Claudio.
If there be any impediment, I pray you discover it.

Don John.
You may think I love you not: let that

appear hereafter, and aim better at me by that I now will manifest. For my brother, I think he holds you well, and in dearness of heart hath holp to effect your ensuing marriage; surely suit ill-spent and labour ill bestowed!

Don Pedro.
Why, what's the matter?

Don John.
I came hither to tell you; and circumstances shortened,—for she has been too long a talking of,—the lady is disloyal.

Claudio.
Who, Hero?

Don John.
Even she: Leonato's Hero, your Hero, every man's Hero.

Claudio.
Disloyal?

Don John.
The word's too good to paint out her wickedness; I could say, she were worse: think you of a worse title, and I will fit her to it. Wonder not till further warrant: go but with me to-night, you shall see her chamber-window entered, even the night before her wedding-day: if you love her then, to-morrow wed her; but it would better fit your honour to change your mind.

Claudio.
May this be so?

Don Pedro.
I will not think it.

Don John.
If you dare not trust that you see, confess not that you know. If you will follow me, I will show you enough; and when you have seen more and heard more, proceed accordingly.

Claudio.
If I see anything to-night why I should not marry her to-morrow, in the congregation, where I should wed, there will I shame her.

Don Pedro.
And, as I wooed for thee to obtain her, I will join with thee to disgrace her.

Don John.
I will disparage her no further till you

are my witnesses: bear it coldly but till midnight, and let the issue show itself.

Don Pedro.
O day untowardly turned!

Claudio.
O mischief strangely thwarting!

Don John.
O plague right well prevented! So will you say when you have seen the sequel.

[Exeunt.]

SCENE III
A street.
[Enter Dogberry *and* Verges, *with the* Watch.]

Dogberry.
Are you good men and true?

Verges.
Yea, or else it were pity but they should suffer salvation, body and soul.

Dogberry.
Nay, that were a punishment too good for them, if they should have any allegiance in them, being chosen for the prince's watch.

Verges.
Well, give them their charge, neighbour Dogberry.

Dogberry.
First, who think you the most desartless man to be constable?

First Watch.
Hugh Oatcake, sir, or George Seacoal; for they can write and read.

Dogberry.
Come hither, neighbour Seacoal. God hath blessed you with a good name: to be a well-favoured man is the gift of fortune; but to write and read comes by nature.

Second Watch.
Both which, Master Constable,—

Dogberry.
You have: I knew it would be your answer. Well, for your favour, sir, why, give God thanks, and make no boast of it; and for your writing and reading, let that appear when there is no need of such vanity. You are thought here to be the most senseless and fit man for the constable of the watch;

therefore bear you the lanthorn. This is your charge: you shall comprehend all vagrom men; you are to bid any man stand, in the prince's name.

Second Watch.
How, if a' will not stand?

Dogberry.
Why, then, take no note of him, but let him go; and presently call the rest of the watch together, and thank God you are rid of a knave.

Verges.
If he will not stand when he is bidden, he is none of the prince's subjects.

Dogberry.
True, and they are to meddle with none but the prince's subjects. You shall also make no noise in the streets: for, for the watch to babble and to talk is most tolerable and not to be endured.

Second Watch.
We will rather sleep than talk: we know what belongs to a watch.

Dogberry.
Why, you speak like an ancient and most quiet watchman, for I cannot see how sleeping should offend; only have a care that your bills be not stolen. Well, you are to call at all the alehouses, and bid those that are drunk get them to bed.

Second Watch.
How if they will not?

Dogberry.
Why, then, let them alone till they are sober: if they make you not then the better answer, you may say they are not the men you took them for.

Second Watch.
Well, sir.

Dogberry.
If you meet a thief, you may suspect him, by virtue of your office, to be no true man; and, for such kind of men, the less you meddle or make with them, why, the more is for your honesty.

Second Watch.
If we know him to be a thief, shall we not lay hands on him?

Dogberry.

Truly, by your office, you may; but I think they that touch pitch will be defiled. The most peaceable way for you, if you do take a thief, is to let him show himself what he is and steal out of your company.

Verges.

You have been always called a merciful man, partner.

Dogberry.

Truly, I would not hang a dog by my will, much more a man who hath any honesty in him.

Verges.

If you hear a child cry in the night, you must call to the nurse and bid her still it.

Second Watch.

How if the nurse be asleep and will not hear us?

Dogberry.

Why then, depart in peace, and let the child wake her with crying; for the ewe that will not hear her lamb when it baes, will never answer a calf when he bleats.

Verges.

'Tis very true.

Dogberry.

This is the end of the charge. You constable, are to present the prince's own person: if you meet the prince in the night, you may stay him.

Verges.

Nay, by'r lady, that I think, a' cannot.

Dogberry.

Five shillings to one on't, with any man that knows the statutes, he may stay him: marry, not without the prince be willing; for, indeed, the watch ought to offend no man, and it is an offence to stay a man against his will.

Verges.

By'r lady, I think it be so.

Dogberry.

Ha, ah, ha! Well, masters, good night: an there be any matter of weight chances, call up me: keep your fellows' counsels and your own, and good night. Come, neighbour.

Second Watch.

Well, masters, we hear our charge: let us go sit here upon the church-bench till two, and then all to bed.

Dogberry.

One word more, honest neighbours. I pray you, watch about Signior Leonato's door; for the wedding being there to-morrow, there is a great coil to-night. Adieu; be vigitant, I beseech you.

[*Exeunt* Dogberry *and* Verges.]
[*Enter* Borachio *and* Conrade.]

Borachio.

What, Conrade!

First Watch. [*Aside.*]

Peace! stir not.

Borachio.

Conrade, I say!

Conrade.

Here, man. I am at thy elbow.

Borachio.

Mass, and my elbow itched; I thought there would a scab follow.

Conrade.

I will owe thee an answer for that; and now forward with thy tale.

Borachio.

Stand thee close then under this penthouse, for it drizzles rain, and I will, like a true drunkard, utter all to thee.

First Watch. [*Aside.*]

Some treason, masters; yet stand close.

Borachio.

Therefore know, I have earned of Don John a thousand ducats.

Conrade.

Is it possible that any villany should be so dear?

Borachio.

Thou shouldst rather ask if it were possible any villany should be so rich; for when rich villains have need of poor ones, poor ones may make what price they will.

Conrade.

I wonder at it.

Borachio.

That shows thou art unconfirmed. Thou knowest that the fashion of a doublet, or a hat, or a cloak, is nothing to a man.

CONRADE.
Yes, it is apparel.

BORACHIO.
I mean, the fashion.

CONRADE.
Yes, the fashion is the fashion.

BORACHIO.
Tush! I may as well say the fool's the fool. But seest thou not what a deformed thief this fashion is?

FIRST WATCH. [*Aside.*]
I know that Deformed; a' has been a vile thief this seven years; a' goes up and down like a gentleman: I remember his name.

BORACHIO.
Didst thou not hear somebody?

CONRADE.
No: 'twas the vane on the house.

BORACHIO.
Seest thou not, I say, what a deformed thief this fashion is? how giddily he turns about all the hot bloods between fourteen and five-and-thirty? sometime fashioning them like Pharaoh's soldiers in the reechy painting; sometime like god Bel's priests in the old church-window; sometime like the shaven Hercules in the smirched worm-eaten tapestry, where his codpiece seems as massy as his club?

CONRADE.
All this I see, and I see that the fashion wears out more apparel than the man. But art not thou thyself giddy with the fashion too, that thou hast shifted out of thy tale into telling me of the fashion?

BORACHIO.
Not so neither; but know, that I have to-night wooed Margaret, the Lady Hero's gentlewoman, by the name of Hero: she leans me out at her mistress' chamber-window, bids me a thousand times good night,—I tell this tale vilely:—I should first tell thee how the prince, Claudio, and my master, planted and placed and possessed by my master Don John, saw afar off in the orchard this amiable encounter.

CONRADE.
And thought they Margaret was Hero?

BORACHIO.
Two of them did, the prince and Claudio; but the devil my master, knew she was Margaret; and partly by his oaths, which first possessed them, partly by the dark night, which did deceive them, but chiefly by my villany, which did confirm any slander that Don John had made, away went Claudio enraged; swore he would meet her, as he was appointed, next morning at the temple, and there, before the whole congregation, shame her with what he saw o'er night, and send her home again without a husband.

FIRST WATCH.
We charge you in the prince's name, stand!

SECOND WATCH.
Call up the right Master Constable. We have here recovered the most dangerous piece of lechery that ever was known in the commonwealth.

FIRST WATCH.
And one Deformed is one of them: I know him, a' wears a lock.

CONRADE.
Masters, masters!

SECOND WATCH.
You'll be made bring Deformed forth, I warrant you.

CONRADE.
Masters,—

FIRST WATCH.
Never speak: we charge you let us obey you to go with us.

BORACHIO.
We are like to prove a goodly commodity, being taken up of these men's bills.

CONRADE.
A commodity in question, I warrant you. Come, we'll obey you.
[*Exeunt.*]

SCENE IV
A room in Leonato's house.
[*Enter* HERO, MARGARET, *and* URSULA.]

HERO.
Good Ursula, wake my cousin Beatrice, and desire her to rise.

URSULA.
I will, lady.
HERO.
And bid her come hither.
URSULA.
Well.

[*Exit.*]

MARGARET.
Troth, I think your other rabato were better.
HERO.
No, pray thee, good Meg, I'll wear this.
MARGARET.
By my troth's not so good; and I warrant your cousin will say so.
HERO.
My cousin's a fool, and thou art another: I'll wear none but this.
MARGARET.
I like the new tire within excellently, if the hair were a thought browner; and your gown's a most rare fashion, i' faith. I saw the Duchess of Milan's gown that they praise so.
HERO.
O! that exceeds, they say.
MARGARET.
By my troth 's but a night-gown in respect of yours: cloth o' gold, and cuts, and laced with silver, set with pearls, down sleeves, side sleeves, and skirts round, underborne with a blush tinsel; but for a fine, quaint, graceful, and excellent fashion, yours is worth ten on't.
HERO.
God give me joy to wear it! for my heart is exceeding heavy.
MARGARET.
'Twill be heavier soon by the weight of a man.
HERO.
Fie upon thee! art not ashamed?
MARGARET.
Of what, lady? of speaking honourably? is not marriage honourable in a beggar? Is not your lord honourable without marriage? I think you would have me say, "saving your reverence, a husband": an bad thinking do not wrest true speaking, I'll offend nobody. Is there any harm in "the heavier for a

husband"? None, I think, an it be the right husband and the right wife; otherwise 'tis light, and not heavy: ask my Lady Beatrice else; here she comes.

[*Enter* BEATRICE.]

HERO.
Good morrow, coz.
BEATRICE.
Good morrow, sweet Hero.
HERO.
Why, how now? do you speak in the sick tune?
BEATRICE.
I am out of all other tune, methinks.
MARGARET.
Clap's into "Light o' love"; that goes without a burden: do you sing it, and I'll dance it.
BEATRICE.
Ye, light o' love with your heels! then, if your husband have stables enough, you'll see he shall lack no barnes.
MARGARET.
O illegitimate construction! I scorn that with my heels.
BEATRICE.
'Tis almost five o'clock, cousin; 'tis time you were ready. By my troth, I am exceeding ill. Heigh-ho!
MARGARET.
For a hawk, a horse, or a husband?
BEATRICE.
For the letter that begins them all, H.
MARGARET.
Well, an you be not turned Turk, there's no more sailing by the star.
BEATRICE.
What means the fool, trow?
MARGARET.
Nothing I; but God send every one their heart's desire!
HERO.
These gloves the count sent me; they are an excellent perfume.
BEATRICE.
I am stuffed, cousin, I cannot smell.
MARGARET.
A maid, and stuffed! there's goodly catching of cold.

BEATRICE.

O, God help me! God help me! how long have you professed apprehension?

MARGARET.

Ever since you left it. Doth not my wit become me rarely!

BEATRICE.

It is not seen enough, you should wear it in your cap. By my troth, I am sick.

MARGARET.

Get you some of this distilled Carduus Benedictus, and lay it to your heart: it is the only thing for a qualm.

HERO.

There thou prick'st her with a thistle.

BEATRICE.

Benedictus! why Benedictus? you have some moral in this Benedictus.

MARGARET.

Moral! no, by my troth, I have no moral meaning; I meant, plain holy-thistle. You may think, perchance, that I think you are in love: nay, by'r lady, I am not such a fool to think what I list; nor I list not to think what I can; nor, indeed, I cannot think, if I would think my heart out of thinking, that you are in love, or that you will be in love, or that you can be in love. Yet Benedick was such another, and now is he become a man: he swore he would never marry; and yet now, in despite of his heart, he eats his meat without grudging: and how you may be converted, I know not; but methinks you look with your eyes as other women do.

BEATRICE.

What pace is this that thy tongue keeps?

MARGARET.

Not a false gallop.

[Re-enter URSULA.]

URSULA.

Madam, withdraw: the prince, the count, Signior Benedick, Don John, and all the gallants of the town, are come to fetch you to church.

HERO.

Help to dress me, good coz, good Meg, good Ursula.

[Exeunt.]

SCENE V

Another room in Leonato's house.
[Enter LEONATO and DOGBERRY and VERGES.]

LEONATO.

What would you with me, honest neighbour?

DOGBERRY.

Marry, sir, I would have some confidence with you, that decerns you nearly.

LEONATO.

Brief, I pray you; for you see it is a busy time with me.

DOGBERRY.

Marry, this it is, sir.

VERGES.

Yes, in truth it is, sir.

LEONATO.

What is it, my good friends?

DOGBERRY.

Goodman Verges, sir, speaks a little off the matter: an old man, sir, and his wits are not so blunt as, God help, I would desire they were; but, in faith, honest as the skin between his brows.

VERGES.

Yes, I thank God, I am as honest as any man living, that is an old man and no honester than I.

DOGBERRY.

Comparisons are odorous: *palabras*, neighbour Verges.

LEONATO.

Neighbours, you are tedious.

DOGBERRY.

It pleases your worship to say so, but we are the poor duke's officers; but truly, for mine own part, if I were as tedious as a king, I could find in my heart to bestow it all of your worship.

LEONATO.

All thy tediousness on me! ha?

DOGBERRY.

Yea, an 'twere a thousand pound more than 'tis; for I hear as good exclamation on your worship, as of any man in the city, and though I be but a poor man, I am glad to hear it.

VERGES.

And so am I.

LEONATO.

I would fain know what you have to say.

VERGES.

Marry, sir, our watch to-night, excepting your worship's presence, ha' ta'en a couple of as arrant knaves as any in Messina.

DOGBERRY.

A good old man, sir; he will be talking; as they say, "when the age is in, the wit is out." God help us! it is a world to see! Well said, i' faith, neighbour Verges: well, God's a good man; an two men ride of a horse, one must ride behind. An honest soul, i' faith, sir; by my troth he is, as ever broke bread; but God is to be worshipped: all men are not alike; alas! good neighbour.

LEONATO.

Indeed, neighbour, he comes too short of you.

DOGBERRY.

Gifts that God gives.

LEONATO.

I must leave you.

DOGBERRY.

One word, sir: our watch, sir, hath indeed comprehended two aspicious persons, and we would have them this morning examined before your worship.

LEONATO.

Take their examination yourself, and bring it me: I am now in great haste, as may appear unto you.

DOGBERRY.

It shall be suffigance.

LEONATO.

Drink some wine ere you go: fare you well.

[*Enter a* MESSENGER.]

MESSENGER.

My lord, they stay for you to give your daughter to her husband.

LEONATO.

I'll wait upon them: I am ready.

[*Exeunt* LEONATO *and* MESSENGER.]

DOGBERRY.

Go, good partner, go, get you to Francis Seacoal; bid him bring his pen and inkhorn

to the gaol: we are now to examination these men.

VERGES.

And we must do it wisely.

DOGBERRY.

We will spare for no wit, I warrant you; here's that shall drive some of them to a non-come: only get the learned writer to set down our excommunication, and meet me at the gaol.

[*Exeunt.*]

ACT IV
SCENE I

The inside of a church.

[*Enter* DON PEDRO, DON JOHN, LEONATO, FRIAR FRANCIS, CLAUDIO, BENEDICK, HERO, BEATRICE, &c.]

LEONATO.

Come, Friar Francis, be brief: only to the plain form of marriage, and you shall recount their particular duties afterwards.

FRIAR.

You come hither, my lord, to marry this lady?

CLAUDIO.

No.

LEONATO.

To be married to her, friar; you come to marry her.

FRIAR.

Lady, you come hither to be married to this count?

HERO.

I do.

FRIAR.

If either of you know any inward impediment, why you should not be conjoined, I charge you, on your souls, to utter it.

CLAUDIO.

Know you any, Hero?

HERO.

None, my lord.

FRIAR.

Know you any, count?

LEONATO.

I dare make his answer; none.

CLAUDIO.

O! what men dare do! what men may do!
what men daily do, not knowing what they
do!

BENEDICK.

How now! Interjections? Why then, some
be of laughing, as ah! ha! he!

CLAUDIO.

Stand thee by, friar. Father, by your leave:
Will you with free and unconstrained soul
Give me this maid, your daughter?

LEONATO.

As freely, son, as God did give her me.

CLAUDIO.

And what have I to give you back whose
worth
May counterpoise this rich and precious
gift?

DON PEDRO.

Nothing, unless you render her again.

CLAUDIO.

Sweet prince, you learn me noble
thankfulness.
There, Leonato, take her back again:
Give not this rotten orange to your
friend;
She's but the sign and semblance of her
honour.
Behold! how like a maid she blushes here.
O! what authority and show of truth
Can cunning sin cover itself withal.
Comes not that blood as modest evidence
To witness simple virtue? Would you not
swear,
All you that see her, that she were a maid,
By these exterior shows? But she is none:
She knows the heat of a luxurious bed;
Her blush is guiltiness, not modesty.

LEONATO.

What do you mean, my lord?

CLAUDIO.

Not to be married, not to knit my soul
To an approved wanton.

LEONATO.

Dear my lord, if you, in your own proof,
Have vanquish'd the resistance of her
youth,
And made defeat of her virginity,—

CLAUDIO.

I know what you would say: if I have
known her,
You'll say she did embrace me as a
husband,
And so extenuate the forehand sin:
No, Leonato,
I never tempted her with word too large;
But, as a brother to his sister, show'd
Bashful sincerity and comely love.

HERO.

And seem'd I ever otherwise to you?

CLAUDIO.

Out on thee! Seeming! I will write against
it:
You seem to me as Dian in her orb,
As chaste as is the bud ere it be blown;
But you are more intemperate in your
blood
Than Venus, or those pamper'd animals
That rage in savage sensuality.

HERO.

Is my lord well, that he doth speak so wide?

LEONATO.

Sweet prince, why speak not you?

DON PEDRO.

                        What should I speak?
I stand dishonour'd, that have gone about
To link my dear friend to a common stale.

LEONATO.

Are these things spoken, or do I but
dream?

DON JOHN.

Sir, they are spoken, and these things are
true.

BENEDICK.

This looks not like a nuptial.

HERO.

                           True! O God!

CLAUDIO.

Leonato, stand I here? Is this the prince?
Is this the prince's brother?
Is this face Hero's? Are our eyes our own?

LEONATO.

All this is so; but what of this, my lord?

CLAUDIO.

Let me but move one question to your
daughter,

And by that fatherly and kindly power
That you have in her, bid her answer truly.
LEONATO.
I charge thee do so, as thou art my child.
HERO.
O, God defend me! how am I beset!
What kind of catechizing call you this?
CLAUDIO.
To make you answer truly to your name.
HERO.
Is it not Hero? Who can blot that name
With any just reproach?
CLAUDIO.
                    Marry, that can Hero:
Hero itself can blot out Hero's virtue.
What man was he talk'd with you
      yesternight
Out at your window, betwixt twelve and
      one?
Now, if you are a maid, answer to this.
HERO.
I talk'd with no man at that hour, my lord.
DON PEDRO.
Why, then are you no maiden.
Leonato, I am sorry you must hear: upon
      my honour,
Myself, my brother, and this grieved count,
Did see her, hear her, at that hour last
      night,
Talk with a ruffian at her chamber-
      window;
Who hath indeed, most like a liberal
      villain,
Confess'd the vile encounters they have
      had
A thousand times in secret.
DON JOHN.
Fie, fie! they are not to be nam'd, my lord,
Not to be spoke of;
There is not chastity enough in language
Without offence to utter them. Thus,
      pretty lady,
I am sorry for thy much misgovernment.
CLAUDIO.
O Hero! what a Hero hadst thou been,
If half thy outward graces had been plac'd
About thy thoughts and counsels of thy
      heart!

But fare thee well, most foul, most fair!
      farewell,
Thou pure impiety, and impious purity!
For thee I'll lock up all the gates of love,
And on my eyelids shall conjecture hang,
To turn all beauty into thoughts of harm,
And never shall it more be gracious.
LEONATO.
Hath no man's dagger here a point for me?
                    [HERO *swoons.*]
BEATRICE.
Why, how now, cousin! wherefore sink you
      down?
DON JOHN.
Come, let us go. These things, come thus
      to light,
Smother her spirits up.
            [*Exeunt* DON PEDRO, DON JOHN,
                    and CLAUDIO.]
BENEDICK.
How doth the lady?
BEATRICE.
                    Dead, I think! help, uncle!
Hero! why, Hero! Uncle! Signior
      Benedick! Friar!
LEONATO.
O Fate! take not away thy heavy hand:
Death is the fairest cover for her shame
That may be wish'd for.
BEATRICE.
                    How now, cousin Hero?
FRIAR.
Have comfort, lady.
LEONATO.
Dost thou look up?
FRIAR.
                    Yea; wherefore should she not?
LEONATO.
Wherefore! Why, doth not every earthly
      thing
Cry shame upon her? Could she here
      deny
The story that is printed in her blood?
Do not live, Hero; do not ope thine eyes;
For, did I think thou wouldst not quickly
      die,
Thought I thy spirits were stronger than
      thy shames,

Myself would, on the rearward of
   reproaches,
Strike at thy life. Griev'd I, I had but one?
Chid I for that at frugal nature's frame?
O! one too much by thee. Why had I one?
Why ever wast thou lovely in mine eyes?
Why had I not with charitable hand
Took up a beggar's issue at my gates,
Who smirched thus, and mir'd with infamy,
I might have said, "No part of it is mine;
This shame derives itself from unknown
   loins?"
But mine, and mine I lov'd, and mine I
   prais'd,
And mine that I was proud on, mine so
   much
That I myself was to myself not mine,
Valuing of her; why, she—O! she is fallen
Into a pit of ink, that the wide sea
Hath drops too few to wash her clean
   again,
And salt too little which may season give
To her foul-tainted flesh.

BENEDICK.

               Sir, sir, be patient.
For my part, I am so attir'd in wonder,
I know not what to say.

BEATRICE.

O! on my soul, my cousin is belied!

BENEDICK.

Lady, were you her bedfellow last night?

BEATRICE.

No, truly, not; although, until last night
I have this twelvemonth been her
   bedfellow.

LEONATO.

Confirm'd, confirm'd! O! that is stronger
   made,
Which was before barr'd up with ribs of
   iron.
Would the two princes lie? and Claudio
   lie,
Who lov'd her so, that, speaking of her
   foulness,
Wash'd it with tears? Hence from her! let
   her die.

FRIAR.

Hear me a little;

For I have only been silent so long,
And given way unto this course of fortune,
By noting of the lady: I have mark'd
A thousand blushing apparitions
To start into her face; a thousand innocent
   shames
In angel whiteness bear away those
   blushes;
And in her eye there hath appear'd a fire,
To burn the errors that these princes hold
Against her maiden truth. Call me a fool;
Trust not my reading nor my observations,
Which with experimental seal doth
   warrant
The tenure of my book; trust not my age,
My reverence, calling, nor divinity,
If this sweet lady lie not guiltless here
Under some biting error.

LEONATO.

             Friar, it cannot be.
Thou seest that all the grace that she hath
   left
Is that she will not add to her damnation
A sin of perjury: she not denies it.
Why seek'st thou then to cover with
   excuse
That which appears in proper nakedness?

FRIAR.

Lady, what man is he you are accus'd of?

HERO.

They know that do accuse me, I know
   none;
If I know more of any man alive
Than that which maiden modesty doth
   warrant,
Let all my sins lack mercy! O, my father!
Prove you that any man with me convers'd
At hours unmeet, or that I yesternight
Maintain'd the change of words with any
   creature,
Refuse me, hate me, torture me to death.

FRIAR.

There is some strange misprision in the
   princes.

BENEDICK.

Two of them have the very bent of
   honour;
And if their wisdoms be misled in this,

The practice of it lives in John the bastard,
Whose spirits toil in frame of villanies.
LEONATO.
I know not. If they speak but truth of her,
These hands shall tear her; if they wrong
    her honour,
The proudest of them shall well hear of it.
Time hath not yet so dried this blood of
    mine,
Nor age so eat up my invention,
Nor fortune made such havoc of my means,
Nor my bad life reft me so much of friends,
But they shall find, awak'd in such a kind,
Both strength of limb and policy of mind,
Ability in means and choice of friends,
To quit me of them throughly.
FRIAR.
                     Pause awhile,
And let my counsel sway you in this case.
Your daughter here the princes left for
    dead;
Let her awhile be secretly kept in,
And publish it that she is dead indeed:
Maintain a mourning ostentation;
And on your family's old monument
Hang mournful epitaphs and do all rites
That appertain unto a burial.
LEONATO.
What shall become of this? What will
    this do?
FRIAR.
Marry, this well carried shall on her behalf
Change slander to remorse; that is some
    good.
But not for that dream I on this strange
    course,
But on this travail look for greater birth.
She dying, as it must be so maintain'd,
Upon the instant that she was accus'd,
Shall be lamented, pitied and excus'd
Of every hearer; for it so falls out
That what we have we prize not to the
    worth
Whiles we enjoy it, but being lack'd and
    lost,
Why, then we rack the value, then we find
The virtue that possession would not show
    us

Whiles it was ours. So will it fare with
    Claudio:
When he shall hear she died upon his
    words,
The idea of her life shall sweetly creep
Into his study of imagination,
And every lovely organ of her life
Shall come apparell'd in more precious
    habit,
More moving-delicate, and full of life
Into the eye and prospect of his soul,
Than when she liv'd indeed: then shall he
    mourn,—
If ever love had interest in his liver,—
And wish he had not so accused her,
No, though be thought his accusation
    true.
Let this be so, and doubt not but success
Will fashion the event in better shape
Than I can lay it down in likelihood.
But if all aim but this be levell'd false,
The supposition of the lady's death
Will quench the wonder of her infamy:
And if it sort not well, you may conceal
    her,—
As best befits her wounded reputation,—
In some reclusive and religious life,
Out of all eyes, tongues, minds, and
    injuries.
BENEDICK.
Signior Leonato, let the friar advise you:
And though you know my inwardness
    and love
Is very much unto the prince and Claudio,
Yet, by mine honour, I will deal in this
As secretly and justly as your soul
Should with your body.
LEONATO.
              Being that I flow in grief,
The smallest twine may lead me.
FRIAR.
'Tis well consented: presently away;
For to strange sores strangely they strain
    the cure.
Come, lady, die to live: this wedding day
Perhaps is but prolong'd: have patience
    and endure.
    [*Exeunt* FRIAR, HERO, *and* LEONATO.]

BENEDICK.
Lady Beatrice, have you wept all this while?

BEATRICE.
Yea, and I will weep a while longer.

BENEDICK.
I will not desire that.

BEATRICE.
You have no reason; I do it freely.

BENEDICK.
Surely I do believe your fair cousin is wronged.

BEATRICE.
Ah! how much might the man deserve of me that would right her.

BENEDICK.
Is there any way to show such friendship?

BEATRICE.
A very even way, but no such friend.

BENEDICK.
May a man do it?

BEATRICE.
It is a man's office, but not yours.

BENEDICK.
I do love nothing in the world so well as you: is not that strange?

BEATRICE.
As strange as the thing I know not. It were as possible for me to say I loved nothing so well as you; but believe me not, and yet I lie not; I confess nothing, nor I deny nothing. I am sorry for my cousin.

BENEDICK.
By my sword, Beatrice, thou lovest me.

BEATRICE.
Do not swear by it, and eat it.

BENEDICK.
I will swear by it that you love me; and I will make him eat it that says I love not you.

BEATRICE.
Will you not eat your word?

BENEDICK.
With no sauce that can be devised to it. I protest I love thee.

BEATRICE.
Why then, God forgive me!

BENEDICK.
What offence, sweet Beatrice?

BEATRICE.
You have stayed me in a happy hour: I was about to protest I loved you.

BENEDICK.
And do it with all thy heart.

BEATRICE.
I love you with so much of my heart that none is left to protest.

BENEDICK.
Come, bid me do anything for thee.

BEATRICE.
Kill Claudio.

BENEDICK.
Ha! not for the wide world.

BEATRICE.
You kill me to deny it. Farewell.

BENEDICK.
Tarry, sweet Beatrice.

BEATRICE.
I am gone, though I am here: there is no love in you: nay, I pray you, let me go.

BENEDICK.
Beatrice,—

BEATRICE.
In faith, I will go.

BENEDICK.
We'll be friends first.

BEATRICE.
You dare easier be friends with me than fight with mine enemy.

BENEDICK.
Is Claudio thine enemy?

BEATRICE.
Is he not approved in the height a villain, that hath slandered, scorned, dishonoured my kinswoman? O! that I were a man. What! bear her in hand until they come to take hands, and then, with public accusation, uncovered slander, unmitigated rancour,—O God, that I were a man! I would eat his heart in the market-place.

BENEDICK.
Hear me, Beatrice,—

BEATRICE.
Talk with a man out at a window! a proper saying!

BENEDICK.
Nay, but Beatrice,—

BEATRICE.
Sweet Hero! she is wronged, she is slandered, she is undone.

BENEDICK.
Beat—

BEATRICE.
Princes and counties! Surely, a princely testimony, a goodly Count Comfect; a sweet gallant, surely! O! that I were a man for his sake, or that I had any friend would be a man for my sake! But manhood is melted into curtsies, valour into compliment, and men are only turned into tongue, and trim ones too: he is now as valiant as Hercules, that only tells a lie and swears it. I cannot be a man with wishing, therefore I will die a woman with grieving.

BENEDICK.
Tarry, good Beatrice. By this hand, I love thee.

BEATRICE.
Use it for my love some other way than swearing by it.

BENEDICK.
Think you in your soul the Count Claudio hath wronged Hero?

BEATRICE.
Yea, as sure is I have a thought or a soul.

BENEDICK.
Enough! I am engaged, I will challenge him. I will kiss your hand, and so leave you. By this hand, Claudio shall render me a dear account. As you hear of me, so think of me. Go, comfort your cousin: I must say she is dead; and so, farewell.

[*Exeunt.*]

SCENE II

A prison.

[*Enter* DOGBERRY, VERGES, *and* SEXTON, *in gowns; and the* WATCH, *with* CONRADE *and* BORACHIO.]

DOGBERRY.
Is our whole dissembly appeared?

VERGES.
O! a stool and a cushion for the sexton.

SEXTON.
Which be the malefactors?

DOGBERRY.
Marry, that am I and my partner.

VERGES.
Nay, that's certain: we have the exhibition to examine.

SEXTON.
But which are the offenders that are to be examined? Let them come before Master constable.

DOGBERRY.
Yea, marry, let them come before me. What is your name, friend?

BORACHIO.
Borachio.

DOGBERRY.
Pray write down Borachio. Yours, sirrah?

CONRADE.
I am a gentleman, sir, and my name is Conrade.

DOGBERRY.
Write down Master gentleman Conrade. Masters, do you serve God?

BOTH.
Yea, sir, we hope.

DOGBERRY.
Write down that they hope they serve God: and write God first; for God defend but God should go before such villains! Masters, it is proved already that you are little better than false knaves, and it will go near to be thought so shortly. How answer you for yourselves?

CONRADE.
Marry, sir, we say we are none.

DOGBERRY.
A marvellous witty fellow, I assure you; but I will go about with him. Come you hither, sirrah; a word in your ear: sir, I say to you, it is thought you are false knaves.

BORACHIO.
Sir, I say to you we are none.

DOGBERRY.
Well, stand aside. 'Fore God, they are both in a tale. Have you writ down, that they are none?

SEXTON.
Master constable, you go not the way to examine: you must call forth the watch that are their accusers.

DOGBERRY.
Yea, marry, that's the eftest way. Let the watch come forth. Masters, I charge you, in the prince's name, accuse these men.

FIRST WATCH.
This man said, sir, that Don John, the prince's brother, was a villain.

DOGBERRY.
Write down Prince John a villain. Why, this is flat perjury, to call a prince's brother villain.

BORACHIO.
Master Constable,—

DOGBERRY.
Pray thee, fellow, peace: I do not like thy look, I promise thee.

SEXTON.
What heard you him say else?

SECOND WATCH.
Marry, that he had received a thousand ducats of Don John for accusing the Lady Hero wrongfully.

DOGBERRY.
Flat burglary as ever was committed.

VERGES.
Yea, by the mass, that it is.

SEXTON.
What else, fellow?

FIRST WATCH.
And that Count Claudio did mean, upon his words, to disgrace Hero before the whole assembly, and not marry her.

DOGBERRY.
O villain! thou wilt be condemned into everlasting redemption for this.

SEXTON.
What else?

SECOND WATCH.
This is all.

SEXTON.
And this is more, masters, than you can deny. Prince John is this morning secretly stolen away: Hero was in this manner accused, in this manner refused, and, upon the grief of this, suddenly died. Master Constable, let these men be bound, and brought to Leonato's: I will go before and show him their examination.

[*Exit.*]

DOGBERRY.
Come, let them be opinioned.

VERGES.
Let them be in the hands—

CONRADE.
Off, coxcomb!

DOGBERRY.
God's my life! where's the sexton? let him write down the prince's officer coxcomb. Come, bind them. Thou naughty varlet!

CONRADE.
Away! you are an ass; you are an ass.

DOGBERRY.
Dost thou not suspect my place? Dost thou not suspect my years? O that he were here to write me down an ass! but, masters, remember that I am an ass; though it be not written down, yet forget not that I am an ass. No, thou villain, thou art full of piety, as shall be proved upon thee by good witness. I am a wise fellow; and, which is more, an officer; and, which is more, a householder; and, which is more, as pretty a piece of flesh as any in Messina; and one that knows the law, go to; and a rich fellow enough, go to; and a fellow that hath had losses; and one that hath two gowns, and everything handsome about him. Bring him away. O that I had been writ down an ass!

[*Exeunt.*]

ACT V
SCENE I

Before Leonato's house.

[*Enter* LEONATO *and* ANTONIO.]

ANTONIO.
If you go on thus, you will kill yourself;
And 'tis not wisdom thus to second grief
Against yourself.

LEONATO.
       I pray thee, cease thy counsel,
Which falls into mine ears as profitless
As water in a sieve: give not me counsel;
Nor let no comforter delight mine ear
But such a one whose wrongs do suit with
     mine:
Bring me a father that so lov'd his child,
Whose joy of her is overwhelm'd like mine,

And bid him speak to me of patience;
Measure his woe the length and breadth
   of mine,
And let it answer every strain for strain,
As thus for thus and such a grief for such,
In every lineament, branch, shape, and
   form:
If such a one will smile, and stroke his
   beard;
Bid sorrow wag, cry "hem" when he should
   groan,
Patch grief with proverbs; make
   misfortune drunk
With candle-wasters; bring him yet to me,
And I of him will gather patience.
But there is no such man; for, brother, men
Can counsel and speak comfort to that
   grief
Which they themselves not feel; but,
   tasting it,
Their counsel turns to passion, which
   before
Would give preceptial medicine to rage,
Fetter strong madness in a silken thread,
Charm ache with air and agony with
   words.
No, no; 'tis all men's office to speak
   patience
To those that wring under the load of
   sorrow,
But no man's virtue nor sufficiency
To be so moral when he shall endure
The like himself. Therefore give me no
   counsel:
My griefs cry louder than advertisement.

ANTONIO.
Therein do men from children nothing
   differ.

LEONATO.
I pray thee peace! I will be flesh and blood;
For there was never yet philosopher
That could endure the toothache patiently,
However they have writ the style of gods
And made a push at chance and
   sufferance.

ANTONIO.
Yet bend not all the harm upon yourself;
Make those that do offend you suffer too.

LEONATO.
There thou speak'st reason: nay, I will do so.
My soul doth tell me Hero is belied;
And that shall Claudio know; so shall the
   prince,
And all of them that thus dishonour her.

ANTONIO.
Here comes the prince and Claudio
   hastily.
   [*Enter* DON PEDRO *and* CLAUDIO.]

DON PEDRO.
Good den, good den.

CLAUDIO.
          Good day to both of you.

LEONATO.
Hear you, my lords,—

DON PEDRO.
        We have some haste, Leonato.

LEONATO.
Some haste, my lord! well, fare you well,
   my lord:
Are you so hasty now?—well, all is one.

DON PEDRO.
Nay, do not quarrel with us, good old man.

ANTONIO.
If he could right himself with quarrelling,
Some of us would lie low.

CLAUDIO.
            Who wrongs him?

LEONATO.
Marry, thou dost wrong me; thou
   dissembler, thou.
Nay, never lay thy hand upon thy sword;
I fear thee not.

CLAUDIO.
        Marry, beshrew my hand,
If it should give your age such cause of
   fear.
In faith, my hand meant nothing to my
   sword.

LEONATO.
Tush, tush, man! never fleer and jest at me:
I speak not like a dotard nor a fool,
As, under privilege of age, to brag
What I have done being young, or what
   would do,
Were I not old. Know, Claudio, to thy
   head,

Thou hast so wrong'd mine innocent child
   and me
That I am forc'd to lay my reverence by,
And, with grey hairs and bruise of many
   days,
Do challenge thee to trial of a man.
I say thou hast belied mine innocent child:
Thy slander hath gone through and
   through her heart,
And she lied buried with her ancestors;
O! in a tomb where never scandal slept,
Save this of hers, fram'd by thy villany!

CLAUDIO.
My villany?

LEONATO.
          Thine, Claudio; thine, I say.

DON PEDRO.
You say not right, old man.

LEONATO.
            My lord, my lord,
I'll prove it on his body, if he dare,
Despite his nice fence and his active
   practice,
His May of youth and bloom of lustihood.

CLAUDIO.
Away! I will not have to do with you.

LEONATO.
Canst thou so daff me? Thou hast kill'd
   my child;
If thou kill'st me, boy, thou shalt kill a
   man.

ANTONIO.
He shall kill two of us, and men indeed:
But that's no matter; let him kill one first:
Win me and wear me; let him answer me.
Come, follow me, boy; come, sir boy, come,
   follow me.
Sir boy, I'll whip you from your foining
   fence;
Nay, as I am a gentleman, I will.

LEONATO.
Brother,—

ANTONIO.
Content yourself. God knows I lov'd my
   niece;
And she is dead, slander'd to death by
   villains,
That dare as well answer a man indeed

As I dare take a serpent by the tongue.
Boys, apes, braggarts, Jacks, milksops!

LEONATO.
             Brother Antony,—

ANTONIO.
Hold your content. What, man! I know
   them, yea,
And what they weigh, even to the utmost
   scruple,
Scambling, out-facing, fashion-monging
   boys,
That lie and cog and flout, deprave and
   slander,
Go antickly, show outward hideousness,
And speak off half a dozen dangerous
   words,
How they might hurt their enemies, if
   they durst;
And this is all!

LEONATO.
But, brother Antony,—

ANTONIO.
           Come, 'tis no matter:
Do not you meddle, let me deal in this.

DON PEDRO.
Gentlemen both, we will not wake your
   patience.
My heart is sorry for your daughter's death;
But, on my honour, she was charg'd with
   nothing
But what was true and very full of proof.

LEONATO.
My lord, my lord—

DON PEDRO.
          I will not hear you.

LEONATO.
               No?
Come, brother, away. I will be heard.—

ANTONIO.
             And shall,
Or some of us will smart for it.
      [*Exeunt* LEONATO *and* ANTONIO.]
            [*Enter* BENEDICK.]

DON PEDRO.
See, see; here comes the man we went to
   seek.

CLAUDIO.
Now, signior, what news?

BENEDICK.
Good day, my lord.

DON PEDRO.
Welcome, signior: you are almost come to part almost a fray.

CLAUDIO.
We had like to have had our two noses snapped off with two old men without teeth.

DON PEDRO.
Leonato and his brother. What think'st thou? Had we fought, I doubt we should have been too young for them.

BENEDICK.
In a false quarrel there is no true valour. I came to seek you both.

CLAUDIO.
We have been up and down to seek thee; for we are high-proof melancholy, and would fain have it beaten away. Wilt thou use thy wit?

BENEDICK.
It is in my scabbard; shall I draw it?

DON PEDRO.
Dost thou wear thy wit by thy side?

CLAUDIO.
Never any did so, though very many have been beside their wit. I will bid thee draw, as we do the minstrels; draw, to pleasure us.

DON PEDRO.
As I am an honest man, he looks pale. Art thou sick, or angry?

CLAUDIO.
What, courage, man! What though care killed a cat, thou hast mettle enough in thee to kill care.

BENEDICK.
Sir, I shall meet your wit in the career, an you charge it against me. I pray you choose another subject.

CLAUDIO.
Nay then, give him another staff: this last was broke cross.

DON PEDRO.
By this light, he changes more and more: I think he be angry indeed.

CLAUDIO.
If he be, he knows how to turn his girdle.

BENEDICK.
Shall I speak a word in your ear?

CLAUDIO.
God bless me from a challenge!

BENEDICK. [*Aside to* CLAUDIO.]
You are a villain, I jest not: I will make it good how you dare, with what you dare, and when you dare. Do me right, or I will protest your cowardice. You have killed a sweet lady, and her death shall fall heavy on you. Let me hear from you.

CLAUDIO.
Well I will meet you, so I may have good cheer.

DON PEDRO.
What, a feast, a feast?

CLAUDIO.
I' faith, I thank him; he hath bid me to a calf's-head and a capon, the which if I do not carve most curiously, say my knife's naught. Shall I not find a woodcock too?

BENEDICK.
Sir, your wit ambles well; it goes easily.

DON PEDRO.
I'll tell thee how Beatrice praised thy wit the other day. I said, thou hadst a fine wit. "True," says she, "a fine little one." "No," said I, "a great wit." "Right," said she, "a great gross one." "Nay," said I, "a good wit." "Just," said she, "it hurts nobody." "Nay," said I, "the gentleman is wise." "Certain," said she, "a wise gentleman." "Nay," said I, "he hath the tongues." "That I believe" said she, "for he swore a thing to me on Monday night, which he forswore on Tuesday morning: there's a double tongue; there's two tongues." Thus did she, an hour together, trans-shape thy particular virtues; yet at last she concluded with a sigh, thou wast the properest man in Italy.

CLAUDIO.
For the which she wept heartily and said she cared not.

DON PEDRO.
Yea, that she did; but yet, for all that, an if she did not hate him deadly, she would love him dearly. The old man's daughter told us all.

CLAUDIO.
All, all; and moreover, God saw him when he was hid in the garden.

DON PEDRO.
But when shall we set the savage bull's horns on the sensible Benedick's head?

CLAUDIO.
Yea, and text underneath, "Here dwells Benedick the married man"?

BENEDICK.
Fare you well, boy: you know my mind. I will leave you now to your gossip-like humour; you break jests as braggarts do their blades, which, God be thanked, hurt not. My lord, for your many courtesies I thank you: I must discontinue your company. Your brother the bastard is fled from Messina: you have, among you, killed a sweet and innocent lady. For my Lord Lack-beard there, he and I shall meet; and till then, peace be with him.

[Exit.]

DON PEDRO.
He is in earnest.

CLAUDIO.
In most profound earnest; and, I'll warrant you, for the love of Beatrice.

DON PEDRO.
And hath challenged thee?

CLAUDIO.
Most sincerely.

DON PEDRO.
What a pretty thing man is when he goes in his doublet and hose and leaves off his wit!

CLAUDIO.
He is then a giant to an ape; but then is an ape a doctor to such a man.

DON PEDRO.
But, soft you; let me be: pluck up, my heart, and be sad! Did he not say my brother was fled?

[Enter DOGBERRY, VERGES, and the WATCH, with CONRADE and BORACHIO.]

DOGBERRY.
Come you, sir: if justice cannot tame you, she shall ne'er weigh more reasons in her balance. Nay, an you be a cursing hypocrite once, you must be looked to.

DON PEDRO.
How now! two of my brother's men bound! Borachio, one!

CLAUDIO.
Hearken after their offence, my lord.

DON PEDRO.
Officers, what offence have these men done?

DOGBERRY.
Marry, sir, they have committed false report; moreover, they have spoken untruths; secondarily, they are slanders; sixth and lastly, they have belied a lady; thirdly, they have verified unjust things; and to conclude, they are lying knaves.

DON PEDRO.
First, I ask thee what they have done; thirdly, I ask thee what's their offence; sixth and lastly, why they are committed; and, to conclude, what you lay to their charge?

CLAUDIO.
Rightly reasoned, and in his own division; and, by my troth, there's one meaning well suited.

DON PEDRO.
Who have you offended, masters, that you are thus bound to your answer? This learned constable is too cunning to be understood. What's your offence?

BORACHIO.
Sweet prince, let me go no further to mine answer: do you hear me, and let this count kill me. I have deceived even your very eyes: what your wisdoms could not discover, these shallow fools have brought to light; who, in the night overheard me confessing to this man how Don John your brother incensed me to slander the Lady Hero; how you were brought into the orchard and saw me court Margaret in Hero's garments; how you disgraced her, when you should marry her. My villany they have upon record; which I had rather seal with my death than repeat over to my shame. The lady is dead upon mine and my master's false accusation; and, briefly, I desire nothing but the reward of a villain.

Don Pedro.
Runs not this speech like iron through your blood?
Claudio.
I have drunk poison whiles he utter'd it.
Don Pedro.
But did my brother set thee on to this?
Borachio.
Yea; and paid me richly for the practice of it.
Don Pedro.
He is compos'd and fram'd of treachery:
And fled he is upon this villany.
Claudio.
Sweet Hero! now thy image doth appear
In the rare semblance that I lov'd it first.
Dogberry.
Come, bring away the plaintiffs: by this time our sexton hath reformed Signior Leonato of the matter. And masters, do not forget to specify, when time and place shall serve, that I am an ass.
Verges.
Here, here comes Master Signior Leonato, and the sexton too.

[*Re-enter* Leonato, Antonio, *and the* Sexton.]

Leonato.
Which is the villain? Let me see his eyes,
That, when I note another man like him,
I may avoid him. Which of these is he?
Borachio.
If you would know your wronger, look on me.
Leonato.
Art thou the slave that with thy breath hast kill'd
Mine innocent child?
Borachio.
                    Yea, even I alone.
Leonato.
No, not so, villain; thou beliest thyself:
Here stand a pair of honourable men;
A third is fled, that had a hand in it.
I thank you, princes, for my daughter's death:
Record it with your high and worthy deeds.

'Twas bravely done, if you bethink you of it.
Claudio.
I know not how to pray your patience;
Yet I must speak. Choose your revenge yourself;
Impose me to what penance your invention
Can lay upon my sin: yet sinn'd I not
But in mistaking.
Don Pedro.
                By my soul, nor I:
And yet, to satisfy this good old man,
I would bend under any heavy weight
That he'll enjoin me to.
Leonato.
I cannot bid you bid my daughter live;
That were impossible; but, I pray you both,
Possess the people in Messina here
How innocent she died; and if your love
Can labour aught in sad invention,
Hang her an epitaph upon her tomb,
And sing it to her bones: sing it to-night.
To-morrow morning come you to my house,
And since you could not be my son-in-law,
Be yet my nephew. My brother hath a daughter,
Almost the copy of my child that's dead,
And she alone is heir to both of us:
Give her the right you should have given her cousin,
And so dies my revenge.
Claudio.
                    O noble sir,
Your over-kindness doth wring tears from me!
I do embrace your offer; and dispose
For henceforth of poor Claudio.
Leonato.
To-morrow then I will expect your coming;
To-night I take my leave. This naughty man
Shall face to face be brought to Margaret,
Who, I believe, was pack'd in all this wrong,
Hir'd to it by your brother.

BORACHIO.

No, by my soul she was not;
Nor knew not what she did when she
   spoke to me;
But always hath been just and virtuous
In anything that I do know by her.

DOGBERRY.

Moreover, sir,—which, indeed, is not under
white and black,—this plaintiff here, the
offender, did call me ass: I beseech you,
let it be remembered in his punishment.
And also, the watch heard them talk of one
Deformed: they say he wears a key in his
ear and a lock hanging by it, and borrows
money in God's name, the which he hath
used so long and never paid, that now men
grow hard-hearted, and will lend nothing
for God's sake. Pray you, examine him
upon that point.

LEONATO.

I thank thee for thy care and honest pains.

DOGBERRY.

Your worship speaks like a most thankful
and reverent youth, and I praise God for
you.

LEONATO.

There's for thy pains.

DOGBERRY.

God save the foundation!

LEONATO.

Go, I discharge thee of thy prisoner, and I
thank thee.

DOGBERRY.

I leave an arrant knave with your worship;
which I beseech your worship to correct
yourself, for the example of others. God keep
your worship! I wish your worship well; God
restore you to health! I humbly give you leave
to depart, and if a merry meeting may be
wished, God prohibit it! Come, neighbour.

   [*Exeunt* DOGBERRY *and* VERGES.]

LEONATO.

Until to-morrow morning, lords, farewell.

ANTONIO.

Farewell, my lords: we look for you to-
morrow.

DON PEDRO.

We will not fail.

CLAUDIO.

To-night I'll mourn with Hero.
   [*Exeunt* DON PEDRO *and* CLAUDIO.]

LEONATO. [*To the* WATCH.]

Bring you these fellows on. We'll talk with
   Margaret,
How her acquaintance grew with this
   lewd fellow.
            [*Exeunt.*]

SCENE II

Leonato's garden.
[*Enter* BENEDICK *and* MARGARET,
               meeting.]

BENEDICK.

Pray thee, sweet Mistress Margaret,
deserve well at my hands by helping me to
the speech of Beatrice.

MARGARET.

Will you then write me a sonnet in praise
of my beauty?

BENEDICK.

In so high a style, Margaret, that no man
living shall come over it; for, in most
comely truth, thou deservest it.

MARGARET.

To have no man come over me! why, shall I
always keep below stairs?

BENEDICK.

Thy wit is as quick as the greyhound's
mouth; it catches.

MARGARET.

And yours as blunt as the fencer's foils,
which hit, but hurt not.

BENEDICK.

A most manly wit, Margaret; it will not
hurt a woman: and so, I pray thee, call
Beatrice. I give thee the bucklers.

MARGARET.

Give us the swords, we have bucklers of our
own.

BENEDICK.

If you use them, Margaret, you must put
in the pikes with a vice; and they are
dangerous weapons for maids.

MARGARET.

Well, I will call Beatrice to you, who I think
hath legs.

BENEDICK.
And therefore will come. [*Exit* MARGARET.]
[*Sings.*]
The god of love,
That sits above,
And knows me, and knows me,
How pitiful I deserve,—
I mean, in singing: but in loving, Leander the good swimmer, Troilus the first employer of panders, and a whole book full of these quondam carpet-mongers, whose names yet run smoothly in the even road of a blank verse, why, they were never so truly turned over and over as my poor self in love. Marry, I cannot show it in rime; I have tried: I can find out no rime to "lady" but "baby," an innocent rhyme; for "scorn," "horn," a hard rime; for "school," "fool," a babbling rhyme; very ominous endings: no, I was not born under a riming planet, nor I cannot woo in festival terms. [*Enter* BEATRICE.] Sweet Beatrice, wouldst thou come when I called thee?

BEATRICE.
Yea, signior; and depart when you bid me.

BENEDICK.
O, stay but till then!

BEATRICE.
"Then" is spoken; fare you well now: and yet, ere I go, let me go with that I came for; which is, with knowing what hath passed between you and Claudio.

BENEDICK.
Only foul words; and thereupon I will kiss thee.

BEATRICE.
Foul words is but foul wind, and foul wind is but foul breath, and foul breath is noisome; therefore I will depart unkissed.

BENEDICK.
Thou hast frighted the word out of his right sense, so forcible is thy wit. But I must tell thee plainly, Claudio undergoes my challenge, and either I must shortly hear from him, or I will subscribe him a coward. And, I pray thee now, tell me, for which of my bad parts didst thou first fall in love with me?

BEATRICE.
For them all together; which maintained so politic a state of evil that they will not admit any good part to intermingle with them. But for which of my good parts did you first suffer love for me?

BENEDICK.
"Suffer love," a good epithet! I do suffer love indeed, for I love thee against my will.

BEATRICE.
In spite of your heart, I think. Alas, poor heart! If you spite it for my sake, I will spite it for yours; for I will never love that which my friend hates.

BENEDICK.
Thou and I are too wise to woo peaceably.

BEATRICE.
It appears not in this confession: there's not one wise man among twenty that will praise himself.

BENEDICK.
An old, an old instance, Beatrice, that lived in the time of good neighbours. If a man do not erect in this age his own tomb ere he dies, he shall live no longer in monument than the bell rings and the widow weeps.

BEATRICE.
And how long is that think you?

BENEDICK.
Question: why, an hour in clamour and a quarter in rheum: therefore is it most expedient for the wise,—if Don Worm, his conscience, find no impediment to the contrary,—to be the trumpet of his own virtues, as I am to myself. So much for praising myself, who, I myself will bear witness, is praiseworthy. And now tell me, how doth your cousin?

BEATRICE.
Very ill.

BENEDICK.
And how do you?

BEATRICE.
Very ill too.

BENEDICK.
Serve God, love me, and mend. There will I leave you too, for here comes one in haste.
[*Enter* URSULA.]

URSULA.
Madam, you must come to your uncle. Yonder's old coil at home: it is proved, my Lady Hero hath been falsely accused, the prince and Claudio mightily abused; and Don John is the author of all, who is fled and gone. Will you come presently?

BEATRICE.
Will you go hear this news, signior?

BENEDICK.
I will live in thy heart, die in thy lap, and be buried in thy eyes; and moreover I will go with thee to thy uncle's.

[*Exeunt.*]

SCENE III
The inside of a church.
[*Enter* DON PEDRO, CLAUDIO, *and* ATTENDANTS, *with music and tapers,*]

CLAUDIO.
Is this the monument of Leonato?

A LORD.
It is, my lord.

CLAUDIO. [*Reads from a scroll.*]
Done to death by slanderous tongues
  Was the Hero that here lies:
Death, in guerdon of her wrongs,
  Gives her fame which never dies.
So the life that died with shame
Lives in death with glorious fame.
Hang thou there upon the tomb,
Praising her when I am dumb.
Now, music, sound, and sing your solemn hymn.

[*Song.*]
Pardon, goddess of the night,
Those that slew thy virgin knight;
For the which, with songs of woe,
Round about her tomb they go.
  Midnight, assist our moan;
  Help us to sigh and groan,
    Heavily, heavily:
  Graves, yawn and yield your dead,
  Till death be uttered,
    Heavily, heavily.

CLAUDIO.
Now, unto thy bones good night!
Yearly will I do this rite.

DON PEDRO.
Good morrow, masters: put your torches out.
The wolves have prey'd; and look, the gentle day,
Before the wheels of Phoebus, round about
Dapples the drowsy east with spots of grey.
Thanks to you all, and leave us: fare you well.

CLAUDIO.
Good morrow, masters: each his several way.

DON PEDRO.
Come, let us hence, and put on other weeds;
And then to Leonato's we will go.

CLAUDIO.
And Hymen now with luckier issue speed's,
Than this for whom we rend'red up this woe!

[*Exeunt.*]

SCENE IV
A room in Leonato's house.
[*Enter* LEONATO, ANTONIO, BENEDICK, BEATRICE, MARGARET, URSULA, FRIAR FRANCIS, *and* HERO.]

FRIAR.
Did I not tell you she was innocent?

LEONATO.
So are the prince and Claudio, who accus'd her
Upon the error that you heard debated:
But Margaret was in some fault for this,
Although against her will, as it appears
In the true course of all the question.

ANTONIO.
Well, I am glad that all things sort so well.

BENEDICK.
And so am I, being else by faith enforc'd
To call young Claudio to a reckoning for it.

LEONATO.
Well, daughter, and you gentlewomen all,
Withdraw into a chamber by yourselves,
And when I send for you, come hither mask'd:

The prince and Claudio promis'd by this
    hour
To visit me.
                [*Exeunt* LADIES.]
            You know your office, brother;
You must be father to your brother's
    daughter,
And give her to young Claudio.
ANTONIO.
Which I will do with confirm'd
    countenance.
BENEDICK.
Friar, I must entreat your pains, I think.
FRIAR.
To do what, signior?
BENEDICK.
To bind me, or undo me; one of them.
Signior Leonato, truth it is, good signior,
Your niece regards me with an eye of
    favour.
LEONATO.
That eye my daughter lent her: 'tis most
    true.
BENEDICK.
And I do with an eye of love requite her.
LEONATO.
The sight whereof I think, you had from
    me,
From Claudio, and the prince. But what's
    your will?
BENEDICK.
Your answer, sir, is enigmatical:
But, for my will, my will is your good
    will
May stand with ours, this day to be
    conjoin'd
In the state of honourable marriage:
In which, good friar, I shall desire your
    help.
LEONATO.
My heart is with your liking.
FRIAR.
                    And my help.
Here comes the prince and Claudio.
    [*Enter* DON PEDRO *and* CLAUDIO,
        with ATTENDANTS.]
DON PEDRO.
Good morrow to this fair assembly.

LEONATO.
Good morrow, prince; good morrow,
    Claudio:
We here attend you. Are you yet
    determin'd
To-day to marry with my brother's
    daughter?
CLAUDIO.
I'll hold my mind, were she an Ethiope.
LEONATO.
Call her forth, brother: here's the friar
    ready.
                [*Exit* ANTONIO.]
DON PEDRO.
Good morrow, Benedick. Why, what's the
    matter,
That you have such a February face,
So full of frost, of storm and cloudiness?
CLAUDIO.
I think he thinks upon the savage bull.
Tush! fear not, man, we'll tip thy horns
    with gold,
And all Europa shall rejoice at thee,
As once Europa did at lusty Jove,
When he would play the noble beast in
    love.
BENEDICK.
Bull Jove, sir, had an amiable low:
And some such strange bull leap'd your
    father's cow,
And got a calf in that same noble feat,
Much like to you, for you have just his
    bleat.
CLAUDIO.
For this I owe you: here comes other
    reckonings.
        [*Re-enter* ANTONIO, *with the*
             LADIES *masked.*]
Which is the lady I must seize upon?
ANTONIO.
This same is she, and I do give you her.
CLAUDIO.
Why then, she's mine. Sweet, let me see
    your face.
LEONATO.
No, that you shall not, till you take her
    hand
Before this friar, and swear to marry her.

CLAUDIO.
Give me your hand: before this holy friar,
I am your husband, if you like of me.

HERO.
And when I liv'd, I was your other wife:
[*Unmasking.*] And when you lov'd, you were my other husband.

CLAUDIO.
Another Hero!

HERO.
         Nothing certainer:
One Hero died defil'd, but I do live,
And surely as I live, I am a maid.

DON PEDRO.
The former Hero! Hero that is dead!

LEONATO.
She died, my lord, but whiles her slander liv'd.

FRIAR.
All this amazement can I qualify:
When after that the holy rites are ended,
I'll tell you largely of fair Hero's death:
Meantime, let wonder seem familiar,
And to the chapel let us presently.

BENEDICK.
Soft and fair, friar. Which is Beatrice?

BEATRICE. [*Unmasking.*]
I answer to that name. What is your will?

BENEDICK.
Do not you love me?

BEATRICE.
         Why, no; no more than reason.

BENEDICK.
Why, then, your uncle and the prince and Claudio
Have been deceived; for they swore you did.

BEATRICE.
Do not you love me?

BENEDICK.
         Troth, no; no more than reason.

BEATRICE.
Why, then my cousin, Margaret, and Ursula,
Are much deceiv'd; for they did swear you did.

BENEDICK.
They swore that you were almost sick for me.

BEATRICE.
They swore that you were well-nigh dead for me.

BENEDICK.
'Tis no such matter. Then you do not love me?

BEATRICE.
No, truly, but in friendly recompense.

LEONATO.
Come, cousin, I am sure you love the gentleman.

CLAUDIO.
And I'll be sworn upon 't that he loves her;
For here's a paper written in his hand,
A halting sonnet of his own pure brain,
Fashion'd to Beatrice.

HERO.
         And here's another,
Writ in my cousin's hand, stolen from her pocket,
Containing her affection unto Benedick.

BENEDICK.
A miracle! here's our own hands against our hearts. Come, I will have thee; but, by this light, I take thee for pity.

BEATRICE.
I would not deny you; but, by this good day, I yield upon great persuasion, and partly to save your life, for I was told you were in a consumption.

BENEDICK.
Peace! I will stop your mouth. [*Kisses her.*]

BENEDICK.
I'll tell thee what, prince; a college of wit-crackers cannot flout me out of my humour. Dost thou think I care for a satire or an epigram? No; if man will be beaten with brains, a' shall wear nothing handsome about him. In brief, since I do purpose to marry, I will think nothing to any purpose that the world can say against it; and therefore never flout at me for what I have said against it, for man is a giddy thing, and this is my conclusion. For thy part, Claudio,

I did think to have beaten thee; but, in that thou art like to be my kinsman, live unbruised, and love my cousin.

CLAUDIO.
I had well hoped thou wouldst have denied Beatrice, that I might have cudgelled thee out of thy single life, to make thee a double-dealer; which, out of question, thou wilt be, if my cousin do not look exceeding narrowly to thee.

BENEDICK.
Come, come, we are friends. Let's have a dance ere we are married, that we may lighten our own hearts and our wives' heels.

LEONATO.
We'll have dancing afterward.

BENEDICK.
First, of my word; therefore play, music! Prince, thou art sad; get thee a wife, get thee a wife: there is no staff more reverent than one tipped with horn.

[*Enter* MESSENGER.]

MESSENGER.
My lord, your brother John is ta'en in
    flight,
And brought with armed men back to
    Messina.

BENEDICK.
Think not on him till to-morrow: I'll devise thee brave punishments for him.—Strike up, pipers!

[*Dance. Exeunt.*]

Love's Labour's Lost

DRAMATIS PERSONAE

FERDINAND, *King of Navarre*
BEROWNE, *lord attending on the king*
LONGAVILLE, *lord attending on the king*
DUMAINE, *lord attending on the king*
BOYET, *lord attending on the Princess of France*
MARCADE, *lord attending on the Princess of France*
DON ADRIANO DE ARMADO, *a fantastical Spaniard*
SIR NATHANIEL, *a curate*
HOLOFERNES, *a schoolmaster*
DULL, *a constable*

COSTARD, *a clown*
MOTH, *page to Armado*
A FORESTER
The PRINCESS OF FRANCE
ROSALINE, *lady attending on the princess*
MARIA, *lady attending on the princess*
KATHARINE, *lady attending on the princess*
JAQUENETTA, *a country wench*
OFFICERS *and* OTHERS, *attendants on the king and princess*

SCENE: *Navarre.*

ACT I
SCENE I

The King of Navarre's park.
[*Enter the* KING, BEROWNE, LONGAVILLE, *and* DUMAINE.]

KING.
Let fame, that all hunt after in their lives,
Live regist'red upon our brazen tombs,
And then grace us in the disgrace of death;
When, spite of cormorant devouring Time,
The endeavour of this present breath may buy
That honour which shall bate his scythe's keen edge,
And make us heirs of all eternity.
Therefore, brave conquerors—for so you are
That war against your own affections
And the huge army of the world's desires—
Our late edict shall strongly stand in force:
Navarre shall be the wonder of the world;
Our court shall be a little academe,
Still and contemplative in living art.
You three, Berowne, Dumain, and Longaville,
Have sworn for three years' term to live with me,
My fellow-scholars, and to keep those statutes
That are recorded in this schedule here:
Your oaths are pass'd; and now subscribe your names,
That his own hand may strike his honour down
That violates the smallest branch herein.
If you are arm'd to do as sworn to do,
Subscribe to your deep oaths, and keep it too.

LONGAVILLE.
I am resolv'd; 'tis but a three years' fast:
The mind shall banquet, though the body pine:
Fat paunches have lean pates; and dainty bits
Make rich the ribs, but bankrupt quite the wits.

DUMAINE.
My loving lord, Dumaine is mortified:
The grosser manner of these world's delights
He throws upon the gross world's baser slaves;

To love, to wealth, to pomp, I pine and die,
With all these living in philosophy.
BEROWNE.
I can but say their protestation over;
So much, dear liege, I have already sworn,
That is, to live and study here three years.
But there are other strict observances:
As, not to see a woman in that term,
Which I hope well is not enrolled there:
And one day in a week to touch no food,
And but one meal on every day beside;
The which I hope is not enrolled there:
And then to sleep but three hours in the
    night
And not be seen to wink of all the day,—
When I was wont to think no harm all
    night,
And make a dark night too of half the
    day,—
Which I hope well is not enrolled there.
O! these are barren tasks, too hard to keep,
Not to see ladies, study, fast, not sleep.
KING.
Your oath is pass'd to pass away from
    these.
BEROWNE.
Let me say no, my liege, an if you please:
I only swore to study with your Grace,
And stay here in your court for three years'
    space.
LONGAVILLE.
You swore to that, Berowne, and to the
    rest.
BEROWNE.
By yea and nay, sir, then I swore in jest.
What is the end of study? let me know.
KING.
Why, that to know which else we should
    not know.
BEROWNE.
Things hid and barr'd, you mean, from
    common sense?
KING.
Ay, that is study's god-like recompense.
BEROWNE.
Come on, then; I will swear to study so,
To know the thing I am forbid to know,
As thus: to study where I well may dine,

When I to feast expressly am forbid;
Or study where to meet some mistress
    fine,
When mistresses from common sense are
    hid;
Or, having sworn too hard-a-keeping oath,
Study to break it, and not break my troth.
If study's gain be thus, and this be so,
Study knows that which yet it doth not
    know.
Swear me to this, and I will ne'er say no.
KING.
These be the stops that hinder study quite,
And train our intellects to vain delight.
BEROWNE.
Why, all delights are vain; but that most
    vain
Which, with pain purchas'd, doth inherit
    pain:
As painfully to pore upon a book,
To seek the light of truth; while truth the
    while
Doth falsely blind the eyesight of his look.
Light, seeking light, doth light of light
    beguile;
So, ere you find where light in darkness
    lies,
Your light grows dark by losing of your
    eyes.
Study me how to please the eye indeed,
By fixing it upon a fairer eye;
Who dazzling so, that eye shall be his
    heed,
And give him light that it was blinded by.
Study is like the heaven's glorious sun,
That will not be deep-search'd with saucy
    looks;
Small have continual plodders ever won,
Save base authority from others' books.
These earthly godfathers of heaven's lights
That give a name to every fixed star
Have no more profit of their shining
    nights
Than those that walk and wot not what
    they are.
Too much to know is to know nought but
    fame;
And every godfather can give a name.

King.
How well he's read, to reason against
  reading!
Dumaine.
Proceeded well, to stop all good proceeding!
Longaville.
He weeds the corn, and still lets grow the
  weeding.
Berowne.
The spring is near, when green geese are
  a-breeding.
Dumaine.
How follows that?
Berowne.
                    Fit in his place and time.
Dumaine.
In reason nothing.
Berowne.
                    Something then in rime.
King.
Berowne is like an envious sneaping frost
That bites the first-born infants of the
  spring.
Berowne.
Well, say I am: why should proud summer
  boast
Before the birds have any cause to sing?
Why should I joy in any abortive birth?
At Christmas I no more desire a rose
Than wish a snow in May's new-fangled
  shows;
But like of each thing that in season
  grows;
So you, to study now it is too late,
Climb o'er the house to unlock the little
  gate.
King.
Well, sit out; go home, Berowne; adieu.
Berowne.
No, my good lord; I have sworn to stay
  with you;
And though I have for barbarism spoke
  more
Than for that angel knowledge you can say,
Yet confident I'll keep what I have swore,
And bide the penance of each three years'
  day.
Give me the paper; let me read the same;

And to the strict'st decrees I'll write my
  name.
King.
How well this yielding rescues thee from
  shame!
Berowne. [*Reads.*]
"*Item.* That no woman shall come within
a mile of my court." Hath this been
proclaimed?
Longaville.
Four days ago.
Berowne.
Let's see the penalty. [*Reads.*] "On pain
of losing her tongue." Who devised this
penalty?
Longaville.
Marry, that did I.
Berowne.
Sweet lord, and why?
Longaville.
To fright them hence with that dread
  penalty.
Berowne.
A dangerous law against gentility! [*Reads.*]
"Item. If any man be seen to talk with a
woman within the term of three years, he
shall endure such public shame as the rest
of the court can possibly devise."
This article, my liege, yourself must break;
For well you know here comes in embassy
The French king's daughter, with yourself
  to speak,
A mild of grace and complete majesty—
About surrender up of Aquitaine
To her decrepit, sick, and bed-rid father:
Therefore this article is made in vain,
Or vainly comes th' admired princess
  hither.
King.
What say you, lords? why, this was quite
  forgot.
Berowne.
So study evermore is over-shot:
While it doth study to have what it would,
It doth forget to do the thing it should;
And when it hath the thing it hunteth
  most,
'Tis won as towns with fire; so won, so lost.

KING.
We must of force dispense with this decree;
She must lie here on mere necessity.
BEROWNE.
Necessity will make us all forsworn
Three thousand times within this three
  years' space;
For every man with his affects is born,
Not by might master'd, but by special
  grace.
If I break faith, this word shall speak for
  me:
I am forsworn "on mere necessity."
So to the laws at large I write my name;
       [*Subscribes.*]
And he that breaks them in the least
  degree
Stands in attainder of eternal shame.
Suggestions are to other as to me;
But I believe, although I seem so loath,
I am the last that will last keep his oath.
But is there no quick recreation granted?
KING.
Ay, that there is. Our court, you know, is
  haunted
With a refined traveller of Spain;
A man in all the world's new fashion-
  planted,
That hath a mint of phrases in his brain;
One who the music of his own vain
  tongue
Doth ravish like enchanting harmony;
A man of complements, whom right and
  wrong
Have chose as umpire of their mutiny:
This child of fancy, that Armado hight,
For interim to our studies shall relate,
In high-born words, the worth of many
  a knight
From tawny Spain lost in the world's
  debate.
How you delight, my lords, I know not, I;
But, I protest, I love to hear him lie,
And I will use him for my minstrelsy.
BEROWNE.
Armado is a most illustrious wight,
A man of fire-new words, fashion's own
  knight.

LONGAVILLE.
Costard the swain and he shall be our
  sport;
And so to study three years is but short.
    [*Enter* DULL, *with a letter, and* COSTARD.]
DULL.
Which is the duke's own person?
BEROWNE.
This, fellow. What wouldst?
DULL.
I myself reprehend his own person, for I am
his Grace's tharborough: but I would see
his own person in flesh and blood.
BEROWNE.
This is he.
DULL.
Signior Arme—Arme—commends you.
There's villainy abroad: this letter will tell
you more.
COSTARD.
Sir, the contempts thereof are as touching
me.
KING.
A letter from the magnificent Armado.
BEROWNE.
How long soever the matter, I hope in God
for high words.
LONGAVILLE.
A high hope for a low heaven: God grant
us patience!
BEROWNE.
To hear, or forbear laughing?
LONGAVILLE.
To hear meekly, sir, and to laugh
moderately; or, to forbear both.
BEROWNE.
Well, sir, be it as the style shall give us cause
to climb in the merriness.
COSTARD.
The matter is to me, sir, as concerning
  Jaquenetta.
The manner of it is, I was taken with the
  manner.
BEROWNE.
In what manner?
COSTARD.
In manner and form following, sir; all those
three: I was seen with her in the manor-

house, sitting with her upon the form, and taken following her into the park; which, put together, is in manner and form following. Now, sir, for the manner,—it is the manner of a man to speak to a woman, for the form,—in some form.

BEROWNE.

For the following, sir?

COSTARD.

As it shall follow in my correction; and God defend the right!

KING.

Will you hear this letter with attention?

BEROWNE.

As we would hear an oracle.

COSTARD.

Such is the simplicity of man to hearken after the flesh.

KING. [*Reads.*]

"Great deputy, the welkin's vicegerent and sole dominator of Navarre, my soul's earth's god and body's fostering patron,—"

COSTARD.

Not a word of Costard yet.

KING. [*Reads.*]

"So it is,—"

COSTARD.

It may be so; but if he say it is so, he is, in telling true, but so.—

KING.

Peace!

COSTARD.

Be to me, and every man that dares not fight!

KING.

No words!

COSTARD.

Of other men's secrets, I beseech you.

KING. [*Reads.*]

"So it is, besieged with sable-coloured melancholy, I did commend the black-oppressing humour to the most wholesome physic of thy health-giving air; and, as I am a gentleman, betook myself to walk. The time when? About the sixth hour; when beasts most graze, birds best peck, and men sit down to that nourishment which is called supper: so much for the time when.

Now for the ground which; which, I mean, I upon; it is ycleped thy park. Then for the place where; where, I mean, I did encounter that obscene and most preposterous event, that draweth from my snow-white pen the ebon-coloured ink which here thou viewest, beholdest, surveyest, or seest. But to the place where, it standeth north-north-east and by east from the west corner of thy curious-knotted garden: there did I see that low-spirited swain, that base minnow of thy mirth,—"

COSTARD.

Me.

KING. [*Reads.*]

"That unlettered small-knowing soul,—"

COSTARD.

Me.

KING.

"That shallow vassal,—"

COSTARD.

Still me.—

KING. [*Reads.*]

"Which, as I remember, hight Costard,—"

COSTARD.

O me.

KING. [*Reads.*]

"Sorted and consorted, contrary to thy established proclaimed edict and continent canon, with—with,—O! with but with this I passion to say wherewith,—"

COSTARD.

With a wench.

KING. [*Reads.*]

"With a child of our grandmother Eve, a female; or, for thy more sweet understanding, a woman. Him, I,—as my ever-esteemed duty pricks me on,—have sent to thee, to receive the meed of punishment, by thy sweet Grace's officer, Antony Dull, a man of good repute, carriage, bearing, and estimation."

DULL.

Me, an't please you; I am Antony Dull.

KING. [*Reads.*]

"For Jaquenetta,—so is the weaker vessel called, which I apprehended with the aforesaid swain,—I keep her as a vessel of

thy law's fury; and shall, at the least of thy
sweet notice, bring her to trial. Thine, in all
compliments of devoted and heart-burning
heat of duty, Don Adriano de Armado."

BEROWNE.

This is not so well as I looked for, but the
best that ever I heard.

KING.

Ay, the best for the worst. But, sirrah, what
say you to this?

COSTARD.

Sir, I confess the wench.

KING.

Did you hear the proclamation?

COSTARD.

I do confess much of the hearing it, but
little of the marking of it.

KING.

It was proclaimed a year's imprisonment to
be taken with a wench.

COSTARD.

I was taken with none, sir: I was taken with
a damosel.

KING.

Well, it was proclaimed "damosel."

COSTARD.

This was no damosel neither, sir; she was
a "virgin."

KING.

It is so varied too; for it was proclaimed
"virgin."

COSTARD.

If it were, I deny her virginity: I was taken
with a maid.

KING.

This maid not serve your turn, sir.

COSTARD.

This maid will serve my turn, sir.

KING.

Sir, I will pronounce your sentence: you
shall fast a week with bran and water.

COSTARD.

I had rather pray a month with mutton and
porridge.

KING.

And Don Armado shall be your keeper.
My Lord Berowne, see him delivered o'er:
And go we, lords, to put in practice that

Which each to other hath so strongly
  sworn.

[*Exeunt* KING, LONGAVILLE, *and*
DUMAINE.]

BEROWNE.

I'll lay my head to any good man's hat
These oaths and laws will prove an idle
  scorn.
Sirrah, come on.

COSTARD.

I suffer for the truth, sir: for true it is I was
taken with Jaquenetta, and Jaquenetta is a
true girl; and therefore welcome the sour
cup of prosperity! Affliction may one day
smile again; and till then, sit thee down,
sorrow!

[*Exeunt.*]

SCENE II

The park.

[*Enter* ARMADO *and* MOTH.]

ARMADO.

Boy, what sign is it when a man of great
spirit grows melancholy?

MOTH.

A great sign, sir, that he will look sad.

ARMADO.

Why, sadness is one and the self-same
thing, dear imp.

MOTH.

No, no; O Lord, sir, no.

ARMADO.

How canst thou part sadness and
melancholy, my tender juvenal?

MOTH.

By a familiar demonstration of the working,
my tough senior.

ARMADO.

Why tough senior? Why tough senior?

MOTH.

Why tender juvenal? Why tender juvenal?

ARMADO.

I spoke it, tender juvenal, as a congruent
epitheton appertaining to thy young days,
which we may nominate tender.

MOTH.

And I, tough senior, as an appertinent title
to your old time, which we may name tough.

ARMADO.
Pretty and apt.

MOTH.
How mean you, sir? I pretty, and my saying apt? or I apt, and my saying pretty?

ARMADO.
Thou pretty, because little.

MOTH.
Little pretty, because little. Wherefore apt?

ARMADO.
And therefore apt, because quick.

MOTH.
Speak you this in my praise, master?

ARMADO.
In thy condign praise.

MOTH.
I will praise an eel with the same praise.

ARMADO.
What! That an eel is ingenious?

MOTH.
That an eel is quick.

ARMADO.
I do say thou art quick in answers: thou heat'st my blood.

MOTH.
I am answered, sir.

ARMADO.
I love not to be crossed.

MOTH. [*Aside.*]
He speaks the mere contrary: crosses love not him.

ARMADO.
I have promised to study three years with the duke.

MOTH.
You may do it in an hour, sir.

ARMADO.
Impossible.

MOTH.
How many is one thrice told?

ARMADO.
I am ill at reck'ning; it fitteth the spirit of a tapster.

MOTH.
You are a gentleman and a gamester, sir.

ARMADO.
I confess both: they are both the varnish of a complete man.

MOTH.
Then I am sure you know how much the gross sum of deuce-ace amounts to.

ARMADO.
It doth amount to one more than two.

MOTH.
Which the base vulgar do call three.

ARMADO.
True.

MOTH.
Why, sir, is this such a piece of study? Now here's three studied ere ye'll thrice wink; and how easy it is to put "years" to the word "three," and study three years in two words, the dancing horse will tell you.

ARMADO.
A most fine figure!

MOTH. [*Aside.*]
To prove you a cipher.

ARMADO.
I will hereupon confess I am in love; and as it is base for a soldier to love, so am I in love with a base wench. If drawing my sword against the humour of affection would deliver me from the reprobate thought of it, I would take Desire prisoner, and ransom him to any French courtier for a new-devised cursty. I think scorn to sigh: methinks I should out-swear Cupid. Comfort me, boy: what great men have been in love?

MOTH.
Hercules, master.

ARMADO.
Most sweet Hercules! More authority, dear boy, name more; and, sweet my child, let them be men of good repute and carriage.

MOTH.
Samson, master: he was a man of good carriage, great carriage, for he carried the town gates on his back like a porter; and he was in love.

ARMADO.
O well-knit Samson! strong-jointed Samson! I do excel thee in my rapier as much as thou didst me in carrying gates. I am in love too. Who was Samson's love, my dear Moth?

Moth.

A woman, master.

Armado.

Of what complexion?

Moth.

Of all the four, or the three, or the two, or one of the four.

Armado.

Tell me precisely of what complexion.

Moth.

Of the sea-water green, sir.

Armado.

Is that one of the four complexions?

Moth.

As I have read, sir; and the best of them too.

Armado.

Green, indeed, is the colour of lovers; but to have a love of that colour, methinks Samson had small reason for it. He surely affected her for her wit.

Moth.

It was so, sir, for she had a green wit.

Armado.

My love is most immaculate white and red.

Moth.

Most maculate thoughts, master, are masked under such colours.

Armado.

Define, define, well-educated infant.

Moth.

My father's wit my mother's tongue assist me!

Armado.

Sweet invocation of a child; most pretty, and pathetical!

Moth.

    If she be made of white and red,
        Her faults will ne'er be known;
    For blushing cheeks by faults are bred,
        And fears by pale white shown.
    Then if she fear, or be to blame,
        By this you shall not know,
    For still her cheeks possess the same
        Which native she doth owe.

A dangerous rhyme, master, against the reason of white and red.

Armado.

Is there not a ballad, boy, of the King and the Beggar?

Moth.

The world was very guilty of such a ballad some three ages since; but I think now 'tis not to be found; or if it were, it would neither serve for the writing nor the tune.

Armado.

I will have that subject newly writ o'er, that I may example my digression by some mighty precedent. Boy, I do love that country girl that I took in the park with the rational hind Costard: she deserves well.

Moth. [*Aside.*]

To be whipped; and yet a better love than my master.

Armado.

Sing, boy: my spirit grows heavy in love.

Moth.

And that's great marvel, loving a light wench.

Armado.

I say, sing.

Moth.

Forbear till this company be past.

    [*Enter* Dull, Costard, *and*
               Jaquenetta.]

Dull.

Sir, the duke's pleasure is, that you keep Costard safe: and you must suffer him to take no delight nor no penance; but a' must fast three days a week. For this damsel, I must keep her at the park; she is allowed for the day-woman. Fare you well.

Armado.

I do betray myself with blushing. Maid!

Jaquenetta.

Man?

Armado.

I will visit thee at the lodge.

Jaquenetta.

That's hereby.

Armado.

I know where it is situate.

Jaquenetta.

Lord, how wise you are!

Armado.

I will tell thee wonders.

Jaquenetta.

With that face?

Armado.

I love thee.

Jaquenetta.

So I heard you say.

Armado.

And so, farewell.

Jaquenetta.

Fair weather after you!

Dull.

Come, Jaquenetta, away!

[*Exit with* Jaquenetta.]

Armado.

Villain, thou shalt fast for thy offences ere thou be pardoned.

Costard.

Well, sir, I hope when I do it I shall do it on a full stomach.

Armado.

Thou shalt be heavily punished.

Costard.

I am more bound to you than your fellows, for they are but lightly rewarded.

Armado.

Take away this villain: shut him up.

Moth.

Come, you transgressing slave: away!

Costard.

Let me not be pent up, sir: I will fast, being loose.

Moth.

No, sir; that were fast and loose: thou shalt to prison.

Costard.

Well, if ever I do see the merry days of desolation that I have seen, some shall see—

Moth.

What shall some see?

Costard.

Nay, nothing, Master Moth, but what they look upon. It is not for prisoners to be too silent in their words, and therefore I will say nothing. I thank God I have as little patience as another man, and therefore I can be quiet.

[*Exeunt* Moth *and* Costard.]

Armado.

I do affect the very ground, which is base, where her shoe, which is baser, guided by her foot, which is basest, doth tread. I shall be forsworn,—which is a great argument of falsehood,—if I love. And how can that be true love which is falsely attempted? Love is a familiar; Love is a devil; there is no evil angel but Love. Yet was Samson so tempted, and he had an excellent strength; yet was Solomon so seduced, and he had a very good wit. Cupid's butt-shaft is too hard for Hercules' club, and therefore too much odds for a Spaniard's rapier. The first and second cause will not serve my turn; the passado he respects not, the duello he regards not; his disgrace is to be called boy, but his glory is to subdue men. Adieu, valour! rust, rapier! be still, drum! for your manager is in love; yea, he loveth. Assist me, some extemporal god of rime, for I am sure I shall turn sonneter. Devise, wit; write, pen; for I am for whole volumes in folio.

[*Exit.*]

ACT II
SCENE I

The King of Navarre's park. A pavilion and tents at a distance.

[*Enter the* Princess of France, Rosaline, Maria, Katharine, Boyet, Lords, *and other* Attendants.]

Boyet.

Now, madam, summon up your dearest spirits:

Consider who the king your father sends,

To whom he sends, and what's his embassy:

Yourself, held precious in the world's esteem,

To parley with the sole inheritor

Of all perfections that a man may owe,

Matchless Navarre; the plea of no less weight

Than Aquitaine, a dowry for a queen.

Be now as prodigal of all dear grace

As Nature was in making graces dear

When she did starve the general world beside,

And prodigally gave them all to you.

Princess.
Good Lord Boyet, my beauty, though but
  mean,
Needs not the painted flourish of your
  praise:
Beauty is bought by judgment of the eye,
Not utt'red by base sale of chapmen's
  tongues.
I am less proud to hear you tell my worth
Than you much willing to be counted wise
In spending your wit in the praise of mine.
But now to task the tasker: good Boyet,
You are not ignorant, all-telling fame
Doth noise abroad, Navarre hath made
  a vow,
Till painful study shall outwear three
  years,
No woman may approach his silent court:
Therefore to's seemeth it a needful course,
Before we enter his forbidden gates,
To know his pleasure; and in that behalf,
Bold of your worthiness, we single you
As our best-moving fair solicitor.
Tell him the daughter of the King of
  France,
On serious business, craving quick dispatch,
Importunes personal conference with his
  Grace.
Haste, signify so much; while we attend,
Like humble-visag'd suitors, his high will.

Boyet.
Proud of employment, willingly I go.

Princess.
All pride is willing pride, and yours is so.
        [*Exit* Boyet.]
Who are the votaries, my loving lords,
That are vow-fellows with this virtuous
  duke?

First Lord.
Lord Longaville is one.

Princess.
                    Know you the man?

Maria.
I know him, madam: at a marriage feast,
Between Lord Perigort and the beauteous
  heir
Of Jacques Falconbridge, solemnized
In Normandy, saw I this Longaville.

A man of sovereign parts, he is esteem'd,
Well fitted in arts, glorious in arms:
Nothing becomes him ill that he would
  well.
The only soil of his fair virtue's gloss,—
If virtue's gloss will stain with any soil,—
Is a sharp wit match'd with too blunt a
  will;
Whose edge hath power to cut, whose will
  still wills
It should none spare that come within his
  power.

Princess.
Some merry mocking lord, belike; is't so?

Maria.
They say so most that most his humours
  know.

Princess.
Such short-liv'd wits do wither as they
  grow.
Who are the rest?

Katharine.
The young Dumaine, a well-accomplish'd
  youth,
Of all that virtue love for virtue lov'd;
Most power to do most harm, least
  knowing ill,
For he hath wit to make an ill shape good,
And shape to win grace though he had
  no wit.
I saw him at the Duke Alençon's once;
And much too little of that good I saw
Is my report to his great worthiness.

Rosaline.
Another of these students at that time
Was there with him, if I have heard a
  truth:
Berowne they call him; but a merrier man,
Within the limit of becoming mirth,
I never spent an hour's talk withal.
His eye begets occasion for his wit,
For every object that the one doth catch
The other turns to a mirth-moving jest,
Which his fair tongue, conceit's expositor,
Delivers in such apt and gracious words
That aged ears play truant at his tales,
And younger hearings are quite ravished;
So sweet and voluble is his discourse.

Princess.
God bless my ladies! Are they all in love,
That every one her own hath garnished
With such bedecking ornaments of praise?
First Lord.
Here comes Boyet.
[*Re-enter* Boyet.]
Princess.
                    Now, what admittance, lord?
Boyet.
Navarre had notice of your fair approach,
And he and his competitors in oath
Were all address'd to meet you, gentle lady,
Before I came. Marry, thus much I have
    learnt;
He rather means to lodge you in the field,
Like one that comes here to besiege his
    court,
Than seek a dispensation for his oath,
To let you enter his unpeeled house.
Here comes Navarre.
[*The* Ladies *mask.*]
[*Enter* King, Longaville, Dumaine,
    Berowne, *and* Attendants.]
King.
Fair princess, welcome to the court of
    Navarre.
Princess.
"Fair" I give you back again; and "welcome"
I have not yet: the roof of this court is too
high to be yours, and welcome to the wide
fields too base to be mine.
King.
You shall be welcome, madam, to my court.
Princess.
I will be welcome then: conduct me
    thither.
King.
Hear me, dear lady; I have sworn an oath.
Princess.
Our Lady help my lord! he'll be forsworn.
King.
Not for the world, fair madam, by my will.
Princess.
Why, will shall break it; will, and nothing
    else.
King.
Your ladyship is ignorant what it is.

Princess.
Were my lord so, his ignorance were
    wise,
Where now his knowledge must prove
    ignorance.
I hear your Grace hath sworn out house-
    keeping:
'Tis deadly sin to keep that oath, my lord,
And sin to break it.
But pardon me, I am too sudden bold:
To teach a teacher ill beseemeth me.
Vouchsafe to read the purpose of my
    coming,
And suddenly resolve me in my suit.
                    [*Gives a paper.*]
King.
Madam, I will, if suddenly I may.
Princess.
You will the sooner that I were away,
For you'll prove perjur'd if you make me
    stay.
Berowne.
Did not I dance with you in Brabant once?
Rosaline.
Did not I dance with you in Brabant once?
Berowne.
I know you did.
Rosaline.
                    How needless was it then,
To ask the question!
Berowne.
                    You must not be so quick.
Rosaline.
'Tis long of you, that spur me with such
    questions.
Berowne.
Your wit's too hot, it speeds too fast, 'twill
    tire.
Rosaline.
Not till it leave the rider in the mire.
Berowne.
What time o' day?
Rosaline.
The hour that fools should ask.
Berowne.
Now fair befall your mask!
Rosaline.
Fair fall the face it covers!

Berowne.
And send you many lovers!
Rosaline.
Amen, so you be none.
Berowne.
Nay, then will I be gone.
King.
Madam, your father here doth intimate
The payment of a hundred thousand
 crowns;
Being but the one half of an entire sum
Disbursed by my father in his wars.
But say that he or we,—as neither have,—
Receiv'd that sum, yet there remains
 unpaid
A hundred thousand more, in surety of
 the which,
One part of Aquitaine is bound to us,
Although not valued to the money's worth.
If then the king your father will restore
But that one half which is unsatisfied,
We will give up our right in Aquitaine,
And hold fair friendship with his majesty.
But that, it seems, he little purposeth,
For here he doth demand to have repaid
A hundred thousand crowns; and not
 demands,
On payment of a hundred thousand
 crowns,
To have his title live in Aquitaine;
Which we much rather had depart withal,
And have the money by our father lent,
Than Aquitaine so gelded as it is.
Dear princess, were not his requests so far
From reason's yielding, your fair self
 should make
A yielding 'gainst some reason in my
 breast,
And go well satisfied to France again.
Princess.
You do the king my father too much wrong,
And wrong the reputation of your name,
In so unseeming to confess receipt
Of that which hath so faithfully been paid.
King.
I do protest I never heard of it;
And, if you prove it, I'll repay it back
Or yield up Aquitaine.

Princess.
     We arrest your word.
Boyet, you can produce acquittances
For such a sum from special officers
Of Charles his father.
King.
    Satisfy me so.
Boyet.
So please your Grace, the packet is not
 come,
Where that and other specialties are bound:
To-morrow you shall have a sight of them.
King.
It shall suffice me; at which interview
All liberal reason I will yield unto.
Meantime receive such welcome at my
 hand
As honour, without breach of honour, may
Make tender of to thy true worthiness.
You may not come, fair princess, in my
 gates;
But here without you shall be so receiv'd
As you shall deem yourself lodg'd in my
 heart,
Though so denied fair harbour in my house.
Your own good thoughts excuse me, and
 farewell:
To-morrow shall we visit you again.
Princess.
Sweet health and fair desires consort your
 Grace!
King.
Thy own wish wish I thee in every place.
  [*Exeunt* King *and his* Train.]
Berowne.
Lady, I will commend you to mine own
 heart.
Rosaline.
Pray you, do my commendations; I would
be glad to see it.
Berowne.
I would you heard it groan.
Rosaline.
Is the fool sick?
Berowne.
Sick at the heart.
Rosaline.
Alack! let it blood.

BEROWNE.
Would that do it good?
ROSALINE.
My physic says "Ay."
BEROWNE.
Will you prick't with your eye?
ROSALINE.
No point, with my knife.
BEROWNE.
Now, God save thy life!
ROSALINE.
And yours from long living!
BEROWNE.
I cannot stay thanksgiving.
              [*Retiring.*]
DUMAINE.
Sir, I pray you, a word: what lady is that
      same?
BOYET.
The heir of Alençon, Katharine her
      name.
DUMAINE.
A gallant lady! Monsieur, fare you well.
              [*Exit.*]
LONGAVILLE.
I beseech you a word: what is she in the
      white?
BOYET.
A woman sometimes, an you saw her in
      the light.
LONGAVILLE.
Perchance light in the light. I desire her
      name.
BOYET.
She hath but one for herself; to desire that
      were a shame.
LONGAVILLE.
Pray you, sir, whose daughter?
BOYET.
Her mother's, I have heard.
LONGAVILLE.
God's blessing on your beard!
BOYET.
Good sir, be not offended.
She is an heir of Falconbridge.
LONGAVILLE.
Nay, my choler is ended.
She is a most sweet lady.

BOYET.
Not unlike, sir; that may be.
              [*Exit* LONGAVILLE.]
BEROWNE.
What's her name in the cap?
BOYET.
Rosaline, by good hap.
BEROWNE.
Is she wedded or no?
BOYET.
To her will, sir, or so.
BEROWNE.
You are welcome, sir. Adieu!
BOYET.
Farewell to me, sir, and welcome to you.
              [*Exit* BEROWNE. LADIES *unmask.*]
MARIA.
That last is Berowne, the merry mad-cap
      lord;
Not a word with him but a jest.
BOYET.
And every jest but a word.
PRINCESS.
It was well done of you to take him at his
      word.
BOYET.
I was as willing to grapple as he was to
      board.
MARIA.
Two hot sheeps, marry!
BOYET.
                    And wherefore not ships?
No sheep, sweet lamb, unless we feed on
      your lips.
MARIA.
You sheep and I pasture: shall that finish
      the jest?
BOYET.
So you grant pasture for me.
              [*Offering to kiss her.*]
MARIA.
                    Not so, gentle beast.
My lips are no common, though several
      they be.
BOYET.
Belonging to whom?
MARIA.
                    To my fortunes and me.

Princess.
Good wits will be jangling; but, gentles,
　　agree;
This civil war of wits were much better us'd
On Navarre and his book-men, for here
　　'tis abus'd.

Boyet.
If my observation,—which very seldom lies,
By the heart's still rhetoric disclosed with
　　eyes,
Deceive me not now, Navarre is infected.

Princess.
With what?

Boyet.
With that which we lovers entitle affected.

Princess.
Your reason.

Boyet.
Why, all his behaviours did make their retire
To the court of his eye, peeping thorough
　　desire;
His heart, like an agate, with your print
　　impress'd,
Proud with his form, in his eye pride
　　express'd;
His tongue, all impatient to speak and
　　not see,
Did stumble with haste in his eyesight
　　to be;
All senses to that sense did make their
　　repair,
To feel only looking on fairest of fair.
Methought all his senses were lock'd in
　　his eye,
As jewels in crystal for some prince to buy;
Who, tend'ring their own worth from
　　where they were glass'd,
Did point you to buy them, along as you
　　pass'd.
His face's own margent did quote such
　　amazes
That all eyes saw his eyes enchanted with
　　gazes.
I'll give you Aquitaine, and all that is his,
An you give him for my sake but one
　　loving kiss.

Princess.
Come, to our pavilion: Boyet is dispos'd.

Boyet.
But to speak that in words which his eye
　　hath disclos'd.
I only have made a mouth of his eye,
By adding a tongue which I know will
　　not lie.

Rosaline.
Thou art an old love-monger, and speak'st
　　skilfully.

Maria.
He is Cupid's grandfather, and learns news
　　of him.

Rosaline.
Then was Venus like her mother; for her
　　father is but grim.

Boyet.
Do you hear, my mad wenches?

Maria.
No.

Boyet.
What, then, do you see?

Rosaline.
Ay, our way to be gone.

Boyet.
You are too hard for me.
　　　　　　　　　　[*Exeunt.*]

ACT III
SCENE I
The King of Navarre's park.
[*Enter* Armado *and* Moth.]

Armado.
Warble, child; make passionate my sense of
hearing.

Moth. [*Singing.*]
Concolinel,—

Armado.
Sweet air! Go, tenderness of years; take this
key, give enlargement to the swain, bring
him festinately hither; I must employ him
in a letter to my love.

Moth.
Master, will you win your love with a
French brawl?

Armado.
How meanest thou? brawling in French?

Moth.
No, my complete master; but to jig off

a tune at the tongue's end, canary to it with your feet, humour it with turning up your eyelids, sigh a note and sing a note, sometime through the throat, as if you swallowed love with singing love, sometime through the nose, as if you snuffed up love by smelling love; with your hat penthouse-like o'er the shop of your eyes, with your arms crossed on your thin-belly doublet, like a rabbit on a spit; or your hands in your pocket, like a man after the old painting; and keep not too long in one tune, but a snip and away. These are complements, these are humours; these betray nice wenches, that would be betrayed without these; and make them men of note,—do you note me?—that most are affected to these.

ARMADO.

How hast thou purchased this experience?

MOTH.

By my penny of observation.

ARMADO.

But O—but O,—

MOTH.

"The hobby-horse is forgot."

ARMADO.

Call'st thou my love "hobby-horse"?

MOTH.

No, master; the hobby-horse is but a colt, and your love perhaps, a hackney. But have you forgot your love?

ARMADO.

Almost I had.

MOTH.

Negligent student! learn her by heart.

ARMADO.

By heart and in heart, boy.

MOTH.

And out of heart, master: all those three I will prove.

ARMADO.

What wilt thou prove?

MOTH.

A man, if I live; and this, by, in, and without, upon the instant: by heart you love her, because your heart cannot come by her; in heart you love her, because your heart is in love with her; and out of heart

you love her, being out of heart that you cannot enjoy her.

ARMADO.

I am all these three.

MOTH.

And three times as much more, and yet nothing at all.

ARMADO.

Fetch hither the swain: he must carry me a letter.

MOTH.

A message well sympathized; a horse to be ambassador for an ass.

ARMADO.

Ha, ha! what sayest thou?

MOTH.

Marry, sir, you must send the ass upon the horse, for he is very slow-gaited. But I go.

ARMADO.

The way is but short: away!

MOTH.

As swift as lead, sir.

ARMADO.

The meaning, pretty ingenious?
Is not lead a metal heavy, dull, and slow?

MOTH.

Minime, honest master; or rather, master, no.

ARMADO.

I say lead is slow.

MOTH.

        You are too swift, sir, to say so:
Is that lead slow which is fir'd from a gun?

ARMADO.

Sweet smoke of rhetoric!
He reputes me a cannon; and the bullet, that's he;
I shoot thee at the swain.

MOTH.

        Thump then, and I flee.
        [*Exit.*]

ARMADO.

A most acute juvenal; volable and free of grace!
By thy favour, sweet welkin, I must sigh in thy face:
Most rude melancholy, valour gives thee place.

My herald is return'd.

   [*Re-enter* Moth *with*
    Costard.*]

Moth.

A wonder, master! here's a Costard broken
 in a shin.

Armado.

Some enigma, some riddle: come, thy
 l'envoy, begin.

Costard.

No egma, no riddle, no *l'envoy*; no salve
in the mail, sir. O! sir, plantain, a plain
plantain; no *l'envoy*, no *l'envoy*; no salve, sir,
but a plantain.

Armado.

By virtue thou enforcest laughter; thy
silly thought, my spleen; the heaving
of my lungs provokes me to ridiculous
smiling: O! pardon me, my stars. Doth the
inconsiderate take salve for *l'envoy*, and the
word *l'envoy* for a salve?

Moth.

Do the wise think them other? Is not
 l'envoy a salve?

Armado.

No, page: it is an epilogue or discourse to
 make plain
Some obscure precedence that hath tofore
 been sain.
I will example it:
 The fox, the ape, and the humble-bee,
 Were still at odds, being but three.
There's the moral. Now the *l'envoy*.

Moth.

I will add the *l'envoy*. Say the moral again.

Armado.

 The fox, the ape, and the humble-bee,
 Were still at odds, being but three.

Moth.

 Until the goose came out of door,
 And stay'd the odds by adding four.
Now will I begin your moral, and do you
follow with my *l'envoy*.
 The fox, the ape, and the humble-bee,
 Were still at odds, being but three.

Armado.

Until the goose came out of door,
Staying the odds by adding four.

Moth.

A good *l'envoy*, ending in the goose; would
 you desire more?

Costard.

The boy hath sold him a bargain, a goose,
 that's flat.
Sir, your pennyworth is good an your
 goose be fat.
To sell a bargain well is as cunning as fast
 and loose:
Let me see: a fat *l'envoy*; ay, that's a fat
 goose.

Armado.

Come hither, come hither. How did this
 argument begin?

Moth.

By saying that a costard was broken in a
 shin.
Then call'd you for the *l'envoy*.

Costard.

True, and I for a plantain: thus came your
 argument in;
Then the boy's fat *l'envoy*, the goose that
 you bought;
And he ended the market.

Armado.

But tell me; how was there a Costard
 broken in a shin?

Moth.

I will tell you sensibly.

Costard.

Thou hast no feeling of it, Moth: I will
 speak that *l'envoy*:
  I, Costard, running out, that was safely
   within,
  Fell over the threshold and broke my
   shin.

Armado.

We will talk no more of this matter.

Costard.

Till there be more matter in the shin.

Armado.

Sirrah Costard, I will enfranchise thee.

Costard.

O! marry me to one Frances: I smell some
 l'envoy, some goose, in this.

Armado.

By my sweet soul, I mean setting thee at

liberty, enfreedoming thy person: thou wert immured, restrained, captivated, bound.

COSTARD.

True, true; and now you will be my purgation, and let me loose.

ARMADO.

I give thee thy liberty, set thee from durance; and, in lieu thereof, impose on thee nothing but this:—[*Giving a letter.*] Bear this significant to the country maid Jaquenetta. [*Giving money.*] There is remuneration; for the best ward of mine honour is rewarding my dependents. Moth, follow.

          [*Exit.*]

MOTH.

Like the sequel, I. Signior Costard, adieu.

COSTARD.

My sweet ounce of man's flesh! my incony Jew!

          [*Exit* MOTH.]

Now will I look to his remuneration. Remuneration! O! that's the Latin word for three farthings: three farthings, remuneration. "What's the price of this inkle?" "One penny." "No, I'll give you a remuneration." Why, it carries it. Remuneration! Why, it is a fairer name than French crown. I will never buy and sell out of this word.

      [*Enter* BEROWNE.]

BEROWNE.

O! My good knave Costard, exceedingly well met.

COSTARD.

Pray you, sir, how much carnation riband may a man buy for a remuneration?

BEROWNE.

What is a remuneration?

COSTARD.

Marry, sir, halfpenny farthing.

BEROWNE.

Why, then, three-farthing worth of silk.

COSTARD.

I thank your worship. God be wi' you!

BEROWNE.

Stay, slave; I must employ thee:
As thou wilt win my favour, good my knave,
Do one thing for me that I shall entreat.

COSTARD.

When would you have it done, sir?

BEROWNE.

O, this afternoon.

COSTARD.

Well, I will do it, sir! fare you well.

BEROWNE.

O, thou knowest not what it is.

COSTARD.

I shall know, sir, when I have done it.

BEROWNE.

Why, villain, thou must know first.

COSTARD.

I will come to your worship to-morrow morning.

BEROWNE.

It must be done this afternoon. Hark, slave, it is but this:
The princess comes to hunt here in the park,
And in her train there is a gentle lady;
When tongues speak sweetly, then they name her name,
And Rosaline they call her: ask for her
And to her white hand see thou do commend
This seal'd-up counsel. There's thy guerdon: go.

      [*Gives him a shilling.*]

COSTARD.

Guerdon, O sweet guerdon! better than remuneration; a 'leven-pence farthing better; most sweet guerdon! I will do it, sir, in print. Guerdon—remuneration!

          [*Exit.*]

BEROWNE.

And I,—
Forsooth, in love; I, that have been love's whip;
A very beadle to a humorous sigh;
A critic, nay, a night-watch constable;
A domineering pedant o'er the boy,
Than whom no mortal so magnificent!
This wimpled, whining, purblind, wayward boy,
This senior-junior, giant-dwarf, Dan Cupid;
Regent of love-rimes, lord of folded arms,

The anointed sovereign of sighs and
    groans,
Liege of all loiterers and malcontents,
Dread prince of plackets, king of
    codpieces,
Sole imperator, and great general
Of trotting 'paritors: O my little heart!
And I to be a corporal of his field,
And wear his colours like a tumbler's
    hoop!
What! I love! I sue, I seek a wife!
A woman, that is like a German clock,
Still a-repairing, ever out of frame,
And never going aright, being a watch,
But being watch'd that it may still go right!
Nay, to be perjur'd, which is worst of all;
And, among three, to love the worst of all,
A wightly wanton with a velvet brow,
With two pitch balls stuck in her face for
    eyes;
Ay, and, by heaven, one that will do the
    deed,
Though Argus were her eunuch and her
    guard:
And I to sigh for her! to watch for her!
To pray for her! Go to; it is a plague
That Cupid will impose for my neglect
Of his almighty dreadful little might.
Well, I will love, write, sigh, pray, sue, and
    groan:
Some men must love my lady, and some
    Joan.

                [*Exit.*]

ACT IV
SCENE I

The King of Navarre's park.
[*Enter the* Princess, Rosaline,
Maria, Katharine, Boyet, Lords,
Attendants, *and a* Forester.]

PRINCESS.
Was that the king that spurr'd his horse
    so hard
Against the steep uprising of the hill?
BOYET.
I know not; but I think it was not he.
PRINCESS.
Whoe'er a' was, a' show'd a mounting mind.

Well, lords, to-day we shall have our
    dispatch;
On Saturday we will return to France.
Then, forester, my friend, where is the
    bush
That we must stand and play the murderer
    in?
FORESTER.
Hereby, upon the edge of yonder coppice;
A stand where you may make the fairest
    shoot.
PRINCESS.
I thank my beauty, I am fair that shoot,
And thereupon thou speak'st the fairest
    shoot.
FORESTER.
Pardon me, madam, for I meant not so.
PRINCESS.
What, what? First praise me, and again
    say no?
O short-liv'd pride! Not fair? Alack for
    woe!
FORESTER.
Yes, madam, fair.
PRINCESS.
              Nay, never paint me now;
Where fair is not, praise cannot mend the
    brow.
Here, good my glass [*Gives money.*]:—take
    this for telling true:
Fair payment for foul words is more than
    due.
FORESTER.
Nothing but fair is that which you inherit.
PRINCESS.
See, see! my beauty will be sav'd by merit.
O heresy in fair, fit for these days!
A giving hand, though foul, shall have fair
    praise.
But come, the bow: now mercy goes to
    kill,
And shooting well is then accounted ill.
Thus will I save my credit in the shoot:
Not wounding, pity would not let me do't;
If wounding, then it was to show my skill,
That more for praise than purpose meant
    to kill.
And out of question so it is sometimes,

Glory grows guilty of detested crimes,
When, for fame's sake, for praise, an
        outward part,
We bend to that the working of the
        heart;
As I for praise alone now seek to spill
The poor deer's blood, that my heart
        means no ill.

BOYET.
Do not curst wives hold that self-
        sovereignty
Only for praise' sake, when they strive to
        be
Lords o'er their lords?

PRINCESS.
Only for praise; and praise we may afford
To any lady that subdues a lord.
                [Enter COSTARD.*]*

BOYET.
Here comes a member of the
        commonwealth.

COSTARD.
God dig-you-den all! Pray you, which is
the head lady?

PRINCESS.
Thou shalt know her, fellow, by the rest that
have no heads.

COSTARD.
Which is the greatest lady, the highest?

PRINCESS.
The thickest and the tallest.

COSTARD.
The thickest and the tallest! It is so; truth
is truth.
An your waist, mistress, were as slender as
my wit,
One o' these maids' girdles for your waist
should be fit.
Are not you the chief woman? You are the
thickest here.

PRINCESS.
What's your will, sir? What's your will?

COSTARD.
I have a letter from Monsieur Berowne to
one Lady Rosaline.

PRINCESS.
O! thy letter, thy letter; he's a good friend
of mine.

Stand aside, good bearer. Boyet, you can
        carve;
Break up this capon.

BOYET.
                        I am bound to serve.
This letter is mistook; it importeth none
        here.
It is writ to Jaquenetta.

PRINCESS.
                        We will read it, I swear.
Break the neck of the wax, and every one
        give ear.

BOYET. *[Reads.]*
"By heaven, that thou art fair is most
infallible; true, that thou art beauteous;
truth itself, that thou art lovely. More
fairer than fair, beautiful than beauteous,
truer than truth itself, have commiseration
on thy heroical vassal! The magnanimous
and most illustrate king Cophetua set
eye upon the pernicious and indubitate
beggar Zenelophon, and he it was that
might rightly say, *Veni, vidi, vici*; which
to anatomize in the vulgar—O base and
obscure vulgar!—*videlicet*, he came, saw,
and overcame: he came, one; saw, two;
overcame, three. Who came? the king:
Why did he come? to see: Why did he see?
to overcome: To whom came he? to the
beggar: What saw he? the beggar. Who
overcame he? the beggar. The conclusion
is victory; on whose side? the king's; the
captive is enriched: on whose side? the
beggar's. The catastrophe is a nuptial: on
whose side? the king's, no, on both in one,
or one in both. I am the king, for so stands
the comparison; thou the beggar, for so
witnesseth thy lowliness. Shall I command
thy love? I may: Shall I enforce thy love?
I could: Shall I entreat thy love? I will.
What shalt thou exchange for rags? robes;
for tittles? titles; for thyself? me. Thus,
expecting thy reply, I profane my lips on thy
foot, my eyes on thy picture, and my heart
on thy every part.
        Thine in the dearest design of industry,
                Don Adriano de Armado."
Thus dost thou hear the Nemean lion roar

'Gainst thee, thou lamb, that standest as
    his prey;
Submissive fall his princely feet before,
And he from forage will incline to play.
But if thou strive, poor soul, what are thou
    then?
Food for his rage, repasture for his den.

PRINCESS.
What plume of feathers is he that indited
    this letter?
What vane? What weathercock? Did you
    ever hear better?

BOYET.
I am much deceiv'd but I remember the
    style.

PRINCESS.
Else your memory is bad, going o'er it
    erewhile.

BOYET.
This Armado is a Spaniard, that keeps
    here in court;
A phantasime, a Monarcho, and one that
    makes sport
To the prince and his book-mates.

PRINCESS.
Thou fellow, a word. Who gave thee this
    letter?

COSTARD.
I told you; my lord.

PRINCESS.
To whom shouldst thou give it?

COSTARD.
From my lord to my lady.

PRINCESS.
From which lord to which lady?

COSTARD.
From my Lord Berowne, a good master
    of mine,
To a lady of France that he call'd
    Rosaline.

PRINCESS.
Thou hast mistaken his letter. Come,
    lords, away.
Here, sweet, put up this: 'twill be thine
    another day.
       [*Exeunt* PRINCESS *and* TRAIN.]

BOYET.
Who is the suitor? who is the suitor?

ROSALINE.
Shall I teach you to know?

BOYET.
Ay, my continent of beauty.

ROSALINE.
Why, she that bears the bow.
Finely put off!

BOYET.
My lady goes to kill horns; but, if thou marry,
Hang me by the neck, if horns that year
    miscarry.
Finely put on!

ROSALINE.
Well then, I am the shooter.

BOYET.
And who is your deer?

ROSALINE.
If we choose by the horns, yourself: come
    not near.
Finely put on indeed!

MARIA.
You still wrangle with her, Boyet, and she
    strikes at the brow.

BOYET.
But she herself is hit lower: have I hit her
    now?

ROSALINE.
Shall I come upon thee with an old saying,
that was a man when King Pepin of France
was a little boy, as touching the hit it?

BOYET.
So I may answer thee with one as old, that
was a woman when Queen Guinever of
Britain was a little wench, as touching the
hit it.

ROSALINE.
Thou canst not hit it, hit it, hit it,
Thou canst not hit it, my good man.

BOYET.
An I cannot, cannot, cannot,
An I cannot, another can.
       [*Exeunt* ROSALINE *and* KATHARINE.]

COSTARD.
By my troth, most pleasant: how both did
    fit it!

MARIA.
A mark marvellous well shot; for they
    both did hit it.

BOYET.
A mark! O! mark but that mark! A mark,
    says my lady!
Let the mark have a prick in't, to mete at,
    if it may be.

MARIA.
Wide o' the bow-hand! I' faith, your hand
    is out.

COSTARD.
Indeed, a' must shoot nearer, or he'll ne'er
    hit the clout.

BOYET.
An' if my hand be out, then belike your
    hand is in.

COSTARD.
Then will she get the upshoot by cleaving
    the pin.

MARIA.
Come, come, you talk greasily; your lips
    grow foul.

COSTARD.
She's too hard for you at pricks, sir;
    challenge her to bowl.

BOYET.
I fear too much rubbing. Good-night, my
    good owl.
        [*Exeunt* BOYET *and* MARIA.]

COSTARD.
By my soul, a swain! a most simple clown!
Lord, Lord! how the ladies and I have put
    him down!
O' my troth, most sweet jests, most incony
    vulgar wit!
When it comes so smoothly off, so
    obscenely, as it were, so fit.
Armado, o' the one side, O! a most dainty
    man!
To see him walk before a lady and to bear
    her fan!
To see him kiss his hand! and how most
    sweetly a' will swear!
And his page o' t'other side, that handful
    of wit!
Ah! heavens, it is a most pathetical nit.
        [*Shouting within.*] Sola, sola!
        [*Exit running.*]

SCENE II

The same.

[*Enter* HOLOFERNES, SIR NATHANIEL,
    and DULL.]

NATHANIEL.
Very reverent sport, truly; and done in the
testimony of a good conscience.

HOLOFERNES.
The deer was, as you know, *sanguis*, in blood;
ripe as the pomewater, who now hangeth
like a jewel in the ear of *coelo*, the sky, the
welkin, the heaven; and anon falleth like a
crab on the face of *terra*, the soil, the land,
the earth.

NATHANIEL.
Truly, Master Holofernes, the epithets are
sweetly varied, like a scholar at the least: but,
sir, I assure ye it was a buck of the first head.

HOLOFERNES.
Sir Nathaniel, *haud credo*.

DULL.
'Twas not a "auld grey doe"; 'twas a pricket.

HOLOFERNES.
Most barbarous intimation! yet a kind of
insinuation, as it were, *in via*, in way, of
explication; *facere*, as it were, replication,
or rather, *ostentare*, to show, as it were,
his inclination,—after his undressed,
unpolished, uneducated, unpruned,
untrained, or rather, unlettered, or ratherest,
unconfirmed fashion,—to insert again my
haud credo for a deer.

DULL.
I said the deer was not a *haud credo*; 'twas
a pricket.

HOLOFERNES.
Twice sod simplicity, *bis coctus*!
O! thou monster Ignorance, how
    deformed dost thou look!

NATHANIEL.
Sir, he hath never fed of the dainties that
    are bred of a book;
He hath not eat paper, as it were; he
hath not drunk ink: his intellect is not
replenished; he is only an animal, only
sensible in the duller parts:
And such barren plants are set before us
    that we thankful should be,—

Which we of taste and feeling are—for
    those parts that do fructify in us more
    than he;
For as it would ill become me to be vain,
    indiscreet, or a fool,
So, were there a patch set on learning, to
    see him in a school.
But, *omne bene*, say I; being of an old
    father's mind:
Many can brook the weather that love not
    the wind.

DULL.
You two are book-men: can you tell me by
    your wit,
What was a month old at Cain's birth,
    that's not five weeks old as yet?

HOLOFERNES.
Dictynna, goodman Dull; *Dictynna*,
    goodman Dull.

DULL.
What is *Dictynna*?

NATHANIEL.
A title to Phoebe, to Luna, to the moon.

HOLOFERNES.
The moon was a month old when Adam
    was no more,
And raught not to five weeks when he
    came to five-score.
The allusion holds in the exchange.

DULL.
'Tis true, indeed; the collusion holds in the
    exchange.

HOLOFERNES.
God comfort thy capacity! I say, the
    allusion holds in the exchange.

DULL.
And I say the pollution holds in the
exchange, for the moon is never but a
month old; and I say beside that 'twas a
pricket that the princess kill'd.

HOLOFERNES.
Sir Nathaniel, will you hear an extempora
epitaph on the death of the deer? And, to
humour the ignorant, I have call'd the deer
the princess kill'd, a pricket.

NATHANIEL.
Perge, good Master Holofernes, *perge*; so it
shall please you to abrogate scurrility.

HOLOFERNES.
I will something affect the letter; for it
    argues facility.
    The preyful Princess pierc'd and prick'd
      a pretty pleasing pricket;
    Some say a sore; but not a sore till now
      made sore with shooting.
    The dogs did yell; put *l* to sore, then
      sorel jumps from thicket;
    Or pricket sore, or else sorel; the people
      fall a-hooting.
    If sore be sore, then *l* to sore makes fifty
      sores one sore *l!*
    Of one sore I an hundred make, by
      adding but one more *l*.

NATHANIEL.
A rare talent!

DULL. [*Aside.*]
If a talent be a claw, look how he claws him
with a talent.

HOLOFERNES.
This is a gift that I have, simple, simple;
a foolish extravagant spirit, full of
forms, figures, shapes, objects, ideas,
apprehensions, motions, revolutions: these
are begot in the ventricle of memory,
nourished in the womb of *pia mater*, and
delivered upon the mellowing of occasion.
But the gift is good in those in whom it is
acute, and I am thankful for it.

NATHANIEL.
Sir, I praise the Lord for you, and so may
my parishioners; for their sons are well
tutored by you, and their daughters profit
very greatly under you: you are a good
member of the commonwealth.

HOLOFERNES.
Mehercle! if their sons be ingenious, they
shall want no instruction; if their daughters
be capable, I will put it to them; but, *vir
sapit qui pauca loquitur*. A soul feminine
saluteth us.

    [*Enter* JAQUENETTA *and* COSTARD.]

JAQUENETTA.
God give you good morrow, Master parson.

HOLOFERNES.
Master parson, *quasi* pers-on. And if one
should be pierced, which is the one?

COSTARD.

Marry, Master schoolmaster, he that is likest to a hogshead.

HOLOFERNES.

Piercing a hogshead! A good lustre or conceit in a turf of earth; fire enough for a flint, pearl enough for a swine; 'tis pretty; it is well.

JAQUENETTA.

Good Master parson, [*Giving a letter to* NATHANIEL.] be so good as read me this letter: it was given me by Costard, and sent me from Don Armado: I beseech you read it.

HOLOFERNES.

Fauste, precor gelida quando pecus omne sub umbra Ruminat, and so forth. Ah! good old Mantuan. I may speak of thee as the traveller doth of Venice:—*Venetia, Venetia, Chi non ti vede, non ti pretia.* Old Mantuan! old Mantuan! Who understandeth thee not, loves thee not. *Ut, re, sol, la, mi, fa.* Under pardon, sir, what are the contents? or rather as Horace says in his—What, my soul, verses?

NATHANIEL.

Ay, sir, and very learned.

HOLOFERNES.

Let me hear a staff, a stanze, a verse; *lege, domine.*

NATHANIEL. [*Reads.*]

If love make me forsworn, how shall I swear to love?

Ah! never faith could hold, if not to beauty vow'd;

Though to myself forsworn, to thee I'll faithful prove;

Those thoughts to me were oaks, to thee like osiers bowed.

Study his bias leaves, and makes his book thine eyes,

Where all those pleasures live that art would comprehend:

If knowledge be the mark, to know thee shall suffice.

Well learned is that tongue that well can thee commend;

All ignorant that soul that sees thee without wonder;

Which is to me some praise that I thy parts admire.

Thy eye Jove's lightning bears, thy voice his dreadful thunder,

Which, not to anger bent, is music and sweet fire.

Celestial as thou art, O! pardon love this wrong,

That sings heaven's praise with such an earthly tongue.

HOLOFERNES.

You find not the apostrophes, and so miss the accent: let me supervise the canzonet. Here are only numbers ratified; but, for the elegancy, facility, and golden cadence of poesy, *caret.* Ovidius Naso was the man: and why, indeed, Naso but for smelling out the odoriferous flowers of fancy, the jerks of invention? *Imitari* is nothing: so doth the hound his master, the ape his keeper, the tired horse his rider. But, damosella virgin, was this directed to you?

JAQUENETTA.

Ay, sir; from one Monsieur Berowne, one of the strange queen's lords.

HOLOFERNES.

I will overglance the superscript: "To the snow-white hand of the most beauteous Lady Rosaline." I will look again on the intellect of the letter, for the nomination of the party writing to the person written unto: "Your Ladyship's in all desired employment, Berowne."—Sir Nathaniel, this Berowne is one of the votaries with the king; and here he hath framed a letter to a sequent of the stranger queen's, which, accidentally, or by the way of progression, hath miscarried. Trip and go, my sweet; deliver this paper into the royal hand of the king; it may concern much. Stay not thy compliment; I forgive thy duty. Adieu.

JAQUENETTA.

Good Costard, go with me. Sir, God save your life!

COSTARD.

Have with thee, my girl.

[*Exeunt* COSTARD *and* JAQUENETTA.]

NATHANIEL.

Sir, you have done this in the fear of God, very religiously; and, as a certain Father saith—

HOLOFERNES.

Sir, tell not me of the Father; I do fear colourable colours. But to return to the verses: did they please you, Sir Nathaniel?

NATHANIEL.

Marvellous well for the pen.

HOLOFERNES.

I do dine to-day at the father's of a certain pupil of mine; where, if, before repast, it shall please you to gratify the table with a grace, I will, on my privilege I have with the parents of the foresaid child or pupil, undertake your *ben venuto*; where I will prove those verses to be very unlearned, neither savouring of poetry, wit, nor invention. I beseech your society.

NATHANIEL.

And thank you too; for society,—saith the text,—is the happiness of life.

HOLOFERNES.

And certes, the text most infallibly concludes it. [*To* DULL.] Sir, I do invite you too; you shall not say me nay: *pauca verba*. Away! the gentles are at their game, and we will to our recreation.

[*Exeunt.*]

SCENE III

The same.

[*Enter* BEROWNE, *with a paper.*]

BEROWNE.

The king he is hunting the deer: I am coursing myself: they have pitched a toil: I am tolling in a pitch,—pitch that defiles: defile! a foul word! Well, sit thee down, sorrow! for so they say the fool said, and so say I, and I am the fool: well proved, wit! By the Lord, this love is as mad as Ajax: it kills sheep; it kills me, I a sheep: well proved again o' my side. I will not love; if I do, hang me; i' faith, I will not. O! but her eye,—by this light, but for her eye, I would not love her; yes, for her two eyes. Well, I do nothing in the world but lie, and lie in

my throat. By heaven, I do love; and it hath taught me to rime, and to be melancholy; and here is part of my rime, and here my melancholy. Well, she hath one o' my sonnets already; the clown bore it, the fool sent it, and the lady hath it: sweet clown, sweeter fool, sweetest lady! By the world, I would not care a pin if the other three were in. Here comes one with a paper; God give him grace to groan!

[*Gets up into a tree.*]

[*Enter the* KING, *with a paper.*]

KING.

Ay me!

BEROWNE. [*Aside.*]

Shot, by heaven! Proceed, sweet Cupid; thou hast thumped him with thy bird-bolt under the left pap. In faith, secrets!

KING. [*Reads.*]

So sweet a kiss the golden sun gives not
To those fresh morning drops upon the
    rose,
As thy eye-beams, when their fresh rays
    have smote
The night of dew that on my cheeks down
    flows;
Nor shines the silver moon one half so
    bright
Through the transparent bosom of the
    deep,
As doth thy face through tears of mine
    give light.
Thou shin'st in every tear that I do weep:
No drop but as a coach doth carry thee;
So ridest thou triumphing in my woe.
Do but behold the tears that swell in me,
And they thy glory through my grief will
    show:
But do not love thyself; then thou wilt
    keep
My tears for glasses, and still make me
    weep.
O queen of queens! how far dost thou
    excel
No thought can think nor tongue of
    mortal tell.

How shall she know my griefs? I'll drop the paper:

Sweet leaves, shade folly. Who is he comes
  here?
[*Steps aside.*] What, Longaville! and
  reading! Listen, ear.
      [*Enter* LONGAVILLE, *with a paper.*]
BEROWNE. [*Aside.*]
Now, in thy likeness, one more fool appear!
LONGAVILLE.
Ay me! I am forsworn.
BEROWNE. [*Aside.*]
Why, he comes in like a perjure, wearing
  papers.
KING. [*Aside.*]
In love, I hope: sweet fellowship in shame!
BEROWNE. [*Aside.*]
One drunkard loves another of the name.
LONGAVILLE.
Am I the first that have been perjur'd so?
BEROWNE. [*Aside.*]
I could put thee in comfort: not by two
  that I know;
Thou makest the triumviry, the corner-cap
  of society,
The shape of love's Tyburn that hangs up
  simplicity.
LONGAVILLE.
I fear these stubborn lines lack power to
  move.
O sweet Maria, empress of my love!
These numbers will I tear, and write in
  prose.
BEROWNE. [*Aside.*]
O! rimes are guards on wanton Cupid's
  hose:
Disfigure not his slop.
LONGAVILLE.
                This same shall go. [*Reads.*]
Did not the heavenly rhetoric of thine eye,
'Gainst whom the world cannot hold
  argument,
Persuade my heart to this false perjury?
Vows for thee broke deserve not
  punishment.
A woman I forswore; but I will prove,
Thou being a goddess, I forswore not thee:
My vow was earthly, thou a heavenly love;
Thy grace being gain'd, cures all disgrace
  in me.

Vows are but breath, and breath a vapour
  is:
Then thou, fair sun, which on my earth
  dost shine,
Exhal'st this vapour-vow; in thee it is:
If broken, then it is no fault of mine:
If by me broke, what fool is not so wise
To lose an oath to win a paradise!
BEROWNE. [*Aside.*]
This is the liver-vein, which makes flesh
  a deity;
A green goose a goddess; pure, pure
  idolatry.
God amend us, God amend! We are much
  out o' the way.
LONGAVILLE.
By whom shall I send this?—Company!
  Stay.
              [*Steps aside.*]
BEROWNE. [*Aside.*]
All hid, all hid; an old infant play.
Like a demigod here sit I in the sky,
And wretched fools' secrets heedfully
  o'er-eye.
More sacks to the mill! O heavens, I have
  my wish.
      [*Enter* DUMAINE, *with a paper.*]
Dumaine transformed: four woodcocks
  in a dish!
DUMAINE.
O most divine Kate!
BEROWNE. [*Aside.*]
O most profane coxcomb!
DUMAINE.
By heaven, the wonder in a mortal eye!
BEROWNE. [*Aside.*]
By earth, she is but corporal; there you
  lie.
DUMAINE.
Her amber hairs for foul hath amber
  quoted.
BEROWNE. [*Aside.*]
An amber-colour'd raven was well noted.
DUMAINE.
As upright as the cedar.
BEROWNE. [*Aside.*]
Stoop, I say;
Her shoulder is with child.

DUMAINE.
As fair as day.
BEROWNE. [*Aside.*]
Ay, as some days; but then no sun must
  shine.
DUMAINE.
O! that I had my wish.
LONGAVILLE. [*Aside.*]
And I had mine!
KING. [*Aside.*]
And I mine too, good Lord!
BEROWNE. [*Aside.*]
Amen, so I had mine. Is not that a good
  word?
DUMAINE.
I would forget her; but a fever she
Reigns in my blood, and will remember'd
  be.
BEROWNE. [*Aside.*]
A fever in your blood! Why, then incision
Would let her out in saucers: sweet
  misprision!
DUMAINE.
Once more I'll read the ode that I have
  writ.
BEROWNE. [*Aside.*]
Once more I'll mark how love can vary wit.
DUMAINE. [*Reads.*]
  On a day, alack the day!
  Love, whose month is ever May,
  Spied a blossom passing fair
  Playing in the wanton air:
  Through the velvet leaves the wind,
  All unseen, 'gan passage find;
  That the lover, sick to death,
  Wish'd himself the heaven's breath.
  Air, quoth he, thy cheeks may blow;
  Air, would I might triumph so!
  But, alack! my hand is sworn
  Ne'er to pluck thee from thy thorn;
  Vow, alack! for youth unmeet,
  Youth so apt to pluck a sweet.
  Do not call it sin in me,
  That I am forsworn for thee;
  Thou for whom e'en Jove would swear
  Juno but an Ethiope were;
  And deny himself for Jove,
  Turning mortal for thy love.

This will I send, and something else more
  plain,
That shall express my true love's fasting
  pain.
O! would the king, Berowne and
  Longaville
Were lovers too. Ill, to example ill,
Would from my forehead wipe a perjur'd
  note;
For none offend where all alike do dote.
LONGAVILLE. [*Advancing.*]
Dumaine, thy love is far from charity,
That in love's grief desir'st society;
You may look pale, but I should blush, I
  know,
To be o'erheard and taken napping so.
KING. [*Advancing.*]
Come, sir, you blush; as his, your case is
  such.
You chide at him, offending twice as
  much:
You do not love Maria; Longaville
Did never sonnet for her sake compile;
Nor never lay his wreathed arms athwart
His loving bosom, to keep down his heart.
I have been closely shrouded in this bush,
And mark'd you both, and for you both
  did blush.
I heard your guilty rimes, observ'd your
  fashion,
Saw sighs reek from you, noted well your
  passion:
Ay me! says one. O Jove! the other cries;
One, her hairs were gold; crystal the
  other's eyes:
[*To* LONGAVILLE.] You would for paradise
  break faith and troth;
[*To* DUMAIN.] And Jove, for your love
  would infringe an oath.
What will Berowne say when that he shall
  hear
Faith infringed which such zeal did swear?
How will he scorn! how will he spend his
  wit!
How will he triumph, leap, and laugh at it!
For all the wealth that ever I did see,
I would not have him know so much by
  me.

BEROWNE.
Now step I forth to whip hypocrisy.
  [*Descends from the tree.*]
Ah! good my liege, I pray thee pardon me:
Good heart! what grace hast thou thus to
    reprove
These worms for loving, that art most in
    love?
Your eyes do make no coaches; in your
    tears
There is no certain princess that appears:
You'll not be perjur'd; 'tis a hateful thing:
Tush! none but minstrels like of sonneting.
But are you not asham'd? nay, are you not,
All three of you, to be thus much o'ershot?
You found his mote; the king your mote
    did see;
But I a beam do find in each of three.
O! what a scene of foolery have I seen,
Of sighs, of groans, of sorrow, and of teen;
O me! with what strict patience have I sat,
To see a king transformed to a gnat;
To see great Hercules whipping a gig,
And profound Solomon to tune a jig,
And Nestor play at push-pin with the
    boys,
And critic Timon laugh at idle toys!
Where lies thy grief, O! tell me, good
    Dumaine?
And, gentle Longaville, where lies thy
    pain?
And where my liege's? all about the breast:
A caudle, ho!
KING.
              Too bitter is thy jest.
Are we betrayed thus to thy over-view?
BEROWNE.
Not you by me, but I betray'd by you.
I that am honest; I that hold it sin
To break the vow I am engaged in;
I am betrayed by keeping company
With men like men, men of inconstancy.
When shall you see me write a thing in
    rime?
Or groan for Joan? or spend a minute's
    time
In pruning me? When shall you hear
    that I

Will praise a hand, a foot, a face, an eye,
A gait, a state, a brow, a breast, a waist,
A leg, a limb?—
KING.
              Soft! whither away so fast?
A true man or a thief that gallops so?
BEROWNE.
I post from love; good lover, let me go.
  [*Enter* JAQUENETTA *and* COSTARD.]
JAQUENETTA.
God bless the king!
KING.
              What present hast thou there?
COSTARD.
Some certain treason.
KING.
              What makes treason here?
COSTARD.
Nay, it makes nothing, sir.
KING.
              If it mar nothing neither,
The treason and you go in peace away
    together.
JAQUENETTA.
I beseech your Grace, let this letter be
    read;
Our parson misdoubts it; 'twas treason,
    he said.
KING.
Berowne, read it over.
        [*Giving the letter to him.*]
Where hadst thou it?
JAQUENETTA.
Of Costard.
KING.
Where hadst thou it?
COSTARD.
Of Dun Adramadio, Dun Adramadio.
        [BEROWNE *tears the letter.*]
KING.
How now! What is in you? Why dost
    thou tear it?
BEROWNE.
A toy, my liege, a toy: your Grace needs
    not fear it.
LONGAVILLE.
It did move him to passion, and therefore
    let's hear it.

DUMAINE. [*Picking up the pieces.*]
It is Berowne's writing, and here is his
    name.
BEROWNE. [*To* COSTARD.]
Ah, you whoreson loggerhead, you were
    born to do me shame.
Guilty, my lord, guilty; I confess, I confess.
KING.
What?
BEROWNE.
That you three fools lack'd me fool to
    make up the mess;
He, he, and you, and you, my liege, and I,
Are pick-purses in love, and we deserve
    to die.
O! dismiss this audience, and I shall tell
    you more.
DUMAINE.
Now the number is even.
BEROWNE.
                    True, true, we are four.
Will these turtles be gone?
KING.
                    Hence, sirs; away!
COSTARD.
Walk aside the true folk, and let the
    traitors stay.
[*Exeunt* COSTARD *and* JAQUENETTA.]
BEROWNE.
Sweet lords, sweet lovers, O! let us embrace!
As true we are as flesh and blood can be:
The sea will ebb and flow, heaven show
    his face;
Young blood doth not obey an old decree:
We cannot cross the cause why we were
    born,
Therefore of all hands must we be
    forsworn.
KING.
What! did these rent lines show some love
    of thine?
BEROWNE.
"Did they?" quoth you? Who sees the
    heavenly Rosaline
That, like a rude and savage man of Inde
At the first op'ning of the gorgeous east,
Bows not his vassal head and, strucken
    blind,

Kisses the base ground with obedient
    breast?
What peremptory eagle-sighted eye
Dares look upon the heaven of her brow,
That is not blinded by her majesty?
KING.
What zeal, what fury hath inspir'd thee
    now?
My love, her mistress, is a gracious moon;
She, an attending star, scarce seen a light.
BEROWNE.
My eyes are then no eyes, nor I Berowne.
O! but for my love, day would turn to
    night.
Of all complexions the cull'd sovereignty
Do meet, as at a fair, in her fair cheek,
Where several worthies make one dignity,
Where nothing wants that want itself
    doth seek.
Lend me the flourish of all gentle
    tongues,—
Fie, painted rhetoric! O! she needs it not:
To things of sale a seller's praise belongs;
She passes praise; then praise too short
    doth blot.
A wither'd hermit, five-score winters worn,
Might shake off fifty, looking in her eye:
Beauty doth varnish age, as if new-born,
And gives the crutch the cradle's infancy.
O! 'tis the sun that maketh all things
    shine!
KING.
By heaven, thy love is black as ebony.
BEROWNE.
Is ebony like her? O wood divine!
A wife of such wood were felicity.
O! who can give an oath? Where is a
    book?
That I may swear beauty doth beauty
    lack,
If that she learn not of her eye to look.
No face is fair that is not full so black.
KING.
O paradox! Black is the badge of hell,
The hue of dungeons, and the school of
    night;
And beauty's crest becomes the heavens
    well.

BEROWNE.
Devils soonest tempt, resembling spirits
    of light.
O! if in black my lady's brows be deck'd,
It mourns that painting and usurping hair
Should ravish doters with a false aspect;
And therefore is she born to make black
    fair.
Her favour turns the fashion of the days,
For native blood is counted painting now;
And therefore red, that would avoid
    dispraise,
Paints itself black, to imitate her brow.

DUMAINE.
To look like her are chimney-sweepers
    black.

LONGAVILLE.
And since her time are colliers counted
    bright.

KING.
And Ethiopes of their sweet complexion
    crack.

DUMAINE.
Dark needs no candles now, for dark is
    light.

BEROWNE.
Your mistresses dare never come in rain,
For fear their colours should be wash'd
    away.

KING.
'Twere good yours did; for, sir, to tell you
    plain,
I'll find a fairer face not wash'd to-day.

BEROWNE.
I'll prove her fair, or talk till doomsday here.

KING.
No devil will fright thee then so much
    as she.

DUMAINE.
I never knew man hold vile stuff so dear.

LONGAVILLE.
Look, here's thy love: [*Showing his shoe.*]
    my foot and her face see.

BEROWNE.
O! if the streets were paved with thine
    eyes,
Her feet were much too dainty for such
    tread.

DUMAINE.
O vile! Then, as she goes, what upward lies
The street should see as she walk'd over
    head.

KING.
But what of this? Are we not all in love?

BEROWNE.
Nothing so sure; and thereby all forsworn.

KING.
Then leave this chat; and, good Berowne,
    now prove
Our loving lawful, and our faith not torn.

DUMAINE.
Ay, marry, there; some flattery for this evil.

LONGAVILLE.
O! some authority how to proceed;
Some tricks, some quillets, how to cheat
    the devil.

DUMAINE.
Some salve for perjury.

BEROWNE.
                            O, 'tis more than need.
Have at you, then, affection's men-at-arms:
Consider what you first did swear unto,
To fast, to study, and to see no woman;
Flat treason 'gainst the kingly state of
    youth.
Say, can you fast? Your stomachs are too
    young,
And abstinence engenders maladies.
And where that you have vow'd to study,
    lords,
In that each of you have forsworn his
    book,
Can you still dream, and pore, and thereon
    look?
For when would you, my lord, or you, or
    you,
Have found the ground of study's
    excellence
Without the beauty of a woman's face?
From women's eyes this doctrine I derive:
They are the ground, the books, the
    academes,
From whence doth spring the true
    Promethean fire.
Why, universal plodding poisons up
The nimble spirits in the arteries,

As motion and long-during action tires
The sinewy vigour of the traveller.
Now, for not looking on a woman's face,
You have in that forsworn the use of eyes,
And study too, the causer of your vow;
For where is author in the world
Teaches such beauty as a woman's eye?
Learning is but an adjunct to ourself,
And where we are our learning likewise is:
Then when ourselves we see in ladies' eyes,
Do we not likewise see our learning there?
O! we have made a vow to study, lords,
And in that vow we have forsworn our
    books:
For when would you, my liege, or you, or
    you,
In leaden contemplation have found out
Such fiery numbers as the prompting eyes
Of beauty's tutors have enrich'd you with?
Other slow arts entirely keep the brain;
And therefore, finding barren practisers,
Scarce show a harvest of their heavy toil;
But love, first learned in a lady's eyes,
Lives not alone immured in the brain,
But with the motion of all elements,
Courses as swift as thought in every
    power,
And gives to every power a double power,
Above their functions and their offices.
It adds a precious seeing to the eye;
A lover's eyes will gaze an eagle blind;
A lover's ear will hear the lowest sound,
When the suspicious head of theft is
    stopp'd:
Love's feeling is more soft and sensible
Than are the tender horns of cockled
    snails:
Love's tongue proves dainty Bacchus gross
    in taste.
For valour, is not Love a Hercules,
Still climbing trees in the Hesperides?
Subtle as Sphinx; as sweet and musical
As bright Apollo's lute, strung with his
    hair;
And when Love speaks, the voice of all
    the gods
Make heaven drowsy with the harmony.
Never durst poet touch a pen to write

Until his ink were temper'd with Love's
    sighs;
O! then his lines would ravish savage ears,
And plant in tyrants mild humility.
From women's eyes this doctrine I derive:
They sparkle still the right Promethean
    fire;
They are the books, the arts, the academes,
That show, contain, and nourish, all the
    world;
Else none at all in aught proves excellent.
Then fools you were these women to
    forswear,
Or, keeping what is sworn, you will prove
    fools.
For wisdom's sake, a word that all men
    love,
Or for love's sake, a word that loves all men,
Or for men's sake, the authors of these
    women;
Or women's sake, by whom we men are
    men,
Let us once lose our oaths to find
    ourselves,
Or else we lose ourselves to keep our
    oaths.
It is religion to be thus forsworn;
For charity itself fulfils the law;
And who can sever love from charity?
KING.
Saint Cupid, then! and, soldiers, to the
    field!
BEROWNE.
Advance your standards, and upon them,
    lords;
Pell-mell, down with them! be first advis'd,
In conflict that you get the sun of them.
LONGAVILLE.
Now to plain-dealing; lay these glozes by:
Shall we resolve to woo these girls of
    France?
KING.
And win them too; therefore let us devise
Some entertainment for them in their
    tents.
BEROWNE.
First, from the park let us conduct them
    thither;

Then homeward every man attach the
   hand
Of his fair mistress: in the afternoon
We will with some strange pastime solace
   them,
Such as the shortness of the time can
   shape;
For revels, dances, masks, and merry hours,
Forerun fair Love, strewing her way with
   flowers.
KING.
Away, away! No time shall be omitted,
That will betime, and may by us be fitted.
BEROWNE.
Allons! *allons*! Sow'd cockle reap'd no
   corn;
And justice always whirls in equal
   measure:
Light wenches may prove plagues to men
   forsworn;
If so, our copper buys no better treasure.
            [*Exeunt.*]

ACT V
SCENE I
The King of Navarre's park.
[*Enter* HOLOFERNES, SIR NATHANIEL,
and DULL.]
HOLOFERNES.
Satis quod sufficit.
NATHANIEL.
I praise God for you, sir: your reasons at
dinner have been sharp and sententious;
pleasant without scurrility, witty without
affection, audacious without impudency,
learned without opinion, and strange
without heresy. I did converse this quondam
day with a companion of the king's who
is intituled, nominated, or called, Don
Adriano de Armado.
HOLOFERNES.
Novi hominem tanquam te: his humour is
lofty, his discourse peremptory, his tongue
filed, his eye ambitious, his gait majestical
and his general behaviour vain, ridiculous,
and thrasonical. He is too picked, too
spruce, too affected, too odd, as it were, too
peregrinate, as I may call it.

NATHANIEL.
A most singular and choice epithet.
         [*Draws out his table-book.*]
HOLOFERNES.
He draweth out the thread of his verbosity
finer than the staple of his argument. I
abhor such fanatical phantasimes, such
insociable and point-devise companions;
such rackers of orthography, as to speak
dout, fine, when he should say doubt; det
when he should pronounce debt,—d, e, b,
t, not d, e, t: he clepeth a calf, cauf; half,
hauf; neighbour *vocatur* nebour, neigh
abbreviated ne. This is abhominable, which
he would call abominable,—it insinuateth
me of insanie: *ne intelligis, domine*? to make
frantic, lunatic.
NATHANIEL.
Laus Deo, bone intelligo.
HOLOFERNES.
Bone? bone for bene: Priscian a little
scratch'd; 'twill serve.
      [*Enter* ARMADO, MOTH, *and* COSTARD.]
NATHANIEL.
Videsne quis venit?
HOLOFERNES.
Video, et gaudeo.
ARMADO. [*To* MOTH.]
Chirrah!
HOLOFERNES.
Quare chirrah, not sirrah?
ARMADO.
Men of peace, well encountered.
HOLOFERNES.
Most military sir, salutation.
MOTH. [*Aside to* COSTARD.]
They have been at a great feast of languages
and stolen the scraps.
COSTARD.
O! they have lived long on the alms-basket
of words. I marvel thy master hath not eaten
thee for a word, for thou are not so long by
the head as *honorificabilitudinitatibus*; thou
art easier swallowed than a flap-dragon.
MOTH.
Peace! the peal begins.
ARMADO. [*To* HOLOFERNES.]
Monsieur, are you not lettered?

MOTH.
Yes, yes; he teaches boys the hornbook. What is a, b, spelt backward with the horn on his head?

HOLOFERNES.
Ba, *pueritia*, with a horn added.

MOTH.
Ba! most silly sheep with a horn. You hear his learning.

HOLOFERNES.
Quis, quis, thou consonant?

MOTH.
The third of the five vowels, if you repeat them; or the fifth, if I.

HOLOFERNES.
I will repeat them,—a, e, i,—

MOTH.
The sheep; the other two concludes it,— o, u.

ARMADO.
Now, by the salt wave of the Mediterraneum, a sweet touch, a quick venue of wit! snip, snap, quick and home! It rejoiceth my intellect: true wit!

MOTH.
Offered by a child to an old man; which is wit-old.

HOLOFERNES.
What is the figure? What is the figure?

MOTH.
Horns.

HOLOFERNES.
Thou disputes like an infant; go, whip thy gig.

MOTH.
Lend me your horn to make one, and I will whip about your infamy *circum circa*. A gig of a cuckold's horn.

COSTARD.
An I had but one penny in the world, thou shouldst have it to buy gingerbread. Hold, there is the very remuneration I had of thy master, thou half-penny purse of wit, thou pigeon-egg of discretion. O! an the heavens were so pleased that thou wert but my bastard, what a joyful father wouldst thou make me. Go to; thou hast it *ad dunghill*, at the fingers' ends, as they say.

HOLOFERNES.
O, I smell false Latin! dunghill for *unguem*.

ARMADO.
Arts-man, *praeambula*; we will be singled from the barbarous. Do you not educate youth at the charge-house on the top of the mountain?

HOLOFERNES.
Or *mons*, the hill.

ARMADO.
At your sweet pleasure, for the mountain.

HOLOFERNES.
I do, sans question.

ARMADO.
Sir, it is the king's most sweet pleasure and affection to congratulate the princess at her pavilion, in the posteriors of this day, which the rude multitude call the afternoon.

HOLOFERNES.
The posterior of the day, most generous sir, is liable, congruent, and measurable, for the afternoon. The word is well culled, chose, sweet, and apt, I do assure you, sir; I do assure.

ARMADO.
Sir, the king is a noble gentleman, and my familiar, I do assure ye, very good friend. For what is inward between us, let it pass: I do beseech thee, remember thy courtsy; I beseech thee, apparel thy head: and among other importunate and most serious designs, and of great import indeed, too, but let that pass: for I must tell thee it will please his Grace, by the world, sometime to lean upon my poor shoulder, and with his royal finger thus dally with my excrement, with my mustachio: but, sweet heart, let that pass. By the world, I recount no fable: some certain special honours it pleaseth his greatness to impart to Armado, a soldier, a man of travel, that hath seen the world: but let that pass. The very all of all is, but, sweet heart, I do implore secrecy, that the king would have me present the princess, sweet chuck, with some delightful ostentation, or show, or pageant, or antic, or firework. Now, understanding that the curate and your sweet self are good at such eruptions and sudden breaking-out

of mirth, as it were, I have acquainted you withal, to the end to crave your assistance.

HOLOFERNES.
Sir, you shall present before her the Nine Worthies. Sir Nathaniel, as concerning some entertainment of time, some show in the posterior of this day, to be rendered by our assistance, the king's command, and this most gallant, illustrate, and learned gentleman, before the princess, I say none so fit as to present the Nine Worthies.

NATHANIEL.
Where will you find men worthy enough to present them?

HOLOFERNES.
Joshua, yourself; myself, Alexander; this gallant gentleman, Judas Maccabaeus; this swain, because of his great limb or joint, shall pass Pompey the Great; the page, Hercules,—

ARMADO.
Pardon, sir; error: he is not quantity enough for that Worthy's thumb; he is not so big as the end of his club.

HOLOFERNES.
Shall I have audience? He shall present Hercules in minority: his enter and exit shall be strangling a snake; and I will have an apology for that purpose.

MOTH.
An excellent device! So, if any of the audience hiss, you may cry "Well done, Hercules; now thou crushest the snake!" That is the way to make an offence gracious, though few have the grace to do it.

ARMADO.
For the rest of the Worthies?—

HOLOFERNES.
I will play three myself.

MOTH.
Thrice-worthy gentleman!

ARMADO.
Shall I tell you a thing?

HOLOFERNES.
We attend.

ARMADO.
We will have, if this fadge not, an antic. I beseech you, follow.

HOLOFERNES.
Via, goodman Dull! Thou has spoken no word all this while.

DULL.
Nor understood none neither, sir.

HOLOFERNES.
Allons! we will employ thee.

DULL.
I'll make one in a dance, or so, or I will play on the tabor to the Worthies, and let them dance the hay.

HOLOFERNES.
Most dull, honest Dull! To our sport, away.
[*Exeunt.*]

SCENE II

The same. Before the princess's pavilion.
[*Enter the* PRINCESS, KATHARINE,
ROSALINE, *and* MARIA.]

PRINCESS.
Sweet hearts, we shall be rich ere we
    depart,
If fairings come thus plentifully in.
A lady wall'd about with diamonds!
Look you what I have from the loving
    king.

ROSALINE.
Madam, came nothing else along with
    that?

PRINCESS.
Nothing but this! Yes, as much love in rime
As would be cramm'd up in a sheet of
    paper
Writ o' both sides the leaf, margent and all,
That he was fain to seal on Cupid's name.

ROSALINE.
That was the way to make his godhead
    wax;
For he hath been five thousand years a boy.

KATHARINE.
Ay, and a shrewd unhappy gallows too.

ROSALINE.
You'll ne'er be friends with him: a' kill'd
    your sister.

KATHARINE.
He made her melancholy, sad, and heavy;
And so she died: had she been light, like
    you,

Of such a merry, nimble, stirring spirit,
She might ha' been a grandam ere she
    died;
And so may you, for a light heart lives
    long.

ROSALINE.
What's your dark meaning, mouse, of this
    light word?

KATHARINE.
A light condition in a beauty dark.

ROSALINE.
We need more light to find your meaning
    out.

KATHARINE.
You'll mar the light by taking it in snuff;
Therefore I'll darkly end the argument.

ROSALINE.
Look what you do, you do it still i' the
    dark.

KATHARINE.
So do not you; for you are a light wench.

ROSALINE.
Indeed, I weigh not you; and therefore
    light.

KATHARINE.
You weigh me not? O! that's you care not
    for me.

ROSALINE.
Great reason; for "past cure is still past
    care."

PRINCESS.
Well bandied both; a set of wit well play'd.
But, Rosaline, you have a favour too:
Who sent it? and what is it?

ROSALINE.
                 I would you knew.
An if my face were but as fair as yours,
My favour were as great: be witness this.
Nay, I have verses too, I thank Berowne;
The numbers true, and, were the
    numbering too,
I were the fairest goddess on the ground:
I am compar'd to twenty thousand fairs.
O! he hath drawn my picture in his letter.

PRINCESS.
Anything like?

ROSALINE.
Much in the letters; nothing in the praise.

PRINCESS.
Beauteous as ink; a good conclusion.

KATHARINE.
Fair as a text B in a copy-book.

ROSALINE.
'Ware pencils! how! let me not die your
    debtor,
My red dominical, my golden letter:
O, that your face were not so full of O's!

KATHARINE.
A pox of that jest! and beshrew all shrows!

PRINCESS.
But, Katharine, what was sent to you from
    fair Dumaine?

KATHARINE.
Madam, this glove.

PRINCESS.
              Did he not send you twain?

KATHARINE.
Yes, madam; and, moreover,
Some thousand verses of a faithful lover;
A huge translation of hypocrisy,
Vilely compil'd, profound simplicity.

MARIA.
This, and these pearl, to me sent
    Longaville;
The letter is too long by half a mile.

PRINCESS.
I think no less. Dost thou not wish in
    heart
The chain were longer and the letter short?

MARIA.
Ay, or I would these hands might never
    part.

PRINCESS.
We are wise girls to mock our lovers so.

ROSALINE.
They are worse fools to purchase mocking
    so.
That same Berowne I'll torture ere I go.
O that I knew he were but in by th' week!
How I would make him fawn, and beg,
    and seek,
And wait the season, and observe the
    times,
And spend his prodigal wits in bootless
    rimes,
And shape his service wholly to my hests,

And make him proud to make me proud
    that jests!
So pertaunt-like would I o'ersway his state
That he should be my fool, and I his fate.

PRINCESS.
None are so surely caught, when they are
    catch'd,
As wit turn'd fool: folly, in wisdom hatch'd,
Hath wisdom's warrant and the help of
    school
And wit's own grace to grace a learned
    fool.

ROSALINE.
The blood of youth burns not with such
    excess
As gravity's revolt to wantonness.

MARIA.
Folly in fools bears not so strong a note
As fool'ry in the wise when wit doth dote;
Since all the power thereof it doth apply
To prove, by wit, worth in simplicity.

               [*Enter* BOYET.]

PRINCESS.
Here comes Boyet, and mirth is in his face.

BOYET.
O! I am stabb'd with laughter! Where's
    her Grace?

PRINCESS.
Thy news, Boyet?

BOYET.
           Prepare, madam, prepare!—
Arm, wenches, arm! encounters mounted
    are
Against your peace: Love doth approach
    disguis'd,
Armed in arguments; you'll be surpris'd:
Muster your wits; stand in your own
    defence;
Or hide your heads like cowards, and fly
    hence.

PRINCESS.
Saint Denis to Saint Cupid! What are they
That charge their breath against us? Say,
    scout, say.

BOYET.
Under the cool shade of a sycamore
I thought to close mine eyes some half an
    hour;

When, lo, to interrupt my purpos'd rest,
Toward that shade I might behold addrest
The king and his companions: warily
I stole into a neighbour thicket by,
And overheard what you shall overhear;
That, by and by, disguis'd they will be here.
Their herald is a pretty knavish page,
That well by heart hath conn'd his
    embassage:
Action and accent did they teach him
    there;
"Thus must thou speak" and "thus thy
    body bear,"
And ever and anon they made a doubt
Presence majestical would put him out;
"For," quoth the king, "an angel shalt thou
    see;
Yet fear not thou, but speak audaciously."'
The boy replied "An angel is not evil;
I should have fear'd her had she been a
    devil."
With that all laugh'd, and clapp'd him on
    the shoulder,
Making the bold wag by their praises
    bolder.
One rubb'd his elbow, thus, and fleer'd,
    and swore
A better speech was never spoke before.
Another with his finger and his thumb
Cried "Via! we will do't, come what will
    come."
The third he caper'd, and cried "All goes
    well."
The fourth turn'd on the toe, and down
    he fell.
With that they all did tumble on the
    ground,
With such a zealous laughter, so profound,
That in this spleen ridiculous appears,
To check their folly, passion's solemn tears.

PRINCESS.
But what, but what, come they to visit us?

BOYET.
They do, they do, and are apparell'd thus,
Like Muscovites or Russians, as I guess.
Their purpose is to parley, court, and
    dance;
And every one his love-feat will advance

Unto his several mistress; which they'll
  know
By favours several which they did bestow.
PRINCESS.
And will they so? The gallants shall be
  task'd:
For, ladies, we will every one be mask'd;
And not a man of them shall have the
  grace,
Despite of suit, to see a lady's face.
Hold, Rosaline, this favour thou shalt wear,
And then the king will court thee for his
  dear;
Hold, take thou this, my sweet, and give
  me thine,
So shall Berowne take me for Rosaline.
And change you favours too; so shall your
  loves
Woo contrary, deceiv'd by these removes.
ROSALINE.
Come on, then, wear the favours most in
  sight.
KATHARINE.
But, in this changing, what is your intent?
PRINCESS.
The effect of my intent is to cross theirs;
They do it but in mocking merriment;
And mock for mock is only my intent.
Their several counsels they unbosom shall
To loves mistook, and so be mock'd withal
Upon the next occasion that we meet
With visages display'd to talk and greet.
ROSALINE.
But shall we dance, if they desire us to't?
PRINCESS.
No, to the death, we will not move a foot,
Nor to their penn'd speech render we no
  grace;
But while 'tis spoke each turn away her
  face.
BOYET.
Why, that contempt will kill the speaker's
  heart,
And quite divorce his memory from his
  part.
PRINCESS.
Therefore I do it; and I make no doubt
The rest will ne'er come in, if he be out.

There's no such sport as sport by sport
  o'erthrown,
To make theirs ours, and ours none but
  our own:
So shall we stay, mocking intended game,
And they well mock'd, depart away with
  shame.
          [*Trumpet sounds within.*]
BOYET.
The trumpet sounds: be mask'd; the
  maskers come.
          [*The* LADIES *mask.*]
[*Enter* BLACKAMOORS *with music;* MOTH,
  the KING, BEROWNE, LONGAVILLE, *and*
  DUMAINE *in Russian habits, and masked.*]
MOTH.
All hail, the richest beauties on the earth!
BOYET.
Beauties no richer than rich taffeta.
MOTH.
A holy parcel of the fairest dames
          [*The* LADIES *turn their backs to him.*]
That ever turn'd their—backs—to mortal
  views!
BEROWNE. [*Aside to* MOTH.]
Their eyes, villain, their eyes.
MOTH.
That ever turn'd their eyes to mortal views!
Out—
BOYET.
True; out, indeed.
MOTH.
Out of your favours, heavenly spirits,
  vouchsafe
Not to behold—
BEROWNE.
Once to behold, rogue.
MOTH.
Once to behold with your sun-beamed
  eyes—
With your sun-beamed eyes—
BOYET.
They will not answer to that epithet;
You were best call it "daughter-beamed
  eyes."
MOTH.
They do not mark me, and that brings me
  out.

BEROWNE.
Is this your perfectness? be gone, you
   rogue.
                 [*Exit* MOTH.]

ROSALINE.
What would these strangers? Know their
   minds, Boyet.
If they do speak our language, 'tis our will
That some plain man recount their
   purposes:
Know what they would.

BOYET.
What would you with the princess?

BEROWNE.
Nothing but peace and gentle visitation.

ROSALINE.
What would they, say they?

BOYET.
Nothing but peace and gentle visitation.

ROSALINE.
Why, that they have; and bid them so be
   gone.

BOYET.
She says you have it, and you may be gone.

KING.
Say to her we have measur'd many miles
To tread a measure with her on this grass.

BOYET.
They say that they have measur'd many
   a mile
To tread a measure with you on this grass.

ROSALINE.
It is not so. Ask them how many inches
Is in one mile? If they have measured
   many,
The measure then of one is easily told.

BOYET.
If to come hither you have measur'd miles,
And many miles, the Princess bids you tell
How many inches doth fill up one mile.

BEROWNE.
Tell her we measure them by weary steps.

BOYET.
She hears herself.

ROSALINE.
            How many weary steps
Of many weary miles you have o'ergone
Are number'd in the travel of one mile?

BEROWNE.
We number nothing that we spend for
   you;
Our duty is so rich, so infinite,
That we may do it still without accompt.
Vouchsafe to show the sunshine of your
   face,
That we, like savages, may worship it.

ROSALINE.
My face is but a moon, and clouded too.

KING.
Blessed are clouds, to do as such clouds do!
Vouchsafe, bright moon, and these thy
   stars, to shine,
Those clouds remov'd, upon our watery
   eyne.

ROSALINE.
O vain petitioner! beg a greater matter;
Thou now requests'st but moonshine in
   the water.

KING.
Then in our measure do but vouchsafe one
   change.
Thou bid'st me beg; this begging is not
   strange.

ROSALINE.
Play, music, then! Nay, you must do it
   soon.
                 [*Music plays.*]
Not yet! No dance! thus change I like the
   moon.

KING.
Will you not dance? How come you thus
   estranged?

ROSALINE.
You took the moon at full; but now she's
   chang'd.

KING.
Yet still she is the moon, and I the man.
The music plays; vouchsafe some motion
   to it.

ROSALINE.
Our ears vouchsafe it.

KING.
              But your legs should do it.

ROSALINE.
Since you are strangers, and come here by
   chance,

We'll not be nice: take hands; we will not
    dance.
KING.
Why take we hands then?
ROSALINE.
                Only to part friends.
Curtsy, sweet hearts; and so the measure
    ends.
KING.
More measure of this measure: be not nice.
ROSALINE.
We can afford no more at such a price.
KING.
Price you yourselves? what buys your
    company?
ROSALINE.
Your absence only.
KING.
                That can never be.
ROSALINE.
Then cannot we be bought: and so adieu;
Twice to your visor, and half once to you!
KING.
If you deny to dance, let's hold more chat.
ROSALINE.
In private then.
KING.
          I am best pleas'd with that.
    [*They converse apart.*]
BEROWNE.
White-handed mistress, one sweet word
    with thee.
PRINCESS.
Honey, and milk, and sugar; there is three.
BEROWNE.
Nay, then, two treys, an if you grow so
    nice,
Metheglin, wort, and malmsey: well run,
    dice!
There's half a dozen sweets.
PRINCESS.
            Seventh sweet, adieu:
Since you can cog, I'll play no more with
    you.
BEROWNE.
One word in secret.
PRINCESS.
          Let it not be sweet.

BEROWNE.
Thou griev'st my gall.
PRINCESS.
          Gall!—bitter.
BEROWNE.
             Therefore meet.
    [*They converse apart.*]
DUMAINE.
Will you vouchsafe with me to change a
    word?
MARIA.
Name it.
DUMAINE.
      Fair lady,—
MARIA.
          Say you so? Fair lord,
Take that for your fair lady.
DUMAINE.
             Please it you,
As much in private, and I'll bid adieu.
    [*They converse apart.*]
KATHARINE.
What, was your visord made without a
    tongue?
LONGAVILLE.
I know the reason, lady, why you ask.
KATHARINE.
O! for your reason! quickly, sir; I long.
LONGAVILLE.
You have a double tongue within your
    mask,
And would afford my speechless visor half.
KATHARINE.
"Veal" quoth the Dutchman. Is not "veal"
    a calf?
LONGAVILLE.
A calf, fair lady!
KATHARINE.
         No, a fair lord calf.
LONGAVILLE.
Let's part the word.
KATHARINE.
        No, I'll not be your half.
Take all and wean it; it may prove an ox.
LONGAVILLE.
Look how you butt yourself in these sharp
    mocks!
Will you give horns, chaste lady? Do not so.

KATHARINE.
Then die a calf, before your horns do grow.
LONGAVILLE.
One word in private with you ere I die.
KATHARINE.
Bleat softly, then; the butcher hears you cry.
          [*They converse apart.*]
BOYET.
The tongues of mocking wenches are as
          keen
As is the razor's edge invisible,
Cutting a smaller hair than may be seen,
Above the sense of sense; so sensible
Seemeth their conference; their conceits
          have wings,
Fleeter than arrows, bullets, wind, thought,
          swifter things.
ROSALINE.
Not one word more, my maids; break off,
          break off.
BEROWNE.
By heaven, all dry-beaten with pure scoff!
KING.
Farewell, mad wenches; you have simple
          wits.
PRINCESS.
Twenty adieus, my frozen Muscovits.
          [*Exeunt* KING, LORDS, MUSIC, *and*
               ATTENDANTS.]
Are these the breed of wits so wondered at?
BOYET.
Tapers they are, with your sweet breaths
          puff'd out.
ROSALINE.
Well-liking wits they have; gross, gross;
          fat, fat.
PRINCESS.
O poverty in wit, kingly-poor flout!
Will they not, think you, hang themselves
          to-night?
Or ever, but in vizors, show their faces?
This pert Berowne was out of countenance
          quite.
ROSALINE.
O! They were all in lamentable cases!
The king was weeping-ripe for a good word.
PRINCESS.
Berowne did swear himself out of all suit.

MARIA.
Dumaine was at my service, and his
          sword:
"No point" quoth I; my servant straight
          was mute.
KATHARINE.
Lord Longaville said, I came o'er his heart;
And trow you what he call'd me?
PRINCESS.
                              Qualm, perhaps.
KATHARINE.
Yes, in good faith.
PRINCESS.
                    Go, sickness as thou art!
ROSALINE.
Well, better wits have worn plain statute-
          caps.
But will you hear? The king is my love
          sworn.
PRINCESS.
And quick Berowne hath plighted faith
          to me.
KATHARINE.
And Longaville was for my service born.
MARIA.
Dumaine is mine, as sure as bark on tree.
BOYET.
Madam, and pretty mistresses, give ear:
Immediately they will again be here
In their own shapes; for it can never be
They will digest this harsh indignity.
PRINCESS.
Will they return?
BOYET.
                    They will, they will, God knows,
And leap for joy, though they are lame
          with blows;
Therefore, change favours; and, when they
          repair,
Blow like sweet roses in this summer air.
PRINCESS.
How blow? how blow? Speak to be
          understood.
BOYET.
Fair ladies mask'd are roses in their bud:
Dismask'd, their damask sweet
          commixture shown,
Are angels vailing clouds, or roses blown.

Princess.
Avaunt, perplexity! What shall we do
If they return in their own shapes to woo?
Rosaline.
Good madam, if by me you'll be advis'd,
Let's mock them still, as well known as
   disguis'd.
Let us complain to them what fools were
   here,
Disguis'd like Muscovites, in shapeless
   gear;
And wonder what they were, and to what
   end
Their shallow shows and prologue vilely
   penn'd,
And their rough carriage so ridiculous,
Should be presented at our tent to us.
Boyet.
Ladies, withdraw: the gallants are at hand.
Princess.
Whip to our tents, as roes run over land.
    [*Exeunt* Princess, Rosaline,
      Katharine, *and* Maria.]
    [*Re-enter the* King, Berowne,
    Longaville, *and* Dumaine *in their*
      proper habits.]
King.
Fair sir, God save you! Where's the
   princess?
Boyet.
Gone to her tent. Please it your Majesty
Command me any service to her thither?
King.
That she vouchsafe me audience for one
   word.
Boyet.
I will; and so will she, I know, my lord.
             [*Exit.*]
Berowne.
This fellow pecks up wit as pigeons pease,
And utters it again when God doth please:
He is wit's pedlar, and retails his wares
At wakes, and wassails, meetings, markets,
   fairs;
And we that sell by gross, the Lord doth
   know,
Have not the grace to grace it with such
   show.

This gallant pins the wenches on his
   sleeve;
Had he been Adam, he had tempted Eve:
He can carve too, and lisp: why this is he
That kiss'd his hand away in courtesy;
This is the ape of form, monsieur the nice,
That, when he plays at tables, chides the
   dice
In honourable terms; nay, he can sing
A mean most meanly; and in ushering
Mend him who can: the ladies call him
   sweet;
The stairs, as he treads on them, kiss his
   feet.
This is the flower that smiles on every one,
To show his teeth as white as whales-
   bone;
And consciences that will not die in debt
Pay him the due of honey-tongued Boyet.
King.
A blister on his sweet tongue, with my
   heart,
That put Armado's page out of his part!
    [*Re-enter the* Princess, *ushered by* Boyet;
      Rosaline, Maria, Katharine, *and*
        Attendants.]
Berowne.
See where it comes! Behaviour, what wert
   thou,
Till this man show'd thee? and what art
   thou now?
King.
All hail, sweet madam, and fair time of
   day!
Princess.
"Fair" in "all hail" is foul, as I conceive.
King.
Construe my speeches better, if you may.
Princess.
Then wish me better: I will give you leave.
King.
We came to visit you, and purpose now
To lead you to our court; vouchsafe it
   then.
Princess.
This field shall hold me, and so hold your
   vow:
Nor God, nor I, delights in perjur'd men.

KING.
Rebuke me not for that which you
    provoke:
The virtue of your eye must break my oath.
PRINCESS.
You nickname virtue: vice you should have
    spoke;
For virtue's office never breaks men's troth.
Now by my maiden honour, yet as pure
As the unsullied lily, I protest,
A world of torments though I should
    endure,
I would not yield to be your house's guest;
So much I hate a breaking cause to be
Of heavenly oaths, vowed with integrity.
KING.
O! you have liv'd in desolation here,
Unseen, unvisited, much to our shame.
PRINCESS.
Not so, my lord; it is not so, I swear;
We have had pastimes here, and pleasant
    game.
A mess of Russians left us but of late.
KING.
How, madam! Russians?
PRINCESS.
              Ay, in truth, my lord;
Trim gallants, full of courtship and of
    state.
ROSALINE.
Madam, speak true. It is not so, my lord:
My lady, to the manner of the days,
In courtesy gives undeserving praise.
We four indeed confronted were with four
In Russian habit: here they stay'd an hour,
And talk'd apace; and in that hour, my
    lord,
They did not bless us with one happy
    word.
I dare not call them fools; but this I think,
When they are thirsty, fools would fain
    have drink.
BEROWNE.
This jest is dry to me. Fair gentle sweet,
Your wit makes wise things foolish: when
    we greet,
With eyes best seeing, heaven's fiery eye,
By light we lose light: your capacity

Is of that nature that to your huge store
Wise things seem foolish and rich things
    but poor.
ROSALINE.
This proves you wise and rich, for in my
    eye—
BEROWNE.
I am a fool, and full of poverty.
ROSALINE.
But that you take what doth to you
    belong,
It were a fault to snatch words from my
    tongue.
BEROWNE.
O! am yours, and all that I possess.
ROSALINE.
All the fool mine?
BEROWNE.
              I cannot give you less.
ROSALINE.
Which of the visors was it that you wore?
BEROWNE.
Where? when? what visor? why demand
    you this?
ROSALINE.
There, then, that visor; that superfluous
    case
That hid the worse, and show'd the better
    face.
KING.
We are descried: they'll mock us now
    downright.
DUMAINE.
Let us confess, and turn it to a jest.
PRINCESS.
Amaz'd, my lord? Why looks your
    Highness sad?
ROSALINE.
Help! hold his brows! he'll swound. Why
    look you pale?
Sea-sick, I think, coming from Muscovy.
BEROWNE.
Thus pour the stars down plagues for
    perjury.
Can any face of brass hold longer out?—
Here stand I, lady; dart thy skill at me;
Bruise me with scorn, confound me with
    a flout;

Thrust thy sharp wit quite through my
    ignorance;
Cut me to pieces with thy keen conceit;
And I will wish thee never more to dance,
Nor never more in Russian habit wait.
O! never will I trust to speeches penn'd,
Nor to the motion of a school-boy's
    tongue,
Nor never come in visor to my friend,
Nor woo in rime, like a blind harper's
    song.
Taffeta phrases, silken terms precise,
Three-pil'd hyperboles, spruce affectation,
Figures pedantical; these summer-flies
Have blown me full of maggot
    ostentation:
I do forswear them; and I here protest,
By this white glove, how white the hand,
    God knows!
Henceforth my wooing mind shall be
    express'd
In russet yeas, and honest kersey noes;
And, to begin, wench,—so God help me,
    la!—
My love to thee is sound, sans crack or
    flaw.

ROSALINE.
Sans "sans," I pray you.

BEROWNE.
                Yet I have a trick
Of the old rage: bear with me, I am sick;
I'll leave it by degrees. Soft! let us see:
Write "Lord have mercy on us" on those
    three;
They are infected; in their hearts it lies;
They have the plague, and caught it of
    your eyes:
These lords are visited; you are not free,
For the Lord's tokens on you do I see.

PRINCESS.
No, they are free that gave these tokens
    to us.

BEROWNE.
Our states are forfeit; seek not to undo us.

ROSALINE.
It is not so. For how can this be true,
That you stand forfeit, being those that
    sue?

BEROWNE.
Peace! for I will not have to do with you.

ROSALINE.
Nor shall not, if I do as I intend.

BEROWNE.
Speak for yourselves: my wit is at an end.

KING.
Teach us, sweet madam, for our rude
    transgression
Some fair excuse.

PRINCESS.
             The fairest is confession.
Were not you here but even now, disguis'd?

KING.
Madam, I was.

PRINCESS.
             And were you well advis'd?

KING.
I was, fair madam.

PRINCESS.
             When you then were here,
What did you whisper in your lady's ear?

KING.
That more than all the world I did respect
    her.

PRINCESS.
When she shall challenge this, you will
    reject her.

KING.
Upon mine honour, no.

PRINCESS.
             Peace! peace! forbear;
Your oath once broke, you force not to
    forswear.

KING.
Despise me when I break this oath of
    mine.

PRINCESS.
I will; and therefore keep it. Rosaline,
What did the Russian whisper in your ear?

ROSALINE.
Madam, he swore that he did hold me
    dear
As precious eyesight, and did value me
Above this world; adding thereto,
    moreover,
That he would wed me, or else die my
    lover.

Princess.

God give thee joy of him! The noble lord
Most honourably doth uphold his word.

King.

What mean you, madam? by my life, my
   troth,
I never swore this lady such an oath.

Rosaline.

By heaven, you did; and, to confirm it
   plain,
You gave me this: but take it, sir, again.

King.

My faith and this the princess I did give;
I knew her by this jewel on her sleeve.

Princess.

Pardon me, sir, this jewel did she wear;
And Lord Berowne, I thank him, is my
   dear.
What, will you have me, or your pearl
   again?

Berowne.

Neither of either; I remit both twain.
I see the trick on't: here was a consent,
Knowing aforehand of our merriment,
To dash it like a Christmas comedy.
Some carry-tale, some please-man, some
   slight zany,
Some mumble-news, some trencher-
   knight, some Dick,
That smiles his cheek in years, and knows
   the trick
To make my lady laugh when she's
   dispos'd,
Told our intents before; which once
   disclos'd,
The ladies did change favours, and then
   we,
Following the signs, woo'd but the sign
   of she.
Now, to our perjury to add more terror,
We are again forsworn, in will and error.
Much upon this it is: [*To* Boyet.] And
   might not you
Forestall our sport, to make us thus
   untrue?
Do not you know my lady's foot by the
   squire,
And laugh upon the apple of her eye?

And stand between her back, sir, and the
   fire,
Holding a trencher, jesting merrily?
You put our page out: go, you are allow'd;
Die when you will, a smock shall be your
   shroud.
You leer upon me, do you? There's an eye
Wounds like a leaden sword.

Boyet.

                 Full merrily
Hath this brave manage, this career, been
   run.

Berowne.

Lo! he is tilting straight! Peace! I have
   done.

            [*Enter* Costard.]

Welcome, pure wit! thou part'st a fair fray.

Costard.

O Lord, sir, they would know
Whether the three Worthies shall come
   in or no?

Berowne.

What, are there but three?

Costard.

          No, sir; but it is vara fine,
For every one pursents three.

Berowne.

          And three times thrice is nine.

Costard.

Not so, sir; under correction, sir, I hope it
   is not so.
You cannot beg us, sir, I can assure you, sir;
   we know what we know:
I hope, sir, three times thrice, sir,—

Berowne.

               Is not nine.

Costard.

Under correction, sir, we know whereuntil
it doth amount.

Berowne.

By Jove, I always took three threes for nine.

Costard.

O Lord, sir! it were pity you should get
your living by reckoning, sir.

Berowne.

How much is it?

Costard.

O Lord, sir, the parties themselves, the

actors, sir, will show whereuntil it doth amount: for mine own part, I am, as they say, but to parfect one man in one poor man, Pompey the Great, sir.

BEROWNE.

Art thou one of the Worthies?

COSTARD.

It pleased them to think me worthy of Pompey the Great; for mine own part, I know not the degree of the Worthy; but I am to stand for him.

BEROWNE.

Go, bid them prepare.

COSTARD.

We will turn it finely off, sir; we will take some care.

[*Exit* COSTARD.]

KING.

Berowne, they will shame us; let them not approach.

BEROWNE.

We are shame-proof, my lord, and 'tis some policy
To have one show worse than the king's and his company.

KING.

I say they shall not come.

PRINCESS.

Nay, my good lord, let me o'errule you now.
That sport best pleases that doth least know how;
Where zeal strives to content, and the contents
Die in the zeal of those which it presents;
Their form confounded makes most form in mirth,
When great things labouring perish in their birth.

BEROWNE.

A right description of our sport, my lord.

[*Enter* ARMADO.]

ARMADO.

Anointed, I implore so much expense of thy royal sweet breath as will utter a brace of words.

[*Converses apart with the* KING, *and delivers a paper to him.*]

PRINCESS.

Doth this man serve God?

BEROWNE.

Why ask you?

PRINCESS.

He speaks not like a man of God his making.

ARMADO.

That is all one, my fair, sweet, honey monarch; for, I protest, the schoolmaster is exceeding fantastical; too-too vain, too-too vain: but we will put it, as they say, to fortuna de la guerra. I wish you the peace of mind, most royal couplement!

[*Exit.*]

KING.

Here is like to be a good presence of Worthies. He presents Hector of Troy; the swain, Pompey the Great; the parish curate, Alexander; Armado's page, Hercules; the pedant, Judas Maccabaeus:
And if these four Worthies in their first show thrive,
These four will change habits and present the other five.

BEROWNE.

There is five in the first show.

KING.

You are deceived, 'tis not so.

BEROWNE.

The pedant, the braggart, the hedge-priest, the fool, and the boy:—
Abate throw at novum, and the whole world again
Cannot pick out five such, take each one in his vein.

KING.

The ship is under sail, and here she comes amain.

[*Enter* COSTARD, *armed for* POMPEY.]

COSTARD.

I Pompey am—

BEROWNE.

You lie, you are not he.

COSTARD.

I Pompey am—

BOYET.

With libbard's head on knee.

BEROWNE.
Well said, old mocker: I must needs be
    friends with thee.

COSTARD.
I Pompey am, Pompey surnam'd the Big—

DUMAINE.
The Great.

COSTARD.
It is "Great," sir; Pompey surnam'd the
    Great,
That oft in field, with targe and shield, did
    make my foe to sweat:
And travelling along this coast, I here am
    come by chance,
And lay my arms before the legs of this
    sweet lass of France.
If your ladyship would say "Thanks,
    Pompey," I had done.

PRINCESS.
Great thanks, great Pompey.

COSTARD.
'Tis not so much worth; but I hope I was
    perfect.
I made a little fault in "Great."

BEROWNE.
My hat to a halfpenny, Pompey proves the
    best Worthy.
        [*Enter* SIR NATHANIEL *armed, for*
                ALEXANDER.]

NATHANIEL.
When in the world I liv'd, I was the
    world's commander;
By east, west, north, and south, I spread
    my conquering might:
My scutcheon plain declares that I am
    Alisander—

BOYET.
Your nose says, no, you are not; for it
    stands to right.

BEROWNE.
Your nose smells "no" in this, most tender-
    smelling knight.

PRINCESS.
The conqueror is dismay'd. Proceed, good
    Alexander.

NATHANIEL.
When in the world I liv'd, I was the
    world's commander;—

BOYET.
Most true; 'tis right, you were so, Alisander.

BEROWNE.
Pompey the Great,—

COSTARD.
Your servant, and Costard.

BEROWNE.
Take away the conqueror, take away
    Alisander.

COSTARD. [*To* SIR NATHANIEL.]
O! sir, you have overthrown Alisander the
conqueror! You will be scraped out of the
painted cloth for this; your lion, that holds
his poll-axe sitting on a close-stool, will be
given to Ajax: he will be the ninth Worthy.
A conqueror, and afeard to speak! Run away
for shame, Alisander. [SIR NATHANIEL
retires.] There, an't shall please you: a foolish
mild man; an honest man, look you, and
soon dashed! He is a marvellous good
neighbour, faith, and a very good bowler;
but for Alisander, alas! you see how 'tis—a
little o'erparted. But there are Worthies
a-coming will speak their mind in some
other sort.

PRINCESS.
Stand aside, good Pompey.
[*Enter* HOLOFERNES *armed, for* JUDAS; *and*
        MOTH *armed, for* HERCULES.]

HOLOFERNES.
Great Hercules is presented by this imp,
Whose club kill'd Cerberus, that three-
    headed canis;
And when he was a babe, a child, a shrimp,
Thus did he strangle serpents in his
    manus.
Quoniam he seemeth in minority,
Ergo I come with this apology.
Keep some state in thy exit, and vanish.—
            [MOTH *retires.*]
Judas I am.—

DUMAINE.
A Judas!

HOLOFERNES.
Not Iscariot, sir. Judas I am, ycliped
    Maccabaeus.

DUMAINE.
Judas Maccabaeus clipt is plain Judas.

BEROWNE.
A kissing traitor. How art thou prov'd
   Judas?
HOLOFERNES.
Judas I am.—
DUMAINE.
The more shame for you, Judas.
HOLOFERNES.
What mean you, sir?
BOYET.
To make Judas hang himself.
HOLOFERNES.
Begin, sir; you are my elder.
BEROWNE.
Well follow'd: Judas was hanged on an
   elder.
HOLOFERNES.
I will not be put out of countenance.
BEROWNE.
Because thou hast no face.
HOLOFERNES.
What is this?
BOYET.
A cittern-head.
DUMAINE.
The head of a bodkin.
BEROWNE.
A death's face in a ring.
LONGAVILLE.
The face of an old Roman coin, scarce seen.
BOYET.
The pommel of Caesar's falchion.
DUMAINE.
The carved-bone face on a flask.
BEROWNE.
Saint George's half-cheek in a brooch.
DUMAINE.
Ay, and in a brooch of lead.
BEROWNE.
Ay, and worn in the cap of a tooth-drawer.
And now, forward; for we have put thee in
   countenance.
HOLOFERNES.
You have put me out of countenance.
BEROWNE.
False: we have given thee faces.
HOLOFERNES.
But you have outfaced them all.

BEROWNE.
An thou wert a lion we would do so.
BOYET.
Therefore, as he is an ass, let him go.
And so adieu, sweet Jude! nay, why dost
   thou stay?
DUMAINE.
For the latter end of his name.
BEROWNE.
For the ass to the Jude? give it him:—
   Jud-as, away!
HOLOFERNES.
This is not generous, not gentle, not
   humble.
BOYET.
A light for Monsieur Judas! It grows dark,
   he may stumble.
PRINCESS.
Alas! poor Maccabaeus, how hath he been
   baited.
         [*Enter* ARMADO *armed, for* HECTOR.]
BEROWNE.
Hide thy head, Achilles: here comes
   Hector in arms.
DUMAINE.
Though my mocks come home by me, I
   will now be merry.
KING.
Hector was but a Troyan in respect of
   this.
BOYET.
But is this Hector?
DUMAINE.
I think Hector was not so clean-timber'd.
LONGAVILLE.
His leg is too big for Hector's.
DUMAINE.
More calf, certain.
BOYET.
No; he is best indued in the small.
BEROWNE.
This cannot be Hector.
DUMAINE.
He's a god or a painter; for he makes faces.
ARMADO.
The armipotent Mars, of lances the
   almighty,
Gave Hector a gift,—

DUMAINE.
A gilt nutmeg.
BEROWNE.
A lemon.
LONGAVILLE.
Stuck with cloves.
DUMAINE.
No, cloven.
ARMADO.
Peace!
The armipotent Mars, of lances the almighty,
  Gave Hector a gift, the heir of Ilion;
    A man so breath'd that certain he would
    fight ye,
From morn till night, out of his pavilion.
I am that flower,—
DUMAINE.
           That mint.
LONGAVILLE.
               That columbine.
ARMADO.
Sweet Lord Longaville, rein thy tongue.
LONGAVILLE.
I must rather give it the rein, for it runs
against Hector.
DUMAINE.
Ay, and Hector's a greyhound.
ARMADO.
The sweet war-man is dead and rotten;
sweet chucks, beat not the bones of the
buried; when he breathed, he was a man.
But I will forward with my device. [*To the*
PRINCESS.] Sweet royalty, bestow on me
the sense of hearing.
PRINCESS.
Speak, brave Hector; we are much
  delighted.
ARMADO.
I do adore thy sweet Grace's slipper.
BOYET. [*Aside to* DUMAINE.]
Loves her by the foot.
DUMAINE. [*Aside to* BOYET.]
He may not by the yard.
ARMADO.
This Hector far surmounted Hannibal,—
COSTARD.
The party is gone; fellow Hector, she is
gone; she is two months on her way.

ARMADO.
What meanest thou?
COSTARD.
Faith, unless you play the honest Troyan,
the poor wench is cast away: she's quick;
the child brags in her belly already; 'tis
yours.
ARMADO.
Dost thou infamonize me among
potentates? Thou shalt die.
COSTARD.
Then shall Hector be whipped for
Jaquenetta that is quick by him, and hanged
for Pompey that is dead by him.
DUMAINE.
Most rare Pompey!
BOYET.
Renowned Pompey!
BEROWNE.
Greater than great, great, great, great
Pompey! Pompey the Huge!
DUMAINE.
Hector trembles.
BEROWNE.
Pompey is moved. More Ates, more Ates!
Stir them on! stir them on!
DUMAINE.
Hector will challenge him.
BEROWNE.
Ay, if a' have no more man's blood in his
belly than will sup a flea.
ARMADO.
By the north pole, I do challenge thee.
COSTARD.
I will not fight with a pole, like a northern
man: I'll slash; I'll do it by the sword. I
bepray you, let me borrow my arms again.
DUMAINE.
Room for the incensed Worthies!
COSTARD.
I'll do it in my shirt.
DUMAINE.
Most resolute Pompey!
MOTH.
Master, let me take you a buttonhole lower.
Do you not see Pompey is uncasing for the
combat? What mean you? You will lose
your reputation.

ARMADO.
Gentlemen and soldiers, pardon me; I will not combat in my shirt.

DUMAINE.
You may not deny it: Pompey hath made the challenge.

ARMADO.
Sweet bloods, I both may and will.

BEROWNE.
What reason have you for 't?

ARMADO.
The naked truth of it is: I have no shirt; I go woolward for penance.

BOYET.
True, and it was enjoined him in Rome for want of linen; since when, I'll be sworn, he wore none but a dish-clout of Jaquenetta's, and that a' wears next his heart for a favour.
[*Enter* MONSIEUR MARCADÉ, *a messenger.*]

MARCADÉ.
God save you, madam!

PRINCESS.
           Welcome, Marcadé;
But that thou interrupt'st our merriment.

MARCADÉ.
I am sorry, madam; for the news I bring
Is heavy in my tongue. The king your
     father—

PRINCESS.
Dead, for my life!

MARCADÉ.
           Even so: my tale is told.

BEROWNE.
Worthies away! the scene begins to cloud.

ARMADO.
For mine own part, I breathe free breath. I have seen the day of wrong through the little hole of discretion, and I will right myself like a soldier.
[*Exeunt* WORTHIES.]

KING.
How fares your Majesty?

PRINCESS.
Boyet, prepare: I will away to-night.

KING.
Madam, not so: I do beseech you stay.

PRINCESS.
Prepare, I say. I thank you, gracious lords,

For all your fair endeavours; and entreat,
Out of a new-sad soul, that you vouchsafe
In your rich wisdom to excuse or hide
The liberal opposition of our spirits,
If over-boldly we have borne ourselves
In the converse of breath; your gentleness
Was guilty of it. Farewell, worthy lord!
A heavy heart bears not a nimble tongue.
Excuse me so, coming so short of thanks
For my great suit so easily obtain'd.

KING.
The extreme parts of time extremely forms
All causes to the purpose of his speed,
And often at his very loose decides
That which long process could not
     arbitrate:
And though the mourning brow of
     progeny
Forbid the smiling courtesy of love
The holy suit which fain it would convince;
Yet, since love's argument was first on foot,
Let not the cloud of sorrow justle it
From what it purpos'd; since, to wail
     friends lost
Is not by much so wholesome-profitable
As to rejoice at friends but newly found.

PRINCESS.
I understand you not: my griefs are double.

BEROWNE.
Honest plain words best pierce the ear of
     grief;
And by these badges understand the king.
For your fair sakes have we neglected time,
Play'd foul play with our oaths. Your
     beauty, ladies,
Hath much deform'd us, fashioning our
     humours
Even to the opposed end of our intents;
And what in us hath seem'd ridiculous,—
As love is full of unbefitting strains;
All wanton as a child, skipping and vain;
Form'd by the eye, and, therefore, like the
     eye,
Full of strange shapes, of habits and of
     forms,
Varying in subjects, as the eye doth roll
To every varied object in his glance:
Which parti-coated presence of loose love

Put on by us, if, in your heavenly eyes,
Have misbecom'd our oaths and gravities,
Those heavenly eyes that look into these
    faults
Suggested us to make. Therefore, ladies,
Our love being yours, the error that love
    makes
Is likewise yours: we to ourselves prove
    false,
By being once false for ever to be true
To those that make us both,—fair ladies,
    you:
And even that falsehood, in itself a sin,
Thus purifies itself and turns to grace.
PRINCESS.
We have receiv'd your letters, full of love;
Your favours, the ambassadors of love;
And, in our maiden council, rated them
At courtship, pleasant jest, and courtesy,
As bombast and as lining to the time;
But more devout than this in our respects
Have we not been; and therefore met your
    loves
In their own fashion, like a merriment.
DUMAINE.
Our letters, madam, show'd much more
    than jest.
LONGAVILLE.
So did our looks.
ROSALINE.
                    We did not quote them so.
KING.
Now, at the latest minute of the hour,
Grant us your loves.
PRINCESS.
                    A time, methinks, too short
To make a world-without-end bargain in.
No, no, my lord, your Grace is perjur'd
    much,
Full of dear guiltiness; and therefore this:
If for my love,—as there is no such
    cause,—
You will do aught, this shall you do for me:
Your oath I will not trust; but go with
    speed
To some forlorn and naked hermitage,
Remote from all the pleasures of the
    world;

There stay until the twelve celestial signs
Have brought about the annual reckoning.
If this austere insociable life
Change not your offer made in heat of
    blood,
If frosts and fasts, hard lodging and thin
    weeds,
Nip not the gaudy blossoms of your love,
But that it bear this trial, and last love,
Then, at the expiration of the year,
Come, challenge me, challenge me by
    these deserts;
And, by this virgin palm now kissing
    thine,
I will be thine; and, till that instant, shut
My woeful self up in a mournful house,
Raining the tears of lamentation
For the remembrance of my father's death.
If this thou do deny, let our hands part,
Neither intitled in the other's heart.
KING.
If this, or more than this, I would deny,
To flatter up these powers of mine with
    rest,
The sudden hand of death close up mine
    eye!
Hence ever then my heart is in thy breast.
BEROWNE.
And what to me, my love? and what to
    me?
ROSALINE.
You must he purged too, your sins are
    rack'd;
You are attaint with faults and perjury;
Therefore, if you my favour mean to get,
A twelvemonth shall you spend, and never
    rest,
But seek the weary beds of people sick.
DUMAINE.
But what to me, my love? but what to me?
KATHARINE.
A wife! A beard, fair health, and honesty;
With three-fold love I wish you all these
    three.
DUMAINE.
O! shall I say I thank you, gentle wife?
KATHARINE.
No so, my lord; a twelvemonth and a day

I'll mark no words that smooth-fac'd
   wooers say.
Come when the king doth to my lady
   come;
Then, if I have much love, I'll give you
   some.

DUMAINE.
I'll serve thee true and faithfully till then.

KATHARINE.
Yet swear not, lest ye be forsworn again.

LONGAVILLE.
What says Maria?

MARIA.
               At the twelvemonth's end
I'll change my black gown for a faithful
   friend.

LONGAVILLE.
I'll stay with patience; but the time is long.

MARIA.
The liker you; few taller are so young.

BEROWNE.
Studies my lady? mistress, look on me;
Behold the window of my heart, mine eye,
What humble suit attends thy answer
   there.
Impose some service on me for thy love.

ROSALINE.
Oft have I heard of you, my Lord
   Berowne,
Before I saw you; and the world's large
   tongue
Proclaims you for a man replete with
   mocks;
Full of comparisons and wounding flouts,
Which you on all estates will execute
That lie within the mercy of your wit:
To weed this wormwood from your
   fruitful brain,
And therewithal to win me, if you
   please,—
Without the which I am not to be won,—
You shall this twelvemonth term, from day
   to day,
Visit the speechless sick, and still converse
With groaning wretches; and your task
   shall be,
With all the fierce endeavour of your wit
To enforce the pained impotent to smile.

BEROWNE.
To move wild laughter in the throat of
   death?
It cannot be; it is impossible:
Mirth cannot move a soul in agony.

ROSALINE.
Why, that's the way to choke a gibing
   spirit,
Whose influence is begot of that loose
   grace
Which shallow laughing hearers give to
   fools.
A jest's prosperity lies in the ear
Of him that hears it, never in the tongue
Of him that makes it: then, if sickly ears,
Deaf'd with the clamours of their own
   dear groans,
Will hear your idle scorns, continue then,
And I will have you and that fault withal;
But if they will not, throw away that spirit,
And I shall find you empty of that fault,
Right joyful of your reformation.

BEROWNE.
A twelvemonth! well, befall what will
   befall,
I'll jest a twelvemonth in an hospital.

PRINCESS. [*To the* KING.]
Ay, sweet my lord; and so I take my leave.

KING.
No, madam; we will bring you on your
   way.

BEROWNE.
Our wooing doth not end like an old play;
Jack hath not Jill; these ladies' courtesy
Might well have made our sport a comedy.

KING.
Come, sir, it wants a twelvemonth and a
   day,
And then 'twill end.

BEROWNE.
             That's too long for a play.
             [*Enter* ARMADO.]

ARMADO.
Sweet Majesty, vouchsafe me,—

PRINCESS.
Was not that not Hector?

DUMAINE.
The worthy knight of Troy.

ARMADO.
I will kiss thy royal finger, and take leave.
I am a votary: I have vowed to Jaquenetta
to hold the plough for her sweet love three
years. But, most esteemed greatness, will
you hear the dialogue that the two learned
men have compiled in praise of the owl and
the cuckoo? It should have followed in the
end of our show.
KING.
Call them forth quickly; we will do so.
ARMADO.
Holla! approach.
  [*Enter* HOLOFERNES, NATHANIEL,
    MOTH, COSTARD, *and* OTHERS.]
This side is Hiems, Winter; this Ver, the
Spring; the one maintained by the owl, the
other by the cuckoo. Ver, begin.
SPRING. [*Sings.*]
  When daisies pied and violets blue
    And lady-smocks all silver-white
  And cuckoo-buds of yellow hue
    Do paint the meadows with delight,
  The cuckoo then on every tree
  Mocks married men, for thus sings he,
            Cuckoo!
  Cuckoo, cuckoo: O, word of fear,
  Unpleasing to a married ear!
  When shepherds pipe on oaten straws,
    And merry larks are ploughmen's
      clocks,
  When turtles tread, and rooks and
      daws,

  And maidens bleach their summer
      smocks,
  The cuckoo then, on every tree,
  Mocks married men, for thus sings he:
            Cuckoo!
  Cuckoo, cuckoo: O, word of fear,
  Unpleasing to a married ear!
WINTER. [*Sings.*]
  When icicles hang by the wall,
    And Dick the shepherd blows his
      nail,
  And Tom bears logs into the hall,
    And milk comes frozen home in pail,
  When blood is nipp'd, and ways be foul,
  Then nightly sings the staring owl:
            Tu-whit;
  Tu-whoo, a merry note,
  While greasy Joan doth keel the pot.

  When all aloud the wind doth blow,
    And coughing drowns the parson's
      saw,
  And birds sit brooding in the snow,
    And Marian's nose looks red and raw,
  When roasted crabs hiss in the bowl,
  Then nightly sings the staring owl:
            Tu-whit;
  Tu-whoo, a merry note,
  While greasy Joan doth keel the pot.
ARMADO.
The words of Mercury are harsh after the
songs of Apollo. You that way: we this way.
            [*Exeunt.*]

A Midsummer Night's Dream

DRAMATIS PERSONAE

THESEUS, *Duke of Athens*
EGEUS, *father to Hermia*
LYSANDER, *in love with Hermia*
DEMETRIUS, *in love with Hermia*
PHILOSTRATE, *master of the revels to Theseus*
QUINCE, *the carpenter*
SNUG, *the joiner*
BOTTOM, *the weaver*
FLUTE, *the bellows-mender*
SNOUT, *the tinker*
STARVELING, *the tailor*
HIPPOLYTA, *queen of the Amazons, bethrothed to Theseus*
HERMIA, *daughter to Egeus, in love with Lysander*
HELENA, *in love with Demetrius*

OBERON, *king of the fairies*
TITANIA, *queen of the fairies*
PUCK, *or* ROBIN GOODFELLOW, *a fairy*
PEASBLOSSOM, *a fairy*
COBWEB, *a fairy*
MOTH, *a fairy*
MUSTARDSEED, *a fairy*
PYRAMUS, THISBE, WALL, MOONSHINE, LION, *characters in the interlude performed by the clowns*
OTHER FAIRIES *attending their king and queen*
ATTENDANTS *on Theseus and Hippolyta*

SCENE: *Athens, and a wood not far from it.*

ACT I
SCENE I

Athens. A room in the palace of Theseus.
[*Enter* THESEUS, HIPPOLYTA, PHILOSTRATE, *and* ATTENDANTS.]
THESEUS.
Now, fair Hippolyta, our nuptial hour
Draws on apace; four happy days bring in
Another moon; but, oh, methinks, how slow
This old moon wanes! She lingers my desires,
Like to a step-dame or a dowager,
Long withering out a young man's revenue.
HIPPOLYTA.
Four days will quickly steep themselves in nights;
Four nights will quickly dream away the time;

And then the moon, like to a silver bow
New bent in heaven, shall behold the night
Of our solemnities.
THESEUS.
        Go, Philostrate,
Stir up the Athenian youth to merriments;
Awake the pert and nimble spirit of mirth;
Turn melancholy forth to funerals—
The pale companion is not for our pomp.—
        [*Exit* PHILOSTRATE.]
Hippolyta, I woo'd thee with my sword,
And won thy love doing thee injuries;
But I will wed thee in another key,
With pomp, with triumph, and with revelling.
        [*Enter* EGEUS, HERMIA, LYSANDER, *and* DEMETRIUS.]

EGEUS.
Happy be Theseus, our renowned duke!
THESEUS.
Thanks, good Egeus: what's the news with
    thee?
EGEUS.
Full of vexation come I, with complaint
Against my child, my daughter Hermia.—
Stand forth, Demetrius.—My noble lord,
This man hath my consent to marry her:—
Stand forth, Lysander;—and, my gracious
    duke,
This man hath bewitch'd the bosom of my
    child.
Thou, thou, Lysander, thou hast given her
    rhymes,
And interchang'd love-tokens with my
    child:
Thou hast by moonlight at her window
    sung,
With feigning voice, verses of feigning
    love;
And stol'n the impression of her fantasy
With bracelets of thy hair, rings, gawds,
    conceits,
Knacks, trifles, nosegays, sweetmeats,—
    messengers
Of strong prevailment in unharden'd
    youth;—
With cunning hast thou filch'd my
    daughter's heart;
Turned her obedience, which is due to me,
To stubborn harshness.—And, my
    gracious duke,
Be it so she will not here before your grace
Consent to marry with Demetrius,
I beg the ancient privilege of Athens,—
As she is mine I may dispose of her:
Which shall be either to this gentleman
Or to her death; according to our law
Immediately provided in that case.
THESEUS.
What say you, Hermia? be advis'd, fair
    maid:
To you your father should be as a god;
One that compos'd your beauties: yea, and
    one
To whom you are but as a form in wax,

By him imprinted, and within his power
To leave the figure, or disfigure it.
Demetrius is a worthy gentleman.
HERMIA.
So is Lysander.
THESEUS.
          In himself he is:
But, in this kind, wanting your father's
    voice,
The other must be held the worthier.
HERMIA.
I would my father look'd but with my eyes.
THESEUS.
Rather your eyes must with his judgment
    look.
HERMIA.
I do entreat your grace to pardon me.
I know not by what power I am made
    bold,
Nor how it may concern my modesty
In such a presence here to plead my
    thoughts:
But I beseech your grace that I may know
The worst that may befall me in this case
If I refuse to wed Demetrius.
THESEUS.
Either to die the death, or to abjure
For ever the society of men.
Therefore, fair Hermia, question your
    desires,
Know of your youth, examine well your
    blood,
Whether, if you yield not to your father's
    choice,
You can endure the livery of a nun;
For aye to be shady cloister mew'd,
To live a barren sister all your life,
Chanting faint hymns to the cold, fruitless
    moon.
Thrice-blessed they that master so their
    blood
To undergo such maiden pilgrimage:
But earthlier happy is the rose distill'd
Than that which, withering on the virgin
    thorn,
Grows, lives, and dies, in single blessedness.
HERMIA.
So will I grow, so live, so die, my lord,

Ere I will yield my virgin patent up
Unto his lordship, whose unwished yoke
My soul consents not to give sovereignty.
Theseus.
Take time to pause; and by the next new
    moon,—
The sealing-day betwixt my love and me
For everlasting bond of fellowship,—
Upon that day either prepare to die
For disobedience to your father's will;
Or else to wed Demetrius, as he would;
Or on Diana's altar to protest
For aye austerity and single life.
Demetrius.
Relent, sweet Hermia;—and, Lysander,
    yield
Thy crazed title to my certain right.
Lysander.
You have her father's love, Demetrius;
Let me have Hermia's: do you marry him.
Egeus.
Scornful Lysander! true, he hath my love;
And what is mine my love shall render
    him;
And she is mine; and all my right of her
I do estate unto Demetrius.
Lysander.
I am, my lord, as well deriv'd as he,
As well possess'd; my love is more than
    his;
My fortunes every way as fairly rank'd,
If not with vantage, as Demetrius's;
And, which is more than all these boasts
    can be,
I am belov'd of beauteous Hermia:
Why should not I then prosecute my
    right?
Demetrius, I'll avouch it to his head,
Made love to Nedar's daughter, Helena,
And won her soul; and she, sweet lady,
    dotes,
Devoutly dotes, dotes in idolatry,
Upon this spotted and inconstant man.
Theseus.
I must confess that I have heard so much,
And with Demetrius thought to have
    spoke thereof;
But, being over-full of self-affairs,

My mind did lose it.—But, Demetrius,
    come;
And come, Egeus; you shall go with me;
I have some private schooling for you
    both.—
For you, fair Hermia, look you arm
    yourself
To fit your fancies to your father's will,
Or else the law of Athens yields you up,—
Which by no means we may extenuate,—
To death, or to a vow of single life.—
Come, my Hippolyta: what cheer, my
    love?
Demetrius, and Egeus, go along;
I must employ you in some business
Against our nuptial, and confer with you
Of something nearly that concerns
    yourselves.
Egeus.
With duty and desire we follow you.
    [*Exeunt* Theseus, Hippolyta, Egeus,
        Demetrius, *and* Train.]
Lysander.
How now, my love! why is your cheek so
    pale?
How chance the roses there do fade so
    fast?
Hermia.
Belike for want of rain, which I could
    well
Beteem them from the tempest of my
    eyes.
Lysander.
Ah me! for aught that I could ever read,
Could ever hear by tale or history,
The course of true love never did run
    smooth:
But either it was different in blood,—
Hermia.
O cross! Too high to be enthrall'd to low!
Lysander.
Or else misgraffed in respect of years;—
Hermia.
O spite! Too old to be engag'd to young!
Lysander.
Or else it stood upon the choice of friends:
Hermia.
O hell! to choose love by another's eye!

LYSANDER.
Or, if there were a sympathy in choice,
War, death, or sickness, did lay siege to it,
Making it momentary as a sound,
Swift as a shadow, short as any dream;
Brief as the lightning in the collied night
That, in a spleen, unfolds both heaven and
   earth,
And ere a man hath power to say, Behold!
The jaws of darkness do devour it up:
So quick bright things come to confusion.
HERMIA.
If then true lovers have ever cross'd,
It stands as an edict in destiny:
Then let us teach our trial patience,
Because it is a customary cross;
As due to love as thoughts, and dreams,
   and sighs,
Wishes and tears, poor fancy's followers.
LYSANDER.
A good persuasion; therefore, hear me,
   Hermia.
I have a widow aunt, a dowager
Of great revenue, and she hath no child:
From Athens is her house remote seven
   leagues;
And she respects me as her only son.
There, gentle Hermia, may I marry thee;
And to that place the sharp Athenian law
Cannot pursue us. If thou lovest me then,
Steal forth thy father's house tomorrow
   night;
And in the wood, a league without the
   town,
Where I did meet thee once with Helena,
To do observance to a morn of May,
There will I stay for thee.
HERMIA.
              My good Lysander!
I swear to thee by Cupid's strongest bow,
By his best arrow, with the golden head,
By the simplicity of Venus' doves,
By that which knitteth souls and prospers
   loves,
And by that fire which burn'd the
   Carthage queen,
When the false Trojan under sail was
   seen,—

By all the vows that ever men have broke,
In number more than ever women
   spoke,—
In that same place thou hast appointed
   me,
Tomorrow truly will I meet with thee.
LYSANDER.
Keep promise, love. Look, here comes
   Helena.
             [*Enter* HELENA.]
HERMIA.
God speed fair Helena! Whither away?
HELENA.
Call you me fair? that fair again unsay.
Demetrius loves your fair. O happy fair!
Your eyes are lode-stars; and your tongue's
   sweet air
More tuneable than lark to shepherd's ear,
When wheat is green, when hawthorn
   buds appear.
Sickness is catching: O, were favour so,
Yours would I catch, fair Hermia, ere I go;
My ear should catch your voice, my eye
   your eye,
My tongue should catch your tongue's
   sweet melody.
Were the world mine, Demetrius being
   bated,
The rest I'd give to be to you translated.
O, teach me how you look; and with what
   art
You sway the motion of Demetrius' heart!
HERMIA.
I frown upon him, yet he loves me still.
HELENA.
O that your frowns would teach my smiles
   such skill!
HERMIA.
I give him curses, yet he gives me love.
HELENA.
O that my prayers could such affection
   move!
HERMIA.
The more I hate, the more he follows me.
HELENA.
The more I love, the more he hateth me.
HERMIA.
His folly, Helena, is no fault of mine.

Helena.
None, but your beauty: would that fault
    were mine!
Hermia.
Take comfort; he no more shall see my
    face;
Lysander and myself will fly this place.—
Before the time I did Lysander see,
Seem'd Athens as a paradise to me:
O, then, what graces in my love do dwell,
That he hath turn'd a heaven unto hell!
Lysander.
Helen, to you our minds we will unfold:
To-morrow night, when Phoebe doth
    behold
Her silver visage in the watery glass,
Decking with liquid pearl the bladed
    grass,—
A time that lovers' flights doth still
    conceal,—
Through Athens' gates have we devis'd to
    steal.
Hermia.
And in the wood where often you and I
Upon faint primrose beds were wont to lie,
Emptying our bosoms of their counsel
    sweet,
There my Lysander and myself shall meet:
And thence from Athens turn away our
    eyes,
To seek new friends and stranger
    companies.
Farewell, sweet playfellow: pray thou for us,
And good luck grant thee thy
    Demetrius!—
Keep word, Lysander: we must starve our
    sight
From lovers' food, till morrow deep
    midnight.
Lysander.
I will, my Hermia. [*Exit* Hermia.]
    Helena, adieu:
As you on him, Demetrius dote on you!
        [*Exit* Lysander.]
Helena.
How happy some o'er other some can be!
Through Athens I am thought as fair as
    she.

But what of that? Demetrius thinks not so;
He will not know what all but he do know.
And as he errs, doting on Hermia's eyes,
So I, admiring of his qualities.
Things base and vile, holding no quantity,
Love can transpose to form and dignity.
Love looks not with the eyes, but with the
    mind;
And therefore is wing'd Cupid painted
    blind.
Nor hath love's mind of any judgment
    taste;
Wings and no eyes figure unheedy haste:
And therefore is love said to be a child,
Because in choice he is so oft beguil'd.
As waggish boys in game themselves
    forswear,
So the boy Love is perjur'd everywhere:
For ere Demetrius look'd on Hermia's
    eyne,
He hail'd down oaths that he was only
    mine;
And when this hail some heat from
    Hermia felt,
So he dissolv'd, and showers of oaths did
    melt.
I will go tell him of fair Hermia's flight;
Then to the wood will he to-morrow night
Pursue her; and for this intelligence
If I have thanks, it is a dear expense:
But herein mean I to enrich my pain,
To have his sight thither and back again.
        [*Exit* Helena.]

SCENE II
The same. A room in a cottage.
[*Enter* Snug, Bottom, Flute, Snout,
    Quince, *and* Starveling.]
Quince.
Is all our company here?
Bottom.
You were best to call them generally, man
by man, according to the scrip.
Quince.
Here is the scroll of every man's name,
which is thought fit, through all Athens, to
play in our interlude before the duke and
duchess on his wedding-day at night.

Bottom.

First, good Peter Quince, say what the play treats on; then read the names of the actors; and so grow to a point.

Quince.

Marry, our play is—The most lamentable comedy and most cruel death of Pyramus and Thisbe.

Bottom.

A very good piece of work, I assure you, and a merry. Now, good Peter Quince, call forth your actors by the scroll. Masters, spread yourselves.

Quince.

Answer, as I call you. Nick Bottom, the weaver.

Bottom.

Ready. Name what part I am for, and proceed.

Quince.

You, Nick Bottom, are set down for Pyramus.

Bottom.

What is Pyramus? a lover, or a tyrant?

Quince.

A lover, that kills himself most gallantly for love.

Bottom.

That will ask some tears in the true performing of it. If I do it, let the audience look to their eyes; I will move storms; I will condole in some measure. To the rest:—yet my chief humour is for a tyrant: I could play Ercles rarely, or a part to tear a cat in, to make all split.

> The raging rocks
> And shivering shocks
> Shall break the locks
>   Of prison gates;
> And Phibbus' car
> Shall shine from far,
> And make and mar
>   The foolish Fates.

This was lofty.—Now name the rest of the players.—This is Ercles' vein, a tyrant's vein;—a lover is more condoling.

Quince.

Francis Flute, the bellows-mender.

Flute.

Here, Peter Quince.

Quince.

Flute, you must take Thisbe on you.

Flute.

What is Thisbe? a wandering knight?

Quince.

It is the lady that Pyramus must love.

Flute.

Nay, faith, let not me play a woman; I have a beard coming.

Quince.

That's all one; you shall play it in a mask, and you may speak as small as you will.

Bottom.

An I may hide my face, let me play Thisbe too: I'll speak in a monstrous little voice;— "Thisne, Thisne!"—"Ah, Pyramus, my lover dear; thy Thisbe dear! and lady dear!"

Quince.

No, no, you must play Pyramus; and, Flute, you Thisbe.

Bottom.

Well, proceed.

Quince

Robin Starveling, the tailor.

Starveling.

Here, Peter Quince.

Quince.

Robin Starveling, you must play Thisbe's mother.—Tom Snout, the tinker.

Snout.

Here, Peter Quince.

Quince.

You, Pyramus' father; myself, Thisbe's father; Snug, the joiner, you, the lion's part:—and, I hope, here is a play fitted.

Snug.

Have you the lion's part written? pray you, if it be, give it me, for I am slow of study.

Quince.

You may do it extempore, for it is nothing but roaring.

Bottom.

Let me play the lion too: I will roar that I will do any man's heart good to hear me; I will roar that I will make the duke say "Let him roar again, let him roar again."

QUINCE.

An you should do it too terribly, you would fright the duchess and the ladies, that they would shriek; and that were enough to hang us all.

ALL.

That would hang us every mother's son.

BOTTOM.

I grant you, friends, if you should fright the ladies out of their wits, they would have no more discretion but to hang us: but I will aggravate my voice so, that I will roar you as gently as any sucking dove; I will roar you an 'twere any nightingale.

QUINCE.

You can play no part but Pyramus; for Pyramus is a sweet-faced man; a proper man, as one shall see in a summer's day; a most lovely gentleman-like man; therefore you must needs play Pyramus.

BOTTOM.

Well, I will undertake it. What beard were I best to play it in?

QUINCE.

Why, what you will.

BOTTOM.

I will discharge it in either your straw-colour beard, your orange-tawny beard, your purple-in-grain beard, or your French-crown-colour beard, your perfect yellow.

QUINCE.

Some of your French crowns have no hair at all, and then you will play bare-faced.— But, masters, here are your parts: and I am to entreat you, request you, and desire you, to con them by to-morrow night; and meet me in the palace wood, a mile without the town, by moonlight; there will we rehearse: for if we meet in the city, we shall be dogg'd with company, and our devices known. In the meantime I will draw a bill of properties, such as our play wants. I pray you, fail me not.

BOTTOM.

We will meet; and there we may rehearse most obscenely and courageously. Take pains; be perfect; adieu.

QUINCE.

At the duke's oak we meet.

BOTTOM.

Enough; hold, or cut bow-strings.

[*Exeunt.*]

ACT II
SCENE I

A wood near Athens.

[*Enter a* FAIRY *at one door, and* PUCK *at another.*]

PUCK.

How now, spirit! whither wander you?

FAIRY.

> Over hill, over dale,
> > Thorough bush, thorough brier,
> Over park, over pale,
> > Thorough flood, thorough fire,
> I do wander everywhere,
> Swifter than the moon's sphere;
> And I serve the fairy queen,
> To dew her orbs upon the green.
> The cowslips tall her pensioners be:
> In their gold coats spots you see;
> Those be rubies, fairy favours,
> In those freckles live their savours;

I must go seek some dew-drops here,
And hang a pearl in every cowslip's ear.
Farewell, thou lob of spirits; I'll be gone:
Our queen and all her elves come here
> anon.

PUCK.

The king doth keep his revels here to-
> night;
Take heed the queen come not within his
> sight.
For Oberon is passing fell and wrath,
Because that she, as her attendant, hath
A lovely boy, stol'n from an Indian king;
She never had so sweet a changeling:
And jealous Oberon would have the child
Knight of his train, to trace the forests
> wild:
But she perforce withholds the loved boy,
Crowns him with flowers, and makes him
> all her joy:
And now they never meet in grove or
> green,

By fountain clear, or spangled starlight
   sheen,
But they do square; that all their elves for
   fear
Creep into acorn cups, and hide them there.

Fairy.
Either I mistake your shape and making
   quite,
Or else you are that shrewd and knavish
   sprite
Call'd Robin Goodfellow: are not you he
That frights the maidens of the villagery;
Skim milk, and sometimes labour in the
   quern,
And bootless make the breathless
   housewife churn;
And sometime make the drink to bear no
   barm;
Mislead night-wanderers, laughing at their
   harm?
Those that Hobgoblin call you, and sweet
   Puck,
You do their work, and they shall have
   good luck:
Are not you he?

Puck.
          Thou speak'st aright;
I am that merry wanderer of the night.
I jest to Oberon, and make him smile,
When I a fat and bean-fed horse beguile,
Neighing in likeness of a filly foal;
And sometime lurk I in a gossip's bowl,
In very likeness of a roasted crab;
And, when she drinks, against her lips I
   bob,
And on her withered dewlap pour the ale.
The wisest aunt, telling the saddest tale,
Sometime for three-foot stool mistaketh
   me;
Then slip I from her bum, down topples
   she,
And "tailor" cries, and falls into a cough;
And then the whole quire hold their hips
   and loffe,
And waxen in their mirth, and neeze, and
   swear
A merrier hour was never wasted there.—
But room, fairy, here comes Oberon.

Fairy.
And here my mistress.—Would that he
   were gone!
[*Enter* Oberon *at one door, with his* Train,
   and Titania, *at another, with hers.*]

Oberon.
Ill met by moonlight, proud Titania.

Titania.
What, jealous Oberon! Fairies, skip hence;
I have forsworn his bed and company.

Oberon.
Tarry, rash wanton: am not I thy lord?

Titania.
Then I must be thy lady; but I know
When thou hast stol'n away from fairy-
   land,
And in the shape of Corin sat all day,
Playing on pipes of corn, and versing love
To amorous Phillida. Why art thou here,
Come from the farthest steep of India,
But that, forsooth, the bouncing Amazon,
Your buskin'd mistress and your warrior
   love,
To Theseus must be wedded; and you
   come
To give their bed joy and prosperity.

Oberon.
How canst thou thus, for shame, Titania,
Glance at my credit with Hippolyta,
Knowing I know thy love to Theseus?
Didst not thou lead him through the
   glimmering night
From Perigenia, whom he ravish'd?
And make him with fair Aegle break his
   faith,
With Ariadne and Antiopa?

Titania.
These are the forgeries of jealousy:
And never, since the middle summer's
   spring,
Met we on hill, in dale, forest, or mead,
By paved fountain, or by rushy brook,
Or on the beached margent of the sea,
To dance our ringlets to the whistling
   wind,
But with thy brawls thou hast disturb'd
   our sport.
Therefore the winds, piping to us in vain,

As in revenge, have suck'd up from the sea
Contagious fogs; which, falling in the
     land,
Hath every pelting river made so proud
That they have overborne their continents:
The ox hath therefore stretch'd his yoke
     in vain,
The ploughman lost his sweat; and the
     green corn
Hath rotted ere his youth attain'd a beard:
The fold stands empty in the drowned
     field,
And crows are fatted with the murrion
     flock;
The nine men's morris is fill'd up with
     mud;
And the quaint mazes in the wanton
     green,
For lack of tread, are undistinguishable:
The human mortals want their winter
     here;
No night is now with hymn or carol
     blest:—
Therefore the moon, the governess of
     floods,
Pale in her anger, washes all the air,
That rheumatic diseases do abound:
And thorough this distemperature we see
The seasons alter: hoary-headed frosts
Fall in the fresh lap of the crimson rose;
And on old Hyem's thin and icy crown
An odorous chaplet of sweet summer buds
Is, as in mockery, set: the spring, the
     summer,
The childing autumn, angry winter, change
Their wonted liveries; and the maz'd world,
By their increase, now knows not which
     is which:
And this same progeny of evils comes
From our debate, from our dissension:
We are their parents and original.

Oberon.
Do you amend it, then: it lies in you:
Why should Titania cross her Oberon?
I do but beg a little changeling boy
To be my henchman.

Titania.
                         Set your heart at rest;

The fairy-land buys not the child of me.
His mother was a vot'ress of my order:
And, in the spiced Indian air, by night,
Full often hath she gossip'd by my side;
And sat with me on Neptune's yellow
     sands,
Marking the embarked traders on the
     flood;
When we have laugh'd to see the sails
     conceive,
And grow big-bellied with the wanton
     wind;
Which she, with pretty and with
     swimming gait
Following,—her womb then rich with my
     young squire,—
Would imitate; and sail upon the land,
To fetch me trifles, and return again,
As from a voyage, rich with merchandise.
But she, being mortal, of that boy did die;
And for her sake do I rear up her boy:
And for her sake I will not part with him.

Oberon.
How long within this wood intend you
     stay?

Titania.
Perchance till after Theseus' wedding-day.
If you will patiently dance in our round,
And see our moonlight revels, go with us;
If not, shun me, and I will spare your
     haunts.

Oberon.
Give me that boy and I will go with thee.

Titania.
Not for thy fairy kingdom. Fairies, away:
We shall chide downright if I longer stay.
          [*Exit* Titania *with her* Train.]

Oberon.
Well, go thy way: thou shalt not from this
     grove
Till I torment thee for this injury.—
My gentle Puck, come hither: thou
     remember'st
Since once I sat upon a promontory,
And heard a mermaid, on a dolphin's back,
Uttering such dulcet and harmonious
     breath,
That the rude sea grew civil at her song,

And certain stars shot madly from their
   spheres
To hear the sea-maid's music.

Puck.

                 I remember.

Oberon.

That very time I saw,—but thou couldst
   not,—
Flying between the cold moon and the
   earth,
Cupid, all arm'd: a certain aim he took
At a fair vestal, throned by the west;
And loos'd his love-shaft smartly from
   his bow,
As it should pierce a hundred thousand
   hearts;
But I might see young Cupid's fiery shaft
Quench'd in the chaste beams of the
   watery moon;
And the imperial votaress passed on,
In maiden meditation, fancy-free.
Yet mark'd I where the bolt of Cupid fell:
It fell upon a little western flower,—
Before milk-white, now purple with love's
   wound,—
And maidens call it love-in-idleness.
Fetch me that flower, the herb I showed
   thee once:
The juice of it on sleeping eyelids laid
Will make or man or woman madly dote
Upon the next live creature that it sees.
Fetch me this herb: and be thou here again
Ere the leviathan can swim a league.

Puck.

I'll put a girdle round about the earth
In forty minutes.

           [*Exit* Puck.]

Oberon.

         Having once this juice,
I'll watch Titania when she is asleep,
And drop the liquor of it in her eyes:
The next thing then she waking looks
   upon,—
Be it on lion, bear, or wolf, or bull,
On meddling monkey, or on busy ape,—
She shall pursue it with the soul of love.
And ere I take this charm from off her
   sight,—

As I can take it with another herb,
I'll make her render up her page to me.
But who comes here? I am invisible;
And I will overhear their conference.

      [*Enter* Demetrius, Helena
          following him.]

Demetrius.

I love thee not, therefore pursue me not.
Where is Lysander and fair Hermia?
The one I'll slay, the other slayeth me.
Thou told'st me they were stol'n into this
   wood,
And here am I, and wode within this
   wood,
Because I cannot meet with Hermia.
Hence, get thee gone, and follow me no
   more.

Helena.

You draw me, you hard-hearted adamant;
But yet you draw not iron, for my heart
Is true as steel. Leave you your power to
   draw,
And I shall have no power to follow you.

Demetrius.

Do I entice you? Do I speak you fair?
Or, rather, do I not in plainest truth
Tell you I do not, nor I cannot love you?

Helena.

And even for that do I love you the more.
I am your spaniel; and, Demetrius,
The more you beat me, I will fawn on you:
Use me but as your spaniel, spurn me,
   strike me,
Neglect me, lose me; only give me leave,
Unworthy as I am, to follow you.
What worser place can I beg in your love,
And yet a place of high respect with me,—
Than to be used as you use your dog?

Demetrius.

Tempt not too much the hatred of my
   spirit;
For I am sick when I do look on thee.

Helena.

And I am sick when I look not on you.

Demetrius.

You do impeach your modesty too much,
To leave the city, and commit yourself
Into the hands of one that loves you not;

To trust the opportunity of night,
And the ill counsel of a desert place,
With the rich worth of your virginity.

HELENA.
Your virtue is my privilege for that.
It is not night when I do see your face,
Therefore I think I am not in the night;
Nor doth this wood lack worlds of
    company;
For you, in my respect, are all the world:
Then how can it be said I am alone
When all the world is here to look on me?

DEMETRIUS.
I'll run from thee, and hide me in the
    brakes,
And leave thee to the mercy of wild
    beasts.

HELENA.
The wildest hath not such a heart as you.
Run when you will, the story shall be
    chang'd;
Apollo flies, and Daphne holds the chase;
The dove pursues the griffin; the mild hind
Makes speed to catch the tiger,—bootless
    speed,
When cowardice pursues and valour flies.

DEMETRIUS.
I will not stay thy questions; let me go:
Or, if thou follow me, do not believe
But I shall do thee mischief in the wood.

HELENA.
Ay, in the temple, in the town, the field,
You do me mischief. Fie, Demetrius!
Your wrongs do set a scandal on my sex:
We cannot fight for love as men may do:
We should be woo'd, and were not made
    to woo.
I'll follow thee, and make a heaven of hell,
To die upon the hand I love so well.
    [*Exeunt* DEMETRIUS *and* HELENA.]

OBERON.
Fare thee well, nymph: ere he do leave this
    grove,
Thou shalt fly him, and he shall seek thy
    love.—
    [*Re-enter* PUCK.]
Hast thou the flower there? Welcome,
    wanderer.

PUCK.
Ay, there it is.

OBERON.
          I pray thee give it me.
I know a bank whereon the wild thyme
    blows,
Where ox-lips and the nodding violet
    grows;
Quite over-canopied with luscious
    woodbine,
With sweet musk-roses, and with
    eglantine:
There sleeps Titania sometime of the night,
Lulled in these flowers with dances and
    delight;
And there the snake throws her enamell'd
    skin,
Weed wide enough to wrap a fairy in:
And with the juice of this I'll streak her
    eyes,
And make her full of hateful fantasies.
Take thou some of it, and seek through
    this grove:
A sweet Athenian lady is in love
With a disdainful youth: anoint his eyes;
But do it when the next thing he espies
May be the lady: thou shalt know the man
By the Athenian garments he hath on.
Effect it with some care, that he may prove
More fond on her than she upon her love:
And look thou meet me ere the first cock
    crow.

PUCK.
Fear not, my lord; your servant shall do so.
    [*Exeunt.*]

SCENE II

Another part of the wood.
[*Enter* TITANIA, *with her* TRAIN.]

TITANIA.
Come, now a roundel and a fairy song;
Then, for the third part of a minute, hence;
Some to kill cankers in the musk-rose
    buds;
Some war with rere-mice for their
    leathern wings,
To make my small elves coats; and some
    keep back

The clamorous owl, that nightly hoots and
　wonders
At our quaint spirits. Sing me now asleep;
Then to your offices, and let me rest.
First Fairy.
　You spotted snakes, with double tongue,
　　Thorny hedgehogs, be not seen;
　Newts and blind-worms do no wrong;
　　Come not near our fairy queen:
Chorus.
　　Philomel, with melody,
　　Sing in our sweet lullaby:
　Lulla, lulla, lullaby; lulla, lulla, lullaby:
　　Never harm, nor spell, nor charm,
　Come our lovely lady nigh;
　So good-night, with lullaby.
Second Fairy.
　Weaving spiders, come not here;
　　Hence, you long-legg'd spinners, hence;
　Beetles black, approach not near;
　　Worm nor snail do no offence.
Chorus.
　　Philomel, with melody,
　　Sing in our sweet lullaby:
　Lulla, lulla, lullaby; lulla, lulla, lullaby:
　　Never harm, nor spell, nor charm,
　Come our lovely lady nigh;
　So good-night, with lullaby.
First Fairy.
Hence away; now all is well.
One, aloof, stand sentinel.
　　　[*Exeunt* Fairies. Titania *sleeps.*]
　　　　[*Enter* Oberon.]
Oberon.
What thou seest when thou dost wake,
　[*Squeezes the flower on* Titania's *eyelids.*]
Do it for thy true-love take;
Love and languish for his sake;
Be it ounce, or cat, or bear,
Pard, or boar with bristled hair,
In thy eye that shall appear
When thou wak'st, it is thy dear;
Wake when some vile thing is near.
　　　　　[*Exit.*]
　　[*Enter* Lysander *and* Hermia.]
Lysander.
Fair love, you faint with wandering in the
　wood;

And, to speak troth, I have forgot our way;
We'll rest us, Hermia, if you think it good,
And tarry for the comfort of the day.
Hermia.
Be it so, Lysander: find you out a bed,
For I upon this bank will rest my head.
Lysander.
One turf shall serve as pillow for us both;
One heart, one bed, two bosoms, and one
　　troth.
Hermia.
Nay, good Lysander; for my sake, my dear,
Lie farther off yet, do not lie so near.
Lysander.
O, take the sense, sweet, of my innocence;
Love takes the meaning in love's
　　conference.
I mean that my heart unto yours is knit;
So that but one heart we can make of it:
Two bosoms interchained with an oath;
So then two bosoms and a single troth.
Then by your side no bed-room me deny;
For lying so, Hermia, I do not lie.
Hermia.
Lysander riddles very prettily:—
Now much beshrew my manners and my
　pride
If Hermia meant to say Lysander lied!
But, gentle friend, for love and courtesy
Lie further off; in human modesty,
Such separation as may well be said
Becomes a virtuous bachelor and a maid:
So far be distant; and good night, sweet
　friend:
Thy love ne'er alter till thy sweet life end!
Lysander.
Amen, amen, to that fair prayer say I;
And then end life when I end loyalty!
Here is my bed: Sleep give thee all his rest!
Hermia.
With half that wish the wisher's eyes be
　pressed!
　　　　[*They sleep.*]
　　　　[*Enter* Puck.]
Puck.
Through the forest have I gone,
But Athenian found I none,
On whose eyes I might approve

This flower's force in stirring love.
Night and silence! Who is here?
Weeds of Athens he doth wear:
This is he, my master said,
Despised the Athenian maid;
And here the maiden, sleeping sound,
On the dank and dirty ground.
Pretty soul! she durst not lie
Near this lack-love, this kill-courtesy.
Churl, upon thy eyes I throw
All the power this charm doth owe;
When thou wak'st let love forbid
Sleep his seat on thy eyelid:
So awake when I am gone;
For I must now to Oberon.
                    [*Exit.*]
        [*Enter* DEMETRIUS *and* HELENA,
                    running.]
HELENA.
Stay, though thou kill me, sweet Demetrius.
DEMETRIUS.
I charge thee, hence, and do not haunt
    me thus.
HELENA.
O, wilt thou darkling leave me? do not so.
DEMETRIUS.
Stay on thy peril; I alone will go.
            [*Exit* DEMETRIUS.]
HELENA.
O, I am out of breath in this fond chase!
The more my prayer, the lesser is my grace.
Happy is Hermia, wheresoe'er she lies,
For she hath blessed and attractive eyes.
How came her eyes so bright? Not with
    salt tears:
If so, my eyes are oftener wash'd than hers.
No, no, I am as ugly as a bear;
For beasts that meet me run away for fear:
Therefore no marvel though Demetrius
Do, as a monster, fly my presence thus.
What wicked and dissembling glass of
    mine
Made me compare with Hermia's sphery
    eyne?—
But who is here?—Lysander! on the
    ground!
Dead? or asleep? I see no blood, no wound.
Lysander, if you live, good sir, awake.

LYSANDER. [*Waking.*]
And run through fire I will for thy sweet
    sake.
Transparent Helena! Nature shows art,
That through thy bosom makes me see
    thy heart.
Where is Demetrius? O, how fit a word
Is that vile name to perish on my sword!
HELENA.
Do not say so, Lysander; say not so:
What though he love your Hermia? Lord,
    what though?
Yet Hermia still loves you: then be
    content.
LYSANDER.
Content with Hermia? No: I do repent
The tedious minutes I with her have spent.
Not Hermia but Helena I love:
Who will not change a raven for a dove?
The will of man is by his reason sway'd;
And reason says you are the worthier
    maid.
Things growing are not ripe until their
    season;
So I, being young, till now ripe not to
    reason;
And touching now the point of human
    skill,
Reason becomes the marshal to my will,
And leads me to your eyes, where I
    o'erlook
Love's stories, written in love's richest
    book.
HELENA.
Wherefore was I to this keen mockery
    born?
When at your hands did I deserve this
    scorn?
Is't not enough, is't not enough, young
    man,
That I did never, no, nor never can
Deserve a sweet look from Demetrius' eye,
But you must flout my insufficiency?
Good troth, you do me wrong,—good
    sooth, you do—
In such disdainful manner me to woo.
But fare you well: perforce I must confess,
I thought you lord of more true gentleness.

O, that a lady of one man refus'd
Should of another therefore be abus'd!
        [*Exit.*]

Lysander.

She sees not Hermia:—Hermia, sleep
   thou there;
And never mayst thou come Lysander
   near!
For, as a surfeit of the sweetest things
The deepest loathing to the stomach
   brings;
Or, as the heresies that men do leave
Are hated most of those they did deceive;
So thou, my surfeit and my heresy,
Of all be hated, but the most of me!
And, all my powers, address your love and
   might
To honour Helen, and to be her knight!
        [*Exit.*]

Hermia. [*Starting.*]

Help me, Lysander, help me! do thy best
To pluck this crawling serpent from my
   breast!
Ay me, for pity!—What a dream was here!
Lysander, look how I do quake with fear!
Methought a serpent eat my heart away,
And you sat smiling at his cruel prey.—
Lysander! what, removed? Lysander! lord!
What, out of hearing? gone? no sound,
   no word?
Alack, where are you? speak, an if you hear;
Speak, of all loves! I swoon almost with
   fear.
No?—then I well perceive you are not
   nigh:
Either death or you I'll find immediately.
        [*Exit.*]

ACT III
SCENE I

The wood. The queen of fairies lying asleep.
[*Enter* Quince, Snug, Bottom, Flute,
Snout, *and* Starveling.]

Bottom.

Are we all met?

Quince.

Pat, pat; and here's a marvellous convenient
place for our rehearsal. This green plot
shall be our stage, this hawthorn brake our
tiring-house; and we will do it in action, as
we will do it before the duke.

Bottom.

Peter Quince,—

Quince.

What sayest thou, bully Bottom?

Bottom.

There are things in this comedy of "Pyramus
and Thisbe" that will never please. First,
Pyramus must draw a sword to kill himself;
which the ladies cannot abide. How answer
you that?

Snout.

By'r lakin, a parlous fear.

Starveling.

I believe we must leave the killing out,
when all is done.

Bottom.

Not a whit: I have a device to make all well.
Write me a prologue; and let the prologue
seem to say we will do no harm with our
swords, and that Pyramus is not killed
indeed; and for the more better assurance,
tell them that I Pyramus am not Pyramus
but Bottom the weaver: this will put them
out of fear.

Quince.

Well, we will have such a prologue; and it
shall be written in eight and six.

Bottom.

No, make it two more; let it be written in
eight and eight.

Snout.

Will not the ladies be afeard of the lion?

Starveling.

I fear it, I promise you.

Bottom.

Masters, you ought to consider with
yourselves: to bring in, God shield us! a lion
among ladies is a most dreadful thing: for
there is not a more fearful wild-fowl than
your lion living; and we ought to look to it.

Snout.

Therefore another prologue must tell he is
not a lion.

Bottom.

Nay, you must name his name, and half his

face must be seen through the lion's neck; and he himself must speak through, saying thus, or to the same defect,—"Ladies," or, "Fair ladies, I would wish you, or, I would request you, or, I would entreat you, not to fear, not to tremble: my life for yours. If you think I come hither as a lion, it were pity of my life. No, I am no such thing; I am a man as other men are":—and there, indeed, let him name his name, and tell them plainly he is Snug the joiner.

QUINCE.

Well, it shall be so. But there is two hard things; that is, to bring the moonlight into a chamber: for, you know, Pyramus and Thisbe meet by moonlight.

SNOUT.

Doth the moon shine that night we play our play?

BOTTOM.

A calendar, a calendar! look in the almanack; find out moonshine, find out moonshine.

QUINCE.

Yes, it doth shine that night.

BOTTOM.

Why, then may you leave a casement of the great chamber-window, where we play, open; and the moon may shine in at the casement.

QUINCE.

Ay; or else one must come in with a bush of thorns and a lantern, and say he comes to disfigure or to present the person of moonshine. Then there is another thing: we must have a wall in the great chamber; for Pyramus and Thisbe, says the story, did talk through the chink of a wall.

SNOUT.

You can never bring in a wall.—What say you, Bottom?

BOTTOM.

Some man or other must present wall: and let him have some plaster, or some loam, or some rough-cast about him, to signify wall; and let him hold his fingers thus, and through that cranny shall Pyramus and Thisbe whisper.

QUINCE.

If that may be, then all is well. Come, sit down, every mother's son, and rehearse your parts. Pyramus, you begin: when you have spoken your speech, enter into that brake; and so every one according to his cue.

[*Enter* PUCK *behind.*]

PUCK.

What hempen homespuns have we
    swaggering here,
So near the cradle of the fairy queen?
What, a play toward! I'll be an auditor;
An actor too perhaps, if I see cause.

QUINCE.

Speak, Pyramus.—Thisbe, stand forth.

PYRAMUS.

"Thisbe, the flowers of odious savours
    sweet,"

QUINCE.

Odours, odours.

PYRAMUS.

           "—odours savours sweet:
So hath thy breath, my dearest Thisbe
    dear.—
But hark, a voice! stay thou but here
    awhile,
And by and by I will to thee appear."
               [*Exit.*]

PUCK. [*Aside.*]

A stranger Pyramus than e'er played here!
               [*Exit.*]

THISBE.

Must I speak now?

QUINCE.

Ay, marry, must you: for you must understand he goes but to see a noise that he heard, and is to come again.

THISBE.

"Most radiant Pyramus, most lily white
    of hue,
Of colour like the red rose on triumphant
    brier,
Most brisky juvenal, and eke most lovely
    Jew,
As true as truest horse, that would never
    tire,
I'll meet thee, Pyramus, at Ninny's tomb."

QUINCE.
Ninus' tomb, man: why, you must not speak
that yet: that you answer to Pyramus. You
speak all your part at once, cues, and all.
Pyramus, enter: your cue is past; it is "never
tire."

THISBE.
O,—"As true as truest horse, that yet
would never tire."

[*Re-enter* PUCK, *and* BOTTOM *with an ass's
head.*]

PYRAMUS.
"If I were fair, Thisbe, I were only thine:—"

QUINCE.
O monstrous! O strange! we are haunted.
Pray, masters! fly, masters! Help!

[*Exeunt* CLOWNS.]

PUCK.
I'll follow you; I'll lead you about a round,
Through bog, through bush, through
    brake, through brier;
Sometime a horse I'll be, sometime a
    hound,
A hog, a headless bear, sometime a fire;
And neigh, and bark, and grunt, and roar,
    and burn,
Like horse, hound, hog, bear, fire, at every
    turn.

[*Exit.*]

BOTTOM.
Why do they run away? This is a knavery of
them to make me afeard.

[*Re-enter* SNOUT.]

SNOUT.
O Bottom, thou art changed! What do I
see on thee?

BOTTOM.
What do you see? you see an ass-head of
your own, do you?

[*Re-enter* QUINCE.]

QUINCE.
Bless thee, Bottom! bless thee! thou art
    translated.

[*Exit.*]

BOTTOM.
I see their knavery: this is to make an ass
of me; to fright me, if they could. But I will
not stir from this place, do what they can: I
will walk up and down here, and I will sing,
that they shall hear I am not afraid. [*Sings.*]
    The ousel cock, so black of hue,
        With orange-tawny bill,
    The throstle with his note so true,
        The wren with little quill.

TITANIA. [*Waking.*]
What angel wakes me from my flowery
    bed?

BOTTOM. [*Sings.*]
    The finch, the sparrow, and the lark,
        The plain-song cuckoo gray,
    Whose note full many a man doth mark,
        And dares not answer nay;—
For, indeed, who would set his wit to so
foolish a bird? Who would give a bird the
lie, though he cry "cuckoo" never so?

TITANIA.
I pray thee, gentle mortal, sing again;
Mine ear is much enamour'd of thy note.
So is mine eye enthralled to thy shape;
And thy fair virtue's force perforce doth
    move me,
On the first view, to say, to swear, I love
    thee.

BOTTOM.
Methinks, mistress, you should have little
reason for that: and yet, to say the truth,
reason and love keep little company together
now-a-days: the more the pity that some
honest neighbours will not make them
friends. Nay, I can gleek upon occasion.

TITANIA.
Thou art as wise as thou art beautiful.

BOTTOM.
Not so, neither: but if I had wit enough to
get out of this wood, I have enough to serve
mine own turn.

TITANIA.
Out of this wood do not desire to go;
Thou shalt remain here whether thou wilt
    or no.
I am a spirit of no common rate,—
The summer still doth tend upon my state;
And I do love thee: therefore, go with me,
I'll give thee fairies to attend on thee;
And they shall fetch thee jewels from the
    deep,

And sing, while thou on pressed flowers
    dost sleep:
And I will purge thy mortal grossness so
That thou shalt like an airy spirit go.—
Peasblossom! Cobweb! Moth! and
    Mustardseed!

[Enter Four Fairies.*]*

First Fairy.
Ready.

Second Fairy.
    And I.

Third Fairy.
        And I.

Fourth Fairy.
            Where shall we go?

Titania.
Be kind and courteous to this gentleman;
Hop in his walks and gambol in his eyes;
Feed him with apricocks and dewberries,
With purple grapes, green figs, and
    mulberries;
The honey bags steal from the humble-
    bees,
And, for night-tapers, crop their waxen
    thighs,
And light them at the fiery glow-worm's
    eyes,
To have my love to bed and to arise;
And pluck the wings from painted
    butterflies,
To fan the moonbeams from his sleeping
    eyes:
Nod to him, elves, and do him courtesies.

First Fairy.
Hail, mortal!

Second Fairy.
Hail!

Third Fairy.
Hail!

Fourth Fairy.
Hail!

Bottom.
I cry your worships mercy, heartily.—I
beseech your worship's name.

Cobweb.
Cobweb.

Bottom.
I shall desire you of more acquaintance,
good Master Cobweb. If I cut my finger,
I shall make bold with you.—Your name,
honest gentleman?

Peasblossom.
Peasblossom.

Bottom.
I pray you, commend me to Mistress Squash,
your mother, and to Master Peascod, your
father. Good Master Peasblossom, I shall
desire you of more acquaintance too.—Your
name, I beseech you, sir?

Mustardseed.
Mustardseed.

Bottom.
Good Master Mustardseed, I know
your patience well: That same cowardly
giant-like ox-beef hath devoured many a
gentleman of your house: I promise you
your kindred hath made my eyes water ere
now. I desire you of more acquaintance,
good Master Mustardseed.

Titania.
Come, wait upon him; lead him to my
    bower.
The moon, methinks, looks with a watery
    eye;
And when she weeps, weeps every little
    flower;
Lamenting some enforced chastity.
Tie up my love's tongue, bring him
    silently.

[Exeunt.]

SCENE II
Another part of the wood.
[Enter Oberon.*]*

Oberon.
I wonder if Titania be awak'd;
Then, what it was that next came in her
    eye,
Which she must dote on in extremity.

[Enter Puck.*]*

Here comes my messenger. How now,
    mad spirit?
What night-rule now about this haunted
    grove?

Puck.
My mistress with a monster is in love.

Near to her close and consecrated bower,
While she was in her dull and sleeping
  hour,
A crew of patches, rude mechanicals,
That work for bread upon Athenian stalls,
Were met together to rehearse a play
Intended for great Theseus' nuptial day.
The shallowest thickskin of that barren
  sort
Who Pyramus presented in their sport,
Forsook his scene and enter'd in a brake;
When I did him at this advantage take,
An ass's nowl I fixed on his head;
Anon, his Thisbe must be answered,
And forth my mimic comes. When they
  him spy,
As wild geese that the creeping fowler eye,
Or russet-pated choughs, many in sort,
Rising and cawing at the gun's report,
Sever themselves and madly sweep the sky,
So at his sight away his fellows fly:
And at our stamp here, o'er and o'er one
  falls;
He murder cries, and help from Athens
  calls.
Their sense thus weak, lost with their fears,
  thus strong,
Made senseless things begin to do them
  wrong;
For briers and thorns at their apparel
  snatch;
Some sleeves, some hats: from yielders all
  things catch.
I led them on in this distracted fear,
And left sweet Pyramus translated there:
When in that moment,—so it came to
  pass,—
Titania wak'd, and straightway lov'd an ass.

OBERON.
This falls out better than I could devise.
But hast thou yet latch'd the Athenian's
  eyes
With the love-juice, as I did bid thee do?

PUCK.
I took him sleeping,—that is finish'd too,—
And the Athenian woman by his side;
That, when he wak'd, of force she must
  be ey'd.

[*Enter* DEMETRIUS *and* HERMIA.]

OBERON.
Stand close; this is the same Athenian.

PUCK.
This is the woman, but not this the man.

DEMETRIUS.
O, why rebuke you him that loves you so?
Lay breath so bitter on your bitter foe.

HERMIA.
Now I but chide, but I should use thee
  worse;
For thou, I fear, hast given me cause to
  curse.
If thou hast slain Lysander in his sleep,
Being o'er shoes in blood, plunge in the
  deep,
And kill me too.
The sun was not so true unto the day
As he to me: would he have stol'n away
From sleeping Hermia? I'll believe as soon
This whole earth may be bor'd; and that
  the moon
May through the centre creep and so
  displease
Her brother's noontide with the antipodes.
It cannot be but thou hast murder'd him;
So should a murderer look; so dead, so
  grim.

DEMETRIUS.
So should the murder'd look; and so
  should I,
Pierc'd through the heart with your stern
  cruelty:
Yet you, the murderer, look as bright, as
  clear,
As yonder Venus in her glimmering
  sphere.

HERMIA.
What's this to my Lysander? where is he?
Ah, good Demetrius, wilt thou give him
  me?

DEMETRIUS.
I had rather give his carcass to my hounds.

HERMIA.
Out, dog! out, cur! thou driv'st me past the
  bounds
Of maiden's patience. Hast thou slain him,
  then?

Henceforth be never number'd among men!
Oh! once tell true; tell true, even for my
sake;
Durst thou have look'd upon him, being
awake,
And hast thou kill'd him sleeping? O
brave touch!
Could not a worm, an adder, do so much?
An adder did it; for with doubler tongue
Than thine, thou serpent, never adder
stung.

DEMETRIUS.
You spend your passion on a mispris'd
mood:
I am not guilty of Lysander's blood;
Nor is he dead, for aught that I can tell.

HERMIA.
I pray thee, tell me, then, that he is well.

DEMETRIUS.
An if I could, what should I get therefore?

HERMIA.
A privilege never to see me more.—
And from thy hated presence part I so:
See me no more whether he be dead or no.
                    [Exit.]

DEMETRIUS.
There is no following her in this fierce
vein:
Here, therefore, for a while I will remain.
So sorrow's heaviness doth heavier grow
For debt that bankrupt sleep doth sorrow
owe;
Which now in some slight measure it will
pay,
If for his tender here I make some stay.
                    [Lies down.]

OBERON.
What hast thou done? thou hast mistaken
quite,
And laid the love-juice on some true-love's
sight:
Of thy misprision must perforce ensue
Some true love turn'd, and not a false
turn'd true.

PUCK.
Then fate o'er-rules, that, one man holding
troth,
A million fail, confounding oath on oath.

OBERON.
About the wood go, swifter than the
wind,
And Helena of Athens look thou find:
All fancy-sick she is, and pale of cheer,
With sighs of love, that costs the fresh
blood dear.
By some illusion see thou bring her here;
I'll charm his eyes against she do appear.

PUCK.
I go, I go; look how I go,—
Swifter than arrow from the Tartar's bow.
                    [Exit.]

OBERON.
    Flower of this purple dye,
    Hit with Cupid's archery,
    Sink in apple of his eye!
    When his love he doth espy,
    Let her shine as gloriously
    As the Venus of the sky.—
    When thou wak'st, if she be by,
    Beg of her for remedy.
                [Re-enter PUCK.]

PUCK.
    Captain of our fairy band,
    Helena is here at hand,
    And the youth mistook by me
    Pleading for a lover's fee;
    Shall we their fond pageant see?
    Lord, what fools these mortals be!

OBERON.
    Stand aside: the noise they make
    Will cause Demetrius to awake.

PUCK.
    Then will two at once woo one,—
    That must needs be sport alone;
    And those things do best please me
    That befall preposterously.
            [Enter LYSANDER and HELENA.]

LYSANDER.
Why should you think that I should woo
in scorn?
Scorn and derision never come in tears.
Look when I vow, I weep; and vows so
born,
In their nativity all truth appears.
How can these things in me seem scorn
to you,

Bearing the badge of faith, to prove them
    true?

HELENA.

You do advance your cunning more and
    more.
When truth kills truth, O devilish-holy
    fray!
These vows are Hermia's: will you give
    her o'er?
Weigh oath with oath, and you will
    nothing weigh:
Your vows to her and me, put in two
    scales,
Will even weigh; and both as light as tales.

LYSANDER.

I had no judgment when to her I swore.

HELENA.

Nor none, in my mind, now you give her
    o'er.

LYSANDER.

Demetrius loves her, and he loves not you.

DEMETRIUS. [*Awaking.*]

O Helen, goddess, nymph, perfect, divine!
To what, my love, shall I compare thine
    eyne?
Crystal is muddy. O, how ripe in show
Thy lips, those kissing cherries, tempting
    grow!
That pure congealed white, high Taurus'
    snow,
Fann'd with the eastern wind, turns to a
    crow
When thou hold'st up thy hand: O, let
    me kiss
This princess of pure white, this seal of
    bliss!

HELENA.

O spite! O hell! I see you all are bent
To set against me for your merriment.
If you were civil, and knew courtesy,
You would not do me thus much injury.
Can you not hate me, as I know you do,
But you must join in souls to mock me
    too?
If you were men, as men you are in show,
You would not use a gentle lady so;
To vow, and swear, and superpraise my
    parts,

When I am sure you hate me with your
    hearts.
You both are rivals, and love Hermia;
And now both rivals, to mock Helena:
A trim exploit, a manly enterprise,
To conjure tears up in a poor maid's eyes
With your derision! None of noble sort
Would so offend a virgin, and extort
A poor soul's patience, all to make you
    sport.

LYSANDER.

You are unkind, Demetrius; be not so;
For you love Hermia: this you know I
    know:
And here, with all good will, with all my
    heart,
In Hermia's love I yield you up my part;
And yours of Helena to me bequeath,
Whom I do love and will do till my death.

HELENA.

Never did mockers waste more idle breath.

DEMETRIUS.

Lysander, keep thy Hermia; I will none:
If e'er I lov'd her, all that love is gone.
My heart to her but as guest-wise
    sojourn'd;
And now to Helen is it home return'd,
There to remain.

LYSANDER.

             Helen, it is not so.

DEMETRIUS.

Disparage not the faith thou dost not
    know,
Lest, to thy peril, thou aby it dear.—
Look where thy love comes; yonder is thy
    dear.

[*Enter* HERMIA.]

HERMIA.

Dark night, that from the eye his function
    takes,
The ear more quick of apprehension
    makes;
Wherein it doth impair the seeing sense,
It pays the hearing double recompense:—
Thou art not by mine eye, Lysander, found;
Mine ear, I thank it, brought me to thy
    sound.
But why unkindly didst thou leave me so?

LYSANDER.
Why should he stay whom love doth press
  to go?
HERMIA.
What love could press Lysander from my
  side?
LYSANDER.
Lysander's love, that would not let him
  bide,—
Fair Helena,—who more engilds the night
Than all yon fiery oes and eyes of light.
Why seek'st thou me? could not this make
  thee know
The hate I bare thee made me leave thee so?
HERMIA.
You speak not as you think; it cannot be.
HELENA.
Lo, she is one of this confederacy!
Now I perceive they have conjoin'd all
  three
To fashion this false sport in spite of me.
Injurious Hermia! most ungrateful maid!
Have you conspir'd, have you with these
  contriv'd,
To bait me with this foul derision?
Is all the counsel that we two have shar'd,
The sisters' vows, the hours that we have
  spent,
When we have chid the hasty-footed time
For parting us,—O, is all forgot?
All school-days' friendship, childhood
  innocence?
We, Hermia, like two artificial gods,
Have with our needles created both one
  flower,
Both on one sampler, sitting on one
  cushion,
Both warbling of one song, both in one
  key;
As if our hands, our sides, voices, and
  minds,
Had been incorporate. So we grew
  together,
Like to a double cherry, seeming parted;
But yet a union in partition,
Two lovely berries moulded on one stem:
So, with two seeming bodies, but one
  heart;

Two of the first, like coats in heraldry,
Due but to one, and crowned with one
  crest.
And will you rent our ancient love
  asunder,
To join with men in scorning your poor
  friend?
It is not friendly, 'tis not maidenly:
Our sex, as well as I, may chide you for it,
Though I alone do feel the injury.
HERMIA.
I am amazed at your passionate words:
I scorn you not; it seems that you scorn
  me.
HELENA.
Have you not set Lysander, as in scorn,
To follow me, and praise my eyes and face?
And made your other love, Demetrius,—
Who even but now did spurn me with his
  foot,—
To call me goddess, nymph, divine, and
  rare,
Precious, celestial? Wherefore speaks he
  this
To her he hates? and wherefore doth
  Lysander
Deny your love, so rich within his soul,
And tender me, forsooth, affection,
But by your setting on, by your consent?
What though I be not so in grace as you,
So hung upon with love, so fortunate;
But miserable most, to love unlov'd?
This you should pity rather than despise.
HERMIA.
I understand not what you mean by this.
HELENA.
Ay, do persever, counterfeit sad looks,
Make mouths upon me when I turn my
  back;
Wink each at other; hold the sweet jest
  up:
This sport, well carried, shall be chronicled.
If you have any pity, grace, or manners,
You would not make me such an
  argument.
But fare ye well: 'tis partly my own fault;
Which death, or absence, soon shall
  remedy.

LYSANDER.
Stay, gentle Helena; hear my excuse;
My love, my life, my soul, fair Helena!

HELENA.
O excellent!

HERMIA.
Sweet, do not scorn her so.

DEMETRIUS.
If she cannot entreat, I can compel.

LYSANDER.
Thou canst compel no more than she entreat;
Thy threats have no more strength than her weak prayers.
Helen, I love thee; by my life I do;
I swear by that which I will lose for thee
To prove him false that says I love thee not.

DEMETRIUS.
I say I love thee more than he can do.

LYSANDER.
If thou say so, withdraw, and prove it too.

DEMETRIUS.
Quick, come,—

HERMIA.
Lysander, whereto tends all this?

LYSANDER.
Away, you Ethiope!

DEMETRIUS.
No, no, sir:—he will
Seem to break loose; take on as you would follow:
But yet come not. You are a tame man; go!

LYSANDER.
Hang off, thou cat, thou burr: vile thing, let loose,
Or I will shake thee from me like a serpent.

HERMIA.
Why are you grown so rude? what change is this,
Sweet love?

LYSANDER.
Thy love! out, tawny Tartar, out!
Out, loathed medicine! hated potion, hence!

HERMIA.
Do you not jest?

HELENA.
Yes, sooth; and so do you.

LYSANDER.
Demetrius, I will keep my word with thee.

DEMETRIUS.
I would I had your bond; for I perceive
A weak bond holds you; I'll not trust your word.

LYSANDER.
What! should I hurt her, strike her, kill her dead?
Although I hate her, I'll not harm her so.

HERMIA.
What! can you do me greater harm than hate?
Hate me! wherefore? O me! what news, my love?
Am not I Hermia? Are not you Lysander?
I am as fair now as I was erewhile.
Since night you lov'd me; yet since night you left me:
Why then, you left me,—O, the gods forbid!—
In earnest, shall I say?

LYSANDER.
Ay, by my life;
And never did desire to see thee more.
Therefore be out of hope, of question, doubt,
Be certain, nothing truer; 'tis no jest
That I do hate thee and love Helena.

HERMIA.
O me! you juggler! you cankerblossom!
You thief of love! What! have you come by night,
And stol'n my love's heart from him?

HELENA.
Fine, i' faith!
Have you no modesty, no maiden shame,
No touch of bashfulness? What! will you tear
Impatient answers from my gentle tongue?
Fie, fie! you counterfeit, you puppet, you!

HERMIA.
Puppet! why so? Ay, that way goes the game.
Now I perceive that she hath made compare

Between our statures; she hath urg'd her
  height;
And with her personage, her tall
  personage,
Her height, forsooth, she hath prevail'd
  with him.—
And are you grown so high in his esteem
Because I am so dwarfish and so low?
How low am I, thou painted maypole?
  speak;
How low am I? I am not yet so low
But that my nails can reach unto thine
  eyes.

HELENA.
I pray you, though you mock me,
  gentlemen,
Let her not hurt me. I was never curst;
I have no gift at all in shrewishness;
I am a right maid for my cowardice;
Let her not strike me. You perhaps may
  think,
Because she is something lower than
  myself,
That I can match her.

HERMIA.
                    Lower! hark, again.

HELENA.
Good Hermia, do not be so bitter with me.
I evermore did love you, Hermia;
Did ever keep your counsels; never
  wrong'd you;
Save that, in love unto Demetrius,
I told him of your stealth unto this wood:
He follow'd you; for love I follow'd him;
But he hath chid me hence, and threaten'd
  me
To strike me, spurn me, nay, to kill me too:
And now, so you will let me quiet go,
To Athens will I bear my folly back,
And follow you no farther. Let me go:
You see how simple and how fond I am.

HERMIA.
Why, get you gone: who is't that hinders
  you?

HELENA.
A foolish heart that I leave here behind.

HERMIA.
What! with Lysander?

HELENA.
                    With Demetrius.

LYSANDER.
Be not afraid; she shall not harm thee,
  Helena.

DEMETRIUS.
No, sir, she shall not, though you take her
  part.

HELENA.
O, when she's angry, she is keen and
  shrewd:
She was a vixen when she went to school;
And, though she be but little, she is fierce.

HERMIA.
Little again! nothing but low and little!—
Why will you suffer her to flout me thus?
Let me come to her.

LYSANDER.
                    Get you gone, you dwarf;
You minimus, of hind'ring knot-grass
  made;
You bead, you acorn.

DEMETRIUS.
                    You are too officious
In her behalf that scorns your services.
Let her alone: speak not of Helena.
Take not her part; for if thou dost intend
Never so little show of love to her,
Thou shalt aby it.

LYSANDER.
                    Now she holds me not;
Now follow, if thou dar'st, to try whose
  right,
Of thine or mine, is most in Helena.

DEMETRIUS.
Follow! nay, I'll go with thee, cheek by
  jole.
                    [Exeunt LYSANDER and DEMETRIUS.]

HERMIA.
You, mistress, all this coil is 'long of you:
Nay, go not back.

HELENA.
                    I will not trust you, I;
Nor longer stay in your curst company.
Your hands than mine are quicker for a
  fray;
My legs are longer though, to run away.
                    [Exit.]

HERMIA.
I am amaz'd, and know not what to say.
        [*Exit, pursuing* HELENA.]
OBERON.
This is thy negligence: still thou mistak'st,
Or else commit'st thy knaveries willfully.
PUCK.
Believe me, king of shadows, I mistook.
Did not you tell me I should know the man
By the Athenian garments he had on?
And so far blameless proves my enterprise
That I have 'nointed an Athenian's eyes:
And so far am I glad it so did sort,
As this their jangling I esteem a sport.
OBERON.
Thou seest these lovers seek a place to
        fight;
Hie therefore, Robin, overcast the night;
The starry welkin cover thou anon
With drooping fog, as black as Acheron,
And lead these testy rivals so astray
As one come not within another's way.
Like to Lysander sometime frame thy
        tongue,
Then stir Demetrius up with bitter wrong;
And sometime rail thou like Demetrius;
And from each other look thou lead them
        thus,
Till o'er their brows death-counterfeiting
        sleep
With leaden legs and batty wings doth
        creep:
Then crush this herb into Lysander's eye;
Whose liquor hath this virtuous property,
To take from thence all error with his
        might
And make his eyeballs roll with wonted
        sight.
When they next wake, all this derision
Shall seem a dream and fruitless vision;
And back to Athens shall the lovers wend
With league whose date till death shall
        never end.
Whiles I in this affair do thee employ,
I'll to my queen, and beg her Indian boy;
And then I will her charmed eye release
From monster's view, and all things shall
        be peace.

PUCK.
My fairy lord, this must be done with haste,
For night's swift dragons cut the clouds
        full fast;
And yonder shines Aurora's harbinger,
At whose approach ghosts, wandering
        here and there,
Troop home to churchyards: damned
        spirits all,
That in cross-ways and floods have burial,
Already to their wormy beds are gone;
For fear lest day should look their shames
        upon
They wilfully exile themselves from light,
And must for aye consort with black-
        brow'd night.
OBERON.
But we are spirits of another sort:
I with the morning's love have oft made
        sport;
And, like a forester, the groves may tread
Even till the eastern gate, all fiery-red,
Opening on Neptune with fair blessed
        beams,
Turns into yellow gold his salt-green
        streams.
But, notwithstanding, haste; make no
        delay:
We may effect this business yet ere day.
        [*Exit* OBERON.]
PUCK.
        Up and down, up and down;
        I will lead them up and down:
        I am fear'd in field and town.
        Goblin, lead them up and down.
Here comes one.
        [*Enter* LYSANDER.]
LYSANDER.
Where art thou, proud Demetrius? speak
        thou now.
PUCK.
Here, villain; drawn and ready. Where art
        thou?
LYSANDER.
I will be with thee straight.
PUCK.
                Follow me, then,
To plainer ground.

[Exit Lysander as following the voice.]
[Enter Demetrius.]

Demetrius.

Lysander! speak again.
Thou runaway, thou coward, art thou fled?
Speak. In some bush? where dost thou
hide thy head?

Puck.

Thou coward, art thou bragging to the
stars,
Telling the bushes that thou look'st for
wars,
And wilt not come? Come, recreant; come,
thou child;
I'll whip thee with a rod: he is defiled
That draws a sword on thee.

Demetrius.

Yea, art thou there?

Puck.

Follow my voice; we'll try no manhood
here.
[Exeunt.]
[Re-enter Lysander.]

Lysander.

He goes before me, and still dares me on;
When I come where he calls, then he is
gone.
The villain is much lighter heeled than I:
I follow'd fast, but faster he did fly;
That fallen am I in dark uneven way,
And here will rest me. Come, thou gentle
day!
[Lies down.]
For if but once thou show me thy grey
light,
I'll find Demetrius, and revenge this spite.
[Sleeps.]
[Re-enter Puck and Demetrius.]

Puck.

Ho, ho, ho, ho! Coward, why com'st thou
not?

Demetrius.

Abide me, if thou dar'st; for well I wot
Thou runn'st before me, shifting every
place;
And dar'st not stand, nor look me in the
face.
Where art thou?

Puck.

Come hither; I am here.

Demetrius.

Nay, then, thou mock'st me. Thou shalt
buy this dear,
If ever I thy face by daylight see:
Now, go thy way. Faintness constraineth
me
To measure out my length on this cold
bed.—
By day's approach look to be visited.
[Lies down and sleeps.]
[Enter Helena.]

Helena.

O weary night, O long and tedious night,
Abate thy hours! Shine comforts from
the east,
That I may back to Athens by daylight,
From these that my poor company
detest:—
And sleep, that sometimes shuts up
sorrow's eye,
Steal me awhile from mine own company.
[Sleeps.]

Puck.

Yet but three? Come one more;
Two of both kinds makes up four.
Here she comes, curst and sad:—
Cupid is a knavish lad,
Thus to make poor females mad.
[Enter Hermia.]

Hermia.

Never so weary, never so in woe,
Bedabbled with the dew, and torn with
briers;
I can no further crawl, no further go;
My legs can keep no pace with my desires.
Here will I rest me till the break of day.
Heavens shield Lysander, if they mean a
fray!
[Lies down.]

Puck.

On the ground
Sleep sound:
I'll apply
To your eye,
Gentle lover, remedy.
[Squeezing the juice on Lysander's eye.]

When thou wak'st,
Thou tak'st
True delight
In the sight
    Of thy former lady's eye:
And the country proverb known,
That every man should take his own,
In your waking shall be shown:
    Jack shall have Jill;
    Nought shall go ill.
The man shall have his mare again, and all
shall be well.

    [*Exit* Puck. Demetrius,
        Helena, &c. *sleep.*]

ACT IV
SCENE I
The wood.
[*Enter* Titania *and* Bottom;
Peasblossom, Cobweb, Moth,
Mustardseed, *and other* Fairies
attending; Oberon *behind, unseen.*]

Titania.
Come, sit thee down upon this flowery bed,
While I thy amiable cheeks do coy,
And stick musk-roses in thy sleek smooth
    head,
And kiss thy fair large ears, my gentle joy.
Bottom.
Where's Peasblossom?
Peasblossom.
Ready.
Bottom.
Scratch my head, Peasblossom.—Where's
Monsieur Cobweb?
Cobweb.
Ready.
Bottom.
Monsieur Cobweb; good monsieur, get you
your weapons in your hand and kill me a
red-hipped humble-bee on the top of a
thistle; and, good monsieur, bring me the
honey-bag. Do not fret yourself too much
in the action, monsieur; and, good monsieur,
have a care the honey-bag break not; I
would be loath to have you overflown with
a honey-bag, signior. Where's Monsieur
Mustardseed?

Mustardseed.
Ready.
Bottom.
Give me your neif, Monsieur Mustardseed.
Pray you, leave your curtsy, good monsieur.
Mustardseed
What's your will?
Bottom.
Nothing, good monsieur, but to help
Cavalero Cobweb to scratch. I must to
the barber's, monsieur; for methinks I am
marvellous hairy about the face; and I am
such a tender ass, if my hair do but tickle
me I must scratch.
Titania.
What, wilt thou hear some music, my
    sweet love?
Bottom.
I have a reasonable good ear in music; let us
have the tongs and the bones.
Titania
Or say, sweet love, what thou desirest to
    eat.
Bottom
Truly, a peck of provender; I could munch
your good dry oats. Methinks I have a great
desire to a bottle of hay: good hay, sweet
hay, hath no fellow.
Titania.
I have a venturous fairy that shall seek
The squirrel's hoard, and fetch thee new
    nuts.
Bottom.
I had rather have a handful or two of dried
peas. But, I pray you, let none of your
people stir me; I have an exposition of sleep
come upon me.
Titania.
Sleep thou, and I will wind thee in my
    arms.
Fairies, be gone, and be all ways away.
So doth the woodbine the sweet
    honeysuckle
Gently entwist,—the female ivy so
Enrings the barky fingers of the elm.
O, how I love thee! how I dote on thee!
        [*They sleep.*]
    [Oberon *advances. Enter* Puck.]

OBERON.

Welcome, good Robin. Seest thou this
    sweet sight?
Her dotage now I do begin to pity.
For, meeting her of late behind the wood,
Seeking sweet favours for this hateful fool,
I did upbraid her and fall out with her:
For she his hairy temples then had
    rounded
With coronet of fresh and fragrant
    flowers;
And that same dew, which sometime on
    the buds
Was wont to swell like round and orient
    pearls,
Stood now within the pretty flow'rets' eyes,
Like tears that did their own disgrace
    bewail.
When I had, at my pleasure, taunted her,
And she, in mild terms, begg'd my
    patience,
I then did ask of her her changeling child;
Which straight she gave me, and her fairy
    sent
To bear him to my bower in fairy-land.
And now I have the boy, I will undo
This hateful imperfection of her eyes.
And, gentle Puck, take this transformed
    scalp
From off the head of this Athenian swain,
That he awaking when the other do,
May all to Athens back again repair,
And think no more of this night's
    accidents
But as the fierce vexation of a dream.
But first I will release the fairy queen.
Be as thou wast wont to be;
      [*Touching her eyes with an herb.*]
See as thou was wont to see.
Dian's bud o'er Cupid's flower
Hath such force and blessed power.
Now, my Titania; wake you, my sweet
    queen.

TITANIA.

My Oberon! what visions have I seen!
Methought I was enamour'd of an ass.

OBERON.

There lies your love.

TITANIA.

How came these things to pass?
O, how mine eyes do loathe his visage
    now!

OBERON.

Silence awhile.—Robin, take off this head.
Titania, music call; and strike more dead
Than common sleep, of all these five, the
    sense.

TITANIA.

Music, ho! music; such as charmeth sleep.

PUCK.

Now when thou wak'st, with thine own
    fool's eyes peep.

OBERON.

Sound music. [*Still music.*] Come, my
    queen, take hands with me,
And rock the ground whereon these
    sleepers be.
Now thou and I are new in amity,
And will to-morrow midnight solemnly
Dance in Duke Theseus' house
    triumphantly,
And bless it to all fair prosperity:
There shall the pairs of faithful lovers be
Wedded, with Theseus, all in jollity.

PUCK.

Fairy king, attend and mark;
I do hear the morning lark.

OBERON.

Then, my queen, in silence sad,
Trip we after night's shade.
We the globe can compass soon,
Swifter than the wand'ring moon.

TITANIA.

Come, my lord; and in our flight,
Tell me how it came this night
That I sleeping here was found
With these mortals on the ground.
      [*Exeunt. Horns sound within.*]
    [*Enter* THESEUS, HIPPOLYTA, EGEUS,
      and TRAIN.]

THESEUS.

Go, one of you, find out the forester;—
For now our observation is perform'd;
And since we have the vaward of the day,
My love shall hear the music of my
    hounds,—

Uncouple in the western valley; go:—
Despatch, I say, and find the forester.—
    [*Exit an* ATTENDANT.]
We will, fair queen, up to the mountain's
    top,
And mark the musical confusion
Of hounds and echo in conjunction.

HIPPOLYTA.

I was with Hercules and Cadmus once
When in a wood of Crete they bay'd the
    bear
With hounds of Sparta: never did I hear
Such gallant chiding; for, besides the
    groves,
The skies, the fountains, every region near
Seem'd all one mutual cry: I never heard
So musical a discord, such sweet thunder.

THESEUS.

My hounds are bred out of the Spartan
    kind,
So flew'd, so sanded; and their heads are
    hung
With ears that sweep away the morning
    dew;
Crook-knee'd and dew-lap'd like
    Thessalian bulls;
Slow in pursuit, but match'd in mouth like
    bells,
Each under each. A cry more tuneable
Was never holla'd to, nor cheer'd with
    horn,
In Crete, in Sparta, nor in Thessaly.
Judge when you hear.—But, soft, what
    nymphs are these?

EGEUS.

My lord, this is my daughter here asleep;
And this Lysander; this Demetrius is;
This Helena, old Nedar's Helena:
I wonder of their being here together.

THESEUS.

No doubt they rose up early to observe
The rite of May; and, hearing our intent,
Came here in grace of our solemnity.—
But speak, Egeus; is not this the day
That Hermia should give answer of her
    choice?

EGEUS.

It is, my lord.

THESEUS.

Go, bid the huntsmen wake them with
    their horns.
    [*Horns, and shout within.* DEMETRIUS,
    LYSANDER, HERMIA, *and* HELENA *awake
        and start up.*]
Good-morrow, friends. Saint Valentine
    is past;
Begin these wood-birds but to couple
    now?

LYSANDER.

Pardon, my lord.
    [*He and the rest kneel to* THESEUS.]

THESEUS.

                    I pray you all, stand up.
I know you two are rival enemies;
How comes this gentle concord in the
    world,
That hatred is so far from jealousy
To sleep by hate, and fear no enmity?

LYSANDER.

My lord, I shall reply amazedly,
Half 'sleep, half waking; but as yet, I swear,
I cannot truly say how I came here:
But, as I think,—for truly would I speak—
And now I do bethink me, so it is,—
I came with Hermia hither: our intent
Was to be gone from Athens, where we
    might be,
Without the peril of the Athenian law.

EGEUS.

Enough, enough, my lord; you have
    enough;
I beg the law, the law upon his head.—
They would have stol'n away, they would,
    Demetrius,
Thereby to have defeated you and me:
You of your wife, and me of my consent,—
Of my consent that she should be your
    wife.

DEMETRIUS.

My lord, fair Helen told me of their
    stealth,
Of this their purpose hither to this wood;
And I in fury hither follow'd them,
Fair Helena in fancy following me.
But, my good lord, I wot not by what
    power,—

But by some power it is,—my love to
    Hermia,
Melted as the snow—seems to me now
As the remembrance of an idle gawd
Which in my childhood I did dote upon:
And all the faith, the virtue of my heart,
The object and the pleasure of mine eye,
Is only Helena. To her, my lord,
Was I betroth'd ere I saw Hermia:
But, like a sickness, did I loathe this food;
But, as in health, come to my natural taste,
Now I do wish it, love it, long for it,
And will for evermore be true to it.

THESEUS.
Fair lovers, you are fortunately met:
Of this discourse we more will hear
    anon.—
Egeus, I will overbear your will;
For in the temple, by and by with us,
These couples shall eternally be knit.
And, for the morning now is something
    worn,
Our purpos'd hunting shall be set aside.—
Away with us to Athens, three and three,
We'll hold a feast in great solemnity.—
Come, Hippolyta.
    [*Exeunt* THESEUS, HIPPOLYTA, EGEUS,
                and TRAIN.]

DEMETRIUS.
These things seem small and
    undistinguishable,
Like far-off mountains turned into
    clouds.

HERMIA.
Methinks I see these things with parted
    eye,
When every thing seems double.

HELENA.
                    So methinks:
And I have found Demetrius like a jewel.
Mine own, and not mine own.

DEMETRIUS.
                    It seems to me
That yet we sleep, we dream.—Do not
    you think
The duke was here, and bid us follow him?

HERMIA.
Yea, and my father.

HELENA.
                And Hippolyta.

LYSANDER.
And he did bid us follow to the temple.

DEMETRIUS.
Why, then, we are awake: let's follow him;
And by the way let us recount our dreams.
                    [*Exeunt.*]
    [*As they go out,* BOTTOM *awakes.*]

BOTTOM.
When my cue comes, call me, and I will
answer. My next is "most fair Pyramus."—
Heigh-ho!—Peter Quince! Flute, the
bellows-mender! Snout, the tinker!
Starveling! God's my life, stol'n hence,
and left me asleep! I have had a most rare
vision. I have had a dream—past the wit of
man to say what dream it was.—Man is but
an ass if he go about to expound this dream.
Methought I was—there is no man can tell
what. Methought I was, and methought
I had,—but man is but a patched fool, if
he will offer to say what methought I had.
The eye of man hath not heard, the ear of
man hath not seen; man's hand is not able
to taste, his tongue to conceive, nor his
heart to report, what my dream was. I will
get Peter Quince to write a ballad of this
dream: it shall be called Bottom's Dream,
because it hath no bottom; and I will sing it
in the latter end of a play, before the duke:
peradventure, to make it the more gracious,
I shall sing it at her death.
                    [*Exit.*]

SCENE II

Athens. A room in Quince's house.
    [*Enter* QUINCE, FLUTE, SNOUT, *and*
                STARVELING.]

QUINCE.
Have you sent to Bottom's house? is he
come home yet?

STARVELING.
He cannot be heard of. Out of doubt, he is
transported.

FLUTE.
If he come not, then the play is marred; it
goes not forward, doth it?

QUINCE.

It is not possible: you have not a man in all Athens able to discharge Pyramus but he.

FLUTE.

No; he hath simply the best wit of any handicraft man in Athens.

QUINCE.

Yea, and the best person too: and he is a very paramour for a sweet voice.

FLUTE.

You must say paragon: a paramour is, God bless us, a thing of naught.

[*Enter* SNUG.]

SNUG.

Masters, the duke is coming from the temple; and there is two or three lords and ladies more married: if our sport had gone forward, we had all been made men.

FLUTE.

O sweet bully Bottom! Thus hath he lost sixpence a day during his life; he could not have 'scaped sixpence a-day; an the duke had not given him sixpence a-day for playing Pyramus, I'll be hanged; he would have deserved it: sixpence a-day in Pyramus, or nothing.

[*Enter* BOTTOM.]

BOTTOM.

Where are these lads? where are these hearts?

QUINCE.

Bottom!—O most courageous day! O most happy hour!

BOTTOM.

Masters, I am to discourse wonders: but ask me not what; for if I tell you, I am not true Athenian. I will tell you everything, right as it fell out.

QUINCE.

Let us hear, sweet Bottom.

BOTTOM.

Not a word of me. All that I will tell you is, that the duke hath dined. Get your apparel together; good strings to your beards, new ribbons to your pumps; meet presently at the palace; every man look over his part; for the short and the long is, our play is preferred. In any case, let Thisbe have clean linen; and let not him that plays the lion pare his nails, for they shall hang out for the lion's claws. And, most dear actors, eat no onions nor garlick, for we are to utter sweet breath; and I do not doubt but to hear them say it is a sweet comedy. No more words: away! go; away!

[*Exeunt.*]

ACT V
SCENE I

Athens. An apartment in the palace of Theseus.

[*Enter* THESEUS, HIPPOLYTA, PHILOSTRATE, LORDS, *and* ATTENDANTS.]

HIPPOLYTA.

'Tis strange, my Theseus, that these lovers
    speak of.

THESEUS.

More strange than true. I never may believe
These antique fables, nor these fairy toys.
Lovers and madmen have such seething
    brains,
Such shaping fantasies, that apprehend
More than cool reason ever comprehends.
The lunatic, the lover, and the poet
Are of imagination all compact:
One sees more devils than vast hell can
    hold;
That is the madman: the lover, all as
    frantic,
Sees Helen's beauty in a brow of Egypt:
The poet's eye, in a fine frenzy rolling,
Doth glance from heaven to earth, from
    earth to heaven;
And as imagination bodies forth
The forms of things unknown, the poet's
    pen
Turns them to shapes, and gives to airy
    nothing
A local habitation and a name.
Such tricks hath strong imagination,
That, if it would but apprehend some joy,
It comprehends some bringer of that joy;
Or in the night, imagining some fear,
How easy is a bush supposed a bear?

HIPPOLYTA.

But all the story of the night told over,

And all their minds transfigur'd so
together,
More witnesseth than fancy's images,
And grows to something of great
constancy;
But, howsoever, strange and admirable.
[*Enter* Lysander, Demetrius, Hermia,
and Helena.]
Theseus.
Here come the lovers, full of joy and
mirth.—
Joy, gentle friends! joy and fresh days of
love
Accompany your hearts!
Lysander.
                 More than to us
Wait in your royal walks, your board, your
bed!
Theseus.
Come now; what masques, what dances
shall we have,
To wear away this long age of three hours
Between our after-supper and bed-time?
Where is our usual manager of mirth?
What revels are in hand? Is there no play
To ease the anguish of a torturing hour?
Call Philostrate.
Philostrate.
                 Here, mighty Theseus.
Theseus.
Say, what abridgment have you for this
evening?
What masque? what music? How shall we
beguile
The lazy time, if not with some delight?
Philostrate.
There is a brief how many sports are ripe;
Make choice of which your highness will
see first.
           [*Giving a paper.*]
Theseus. [*Reads.*]
    "The battle with the Centaurs, to be
sung
    By an Athenian eunuch to the harp."
We'll none of that: that have I told my
love,
In glory of my kinsman Hercules.
    "The riot of the tipsy Bacchanals,

Tearing the Thracian singer in their
rage."
That is an old device, and it was play'd
When I from Thebes came last a
conqueror.
    "The thrice three Muses mourning for
the death
Of learning, late deceas'd in beggary."
That is some satire, keen and critical,
Not sorting with a nuptial ceremony.
    "A tedious brief scene of young
Pyramus
And his love Thisbe; very tragical
mirth."
Merry and tragical! tedious and brief!
That is hot ice and wondrous strange snow.
How shall we find the concord of this
discord?
Philostrate.
A play there is, my lord, some ten words
long,
Which is as brief as I have known a play;
But by ten words, my lord, it is too long,
Which makes it tedious: for in all the play
There is not one word apt, one player
fitted:
And tragical, my noble lord, it is;
For Pyramus therein doth kill himself:
Which when I saw rehears'd, I must
confess,
Made mine eyes water; but more merry
tears
The passion of loud laughter never shed.
Theseus.
What are they that do play it?
Philostrate.
Hard-handed men that work in Athens
here,
Which never labour'd in their minds till
now;
And now have toil'd their unbreath'd
memories
With this same play against your nuptial.
Theseus.
And we will hear it.
Philostrate.
                No, my noble lord,
It is not for you: I have heard it over,

And it is nothing, nothing in the world;
Unless you can find sport in their intents,
Extremely stretch'd and conn'd with cruel
    pain,
To do you service.

THESEUS.
            I will hear that play;
For never anything can be amiss
When simpleness and duty tender it.
Go, bring them in: and take your places,
    ladies.
           [Exit PHILOSTRATE.*]*

HIPPOLYTA.
I love not to see wretchedness o'er-charged,
And duty in his service perishing.

THESEUS.
Why, gentle sweet, you shall see no such
    thing.

HIPPOLYTA.
He says they can do nothing in this kind.

THESEUS.
The kinder we, to give them thanks for
    nothing.
Our sport shall be to take what they
    mistake:
And what poor duty cannot do,
Noble respect takes it in might, not merit.
Where I have come, great clerks have
    purposed
To greet me with premeditated welcomes;
Where I have seen them shiver and look
    pale,
Make periods in the midst of sentences,
Throttle their practis'd accent in their fears,
And, in conclusion, dumbly have broke off,
Not paying me a welcome. Trust me, sweet,
Out of this silence yet I pick'd a welcome;
And in the modesty of fearful duty
I read as much as from the rattling tongue
Of saucy and audacious eloquence.
Love, therefore, and tongue-tied simplicity
In least speak most to my capacity.
           [Enter PHILOSTRATE.*]*

PHILOSTRATE.
So please your grace, the prologue is
    address'd.

THESEUS.
Let him approach.

[Flourish of trumpets. Enter PROLOGUE.*]*

PROLOGUE.
If we offend, it is with our good will.
That you should think, we come not to
    offend,
But with good will. To show our simple
    skill,
That is the true beginning of our end.
Consider then, we come but in despite.
We do not come, as minding to content
    you,
Our true intent is. All for your delight
We are not here. That you should here
    repent you,
The actors are at hand: and, by their show,
You shall know all that you are like to know.

THESEUS.
This fellow doth not stand upon points.

LYSANDER.
He hath rid his prologue like a rough colt;
he knows not the stop. A good moral, my
lord: it is not enough to speak, but to speak
true.

HIPPOLYTA.
Indeed he hath played on this prologue like
a child on a recorder; a sound, but not in
government.

THESEUS.
His speech was like a tangled chain;
nothing impaired, but all disordered. Who
is next?
    [Enter PYRAMUS *and* THISBE, WALL,
    MOONSHINE, *and* LION, *as in dumb show.*]*

PROLOGUE.
Gentles, perchance you wonder at this
    show;
But wonder on, till truth make all things
    plain.
This man is Pyramus, if you would know;
This beauteous lady Thisbe is certain.
This man, with lime and rough-cast, doth
    present
Wall, that vile Wall which did these lovers
    sunder;
And through Wall's chink, poor souls, they
    are content
To whisper, at the which let no man
    wonder.

This man, with lanthorn, dog, and bush
  of thorn,
Presenteth Moonshine: for, if you will
  know,
By moonshine did these lovers think no
  scorn
To meet at Ninus' tomb, there, there to woo.
This grisly beast, which by name Lion
  hight,
The trusty Thisbe, coming first by night,
Did scare away, or rather did affright;
And as she fled, her mantle she did fall;
Which Lion vile with bloody mouth did
  stain:
Anon comes Pyramus, sweet youth, and
  tall,
And finds his trusty Thisbe's mantle slain;
Whereat with blade, with bloody blameful
  blade,
He bravely broach'd his boiling bloody
  breast;
And Thisbe, tarrying in mulberry shade,
His dagger drew, and died. For all the rest,
Let Lion, Moonshine, Wall, and lovers
  twain,
At large discourse while here they do
  remain.
        [*Exeunt* PROLOGUE, THISBE, LION, *and*
                MOONSHINE.]
THESEUS.
I wonder if the lion be to speak.
DEMETRIUS.
No wonder, my lord: one lion may, when
many asses do.
WALL.
In this same interlude it doth befall
That I, one Snout by name, present a wall:
And such a wall as I would have you think
That had in it a crannied hole or chink,
Through which the lovers, Pyramus and
  Thisbe,
Did whisper often very secretly.
This loam, this rough-cast, and this stone,
  doth show
That I am that same wall; the truth is so:
And this the cranny is, right and sinister,
Through which the fearful lovers are to
  whisper.

THESEUS.
Would you desire lime and hair to speak
  better?
DEMETRIUS.
It is the wittiest partition that ever I heard
discourse, my lord.
THESEUS.
Pyramus draws near the wall; silence.
                [*Enter* PYRAMUS.]
PYRAMUS.
O grim-look'd night! O night with hue
  so black!
  O night, which ever art when day is
    not!
O night, O night, alack, alack, alack,
  I fear my Thisbe's promise is forgot!—
And thou, O wall, O sweet, O lovely wall,
  That stand'st between her father's
    ground and mine;
Thou wall, O wall, O sweet and lovely wall,
  Show me thy chink, to blink through
    with mine eyne.
            [WALL *holds up his fingers.*]
Thanks, courteous wall: Jove shield thee
  well for this!
  But what see what see I? No Thisbe
    do I see.
O wicked wall, through whom I see no
  bliss,
  Curs'd be thy stones for thus deceiving
    me!
THESEUS.
The wall, methinks, being sensible, should
curse again.
PYRAMUS.
No, in truth, sir, he should not. "Deceiving
me" is Thisbe's cue: she is to enter now, and
I am to spy her through the wall. You shall
see it will fall pat as I told you.—Yonder
she comes.
                [*Enter* THISBE.]
THISBE.
O wall, full often hast thou heard my
  moans,
For parting my fair Pyramus and me:
My cherry lips have often kiss'd thy stones:
Thy stones with lime and hair knit up in
  thee.

Pyramus.
I see a voice; now will I to the chink,
To spy an I can hear my Thisbe's face.
Thisbe!
Thisbe.
My love! thou art my love, I think.
Pyramus.
Think what thou wilt, I am thy lover's
    grace;
And like Limander am I trusty still.
Thisbe.
And I like Helen, till the fates me kill.
Pyramus.
Not Shafalus to Procrus was so true.
Thisbe.
As Shafalus to Procrus, I to you.
Pyramus.
O, kiss me through the hole of this vile
    wall.
Thisbe.
I kiss the wall's hole, not your lips at all.
Pyramus.
Wilt thou at Ninny's tomb meet me
    straightway?
Thisbe.
'Tide life, 'tide death, I come without delay.
Wall.
Thus have I, wall, my part discharged so;
And, being done, thus Wall away doth go.
    [*Exeunt* Wall, Pyramus, *and* Thisbe.]
Theseus.
Now is the mural down between the two
neighbours.
Demetrius.
No remedy, my lord, when walls are so
wilful to hear without warning.
Hippolyta.
This is the silliest stuff that ever I heard.
Theseus.
The best in this kind are but shadows;
and the worst are no worse, if imagination
amend them.
Hippolyta.
It must be your imagination then, and not
theirs.
Theseus.
If we imagine no worse of them than they
of themselves, they may pass for excellent

men. Here come two noble beasts in, a
moon and a lion.
    [*Enter* Lion *and* Moonshine.]
Lion.
You, ladies, you, whose gentle hearts do fear
The smallest monstrous mouse that creeps
    on floor,
May now, perchance, both quake and
    tremble here,
When lion rough in wildest rage doth roar.
Then know that I, one Snug the joiner, am
A lion fell, nor else no lion's dam:
For, if I should as lion come in strife
Into this place, 'twere pity on my life.
Theseus.
A very gentle beast, and of a good
    conscience.
Demetrius.
The very best at a beast, my lord, that e'er
    I saw.
Lysander.
This lion is a very fox for his valour.
Theseus.
True; and a goose for his discretion.
Demetrius.
Not so, my lord; for his valour cannot carry
his discretion, and the fox carries the goose.
Theseus.
His discretion, I am sure, cannot carry his
valour; for the goose carries not the fox. It
is well; leave it to his discretion, and let us
listen to the moon.
Moonshine.
This lanthorn doth the horned moon
    present.
Demetrius.
He should have worn the horns on his head.
Theseus.
He is no crescent, and his horns are
invisible within the circumference.
Moonshine.
This lanthorn doth the horned moon
    present;
Myself the man i' the moon do seem to be.
Theseus.
This is the greatest error of all the rest: the
man should be put into the lantern. How is
it else the man i' the moon?

DEMETRIUS.
He dares not come there for the candle: for,
you see, it is already in snuff.

HIPPOLYTA.
I am aweary of this moon: would he would
change!

THESEUS.
It appears, by his small light of discretion,
that he is in the wane: but yet, in courtesy,
in all reason, we must stay the time.

LYSANDER.
Proceed, moon.

MOON.
All that I have to say, is to tell you that the
lantern is the moon; I, the man i' the moon;
this thorn-bush, my thorn-bush; and this
dog, my dog.

DEMETRIUS.
Why, all these should be in the lantern; for
all these are in the moon. But silence; here
comes Thisbe.

[*Enter* THISBE.]

THISBE.
This is old Ninny's tomb. Where is my
love?

LION.
Oh!

[*The* LION *roars.* THISBE *runs off.*]

DEMETRIUS.
Well roared, lion.

THESEUS.
Well run, Thisbe.

HIPPOLYTA.
Well shone, moon. Truly, the moon shines
with a good grace.

[*The* LION *tears* THISBE'S *mantle, and exit.*]

THESEUS.
Well moused, lion.

DEMETRIUS.
And so comes Pyramus.

LYSANDER.
And then the lion vanishes.

[*Enter* PYRAMUS.]

PYRAMUS.
Sweet moon, I thank thee for thy sunny
beams;
   I thank thee, moon, for shining now
   so bright:

For, by thy gracious golden, glittering
streams,
   I trust to take of truest Thisbe's sight.
      But stay;—O spite!
      But mark,—poor knight,
   What dreadful dole is here!
      Eyes, do you see?
      How can it be?
   O dainty duck! O dear!
      Thy mantle good,
      What! stained with blood?
   Approach, ye furies fell!
      O fates! come, come;
      Cut thread and thrum;
   Quail, rush, conclude, and quell!

THESEUS.
This passion, and the death of a dear friend,
would go near to make a man look sad.

HIPPOLYTA.
Beshrew my heart, but I pity the man.

PYRAMUS.
O wherefore, nature, didst thou lions
   frame?
   Since lion vile hath here deflower'd
   my dear;
Which is—no, no—which was the fairest
   dame
   That liv'd, that lov'd, that lik'd, that
   look'd with cheer.
      Come, tears, confound;
      Out, sword, and wound
   The pap of Pyramus:
      Ay, that left pap,
      Where heart doth hop:—
   Thus die I, thus, thus, thus.
      Now am I dead,
      Now am I fled;
   My soul is in the sky:
      Tongue, lose thy light!
      Moon, take thy flight!
   Now die, die, die, die, die.

[*Dies. Exit* MOONSHINE.]

DEMETRIUS.
No die, but an ace, for him; for he is but
one.

LYSANDER.
Less than an ace, man; for he is dead; he
is nothing.

THESEUS.
With the help of a surgeon he might yet recover and prove an ass.

HIPPOLYTA.
How chance moonshine is gone before Thisbe comes back and finds her lover?

THESEUS.
She will find him by starlight. Here she comes; and her passion ends the play.

[*Enter* THISBE.]

HIPPOLYTA.
Methinks she should not use a long one for such a Pyramus: I hope she will be brief.

DEMETRIUS.
A mote will turn the balance, which Pyramus, which Thisbe, is the better.

LYSANDER.
She hath spied him already with those sweet eyes.

DEMETRIUS.
And thus she moans, *videlicet.*—

THISBE.
Asleep, my love?
    What, dead, my dove?
O Pyramus, arise,
    Speak, speak. Quite dumb?
    Dead, dead? A tomb
Must cover thy sweet eyes.
    These lily lips,
    This cherry nose,
These yellow cowslip cheeks,
    Are gone, are gone:
    Lovers, make moan!
His eyes were green as leeks.
    O Sisters Three,
    Come, come to me,
With hands as pale as milk;
    Lay them in gore,
    Since you have shore
With shears his thread of silk.
    Tongue, not a word:—
    Come, trusty sword;
Come, blade, my breast imbrue;
    And farewell, friends:—
    Thus Thisbe ends;
Adieu, adieu, adieu.

[*Dies.*]

THESEUS.
Moonshine and lion are left to bury the dead.

DEMETRIUS.
Ay, and wall too.

BOTTOM.
No, I assure you; the wall is down that parted their fathers. Will it please you to see the epilogue, or to hear a Bergomask dance between two of our company?

THESEUS.
No epilogue, I pray you; for your play needs no excuse. Never excuse; for when the players are all dead there need none to be blamed. Marry, if he that writ it had played Pyramus, and hang'd himself in Thisbe's garter, it would have been a fine tragedy: and so it is, truly; and very notably discharged. But come, your Bergomask; let your epilogue alone.

[*Here a dance of* CLOWNS.]

The iron tongue of midnight hath told
    twelve:—
Lovers, to bed; 'tis almost fairy time.
I fear we shall out-sleep the coming morn,
As much as we this night have
    overwatch'd.
This palpable-gross play hath well beguil'd
The heavy gait of night.—Sweet friends,
    to bed.—
A fortnight hold we this solemnity,
In nightly revels and new jollity.

[*Exeunt.*]

SCENE II

[*Enter* PUCK.]

PUCK.
    Now the hungry lion roars,
        And the wolf behowls the moon;
    Whilst the heavy ploughman snores,
        All with weary task fordone.
    Now the wasted brands do glow,
        Whilst the scritch-owl, scritching
            loud,
    Puts the wretch that lies in woe
        In remembrance of a shroud.
    Now it is the time of night
        That the graves, all gaping wide,

Every one lets forth its sprite,
      In the church-way paths to glide:
And we fairies, that do run
      By the triple Hecate's team
From the presence of the sun,
      Following darkness like a dream,
Now are frolic; not a mouse
Shall disturb this hallow'd house:
I am sent with broom before,
To sweep the dust behind the door.
            [*Enter* OBERON *and* TITANIA,
                  with their TRAIN.]

OBERON.

Through the house give glimmering
      light,
      By the dead and drowsy fire:
Every elf and fairy sprite
      Hop as light as bird from brier:
And this ditty, after me,
Sing and dance it trippingly.

TITANIA.

First, rehearse your song by rote,
To each word a warbling note;
Hand in hand, with fairy grace,
Will we sing, and bless this place.
            [*Song and dance.*]

OBERON.

Now, until the break of day,
Through this house each fairy stray,
To the best bride-bed will we,
Which by us shall blessed be;
And the issue there create
Ever shall be fortunate.
So shall all the couples three
Ever true in loving be;

And the blots of Nature's hand
Shall not in their issue stand:
Never mole, hare-lip, nor scar,
Nor mark prodigious, such as are
Despised in nativity,
Shall upon their children be.—
With this field-dew consecrate,
Every fairy take his gate;
And each several chamber bless,
Through this palace, with sweet peace;
E'er shall it in safety rest,
And the owner of it blest.
      Trip away:
      Make no stay:
Meet me all by break of day.
            [*Exeunt* OBERON, TITANIA,
                  and TRAIN.]

PUCK.

If we shadows have offended,
Think but this,—and all is mended,—
That you have but slumber'd here
While these visions did appear.
And this weak and idle theme,
No more yielding but a dream,
Gentles, do not reprehend;
If you pardon, we will mend.
And, as I am an honest Puck,
If we have unearned luck
Now to 'scape the serpent's tongue,
We will make amends ere long;
Else the Puck a liar call:
So, good night unto you all.
Give me your hands, if we be friends,
And Robin shall restore amends.
            [*Exit.*]

The Merchant of Venice

DRAMATIS PERSONAE

DUKE OF VENICE
PRINCE OF MOROCCO, *suitor to Portia*
PRINCE OF ARRAGON, *suitor to Portia*
ANTONIO, *a merchant of Venice*
BASSANIO, *his friend*
SALANIO, *friend to Antonio and Bassanio*
SALARINO, *friend to Antonio and Bassanio*
GRATIANO, *friend to Antonio and Bassanio*
LORENZO, *in love with Jessica*
SHYLOCK, *a rich Jew*
TUBAL, *a Jew, his friend*
LAUNCELOT GOBBO, *a clown, servant to Shylock*

OLD GOBBO, *father to Launcelot*
LEONARDO, *servant to Bassanio*
BALTHASAR, *servant to Portia*
STEPHANO, *servant to Portia*
PORTIA, *a rich heiress*
NERISSA, *her waiting-maid*
JESSICA, *daughter to Shylock*
MAGNIFICOES *of Venice*, OFFICERS *of the Court of Justice*, GAOLER, SERVANTS *to Portia, and other* ATTENDANTS

SCENE: *Partly at Venice, and partly at Belmont, the seat of Portia, on the Continent.*

ACT I
SCENE I
Venice. A street.
[*Enter* ANTONIO, SALARINO, *and* SALANIO.]

ANTONIO.
In sooth, I know not why I am so sad;
It wearies me; you say it wearies you;
But how I caught it, found it, or came by it,
What stuff 'tis made of, whereof it is born,
I am to learn;
And such a want-wit sadness makes of me
That I have much ado to know myself.

SALARINO.
Your mind is tossing on the ocean;
There where your argosies, with portly sail—
Like signiors and rich burghers on the flood,
Or as it were the pageants of the sea—
Do overpeer the petty traffickers,
That curtsy to them, do them reverence,
As they fly by them with their woven wings.

SALANIO.
Believe me, sir, had I such venture forth,
The better part of my affections would
Be with my hopes abroad. I should be still
Plucking the grass to know where sits the wind,
Peering in maps for ports, and piers, and roads;
And every object that might make me fear
Misfortune to my ventures, out of doubt
Would make me sad.

SALARINO.
          My wind, cooling my broth
Would blow me to an ague, when I thought
What harm a wind too great might do at sea.
I should not see the sandy hour-glass run
But I should think of shallows and of flats,
And see my wealthy Andrew dock'd in sand,

Vailing her high top lower than her ribs
To kiss her burial. Should I go to church
And see the holy edifice of stone,
And not bethink me straight of dangerous
   rocks,
Which, touching but my gentle vessel's side,
Would scatter all her spices on the stream,
Enrobe the roaring waters with my silks,
And, in a word, but even now worth this,
And now worth nothing? Shall I have the
   thought
To think on this, and shall I lack the
   thought
That such a thing bechanc'd would make
   me sad?
But tell not me; I know Antonio
Is sad to think upon his merchandise.
ANTONIO.
Believe me, no; I thank my fortune for it,
My ventures are not in one bottom trusted,
Nor to one place; nor is my whole estate
Upon the fortune of this present year;
Therefore my merchandise makes me not
   sad.
SALARINO.
Why, then you are in love.
ANTONIO.
                Fie, fie!
SALARINO.
Not in love neither? Then let us say you
   are sad
Because you are not merry; and 'twere as
   easy
For you to laugh and leap and say you are
   merry,
Because you are not sad. Now, by two-
   headed Janus,
Nature hath fram'd strange fellows in her
   time:
Some that will evermore peep through
   their eyes,
And laugh like parrots at a bag-piper;
And other of such vinegar aspect
That they'll not show their teeth in way
   of smile
Though Nestor swear the jest be laughable.
     [*Enter* BASSANIO, LORENZO, *and*
           GRATIANO.]

SALANIO.
Here comes Bassanio, your most noble
   kinsman,
Gratiano, and Lorenzo. Fare ye well;
We leave you now with better company.
SALARINO.
I would have stay'd till I had made you
   merry,
If worthier friends had not prevented me.
ANTONIO.
Your worth is very dear in my regard.
I take it your own business calls on you,
And you embrace th' occasion to depart.
SALARINO.
Good morrow, my good lords.
BASSANIO.
Good signiors both, when shall we laugh?
   Say when.
You grow exceeding strange; must it be so?
SALARINO.
We'll make our leisures to attend on yours.
    [*Exeunt* SALARINO *and* SALANIO.]
LORENZO.
My Lord Bassanio, since you have found
   Antonio,
We two will leave you; but at dinner-time,
I pray you, have in mind where we must
   meet.
BASSANIO.
I will not fail you.
GRATIANO.
You look not well, Signior Antonio;
You have too much respect upon the world;
They lose it that do buy it with much care.
Believe me, you are marvellously chang'd.
ANTONIO.
I hold the world but as the world,
   Gratiano;
A stage, where every man must play a part,
And mine a sad one.
GRATIANO.
              Let me play the fool;
With mirth and laughter let old wrinkles
   come;
And let my liver rather heat with wine
Than my heart cool with mortifying groans.
Why should a man whose blood is warm
   within

Sit like his grandsire cut in alabaster,
Sleep when he wakes, and creep into the
    jaundice
By being peevish? I tell thee what,
    Antonio—
I love thee, and 'tis my love that speaks—
There are a sort of men whose visages
Do cream and mantle like a standing pond,
And do a wilful stillness entertain,
With purpose to be dress'd in an opinion
Of wisdom, gravity, profound conceit;
As who should say "I am Sir Oracle,
And when I ope my lips let no dog bark."
O my Antonio, I do know of these
That therefore only are reputed wise
For saying nothing; when, I am very sure,
If they should speak, would almost damn
    those ears
Which, hearing them, would call their
    brothers fools.
I'll tell thee more of this another time.
But fish not with this melancholy bait,
For this fool gudgeon, this opinion.
Come, good Lorenzo. Fare ye well awhile;
I'll end my exhortation after dinner.

LORENZO.

Well, we will leave you then till dinner-
    time.
I must be one of these same dumb wise
    men,
For Gratiano never lets me speak.

GRATIANO.

Well, keep me company but two years moe,
Thou shalt not know the sound of thine
    own tongue.

ANTONIO.

Fare you well; I'll grow a talker for this
    gear.

GRATIANO.

Thanks, i' faith, for silence is only
    commendable
In a neat's tongue dried, and a maid not
    vendible.
    [*Exeunt* GRATIANO *and* LORENZO.]

ANTONIO.

Is that anything now?

BASSANIO.

Gratiano speaks an infinite deal of nothing,
more than any man in all Venice. His
reasons are as two grains of wheat hid in,
two bushels of chaff: you shall seek all day
ere you find them, and when you have them
they are not worth the search.

ANTONIO.

Well; tell me now what lady is the same
To whom you swore a secret pilgrimage,
That you to-day promis'd to tell me of?

BASSANIO.

'Tis not unknown to you, Antonio,
How much I have disabled mine estate
By something showing a more swelling
    port
Than my faint means would grant
    continuance;
Nor do I now make moan to be abridg'd
From such a noble rate; but my chief care
Is to come fairly off from the great debts
Wherein my time, something too prodigal,
Hath left me gag'd. To you, Antonio,
I owe the most, in money and in love;
And from your love I have a warranty
To unburden all my plots and purposes
How to get clear of all the debts I owe.

ANTONIO.

I pray you, good Bassanio, let me know it;
And if it stand, as you yourself still do,
Within the eye of honour, be assur'd
My purse, my person, my extremest means,
Lie all unlock'd to your occasions.

BASSANIO.

In my school-days, when I had lost one
    shaft,
I shot his fellow of the self-same flight
The self-same way, with more advised
    watch,
To find the other forth; and by
    adventuring both
I oft found both. I urge this childhood
    proof,
Because what follows is pure innocence.
I owe you much; and, like a wilful youth,
That which I owe is lost; but if you please
To shoot another arrow that self way
Which you did shoot the first, I do not
    doubt,
As I will watch the aim, or to find both,

Or bring your latter hazard back again
And thankfully rest debtor for the first.

ANTONIO.

You know me well, and herein spend but
    time
To wind about my love with circumstance;
And out of doubt you do me now more
    wrong
In making question of my uttermost
Than if you had made waste of all I have.
Then do but say to me what I should do
That in your knowledge may by me be
    done,
And I am prest unto it; therefore, speak.

BASSANIO.

In Belmont is a lady richly left,
And she is fair and, fairer than that word,
Of wondrous virtues. Sometimes from
    her eyes
I did receive fair speechless messages:
Her name is Portia—nothing undervalu'd
To Cato's daughter, Brutus' Portia:
Nor is the wide world ignorant of her
    worth,
For the four winds blow in from every
    coast
Renowned suitors, and her sunny locks
Hang on her temples like a golden fleece;
Which makes her seat of Belmont
    Colchos' strond,
And many Jasons come in quest of her.
O my Antonio! had I but the means
To hold a rival place with one of them,
I have a mind presages me such thrift
That I should questionless be fortunate.

ANTONIO.

Thou know'st that all my fortunes are at
    sea;
Neither have I money nor commodity
To raise a present sum; therefore go forth,
Try what my credit can in Venice do;
That shall be rack'd, even to the uttermost,
To furnish thee to Belmont to fair Portia.
Go presently inquire, and so will I,
Where money is; and I no question make
To have it of my trust or for my sake.

[Exeunt.]

SCENE II

Belmont. A room in Portia's house.

[Enter PORTIA *and* NERISSA.]

PORTIA.

By my troth, Nerissa, my little body is
aweary of this great world.

NERISSA.

You would be, sweet madam, if your
miseries were in the same abundance as
your good fortunes are; and yet, for aught
I see, they are as sick that surfeit with too
much as they that starve with nothing. It is
no mean happiness, therefore, to be seated
in the mean: superfluity come sooner by
white hairs, but competency lives longer.

PORTIA.

Good sentences, and well pronounced.

NERISSA.

They would be better, if well followed.

PORTIA.

If to do were as easy as to know what were
good to do, chapels had been churches,
and poor men's cottages princes' palaces.
It is a good divine that follows his own
instructions; I can easier teach twenty
what were good to be done than to be
one of the twenty to follow mine own
teaching. The brain may devise laws for
the blood, but a hot temper leaps o'er a
cold decree; such a hare is madness the
youth, to skip o'er the meshes of good
counsel the cripple. But this reasoning is
not in the fashion to choose me a husband.
O me, the word "choose"! I may neither
choose who I would nor refuse who I
dislike; so is the will of a living daughter
curb'd by the will of a dead father. Is it not
hard, Nerissa, that I cannot choose one,
nor refuse none?

NERISSA.

Your father was ever virtuous, and holy
men at their death have good inspirations;
therefore the lott'ry that he hath devised in
these three chests of gold, silver, and lead,
whereof who chooses his meaning chooses
you, will no doubt never be chosen by any
rightly but one who you shall rightly love.
But what warmth is there in your affection

towards any of these princely suitors that are already come?

PORTIA.
I pray thee over-name them; and as thou namest them, I will describe them; and according to my description, level at my affection.

NERISSA.
First, there is the Neapolitan prince.

PORTIA.
Ay, that's a colt indeed, for he doth nothing but talk of his horse; and he makes it a great appropriation to his own good parts that he can shoe him himself; I am much afeard my lady his mother play'd false with a smith.

NERISSA.
Then is there the County Palatine.

PORTIA.
He doth nothing but frown, as who should say "An you will not have me, choose." He hears merry tales and smiles not: I fear he will prove the weeping philosopher when he grows old, being so full of unmannerly sadness in his youth. I had rather be married to a death's-head with a bone in his mouth than to either of these. God defend me from these two!

NERISSA.
How say you by the French lord, Monsieur Le Bon?

PORTIA.
God made him, and therefore let him pass for a man. In truth, I know it is a sin to be a mocker, but he! why, he hath a horse better than the Neapolitan's, a better bad habit of frowning than the Count Palatine; he is every man in no man. If a throstle sing he falls straight a-capering; he will fence with his own shadow; if I should marry him, I should marry twenty husbands. If he would despise me, I would forgive him; for if he love me to madness, I shall never requite him.

NERISSA.
What say you, then, to Falconbridge, the young baron of England?

PORTIA.
You know I say nothing to him, for he understands not me, nor I him: he hath neither Latin, French, nor Italian, and you will come into the court and swear that I have a poor pennyworth in the English. He is a proper man's picture; but alas, who can converse with a dumb-show? How oddly he is suited! I think he bought his doublet in Italy, his round hose in France, his bonnet in Germany, and his behaviour everywhere.

NERISSA.
What think you of the Scottish lord, his neighbour?

PORTIA.
That he hath a neighbourly charity in him, for he borrowed a box of the ear of the Englishman, and swore he would pay him again when he was able; I think the Frenchman became his surety, and sealed under for another.

NERISSA.
How like you the young German, the Duke of Saxony's nephew?

PORTIA.
Very vilely in the morning when he is sober, and most vilely in the afternoon when he is drunk: when he is best, he is a little worse than a man, and when he is worst, he is little better than a beast. An the worst fall that ever fell, I hope I shall make shift to go without him.

NERISSA.
If he should offer to choose, and choose the right casket, you should refuse to perform your father's will, if you should refuse to accept him.

PORTIA.
Therefore, for fear of the worst, I pray thee set a deep glass of Rhenish wine on the contrary casket; for if the devil be within and that temptation without, I know he will choose it. I will do anything, Nerissa, ere I will be married to a sponge.

NERISSA.
You need not fear, lady, the having any of these lords; they have acquainted me with their determinations, which is indeed to return to their home, and to trouble you with no more suit, unless you may be

won by some other sort than your father's imposition, depending on the caskets.

PORTIA.

If I live to be as old as Sibylla, I will die as chaste as Diana, unless I be obtained by the manner of my father's will. I am glad this parcel of wooers are so reasonable; for there is not one among them but I dote on his very absence, and I pray God grant them a fair departure.

NERISSA.

Do you not remember, lady, in your father's time, a Venetian, a scholar and a soldier, that came hither in company of the Marquis of Montferrat?

PORTIA.

Yes, yes, it was Bassanio; as I think, so was he called.

NERISSA.

True, madam; he, of all the men that ever my foolish eyes looked upon, was the best deserving a fair lady.

PORTIA.

I remember him well, and I remember him worthy of thy praise. [*Enter a* SERVANT.] How now! what news?

SERVANT.

The four strangers seek for you, madam, to take their leave; and there is a forerunner come from a fifth, the Prince of Morocco, who brings word the prince his master will be here to-night.

PORTIA.

If I could bid the fifth welcome with so good heart as I can bid the other four farewell, I should be glad of his approach; if he have the condition of a saint and the complexion of a devil, I had rather he should shrive me than wive me.

Come, Nerissa. [*To* SERVANT.] Sirrah, go before.

Whiles we shut the gate upon one wooer, Another knocks at the door.

[*Exeunt.*]

SCENE III

Venice. A public place.
[*Enter* BASSANIO *and* SHYLOCK.]

SHYLOCK.

Three thousand ducats; well?

BASSANIO.

Ay, sir, for three months.

SHYLOCK.

For three months; well?

BASSANIO.

For the which, as I told you, Antonio shall be bound.

SHYLOCK.

Antonio shall become bound; well?

BASSANIO.

May you stead me? Will you pleasure me? Shall I know your answer?

SHYLOCK.

Three thousand ducats, for three months, and Antonio bound.

BASSANIO.

Your answer to that.

SHYLOCK.

Antonio is a good man.

BASSANIO.

Have you heard any imputation to the contrary?

SHYLOCK.

Ho, no, no, no, no: my meaning in saying he is a good man is to have you understand me that he is sufficient; yet his means are in supposition: he hath an argosy bound to Tripolis, another to the Indies; I understand, moreover, upon the Rialto, he hath a third at Mexico, a fourth for England, and other ventures he hath, squandered abroad. But ships are but boards, sailors but men; there be land-rats and water-rats, land-thieves and water-thieves,—I mean pirates,—and then there is the peril of waters, winds, and rocks. The man is, notwithstanding, sufficient. Three thousand ducats—I think I may take his bond.

BASSANIO.

Be assured you may.

SHYLOCK.

I will be assured I may; and, that I may be assured, I will bethink me. May I speak with Antonio?

BASSANIO.

If it please you to dine with us.

SHYLOCK.
Yes, to smell pork; to eat of the habitation
which your prophet, the Nazarite, conjured
the devil into. I will buy with you, sell with
you, talk with you, walk with you, and so
following; but I will not eat with you, drink
with you, nor pray with you. What news on
the Rialto? Who is he comes here?
[*Enter* ANTONIO.]
BASSANIO.
This is Signior Antonio.
SHYLOCK. [*Aside.*]
How like a fawning publican he looks!
I hate him for he is a Christian;
But more for that in low simplicity
He lends out money gratis, and brings
down
The rate of usance here with us in Venice.
If I can catch him once upon the hip,
I will feed fat the ancient grudge I bear
him.
He hates our sacred nation; and he rails,
Even there where merchants most do
congregate,
On me, my bargains, and my well-won
thrift,
Which he calls interest. Cursed be my
tribe
If I forgive him!
BASSANIO.
Shylock, do you hear?
SHYLOCK.
I am debating of my present store,
And, by the near guess of my memory,
I cannot instantly raise up the gross
Of full three thousand ducats. What of
that?
Tubal, a wealthy Hebrew of my tribe,
Will furnish me. But soft! how many
months
Do you desire? [*To* ANTONIO.] Rest you
fair, good signior;
Your worship was the last man in our
mouths.
ANTONIO.
Shylock, albeit I neither lend nor borrow
By taking nor by giving of excess,
Yet, to supply the ripe wants of my friend,

I'll break a custom. [*To* BASSANIO.] Is he
yet possess'd
How much ye would?
SHYLOCK.
Ay, ay, three thousand ducats.
ANTONIO.
And for three months.
SHYLOCK.
I had forgot; three months; you told me so.
Well then, your bond; and, let me see. But
hear you,
Methought you said you neither lend nor
borrow
Upon advantage.
ANTONIO.
I do never use it.
SHYLOCK.
When Jacob graz'd his uncle Laban's
sheep,—
This Jacob from our holy Abram was,
As his wise mother wrought in his
behalf,
The third possessor; ay, he was the third,—
ANTONIO.
And what of him? Did he take interest?
SHYLOCK.
No, not take interest; not, as you would
say,
Directly interest; mark what Jacob did.
When Laban and himself were
compromis'd
That all the eanlings which were streak'd
and pied
Should fall as Jacob's hire, the ewes, being
rank,
In end of autumn turned to the rams;
And when the work of generation was
Between these woolly breeders in the act,
The skilful shepherd peel'd me certain
wands,
And, in the doing of the deed of kind,
He stuck them up before the fulsome
ewes,
Who, then conceiving, did in eaning time
Fall parti-colour'd lambs, and those were
Jacob's.
This was a way to thrive, and he was blest;
And thrift is blessing, if men steal it not.

ANTONIO.
This was a venture, sir, that Jacob serv'd for;
A thing not in his power to bring to pass,
But sway'd and fashion'd by the hand of
   heaven.
Was this inserted to make interest good?
Or is your gold and silver ewes and rams?
SHYLOCK.
I cannot tell; I make it breed as fast.
But note me, signior.
ANTONIO.
             Mark you this, Bassanio,
The devil can cite Scripture for his
   purpose.
An evil soul producing holy witness
Is like a villain with a smiling cheek,
A goodly apple rotten at the heart.
O, what a goodly outside falsehood hath!
SHYLOCK.
Three thousand ducats; 'tis a good round
   sum.
Three months from twelve; then let me see
   the rate.
ANTONIO.
Well, Shylock, shall we be beholding to
   you?
SHYLOCK.
Signior Antonio, many a time and oft
In the Rialto you have rated me
About my moneys and my usances;
Still have I borne it with a patient shrug,
For suff'rance is the badge of all our tribe;
You call me misbeliever, cut-throat dog,
And spet upon my Jewish gaberdine,
And all for use of that which is mine own.
Well then, it now appears you need my
   help;
Go to, then; you come to me, and you say
"Shylock, we would have moneys." You
   say so:
You that did void your rheum upon my
   beard,
And foot me as you spurn a stranger cur
Over your threshold; moneys is your suit.
What should I say to you? Should I not
   say
"Hath a dog money? Is it possible
A cur can lend three thousand ducats?" Or

Shall I bend low and, in a bondman's key,
With bated breath and whisp'ring
   humbleness,
Say this:—"Fair sir, you spit on me on
   Wednesday last;
You spurn'd me such a day; another time
You call'd me dog; and for these courtesies
I'll lend you thus much moneys"?
ANTONIO.
I am as like to call thee so again,
To spet on thee again, to spurn thee too.
If thou wilt lend this money, lend it not
As to thy friends,—for when did
   friendship take
A breed for barren metal of his friend?—
But lend it rather to thine enemy;
Who if he break thou mayst with better
   face
Exact the penalty.
SHYLOCK.
           Why, look you, how you storm!
I would be friends with you, and have your
   love,
Forget the shames that you have stain'd
   me with,
Supply your present wants, and take no
   doit
Of usance for my moneys, and you'll not
   hear me:
This is kind I offer.
BASSANIO.
This were kindness.
SHYLOCK.
           This kindness will I show.
Go with me to a notary, seal me there
Your single bond; and, in a merry sport,
If you repay me not on such a day,
In such a place, such sum or sums as are
Express'd in the condition, let the forfeit
Be nominated for an equal pound
Of your fair flesh, to be cut off and taken
In what part of your body pleaseth me.
ANTONIO.
Content, in faith; I'll seal to such a bond,
And say there is much kindness in the Jew.
BASSANIO.
You shall not seal to such a bond for me;
I'll rather dwell in my necessity.

ANTONIO.
Why, fear not, man; I will not forfeit it;
Within these two months, that's a month before
This bond expires, I do expect return
Of thrice three times the value of this bond.

SHYLOCK.
O father Abram, what these Christians are,
Whose own hard dealings teaches them suspect
The thoughts of others. Pray you, tell me this;
If he should break his day, what should I gain
By the exaction of the forfeiture?
A pound of man's flesh, taken from a man,
Is not so estimable, profitable neither,
As flesh of muttons, beefs, or goats. I say,
To buy his favour, I extend this friendship;
If he will take it, so; if not, adieu;
And, for my love, I pray you wrong me not.

ANTONIO.
Yes, Shylock, I will seal unto this bond.

SHYLOCK.
Then meet me forthwith at the notary's;
Give him direction for this merry bond,
And I will go and purse the ducats straight,
See to my house, left in the fearful guard
Of an unthrifty knave, and presently
I'll be with you.

ANTONIO.
                    Hie thee, gentle Jew.
                    [*Exit* SHYLOCK.]
This Hebrew will turn Christian: he grows kind.

BASSANIO.
I like not fair terms and a villain's mind.

ANTONIO.
Come on; in this there can be no dismay;
My ships come home a month before the day.
                    [*Exeunt.*]

ACT II
SCENE I
Belmont. A room in Portia's house.
[*Flourish of cornets. Enter the* PRINCE OF MOROCCO, *and his* FOLLOWERS; PORTIA, NERISSA, *and* OTHERS *of her train.*]

PRINCE OF MOROCCO.
Mislike me not for my complexion,
The shadow'd livery of the burnish'd sun,
To whom I am a neighbour, and near bred.
Bring me the fairest creature northward born,
Where Phoebus' fire scarce thaws the icicles,
And let us make incision for your love
To prove whose blood is reddest, his or mine.
I tell thee, lady, this aspect of mine
Hath fear'd the valiant; by my love, I swear
The best-regarded virgins of our clime
Have lov'd it too. I would not change this hue,
Except to steal your thoughts, my gentle queen.

PORTIA.
In terms of choice I am not solely led
By nice direction of a maiden's eyes;
Besides, the lottery of my destiny
Bars me the right of voluntary choosing;
But, if my father had not scanted me
And hedg'd me by his wit, to yield myself
His wife who wins me by that means I told you,
Yourself, renowned prince, then stood as fair
As any comer I have look'd on yet
For my affection.

PRINCE OF MOROCCO.
                    Even for that I thank you:
Therefore, I pray you, lead me to the caskets
To try my fortune. By this scimitar,—
That slew the Sophy and a Persian prince,
That won three fields of Sultan Solyman,—
I would o'erstare the sternest eyes that look,
Outbrave the heart most daring on the earth,

Pluck the young sucking cubs from the
   she-bear,
Yea, mock the lion when he roars for
   prey,
To win thee, lady. But, alas the while!
If Hercules and Lichas play at dice
Which is the better man, the greater
   throw
May turn by fortune from the weaker
   hand:
So is Alcides beaten by his page;
And so may I, blind Fortune leading me,
Miss that which one unworthier may
   attain,
And die with grieving.

PORTIA.
             You must take your chance,
And either not attempt to choose at all,
Or swear before you choose, if you choose
   wrong,
Never to speak to lady afterward
In way of marriage; therefore be advis'd.

PRINCE OF MOROCCO.
Nor will not; come, bring me unto my
   chance.

PORTIA.
First, forward to the temple: after dinner
Your hazard shall be made.

PRINCE OF MOROCCO.
             Good fortune then!
To make me blest or cursed'st among men!
     [*Cornets, and exeunt.*]

SCENE II
Venice. A street.
[*Enter* LAUNCELOT GOBBO.]

LAUNCELOT.
Certainly my conscience will serve me to
run from this Jew my master. The fiend
is at mine elbow and tempts me, saying
to me "Gobbo, Launcelot Gobbo, good
Launcelot" or "good Gobbo" or "good
Launcelot Gobbo, use your legs, take the
start, run away." My conscience says "No;
take heed, honest Launcelot, take heed,
honest Gobbo" or, as aforesaid, "honest
Launcelot Gobbo, do not run; scorn running
with thy heels." Well, the most courageous

fiend bids me pack. "Via!" says the fiend;
"away!" says the fiend. "For the heavens,
rouse up a brave mind," says the fiend "and
run." Well, my conscience, hanging about
the neck of my heart, says very wisely to
me "My honest friend Launcelot, being an
honest man's son"—or rather "an honest
woman's son";—for indeed my father did
something smack, something grow to, he
had a kind of taste;—well, my conscience
says "Launcelot, budge not." "Budge," says
the fiend. "Budge not," says my conscience.
"Conscience," say I, "you counsel well."
"Fiend," say I, "you counsel well." To be
ruled by my conscience, I should stay with
the Jew my master, who, God bless the
mark! is a kind of devil; and, to run away
from the Jew, I should be ruled by the
fiend, who, saving your reverence! is the
devil himself. Certainly the Jew is the very
devil incarnal; and, in my conscience, my
conscience is but a kind of hard conscience,
to offer to counsel me to stay with the Jew.
The fiend gives the more friendly counsel:
I will run, fiend; my heels are at your
commandment; I will run.
     [*Enter* OLD GOBBO, *with a basket.*]

OLD GOBBO.
Master young man, you, I pray you; which
is the way to Master Jew's?

LAUNCELOT. [*Aside.*]
O heavens! This is my true-begotten
father, who, being more than sand-blind,
high-gravel blind, knows me not: I will try
confusions with him.

OLD GOBBO.
Master young gentleman, I pray you, which
is the way to Master Jew's?

LAUNCELOT.
Turn up on your right hand at the next
turning, but, at the next turning of all, on
your left; marry, at the very next turning,
turn of no hand, but turn down indirectly
to the Jew's house.

OLD GOBBO.
Be God's sonties, 'twill be a hard way to hit.
Can you tell me whether one Launcelot,
that dwells with him, dwell with him or no?

LAUNCELOT.
Talk you of young Master Launcelot?
[*Aside.*] Mark me now; now will I
raise the waters. Talk you of young
Master Launcelot?

OLD GOBBO.
No master, sir, but a poor man's son;
his father, though I say't, is an honest
exceeding poor man, and, God be thanked,
well to live.

LAUNCELOT.
Well, let his father be what a' will, we talk of
young Master Launcelot.

OLD GOBBO.
Your worship's friend, and Launcelot, sir.

LAUNCELOT.
But I pray you, ergo, old man, ergo, I beseech
you, talk you of young Master Launcelot?

OLD GOBBO.
Of Launcelot, an't please your mastership.

LAUNCELOT.
Ergo, Master Launcelot. Talk not of
Master Launcelot, father; for the young
gentleman,—according to Fates and
Destinies and such odd sayings, the Sisters
Three and such branches of learning,—is
indeed deceased; or, as you would say in
plain terms, gone to heaven.

OLD GOBBO.
Marry, God forbid! The boy was the very
staff of my age, my very prop.

LAUNCELOT.
Do I look like a cudgel or a hovel-post, a
staff or a prop? Do you know me, father?

OLD GOBBO.
Alack the day! I know you not, young
gentleman; but I pray you tell me, is my
boy—God rest his soul!—alive or dead?

LAUNCELOT.
Do you not know me, father?

OLD GOBBO.
Alack, sir, I am sand-blind; I know you not.

LAUNCELOT.
Nay, indeed, if you had your eyes, you might
fail of the knowing me: it is a wise father
that knows his own child. Well, old man, I
will tell you news of your son. Give me your
blessing; truth will come to light; murder

cannot be hid long; a man's son may, but in
the end truth will out.

OLD GOBBO.
Pray you, sir, stand up; I am sure you are not
Launcelot, my boy.

LAUNCELOT.
Pray you, let's have no more fooling
about it, but give me your blessing; I am
Launcelot, your boy that was, your son that
is, your child that shall be.

OLD GOBBO.
I cannot think you are my son.

LAUNCELOT.
I know not what I shall think of that; but
I am Launcelot, the Jew's man, and I am
sure Margery your wife is my mother.

OLD GOBBO.
Her name is Margery, indeed: I'll be sworn,
if thou be Launcelot, thou art mine own
flesh and blood. Lord worshipped might he
be, what a beard hast thou got! Thou hast
got more hair on thy chin than Dobbin my
thill-horse has on his tail.

LAUNCELOT.
It should seem, then, that Dobbin's tail
grows backward; I am sure he had more
hair on his tail than I have on my face when
I last saw him.

OLD GOBBO.
Lord! how art thou changed! How dost
thou and thy master agree? I have brought
him a present. How 'gree you now?

LAUNCELOT.
Well, well; but, for mine own part, as I have
set up my rest to run away, so I will not rest
till I have run some ground. My master's
a very Jew. Give him a present! Give him
a halter. I am famished in his service; you
may tell every finger I have with my ribs.
Father, I am glad you are come; give me
your present to one Master Bassanio, who
indeed gives rare new liveries. If I serve
not him, I will run as far as God has any
ground. O rare fortune! Here comes the
man: to him, father; for I am a Jew, if I serve
the Jew any longer.

[*Enter* BASSANIO, *with* LEONARDO, *and
other* FOLLOWERS.]

BASSANIO.
You may do so; but let it be so hasted that
supper be ready at the farthest by five of
the clock. See these letters delivered, put
the liveries to making, and desire Gratiano
to come anon to my lodging.
[*Exit a* SERVANT.]

LAUNCELOT.
To him, father.

OLD GOBBO.
God bless your worship!

BASSANIO.
Gramercy; wouldst thou aught with me?

OLD GOBBO.
Here's my son, sir, a poor boy—

LAUNCELOT.
Not a poor boy, sir, but the rich Jew's
man, that would, sir,—as my father shall
specify—

OLD GOBBO.
He hath a great infection, sir, as one would
say, to serve—

LAUNCELOT.
Indeed the short and the long is, I serve the
Jew, and have a desire, as my father shall
specify—

OLD GOBBO.
His master and he, saving your worship's
reverence, are scarce cater-cousins—

LAUNCELOT.
To be brief, the very truth is that the Jew,
having done me wrong, doth cause me,—as
my father, being I hope an old man, shall
frutify unto you—

OLD GOBBO.
I have here a dish of doves that I would
bestow upon your worship; and my suit is—

LAUNCELOT.
In very brief, the suit is impertinent to
myself, as your worship shall know by
this honest old man; and, though I say it,
though old man, yet poor man, my father.

BASSANIO.
One speak for both. What would you?

LAUNCELOT.
Serve you, sir.

OLD GOBBO.
That is the very defect of the matter, sir.

BASSANIO.
I know thee well; thou hast obtain'd thy
suit.
Shylock thy master spoke with me this day,
And hath preferr'd thee, if it be preferment
To leave a rich Jew's service to become
The follower of so poor a gentleman.

LAUNCELOT.
The old proverb is very well parted between
my master Shylock and you, sir: you have
the grace of God, sir, and he hath enough.

BASSANIO.
Thou speak'st it well. Go, father, with thy
son.
Take leave of thy old master, and inquire
My lodging out. [*To a* SERVANT] Give him
a livery
More guarded than his fellows'; see it
done.

LAUNCELOT.
Father, in. I cannot get a service, no! I have
ne'er a tongue in my head! [*Looking on his
palm.*] Well; if any man in Italy have a
fairer table which doth offer to swear upon
a book, I shall have good fortune. Go to;
here's a simple line of life: here's a small
trifle of wives; alas, fifteen wives is nothing;
a'leven widows and nine maids is a simple
coming-in for one man. And then to 'scape
drowning thrice, and to be in peril of my
life with the edge of a feather-bed; here
are simple 'scapes. Well, if Fortune be a
woman, she's a good wench for this gear.
Father, come; I'll take my leave of the Jew
in the twinkling of an eye.
[*Exeunt* LAUNCELOT *and* OLD GOBBO.]

BASSANIO.
I pray thee, good Leonardo, think on this:
These things being bought and orderly
bestow'd,
Return in haste, for I do feast to-night
My best esteem'd acquaintance; hie thee,
go.

LEONARDO.
My best endeavours shall be done herein.
[*Enter* GRATIANO.]

GRATIANO.
Where's your master?

LEONARDO.
                    Yonder, sir, he walks.
                    [*Exit.*]
GRATIANO.
Signior Bassanio!
BASSANIO.
                    Gratiano!
GRATIANO.
I have suit to you.
BASSANIO.
                    You have obtain'd it.
GRATIANO.
You must not deny me: I must go with you
    to Belmont.
BASSANIO.
Why, then you must. But hear thee,
    Gratiano;
Thou art too wild, too rude, and bold of
    voice;
Parts that become thee happily enough,
And in such eyes as ours appear not
    faults;
But where thou art not known, why there
    they show
Something too liberal. Pray thee, take
    pain
To allay with some cold drops of modesty
Thy skipping spirit, lest through thy wild
    behaviour
I be misconstrued in the place I go to,
And lose my hopes.
GRATIANO.
                Signior Bassanio, hear me:
If I do not put on a sober habit,
Talk with respect, and swear but now and
    then,
Wear prayer-books in my pocket, look
    demurely,
Nay more, while grace is saying, hood
    mine eyes
Thus with my hat, and sigh, and say
    "amen";
Use all the observance of civility,
Like one well studied in a sad ostent
To please his grandam, never trust me
    more.
BASSANIO.
Well, we shall see your bearing.

GRATIANO.
Nay, but I bar to-night; you shall not
    gauge me
By what we do to-night.
BASSANIO.
                        No, that were pity;
I would entreat you rather to put on
Your boldest suit of mirth, for we have
    friends
That purpose merriment. But fare you well;
I have some business.
GRATIANO.
And I must to Lorenzo and the rest;
But we will visit you at supper-time.
                    [*Exeunt.*]

SCENE III
The same. A room in Shylock's house.
[*Enter* JESSICA *and* LAUNCELOT.]
JESSICA.
I am sorry thou wilt leave my father so:
Our house is hell, and thou, a merry devil,
Didst rob it of some taste of tediousness.
But fare thee well; there is a ducat for thee;
And, Launcelot, soon at supper shalt thou
    see
Lorenzo, who is thy new master's guest:
Give him this letter; do it secretly.
And so farewell. I would not have my
    father
See me in talk with thee.
LAUNCELOT.
Adieu! tears exhibit my tongue. Most
beautiful pagan, most sweet Jew! If a
Christian do not play the knave and get
thee, I am much deceived. But, adieu! these
foolish drops do something drown my
manly spirit; adieu!
JESSICA.
Farewell, good Launcelot.
                [*Exit* LAUNCELOT.]
Alack, what heinous sin is it in me
To be asham'd to be my father's child!
But though I am a daughter to his blood,
I am not to his manners. O Lorenzo!
If thou keep promise, I shall end this strife,
Become a Christian and thy loving wife.
                    [*Exit.*]

SCENE IV

The same. A street.

[*Enter* Gratiano, Lorenzo, Salarino, *and* Salanio.]

Lorenzo.
Nay, we will slink away in supper-time,
Disguise us at my lodging, and return
All in an hour.

Gratiano.
We have not made good preparation.

Salarino.
We have not spoke us yet of torch-bearers.

Salanio.
'Tis vile, unless it may be quaintly order'd,
And better in my mind not undertook.

Lorenzo.
'Tis now but four o'clock; we have two hours
To furnish us. [*Enter* Launcelot, *with a letter.*]
Friend Launcelot, what's the news?

Launcelot.
An it shall please you to break up this, it shall seem to signify.

Lorenzo.
I know the hand; in faith, 'tis a fair hand,
And whiter than the paper it writ on
Is the fair hand that writ.

Gratiano.
                    Love news, in faith.

Launcelot.
By your leave, sir.

Lorenzo.
Whither goest thou?

Launcelot.
Marry, sir, to bid my old master, the Jew, to sup to-night with my new master, the Christian.

Lorenzo.
Hold, here, take this. Tell gentle Jessica
I will not fail her; speak it privately.
Go, gentlemen,
                    [*Exit* Launcelot.]
Will you prepare you for this masque to-night?
I am provided of a torch-bearer.

Salarino.
Ay, marry, I'll be gone about it straight.

Salanio.
And so will I.

Lorenzo.
                    Meet me and Gratiano
At Gratiano's lodging some hour hence.

Salarino.
'Tis good we do so.
                    [*Exeunt* Salarino *and* Salanio.]

Gratiano.
Was not that letter from fair Jessica?

Lorenzo.
I must needs tell thee all. She hath directed
How I shall take her from her father's house;
What gold and jewels she is furnish'd with;
What page's suit she hath in readiness.
If e'er the Jew her father come to heaven,
It will be for his gentle daughter's sake;
And never dare misfortune cross her foot,
Unless she do it under this excuse,
That she is issue to a faithless Jew.
Come, go with me, peruse this as thou goest;
Fair Jessica shall be my torch-bearer.
                    [*Exeunt*]

SCENE V

The same. Before Shylock's house.

[*Enter* Shylock *and* Launcelot.]

Shylock.
Well, thou shalt see; thy eyes shall be thy judge,
The difference of old Shylock and Bassanio:—
What, Jessica!—Thou shalt not gormandize,
As thou hast done with me;—What, Jessica!—
And sleep and snore, and rend apparel out—
Why, Jessica, I say!

Launcelot.
                    Why, Jessica!

Shylock.
Who bids thee call? I do not bid thee call.

LAUNCELOT.
Your worship was wont to tell me I could
do nothing without bidding.
                    [*Enter* JESSICA.]
JESSICA.
Call you? What is your will?
SHYLOCK.
I am bid forth to supper, Jessica:
There are my keys. But wherefore should
    I go?
I am not bid for love; they flatter me;
But yet I'll go in hate, to feed upon
The prodigal Christian. Jessica, my girl,
Look to my house. I am right loath to go;
There is some ill a-brewing towards my rest,
For I did dream of money-bags to-night.
LAUNCELOT.
I beseech you, sir, go: my young master
doth expect your reproach.
SHYLOCK.
So do I his.
LAUNCELOT.
And they have conspired together; I will
not say you shall see a masque, but if you
do, then it was not for nothing that my
nose fell a-bleeding on Black Monday last
at six o'clock i' the morning, falling out that
year on Ash-Wednesday was four year in
the afternoon.
SHYLOCK.
What! are there masques? Hear you me,
    Jessica:
Lock up my doors, and when you hear the
    drum,
And the vile squealing of the wry-neck'd
    fife,
Clamber not you up to the casements
    then,
Nor thrust your head into the public street
To gaze on Christian fools with varnish'd
    faces;
But stop my house's ears—I mean my
    casements;
Let not the sound of shallow fopp'ry enter
My sober house. By Jacob's staff, I swear
I have no mind of feasting forth to-night;
But I will go. Go you before me, sirrah;
Say I will come.

LAUNCELOT.
            I will go before, sir.
Mistress, look out at window for all this;
There will come a Christian by
Will be worth a Jewess' eye.
                    [*Exit* LAUNCELOT.]
SHYLOCK.
What says that fool of Hagar's offspring,
    ha?
JESSICA.
His words were "Farewell, mistress";
    nothing else.
SHYLOCK.
The patch is kind enough, but a huge
    feeder;
Snail-slow in profit, and he sleeps by day
More than the wild-cat; drones hive not
    with me,
Therefore I part with him; and part with
    him
To one that I would have him help to waste
His borrow'd purse. Well, Jessica, go in;
Perhaps I will return immediately:
Do as I bid you, shut doors after you:
"Fast bind, fast find,"
A proverb never stale in thrifty mind.
                    [*Exit.*]
JESSICA.
Farewell; and if my fortune be not crost,
I have a father, you a daughter, lost.
                    [*Exit.*]

SCENE VI
The same.
[*Enter* GRATIANO *and* SALARINO,
            masqued.]

GRATIANO.
This is the pent-house under which
    Lorenzo
Desir'd us to make stand.
SALARINO.
                    His hour is
    almost past.
GRATIANO.
And it is marvel he out-dwells his hour,
For lovers ever run before the clock.
SALARINO.
O! ten times faster Venus' pigeons fly

To seal love's bonds new made than they
are wont

To keep obliged faith unforfeited!

GRATIANO.

That ever holds: who riseth from a feast

With that keen appetite that he sits down?

Where is the horse that doth untread
again

His tedious measures with the unbated fire

That he did pace them first? All things
that are

Are with more spirit chased than enjoy'd.

How like a younker or a prodigal

The scarfed bark puts from her native bay,

Hugg'd and embraced by the strumpet
wind!

How like the prodigal doth she return,

With over-weather'd ribs and ragged sails,

Lean, rent, and beggar'd by the strumpet
wind!

SALARINO.

Here comes Lorenzo; more of this
hereafter.

        [Enter LORENZO.*]*

LORENZO.

Sweet friends, your patience for my long
abode;

Not I, but my affairs, have made you wait:

When you shall please to play the thieves
for wives,

I'll watch as long for you then. Approach;

Here dwells my father Jew. Ho! who's
within?

   [Enter JESSICA, *above, in boy's clothes.]*

JESSICA.

Who are you? Tell me, for more certainty,

Albeit I'll swear that I do know your
tongue.

LORENZO.

Lorenzo, and thy love.

JESSICA.

Lorenzo, certain; and my love indeed,

For who love I so much? And now who
knows

But you, Lorenzo, whether I am yours?

LORENZO.

Heaven and thy thoughts are witness that
thou art.

JESSICA.

Here, catch this casket; it is worth the
pains.

I am glad 'tis night, you do not look on me,

For I am much asham'd of my exchange;

But love is blind, and lovers cannot see

The pretty follies that themselves commit,

For, if they could, Cupid himself would
blush

To see me thus transformed to a boy.

LORENZO.

Descend, for you must be my torch-bearer.

JESSICA.

What! must I hold a candle to my shames?

They in themselves, good sooth, are too-
too light.

Why, 'tis an office of discovery, love,

And I should be obscur'd.

LORENZO.

                      So are you, sweet,

Even in the lovely garnish of a boy.

But come at once;

For the close night doth play the runaway,

And we are stay'd for at Bassanio's feast.

JESSICA.

I will make fast the doors, and gild myself

With some moe ducats, and be with you
straight.

        [Exit above.]

GRATIANO.

Now, by my hood, a Gentile, and no Jew.

LORENZO.

Beshrew me, but I love her heartily;

For she is wise, if I can judge of her,

And fair she is, if that mine eyes be true,

And true she is, as she hath prov'd herself;

And therefore, like herself, wise, fair, and
true,

Shall she be placed in my constant soul.

        [Enter JESSICA.*]*

What, art thou come? On, gentlemen,
away!

Our masquing mates by this time for us
stay.

  [Exit with JESSICA *and* SALARINO.*]*

         [Enter ANTONIO.*]*

ANTONIO.

Who's there?

GRATIANO.
        Signior Antonio!
ANTONIO.
Fie, fie, Gratiano! where are all the rest?
'Tis nine o'clock; our friends all stay for
   you.
No masque to-night: the wind is come
   about;
Bassanio presently will go aboard:
I have sent twenty out to seek for you.
GRATIANO.
I am glad on't: I desire no more delight
Than to be under sail and gone to-night.
        [Exeunt.]

SCENE VII

Belmont. A room in Portia's house.
[*Flourish of cornets. Enter* PORTIA, *with the*
PRINCE OF MOROCCO, *and their* TRAINS.]
PORTIA.
Go draw aside the curtains and discover
The several caskets to this noble prince.
Now make your choice.
PRINCE OF MOROCCO.
The first, of gold, who this inscription
   bears:
"Who chooseth me shall gain what many
   men desire."
The second, silver, which this promise
   carries:
"Who chooseth me shall get as much as
   he deserves."
This third, dull lead, with warning all as
   blunt:
"Who chooseth me must give and hazard
   all he hath."
How shall I know if I do choose the right?
PORTIA.
The one of them contains my picture,
   prince;
If you choose that, then I am yours withal.
PRINCE OF MOROCCO.
Some god direct my judgment! Let me
   see;
I will survey the inscriptions back again.
What says this leaden casket?
"Who chooseth me must give and hazard
   all he hath."

Must give: for what? For lead? Hazard
   for lead!
This casket threatens; men that hazard all
Do it in hope of fair advantages:
A golden mind stoops not to shows of
   dross;
I'll then nor give nor hazard aught for lead.
What says the silver with her virgin hue?
"Who chooseth me shall get as much as
   he deserves."
As much as he deserves! Pause there,
   Morocco,
And weigh thy value with an even hand.
If thou be'st rated by thy estimation,
Thou dost deserve enough, and yet enough
May not extend so far as to the lady;
And yet to be afeard of my deserving
Were but a weak disabling of myself.
As much as I deserve! Why, that's the lady:
I do in birth deserve her, and in fortunes,
In graces, and in qualities of breeding;
But more than these, in love I do deserve.
What if I stray'd no farther, but chose
   here?
Let's see once more this saying grav'd in
   gold:
"Who chooseth me shall gain what many
   men desire."
Why, that's the lady: all the world desires
   her;
From the four corners of the earth they
   come,
To kiss this shrine, this mortal-breathing
   saint:
The Hyrcanian deserts and the vasty wilds
Of wide Arabia are as throughfares now
For princes to come view fair Portia:
The watery kingdom, whose ambitious
   head
Spits in the face of heaven, is no bar
To stop the foreign spirits, but they come
As o'er a brook to see fair Portia.
One of these three contains her heavenly
   picture.
Is't like that lead contains her? 'Twere
   damnation
To think so base a thought; it were too
   gross

To rib her cerecloth in the obscure grave.
Or shall I think in silver she's immur'd,
Being ten times undervalu'd to tried gold?
O sinful thought! Never so rich a gem
Was set in worse than gold. They have in
   England
A coin that bears the figure of an angel
Stamped in gold; but that's insculp'd upon;
But here an angel in a golden bed
Lies all within. Deliver me the key;
Here do I choose, and thrive I as I may!

PORTIA.

There, take it, prince, and if my form lie
   there,
Then I am yours.

    [*He unlocks the golden casket.*]

PRINCE OF MOROCCO.

             O hell! what have we here?
A carrion Death, within whose empty eye
There is a written scroll! I'll read the
   writing. [*Reads.*]
   "All that glisters is not gold,
   Often have you heard that told;
   Many a man his life hath sold
   But my outside to behold:
   Gilded tombs do worms infold.
   Had you been as wise as bold,
   Young in limbs, in judgment old,
   Your answer had not been inscroll'd:
   Fare you well, your suit is cold."
Cold indeed; and labour lost:
Then, farewell, heat, and welcome, frost!
Portia, adieu! I have too griev'd a heart
To take a tedious leave; thus losers part.

    [*Exit with his* TRAIN. *Flourish of cornets.*]

PORTIA.

A gentle riddance. Draw the curtains: go.
Let all of his complexion choose me so.

           [*Exeunt.*]

SCENE VIII

Venice. A street.

[*Enter* SALARINO *and* SALANIO.]

SALARINO.

Why, man, I saw Bassanio under sail;
With him is Gratiano gone along;
And in their ship I am sure Lorenzo is
   not.

SALANIO.

The villain Jew with outcries rais'd the
   duke,
Who went with him to search Bassanio's
   ship.

SALARINO.

He came too late, the ship was under sail;
But there the duke was given to
   understand
That in a gondola were seen together
Lorenzo and his amorous Jessica.
Besides, Antonio certified the duke
They were not with Bassanio in his ship.

SALANIO.

I never heard a passion so confus'd,
So strange, outrageous, and so variable,
As the dog Jew did utter in the streets.
"My daughter! O my ducats! O my
   daughter!
Fled with a Christian! O my Christian
   ducats!
Justice! the law! my ducats and my
   daughter!
A sealed bag, two sealed bags of ducats,
Of double ducats, stol'n from me by my
   daughter!
And jewels! two stones, two rich and
   precious stones,
Stol'n by my daughter! Justice! find the
   girl!
She hath the stones upon her and the
   ducats."

SALARINO.

Why, all the boys in Venice follow him,
Crying, his stones, his daughter, and his
   ducats.

SALANIO.

Let good Antonio look he keep his day,
Or he shall pay for this.

SALARINO.

           Marry, well remember'd.
I reason'd with a Frenchman yesterday,
Who told me,—in the narrow seas that
   part
The French and English,—there miscarried
A vessel of our country richly fraught.
I thought upon Antonio when he told me,
And wish'd in silence that it were not his.

SALANIO.
You were best to tell Antonio what you
    hear;
Yet do not suddenly, for it may grieve him.
SALARINO.
A kinder gentleman treads not the earth.
I saw Bassanio and Antonio part:
Bassanio told him he would make some
    speed
Of his return. He answer'd "Do not so;
Slubber not business for my sake, Bassanio,
But stay the very riping of the time;
And for the Jew's bond which he hath
    of me,
Let it not enter in your mind of love:
Be merry, and employ your chiefest
    thoughts
To courtship, and such fair ostents of love
As shall conveniently become you there."
And even there, his eye being big with
    tears,
Turning his face, he put his hand behind
    him,
And with affection wondrous sensible
He wrung Bassanio's hand; and so they
    parted.
SALANIO.
I think he only loves the world for him.
I pray thee, let us go and find him out,
And quicken his embraced heaviness
With some delight or other.
SALARINO.
                                        Do we so.
            [*Exeunt.*]

SCENE IX
Belmont. A room in Portia's house.
    [*Enter* NERISSA, *with a* SERVITOR.]
NERISSA.
Quick, quick, I pray thee, draw the curtain
    straight;
The Prince of Arragon hath ta'en his oath,
And comes to his election presently.
    [*Flourish of cornets. Enter the* PRINCE OF
    ARRAGON, PORTIA, *and their* TRAINS.]
PORTIA.
Behold, there stand the caskets, noble
    prince:

If you choose that wherein I am contain'd,
Straight shall our nuptial rites be
    solemniz'd;
But if you fail, without more speech, my
    lord,
You must be gone from hence
    immediately.
ARRAGON.
I am enjoin'd by oath to observe three
    things:
First, never to unfold to any one
Which casket 'twas I chose; next, if I fail
Of the right casket, never in my life
To woo a maid in way of marriage;
Lastly, if I do fail in fortune of my choice,
Immediately to leave you and be gone.
PORTIA.
To these injunctions every one doth swear
That comes to hazard for my worthless
    self.
ARRAGON.
And so have I address'd me. Fortune now
To my heart's hope! Gold, silver, and base
    lead.
"Who chooseth me must give and hazard
    all he hath."
You shall look fairer ere I give or hazard.
What says the golden chest? Ha! let me
    see:
"Who chooseth me shall gain what many
    men desire."
What many men desire! that "many" may
    be meant
By the fool multitude, that choose by
    show,
Not learning more than the fond eye doth
    teach;
Which pries not to th' interior, but, like
    the martlet,
Builds in the weather on the outward wall,
Even in the force and road of casualty.
I will not choose what many men desire,
Because I will not jump with common
    spirits
And rank me with the barbarous
    multitudes.
Why, then to thee, thou silver treasure-
    house;

Tell me once more what title thou dost
    bear:
"Who chooseth me shall get as much as
    he deserves."
And well said too; for who shall go about
To cozen fortune, and be honourable
Without the stamp of merit? Let none
    presume
To wear an undeserved dignity.
O! that estates, degrees, and offices
Were not deriv'd corruptly, and that clear
    honour
Were purchas'd by the merit of the wearer!
How many then should cover that stand
    bare;
How many be commanded that command;
How much low peasantry would then be
    glean'd
From the true seed of honour; and how
    much honour
Pick'd from the chaff and ruin of the
    times
To be new varnish'd! Well, but to my
    choice:
"Who chooseth me shall get as much as
    he deserves."
I will assume desert. Give me a key for
    this,
And instantly unlock my fortunes here.
       [*He opens the silver casket.*]
PORTIA.
Too long a pause for that which you find
    there.
ARRAGON.
What's here? The portrait of a blinking
    idiot,
Presenting me a schedule! I will read it.
How much unlike art thou to Portia!
How much unlike my hopes and my
    deservings!
"Who chooseth me shall have as much as
    he deserves.'"
Did I deserve no more than a fool's head?
Is that my prize? Are my deserts no
    better?
PORTIA.
To offend, and judge, are distinct offices,
And of opposed natures.

ARRAGON.
                  What is here?
    [*Reads.*]
    "The fire seven times tried this;
    Seven times tried that judgment is
    That did never choose amiss.
    Some there be that shadows kiss;
    Such have but a shadow's bliss;
    There be fools alive, I wis,
    Silver'd o'er, and so was this.
    Take what wife you will to bed,
    I will ever be your head:
    So be gone; you are sped."
Still more fool I shall appear
By the time I linger here;
With one fool's head I came to woo,
But I go away with two.
Sweet, adieu! I'll keep my oath,
Patiently to bear my wroth.
       [*Exit* ARRAGON *with his* TRAIN.]
PORTIA.
Thus hath the candle sing'd the moth.
O, these deliberate fools! When they do
    choose,
They have the wisdom by their wit to
    lose.
NERISSA.
The ancient saying is no heresy:
"Hanging and wiving goes by destiny."
PORTIA.
Come, draw the curtain, Nerissa.
       [*Enter a* SERVANT.]
SERVANT.
Where is my lady?
PORTIA.
           Here; what would my lord?
SERVANT.
Madam, there is alighted at your gate
A young Venetian, one that comes before
To signify th' approaching of his lord;
From whom he bringeth sensible regreets;
To wit, besides commends and courteous
    breath,
Gifts of rich value. Yet I have not seen
So likely an ambassador of love.
A day in April never came so sweet,
To show how costly summer was at hand,
As this fore-spurrer comes before his lord.

Portia.
No more, I pray thee; I am half afeard
Thou wilt say anon he is some kin to thee,
Thou spend'st such high-day wit in
   praising him.
Come, come, Nerissa, for I long to see
Quick Cupid's post that comes so
   mannerly.
Nerissa.
Bassanio, lord Love, if thy will it be!
                              [*Exeunt.*]

ACT III
SCENE I
Venice. A street.
[*Enter* Salanio *and* Salarino.]
Salanio.
Now, what news on the Rialto?
Salarino.
Why, yet it lives there unchecked that
Antonio hath a ship of rich lading wrack'd
on the narrow seas; the Goodwins, I think
they call the place, a very dangerous flat and
fatal, where the carcasses of many a tall ship
lie buried, as they say, if my gossip Report
be an honest woman of her word.
Salanio.
I would she were as lying a gossip in
that as ever knapped ginger or made
her neighbours believe she wept for the
death of a third husband. But it is true,—
without any slips of prolixity or crossing
the plain highway of talk,—that the good
Antonio, the honest Antonio,—O that I
had a title good enough to keep his name
company!—
Salarino.
Come, the full stop.
Salanio.
Ha! What sayest thou? Why, the end is, he
hath lost a ship.
Salarino.
I would it might prove the end of his losses.
Salanio.
Let me say "amen" betimes, lest the devil
cross my prayer, for here he comes in the
likeness of a Jew.
                      [*Enter* Shylock.]

How now, Shylock! What news among the
merchants?
Shylock.
You knew, none so well, none so well as you,
of my daughter's flight.
Salarino.
That's certain; I, for my part, knew the
tailor that made the wings she flew withal.
Salanio.
And Shylock, for his own part, knew
the bird was fledged; and then it is the
complexion of them all to leave the dam.
Shylock.
She is damned for it.
Salarino.
That's certain, if the devil may be her judge.
Shylock.
My own flesh and blood to rebel!
Salanio.
Out upon it, old carrion! Rebels it at these
years?
Shylock.
I say my daughter is my flesh and my blood.
Salarino.
There is more difference between thy flesh
and hers than between jet and ivory; more
between your bloods than there is between
red wine and Rhenish. But tell us, do you
hear whether Antonio have had any loss at
sea or no?
Shylock.
There I have another bad match: a bankrupt,
a prodigal, who dare scarce show his head
on the Rialto; a beggar, that used to come
so smug upon the mart; let him look to his
bond: he was wont to call me usurer; let
him look to his bond: he was wont to lend
money for a Christian courtesy; let him
look to his bond.
Salarino.
Why, I am sure, if he forfeit, thou wilt not
take his flesh: what's that good for?
Shylock.
To bait fish withal: if it will feed nothing
else, it will feed my revenge. He hath
disgrac'd me and hind'red me half a million;
laugh'd at my losses, mock'd at my gains,
scorned my nation, thwarted my bargains,

cooled my friends, heated mine enemies. And what's his reason? I am a Jew. Hath not a Jew eyes? Hath not a Jew hands, organs, dimensions, senses, affections, passions, fed with the same food, hurt with the same weapons, subject to the same diseases, healed by the same means, warmed and cooled by the same winter and summer, as a Christian is? If you prick us, do we not bleed? If you tickle us, do we not laugh? If you poison us, do we not die? And if you wrong us, shall we not revenge? If we are like you in the rest, we will resemble you in that. If a Jew wrong a Christian, what is his humility? Revenge. If a Christian wrong a Jew, what should his sufferance be by Christian example? Why, revenge. The villainy you teach me I will execute; and it shall go hard but I will better the instruction.

[*Enter a* SERVANT.]

SERVANT.

Gentlemen, my master Antonio is at his house, and desires to speak with you both.

SALARINO.

We have been up and down to seek him.

[*Enter* TUBAL.]

SALANIO.

Here comes another of the tribe: a third cannot be match'd, unless the devil himself turn Jew.

[*Exeunt* SALANIO, SALARINO, *and* SERVANT.]

SHYLOCK.

How now, Tubal! what news from Genoa? Hast thou found my daughter?

TUBAL.

I often came where I did hear of her, but cannot find her.

SHYLOCK.

Why there, there, there, there! A diamond gone, cost me two thousand ducats in Frankfort! The curse never fell upon our nation till now; I never felt it till now. Two thousand ducats in that, and other precious, precious jewels. I would my daughter were dead at my foot, and the jewels in her ear; would she were hearsed at my foot, and the ducats in her coffin! No news of them?

Why, so: and I know not what's spent in the search. Why, thou—loss upon loss! The thief gone with so much, and so much to find the thief; and no satisfaction, no revenge; nor no ill luck stirring but what lights on my shoulders; no sighs but of my breathing; no tears but of my shedding.

TUBAL.

Yes, other men have ill luck too. Antonio, as I heard in Genoa,—

SHYLOCK.

What, what, what? Ill luck, ill luck?

TUBAL.

Hath an argosy cast away, coming from Tripolis.

SHYLOCK.

I thank God! I thank God! Is it true, is it true?

TUBAL.

I spoke with some of the sailors that escaped the wrack.

SHYLOCK.

I thank thee, good Tubal. Good news, good news! ha, ha! Where? in Genoa?

TUBAL.

Your daughter spent in Genoa, as I heard, one night, fourscore ducats.

SHYLOCK.

Thou stick'st a dagger in me: I shall never see my gold again: fourscore ducats at a sitting! Fourscore ducats!

TUBAL.

There came divers of Antonio's creditors in my company to Venice that swear he cannot choose but break.

SHYLOCK.

I am very glad of it; I'll plague him, I'll torture him; I am glad of it.

TUBAL.

One of them showed me a ring that he had of your daughter for a monkey.

SHYLOCK.

Out upon her! Thou torturest me, Tubal: It was my turquoise; I had it of Leah when I was a bachelor; I would not have given it for a wilderness of monkeys.

TUBAL.

But Antonio is certainly undone.

SHYLOCK.
Nay, that's true; that's very true. Go, Tubal,
fee me an officer; bespeak him a fortnight
before. I will have the heart of him, if he
forfeit; for, were he out of Venice, I can
make what merchandise I will. Go, Tubal,
and meet me at our synagogue; go, good
Tubal; at our synagogue, Tubal.
                    [*Exeunt.*]

SCENE II

Belmont. A room in Portia's house.
[*Enter* BASSANIO, PORTIA, GRATIANO,
    NERISSA, *and* ATTENDANTS.]
PORTIA.
I pray you tarry; pause a day or two
Before you hazard; for, in choosing wrong,
I lose your company; therefore forbear a
    while.
There's something tells me, but it is not
    love,
I would not lose you; and you know
    yourself
Hate counsels not in such a quality.
But lest you should not understand me
    well,—
And yet a maiden hath no tongue but
    thought,—
I would detain you here some month or
    two
Before you venture for me. I could teach
    you
How to choose right, but then I am
    forsworn;
So will I never be; so may you miss me;
But if you do, you'll make me wish a sin,
That I had been forsworn. Beshrew your
    eyes,
They have o'erlook'd me and divided me:
One half of me is yours, the other half
    yours,
Mine own, I would say; but if mine, then
    yours,
And so all yours. O! these naughty times
Puts bars between the owners and their
    rights;
And so, though yours, not yours. Prove
    it so,

Let fortune go to hell for it, not I.
I speak too long, but 'tis to peise the time,
To eke it, and to draw it out in length,
To stay you from election.
BASSANIO.
                    Let me choose;
For as I am, I live upon the rack.
PORTIA.
Upon the rack, Bassanio! Then confess
What treason there is mingled with your
    love.
BASSANIO.
None but that ugly treason of mistrust,
Which makes me fear th' enjoying of my
    love:
There may as well be amity and life
'Tween snow and fire as treason and my
    love.
PORTIA.
Ay, but I fear you speak upon the rack,
Where men enforced do speak anything.
BASSANIO.
Promise me life, and I'll confess the truth.
PORTIA.
Well then, confess and live.
BASSANIO.
                    "Confess" and "love"
Had been the very sum of my confession:
O happy torment, when my torturer
Doth teach me answers for deliverance!
But let me to my fortune and the caskets.
PORTIA.
Away, then! I am lock'd in one of them:
If you do love me, you will find me out.
Nerissa and the rest, stand all aloof;
Let music sound while he doth make his
    choice;
Then, if he lose, he makes a swan-like end,
Fading in music: that the comparison
May stand more proper, my eye shall be
    the stream
And watery death-bed for him. He may
    win;
And what is music then? Then music is
Even as the flourish when true subjects
    bow
To a new-crowned monarch; such it is
As are those dulcet sounds in break of day

That creep into the dreaming bridegroom's
    ear
And summon him to marriage. Now he
    goes,
With no less presence, but with much
    more love,
Than young Alcides when he did redeem
The virgin tribute paid by howling Troy
To the sea-monster: I stand for sacrifice;
The rest aloof are the Dardanian wives,
With bleared visages come forth to view
The issue of th' exploit. Go, Hercules!
Live thou, I live. With much much more
    dismay
I view the fight than thou that mak'st the
    fray.
      [*A song, whilst* BASSANIO *comments*
          on the caskets to himself.]
    Tell me where is fancy bred,
    Or in the heart or in the head,
    How begot, how nourished?
        Reply, reply.
    It is engendered in the eyes,
    With gazing fed; and fancy dies
    In the cradle where it lies.
        Let us all ring fancy's knell:
        I'll begin it: Ding, dong, bell.
ALL.
    Ding, dong, bell.
BASSANIO.
So may the outward shows be least
    themselves:
The world is still deceiv'd with ornament.
In law, what plea so tainted and corrupt
But, being season'd with a gracious voice,
Obscures the show of evil? In religion,
What damned error but some sober brow
Will bless it, and approve it with a text,
Hiding the grossness with fair ornament?
There is no vice so simple but assumes
Some mark of virtue on his outward parts.
How many cowards, whose hearts are all
    as false
As stairs of sand, wear yet upon their chins
The beards of Hercules and frowning
    Mars;
Who, inward search'd, have livers white
    as milk;

And these assume but valour's excrement
To render them redoubted! Look on
    beauty
And you shall see 'tis purchas'd by the
    weight;
Which therein works a miracle in nature,
Making them lightest that wear most of it:
So are those crisped snaky golden locks
Which make such wanton gambols with
    the wind,
Upon supposed fairness, often known
To be the dowry of a second head,
The skull that bred them, in the sepulchre.
Thus ornament is but the guiled shore
To a most dangerous sea; the beauteous
    scarf
Veiling an Indian beauty; in a word,
The seeming truth which cunning times
    put on
To entrap the wisest. Therefore, thou
    gaudy gold,
Hard food for Midas, I will none of thee;
Nor none of thee, thou pale and common
    drudge
'Tween man and man: but thou, thou
    meagre lead,
Which rather threaten'st than dost
    promise aught,
Thy plainness moves me more than
    eloquence,
And here choose I: joy be the
    consequence!
PORTIA. [*Aside.*]
How all the other passions fleet to air,
As doubtful thoughts, and rash-embrac'd
    despair,
And shuddering fear, and green-ey'd
    jealousy!
O love! be moderate; allay thy ecstasy;
In measure rain thy joy; scant this excess;
I feel too much thy blessing; make it less,
For fear I surfeit!
BASSANIO. [*Opening the leaden casket.*]
              What find I here?
Fair Portia's counterfeit! What demi-god
Hath come so near creation? Move these
    eyes?
Or whether riding on the balls of mine,

Seem they in motion? Here are sever'd
   lips,
Parted with sugar breath; so sweet a bar
Should sunder such sweet friends. Here in
   her hairs
The painter plays the spider, and hath
   woven
A golden mesh t' entrap the hearts of men
Faster than gnats in cobwebs: but her
   eyes!—
How could he see to do them? Having
   made one,
Methinks it should have power to steal
   both his,
And leave itself unfurnish'd: yet look, how
   far
The substance of my praise doth wrong
   this shadow
In underprizing it, so far this shadow
Doth limp behind the substance. Here's
   the scroll,
The continent and summary of my
   fortune.
   "You that choose not by the view,
   Chance as fair and choose as true!
   Since this fortune falls to you,
   Be content and seek no new.
   If you be well pleas'd with this,
   And hold your fortune for your bliss,
   Turn to where your lady is
   And claim her with a loving kiss."
A gentle scroll. Fair lady, by your leave;
         [*Kissing her.*]
I come by note, to give and to receive.
Like one of two contending in a prize,
That thinks he hath done well in people's
   eyes,
Hearing applause and universal shout,
Giddy in spirit, still gazing in a doubt
Whether those peals of praise be his or no;
So, thrice-fair lady, stand I, even so,
As doubtful whether what I see be true,
Until confirm'd, sign'd, ratified by you.
PORTIA.
You see me, Lord Bassanio, where I stand,
Such as I am: though for myself alone
I would not be ambitious in my wish
To wish myself much better, yet for you

I would be trebled twenty times myself,
A thousand times more fair, ten thousand
   times more rich;
That only to stand high in your account,
I might in virtues, beauties, livings, friends,
Exceed account. But the full sum of me
Is sum of something which, to term in
   gross,
Is an unlesson'd girl, unschool'd,
   unpractis'd;
Happy in this, she is not yet so old
But she may learn; happier than this,
She is not bred so dull but she can learn;
Happiest of all is that her gentle spirit
Commits itself to yours to be directed,
As from her lord, her governor, her king.
Myself and what is mine to you and yours
Is now converted. But now I was the lord
Of this fair mansion, master of my
   servants,
Queen o'er myself; and even now, but now,
This house, these servants, and this same
   myself,
Are yours, my lord. I give them with this
   ring,
Which when you part from, lose, or give
   away,
Let it presage the ruin of your love,
And be my vantage to exclaim on you.
BASSANIO.
Madam, you have bereft me of all words,
Only my blood speaks to you in my veins;
And there is such confusion in my powers
As, after some oration fairly spoke
By a beloved prince, there doth appear
Among the buzzing pleased multitude;
Where every something, being blent
   together,
Turns to a wild of nothing, save of joy,
Express'd and not express'd. But when
   this ring
Parts from this finger, then parts life from
   hence:
O! then be bold to say Bassanio's dead.
NERISSA.
My lord and lady, it is now our time,
That have stood by and seen our wishes
   prosper,

To cry, good joy. Good joy, my lord and
    lady!

GRATIANO.

My Lord Bassanio, and my gentle lady,
I wish you all the joy that you can wish;
For I am sure you can wish none from me;
And when your honours mean to solemnize
The bargain of your faith, I do beseech you
Even at that time I may be married too.

BASSANIO.

With all my heart, so thou canst get a wife.

GRATIANO.

I thank your lordship, you have got me
    one.
My eyes, my lord, can look as swift as
    yours:
You saw the mistress, I beheld the maid;
You lov'd, I lov'd; for intermission
No more pertains to me, my lord, than
    you.
Your fortune stood upon the caskets there,
And so did mine too, as the matter falls;
For wooing here until I sweat again,
And swearing till my very roof was dry
With oaths of love, at last, if promise last,
I got a promise of this fair one here
To have her love, provided that your
    fortune
Achiev'd her mistress.

PORTIA.

                      Is this true, Nerissa?

NERISSA.

Madam, it is, so you stand pleas'd withal.

BASSANIO.

And do you, Gratiano, mean good faith?

GRATIANO.

Yes, faith, my lord.

BASSANIO.

Our feast shall be much honour'd in your
marriage.

GRATIANO.

We'll play with them the first boy for a
thousand ducats.

NERISSA.

What! and stake down?

GRATIANO.

No; we shall ne'er win at that sport, and
    stake down.

But who comes here? Lorenzo and his
    infidel?
What, and my old Venetian friend, Salanio!
[*Enter* LORENZO, JESSICA, *and* SALANIO.]

BASSANIO.

Lorenzo and Salanio, welcome hither,
If that the youth of my new interest here
Have power to bid you welcome. By your
    leave,
I bid my very friends and countrymen,
Sweet Portia, welcome.

PORTIA.

So do I, my lord;
They are entirely welcome.

LORENZO.

I thank your honour. For my part, my lord,
My purpose was not to have seen you here;
But meeting with Salanio by the way,
He did entreat me, past all saying nay,
To come with him along.

SALANIO.

                      I did, my lord,
And I have reason for it. Signior Antonio
Commends him to you.
            [*Gives* BASSANIO *a letter.*]

BASSANIO.

                      Ere I ope his letter,
I pray you tell me how my good friend
    doth.

SALANIO.

Not sick, my lord, unless it be in mind;
Nor well, unless in mind; his letter there
Will show you his estate.

GRATIANO.

Nerissa, cheer yon stranger; bid her
    welcome.
Your hand, Salanio. What's the news from
    Venice?
How doth that royal merchant, good
    Antonio?
I know he will be glad of our success:
We are the Jasons, we have won the fleece.

SALANIO.

I would you had won the fleece that he
    hath lost.

PORTIA.

There are some shrewd contents in yon
    same paper.

That steal the colour from Bassanio's
    cheek:
Some dear friend dead, else nothing in
    the world
Could turn so much the constitution
Of any constant man. What, worse and
    worse!
With leave, Bassanio: I am half yourself,
And I must freely have the half of anything
That this same paper brings you.

BASSANIO.

              O sweet Portia!
Here are a few of the unpleasant'st words
That ever blotted paper. Gentle lady,
When I did first impart my love to you,
I freely told you all the wealth I had
Ran in my veins, I was a gentleman;
And then I told you true. And yet, dear
    lady,
Rating myself at nothing, you shall see
How much I was a braggart. When I told
    you
My state was nothing, I should then have
    told you
That I was worse than nothing; for indeed
I have engag'd myself to a dear friend,
Engag'd my friend to his mere enemy,
To feed my means. Here is a letter, lady,
The paper as the body of my friend,
And every word in it a gaping wound
Issuing life-blood. But is it true, Salanio?
Hath all his ventures fail'd? What, not
    one hit?
From Tripolis, from Mexico, and England,
From Lisbon, Barbary, and India?
And not one vessel scape the dreadful
    touch
Of merchant-marring rocks?

SALANIO.

              Not one, my lord.
Besides, it should appear that, if he had
The present money to discharge the Jew,
He would not take it. Never did I know
A creature that did bear the shape of man,
So keen and greedy to confound a man.
He plies the duke at morning and at night,
And doth impeach the freedom of the
    state,

If they deny him justice. Twenty merchants,
The duke himself, and the magnificoes
Of greatest port, have all persuaded with
    him;
But none can drive him from the envious
    plea
Of forfeiture, of justice, and his bond.

JESSICA.

When I was with him, I have heard him
    swear
To Tubal and to Chus, his countrymen,
That he would rather have Antonio's flesh
Than twenty times the value of the sum
That he did owe him; and I know, my lord,
If law, authority, and power, deny not,
It will go hard with poor Antonio.

PORTIA.

Is it your dear friend that is thus in trouble?

BASSANIO.

The dearest friend to me, the kindest man,
The best condition'd and unwearied spirit
In doing courtesies; and one in whom
The ancient Roman honour more appears
Than any that draws breath in Italy.

PORTIA.

What sum owes he the Jew?

BASSANIO.

For me, three thousand ducats.

PORTIA.

              What! no more?
Pay him six thousand, and deface the
    bond;
Double six thousand, and then treble that,
Before a friend of this description
Shall lose a hair through Bassanio's fault.
First go with me to church and call me
    wife,
And then away to Venice to your friend;
For never shall you lie by Portia's side
With an unquiet soul. You shall have gold
To pay the petty debt twenty times over:
When it is paid, bring your true friend
    along.
My maid Nerissa and myself meantime,
Will live as maids and widows. Come,
    away!
For you shall hence upon your wedding
    day.

Bid your friends welcome, show a merry
    cheer;
Since you are dear bought, I will love you
    dear.
But let me hear the letter of your friend.
BASSANIO. [*Reads.*]
"Sweet Bassanio, my ships have all
miscarried, my creditors grow cruel, my
estate is very low, my bond to the Jew
is forfeit; and since, in paying it, it is
impossible I should live, all debts are clear'd
between you and I, if I might but see you
at my death. Notwithstanding, use your
pleasure; if your love do not persuade you
to come, let not my letter."
PORTIA.
O love, dispatch all business and be gone!
BASSANIO.
Since I have your good leave to go away,
I will make haste; but, till I come again,
No bed shall e'er be guilty of my stay,
Nor rest be interposer 'twixt us twain.
          [*Exeunt.*]

SCENE III
Venice. A street.
[*Enter* SHYLOCK, SALARINO, ANTONIO,
and GAOLER.]
SHYLOCK.
Gaoler, look to him. Tell not me of mercy;
This is the fool that lent out money gratis:
Gaoler, look to him.
ANTONIO.
          Hear me yet, good Shylock.
SHYLOCK.
I'll have my bond; speak not against my
    bond.
I have sworn an oath that I will have my
    bond.
Thou call'dst me dog before thou hadst a
    cause,
But, since I am a dog, beware my fangs;
The duke shall grant me justice. I do
    wonder,
Thou naughty gaoler, that thou art so fond
To come abroad with him at his request.
ANTONIO.
I pray thee hear me speak.

SHYLOCK.
I'll have my bond. I will not hear thee
    speak;
I'll have my bond; and therefore speak no
    more.
I'll not be made a soft and dull-eyed fool,
To shake the head, relent, and sigh, and
    yield
To Christian intercessors. Follow not;
I'll have no speaking; I will have my bond.
          [*Exit.*]
SALARINO.
It is the most impenetrable cur
That ever kept with men.
ANTONIO.
          Let him alone;
I'll follow him no more with bootless
    prayers.
He seeks my life; his reason well I know:
I oft deliver'd from his forfeitures
Many that have at times made moan to me;
Therefore he hates me.
SALARINO.
          I am sure the duke
Will never grant this forfeiture to hold.
ANTONIO.
The duke cannot deny the course of law;
For the commodity that strangers have
With us in Venice, if it be denied,
'Twill much impeach the justice of the
    state,
Since that the trade and profit of the city
Consisteth of all nations. Therefore, go;
These griefs and losses have so bated me
That I shall hardly spare a pound of flesh
To-morrow to my bloody creditor.
Well, gaoler, on; pray God Bassanio come
To see me pay his debt, and then I care not.
          [*Exeunt.*]

SCENE IV
Belmont. A room in Portia's house.
[*Enter* PORTIA, NERISSA, LORENZO,
JESSICA, *and* BALTHASAR.]
LORENZO.
Madam, although I speak it in your
    presence,
You have a noble and a true conceit

Of godlike amity, which appears most
   strongly
In bearing thus the absence of your lord.
But if you knew to whom you show this
   honour,
How true a gentleman you send relief,
How dear a lover of my lord your husband,
I know you would be prouder of the work
Than customary bounty can enforce you.

PORTIA.
I never did repent for doing good,
Nor shall not now; for in companions
That do converse and waste the time
   together,
Whose souls do bear an equal yoke of love,
There must be needs a like proportion
Of lineaments, of manners, and of spirit,
Which makes me think that this Antonio,
Being the bosom lover of my lord,
Must needs be like my lord. If it be so,
How little is the cost I have bestowed
In purchasing the semblance of my soul
From out the state of hellish cruelty!
This comes too near the praising of myself;
Therefore, no more of it; hear other things.
Lorenzo, I commit into your hands
The husbandry and manage of my house
Until my lord's return; for mine own part,
I have toward heaven breath'd a secret vow
To live in prayer and contemplation,
Only attended by Nerissa here,
Until her husband and my lord's return.
There is a monastery two miles off,
And there we will abide. I do desire you
Not to deny this imposition,
The which my love and some necessity
Now lays upon you.

LORENZO.
           Madam, with all my heart
I shall obey you in all fair commands.

PORTIA.
My people do already know my mind,
And will acknowledge you and Jessica
In place of Lord Bassanio and myself.
So fare you well till we shall meet again.

LORENZO.
Fair thoughts and happy hours attend on
   you!

JESSICA.
I wish your ladyship all heart's content.

PORTIA.
I thank you for your wish, and am well
   pleas'd
To wish it back on you. Fare you well,
   Jessica.
       [Exeunt JESSICA *and* LORENZO.]
Now, Balthasar,
As I have ever found thee honest-true,
So let me find thee still. Take this same
   letter,
And use thou all th' endeavour of a man
In speed to Padua; see thou render this
Into my cousin's hands, Doctor Bellario;
And look what notes and garments he
   doth give thee,
Bring them, I pray thee, with imagin'd
   speed
Unto the traject, to the common ferry
Which trades to Venice. Waste no time
   in words,
But get thee gone; I shall be there before
   thee.

BALTHASAR.
Madam, I go with all convenient speed.
           [Exit.]

PORTIA.
Come on, Nerissa, I have work in hand
That you yet know not of; we'll see our
   husbands
Before they think of us.

NERISSA.
               Shall they see us?

PORTIA.
They shall, Nerissa; but in such a habit
That they shall think we are accomplished
With that we lack. I'll hold thee any
   wager,
When we are both accoutred like young
   men,
I'll prove the prettier fellow of the two,
And wear my dagger with the braver
   grace,
And speak between the change of man
   and boy
With a reed voice; and turn two mincing
   steps

Into a manly stride; and speak of frays
Like a fine bragging youth; and tell quaint
    lies,
How honourable ladies sought my love,
Which I denying, they fell sick and died;
I could not do withal. Then I'll repent,
And wish for all that, that I had not kill'd
    them.
And twenty of these puny lies I'll tell,
That men shall swear I have discontinu'd
    school
About a twelvemonth. I have within my
    mind
A thousand raw tricks of these bragging
    Jacks,
Which I will practise.

Nerissa.
Why, shall we turn to men?

Portia.
Fie, what a question's that,
If thou wert near a lewd interpreter!
But come, I'll tell thee all my whole device
When I am in my coach, which stays for us
At the park gate; and therefore haste away,
For we must measure twenty miles to-day.

[Exeunt.]

SCENE V

The same. A garden.

[Enter Launcelot *and* Jessica.*]*

Launcelot.
Yes, truly; for, look you, the sins of the
father are to be laid upon the children;
therefore, I promise you, I fear you. I was
always plain with you, and so now I speak
my agitation of the matter; therefore be of
good cheer, for truly I think you are damn'd.
There is but one hope in it that can do you
any good, and that is but a kind of bastard
hope neither.

Jessica.
And what hope is that, I pray thee?

Launcelot.
Marry, you may partly hope that your
father got you not, that you are not the
Jew's daughter.

Jessica.
That were a kind of bastard hope indeed;

so the sins of my mother should be visited
upon me.

Launcelot.
Truly then I fear you are damn'd both
by father and mother; thus when I shun
Scylla, your father, I fall into Charybdis,
your mother; well, you are gone both ways.

Jessica.
I shall be saved by my husband; he hath
made me a Christian.

Launcelot.
Truly, the more to blame he; we were
Christians enow before, e'en as many as
could well live one by another. This making
of Christians will raise the price of hogs;
if we grow all to be pork-eaters, we shall
not shortly have a rasher on the coals for
money.

Jessica.
I'll tell my husband, Launcelot, what you
say; here he comes.

[Enter Lorenzo.*]*

Lorenzo.
I shall grow jealous of you shortly,
Launcelot, if you thus get my wife into
corners.

Jessica.
Nay, you need nor fear us, Lorenzo;
Launcelot and I are out; he tells me flatly
there's no mercy for me in heaven, because
I am a Jew's daughter; and he says you are
no good member of the commonwealth,
for in converting Jews to Christians you
raise the price of pork.

Lorenzo.
I shall answer that better to the
commonwealth than you can the getting
up of the negro's belly; the Moor is with
child by you, Launcelot.

Launcelot.
It is much that the Moor should be more
than reason; but if she be less than an
honest woman, she is indeed more than I
took her for.

Lorenzo.
How every fool can play upon the word!
I think the best grace of wit will shortly
turn into silence, and discourse grow

commendable in none only but parrots. Go
in, sirrah; bid them prepare for dinner.
LAUNCELOT.
That is done, sir; they have all stomachs.
LORENZO.
Goodly Lord, what a wit-snapper are you!
Then bid them prepare dinner.
LAUNCELOT.
That is done too, sir, only "cover" is the
word.
LORENZO.
Will you cover, then, sir?
LAUNCELOT.
Not so, sir, neither; I know my duty.
LORENZO.
Yet more quarrelling with occasion! Wilt
thou show the whole wealth of thy wit in
an instant? I pray thee understand a plain
man in his plain meaning: go to thy fellows,
bid them cover the table, serve in the meat,
and we will come in to dinner.
LAUNCELOT.
For the table, sir, it shall be served in; for
the meat, sir, it shall be covered; for your
coming in to dinner, sir, why, let it be as
humours and conceits shall govern.
                    [*Exit.*]
LORENZO.
O dear discretion, how his words are
    suited!
The fool hath planted in his memory
An army of good words; and I do know
A many fools that stand in better place,
Garnish'd like him, that for a tricksy word
Defy the matter. How cheer'st thou,
    Jessica?
And now, good sweet, say thy opinion,
How dost thou like the Lord Bassanio's
    wife?
JESSICA.
Past all expressing. It is very meet
The Lord Bassanio live an upright life,
For, having such a blessing in his lady,
He finds the joys of heaven here on earth;
And if on earth he do not merit it,
In reason he should never come to heaven.
Why, if two gods should play some
    heavenly match,

And on the wager lay two earthly women,
And Portia one, there must be something
    else
Pawn'd with the other; for the poor rude
    world
Hath not her fellow.
LORENZO.
                    Even such a husband
Hast thou of me as she is for a wife.
JESSICA.
Nay, but ask my opinion too of that.
LORENZO.
I will anon; first let us go to dinner.
JESSICA.
Nay, let me praise you while I have a
    stomach.
LORENZO.
No, pray thee, let it serve for table-talk;
Then howsoe'er thou speak'st, 'mong other
    things
I shall digest it.
JESSICA.
                    Well, I'll set you forth.
                    [*Exeunt.*]

ACT IV
SCENE I
Venice. A court of justice.
[*Enter the* DUKE, *the* MAGNIFICOES,
    ANTONIO, BASSANIO, GRATIANO,
    SALARINO, SALANIO, *and* OTHERS.]
DUKE.
What, is Antonio here?
ANTONIO.
                    Ready, so please
    your Grace.
DUKE.
I am sorry for thee; thou art come to
    answer
A stony adversary, an inhuman wretch,
Uncapable of pity, void and empty
From any dram of mercy.
ANTONIO.
                    I have heard
Your Grace hath ta'en great pains to
    qualify
His rigorous course; but since he stands
    obdurate,

And that no lawful means can carry me
Out of his envy's reach, I do oppose
My patience to his fury, and am arm'd
To suffer with a quietness of spirit
The very tyranny and rage of his.
Duke.
Go one, and call the Jew into the court.
Salarino.
He is ready at the door; he comes, my lord.
                        [*Enter* Shylock.]
Duke.
Make room, and let him stand before our
    face.
Shylock, the world thinks, and I think so
    too,
That thou but leadest this fashion of thy
    malice
To the last hour of act; and then, 'tis
    thought,
Thou'lt show thy mercy and remorse, more
    strange
Than is thy strange apparent cruelty;
And where thou now exacts the penalty,—
Which is a pound of this poor merchant's
    flesh,—
Thou wilt not only loose the forfeiture,
But, touch'd with human gentleness and
    love,
Forgive a moiety of the principal,
Glancing an eye of pity on his losses,
That have of late so huddled on his back,
Enow to press a royal merchant down,
And pluck commiseration of his state
From brassy bosoms and rough hearts of
    flint,
From stubborn Turks and Tartars, never
    train'd
To offices of tender courtesy.
We all expect a gentle answer, Jew.
Shylock.
I have possess'd your Grace of what I
    purpose,
And by our holy Sabbath have I sworn
To have the due and forfeit of my bond.
If you deny it, let the danger light
Upon your charter and your city's freedom.
You'll ask me why I rather choose to have
A weight of carrion flesh than to receive

Three thousand ducats. I'll not answer
    that,
But say it is my humour: is it answer'd?
What if my house be troubled with a rat,
And I be pleas'd to give ten thousand
    ducats
To have it ban'd? What, are you answer'd
    yet?
Some men there are love not a gaping pig;
Some that are mad if they behold a cat;
And others, when the bagpipe sings i' the
    nose,
Cannot contain their urine; for affection,
Mistress of passion, sways it to the mood
Of what it likes or loathes. Now, for your
    answer:
As there is no firm reason to be render'd,
Why he cannot abide a gaping pig;
Why he, a harmless necessary cat;
Why he, a wauling bagpipe; but of force
Must yield to such inevitable shame
As to offend, himself being offended;
So can I give no reason, nor I will not,
More than a lodg'd hate and a certain
    loathing
I bear Antonio, that I follow thus
A losing suit against him. Are you
    answered?
Bassanio.
This is no answer, thou unfeeling man,
To excuse the current of thy cruelty.
Shylock.
I am not bound to please thee with my
    answer.
Bassanio.
Do all men kill the things they do not
    love?
Shylock.
Hates any man the thing he would not
    kill?
Bassanio.
Every offence is not a hate at first.
Shylock.
What! wouldst thou have a serpent sting
    thee twice?
Antonio.
I pray you, think you question with the
    Jew:

You may as well go stand upon the beach,
And bid the main flood bate his usual
    height;
You may as well use question with the
    wolf,
Why he hath made the ewe bleat for the
    lamb;
You may as well forbid the mountain pines
To wag their high tops and to make no
    noise
When they are fretten with the gusts of
    heaven;
You may as well do anything most hard
As seek to soften that—than which what's
    harder?—
His Jewish heart: therefore, I do beseech
    you,
Make no more offers, use no farther
    means,
But with all brief and plain conveniency.
Let me have judgment, and the Jew his
    will.

BASSANIO.
For thy three thousand ducats here is six.

SHYLOCK.
If every ducat in six thousand ducats
Were in six parts, and every part a ducat,
I would not draw them; I would have my
    bond.

DUKE.
How shalt thou hope for mercy, rendering
    none?

SHYLOCK.
What judgment shall I dread, doing no
    wrong?
You have among you many a purchas'd
    slave,
Which, like your asses and your dogs and
    mules,
You use in abject and in slavish parts,
Because you bought them; shall I say to
    you,
"Let them be free, marry them to your
    heirs?
Why sweat they under burdens? let their
    beds
Be made as soft as yours, and let their
    palates

Be season'd with such viands?" You will
    answer,
"The slaves are ours." So do I answer you:
The pound of flesh which I demand of him
Is dearly bought; 'tis mine, and I will have
    it.
If you deny me, fie upon your law!
There is no force in the decrees of Venice.
I stand for judgment: answer; shall I have
    it?

DUKE.
Upon my power I may dismiss this court,
Unless Bellario, a learned doctor,
Whom I have sent for to determine this,
Come here to-day.

SALARINO.
                My lord, here stays without
A messenger with letters from the doctor,
New come from Padua.

DUKE.
Bring us the letters; call the messenger.

BASSANIO.
Good cheer, Antonio! What, man, courage
    yet!
The Jew shall have my flesh, blood, bones,
    and all,
Ere thou shalt lose for me one drop of
    blood.

ANTONIO.
I am a tainted wether of the flock,
Meetest for death; the weakest kind of
    fruit
Drops earliest to the ground, and so let me.
You cannot better be employ'd, Bassanio,
Than to live still, and write mine epitaph.
[*Enter* NERISSA *dressed like a lawyer's clerk.*]

DUKE.
Came you from Padua, from Bellario?

NERISSA.
From both, my lord. Bellario greets your
    Grace.
                [*Presents a letter.*]

BASSANIO.
Why dost thou whet thy knife so
    earnestly?

SHYLOCK.
To cut the forfeiture from that bankrupt
    there.

GRATIANO.
Not on thy sole, but on thy soul, harsh Jew,
Thou mak'st thy knife keen; but no metal
    can,
No, not the hangman's axe, bear half the
    keenness
Of thy sharp envy. Can no prayers pierce
    thee?
SHYLOCK.
No, none that thou hast wit enough to
    make.
GRATIANO.
O, be thou damn'd, inexecrable dog!
And for thy life let justice be accus'd.
Thou almost mak'st me waver in my faith,
To hold opinion with Pythagoras
That souls of animals infuse themselves
Into the trunks of men. Thy currish spirit
Govern'd a wolf who, hang'd for human
    slaughter,
Even from the gallows did his fell soul
    fleet,
And, whilst thou lay'st in thy unhallow'd
    dam,
Infus'd itself in thee; for thy desires
Are wolfish, bloody, starv'd and ravenous.
SHYLOCK.
Till thou canst rail the seal from off my
    bond,
Thou but offend'st thy lungs to speak so
    loud;
Repair thy wit, good youth, or it will fall
To cureless ruin. I stand here for law.
DUKE.
This letter from Bellario doth commend
A young and learned doctor to our court.
Where is he?
NERISSA.
                He attendeth here hard by,
To know your answer, whether you'll
    admit him.
DUKE OF VENICE.
With all my heart: some three or four of
    you
Go give him courteous conduct to this
    place.
Meantime, the court shall hear Bellario's
    letter.

CLERK. [*Reads.*]
"Your Grace shall understand that at the
receipt of your letter I am very sick; but
in the instant that your messenger came,
in loving visitation was with me a young
doctor of Rome; his name is Balthazar.
I acquainted him with the cause in
controversy between the Jew and Antonio
the merchant; we turn'd o'er many books
together; he is furnished with my opinion
which, bettered with his own learning,—
the greatness whereof I cannot enough
commend,—comes with him at my
importunity to fill up your Grace's request
in my stead. I beseech you let his lack of
years be no impediment to let him lack a
reverend estimation, for I never knew so
young a body with so old a head. I leave him
to your gracious acceptance, whose trial
shall better publish his commendation."
DUKE.
You hear the learn'd Bellario, what he
    writes;
And here, I take it, is the doctor come.
[*Enter* PORTIA, *dressed like a doctor of laws.*]
Give me your hand; come you from old
    Bellario?
PORTIA.
I did, my lord.
DUKE.
                You are welcome; take your place.
Are you acquainted with the difference
That holds this present question in the
    court?
PORTIA.
I am informed throughly of the cause.
Which is the merchant here, and which
    the Jew?
DUKE OF VENICE.
Antonio and old Shylock, both stand forth.
PORTIA.
Is your name Shylock?
SHYLOCK.
                Shylock is my name.
PORTIA.
Of a strange nature is the suit you follow;
Yet in such rule that the Venetian law
Cannot impugn you as you do proceed.

[*To* ANTONIO.] You stand within his
    danger, do you not?

ANTONIO.
Ay, so he says.

PORTIA.
                    Do you confess the bond?

ANTONIO.
I do.

PORTIA.
    Then must the Jew be merciful.

SHYLOCK.
On what compulsion must I? Tell me that.

PORTIA.
The quality of mercy is not strain'd;
It droppeth as the gentle rain from heaven
Upon the place beneath. It is twice blest:
It blesseth him that gives and him that
    takes.
'Tis mightiest in the mightiest; it becomes
The throned monarch better than his
    crown;
His sceptre shows the force of temporal
    power,
The attribute to awe and majesty,
Wherein doth sit the dread and fear of
    kings;
But mercy is above this sceptred sway,
It is enthroned in the hearts of kings,
It is an attribute to God himself;
And earthly power doth then show likest
    God's
When mercy seasons justice. Therefore,
    Jew,
Though justice be thy plea, consider this,
That in the course of justice none of us
Should see salvation; we do pray for mercy,
And that same prayer doth teach us all to
    render
The deeds of mercy. I have spoke thus
    much
To mitigate the justice of thy plea,
Which if thou follow, this strict court of
    Venice
Must needs give sentence 'gainst the
    merchant there.

SHYLOCK.
My deeds upon my head! I crave the law,
The penalty and forfeit of my bond.

PORTIA.
Is he not able to discharge the money?

BASSANIO.
Yes; here I tender it for him in the court;
Yea, twice the sum; if that will not suffice,
I will be bound to pay it ten times o'er
On forfeit of my hands, my head, my
    heart;
If this will not suffice, it must appear
That malice bears down truth. And, I
    beseech you,
Wrest once the law to your authority;
To do a great right do a little wrong,
And curb this cruel devil of his will.

PORTIA.
It must not be; there is no power in Venice
Can alter a decree established;
'Twill be recorded for a precedent,
And many an error by the same example
Will rush into the state. It cannot be.

SHYLOCK.
A Daniel come to judgment! Yea, a
    Daniel!
O wise young judge, how I do honour
    thee!

PORTIA.
I pray you, let me look upon the bond.

SHYLOCK.
Here 'tis, most reverend doctor; here it is.

PORTIA.
Shylock, there's thrice thy money offer'd
    thee.

SHYLOCK.
An oath, an oath! I have an oath in
    heaven.
Shall I lay perjury upon my soul?
No, not for Venice.

PORTIA.
                    Why, this bond is forfeit;
And lawfully by this the Jew may claim
A pound of flesh, to be by him cut off
Nearest the merchant's heart. Be merciful.
Take thrice thy money; bid me tear the
    bond.

SHYLOCK.
When it is paid according to the tenour.
It doth appear you are a worthy judge;
You know the law; your exposition

Hath been most sound; I charge you by
    the law,
Whereof you are a well-deserving pillar,
Proceed to judgment. By my soul I swear
There is no power in the tongue of man
To alter me. I stay here on my bond.
ANTONIO.
Most heartily I do beseech the court
To give the judgment.
PORTIA.
               Why then, thus it is:
You must prepare your bosom for his
    knife.
SHYLOCK.
O noble judge! O excellent young man!
PORTIA.
For the intent and purpose of the law
Hath full relation to the penalty,
Which here appeareth due upon the
    bond.
SHYLOCK.
'Tis very true. O wise and upright judge,
How much more elder art thou than thy
    looks!
PORTIA.
Therefore, lay bare your bosom.
SHYLOCK.
             Ay, "his breast":
So says the bond: doth it not, noble judge?
"Nearest his heart": those are the very
    words.
PORTIA.
It is so. Are there balance here to weigh
The flesh?
SHYLOCK.
I have them ready.
PORTIA.
Have by some surgeon, Shylock, on your
    charge,
To stop his wounds, lest he do bleed to
    death.
SHYLOCK.
Is it so nominated in the bond?
PORTIA.
It is not so express'd; but what of that?
'Twere good you do so much for charity.
SHYLOCK.
I cannot find it; 'tis not in the bond.

PORTIA.
You, merchant, have you anything to say?
ANTONIO.
But little: I am arm'd and well prepar'd.
Give me your hand, Bassanio: fare you
    well!
Grieve not that I am fallen to this for you,
For herein Fortune shows herself more
    kind
Than is her custom: it is still her use
To let the wretched man outlive his
    wealth,
To view with hollow eye and wrinkled brow
An age of poverty; from which lingering
    penance
Of such misery doth she cut me off.
Commend me to your honourable wife:
Tell her the process of Antonio's end;
Say how I lov'd you; speak me fair in
    death;
And, when the tale is told, bid her be
    judge
Whether Bassanio had not once a love.
Repent but you that you shall lose your
    friend,
And he repents not that he pays your debt;
For if the Jew do cut but deep enough,
I'll pay it instantly with all my heart.
BASSANIO.
Antonio, I am married to a wife
Which is as dear to me as life itself;
But life itself, my wife, and all the world,
Are not with me esteem'd above thy life;
I would lose all, ay, sacrifice them all
Here to this devil, to deliver you.
PORTIA.
Your wife would give you little thanks for
    that,
If she were by to hear you make the offer.
GRATIANO.
I have a wife whom, I protest, I love;
I would she were in heaven, so she could
Entreat some power to change this currish
    Jew.
NERISSA.
'Tis well you offer it behind her back;
The wish would make else an unquiet
    house.

SHYLOCK.
These be the Christian husbands! I have a
    daughter;
Would any of the stock of Barabbas
Had been her husband, rather than a
    Christian!
We trifle time; I pray thee, pursue sentence.

PORTIA.
A pound of that same merchant's flesh is
    thine.
The court awards it and the law doth give it.

SHYLOCK.
Most rightful judge!

PORTIA.
And you must cut this flesh from off his
    breast.
The law allows it and the court awards it.

SHYLOCK.
Most learned judge! A sentence! Come,
    prepare.

PORTIA.
Tarry a little; there is something else.
This bond doth give thee here no jot of
    blood;
The words expressly are "a pound of flesh":
Take then thy bond, take thou thy pound
    of flesh;
But, in the cutting it, if thou dost shed
One drop of Christian blood, thy lands
    and goods
Are, by the laws of Venice, confiscate
Unto the state of Venice.

GRATIANO.
               O upright judge!
Mark, Jew: O learned judge!

SHYLOCK.
Is that the law?

PORTIA.
Thyself shalt see the act;
For, as thou urgest justice, be assur'd
Thou shalt have justice, more than thou
    desir'st.

GRATIANO.
O learned judge! Mark, Jew:—a learned
    judge!

SHYLOCK.
I take this offer then: pay the bond thrice,
And let the Christian go.

BASSANIO.
               Here is the money.

PORTIA.
Soft! The Jew shall have all justice; soft!
    no haste:—
He shall have nothing but the penalty.

GRATIANO.
O Jew! an upright judge, a learned judge!

PORTIA.
Therefore, prepare thee to cut off the flesh.
Shed thou no blood; nor cut thou less nor
    more,
But just a pound of flesh: if thou tak'st
    more,
Or less, than a just pound, be it but so
    much
As makes it light or heavy in the substance,
Or the division of the twentieth part
Of one poor scruple; nay, if the scale do
    turn
But in the estimation of a hair,
Thou diest, and all thy goods are
    confiscate.

GRATIANO.
A second Daniel, a Daniel, Jew!
Now, infidel, I have you on the hip.

PORTIA.
Why doth the Jew pause? Take thy
    forfeiture.

SHYLOCK.
Give me my principal, and let me go.

BASSANIO.
I have it ready for thee; here it is.

PORTIA.
He hath refus'd it in the open court;
He shall have merely justice, and his bond.

GRATIANO.
A Daniel still say I; a second Daniel!
I thank thee, Jew, for teaching me that
    word.

SHYLOCK.
Shall I not have barely my principal?

PORTIA.
Thou shalt have nothing but the forfeiture
To be so taken at thy peril, Jew.

SHYLOCK.
Why, then the devil give him good of it!
I'll stay no longer question.

PORTIA.
                                Tarry, Jew.
The law hath yet another hold on you.
It is enacted in the laws of Venice,
If it be prov'd against an alien
That by direct or indirect attempts
He seek the life of any citizen,
The party 'gainst the which he doth contrive
Shall seize one half his goods; the other
    half
Comes to the privy coffer of the state;
And the offender's life lies in the mercy
Of the duke only, 'gainst all other voice.
In which predicament, I say, thou stand'st;
For it appears by manifest proceeding
That indirectly, and directly too,
Thou hast contrived against the very life
Of the defendant; and thou hast incurr'd
The danger formerly by me rehears'd.
Down, therefore, and beg mercy of the
    duke.

GRATIANO.
Beg that thou mayst have leave to hang
    thyself;
And yet, thy wealth being forfeit to the
    state,
Thou hast not left the value of a cord;
Therefore thou must be hang'd at the
    state's charge.

DUKE.
That thou shalt see the difference of our
    spirits,
I pardon thee thy life before thou ask it.
For half thy wealth, it is Antonio's;
The other half comes to the general state,
Which humbleness may drive unto a fine.

PORTIA.
Ay, for the state; not for Antonio.

SHYLOCK.
Nay, take my life and all, pardon not that:
You take my house when you do take the
    prop
That doth sustain my house; you take my
    life
When you do take the means whereby I
    live.

PORTIA.
What mercy can you render him, Antonio?

GRATIANO.
A halter gratis; nothing else, for God's
    sake!

ANTONIO.
So please my lord the duke and all the
    court
To quit the fine for one half of his goods;
I am content, so he will let me have
The other half in use, to render it
Upon his death unto the gentleman
That lately stole his daughter:
Two things provided more, that, for this
    favour,
He presently become a Christian;
The other, that he do record a gift,
Here in the court, of all he dies possess'd
Unto his son Lorenzo and his daughter.

DUKE.
He shall do this, or else I do recant
The pardon that I late pronounced here.

PORTIA.
Art thou contented, Jew? What dost thou
    say?

SHYLOCK.
I am content.

PORTIA.
Clerk, draw a deed of gift.

SHYLOCK.
I pray you, give me leave to go from
    hence;
I am not well; send the deed after me
And I will sign it.

DUKE.
                            Get thee gone, but do it.

GRATIANO.
In christening shalt thou have two god-
    fathers;
Had I been judge, thou shouldst have had
    ten more,
To bring thee to the gallows, not to the
    font.
                        [*Exit* SHYLOCK.]

DUKE.
Sir, I entreat you home with me to dinner.

PORTIA.
I humbly do desire your Grace of pardon;
I must away this night toward Padua,
And it is meet I presently set forth.

DUKE.

I am sorry that your leisure serves you not.
Antonio, gratify this gentleman,
For in my mind you are much bound to
    him.

[*Exeunt* DUKE, MAGNIFICOES, *and* TRAIN.]

BASSANIO.

Most worthy gentleman, I and my friend
Have by your wisdom been this day
    acquitted
Of grievous penalties; in lieu whereof
Three thousand ducats, due unto the Jew,
We freely cope your courteous pains withal.

ANTONIO.

And stand indebted, over and above,
In love and service to you evermore.

PORTIA.

He is well paid that is well satisfied;
And I, delivering you, am satisfied,
And therein do account myself well paid:
My mind was never yet more mercenary.
I pray you, know me when we meet again:
I wish you well, and so I take my leave.

BASSANIO.

Dear sir, of force I must attempt you
    further;
Take some remembrance of us, as a tribute,
Not as fee. Grant me two things, I pray
    you,
Not to deny me, and to pardon me.

PORTIA.

You press me far, and therefore I will yield.
[*To* ANTONIO.] Give me your gloves, I'll
    wear them for your sake.
[*To* BASSANIO.] And, for your love, I'll take
    this ring from you.
Do not draw back your hand; I'll take no
    more;
And you in love shall not deny me this.

BASSANIO.

This ring, good sir? alas, it is a trifle;
I will not shame myself to give you this.

PORTIA.

I will have nothing else but only this;
And now, methinks, I have a mind to it.

BASSANIO.

There's more depends on this than on the
    value.

The dearest ring in Venice will I give you,
And find it out by proclamation:
Only for this, I pray you, pardon me.

PORTIA.

I see, sir, you are liberal in offers;
You taught me first to beg, and now
    methinks
You teach me how a beggar should be
    answer'd.

BASSANIO.

Good sir, this ring was given me by my
    wife;
And, when she put it on, she made me vow
That I should neither sell, nor give, nor
    lose it.

PORTIA.

That 'scuse serves many men to save their
    gifts.
And if your wife be not a mad-woman,
And know how well I have deserv'd this
    ring,
She would not hold out enemy for ever
For giving it to me. Well, peace be with
    you!

[*Exeunt* PORTIA *and* NERISSA.]

ANTONIO.

My Lord Bassanio, let him have the ring:
Let his deservings, and my love withal,
Be valued 'gainst your wife's
    commandment.

BASSANIO.

Go, Gratiano, run and overtake him;
Give him the ring, and bring him, if thou
    canst,
Unto Antonio's house. Away! make haste.
[*Exit* GRATIANO.]
Come, you and I will thither presently;
And in the morning early will we both
Fly toward Belmont. Come, Antonio.
[*Exeunt.*]

SCENE II

The same. A street.

[*Enter* PORTIA *and* NERISSA.]

PORTIA.

Inquire the Jew's house out, give him this
    deed,
And let him sign it; we'll away tonight,

And be a day before our husbands home.
This deed will be well welcome to
   Lorenzo.
        [Enter GRATIANO.*]*
GRATIANO.
Fair sir, you are well o'erta'en.
My Lord Bassanio, upon more advice,
Hath sent you here this ring, and doth
   entreat
Your company at dinner.
PORTIA.
            That cannot be:
His ring I do accept most thankfully;
And so, I pray you, tell him: furthermore,
I pray you show my youth old Shylock's
   house.
GRATIANO.
That will I do.
NERISSA.
         Sir, I would speak with you.
[Aside to PORTIA.*]* I'll see if I can get my
   husband's ring,
Which I did make him swear to keep for
   ever.
PORTIA. *[To* NERISSA.*]*
Thou mayst, I warrant. We shall have old
   swearing
That they did give the rings away to men;
But we'll outface them, and outswear
   them too.
Away! make haste: thou know'st where I
   will tarry.
NERISSA.
Come, good sir, will you show me to this
   house?
             [Exeunt.]

ACT V
SCENE I
Belmont. The avenue to Portia's house.
  [Enter LORENZO *and* JESSICA.*]*
LORENZO.
The moon shines bright: in such a night
   as this,
When the sweet wind did gently kiss the
   trees,
And they did make no noise, in such a
   night,

Troilus methinks mounted the Troyan
   walls,
And sigh'd his soul toward the Grecian
   tents,
Where Cressid lay that night.
JESSICA.
            In such a night
Did Thisby fearfully o'ertrip the dew,
And saw the lion's shadow ere himself,
And ran dismay'd away.
LORENZO.
            In such a night
Stood Dido with a willow in her hand
Upon the wild sea-banks, and waft her
   love
To come again to Carthage.
JESSICA.
            In such a night
Medea gather'd the enchanted herbs
That did renew old Aeson.
LORENZO.
            In such a night
Did Jessica steal from the wealthy Jew,
And with an unthrift love did run from
   Venice
As far as Belmont.
JESSICA.
            In such a night
Did young Lorenzo swear he lov'd her
   well,
Stealing her soul with many vows of
   faith,—
And ne'er a true one.
LORENZO.
            In such a night
Did pretty Jessica, like a little shrew,
Slander her love, and he forgave it her.
JESSICA.
I would out-night you, did no body come;
But, hark, I hear the footing of a man.
          [Enter STEPHANO.*]*
LORENZO.
Who comes so fast in silence of the night?
STEPHANO.
A friend.
LORENZO.
A friend! What friend? Your name, I pray
   you, friend?

STEPHANO.
Stephano is my name, and I bring word
My mistress will before the break of day
Be here at Belmont; she doth stray about
By holy crosses, where she kneels and
   prays
For happy wedlock hours.

LORENZO.
               Who comes with her?

STEPHANO.
None but a holy hermit and her maid.
I pray you, is my master yet return'd?

LORENZO.
He is not, nor we have not heard from
   him.
But go we in, I pray thee, Jessica,
And ceremoniously let us prepare
Some welcome for the mistress of the
   house.
           [Enter LAUNCELOT.*]*

LAUNCELOT.
Sola, sola! wo ha, ho! sola, sola!

LORENZO.
Who calls?

LAUNCELOT.
Sola! Did you see Master Lorenzo? Master
Lorenzo! Sola, sola!

LORENZO.
Leave holloaing, man. Here!

LAUNCELOT.
Sola! Where? where?

LORENZO.
Here!

LAUNCELOT.
Tell him there's a post come from my
master with his horn full of good news; my
master will be here ere morning.
           [Exit.]

LORENZO.
Sweet soul, let's in, and there expect their
   coming.
And yet no matter; why should we go in?
My friend Stephano, signify, I pray you,
Within the house, your mistress is at hand;
And bring your music forth into the air.
         [Exit STEPHANO.*]*
How sweet the moonlight sleeps upon
   this bank!

Here will we sit and let the sounds of
   music
Creep in our ears; soft stillness and the
   night
Become the touches of sweet harmony.
Sit, Jessica: look how the floor of heaven
Is thick inlaid with patines of bright gold;
There's not the smallest orb which thou
   behold'st
But in his motion like an angel sings,
Still quiring to the young-eyed cherubins;
Such harmony is in immortal souls;
But, whilst this muddy vesture of decay
Doth grossly close it in, we cannot hear it.
         [Enter MUSICIANS.*]*
Come, ho! and wake Diana with a hymn;
With sweetest touches pierce your
   mistress' ear.
And draw her home with music.
               [Music.]

JESSICA.
I am never merry when I hear sweet
   music.

LORENZO.
The reason is, your spirits are attentive;
For do but note a wild and wanton herd,
Or race of youthful and unhandled colts,
Fetching mad bounds, bellowing and
   neighing loud,
Which is the hot condition of their blood;
If they but hear perchance a trumpet
   sound,
Or any air of music touch their ears,
You shall perceive them make a mutual
   stand,
Their savage eyes turn'd to a modest gaze
By the sweet power of music: therefore
   the poet
Did feign that Orpheus drew trees, stones,
   and floods;
Since nought so stockish, hard, and full
   of rage,
But music for the time doth change his
   nature.
The man that hath no music in himself,
Nor is not mov'd with concord of sweet
   sounds,
Is fit for treasons, stratagems, and spoils;

The motions of his spirit are dull as night,
And his affections dark as Erebus.
Let no such man be trusted. Mark the
    music.
[*Enter* PORTIA *and* NERISSA, *at a distance.*]

PORTIA.
That light we see is burning in my hall.
How far that little candle throws his beams!
So shines a good deed in a naughty world.

NERISSA.
When the moon shone, we did not see the
    candle.

PORTIA.
So doth the greater glory dim the less:
A substitute shines brightly as a king
Until a king be by, and then his state
Empties itself, as doth an inland brook
Into the main of waters. Music! hark!

NERISSA.
It is your music, madam, of the house.

PORTIA.
Nothing is good, I see, without respect:
Methinks it sounds much sweeter than
    by day.

NERISSA.
Silence bestows that virtue on it, madam.

PORTIA.
The crow doth sing as sweetly as the lark
When neither is attended; and I think
The nightingale, if she should sing by day,
When every goose is cackling, would be
    thought
No better a musician than the wren.
How many things by season season'd are
To their right praise and true perfection!
Peace, ho! The moon sleeps with
    Endymion,
And would not be awak'd!
           [*Music ceases.*]

LORENZO.
                That is the voice,
Or I am much deceiv'd, of Portia.

PORTIA.
He knows me as the blind man knows the
    cuckoo,
By the bad voice.

LORENZO.
           Dear lady, welcome home.

PORTIA.
We have been praying for our husbands'
    welfare,
Which speed, we hope, the better for our
    words.
Are they return'd?

LORENZO.
          Madam, they are not yet;
But there is come a messenger before,
To signify their coming.

PORTIA.
             Go in, Nerissa:
Give order to my servants that they take
No note at all of our being absent hence;
Nor you, Lorenzo; Jessica, nor you.
           [*A tucket sounds.*]

LORENZO.
Your husband is at hand; I hear his
    trumpet.
We are no tell-tales, madam, fear you not.

PORTIA.
This night methinks is but the daylight
    sick;
It looks a little paler; 'tis a day
Such as the day is when the sun is hid.
[*Enter* BASSANIO, ANTONIO, GRATIANO,
           and their FOLLOWERS.]

BASSANIO.
We should hold day with the Antipodes,
If you would walk in absence of the sun.

PORTIA.
Let me give light, but let me not be light,
For a light wife doth make a heavy
    husband,
And never be Bassanio so for me:
But God sort all! You are welcome home,
    my lord.

BASSANIO.
I thank you, madam; give welcome to my
    friend:
This is the man, this is Antonio,
To whom I am so infinitely bound.

PORTIA.
You should in all sense be much bound
    to him,
For, as I hear, he was much bound for you.

ANTONIO.
No more than I am well acquitted of.

PORTIA.
Sir, you are very welcome to our house.
It must appear in other ways than words,
Therefore I scant this breathing courtesy.
GRATIANO. [*To* NERISSA.]
By yonder moon I swear you do me
 wrong;
In faith, I gave it to the judge's clerk.
Would he were gelt that had it, for my
 part,
Since you do take it, love, so much at
 heart.
PORTIA.
A quarrel, ho, already! What's the matter?
GRATIANO.
About a hoop of gold, a paltry ring
That she did give me, whose posy was
For all the world like cutlers' poetry
Upon a knife, "Love me, and leave me
 not."
NERISSA.
What talk you of the posy, or the value?
You swore to me, when I did give it you,
That you would wear it till your hour of
 death,
And that it should lie with you in your
 grave;
Though not for me, yet for your vehement
 oaths,
You should have been respective and have
 kept it.
Gave it a judge's clerk! No, God's my
 judge,
The clerk will ne'er wear hair on's face that
 had it.
GRATIANO.
He will, an if he live to be a man.
NERISSA.
Ay, if a woman live to be a man.
GRATIANO.
Now, by this hand, I gave it to a youth,
A kind of boy, a little scrubbed boy
No higher than thyself, the judge's clerk;
A prating boy that begg'd it as a fee;
I could not for my heart deny it him.
PORTIA.
You were to blame,—I must be plain with
 you,—

To part so slightly with your wife's first
 gift,
A thing stuck on with oaths upon your
 finger,
And so riveted with faith unto your flesh.
I gave my love a ring, and made him swear
Never to part with it, and here he stands,
I dare be sworn for him he would not
 leave it
Nor pluck it from his finger for the wealth
That the world masters. Now, in faith,
 Gratiano,
You give your wife too unkind a cause of
 grief;
An 'twere to me, I should be mad at it.
BASSANIO. [*Aside.*]
Why, I were best to cut my left hand off,
And swear I lost the ring defending it.
GRATIANO.
My Lord Bassanio gave his ring away
Unto the judge that begg'd it, and indeed
Deserv'd it too; and then the boy, his clerk,
That took some pains in writing, he begg'd
 mine;
And neither man nor master would take
 aught
But the two rings.
PORTIA.
                    What ring gave you, my lord?
Not that, I hope, which you receiv'd of me.
BASSANIO.
If I could add a lie unto a fault,
I would deny it; but you see my finger
Hath not the ring upon it; it is gone.
PORTIA.
Even so void is your false heart of truth;
By heaven, I will ne'er come in your bed
Until I see the ring.
NERISSA.
                    Nor I in yours
Till I again see mine.
BASSANIO.
                    Sweet Portia,
If you did know to whom I gave the ring,
If you did know for whom I gave the ring,
And would conceive for what I gave the
 ring,
And how unwillingly I left the ring,

When nought would be accepted but the
    ring,
You would abate the strength of your
    displeasure.

PORTIA.
If you had known the virtue of the ring,
Or half her worthiness that gave the ring,
Or your own honour to contain the ring,
You would not then have parted with the
    ring.
What man is there so much unreasonable,
If you had pleas'd to have defended it
With any terms of zeal, wanted the
    modesty
To urge the thing held as a ceremony?
Nerissa teaches me what to believe:
I'll die for't but some woman had the ring.

BASSANIO.
No, by my honour, madam, by my soul,
No woman had it, but a civil doctor,
Which did refuse three thousand ducats
    of me,
And begg'd the ring; the which I did deny
    him,
And suffer'd him to go displeas'd away;
Even he that had held up the very life
Of my dear friend. What should I say,
    sweet lady?
I was enforc'd to send it after him;
I was beset with shame and courtesy;
My honour would not let ingratitude
So much besmear it. Pardon me, good lady;
For, by these blessed candles of the night,
Had you been there, I think you would
    have begg'd
The ring of me to give the worthy doctor.

PORTIA.
Let not that doctor e'er come near my
    house;
Since he hath got the jewel that I loved,
And that which you did swear to keep
    for me,
I will become as liberal as you;
I'll not deny him anything I have,
No, not my body, nor my husband's bed.
Know him I shall, I am well sure of it.
Lie not a night from home; watch me like
    Argus;

If you do not, if I be left alone,
Now, by mine honour which is yet mine
    own,
I'll have that doctor for mine bedfellow.

NERISSA.
And I his clerk; therefore be well advis'd
How you do leave me to mine own
    protection.

GRATIANO.
Well, do you so: let not me take him then;
For, if I do, I'll mar the young clerk's pen.

ANTONIO.
I am the unhappy subject of these quarrels.

PORTIA.
Sir, grieve not you; you are welcome
    notwithstanding.

BASSANIO.
Portia, forgive me this enforced wrong;
And in the hearing of these many friends
I swear to thee, even by thine own fair
    eyes,
Wherein I see myself—

PORTIA.
                 Mark you but that!
In both my eyes he doubly sees himself,
In each eye one; swear by your double self,
And there's an oath of credit.

BASSANIO.
                 Nay, but hear me:
Pardon this fault, and by my soul I swear
I never more will break an oath with thee.

ANTONIO.
I once did lend my body for his wealth,
Which, but for him that had your
    husband's ring,
Had quite miscarried; I dare be bound
    again,
My soul upon the forfeit, that your lord
Will never more break faith advisedly.

PORTIA.
Then you shall be his surety. Give him this,
And bid him keep it better than the other.

ANTONIO.
Here, Lord Bassanio, swear to keep this
    ring.

BASSANIO.
By heaven! it is the same I gave the
    doctor!

PORTIA.
I had it of him: pardon me, Bassanio,
For, by this ring, the doctor lay with me.
NERISSA.
And pardon me, my gentle Gratiano,
For that same scrubbed boy, the doctor's
        clerk,
In lieu of this, last night did lie with me.
GRATIANO.
Why, this is like the mending of high
        ways
In summer, where the ways are fair
        enough.
What! are we cuckolds ere we have
        deserv'd it?
PORTIA.
Speak not so grossly. You are all amaz'd:
Here is a letter; read it at your leisure;
It comes from Padua, from Bellario:
There you shall find that Portia was the
        doctor,
Nerissa there, her clerk: Lorenzo here
Shall witness I set forth as soon as you,
And even but now return'd; I have not yet
Enter'd my house. Antonio, you are
        welcome;
And I have better news in store for you
Than you expect: unseal this letter soon;
There you shall find three of your argosies
Are richly come to harbour suddenly.
You shall not know by what strange
        accident
I chanced on this letter.
ANTONIO.
                              I am dumb!
BASSANIO.
Were you the doctor, and I knew you
        not?
GRATIANO.
Were you the clerk that is to make me
        cuckold?

NERISSA.
Ay, but the clerk that never means to do it,
Unless he live until he be a man.
BASSANIO.
Sweet doctor, you shall be my bedfellow:
When I am absent, then lie with my wife.
ANTONIO.
Sweet lady, you have given me life and
        living;
For here I read for certain that my ships
Are safely come to road.
PORTIA.
                        How now, Lorenzo!
My clerk hath some good comforts too
        for you.
NERISSA.
Ay, and I'll give them him without a fee.
There do I give to you and Jessica,
From the rich Jew, a special deed of gift,
After his death, of all he dies possess'd of.
LORENZO.
Fair ladies, you drop manna in the way
Of starved people.
PORTIA.
                      It is almost morning,
And yet I am sure you are not satisfied
Of these events at full. Let us go in;
And charge us there upon inter'gatories,
And we will answer all things faithfully.
GRATIANO.
Let it be so: the first inter'gatory
That my Nerissa shall be sworn on is,
Whether till the next night she had rather
        stay,
Or go to bed now, being two hours to day:
But were the day come, I should wish it
        dark,
Till I were couching with the doctor's clerk.
Well, while I live, I'll fear no other thing
So sore as keeping safe Nerissa's ring.
                              [*Exeunt.*]

As You Like It

Dramatis Personae

DUKE, *living in exile*

FREDERICK, *brother to the duke, and usurper of his dominions*

AMIENS, *lord attending on the duke in his banishment*

JAQUES, *lord attending on the duke in his banishment*

LE BEAU, *a courtier attending upon Frederick*

CHARLES, *his wrestler*

OLIVER, *son of Sir Rowland de Boys*

JAQUES, *son of Sir Rowland de Boys*

ORLANDO, *son of Sir Rowland de Boys*

ADAM, *servant to Oliver*

DENNIS, *servant to Oliver*

TOUCHSTONE, *a clown*

SIR OLIVER MARTEXT, *a vicar*

CORIN, *a shepherd*

SILVIUS, *a shepherd*

WILLIAM, *a country fellow, in love with Audrey*

A PERSON *representing Hymen*

ROSALIND, *daughter to the banished duke*

CELIA, *daughter to Frederick*

PHEBE, *a shepherdess*

AUDREY, *a country wench*

LORDS *belonging to the two dukes;* PAGES, FORESTERS, *and other* ATTENDANTS

SCENE: *Near Oliver's house; afterwards partly in the usurper's court; and partly in the Forest of Arden.*

ACT I
SCENE I

An orchard near Oliver's house.

[*Enter* ORLANDO *and* ADAM.]

ORLANDO.

As I remember, Adam, it was upon this fashion,—bequeathed me by will but poor a thousand crowns, and, as thou say'st, charged my brother, on his blessing, to breed me well: and there begins my sadness. My brother Jaques he keeps at school, and report speaks goldenly of his profit: for my part, he keeps me rustically at home, or, to speak more properly, stays me here at home unkept: for call you that keeping for a gentleman of my birth that differs not from the stalling of an ox? His horses are bred better; for, besides that they are fair with their feeding, they are taught their manage, and to that end riders dearly hired; but I, his brother, gain nothing under him but growth; for the which his animals on his dunghills are as much bound to him as I. Besides this nothing that he so plentifully gives me, the something that nature gave me, his countenance seems to take from me: he lets me feed with his hinds, bars me the place of a brother, and as much as in him lies, mines my gentility with my education. This is it, Adam, that grieves me; and the spirit of my father, which I think is within me, begins to mutiny against this servitude; I will no longer endure it, though yet I know no wise remedy how to avoid it.

ADAM.

Yonder comes my master, your brother.

ORLANDO.

Go apart, Adam, and thou shalt hear how he will shake me up.

[ADAM *retires.*]

[*Enter* OLIVER.]

OLIVER.

Now, sir! what make you here?

Orlando.
Nothing: I am not taught to make anything.

Oliver.
What mar you then, sir?

Orlando.
Marry, sir, I am helping you to mar that which God made, a poor unworthy brother of yours, with idleness.

Oliver.
Marry, sir, be better employed, and be naught awhile.

Orlando.
Shall I keep your hogs, and eat husks with them? What prodigal portion have I spent that I should come to such penury?

Oliver.
Know you where you are, sir?

Orlando.
O, sir, very well: here in your orchard.

Oliver.
Know you before whom, sir?

Orlando.
Ay, better than him I am before knows me. I know you are my eldest brother: and in the gentle condition of blood, you should so know me. The courtesy of nations allows you my better in that you are the first-born; but the same tradition takes not away my blood, were there twenty brothers betwixt us: I have as much of my father in me as you, albeit, I confess, your coming before me is nearer to his reverence.

Oliver.
What, boy!

Orlando.
Come, come, elder brother, you are too young in this.

Oliver.
Wilt thou lay hands on me, villain?

Orlando.
I am no villain: I am the youngest son of Sir Rowland de Boys: he was my father; and he is thrice a villain that says such a father begot villains. Wert thou not my brother, I would not take this hand from thy throat till this other had pulled out thy tongue for saying so: thou has railed on thyself.

Adam. [*Coming forward.*]
Sweet masters, be patient; for your father's remembrance, be at accord.

Oliver.
Let me go, I say.

Orlando.
I will not, till I please: you shall hear me. My father charged you in his will to give me good education: you have trained me like a peasant, obscuring and hiding from me all gentleman-like qualities: the spirit of my father grows strong in me, and I will no longer endure it: therefore, allow me such exercises as may become a gentleman, or give me the poor allottery my father left me by testament; with that I will go buy my fortunes.

Oliver.
And what wilt thou do? beg, when that is spent? Well, sir, get you in; I will not long be troubled with you: you shall have some part of your will: I pray you leave me.

Orlando.
I no further offend you than becomes me for my good.

Oliver.
Get you with him, you old dog.

Adam.
Is "old dog" my reward? Most true, I have lost my teeth in your service.—God be with my old master! he would not have spoke such a word.

[*Exeunt* Orlando *and* Adam.]

Oliver.
Is it even so? begin you to grow upon me? I will physic your rankness, and yet give no thousand crowns neither. Holla, Dennis!

[*Enter* Dennis.]

Dennis.
Calls your worship?

Oliver.
Was not Charles, the duke's wrestler, here to speak with me?

Dennis.
So please you, he is here at the door and importunes access to you.

Oliver.
Call him in.

[Exit Dennis.]

'Twill be a good way; and to-morrow the wrestling is.

[Enter Charles.]

Charles.

Good morrow to your worship.

Oliver.

Good Monsieur Charles!—what's the new news at the new court?

Charles.

There's no news at the court, sir, but the old news; that is, the old duke is banished by his younger brother the new duke; and three or four loving lords have put themselves into voluntary exile with him, whose lands and revenues enrich the new duke; therefore he gives them good leave to wander.

Oliver.

Can you tell if Rosalind, the duke's daughter, be banished with her father?

Charles.

O, no; for the duke's daughter, her cousin, so loves her,—being ever from their cradles bred together,—that she would have followed her exile, or have died to stay behind her. She is at the court, and no less beloved of her uncle than his own daughter; and never two ladies loved as they do.

Oliver.

Where will the old duke live?

Charles.

They say he is already in the Forest of Arden, and a many merry men with him; and there they live like the old Robin Hood of England: they say many young gentlemen flock to him every day, and fleet the time carelessly, as they did in the golden world.

Oliver.

What, you wrestle to-morrow before the new duke?

Charles.

Marry, do I, sir; and I came to acquaint you with a matter. I am given, sir, secretly to understand that your younger brother, Orlando, hath a disposition to come in disguis'd against me to try a fall. To-morrow, sir, I wrestle for my credit; and he that escapes me without some broken limb shall acquit him well. Your brother is but young and tender; and, for your love, I would be loath to foil him, as I must, for my own honour, if he come in: therefore, out of my love to you, I came hither to acquaint you withal; that either you might stay him from his intendment, or brook such disgrace well as he shall run into; in that it is thing of his own search, and altogether against my will.

Oliver.

Charles, I thank thee for thy love to me, which thou shalt find I will most kindly requite. I had myself notice of my brother's purpose herein, and have by underhand means laboured to dissuade him from it; but he is resolute. I'll tell thee, Charles, it is the stubbornest young fellow of France; full of ambition, an envious emulator of every man's good parts, a secret and villainous contriver against me his natural brother: therefore use thy discretion: I had as lief thou didst break his neck as his finger. And thou wert best look to't; for if thou dost him any slight disgrace, or if he do not mightily grace himself on thee, he will practise against thee by poison, entrap thee by some treacherous device, and never leave thee till he hath ta'en thy life by some indirect means or other: for, I assure thee, and almost with tears I speak it, there is not one so young and so villainous this day living. I speak but brotherly of him; but should I anatomize him to thee as he is, I must blush and weep, and thou must look pale and wonder.

Charles.

I am heartily glad I came hither to you. If he come to-morrow I'll give him his payment. If ever he go alone again I'll never wrestle for prize more: and so, God keep your worship!

[Exit.]

Oliver.

Farewell, good Charles.—Now will I stir this gamester: I hope I shall see an end of him: for my soul, yet I know not why, hates nothing more than he. Yet he's gentle; never schooled and yet learned; full of noble device; of all sorts enchantingly beloved; and, indeed, so much in the heart of the world, and especially of my own people, who best know him, that I am altogether misprised: but it shall not be so long; this wrestler shall clear all: nothing remains but that I kindle the boy thither, which now I'll go about.

[Exit.]

SCENE II

A lawn before the duke's palace.
[Enter Rosalind and Celia.]

CELIA.

I pray thee, Rosalind, sweet my coz, be merry.

ROSALIND.

Dear Celia, I show more mirth than I am mistress of; and would you yet I were merrier? Unless you could teach me to forget a banished father, you must not learn me how to remember any extraordinary pleasure.

CELIA.

Herein I see thou lov'st me not with the full weight that I love thee; if my uncle, thy banished father, had banished thy uncle, the duke my father, so thou hadst been still with me, I could have taught my love to take thy father for mine; so wouldst thou, if the truth of thy love to me were so righteously tempered as mine is to thee.

ROSALIND.

Well, I will forget the condition of my estate, to rejoice in yours.

CELIA.

You know my father hath no child but I, nor none is like to have; and, truly, when he dies thou shalt be his heir: for what he hath taken away from thy father perforce, I will render thee again in affection: by mine honour, I will; and when I break that oath, let me turn monster; therefore, my sweet Rose, my dear Rose, be merry.

ROSALIND.

From henceforth I will, coz, and devise sports: let me see; what think you of falling in love?

CELIA.

Marry, I pr'ythee, do, to make sport withal: but love no man in good earnest, nor no further in sport neither than with safety of a pure blush thou mayst in honour come off again.

ROSALIND.

What shall be our sport, then?

CELIA.

Let us sit and mock the good housewife Fortune from her wheel, that her gifts may henceforth be bestowed equally.

ROSALIND.

I would we could do so; for her benefits are mightily misplaced: and the bountiful blind woman doth most mistake in her gifts to women.

CELIA.

'Tis true; for those that she makes fair she scarce makes honest; and those that she makes honest she makes very ill-favouredly.

ROSALIND.

Nay; now thou goest from Fortune's office to Nature's: Fortune reigns in gifts of the world, not in the lineaments of Nature.

CELIA.

No; when Nature hath made a fair creature, may she not by Fortune fall into the fire?— Though Nature hath given us wit to flout at Fortune, hath not Fortune sent in this fool to cut off the argument?

[Enter Touchstone.]

ROSALIND.

Indeed, there is Fortune too hard for Nature, when Fortune makes Nature's natural the cutter-off of Nature's wit.

CELIA.

Peradventure this is not Fortune's work neither, but Nature's, who perceiveth our natural wits too dull to reason of such goddesses, and hath sent this natural for our whetstone: for always the dullness of the fool is the whetstone of the wits.— How now, wit? whither wander you?

TOUCHSTONE.

Mistress, you must come away to your father.

CELIA.
Were you made the messenger?

TOUCHSTONE.
No, by mine honour; but I was bid to come for you.

ROSALIND.
Where learned you that oath, fool?

TOUCHSTONE.
Of a certain knight that swore by his honour they were good pancakes, and swore by his honour the mustard was naught: now, I'll stand to it, the pancakes were naught and the mustard was good: and yet was not the knight forsworn.

CELIA.
How prove you that, in the great heap of your knowledge?

ROSALIND.
Ay, marry; now unmuzzle your wisdom.

TOUCHSTONE.
Stand you both forth now: stroke your chins, and swear by your beards that I am a knave.

CELIA.
By our beards, if we had them, thou art.

TOUCHSTONE.
By my knavery, if I had it, then I were: but if you swear by that that is not, you are not forsworn: no more was this knight, swearing by his honour, for he never had any; or if he had, he had sworn it away before ever he saw those pancackes or that mustard.

CELIA.
Pr'ythee, who is't that thou mean'st?

TOUCHSTONE.
One that old Frederick, your father, loves.

CELIA.
My father's love is enough to honour him enough: speak no more of him: you'll be whipp'd for taxation one of these days.

TOUCHSTONE.
The more pity that fools may not speak wisely what wise men do foolishly.

CELIA.
By my troth, thou sayest true: for since the little wit that fools have was silenced, the little foolery that wise men have makes a great show. Here comes Monsieur Le Beau.

ROSALIND.
With his mouth full of news.

CELIA.
Which he will put on us as pigeons feed their young.

ROSALIND.
Then shall we be news-crammed.

CELIA.
All the better; we shall be the more marketable. [*Enter* LE BEAU.] *Bon jour,* Monsieur Le Beau. What's the news?

LE BEAU.
Fair princess, you have lost much good sport.

CELIA.
Sport! of what colour?

LE BEAU.
What colour, madam? How shall I answer you?

ROSALIND.
As wit and fortune will.

TOUCHSTONE.
Or as the destinies decrees.

CELIA.
Well said: that was laid on with a trowel.

TOUCHSTONE.
Nay, if I keep not my rank,—

ROSALIND.
Thou losest thy old smell.

LE BEAU.
You amaze me, ladies; I would have told you of good wrestling, which you have lost the sight of.

ROSALIND.
Yet tell us the manner of the wrestling.

LE BEAU.
I will tell you the beginning, and, if it please your ladyships, you may see the end; for the best is yet to do; and here, where you are, they are coming to perform it.

CELIA.
Well,—the beginning, that is dead and buried.

LE BEAU.
There comes an old man and his three sons,—

CELIA.
I could match this beginning with an old tale.

LE BEAU.

Three proper young men, of excellent growth and presence, with bills on their necks,—

ROSALIND.

"Be it known unto all men by these presents,"—

LE BEAU.

The eldest of the three wrestled with Charles, the duke's wrestler; which Charles in a moment threw him, and broke three of his ribs, that there is little hope of life in him: so he served the second, and so the third. Yonder they lie; the poor old man, their father, making such pitiful dole over them that all the beholders take his part with weeping.

ROSALIND.

Alas!

TOUCHSTONE.

But what is the sport, monsieur, that the ladies have lost?

LE BEAU.

Why, this that I speak of.

TOUCHSTONE.

Thus men may grow wiser every day! It is the first time that ever I heard breaking of ribs was sport for ladies.

CELIA.

Or I, I promise thee.

ROSALIND.

But is there any else longs to see this broken music in his sides? is there yet another dotes upon rib-breaking?—Shall we see this wrestling, cousin?

LE BEAU.

You must, if you stay here: for here is the place appointed for the wrestling, and they are ready to perform it.

CELIA.

Yonder, sure, they are coming: let us now stay and see it.

[*Flourish. Enter* DUKE FREDERICK, LORDS, ORLANDO, CHARLES, *and* ATTENDANTS.]

DUKE FREDERICK.

Come on; since the youth will not be entreated, his own peril on his forwardness.

ROSALIND.

Is yonder the man?

LE BEAU.

Even he, madam.

CELIA.

Alas, he is too young: yet he looks successfully.

DUKE FREDERICK.

How now, daughter and cousin? are you crept hither to see the wrestling?

ROSALIND.

Ay, my liege; so please you give us leave.

DUKE FREDERICK.

You will take little delight in it, I can tell you, there is such odds in the men. In pity of the challenger's youth I would fain dissuade him, but he will not be entreated. Speak to him, ladies; see if you can move him.

CELIA.

Call him hither, good Monsieur Le Beau.

DUKE FREDERICK.

Do so; I'll not be by.

[DUKE FREDERICK *goes apart.*]

LE BEAU.

Monsieur the challenger, the princesses call for you.

ORLANDO.

I attend them with all respect and duty.

ROSALIND.

Young man, have you challenged Charles the wrestler?

ORLANDO.

No, fair princess; he is the general challenger: I come but in, as others do, to try with him the strength of my youth.

CELIA.

Young gentleman, your spirits are too bold for your years. You have seen cruel proof of this man's strength: if you saw yourself with your eyes, or knew yourself with your judgment, the fear of your adventure would counsel you to a more equal enterprise. We pray you, for your own sake, to embrace your own safety and give over this attempt.

ROSALIND.

Do, young sir; your reputation shall not therefore be misprised: we will make it our suit to the duke that the wrestling might not go forward.

ORLANDO.
I beseech you, punish me not with your hard thoughts: wherein I confess me much guilty to deny so fair and excellent ladies anything. But let your fair eyes and gentle wishes go with me to my trial: wherein if I be foiled there is but one shamed that was never gracious; if killed, but one dead that is willing to be so: I shall do my friends no wrong, for I have none to lament me: the world no injury, for in it I have nothing; only in the world I fill up a place, which may be better supplied when I have made it empty.

ROSALIND.
The little strength that I have, I would it were with you.

CELIA.
And mine to eke out hers.

ROSALIND.
Fare you well. Pray heaven, I be deceived in you!

CELIA.
Your heart's desires be with you.

CHARLES.
Come, where is this young gallant that is so desirous to lie with his mother earth?

ORLANDO.
Ready, sir; but his will hath in it a more modest working.

DUKE FREDERICK.
You shall try but one fall.

CHARLES.
No; I warrant your grace, you shall not entreat him to a second, that have so mightily persuaded him from a first.

ORLANDO.
You mean to mock me after; you should not have mocked me before; but come your ways.

ROSALIND.
Now, Hercules be thy speed, young man!

CELIA.
I would I were invisible, to catch the strong fellow by the leg.
[CHARLES *and* ORLANDO *wrestle.*]

ROSALIND.
O excellent young man!

CELIA.
If I had a thunderbolt in mine eye, I can tell who should down.
[CHARLES *is thrown. Shout.*]

DUKE FREDERICK.
No more, no more.

ORLANDO.
Yes, I beseech your grace; I am not yet well breathed.

DUKE FREDERICK.
How dost thou, Charles?

LE BEAU.
He cannot speak, my lord.

DUKE FREDERICK.
Bear him away. [CHARLES *is borne out.*]
What is thy name, young man?

ORLANDO.
Orlando, my liege; the youngest son of Sir Rowland de Boys.

DUKE FREDERICK.
I would thou hadst been son to some man
     else.
The world esteem'd thy father honourable,
But I did find him still mine enemy:
Thou shouldst have better pleas'd me with
     this deed
Hadst thou descended from another
     house.
But fare thee well; thou art a gallant youth;
I would thou hadst told me of another
     father.
     [*Exeunt* DUKE FREDERICK, TRAIN,
          and LE BEAU.]

CELIA.
Were I my father, coz, would I do this?

ORLANDO.
I am more proud to be Sir Rowland's son,
His youngest son;—and would not change
     that calling
To be adopted heir to Frederick.

ROSALIND.
My father loved Sir Rowland as his soul,
And all the world was of my father's
     mind:
Had I before known this young man his
     son,

I should have given him tears unto
   entreaties
Ere he should thus have ventur'd.
CELIA.
                 Gentle cousin,
Let us go thank him, and encourage him:
My father's rough and envious disposition
Sticks me at heart.—Sir, you have well
   deserv'd:
If you do keep your promises in love
But justly, as you have exceeded promise,
Your mistress shall be happy.
ROSALIND.
                Gentleman,
  [*Giving him a chain from her neck.*]
Wear this for me; one out of suits with
   fortune,
That could give more, but that her hand
   lacks means.—
Shall we go, coz?
CELIA.
      Ay.—Fare you well, fair gentleman.
ORLANDO.
Can I not say, I thank you? My better parts
Are all thrown down; and that which here
   stands up
Is but a quintain, a mere lifeless block.
ROSALIND.
He calls us back: my pride fell with my
   fortunes:
I'll ask him what he would.—Did you call,
   sir?—
Sir, you have wrestled well, and overthrown
More than your enemies.
CELIA.
              Will you go, coz?
ROSALIND.
Have with you.—Fare you well.
   [*Exeunt* ROSALIND *and* CELIA.]
ORLANDO.
What passion hangs these weights upon
   my tongue?
I cannot speak to her, yet she urg'd
   conference.
O poor Orlando! thou art overthrown:
Or Charles, or something weaker, masters
   thee.
   [*Re-enter* LE BEAU.]

LE BEAU.
Good sir, I do in friendship counsel you
To leave this place. Albeit you have
   deserv'd
High commendation, true applause, and
   love,
Yet such is now the duke's condition,
That he misconstrues all that you have
   done.
The duke is humourous; what he is, indeed,
More suits you to conceive than I to speak
   of.
ORLANDO.
I thank you, sir: and pray you tell me this;
Which of the two was daughter of the
   duke
That here was at the wrestling?
LE BEAU.
Neither his daughter, if we judge by
   manners;
But yet, indeed, the smaller is his
   daughter:
The other is daughter to the banish'd duke,
And here detain'd by her usurping uncle,
To keep his daughter company; whose
   loves
Are dearer than the natural bond of sisters.
But I can tell you that of late this duke
Hath ta'en displeasure 'gainst his gentle
   niece,
Grounded upon no other argument
But that the people praise her for her
   virtues
And pity her for her good father's sake;
And, on my life, his malice 'gainst the lady
Will suddenly break forth.—Sir, fare you
   well!
Hereafter, in a better world than this,
I shall desire more love and knowledge
   of you.
ORLANDO.
I rest much bounden to you: fare you well!
             [*Exit* LE BEAU.]
Thus must I from the smoke into the
   smother;
From tyrant duke unto a tyrant brother:—
But heavenly Rosalind!
             [*Exit.*]

SCENE III

A room in the palace.
[*Enter* CELIA *and* ROSALIND.]
CELIA.
Why, cousin; why, Rosalind;—Cupid have
mercy!—Not a word?
ROSALIND.
Not one to throw at a dog.
CELIA.
No, thy words are too precious to be cast
away upon curs, throw some of them at me;
come, lame me with reasons.
ROSALIND.
Then there were two cousins laid up; when
the one should be lamed with reasons and
the other mad without any.
CELIA.
But is all this for your father?
ROSALIND.
No, some of it is for my child's father. O,
how full of briers is this working-day
world!
CELIA.
They are but burs, cousin, thrown upon
thee in holiday foolery; if we walk not in
the trodden paths, our very petticoats will
catch them.
ROSALIND.
I could shake them off my coat: these burs
are in my heart.
CELIA.
Hem them away.
ROSALIND.
I would try, if I could cry hem and have him.
CELIA.
Come, come, wrestle with thy affections.
ROSALIND.
O, they take the part of a better wrestler
than myself.
CELIA.
O, a good wish upon you! you will try in
time, in despite of a fall.—But, turning
these jests out of service, let us talk in good
earnest: is it possible, on such a sudden, you
should fall into so strong a liking with old
Sir Rowland's youngest son?
ROSALIND.
The duke my father loved his father dearly.

CELIA.
Doth it therefore ensue that you should
love his son dearly? By this kind of chase
I should hate him, for my father hated his
father dearly; yet I hate not Orlando.
ROSALIND.
No, 'faith, hate him not, for my sake.
CELIA.
Why should I not? doth he not deserve
well?
ROSALIND.
Let me love him for that; and do you love
him because I do.—Look, here comes the
duke.
CELIA.
With his eyes full of anger.
[*Enter* DUKE FREDERICK, *with* LORDS.]
DUKE FREDERICK.
Mistress, despatch you with your safest
    haste,
And get you from our court.
ROSALIND.
                                Me, uncle?
DUKE FREDERICK.
                                You, cousin:
Within these ten days if that thou be'st
    found
So near our public court as twenty miles,
Thou diest for it.
ROSALIND.
                        I do beseech your grace,
Let me the knowledge of my fault bear
    with me:
If with myself I hold intelligence,
Or have acquaintance with mine own
    desires;
If that I do not dream, or be not frantic,—
As I do trust I am not,—then, dear uncle,
Never so much as in a thought unborn
Did I offend your highness.
DUKE FREDERICK.
                                Thus do all traitors;
If their purgation did consist in words,
They are as innocent as grace itself:—
Let it suffice thee that I trust thee not.
ROSALIND.
Yet your mistrust cannot make me a traitor:
Tell me whereon the likelihood depends.

Duke Frederick.
Thou art thy father's daughter; there's
    enough.
Rosalind.
So was I when your highness took his
    dukedom;
So was I when your highness banish'd
    him:
Treason is not inherited, my lord:
Or, if we did derive it from our friends,
What's that to me? my father was no
    traitor!
Then, good my liege, mistake me not so
    much
To think my poverty is treacherous.
Celia.
Dear sovereign, hear me speak.
Duke Frederick.
Ay, Celia: we stay'd her for your sake,
Else had she with her father rang'd along.
Celia.
I did not then entreat to have her stay;
It was your pleasure, and your own
    remorse:
I was too young that time to value her;
But now I know her: if she be a traitor,
Why so am I: we still have slept together,
Rose at an instant, learn'd, play'd, eat
    together;
And wheresoe'er we went, like Juno's
    swans,
Still we went coupled and inseparable.
Duke Frederick.
She is too subtle for thee; and her
    smoothness,
Her very silence, and her patience
Speak to the people, and they pity her.
Thou art a fool: she robs thee of thy name;
And thou wilt show more bright and seem
    more virtuous
When she is gone: then open not thy lips;
Firm and irrevocable is my doom
Which I have pass'd upon her;—she is
    banish'd.
Celia.
Pronounce that sentence, then, on me, my
    liege:
I cannot live out of her company.

Duke Frederick.
You are a fool.—You, niece, provide
    yourself:
If you outstay the time, upon mine honour,
And in the greatness of my word, you die.
    [*Exeunt* Duke Frederick *and* Lords.]
Celia.
O my poor Rosalind! whither wilt thou
    go?
Wilt thou change fathers? I will give thee
    mine.
I charge thee be not thou more griev'd
    than I am.
Rosalind.
I have more cause.
Celia.
                Thou hast not, cousin;
Pr'ythee be cheerful: know'st thou not the
    duke
Hath banish'd me, his daughter?
Rosalind.
                   That he hath not.
Celia.
No! hath not? Rosalind lacks, then, the
    love
Which teacheth thee that thou and I am
    one:
Shall we be sund'red? shall we part, sweet
    girl?
No; let my father seek another heir.
Therefore devise with me how we may fly,
Whither to go, and what to bear with us:
And do not seek to take your charge upon
    you,
To bear your griefs yourself, and leave me
    out;
For, by this heaven, now at our sorrows
    pale,
Say what thou canst, I'll go along with thee.
Rosalind.
Why, whither shall we go?
Celia.
To seek my uncle in the Forest of Arden.
Rosalind.
Alas! what danger will it be to us,
Maids as we are, to travel forth so far?
Beauty provoketh thieves sooner than
    gold.

Celia.

I'll put myself in poor and mean attire,
And with a kind of umber smirch my face;
The like do you; so shall we pass along,
And never stir assailants.

Rosalind.

             Were it not better,
Because that I am more than common tall,
That I did suit me all points like a man?
A gallant curtle-axe upon my thigh,
A boar spear in my hand; and,—in my
    heart
Lie there what hidden woman's fear there
    will,—
We'll have a swashing and a martial
    outside,
As many other mannish cowards have
That do outface it with their semblances.

Celia.

What shall I call thee when thou art a
    man?

Rosalind.

I'll have no worse a name than Jove's own
    page,
And, therefore, look you call me
    Ganymede.
But what will you be call'd?

Celia.

Something that hath a reference to my
    state:
No longer Celia, but Aliena.

Rosalind.

But, cousin, what if we assay'd to steal
The clownish fool out of your father's
    court?
Would he not be a comfort to our travel?

Celia.

He'll go along o'er the wide world with
    me;
Leave me alone to woo him. Let's away,
And get our jewels and our wealth
    together;
Devise the fittest time and safest way
To hide us from pursuit that will be made
After my flight. Now go we in content
To liberty, and not to banishment.

             [*Exeunt.*]

ACT II
SCENE I
The Forest of Arden.
[*Enter* Duke Senior, Amiens, *and other*
Lords, *in the dress of foresters.*]

Duke Senior.

Now, my co-mates and brothers in exile,
Hath not old custom made this life more
    sweet
Than that of painted pomp? Are not these
    woods
More free from peril than the envious
    court?
Here feel we not the penalty of Adam,—
The seasons' difference: as the icy fang
And churlish chiding of the winter's wind,
Which when it bites and blows upon my
    body,
Even till I shrink with cold, I smile and
    say,
"This is no flattery: these are counsellors
That feelingly persuade me what I am."
Sweet are the uses of adversity;
Which, like the toad, ugly and venomous,
Wears yet a precious jewel in his head;
And this our life, exempt from public
    haunt,
Finds tongues in trees, books in the
    running brooks,
Sermons in stones, and good in everything.
I would not change it.

Amiens.

             Happy is your grace,
That can translate the stubbornness of
    fortune
Into so quiet and so sweet a style.

Duke Senior.

Come, shall we go and kill us venison?
And yet it irks me, the poor dappled fools,
Being native burghers of this desert city,
Should, in their own confines, with forked
    heads
Have their round haunches gor'd.

First Lord.

             Indeed, my lord,
The melancholy Jaques grieves at that;
And, in that kind, swears you do more
    usurp

Than doth your brother that hath banish'd
    you.
To-day my lord of Amiens and myself
Did steal behind him as he lay along
Under an oak, whose antique root peeps
    out
Upon the brook that brawls along this
    wood:
To the which place a poor sequester'd stag,
That from the hunter's aim had ta'en a hurt,
Did come to languish; and, indeed, my
    lord,
The wretched animal heav'd forth such
    groans,
That their discharge did stretch his
    leathern coat
Almost to bursting; and the big round
    tears
Cours'd one another down his innocent
    nose
In piteous chase: and thus the hairy fool,
Much marked of the melancholy Jaques,
Stood on the extremest verge of the swift
    brook,
Augmenting it with tears.

DUKE SENIOR.
                    But what said Jaques?
Did he not moralize this spectacle?

FIRST LORD.
O, yes, into a thousand similes.
First, for his weeping into the needless
    stream;
"Poor deer," quoth he, "thou mak'st a
    testament
As worldlings do, giving thy sum of more
To that which had too much": then, being
    there alone,
Left and abandoned of his velvet friends;
" 'Tis right"; quoth he; "thus misery doth
    part
The flux of company": anon, a careless
    herd,
Full of the pasture, jumps along by him
And never stays to greet him; "Ay," quoth
    Jaques,
"Sweep on, you fat and greasy citizens;
'Tis just the fashion; wherefore do you
    look

Upon that poor and broken bankrupt
    there?"
Thus most invectively he pierceth through
The body of the country, city, court,
Yea, and of this our life: swearing that we
Are mere usurpers, tyrants, and what's
    worse,
To fright the animals, and to kill them up
In their assign'd and native dwelling-place.

DUKE SENIOR.
And did you leave him in this
    contemplation?

SECOND LORD.
We did, my lord, weeping and
    commenting
Upon the sobbing deer.

DUKE SENIOR.
                    Show me the place:
I love to cope him in these sullen fits,
For then he's full of matter.

FIRST LORD.
I'll bring you to him straight.
                    [*Exeunt.*]

SCENE II
A room in the palace.
[*Enter* DUKE FREDERICK, LORDS,
    and ATTENDANTS.]

DUKE FREDERICK.
Can it be possible that no man saw them?
It cannot be: some villains of my court
Are of consent and sufferance in this.

FIRST LORD.
I cannot hear of any that did see her.
The ladies, her attendants of her chamber,
Saw her a-bed; and in the morning early
They found the bed untreasur'd of their
    mistress.

SECOND LORD.
My lord, the roynish clown, at whom so oft
Your grace was wont to laugh, is also
    missing.
Hesperia, the princess' gentlewoman,
Confesses that she secretly o'erheard
Your daughter and her cousin much
    commend
The parts and graces of the wrestler
That did but lately foil the sinewy Charles;

And she believes, wherever they are gone,
That youth is surely in their company.
DUKE FREDERICK.
Send to his brother; fetch that gallant
    hither:
If he be absent, bring his brother to me,
I'll make him find him: do this suddenly;
And let not search and inquisition quail
To bring again these foolish runaways.
                    [*Exeunt.*]

SCENE III

Before Oliver's house.
[*Enter* ORLANDO *and* ADAM, *meeting.*]
ORLANDO.
Who's there?
ADAM.
What, my young master?—O my gentle
    master!
O my sweet master! O you memory
Of old Sir Rowland! why, what make you
    here?
Why are you virtuous? why do people love
    you?
And wherefore are you gentle, strong, and
    valiant?
Why would you be so fond to overcome
The bonny prizer of the humourous duke?
Your praise is come too swiftly home
    before you.
Know you not, master, to some kind of
    men
Their graces serve them but as enemies?
No more do yours; your virtues, gentle
    master,
Are sanctified and holy traitors to you.
O, what a world is this, when what is
    comely
Envenoms him that bears it!
ORLANDO.
Why, what's the matter?
ADAM.
                        O unhappy youth,
Come not within these doors; within this
    roof
The enemy of all your graces lives:
Your brother,—no, no brother; yet the
    son—

Yet not the son; I will not call him son—
Of him I was about to call his father,—
Hath heard your praises; and this night
    he means
To burn the lodging where you use to lie,
And you within it: if he fail of that,
He will have other means to cut you off;
I overheard him and his practices.
This is no place; this house is but a
    butchery:
Abhor it, fear it, do not enter it.
ORLANDO.
Why, whither, Adam, wouldst thou have
    me go?
ADAM.
No matter whither, so you come not here.
ORLANDO.
What, wouldst thou have me go and beg
    my food?
Or with a base and boisterous sword
    enforce
A thievish living on the common road?
This I must do, or know not what to do:
Yet this I will not do, do how I can:
I rather will subject me to the malice
Of a diverted blood and bloody brother.
ADAM.
But do not so. I have five hundred crowns,
The thrifty hire I sav'd under your father,
Which I did store to be my foster-nurse,
When service should in my old limbs lie
    lame,
And unregarded age in corners thrown;
Take that: and He that doth the ravens
    feed,
Yea, providently caters for the sparrow,
Be comfort to my age! Here is the gold;
All this I give you. Let me be your servant;
Though I look old, yet I am strong and
    lusty:
For in my youth I never did apply
Hot and rebellious liquors in my blood;
Nor did not with unbashful forehead woo
The means of weakness and debility;
Therefore my age is as a lusty winter,
Frosty, but kindly: let me go with you;
I'll do the service of a younger man
In all your business and necessities.

ORLANDO.

O good old man; how well in thee appears
The constant service of the antique world,
When service sweat for duty, not for meed!
Thou art not for the fashion of these times,
Where none will sweat but for promotion;
And having that, do choke their service up
Even with the having: it is not so with
    thee.
But, poor old man, thou prun'st a rotten
    tree,
That cannot so much as a blossom yield
In lieu of all thy pains and husbandry:
But come thy ways, we'll go along
    together;
And ere we have thy youthful wages spent
We'll light upon some settled low content.

ADAM.

Master, go on; and I will follow thee
To the last gasp, with truth and loyalty.—
From seventeen years till now almost
    fourscore
Here lived I, but now live here no more.
At seventeen years many their fortunes
    seek;
But at fourscore it is too late a week:
Yet fortune cannot recompense me better
Than to die well and not my master's
    debtor.

    [Exeunt.]

SCENE IV

The Forest of Arden.
[Enter ROSALIND *in boy's clothes,*
CELIA *dressed like a shepherdess, and*
TOUCHSTONE.*]*

ROSALIND.

O Jupiter! how weary are my spirits!

TOUCHSTONE.

I care not for my spirits, if my legs were
not weary.

ROSALIND.

I could find in my heart to disgrace my
man's apparel, and to cry like a woman;
but I must comfort the weaker vessel, as
doublet and hose ought to show itself
courageous to petticoat; therefore, courage,
good Aliena.

CELIA.

I pray you bear with me; I can go no further.

TOUCHSTONE.

For my part, I had rather bear with you
than bear you: yet I should bear no cross
if I did bear you; for I think you have no
money in your purse.

ROSALIND.

Well, this is the forest of Arden.

TOUCHSTONE.

Ay, now am I in Arden: the more fool I;
when I was at home I was in a better place;
but travellers must be content.

ROSALIND.

Ay, be so, good Touchstone.—Look you,
who comes here?—a young man and an
old in solemn talk.

    [Enter CORIN *and* SILVIUS.*]*

CORIN.

That is the way to make her scorn you still.

SILVIUS.

O Corin, that thou knew'st how I do love
    her!

CORIN.

I partly guess; for I have lov'd ere now.

SILVIUS.

No, Corin, being old, thou canst not guess;
Though in thy youth thou wast as true a
    lover
As ever sigh'd upon a midnight pillow:
But if thy love were ever like to mine,—
As sure I think did never man love so,—
How many actions most ridiculous
Hast thou been drawn to by thy fantasy?

CORIN.

Into a thousand that I have forgotten.

SILVIUS.

O, thou didst then never love so heartily:
If thou remember'st not the slightest folly
That ever love did make thee run into,
Thou hast not lov'd:
Or if thou hast not sat as I do now,
Wearing thy hearer in thy mistress' praise,
Thou hast not lov'd:
Or if thou hast not broke from company
Abruptly, as my passion now makes me,
Thou hast not lov'd: O Phebe, Phebe,
    Phebe!

AS YOU LIKE IT

[*Exit* SILVIUS.]

ROSALIND.

Alas, poor shepherd! searching of thy wound, I have by hard adventure found mine own.

TOUCHSTONE.

And I mine. I remember, when I was in love, I broke my sword upon a stone, and bid him take that for coming a-night to Jane Smile: and I remember the kissing of her batlet, and the cow's dugs that her pretty chapp'd hands had milk'd: and I remember the wooing of a peascod instead of her; from whom I took two cods, and giving her them again, said with weeping tears, "Wear these for my sake." We that are true lovers run into strange capers; but as all is mortal in nature, so is all nature in love mortal in folly.

ROSALIND.

Thou speak'st wiser than thou art 'ware of.

TOUCHSTONE.

Nay, I shall ne'er be 'ware of mine own wit till I break my shins against it.

ROSALIND.

Jove, Jove! this shepherd's passion
Is much upon my fashion.

TOUCHSTONE.

And mine: but it grows something stale with me.

CELIA.

I pray you, one of you question yond man If he for gold will give us any food: I faint almost to death.

TOUCHSTONE.

Holla, you clown!

ROSALIND.

Peace, fool; he's not thy kinsman.

CORIN.

Who calls?

TOUCHSTONE.

Your betters, sir.

CORIN.

Else are they very wretched.

ROSALIND.

Peace, I say.—Good even to you, friend.

CORIN.

And to you, gentle sir, and to you all.

ROSALIND.

I pr'ythee, shepherd, if that love or gold Can in this desert place buy entertainment, Bring us where we may rest ourselves and feed: Here's a young maid with travel much oppress'd, And faints for succour.

CORIN.

Fair sir, I pity her, And wish, for her sake more than for mine own, My fortunes were more able to relieve her: But I am shepherd to another man, And do not shear the fleeces that I graze: My master is of churlish disposition And little recks to find the way to heaven By doing deeds of hospitality: Besides, his cote, his flocks, and bounds of feed, Are now on sale; and at our sheepcote now, By reason of his absence, there is nothing That you will feed on; but what is, come see, And in my voice most welcome shall you be.

ROSALIND.

What is he that shall buy his flock and pasture?

CORIN.

That young swain that you saw here but erewhile, That little cares for buying anything.

ROSALIND.

I pray thee, if it stand with honesty, Buy thou the cottage, pasture, and the flock, And thou shalt have to pay for it of us.

CELIA.

And we will mend thy wages. I like this place, And willingly could waste my time in it.

CORIN.

Assuredly the thing is to be sold: Go with me: if you like, upon report,

The soil, the profit, and this kind of
    life,
I will your very faithful feeder be,
And buy it with your gold right
    suddenly.
                [*Exeunt.*]

SCENE V
Another part of the forest.
[*Enter* AMIENS, JAQUES, *and* OTHERS.]
AMIENS. [*Sings.*]
      Under the greenwood tree,
      Who loves to lie with me,
      And turn his merry note
      Unto the sweet bird's throat,
    Come hither, come hither, come hither;
      Here shall he see
      No enemy
    But winter and rough weather.
JAQUES.
More, more, I pr'ythee, more.
AMIENS.
It will make you melancholy, Monsieur
Jaques.
JAQUES.
I thank it. More, I pr'ythee, more. I can
suck melancholy out of a song, as a weasel
sucks eggs. More, I pr'ythee, more.
AMIENS.
My voice is ragged; I know I cannot please
you.
JAQUES.
I do not desire you to please me; I do desire
you to sing. Come, more: another stanza.
Call you them stanzas?
AMIENS.
What you will, Monsieur Jaques.
JAQUES.
Nay, I care not for their names; they owe
me nothing. Will you sing?
AMIENS.
More at your request than to please myself.
JAQUES.
Well then, if ever I thank any man, I'll
thank you: but that they call compliment
is like the encounter of two dog-apes; and
when a man thanks me heartily, methinks
have given him a penny, and he renders me

the beggarly thanks. Come, sing; and you
that will not, hold your tongues.
AMIENS.
Well, I'll end the song.—Sirs, cover the
while: the duke will drink under this
tree:—he hath been all this day to look you.
JAQUES.
And I have been all this day to avoid him.
He is too disputable for my company: I
think of as many matters as he; but I give
heaven thanks, and make no boast of them.
Come, warble, come.
        [*Song. All together here.*]
      Who doth ambition shun,
      And loves to live i' the sun,
      Seeking the food he eats,
      And pleas'd with what he gets,
    Come hither, come hither, come hither.
      Here shall he see
      No enemy
    But winter and rough weather.
JAQUES.
I'll give you a verse to this note that I made
yesterday in despite of my invention.
AMIENS.
And I'll sing it.
JAQUES.
Thus it goes:
      If it do come to pass
      That any man turn ass,
      Leaving his wealth and ease
      A stubborn will to please,
    Ducdame, ducdame, ducdame;
      Here shall he see
      Gross fools as he,
    An if he will come to me.
AMIENS.
What's that "ducdame"?
JAQUES.
'Tis a Greek invocation, to call fools into a
circle. I'll go sleep, if I can; if I cannot, I'll
rail against all the first-born of Egypt.
AMIENS.
And I'll go seek the duke; his banquet is
    prepared.
          [*Exeunt severally.*]

ACT II, SCENE VII   AS YOU LIKE IT

SCENE VI
Another part of the forest.
[*Enter* ORLANDO *and* ADAM.]
ADAM.
Dear master, I can go no further: O, I die
for food! Here lie I down, and measure out
my grave. Farewell, kind master.
ORLANDO.
Why, how now, Adam! no greater heart in
thee? Live a little; comfort a little; cheer
thyself a little. If this uncouth forest yield
anything savage, I will either be food for
it or bring it for food to thee. Thy conceit
is nearer death than thy powers. For my
sake be comfortable: hold death awhile
at the arm's end: I will here be with thee
presently; and if I bring thee not something
to eat, I'll give thee leave to die: but if thou
diest before I come, thou art a mocker of
my labour. Well said! thou look'st cheerily:
and I'll be with thee quickly.—Yet thou
liest in the bleak air: come, I will bear thee
to some shelter; and thou shalt not die for
lack of a dinner if there live anything in this
desert. Cheerily, good Adam!
[*Exeunt.*]

SCENE VII
Another part of the forest.
[*A table set. Enter* DUKE SENIOR, AMIENS,
and OTHERS.]
DUKE SENIOR.
I think he be transform'd into a beast;
For I can nowhere find him like a man.
FIRST LORD.
My lord, he is but even now gone hence;
Here was he merry, hearing of a song.
DUKE SENIOR.
If he, compact of jars, grow musical,
We shall have shortly discord in the
spheres.
Go, seek him; tell him I would speak with
him.
FIRST LORD.
He saves my labour by his own approach.
[*Enter* JAQUES.]
DUKE SENIOR.
Why, how now, monsieur! what a life is this,

That your poor friends must woo your
company?
What! you look merrily!
JAQUES.
A fool, a fool!—I met a fool i' the forest,
A motley fool;—a miserable world!—
As I do live by food, I met a fool,
Who laid him down and bask'd him in
the sun,
And rail'd on Lady Fortune in good terms,
In good set terms,—and yet a motley fool.
"Good morrow, fool," quoth I: "No, sir,"
quoth he,
"Call me not fool till heaven hath sent me
fortune."
And then he drew a dial from his poke,
And, looking on it with lack-lustre eye,
Says very wisely, "It is ten o'clock:
Thus we may see," quoth he, "how the
world wags;
'Tis but an hour ago since it was nine;
And after one hour more 'twill be eleven;
And so, from hour to hour, we ripe and
ripe,
And then, from hour to hour, we rot and
rot;
And thereby hangs a tale." When I did
hear
The motley fool thus moral on the time,
My lungs began to crow like chanticleer,
That fools should be so deep contemplative;
And I did laugh sans intermission
An hour by his dial.—O noble fool!
A worthy fool!—Motley's the only wear.
DUKE SENIOR.
What fool is this?
JAQUES.
O worthy fool!—One that hath been a
courtier,
And says, if ladies be but young and fair,
They have the gift to know it: and in his
brain,—
Which is as dry as the remainder biscuit
After a voyage,—he hath strange places
cramm'd
With observation, the which he vents
In mangled forms.—O that I were a fool!
I am ambitious for a motley coat.

DUKE SENIOR.
Thou shalt have one.
JAQUES.
                    It is my only suit,
Provided that you weed your better
    judgments
Of all opinion that grows rank in them
That I am wise. I must have liberty
Withal, as large a charter as the wind,
To blow on whom I please; for so fools
    have:
And they that are most galled with my
    folly,
They most must laugh. And why, sir, must
    they so?
The "why" is plain as way to parish church:
He that a fool doth very wisely hit
Doth very foolishly, although he smart,
Not to seem senseless of the bob; if not,
The wise man's folly is anatomiz'd
Even by the squandering glances of the
    fool.
Invest me in my motley; give me leave
To speak my mind, and I will through and
    through
Cleanse the foul body of the infected
    world,
If they will patiently receive my medicine.
DUKE SENIOR.
Fie on thee! I can tell what thou wouldst
    do.
JAQUES.
What, for a counter, would I do but good?
DUKE SENIOR.
Most mischievous foul sin, in chiding sin;
For thou thyself hast been a libertine,
As sensual as the brutish sting itself;
And all the embossed sores and headed
    evils
That thou with license of free foot hast
    caught
Wouldst thou disgorge into the general
    world.
JAQUES.
Why, who cries out on pride
That can therein tax any private party?
Doth it not flow as hugely as the sea,
Till that the weary very means do ebb?

What woman in the city do I name
When that I say, the city-woman bears
The cost of princes on unworthy shoulders?
Who can come in and say that I mean her,
When such a one as she, such is her
    neighbour?
Or what is he of basest function
That says his bravery is not on my cost,—
Thinking that I mean him,—but therein
    suits
His folly to the metal of my speech?
There then; how then? what then? Let me
    see wherein
My tongue hath wrong'd him: if it do him
    right,
Then he hath wrong'd himself; if he be
    free,
Why then, my taxing like a wild-goose
    flies,
Unclaim'd of any man.—But who comes
    here?
[*Enter* ORLANDO, *with his sword drawn.*]
ORLANDO.
Forbear, and eat no more.
JAQUES.
                    Why, I have eat none yet.
ORLANDO.
Nor shalt not, till necessity be serv'd.
JAQUES.
Of what kind should this cock come of?
DUKE SENIOR.
Art thou thus bolden'd, man, by thy
    distress:
Or else a rude despiser of good manners,
That in civility thou seem'st so empty?
ORLANDO.
You touch'd my vein at first: the thorny
    point
Of bare distress hath ta'en from me the
    show
Of smooth civility: yet am I inland bred,
And know some nurture. But forbear, I
    say;
He dies that touches any of this fruit
Till I and my affairs are answered.
JAQUES.
An you will not be answered with reason,
I must die.

DUKE SENIOR.
What would you have? your gentleness
    shall force
More than your force move us to
    gentleness.
ORLANDO.
I almost die for food, and let me have it.
DUKE SENIOR.
Sit down and feed, and welcome to our
    table.
ORLANDO.
Speak you so gently? Pardon me, I pray you:
I thought that all things had been savage
    here;
And therefore put I on the countenance
Of stern commandment. But whate'er
    you are
That in this desert inaccessible,
Under the shade of melancholy boughs,
Lose and neglect the creeping hours of
    time;
If ever you have look'd on better days,
If ever been where bells have knoll'd to
    church,
If ever sat at any good man's feast,
If ever from your eyelids wip'd a tear,
And know what 'tis to pity and be pitied,
Let gentleness my strong enforcement be:
In the which hope I blush, and hide my
    sword.
DUKE SENIOR.
True is it that we have seen better days,
And have with holy bell been knoll'd to
    church,
And sat at good men's feasts, and wip'd
    our eyes
Of drops that sacred pity hath engender'd:
And therefore sit you down in gentleness,
And take upon command what help we
    have,
That to your wanting may be minister'd.
ORLANDO.
Then but forbear your food a little while,
Whiles, like a doe, I go to find my fawn,
And give it food. There is an old poor man
Who after me hath many a weary step
Limp'd in pure love: till he be first
    suffic'd,—

Oppress'd with two weak evils, age and
    hunger,—
I will not touch a bit.
DUKE SENIOR.
                          Go find him out.
And we will nothing waste till you return.
ORLANDO.
I thank ye; and be blest for your good
    comfort!
                          [*Exit.*]
DUKE SENIOR.
Thou seest we are not all alone unhappy;
This wide and universal theatre
Presents more woeful pageants than the
    scene
Wherein we play in.
JAQUES.
                          All the world's a stage,
And all the men and women merely
    players;
They have their exits and their entrances;
And one man in his time plays many parts,
His acts being seven ages. At first the
    infant,
Mewling and puking in the nurse's arms;
Then the whining school-boy, with his
    satchel
And shining morning face, creeping like
    snail
Unwillingly to school. And then the lover,
Sighing like furnace, with a woeful ballad
Made to his mistress' eyebrow. Then a
    soldier,
Full of strange oaths, and bearded like the
    pard,
Jealous in honour, sudden and quick in
    quarrel,
Seeking the bubble reputation
Even in the cannon's mouth. And then
    the justice,
In fair round belly with good capon lin'd,
With eyes severe and beard of formal cut,
Full of wise saws and modern instances;
And so he plays his part. The sixth age
    shifts
Into the lean and slipper'd pantaloon,
With spectacles on nose and pouch on
    side;

His youthful hose, well sav'd, a world too
wide
For his shrunk shank; and his big manly
voice,
Turning again toward childish treble, pipes
And whistles in his sound. Last scene of
all,
That ends this strange eventful history,
Is second childishness and mere oblivion;
Sans teeth, sans eyes, sans taste, sans
everything.
        [*Re-enter* ORLANDO *with* ADAM.]
DUKE SENIOR.
Welcome. Set down your venerable
burden,
And let him feed.
ORLANDO.
I thank you most for him.
ADAM.
                        So had you need;
I scarce can speak to thank you for myself.
DUKE SENIOR.
Welcome; fall to: I will not trouble you
As yet, to question you about your
fortunes.—
Give us some music; and, good cousin,
sing.
AMIENS. [*Sings.*]
        Blow, blow, thou winter wind,
        Thou art not so unkind
                As man's ingratitude;
        Thy tooth is not so keen,
        Because thou art not seen,
                Although thy breath be rude.
Heigh-ho! sing heigh-ho! unto the green
holly:
Most friendship is feigning, most loving
mere folly:
        Then, heigh-ho, the holly!
        This life is most jolly.
        Freeze, freeze, thou bitter sky,
        That dost not bite so nigh
                As benefits forgot:
        Though thou the waters warp,
        Thy sting is not so sharp
                As friend remember'd not.
Heigh-ho! sing heigh-ho! unto the green
holly:

Most friendship is feigning, most loving
mere folly:
        Then, heigh-ho, the holly!
        This life is most jolly.
DUKE SENIOR.
If that you were the good Sir Rowland's
son,—
As you have whisper'd faithfully you were,
And as mine eye doth his effigies witness
Most truly limn'd and living in your face,—
Be truly welcome hither: I am the duke
That lov'd your father. The residue of your
fortune,
Go to my cave and tell me.—Good old
man,
Thou art right welcome as thy master is;
Support him by the arm.—Give me your
hand,
And let me all your fortunes understand.
                        [*Exeunt.*]

ACT III
SCENE I
A room in the palace.
[*Enter* DUKE FREDERICK, OLIVER, LORDS,
and ATTENDANTS.]
DUKE FREDERICK.
Not see him since? Sir, sir, that cannot be:
But were I not the better part made mercy,
I should not seek an absent argument
Of my revenge, thou present. But look
to it:
Find out thy brother wheresoe'er he is:
Seek him with candle; bring him dead or
living
Within this twelvemonth, or turn thou
no more
To seek a living in our territory.
Thy lands, and all things that thou dost
call thine
Worth seizure, do we seize into our hands,
Till thou canst quit thee by thy brother's
mouth
Of what we think against thee.
OLIVER.
O that your highness knew my heart in
this!
I never lov'd my brother in my life.

Duke Frederick.

More villain thou.—Well, push him out
of doors,
And let my officers of such a nature
Make an extent upon his house and lands:
Do this expediently, and turn him going.

[*Exeunt.*]

SCENE II

The Forest of Arden.

[*Enter* Orlando, *with a paper.*]

Orlando.

Hang there, my verse, in witness of my love;
And thou, thrice-crowned queen of night,
survey
With thy chaste eye, from thy pale sphere
above,
Thy huntress' name, that my full life doth
sway.
O Rosalind! these trees shall be my books,
And in their barks my thoughts I'll
character,
That every eye which in this forest looks
Shall see thy virtue witness'd every where.
Run, run, Orlando; carve on every tree,
The fair, the chaste, and unexpressive she.

[*Exit.*]

[*Enter* Corin *and* Touchstone.]

Corin.

And how like you this shepherd's life,
Master Touchstone?

Touchstone.

Truly, shepherd, in respect of itself, it
is a good life; but in respect that it is a
shepherd's life, it is naught. In respect
that it is solitary, I like it very well; but in
respect that it is private, it is a very vile life.
Now in respect it is in the fields, it pleaseth
me well; but in respect it is not in the court,
it is tedious. As it is a spare life, look you,
it fits my humour well; but as there is no
more plenty in it, it goes much against
my stomach. Hast any philosophy in thee,
shepherd?

Corin.

No more but that I know the more one
sickens, the worse at ease he is; and that
he that wants money, means, and content,

is without three good friends; that the
property of rain is to wet, and fire to burn;
that good pasture makes fat sheep; and that
a great cause of the night is lack of the sun;
that he that hath learned no wit by nature
nor art may complain of good breeding, or
comes of a very dull kindred.

Touchstone.

Such a one is a natural philosopher. Wast
ever in court, shepherd?

Corin.

No, truly.

Touchstone.

Then thou art damned.

Corin.

Nay, I hope,—

Touchstone.

Truly, thou art damned, like an ill-roasted
egg, all on one side.

Corin.

For not being at court? Your reason.

Touchstone.

Why, if thou never wast at court, thou
never saw'st good manners; if thou never
saw'st good manners, then thy manners
must be wicked; and wickedness is sin,
and sin is damnation. Thou art in a parlous
state, shepherd.

Corin.

Not a whit, Touchstone; those that are
good manners at the court are as ridiculous
in the country as the behaviour of the
country is most mockable at the court. You
told me you salute not at the court, but you
kiss your hands; that courtesy would be
uncleanly if courtiers were shepherds.

Touchstone.

Instance, briefly; come, instance.

Corin.

Why, we are still handling our ewes; and
their fells, you know, are greasy.

Touchstone.

Why, do not your courtier's hands sweat?
and is not the grease of a mutton as
wholesome as the sweat of a man? Shallow,
shallow: a better instance, I say; come.

Corin.

Besides, our hands are hard.

TOUCHSTONE.
Your lips will feel them the sooner. Shallow again: a more sounder instance; come.

CORIN.
And they are often tarred over with the surgery of our sheep; and would you have us kiss tar? The courtier's hands are perfumed with civet.

TOUCHSTONE.
Most shallow man! thou worm's-meat in respect of a good piece of flesh indeed!—Learn of the wise, and perpend: civet is of a baser birth than tar,—the very uncleanly flux of a cat. Mend the instance, shepherd.

CORIN.
You have too courtly a wit for me: I'll rest.

TOUCHSTONE.
Wilt thou rest damned? God help thee, shallow man! God make incision in thee! thou art raw.

CORIN.
Sir, I am a true labourer: I earn that I eat, get that I wear, owe no man hate, envy no man's happiness, glad of other men's good, content with my harm; and the greatest of my pride is to see my ewes graze and my lambs suck.

TOUCHSTONE .
That is another simple sin in you: to bring the ewes and the rams together, and to offer to get your living by the copulation of cattle; to be bawd to a bell-wether; and to betray a she-lamb of a twelvemonth to crooked-pated, old, cuckoldly ram, out of all reasonable match. If thou be'st not damned for this, the devil himself will have no shepherds; I cannot see else how thou shouldst 'scape.

CORIN.
Here comes young Master Ganymede, my new mistress's brother.

[*Enter* ROSALIND, *reading a paper.*]

ROSALIND. [*Reads.*]
"From the east to western Ind,
No jewel is like Rosalind.
Her worth, being mounted on the wind,
Through all the world bears Rosalind.
All the pictures fairest lin'd

Are but black to Rosalind.
Let no face be kept in mind
But the fair of Rosalind."

TOUCHSTONE.
I'll rhyme you so eight years together, dinners, and suppers, and sleeping hours excepted. It is the right butter-women's rank to market.

ROSALIND.
Out, fool!

TOUCHSTONE.
For a taste:—
If a hart do lack a hind,
Let him seek out Rosalind.
If the cat will after kind,
So be sure will Rosalind.
Winter garments must be lin'd,
So must slender Rosalind.
They that reap must sheaf and bind,—
Then to cart with Rosalind.
Sweetest nut hath sourest rind,
Such a nut is Rosalind.
He that sweetest rose will find
Must find love's prick, and Rosalind.
This is the very false gallop of verses: why do you infect yourself with them?

ROSALIND.
Peace, you dull fool! I found them on a tree.

TOUCHSTONE.
Truly, the tree yields bad fruit.

ROSALIND.
I'll graff it with you, and then I shall graff it with a medlar. Then it will be the earliest fruit in the country: for you'll be rotten ere you be half ripe, and that's the right virtue of the medlar.

TOUCHSTONE.
You have said; but whether wisely or no, let the forest judge.

[*Enter* CELIA, *reading a paper.*]

ROSALIND.
Peace!
Here comes my sister, reading: stand aside.

CELIA. [*Reads.*]
"Why should this a desert be?
For it is unpeopled? No;
Tongues I'll hang on every tree
That shall civil sayings show:
Some, how brief the life of man

Runs his erring pilgrimage,
That the streching of a span
    Buckles in his sum of age.
Some, of violated vows
    'Twixt the souls of friend and friend;
But upon the fairest boughs,
    Or at every sentence end,
Will I Rosalinda write,
    Teaching all that read to know
The quintessence of every sprite
    Heaven would in little show.
Therefore heaven nature charg'd
    That one body should be fill'd
With all graces wide-enlarg'd:
    Nature presently distill'd
Helen's cheek, but not her heart;
    Cleopatra's majesty;
Atalanta's better part;
    Sad Lucretia's modesty.
Thus Rosalind of many parts
    By heavenly synod was devis'd,
Of many faces, eyes, and hearts,
    To have the touches dearest priz'd.
Heaven would that she these gifts should
    have,
And I to live and die her slave."

Rosalind.
O most gentle Jupiter!—What tedious homily of love have you wearied your parishioners withal, and never cried "Have patience, good people!"

Celia.
How now! back, friends; shepherd, go off a little:—go with him, sirrah.

Touchstone.
Come, shepherd, let us make an honourable retreat; though not with bag and baggage, yet with scrip and scrippage.
    [*Exeunt* Corin *and* Touchstone.]

Celia.
Didst thou hear these verses?

Rosalind.
O, yes, I heard them all, and more too; for some of them had in them more feet than the verses would bear.

Celia.
That's no matter; the feet might bear the verses.

Rosalind.
Ay, but the feet were lame, and could not bear themselves without the verse, and therefore stood lamely in the verse.

Celia.
But didst thou hear without wondering how thy name should be hanged and carved upon these trees?

Rosalind.
I was seven of the nine days out of the wonder before you came; for look here what I found on a palm-tree: I was never so berhymed since Pythagoras' time, that I was an Irish rat, which I can hardly remember.

Celia.
Trow you who hath done this?

Rosalind.
Is it a man?

Celia.
And a chain, that you once wore, about his neck. Change you colour?

Rosalind.
I pray thee, who?

Celia.
O lord, lord! it is a hard matter for friends to meet; but mountains may be removed with earthquakes, and so encounter.

Rosalind.
Nay, but who is it?

Celia.
Is it possible?

Rosalind.
Nay, I pr'ythee now, with most petitionary vehemence, tell me who it is.

Celia.
O wonderful, wonderful, most wonderful wonderful! and yet again wonderful, and after that, out of all whooping!

Rosalind.
Good my complexion! dost thou think, though I am caparisoned like a man, I have a doublet and hose in my disposition? One inch of delay more is a South-sea of discovery. I pr'ythee tell me who is it? quickly, and speak apace. I would thou couldst stammer, that thou mightst pour this concealed man out of thy mouth, as wine comes out of narrow-mouth'd bottle;

either too much at once or none at all. I pr'ythee take the cork out of thy mouth that I may drink thy tidings.

CELIA.

So you may put a man in your belly.

ROSALIND.

Is he of God's making? What manner of man? Is his head worth a hat or his chin worth a beard?

CELIA.

Nay, he hath but a little beard.

ROSALIND.

Why, God will send more if the man will be thankful: let me stay the growth of his beard, if thou delay me not the knowledge of his chin.

CELIA.

It is young Orlando, that tripped up the wrestler's heels and your heart both in an instant.

ROSALIND.

Nay, but the devil take mocking: speak sad brow and true maid.

CELIA.

I' faith, coz, 'tis he.

ROSALIND.

Orlando?

CELIA.

Orlando.

ROSALIND.

Alas the day! what shall I do with my doublet and hose?—What did he when thou saw'st him? What said he? How look'd he? Wherein went he? What makes he here? Did he ask for me? Where remains he? How parted he with thee? and when shalt thou see him again? Answer me in one word.

CELIA.

You must borrow me Gargantua's mouth first: 'tis a word too great for any mouth of this age's size. To say ay and no to these particulars is more than to answer in a catechism.

ROSALIND.

But doth he know that I am in this forest, and in man's apparel? Looks he as freshly as he did the day he wrestled?

CELIA.

It is as easy to count atomies as to resolve the propositions of a lover:—but take a taste of my finding him, and relish it with good observance. I found him under a tree, like a dropp'd acorn.

ROSALIND.

It may well be called Jove's tree, when it drops forth such fruit.

CELIA.

Give me audience, good madam.

ROSALIND.

Proceed.

CELIA.

There lay he, stretched along like a wounded knight.

ROSALIND.

Though it be pity to see such a sight, it well becomes the ground.

CELIA.

Cry, "holla!" to thy tongue, I pr'ythee; it curvets unseasonably. He was furnished like a hunter.

ROSALIND.

O, ominous! he comes to kill my heart.

CELIA.

I would sing my song without a burden: thou bring'st me out of tune.

ROSALIND.

Do you not know I am a woman? when I think, I must speak. Sweet, say on.

CELIA.

You bring me out.—Soft! comes he not here?

ROSALIND.

'Tis he: slink by, and note him.

[CELIA *and* ROSALIND *retire.*]

[*Enter* ORLANDO *and* JAQUES.]

JAQUES.

I thank you for your company; but, good faith, I had as lief have been myself alone.

ORLANDO.

And so had I; but yet, for fashion's sake, I thank you too for your society.

JAQUES.

God buy you: let's meet as little as we can.

ORLANDO.

I do desire we may be better strangers.

JAQUES.
I pray you, mar no more trees with writing love songs in their barks.

ORLANDO.
I pray you, mar no more of my verses with reading them ill-favouredly.

JAQUES.
Rosalind is your love's name?

ORLANDO.
Yes, just.

JAQUES.
I do not like her name.

ORLANDO.
There was no thought of pleasing you when she was christened.

JAQUES.
What stature is she of?

ORLANDO.
Just as high as my heart.

JAQUES.
You are full of pretty answers. Have you not been acquainted with goldsmiths' wives, and conned them out of rings?

ORLANDO.
Not so; but I answer you right painted cloth, from whence you have studied your questions.

JAQUES.
You have a nimble wit: I think 'twas made of Atalanta's heels. Will you sit down with me? and we two will rail against our mistress the world, and all our misery.

ORLANDO.
I will chide no breather in the world but myself, against whom I know most faults.

JAQUES.
The worst fault you have is to be in love.

ORLANDO.
'Tis a fault I will not change for your best virtue. I am weary of you.

JAQUES.
By my troth, I was seeking for a fool when I found you.

ORLANDO.
He is drowned in the brook; look but in, and you shall see him.

JAQUES.
There I shall see mine own figure.

ORLANDO.
Which I take to be either a fool or a cipher.

JAQUES.
I'll tarry no longer with you: farewell, good Signior Love.

ORLANDO.
I am glad of your departure: adieu, good Monsieur Melancholy.

[*Exit* JAQUES. CELIA *and* ROSALIND *come forward.*]

ROSALIND.
I will speak to him like a saucy lackey, and under that habit play the knave with him.—Do you hear, forester?

ORLANDO.
Very well: what would you?

ROSALIND.
I pray you, what is't o'clock?

ORLANDO.
You should ask me what time o' day; there's no clock in the forest.

ROSALIND.
Then there is no true lover in the forest, else sighing every minute and groaning every hour would detect the lazy foot of Time as well as a clock.

ORLANDO.
And why not the swift foot of Time? had not that been as proper?

ROSALIND.
By no means, sir. Time travels in divers paces with divers persons. I'll tell you who time ambles withal, who Time trots withal, who Time gallops withal, and who he stands still withal.

ORLANDO.
I pr'ythee, who doth he trot withal?

ROSALIND.
Marry, he trots hard with a young maid between the contract of her marriage and the day it is solemnized; if the interim be but a se'nnight, Time's pace is so hard that it seems the length of seven year.

ORLANDO.
Who ambles time withal?

ROSALIND.
With a priest that lacks Latin and a rich man that hath not the gout: for the one

sleeps easily because he cannot study, and the other lives merrily because he feels no pain; the one lacking the burden of lean and wasteful learning, the other knowing no burden of heavy tedious penury. These Time ambles withal.

ORLANDO.
Who doth he gallop withal?

ROSALIND.
With a thief to the gallows; for though he go as softly as foot can fall, he thinks himself too soon there.

ORLANDO.
Who stays it still withal?

ROSALIND.
With lawyers in the vacation; for they sleep between term and term, and then they perceive not how Time moves.

ORLANDO.
Where dwell you, pretty youth?

ROSALIND.
With this shepherdess, my sister; here in the skirts of the forest, like fringe upon a petticoat.

ORLANDO.
Are you native of this place?

ROSALIND.
As the cony, that you see dwell where she is kindled.

ORLANDO.
Your accent is something finer than you could purchase in so removed a dwelling.

ROSALIND.
I have been told so of many: but indeed an old religious uncle of mine taught me to speak, who was in his youth an inland man; one that knew courtship too well, for there he fell in love. I have heard him read many lectures against it; and I thank God I am not a woman, to be touched with so many giddy offences as he hath generally taxed their whole sex withal.

ORLANDO.
Can you remember any of the principal evils that he laid to the charge of women?

ROSALIND.
There were none principal; they were all like one another as halfpence are; every one

fault seeming monstrous till his fellow fault came to match it.

ORLANDO.
I pr'ythee recount some of them.

ROSALIND.
No; I will not cast away my physic but on those that are sick. There is a man haunts the forest that abuses our young plants with carving "Rosalind" on their barks; hangs odes upon hawthorns, and elegies on brambles; all, forsooth, deifying the name of Rosalind: if I could meet that fancy-monger, I would give him some good counsel, for he seems to have the quotidian of love upon him.

ORLANDO.
I am he that is so love-shaked: I pray you tell me your remedy.

ROSALIND.
There is none of my uncle's marks upon you; he taught me how to know a man in love; in which cage of rushes I am sure you are not prisoner.

ORLANDO.
What were his marks?

ROSALIND.
A lean cheek; which you have not: a blue eye and sunken; which you have not: an unquestionable spirit; which you have not: a beard neglected; which you have not: but I pardon you for that, for simply your having in beard is a younger brother's revenue:— then your hose should be ungartered, your bonnet unbanded, your sleeve unbuttoned, your shoe untied, and every thing about you demonstrating a careless desolation. But you are no such man; you are rather point-device in your accoutrements, as loving yourself than seeming the lover of any other.

ORLANDO.
Fair youth, I would I could make thee believe I love.

ROSALIND.
Me believe it! you may as soon make her that you love believe it; which, I warrant, she is apter to do than to confess she does: that is one of the points in the which women still give the lie to their consciences.

But, in good sooth, are you he that hangs the verses on the trees, wherein Rosalind is so admired?

ORLANDO.

I swear to thee, youth, by the white hand of Rosalind, I am that he, that unfortunate he.

ROSALIND.

But are you so much in love as your rhymes speak?

ORLANDO.

Neither rhyme nor reason can express how much.

ROSALIND.

Love is merely a madness; and, I tell you, deserves as well a dark house and a whip as madmen do: and the reason why they are not so punished and cured is, that the lunacy is so ordinary that the whippers are in love too. Yet I profess curing it by counsel.

ORLANDO.

Did you ever cure any so?

ROSALIND.

Yes, one; and in this manner. He was to imagine me his love, his mistress; and I set him every day to woo me: at which time would I, being but a moonish youth, grieve, be effeminate, changeable, longing and liking; proud, fantastical, apish, shallow, inconstant, full of tears, full of smiles; for every passion something and for no passion truly anything, as boys and women are for the most part cattle of this colour; would now like him, now loathe him; then entertain him, then forswear him; now weep for him, then spit at him; that I drave my suitor from his mad humour of love to a living humour of madness; which was, to forswear the full stream of the world and to live in a nook merely monastic. And thus I cured him; and this way will I take upon me to wash your liver as clean as a sound sheep's heart, that there shall not be one spot of love in 't.

ORLANDO.

I would not be cured, youth.

ROSALIND.

I would cure you, if you would but call me Rosalind, and come every day to my cote and woo me.

ORLANDO.

Now, by the faith of my love, I will: tell me where it is.

ROSALIND.

Go with me to it, and I'll show it you: and, by the way, you shall tell me where in the forest you live. Will you go?

ORLANDO.

With all my heart, good youth.

ROSALIND.

Nay, you must call me Rosalind.—Come, sister, will you go?

[*Exeunt.*]

SCENE III

Another part of the forest.

[*Enter* TOUCHSTONE *and* AUDREY; JAQUES *at a distance observing them.*]

TOUCHSTONE.

Come apace, good Audrey; I will fetch up your goats, Audrey. And how, Audrey? am I the man yet? Doth my simple feature content you?

AUDREY.

Your features! Lord warrant us! what features?

TOUCHSTONE.

I am here with thee and thy goats, as the most capricious poet, honest Ovid, was among the Goths.

JAQUES. [*Aside.*]

O knowledge ill-inhabited! worse than Jove in a thatch'd house!

TOUCHSTONE.

When a man's verses cannot be understood, nor a man's good wit seconded with the forward child understanding, it strikes a man more dead than a great reckoning in a little room.—Truly, I would the gods had made thee poetical.

AUDREY.

I do not know what "poetical" is: is it honest in deed and word? is it a true thing?

TOUCHSTONE.

No, truly: for the truest poetry is the most feigning; and lovers are given to poetry;

and what they swear in poetry may be said, as lovers, they do feign.

AUDREY.

Do you wish, then, that the gods had made me poetical?

TOUCHSTONE.

I do, truly, for thou swear'st to me thou art honest; now, if thou wert a poet, I might have some hope thou didst feign.

AUDREY.

Would you not have me honest?

TOUCHSTONE.

No, truly, unless thou wert hard-favoured; for honesty coupled to beauty is to have honey a sauce to sugar.

JAQUES. [*Aside.*]

A material fool!

AUDREY.

Well, I am not fair; and therefore I pray the gods make me honest!

TOUCHSTONE.

Truly, and to cast away honesty upon a foul slut were to put good meat into an unclean dish.

AUDREY.

I am not a slut, though I thank the gods I am foul.

TOUCHSTONE.

Well, praised be the gods for thy foulness! sluttishness may come hereafter. But be it as it may be, I will marry thee: and to that end I have been with Sir Oliver Martext, the vicar of the next village; who hath promised to meet me in this place of the forest, and to couple us.

JAQUES. [*Aside.*]

I would fain see this meeting.

AUDREY.

Well, the gods give us joy!

TOUCHSTONE.

Amen. A man may, if he were of a fearful heart, stagger in this attempt; for here we have no temple but the wood, no assembly but horn-beasts. But what though? Courage! As horns are odious, they are necessary. It is said, "Many a man knows no end of his goods"; right! many a man has good horns and knows no end of

them. Well, that is the dowry of his wife; 'tis none of his own getting. Horns? Ever to poor men alone?—No, no; the noblest deer hath them as huge as the rascal. Is the single man therefore blessed? No: as a walled town is more worthier than a village, so is the forehead of a married man more honourable than the bare brow of a bachelor: and by how much defence is better than no skill, by so much is horn more precious than to want. Here comes Sir Oliver.

[*Enter* SIR OLIVER MARTEXT.]

Sir Oliver Martext, you are well met. Will you despatch us here under this tree, or shall we go with you to your chapel?

MARTEXT.

Is there none here to give the woman?

TOUCHSTONE.

I will not take her on gift of any man.

MARTEXT.

Truly, she must be given, or the marriage is not lawful.

JAQUES. [*Discovering himself.*]

Proceed, proceed; I'll give her.

TOUCHSTONE.

Good even, good Master "What-ye-call't": how do you, sir? You are very well met: God 'ild you for your last company: I am very glad to see you:—even a toy in hand here, sir:—nay; pray be covered.

JAQUES.

Will you be married, motley?

TOUCHSTONE.

As the ox hath his bow, sir, the horse his curb, and the falcon her bells, so man hath his desires; and as pigeons bill, so wedlock would be nibbling.

JAQUES.

And will you, being a man of your breeding, be married under a bush, like a beggar? Get you to church and have a good priest that can tell you what marriage is: this fellow will but join you together as they join wainscot; then one of you will prove a shrunk panel, and like green timber, warp, warp.

TOUCHSTONE. [*Aside.*]

I am not in the mind but I were better to

be married of him than of another: for he is not like to marry me well; and not being well married, it will be a good excuse for me hereafter to leave my wife.

JAQUES.
Go thou with me, and let me counsel thee.

TOUCHSTONE.
Come, sweet Audrey;
We must be married or we must live in
    bawdry.
Farewell, good Master Oliver!—Not—
      "O sweet Oliver,
      O brave Oliver,
      Leave me not behind thee."
But,—
      "Wind away,—
      Begone, I say,
      I will not to wedding with thee."
      [*Exeunt* JAQUES, TOUCHSTONE, *and*
            AUDREY.]

MARTEXT.
'Tis no matter; ne'er a fantastical knave of them all shall flout me out of my calling.
          [*Exit.*]

SCENE IV

Another part of the forest. Before a cottage.
[*Enter* ROSALIND *and* CELIA.]

ROSALIND.
Never talk to me; I will weep.

CELIA.
Do, I pr'ythee; but yet have the grace to consider that tears do not become a man.

ROSALIND.
But have I not cause to weep?

CELIA.
As good cause as one would desire; therefore weep.

ROSALIND.
His very hair is of the dissembling colour.

CELIA.
Something browner than Judas's: marry, his kisses are Judas's own children.

ROSALIND.
I' faith, his hair is of a good colour.

CELIA.
An excellent colour: your chestnut was ever the only colour.

ROSALIND.
And his kissing is as full of sanctity as the touch of holy bread.

CELIA.
He hath bought a pair of cast lips of Diana: a nun of winter's sisterhood kisses not more religiously; the very ice of chastity is in them.

ROSALIND.
But why did he swear he would come this morning, and comes not?

CELIA.
Nay, certainly, there is no truth in him.

ROSALIND.
Do you think so?

CELIA.
Yes; I think he is not a pick-purse nor a horse-stealer; but for his verity in love, I do think him as concave as a covered goblet or a worm-eaten nut.

ROSALIND.
Not true in love?

CELIA.
Yes, when he is in; but I think he is not in.

ROSALIND.
You have heard him swear downright he was.

CELIA.
"Was" is not "is": besides, the oath of a lover is no stronger than the word of a tapster; they are both the confirmer of false reckonings. He attends here in the forest on the duke, your father.

ROSALIND.
I met the duke yesterday, and had much question with him. He asked me of what parentage I was; I told him, of as good as he; so he laughed and let me go. But what talk we of fathers when there is such a man as Orlando?

CELIA.
O, that's a brave man! he writes brave verses, speaks brave words, swears brave oaths, and breaks them bravely, quite traverse, athwart the heart of his lover; as a puny tilter, that spurs his horse but on one side, breaks his staff like a noble goose: but all's brave that youth mounts and folly guides.—Who comes here?

[*Enter* CORIN.]

CORIN.

Mistress and master, you have oft enquired
After the shepherd that complain'd of love,
Who you saw sitting by me on the turf,
Praising the proud disdainful shepherdess
That was his mistress.

CELIA.

Well, and what of him?

CORIN.

If you will see a pageant truly play'd
Between the pale complexion of true love
And the red glow of scorn and proud
    disdain,
Go hence a little, and I shall conduct you,
If you will mark it.

ROSALIND.

O, come, let us remove:
The sight of lovers feedeth those in love.
Bring us to this sight, and you shall say
I'll prove a busy actor in their play.

[*Exeunt.*]

SCENE V

Another part of the forest.

[*Enter* SILVIUS *and* PHEBE.]

SILVIUS.

Sweet Phebe, do not scorn me; do not,
    Phebe;
Say that you love me not; but say not so
In bitterness. The common executioner,
Whose heart the accustom'd sight of death
    makes hard,
Falls not the axe upon the humbled neck
But first begs pardon. Will you sterner be
Than he that dies and lives by bloody
    drops?

[*Enter* ROSALIND, CELIA, *and* CORIN,
    at a distance.]

PHEBE.

I would not be thy executioner:
I fly thee, for I would not injure thee.
Thou tell'st me there is murder in mine eye:
'Tis pretty, sure, and very probable,
That eyes,—that are the frail'st and softest
    things,
Who shut their coward gates on
    atomies,—

Should be called tyrants, butchers,
    murderers!
Now I do frown on thee with all my heart;
And if mine eyes can wound, now let them
    kill thee:
Now counterfeit to swoon; why, now fall
    down;
Or, if thou canst not, O, for shame, for
    shame,
Lie not, to say mine eyes are murderers.
Now show the wound mine eye hath made
    in thee:
Scratch thee but with a pin, and there
    remains
Some scar of it; lean upon a rush,
The cicatrice and capable impressure
Thy palm some moment keeps; but now
    mine eyes,
Which I have darted at thee, hurt thee
    not;
Nor, I am sure, there is not force in eyes
That can do hurt.

SILVIUS.

O dear Phebe,
If ever,—as that ever may be near,—
You meet in some fresh cheek the power
    of fancy,
Then shall you know the wounds invisible
That love's keen arrows make.

PHEBE.

But till that time
Come not thou near me; and when that
    time comes
Afflict me with thy mocks, pity me not;
As till that time I shall not pity thee.

ROSALIND. [*Advancing.*]

And why, I pray you? Who might be your
    mother,
That you insult, exult, and all at once,
Over the wretched? What though you
    have no beauty,—
As, by my faith, I see no more in you
Than without candle may go dark to
    bed,—
Must you be therefore proud and pitiless?
Why, what means this? Why do you look
    on me?
I see no more in you than in the ordinary

Of nature's sale-work:—Od's my little life,
I think she means to tangle my eyes too!—
No, faith, proud mistress, hope not after it;
'Tis not your inky brows, your black silk
    hair,
Your bugle eyeballs, nor your cheek of
    cream,
That can entame my spirits to your
    worship.—
You foolish shepherd, wherefore do you
    follow her,
Like foggy south, puffing with wind and
    rain?
You are a thousand times a properer man
Than she a woman. 'Tis such fools as you
That makes the world full of ill-favour'd
    children:
'Tis not her glass, but you, that flatters
    her;
And out of you she sees herself more
    proper
Than any of her lineaments can show
    her;—
But, mistress, know yourself; down on
    your knees,
And thank heaven, fasting, for a good
    man's love:
For I must tell you friendly in your ear,—
Sell when you can; you are not for all
    markets:
Cry the man mercy; love him; take his
    offer;
Foul is most foul, being foul to be a scoffer.
So take her to thee, shepherd;—fare you
    well.

PHEBE.
Sweet youth, I pray you chide a year
    together:
I had rather hear you chide than this man
    woo.

ROSALIND.
He's fall'n in love with your foulness, and
she'll fall in love with my anger. If it be so,
as fast as she answers thee with frowning
looks, I'll sauce her with bitter words.—
Why look you so upon me?

PHEBE.
For no ill-will I bear you.

ROSALIND.
I pray you do not fall in love with me,
For I am falser than vows made in wine:
Besides, I like you not.—If you will know
    my house,
'Tis at the tuft of olives here hard by.—
Will you go, sister?—Shepherd, ply her
    hard.—
Come, sister.—Shepherdess, look on him
    better,
And be not proud; though all the world
    could see,
None could be so abused in sight as he.
Come to our flock.
    [*Exeunt* ROSALIND, CELIA, *and* CORIN.]

PHEBE.
Dead shepherd! now I find thy saw of
    might;
"Who ever loved that loved not at first
    sight?"

SILVIUS.
Sweet Phebe,—

PHEBE.
                Ha! what say'st thou, Silvius?

SILVIUS.
Sweet Phebe, pity me.

PHEBE.
Why, I am sorry for thee, gentle Silvius.

SILVIUS.
Wherever sorrow is, relief would be:
If you do sorrow at my grief in love,
By giving love, your sorrow and my grief
Were both extermin'd.

PHEBE.
Thou hast my love: is not that
    neighbourly?

SILVIUS.
I would have you.

PHEBE.
                Why, that were covetousness.
Silvius, the time was that I hated thee;
And yet it is not that I bear thee love:
But since that thou canst talk of love so
    well,
Thy company, which erst was irksome to
    me,
I will endure; and I'll employ thee too:
But do not look for further recompense

Than thine own gladness that thou art
  employ'd.
SILVIUS.
So holy and so perfect is my love,
And I in such a poverty of grace,
That I shall think it a most plenteous crop
To glean the broken ears after the man
That the main harvest reaps: lose now and
  then
A scatter'd smile, and that I'll live upon.
PHEBE.
Know'st thou the youth that spoke to me
  erewhile?
SILVIUS.
Not very well; but I have met him oft;
And he hath bought the cottage and the
  bounds
That the old carlot once was master of.
PHEBE.
Think not I love him, though I ask for
  him;
'Tis but a peevish boy:—yet he talks
  well;—
But what care I for words? yet words do
  well
When he that speaks them pleases those
  that hear.
It is a pretty youth:—not very pretty:—
But, sure, he's proud; and yet his pride
  becomes him:
He'll make a proper man: the best thing
  in him
Is his complexion; and faster than his
  tongue
Did make offence, his eye did heal it up.
He is not very tall; yet for his years he's
  tall;
His leg is but so-so; and yet 'tis well:
There was a pretty redness in his lip;
A little riper and more lusty red
Than that mix'd in his cheek; 'twas just the
  difference
Betwixt the constant red and mingled
  damask.
There be some women, Silvius, had they
  mark'd him
In parcels as I did, would have gone near
To fall in love with him: but, for my part,

I love him not, nor hate him not; and yet
I have more cause to hate him than to
  love him:
For what had he to do to chide at me?
He said mine eyes were black, and my
  hair black;
And, now I am remember'd, scorn'd at me:
I marvel why I answer'd not again:
But that's all one; omittance is no
  quittance.
I'll write to him a very taunting letter,
And thou shalt bear it: wilt thou, Silvius?
SILVIUS.
Phebe, with all my heart.
PHEBE.
               I'll write it straight,
The matter's in my head and in my heart:
I will be bitter with him and passing short:
Go with me, Silvius.
               [Exeunt.]

ACT IV
SCENE I
The Forest of Arden.
[*Enter* ROSALIND, CELIA, *and* JAQUES.]
JAQUES.
I pr'ythee, pretty youth, let me be better
acquainted with thee.
ROSALIND.
They say you are a melancholy fellow.
JAQUES.
I am so; I do love it better than laughing.
ROSALIND.
Those that are in extremity of either are
abominable fellows, and betray themselves to
every modern censure worse than drunkards.
JAQUES.
Why, 'tis good to be sad and say nothing.
ROSALIND.
Why then, 'tis good to be a post.
JAQUES.
I have neither the scholar's melancholy,
which is emulation; nor the musician's,
which is fantastical; nor the courtier's,
which is proud; nor the soldier's, which is
ambitious; nor the lawyer's, which is politic;
nor the lady's, which is nice; nor the lover's,
which is all these: but it is a melancholy of

mine own, compounded of many simples, extracted from many objects: and, indeed, the sundry contemplation of my travels; in which my often rumination wraps me in a most humourous sadness.

ROSALIND.
A traveller! By my faith, you have great reason to be sad: I fear you have sold your own lands to see other men's; then to have seen much and to have nothing is to have rich eyes and poor hands.

JAQUES.
Yes, I have gained my experience.

ROSALIND.
And your experience makes you sad: I had rather have a fool to make me merry than experience to make me sad; and to travel for it too.

[*Enter* ORLANDO.]

ORLANDO.
Good day, and happiness, dear Rosalind!

JAQUES.
Nay, then, God be wi' you, an you talk in blank verse.

ROSALIND.
Farewell, monsieur traveller: look you lisp and wear strange suits; disable all the benefits of your own country; be out of love with your nativity, and almost chide God for making you that countenance you are; or I will scarce think you have swam in a gondola. [*Exit* JAQUES.] Why, how now, Orlando! where have you been all this while? You a lover!—An you serve me such another trick, never come in my sight more.

ORLANDO.
My fair Rosalind, I come within an hour of my promise.

ROSALIND.
Break an hour's promise in love! He that will divide a minute into a thousand parts, and break but a part of the thousand part of a minute in the affairs of love, it may be said of him that Cupid hath clapped him o' the shoulder, but I'll warrant him heart-whole.

ORLANDO.
Pardon me, dear Rosalind.

ROSALIND.
Nay, an you be so tardy, come no more in my sight: I had as lief be wooed of a snail.

ORLANDO.
Of a snail!

ROSALIND.
Ay, of a snail; for though he comes slowly, he carries his house on his head; a better jointure, I think, than you make a woman: besides, he brings his destiny with him.

ORLANDO.
What's that?

ROSALIND.
Why, horns; which such as you are fain to be beholding to your wives for: but he comes armed in his fortune, and prevents the slander of his wife.

ORLANDO.
Virtue is no horn-maker; and my Rosalind is virtuous.

ROSALIND.
And I am your Rosalind.

CELIA.
It pleases him to call you so; but he hath a Rosalind of a better leer than you.

ROSALIND.
Come, woo me, woo me; for now I am in a holiday humour, and like enough to consent.—What would you say to me now, an I were your very very Rosalind?

ORLANDO.
I would kiss before I spoke.

ROSALIND.
Nay, you were better speak first; and when you were gravelled for lack of matter, you might take occasion to kiss. Very good orators, when they are out, they will spit; and for lovers lacking,—God warn us!—matter, the cleanliest shift is to kiss.

ORLANDO.
How if the kiss be denied?

ROSALIND.
Then she puts you to entreaty, and there begins new matter.

ORLANDO.
Who could be out, being before his beloved mistress?

Rosalind.
Marry, that should you, if I were your mistress; or I should think my honesty ranker than my wit.

Orlando.
What, of my suit?

Rosalind.
Not out of your apparel, and yet out of your suit. Am not I your Rosalind?

Orlando.
I take some joy to say you are, because I would be talking of her.

Rosalind.
Well, in her person, I say I will not have you.

Orlando.
Then, in mine own person, I die.

Rosalind.
No, faith, die by attorney. The poor world is almost six thousand years old, and in all this time there was not any man died in his own person, videlicet, in a love-cause. Troilus had his brains dashed out with a Grecian club; yet he did what he could to die before; and he is one of the patterns of love. Leander, he would have lived many a fair year, though Hero had turned nun, if it had not been for a hot midsummer night; for, good youth, he went but forth to wash him in the Hellespont, and, being taken with the cramp, was drowned; and the foolish chroniclers of that age found it was—Hero of Sestos. But these are all lies; men have died from time to time, and worms have eaten them, but not for love.

Orlando.
I would not have my right Rosalind of this mind; for, I protest, her frown might kill me.

Rosalind.
By this hand, it will not kill a fly. But come, now I will be your Rosalind in a more coming-on disposition; and ask me what you will, I will grant it.

Orlando.
Then love me, Rosalind.

Rosalind.
Yes, faith, will I, Fridays and Saturdays, and all.

Orlando.
And wilt thou have me?

Rosalind.
Ay, and twenty such.

Orlando.
What sayest thou?

Rosalind.
Are you not good?

Orlando.
I hope so.

Rosalind.
Why then, can one desire too much of a good thing?—Come, sister, you shall be the priest, and marry us.—Give me your hand, Orlando:—What do you say, sister?

Orlando.
Pray thee, marry us.

Celia.
I cannot say the words.

Rosalind.
You must begin,—"Will you, Orlando"—

Celia.
Go to:—Will you, Orlando, have to wife this Rosalind?

Orlando.
I will.

Rosalind.
Ay, but when?

Orlando.
Why, now; as fast as she can marry us.

Rosalind.
Then you must say,—"I take thee, Rosalind, for wife."

Orlando.
I take thee, Rosalind, for wife.

Rosalind.
I might ask you for your commission; but,—I do take thee, Orlando, for my husband:—there's a girl goes before the priest; and, certainly, a woman's thought runs before her actions.

Orlando.
So do all thoughts; they are winged.

Rosalind.
Now tell me how long you would have her, after you have possessed her.

Orlando.
For ever and a day.

ROSALIND.
Say "a day," without the "ever." No, no, Orlando: men are April when they woo, December when they wed: maids are May when they are maids, but the sky changes when they are wives. I will be more jealous of thee than a Barbary cock-pigeon over his hen; more clamorous than a parrot against rain; more new-fangled than an ape; more giddy in my desires than a monkey: I will weep for nothing, like Diana in the fountain, and I will do that when you are disposed to be merry; I will laugh like a hyen, and that when thou are inclined to sleep.

ORLANDO.
But will my Rosalind do so?

ROSALIND.
By my life, she will do as I do.

ORLANDO.
O, but she is wise.

ROSALIND.
Or else she could not have the wit to do this: the wiser, the waywarder: make the doors upon a woman's wit, and it will out at the casement; shut that, and it will out at the keyhole; stop that, 'twill fly with the smoke out at the chimney.

ORLANDO.
A man that had a wife with such a wit, he might say,—"Wit, whither wilt?"

ROSALIND.
Nay, you might keep that check for it, till you met your wife's wit going to your neighbour's bed.

ORLANDO.
And what wit could wit have to excuse that?

ROSALIND.
Marry, to say,—she came to seek you there. You shall never take her without her answer, unless you take her without her tongue. O, that woman that cannot make her fault her husband's occasion, let her never nurse her child herself, for she will breed it like a fool.

ORLANDO.
For these two hours, Rosalind, I will leave thee.

ROSALIND.
Alas, dear love, I cannot lack thee two hours!

ORLANDO.
I must attend the duke at dinner; by two o'clock I will be with thee again.

ROSALIND.
Ay, go your ways, go your ways; I knew what you would prove; my friends told me as much, and I thought no less:—that flattering tongue of yours won me:—'tis but one cast away, and so,—come death!— Two o'clock is your hour?

ORLANDO.
Ay, sweet Rosalind.

ROSALIND.
By my troth, and in good earnest, and so God mend me, and by all pretty oaths that are not dangerous, if you break one jot of your promise, or come one minute behind your hour, I will think you the most pathetical break-promise, and the most hollow lover, and the most unworthy of her you call Rosalind, that may be chosen out of the gross band of the unfaithful: therefore beware my censure, and keep your promise.

ORLANDO.
With no less religion than if thou wert indeed my Rosalind: so, adieu!

ROSALIND.
Well, Time is the old justice that examines all such offenders, and let time try: adieu!
                         [*Exit* ORLANDO.]

CELIA.
You have simply misus'd our sex in your love-prate: we must have your doublet and hose plucked over your head, and show the world what the bird hath done to her own nest.

ROSALIND.
O coz, coz, coz, my pretty little coz, that thou didst know how many fathom deep I am in love! But it cannot be sounded: my affection hath an unknown bottom, like the bay of Portugal.

CELIA.
Or rather, bottomless; that as fast as you pour affection in, it runs out.

ROSALIND.
No; that same wicked bastard of Venus,
that was begot of thought, conceived of
spleen, and born of madness; that blind
rascally boy, that abuses every one's eyes,
because his own are out, let him be judge
how deep I am in love.—I'll tell thee,
Aliena, I cannot be out of the sight of
Orlando: I'll go find a shadow, and sigh till
he come.

CELIA.
And I'll sleep.

[*Exeunt.*]

SCENE II
Another part of the forest.
[*Enter* JAQUES *and* LORDS, *in the habit
of foresters.*]

JAQUES.
Which is he that killed the deer?

LORD.
Sir, it was I.

JAQUES.
Let's present him to the duke, like a Roman
conqueror; and it would do well to set the
deer's horns upon his head for a branch of
victory.—Have you no song, forester, for
this purpose?

LORD.
Yes, sir.

JAQUES.
Sing it; 'tis no matter how it be in tune, so
it make noise enough.

[*Sings.*]
What shall he have that kill'd the deer?
His leather skin and horns to wear.
    Then sing him home:
    The rest shall bear this burden.
Take thou no scorn to wear the horn;
It was a crest ere thou wast born.
    Thy father's father wore it;
    And thy father bore it;
The horn, the horn, the lusty horn,
Is not a thing to laugh to scorn.

[*Exeunt.*]

SCENE III
Another part of the forest.
[*Enter* ROSALIND *and* CELIA.]

ROSALIND.
How say you now? Is it not past two
o'clock? And here much Orlando!

CELIA.
I warrant you, with pure love and troubled
brain, he hath ta'en his bow and arrows, and
is gone forth—to sleep. Look, who comes
here.

[*Enter* SILVIUS.]

SILVIUS.
My errand is to you, fair youth;—
My gentle Phebe did bid me give you this:
    [*Giving a letter.*]
I know not the contents; but, as I guess
By the stern brow and waspish action
Which she did use as she was writing of it,
It bears an angry tenor: pardon me,
I am but as a guiltless messenger.

ROSALIND.
Patience herself would startle at this letter,
And play the swaggerer; bear this, bear all:
She says I am not fair; that I lack manners;
She calls me proud, and that she could not
    love me,
Were man as rare as Phoenix. Od's my
    will!
Her love is not the hare that I do hunt;
Why writes she so to me?—Well,
    shepherd, well,
This is a letter of your own device.

SILVIUS.
No, I protest, I know not the contents:
Phebe did write it.

ROSALIND.
            Come, come, you are a fool,
And turn'd into the extremity of love.
I saw her hand: she has a leathern hand,
A freestone-colour'd hand: I verily did
    think
That her old gloves were on, but 'twas her
    hands;
She has a housewife's hand: but that's no
    matter:
I say she never did invent this letter:
This is a man's invention, and his hand.

SILVIUS.
Sure, it is hers.
ROSALIND.
Why, 'tis a boisterous and a cruel style;
A style for challengers: why, she defies me,
Like Turk to Christian: women's gentle
    brain
Could not drop forth such giant-rude
    invention,
Such Ethiop words, blacker in their effect
Than in their countenance.—Will you
    hear the letter?
SILVIUS.
So please you, for I never heard it yet;
Yet heard too much of Phebe's cruelty.
ROSALIND.
She Phebes me: mark how the tyrant
    writes.
    "Art thou god to shepherd turn'd,
    That a maiden's heart hath burn'd?"
Can a woman rail thus?
SILVIUS.
Call you this railing?
ROSALIND. [Reads.]
    "Why, thy godhead laid apart,
    Warr'st thou with a woman's heart?"
Did you ever hear such railing?
    "Whiles the eye of man did woo me,
    That could do no vengeance to me."—
Meaning me a beast.—
    "If the scorn of your bright eyne
    Have power to raise such love in mine,
    Alack, in me what strange effect
    Would they work in mild aspect?
    Whiles you chid me, I did love;
    How then might your prayers move?
    He that brings this love to thee
    Little knows this love in me:
    And by him seal up thy mind;
    Whether that thy youth and kind
    Will the faithful offer take
    Of me and all that I can make;
    Or else by him my love deny,
    And then I'll study how to die."
SILVIUS.
Call you this chiding?
CELIA.
Alas, poor shepherd!

ROSALIND.
Do you pity him? no, he deserves no pity.—
Wilt thou love such a woman?—What, to
make thee an instrument, and play false
strains upon thee! Not to be endured!—
Well, go your way to her,—for I see love
hath made thee a tame snake,—and say
this to her;—that if she love me, I charge
her to love thee; if she will not, I will never
have her unless thou entreat for her.—If
you be a true lover, hence, and not a word;
for here comes more company.
        [Exit SILVIUS.]
        [Enter OLIVER.]
OLIVER.
Good morrow, fair ones: pray you, if you
    know,
Where in the purlieus of this forest stands
A sheep-cote fenc'd about with olive trees?
CELIA.
West of this place, down in the neighbour
    bottom:
The rank of osiers, by the murmuring
    stream,
Left on your right hand, brings you to the
    place.
But at this hour the house doth keep itself;
There's none within.
OLIVER.
If that an eye may profit by a tongue,
Then should I know you by description;
Such garments, and such years: "The boy
    is fair,
Of female favour, and bestows himself
Like a ripe sister: the woman low,
And browner than her brother." Are not
    you
The owner of the house I did inquire for?
CELIA.
It is no boast, being ask'd, to say we are.
OLIVER
Orlando doth commend him to you both;
And to that youth he calls his Rosalind
He sends this bloody napkin:—are you he?
ROSALIND.
I am: what must we understand by this?
OLIVER.
Some of my shame; if you will know of me

What man I am, and how, and why, and
   where,
This handkerchief was stain'd.

CELIA.
               I pray you, tell it.

OLIVER.
When last the young Orlando parted from
   you,
He left a promise to return again
Within an hour; and, pacing through the
   forest,
Chewing the food of sweet and bitter
   fancy,
Lo, what befell! he threw his eye aside,
And, mark, what object did present itself!
Under an oak, whose boughs were moss'd
   with age,
And high top bald with dry antiquity,
A wretched ragged man, o'ergrown with
   hair,
Lay sleeping on his back: about his neck
A green and gilded snake had wreath'd
   itself,
Who, with her head nimble in threats,
   approach'd
The opening of his mouth; but suddenly,
Seeing Orlando, it unlink'd itself,
And with indented glides did slip away
Into a bush: under which bush's shade
A lioness, with udders all drawn dry,
Lay couching, head on ground, with cat-
   like watch,
When that the sleeping man should stir;
   for 'tis
The royal disposition of that beast
To prey on nothing that doth seem as
   dead:
This seen, Orlando did approach the man,
And found it was his brother, his elder
   brother.

CELIA.
O, I have heard him speak of that same
   brother;
And he did render him the most unnatural
That liv'd amongst men.

OLIVER.
             And well he might so do,
For well I know he was unnatural.

ROSALIND.
But, to Orlando:—did he leave him there,
Food to the suck'd and hungry lioness?

OLIVER.
Twice did he turn his back, and purpos'd so;
But kindness, nobler ever than revenge,
And nature, stronger than his just
   occasion,
Made him give battle to the lioness,
Who quickly fell before him; in which
   hurtling
From miserable slumber I awak'd.

CELIA.
Are you his brother?

ROSALIND.
               Was it you he rescued?

CELIA.
Was't you that did so oft contrive to kill
   him?

OLIVER.
'Twas I; but 'tis not I: I do not shame
To tell you what I was, since my
   conversion
So sweetly tastes, being the thing I am.

ROSALIND.
But, for the bloody napkin?—

OLIVER.
                  By and by.
When from the first to last, betwixt us
   two,
Tears our recountments had most kindly
   bath'd,
As, how I came into that desert place;—
In brief, he led me to the gentle duke,
Who gave me fresh array and
   entertainment,
Committing me unto my brother's love,
Who led me instantly unto his cave,
There stripp'd himself, and here upon his
   arm
The lioness had torn some flesh away,
Which all this while had bled; and now
   he fainted,
And cried, in fainting, upon Rosalind.
Brief, I recover'd him, bound up his
   wound,
And, after some small space, being strong
   at heart,

He sent me hither, stranger as I am,
To tell this story, that you might excuse
His broken promise, and to give this
     napkin,
Dy'd in his blood, unto the shepherd-youth
That he in sport doth call his Rosalind.
              [ROSALIND *faints.*]
CELIA.
Why, how now, Ganymede! sweet
     Ganymede!
OLIVER.
Many will swoon when they do look on
     blood.
CELIA.
There is more in it:—Cousin—Ganymede!
OLIVER.
Look, he recovers.
ROSALIND.
I would I were at home.
CELIA.
                    We'll lead you thither:—
I pray you, will you take him by the arm?
OLIVER.
Be of good cheer, youth:—you a man?—
You lack a man's heart.
ROSALIND.
I do so, I confess it. Ah, sir, a body
would think this was well counterfeited.
I pray you tell your brother how well I
counterfeited.—Heigh-ho!
OLIVER.
This was not counterfeit; there is too great
testimony in your complexion that it was a
passion of earnest.
ROSALIND.
Counterfeit, I assure you.
OLIVER.
Well then, take a good heart, and counterfeit
to be a man.
ROSALIND.
So I do: but, i' faith, I should have been a
woman by right.
CELIA.
Come, you look paler and paler: pray you
draw homewards.—Good sir, go with us.
OLIVER.
That will I, for I must bear answer back
How you excuse my brother, Rosalind.

ROSALIND.
I shall devise something: but, I pray you,
commend my counterfeiting to him.—
Will you go?
              [*Exeunt.*]

ACT V
SCENE I
The Forest of Arden.
[*Enter* TOUCHSTONE *and* AUDREY.]
TOUCHSTONE.
We shall find a time, Audrey; patience,
gentle Audrey.
AUDREY.
Faith, the priest was good enough, for all
the old gentleman's saying.
TOUCHSTONE.
A most wicked Sir Oliver, Audrey, a most
vile Martext. But, Audrey, there is a youth
here in the forest lays claim to you.
AUDREY.
Ay, I know who 'tis: he hath no interest in
me in the world: here comes the man you
mean.
              [*Enter* WILLIAM.]
TOUCHSTONE.
It is meat and drink to me to see a clown:
By my troth, we that have good wits have
much to answer for; we shall be flouting;
we cannot hold.
WILLIAM.
Good even, Audrey.
AUDREY.
God ye good even, William.
WILLIAM.
And good even to you, sir.
TOUCHSTONE.
Good even, gentle friend. Cover thy head,
cover thy head; nay, pr'ythee, be covered.
How old are you, friend?
WILLIAM.
Five and twenty, sir.
TOUCHSTONE.
A ripe age. Is thy name William?
WILLIAM.
William, sir.
TOUCHSTONE.
A fair name. Wast born i' the forest here?

WILLIAM.
Ay, sir, I thank God.
TOUCHSTONE.
"Thank God"—a good answer. Art rich?
WILLIAM.
Faith, sir, so-so.
TOUCHSTONE.
"So-so" is good, very good, very excellent
good:—and yet it is not; it is but so-so. Art
thou wise?
WILLIAM.
Ay, sir, I have a pretty wit.
TOUCHSTONE.
Why, thou say'st well. I do now remember
a saying: "The fool doth think he is wise,
but the wise man knows himself to be a
fool." The heathen philosopher, when he
had a desire to eat a grape, would open
his lips when he put it into his mouth;
meaning thereby that grapes were made
to eat and lips to open. You do love this
maid?
WILLIAM.
I do, sir.
TOUCHSTONE.
Give me your hand. Art thou learned?
WILLIAM.
No, sir.
TOUCHSTONE.
Then learn this of me:—to have is to have;
for it is a figure in rhetoric that drink, being
poured out of cup into a glass, by filling
the one doth empty the other; for all your
writers do consent that *ipse* is he; now, you
are not *ipse*, for I am he.
WILLIAM.
Which he, sir?
TOUCHSTONE.
He, sir, that must marry this woman.
Therefore, you clown, abandon,—which is
in the vulgar, leave,—the society,—which in
the boorish is company,—of this female,—
which in the common is woman,—which
together is abandon the society of this
female; or, clown, thou perishest; or, to thy
better understanding, diest; or, to wit, I kill
thee, make thee away, translate thy life into
death, thy liberty into bondage: I will deal

in poison with thee, or in bastinado, or in
steel; I will bandy with thee in faction; will
o'er-run thee with policy; I will kill thee a
hundred and fifty ways; therefore tremble
and depart.
AUDREY.
Do, good William.
WILLIAM.
God rest you merry, sir.
                    [*Exit.*]
                [*Enter* CORIN.]
CORIN.
Our master and mistress seek you; come
away, away!
TOUCHSTONE.
Trip, Audrey, trip, Audrey;—I attend, I
attend.
                [*Exeunt.*]

SCENE II
Another part of the forest.
[*Enter* ORLANDO *and* OLIVER.]
ORLANDO.
Is't possible that on so little acquaintance
you should like her? that but seeing you
should love her? and loving woo? and,
wooing, she should grant? and will you
persever to enjoy her?
OLIVER.
Neither call the giddiness of it in question,
the poverty of her, the small acquaintance,
my sudden wooing, nor her sudden
consenting; but say with me, I love Aliena;
say, with her, that she loves me; consent
with both, that we may enjoy each other:
it shall be to your good; for my father's
house, and all the revenue that was old Sir
Rowland's will I estate upon you, and here
live and die a shepherd.
ORLANDO.
You have my consent. Let your wedding be
to-morrow: thither will I invite the duke
and all's contented followers. Go you and
prepare Aliena; for, look you, here comes
my Rosalind.
                [*Enter* ROSALIND.]
ROSALIND.
God save you, brother.

Oliver.
And you, fair sister.
[*Exit.*]
Rosalind.
O, my dear Orlando, how it grieves me to see thee wear thy heart in a scarf!
Orlando.
It is my arm.
Rosalind.
I thought thy heart had been wounded with the claws of a lion.
Orlando.
Wounded it is, but with the eyes of a lady.
Rosalind.
Did your brother tell you how I counterfeited to swoon when he show'd me your handkercher?
Orlando.
Ay, and greater wonders than that.
Rosalind.
O, I know where you are:—nay, 'tis true: there was never anything so sudden but the fight of two rams and Caesar's thrasonical brag of "I came, saw, and overcame": for your brother and my sister no sooner met, but they looked; no sooner looked, but they loved; no sooner loved, but they sighed; no sooner sighed, but they asked one another the reason; no sooner knew the reason, but they sought the remedy: and in these degrees have they made pair of stairs to marriage, which they will climb incontinent, or else be incontinent before marriage: they are in the very wrath of love, and they will together: clubs cannot part them.
Orlando.
They shall be married to-morrow; and I will bid the duke to the nuptial. But O, how bitter a thing it is to look into happiness through another man's eyes! By so much the more shall I to-morrow be at the height of heart-heaviness, by how much I shall think my brother happy in having what he wishes for.
Rosalind.
Why, then, to-morrow I cannot serve your turn for Rosalind?

Orlando.
I can live no longer by thinking.
Rosalind.
I will weary you, then, no longer with idle talking. Know of me then,—for now I speak to some purpose,—that I know you are a gentleman of good conceit: I speak not this that you should bear a good opinion of my knowledge, insomuch I say I know you are; neither do I labour for a greater esteem than may in some little measure draw a belief from you, to do yourself good, and not to grace me. Believe then, if you please, that I can do strange things: I have, since I was three year old, conversed with a magician, most profound in his art and yet not damnable. If you do love Rosalind so near the heart as your gesture cries it out, when your brother marries Aliena, shall you marry her:—I know into what straits of fortune she is driven; and it is not impossible to me, if it appear not inconvenient to you, to set her before your eyes to-morrow, human as she is, and without any danger.
Orlando.
Speak'st thou in sober meanings?
Rosalind.
By my life, I do; which I tender dearly, though I say I am a magician. Therefore put you in your best array, bid your friends; for if you will be married to-morrow, you shall; and to Rosalind, if you will. Look, here comes a lover of mine, and a lover of hers.
[*Enter* Silvius *and* Phebe.]
Phebe.
Youth, you have done me much ungentleness,
To show the letter that I writ to you.
Rosalind.
I care not if I have: it is my study
To seem despiteful and ungentle to you:
You are there follow'd by a faithful shepherd;
Look upon him, love him; he worships you.
Phebe.
Good shepherd, tell this youth what 'tis to love.

SILVIUS.
It is to be all made of sighs and tears;—
And so am I for Phebe.
PHEBE.
And I for Ganymede.
ORLANDO.
And I for Rosalind.
ROSALIND.
And I for no woman.
SILVIUS.
It is to be all made of faith and service;—
And so am I for Phebe.
PHEBE.
And I for Ganymede.
ORLANDO.
And I for Rosalind.
ROSALIND.
And I for no woman.
SILVIUS.
It is to be all made of fantasy,
All made of passion, and all made of
    wishes;
All adoration, duty, and observance,
All humbleness, all patience, and
    impatience,
All purity, all trial, all observance;—
And so am I for Phebe.
PHEBE.
And so am I for Ganymede.
ORLANDO.
And so am I for Rosalind.
ROSALIND.
And so am I for no woman.
PHEBE. [*To* ROSALIND.]
If this be so, why blame you me to love you?
SILVIUS. [*To* PHEBE.]
If this be so, why blame you me to love you?
ORLANDO.
If this be so, why blame you me to love you?
ROSALIND.
Why do you speak too,—"Why blame you
me to love you?"
ORLANDO.
To her that is not here, nor doth not hear.
ROSALIND.
Pray you, no more of this; 'tis like the
howling of Irish wolves against the moon.
[*To* SILVIUS.] I will help you if I can. [*To*

PHEBE.] I would love you if I could.—To-
morrow meet me all together. [*To* PHEBE.]
I will marry you if ever I marry woman, and
I'll be married to-morrow. [*To* ORLANDO.]
I will satisfy you if ever I satisfied man,
and you shall be married to-morrow. [*To*
SILVIUS.] I will content you if what pleases
you contents you, and you shall be married
to-morrow. [*To* ORLANDO.] As you love
Rosalind, meet. [*To* SILVIUS.] As you love
Phebe, meet;—and as I love no woman, I'll
meet.—So, fare you well; I have left you
commands.
SILVIUS.
I'll not fail, if I live.
PHEBE.
Nor I.
ORLANDO.
Nor I.
[*Exeunt.*]

SCENE III
Another part of the forest.
[*Enter* TOUCHSTONE *and* AUDREY.]
TOUCHSTONE.
To-morrow is the joyful day, Audrey; to-
morrow will we be married.
AUDREY.
I do desire it with all my heart; and I hope
it is no dishonest desire to desire to be a
woman of the world. Here come two of the
banished duke's pages.
[*Enter two* PAGES.]
FIRST PAGE.
Well met, honest gentleman.
TOUCHSTONE.
By my troth, well met. Come sit, sit, and
    a song.
SSECOND PAGE.
We are for you: sit i' the middle.
FIRST PAGE.
Shall we clap into't roundly, without
hawking, or spitting, or saying we are hoarse,
which are the only prologues to a bad voice?
SSECOND PAGE.
I'faith, i'faith; and both in a tune, like two
gipsies on a horse.
[*Sings.*]

It was a lover and his lass,
  With a hey, and a ho, and a hey nonino,
That o'er the green corn-field did pass
    In the spring time, the only pretty ring
    time,
When birds do sing, hey ding a ding, ding:
Sweet lovers love the spring.
Between the acres of the rye,
  With a hey, and a ho, and a hey nonino,
These pretty country folks would lie,
    In the spring time, the only pretty ring
    time,
When birds do sing, hey ding a ding, ding:
Sweet lovers love the spring.
This carol they began that hour,
  With a hey, and a ho, and a hey nonino,
How that a life was but a flower,
    In the spring time, the only pretty ring
    time,
When birds do sing, hey ding a ding, ding:
Sweet lovers love the spring.
And therefore take the present time,
  With a hey, and a ho, and a hey nonino,
For love is crowned with the prime,
    In the spring time, the only pretty ring
    time,
When birds do sing, hey ding a ding, ding:
Sweet lovers love the spring.

TOUCHSTONE.
Truly, young gentlemen, though there was
no great matter in the ditty, yet the note
was very untimeable.

FIRST PAGE.
You are deceived, sir; we kept time, we lost
not our time.

TOUCHSTONE.
By my troth, yes; I count it but time lost to
hear such a foolish song. God be with you;
and God mend your voices! Come, Audrey.
                              [*Exeunt.*]

SCENE IV

Another part of the forest.
[*Enter* DUKE SENIOR, AMIENS, JAQUES,
  ORLANDO, OLIVER, *and* CELIA.]

DUKE SENIOR.
Dost thou believe, Orlando, that the boy
Can do all this that he hath promised?

ORLANDO.
I sometimes do believe and sometimes
    do not:
As those that fear they hope, and know
    they fear.
  [*Enter* ROSALIND, SILVIUS, *and* PHEBE.]

ROSALIND.
Patience once more, whiles our compact
    is urg'd:—
[*To the* DUKE.] You say, if I bring in your
    Rosalind,
You will bestow her on Orlando here?

DUKE SENIOR.
That would I, had I kingdoms to give with
    her.

ROSALIND. [*To* ORLANDO.]
And you say you will have her when I
    bring her?

ORLANDO.
That would I, were I of all kingdoms king.

ROSALIND. [*To* PHEBE.]
You say you'll marry me, if I be willing?

PHEBE.
That will I, should I die the hour after.

ROSALIND.
But if you do refuse to marry me,
You'll give yourself to this most faithful
    shepherd?

PHEBE.
So is the bargain.

ROSALIND. [*To* SILVIUS.]
You say that you'll have Phebe, if she will?

SILVIUS.
Though to have her and death were both
one thing.

ROSALIND.
I have promis'd to make all this matter
    even.
Keep you your word, O duke, to give your
    daughter;—
You yours, Orlando, to receive his
    daughter;—
Keep your word, Phebe, that you'll marry
    me;
Or else, refusing me, to wed this
    shepherd:—
Keep your word, Silvius, that you'll marry
    her

If she refuse me:—and from hence I go,
To make these doubts all even.

    [*Exeunt* ROSALIND *and* CELIA.]

DUKE SENIOR.
I do remember in this shepherd-boy
Some lively touches of my daughter's
    favour.

ORLANDO.
My lord, the first time that I ever saw him
Methought he was a brother to your
    daughter:
But, my good lord, this boy is forest-born,
And hath been tutor'd in the rudiments
Of many desperate studies by his uncle,
Whom he reports to be a great magician,
Obscured in the circle of this forest.

JAQUES.
There is, sure, another flood toward, and
these couples are coming to the ark. Here
comes a pair of very strange beasts which
in all tongues are called fools.

    [*Enter* TOUCHSTONE *and* AUDREY.]

TOUCHSTONE.
Salutation and greeting to you all!

JAQUES.
Good my lord, bid him welcome. This is
the motley-minded gentleman that I have
so often met in the forest: he hath been a
courtier, he swears.

TOUCHSTONE.
If any man doubt that, let him put me to
my purgation. I have trod a measure; I have
flattered a lady; I have been politic with
my friend, smooth with mine enemy; I
have undone three tailors; I have had four
quarrels, and like to have fought one.

JAQUES.
And how was that ta'en up?

TOUCHSTONE.
Faith, we met, and found the quarrel was
upon the seventh cause.

JAQUES.
How seventh cause? Good my lord, like
this fellow?

DUKE SENIOR.
I like him very well.

TOUCHSTONE.
God 'ild you, sir; I desire you of the like.

I press in here, sir, amongst the rest of
the country copulatives, to swear and to
forswear; according as marriage binds and
blood breaks:—A poor virgin, sir, an ill-
favoured thing, sir, but mine own; a poor
humour of mine, sir, to take that that no
man else will; rich honesty dwells like a
miser, sir, in a poor-house; as your pearl in
your foul oyster.

DUKE SENIOR.
By my faith, he is very swift and sententious.

TOUCHSTONE.
According to the fool's bolt, sir, and such
dulcet diseases.

JAQUES.
But, for the seventh cause; how did you
find the quarrel on the seventh cause?

TOUCHSTONE.
Upon a lie seven times removed;—bear
your body more seeming, Audrey:—as
thus, sir, I did dislike the cut of a certain
courtier's beard; he sent me word, if I
said his beard was not cut well, he was in
the mind it was: this is called the Retort
courteous. If I sent him word again it was
not well cut, he would send me word he
cut it to please himself: this is called the
Quip modest. If again, it was not well cut,
he disabled my judgment: this is called the
Reply churlish. If again, it was not well cut,
he would answer I spake not true: this is
called the Reproof valiant. If again, it was
not well cut, he would say I lie: this is called
the Countercheck quarrelsome: and so, to
the Lie circumstantial, and the Lie direct.

JAQUES.
And how oft did you say his beard was not
well cut?

TOUCHSTONE.
I durst go no further than the Lie
circumstantial, nor he durst not give me
the Lie direct; and so we measured swords
and parted.

JAQUES.
Can you nominate in order now the
degrees of the lie?

TOUCHSTONE.
O, sir, we quarrel in print by the book,

as you have books for good manners: I will name you the degrees. The first, the Retort courteous; the second, the Quip modest; the third, the Reply churlish; the fourth, the Reproof valiant; the fifth, the Countercheck quarrelsome; the sixth, the Lie with circumstance; the seventh, the Lie direct. All these you may avoid but the Lie direct; and you may avoid that too with an "If." I knew when seven justices could not take up a quarrel; but when the parties were met themselves, one of them thought but of an "If," as: "If you said so, then I said so"; and they shook hands, and swore brothers. Your "If" is the only peace-maker;—much virtue in "If."

JAQUES.

Is not this a rare fellow, my lord? he's as good at anything, and yet a fool.

DUKE SENIOR.

He uses his folly like a stalking-horse, and under the presentation of that he shoots his wit.

   [*Enter* HYMEN, *leading* ROSALIND *in woman's clothes; and* CELIA.]
       [*Still music.*]

HYMEN.

Then is there mirth in heaven,
  When earthly things made even
    Atone together.
  Good duke, receive thy daughter;
  Hymen from heaven brought her,
    Yea, brought her hither,
  That thou mightst join her hand with his,
  Whose heart within his bosom is.

ROSALIND. [*To* DUKE SENIOR.]

To you I give myself, for I am yours.
[*To* ORLANDO.] To you I give myself, for I
  am yours.

DUKE SENIOR.

If there be truth in sight, you are my
  daughter.

ORLANDO.

If there be truth in sight, you are my
  Rosalind.

PHEBE.

If sight and shape be true,
Why then, my love, adieu!

ROSALIND. [*To* DUKE SENIOR.]

I'll have no father, if you be not he;—
      [*To* ORLANDO.]
I'll have no husband, if you be not he;—
      [*To* PHEBE.]
Nor ne'er wed woman, if you be not
  she.

HYMEN.

Peace, ho! I bar confusion:
'Tis I must make conclusion
  Of these most strange events:
Here's eight that must take hands
To join in Hymen's bands,
  If truth holds true contents.
   [*To* ORLANDO *and* ROSALIND.]
You and you no cross shall part:
   [*To* OLIVER *and* CELIA.]
You and you are heart in heart;
      [*To* PHEBE.]
You to his love must accord,
Or have a woman to your lord:—
   [*To* TOUCHSTONE *and* AUDREY.]
You and you are sure together,
As the winter to foul weather.
Whiles a wedlock-hymn we sing,
Feed yourselves with questioning,
That reason wonder may diminish,
How thus we met, and these things
  finish.
       [*Sings.*]
Wedding is great Juno's crown;
  O blessed bond of board and bed!
'Tis Hymen peoples every town;
  High wedlock then be honoured;
Honour, high honour, and renown,
To Hymen, god of every town!

DUKE SENIOR.

O my dear niece, welcome thou art to me!
Even daughter, welcome in no less degree.

PHEBE. [*To* SILVIUS.]

I will not eat my word, now thou art mine;
Thy faith my fancy to thee doth combine.
     [*Enter* JAQUES DE BOYS.]

JAQUES DE BOYS.

Let me have audience for a word or two;
I am the second son of old Sir Rowland,
That bring these tidings to this fair
  assembly:—

Duke Frederick, hearing how that every
    day
Men of great worth resorted to this forest,
Address'd a mighty power; which were
    on foot,
In his own conduct, purposely to take
His brother here, and put him to the
    sword:
And to the skirts of this wild wood he
    came;
Where, meeting with an old religious man,
After some question with him, was
    converted
Both from his enterprise and from the
    world;
His crown bequeathing to his banish'd
    brother,
And all their lands restored to them again
That were with him exil'd. This to be true
I do engage my life.

DUKE SENIOR.
               Welcome, young man:
Thou offer'st fairly to thy brother's
    wedding:
To one, his lands withheld; and to the
    other,
A land itself at large, a potent dukedom.
First, in this forest, let us do those ends
That here were well begun and well begot:
And after, every of this happy number,
That have endur'd shrewd days and nights
    with us,
Shall share the good of our returned
    fortune,
According to the measure of their states.
Meantime, forget this new-fall'n dignity,
And fall into our rustic revelry:—
Play, music!—and you brides and
    bridegrooms all, .
With measure heap'd in joy, to the
    measures fall.

JAQUES.
Sir, by your patience. If I heard you rightly,
The duke hath put on a religious life,
And thrown into neglect the pompous
    court?

JAQUES DE BOYS.
He hath.

JAQUES.
To him will I: out of these convertites
There is much matter to be heard and
    learn'd.—
           [*To* DUKE SENIOR.]
You to your former honour I bequeath;
Your patience and your virtue well
    deserves it:—
           [*To* ORLANDO.]
You to a love that your true faith doth
    merit:—
           [*To* OLIVER.]
You to your land, and love, and great
    allies:—
           [*To* SILVIUS.]
You to a long and well-deserved bed:—
           [*To* TOUCHSTONE.]
And you to wrangling; for thy loving
    voyage
Is but for two months victuall'd.—So to
    your pleasures;
I am for other than for dancing measures.

DUKE SENIOR.
Stay, Jaques, stay.

JAQUES.
To see no pastime I; what you would have
I'll stay to know at your abandon'd cave.
           [*Exit.*]

DUKE SENIOR.
Proceed, proceed: we will begin these rites,
As we do trust they'll end, in true delights.
           [*A dance.*]

EPILOGUE

ROSALIND.
It is not the fashion to see the lady the
epilogue; but it is no more unhandsome
than to see the lord the prologue. If it be
true that good wine needs no bush, 'tis true
that a good play needs no epilogue. Yet to
good wine they do use good bushes; and
good plays prove the better by the help of
good epilogues. What a case am I in, then,
that am neither a good epilogue nor cannot
insinuate with you in the behalf of a good
play! I am not furnished like a beggar;
therefore to beg will not become me: my
way is to conjure you; and I'll begin with

the women. I charge you, O women, for the love you bear to men, to like as much of this play as please you: and I charge you, O men, for the love you bear to women;—as I perceive by your simpering, none of you hates them,—that between you and the women the play may please. If I were a woman, I would kiss as many of you as had beards that pleased me, complexions that liked me, and breaths that I defied not; and, I am sure, as many as have good beards, or good faces, or sweet breaths, will, for my kind offer, when I make curtsy, bid me farewell.

[*Exeunt.*]

The Taming of the Shrew

DRAMATIS PERSONAE

A LORD
CHRISTOPHER SLY, *a tinker*
HOSTESS, PAGE, PLAYERS,
  HUNTSMEN, *and* SERVANTS
BAPTISTA MINOLA, *a rich man of*
  Padua
VINCENTIO, *an old gentleman of Pisa*
LUCENTIO, *son to Vincentio; in love with*
  Bianca
PETRUCHIO, *a gentleman of Verona;*
  suitor to Katherina
GREMIO *and* HORTENSIO, *suitors to*
  Bianca
TRANIO *and* BIONDELLO, *servants*
  to Lucentio

GRUMIO, CURTIS, *and* PEDANT,
  servants to Petruchio
KATHERINA, *the shrew, daughter to*
  Baptista
BIANCA, *daughter to Baptista*
A WIDOW
TAILOR, HABERDASHER, *and*
  SERVANTS

SCENE: *Sometimes in Padua, and*
  sometimes in Petruchio's house in the
  country.

INDUCTION
SCENE I
Before an alehouse on a heath.
[*Enter* HOSTESS *and* SLY.]

SLY.
I'll pheeze you, in faith.

HOSTESS.
A pair of stocks, you rogue!

SLY.
Y'are a baggage; the Slys are no rogues;
look in the chronicles: we came in with
Richard Conqueror. Therefore, *paucas*
pallabris; let the world slide. Sessa!

HOSTESS.
You will not pay for the glasses you have
burst?

SLY.
No, not a denier. Go by, Saint Jeronimy, go
to thy cold bed and warm thee.

HOSTESS.
I know my remedy; I must go fetch the
third-borough.
                [*Exit.*]

SLY.
Third, or fourth, or fifth borough, I'll

answer him by law. I'll not budge an inch,
boy: let him come, and kindly.
  [*Lies down on the ground, and falls asleep.*]
  [*Horns winded. Enter a* LORD *from hunting,*
      with HUNTSMEN *and* SERVANTS.]

LORD.
Huntsman, I charge thee, tender well my
  hounds;
Brach Merriman, the poor cur, is emboss'd,
And couple Clowder with the deep-
  mouth'd brach.
Saw'st thou not, boy, how Silver made it
  good
At the hedge-corner, in the coldest fault?
I would not lose the dog for twenty
  pound.

FIRST HUNTSMAN.
Why, Bellman is as good as he, my lord;
He cried upon it at the merest loss,
And twice to-day pick'd out the dullest
  scent;
Trust me, I take him for the better dog.

LORD.
Thou art a fool: if Echo were as fleet,
I would esteem him worth a dozen such.

But sup them well, and look unto them all;
To-morrow I intend to hunt again.
First Huntsman.
I will, my lord.
Lord. [*Sees* Sly.]
What's here? One dead, or drunk?
See, doth he breathe?
Second Huntsman.
He breathes, my lord. Were he not warm'd with ale,
This were a bed but cold to sleep so soundly.
Lord.
O monstrous beast! how like a swine he lies!
Grim death, how foul and loathsome is thine image!
Sirs, I will practise on this drunken man.
What think you, if he were convey'd to bed,
Wrapp'd in sweet clothes, rings put upon his fingers,
A most delicious banquet by his bed,
And brave attendants near him when he wakes,
Would not the beggar then forget himself?
First Huntsman.
Believe me, lord, I think he cannot choose.
Second Huntsman.
It would seem strange unto him when he wak'd.
Lord.
Even as a flattering dream or worthless fancy.
Then take him up, and manage well the jest.
Carry him gently to my fairest chamber,
And hang it round with all my wanton pictures;
Balm his foul head in warm distilled waters,
And burn sweet wood to make the lodging sweet.
Procure me music ready when he wakes,
To make a dulcet and a heavenly sound;
And if he chance to speak, be ready straight,
And with a low submissive reverence

Say "What is it your honour will command?"
Let one attend him with a silver basin
Full of rose-water and bestrew'd with flowers;
Another bear the ewer, the third a diaper,
And say "Will't please your lordship cool your hands?"
Some one be ready with a costly suit,
And ask him what apparel he will wear;
Another tell him of his hounds and horse,
And that his lady mourns at his disease.
Persuade him that he hath been lunatic;
And, when he says he is—say that he dreams,
For he is nothing but a mighty lord.
This do, and do it kindly, gentle sirs;
It will be pastime passing excellent,
If it be husbanded with modesty.
First Huntsman.
My lord, I warrant you we will play our part,
As he shall think by our true diligence,
He is no less than what we say he is.
Lord.
Take him up gently, and to bed with him,
And each one to his office when he wakes.
    [Sly *is bourne out. A trumpet sounds.*]
Sirrah, go see what trumpet 'tis that sounds:
        [*Exit* Servant.]
Belike some noble gentleman that means,
Travelling some journey, to repose him here.
        [*Re-enter* Servant.]
How now! who is it?
Servant.
        An it please your honour, players
That offer service to your lordship.
Lord.
Bid them come near. [*Enter* Players.]
    Now, fellows, you are welcome.
Players.
We thank your honour.
Lord.
Do you intend to stay with me to-night?
Player.
So please your lordship to accept our duty.

Lord.
With all my heart. This fellow I remember
Since once he play'd a farmer's eldest son;
'Twas where you woo'd the gentlewoman
    so well.
I have forgot your name; but, sure, that
    part
Was aptly fitted and naturally perform'd.
Player.
I think 'twas Soto that your honour means.
Lord.
'Tis very true; thou didst it excellent.
Well, you are come to me in happy time,
The rather for I have some sport in hand
Wherein your cunning can assist me
    much.
There is a lord will hear you play to-night;
But I am doubtful of your modesties,
Lest, over-eying of his odd behaviour,—
For yet his honour never heard a play,—
You break into some merry passion
And so offend him; for I tell you, sirs,
If you should smile, he grows impatient.
Player.
Fear not, my lord; we can contain ourselves,
Were he the veriest antick in the world.
Lord.
Go, sirrah, take them to the buttery,
And give them friendly welcome every
    one:
Let them want nothing that my house
    affords.
    [*Exit one with the* Players.]
Sirrah, go you to Barthol'mew my page,
And see him dress'd in all suits like a lady;
That done, conduct him to the drunkard's
    chamber,
And call him "madam," do him obeisance.
Tell him from me—as he will win my
    love,—
He bear himself with honourable action,
Such as he hath observ'd in noble ladies
Unto their lords, by them accomplished;
Such duty to the drunkard let him do,
With soft low tongue and lowly courtesy,
And say "What is't your honour will
    command,
Wherein your lady and your humble wife

May show her duty and make known her
    love?"
And then with kind embracements,
    tempting kisses,
And with declining head into his bosom,
Bid him shed tears, as being overjoy'd
To see her noble lord restor'd to health,
Who for this seven years hath esteemed
    him
No better than a poor and loathsome
    beggar.
And if the boy have not a woman's gift
To rain a shower of commanded tears,
An onion will do well for such a shift,
Which, in a napkin being close convey'd,
Shall in despite enforce a watery eye.
See this dispatch'd with all the haste thou
    canst;
Anon I'll give thee more instructions.
    [*Exit* Servant.]
I know the boy will well usurp the grace,
Voice, gait, and action, of a gentlewoman;
I long to hear him call the drunkard
    husband;
And how my men will stay themselves
    from laughter
When they do homage to this simple
    peasant.
I'll in to counsel them; haply my presence
May well abate the over-merry spleen,
Which otherwise would grow into
    extremes.
    [*Exeunt.*]

SCENE II

A bedchamber in the lord's house.
[Sly *is discovered in a rich nightgown, with*
Attendants: *some with apparel, basin,*
ewer, and other appurtenances; and Lord,
dressed like a servant.]
Sly.
For God's sake! a pot of small ale.
First Servant.
Will't please your lordship drink a cup of
    sack?
Second Servant.
Will't please your honour taste of these
    conserves?

THIRD SERVANT.
What raiment will your honour wear
    to-day?
SLY.
I am Christophero Sly; call not me honour
nor lordship. I ne'er drank sack in my life;
and if you give me any conserves, give me
conserves of beef. Ne'er ask me what raiment
I'll wear, for I have no more doublets than
backs, no more stockings than legs, nor no
more shoes than feet: nay, sometime more
feet than shoes, or such shoes as my toes
look through the overleather.
LORD.
Heaven cease this idle humour in your
    honour!
O, that a mighty man of such descent,
Of such possessions, and so high esteem,
Should be infused with so foul a spirit!
SLY.
What! would you make me mad? Am not
I Christopher Sly, old Sly's son of Burton-
heath; by birth a pedlar, by education a
card-maker, by transmutation a bear-herd,
and now by present profession a tinker?
Ask Marian Hacket, the fat ale-wife of
Wincot, if she know me not: if she say I am
not fourteen pence on the score for sheer
ale, score me up for the lyingest knave in
Christendom. What! I am not bestraught.
Here's—
THIRD SERVANT.
O! this it is that makes your lady mourn.
SECOND SERVANT.
O! this is it that makes your servants droop.
LORD.
Hence comes it that your kindred shuns
    your house,
As beaten hence by your strange lunacy.
O noble lord, bethink thee of thy birth,
Call home thy ancient thoughts from
    banishment,
And banish hence these abject lowly
    dreams.
Look how thy servants do attend on thee,
Each in his office ready at thy beck:
Wilt thou have music? Hark! Apollo plays,
            [*Music.*]

And twenty caged nightingales do sing:
Or wilt thou sleep? We'll have thee to a
    couch
Softer and sweeter than the lustful bed
On purpose trimm'd up for Semiramis.
Say thou wilt walk: we will bestrew the
    ground:
Or wilt thou ride? Thy horses shall be
    trapp'd,
Their harness studded all with gold and
    pearl.
Dost thou love hawking? Thou hast hawks
    will soar
Above the morning lark: or wilt thou
    hunt?
Thy hounds shall make the welkin answer
    them
And fetch shrill echoes from the hollow
    earth.
FIRST SERVANT.
Say thou wilt course; thy greyhounds are
    as swift
As breathed stags; ay, fleeter than the roe.
SECOND SERVANT.
Dost thou love pictures? We will fetch
    thee straight
Adonis painted by a running brook,
And Cytherea all in sedges hid,
Which seem to move and wanton with
    her breath
Even as the waving sedges play with
    wind.
LORD.
We'll show thee Io as she was a maid
And how she was beguiled and surpris'd,
As lively painted as the deed was done.
THIRD SERVANT.
Or Daphne roaming through a thorny
    wood,
Scratching her legs, that one shall swear
    she bleeds
And at that sight shall sad Apollo weep,
So workmanly the blood and tears are
    drawn.
LORD.
Thou art a lord, and nothing but a lord:
Thou hast a lady far more beautiful
Than any woman in this waning age.

FIRST SERVANT.
And, till the tears that she hath shed for
    thee
Like envious floods o'er-run her lovely
    face,
She was the fairest creature in the world;
And yet she is inferior to none.
SLY.
Am I a lord? and have I such a lady?
Or do I dream? Or have I dream'd till
    now?
I do not sleep: I see, I hear, I speak;
I smell sweet savours, and I feel soft
    things:
Upon my life, I am a lord indeed;
And not a tinker, nor Christophero Sly.
Well, bring our lady hither to our sight;
And once again, a pot o' the smallest ale.
SECOND SERVANT.
Will't please your mightiness to wash your
    hands?
    [SERVANTS *present a ewer, basin, and*
        napkin.]
O, how we joy to see your wit restor'd!
O, that once more you knew but what
    you are!
These fifteen years you have been in a
    dream,
Or, when you wak'd, so wak'd as if you
    slept.
SLY.
These fifteen years! by my fay, a goodly
    nap.
But did I never speak of all that time?
FIRST SERVANT.
O! yes, my lord, but very idle words;
For though you lay here in this goodly
    chamber,
Yet would you say ye were beaten out of
    door,
And rail upon the hostess of the house,
And say you would present her at the leet,
Because she brought stone jugs and no
    seal'd quarts.
Sometimes you would call out for Cicely
    Hacket.
SLY.
Ay, the woman's maid of the house.

THIRD SERVANT.
Why, sir, you know no house nor no such
    maid,
Nor no such men as you have reckon'd up,
As Stephen Sly, and old John Naps of
    Greece,
And Peter Turf, and Henry Pimpernell;
And twenty more such names and men
    as these,
Which never were, nor no man ever saw.
SLY.
Now, Lord be thanked for my good
    amends!
ALL.
Amen.
SLY.
I thank thee; thou shalt not lose by it.
    [*Enter the* PAGE, *as a lady, with*
        ATTENDANTS.]
PAGE.
How fares my noble lord?
SLY.
                        Marry, I fare well;
For here is cheer enough. Where is my
    wife?
PAGE.
Here, noble lord: what is thy will with her?
SLY.
Are you my wife, and will not call me
    husband?
My men should call me lord: I am your
    goodman.
PAGE.
My husband and my lord, my lord and
    husband;
I am your wife in all obedience.
SLY.
I know it well. What must I call her?
LORD.
                        Madam.
SLY.
Al'ce madam, or Joan madam?
LORD.
Madam, and nothing else; so lords call
    ladies.
SLY.
Madam wife, they say that I have dream'd
And slept above some fifteen year or more.

PAGE.

Ay, and the time seems thirty unto me,
Being all this time abandon'd from your
  bed.

SLY.

'Tis much. Servants, leave me and her
  alone.
Madam, undress you, and come now to
  bed.

PAGE.

Thrice noble lord, let me entreat of you
To pardon me yet for a night or two;
Or, if not so, until the sun be set:
For your physicians have expressly charg'd,
In peril to incur your former malady,
That I should yet absent me from your
  bed:
I hope this reason stands for my excuse.

SLY.

Ay, it stands so that I may hardly tarry
so long; but I would be loath to fall into
my dreams again: I will therefore tarry, in
despite of the flesh and the blood.

    [*Enter a* SERVANT.]

SERVANT.

Your honour's players, hearing your
  amendment,
Are come to play a pleasant comedy;
For so your doctors hold it very meet,
Seeing too much sadness hath congeal'd
  your blood,
And melancholy is the nurse of frenzy:
Therefore they thought it good you hear
  a play,
And frame your mind to mirth and
  merriment,
Which bars a thousand harms and
  lengthens life.

SLY.

Marry, I will; let them play it. Is not a
commonty a Christmas gambol or a
tumbling-trick?

PAGE.

No, my good lord; it is more pleasing stuff.

SLY.

What! household stuff?

PAGE.

                    It is a kind of history.

SLY.

Well, we'll see't. Come, madam wife, sit by
my side and let the world slip: we shall ne'er
be younger.

            [*Flourish.*]

ACT I
SCENE I
Padua. A public place.
[*Enter* LUCENTIO *and* TRANIO.]

LUCENTIO.

Tranio, since for the great desire I had
To see fair Padua, nursery of arts,
I am arriv'd for fruitful Lombardy,
The pleasant garden of great Italy,
And by my father's love and leave am
  arm'd
With his good will and thy good company,
My trusty servant well approv'd in all,
Here let us breathe, and haply institute
A course of learning and ingenious studies.
Pisa, renowned for grave citizens,
Gave me my being and my father first,
A merchant of great traffic through the
  world,
Vincentio, come of the Bentivolii.
Vincentio's son, brought up in Florence,
It shall become to serve all hopes
  conceiv'd,
To deck his fortune with his virtuous
  deeds:
And therefore, Tranio, for the time I study,
Virtue and that part of philosophy
Will I apply that treats of happiness
By virtue specially to be achiev'd.
Tell me thy mind; for I have Pisa left
And am to Padua come as he that leaves
A shallow plash to plunge him in the deep,
And with satiety seeks to quench his
  thirst.

TRANIO.

Mi perdonato, gentle master mine;
I am in all affected as yourself;
Glad that you thus continue your resolve
To suck the sweets of sweet philosophy.
Only, good master, while we do admire
This virtue and this moral discipline,
Let's be no stoics nor no stocks, I pray;

Or so devote to Aristotle's checks
As Ovid be an outcast quite abjur'd.
Balk logic with acquaintance that you have,
And practise rhetoric in your common
    talk;
Music and poesy use to quicken you;
The mathematics and the metaphysics,
Fall to them as you find your stomach
    serves you:
No profit grows where is no pleasure ta'en;
In brief, sir, study what you most affect.
LUCENTIO.
Gramercies, Tranio, well dost thou advise.
If, Biondello, thou wert come ashore,
We could at once put us in readiness,
And take a lodging fit to entertain
Such friends as time in Padua shall beget.
But stay awhile; what company is this?
TRANIO.
Master, some show to welcome us to town.
    [*Enter* BAPTISTA, KATHERINA, BIANCA,
    GREMIO, *and* HORTENSIO. LUCENTIO and
            TRANIO *stand aside.*]
BAPTISTA.
Gentlemen, importune me no further,
For how I firmly am resolv'd you know;
That is, not to bestow my youngest
    daughter
Before I have a husband for the elder.
If either of you both love Katherina,
Because I know you well and love you
    well,
Leave shall you have to court her at your
    pleasure.
GREMIO.
To cart her rather: she's too rough for me.
There, there, Hortensio, will you any wife?
KATHERINA. [*To* BAPTISTA.]
I pray you, sir, is it your will
To make a stale of me amongst these
    mates?
HORTENSIO.
Mates, maid! How mean you that? No
    mates for you,
Unless you were of gentler, milder mould.
KATHERINA.
I' faith, sir, you shall never need to fear;
I wis it is not halfway to her heart;

But if it were, doubt not her care should be
To comb your noddle with a three-legg'd
    stool,
And paint your face, and use you like a
    fool.
HORTENSIO.
From all such devils, good Lord deliver us!
GREMIO.
And me, too, good Lord!
TRANIO.
Husht, master! Here's some good pastime
    toward:
That wench is stark mad or wonderful
    froward.
LUCENTIO.
But in the other's silence do I see
Maid's mild behaviour and sobriety.
Peace, Tranio!
TRANIO.
Well said, master; mum! and gaze your fill.
BAPTISTA.
Gentlemen, that I may soon make good
What I have said,—Bianca, get you in:
And let it not displease thee, good Bianca,
For I will love thee ne'er the less, my girl.
KATHERINA.
A pretty peat! it is best
Put finger in the eye, an she knew why.
BIANCA.
Sister, content you in my discontent.
Sir, to your pleasure humbly I subscribe:
My books and instruments shall be my
    company,
On them to look, and practise by myself.
LUCENTIO.
Hark, Tranio! thou mayst hear Minerva
    speak.
HORTENSIO.
Signior Baptista, will you be so strange?
Sorry am I that our good will effects
Bianca's grief.
GREMIO.
                Why will you mew her up,
Signior Baptista, for this fiend of hell,
And make her bear the penance of her
    tongue?
BAPTISTA.
Gentlemen, content ye; I am resolv'd.

Go in, Bianca. [*Exit* BIANCA.]
And for I know she taketh most delight
In music, instruments, and poetry,
Schoolmasters will I keep within my
    house
Fit to instruct her youth. If you, Hortensio,
Or, Signior Gremio, you, know any such,
Prefer them hither; for to cunning men
I will be very kind, and liberal
To mine own children in good bringing
    up;
And so, farewell. Katherina, you may stay;
For I have more to commune with Bianca.
                    [*Exit.*]

KATHERINA.
Why, and I trust I may go too, may I
not? What! shall I be appointed hours, as
though, belike, I knew not what to take and
what to leave? Ha!
                    [*Exit.*]

GREMIO.
You may go to the devil's dam: your gifts are
so good here's none will hold you. Our love
is not so great, Hortensio, but we may blow
our nails together, and fast it fairly out; our
cake's dough on both sides. Farewell: yet, for
the love I bear my sweet Bianca, if I can by
any means light on a fit man to teach her
that wherein she delights, I will wish him
to her father.

HORTENSIO.
So will I, Signior Gremio: but a word, I
pray. Though the nature of our quarrel
yet never brooked parle, know now, upon
advice, it toucheth us both,—that we may
yet again have access to our fair mistress,
and be happy rivals in Bianca's love,—to
labour and effect one thing specially.

GREMIO.
What's that, I pray?

HORTENSIO.
Marry, sir, to get a husband for her sister.

GREMIO.
A husband! a devil.

HORTENSIO.
I say, a husband.

GREMIO.
I say, a devil. Thinkest thou, Hortensio,

though her father be very rich, any man is
so very a fool to be married to hell?

HORTENSIO.
Tush, Gremio! Though it pass your patience
and mine to endure her loud alarums, why,
man, there be good fellows in the world, an
a man could light on them, would take her
with all faults, and money enough.

GREMIO.
I cannot tell; but I had as lief take her
dowry with this condition: to be whipp'd at
the high cross every morning.

HORTENSIO.
Faith, as you say, there's small choice in
rotten apples. But, come; since this bar
in law makes us friends, it shall be so far
forth friendly maintained, till by helping
Baptista's eldest daughter to a husband,
we set his youngest free for a husband, and
then have to't afresh. Sweet Bianca! Happy
man be his dole! He that runs fastest gets
the ring. How say you, Signior Gremio?

GREMIO.
I am agreed; and would I had given him the
best horse in Padua to begin his wooing,
that would thoroughly woo her, wed her,
and bed her, and rid the house of her. Come
on.
        [*Exeunt* GREMIO *and* HORTENSIO.]

TRANIO.
I pray, sir, tell me, is it possible
That love should of a sudden take such
    hold?

LUCENTIO.
O Tranio! till I found it to be true,
I never thought it possible or likely;
But see, while idly I stood looking on,
I found the effect of love in idleness;
And now in plainness do confess to thee,
That art to me as secret and as dear
As Anna to the Queen of Carthage was,
Tranio, I burn, I pine, I perish, Tranio,
If I achieve not this young modest girl.
Counsel me, Tranio, for I know thou canst:
Assist me, Tranio, for I know thou wilt.

TRANIO.
Master, it is no time to chide you now;
Affection is not rated from the heart:

If love have touch'd you, nought remains
   but so:
Redime te captum quam queas minimo.
LUCENTIO.
Gramercies, lad; go forward; this contents;
The rest will comfort, for thy counsel's
   sound.
TRANIO.
Master, you look'd so longly on the maid.
Perhaps you mark'd not what's the pith
   of all.
LUCENTIO.
O, yes, I saw sweet beauty in her face,
Such as the daughter of Agenor had,
That made great Jove to humble him to
   her hand,
When with his knees he kiss'd the Cretan
   strand.
TRANIO.
Saw you no more? mark'd you not how
   her sister
Began to scold and raise up such a storm
That mortal ears might hardly endure the
   din?
LUCENTIO.
Tranio, I saw her coral lips to move,
And with her breath she did perfume the
   air;
Sacred and sweet was all I saw in her.
TRANIO.
Nay, then, 'tis time to stir him from his
   trance.
I pray, awake, sir: if you love the maid,
Bend thoughts and wits to achieve her.
Thus it stands:
Her elder sister is so curst and shrewd,
That till the father rid his hands of her,
Master, your love must live a maid at
   home;
And therefore has he closely mew'd her
   up,
Because she will not be annoy'd with
   suitors.
LUCENTIO.
Ah, Tranio, what a cruel father's he!
But art thou not advis'd he took some care
To get her cunning schoolmasters to
   instruct her?

TRANIO.
Ay, marry, am I, sir, and now 'tis plotted.
LUCENTIO.
I have it, Tranio.
TRANIO.
          Master, for my hand,
Both our inventions meet and jump in one.
LUCENTIO.
Tell me thine first.
TRANIO.
          You will be schoolmaster,
And undertake the teaching of the maid:
That's your device.
LUCENTIO.
         It is: may it be done?
TRANIO.
Not possible; for who shall bear your part
And be in Padua here Vincentio's son;
Keep house and ply his book, welcome his
   friends;
Visit his countrymen, and banquet them?
LUCENTIO.
Basta; content thee, for I have it full.
We have not yet been seen in any house,
Nor can we be distinguish'd by our faces
For man or master: then it follows thus:
Thou shalt be master, Tranio, in my stead,
Keep house and port and servants, as I
   should;
I will some other be; some Florentine,
Some Neapolitan, or meaner man of Pisa.
'Tis hatch'd, and shall be so: Tranio, at
   once
Uncase thee; take my colour'd hat and
   cloak.
When Biondello comes, he waits on thee;
But I will charm him first to keep his
   tongue.
TRANIO.
So had you need. [*They exchange habits.*]
In brief, sir, sith it your pleasure is,
And I am tied to be obedient;
For so your father charg'd me at our
   parting,
"Be serviceable to my son," quoth he,
Although I think 'twas in another sense:
I am content to be Lucentio,
Because so well I love Lucentio.

Lucentio.

Tranio, be so, because Lucentio loves;

And let me be a slave, to achieve that maid

Whose sudden sight hath thrall'd my
wounded eye.

[*Enter* Biondello.]

Here comes the rogue. Sirrah, where have
you been?

Biondello.

Where have *I* been! Nay, how now! where
are *you*? Master, has my fellow Tranio stol'n
your clothes? Or you stol'n his? or both?
Pray, what's the news?

Lucentio.

Sirrah, come hither: 'tis no time to jest,

And therefore frame your manners to the
time.

Your fellow Tranio here, to save my life,

Puts my apparel and my count'nance on,

And I for my escape have put on his;

For in a quarrel since I came ashore

I kill'd a man, and fear I was descried.

Wait you on him, I charge you, as
becomes,

While I make way from hence to save
my life.

You understand me?

Biondello.

                I, sir! Ne'er a whit.

Lucentio.

And not a jot of Tranio in your mouth:

Tranio is changed to Lucentio.

Biondello.

The better for him: would I were so too!

Tranio.

So could I, faith, boy, to have the next wish
after,

That Lucentio indeed had Baptista's
youngest daughter.

But, sirrah, not for my sake but your
master's, I advise

You use your manners discreetly in all kind
of companies:

When I am alone, why, then I am Tranio;

But in all places else your master, Lucentio.

Lucentio.

Tranio, let's go.

One thing more rests, that thyself execute,

To make one among these wooers: if thou
ask me why,

Sufficeth my reasons are both good and
weighty.

[*Exeunt.*]

[*The* Presenters *above speak.*]

First Servant.

My lord, you nod; you do not mind the play.

Sly.

Yes, by Saint Anne, I do. A good matter,
surely: comes there any more of it?

Page.

My lord, 'tis but begun.

Sly.

'Tis a very excellent piece of work, madam
lady: would 'twere done!

[*They sit and mark.*]

SCENE II

Padua. Before Hortensio's house.

[*Enter* Petruchio *and his man* Grumio.]

Petruchio.

Verona, for a while I take my leave,

To see my friends in Padua; but of all

My best beloved and approved friend,

Hortensio; and I trow this is his house.

Here, sirrah Grumio, knock, I say.

Grumio.

Knock, sir! Whom should I knock? Is there
any man has rebused your worship?

Petruchio.

Villain, I say, knock me here soundly.

Grumio.

Knock you here, sir! Why, sir, what am I, sir,
that I should knock you here, sir?

Petruchio.

Villain, I say, knock me at this gate;

And rap me well, or I'll knock your knave's
pate.

Grumio.

My master is grown quarrelsome. I should
knock you first,

And then I know after who comes by the
worst.

Petruchio.

Will it not be?

Faith, sirrah, an you'll not knock, I'll ring
it;

I'll try how you can *sol, fa,* and sing it.
  [*He wrings* GRUMIO *by the ears.*]
GRUMIO.
Help, masters, help! my master is mad.
PETRUCHIO.
Now, knock when I bid you, sirrah villain!
  [*Enter* HORTENSIO.]
HORTENSIO.
How now! what's the matter? My old friend
Grumio! and my good friend Petruchio!
How do you all at Verona?
PETRUCHIO.
Signior Hortensio, come you to part the
  fray?
Con tutto il cuore ben trovato, may I say.
HORTENSIO.
*Alla nostra casa ben venuto; molto honorato
  signor mio Petruchio.*
Rise, Grumio, rise: we will compound this
  quarrel.
GRUMIO.
Nay, 'tis no matter, sir, what he 'leges in
Latin. If this be not a lawful cause for me
to leave his service, look you, sir, he bid me
knock him and rap him soundly, sir: well,
was it fit for a servant to use his master so;
being, perhaps, for aught I see, two-and-
thirty, a pip out?
Whom would to God I had well knock'd
  at first,
Then had not Grumio come by the worst.
PETRUCHIO.
A senseless villain! Good Hortensio,
I bade the rascal knock upon your gate,
And could not get him for my heart to
  do it.
GRUMIO.
Knock at the gate! O heavens! Spake you
not these words plain: "Sirrah knock me
here, rap me here, knock me well, and
knock me soundly"? And come you now
with "knocking at the gate"?
PETRUCHIO.
Sirrah, be gone, or talk not, I advise you.
HORTENSIO.
Petruchio, patience; I am Grumio's pledge;
Why, this's a heavy chance 'twixt him and
  you,

Your ancient, trusty, pleasant servant
  Grumio.
And tell me now, sweet friend, what happy
  gale
Blows you to Padua here from old Verona?
PETRUCHIO.
Such wind as scatters young men through
  the world
To seek their fortunes farther than at
  home,
Where small experience grows. But in a
  few,
Signior Hortensio, thus it stands with me:
Antonio, my father, is deceas'd,
And I have thrust myself into this maze,
Haply to wive and thrive as best I may;
Crowns in my purse I have, and goods at
  home,
And so am come abroad to see the world.
HORTENSIO.
Petruchio, shall I then come roundly to
  thee
And wish thee to a shrewd ill-favour'd
  wife?
Thou'dst thank me but a little for my
  counsel;
And yet I'll promise thee she shall be rich,
And very rich: but th'art too much my
  friend,
And I'll not wish thee to her.
PETRUCHIO.
Signior Hortensio, 'twixt such friends as
  we
Few words suffice; and therefore, if thou
  know
One rich enough to be Petruchio's wife,
As wealth is burden of my wooing dance,
Be she as foul as was Florentius' love,
As old as Sibyl, and as curst and shrewd
As Socrates' Xanthippe or a worse,
She moves me not, or not removes, at
  least,
Affection's edge in me, were she as rough
As are the swelling Adriatic seas:
I come to wive it wealthily in Padua;
If wealthily, then happily in Padua.
GRUMIO.
Nay, look you, sir, he tells you flatly what

his mind is: why, give him gold enough and
marry him to a puppet or an aglet-baby; or
an old trot with ne'er a tooth in her head,
though she has as many diseases as two-
and-fifty horses: why, nothing comes amiss,
so money comes withal.

HORTENSIO.

Petruchio, since we are stepp'd thus far in,
I will continue that I broach'd in jest.
I can, Petruchio, help thee to a wife
With wealth enough, and young and
    beauteous;
Brought up as best becomes a
    gentlewoman:
Her only fault,—and that is faults
    enough,—
Is, that she is intolerable curst
And shrewd and froward, so beyond all
    measure,
That, were my state far worser than it is,
I would not wed her for a mine of gold.

PETRUCHIO.

Hortensio, peace! thou know'st not gold's
    effect:
Tell me her father's name, and 'tis enough;
For I will board her, though she chide as
    loud
As thunder when the clouds in autumn
    crack.

HORTENSIO.

Her father is Baptista Minola,
An affable and courteous gentleman;
Her name is Katherina Minola,
Renown'd in Padua for her scolding
    tongue.

PETRUCHIO.

I know her father, though I know not her;
And he knew my deceased father well.
I will not sleep, Hortensio, till I see her;
And therefore let me be thus bold with you,
To give you over at this first encounter,
Unless you will accompany me thither.

GRUMIO.

I pray you, sir, let him go while the humour
lasts. O' my word, an she knew him as well
as I do, she would think scolding would do
little good upon him. She may perhaps call
him half a score knaves or so; why, that's

nothing; and he begin once, he'll rail in
his rope-tricks. I'll tell you what, sir, an she
stand him but a little, he will throw a figure
in her face, and so disfigure her with it that
she shall have no more eyes to see withal
than a cat. You know him not, sir.

HORTENSIO.

Tarry, Petruchio, I must go with thee,
For in Baptista's keep my treasure is:
He hath the jewel of my life in hold,
His youngest daughter, beautiful Bianca,
And her withholds from me and other
    more,
Suitors to her and rivals in my love;
Supposing it a thing impossible,
For those defects I have before rehears'd,
That ever Katherina will be woo'd:
Therefore this order hath Baptista ta'en,
That none shall have access unto Bianca
Till Katherine the curst have got a
    husband.

GRUMIO.

Katherine the curst!
A title for a maid of all titles the worst.

HORTENSIO.

Now shall my friend Petruchio do me
    grace,
And offer me disguis'd in sober robes,
To old Baptista as a schoolmaster
Well seen in music, to instruct Bianca;
That so I may, by this device at least
Have leave and leisure to make love to her,
And unsuspected court her by herself.

GRUMIO.

Here's no knavery! See, to beguile the old
folks, how the young folks lay their heads
together!

[*Enter* GREMIO, *and* LUCENTIO *disguised,
    with books under his arm.*]

Master, master, look about you: who goes
there, ha?

HORTENSIO.

Peace, Grumio! 'tis the rival of my love.
Petruchio, stand by awhile.

GRUMIO.

A proper stripling, and an amorous!

GREMIO.

O! very well; I have perus'd the note.

Hark you, sir; I'll have them very fairly
  bound:
All books of love, see that at any hand,
And see you read no other lectures to her.
You understand me. Over and beside
Signior Baptista's liberality,
I'll mend it with a largess. Take your
  papers too,
And let me have them very well perfum'd;
For she is sweeter than perfume itself
To whom they go to. What will you read
  to her?

LUCENTIO.
Whate'er I read to her, I'll plead for you,
As for my patron, stand you so assur'd,
As firmly as yourself were still in place;
Yea, and perhaps with more successful
  words
Than you, unless you were a scholar, sir.

GREMIO.
O! this learning, what a thing it is.

GRUMIO.
O! this woodcock, what an ass it is.

PETRUCHIO.
Peace, sirrah!

HORTENSIO.
Grumio, mum! God save you, Signior
  Gremio!

GREMIO.
And you are well met, Signior Hortensio.
Trow you whither I am going? To Baptista
  Minola.
I promis'd to enquire carefully
About a schoolmaster for the fair Bianca;
And by good fortune I have lighted well
On this young man; for learning and
  behaviour
Fit for her turn, well read in poetry
And other books, good ones, I warrant ye.

HORTENSIO.
'Tis well; and I have met a gentleman
Hath promis'd me to help me to another,
A fine musician to instruct our mistress:
So shall I no whit be behind in duty
To fair Bianca, so belov'd of me.

GREMIO.
Belov'd of me, and that my deeds shall
  prove.

GRUMIO. [*Aside.*]
And that his bags shall prove.

HORTENSIO.
Gremio, 'tis now no time to vent our love:
Listen to me, and if you speak me fair,
I'll tell you news indifferent good for
  either.
Here is a gentleman whom by chance I
  met,
Upon agreement from us to his liking,
Will undertake to woo curst Katherine;
Yea, and to marry her, if her dowry please.

GREMIO.
So said, so done, is well.—
Hortensio, have you told him all her
  faults?

PETRUCHIO.
I know she is an irksome brawling scold;
If that be all, masters, I hear no harm.

GREMIO.
No, say'st me so, friend? What
  countryman?

PETRUCHIO.
Born in Verona, old Antonio's son.
My father dead, my fortune lives for me;
And I do hope good days and long to see.

GREMIO.
O sir, such a life, with such a wife, were
  strange!
But if you have a stomach, to't i' God's
  name;
You shall have me assisting you in all.
But will you woo this wild-cat?

PETRUCHIO.
                          Will I live?

GRUMIO.
Will he woo her? Ay, or I'll hang her.

PETRUCHIO.
Why came I hither but to that intent?
Think you a little din can daunt mine ears?
Have I not in my time heard lions roar?
Have I not heard the sea, puff'd up with
  winds,
Rage like an angry boar chafed with
  sweat?
Have I not heard great ordnance in the
  field,
And heaven's artillery thunder in the skies?

Have I not in a pitched battle heard
Loud 'larums, neighing steeds, and
    trumpets' clang?
And do you tell me of a woman's tongue,
That gives not half so great a blow to hear
As will a chestnut in a farmer's fire?
Tush, tush! fear boys with bugs.

Grumio. [*Aside.*]
For he fears none.

Gremio.
Hortensio, hark:
This gentleman is happily arriv'd,
My mind presumes, for his own good and
    ours.

Hortensio.
I promis'd we would be contributors,
And bear his charge of wooing, whatsoe'er.

Gremio.
And so we will, provided that he win her.

Grumio.
I would I were as sure of a good dinner.

    [*Enter* Tranio, *bravely apparelled; and*
          Biondello.]

Tranio.
Gentlemen, God save you! If I may be bold,
Tell me, I beseech you, which is the
    readiest way
To the house of Signior Baptista Minola?

Biondello.
He that has the two fair daughters; is't he
    you mean?

Tranio.
Even he, Biondello!

Gremio.
Hark you, sir, you mean not her to—

Tranio.
Perhaps him and her, sir; what have you
    to do?

Petruchio.
Not her that chides, sir, at any hand, I pray.

Tranio.
I love no chiders, sir. Biondello, let's away.

Lucentio. [*Aside.*]
Well begun, Tranio.

Hortensio.
             Sir, a word ere you go.
Are you a suitor to the maid you talk of,
    yea or no?

Tranio.
And if I be, sir, is it any offence?

Gremio.
No; if without more words you will get
    you hence.

Tranio.
Why, sir, I pray, are not the streets as free
For me as for you?

Gremio.
             But so is not she.

Tranio.
For what reason, I beseech you?

Gremio.
For this reason, if you'll know,
That she's the choice love of Signior
    Gremio.

Hortensio.
That she's the chosen of Signior Hortensio.

Tranio.
Softly, my masters! If you be gentlemen,
Do me this right; hear me with patience.
Baptista is a noble gentleman,
To whom my father is not all unknown;
And were his daughter fairer than she is,
She may more suitors have, and me for
    one.
Fair Leda's daughter had a thousand
    wooers;
Then well one more may fair Bianca have;
And so she shall: Lucentio shall make one,
Though Paris came in hope to speed alone.

Gremio.
What! this gentleman will out-talk us all.

Lucentio.
Sir, give him head; I know he'll prove a
    jade.

Petruchio.
Hortensio, to what end are all these
    words?

Hortensio.
Sir, let me be so bold as ask you,
Did you yet ever see Baptista's daughter?

Tranio.
No, sir, but hear I do that he hath two,
The one as famous for a scolding tongue
As is the other for beauteous modesty.

Petruchio.
Sir, sir, the first's for me; let her go by.

GREMIO.
Yea, leave that labour to great Hercules,
And let it be more than Alcides' twelve.
PETRUCHIO.
Sir, understand you this of me, in sooth:
The youngest daughter, whom you hearken
    for,
Her father keeps from all access of suitors,
And will not promise her to any man
Until the elder sister first be wed;
The younger then is free, and not before.
TRANIO.
If it be so, sir, that you are the man
Must stead us all, and me amongst the
    rest;
And if you break the ice, and do this feat,
Achieve the elder, set the younger free
For our access, whose hap shall be to have
    her
Will not so graceless be to be ingrate.
HORTENSIO.
Sir, you say well, and well you do conceive;
And since you do profess to be a suitor,
You must, as we do, gratify this gentleman,
To whom we all rest generally beholding.
TRANIO.
Sir, I shall not be slack; in sign whereof,
Please ye we may contrive this afternoon,
And quaff carouses to our mistress' health;
And do as adversaries do in law,
Strive mightily, but eat and drink as
    friends.
GRUMIO AND BIONDELLO.
O excellent motion! Fellows, let's be gone.
HORTENSIO.
The motion's good indeed, and be it so:—
Petruchio, I shall be your *ben venuto*.
                    [*Exeunt.*]

ACT II
SCENE I
Padua. A room in Baptista's house.
[*Enter* KATHERINA *and* BIANCA.]
BIANCA.
Good sister, wrong me not, nor wrong
    yourself,
To make a bondmaid and a slave of me;
That I disdain; but for these other gawds,

Unbind my hands, I'll pull them off
    myself,
Yea, all my raiment, to my petticoat;
Or what you will command me will I do,
So well I know my duty to my elders.
KATHERINA.
Of all thy suitors here I charge thee tell
Whom thou lov'st best: see thou dissemble
    not.
BIANCA.
Believe me, sister, of all the men alive
I never yet beheld that special face
Which I could fancy more than any other.
KATHERINA.
Minion, thou liest. Is't not Hortensio?
BIANCA.
If you affect him, sister, here I swear
I'll plead for you myself but you shall have
    him.
KATHERINA.
O! then, belike, you fancy riches more:
You will have Gremio to keep you fair.
BIANCA.
Is it for him you do envy me so?
Nay, then you jest; and now I well perceive
You have but jested with me all this while:
I prithee, sister Kate, untie my hands.
KATHERINA.
If that be jest, then an the rest was so.
                    [*Strikes her.*]
                    [*Enter* BAPTISTA.]
BAPTISTA.
Why, how now, dame! Whence grows this
    insolence?
Bianca, stand aside. Poor girl! she weeps.
Go ply thy needle; meddle not with her.
For shame, thou hilding of a devilish
    spirit,
Why dost thou wrong her that did ne'er
    wrong thee?
When did she cross thee with a bitter
    word?
KATHERINA.
Her silence flouts me, and I'll be reveng'd.
                    [*Flies after* BIANCA.]
BAPTISTA.
What! in my sight? Bianca, get thee in.
                    [*Exit* BIANCA.]

KATHERINA.

What! will you not suffer me? Nay, now
I see

She is your treasure, she must have a
husband;

I must dance bare-foot on her wedding-
day,

And, for your love to her, lead apes in hell.

Talk not to me: I will go sit and weep

Till I can find occasion of revenge.

[*Exit.*]

BAPTISTA.

Was ever gentleman thus griev'd as I?

But who comes here?

[*Enter* GREMIO, *with* LUCENTIO *in the
habit of a mean man;* PETRUCHIO, *with*
HORTENSIO *as a musician; and* TRANIO,
with BIONDELLO *bearing a lute and books.*]

GREMIO.

Good morrow, neighbour Baptista.

BAPTISTA.

Good morrow, neighbour Gremio. God
save you, gentlemen!

PETRUCHIO.

And you, good sir! Pray, have you not a
daughter

Call'd Katherina, fair and virtuous?

BAPTISTA.

I have a daughter, sir, call'd Katherina.

GREMIO.

You are too blunt: go to it orderly.

PETRUCHIO.

You wrong me, Signior Gremio: give me
leave.

I am a gentleman of Verona, sir,

That, hearing of her beauty and her wit,

Her affability and bashful modesty,

Her wondrous qualities and mild
behaviour,

Am bold to show myself a forward guest

Within your house, to make mine eye the
witness

Of that report which I so oft have heard.

And, for an entrance to my entertainment,

I do present you with a man of mine,

[*Presenting* HORTENSIO.]

Cunning in music and the mathematics,

To instruct her fully in those sciences,

Whereof I know she is not ignorant.

Accept of him, or else you do me wrong:

His name is Licio, born in Mantua.

BAPTISTA.

You're welcome, sir, and he for your good
sake;

But for my daughter Katherine, this I
know,

She is not for your turn, the more my
grief.

PETRUCHIO.

I see you do not mean to part with her;

Or else you like not of my company.

BAPTISTA.

Mistake me not; I speak but as I find.

Whence are you, sir? What may I call your
name?

PETRUCHIO.

Petruchio is my name, Antonio's son;

A man well known throughout all Italy.

BAPTISTA.

I know him well: you are welcome for his
sake.

GREMIO.

Saving your tale, Petruchio, I pray,

Let us, that are poor petitioners, speak too.

Backare! you are marvellous forward.

PETRUCHIO.

O, pardon me, Signior Gremio; I would
fain be doing.

GREMIO.

I doubt it not, sir; but you will curse
your wooing. Neighbour, this is a gift
very grateful, I am sure of it. To express
the like kindness, myself, that have been
more kindly beholding to you than any,
freely give unto you this young scholar—
[*Presenting* LUCENTIO.] that has been long
studying at Rheims; as cunning in Greek,
Latin, and other languages, as the other
in music and mathematics. His name is
Cambio; pray accept his service.

BAPTISTA.

A thousand thanks, Signior Gremio;
welcome, good Cambio. [*To* TRANIO.] But,
gentle sir, methinks you walk like a stranger:
may I be so bold to know the cause of your
coming?

Tranio.
Pardon me, sir, the boldness is mine own,
That, being a stranger in this city here,
Do make myself a suitor to your daughter,
Unto Bianca, fair and virtuous.
Nor is your firm resolve unknown to me,
In the preferment of the eldest sister.
This liberty is all that I request,
That, upon knowledge of my parentage,
I may have welcome 'mongst the rest that
    woo,
And free access and favour as the rest:
And, toward the education of your
    daughters,
I here bestow a simple instrument,
And this small packet of Greek and Latin
    books:
If you accept them, then their worth is
    great.
Baptista.
Lucentio is your name, of whence, I pray?
Tranio.
Of Pisa, sir; son to Vincentio.
Baptista.
A mighty man of Pisa: by report
I know him well: you are very welcome, sir.
[*To* Hortensio.] Take you the lute, [*To*
    Lucentio.] and you the set of books;
You shall go see your pupils presently.
Holla, within! [*Enter a* Servant.] Sirrah,
    lead these gentlemen
To my two daughters, and tell them both
These are their tutors: bid them use them
    well.
        [*Exit* Servant, *with* Hortensio,
        Lucentio, *and* Biondello.]
We will go walk a little in the orchard,
And then to dinner. You are passing
    welcome,
And so I pray you all to think yourselves.
Petruchio.
Signior Baptista, my business asketh
    haste,
And every day I cannot come to woo.
You knew my father well, and in him me,
Left solely heir to all his lands and goods,
Which I have bettered rather than
    decreas'd:

Then tell me, if I get your daughter's love,
What dowry shall I have with her to wife?
Baptista.
After my death, the one half of my lands,
And in possession twenty thousand
    crowns.
Petruchio.
And, for that dowry, I'll assure her of
Her widowhood, be it that she survive me,
In all my lands and leases whatsoever.
Let specialities be therefore drawn
    between us,
That covenants may be kept on either
    hand.
Baptista.
Ay, when the special thing is well obtain'd,
That is, her love; for that is all in all.
Petruchio.
Why, that is nothing; for I tell you, father,
I am as peremptory as she proud-minded;
And where two raging fires meet together,
They do consume the thing that feeds
    their fury:
Though little fire grows great with little
    wind,
Yet extreme gusts will blow out fire and
    all;
So I to her, and so she yields to me;
For I am rough and woo not like a babe.
Baptista.
Well mayst thou woo, and happy be thy
    speed!
But be thou arm'd for some unhappy
    words.
Petruchio.
Ay, to the proof, as mountains are for
    winds,
That shake not though they blow
    perpetually.
[*Re-enter* Hortensio, *with his head broke.*]
Baptista.
How now, my friend! Why dost thou look
    so pale?
Hortensio.
For fear, I promise you, if I look pale.
Baptista.
What, will my daughter prove a good
    musician?

Hortensio.
I think she'll sooner prove a soldier:
Iron may hold with her, but never lutes.
Baptista.
Why, then thou canst not break her to
     the lute?
Hortensio.
Why, no; for she hath broke the lute to me.
I did but tell her she mistook her frets,
And bow'd her hand to teach her
     fingering;
When, with a most impatient devilish
     spirit,
"Frets, call you these?" quoth she "I'll fume
     with them";
And with that word she struck me on the
     head,
And through the instrument my pate
     made way;
And there I stood amazed for a while,
As on a pillory, looking through the lute;
While she did call me rascal fiddler,
And twangling Jack, with twenty such vile
     terms,
As she had studied to misuse me so.
Petruchio.
Now, by the world, it is a lusty wench!
I love her ten times more than e'er I did:
O! how I long to have some chat with her!
Baptista. [*To* Hortensio.]
Well, go with me, and be not so
     discomfited;
Proceed in practice with my younger
     daughter;
She's apt to learn, and thankful for good
     turns.
Signior Petruchio, will you go with us,
Or shall I send my daughter Kate to you?
Petruchio.
I pray you do. I will attend her here.
     [*Exeunt* Baptista, Gremio, Tranio,
          and Hortensio.]
And woo her with some spirit when she
     comes.
Say that she rail; why, then I'll tell her plain
She sings as sweetly as a nightingale:
Say that she frown; I'll say she looks as
     clear

As morning roses newly wash'd with dew:
Say she be mute, and will not speak a
     word;
Then I'll commend her volubility,
And say she uttereth piercing eloquence:
If she do bid me pack, I'll give her thanks,
As though she bid me stay by her a week:
If she deny to wed, I'll crave the day
When I shall ask the banns, and when be
     married.
But here she comes; and now, Petruchio,
     speak.
          [*Enter* Katherina.]
Good morrow, Kate; for that's your name,
     I hear.
Katherina.
Well have you heard, but something hard
     of hearing:
They call me Katherine that do talk of me.
Petruchio.
You lie, in faith, for you are call'd plain Kate,
And bonny Kate, and sometimes Kate the
     curst;
But, Kate, the prettiest Kate in
     Christendom,
Kate of Kate Hall, my super-dainty Kate,
For dainties are all cates: and therefore,
     Kate,
Take this of me, Kate of my consolation;
Hearing thy mildness prais'd in every
     town,
Thy virtues spoke of, and thy beauty
     sounded,—
Yet not so deeply as to thee belongs,—
Myself am mov'd to woo thee for my wife.
Katherina.
Mov'd! in good time: let him that mov'd
     you hither
Remove you hence. I knew you at the first,
You were a moveable.
Petruchio.
                    Why, what's a moveable?
Katherina.
A joint-stool.
Petruchio.
               Thou hast hit it: come, sit on me.
Katherina.
Asses are made to bear, and so are you.

PETRUCHIO.
Women are made to bear, and so are you.
KATHERINA.
No such jade as bear you, if me you mean.
PETRUCHIO.
Alas! good Kate, I will not burden thee;
For, knowing thee to be but young and
   light,—
KATHERINA.
Too light for such a swain as you to catch;
And yet as heavy as my weight should be.
PETRUCHIO.
Should be! should buzz!
KATHERINA.
                    Well ta'en, and like a buzzard.
PETRUCHIO.
O, slow-wing'd turtle! shall a buzzard take
   thee?
KATHERINA.
Ay, for a turtle, as he takes a buzzard.
PETRUCHIO.
Come, come, you wasp; i' faith, you are
   too angry.
KATHERINA.
If I be waspish, best beware my sting.
PETRUCHIO.
My remedy is, then, to pluck it out.
KATHERINA.
Ay, if the fool could find it where it lies.
PETRUCHIO.
Who knows not where a wasp does wear
   his sting?
In his tail.
KATHERINA.
          In his tongue.
PETRUCHIO.
                    Whose tongue?
KATHERINA.
Yours, if you talk of tales; and so farewell.
PETRUCHIO.
What! with my tongue in your tail? Nay,
   come again,
Good Kate; I am a gentleman.
KATHERINA.
                              That I'll try.
          [Striking him.]
PETRUCHIO.
I swear I'll cuff you if you strike again.

KATHERINA.
So may you lose your arms:
If you strike me, you are no gentleman;
And if no gentleman, why then no arms.
PETRUCHIO.
A herald, Kate? O! put me in thy books.
KATHERINA.
What is your crest? a coxcomb?
PETRUCHIO.
A combless cock, so Kate will be my
   hen.
KATHERINA.
No cock of mine; you crow too like a
   craven.
PETRUCHIO.
Nay, come, Kate, come; you must not
   look so sour.
KATHERINA.
It is my fashion when I see a crab.
PETRUCHIO.
Why, here's no crab, and therefore look
   not sour.
KATHERINA.
There is, there is.
PETRUCHIO.
Then show it me.
KATHERINA.
Had I a glass I would.
PETRUCHIO.
What, you mean my face?
KATHERINA.
Well aim'd of such a young one.
PETRUCHIO.
Now, by Saint George, I am too young
   for you.
KATHERINA.
Yet you are wither'd.
PETRUCHIO.
                    'Tis with cares.
KATHERINA.
                              I care not.
PETRUCHIO.
Nay, hear you, Kate: in sooth, you 'scape
   not so.
KATHERINA.
I chafe you, if I tarry; let me go.
PETRUCHIO.
No, not a whit; I find you passing gentle.

'Twas told me you were rough, and coy,
   and sullen,
And now I find report a very liar;
For thou art pleasant, gamesome, passing
   courteous,
But slow in speech, yet sweet as spring-
   time flowers.
Thou canst not frown, thou canst not look
   askance,
Nor bite the lip, as angry wenches will,
Nor hast thou pleasure to be cross in talk;
But thou with mildness entertain'st thy
   wooers;
With gentle conference, soft and affable.
Why does the world report that Kate doth
   limp?
O sland'rous world! Kate like the hazel-
   twig
Is straight and slender, and as brown in
   hue
As hazel-nuts, and sweeter than the
   kernels.
O! let me see thee walk: thou dost not
   halt.

KATHERINA.
Go, fool, and whom thou keep'st command.

PETRUCHIO.
Did ever Dian so become a grove
As Kate this chamber with her princely
   gait?
O! be thou Dian, and let her be Kate,
And then let Kate be chaste, and Dian
   sportful!

KATHERINA.
Where did you study all this goodly
   speech?

PETRUCHIO.
It is extempore, from my mother-wit.

KATHERINA.
A witty mother! witless else her son.

PETRUCHIO.
Am I not wise?

KATHERINA.
               Yes; keep you warm.

PETRUCHIO.
Marry, so I mean, sweet Katherine, in thy
   bed;
And therefore, setting all this chat aside,

Thus in plain terms: your father hath
   consented
That you shall be my wife your dowry
   'greed on;
And will you, nill you, I will marry you.
Now, Kate, I am a husband for your turn;
For, by this light, whereby I see thy
   beauty,—
Thy beauty that doth make me like thee
   well,—
Thou must be married to no man but me;
For I am he am born to tame you, Kate,
And bring you from a wild Kate to a Kate
Conformable as other household Kates.
Here comes your father. Never make
   denial;
I must and will have Katherine to my wife.
   [*Re-enter* BAPTISTA, GREMIO, *and*
                  TRANIO.]

BAPTISTA.
Now, Signior Petruchio, how speed you
   with my daughter?

PETRUCHIO.
How but well, sir? how but well?
It were impossible I should speed amiss.

BAPTISTA.
Why, how now, daughter Katherine, in
   your dumps?

KATHERINA.
Call you me daughter? Now I promise you
You have show'd a tender fatherly regard
To wish me wed to one half lunatic,
A mad-cap ruffian and a swearing Jack,
That thinks with oaths to face the matter
   out.

PETRUCHIO.
Father, 'tis thus: yourself and all the world
That talk'd of her have talk'd amiss of her:
If she be curst, it is for policy,
For she's not froward, but modest as the
   dove;
She is not hot, but temperate as the morn;
For patience she will prove a second
   Grissel,
And Roman Lucrece for her chastity;
And to conclude, we have 'greed so well
   together
That upon Sunday is the wedding-day.

KATHERINA.
I'll see thee hang'd on Sunday first.
GREMIO.
Hark, Petruchio; she says she'll see thee
    hang'd first.
TRANIO.
Is this your speeding? Nay, then good-
    night our part!
PETRUCHIO.
Be patient, gentlemen. I choose her for
    myself;
If she and I be pleas'd, what's that to you?
'Tis bargain'd 'twixt us twain, being alone,
That she shall still be curst in company.
I tell you, 'tis incredible to believe
How much she loves me: O! the kindest
    Kate
She hung about my neck, and kiss on kiss
She vied so fast, protesting oath on oath,
That in a twink she won me to her love.
O! you are novices: 'tis a world to see,
How tame, when men and women are
    alone,
A meacock wretch can make the curstest
    shrew.
Give me thy hand, Kate; I will unto
    Venice,
To buy apparel 'gainst the wedding-day.
Provide the feast, father, and bid the
    guests;
I will be sure my Katherine shall be fine.
BAPTISTA.
I know not what to say; but give me your
    hands.
God send you joy, Petruchio! 'Tis a match.
GREMIO, TRANIO.
Amen, say we; we will be witnesses.
PETRUCHIO.
Father, and wife, and gentlemen, adieu.
I will to Venice; Sunday comes apace;
We will have rings and things, and fine
    array;
And kiss me, Kate; we will be married o'
    Sunday.
     [*Exeunt* PETRUCHIO *and* KATHERINA,
         severally.]
GREMIO.
Was ever match clapp'd up so suddenly?

BAPTISTA.
Faith, gentlemen, now I play a merchant's
    part,
And venture madly on a desperate mart.
TRANIO.
'Twas a commodity lay fretting by you;
'Twill bring you gain, or perish on the seas.
BAPTISTA.
The gain I seek is, quiet in the match.
GREMIO.
No doubt but he hath got a quiet catch.
But now, Baptista, to your younger
    daughter:
Now is the day we long have looked for;
I am your neighbour, and was suitor first.
TRANIO.
And I am one that love Bianca more
Than words can witness or your thoughts
    can guess.
GREMIO.
Youngling, thou canst not love so dear as I.
TRANIO.
Greybeard, thy love doth freeze.
GREMIO.
                   But thine doth fry.
Skipper, stand back; 'tis age that
    nourisheth.
TRANIO.
But youth in ladies' eyes that flourisheth.
BAPTISTA.
Content you, gentlemen; I'll compound
    this strife:
'Tis deeds must win the prize, and he of
    both
That can assure my daughter greatest
    dower
Shall have my Bianca's love.
Say, Signior Gremio, what can you assure
    her?
GREMIO.
First, as you know, my house within the
    city
Is richly furnished with plate and gold:
Basins and ewers to lave her dainty hands;
My hangings all of Tyrian tapestry;
In ivory coffers I have stuff'd my crowns;
In cypress chests my arras counterpoints,
Costly apparel, tents, and canopies,

Fine linen, Turkey cushions boss'd with
    pearl,
Valance of Venice gold in needle-work;
Pewter and brass, and all things that
    belong
To house or housekeeping: then, at my
    farm
I have a hundred milch-kine to the pail,
Six score fat oxen standing in my stalls,
And all things answerable to this portion.
Myself am struck in years, I must confess;
And if I die to-morrow this is hers,
If whilst I live she will be only mine.

TRANIO.
That "only" came well in. Sir, list to me:
I am my father's heir and only son;
If I may have your daughter to my wife,
I'll leave her houses three or four as good
Within rich Pisa's walls as any one
Old Signior Gremio has in Padua;
Besides two thousand ducats by the year
Of fruitful land, all which shall be her
    jointure.
What, have I pinch'd you, Signior
    Gremio?

GREMIO.
Two thousand ducats by the year of land!
My land amounts not to so much in all:
That she shall have, besides an argosy
That now is lying in Marseilles' road.
What, have I chok'd you with an argosy?

TRANIO.
Gremio, 'tis known my father hath no less
Than three great argosies, besides two
    galliasses,
And twelve tight galleys; these I will
    assure her,
And twice as much, whate'er thou offer'st
    next.

GREMIO.
Nay, I have offer'd all; I have no more;
And she can have no more than all I have;
If you like me, she shall have me and
    mine.

TRANIO.
Why, then the maid is mine from all the
    world,
By your firm promise; Gremio is out-vied.

BAPTISTA.
I must confess your offer is the best;
And let your father make her the
    assurance,
She is your own; else, you must pardon
    me;
If you should die before him, where's her
    dower?

TRANIO.
That's but a cavil; he is old, I young.

GREMIO.
And may not young men die as well as
    old?

BAPTISTA.
Well, gentlemen,
I am thus resolv'd. On Sunday next, you
    know,
My daughter Katherine is to be married;
Now, on the Sunday following, shall
    Bianca
Be bride to you, if you make this
    assurance;
If not, to Signior Gremio.
And so I take my leave, and thank you
    both.

GREMIO.
Adieu, good neighbour.
                    [*Exit* BAPTISTA.]
                        Now, I fear thee not:
Sirrah young gamester, your father were
    a fool
To give thee all, and in his waning age
Set foot under thy table. Tut! a toy!
An old Italian fox is not so kind, my boy.
                        [*Exit.*]

TRANIO.
A vengeance on your crafty wither'd hide!
Yet I have fac'd it with a card of ten.
'Tis in my head to do my master good:
I see no reason but suppos'd Lucentio
Must get a father, call'd "suppos'd
    Vincentio";
And that's a wonder: fathers commonly
Do get their children; but in this case of
    wooing
A child shall get a sire, if I fail not of my
    cunning.
                        [*Exit.*]

ACT III
SCENE I

Padua. A room in Baptista's house.
[*Enter* Lucentio, Hortensio, *and*
Bianca.]

Lucentio.
Fiddler, forbear; you grow too forward, sir.
Have you so soon forgot the
    entertainment
Her sister Katherine welcome'd you
    withal?

Hortensio.
But, wrangling pedant, this is
The patroness of heavenly harmony:
Then give me leave to have prerogative;
And when in music we have spent an hour,
Your lecture shall have leisure for as much.

Lucentio.
Preposterous ass, that never read so far
To know the cause why music was
    ordain'd!
Was it not to refresh the mind of man
After his studies or his usual pain?
Then give me leave to read philosophy,
And while I pause serve in your harmony.

Hortensio.
Sirrah, I will not bear these braves of
    thine.

Bianca.
Why, gentlemen, you do me double wrong,
To strive for that which resteth in my
    choice.
I am no breeching scholar in the schools,
I'll not be tied to hours nor 'pointed times,
But learn my lessons as I please myself.
And, to cut off all strife, here sit we down;
Take you your instrument, play you the
    whiles;
His lecture will be done ere you have tun'd.

Hortensio.
You'll leave his lecture when I am in tune?
                    [*Retires.*]

Lucentio.
That will be never: tune your instrument.

Bianca.
Where left we last?

Lucentio.
Here, madam:— [*Reads.*]

Hic ibat Simois; hic est Sigeia tellus;
Hic steterat Priami regia celsa senis.

Bianca.
Construe them.

Lucentio.
Hic ibat, as I told you before; *Simois,* I
am Lucentio; *hic est,* son unto Vincentio
of Pisa; *Sigeia tellus,* disguised thus to get
your love; *Hic steterat,* and that Lucentio
that comes a-wooing; *Priami,* is my man
Tranio; *regia,* bearing my port; *celsa senis,*
that we might beguile the old pantaloon.

Hortensio. [*Returning.*]
Madam, my instrument's in tune.

Bianca.
Let's hear.—
                [Hortensio *plays.*]
O fie! the treble jars.

Lucentio.
Spit in the hole, man, and tune again.

Bianca.
Now let me see if I can construe it:
Hic ibat Simois, I know you not; *Hic est*
Sigeia tellus, I trust you not; *Hic steterat*
Priami, take heed he hear us not; *regia,*
presume not; *celsa senis,* despair not.

Hortensio.
Madam, 'tis now in tune.

Lucentio.
All but the base.

Hortensio.
The base is right; 'tis the base knave that
    jars.
How fiery and forward our pedant is!
[*Aside.*] Now, for my life, the knave doth
    court my love:
Pedascule, I'll watch you better yet.

Bianca.
In time I may believe, yet I mistrust.

Lucentio.
Mistrust it not; for sure, Aeacides
Was Ajax, call'd so from his grandfather.

Bianca.
I must believe my master; else, I promise
    you,
I should be arguing still upon that doubt;
But let it rest. Now, Licio, to you.
Good master, take it not unkindly, pray,

That I have been thus pleasant with you both.

HORTENSIO. [*To* LUCENTIO.]
You may go walk and give me leave awhile;
My lessons make no music in three parts.

LUCENTIO.
Are you so formal, sir? [*Aside.*] Well, I must wait,
And watch withal; for, but I be deceiv'd,
Our fine musician groweth amorous.

HORTENSIO.
Madam, before you touch the instrument,
To learn the order of my fingering,
I must begin with rudiments of art;
To teach you gamut in a briefer sort,
More pleasant, pithy, and effectual,
Than hath been taught by any of my trade:
And there it is in writing, fairly drawn.

BIANCA.
Why, I am past my gamut long ago.

HORTENSIO.
Yet read the gamut of Hortensio.

BIANCA. [*Reads.*]
    "*Gamut* I am, the ground of all accord,
        A re, to plead Hortensio's passion;
    B mi, Bianca, take him for thy lord,
        C fa ut, that loves with all affection:
    D sol re, one clef, two notes have I
    E la mi, show pity or I die."
Call you this gamut? Tut, I like it not:
Old fashions please me best; I am not so nice,
To change true rules for odd inventions.
            [*Enter a* SERVANT.]

SERVANT.
Mistress, your father prays you leave your books,
And help to dress your sister's chamber up:
You know to-morrow is the wedding-day.

BIANCA.
Farewell, sweet masters, both: I must be gone.
        [*Exeunt* BIANCA *and* SERVANT.]

LUCENTIO.
Faith, mistress, then I have no cause to stay.
            [*Exit.*]

HORTENSIO.
But I have cause to pry into this pedant:

Methinks he looks as though he were in love.
Yet if thy thoughts, Bianca, be so humble
To cast thy wand'ring eyes on every stale,
Seize thee that list: if once I find thee ranging,
Hortensio will be quit with thee by changing.
            [*Exit.*]

SCENE II
The same. Before Baptista's house.
[*Enter* BAPTISTA, GREMIO, TRANIO,
KATHERINA, BIANCA, LUCENTIO, *and*
ATTENDANTS.]

BAPTISTA. [*To* TRANIO.]
Signior Lucentio, this is the 'pointed day
That Katherine and Petruchio should be married,
And yet we hear not of our son-in-law.
What will be said? What mockery will it be
To want the bridegroom when the priest attends
To speak the ceremonial rites of marriage!
What says Lucentio to this shame of ours?

KATHERINA.
No shame but mine; I must, forsooth, be forc'd
To give my hand, oppos'd against my heart,
Unto a mad-brain rudesby, full of spleen;
Who woo'd in haste and means to wed at leisure.
I told you, I, he was a frantic fool,
Hiding his bitter jests in blunt behaviour;
And to be noted for a merry man,
He'll woo a thousand, 'point the day of marriage,
Make friends invited, and proclaim the banns;
Yet never means to wed where he hath woo'd.
Now must the world point at poor Katherine,
And say "Lo! there is mad Petruchio's wife,
If it would please him come and marry her."

TRANIO.
Patience, good Katherine, and Baptista
    too.
Upon my life, Petruchio means but well,
Whatever fortune stays him from his
    word:
Though he be blunt, I know him passing
    wise;
Though he be merry, yet withal he's
    honest.
KATHERINA.
Would Katherine had never seen him
    though!
    [*Exit, weeping, followed by* BIANCA *and*
        OTHERS.]
BAPTISTA.
Go, girl, I cannot blame thee now to weep,
For such an injury would vex a very saint;
Much more a shrew of thy impatient
    humour.
            [*Enter* BIONDELLO.]
BIONDELLO.
Master, master! News! old news, and such
news as you never heard of!
BAPTISTA.
Is it new and old too? How may that be?
BIONDELLO.
Why, is it not news to hear of Petruchio's
coming?
BAPTISTA.
Is he come?
BIONDELLO.
Why, no, sir.
BAPTISTA.
What then?
BIONDELLO.
He is coming.
BAPTISTA.
When will he be here?
BIONDELLO.
When he stands where I am and sees you
there.
TRANIO.
But, say, what to thine old news?
BIONDELLO.
Why, Petruchio is coming, in a new hat
and an old jerkin; a pair of old breeches
thrice turned; a pair of boots that have been

candle-cases, one buckled, another laced;
an old rusty sword ta'en out of the town
armoury, with a broken hilt, and chapeless;
with two broken points: his horse hipped
with an old mothy saddle and stirrups of
no kindred; besides, possessed with the
glanders and like to mose in the chine;
troubled with the lampass, infected with
the fashions, full of windgalls, sped with
spavins, rayed with the yellows, past cure
of the fives, stark spoiled with the staggers,
begnawn with the bots, swayed in the
back and shoulder-shotten; near-legged
before, and with a half-checked bit, and a
head-stall of sheep's leather, which, being
restrained to keep him from stumbling,
hath been often burst, and now repaired
with knots; one girth six times pieced, and
a woman's crupper of velure, which hath
two letters for her name fairly set down in
studs, and here and there pieced with pack-
thread.
BAPTISTA.
Who comes with him?
BIONDELLO.
O, sir! his lackey, for all the world
caparisoned like the horse; with a linen
stock on one leg and a kersey boot-hose
on the other, gartered with a red and blue
list; an old hat, and the *The Humour of Forty
Fancies* prick'd in't for a feather: a monster,
a very monster in apparel, and not like a
Christian footboy or a gentleman's lackey.
TRANIO.
'Tis some odd humour pricks him to this
    fashion;
Yet oftentimes he goes but mean-
    apparell'd.
BAPTISTA.
I am glad he's come, howsoe'er he comes.
BIONDELLO.
Why, sir, he comes not.
BAPTISTA.
Didst thou not say he comes?
BIONDELLO.
Who? that Petruchio came?
BAPTISTA.
Ay, that Petruchio came.

BIONDELLO.

No, sir; I say his horse comes, with him on
 his back.

BAPTISTA.

Why, that's all one.

BIONDELLO.

> Nay, by Saint Jamy,
> I hold you a penny,
>> A horse and a man
>> Is more than one,
> And yet not many.

[*Enter* PETRUCHIO *and* GRUMIO.]

PETRUCHIO.

Come, where be these gallants? Who is
 at home?

BAPTISTA.

You are welcome, sir.

PETRUCHIO.

And yet I come not well.

BAPTISTA.

And yet you halt not.

TRANIO.

Not so well apparell'd
As I wish you were.

PETRUCHIO.

Were it better, I should rush in thus.
But where is Kate? Where is my lovely
 bride?
How does my father? Gentles, methinks
 you frown;
And wherefore gaze this goodly company,
As if they saw some wondrous monument,
Some comet or unusual prodigy?

BAPTISTA.

Why, sir, you know this is your wedding-
 day:
First were we sad, fearing you would not
 come;
Now sadder, that you come so unprovided.
Fie! doff this habit, shame to your estate,
An eye-sore to our solemn festival.

TRANIO.

And tell us what occasion of import
Hath all so long detain'd you from your
 wife,
And sent you hither so unlike yourself?

PETRUCHIO.

Tedious it were to tell, and harsh to hear;

Sufficeth, I am come to keep my word,
Though in some part enforced to digress;
Which at more leisure I will so excuse
As you shall well be satisfied withal.
But where is Kate? I stay too long from
 her;
The morning wears, 'tis time we were at
 church.

TRANIO.

See not your bride in these unreverent
 robes;
Go to my chamber, put on clothes of
 mine.

PETRUCHIO.

Not I, believe me: thus I'll visit her.

BAPTISTA.

But thus, I trust, you will not marry her.

PETRUCHIO.

Good sooth, even thus; therefore ha' done
 with words;
To me she's married, not unto my clothes.
Could I repair what she will wear in me
As I can change these poor accoutrements,
'Twere well for Kate and better for myself.
But what a fool am I to chat with you
When I should bid good-morrow to my
 bride,
And seal the title with a lovely kiss!

[*Exeunt* PETRUCHIO, GRUMIO, *and*
 BIODELLO.]

TRANIO.

He hath some meaning in his mad attire.
We will persuade him, be it possible,
To put on better ere he go to church.

BAPTISTA.

I'll after him and see the event of this.

[*Exeunt* BAPTISTA, GREMIO, *and*
 ATTENDANTS.]

TRANIO.

But to her love concerneth us to add
Her father's liking; which to bring to pass,
As I before imparted to your worship,
I am to get a man,—whate'er he be
It skills not much; we'll fit him to our
 turn,—
And he shall be Vincentio of Pisa,
And make assurance here in Padua,
Of greater sums than I have promised.

So shall you quietly enjoy your hope,
And marry sweet Bianca with consent.
LUCENTIO.
Were it not that my fellow schoolmaster
Doth watch Bianca's steps so narrowly,
'Twere good, methinks, to steal our
    marriage;
Which once perform'd, let all the world
    say no,
I'll keep mine own despite of all the world.
TRANIO.
That by degrees we mean to look into,
And watch our vantage in this business.
We'll over-reach the greybeard, Gremio,
The narrow-prying father, Minola,
The quaint musician, amorous Licio;
All for my master's sake, Lucentio.
        [*Re-enter* GREMIO.]
Signior Gremio, came you from the
    church?
GREMIO.
As willingly as e'er I came from school.
TRANIO.
And is the bride and bridegroom coming
    home?
GREMIO.
A bridegroom, say you? 'Tis a groom
    indeed,
A grumbling groom, and that the girl shall
    find.
TRANIO.
Curster than she? Why, 'tis impossible.
GREMIO.
Why, he's a devil, a devil, a very fiend.
TRANIO.
Why, she's a devil, a devil, the devil's dam.
GREMIO.
Tut! she's a lamb, a dove, a fool, to him.
I'll tell you, Sir Lucentio: when the priest
Should ask if Katherine should be his
    wife,
"Ay, by gogs-wouns" quoth he, and swore
    so loud
That, all amaz'd, the priest let fall the
    book;
And as he stoop'd again to take it up,
The mad-brain'd bridegroom took him
    such a cuff

That down fell priest and book, and book
    and priest:
"Now take them up," quoth he "if any list."
TRANIO.
What said the wench, when he rose again?
GREMIO.
Trembled and shook, for why, he stamp'd
    and swore
As if the vicar meant to cozen him.
But after many ceremonies done,
He calls for wine: "A health!" quoth he,
    as if
He had been abroad, carousing to his mates
After a storm; quaff'd off the muscadel,
And threw the sops all in the sexton's face,
Having no other reason
But that his beard grew thin and hungerly
And seem'd to ask him sops as he was
    drinking.
This done, he took the bride about the
    neck,
And kiss'd her lips with such a clamorous
    smack
That at the parting all the church did echo.
And I, seeing this, came thence for very
    shame;
And after me, I know, the rout is coming.
Such a mad marriage never was before.
Hark, hark! I hear the minstrels play.
        [*Music.*]
[*Enter* PETRUCHIO, KATHERINA, BIANCA,
    BAPTISTA, HORTENSIO, GRUMIO, *and*
        TRAIN.]
PETRUCHIO.
Gentlemen and friends, I thank you for
    your pains:
I know you think to dine with me to-day,
And have prepar'd great store of wedding
    cheer
But so it is, my haste doth call me hence,
And therefore here I mean to take my
    leave.
BAPTISTA.
Is't possible you will away to-night?
PETRUCHIO.
I must away to-day before night come.
Make it no wonder: if you knew my
    business,

You would entreat me rather go than stay.
And, honest company, I thank you all,
That have beheld me give away myself
To this most patient, sweet, and virtuous
   wife.
Dine with my father, drink a health to me.
For I must hence; and farewell to you all.

TRANIO.
Let us entreat you stay till after dinner.

PETRUCHIO.
It may not be.

GREMIO.
         Let me entreat you.

PETRUCHIO.
It cannot be.

KATHERINA.
         Let me entreat you.

PETRUCHIO.
I am content.

KATHERINA.
       Are you content to stay?

PETRUCHIO.
I am content you shall entreat me stay;
But yet not stay, entreat me how you can.

KATHERINA.
Now, if you love me, stay.

PETRUCHIO.
         Grumio, my horse!

GRUMIO.
Ay, sir, they be ready; the oats have eaten
   the horses.

KATHERINA.
Nay, then, do what thou canst, I will not
   go to-day;
No, nor to-morrow, not till I please myself.
The door is open, sir; there lies your way;
You may be jogging whiles your boots are
   green;
For me, I'll not be gone till I please myself.
'Tis like you'll prove a jolly surly groom
That take it on you at the first so roundly.

PETRUCHIO.
O Kate! content thee: prithee be not angry.

KATHERINA.
I will be angry: what hast thou to do?
Father, be quiet; he shall stay my leisure.

GREMIO.
Ay, marry, sir, now it begins to work.

KATHERINA.
Gentlemen, forward to the bridal dinner:
I see a woman may be made a fool,
If she had not a spirit to resist.

PETRUCHIO.
They shall go forward, Kate, at thy
   command.
Obey the bride, you that attend on her;
Go to the feast, revel and domineer,
Carouse full measure to her maidenhead,
Be mad and merry, or go hang yourselves:
But for my bonny Kate, she must with me.
Nay, look not big, nor stamp, nor stare,
   nor fret;
I will be master of what is mine own.
She is my goods, my chattels; she is my
   house,
My household stuff, my field, my barn,
My horse, my ox, my ass, my anything;
And here she stands, touch her whoever
   dare;
I'll bring mine action on the proudest he
That stops my way in Padua. Grumio,
Draw forth thy weapon; we are beset with
   thieves;
Rescue thy mistress, if thou be a man.
Fear not, sweet wench; they shall not
   touch thee, Kate;
I'll buckler thee against a million.
     [*Exeunt* PETRUCHIO, KATHERINA,
          and GRUMIO.]

BAPTISTA.
Nay, let them go, a couple of quiet ones.

GREMIO.
Went they not quickly, I should die with
   laughing.

TRANIO.
Of all mad matches, never was the like.

LUCENTIO.
Mistress, what's your opinion of your
   sister?

BIANCA.
That, being mad herself, she's madly mated.

GREMIO.
I warrant him, Petruchio is Kated.

BAPTISTA.
Neighbours and friends, though bride and
   bridegroom wants

For to supply the places at the table,
You know there wants no junkets at the
    feast.
Lucentio, you shall supply the
    bridegroom's place;
And let Bianca take her sister's room.

TRANIO.
Shall sweet Bianca practise how to bride it?

BAPTISTA.
She shall, Lucentio. Come, gentlemen,
    let's go.

[Exeunt.]

ACT IV
SCENE I
A hall in Petruchio's country house.
[Enter GRUMIO.*]*

GRUMIO.
Fie, fie on all tired jades, on all mad masters,
and all foul ways! Was ever man so beaten?
Was ever man so ray'd? Was ever man so
weary? I am sent before to make a fire, and
they are coming after to warm them. Now,
were not I a little pot and soon hot, my very
lips might freeze to my teeth, my tongue to
the roof of my mouth, my heart in my belly,
ere I should come by a fire to thaw me. But
I with blowing the fire shall warm myself;
for, considering the weather, a taller man
than I will take cold. Holla, ho! Curtis!

[Enter CURTIS.*]*

CURTIS.
Who is that calls so coldly?

GRUMIO.
A piece of ice: if thou doubt it, thou mayst
slide from my shoulder to my heel with no
greater a run but my head and my neck. A
fire, good Curtis.

CURTIS.
Is my master and his wife coming, Grumio?

GRUMIO.
O, ay! Curtis, ay; and therefore fire, fire;
cast on no water.

CURTIS.
Is she so hot a shrew as she's reported?

GRUMIO.
She was, good Curtis, before this frost; but
thou knowest winter tames man, woman,

and beast; for it hath tamed my old master,
and my new mistress, and myself, fellow
Curtis.

CURTIS.
Away, you three-inch fool! I am no beast.

GRUMIO.
Am I but three inches? Why, thy horn is
a foot; and so long am I at the least. But
wilt thou make a fire, or shall I complain
on thee to our mistress, whose hand,—she
being now at hand,—thou shalt soon feel,
to thy cold comfort, for being slow in thy
hot office?

CURTIS.
I prithee, good Grumio, tell me, how goes
the world?

GRUMIO.
A cold world, Curtis, in every office but
thine; and therefore fire. Do thy duty, and
have thy duty, for my master and mistress
are almost frozen to death.

CURTIS.
There's fire ready; and therefore, good
Grumio, the news?

GRUMIO.
Why, "Jack boy! ho, boy!" and as much news
as thou wilt.

CURTIS.
Come, you are so full of cony-catching.

GRUMIO.
Why, therefore, fire; for I have caught
extreme cold. Where's the cook? Is supper
ready, the house trimmed, rushes strewed,
cobwebs swept, the serving-men in their
new fustian, their white stockings, and
every officer his wedding-garment on? Be
the Jacks fair within, the Jills fair without,
and carpets laid, and everything in order?

CURTIS.
All ready; and therefore, I pray thee, news?

GRUMIO.
First, know my horse is tired; my master
and mistress fallen out.

CURTIS.
How?

GRUMIO.
Out of their saddles into the dirt; and
thereby hangs a tale.

CURTIS.
Let's ha't, good Grumio.

GRUMIO.
Lend thine ear.

CURTIS.
Here.

GRUMIO. [*Striking him.*]
There.

CURTIS.
This 'tis to feel a tale, not to hear a tale.

GRUMIO.
And therefore 'tis called a sensible tale; and this cuff was but to knock at your ear and beseech listening. Now I begin: *Imprimis,* we came down a foul hill, my master riding behind my mistress,—

CURTIS.
Both of one horse?

GRUMIO.
What's that to thee?

CURTIS.
Why, a horse.

GRUMIO.
Tell thou the tale: but hadst thou not crossed me, thou shouldst have heard how her horse fell and she under her horse; thou shouldst have heard in how miry a place, how she was bemoiled; how he left her with the horse upon her; how he beat me because her horse stumbled; how she waded through the dirt to pluck him off me: how he swore; how she prayed, that never prayed before; how I cried; how the horses ran away; how her bridle was burst; how I lost my crupper; with many things of worthy memory, which now shall die in oblivion, and thou return unexperienced to thy grave.

CURTIS.
By this reckoning he is more shrew than she.

GRUMIO.
Ay; and that thou and the proudest of you all shall find when he comes home. But what talk I of this? Call forth Nathaniel, Joseph, Nicholas, Philip, Walter, Sugarsop, and the rest; let their heads be sleekly combed, their blue coats brush'd and their garters of an indifferent knit; let them curtsy with their left legs, and not presume to touch a hair of my master's horse-tail till they kiss their hands. Are they all ready?

CURTIS.
They are.

GRUMIO.
Call them forth.

CURTIS.
Do you hear? ho! You must meet my master to countenance my mistress.

GRUMIO.
Why, she hath a face of her own.

CURTIS.
Who knows not that?

GRUMIO.
Thou, it seems, that calls for company to countenance her.

CURTIS.
I call them forth to credit her.

GRUMIO.
Why, she comes to borrow nothing of them.

[*Enter several* SERVANTS.]

NATHANIEL.
Welcome home, Grumio!

PHILIP.
How now, Grumio!

JOSEPH.
What, Grumio!

NICHOLAS.
Fellow Grumio!

NATHANIEL.
How now, old lad!

GRUMIO.
Welcome, you; how now, you; what, you; fellow, you; and thus much for greeting. Now, my spruce companions, is all ready, and all things neat?

NATHANIEL.
All things is ready. How near is our master?

GRUMIO.
E'en at hand, alighted by this; and therefore be not,—Cock's passion, silence!—I hear my master.

[*Enter* PETRUCHIO *and* KATHERINA.]

PETRUCHIO.
Where be these knaves? What! no man
     at door

To hold my stirrup nor to take my
    horse?
Where is Nathaniel, Gregory, Philip?—
ALL SERVANTS.
Here, here, sir; here, sir.
PETRUCHIO.
Here, sir! here, sir! here, sir! here, sir!
You logger-headed and unpolish'd grooms!
What, no attendance? no regard? no duty?
Where is the foolish knave I sent before?
GRUMIO.
Here, sir; as foolish as I was before.
PETRUCHIO.
You peasant swain! you whoreson malt-
    horse drudge!
Did I not bid thee meet me in the park,
And bring along these rascal knaves with
    thee?
GRUMIO.
Nathaniel's coat, sir, was not fully made,
And Gabriel's pumps were all unpink'd i'
    the heel;
There was no link to colour Peter's hat,
And Walter's dagger was not come from
    sheathing;
There was none fine but Adam, Ralph, and
    Gregory;
The rest were ragged, old, and beggarly;
Yet, as they are, here are they come to
    meet you.
PETRUCHIO.
Go, rascals, go and fetch my supper in.
       [*Exeunt some of the* SERVANTS.]
             [*Sings.*]
    Where is the life that late I led?
    Where are those—?
Sit down, Kate, and welcome. Soud, soud,
    soud, soud!
      [*Re-enter* SERVANTS *with supper.*]
Why, when, I say?—Nay, good sweet Kate,
    be merry.—
Off with my boots, you rogues! you
    villains! when?
             [*Sings.*]
    It was the friar of orders grey,
    As he forth walked on his way:
Out, you rogue! you pluck my foot awry:
        [*Strikes him.*]

Take that, and mend the plucking off the
    other.
Be merry, Kate. Some water, here; what,
    ho!
Where's my spaniel Troilus? Sirrah, get
    you hence
And bid my cousin Ferdinand come
    hither:
           [*Exit* SERVANT.]
One, Kate, that you must kiss and be
    acquainted with.
Where are my slippers? Shall I have some
    water?
Come, Kate, and wash, and welcome
    heartily.—
    [SERVANT *lets the ewer fall.* PETRUCHIO
                strikes him.]
You whoreson villain! will you let it fall?
KATHERINA.
Patience, I pray you; 'twas a fault unwilling.
PETRUCHIO.
A whoreson, beetle-headed, flap-ear'd
    knave!
Come, Kate, sit down; I know you have a
    stomach.
Will you give thanks, sweet Kate, or else
    shall I?—
What's this? Mutton?
FIRST SERVANT.
               Ay.
PETRUCHIO.
             Who brought it?
PETER.
                        I.
PETRUCHIO.
'Tis burnt; and so is all the meat.
What dogs are these! Where is the rascal
    cook?
How durst you, villains, bring it from the
    dresser,
And serve it thus to me that love it not?
       [*Throws the meat, etc., at them.*]
There, take it to you, trenchers, cups, and
    all.
You heedless joltheads and unmanner'd
    slaves!
What! do you grumble? I'll be with you
    straight.

KATHERINA.
I pray you, husband, be not so disquiet;
The meat was well, if you were so
  contented.
PETRUCHIO.
I tell thee, Kate, 'twas burnt and dried
  away,
And I expressly am forbid to touch it;
For it engenders choler, planteth anger;
And better 'twere that both of us did fast,
Since, of ourselves, ourselves are choleric,
Than feed it with such over-roasted flesh.
Be patient; to-morrow 't shall be mended.
And for this night we'll fast for company:
Come, I will bring thee to thy bridal
  chamber.
      [*Exeunt* PETRUCHIO, KATHERINA,
          and CURTIS.]
NATHANIEL.
Peter, didst ever see the like?
PETER.
He kills her in her own humour.
          [*Re-enter* CURTIS.]
GRUMIO.
Where is he?
CURTIS.
In her chamber, making a sermon of
  continency to her;
And rails, and swears, and rates, that she,
  poor soul,
Knows not which way to stand, to look,
  to speak,
And sits as one new risen from a dream.
Away, away! for he is coming hither.
          [*Exeunt.*]
          [*Re-enter* PETRUCHIO.]
PETRUCHIO.
Thus have I politicly begun my reign,
And 'tis my hope to end successfully.
My falcon now is sharp and passing empty.
And till she stoop she must not be full-
  gorg'd,
For then she never looks upon her lure.
Another way I have to man my haggard,
To make her come, and know her keeper's
  call,
That is, to watch her, as we watch these
  kites

That bate and beat, and will not be
  obedient.
She eat no meat to-day, nor none shall eat;
Last night she slept not, nor to-night she
  shall not;
As with the meat, some undeserved fault
I'll find about the making of the bed;
And here I'll fling the pillow, there the
  bolster,
This way the coverlet, another way the
  sheets;
Ay, and amid this hurly I intend
That all is done in reverend care of her;
And, in conclusion, she shall watch all
  night:
And if she chance to nod I'll rail and
  brawl,
And with the clamour keep her still
  awake.
This is a way to kill a wife with kindness;
And thus I'll curb her mad and headstrong
  humour.
He that knows better how to tame a
  shrew,
Now let him speak; 'tis charity to show.
          [*Exit.*]

SCENE II

Padua. Before Baptista's house.
      [*Enter* TRANIO *and* HORTENSIO.]
TRANIO.
Is 't possible, friend Licio, that Mistress
  Bianca
Doth fancy any other but Lucentio?
I tell you, sir, she bears me fair in hand.
HORTENSIO.
Sir, to satisfy you in what I have said,
Stand by and mark the manner of his
  teaching.
          [*They stand aside.*]
      [*Enter* BIANCA *and* LUCENTIO.]
LUCENTIO.
Now, mistress, profit you in what you read?
BIANCA.
What, master, read you? First resolve me
  that.
LUCENTIO.
I read that I profess, *The Art to Love.*

Bianca.

And may you prove, sir, master of your art!

Lucentio.

While you, sweet dear, prove mistress of
  my heart.

[They retire.]

Hortensio.

Quick proceeders, marry! Now tell me, I
  pray,

You that durst swear that your Mistress
  Bianca

Lov'd none in the world so well as
  Lucentio.

Tranio.

O despiteful love! unconstant womankind!

I tell thee, Licio, this is wonderful.

Hortensio.

Mistake no more; I am not Licio.

Nor a musician as I seem to be;

But one that scorn to live in this disguise

For such a one as leaves a gentleman

And makes a god of such a cullion:

Know, sir, that I am call'd Hortensio.

Tranio.

Signior Hortensio, I have often heard

Of your entire affection to Bianca;

And since mine eyes are witness of her
  lightness,

I will with you, if you be so contented,

Forswear Bianca and her love for ever.

Hortensio.

See, how they kiss and court! Signior
  Lucentio,

Here is my hand, and here I firmly vow

Never to woo her more, but do forswear
  her,

As one unworthy all the former favours

That I have fondly flatter'd her withal.

Tranio.

And here I take the like unfeigned oath,

Never to marry with her though she
  would entreat;

Fie on her! See how beastly she doth court
  him!

Hortensio.

Would all the world but he had quite
  forsworn!

For me, that I may surely keep mine oath,

I will be married to a wealthy widow

Ere three days pass, which hath as long
  lov'd me

As I have lov'd this proud disdainful
  haggard.

And so farewell, Signior Lucentio.

Kindness in women, not their beauteous
  looks,

Shall win my love; and so I take my leave,

In resolution as I swore before.

[Exit Hortensio. Lucentio and
Bianca advance.]

Tranio.

Mistress Bianca, bless you with such grace

As 'longeth to a lover's blessed case!

Nay, I have ta'en you napping, gentle love,

And have forsworn you with Hortensio.

Bianca.

Tranio, you jest; but have you both
  forsworn me?

Tranio.

Mistress, we have.

Lucentio.

                    Then we are rid of Licio.

Tranio.

I' faith, he'll have a lusty widow now,

That shall be woo'd and wedded in a day.

Bianca.

God give him joy!

Tranio.

Ay, and he'll tame her.

Bianca.

He says so, Tranio.

Tranio.

Faith, he is gone unto the taming-school.

Bianca.

The taming-school! What, is there such
  a place?

Tranio.

Ay, mistress; and Petruchio is the master,

That teacheth tricks eleven and twenty
  long,

To tame a shrew and charm her chattering
  tongue.

[Enter Biondello, running.]

Biondello.

O master, master! I have watch'd so long

That I am dog-weary; but at last I spied

An ancient angel coming down the hill
Will serve the turn.

TRANIO.

What is he, Biondello?

BIONDELLO.

Master, a mercatante or a pedant,
I know not what; but formal in apparel,
In gait and countenance surely like a
    father.

LUCENTIO.

And what of him, Tranio?

TRANIO.

If he be credulous and trust my tale,
I'll make him glad to seem Vincentio,
And give assurance to Baptista Minola,
As if he were the right Vincentio.
Take in your love, and then let me alone.

[*Exeunt* LUCENTIO *and* BIANCA.]

[*Enter a* PEDANT.]

PEDANT.

God save you, sir!

TRANIO.

And you, sir! you are welcome.
Travel you far on, or are you at the
    farthest?

PEDANT.

Sir, at the farthest for a week or two;
But then up farther, and as far as Rome;
And so to Tripoli, if God lend me life.

TRANIO.

What countryman, I pray?

PEDANT.

Of Mantua.

TRANIO.

Of Mantua, sir? Marry, God forbid,
And come to Padua, careless of your life!

PEDANT.

My life, sir! How, I pray? for that goes
    hard.

TRANIO.

'Tis death for any one in Mantua
To come to Padua. Know you not the
    cause?
Your ships are stay'd at Venice; and the
    duke,—
For private quarrel 'twixt your duke and
    him,—
Hath publish'd and proclaim'd it openly.

'Tis marvel, but that you are but newly
    come
You might have heard it else proclaim'd
    about.

PEDANT.

Alas, sir! it is worse for me than so;
For I have bills for money by exchange
From Florence, and must here deliver them.

TRANIO.

Well, sir, to do you courtesy,
This will I do, and this I will advise you:
First, tell me, have you ever been at Pisa?

PEDANT.

Ay, sir, in Pisa have I often been,
Pisa renowned for grave citizens.

TRANIO.

Among them know you one Vincentio?

PEDANT.

I know him not, but I have heard of him,
A merchant of incomparable wealth.

TRANIO.

He is my father, sir; and, sooth to say,
In countenance somewhat doth resemble
    you.

BIONDELLO. [*Aside.*]

As much as an apple doth an oyster, and
    all one.

TRANIO.

To save your life in this extremity,
This favour will I do you for his sake;
And think it not the worst of all your
    fortunes
That you are like to Sir Vincentio.
His name and credit shall you undertake,
And in my house you shall be friendly
    lodg'd;
Look that you take upon you as you should!
You understand me, sir; so shall you stay
Till you have done your business in the
    city.
If this be courtesy, sir, accept of it.

PEDANT.

O, sir, I do; and will repute you ever
The patron of my life and liberty.

TRANIO.

Then go with me to make the matter good.
This, by the way, I let you understand:
My father is here look'd for every day

To pass assurance of a dower in marriage
'Twixt me and one Baptista's daughter
      here:
In all these circumstances I'll instruct you.
Go with me to clothe you as becomes you.
                                    [*Exeunt.*]

SCENE III

A room in Petruchio's house.
[*Enter* KATHERINA *and* GRUMIO.]
GRUMIO.
No, no, forsooth; I dare not for my life.
KATHERINA.
The more my wrong, the more his spite
      appears.
What, did he marry me to famish me?
Beggars that come unto my father's door
Upon entreaty have a present alms;
If not, elsewhere they meet with charity;
But I, who never knew how to entreat,
Nor never needed that I should entreat,
Am starv'd for meat, giddy for lack of
      sleep;
With oaths kept waking, and with
      brawling fed.
And that which spites me more than all
      these wants,
He does it under name of perfect love;
As who should say, if I should sleep or eat
'Twere deadly sickness, or else present
      death.
I prithee go and get me some repast;
I care not what, so it be wholesome food.
GRUMIO.
What say you to a neat's foot?
KATHERINA.
'Tis passing good; I prithee let me have it.
GRUMIO.
I fear it is too choleric a meat.
How say you to a fat tripe finely broil'd?
KATHERINA.
I like it well; good Grumio, fetch it me.
GRUMIO.
I cannot tell; I fear 'tis choleric.
What say you to a piece of beef and
      mustard?
KATHERINA.
A dish that I do love to feed upon.

GRUMIO.
Ay, but the mustard is too hot a little.
KATHERINA.
Why then the beef, and let the mustard
      rest.
GRUMIO.
Nay, then I will not: you shall have the
      mustard,
Or else you get no beef of Grumio.
KATHERINA.
Then both, or one, or anything thou wilt.
GRUMIO.
Why then the mustard without the beef.
KATHERINA.
Go, get thee gone, thou false deluding
      slave,
[*Beats him.*] That feed'st me with the very
      name of meat.
Sorrow on thee and all the pack of you
That triumph thus upon my misery!
Go, get thee gone, I say.
            [*Enter* PETRUCHIO *with a dish of meat;
                        and* HORTENSIO.]
PETRUCHIO.
How fares my Kate? What, sweeting, all
      amort?
HORTENSIO.
Mistress, what cheer?
KATHERINA.
                              Faith, as cold as can be.
PETRUCHIO.
Pluck up thy spirits; look cheerfully upon
      me.
Here, love; thou seest how diligent I am,
To dress thy meat myself, and bring it thee:
            [*Sets the dish on a table.*]
I am sure, sweet Kate, this kindness merits
      thanks.
What! not a word? Nay, then thou lov'st
      it not,
And all my pains is sorted to no proof.
Here, take away this dish.
KATHERINA.
                              I pray you, let it stand.
PETRUCHIO.
The poorest service is repaid with thanks;
And so shall mine, before you touch the
      meat.

KATHERINA.
I thank you, sir.
HORTENSIO.
Signior Petruchio, fie! you are to blame.
Come, Mistress Kate, I'll bear you company.
PETRUCHIO. [*Aside.*]
Eat it up all, Hortensio, if thou lovest me.
Much good do it unto thy gentle heart!
Kate, eat apace: and now, my honey love,
Will we return unto thy father's house
And revel it as bravely as the best,
With silken coats and caps, and golden
     rings,
With ruffs and cuffs and farthingales and
     things;
With scarfs and fans and double change
     of bravery,
With amber bracelets, beads, and all this
     knavery.
What! hast thou din'd? The tailor stays thy
     leisure,
To deck thy body with his ruffling treasure.
          [*Enter* TAILOR.]
Come, tailor, let us see these ornaments;
Lay forth the gown.
          [*Enter* HABERDASHER.]
               What news with you, sir?
HABERDASHER.
Here is the cap your worship did bespeak.
PETRUCHIO.
Why, this was moulded on a porringer;
A velvet dish: fie, fie! 'tis lewd and filthy:
Why, 'tis a cockle or a walnut-shell,
A knack, a toy, a trick, a baby's cap:
Away with it! come, let me have a bigger.
KATHERINA.
I'll have no bigger; this doth fit the time,
And gentlewomen wear such caps as these.
PETRUCHIO.
When you are gentle, you shall have one
     too,
And not till then.
HORTENSIO. [*Aside.*]
               That will not be in haste.
KATHERINA.
Why, sir, I trust I may have leave to speak;
And speak I will. I am no child, no babe.
Your betters have endur'd me say my mind,

And if you cannot, best you stop your ears.
My tongue will tell the anger of my heart,
Or else my heart, concealing it, will break;
And rather than it shall, I will be free
Even to the uttermost, as I please, in
     words.
PETRUCHIO.
Why, thou say'st true; it is a paltry cap,
A custard-coffin, a bauble, a silken pie;
I love thee well in that thou lik'st it not.
KATHERINA.
Love me or love me not, I like the cap;
And it I will have, or I will have none.
          [*Exit* HABERDASHER.]
PETRUCHIO.
Thy gown? Why, ay: come, tailor, let us
     see't.
O mercy, God! what masquing stuff is
     here?
What's this? A sleeve? 'Tis like a demi-
     cannon.
What, up and down, carv'd like an
     appletart?
Here's snip and nip and cut and slish and
     slash,
Like to a censer in a barber's shop.
Why, what i' devil's name, tailor, call'st
     thou this?
HORTENSIO. [*Aside.*]
I see she's like to have neither cap nor
     gown.
TAILOR.
You bid me make it orderly and well,
According to the fashion and the time.
PETRUCHIO.
Marry, and did; but if you be remember'd,
I did not bid you mar it to the time.
Go, hop me over every kennel home,
For you shall hop without my custom, sir.
I'll none of it: hence! make your best of it.
KATHERINA.
I never saw a better fashion'd gown,
More quaint, more pleasing, nor more
     commendable;
Belike you mean to make a puppet of me.
PETRUCHIO.
Why, true; he means to make a puppet
     of thee.

TAILOR.
She says your worship means to make a
  puppet of her.
PETRUCHIO.
O monstrous arrogance! Thou liest, thou
  thread,
Thou thimble,
Thou yard, three-quarters, half-yard,
  quarter, nail!
Thou flea, thou nit, thou winter-cricket
  thou!
Brav'd in mine own house with a skein of
  thread!
Away! thou rag, thou quantity, thou
  remnant,
Or I shall so be-mete thee with thy yard
As thou shalt think on prating whilst thou
  liv'st!
I tell thee, I, that thou hast marr'd her
  gown.
TAILOR.
Your worship is deceiv'd: the gown is
  made
Just as my master had direction.
Grumio gave order how it should be done.
GRUMIO.
I gave him no order; I gave him the stuff.
TAILOR.
But how did you desire it should be made?
GRUMIO.
Marry, sir, with needle and thread.
TAILOR.
But did you not request to have it cut?
GRUMIO.
Thou hast faced many things.
TAILOR.
I have.
GRUMIO.
Face not me. Thou hast braved many men;
brave not me: I will neither be fac'd nor
brav'd. I say unto thee, I bid thy master cut
out the gown; but I did not bid him cut it
to pieces: ergo, thou liest.
TAILOR.
Why, here is the note of the fashion to
  testify.
PETRUCHIO.
Read it.

GRUMIO.
The note lies in 's throat, if he say I said so.
TAILOR. [Reads.]
"Imprimis, a loose-bodied gown."
GRUMIO.
Master, if ever I said loose-bodied gown,
sew me in the skirts of it and beat me to
death with a bottom of brown thread; I
said a gown.
PETRUCHIO.
Proceed.
TAILOR. [Reads.]
"With a small compassed cape."
GRUMIO.
I confess the cape.
TAILOR. [Reads.]
"With a trunk sleeve."
GRUMIO.
I confess two sleeves.
TAILOR. [Reads.]
"The sleeves curiously cut."
PETRUCHIO.
Ay, there's the villainy.
GRUMIO.
Error i' the bill, sir; error i' the bill. I
commanded the sleeves should be cut out,
and sew'd up again; and that I'll prove upon
thee, though thy little finger be armed in a
thimble.
TAILOR.
This is true that I say; an I had thee in place
where thou shouldst know it.
GRUMIO.
I am for thee straight; take thou the bill,
give me thy mete-yard, and spare not me.
HORTENSIO.
God-a-mercy, Grumio! Then he shall have
no odds.
PETRUCHIO.
Well, sir, in brief, the gown is not for me.
GRUMIO.
You are i' the right, sir; 'tis for my
  mistress.
PETRUCHIO.
Go, take it up unto thy master's use.
GRUMIO.
Villain, not for thy life! Take up my
mistress' gown for thy master's use!

PETRUCHIO.
Why, sir, what's your conceit in that?
GRUMIO.
O, sir, the conceit is deeper than you think
   for. Take up my mistress' gown to his
   master's use! O fie, fie, fie!
PETRUCHIO. [*Aside.*]
Hortensio, say thou wilt see the tailor paid.
[*To* TAILOR.] Go take it hence; be gone,
   and say no more.
HORTENSIO. [*Aside to* TAILOR.]
Tailor, I'll pay thee for thy gown to-
   morrow;
Take no unkindness of his hasty words.
Away, I say! commend me to thy master.
           [*Exit* TAILOR.]
PETRUCHIO.
Well, come, my Kate; we will unto your
   father's
Even in these honest mean habiliments.
Our purses shall be proud, our garments
   poor
For 'tis the mind that makes the body rich;
And as the sun breaks through the darkest
   clouds,
So honour peereth in the meanest habit.
What, is the jay more precious than the
   lark
Because his feathers are more beautiful?
Or is the adder better than the eel
Because his painted skin contents the
   eye?
O no, good Kate; neither art thou the
   worse
For this poor furniture and mean array.
If thou account'st it shame, lay it on me;
And therefore frolic; we will hence
   forthwith,
To feast and sport us at thy father's house.
Go call my men, and let us straight to
   him;
And bring our horses unto Long-lane end;
There will we mount, and thither walk on
   foot.
Let's see; I think 'tis now some seven
   o'clock,
And well we may come there by dinner-
   time.

KATHERINA.
I dare assure you, sir, 'tis almost two,
And 'twill be supper-time ere you come
   there.
PETRUCHIO.
It shall be seven ere I go to horse.
Look what I speak, or do, or think to do,
You are still crossing it. Sirs, let 't alone:
I will not go to-day; and ere I do,
It shall be what o'clock I say it is.
HORTENSIO.
Why, so this gallant will command the
   sun.
           [*Exeunt.*]

SCENE IV
Padua. Before Baptista's house.
[*Enter* TRANIO, *and the* PEDANT *dressed
like Vincentio.*]
TRANIO.
Sir, this is the house; please it you that I
   call?
PEDANT.
Ay, what else? and, but I be deceived,
Signior Baptista may remember me,
Near twenty years ago in Genoa,
Where we were lodgers at the Pegasus.
TRANIO.
'Tis well; and hold your own, in any case,
With such austerity as 'longeth to a
   father.
PEDANT.
I warrant you. But, sir, here comes your
   boy;
'Twere good he were school'd.
           [*Enter* BIONDELLO.]
TRANIO.
Fear you not him. Sirrah Biondello,
Now do your duty throughly, I advise you.
Imagine 'twere the right Vincentio.
BIONDELLO.
Tut! fear not me.
TRANIO.
But hast thou done thy errand to Baptista?
BIONDELLO.
I told him that your father was at Venice,
And that you look'd for him this day in
   Padua.

Tranio.
Thou'rt a tall fellow; hold thee that to
    drink.
Here comes Baptista.—Set your
    countenance, sir.
    [*Enter* Baptista *and* Lucentio.]
Signior Baptista, you are happily met.
[*To the* Pedant.] Sir, this is the gentleman
    I told you of;
I pray you stand good father to me now;
Give me Bianca for my patrimony.
Pedant.
Soft, son!
Sir, by your leave: having come to Padua
To gather in some debts, my son Lucentio
Made me acquainted with a weighty cause
Of love between your daughter and
    himself:
And,—for the good report I hear of you,
And for the love he beareth to your
    daughter,
And she to him,—to stay him not too long,
I am content, in a good father's care,
To have him match'd; and, if you please
    to like
No worse than I, upon some agreement
Me shall you find ready and willing
With one consent to have her so bestow'd;
For curious I cannot be with you,
Signior Baptista, of whom I hear so well.
Baptista.
Sir, pardon me in what I have to say.
Your plainness and your shortness please
    me well.
Right true it is your son Lucentio here
Doth love my daughter, and she loveth
    him,
Or both dissemble deeply their affections;
And therefore, if you say no more than
    this,
That like a father you will deal with him,
And pass my daughter a sufficient dower,
The match is made, and all is done:
Your son shall have my daughter with
    consent.
Tranio.
I thank you, sir. Where then do you know
    best

We be affied, and such assurance ta'en
As shall with either part's agreement
    stand?
Baptista.
Not in my house, Lucentio, for you know
Pitchers have ears, and I have many
    servants;
Besides, old Gremio is hearkening still,
And happily we might be interrupted.
Tranio.
Then at my lodging, an it like you:
There doth my father lie; and there this
    night
We'll pass the business privately and well.
Send for your daughter by your servant
    here;
My boy shall fetch the scrivener presently.
The worst is this, that at so slender warning
You are like to have a thin and slender
    pittance.
Baptista.
It likes me well. Cambio, hie you home,
And bid Bianca make her ready straight;
And, if you will, tell what hath happened:
Lucentio's father is arriv'd in Padua,
And how she's like to be Lucentio's wife.
Lucentio.
I pray the gods she may, with all my heart!
Tranio.
Dally not with the gods, but get thee gone.
Signior Baptista, shall I lead the way?
Welcome! One mess is like to be your
    cheer;
Come, sir; we will better it in Pisa.
Baptista.
I follow you.
    [*Exeunt* Tranio, Pedant, *and* Baptista.]
Biondello.
Cambio!
Lucentio.
What say'st thou, Biondello?
Biondello.
You saw my master wink and laugh upon
    you?
Lucentio.
Biondello, what of that?
Biondello.
Faith, nothing; but has left me here behind

to expound the meaning or moral of his
signs and tokens.

LUCENTIO.
I pray thee moralize them.

BIONDELLO.
Then thus: Baptista is safe, talking with the
deceiving father of a deceitful son.

LUCENTIO.
And what of him?

BIONDELLO.
His daughter is to be brought by you to the
supper.

LUCENTIO.
And then?

BIONDELLO.
The old priest at Saint Luke's church is at
your command at all hours.

LUCENTIO.
And what of all this?

BIONDELLO.
I cannot tell, except they are busied about a
counterfeit assurance. Take your assurance
of her, *cum privilegio ad imprimendum
solum*; to the church! take the priest, clerk,
and some sufficient honest witnesses.
If this be not that you look for, I have
    more to say,
But bid Bianca farewell for ever and a day.

LUCENTIO.
Hear'st thou, Biondello?

BIONDELLO.
I cannot tarry: I knew a wench married in
an afternoon as she went to the garden for
parsley to stuff a rabbit; and so may you, sir;
and so adieu, sir. My master hath appointed
me to go to Saint Luke's to bid the priest be
ready to come against you come with your
appendix.
                    [*Exit.*]

LUCENTIO.
I may, and will, if she be so contented.
She will be pleas'd; then wherefore should
    I doubt?
Hap what hap may, I'll roundly go about
    her;
It shall go hard if Cambio go without
    her:
                    [*Exit.*]

SCENE V
A public road.
[*Enter* PETRUCHIO, KATHERINA,
    HORTENSIO, *and* SERVANTS.]

PETRUCHIO.
Come on, i' God's name; once more
    toward our father's.
Good Lord, how bright and goodly shines
    the moon!

KATHERINA.
The moon! The sun; it is not moonlight
    now.

PETRUCHIO.
I say it is the moon that shines so bright.

KATHERINA.
I know it is the sun that shines so bright.

PETRUCHIO.
Now by my mother's son, and that's
    myself,
It shall be moon, or star, or what I list,
Or ere I journey to your father's house.
Go on and fetch our horses back again.
Evermore cross'd and cross'd; nothing but
    cross'd!

HORTENSIO.
Say as he says, or we shall never go.

KATHERINA.
Forward, I pray, since we have come so
    far,
And be it moon, or sun, or what you
    please;
And if you please to call it a rush-candle,
Henceforth I vow it shall be so for me.

PETRUCHIO.
I say it is the moon.

KATHERINA.
I know it is the moon.

PETRUCHIO.
Nay, then you lie; it is the blessed sun.

KATHERINA.
Then, God be bless'd, it is the blessed
    sun;
But sun it is not when you say it is not,
And the moon changes even as your
    mind.
What you will have it nam'd, even that
    it is,
And so it shall be so for Katherine.

HORTENSIO.
Petruchio, go thy ways; the field is won.
PETRUCHIO.
Well, forward, forward! thus the bowl
    should run,
And not unluckily against the bias.
But, soft! Company is coming here.
        [Enter VINCENTIO, in a travelling
                dress.]
[To VINCENTIO.] Good-morrow, gentle
    mistress; where away?
Tell me, sweet Kate, and tell me truly too,
Hast thou beheld a fresher gentlewoman?
Such war of white and red within her
    cheeks!
What stars do spangle heaven with such
    beauty
As those two eyes become that heavenly
    face?
Fair lovely maid, once more good day to
    thee.
Sweet Kate, embrace her for her beauty's
    sake.
HORTENSIO.
A' will make the man mad, to make a
    woman of him.
KATHERINA.
Young budding virgin, fair and fresh and
    sweet,
Whither away, or where is thy abode?
Happy the parents of so fair a child;
Happier the man whom favourable stars
Allot thee for his lovely bed-fellow.
PETRUCHIO.
Why, how now, Kate! I hope thou art not
    mad:
This is a man, old, wrinkled, faded,
    wither'd,
And not a maiden, as thou sayst he is.
KATHERINA.
Pardon, old father, my mistaking eyes,
That have been so bedazzled with the sun
That everything I look on seemeth green:
Now I perceive thou art a reverend father;
Pardon, I pray thee, for my mad mistaking.
PETRUCHIO.
Do, good old grandsire, and withal make
    known

Which way thou travellest: if along with
    us,
We shall be joyful of thy company.
VINCENTIO.
Fair sir, and you my merry mistress,
That with your strange encounter much
    amaz'd me,
My name is called Vincentio; my dwelling
    Pisa;
And bound I am to Padua, there to visit
A son of mine, which long I have not
    seen.
PETRUCHIO.
What is his name?
VINCENTIO.
                    Lucentio, gentle sir.
PETRUCHIO.
Happily met; the happier for thy son.
And now by law, as well as reverend
    age,
I may entitle thee my loving father:
The sister to my wife, this gentlewoman,
Thy son by this hath married. Wonder
    not,
Nor be not griev'd: she is of good esteem,
Her dowry wealthy, and of worthy birth;
Beside, so qualified as may beseem
The spouse of any noble gentleman.
Let me embrace with old Vincentio;
And wander we to see thy honest son,
Who will of thy arrival be full joyous.
VINCENTIO.
But is this true? or is it else your pleasure,
Like pleasant travellers, to break a jest
Upon the company you overtake?
HORTENSIO.
I do assure thee, father, so it is.
PETRUCHIO.
Come, go along, and see the truth hereof;
For our first merriment hath made thee
    jealous.
        [Exeunt all but HORTENSIO.]
HORTENSIO.
Well, Petruchio, this has put me in heart.
Have to my widow! and if she be froward,
Then hast thou taught Hortensio to be
    untoward.
                    [Exit.]

ACT V
SCENE I

Padua. Before Lucentio's house.
[*Enter on one side* BIONDELLO, LUCENTIO, *and* BIANCA; GREMIO *walking on other side.*]

BIONDELLO.
Softly and swiftly, sir, for the priest is ready.

LUCENTIO.
I fly, Biondello; but they may chance to need thee at home, therefore leave us.

BIONDELLO.
Nay, faith, I'll see the church o' your back; and then come back to my master's as soon as I can.

[*Exeunt* LUCENTIO, BIANCA, *and* BIONDELLO.]

GREMIO.
I marvel Cambio comes not all this while.

[*Enter* PETRUCHIO, KATHERINA, VINCENTIO, *and* ATTENDANTS.]

PETRUCHIO.
Sir, here's the door; this is Lucentio's house:
My father's bears more toward the market-place;
Thither must I, and here I leave you, sir.

VINCENTIO.
You shall not choose but drink before you go.
I think I shall command your welcome here,
And by all likelihood some cheer is toward.
[*Knocks.*]

GREMIO.
They're busy within; you were best knock louder.

[*Enter* PEDANT *above, at a window.*]

PEDANT.
What's he that knocks as he would beat down the gate?

VINCENTIO.
Is Signior Lucentio within, sir?

PEDANT.
He's within, sir, but not to be spoken withal.

VINCENTIO.
What if a man bring him a hundred pound or two to make merry withal?

PEDANT.
Keep your hundred pounds to yourself: he shall need none so long as I live.

PETRUCHIO.
Nay, I told you your son was well beloved in Padua. Do you hear, sir? To leave frivolous circumstances, I pray you tell Signior Lucentio that his father is come from Pisa, and is here at the door to speak with him.

PEDANT.
Thou liest: his father is come from Padua, and here looking out at the window.

VINCENTIO.
Art thou his father?

PEDANT.
Ay, sir; so his mother says, if I may believe her.

PETRUCHIO. [*To* VINCENTIO.]
Why, how now, gentleman! why, this is flat knavery to take upon you another man's name.

PEDANT.
Lay hands on the villain: I believe a' means to cozen somebody in this city under my countenance.

[*Re-enter* BIONDELLO.]

BIONDELLO.
I have seen them in the church together: God send 'em good shipping! But who is here? Mine old master, Vincentio! Now we are undone and brought to nothing.

VINCENTIO. [*Seeing* BIONDELLO.]
Come hither, crack-hemp.

BIONDELLO.
I hope I may choose, sir.

VINCENTIO.
Come hither, you rogue. What, have you forgot me?

BIONDELLO.
Forgot you! No, sir: I could not forget you, for I never saw you before in all my life.

VINCENTIO.
What, you notorious villain! didst thou never see thy master's father, Vincentio?

BIONDELLO.
What, my old worshipful old master? Yes, marry, sir; see where he looks out of the window.

VINCENTIO.

Is't so, indeed?

[*He beats* BIONDELLO.]

BIONDELLO.

Help, help, help! here's a madman will murder me.

[*Exit.*]

PEDANT.

Help, son! help, Signior Baptista!

[*Exit from the window.*]

PETRUCHIO.

Prithee, Kate, let's stand aside and see the end of this controversy.

[*They retire.*]

[*Re-enter* PEDANT *below;* BAPTISTA, TRANIO, *and* SERVANTS.]

TRANIO.

Sir, what are you that offer to beat my servant?

VINCENTIO.

What am I, sir! nay, what are you, sir? O immortal gods! O fine villain! A silken doublet, a velvet hose, a scarlet cloak, and a copatain hat! O, I am undone! I am undone! While I play the good husband at home, my son and my servant spend all at the university.

TRANIO.

How now! what's the matter?

BAPTISTA.

What, is the man lunatic?

TRANIO.

Sir, you seem a sober ancient gentleman by your habit, but your words show you a madman. Why, sir, what 'cerns it you if I wear pearl and gold? I thank my good father, I am able to maintain it.

VINCENTIO.

Thy father! O villain! he is a sailmaker in Bergamo.

BAPTISTA.

You mistake, sir; you mistake, sir. Pray, what do you think is his name?

VINCENTIO.

His name! As if I knew not his name! I have brought him up ever since he was three years old, and his name is Tranio.

PEDANT.

Away, away, mad ass! His name is Lucentio; and he is mine only son, and heir to the lands of me, Signior Vicentio.

VINCENTIO.

Lucentio! O, he hath murdered his master! Lay hold on him, I charge you, in the duke's name. O, my son, my son! Tell me, thou villain, where is my son, Lucentio?

TRANIO.

Call forth an officer. [*Enter one with an* OFFICER.] Carry this mad knave to the gaol. Father Baptista, I charge you see that he be forthcoming.

VINCENTIO.

Carry me to the gaol!

GREMIO.

Stay, officer; he shall not go to prison.

BAPTISTA.

Talk not, Signior Gremio; I say he shall go to prison.

GREMIO.

Take heed, Signior Baptista, lest you be cony-catched in this business; I dare swear this is the right Vincentio.

PEDANT.

Swear if thou darest.

GREMIO.

Nay, I dare not swear it.

TRANIO.

Then thou wert best say that I am not Lucentio.

GREMIO.

Yes, I know thee to be Signior Lucentio.

BAPTISTA.

Away with the dotard! to the gaol with him!

VINCENTIO.

Thus strangers may be haled and abus'd: O monstrous villain!

[*Re-enter* BIONDELLO, *with* LUCENTIO *and* BIANCA.]

BIONDELLO.

O! we are spoiled; and yonder he is: deny him, forswear him, or else we are all undone.

LUCENTIO. [*Kneeling.*]

Pardon, sweet father.

VINCENTIO.

Lives my sweetest son?

[BIONDELLO, TRANIO, *and* PEDANT
run out.]
BIANCA. [*Kneeling.*]
Pardon, dear father.
BAPTISTA.
How hast thou offended?
Where is Lucentio?
LUCENTIO.
Here's Lucentio,
Right son to the right Vincentio;
That have by marriage made thy daughter
    mine,
While counterfeit supposes blear'd thine
    eyne.
GREMIO.
Here's packing, with a witness, to deceive
    us all!
VINCENTIO.
Where is that damned villain, Tranio,
That fac'd and brav'd me in this matter so?
BAPTISTA.
Why, tell me, is not this my Cambio?
BIANCA.
Cambio is chang'd into Lucentio.
LUCENTIO.
Love wrought these miracles. Bianca's love
Made me exchange my state with Tranio,
While he did bear my countenance in the
    town;
And happily I have arriv'd at the last
Unto the wished haven of my bliss.
What Tranio did, myself enforc'd him to;
Then pardon him, sweet father, for my
    sake.
VINCENTIO.
I'll slit the villain's nose that would have
sent me to the gaol.
BAPTISTA. [*To* LUCENTIO.]
But do you hear, sir? Have you married my
daughter without asking my good will?
VINCENTIO.
Fear not, Baptista; we will content you,
go to: but I will in, to be revenged for this
villainy.
                    [*Exit.*]
BAPTISTA.
And I to sound the depth of this knavery.
                    [*Exit.*]

LUCENTIO.
Look not pale, Bianca; thy father will not
    frown.
            [*Exeunt* LUCENTIO *and* BIANCA.]
GREMIO.
My cake is dough, but I'll in among the
    rest;
Out of hope of all but my share of the
    feast.
                    [*Exit.*]
        [PETRUCHIO *and* KATHERINA *advance.*]
KATHERINA.
Husband, let's follow to see the end of
    this ado.
PETRUCHIO.
First kiss me, Kate, and we will.
KATHERINA.
What! in the midst of the street?
PETRUCHIO.
What! art thou ashamed of me?
KATHERINA.
No, sir; God forbid; but ashamed to kiss.
PETRUCHIO.
Why, then, let's home again. Come, sirrah,
    let's away.
KATHERINA.
Nay, I will give thee a kiss: now pray thee,
    love, stay.
PETRUCHIO.
Is not this well? Come, my sweet Kate:
Better once than never, for never too late.
                    [*Exeunt.*]

SCENE II
A room in Lucentio's house.
[*Enter* BAPTISTA, VINCENTIO, GREMIO,
PEDANT, LUCENTIO, BIANCA, PETRUCHIO,
KATHERINA, HORTENSIO, *and* WIDOW;
TRANIO, BIONDELLO, GRUMIO, *and*
OTHERS *attending.*]
LUCENTIO.
At last, though long, our jarring notes
    agree:
And time it is when raging war is done,
To smile at 'scapes and perils overblown.
My fair Bianca, bid my father welcome,
While I with self-same kindness welcome
    thine.

Brother Petruchio, sister Katherina,
And thou, Hortensio, with thy loving
    widow,
Feast with the best, and welcome to my
    house:
My banquet is to close our stomachs up,
After our great good cheer. Pray you, sit
    down;
For now we sit to chat as well as eat.
    [*They sit at table.*]

PETRUCHIO.
Nothing but sit and sit, and eat and eat!

BAPTISTA.
Padua affords this kindness, son Petruchio.

PETRUCHIO.
Padua affords nothing but what is kind.

HORTENSIO.
For both our sakes I would that word were
    true.

PETRUCHIO.
Now, for my life, Hortensio fears his widow.

WIDOW.
Then never trust me if I be afeard.

PETRUCHIO.
You are very sensible, and yet you miss my
    sense:
I mean Hortensio is afeard of you.

WIDOW.
He that is giddy thinks the world turns
    round.

PETRUCHIO.
Roundly replied.

KATHERINA.
Mistress, how mean you that?

WIDOW.
Thus I conceive by him.

PETRUCHIO.
Conceives by me! How likes Hortensio
    that?

HORTENSIO.
My widow says thus she conceives her tale.

PETRUCHIO.
Very well mended. Kiss him for that, good
    widow.

KATHERINA.
"He that is giddy thinks the world turns
    round":
I pray you tell me what you meant by that.

WIDOW.
Your husband, being troubled with a
    shrew,
Measures my husband's sorrow by his woe;
And now you know my meaning.

KATHERINA.
A very mean meaning.

WIDOW.
Right, I mean you.

KATHERINA.
And I am mean, indeed, respecting you.

PETRUCHIO.
To her, Kate!

HORTENSIO.
To her, widow!

PETRUCHIO.
A hundred marks, my Kate does put her
    down.

HORTENSIO.
That's my office.

PETRUCHIO.
Spoke like an officer: ha' to thee, lad.
    [*Drinks to* HORTENSIO.]

BAPTISTA.
How likes Gremio these quick-witted
    folks?

GREMIO.
Believe me, sir, they butt together well.

BIANCA.
Head and butt! An hasty-witted body
Would say your head and butt were head
    and horn.

VINCENTIO.
Ay, mistress bride, hath that awaken'd you?

BIANCA.
Ay, but not frighted me; therefore I'll sleep
    again.

PETRUCHIO.
Nay, that you shall not; since you have
    begun,
Have at you for a bitter jest or two.

BIANCA.
Am I your bird? I mean to shift my bush,
And then pursue me as you draw your
    bow.
You are welcome all.
    [*Exeunt* BIANCA, KATHERINA, *and*
    WIDOW.]

PETRUCHIO.

She hath prevented me. Here, Signior
  Tranio;

This bird you aim'd at, though you hit her
  not:

Therefore a health to all that shot and
  miss'd.

TRANIO.

O, sir! Lucentio slipp'd me like his
  greyhound,

Which runs himself, and catches for his
  master.

PETRUCHIO.

A good swift simile, but something
  currish.

TRANIO.

'Tis well, sir, that you hunted for yourself:

'Tis thought your deer does hold you at
  a bay.

BAPTISTA.

O ho, Petruchio! Tranio hits you now.

LUCENTIO.

I thank thee for that gird, good Tranio.

HORTENSIO.

Confess, confess; hath he not hit you here?

PETRUCHIO.

A' has a little gall'd me, I confess;

And, as the jest did glance away from me,

'Tis ten to one it maim'd you two outright.

BAPTISTA.

Now, in good sadness, son Petruchio,

I think thou hast the veriest shrew of all.

PETRUCHIO.

Well, I say no; and therefore, for assurance,

Let's each one send unto his wife,

And he whose wife is most obedient,

To come at first when he doth send for her,

Shall win the wager which we will propose.

HORTENSIO.

Content. What's the wager?

LUCENTIO.

Twenty crowns.

PETRUCHIO.

Twenty crowns!

I'll venture so much of my hawk or hound,

But twenty times so much upon my wife.

LUCENTIO.

A hundred then.

HORTENSIO.

Content.

PETRUCHIO.

A match! 'tis done.

HORTENSIO.

Who shall begin?

LUCENTIO.

That will I.

Go, Biondello, bid your mistress come to
  me.

BIONDELLO.

I go.

                    [*Exit.*]

BAPTISTA.

Son, I'll be your half, Bianca comes.

LUCENTIO.

I'll have no halves; I'll bear it all myself.

            [*Re-enter* BIONDELLO.]

How now! what news?

BIONDELLO.

Sir, my mistress sends you word

That she is busy and she cannot come.

PETRUCHIO.

How! She's busy, and she cannot come!

Is that an answer?

GREMIO.

                    Ay, and a kind one too:

Pray God, sir, your wife send you not a
  worse.

PETRUCHIO.

I hope, better.

HORTENSIO.

            Sirrah Biondello,

Go and entreat my wife to come to me
  forthwith.

            [*Exit* BIONDELLO.]

PETRUCHIO.

O, ho! entreat her! Nay, then she must
  needs come.

HORTENSIO.

I am afraid, sir, do what you can,

            [*Re-enter* BIONDELLO.]

Yours will not be entreated. Now, where's
  my wife?

BIONDELLO.

She says you have some goodly jest in hand:

She will not come; she bids you come to
  her.

PETRUCHIO.
Worse and worse; she will not come! O
   vile,
Intolerable, not to be endur'd!
Sirrah Grumio, go to your mistress; say,
I command her come to me.
              [Exit GRUMIO.]

HORTENSIO.
I know her answer.

PETRUCHIO.
          What?

HORTENSIO.
               She will not.

PETRUCHIO.
The fouler fortune mine, and there an end.
        [Re-enter KATHERINA.]

BAPTISTA.
Now, by my holidame, here comes
   Katherina!

KATHERINA.
What is your sir, that you send for me?

PETRUCHIO.
Where is your sister, and Hortensio's wife?

KATHERINA.
They sit conferring by the parlour fire.

PETRUCHIO.
Go, fetch them hither; if they deny to
   come,
Swinge me them soundly forth unto their
   husbands.
Away, I say, and bring them hither straight.
        [Exit KATHERINA.]

LUCENTIO.
Here is a wonder, if you talk of a wonder.

HORTENSIO.
And so it is. I wonder what it bodes.

PETRUCHIO.
Marry, peace it bodes, and love, and quiet
   life,
An awful rule, and right supremacy;
And, to be short, what not that's sweet
   and happy.

BAPTISTA.
Now fair befall thee, good Petruchio!
The wager thou hast won; and I will add
Unto their losses twenty thousand crowns;
Another dowry to another daughter,
For she is chang'd, as she had never been.

PETRUCHIO.
Nay, I will win my wager better yet,
And show more sign of her obedience,
Her new-built virtue and obedience.
See where she comes, and brings your
   froward wives
As prisoners to her womanly persuasion.
    [Re-enter KATHERINA *with* BIANCA
              and WIDOW.]
Katherine, that cap of yours becomes you
   not:
Off with that bauble, throw it underfoot.
   [KATHERINA *pulls off her cap and throws
               it down.*]

WIDOW.
Lord, let me never have a cause to sigh
Till I be brought to such a silly pass!

BIANCA.
Fie! what a foolish duty call you this?

LUCENTIO.
I would your duty were as foolish too;
The wisdom of your duty, fair Bianca,
Hath cost me a hundred crowns since
   supper-time!

BIANCA.
The more fool you for laying on my duty.

PETRUCHIO.
Katherine, I charge thee, tell these
   headstrong women
What duty they do owe their lords and
   husbands.

WIDOW.
Come, come, you're mocking; we will have
no telling.

PETRUCHIO.
Come on, I say; and first begin with her.

WIDOW.
She shall not.

PETRUCHIO.
I say she shall: and first begin with her.

KATHERINA.
Fie, fie! unknit that threatening unkind
   brow,
And dart not scornful glances from those
   eyes
To wound thy lord, thy king, thy governor:
It blots thy beauty as frosts do bite the
   meads,

Confounds thy fame as whirlwinds shake
    fair buds,
And in no sense is meet or amiable.
A woman mov'd is like a fountain
    troubled,
Muddy, ill-seeming, thick, bereft of
    beauty;
And while it is so, none so dry or thirsty
Will deign to sip or touch one drop of it.
Thy husband is thy lord, thy life, thy
    keeper,
Thy head, thy sovereign; one that cares
    for thee,
And for thy maintenance commits his
    body
To painful labour both by sea and land,
To watch the night in storms, the day in
    cold,
Whilst thou liest warm at home, secure
    and safe;
And craves no other tribute at thy hands
But love, fair looks, and true obedience;
Too little payment for so great a debt.
Such duty as the subject owes the prince,
Even such a woman oweth to her husband;
And when she is froward, peevish, sullen,
    sour,
And not obedient to his honest will,
What is she but a foul contending rebel
And graceless traitor to her loving lord?—
I am asham'd that women are so simple
To offer war where they should kneel for
    peace,
Or seek for rule, supremacy, and sway,
When they are bound to serve, love, and
    obey.
Why are our bodies soft and weak and
    smooth,
Unapt to toil and trouble in the world,
But that our soft conditions and our hearts
Should well agree with our external parts?
Come, come, you froward and unable
    worms!

My mind hath been as big as one of yours,
My heart as great, my reason haply more,
To bandy word for word and frown for
    frown;
But now I see our lances are but straws,
Our strength as weak, our weakness past
    compare,
That seeming to be most which we indeed
    least are.
Then vail your stomachs, for it is no boot,
And place your hands below your
    husband's foot:
In token of which duty, if he please,
My hand is ready; may it do him ease.

PETRUCHIO.
Why, there's a wench! Come on, and kiss
    me, Kate.

LUCENTIO.
Well, go thy ways, old lad, for thou shalt
    ha't.

VINCENTIO.
'Tis a good hearing when children are
    toward.

LUCENTIO.
But a harsh hearing when women are
    froward.

PETRUCHIO.
Come, Kate, we'll to bed.
We three are married, but you two are
    sped.
'Twas I won the wager [*To* LUCENTIO.]
    though you hit the white;
And being a winner, God give you good
    night!
    [*Exeunt* PETRUCHIO *and* KATHERINA.]

HORTENSIO.
Now go thy ways; thou hast tam'd a curst
    shrew.

LUCENTIO.
'Tis a wonder, by your leave, she will be
    tam'd so.
           [*Exeunt.*]

All's Well That Ends Well

DRAMATIS PERSONAE

KING OF FRANCE
DUKE OF FLORENCE
BERTRAM, *Count of Rousillon*
LAFEU, *an old lord*
PAROLLES, *a follower of Bertram*
Several young FRENCH LORDS, *who serve with Bertram in the Florentine War*
STEWARD, *servant to the Countess of Rousillon*
CLOWN, *servant to the Countess of Rousillon*
A PAGE, *servant to the Countess of Rousillon*
COUNTESS OF ROUSILLON, *mother to Bertram*

HELENA, *a gentlewoman protected by the countess*
A WIDOW *of Florence*
DIANA, *daughter to the widow*
VIOLENTA, *neighbour and friend to the widow*
MARIANA, *neighbour and friend to the widow*
LORDS *attending on the king;*
OFFICERS; SOLDIERS, &C.,
French and Florentine

SCENE: *Partly in France, and partly in Tuscany.*

ACT I
SCENE I

Rousillon. A room in the countess's palace.
[*Enter* BERTRAM, *the* COUNTESS OF ROUSILLON, HELENA, *and* LAFEU, *all in black.*]

COUNTESS.
In delivering my son from me, I bury a second husband.

BERTRAM.
And I in going, madam, weep o'er my father's death anew; but I must attend his majesty's command, to whom I am now in ward, evermore in subjection.

LAFEU.
You shall find of the king a husband, madam;—you, sir, a father: he that so generally is at all times good, must of necessity hold his virtue to you; whose worthiness would stir it up where it wanted, rather than lack it where there is such abundance.

COUNTESS.
What hope is there of his majesty's amendment?

LAFEU.
He hath abandoned his physicians, madam; under whose practices he hath persecuted time with hope; and finds no other advantage in the process but only the losing of hope by time.

COUNTESS.
This young gentlewoman had a father—O, that "had!" how sad a passage 'tis!—whose skill was almost as great as his honesty; had it stretched so far, would have made nature immortal, and death should have play for lack of work. Would, for the king's sake, he were living! I think it would be the death of the king's disease.

LAFEU.
How called you the man you speak of, madam?

COUNTESS.
He was famous, sir, in his profession, and it was his great right to be so—Gerard de Narbon.

LAFEU.
He was excellent indeed, madam; the king very lately spoke of him admiringly

and mourningly; he was skilful enough to have liv'd still, if knowledge could be set up against mortality.

BERTRAM.

What is it, my good lord, the king languishes of?

LAFEU.

A fistula, my lord.

BERTRAM.

I heard not of it before.

LAFEU.

I would it were not notorious. Was this gentlewoman the daughter of Gerard de Narbon?

COUNTESS.

His sole child, my lord, and bequeathed to my overlooking. I have those hopes of her good that her education promises; her dispositions she inherits, which makes fair gifts fairer; for where an unclean mind carries virtuous qualities, there commendations go with pity,—they are virtues and traitors too: in her they are the better for their simpleness; she derives her honesty, and achieves her goodness.

LAFEU.

Your commendations, madam, get from her tears.

COUNTESS.

'Tis the best brine a maiden can season her praise in. The remembrance of her father never approaches her heart but the tyranny of her sorrows takes all livelihood from her cheek. No more of this, Helena,—go to, no more, lest it be rather thought you affect a sorrow than to have.

HELENA.

I do affect a sorrow indeed; but I have it too.

LAFEU.

Moderate lamentation is the right of the dead; excessive grief the enemy to the living.

COUNTESS.

If the living be enemy to the grief, the excess makes it soon mortal.

BERTRAM.

Madam, I desire your holy wishes.

LAFEU.

How understand we that?

COUNTESS.

Be thou blest, Bertram, and succeed thy father

In manners, as in shape! thy blood and virtue

Contend for empire in thee, and thy goodness

Share with thy birthright! Love all, trust a few,

Do wrong to none: be able for thine enemy

Rather in power than use; and keep thy friend

Under thy own life's key: be check'd for silence,

But never tax'd for speech. What heaven more will,

That thee may furnish and my prayers pluck down,

Fall on thy head! Farewell.—My lord,

'Tis an unseason'd courtier; good my lord,

Advise him.

LAFEU.

    He cannot want the best

That shall attend his love.

COUNTESS.

Heaven bless him!—Farewell, Bertram.

    [*Exit* COUNTESS.]

BERTRAM. [*To* HELENA.]

The best wishes that can be forg'd in your thoughts be servants to you! Be comfortable to my mother, your mistress, and make much of her.

LAFEU.

Farewell, pretty lady: you must hold the credit of your father.

    [*Exeunt* BERTRAM *and* LAFEU.]

HELENA.

O, were that all!—I think not on my father;

And these great tears grace his remembrance more

Than those I shed for him. What was he like?

I have forgot him; my imagination

Carries no favour in't but Bertram's.

I am undone: there is no living, none,
If Bertram be away. It were all one
That I should love a bright particular star,
And think to wed it, he is so above me:
In his bright radiance and collateral light
Must I be comforted, not in his sphere.
The ambition in my love thus plagues
  itself:
The hind that would be mated by the lion
Must die for love. 'Twas pretty, though a
  plague,
To see him every hour; to sit and draw
His arched brows, his hawking eye, his
  curls,
In our heart's table,—heart too capable
Of every line and trick of his sweet favour:
But now he's gone, and my idolatrous
  fancy
Must sanctify his relics. Who comes here?
One that goes with him: I love him for
  his sake;
And yet I know him a notorious liar,
Think him a great way fool, solely a
  coward;
Yet these fix'd evils sit so fit in him
That they take place when virtue's steely
  bones
Looks bleak i' the cold wind: withal, full
  oft we see
Cold wisdom waiting on superfluous folly.
        [*Enter* PAROLLES.]

PAROLLES.
Save you, fair queen!

HELENA.
And you, monarch!

PAROLLES.
No.

HELENA.
And no.

PAROLLES.
Are you meditating on virginity?

HELENA.
Ay. You have some stain of soldier in you:
let me ask you a question. Man is enemy to
virginity; how may we barricado it against
him?

PAROLLES.
Keep him out.

HELENA.
But he assails; and our virginity, though
valiant in the defence, yet is weak: unfold
to us some warlike resistance.

PAROLLES.
There is none: man, setting down before
you, will undermine you and blow you up.

HELENA.
Bless our poor virginity from underminers
and blowers-up!—Is there no military
policy how virgins might blow up men?

PAROLLES.
Virginity being blown down, man will
quicklier be blown up: marry, in blowing
him down again, with the breach yourselves
made, you lose your city. It is not politic in
the commonwealth of nature to preserve
virginity. Loss of virginity is rational
increase; and there was never virgin got till
virginity was first lost. That you were made
of is metal to make virgins. Virginity by
being once lost may be ten times found; by
being ever kept, it is ever lost: 'tis too cold a
companion; away with it!

HELENA.
I will stand for 't a little, though therefore
I die a virgin.

PAROLLES.
There's little can be said in't; 'tis against
the rule of nature. To speak on the part of
virginity is to accuse your mothers; which is
most infallible disobedience. He that hangs
himself is a virgin: virginity murders itself;
and should be buried in highways, out of
all sanctified limit, as a desperate offendress
against nature. Virginity breeds mites,
much like a cheese; consumes itself to the
very paring, and so dies with feeding his
own stomach. Besides, virginity is peevish,
proud, idle, made of self-love, which is the
most inhibited sin in the canon. Keep it not;
you cannot choose but lose by't: out with't!
within ten years it will make itself ten,
which is a goodly increase; and the principal
itself not much the worse: away with it!

HELENA.
How might one do, sir, to lose it to her own
liking?

PAROLLES.

Let me see: marry, ill to like him that ne'er
it likes. 'Tis a commodity will lose the
gloss with lying; the longer kept, the less
worth: off with't while 'tis vendible; answer
the time of request. Virginity, like an old
courtier, wears her cap out of fashion; richly
suited, but unsuitable: just like the brooch
and the toothpick, which wear not now.
Your date is better in your pie and your
porridge than in your cheek. And your
virginity, your old virginity, is like one of
our French withered pears; it looks ill, it
eats drily; marry, 'tis a wither'd pear; it was
formerly better; marry, yet 'tis a wither'd
pear. Will you anything with it?

HELENA.

Not my virginity yet . . .
There shall your master have a thousand
    loves,
A mother, and a mistress, and a friend,
A phoenix, captain, and an enemy,
A guide, a goddess, and a sovereign,
A counsellor, a traitress, and a dear:
His humble ambition, proud humility,
His jarring concord, and his discord
    dulcet,
His faith, his sweet disaster; with a world
Of pretty, fond, adoptious christendoms,
That blinking Cupid gossips. Now shall
    he—
I know not what he shall:—God send him
    well!—
The court's a learning-place;—and he is
    one,—

PAROLLES.

What one, i' faith?

HELENA.

That I wish well.—'Tis pity—

PAROLLES.

What's pity?

HELENA.

That wishing well had not a body in't
Which might be felt; that we, the poorer
    born,
Whose baser stars do shut us up in wishes,
Might with effects of them follow our
    friends

And show what we alone must think;
    which never
Returns us thanks.

        [*Enter a* PAGE.]

PAGE.

Monsieur Parolles, my lord calls for you.

        [*Exit* PAGE.]

PAROLLES.

Little Helen, farewell: if I can remember
thee, I will think of thee at court.

HELENA.

Monsieur Parolles, you were born under a
charitable star.

PAROLLES.

Under Mars, I.

HELENA.

I especially think, under Mars.

PAROLLES.

Why under Mars?

HELENA.

The wars hath so kept you under that you
must needs be born under Mars.

PAROLLES.

When he was predominant.

HELENA.

When he was retrograde, I think, rather.

PAROLLES.

Why think you so?

HELENA.

You go so much backward when you fight.

PAROLLES.

That's for advantage.

HELENA.

So is running away, when fear proposes
the safety: but the composition that your
valour and fear makes in you is a virtue of a
good wing, and I like the wear well.

PAROLLES.

I am so full of business I cannot answer
thee acutely. I will return perfect courtier;
in the which my instruction shall serve to
naturalize thee, so thou wilt be capable of
a courtier's counsel, and understand what
advice shall thrust upon thee; else thou
diest in thine unthankfulness, and thine
ignorance makes thee away: farewell.
When thou hast leisure, say thy prayers;
when thou hast none, remember thy

friends: get thee a good husband, and use
him as he uses thee: so, farewell.

        [Exit.]

HELENA.

Our remedies oft in ourselves do lie,
Which we ascribe to heaven: the fated sky
Gives us free scope; only doth backward
    pull
Our slow designs when we ourselves are
    dull.
What power is it which mounts my love
    so high,—
That makes me see, and cannot feed mine
    eye?
The mightiest space in fortune nature
    brings
To join like likes, and kiss like native
    things.
Impossible be strange attempts to those
That weigh their pains in sense, and do
    suppose
What hath been cannot be: who ever
    strove
To show her merit that did miss her love?
The king's disease,—my project may
    deceive me,
But my intents are fix'd, and will not leave
    me.

        [Exit.]

SCENE II

Paris. A room in the king's palace.
[Flourish of cornets. Enter the KING OF
FRANCE, *with letters;* LORDS *and* OTHERS
attending.]

KING.

The Florentines and Senoys are by the ears;
Have fought with equal fortune, and
    continue
A braving war.

FIRST LORD.

So 'tis reported, sir.

KING.

Nay, 'tis most credible; we here receive it,
A certainty, vouch'd from our cousin
    Austria,
With caution, that the Florentine will
    move us

For speedy aid; wherein our dearest friend
Prejudicates the business, and would seem
To have us make denial.

FIRST LORD.

           His love and wisdom,
Approv'd so to your majesty, may plead
For amplest credence.

KING.

           He hath arm'd our answer,
And Florence is denied before he comes:
Yet, for our gentlemen that mean to see
The Tuscan service, freely have they leave
To stand on either part.

SECOND LORD.

           It well may serve
A nursery to our gentry, who are sick
For breathing and exploit.

KING.

           What's he comes here?
[Enter BERTRAM, LAFEU, *and* PAROLLES.]

FIRST LORD.

It is the Count Rousillon, my good lord,
Young Bertram.

KING.

           Youth, thou bear'st thy father's face;
Frank nature, rather curious than in haste,
Hath well compos'd thee. Thy father's
    moral parts
Mayst thou inherit too! Welcome to Paris.

BERTRAM.

My thanks and duty are your majesty's.

KING.

I would I had that corporal soundness
    now,
As when thy father and myself in
    friendship
First tried our soldiership! He did look far
Into the service of the time, and was
Discipled of the bravest: he lasted long;
But on us both did haggish age steal on,
And wore us out of act. It much repairs me
To talk of your good father. In his youth
He had the wit which I can well observe
To-day in our young lords; but they may
    jest
Till their own scorn return to them
    unnoted,
Ere they can hide their levity in honour

So like a courtier: contempt nor bitterness
Were in his pride or sharpness; if they were,
His equal had awak'd them; and his honour,
Clock to itself, knew the true minute when
Exception bid him speak, and at this time
His tongue obey'd his hand: who were
     below him
He us'd as creatures of another place;
And bow'd his eminent top to their low
     ranks,
Making them proud of his humility,
In their poor praise he humbled. Such a
     man
Might be a copy to these younger times;
Which, follow'd well, would demonstrate
     them now
But goers backward.

BERTRAM.
                 His good remembrance, sir,
Lies richer in your thoughts than on his
     tomb;
So in approof lives not his epitaph
As in your royal speech.

KING.
Would I were with him! He would always
     say,—
Methinks I hear him now; his plausive
     words
He scatter'd not in ears, but grafted them
To grow there, and to bear,—"Let me not
     live,"—
This his good melancholy oft began,
On the catastrophe and heel of pastime,
When it was out,—"Let me not live"
     quoth he,
"After my flame lacks oil, to be the snuff
Of younger spirits, whose apprehensive
     senses
All but new things disdain; whose
     judgments are
Mere fathers of their garments; whose
     constancies
Expire before their fashions":—This he
     wish'd:
I, after him, do after him wish too,
Since I nor wax nor honey can bring home,
I quickly were dissolved from my hive,
To give some labourers room.

SECOND LORD.
                     You're lov'd, sir;
They that least lend it you shall lack you
     first.

KING.
I fill a place, I know't.—How long is't,
     count,
Since the physician at your father's died?
He was much fam'd.

BERTRAM.
              Some six months since, my lord.

KING.
If he were living, I would try him yet;—
Lend me an arm;—the rest have worn
     me out
With several applications:—nature and
     sickness
Debate it at their leisure. Welcome,
     count;
My son's no dearer.

BERTRAM.
                 Thank your majesty.
         [*Exeunt. Flourish.*]

SCENE III
Rousillon. A room in the palace.
[*Enter* COUNTESS, STEWARD, *and*
CLOWN.]

COUNTESS.
I will now hear: what say you of this
gentlewoman?

STEWARD.
Madam, the care I have had to even your
content, I wish might be found in the
calendar of my past endeavours; for then
we wound our modesty, and make foul
the clearness of our deservings, when of
ourselves we publish them.

COUNTESS.
What does this knave here? Get you gone,
sirrah: the complaints I have heard of you
I do not all believe; 'tis my slowness that
I do not; for I know you lack not folly to
commit them, and have ability enough to
make such knaveries yours.

CLOWN.
'Tis not unknown to you, madam, I am a
poor fellow.

COUNTESS.
Well, sir.

CLOWN.
No, madam, 'tis not so well that I am poor, though many of the rich are damned: but if I may have your ladyship's good will to go to the world, Isbel the woman and I will do as we may.

COUNTESS.
Wilt thou needs be a beggar?

CLOWN.
I do beg your good will in this case.

COUNTESS.
In what case?

CLOWN.
In Isbel's case and mine own. Service is no heritage: and I think I shall never have the blessing of God till I have issue of my body; for they say barns are blessings.

COUNTESS.
Tell me thy reason why thou wilt marry.

CLOWN.
My poor body, madam, requires it: I am driven on by the flesh; and he must needs go that the devil drives.

COUNTESS.
Is this all your worship's reason?

CLOWN.
Faith, madam, I have other holy reasons, such as they are.

COUNTESS.
May the world know them?

CLOWN.
I have been, madam, a wicked creature, as you and all flesh and blood are; and, indeed, I do marry that I may repent.

COUNTESS.
Thy marriage, sooner than thy wickedness.

CLOWN.
I am out of friends, madam, and I hope to have friends for my wife's sake.

COUNTESS.
Such friends are thine enemies, knave.

CLOWN.
Y'are shallow, madam, in great friends: for the knaves come to do that for me which I am a-weary of. He that ears my land spares my team, and gives me leave to in the crop:

if I be his cuckold, he's my drudge: he that comforts my wife is the cherisher of my flesh and blood; he that cherishes my flesh and blood loves my flesh and blood; he that loves my flesh and blood is my friend; ergo, he that kisses my wife is my friend. If men could be contented to be what they are, there were no fear in marriage; for young Charbon the puritan and old Poysam the papist, howsome'er their hearts are severed in religion, their heads are both one; they may jowl horns together like any deer i' the herd.

COUNTESS.
Wilt thou ever be a foul-mouth'd and calumnious knave?

CLOWN.
A prophet I, madam; and I speak the truth the next way:
    For I the ballad will repeat,
        Which men full true shall find;
    Your marriage comes by destiny,
        Your cuckoo sings by kind.

COUNTESS.
Get you gone, sir; I'll talk with you more anon.

STEWARD.
May it please you, madam, that he bid Helen come to you; of her I am to speak.

COUNTESS.
Sirrah, tell my gentlewoman I would speak with her; Helen I mean.

CLOWN. [*Sings.*]
    Was this fair face the cause, quoth she
        Why the Grecians sacked Troy?
    Fond done, done fond,
        Was this King Priam's joy?
    With that she sighed as she stood,
    With that she sighed as she stood,
        And gave this sentence then:—
    Among nine bad if one be good,
    Among nine bad if one be good,
        There's yet one good in ten.

COUNTESS.
What, one good in ten? you corrupt the song, sirrah.

CLOWN.
One good woman in ten, madam, which is

a purifying o' the song: would God would
serve the world so all the year! we'd find no
fault with the tithe-woman, if I were the
parson: one in ten, quoth a'! an we might
have a good woman born before every
blazing star, or at an earthquake, 'twould
mend the lottery well: a man may draw his
heart out ere he pluck one.

COUNTESS.
You'll be gone, sir knave, and do as I
command you!

CLOWN.
That man should be at woman's command,
and yet no hurt done!—Though honesty
be no puritan, yet it will do no hurt; it will
wear the surplice of humility over the black
gown of a big heart.—I am going, forsooth:
the business is for Helen to come hither.

[*Exit.*]

COUNTESS.
Well, now.

STEWARD.
I know, madam, you love your gentlewoman
entirely.

COUNTESS.
Faith I do: her father bequeathed her to me;
and she herself, without other advantage,
may lawfully make title to as much love as
she finds: there is more owing her than is
paid; and more shall be paid her than she'll
demand.

STEWARD.
Madam, I was very late more near her than
I think she wished me: alone she was, and
did communicate to herself her own words
to her own ears; she thought, I dare vow
for her, they touched not any stranger
sense. Her matter was, she loved your son:
Fortune, she said, was no goddess, that
had put such difference betwixt their two
estates; Love no god, that would not extend
his might only where qualities were level;
Diana no queen of virgins, that would suffer
her poor knight surprise, without rescue in
the first assault, or ransom afterward. This
she delivered in the most bitter touch of
sorrow that e'er I heard virgin exclaim in;
which I held my duty speedily to acquaint

you withal; sithence, in the loss that may
happen, it concerns you something to know
it.

COUNTESS.
You have discharged this honestly; keep
it to yourself; many likelihoods informed
me of this before, which hung so tottering
in the balance that I could neither believe
nor misdoubt. Pray you leave me: stall this
in your bosom; and I thank you for your
honest care: I will speak with you further
anon.

[*Exit* STEWARD.]

Even so it was with me when I was young:
If ever we are nature's, these are ours; this
   thorn
Doth to our rose of youth rightly belong;
Our blood to us, this to our blood is born;
It is the show and seal of nature's truth,
Where love's strong passion is impress'd
   in youth:
By our remembrances of days foregone,
Such were our faults:—or then we thought
   them none.

[*Enter* HELENA.]

Her eye is sick on't;—I observe her now.

HELENA.
What is your pleasure, madam?

COUNTESS.
               You know, Helen,
I am a mother to you.

HELENA.
Mine honourable mistress.

COUNTESS.
               Nay, a mother.
Why not a mother? When I said a mother,
Methought you saw a serpent: what's in
   mother,
That you start at it? I say I am your
   mother;
And put you in the catalogue of those
That were enwombed mine. 'Tis often seen
Adoption strives with nature; and choice
   breeds
A native slip to us from foreign seeds:
You ne'er oppress'd me with a mother's
   groan,
Yet I express to you a mother's care:—

God's mercy, maiden! does it curd thy
    blood
To say I am thy mother? What's the
    matter,
That this distemper'd messenger of wet,
The many-colour'd iris, rounds thine eye?
Why,—that you are my daughter?
Helena.
                    That I am not.
Countess.
I say, I am your mother.
Helena.
               Pardon, madam;
The Count Rousillon cannot be my
    brother:
I am from humble, he from honour'd
    name;
No note upon my parents, his all noble;
My master, my dear lord he is; and I
His servant live, and will his vassal die:
He must not be my brother.
Countess.
             Nor I your mother?
Helena.
You are my mother, madam; would you
    were,—
So that my lord your son were not my
    brother,—
Indeed my mother!—or were you both our
    mothers,
I care no more for than I do for heaven,
So I were not his sister. Can't no other,
But, I your daughter, he must be my
    brother?
Countess.
Yes, Helen, you might be my daughter-
    in-law:
God shield you mean it not! daughter and
    mother
So strive upon your pulse. What! pale
    again?
My fear hath catch'd your fondness: now
    I see
The mystery of your loneliness, and find
Your salt tears' head. Now to all sense 'tis
    gross
You love my son; invention is asham'd,
Against the proclamation of thy passion,

To say thou dost not: therefore tell me
    true;
But tell me then, 'tis so;—for, look, thy
    cheeks
Confess it, one to the other; and thine eyes
See it so grossly shown in thy behaviours,
That in their kind they speak it; only sin
And hellish obstinacy tie thy tongue,
That truth should be suspected. Speak,
    is't so?
If it be so, you have wound a goodly clue;
If it be not, forswear't: howe'er, I charge
    thee,
As heaven shall work in me for thine avail,
To tell me truly.
Helena.
             Good madam, pardon me!
Countess.
Do you love my son?
Helena.
          Your pardon, noble mistress!
Countess.
Love you my son?
Helena.
         Do not you love him, madam?
Countess.
Go not about; my love hath in't a bond
Whereof the world takes note: come,
    come, disclose
The state of your affection; for your
    passions
Have to the full appeach'd.
Helena.
                Then I confess,
Here on my knee, before high heaven and
    you,
That before you, and next unto high
    heaven,
I love your son:—
My friends were poor, but honest; so's my
    love:
Be not offended; for it hurts not him
That he is lov'd of me: I follow him not
By any token of presumptuous suit;
Nor would I have him till I do deserve
    him;
Yet never know how that desert should be.
I know I love in vain, strive against hope;

Yet in this captious and intenible sieve
I still pour in the waters of my love,
And lack not to lose still: thus, Indian-like,
Religious in mine error, I adore
The sun, that looks upon his worshipper,
But knows of him no more. My dearest
    madam,
Let not your hate encounter with my love,
For loving where you do; but if yourself,
Whose aged honour cites a virtuous youth,
Did ever, in so true a flame of liking,
Wish chastely, and love dearly, that your
    Dian
Was both herself and love; O, then, give
    pity
To her whose state is such that cannot
    choose
But lend and give where she is sure to lose;
That seeks not to find that her search
    implies,
But, riddle-like, lives sweetly where she
    dies!

COUNTESS.
Had you not lately an intent,—speak
    truly,—
To go to Paris?

HELENA.
                    Madam, I had.

COUNTESS.
                              Wherefore?
Tell true.

HELENA.
I will tell truth; by grace itself I swear.
You know my father left me some
    prescriptions
Of rare and prov'd effects, such as his
    reading
And manifest experience had collected
For general sovereignty; and that he will'd
    me
In heedfullest reservation to bestow them,
As notes whose faculties inclusive were
More than they were in note: amongst
    the rest
There is a remedy, approv'd, set down,
To cure the desperate languishings
    whereof
The king is render'd lost.

COUNTESS.
                              This was your motive
For Paris, was it? speak.

HELENA.
My lord your son made me to think of this;
Else Paris, and the medicine, and the king,
Had from the conversation of my thoughts
Haply been absent then.

COUNTESS.
                              But think you, Helen,
If you should tender your supposed aid,
He would receive it? He and his physicians
Are of a mind; he, that they cannot help
    him;
They, that they cannot help: how shall they
    credit
A poor unlearned virgin, when the schools,
Embowell'd of their doctrine, have let off
The danger to itself?

HELENA.
                              There's something hints
More than my father's skill, which was the
    greatest
Of his profession, that his good receipt
Shall, for my legacy, be sanctified
By th' luckiest stars in heaven: and, would
    your honour
But give me leave to try success, I'd
    venture
The well-lost life of mine on his grace's
    cure
By such a day and hour.

COUNTESS.
                              Dost thou believe't?

HELENA.
Ay, madam, knowingly.

COUNTESS.
Why, Helen, thou shalt have my leave,
    and love,
Means, and attendants, and my loving
    greetings
To those of mine in court: I'll stay at
    home,
And pray God's blessing into thy attempt:
Be gone to-morrow; and be sure of this,
What I can help thee to thou shalt not
    miss.
                              [*Exeunt.*]

ACT II
SCENE I

Paris. A room in the king's palace.
[*Flourish. Enter the* KING, *with young*
LORDS *taking leave for the Florentine war;*
BERTRAM, PAROLLES, *and* ATTENDANTS.]
KING.
Farewell, young lord; these war-like
　principles
Do not throw from you:—and you, my
　lord, farewell;—
Share the advice betwixt you; if both gain
　all,
The gift doth stretch itself as 'tis received,
And is enough for both.
FIRST LORD.
　　　　　　It is our hope, sir,
After well-enter'd soldiers, to return
And find your grace in health.
KING.
No, no, it cannot be; and yet my heart
Will not confess he owes the malady
That doth my life besiege. Farewell, young
　lords;
Whether I live or die, be you the sons
Of worthy Frenchmen; let higher Italy,—
Those bated that inherit but the fall
Of the last monarchy,—see that you come
Not to woo honour, but to wed it; when
The bravest questant shrinks, find what
　you seek,
That fame may cry you aloud: I say
　farewell.
SECOND LORD.
Health, at your bidding, serve your majesty!
KING.
Those girls of Italy, take heed of them;
They say our French lack language to deny,
If they demand: beware of being captives
Before you serve.
BOTH.
　　　　　　Our hearts receive your warnings.
KING.
Farewell.—Come hither to me.
　　　　[*The* KING *retires to a couch.*]
FIRST LORD.
O my sweet lord, that you will stay behind
　us!

PAROLLES.
'Tis not his fault; the spark—
SECOND LORD.
　　　　　　　　O, 'tis brave wars!
PAROLLES.
Most admirable: I have seen those wars.
BERTRAM.
I am commanded here and kept a coil with,
"Too young" and "the next year" and "'tis
　too early."
PAROLLES.
An thy mind stand to it, boy, steal away
　bravely.
BERTRAM.
I shall stay here the forehorse to a smock,
Creaking my shoes on the plain masonry,
Till honour be bought up, and no sword
　worn
But one to dance with! By heaven, I'll steal
　away.
FIRST LORD.
There's honour in the theft.
PAROLLES.
　　　　　　　　Commit it, count.
SECOND LORD.
I am your accessary; and so farewell.
BERTRAM.
I grow to you, and our parting is a tortured
　body.
FIRST LORD.
Farewell, captain.
SECOND LORD.
Sweet Monsieur Parolles!
PAROLLES.
Noble heroes, my sword and yours are kin.
Good sparks and lustrous, a word, good
metals.—You shall find in the regiment
of the Spinii one Captain Spurio, with
his cicatrice, an emblem of war, here on
his sinister cheek; it was this very sword
entrenched it: say to him I live; and observe
his reports for me.
FIRST LORD.
We shall, noble captain.
PAROLLES.
Mars dote on you for his novices!
　　　　　[*Exeunt* LORDS.]
What will ye do?

BERTRAM.
Stay; the king—
PAROLLES.
Use a more spacious ceremony to the noble lords; you have restrained yourself within the list of too cold an adieu: be more expressive to them; for they wear themselves in the cap of the time; there do muster true gait; eat, speak, and move, under the influence of the most received star; and though the devil lead the measure, such are to be followed: after them, and take a more dilated farewell.
BERTRAM.
And I will do so.
PAROLLES.
Worthy fellows; and like to prove most sinewy sword-men.
    [*Exeunt* BERTRAM *and* PAROLLES.]
        [*Enter* LAFEU.]
LAFEU. [*Kneeling.*]
Pardon, my lord, for me and for my tidings.
KING.
I'll fee thee to stand up.
LAFEU.
Then here's a man stands that has bought his pardon.
I would you had kneel'd, my lord, to ask me mercy;
And that at my bidding you could so stand up.
KING.
I would I had; so I had broke thy pate,
And ask'd thee mercy for't.
LAFEU.
Good faith, across; but, my good lord, 'tis thus:
Will you be cured of your infirmity?
KING.
No.
LAFEU.
O, will you eat no grapes, my royal fox?
Yes, but you will my noble grapes, and if
My royal fox could reach them: I have seen a medicine
That's able to breathe life into a stone,
Quicken a rock, and make you dance canary

With spritely fire and motion; whose simple touch
Is powerful to araise King Pipin, nay,
To give great Charlemain a pen in his hand
And write to her a love-line.
KING.
              What "her" is that?
LAFEU.
Why, doctor "she": my lord, there's one arriv'd,
If you will see her,—now, by my faith and honour,
If seriously I may convey my thoughts
In this my light deliverance, I have spoke
With one that in her sex, her years, profession,
Wisdom, and constancy, hath amaz'd me more
Than I dare blame my weakness: will you see her,—
For that is her demand,—and know her business?
That done, laugh well at me.
KING.
              Now, good Lafeu,
Bring in the admiration; that we with thee
May spend our wonder too, or take off thine
By wondering how thou took'st it.
LAFEU.
              Nay, I'll fit you,
And not be all day neither.
        [*Exit* LAFEU.]
KING.
Thus he his special nothing ever prologues.
    [*Re-enter* LAFEU *with* HELENA.]
LAFEU.
Nay, come your ways.
KING.
         This haste hath wings indeed.
LAFEU.
Nay, come your ways;
This is his majesty: say your mind to him.
A traitor you do look like; but such traitors
His majesty seldom fears: I am Cressid's uncle,
That dare leave two together: fare you well.
        [*Exit.*]

King.
Now, fair one, does your business follow us?
Helena.
Ay, my good lord.
Gerard de Narbon was my father;
In what he did profess, well found.
King.
                                            I knew him.
Helena.
The rather will I spare my praises towards
    him.
Knowing him is enough. On his bed of
    death
Many receipts he gave me; chiefly one,
Which, as the dearest issue of his practice,
And of his old experience the only darling,
He bade me store up as a triple eye,
Safer than mine own two, more dear: I
    have so:
And, hearing your high majesty is touch'd
With that malignant cause wherein the
    honour
Of my dear father's gift stands chief in
    power,
I come to tender it, and my appliance,
With all bound humbleness.
King.
                          We thank you, maiden:
But may not be so credulous of cure,—
When our most learned doctors leave us,
    and
The congregated college have concluded
That labouring art can never ransom
    nature
From her inaidable estate,—I say we must
    not
So stain our judgment, or corrupt our hope,
To prostitute our past-cure malady
To empirics; or to dissever so
Our great self and our credit, to esteem
A senseless help, when help past sense we
    deem.
Helena.
My duty, then, shall pay me for my pains:
I will no more enforce mine office on you;
Humbly entreating from your royal
    thoughts
A modest one to bear me back again.

King.
I cannot give thee less, to be call'd grateful.
Thou thought'st to help me; and such
    thanks I give
As one near death to those that wish him
    live:
But what at full I know, thou know'st no
    part;
I knowing all my peril, thou no art.
Helena.
What I can do can do no hurt to try,
Since you set up your rest 'gainst remedy.
He that of greatest works is finisher
Oft does them by the weakest minister:
So holy writ in babes hath judgment
    shown,
When judges have been babes. Great
    floods have flown
From simple sources; and great seas have
    dried
When miracles have by the greatest been
    denied.
Oft expectation fails, and most oft there
Where most it promises; and oft it hits
Where hope is coldest, and despair most
    fits.
King.
I must not hear thee: fare thee well, kind
    maid;
Thy pains, not used, must by thyself be
    paid:
Proffers, not took, reap thanks for their
    reward.
Helena.
Inspired merit so by breath is barred:
It is not so with Him that all things knows,
As 'tis with us that square our guess by
    shows:
But most it is presumption in us when
The help of heaven we count the act of
    men.
Dear sir, to my endeavours give consent:
Of heaven, not me, make an experiment.
I am not an impostor, that proclaim
Myself against the level of mine aim;
But know I think, and think I know most
    sure,
My art is not past power nor you past cure.

KING.
Art thou so confident? Within what space
Hop'st thou my cure?
HELENA.
           The greatest grace lending grace.
Ere twice the horses of the sun shall bring
Their fiery torcher his diurnal ring;
Ere twice in murk and occidental damp
Moist Hesperus hath quench'd his sleepy
     lamp;
Or four-and-twenty times the pilot's glass
Hath told the thievish minutes how they
     pass;
What is infirm from your sound parts
     shall fly,
Health shall live free, and sickness freely
     die.
KING.
Upon thy certainty and confidence
What dar'st thou venture?
HELENA.
           Tax of impudence,—
A strumpet's boldness, a divulged shame,—
Traduc'd by odious ballads; my maiden's
     name
Sear'd otherwise; nay worse of worst
     extended,
With vilest torture let my life be ended.
KING.
Methinks in thee some blessed spirit doth
     speak;
His powerful sound within an organ weak:
And what impossibility would slay
In common sense, sense saves another way.
Thy life is dear; for all that life can rate
Worth name of life in thee hath estimate:
Youth, beauty, wisdom, courage, all
That happiness and prime can happy call;
Thou this to hazard needs must intimate
Skill infinite or monstrous desperate.
Sweet practiser, thy physic I will try:
That ministers thine own death if I die.
HELENA.
If I break time, or flinch in property
Of what I spoke, unpitied let me die;
And well deserv'd. Not helping, death's
     my fee;
But, if I help, what do you promise me?

KING.
Make thy demand.
HELENA.
           But will you make it even?
KING.
Ay, by my sceptre and my hopes of heaven.
HELENA.
Then shalt thou give me, with thy kingly
     hand
What husband in thy power I will
     command:
Exempted be from me the arrogance
To choose from forth the royal blood of
     France,
My low and humble name to propagate
With any branch or image of thy state:
But such a one, thy vassal, whom I know
Is free for me to ask, thee to bestow.
KING.
Here is my hand; the premises observ'd,
Thy will by my performance shall be
     serv'd;
So make the choice of thy own time, for I,
Thy resolv'd patient, on thee still rely.
More should I question thee, and more I
     must,—
Though more to know could not be more
     to trust,—
From whence thou cam'st, how tended on:
     but rest
Unquestion'd welcome and undoubted
     blest.—
Give me some help here, ho!—If thou
     proceed
As high as word, my deed shall match thy
     deed.
          [*Flourish. Exeunt.*]

SCENE II

Rousillon. A room in the countess's palace.
     [*Enter* COUNTESS *and* CLOWN.]
COUNTESS.
Come on, sir; I shall now put you to the
height of your breeding.
CLOWN.
I will show myself highly fed and lowly
taught: I know my business is but to the
court.

COUNTESS.
To the court! why, what place make you special, when you put off that with such contempt? But to the court!

CLOWN.
Truly, madam, if God have lent a man any manners, he may easily put it off at court: he that cannot make a leg, put off's cap, kiss his hand, and say nothing, has neither leg, hands, lip, nor cap; and indeed such a fellow, to say precisely, were not for the court; but for me, I have an answer will serve all men.

COUNTESS.
Marry, that's a bountiful answer that fits all questions.

CLOWN.
It is like a barber's chair, that fits all buttocks—the pin-buttock, the quatch-buttock, the brawn-buttock, or any buttock.

COUNTESS.
Will your answer serve fit to all questions?

CLOWN.
As fit as ten groats is for the hand of an attorney, as your French crown for your taffety punk, as Tib's rush for Tom's forefinger, as a pancake for Shrove-Tuesday, a morris for Mayday, as the nail to his hole, the cuckold to his horn, as a scolding quean to a wrangling knave, as the nun's lip to the friar's mouth; nay, as the pudding to his skin.

COUNTESS.
Have you, I, say, an answer of such fitness for all questions?

CLOWN.
From below your duke to beneath your constable, it will fit any question.

COUNTESS.
It must be an answer of most monstrous size that must fit all demands.

CLOWN.
But a trifle neither, in good faith, if the learned should speak truth of it: here it is, and all that belongs to't. Ask me if I am a courtier: it shall do you no harm to learn.

COUNTESS.
To be young again, if we could: I will be a fool in question, hoping to be the wiser by your answer. I pray you, sir, are you a courtier?

CLOWN.
O Lord, sir!—There's a simple putting off. More, more, a hundred of them.

COUNTESS.
Sir, I am a poor friend of yours, that loves you.

CLOWN.
O Lord, sir!—Thick, thick; spare not me.

COUNTESS.
I think, sir, you can eat none of this
    homely meat.

CLOWN.
O Lord, sir!—Nay, put me to't, I warrant you.

COUNTESS.
You were lately whipped, sir, as I think.

CLOWN.
O Lord, sir!—Spare not me.

COUNTESS.
Do you cry "O Lord, sir!" at your whipping, and "spare not me"? Indeed your "O Lord, sir!" is very sequent to your whipping. You would answer very well to a whipping, if you were but bound to't.

CLOWN.
I ne'er had worse luck in my life in my—"O Lord, sir!" I see thing's may serve long, but not serve ever.

COUNTESS.
I play the noble housewife with the time, to entertain it so merrily with a fool.

CLOWN.
O Lord, sir!—Why, there't serves well again.

COUNTESS.
An end, sir! To your business. Give Helen this,
And urge her to a present answer back:
Commend me to my kinsmen and my son:
This is not much.

CLOWN.
Not much commendation to them.

COUNTESS.
Not much employment for you: you understand me?

CLOWN.
Most fruitfully: I am there before my legs.
COUNTESS.
Haste you again.
          [*Exeunt severally.*]

SCENE III
Paris. The king's palace.
[*Enter* BERTRAM, LAFEU, *and* PAROLLES.]
LAFEU.
They say miracles are past; and we have our philosophical persons to make modern and familiar things supernatural and causeless. Hence is it that we make trifles of terrors, ensconcing ourselves into seeming knowledge when we should submit ourselves to an unknown fear.
PAROLLES.
Why, 'tis the rarest argument of wonder that hath shot out in our latter times.
BERTRAM.
And so 'tis.
LAFEU.
To be relinquish'd of the artists,—
PAROLLES.
So I say; both of Galen and Paracelsus.
LAFEU.
Of all the learned and authentic fellows,—
PAROLLES.
Right; so I say.
LAFEU.
That gave him out incurable,—
PAROLLES.
Why, there 'tis; so say I too.
LAFEU.
Not to be helped,—
PAROLLES.
Right; as 'twere a man assured of a,—
LAFEU.
Uncertain life and sure death.
PAROLLES.
Just; you say well: so would I have said.
LAFEU.
I may truly say, it is a novelty to the world.
PAROLLES.
It is indeed: if you will have it in showing, you shall read it in,—What do you call there?—

LAFEU.
A showing of a heavenly effect in an earthly actor.
PAROLLES.
That's it; I would have said the very same.
LAFEU.
Why, your dolphin is not lustier: 'fore me, I speak in respect,—
PAROLLES.
Nay, 'tis strange, 'tis very strange; that is the brief and the tedious of it; and he's of a most facinerious spirit that will not acknowledge it to be the,—
LAFEU.
Very hand of heaven.
PAROLLES.
Ay; so I say.
LAFEU.
In a most weak,—
PAROLLES.
And debile minister, great power, great transcendence: which should, indeed, give us a further use to be made than alone the recov'ry of the king, as to be,—
LAFEU.
Generally thankful.
PAROLLES.
I would have said it; you say well. Here comes the king.
[*Enter* KING, HELENA, *and* ATTENDANTS.]
LAFEU.
Lustic, as the Dutchman says: I'll like a maid the better, whilst I have a tooth in my head: why, he's able to lead her a coranto.
PAROLLES.
Mort du vinaigre! Is not this Helen?
LAFEU.
'Fore God, I think so.
KING.
Go, call before me all the lords in court.—
          [*Exit an* ATTENDANT.]
Sit, my preserver, by thy patient's side;
And with this healthful hand, whose banish'd sense
Thou has repeal'd, a second time receive
The confirmation of my promis'd gift,
Which but attends thy naming.
          [*Enter several* LORDS.]

Fair maid, send forth thine eye: this
    youthful parcel
Of noble bachelors stand at my bestowing,
O'er whom both sovereign power and
    father's voice
I have to use: thy frank election make;
Thou hast power to choose, and they none
    to forsake.

HELENA.
To each of you one fair and virtuous
    mistress
Fall, when love please!—marry, to each,
    but one!

LAFEU.
I'd give bay Curtal and his furniture,
My mouth no more were broken than
    these boys',
And writ as little beard.

KING.
                          Peruse them well:
Not one of those but had a noble father.

HELENA.
Gentlemen,
Heaven hath through me restor'd the king
    to health.

ALL.
We understand it, and thank heaven for
    you.

HELENA.
I am a simple maid, and therein wealthiest
That I protest I simply am a maid.—
Please it, your majesty, I have done already:
The blushes in my cheeks thus whisper
    me—
"We blush that thou shouldst choose; but,
    be refus'd,
Let the white death sit on thy cheek for
    ever;
We'll ne'er come there again."

KING.
                          Make choice; and, see:
Who shuns thy love shuns all his love in
    me.

HELENA.
Now, Dian, from thy altar do I fly,
And to imperial Love, that god most high,
Do my sighs stream.—Sir, will you hear
    my suit?

FIRST LORD.
And grant it.

HELENA.
                          Thanks, sir; all the rest is mute.

LAFEU.
I had rather be in this choice than throw
ames-ace for my life.

HELENA.
The honour, sir, that flames in your fair
    eyes,
Before I speak, too threateningly replies:
Love make your fortunes twenty times
    above
Her that so wishes, and her humble love!

SECOND LORD.
No better, if you please.

HELENA.
                          My wish receive,
Which great Love grant; and so I take
    my leave.

LAFEU.
Do all they deny her? An they were sons
of mine I'd have them whipped; or I would
send them to the Turk to make eunuchs of.

HELENA. [*To* THIRD LORD.]
Be not afraid that I your hand should take;
I'll never do you wrong for your own sake:
Blessing upon your vows! and in your bed
Find fairer fortune, if you ever wed!

LAFEU.
These boys are boys of ice: they'll none have
her: sure, they are bastards to the English;
the French ne'er got 'em.

HELENA.
You are too young, too happy, and too
    good,
To make yourself a son out of my blood.

FOURTH LORD.
Fair one, I think not so.

LAFEU.
There's one grape yet,—I am sure thy father
drank wine.—But if thou beest not an ass, I
am a youth of fourteen; I have known thee
already.

HELENA. [*To* BERTRAM.]
I dare not say I take you; but I give
Me and my service, ever whilst I live,
Into your guiding power.—This is the man.

KING.
Why, then, young Bertram, take her; she's
    thy wife.
BERTRAM.
My wife, my liege! I shall beseech your
    highness,
In such a business give me leave to use
The help of mine own eyes.
KING.
                        Know'st thou not, Bertram,
What she has done for me?
BERTRAM.
                        Yes, my good lord;
But never hope to know why I should
    marry her.
KING.
Thou know'st she has rais'd me from my
    sickly bed.
BERTRAM.
But follows it, my lord, to bring me down
Must answer for your raising? I know her
    well;
She had her breeding at my father's charge:
A poor physician's daughter my wife!—
    Disdain
Rather corrupt me ever!
KING.
'Tis only title thou disdain'st in her, the
    which
I can build up. Strange is it that our bloods,
Of colour, weight, and heat, pour'd all
    together,
Would quite confound distinction, yet
    stand off
In differences so mighty. If she be
All that is virtuous,—save what thou
    dislik'st,
A poor physician's daughter,—thou
    dislik'st
Of virtue for the name: but do not so:
From lowest place when virtuous things
    proceed,
The place is dignified by the doer's deed:
Where great additions swell's, and virtue
    none,
It is a dropsied honour: good alone
Is good without a name; vileness is so:
The property by what it is should go,

Not by the title. She is young, wise, fair;
In these to nature she's immediate heir;
And these breed honour: that is honour's
    scorn
Which challenges itself as honour's born,
And is not like the sire: honours thrive
When rather from our acts we them derive
Than our fore-goers: the mere word's a
    slave,
Debauch'd on every tomb; on every grave
A lying trophy; and as oft is dumb
Where dust and damn'd oblivion is the
    tomb
Of honour'd bones indeed. What should
    be said?
If thou canst like this creature as a maid,
I can create the rest: virtue and she
Is her own dower; honour and wealth
    from me.
BERTRAM.
I cannot love her, nor will strive to do 't.
KING.
Thou wrong'st thyself, if thou shouldst
    strive to choose.
HELENA.
That you are well restor'd, my lord, I am
    glad:
Let the rest go.
KING.
My honour's at the stake; which to defeat,
I must produce my power. Here, take her
    hand,
Proud scornful boy, unworthy this good
    gift;
That dost in vile misprision shackle up
My love and her desert; that canst not
    dream
We, poising us in her defective scale,
Shall weigh thee to the beam; that wilt
    not know
It is in us to plant thine honour where
We please to have it grow. Check thy
    contempt:
Obey our will, which travails in thy good;
Believe not thy disdain, but presently
Do thine own fortunes that obedient right
Which both thy duty owes and our power
    claims

Or I will throw thee from my care for ever,
Into the staggers and the careless lapse
Of youth and ignorance; both my revenge
    and hate
Loosing upon thee in the name of justice,
Without all terms of pity. Speak! thine
    answer!

BERTRAM.
Pardon, my gracious lord; for I submit
My fancy to your eyes: when I consider
What great creation, and what dole of
    honour
Flies where you bid it, I find that she,
    which late
Was in my nobler thoughts most base, is
    now
The praised of the king; who, so ennobled,
Is as 'twere born so.

KING.
                            Take her by the hand,
And tell her she is thine: to whom I
    promise
A counterpoise; if not to thy estate,
A balance more replete.

BERTRAM.
                            I take her hand.

KING.
Good fortune and the favour of the king
Smile upon this contract; whose ceremony
Shall seem expedient on the now-born
    brief,
And be perform'd to-night: the solemn
    feast
Shall more attend upon the coming space,
Expecting absent friends. As thou lov'st
    her,
Thy love's to me religious; else, does err.
    [*Exeunt* KING, BERTRAM, HELENA,
        LORDS, *and* ATTENDANTS.]

LAFEU.
Do you hear, monsieur? a word with you.

PAROLLES.
Your pleasure, sir?

LAFEU.
Your lord and master did well to make his
recantation.

PAROLLES.
Recantation!—my lord! my master!

LAFEU.
Ay; is it not a language I speak?

PAROLLES.
A most harsh one, and not to be understood
without bloody succeeding. My master!

LAFEU.
Are you companion to the Count
        Rousillon?

PAROLLES.
To any count; to all counts; to what is
        man.

LAFEU.
To what is count's man: count's master is
of another style.

PAROLLES.
You are too old, sir; let it satisfy you, you
are too old.

LAFEU.
I must tell thee, sirrah, I write man; to
which title age cannot bring thee.

PAROLLES.
What I dare too well do, I dare not do.

LAFEU.
I did think thee, for two ordinaries, to
be a pretty wise fellow; thou didst make
tolerable vent of thy travel; it might pass:
yet the scarfs and the bannerets about thee
did manifoldly dissuade me from believing
thee a vessel of too great a burden. I have
now found thee; when I lose thee again I
care not: yet art thou good for nothing but
taking up; and that thou art scarce worth.

PAROLLES.
Hadst thou not the privilege of antiquity
upon thee,—

LAFEU.
Do not plunge thyself too far in anger,
lest thou hasten thy trial; which if—Lord
have mercy on thee for a hen! So, my
good window of lattice, fare thee well:
thy casement I need not open, for I look
through thee. Give me thy hand.

PAROLLES.
My lord, you give me most egregious
indignity.

LAFEU.
Ay, with all my heart; and thou art worthy
of it.

PAROLLES.
I have not, my lord, deserved it.
LAFEU.
Yes, good faith, every dram of it: and I will
not bate thee a scruple.
PAROLLES.
Well, I shall be wiser.
LAFEU.
E'en as soon as thou canst, for thou hast
to pull at a smack o' th' contrary. If ever
thou beest bound in thy scarf and beaten,
thou shalt find what it is to be proud of
thy bondage. I have a desire to hold my
acquaintance with thee, or rather my
knowledge, that I may say in the default, he
is a man I know.
PAROLLES.
My lord, you do me most insupportable
vexation.
LAFEU.
I would it were hell-pains for thy sake, and
my poor doing eternal: for doing I am past;
as I will by thee, in what motion age will
give me leave.
                    [*Exit.*]
PAROLLES.
Well, thou hast a son shall take this disgrace
off me; scurvy, old, filthy, scurvy lord!—
Well, I must be patient; there is no fettering
of authority. I'll beat him, by my life, if I can
meet him with any convenience, an he were
double and double a lord. I'll have no more
pity of his age than I would have of—I'll
beat him, an if I could but meet him again.
                [*Re-enter* LAFEU.]
LAFEU.
Sirrah, your lord and master's married;
there's news for you; you have a new
mistress.
PAROLLES.
I most unfeignedly beseech your lordship
to make some reservation of your wrongs:
he is my good lord: whom I serve above is
my master.
LAFEU.
Who? God?
PAROLLES.
Ay, sir.

LAFEU.
The devil it is that's thy master. Why dost
thou garter up thy arms o' this fashion? dost
make hose of thy sleeves? do other servants
so? Thou wert best set thy lower part where
thy nose stands. By mine honour, if I
were but two hours younger, I'd beat thee:
methink'st thou art a general offence, and
every man should beat thee. I think thou
wast created for men to breathe themselves
upon thee.
PAROLLES.
This is hard and undeserved measure, my
lord.
LAFEU.
Go to, sir; you were beaten in Italy for
picking a kernel out of a pomegranate; you
are a vagabond, and no true traveller: you
are more saucy with lords and honourable
personages than the heraldry of your birth
and virtue gives you commission. You are
not worth another word, else I'd call you
knave. I leave you.
                    [*Exit.*]
PAROLLES.
Good, very good, it is so then.—Good, very
good; let it be concealed awhile.
                [*Enter* BERTRAM.]
BERTRAM.
Undone, and forfeited to cares for ever!
PAROLLES.
What's the matter, sweet heart?
BERTRAM.
Although before the solemn priest I have
        sworn,
I will not bed her.
PAROLLES.
What, what, sweet heart?
BERTRAM.
O my Parolles, they have married me!—
I'll to the Tuscan wars, and never bed her.
PAROLLES.
France is a dog-hole, and it no more merits
The tread of a man's foot:—to the wars!
BERTRAM.
There's letters from my mother; what the
        import is,
I know not yet.

PAROLLES.

Ay, that would be known. To the wars, my
    boy, to the wars!
He wears his honour in a box unseen
That hugs his kicksy-wicksy here at home,
Spending his manly marrow in her arms,
Which should sustain the bound and high
    curvet
Of Mars's fiery steed. To other regions!
France is a stable; we that dwell in't, jades;
Therefore, to the wars!

BERTRAM.

It shall be so; I'll send her to my house,
Acquaint my mother with my hate to her,
And wherefore I am fled; write to the king
That which I durst not speak: his present
    gift
Shall furnish me to those Italian fields
Where noble fellows strike: war is no
    strife
To the dark house and the detested wife.

PAROLLES.

Will this caprichio hold in thee, art sure?

BERTRAM.

Go with me to my chamber and advise
    me.
I'll send her straight away: to-morrow
I'll to the wars, she to her single sorrow.

PAROLLES.

Why, these balls bound; there's noise in it.
    'Tis hard:
A young man married is a man that's
    marr'd:
Therefore away, and leave her bravely; go:
The king has done you wrong: but, hush,
    'tis so.

[*Exeunt.*]

SCENE IV

The same. Another room in the palace.
[*Enter* HELENA *and* CLOWN.]

HELENA.

My mother greets me kindly: is she well?

CLOWN.

She is not well, but yet she has her health:
she's very merry, but yet she is not well: but
thanks be given, she's very well, and wants
nothing i' the world; but yet she is not well.

HELENA.

If she be very well, what does she ail that
she's not very well?

CLOWN.

Truly, she's very well indeed, but for two
things.

HELENA.

What two things?

CLOWN.

One, that she's not in heaven, whither
God send her quickly! The other, that
she's in earth, from whence God send her
quickly!

[*Enter* PAROLLES.]

PAROLLES.

Bless you, my fortunate lady!

HELENA.

I hope, sir, I have your good will to have
mine own good fortunes.

PAROLLES.

You had my prayers to lead them on; and
to keep them on, have them still. O, my
knave,—how does my old lady?

CLOWN.

So that you had her wrinkles and I her
money, I would she did as you say.

PAROLLES.

Why, I say nothing.

CLOWN.

Marry, you are the wiser man; for many
a man's tongue shakes out his master's
undoing: to say nothing, to do nothing, to
know nothing, and to have nothing, is to be
a great part of your title; which is within a
very little of nothing.

PAROLLES.

Away! thou art a knave.

CLOWN.

You should have said, sir, before a knave
thou art a knave; that is before me thou art
a knave: this had been truth, sir.

PAROLLES.

Go to, thou art a witty fool; I have found
thee.

CLOWN.

Did you find me in yourself, sir? or were
you taught to find me? The search, sir, was
profitable; and much fool may you find in

you, even to the world's pleasure and the increase of laughter.

PAROLLES.
A good knave, i' faith, and well fed.—
Madam, my lord will go away to-night:
A very serious business calls on him.
The great prerogative and right of love,
Which, as your due, time claims, he does
   acknowledge;
But puts it off to a compell'd restraint;
Whose want, and whose delay, is strew'd
   with sweets;
Which they distil now in the curbed time,
To make the coming hour o'erflow with joy
And pleasure drown the brim.

HELENA.
                What's his will else?

PAROLLES.
That you will take your instant leave o' the
   king,
And make this haste as your own good
   proceeding,
Strengthen'd with what apology you think
May make it probable need.

HELENA.
             What more commands he?

PAROLLES.
That, having this obtain'd, you presently
Attend his further pleasure.

HELENA.
In everything I wait upon his will.

PAROLLES.
I shall report it so.

HELENA.
                  I pray you.
Come, sirrah.

                   [*Exeunt.*]

SCENE V

Another room in the palace.
[*Enter* LAFEU *and* BERTRAM.]

LAFEU.
But I hope your lordship thinks not him
   a soldier.

BERTRAM.
Yes, my lord, and of very valiant approof.

LAFEU.
You have it from his own deliverance.

BERTRAM.
And by other warranted testimony.

LAFEU.
Then my dial goes not true: I took this lark
for a bunting.

BERTRAM.
I do assure you, my lord, he is very great in
knowledge, and accordingly valiant.

LAFEU.
I have, then, sinned against his experience
and transgressed against his valour; and my
state that way is dangerous, since I cannot
yet find in my heart to repent. Here he
comes; I pray you make us friends; I will
pursue the amity.

           [*Enter* PAROLLES.]

PAROLLES. [*To* BERTRAM.]
These things shall be done, sir.

LAFEU.
Pray you, sir, who's his tailor?

PAROLLES.
Sir!

LAFEU.
O, I know him well, I, sir; he, sir, is a good
workman, a very good tailor.

BERTRAM. [*Aside to* PAROLLES.]
Is she gone to the king?

PAROLLES.
She is.

BERTRAM.
Will she away to-night?

PAROLLES.
As you'll have her.

BERTRAM.
I have writ my letters, casketed my treasure,
Given order for our horses; and to-night,
When I should take possession of the
   bride,
End ere I do begin.

LAFEU.
A good traveller is something at the latter
end of a dinner; but one that lies three-thirds
and uses a known truth to pass a thousand
nothings with, should be once heard and
thrice beaten.—God save you, captain.

BERTRAM.
Is there any unkindness between my lord
and you, monsieur?

PAROLLES.
I know not how I have deserved to run into my lord's displeasure.

LAFEU.
You have made shift to run into 't, boots and spurs and all, like him that leapt into the custard; and out of it you'll run again, rather than suffer question for your residence.

BERTRAM.
It may be you have mistaken him, my lord.

LAFEU.
And shall do so ever, though I took him at his prayers. Fare you well, my lord; and believe this of me, there can be no kernal in this light nut; the soul of this man is his clothes; trust him not in matter of heavy consequence; I have kept of them tame, and know their natures.—Farewell, monsieur; I have spoken better of you than you have or will to deserve at my hand; but we must do good against evil.

[*Exit.*]

PAROLLES.
An idle lord, I swear.

BERTRAM.
I think so.

PAROLLES.
Why, do you not know him?

BERTRAM.
Yes, I do know him well; and common speech
Gives him a worthy pass. Here comes my clog.

[*Enter* HELENA.]

HELENA.
I have, sir, as I was commanded from you,
Spoke with the king, and have procur'd his leave
For present parting; only he desires
Some private speech with you.

BERTRAM.
            I shall obey his will.
You must not marvel, Helen, at my course,
Which holds not colour with the time, nor does
The ministration and required office
On my particular. Prepared I was not

For such a business; therefore am I found
So much unsettled: this drives me to entreat you:
That presently you take your way for home,
And rather muse than ask why I entreat you:
For my respects are better than they seem;
And my appointments have in them a need
Greater than shows itself at the first view
To you that know them not. This to my mother:

[*Giving a letter.*]

'Twill be two days ere I shall see you; so
I leave you to your wisdom.

HELENA.
            Sir, I can nothing say
But that I am your most obedient servant.

BERTRAM.
Come, come, no more of that.

HELENA.
            And ever shall
With true observance seek to eke out that
Wherein toward me my homely stars have fail'd
To equal my great fortune.

BERTRAM.
            Let that go:
My haste is very great. Farewell; hie home.

HELENA.
Pray, sir, your pardon.

BERTRAM.
            Well, what would you say?

HELENA.
I am not worthy of the wealth I owe;
Nor dare I say 'tis mine, and yet it is;
But, like a timorous thief, most fain would steal
What law does vouch mine own.

BERTRAM.
What would you have?

HELENA.
Something; and scarce so much:— nothing, indeed.—
I would not tell you what I would, my lord:—Faith, yes;—
Strangers and foes do sunder and not kiss.

BERTRAM.

I pray you, stay not, but in haste to horse.

HELENA.

I shall not break your bidding, good my lord.

BERTRAM.

Where are my other men, monsieur?—
  Farewell.

[*Exit* HELENA.]

Go thou toward home, where I will never
  come
Whilst I can shake my sword or hear the
  drum:—
Away, and for our flight.

PAROLLES.

Bravely, coragio!

[*Exeunt.*]

ACT III
SCENE I

Florence. A room in the duke's palace.
[*Flourish. Enter the* DUKE OF FLORENCE,
attended; two FRENCH LORDS, *and*
SOLDIERS.]

DUKE.

So that, from point to point, now have
  you heard
The fundamental reasons of this war;
Whose great decision hath much blood
  let forth,
And more thirsts after.

FIRST LORD.

Holy seems the quarrel
Upon your grace's part; black and fearful
On the opposer.

DUKE.

Therefore we marvel much our cousin
  France
Would, in so just a business, shut his bosom
Against our borrowing prayers.

SECOND LORD.

Good my lord,
The reasons of our state I cannot yield,
But like a common and an outward man
That the great figure of a council frames
By self-unable motion; therefore dare not
Say what I think of it, since I have found
Myself in my incertain grounds to fail
As often as I guess'd.

DUKE.

Be it his pleasure.

FIRST LORD.

But I am sure the younger of our nature,
That surfeit on their ease, will day by day
Come here for physic.

DUKE.

Welcome shall they be;
And all the honours that can fly from us
Shall on them settle. You know your places
  well;
When better fall, for your avails they fell:
To-morrow to th' field.

[*Flourish. Exeunt.*]

SCENE II

Rousillon. A room in the countess's palace.
[*Enter* COUNTESS *and* CLOWN.]

COUNTESS.

It hath happened all as I would have had
it, save that he comes not along with her.

CLOWN.

By my troth, I take my young lord to be a
very melancholy man.

COUNTESS.

By what observance, I pray you?

CLOWN.

Why, he will look upon his boot and sing;
mend the ruff and sing; ask questions and
sing; pick his teeth and sing. I know a man
that had this trick of melancholy sold a
goodly manor for a song.

COUNTESS.

Let me see what he writes, and when he
means to come.

[*Opening a letter.*]

CLOWN.

I have no mind to Isbel since I was at court.
Our old ling and our Isbels o' the country
are nothing like your old ling and your
Isbels o' the court. The brains of my Cupid's
knocked out; and I begin to love, as an old
man loves money, with no stomach.

COUNTESS.

What have we here?

CLOWN.

E'en that you have there.

[*Exit.*]

Countess. [*Reads.*]
"I have sent you a daughter-in-law; she hath recovered the king and undone me. I have wedded her, not bedded her; and sworn to make the 'not' eternal. You shall hear I am run away: know it before the report come. If there be breadth enough in the world, I will hold a long distance. My duty to you. Your unfortunate son,
Bertram."
This is not well, rash and unbridled boy,
To fly the favours of so good a king;
To pluck his indignation on thy head
By the misprizing of a maid too virtuous
For the contempt of empire.

[*Re-enter* Clown.]

Clown.
O madam, yonder is heavy news within between two soldiers and my young lady.

Countess.
What is the matter?

Clown.
Nay, there is some comfort in the news, some comfort; your son will not be killed so soon as I thought he would.

Countess.
Why should he be killed?

Clown.
So say I, madam, if he run away, as I hear he does: the danger is in standing to 't; that's the loss of men, though it be the getting of children. Here they come will tell you more: for my part, I only hear your son was run away.

[*Exit.*]
[*Enter* Helena *and the two* Gentlemen.]

Second Gentleman.
Save you, good madam.

Helena.
Madam, my lord is gone, for ever gone.

First Gentleman.
Do not say so.

Countess.
Think upon patience.—Pray you, gentlemen,—
I have felt so many quirks of joy and grief
That the first face of neither, on the start,

Can woman me unto 't.—Where is my son, I pray you?

First Gentleman.
Madam, he's gone to serve the Duke of Florence:
We met him thitherward; for thence we came,
And, after some despatch in hand at court,
Thither we bend again.

Helena.
Look on this letter, madam; here's my passport.[*Reads.*] "When thou canst get the ring upon my finger, which never shall come off, and show me a child begotten of thy body that I am father to, then call me husband; but in such a 'then' I write a 'never.'"
This is a dreadful sentence.

Countess.
Brought you this letter, gentlemen?

First Gentleman.
                              Ay, madam;
And for the contents' sake, are sorry for our pains.

Countess.
I pr'ythee, lady, have a better cheer;
If thou engrossest all the griefs are thine,
Thou robb'st me of a moiety. He was my son:
But I do wash his name out of my blood,
And thou art all my child.—Towards Florence is he?

First Gentleman.
Ay, madam.

Countess.
                    And to be a soldier?

First Gentleman.
Such is his noble purpose: and, believe 't,
The duke will lay upon him all the honour
That good convenience claims.

Countess.
                        Return you thither?

Second Gentleman.
Ay, madam, with the swiftest wing of speed.

Helena. [*Reads.*]
"Till I have no wife, I have nothing in France."
'Tis bitter.

Countess.
Find you that there?
Helena.
                              Ay, madam.
Second Gentleman.
'Tis but the boldness of his hand haply,
which his heart was not consenting to.
Countess.
Nothing in France until he have no wife!
There's nothing here that is too good for
      him
But only she; and she deserves a lord
That twenty such rude boys might tend
      upon,
And call her hourly mistress. Who was
      with him?
Second Gentleman.
A servant only, and a gentleman
Which I have sometime known.
Countess.
                              Parolles, was it not?
Second Gentleman.
Ay, my good lady, he.
Countess.
A very tainted fellow, and full of wickedness.
My son corrupts a well-derived nature
With his inducement.
Second Gentleman.
                              Indeed, good lady,
The fellow has a deal of that too much
Which holds him much to have.
Countess.
You are welcome, gentlemen.
I will entreat you, when you see my son,
To tell him that his sword can never win
The honour that he loses: more I'll entreat
      you
Written to bear along.
First Gentleman.
                              We serve you, madam,
In that and all your worthiest affairs.
Countess.
Not so, but as we change our courtesies.
Will you draw near?
      [*Exeunt* Countess *and* Gentlemen.]
Helena.
"Till I have no wife, I have nothing in
      France."

Nothing in France until he has no wife!
Thou shalt have none, Rousillon, none in
      France;
Then hast thou all again. Poor lord! is't I
That chase thee from thy country, and
      expose
Those tender limbs of thine to the event
Of the none-sparing war? and is it I
That drive thee from the sportive court,
      where thou
Wast shot at with fair eyes, to be the mark
Of smoky muskets? O you leaden
      messengers,
That ride upon the violent speed of fire,
Fly with false aim: move the still-peering
      air,
That sings with piercing; do not touch
      my lord!
Whoever shoots at him, I set him there;
Whoever charges on his forward breast,
I am the caitiff that do hold him to it;
And though I kill him not, I am the cause
His death was so effected: better 'twere
I met the ravin lion when he roar'd
With sharp constraint of hunger; better
      'twere
That all the miseries which nature owes
Were mine at once. No; come thou home,
      Rousillon,
Whence honour but of danger wins a scar,
As oft it loses all. I will be gone:
My being here it is that holds thee hence:
Shall I stay here to do't? no, no, although
The air of paradise did fan the house,
And angels offic'd all: I will be gone,
That pitiful rumour may report my flight
To consolate thine ear. Come, night; end,
      day!
For with the dark, poor thief, I'll steal away.
                              [*Exit.*]

SCENE III

Florence. Before the duke's palace.
[*Flourish. Enter the* Duke of Florence,
Bertram, Parolles, Lords, Soldiers,
                  and Others.]

Duke.
The general of our horse thou art; and we,

Great in our hope, lay our best love and
  credence
Upon thy promising fortune.
BERTRAM.
                              Sir, it is
A charge too heavy for my strength; but
  yet
We'll strive to bear it, for your worthy sake
To the extreme edge of hazard.
DUKE.
                    Then go thou forth;
And fortune play upon thy prosperous
  helm,
As thy auspicious mistress!
BERTRAM.
                        This very day,
Great Mars, I put myself into thy file;
Make me but like my thoughts, and I shall
  prove
A lover of thy drum, hater of love.
                              [*Exeunt.*]

SCENE IV

Rousillon. A room in the countess's palace.
  [*Enter* COUNTESS *and* STEWARD.]
COUNTESS.
Alas! and would you take the letter of her?
Might you not know she would do as she
  has done,
By sending me a letter? Read it again.
STEWARD. [*Reads.*]
"I am Saint Jaques' pilgrim, thither gone:
Ambitious love hath so in me offended
That barefoot plod I the cold ground upon,
With sainted vow my faults to have
  amended.
Write, write, that from the bloody course
  of war
My dearest master, your dear son, may hie:
Bless him at home in peace, whilst I from
  far
His name with zealous fervour sanctify:
His taken labours bid him me forgive;
I, his despiteful Juno, sent him forth
From courtly friends, with camping foes
  to live,
Where death and danger dog the heels of
  worth:

He is too good and fair for death and me;
Whom I myself embrace to set him free."
COUNTESS.
Ah, what sharp stings are in her mildest
  words!—
Rinaldo, you did never lack advice so
  much
As letting her pass so; had I spoke with
  her,
I could have well diverted her intents,
Which thus she hath prevented.
STEWARD.
                        Pardon me, madam:
If I had given you this at over-night,
She might have been o'er ta'en; and yet she
  writes,
Pursuit would be but vain.
COUNTESS.
                          What angel shall
Bless this unworthy husband? he cannot
  thrive,
Unless her prayers, whom heaven delights
  to hear
And loves to grant, reprieve him from the
  wrath
Of greatest justice.—Write, write, Rinaldo,
To this unworthy husband of his wife:
Let every word weigh heavy of her worth,
That he does weigh too light: my greatest
  grief,
Though little he do feel it, set down
  sharply.
Dispatch the most convenient
  messenger:—
When, haply, he shall hear that she is gone
He will return; and hope I may that she,
Hearing so much, will speed her foot
  again,
Led hither by pure love: which of them
  both
Is dearest to me I have no skill in sense
To make distinction:—provide this
  messenger:—
My heart is heavy, and mine age is weak;
Grief would have tears, and sorrow bids
  me speak.
                              [*Exeunt.*]

SCENE V
Without the walls of Florence.
[*Enter an old* Widow of Florence,
Diana, Violenta, Mariana, *and other*
Citizens.]

Widow.
Nay, come; for if they do approach the city
we shall lose all the sight.

Diana.
They say the French count has done most
honourable service.

Widow.
It is reported that he has taken their
greatest commander; and that with his own
hand he slew the duke's brother. [*A tucket
far off.*] We have lost our labour; they are
gone a contrary way: hark! you may know
by their trumpets.

Mariana.
Come, let's return again, and suffice
ourselves with the report of it. Well, Diana,
take heed of this French earl: the honour
of a maid is her name; and no legacy is so
rich as honesty.

Widow.
I have told my neighbour how you
have been solicited by a gentleman his
companion.

Mariana.
I know that knave; hang him! one Parolles:
a filthy officer he is in those suggestions for
the young earl.—Beware of them, Diana;
their promises, enticements, oaths, tokens,
and all these engines of lust, are not the
things they go under; many a maid hath
been seduced by them; and the misery is,
example, that so terrible shows in the wreck
of maidenhood, cannot for all that dissuade
succession, but that they are limed with the
twigs that threaten them. I hope I need not
to advise you further; but I hope your own
grace will keep you where you are, though
there were no further danger known but
the modesty which is so lost.

Diana.
You shall not need to fear me.

Widow.
I hope so.—Look, here comes a pilgrim. I

know she will lie at my house: thither they
send one another; I'll question her. [*Enter*
Helena *in the dress of a pilgrim.*] God save
you, pilgrim! Whither are you bound?

Helena.
To Saint Jaques-le-Grand.
Where do the palmers lodge, I do beseech
    you?

Widow.
At the Saint Francis here, beside the port.

Helena.
Is this the way?

Widow.
Ay, marry, is't. Hark you! They come this
    way.
                            [*A march afar off.*]
If you will tarry, holy pilgrim,
But till the troops come by,
I will conduct you where you shall be
    lodg'd;
The rather for I think I know your hostess
As ample as myself.

Helena.
                            Is it yourself?

Widow.
If you shall please so, pilgrim.

Helena.
I thank you, and will stay upon your leisure.

Widow.
You came, I think, from France?

Helena.
                                    I did so.

Widow.
Here you shall see a countryman of yours
That has done worthy service.

Helena.
                            His name, I pray you.

Diana.
The Count Rousillon: know you such a
    one?

Helena.
But by the ear, that hears most nobly of
    him:
His face I know not.

Diana.
                            Whatsoe'er he is,
He's bravely taken here. He stole from
    France,

As 'tis reported, for the king had married
     him
Against his liking: think you it is so?

HELENA.

Ay, surely, mere the truth; I know his lady.

DIANA.

There is a gentleman that serves the count
Reports but coarsely of her.

HELENA.
                    What's his name?

DIANA.

Monsieur Parolles.

HELENA.
                    O, I believe with him,
In argument of praise, or to the worth
Of the great count himself, she is too
     mean
To have her name repeated; all her
     deserving
Is a reserved honesty, and that
I have not heard examin'd.

DIANA.
                    Alas, poor lady!
'Tis a hard bondage to become the wife
Of a detesting lord.

WIDOW.

Ay, right; good creature, wheresoe'er she is
Her heart weighs sadly: this young maid
     might do her
A shrewd turn, if she pleas'd.

HELENA.
                    How do you mean?
May be, the amorous count solicits her
In the unlawful purpose.

WIDOW.
                    He does, indeed;
And brokes with all that can in such a suit
Corrupt the tender honour of a maid;
But she is arm'd for him, and keeps her
     guard
In honestest defence.

MARIANA.
                    The gods forbid else!

WIDOW.

So, now they come:—
[*Enter, with a drum and colours, a* PARTY OF
     THE FLORENTINE ARMY, BERTRAM, *and*
          PAROLLES.]

That is Antonio, the duke's eldest son;
That, Escalus.

HELENA.
                    Which is the Frenchman?

DIANA.
                                        He;
That with the plume: 'tis a most gallant
     fellow.
I would he lov'd his wife: if he were
     honester
He were much goodlier: is't not a
     handsome gentleman?

HELENA.

I like him well.

DIANA.

'Tis pity he is not honest? yond's that
     same knave
That leads him to these places; were I his
     lady
I would poison that vile rascal.

HELENA.
                    Which is he?

DIANA.

That jack-an-apes with scarfs. Why is he
     melancholy?

HELENA.

Perchance he's hurt i' the battle.

PAROLLES.

Lose our drum! well.

MARIANA.

He's shrewdly vex'd at something.
Look, he has spied us.

WIDOW.

Marry, hang you!

MARIANA.

And your courtesy, for a ring-carrier!
[*Exeunt* BERTRAM, PAROLLES, OFFICERS,
          and SOLDIERS.]

WIDOW.

The troop is past. Come, pilgrim, I will
     bring you
Where you shall host: of enjoin'd penitents
There's four or five, to great Saint Jaques
     bound,
Already at my house.

HELENA.
                    I humbly thank you:
Please it this matron and this gentle maid

To eat with us to-night; the charge and
   thanking
Shall be for me: and, to requite you further,
I will bestow some precepts of this virgin,
Worthy the note.

Both.

We'll take your offer kindly.
[*Exeunt.*]

SCENE VI

Camp before Florence.

[*Enter* Bertram, *and the two* French
Lords.]

First Lord.

Nay, good my lord, put him to't; let him
have his way.

Second Lord.

If your lordship find him not a hilding,
hold me no more in your respect.

First Lord.

On my life, my lord, a bubble.

Bertram.

Do you think I am so far deceived in him?

First Lord.

Believe it, my lord, in mine own direct
knowledge, without any malice, but to
speak of him as my kinsman, he's a most
notable coward, an infinite and endless liar,
an hourly promise-breaker, the owner of
no one good quality worthy your lordship's
entertainment.

Second Lord.

It were fit you knew him; lest, reposing
too far in his virtue, which he hath not, he
might at some great and trusty business, in
a main danger fail you.

Bertram.

I would I knew in what particular action
to try him.

Second Lord.

None better than to let him fetch off his
drum, which you hear him so confidently
undertake to do.

First Lord.

I with a troop of Florentines will suddenly
surprise him; such I will have whom I am
sure he knows not from the enemy; we will
bind and hoodwink him so that he shall

suppose no other but that he is carried
into the leaguer of the adversaries when we
bring him to our own tents. Be but your
lordship present at his examination; if he
do not, for the promise of his life, and in
the highest compulsion of base fear, offer to
betray you, and deliver all the intelligence
in his power against you, and that with the
divine forfeit of his soul upon oath, never
trust my judgment in anything.

Second Lord.

O, for the love of laughter, let him fetch his
drum; he says he has a stratagem for't: when
your lordship sees the bottom of his success
in't, and to what metal this counterfeit lump
of ore will be melted, if you give him not
John Drum's entertainment, your inclining
cannot be removed. Here he comes.

First Lord.

O, for the love of laughter, hinder not the
honour of his design: let him fetch off his
drum in any hand.

[*Enter* Parolles.]

Bertram.

How now, monsieur! this drum sticks
sorely in your disposition.

Second Lord.

A pox on 't; let it go; 'tis but a drum.

Parolles.

But a drum! Is't but a drum? A drum so
lost!—There was excellent command! to
charge in with our horse upon our own
wings, and to rend our own soldiers.

Second Lord.

That was not to be blamed in the command
of the service; it was a disaster of war that
Caesar himself could not have prevented, if
he had been there to command.

Bertram.

Well, we cannot greatly condemn our
success: some dishonour we had in the loss
of that drum; but it is not to be recovered.

Parolles.

It might have been recovered.

Bertram.

It might, but it is not now.

Parolles.

It is to be recovered: but that the merit of

service is seldom attributed to the true and exact performer, I would have that drum or another, or *hic jacet*.

BERTRAM.

Why, if you have a stomach, to't, monsieur, if you think your mystery in stratagem can bring this instrument of honour again into his native quarter, be magnanimous in the enterprise, and go on; I will grace the attempt for a worthy exploit; if you speed well in it, the duke shall both speak of it and extend to you what further becomes his greatness, even to the utmost syllable of your worthiness.

PAROLLES.

By the hand of a soldier, I will undertake it.

BERTRAM.

But you must not now slumber in it.

PAROLLES.

I'll about it this evening: and I will presently pen down my dilemmas, encourage myself in my certainty, put myself into my mortal preparation; and, by midnight, look to hear further from me.

BERTRAM.

May I be bold to acquaint his grace you are gone about it?

PAROLLES.

I know not what the success will be, my lord, but the attempt I vow.

BERTRAM.

I know thou art valiant; and, to the possibility of thy soldiership, will subscribe for thee. Farewell.

PAROLLES.

I love not many words.

[*Exit.*]

FIRST LORD.

No more than a fish loves water.—Is not this a strange fellow, my lord? that so confidently seems to undertake this business, which he knows is not to be done; damns himself to do, and dares better be damned than to do't.

SECOND LORD.

You do not know him, my lord, as we do: certain it is that he will steal himself into a man's favour, and for a week escape a great deal of discoveries; but when you find him out, you have him ever after.

BERTRAM.

Why, do you think he will make no deed at all of this, that so seriously he does address himself unto?

FIRST LORD.

None in the world: but return with an invention, and clap upon you two or three probable lies: but we have almost embossed him,—you shall see his fall to-night: for indeed he is not for your lordship's respect.

SECOND LORD.

We'll make you some sport with the fox ere we case him. He was first smok'd by the old Lord Lafeu: when his disguise and he is parted, tell me what a sprat you shall find him; which you shall see this very night.

FIRST LORD.

I must go look my twigs; he shall be caught.

BERTRAM.

Your brother, he shall go along with me.

FIRST LORD.

As't please your lordship: I'll leave you.

[*Exit.*]

BERTRAM.

Now will I lead you to the house, and show you

The lass I spoke of.

SECOND LORD.

But you say she's honest.

BERTRAM.

That's all the fault: I spoke with her but once,

And found her wondrous cold; but I sent to her,

By this same coxcomb that we have i' the wind,

Tokens and letters which she did re-send;

And this is all I have done. She's a fair creature;

Will you go see her?

SECOND LORD.

With all my heart, my lord.

[*Exeunt.*]

SCENE VII

Florence. A room in the widow's house.
[*Enter* Helena *and* Widow.]

Helena.
If you misdoubt me that I am not she,
I know not how I shall assure you further,
But I shall lose the grounds I work upon.

Widow.
Though my estate be fallen, I was well
    born,
Nothing acquainted with these businesses;
And would not put my reputation now
In any staining act.

Helena.
                    Nor would I wish you.
First give me trust, the count he is my
    husband,
And what to your sworn counsel I have
    spoken
Is so from word to word; and then you
    cannot,
By the good aid that I of you shall borrow,
Err in bestowing it.

Widow.
                    I should believe you;
For you have show'd me that which well
    approves
You're great in fortune.

Helena.
                    Take this purse of gold,
And let me buy your friendly help thus far,
Which I will over-pay, and pay again
When I have found it. The count he woos
    your daughter
Lays down his wanton siege before her
    beauty,
Resolv'd to carry her: let her in fine,
    consent,
As we'll direct her how 'tis best to bear it,
Now his important blood will naught deny
That she'll demand: a ring the county
    wears,
That downward hath succeeded in his
    house
From son to son, some four or five
    descents
Since the first father wore it: this ring he
    holds

In most rich choice; yet, in his idle fire,
To buy his will, it would not seem too
    dear,
Howe'er repented after.

Widow.
                    Now I see
The bottom of your purpose.

Helena.
You see it lawful then: it is no more
But that your daughter, ere she seems as
    won,
Desires this ring; appoints him an
    encounter;
In fine, delivers me to fill the time,
Herself most chastely absent; after this,
To marry her, I'll add three thousand
    crowns
To what is pass'd already.

Widow.
                    I have yielded:
Instruct my daughter how she shall
    persever,
That time and place, with this deceit so
    lawful,
May prove coherent. Every night he comes
With musics of all sorts, and songs
    compos'd
To her unworthiness: it nothing steads us
To chide him from our eaves; for he
    persists,
As if his life lay on't.

Helena.
                    Why, then, to-night
Let us assay our plot; which, if it speed,
Is wicked meaning in a lawful deed,
And lawful meaning in a lawful act;
Where both not sin, and yet a sinful fact:
But let's about it.
                    [*Exeunt.*]

ACT IV
SCENE I

Without the Florentine camp.
[*Enter first* Lord *with five or six*
    Soldiers *in ambush.*]

First Lord.
He can come no other way but by this
hedge-corner. When you sally upon him,

speak what terrible language you will; though you understand it not yourselves, no matter; for we must not seem to understand him, unless some one among us, whom we must produce for an interpreter.

FIRST SOLDIER.
Good captain, let me be the interpreter.

FIRST LORD.
Art not acquainted with him? knows he not thy voice?

FIRST SOLDIER.
No, sir, I warrant you.

FIRST LORD.
But what linsey-woolsey has thou to speak to us again?

FIRST SOLDIER.
E'en such as you speak to me.

FIRST LORD.
He must think us some band of strangers i' the adversary's entertainment. Now he hath a smack of all neighbouring languages, therefore we must every one be a man of his own fancy; not to know what we speak one to another, so we seem to know, is to know straight our purpose: choughs' language, gabble enough, and good enough. As for you, interpreter, you must seem very politic. But couch, ho! here he comes; to beguile two hours in a sleep, and then to return and swear the lies he forges.

[*Enter* PAROLLES.]

PAROLLES.
Ten o'clock. Within these three hours 'twill be time enough to go home. What shall I say I have done? It must be a very plausive invention that carries it; they begin to smoke me: and disgraces have of late knocked too often at my door. I find my tongue is too foolhardy; but my heart hath the fear of Mars before it, and of his creatures, not daring the reports of my tongue.

FIRST LORD. [*Aside.*]
This is the first truth that e'er thine own tongue was guilty of.

PAROLLES.
What the devil should move me to undertake the recovery of this drum: being not ignorant of the impossibility, and

knowing I had no such purpose? I must give myself some hurts, and say I got them in exploit: yet slight ones will not carry it: they will say "Came you off with so little?" and great ones I dare not give. Wherefore, what's the instance? Tongue, I must put you into a butter-woman's mouth, and buy myself another of Bajazet's mule, if you prattle me into these perils.

FIRST LORD. [*Aside.*]
Is it possible he should know what he is, and be that he is?

PAROLLES.
I would the cutting of my garments would serve the turn, or the breaking of my Spanish sword.

FIRST LORD. [*Aside.*]
We cannot afford you so.

PAROLLES.
Or the baring of my beard; and to say it was in stratagem.

FIRST LORD. [*Aside.*]
'Twould not do.

PAROLLES.
Or to drown my clothes, and say I was stripped.

FIRST LORD. [*Aside.*]
Hardly serve.

PAROLLES.
Though I swore I leap'd from the window of the citadel,—

FIRST LORD. [*Aside.*]
How deep?

PAROLLES.
Thirty fathom.

FIRST LORD. [*Aside.*]
Three great oaths would scarce make that be believed.

PAROLLES.
I would I had any drum of the enemy's; I would swear I recovered it.

FIRST LORD. [*Aside.*]
You shall hear one anon.

PAROLLES.
A drum now of the enemy's!
[*Alarum within.*]

FIRST LORD.
Throca movousus, cargo, cargo, cargo.

ALL.
Cargo, cargo, cargo, villianda par corbo, cargo.
PAROLLES.
O, ransom, ransom! Do not hide mine eyes.
          [*They seize and blindfold him.*]
FIRST SOLDIER.
Boskos thromuldo boskos.
PAROLLES.
I know you are the Muskos' regiment,
And I shall lose my life for want of
          language:
If there be here German, or Dane, low
          Dutch,
Italian, or French, let him speak to me;
I'll discover that which shall undo the
          Florentine.
SECOND SOLDIER.
Boskos vauvado:—
I understand thee, and can speak thy
          tongue.
Kerelybonto:—Sir,
Betake thee to thy faith, for seventeen
          poniards
Are at thy bosom.
PAROLLES.
                              O!
FIRST SOLDIER.
                    O, pray, pray, pray!—
Manka revania dulche.
FIRST LORD.
Oscorbi dulchos volivorco.
FIRST SOLDIER.
The general is content to spare thee yet;
And, hoodwink'd as thou art, will lead
          thee on
To gather from thee: haply thou mayst
          inform
Something to save thy life.
PAROLLES.
                              O, let me live,
And all the secrets of our camp I'll show,
Their force, their purposes: nay, I'll speak
          that
Which you will wonder at.
FIRST SOLDIER.
                    But wilt thou faithfully?
PAROLLES.
If I do not, damn me.

FIRST SOLDIER.
                    Acordo linta.—
Come on; thou art granted space.
          [*Exit, with* PAROLLES *guarded.*]
FIRST LORD.
Go, tell the Count Rousillon and my
          brother
We have caught the woodcock, and will
          keep him muffled
Till we do hear from them.
SECOND SOLDIER.
                              Captain, I will.
FIRST LORD.
A' will betray us all unto ourselves;—
Inform 'em that.
SECOND SOLDIER.
                    So I will, sir.
FIRST LORD.
Till then I'll keep him dark, and safely
          lock'd.

          [*Exeunt.*]

SCENE II

Florence. A room in the widow's house.
          [*Enter* BERTRAM *and* DIANA.]
BERTRAM.
They told me that your name was
          Fontibell.
DIANA.
No, my good lord, Diana.
BERTRAM.
                              Titled goddess;
And worth it, with addition! But, fair soul,
In your fine frame hath love no quality?
If the quick fire of youth light not your
          mind,
You are no maiden, but a monument;
When you are dead, you should be such
          a one
As you are now, for you are cold and stern;
And now you should be as your mother was
When your sweet self was got.
DIANA.
She then was honest.
BERTRAM.
                    So should you be.
DIANA.
                                        No:

522

My mother did but duty; such, my lord,
As you owe to your wife.
Bertram.
                 No more of that!
I pr'ythee, do not strive against my vows:
I was compell'd to her; but I love thee
By love's own sweet constraint, and will
    for ever
Do thee all rights of service.
Diana.
                 Ay, so you serve us
Till we serve you; but when you have our
    roses
You barely leave our thorns to prick
    ourselves,
And mock us with our bareness.
Bertram.
                 How have I sworn?
Diana.
'Tis not the many oaths that makes the
    truth,
But the plain single vow that is vow'd true.
What is not holy, that we swear not by,
But take the Highest to witness: then, pray
    you, tell me,
If I should swear by Jove's great attributes
I lov'd you dearly, would you believe my
    oaths
When I did love you ill? This has no
    holding,
To swear by him whom I protest to love
That I will work against him: therefore
    your oaths
Are words and poor conditions; but
    unseal'd,—
At least in my opinion.
Bertram.
                 Change it, change it;
Be not so holy-cruel. Love is holy;
And my integrity ne'er knew the crafts
That you do charge men with. Stand no
    more off,
But give thyself unto my sick desires,
Who then recover: say thou art mine, and
    ever
My love as it begins shall so persever.
Diana.
I see that men make hopes in such a case,

That we'll forsake ourselves. Give me that
    ring.
Bertram.
I'll lend it thee, my dear, but have no power
To give it from me.
Diana.
                 Will you not, my lord?
Bertram.
It is an honour 'longing to our house,
Bequeathed down from many ancestors;
Which were the greatest obloquy i' the
    world
In me to lose.
Diana.
                 Mine honour's such a ring:
My chastity's the jewel of our house,
Bequeathed down from many ancestors;
Which were the greatest obloquy i' the
    world
In me to lose. Thus your own proper
    wisdom
Brings in the champion honour on my
    part
Against your vain assault.
Bertram.
                 Here, take my ring:
My house, mine honour, yea, my life, be
    thine,
And I'll be bid by thee.
Diana.
When midnight comes, knock at my
    chamber-window;
I'll order take my mother shall not hear.
Now will I charge you in the band of
    truth,
When you have conquer'd my yet maiden-
    bed,
Remain there but an hour, nor speak to
    me:
My reasons are most strong; and you shall
    know them
When back again this ring shall be
    deliver'd;
And on your finger in the night, I'll put
Another ring; that what in time proceeds
May token to the future our past deeds.
Adieu till then; then fail not. You have
    won

A wife of me, though there my hope be
    done.

BERTRAM.

A heaven on earth I have won by wooing
    thee.

                 [Exit.]

DIANA.

For which live long to thank both heaven
    and me!

You may so in the end.—

My mother told me just how he would
    woo,

As if she sat in's heart; she says all men

Have the like oaths: he had sworn to
    marry me

When his wife's dead; therefore I'll lie
    with him

When I am buried. Since Frenchmen are
    so braid,

Marry that will, I live and die a maid:

Only, in this disguise, I think't no sin

To cozen him that would unjustly win.

                 [Exit.]

SCENE III

The Florentine camp.
[Enter the two FRENCH LORDS, *and
two or three* SOLDIERS.]

FIRST LORD.

You have not given him his mother's letter?

SECOND LORD.

I have deliv'red it an hour since: there is
something in't that stings his nature; for
on the reading, it he changed almost into
another man.

FIRST LORD.

He has much worthy blame laid upon him
for shaking off so good a wife and so sweet
a lady.

SECOND LORD.

Especially he hath incurred the everlasting
displeasure of the king, who had even
tuned his bounty to sing happiness to him.
I will tell you a thing, but you shall let it
dwell darkly with you.

FIRST LORD.

When you have spoken it, 'tis dead, and I
am the grave of it.

SECOND LORD.

He hath perverted a young gentlewoman
here in Florence, of a most chaste renown;
and this night he fleshes his will in the
spoil of her honour: he hath given her his
monumental ring, and thinks himself made
in the unchaste composition.

FIRST LORD.

Now, God delay our rebellion: as we are
ourselves, what things are we!

SECOND LORD.

Merely our own traitors. And as in the
common course of all treasons, we still
see them reveal themselves till they attain
to their abhorred ends; so he that in this
action contrives against his own nobility, in
his proper stream, o'erflows himself.

FIRST LORD.

Is it not meant damnable in us to be
trumpeters of our unlawful intents? We
shall not then have his company to-night?

SECOND LORD.

Not till after midnight; for he is dieted to
his hour.

FIRST LORD.

That approaches apace: I would gladly
have him see his company anatomized,
that he might take a measure of his own
judgments, wherein so curiously he had set
this counterfeit.

SECOND LORD.

We will not meddle with him till he come;
for his presence must be the whip of the
other.

FIRST LORD.

In the meantime, what hear you of these
wars?

SECOND LORD.

I hear there is an overture of peace.

FIRST LORD.

Nay, I assure you, a peace concluded.

SECOND LORD.

What will Count Rousillon do then?
will he travel higher, or return again into
France?

FIRST LORD.

I perceive, by this demand, you are not
altogether of his counsel.

SECOND LORD.

Let it be forbid, sir: so should I be a great deal of his act.

FIRST LORD.

Sir, his wife, some two months since, fled from his house: her pretence is a pilgrimage to Saint Jaques-le-Grand: which holy undertaking with most austere sanctimony she accomplished; and, there residing, the tenderness of her nature became as a prey to her grief; in fine, made a groan of her last breath; and now she sings in heaven.

SECOND LORD.

How is this justified?

FIRST LORD.

The stronger part of it by her own letters, which makes her story true, even to the point of her death: her death itself which could not be her office to say is come, was faithfully confirmed by the rector of the place.

SECOND LORD.

Hath the count all this intelligence?

FIRST LORD.

Ay, and the particular confirmations, point from point, to the full arming of the verity.

SECOND LORD.

I am heartily sorry that he'll be glad of this.

FIRST LORD.

How mightily, sometimes, we make us comforts of our losses!

SECOND LORD.

And how mightily, some other times, we drown our gain in tears! The great dignity that his valour hath here acquired for him shall at home be encountered with a shame as ample.

FIRST LORD.

The web of our life is of a mingled yarn, good and ill together: our virtues would be proud if our faults whipped them not; and our crimes would despair if they were not cherished by our virtues. [*Enter a* SERVANT.] How now? where's your master?

SERVANT.

He met the duke in the street, sir; of whom he hath taken a solemn leave: his lordship will next morning for France. The duke hath offered him letters of commendations to the king.

SECOND LORD.

They shall be no more than needful there, if they were more than they can commend.

FIRST LORD.

They cannot be too sweet for the king's tartness. Here's his lordship now. [*Enter* BERTRAM.] How now, my lord, is't not after midnight?

BERTRAM.

I have to-night despatch'd sixteen businesses, a month's length apiece; by an abstract of success: I have conge'd with the duke, done my adieu with his nearest; buried a wife, mourned for her; writ to my lady mother I am returning; entertained my convoy; and between these main parcels of despatch effected many nicer needs: the last was the greatest, but that I have not ended yet.

SECOND LORD.

If the business be of any difficulty and this morning your departure hence, it requires haste of your lordship.

BERTRAM.

I mean the business is not ended, as fearing to hear of it hereafter. But shall we have this dialogue between the fool and the soldier?—Come, bring forth this counterfeit module has deceived me like a double-meaning prophesier.

SECOND LORD.

Bring him forth. [*Exeunt* SOLDIERS.] Has sat i' the stocks all night, poor gallant knave.

BERTRAM.

No matter; his heels have deserved it, in usurping his spurs so long. How does he carry himself?

FIRST LORD.

I have told your lordship already; the stocks carry him. But to answer you as you would be understood: he weeps like a wench that had shed her milk; he hath confessed himself to Morgan, whom he supposes to be a friar, from the time of his remembrance to this very instant disaster of his setting i' the stocks: and what think you he hath confessed?

Bertram.
Nothing of me, has he?

Second Lord.
His confession is taken, and it shall be read to his face; if your lordship be in't, as I believe you are, you must have the patience to hear it.

[*Re-enter* Soldiers, *with* Parolles.]

Bertram.
A plague upon him! muffled! he can say nothing of me; hush, hush!

First Lord.
Hoodman comes! *Porto tartarossa.*

First Soldier.
He calls for the tortures: what will you say without 'em?

Parolles.
I will confess what I know without constraint; if ye pinch me like a pasty I can say no more.

First Soldier.
Bosko chimurcho.

First Lord.
Boblibindo chicurmurco.

First Soldier.
You are a merciful general:—Our general bids you answer to what I shall ask you out of a note.

Parolles.
And truly, as I hope to live.

First Soldier. [*Reads.*]
"First demand of him how many horse the duke is strong." What say you to that?

Parolles.
Five or six thousand; but very weak and unserviceable: the troops are all scattered, and the commanders very poor rogues, upon my reputation and credit, and as I hope to live.

First Soldier.
Shall I set down your answer so?

Parolles.
Do; I'll take the sacrament on 't, how and which way you will.

Bertram.
All's one to him. What a past-saving slave is this!

First Lord.
You are deceived, my lord; this is Monsieur Parolles, the gallant militarist—that was his own phrase—that had the whole theoric of war in the knot of his scarf, and the practice in the chape of his dagger.

Second Lord.
I will never trust a man again for keeping his sword clean; nor believe he can have everything in him by wearing his apparel neatly.

First Soldier.
Well, that's set down.

Parolles.
"Five or six thousand horse" I said—I will say true—or thereabouts, set down,—for I'll speak truth.

First Lord.
He's very near the truth in this.

Bertram.
But I con him no thanks for't in the nature he delivers it.

Parolles.
Poor rogues, I pray you say.

First Soldier.
Well, that's set down.

Parolles.
I humbly thank you, sir: a truth's a truth, the rogues are marvellous poor.

First Soldier. [*Reads.*]
"Demand of him of what strength they are a-foot." What say you to that?

Parolles.
By my troth, sir, if I were to live this present hour, I will tell true. Let me see: Spurio, a hundred and fifty, Sebastian, so many; Corambus, so many; Jaques, so many; Guiltian, Cosmo, Lodowick, and Gratii, two hundred fifty each; mine own company, Chitopher, Vaumond, Bentii, two hundred fifty each: so that the muster-file, rotten and sound, upon my life, amounts not to fifteen thousand poll; half of the which dare not shake the snow from off their cassocks lest they shake themselves to pieces.

BERTRAM.
What shall be done to him?

FIRST LORD.
Nothing, but let him have thanks. Demand of him my condition, and what credit I have with the duke.

FIRST SOLDIER.
Well, that's set down. [*Reads.*] "You shall demand of him whether one Captain Dumain be i' the camp, a Frenchman; what his reputation is with the duke, what his valour, honesty, expertness in wars; or whether he thinks it were not possible, with well-weighing sums of gold, to corrupt him to a revolt." What say you to this? what do you know of it?

PAROLLES.
I beseech you, let me answer to the particular of the inter'gatories: demand them singly.

FIRST SOLDIER.
Do you know this Captain Dumain?

PAROLLES.
I know him: he was a botcher's 'prentice in Paris, from whence he was whipped for getting the shrieve's fool with child: a dumb innocent that could not say him nay.
[FIRST LORD *lifts up his hand in anger.*]

BERTRAM.
Nay, by your leave, hold your hands; though I know his brains are forfeit to the next tile that falls.

FIRST SOLDIER.
Well, is this captain in the Duke of Florence's camp?

PAROLLES.
Upon my knowledge, he is, and lousy.

FIRST LORD.
Nay, look not so upon me; we shall hear of your lordship anon.

FIRST SOLDIER.
What is his reputation with the duke?

PAROLLES.
The duke knows him for no other but a poor officer of mine; and writ to me this other day to turn him out o' the band: I think I have his letter in my pocket.

FIRST SOLDIER.
Marry, we'll search.

PAROLLES.
In good sadness, I do not know; either it is there or it is upon a file, with the duke's other letters, in my tent.

FIRST SOLDIER.
Here 'tis; here's a paper. Shall I read it to you?

PAROLLES.
I do not know if it be it or no.

BERTRAM.
Our interpreter does it well.

FIRST LORD.
Excellently.

FIRST SOLDIER. [*Reads.*]
"Dian, the count's a fool, and full of
    gold,—"

PAROLLES.
That is not the duke's letter, sir; that is an advertisement to a proper maid in Florence, one Diana, to take heed of the allurement of one Count Rousillon, a foolish idle boy, but for all that very ruttish: I pray you, sir, put it up again.

FIRST SOLDIER.
Nay, I'll read it first by your favour.

PAROLLES.
My meaning in't, I protest, was very honest in the behalf of the maid; for I knew the young count to be a dangerous and lascivious boy, who is a whale to virginity, and devours up all the fry it finds.

BERTRAM.
Damnable! both sides rogue!

FIRST SOLDIER. [*Reads.*]
"When he swears oaths, bid him drop
    gold, and take it:
After he scores, he never pays the score;
Half won is match well made; match, and
    well make it;
He ne'er pays after-debts, take it before;
And say a soldier, 'Dian,' told thee this:
Men are to mell with, boys are not to kiss;
For count of this, the count's a fool, I
    know it,
Who pays before, but not when he does
    owe it.
Thine, as he vow'd to thee in thine ear,
                                    Parolles."

BERTRAM.

He shall be whipped through the army with this rhyme in his forehead.

SECOND LORD.

This is your devoted friend, sir, the manifold linguist, and the armipotent soldier.

BERTRAM.

I could endure anything before but a cat, and now he's a cat to me.

FIRST SOLDIER.

I perceive, sir, by our general's looks we shall be fain to hang you.

PAROLLES.

My life, sir, in any case: not that I am afraid to die, but that, my offences being many, I would repent out the remainder of nature: let me live, sir, in a dungeon, i' the stocks, or anywhere, so I may live.

FIRST SOLDIER.

We'll see what may be done, so you confess freely; therefore, once more to this Captain Dumain: you have answered to his reputation with the duke, and to his valour: what is his honesty?

PAROLLES.

He will steal, sir, an egg out of a cloister: for rapes and ravishments he parallels Nessus. He professes not keeping of oaths; in breaking them he is stronger than Hercules. He will lie, sir, with such volubility that you would think truth were a fool: drunkenness is his best virtue, for he will be swine-drunk; and in his sleep he does little harm, save to his bedclothes about him; but they know his conditions and lay him in straw. I have but little more to say, sir, of his honesty; he has everything that an honest man should not have; what an honest man should have he has nothing.

FIRST LORD.

I begin to love him for this.

BERTRAM.

For this description of thine honesty? A pox upon him for me; he's more and more a cat.

FIRST SOLDIER.

What say you to his expertness in war?

PAROLLES.

Faith, sir, has led the drum before the English tragedians,—to belie him I will not,—and more of his soldiership I know not, except in that country he had the honour to be the officer at a place there called Mile-end to instruct for the doubling of files: I would do the man what honour I can, but of this I am not certain.

FIRST LORD.

He hath out-villanied villainy so far that the rarity redeems him.

BERTRAM.

A pox on him! he's a cat still.

FIRST SOLDIER.

His qualities being at this poor price, I need not to ask you if gold will corrupt him to revolt.

PAROLLES.

Sir, for a cardecu he will sell the fee-simple of his salvation, the inheritance of it; and cut the entail from all remainders and a perpetual succession for it perpetually.

FIRST SOLDIER.

What's his brother, the other Captain Dumain?

SECOND LORD.

Why does he ask him of me?

FIRST SOLDIER.

What's he?

PAROLLES.

E'en a crow o' the same nest; not altogether so great as the first in goodness, but greater a great deal in evil. He excels his brother for a coward, yet his brother is reputed one of the best that is; in a retreat he outruns any lackey: marry, in coming on he has the cramp.

FIRST SOLDIER.

If your life be saved, will you undertake to betray the Florentine?

PAROLLES.

Ay, and the captain of his horse, Count Rousillon.

FIRST SOLDIER.

I'll whisper with the general, and know his pleasure.

PAROLLES. [*Aside.*]

I'll no more drumming; a plague of all drums! Only to seem to deserve well, and to beguile the supposition of that lascivious young boy the count, have I run into this danger: yet who would have suspected an ambush where I was taken?

FIRST SOLDIER.

There is no remedy, sir, but you must die: the general says you that have so traitorously discovered the secrets of your army, and made such pestiferous reports of men very nobly held, can serve the world for no honest use; therefore you must die. Come, headsman, off with his head.

PAROLLES.

O Lord! sir, let me live, or let me see my death.

FIRST SOLDIER.

That shall you, and take your leave of all your friends. [*Unmuffling him.*] So look about you; know you any here?

BERTRAM.

Good morrow, noble captain.

SECOND LORD.

God bless you, Captain Parolles.

FIRST LORD.

God save you, noble captain.

SECOND LORD.

Captain, what greeting will you to my Lord Lafeu? I am for France.

FIRST LORD.

Good captain, will you give me a copy of the sonnet you writ to Diana in behalf of the Count Rousillon? an I were not a very coward I'd compel it of you; but fare you well.

[*Exeunt* BERTRAM, LORDS, &c.]

FIRST SOLDIER.

You are undone, captain: all but your scarf; that has a knot on't yet.

PAROLLES.

Who cannot be crushed with a plot?

FIRST SOLDIER.

If you could find out a country where but women were that had received so much shame, you might begin an impudent nation. Fare ye well, sir; I am for France too: we shall speak of you there.

[*Exit.*]

PAROLLES.

Yet am I thankful: if my heart were great,

'Twould burst at this. Captain I'll be no more;
But I will eat, and drink, and sleep as soft
As captain shall: simply the thing I am
Shall make me live. Who knows himself
    a braggart,
Let him fear this; for it will come to pass
That every braggart shall be found an ass.
Rust, sword! cool, blushes! and, Parolles,
    live
Safest in shame! being fool'd, by foolery
    thrive.
There's place and means for every man
    alive.
I'll after them.

[*Exit.*]

SCENE IV

Florence. A room in the widow's house.

[*Enter* HELENA, WIDOW, *and* DIANA.]

HELENA.

That you may well perceive I have not
    wrong'd you!
One of the greatest in the Christian world
Shall be my surety; 'fore whose throne 'tis
    needful,
Ere I can perfect mine intents, to kneel:
Time was I did him a desired office,
Dear almost as his life; which gratitude
Through flinty Tartar's bosom would peep
    forth,
And answer, thanks: I duly am informed
His grace is at Marseilles; to which place
We have convenient convoy. You must
    know
I am supposed dead: the army breaking,
My husband hies him home; where,
    heaven aiding,
And by the leave of my good lord the king,
We'll be before our welcome.

WIDOW.

                         Gentle madam,
You never had a servant to whose trust
Your business was more welcome.

HELENA.

                         Nor you, mistress,
Ever a friend whose thoughts more truly
    labour

To recompense your love: doubt not but
   heaven
Hath brought me up to be your daughter's
   dower,
As it hath fated her to be my motive
And helper to a husband. But, O strange
   men!
That can such sweet use make of what
   they hate,
When saucy trusting of the cozen'd
   thoughts
Defiles the pitchy night! so lust doth play
With what it loathes, for that which is
   away:
But more of this hereafter.—You, Diana,
Under my poor instructions yet must suffer
Something in my behalf.

DIANA.
                 Let death and honesty
Go with your impositions, I am yours
Upon your will to suffer.

HELENA.
                    Yet, I pray you:
But with the word the time will bring on
   summer,
When briers shall have leaves as well as
   thorns,
And be as sweet as sharp. We must away;
Our waggon is prepar'd, and time revives
   us:
All's well that ends well: still the fine's the
   crown;
Whate'er the course, the end is the
   renown.

                 [*Exeunt.*]

SCENE V

Rousillon. A room in the countess's palace.
[*Enter* COUNTESS, LAFEU, *and* CLOWN.]

LAFEU.
No, no, no, son was misled with a snipt-taffeta fellow there, whose villanous saffron would have made all the unbaked and doughy youth of a nation in his colour: your daughter-in-law had been alive at this hour, and your son here at home, more advanced by the king than by that red-tail'd humble-bee I speak of.

COUNTESS.
I would I had not known him! It was the death of the most virtuous gentlewoman that ever nature had praise for creating: if she had partaken of my flesh, and cost me the dearest groans of a mother, I could not have owed her a more rooted love.

LAFEU.
'Twas a good lady, 'twas a good lady: we may pick a thousand salads ere we light on such another herb.

CLOWN.
Indeed, sir, she was the sweet marjoram of the salad, or, rather, the herb of grace.

LAFEU.
They are not salad-herbs, you knave; they are nose-herbs.

CLOWN.
I am no great Nebuchadnezzar, sir; I have not much skill in grass.

LAFEU.
Whether dost thou profess thyself, a knave or a fool?

CLOWN.
A fool, sir, at a woman's service, and a knave at a man's.

LAFEU.
Your distinction?

CLOWN.
I would cozen the man of his wife, and do his service.

LAFEU.
So you were a knave at his service, indeed.

CLOWN.
And I would give his wife my bauble, sir, to do her service.

LAFEU.
I will subscribe for thee; thou art both knave and fool.

CLOWN.
At your service.

LAFEU.
No, no, no.

CLOWN.
Why, sir, if I cannot serve you, I can serve as great a prince as you are.

LAFEU.
Who's that? a Frenchman?

CLOWN.
Faith, sir, a' has an English name; but his phisnomy is more hotter in France than there.

LAFEU.
What prince is that?

CLOWN.
The black prince, sir; alias, the prince of darkness; alias, the devil.

LAFEU.
Hold thee, there's my purse: I give thee not this to suggest thee from thy master thou talkest of; serve him still.

CLOWN.
I am a woodland fellow, sir, that always loved a great fire; and the master I speak of ever keeps a good fire. But, sure, he is the prince of the world; let his nobility remain in his court. I am for the house with the narrow gate, which I take to be too little for pomp to enter: some that humble themselves may; but the many will be too chill and tender; and they'll be for the flow'ry way that leads to the broad gate and the great fire.

LAFEU.
Go thy ways, I begin to be a-weary of thee; and I tell thee so before, because I would not fall out with thee. Go thy ways; let my horses be well looked to, without any tricks.

CLOWN.
If I put any tricks upon 'em, sir, they shall be jades' tricks, which are their own right by the law of nature.

[Exit.]

LAFEU.
A shrewd knave, and an unhappy.

COUNTESS.
So he is. My lord that's gone made himself much sport out of him; by his authority he remains here, which he thinks is a patent for his sauciness; and indeed he has no pace, but runs where he will.

LAFEU.
I like him well; 'tis not amiss. And I was about to tell you, since I heard of the good lady's death, and that my lord your son was

upon his return home, I moved the king my master to speak in the behalf of my daughter; which, in the minority of them both, his majesty out of a self-gracious remembrance did first propose: His highness hath promised me to do it; and, to stop up the displeasure he hath conceived against your son, there is no fitter matter. How does your ladyship like it?

COUNTESS.
With very much content, my lord; and I wish it happily effected.

LAFEU.
His highness comes post from Marseilles, of as able body as when he numbered thirty; he will be here to-morrow, or I am deceived by him that in such intelligence hath seldom failed.

COUNTESS.
It rejoices me that I hope I shall see him ere I die. I have letters that my son will be here to-night: I shall beseech your lordship to remain with me till they meet together.

LAFEU.
Madam, I was thinking with what manners I might safely be admitted.

COUNTESS.
You need but plead your honourable privilege.

LAFEU.
Lady, of that I have made a bold charter; but, I thank my God, it holds yet.

[Re-enter CLOWN.]

CLOWN.
O madam, yonder's my lord your son with a patch of velvet on's face; whether there be a scar under it or no, the velvet knows; but 'tis a goodly patch of velvet: his left cheek is a cheek of two pile and a half, but his right cheek is worn bare.

LAFEU.
A scar nobly got, or a noble scar, is a good livery of honour; so belike is that.

CLOWN.
But it is your carbonadoed face.

LAFEU.
Let us go see your son, I pray you; I long to talk with the young noble soldier.

Clown.

Faith, there's a dozen of 'em, with delicate fine hats, and most courteous feathers, which bow the head and nod at every man.

[Exeunt.]

ACT V
SCENE I

Marseilles. A street.

[Enter Helena, Widow, *and* Diana, *with two* Attendants.*]*

Helena.

But this exceeding posting day and night
Must wear your spirits low: we cannot help it.
But since you have made the days and nights as one,
To wear your gentle limbs in my affairs,
Be bold you do so grow in my requital
As nothing can unroot you. In happy time;—

[Enter a Gentleman.*]*

This man may help me to his majesty's ear,
If he would spend his power.—God save you, sir.

Gentleman.

And you.

Helena.

Sir, I have seen you in the court of France.

Gentleman.

I have been sometimes there.

Helena.

I do presume, sir, that you are not fallen
From the report that goes upon your goodness;
And therefore, goaded with most sharp occasions,
Which lay nice manners by, I put you to
The use of your own virtues, for the which
I shall continue thankful.

Gentleman.

          What's your will?

Helena.

That it will please you
To give this poor petition to the king;
And aid me with that store of power you have
To come into his presence.

Gentleman.

The king's not here.

Helena.

          Not here, sir?

Gentleman.

          Not, indeed.
He hence remov'd last night, and with more haste
Than is his use.

Widow.

          Lord, how we lose our pains!

Helena.

All's well that ends well yet,
Though time seem so adverse and means unfit.
I do beseech you, whither is he gone?

Gentleman.

Marry, as I take it, to Rousillon;
Whither I am going.

Helena.

          I do beseech you, sir,
Since you are like to see the king before me,
Commend the paper to his gracious hand;
Which I presume shall render you no blame,
But rather make you thank your pains for it:
I will come after you with what good speed
Our means will make us means.

Gentleman.

          This I'll do for you.

Helena.

And you shall find yourself to be well thank'd,
Whate'er falls more.—We must to horse again;—
Go, go, provide.

[Exeunt.]

SCENE II

Rousillon. The inner court of the countess's palace.

[Enter Clown *and* Parolles.*]*

Parolles.

Good Monsieur Lavache, give my Lord Lafeu this letter: I have ere now, sir, been better known to you, when I have held familiarity with fresher clothes; but I am now, sir, muddied in fortune's mood, and smell somewhat strong of her strong displeasure.

CLOWN.
Truly, Fortune's displeasure is but sluttish, if it smell so strongly as thou speak'st of: I will henceforth eat no fish of fortune's buttering. Pr'ythee, allow the wind.

PAROLLES.
Nay, you need not to stop your nose, sir; I spake but by a metaphor.

CLOWN.
Indeed, sir, if your metaphor stink, I will stop my nose; or against any man's metaphor. Pr'ythee, get thee further.

PAROLLES.
Pray you, sir, deliver me this paper.

CLOWN.
Foh, pr'ythee stand away. A paper from Fortune's close-stool to give to a nobleman! Look here he comes himself. [*Enter* LAFEU.] Here is a pur of fortune's, sir, or of fortune's cat—but not a musk-cat—that has fallen into the unclean fishpond of her displeasure, and, as he says, is muddied withal: pray you, sir, use the carp as you may; for he looks like a poor, decayed, ingenious, foolish, rascally knave. I do pity his distress in my similes of comfort, and leave him to your lordship. [*Exit.*]

PAROLLES.
My lord, I am a man whom fortune hath cruelly scratched.

LAFEU.
And what would you have me to do? 'tis too late to pare her nails now. Wherein have you played the knave with fortune, that she should scratch you, who of herself is a good lady, and would not have knaves thrive long under her? There's a cardecu for you: let the justices make you and fortune friends; I am for other business.

PAROLLES.
I beseech your honour to hear me one single word.

LAFEU.
You beg a single penny more: come, you shall ha't: save your word.

PAROLLES.
My name, my good lord, is Parolles.

LAFEU.
You beg more than "word" then.—Cox my passion! give me your hand:—how does your drum?

PAROLLES.
O my good lord, you were the first that found me.

LAFEU.
Was I, in sooth? and I was the first that lost thee.

PAROLLES.
It lies in you, my lord, to bring me in some grace, for you did bring me out.

LAFEU.
Out upon thee, knave! dost thou put upon me at once both the office of God and the devil? one brings thee in grace, and the other brings thee out. [*Trumpets sound.*] The king's coming; I know by his trumpets.— Sirrah, inquire further after me; I had talk of you last night: though you are a fool and a knave, you shall eat: go to; follow.

PAROLLES.
I praise God for you.
                    [*Exeunt.*]

SCENE III

The same. A room in the countess's palace.
[*Flourish. Enter* KING, COUNTESS, LAFEU, LORDS, GENTLEMEN, GUARDS, &C.]

KING.
We lost a jewel of her; and our esteem
Was made much poorer by it: but your son,
As mad in folly, lack'd the sense to know
Her estimation home.

COUNTESS.
                    'Tis past, my liege:
And I beseech your majesty to make it
Natural rebellion, done i' the blaze of
        youth,
When oil and fire, too strong for reason's
        force,
O'erbears it and burns on.

KING.

My honour'd lady,
I have forgiven and forgotten all;
Though my revenges were high bent upon
him,
And watch'd the time to shoot.

LAFEU.

This I must say,—
But first, I beg my pardon,—the young
lord
Did to his majesty, his mother, and his lady,
Offence of mighty note; but to himself
The greatest wrong of all: he lost a wife
Whose beauty did astonish the survey
Of richest eyes; whose words all ears took
captive;
Whose dear perfection hearts that scorn'd
to serve
Humbly call'd mistress.

KING.

Praising what is lost
Makes the remembrance dear. Well, call
him hither;
We are reconcil'd, and the first view shall
kill
All repetition:—let him not ask our
pardon;
The nature of his great offence is dead,
And deeper than oblivion do we bury
Th' incensing relics of it; let him approach,
A stranger, no offender; and inform him,
So 'tis our will he should.

GENTLEMAN.

I shall, my liege.

[*Exit* GENTLEMAN.]

KING.

What says he to your daughter? have you
spoke?

LAFEU.

All that he is hath reference to your
highness.

KING.

Then shall we have a match. I have letters
sent me
That sets him high in fame.

[*Enter* BERTRAM.]

LAFEU.

He looks well on 't.

KING.

I am not a day of season,
For thou mayst see a sunshine and a hail
In me at once: but to the brightest beams
Distracted clouds give way; so stand thou
forth;
The time is fair again.

BERTRAM.

My high-repented blames,
Dear sovereign, pardon to me.

KING.

All is whole;
Not one word more of the consumed time.
Let's take the instant by the forward top;
For we are old, and on our quick'st decrees
The inaudible and noiseless foot of time
Steals ere we can effect them. You
remember
The daughter of this lord?

BERTRAM.

Admiringly, my liege: at first
I stuck my choice upon her, ere my heart
Durst make too bold herald of my tongue:
Where the impression of mine eye infixing,
Contempt his scornful perspective did
lend me,
Which warp'd the line of every other
favour;
Scorned a fair colour, or express'd it stolen;
Extended or contracted all proportions
To a most hideous object: thence it came
That she whom all men prais'd, and whom
myself,
Since I have lost, have lov'd, was in mine
eye
The dust that did offend it.

KING.

Well excus'd:
That thou didst love her, strikes some
scores away
From the great compt: but love that comes
too late,
Like a remorseful pardon slowly carried,
To the great sender turns a sour offence,
Crying, "That's good that's gone." Our
rasher faults
Make trivial price of serious things we
have,

Not knowing them until we know their
    grave:
Oft our displeasures, to ourselves unjust,
Destroy our friends, and after weep their
    dust:
Our own love waking cries to see what's
    done,
While shameful hate sleeps out the
    afternoon.
Be this sweet Helen's knell, and now
    forget her.
Send forth your amorous token for fair
    Maudlin:
The main consents are had; and here we'll
    stay
To see our widower's second marriage-day.
COUNTESS.
Which better than the first, O dear
    heaven, bless!
Or, ere they meet, in me, O nature, cesse!
LAFEU.
Come on, my son, in whom my house's
    name
Must be digested, give a favour from you,
To sparkle in the spirits of my daughter,
That she may quickly come.—
    [BERTRAM *gives a ring to* LAFEU.]
                By my old beard,
And every hair that's on 't, Helen, that's
    dead,
Was a sweet creature: such a ring as this,
The last that e'er I took her leave at court,
I saw upon her finger.
BERTRAM.
                Hers it was not.
KING.
Now, pray you, let me see it; for mine eye,
While I was speaking, oft was fasten'd to
    it.—
This ring was mine; and when I gave it
    Helen
I bade her, if her fortunes ever stood
Necessitied to help, that by this token
I would relieve her. Had you that craft to
    'reave her
Of what should stead her most?
BERTRAM.
              My gracious sovereign,

Howe'er it pleases you to take it so,
The ring was never hers.
COUNTESS.
              Son, on my life,
I have seen her wear it; and she reckon'd it
At her life's rate.
LAFEU.
           I am sure I saw her wear it.
BERTRAM.
You are deceiv'd, my lord; she never saw it:
In Florence was it from a casement
    thrown me,
Wrapp'd in a paper, which contain'd the
    name
Of her that threw it: noble she was, and
    thought
I stood engag'd: but when I had subscrib'd
To mine own fortune, and inform'd her
    fully
I could not answer in that course of
    honour
As she had made the overture, she ceas'd,
In heavy satisfaction, and would never
Receive the ring again.
KING.
             Plutus himself,
That knows the tinct and multiplying
    medicine,
Hath not in nature's mystery more science
Than I have in this ring: 'twas mine, 'twas
    Helen's,
Whoever gave it you. Then, if you know
That you are well acquainted with yourself,
Confess 'twas hers, and by what rough
    enforcement
You got it from her: she call'd the saints
    to surety
That she would never put it from her
    finger
Unless she gave it to yourself in bed,—
Where you have never come,—or sent
    it us
Upon her great disaster.
BERTRAM.
             She never saw it.
KING.
Thou speak'st it falsely, as I love mine
    honour;

And mak'st conjectural fears to come into
    me
Which I would fain shut out. If it should
    prove
That thou art so inhuman,—'twill not
    prove so:—
And yet I know not:—thou didst hate her
    deadly.
And she is dead; which nothing, but to
    close
Her eyes myself, could win me to believe
More than to see this ring.—Take him
    away.
        [GUARDS *seize* BERTRAM.]
My fore-past proofs, howe'er the matter
    fall,
Shall tax my fears of little vanity,
Having vainly fear'd too little.—Away
    with him!—
We'll sift this matter further.

BERTRAM.
                If you shall prove
This ring was ever hers, you shall as easy
Prove that I husbanded her bed in
    Florence,
Where she yet never was.
        [*Exit, guarded.*]

KING.
I am wrapp'd in dismal thinkings.
        [*Enter a* GENTLEMAN.]

GENTLEMAN.
             Gracious sovereign,
Whether I have been to blame or no, I
    know not:
Here's a petition from a Florentine,
Who hath, for four or five removes, come
    short
To tender it herself. I undertook it,
Vanquish'd thereto by the fair grace and
    speech
Of the poor suppliant, who by this, I know,
Is here attending: her business looks in her
With an importing visage; and she told me
In a sweet verbal brief, it did concern
Your highness with herself.

KING. [*Reads.*]
"Upon his many protestations to marry me,
when his wife was dead, I blush to say it,

he won me. Now is the Count Rousillon a
widower; his vows are forfeited to me, and
my honour's paid to him. He stole from
Florence, taking no leave, and I follow him
to his country for justice: grant it me, O
king; in you it best lies; otherwise a seducer
flourishes, and a poor maid is undone.
                        Diana Capulet."

LAFEU.
I will buy me a son-in-law in a fair, and toll
this: I'll none of him.

KING.
The heavens have thought well on thee,
    Lafeu,
To bring forth this discovery.—Seek these
    suitors:—
Go speedily, and bring again the count.
        [*Exeunt* GENTLEMAN, *and some*
                ATTENDANTS.]
I am afeard the life of Helen, lady,
Was foully snatch'd.

COUNTESS.
             Now, justice on the doers!
        [*Enter* BERTRAM, *guarded.*]

KING.
I wonder, sir, since wives are monsters to
    you.
And that you fly them as you swear them
    lordship,
Yet you desire to marry.—What woman's
    that?
        [*Re-enter* WIDOW *and* DIANA.]

DIANA.
I am, my lord, a wretched Florentine,
Derived from the ancient Capulet;
My suit, as I do understand, you know,
And therefore know how far I may be
    pitied.

WIDOW.
I am her mother, sir, whose age and
    honour
Both suffer under this complaint we bring,
And both shall cease, without your remedy.

KING.
Come hither, count; do you know these
    women?

BERTRAM.
My lord, I neither can nor will deny

But that I know them: do they charge me
    further?
DIANA.
Why do you look so strange upon your
    wife?
BERTRAM.
She's none of mine, my lord.
DIANA.
                    If you shall marry,
You give away this hand, and that is mine;
You give away heaven's vows, and those
    are mine;
You give away myself, which is known
    mine;
For I by vow am so embodied yours
That she which marries you must marry
    me,
Either both or none.
LAFEU. [*To* BERTRAM.]
Your reputation comes too short for my
daughter; you are no husband for her.
BERTRAM.
My lord, this is a fond and desperate
    creature
Whom sometime I have laugh'd with: let
    your highness
Lay a more noble thought upon mine
    honour
Than for to think that I would sink it here.
KING.
Sir, for my thoughts, you have them ill to
    friend
Till your deeds gain them: fairer prove
    your honour
Than in my thought it lies!
DIANA.
                    Good my lord,
Ask him upon his oath, if he does think
He had not my virginity.
KING.
What say'st thou to her?
BERTRAM.
                    She's impudent, my lord;
And was a common gamester to the camp.
DIANA.
He does me wrong, my lord; if I were so
He might have bought me at a common
    price:

Do not believe him. O, behold this ring,
Whose high respect and rich validity
Did lack a parallel; yet, for all that,
He gave it to a commoner o' the camp,
If I be one.
COUNTESS.
                    He blushes, and 'tis his:
Of six preceding ancestors, that gem,
Conferr'd by testament to the sequent
    issue,
Hath it been ow'd and worn. This is his
    wife;
That ring's a thousand proofs.
KING.
                    Methought you said
You saw one here in court could witness it.
DIANA.
I did, my lord, but loath am to produce
So bad an instrument; his name's Parolles.
LAFEU.
I saw the man to-day, if man he be.
KING.
Find him, and bring him hither.
                    [*Exit an* ATTENDANT.]
BERTRAM.
                    What of him?
He's quoted for a most perfidious slave,
With all the spots o' the world tax'd and
    debauch'd:
Whose nature sickens but to speak a truth:
Am I or that or this for what he'll utter,
That will speak anything?
KING.
                    She hath that ring of yours.
BERTRAM.
I think she has: certain it is I lik'd her,
And boarded her i' the wanton way of
    youth:
She knew her distance, and did angle for
    me,
Madding my eagerness with her restraint,
As all impediments in fancy's course
Are motives of more fancy; and, in fine,
Her infinite cunning with her modern
    grace,
Subdu'd me to her rate: she got the ring;
And I had that which any inferior might
At market-price have bought.

DIANA.

I must be patient:
You that have turn'd off a first so noble
wife
May justly diet me. I pray you yet,—
Since you lack virtue, I will lose a
husband,—
Send for your ring, I will return it home,
And give me mine again.

BERTRAM.

I have it not.

KING.

What ring was yours, I pray you?

DIANA.

Sir, much like
The same upon your finger.

KING.

Know you this ring? this ring was his of
late.

DIANA.

And this was it I gave him, being a-bed.

KING.

The story, then, goes false you threw it him
Out of a casement.

DIANA.

I have spoke the truth.

BERTRAM.

My lord, I do confess the ring was hers.

KING.

You boggle shrewdly; every feather starts
you.—

[*Re-enter* ATTENDANT, *with* PAROLLES.]
Is this the man you speak of?

DIANA.

Ay, my lord.

KING.

Tell me, sirrah, but tell me true I charge
you,
Not fearing the displeasure of your
master,—
Which, on your just proceeding, I'll keep
off,—
By him and by this woman here what
know you?

PAROLLES.

So please your majesty, my master hath
been an honourable gentleman; tricks he
hath had in him, which gentlemen have.

KING.

Come, come, to the purpose: did he love
this woman?

PAROLLES.

Faith, sir, he did love her; but how?

KING.

How, I pray you?

PAROLLES.

He did love her, sir, as a gentleman loves
a woman.

KING.

How is that?

PAROLLES.

He loved her, sir, and loved her not.

KING.

As thou art a knave and no knave.—
What an equivocal companion is this!

PAROLLES.

I am a poor man, and at your majesty's
command.

LAFEU.

He's a good drum, my lord, but a naughty
orator.

DIANA.

Do you know he promised me marriage?

PAROLLES.

Faith, I know more than I'll speak.

KING.

But wilt thou not speak all thou know'st?

PAROLLES.

Yes, so please your majesty; I did go
between them, as I said; but more than
that, he loved her,—for indeed he was mad
for her, and talked of Satan, and of limbo,
and of furies, and I know not what: yet I
was in that credit with them at that time
that I knew of their going to bed; and of
other motions, as promising her marriage,
and things which would derive me ill-will
to speak of; therefore I will not speak what
I know.

KING.

Thou hast spoken all already, unless thou
canst say they are married: but thou art too
fine in thy evidence; therefore stand aside.—
This ring, you say, was yours?

DIANA.

Ay, my good lord.

KING.
Where did you buy it? or who gave it you?
DIANA.
It was not given me, nor I did not buy it.
KING.
Who lent it you?
DIANA.
                    It was not lent me neither.
KING.
Where did you find it then?
DIANA.
                        I found it not.
KING.
If it were yours by none of all these ways,
How could you give it him?
DIANA.
                        I never gave it him.
LAFEU.
This woman's an easy glove, my lord; she
goes off and on at pleasure.
KING.
This ring was mine, I gave it his first wife.
DIANA.
It might be yours or hers, for aught I
    know.
KING.
Take her away, I do not like her now;
To prison with her: and away with him.—
Unless thou tell'st me where thou hadst
    this ring,
Thou diest within this hour.
DIANA.
                    I'll never tell you.
KING.
Take her away.
DIANA.
                I'll put in bail, my liege.
KING.
I think thee now some common customer.
DIANA.
By Jove, if ever I knew man, 'twas you.
KING.
Wherefore hast thou accus'd him all this
    while?
DIANA.
Because he's guilty, and he is not guilty:
He knows I am no maid, and he'll swear
    to't:

I'll swear I am a maid, and he knows not.
Great king, I am no strumpet, by my life;
I am either maid, or else this old man's
    wife.
                [*Pointing to* LAFEU.]
KING.
She does abuse our ears; to prison with
    her.
DIANA.
Good mother, fetch my bail.—Stay, royal
    sir.
                    [*Exit* WIDOW.]
The jeweller that owes the ring is sent for,
And he shall surety me. But for this lord
Who hath abus'd me as he knows himself,
Though yet he never harm'd me, here I
    quit him:
He knows himself my bed he hath defil'd;
And at that time he got his wife with child.
Dead though she be, she feels her young
    one kick;
So there's my riddle:—One that's dead is
    quick;
And now behold the meaning.
        [*Re-enter* WIDOW *with* HELENA.]
KING.
                        Is there no exorcist
Beguiles the truer office of mine eyes?
Is't real that I see?
HELENA.
                No, my good lord;
'Tis but the shadow of a wife you see—
The name, and not the thing.
BERTRAM.
                        Both, both; O, pardon!
HELENA.
O, my good lord, when I was like this
    maid;
I found you wondrous kind. There is your
    ring,
And, look you, here's your letter. This it
    says,
"When from my finger you can get this
    ring,
And are by me with child, etc."—This is
    done:
Will you be mine now you are doubly
    won?

BERTRAM.

If she, my liege, can make me know this
   clearly,

I'll love her dearly, ever, ever dearly.

HELENA.

If it appear not plain, and prove untrue,

Deadly divorce step between me and
   you!—

O my dear mother, do I see you living?

LAFEU.

Mine eyes smell onions; I shall weep
   anon:—

         [*To* PAROLLES.]

Good Tom Drum, lend me a handkercher:
so, I thank thee; wait on me home, I'll make
sport with thee: let thy courtesies alone,
they are scurvy ones.

KING.

Let us from point to point this story
   know,

To make the even truth in pleasure
   flow:—

         [*To* DIANA.]

If thou beest yet a fresh uncropped flower,

Choose thou thy husband, and I'll pay thy
   dower;

For I can guess that, by thy honest aid,

Thou kept'st a wife herself, thyself a maid.

Of that and all the progress, more and less,

Resolvedly more leisure shall express:

All yet seems well; and if it end so meet,

The bitter past, more welcome is the sweet.

         [*Flourish.*]

EPILOGUE

[*Spoken by the* KING.]

The king's a beggar, now the play is
   done;

All is well ended if this suit be won,

That you express content; which we will
   pay

With strife to please you, day exceeding
   day:

Ours be your patience then, and yours
   our parts;

Your gentle hands lend us, and take our
   hearts.

         [*Exeunt.*]

Twelfth Night, or What You Will

DRAMATIS PERSONAE

ORSINO, *Duke of Illyria*
SEBASTIAN, *a young gentleman, brother to Viola*
ANTONIO, *a sea captain, friend to Sebastian*
A SEA CAPTAIN, *friend to Viola*
VALENTINE, *gentleman attending on the duke*
CURIO, *gentleman attending on the duke*
SIR TOBY BELCH, *uncle of Olivia*
SIR ANDREW AGUECHEEK
MALVOLIO, *steward to Olivia*

FABIAN, *servant to Olivia*
CLOWN, *servant to Olivia*
OLIVIA, *a rich countess*
VIOLA, *in love with the duke*
MARIA, *Olivia's woman*
LORDS, PRIESTS, SAILORS, OFFICERS, MUSICIANS, *and other* ATTENDANTS

SCENE: *A city in Illyria; and the sea coast near it.*

ACT I
SCENE I

An apartment in the duke's palace.
[*Enter* DUKE, CURIO, LORDS; MUSICIANS *attending.*]

DUKE.

If music be the food of love, play on,
Give me excess of it; that, surfeiting,
The appetite may sicken and so die.—
That strain again;—it had a dying fall;
O, it came o'er my ear like the sweet sound,
That breathes upon a bank of violets,
Stealing and giving odour.—Enough; no more;
'Tis not so sweet now as it was before.
O spirit of love, how quick and fresh art thou!
That, notwithstanding thy capacity
Receiveth as the sea, nought enters there,
Of what validity and pitch soever,
But falls into abatement and low price
Even in a minute! so full of shapes is fancy,
That it alone is high-fantastical.

CURIO.

Will you go hunt, my lord?

DUKE.

What, Curio?

CURIO.

The hart.

DUKE.

Why, so I do, the noblest that I have:
O, when mine eyes did see Olivia first,
Methought she purg'd the air of pestilence;
That instant was I turn'd into a hart;
And my desires, like fell and cruel hounds,
E'er since pursue me.—
[*Enter* VALENTINE.]
How now! what news from her?

VALENTINE.

So please my lord, I might not be admitted,
But from her handmaid do return this answer:
The element itself, till seven years' hence,
Shall not behold her face at ample view;
But like a cloistress she will veiled walk,

And water once a-day her chamber round
With eye-offending brine: all this to
  season
A brother's dead love, which she would
  keep fresh
And lasting in her sad remembrance.

Duke.
O, she that hath a heart of that fine frame
To pay this debt of love but to a brother,
How will she love when the rich golden
  shaft
Hath kill'd the flock of all affections else
That live in her; when liver, brain, and
  heart,
These sovereign thrones, are all supplied
  and fill'd,—
Her sweet perfections,—with one self
  king!—
Away before me to sweet beds of flowers:
Love-thoughts lie rich when canopied
  with bowers.

[Exeunt.]

SCENE II
The sea coast.
[Enter Viola, Captain, *and* Sailors.*]*

Viola.
What country, friends, is this?

Captain.
This is Illyria, lady.

Viola.
And what should I do in Illyria?
My brother he is in Elysium.
Perchance he is not drown'd—What think
  you, sailors?

Captain.
It is perchance that you yourself were sav'd.

Viola.
O my poor brother! and so perchance may
  he be.

Captain.
True, madam; and, to comfort you with
  chance,
Assure yourself, after our ship did split,
When you, and those poor number sav'd
  with you,
Hung on our driving boat, I saw your
  brother,

Most provident in peril, bind himself,—
Courage and hope both teaching him the
  practice,—
To a strong mast that liv'd upon the sea;
Where, like Arion on the dolphin's back,
I saw him hold acquaintance with the
  waves
So long as I could see.

Viola.
For saying so, there's gold!
Mine own escape unfoldeth to my hope,
Whereto thy speech serves for authority,
The like of him. Know'st thou this
  country?

Captain.
Ay, madam, well; for I was bred and born
Not three hours' travel from this very
  place.

Viola.
Who governs here?

Captain.
A noble duke, in nature as in name.

Viola.
What is his name?

Captain.
Orsino.

Viola.
Orsino! I have heard my father name him.
He was a bachelor then.

Captain.
And so is now, or was so very late;
For but a month ago I went from hence;
And then 'twas fresh in murmur,—as, you
  know,
What great ones do, the less will prattle
  of,—
That he did seek the love of fair Olivia.

Viola.
What's she?

Captain.
A virtuous maid, the daughter of a count
That died some twelvemonth since; then
  leaving her
In the protection of his son, her brother,
Who shortly also died; for whose dear
  love,
They say, she hath abjured the company
And sight of men.

VIOLA.
           O that I served that lady!
And might not be delivered to the world,
Till I had made mine own occasion mellow,
What my estate is.

CAPTAIN.
           That were hard to compass:
Because she will admit no kind of suit,
No, not the duke's.

VIOLA.
There is a fair behaviour in thee, captain;
And though that nature with a beauteous wall
Doth oft close in pollution, yet of thee
I will believe thou hast a mind that suits
With this thy fair and outward character.
I pray thee, and I'll pay thee bounteously,
Conceal me what I am; and be my aid
For such disguise as, haply, shall become
The form of my intent. I'll serve this duke;
Thou shalt present me as an eunuch to him;
It may be worth thy pains, for I can sing,
And speak to him in many sorts of music,
That will allow me very worth his service.
What else may hap to time I will commit;
Only shape thou silence to my wit.

CAPTAIN.
Be you his eunuch and your mute I'll be;
When my tongue blabs, then let mine eyes not see.

VIOLA.
I thank thee. Lead me on.
           [*Exeunt.*]

SCENE III

A room in Olivia's house.

[*Enter* SIR TOBY BELCH *and* MARIA.]

SIR TOBY.
What a plague means my niece, to take the death of her brother thus? I am sure care's an enemy to life.

MARIA.
By my troth, Sir Toby, you must come in earlier o' nights; your cousin, my lady, takes great exceptions to your ill hours.

SIR TOBY.
Why, let her except, before excepted.

MARIA.
Ay, but you must confine yourself within the modest limits of order.

SIR TOBY.
Confine? I'll confine myself no finer than I am: these clothes are good enough to drink in, and so be these boots too; an they be not, let them hang themselves in their own straps.

MARIA.
That quaffing and drinking will undo you: I heard my lady talk of it yesterday; and of a foolish knight that you brought in one night here to be her wooer.

SIR TOBY.
Who? Sir Andrew Aguecheek?

MARIA.
Ay, he.

SIR TOBY.
He's as tall a man as any's in Illyria.

MARIA.
What's that to the purpose?

SIR TOBY.
Why, he has three thousand ducats a year.

MARIA.
Ay, but he'll have but a year in all these ducats; he's a very fool, and a prodigal.

SIR TOBY.
Fye that you'll say so! he plays o' the viol-de-gambo, and speaks three or four languages word for word without book, and hath all the good gifts of nature.

MARIA.
He hath indeed,—almost natural: for, besides that he's a fool, he's a great quarreller; and, but that he hath the gift of a coward to allay the gust he hath in quarrelling, 'tis thought among the prudent he would quickly have the gift of a grave.

SIR TOBY.
By this hand, they are scoundrels and subtractors that say so of him. Who are they?

MARIA.
They that add, moreover, he's drunk nightly in your company.

SIR TOBY.
With drinking healths to my niece; I'll

drink to her as long as there is a passage in my throat and drink in Illyria. He's a coward and a coystril that will not drink to my niece till his brains turn o' the toe like a parish-top. What, wench! *Castiliano–vulgo!* for here comes Sir Andrew Ague-face.

[*Enter* Sir Andrew Aguecheek.]

Sir Andrew.
Sir Toby Belch! how now, Sir Toby Belch!

Sir Toby.
Sweet Sir Andrew?

Sir Andrew.
Bless you, fair shrew.

Maria.
And you too, sir.

Sir Toby.
Accost, Sir Andrew, accost.

Sir Andrew.
What's that?

Sir Toby.
My niece's chamber-maid.

Sir Andrew.
Good Mistress Accost, I desire better acquaintance.

Maria.
My name is Mary, sir.

Sir Andrew.
Good Mistress Mary Accost,—

Sir Toby.
You mistake, knight: accost is, front her, board her, woo her, assail her.

Sir Andrew.
By my troth, I would not undertake her in this company. Is that the meaning of accost?

Maria.
Fare you well, gentlemen.

Sir Toby.
An thou let part so, Sir Andrew, would thou mightst never draw sword again.

Sir Andrew.
An you part so, mistress, I would I might never draw sword again. Fair lady, do you think you have fools in hand?

Maria.
Sir, I have not you by the hand.

Sir Andrew.
Marry, but you shall have; and here's my hand.

Maria.
Now, sir, thought is free. I pray you, bring your hand to the buttery-bar and let it drink.

Sir Andrew.
Wherefore, sweetheart? what's your metaphor?

Maria.
It's dry, sir.

Sir Andrew.
Why, I think so; I am not such an ass but I can keep my hand dry. But what's your jest?

Maria.
A dry jest, sir.

Sir Andrew.
Are you full of them?

Maria.
Ay, sir, I have them at my fingers' ends: marry, now I let go your hand I am barren.
[*Exit* Maria.]

Sir Toby.
O knight, thou lack'st a cup of canary: When did I see thee so put down?

Sir Andrew.
Never in your life, I think; unless you see canary put me down. Methinks sometimes I have no more wit than a Christian or an ordinary man has; but I am great eater of beef, and, I believe, that does harm to my wit.

Sir Toby.
No question.

Sir Andrew.
An I thought that, I'd forswear it. I'll ride home to-morrow, Sir Toby.

Sir Toby.
Pourquoy, my dear knight?

Sir Andrew.
What is *pourquoy?* do or not do? I would I had bestowed that time in the tongues that I have in fencing, dancing, and bear-baiting. Oh, had I but followed the arts!

Sir Toby.
Then hadst thou had an excellent head of hair.

Sir Andrew.
Why, would that have mended my hair?

Sir Toby.

Past question; for thou seest it will not curl by nature.

Sir Andrew.

But it becomes me well enough, does't not?

Sir Toby.

Excellent; it hangs like flax on a distaff; and I hope to see a housewife take thee between her legs and spin it off.

Sir Andrew.

Faith, I'll home to-morrow, Sir Toby; your niece will not be seen; or, if she be, it's four to one she'll none of me; the count himself here hard by woos her.

Sir Toby.

She'll none o' the count; she'll not match above her degree, neither in estate, years, nor wit; I have heard her swear't. Tut, there's life in't, man.

Sir Andrew.

I'll stay a month longer. I am a fellow o' the strangest mind i' the world; I delight in masques and revels sometimes altogether.

Sir Toby.

Art thou good at these kick-shaws, knight?

Sir Andrew.

As any man in Illyria, whatsoever he be, under the degree of my betters; and yet I will not compare with an old man.

Sir Toby.

What is thy excellence in a galliard, knight?

Sir Andrew.

Faith, I can cut a caper.

Sir Toby.

And I can cut the mutton to't.

Sir Andrew.

And, I think, I have the back-trick simply as strong as any man in Illyria.

Sir Toby.

Wherefore are these things hid? wherefore have these gifts a curtain before them? are they like to take dust, like Mistress Mall's picture? why dost thou not go to church in a galliard and come home in a coranto? My very walk should be a jig; I would not so much as make water but in a sink-a-pace. What dost thou mean? is it a world to hide

virtues in? I did think, by the excellent constitution of thy leg, it was formed under the star of a galliard.

Sir Andrew.

Ay, 'tis strong, and it does indifferent well in flame-colour'd stock. Shall we set about some revels?

Sir Toby.

What shall we do else? were we not born under Taurus?

Sir Andrew.

Taurus? that's sides and heart.

Sir Toby.

No, sir; it is legs and thighs. Let me see thee caper: ha, higher: ha, ha!—excellent!

[*Exeunt.*]

SCENE IV

A room in the duke's palace.

[*Enter* Valentine, *and* Viola *in man's attire.*]

Valentine.

If the duke continue these favours towards you, Cesario, you are like to be much advanced; he hath known you but three days, and already you are no stranger.

Viola.

You either fear his humour or my negligence, that you call in question the continuance of his love. Is he inconstant, sir, in his favours?

Valentine.

No, believe me.

[*Enter* Duke, Curio, *and* Attendants.]

Viola.

I thank you. Here comes the count.

Duke.

Who saw Cesario, ho?

Viola.

On your attendance, my lord; here.

Duke.

Stand you awhile aloof.—Cesario,
Thou know'st no less but all; I have unclasp'd
To thee the book even of my secret soul:
Therefore, good youth, address thy gait
    unto her;

Be not denied access, stand at her doors,
And tell them there thy fixed foot shall
    grow
Till thou have audience.

VIOLA.

                Sure, my noble lord,
If she be so abandon'd to her sorrow
As it is spoke, she never will admit me.

DUKE.

Be clamorous and leap all civil bounds,
Rather than make unprofited return.

VIOLA.

Say I do speak with her, my lord. What
    then?

DUKE.

O, then unfold the passion of my love,
Surprise her with discourse of my dear
    faith:
It shall become thee well to act my
    woes;
She will attend it better in thy youth
Than in a nuncio of more grave aspect.

VIOLA.

I think not so, my lord.

DUKE.

              Dear lad, believe it,
For they shall yet belie thy happy years
That say thou art a man: Diana's lip
Is not more smooth and rubious; thy small
    pipe
Is as the maiden's organ, shrill and sound,
And all is semblative a woman's part.
I know thy constellation is right apt
For this affair:—some four or five attend
    him:
All, if you will; for I myself am best
When least in company:—prosper well
    in this,
And thou shalt live as freely as thy lord,
To call his fortunes thine.

VIOLA.

                  I'll do my best
To woo your lady. [*Aside.*] Yet, a barful
    strife!
Whoe'er I woo, myself would be his
    wife.

              [*Exit.*]

SCENE V

A room in Olivia's house.

[*Enter* MARIA *and* CLOWN.]

MARIA.

Nay; either tell me where thou hast been, or
I will not open my lips so wide as a bristle
may enter in way of thy excuse: my lady will
hang thee for thy absence.

CLOWN.

Let her hang me: he that is well hanged in
this world needs to fear no colours.

MARIA.

Make that good.

CLOWN.

He shall see none to fear.

MARIA.

A good lenten answer: I can tell thee where
that saying was born, of, I fear no colours.

CLOWN.

Where, good Mistress Mary?

MARIA.

In the wars; and that may you be bold to
say in your foolery.

CLOWN.

Well, God give them wisdom that have it;
and those that are fools, let them use their
talents.

MARIA.

Yet you will be hanged for being so long
absent: or to be turned away; is not that as
good as a hanging to you?

CLOWN.

Many a good hanging prevents a bad
marriage; and for turning away, let summer
bear it out.

MARIA.

You are resolute, then?

CLOWN.

Not so, neither: but I am resolved on two
    points.

MARIA.

That if one break, the other will hold; or if
both break, your gaskins fall.

CLOWN.

Apt, in good faith, very apt! Well, go thy
way; if Sir Toby would leave drinking, thou
wert as witty a piece of Eve's flesh as any
in Illyria.

MARIA.

Peace, you rogue; no more o' that; here comes my lady: make your excuse wisely; you were best.

[*Exit.*]

[*Enter* OLIVIA *and* MALVOLIO.]

CLOWN.

Wit, and't be thy will, put me into good fooling! Those wits that think they have thee do very oft prove fools; and I, that am sure I lack thee, may pass for a wise man. For what says Quinapalus? Better a witty fool than a foolish wit.—God bless thee, lady!

OLIVIA.

Take the fool away.

CLOWN.

Do you not hear, fellows? Take away the lady.

OLIVIA.

Go to, you're a dry fool; I'll no more of you: besides, you grow dishonest.

CLOWN.

Two faults, madonna, that drink and good counsel will amend: for give the dry fool drink, then is the fool not dry; bid the dishonest man mend himself: if he mend, he is no longer dishonest; if he cannot, let the botcher mend him. Anything that's mended is but patched; virtue that transgresses is but patched with sin, and sin that amends is but patched with virtue. If that this simple syllogism will serve, so; if it will not, what remedy? As there is no true cuckold but calamity, so beauty's a flower:—the lady bade take away the fool; therefore, I say again, take her away.

OLIVIA.

Sir, I bade them take away you.

CLOWN.

Misprision in the highest degree!—Lady, *Cucullus non facit monachum;* that's as much to say, I wear not motley in my brain. Good madonna, give me leave to prove you a fool.

OLIVIA.

Can you do it?

CLOWN.

Dexteriously, good madonna.

OLIVIA.

Make your proof.

CLOWN.

I must catechize you for it, madonna. Good my mouse of virtue, answer me.

OLIVIA.

Well, sir, for want of other idleness, I'll 'bide your proof.

CLOWN.

Good madonna, why mourn'st thou?

OLIVIA.

Good fool, for my brother's death.

CLOWN.

I think his soul is in hell, madonna.

OLIVIA.

I know his soul is in heaven, fool.

CLOWN.

The more fool you, madonna, to mourn for your brother's soul being in heaven.—Take away the fool, gentlemen.

OLIVIA.

What think you of this fool, Malvolio? doth he not mend?

MALVOLIO.

Yes; and shall do, till the pangs of death shake him. Infirmity, that decays the wise, doth ever make the better fool.

CLOWN.

God send you, sir, a speedy infirmity, for the better increasing your folly! Sir Toby will be sworn that I am no fox; but he will not pass his word for twopence that you are no fool.

OLIVIA.

How say you to that, Malvolio?

MALVOLIO.

I marvel your ladyship takes delight in such a barren rascal; I saw him put down the other day with an ordinary fool that has no more brain than a stone. Look you now, he's out of his guard already; unless you laugh and minister occasion to him, he is gagged. I protest I take these wise men that crow so at these set kind of fools, no better than the fools' zanies.

OLIVIA.

O, you are sick of self-love, Malvolio, and taste with a distempered appetite. To be generous, guiltless, and of free disposition, is to take those things for bird-bolts that you deem cannon bullets. There is no slander in an allowed fool, though he do nothing but rail; nor no railing in known discreet man, though he do nothing but reprove.

Clown.
Now Mercury endue thee with leasing, for thou speakest well of fools!

        [Re-enter Maria.*]*

Maria.
Madam, there is at the gate a young gentleman much desires to speak with you.

Olivia.
From the Count Orsino, is it?

Maria.
I know not, madam; 'tis a fair young man, and well attended.

Olivia.
Who of my people hold him in delay?

Maria.
Sir Toby, madam, your kinsman.

Olivia.
Fetch him off, I pray you; he speaks nothing but madman. Fie on him! *[Exit* Maria.*]* Go you, Malvolio: if it be a suit from the count, I am sick, or not at home; what you will to dismiss it. *[Exit* Malvolio.*]* Now you see, sir, how your fooling grows old, and people dislike it.

Clown.
Thou hast spoke for us, madonna, as if thy eldest son should be a fool: whose skull Jove cram with brains, for here he comes— one of thy kin, has a most weak *pia mater.*

        [Enter Sir Toby Belch.*]*

Olivia.
By mine honour, half drunk!—What is he at the gate, cousin?

Sir Toby.
A gentleman.

Olivia.
A gentleman? What gentleman?

Sir Toby.
'Tis a gentleman here.—A plague o' these pickle-herrings!—How now, sot?

Clown.
Good Sir Toby,—

Olivia.
Cousin, cousin, how have you come so early by this lethargy?

Sir Toby.
Lechery! I defy lechery. There's one at the gate.

Olivia.
Ay, marry; what is he?

Sir Toby.
Let him be the devil an he will, I care not: give me faith, say I. Well, it's all one.

        [Exit.]

Olivia.
What's a drunken man like, fool?

Clown.
Like a drowned man, a fool, and a madman: one draught above heat makes him a fool; the second mads him; and a third drowns him.

Olivia.
Go thou and seek the coroner, and let him sit o' my coz; for he's in the third degree of drink; he's drowned: go, look after him.

Clown.
He is but mad yet, madonna; and the fool shall look to the madman.

        [Exit Clown.*]*
        [Re-enter Malvolio.*]*

Malvolio.
Madam, yond young fellow swears he will speak with you. I told him you were sick; he takes on him to understand so much, and therefore comes to speak with you; I told him you were asleep; he seems to have a foreknowledge of that too, and therefore comes to speak with you. What is to be said to him, lady? he's fortified against any denial.

Olivia.
Tell him, he shall not speak with me.

Malvolio.
Has been told so; and he says he'll stand at your door like a sheriff's post, and be the supporter of a bench, but he'll speak with you.

Olivia.
What kind of man is he?

Malvolio.
Why, of mankind.

OLIVIA.

What manner of man?

MALVOLIO.

Of very ill manner; he'll speak with you, will you or no.

OLIVIA.

Of what personage and years is he?

MALVOLIO.

Not yet old enough for a man, nor young enough for a boy; as a squash is before 'tis a peascod, or a codling, when 'tis almost an apple: 'tis with him e'en standing water, between boy and man. He is very well-favoured, and he speaks very shrewishly; one would think his mother's milk were scarce out of him.

OLIVIA.

Let him approach. Call in my gentlewoman.

MALVOLIO.

Gentlewoman, my lady calls.

[Exit.]

[Re-enter MARIA.]

OLIVIA.

Give me my veil; come, throw it o'er my face. We'll once more hear Orsino's embassy.

[Enter VIOLA.]

VIOLA.

The honourable lady of the house, which is she?

OLIVIA.

Speak to me; I shall answer for her. Your will?

VIOLA.

Most radiant, exquisite, and unmatchable beauty,—I pray you, tell me if this be the lady of the house, for I never saw her: I would be loath to cast away my speech; for, besides that it is excellently well penned, I have taken great pains to con it. Good beauties, let me sustain no scorn; I am very comptible, even to the least sinister usage.

OLIVIA.

Whence came you, sir?

VIOLA.

I can say little more than I have studied, and that question's out of my part. Good gentle one, give me modest assurance, if you be the lady of the house, that I may proceed in my speech.

OLIVIA.

Are you a comedian?

VIOLA.

No, my profound heart: and yet, by the very fangs of malice I swear, I am not that I play. Are you the lady of the house?

OLIVIA.

If I do not usurp myself, I am.

VIOLA.

Most certain, if you are she, you do usurp yourself; for what is yours to bestow is not yours to reserve. But this is from my commission: I will on with my speech in your praise, and then show you the heart of my message.

OLIVIA.

Come to what is important in't: I forgive you the praise.

VIOLA.

Alas, I took great pains to study it, and 'tis poetical.

OLIVIA.

It is the more like to be feigned; I pray you keep it in. I heard you were saucy at my gates; and allowed your approach, rather to wonder at you than to hear you. If you be not mad, be gone; if you have reason, be brief: 'tis not that time of moon with me to make one in so skipping a dialogue.

MARIA.

Will you hoist sail, sir? here lies your way.

VIOLA.

No, good swabber; I am to hull here a little longer.—Some mollification for your giant, sweet lady.

OLIVIA.

Tell me your mind.

VIOLA.

I am a messenger.

OLIVIA.

Sure, you have some hideous matter to deliver, when the courtesy of it is so fearful. Speak your office.

VIOLA.

It alone concerns your ear. I bring no overture of war, no taxation of homage; I hold the olive in my hand: my words are as full of peace as matter.

Olivia.

Yet you began rudely. What are you? what would you?

Viola.

The rudeness that hath appeared in me have I learned from my entertainment. What I am and what I would are as secret as maidenhead: to your ears, divinity; to any other's, profanation.

Olivia.

Give us the place alone: we will hear this divinity.[*Exit* Maria.] Now, sir, what is your text?

Viola.

Most sweet lady,—

Olivia.

A comfortable doctrine, and much may be said of it. Where lies your text?

Viola.

In Orsino's bosom.

Olivia.

In his bosom? In what chapter of his bosom?

Viola.

To answer by the method, in the first of his heart.

Olivia.

O, I have read it; it is heresy. Have you no more to say?

Viola.

Good madam, let me see your face.

Olivia.

Have you any commission from your lord to negotiate with my face? you are now out of your text: but we will draw the curtain and show you the picture. Look you, sir, such a one I was this present. Is't not well done? [*Unveiling.*]

Viola.

Excellently done, if God did all.

Olivia.

'Tis in grain, sir; 'twill endure wind and weather.

Viola.

'Tis beauty truly blent, whose red and white

Nature's own sweet and cunning hand laid on:

Lady, you are the cruel'st she alive,

If you will lead these graces to the grave,

And leave the world no copy.

Olivia.

O, sir, I will not be so hard-hearted; I will give out divers schedules of my beauty. It shall be inventoried; and every particle and utensil labelled to my will: as, item, two lips indifferent red; item, two grey eyes with lids to them; item, one neck, one chin, and so forth. Were you sent hither to praise me?

Viola.

I see you what you are: you are too proud;

But, if you were the devil, you are fair.

My lord and master loves you. O, such love

Could be but recompens'd though you were crown'd

The nonpareil of beauty!

Olivia.

                 How does he love me?

Viola.

With adorations, fertile tears,

With groans that thunder love, with sighs of fire.

Olivia.

Your lord does know my mind; I cannot love him:

Yet I suppose him virtuous, know him noble,

Of great estate, of fresh and stainless youth;

In voices well divulged, free, learn'd, and valiant,

And, in dimension and the shape of nature,

A gracious person: but yet I cannot love him;

He might have took his answer long ago.

Viola.

If I did love you in my master's flame,

With such a suffering, such a deadly life,

In your denial I would find no sense,

I would not understand it.

OLIVIA.

Why, what would you?

VIOLA.

Make me a willow cabin at your gate,
And call upon my soul within the house;
Write loyal cantons of contemned love,
And sing them loud, even in the dead of
    night;
Holla your name to the reverberate hills,
And make the babbling gossip of the air
Cry out Olivia! O, you should not rest
Between the elements of air and earth,
But you should pity me.

OLIVIA.

You might do much. What is your
    parentage?

VIOLA.

Above my fortunes, yet my state is well:
I am a gentleman.

OLIVIA.

Get you to your lord;
I cannot love him: let him send no more;
Unless, perchance, you come to me again,
To tell me how he takes it. Fare you well:
I thank you for your pains: spend this for
    me.

VIOLA.

I am no fee'd post, lady; keep your purse;
My master, not myself, lacks recompense.
Love make his heart of flint that you shall
    love;
And let your fervour, like my master's, be
Placed in contempt! Farewell, fair cruelty.
                                    [*Exit.*]

OLIVIA.

"What is your parentage?"
"Above my fortunes, yet my state is well:
I am a gentleman." I'll be sworn thou art;
Thy tongue, thy face, thy limbs, actions,
    and spirit,
Do give thee five-fold blazon. Not too
    fast:—
Soft, soft!
Unless the master were the man.—How
    now?
Even so quickly may one catch the plague?
Methinks I feel this youth's perfections
With an invisible and subtle stealth

To creep in at mine eyes. Well, let it be.—
What, ho, Malvolio!
                    [*Re-enter* MALVOLIO.]

MALVOLIO.

Here, madam, at your service.

OLIVIA.

Run after that same peevish messenger,
The county's man: he left this ring behind
    him,
Would I or not; tell him I'll none of it.
Desire him not to flatter with his lord,
Nor hold him up with hopes; I am not
    for him:
If that the youth will come this way to-
    morrow,
I'll give him reasons for't. Hie thee,
    Malvolio.

MALVOLIO.

Madam, I will.
                                    [*Exit.*]

OLIVIA.

I do I know not what: and fear to find
Mine eye too great a flatterer for my mind.
Fate, show thy force. Ourselves we do not
    owe:
What is decreed must be; and be this so!
                                    [*Exit.*]

ACT II
SCENE I

The sea coast.

[*Enter* ANTONIO *and* SEBASTIAN.]

ANTONIO.

Will you stay no longer; nor will you not
that I go with you?

SEBASTIAN.

By your patience, no; my stars shine darkly
over me; the malignancy of my fate might,
perhaps, distemper yours; therefore I shall
crave of you your leave that I may bear my
evils alone. It were a bad recompense for
your love, to lay any of them on you.

ANTONIO.

Let me know of you whither you are bound.

SEBASTIAN.

No, 'sooth, sir; my determinate voyage is
mere extravagancy. But I perceive in you so
excellent a touch of modesty, that you will

not extort from me what I am willing to keep in; therefore it charges me in manners the rather to express myself. You must know of me then, Antonio, my name is Sebastian, which I called Rodorigo; my father was that Sebastian of Messaline whom I know you have heard of: he left behind him myself and a sister, both born in an hour; if the heavens had been pleased, would we had so ended! but you, sir, altered that; for some hours before you took me from the breach of the sea was my sister drowned.

Antonio.

Alas the day!

Sebastian.

A lady, sir, though it was said she much resembled me, was yet of many accounted beautiful: but though I could not, with such estimable wonder, overfar believe that, yet thus far I will boldly publish her,—she bore mind that envy could not but call fair. She is drowned already, sir, with salt water, though I seem to drown her remembrance again with more.

Antonio.

Pardon me, sir, your bad entertainment.

Sebastian.

O, good Antonio, forgive me your trouble.

Antonio.

If you will not murder me for my love, let me be your servant.

Sebastian.

If you will not undo what you have done—that is, kill him whom you have recovered—desire it not. Fare ye well at once; my bosom is full of kindness; and I am yet so near the manners of my mother that, upon the least occasion more, mine eyes will tell tales of me. I am bound to the Count Orsino's court: farewell.

[*Exit.*]

Antonio.

The gentleness of all the gods go with thee! I have many enemies in Orsino's court, Else would I very shortly see thee there: But come what may, I do adore thee so That danger shall seem sport, and I will go.

[*Exit.*]

SCENE II

A street.

[*Enter* Viola; Malvolio *following.*]

Malvolio.

Were you not even now with the Countess Olivia?

Viola.

Even now, sir; on a moderate pace I have since arrived but hither.

Malvolio.

She returns this ring to you, sir; you might have saved me my pains, to have taken it away yourself. She adds moreover, that you should put your lord into a desperate assurance she will none of him: and one thing more: that you be never so hardy to come again in his affairs, unless it be to report your lord's taking of this. Receive it so.

Viola.

She took the ring of me: I'll none of it.

Malvolio.

Come, sir, you peevishly threw it to her; and her will is it should be so returned. If it be worth stooping for, there it lies in your eye; if not, be it his that finds it.

[*Exit.*]

Viola.

I left no ring with her; what means this lady?
Fortune forbid my outside have not charm'd her!
She made good view of me; indeed, so much,
That methought her eyes had lost her tongue,
For she did speak in starts distractedly.
She loves me, sure: the cunning of her passion
Invites me in this churlish messenger.
None of my lord's ring! why, he sent her none.
I am the man;—if it be so,—as 'tis,—
Poor lady, she were better love a dream.
Disguise, I see thou art a wickedness
Wherein the pregnant enemy does much.
How easy is it for the proper-false
In women's waxen hearts to set their forms!
Alas, our frailty is the cause, not we;

For such as we are made of, such we be.
How will this fadge? My master loves her
    dearly,
And I, poor monster, fond as much on him;
And she, mistaken, seems to dote on me.
What will become of this? As I am man,
My state is desperate for my master's love;
As I am woman, now alas the day!
What thriftless sighs shall poor Olivia
    breathe!
O time, thou must untangle this, not I;
It is too hard a knot for me to untie!
                    [*Exit.*]

SCENE III
A room in Olivia's house.
[*Enter* SIR TOBY BELCH *and*
SIR ANDREW AGUECHEEK.]

SIR TOBY.
Approach, Sir Andrew; not to be a-bed
after midnight is to be up betimes; and
diluculo surgere, thou know'st.

SIR ANDREW.
Nay; by my troth, I know not; but I know
to be up late is to be up late.

SIR TOBY.
A false conclusion; I hate it as an unfilled
can. To be up after midnight, and to go to
bed then is early: so that to go to bed after
midnight is to go to bed betimes. Do not
our lives consist of the four elements?

SIR ANDREW.
Faith, so they say; but I think it rather
consists of eating and drinking.

SIR TOBY.
Thou art a scholar; let us therefore eat and
drink.—Marian, I say!—a stoup of wine.
                [*Enter* CLOWN.]

SIR ANDREW.
Here comes the fool, i' faith.

CLOWN.
How now, my hearts? Did you never see
the picture of we three?

SIR TOBY.
Welcome, ass. Now let's have a catch.

SIR ANDREW.
By my troth, the fool has an excellent
breast. I had rather than forty shillings I

had such a leg; and so sweet a breath to
sing, as the fool has. In sooth, thou wast in
very gracious fooling last night when thou
spokest of Pigrogromitus, of the Vapians
passing the equinoctial of Queubus; 'twas
very good, i' faith. I sent thee sixpence for
thy leman. Hadst it?

CLOWN.
I did impeticos thy gratillity; for Malvolio's
nose is no whipstock. My lady has a white
hand, and the Myrmidons are no bottle-ale
houses.

SIR ANDREW.
Excellent! Why, this is the best fooling,
when all is done. Now, a song.

SIR TOBY.
Come on; there is sixpence for you: let's
have a song.

SIR ANDREW.
There's a testril of me too: if one knight
give a—

CLOWN.
Would you have a love-song, or a song of
good life?

SIR TOBY.
A love-song, a love-song.

SIR ANDREW.
Ay, ay; I care not for good life.

CLOWN. [*Sings.*]
    O, mistress mine, where are you roaming?
    O, stay and hear; your true love's coming,
        That can sing both high and low:
    Trip no further, pretty sweeting;
    Journeys end in lovers meeting,
        Every wise man's son doth know.

SIR ANDREW.
Excellent good, i' faith.

SIR TOBY.
Good, good.

CLOWN. [*Sings.*]
    What is love? 'tis not hereafter;
    Present mirth hath present laughter;
        What's to come is still unsure.
    In delay there lies no plenty;
    Then come kiss me, sweet and twenty;
        Youth's a stuff will not endure.

SIR ANDREW.
A mellifluous voice, as I am true knight.

Sir Toby.
A contagious breath.

Sir Andrew.
Very sweet and contagious, i' faith.

Sir Toby.
To hear by the nose, it is dulcet in contagion. But shall we make the welkin dance indeed? Shall we rouse the night-owl in a catch that will draw three souls out of one weaver? shall we do that?

Sir Andrew.
An you love me, let's do't: I am dog at a catch.

Clown.
By'r lady, sir, and some dogs will catch well.

Sir Andrew.
Most certain: let our catch be, "Thou knave."

Clown.
"Hold thy peace, thou knave" knight? I shall be constrain'd in't to call thee knave, knight.

Sir Andrew.
'Tis not the first time I have constrained one to call me knave. Begin, fool; it begins "Hold thy peace."

Clown.
I shall never begin if I hold my peace.

Sir Andrew.
Good, i' faith! Come, begin.
    [They sing a catch.]
    [Enter Maria.]*

Maria.
What a caterwauling do you keep here! If my lady have not called up her steward Malvolio, and bid him turn you out of doors, never trust me.

Sir Toby.
My lady's a Cataian, we are politicians; Malvolio's a Peg-a-Ramsey, and "Three merry men be we." Am not I consanguineous? am I not of her blood? Tilly-valley, lady. *[Sings.]* "There dwelt a man in Babylon, lady, lady."

Clown.
Beshrew me, the knight's in admirable fooling.

Sir Andrew.
Ay, he does well enough if he be disposed, and so do I too; he does it with a better grace, but I do it more natural.

Sir Toby.
"O, the twelfth day of December,—"

Maria.
For the love o' God, peace!
    [Enter Malvolio.]*

Malvolio.
My masters, are you mad? or what are you? Have you no wit, manners, nor honesty, but to gabble like tinkers at this time of night? Do ye make an ale-house of my lady's house, that ye squeak out your coziers' catches without any mitigation or remorse of voice? Is there no respect of place, persons, nor time, in you?

Sir Toby.
We did keep time, sir, in our catches. Sneck up!

Malvolio.
Sir Toby, I must be round with you. My lady bade me tell you that, though she harbours you as her kinsman she's nothing allied to your disorders. If you can separate yourself and your misdemeanours, you are welcome to the house; if not, an it would please you to take leave of her, she is very willing to bid you farewell.

Sir Toby.
"Farewell, dear heart, since I must needs be gone."

Maria.
Nay, good Sir Toby.

Clown.
"His eyes do show his days are almost done."

Malvolio.
Is't even so?

Sir Toby.
"But I will never die."

Clown.
Sir Toby, there you lie.

Malvolio.
This is much credit to you.

Sir Toby.
"Shall I bid him go?"

Clown.
"What an if you do?"

SIR TOBY.
"Shall I bid him go, and spare not?"
CLOWN.
"O, no, no, no, no, you dare not."
SIR TOBY.
Out o' tune? sir, ye lie. Art any more than a steward? Dost thou think, because thou art virtuous, there shall be no more cakes and ale?
CLOWN.
Yes, by Saint Anne; and ginger shall be hot i' the mouth too.
SIR TOBY.
Thou'art i' the right.—Go, sir, rub your chain with crumbs: A stoup of wine, Maria!
MALVOLIO.
Mistress Mary, if you prized my lady's favour at anything more than contempt, you would not give means for this uncivil rule; she shall know of it, by this hand.
                    [*Exit.*]
MARIA.
Go shake your ears.
SIR ANDREW.
'Twere as good a deed as to drink when a man's a-hungry, to challenge him the field, and then to break promise with him and make a fool of him.
SIR TOBY.
Do't, knight; I'll write thee a challenge; or I'll deliver thy indignation to him by word of mouth.
MARIA.
Sweet Sir Toby, be patient for to-night; since the youth of the count's was to-day with my lady, she is much out of quiet. For Monsieur Malvolio, let me alone with him: if I do not gull him into a nayword, and make him a common recreation, do not think I have wit enough to lie straight in my bed. I know I can do it.
SIR TOBY.
Possess us, possess us; tell us something of him.
MARIA.
Marry, sir, sometimes he is a kind of Puritan.

SIR ANDREW.
O, if I thought that, I'd beat him like a dog.
SIR TOBY.
What, for being a Puritan? thy exquisite reason, dear knight?
SIR ANDREW.
I have no exquisite reason for't, but I have reason good enough.
MARIA.
The devil a Puritan that he is, or anything constantly but a time-pleaser: an affectioned ass that cons state without book and utters it by great swarths; the best persuaded of himself, so crammed, as he thinks, with excellences, that it is his grounds of faith that all that look on him love him; and on that vice in him will my revenge find notable cause to work.
SIR TOBY.
What wilt thou do?
MARIA.
I will drop in his way some obscure epistles of love; wherein, by the colour of his beard, the shape of his leg, the manner of his gait, the expressure of his eye, forehead, and complexion, he shall find himself most feelingly personated. I can write very like my lady, your niece; on a forgotten matter we can hardly make distinction of our hands.
SIR TOBY.
Excellent! I smell a device.
SIR ANDREW.
I have't in my nose too.
SIR TOBY.
He shall think, by the letters that thou wilt drop, that they come from my niece, and that she is in love with him.
MARIA.
My purpose is, indeed, a horse of that
    colour.
SIR ANDREW.
And your horse now would make him an
    ass.
MARIA.
Ass, I doubt not.
SIR ANDREW.
O 'twill be admirable!

Maria.

Sport royal, I warrant you. I know my physic will work with him. I will plant you two, and let the fool make a third, where he shall find the letter; observe his construction of it. For this night, to bed, and dream on the event. Farewell.

                    [*Exit.*]

Sir Toby.

Good night, Penthesilea.

Sir Andrew.

Before me, she's a good wench.

Sir Toby.

She's a beagle true bred, and one that adores me. What o' that?

Sir Andrew.

I was adored once too.

Sir Toby.

Let's to bed, knight.—Thou hadst need send for more money.

Sir Andrew.

If I cannot recover your niece I am a foul way out.

Sir Toby.

Send for money, knight; if thou hast her not i' the end, call me Cut.

Sir Andrew.

If I do not, never trust me; take it how you will.

Sir Toby.

Come, come; I'll go burn some sack; 'tis too late to go to bed now: come, knight; come, knight.

                    [*Exeunt.*]

SCENE IV

A room in the duke's palace.
[*Enter* Duke, Viola, Curio, *and*
                    Others.]

Duke.

Give me some music:—Now, good
    morrow, friends:—
Now, good Cesario, but that piece of song,
That old and antique song we heard last
    night;
Methought it did relieve my passion
    much;
More than light airs and recollected terms

Of these most brisk and giddy-paced
    times:—
Come, but one verse.

Curio.

He is not here, so please your lordship, that
should sing it.

Duke.

Who was it?

Curio.

Feste, the jester, my lord; a fool that the
Lady Olivia's father took much delight in:
he is about the house.

Duke.

Seek him out, and play the tune the while.
                    [*Exit* Curio. *Music.*]
Come hither, boy. If ever thou shalt love,
In the sweet pangs of it remember me:
For, such as I am, all true lovers are;
Unstaid and skittish in all motions else,
Save in the constant image of the creature
That is belov'd.—How dost thou like this
    tune?

Viola.

It gives a very echo to the seat
Where Love is throned.

Duke.
                    Thou dost speak masterly:
My life upon't, young though thou art,
    thine eye
Hath stayed upon some favour that it loves;
Hath it not, boy?

Viola.
                    A little, by your favour.

Duke.

What kind of woman is't?

Viola.
                    Of your complexion.

Duke.

She is not worth thee, then. What years,
    i' faith?

Viola.

About your years, my lord.

Duke.

Too old, by heaven! Let still the woman
    take
An elder than herself; so wears she to him,
So sways she level in her husband's heart.
For, boy, however we do praise ourselves,

Our fancies are more giddy and unfirm,
More longing, wavering, sooner lost and
  won,
Than women's are.
VIOLA.
              I think it well, my lord.
DUKE.
Then let thy love be younger than thyself,
Or thy affection cannot hold the bent:
For women are as roses, whose fair flower,
Being once display'd, doth fall that very
  hour.
VIOLA.
And so they are: alas, that they are so;
To die, even when they to perfection grow!
    [*Re-enter* CURIO *and* CLOWN.]
DUKE.
O, fellow, come, the song we had last
  night:—
Mark it, Cesario; it is old and plain:
The spinsters and the knitters in the sun,
And the free maids, that weave their
  thread with bones,
Do use to chant it: it is silly sooth,
And dallies with the innocence of love
Like the old age.
CLOWN.
Are you ready, sir?
DUKE.
Ay; pr'ythee, sing. [*Music.*]
CLOWN. [*Sings.*]
  Come away, come away, death.
    And in sad cypress let me be laid;
  Fly away, fly away, breath;
    I am slain by a fair cruel maid.
  My shroud of white, stuck all with yew,
    O, prepare it!
  My part of death no one so true
    Did share it.
  Not a flower, not a flower sweet,
    On my black coffin let there be strown:
  Not a friend, not a friend greet
    My poor corpse where my bones shall
    be thrown:
  A thousand thousand sighs to save,
    Lay me, O, where
  Sad true lover never find my grave,
    To weep there!

DUKE.
There's for thy pains.
CLOWN.
No pains, sir; I take pleasure in singing, sir.
DUKE.
I'll pay thy pleasure, then.
CLOWN.
Truly, sir, and pleasure will be paid one time
or another.
DUKE.
Give me now leave to leave thee.
CLOWN.
Now the melancholy god protect thee; and
the tailor make thy doublet of changeable
taffeta, for thy mind is a very opal!—I
would have men of such constancy put
to sea, that their business might be
everything, and their intent everywhere; for
that's it that always makes a good voyage of
nothing.—Farewell.
        [*Exit* CLOWN.]
DUKE.
Let all the rest give place.—
    [*Exeunt* CURIO *and* ATTENDANTS.]
           Once more, Cesario,
Get thee to yond same sovereign cruelty:
Tell her my love, more noble than the
  world,
Prizes not quantity of dirty lands;
The parts that fortune hath bestow'd upon
  her,
Tell her, I hold as giddily as fortune;
But 'tis that miracle and queen of gems
That Nature pranks her in attracts my soul.
VIOLA.
But if she cannot love you, sir?
DUKE.
I cannot be so answer'd.
VIOLA.
            'Sooth, but you must.
Say that some lady, as perhaps there is,
Hath for your love as great a pang of heart
As you have for Olivia: you cannot love
  her;
You tell her so. Must she not then be
  answer'd?
DUKE.
There is no woman's sides

Can bide the beating of so strong a
    passion
As love doth give my heart: no woman's
    heart
So big to hold so much; they lack
    retention.
Alas, their love may be called appetite,—
No motion of the liver, but the palate,—
That suffer surfeit, cloyment, and revolt;
But mine is all as hungry as the sea,
And can digest as much: make no compare
Between that love a woman can bear me
And that I owe Olivia.

VIOLA.

              Ay, but I know,—

DUKE.

What dost thou know?

VIOLA.

Too well what love women to men may
    owe.
In faith, they are as true of heart as we.
My father had a daughter loved a man,
As it might be perhaps, were I a woman,
I should your lordship.

DUKE.

           And what's her history?

VIOLA.

A blank, my lord. She never told her love,
But let concealment, like a worm i' the
    bud,
Feed on her damask cheek: she pined in
    thought;
And with a green and yellow melancholy,
She sat like patience on a monument,
Smiling at grief. Was not this love, indeed?
We men may say more, swear more; but
    indeed,
Our shows are more than will; for still we
    prove
Much in our vows, but little in our love.

DUKE.

But died thy sister of her love, my boy?

VIOLA.

I am all the daughters of my father's
    house,
And all the brothers too;—and yet I know
    not.—
Sir, shall I to this lady?

DUKE.

              Ay, that's the theme.
To her in haste: give her this jewel; say
My love can give no place, bide no denay.
           [Exeunt.]

SCENE V

Olivia's garden.

[*Enter* SIR TOBY BELCH, SIR ANDREW
AGUECHEEK, *and* FABIAN.]

SIR TOBY.

Come thy ways, Signior Fabian.

FABIAN.

Nay, I'll come; if I lose a scruple of this sport
let me be boiled to death with melancholy.

SIR TOBY.

Wouldst thou not be glad to have the
niggardly rascally sheep-biter come by
some notable shame?

FABIAN.

I would exult, man; you know he brought
me out o' favour with my lady about a bear-
baiting here.

SIR TOBY.

To anger him we'll have the bear again; and
we will fool him black and blue:—shall we
not, Sir Andrew?

SIR ANDREW.

An we do not, it is pity of our lives.
           [*Enter* MARIA.]

SIR TOBY.

Here comes the little villain:—How now,
my nettle of India?

MARIA.

Get ye all three into the box-tree: Malvolio's
coming down this walk; he has been yonder
i' the sun practising behaviour to his own
shadow this half hour: observe him, for
the love of mockery; for I know this letter
will make a contemplative idiot of him.
Close, in the name of jesting! [*The men hide
themselves.*] Lie thou there; [*Throws down a
letter.*] for here comes the trout that must
be caught with tickling.
           [*Exit* MARIA.]
           [*Enter* MALVOLIO.]

MALVOLIO.

'Tis but fortune; all is fortune. Maria once

told me she did affect me: and I have heard herself come thus near, that, should she fancy, it should be one of my complexion. Besides, she uses me with a more exalted respect than any one else that follows her. What should I think on't?

SIR TOBY.
Here's an overweening rogue!

FABIAN.
O, peace! Contemplation makes a rare turkey-cock of him; how he jets under his advanced plumes!

SIR ANDREW.
'Slight, I could so beat the rogue:—

SIR TOBY.
Peace, I say.

MALVOLIO.
To be Count Malvolio;—

SIR TOBY.
Ah, rogue!

SIR ANDREW.
Pistol him, pistol him.

SIR TOBY.
Peace, peace.

MALVOLIO.
There is example for't; the lady of the Strachy married the yeoman of the wardrobe.

SIR ANDREW.
Fie on him, Jezebel!

FABIAN.
O, peace! now he's deeply in; look how imagination blows him.

MALVOLIO.
Having been three months married to her, sitting in my state,—

SIR TOBY.
O for a stone-bow to hit him in the eye!

MALVOLIO.
Calling my officers about me, in my branched velvet gown; having come from a day-bed, where I have left Olivia sleeping.

SIR TOBY.
Fire and brimstone!

FABIAN.
O, peace, peace.

MALVOLIO.
And then to have the humour of state: and after a demure travel of regard,—telling

them I know my place as I would they should do theirs,—to ask for my kinsman Toby.

SIR TOBY.
Bolts and shackles!

FABIAN.
O, peace, peace, peace! Now, now.

MALVOLIO.
Seven of my people, with an obedient start, make out for him: I frown the while, and perchance, wind up my watch, or play with some rich jewel. Toby approaches; court'sies there to me:—

SIR TOBY.
Shall this fellow live?

FABIAN.
Though our silence be drawn from us with cars, yet peace.

MALVOLIO.
I extend my hand to him thus, quenching my familiar smile with an austere regard of control:—

SIR TOBY.
And does not Toby take you a blow o' the lips then?

MALVOLIO.
Saying "Cousin Toby, my fortunes having cast me on your niece, give me this prerogative of speech":—

SIR TOBY.
What, what?

MALVOLIO.
"You must amend your drunkenness."

SIR TOBY.
Out, scab!

FABIAN.
Nay, patience, or we break the sinews of our plot.

MALVOLIO.
"Besides, you waste the treasure of your time with a foolish knight,"—

SIR ANDREW.
That's me, I warrant you.

MALVOLIO.
"One Sir Andrew,"—

SIR ANDREW.
I knew 'twas I; for many do call me fool.

MALVOLIO.
What employment have we here?

[Taking up the letter.]

FABIAN.

Now is the woodcock near the gin.

SIR TOBY.

O, peace! And the spirit of humours intimate reading aloud to him!

MALVOLIO.

By my life, this is my lady's hand: these be her very C's, her U's, and her T's; and thus makes she her great P's. It is in contempt of question, her hand.

SIR ANDREW.

Her C's, her U's, and her T's. Why that?

MALVOLIO. *[Reads.]*

"To the unknown beloved, this, and my good wishes." Her very phrases!—By your leave, wax.—Soft!—and the impressure her Lucrece, with which she uses to seal: 'tis my lady. To whom should this be?

FABIAN.

This wins him, liver and all.

MALVOLIO. *[Reads.]*

Jove knows I love,
    But who?
Lips, do not move,
No man must know.

"No man must know."—What follows? the numbers alter'd!—"No man must know":—If this should be thee, Malvolio?

SIR TOBY.

Marry, hang thee, brock!

MALVOLIO. *[Reads.]*

I may command where I adore:
    But silence, like a Lucrece knife,
With bloodless stroke my heart doth gore;
    M, O, A, I, doth sway my life.

FABIAN.

A fustian riddle!

SIR TOBY.

Excellent wench, say I.

MALVOLIO.

"M, O, A, I, doth sway my life."—Nay, but first let me see,—let me see,—let me see.

FABIAN.

What dish of poison has she dressed him!

SIR TOBY.

And with what wing the staniel checks at it!

MALVOLIO.

"I may command where I adore." Why, she may command me: I serve her, she is my lady. Why, this is evident to any formal capacity; there is no obstruction in this;—And the end,—What should that alphabetical position portend? If I could make that resemble something in me.—Softly!—M, O, A, I,—

SIR TOBY.

O, ay, make up that:—he is now at a cold scent.

FABIAN.

Sowter will cry upon't for all this, though it be as rank as a fox.

MALVOLIO.

M,—Malvolio; M,—why, that begins my name.

FABIAN.

Did not I say he would work it out? The cur is excellent at faults.

MALVOLIO.

M,—But then there is no consonancy in the sequel; that suffers under probation: A should follow, but O does.

FABIAN.

And O shall end, I hope.

SIR TOBY.

Ay, or I'll cudgel him, and make him cry "O!"

MALVOLIO.

And then I comes behind.

FABIAN.

Ay, an you had any eye behind you, you might see more detraction at your heels than fortunes before you.

MALVOLIO.

M, O, A, I;—This simulation is not as the former:—and yet, to crush this a little, it would bow to me, for every one of these letters are in my name. Soft; here follows prose. *[Reads.]* "If this fall into thy hand, revolve. In my stars I am above thee; but be not afraid of greatness. Some are born great, some achieve greatness, and some have greatness thrust upon them. Thy fates open their hands; let thy blood and spirit embrace them. And, to inure thyself to what thou art like to be, cast thy humble slough and appear fresh. Be opposite with a kinsman, surly with servants: let thy tongue tang arguments of state; put thyself into the trick of singularity: She thus advises thee that sighs for thee. Remember who commended thy yellow stockings, and wished to see thee ever cross-gartered. I say, remember. Go to; thou art made, if thou desirest to be so; if not, let me see thee a steward still, the fellow of servants, and not worthy to touch fortune's fingers. Farewell. She that would alter services with thee,

                The fortunate-unhappy."
Daylight and champain discovers not more: this is open. I will be proud, I will read politic authors, I will baffle Sir Toby, I will wash off gross acquaintance, I will be point-device, the very man. I do not now fool myself to let imagination jade me; for every reason excites to this, that my lady loves me. She did commend my yellow stockings of late, she did praise my leg being cross-gartered; and in this she manifests herself to my love, and with a kind of injunction, drives me to these habits of her liking. I thank my stars I am happy. I will be strange, stout, in yellow stockings, and cross-gartered, even with the swiftness of putting on. Jove and my stars be praised!—Here is yet a postscript. [*Reads.*] "Thou canst not choose but know who I am. If thou entertainest my love, let it appear in thy smiling; thy smiles become thee well: therefore in my presence still smile, dear my sweet, I pr'ythee."

Jove, I thank thee. I will smile; I will do everything that thou wilt have me.

                    [*Exit.*]

FABIAN.

I will not give my part of this sport for a pension of thousands to be paid from the Sophy.

SIR TOBY.

I could marry this wench for this device:—

SIR ANDREW.

So could I too.

SIR TOBY.

And ask no other dowry with her but such another jest.

                    [*Enter* MARIA.]

SIR ANDREW.

Nor I neither.

FABIAN.

Here comes my noble gull-catcher.

SIR TOBY.

Wilt thou set thy foot o' my neck?

SIR ANDREW.

Or o' mine either?

SIR TOBY.

Shall I play my freedom at tray-trip, and become thy bond-slave?

SIR ANDREW.

I' faith, or I either?

SIR TOBY.

Why, thou hast put him in such a dream, that, when the image of it leaves him, he must run mad.

MARIA.

Nay, but say true; does it work upon him?

SIR TOBY.

Like aqua-vitae with a midwife.

MARIA.

If you will then see the fruits of the sport, mark his first approach before my lady: he will come to her in yellow stockings, and 'tis a colour she abhors, and cross-gartered, a fashion she detests; and he will smile upon her, which will now be so unsuitable to her disposition, being addicted to a melancholy as she is, that it cannot but turn him into a notable contempt; if you will see it, follow me.

SIR TOBY.

To the gates of Tartar, thou most excellent devil of wit!

SIR ANDREW.

I'll make one too.

                    [*Exeunt.*]

ACT III
SCENE I
Olivia's garden.
[*Enter* VIOLA, *and* CLOWN *with
a tabor.*]

VIOLA.

Save thee, friend, and thy music. Dost thou live by thy tabor?

Clown.
No, sir, I live by the church.
Viola.
Art thou a churchman?
Clown.
No such matter, sir: I do live by the church; for I do live at my house, and my house doth stand by the church.
Viola.
So thou mayst say the king lies by a beggar, if a beggar dwell near him; or the church stands by thy tabor, if thy tabor stand by the church.
Clown.
You have said, sir.—To see this age!—A sentence is but a cheveril glove to a good wit. How quickly the wrong side may be turned outward!
Viola.
Nay, that's certain; they that dally nicely with words may quickly make them wanton.
Clown.
I would, therefore, my sister had had no name, sir.
Viola.
Why, man?
Clown.
Why, sir, her name's a word; and to dally with that word might make my sister wanton. But indeed words are very rascals, since bonds disgraced them.
Viola.
Thy reason, man?
Clown.
Troth, sir, I can yield you none without words; and words are grown so false I am loath to prove reason with them.
Viola.
I warrant, thou art a merry fellow, and carest for nothing.
Clown.
Not so, sir, I do care for something: but in my conscience, sir, I do not care for you; if that be to care for nothing, sir, I would it would make you invisible.
Viola.
Art not thou the Lady Olivia's fool?

Clown.
No, indeed, sir; the Lady Olivia has no folly: she will keep no fool, sir, till she be married; and fools are as like husbands as pilchards are to herrings, the husband's the bigger; I am, indeed, not her fool, but her corrupter of words.
Viola.
I saw thee late at the Count Orsino's.
Clown.
Foolery, sir, does walk about the orb like the sun; it shines everywhere. I would be sorry, sir, but the fool should be as oft with your master as with my mistress: I think I saw your wisdom there.
Viola.
Nay, an thou pass upon me, I'll no more with thee.
Hold, there's expenses for thee.
Clown.
Now Jove, in his next commodity of hair, send thee a beard!
Viola.
By my troth, I'll tell thee, I am almost sick for one; though I would not have it grow on my chin. Is thy lady within?
Clown.
Would not a pair of these have bred, sir?
Viola.
Yes, being kept together and put to use.
Clown.
I would play Lord Pandarus of Phrygia, sir, to bring a Cressida to this Troilus.
Viola.
I understand you, sir; 'tis well begged.
Clown.
The matter, I hope, is not great, sir, begging but a beggar: Cressida was a beggar. My lady is within, sir. I will construe to them whence you come; who you are and what you would are out of my welkin: I might say element; but the word is overworn.
[*Exit.*]
Viola.
This fellow's wise enough to play the fool;
And, to do that well, craves a kind of wit:

He must observe their mood on whom
    he jests,
The quality of persons, and the time;
And, like the haggard, check at every
    feather
That comes before his eye. This is a practice
As full of labour as a wise man's art:
For folly, that he wisely shows, is fit;
But wise men, folly-fallen, quite taint
    their wit.

        [*Enter* SIR TOBY BELCH *and*
        SIR ANDREW AGUECHEEK.*]

SIR TOBY.
Save you, gentleman.

VIOLA.
And you, sir.

SIR ANDREW.
Dieu vous garde, monsieur.

VIOLA.
Et vous aussi; votre serviteur.

SIR ANDREW.
I hope, sir, you are; and I am yours.

SIR TOBY.
Will you encounter the house? my niece is
desirous you should enter, if your trade be
to her.

VIOLA.
I am bound to your niece, sir: I mean, she is
the list of my voyage.

SIR TOBY.
Taste your legs, sir; put them to motion.

VIOLA.
My legs do better understand me, sir, than
I understand what you mean by bidding me
taste my legs.

SIR TOBY.
I mean, to go, sir, to enter.

VIOLA.
I will answer you with gait and entrance:
but we are prevented. [*Enter* OLIVIA *and*
MARIA.] Most excellent accomplished lady,
the heavens rain odours on you!

SIR ANDREW.
That youth's a rare courtier—"Rain odours":
well.

VIOLA.
My matter hath no voice, lady, but to your
own most pregnant and vouchsafed ear.

SIR ANDREW.
"Odours," "pregnant," and "vouchsafed":—
I'll get 'em all three ready.

OLIVIA.
Let the garden door be shut, and leave
me to my hearing. [*Exeunt* SIR TOBY, SIR
ANDREW, *and* MARIA.] Give me your hand,
sir.

VIOLA.
My duty, madam, and most humble
    service.

OLIVIA.
What is your name?

VIOLA.
Cesario is your servant's name, fair
    princess.

OLIVIA.
My servant, sir! 'Twas never merry world,
Since lowly feigning was call'd
    compliment:
You are servant to the Count Orsino,
    youth.

VIOLA.
And he is yours, and his must needs be
    yours;
Your servant's servant is your servant,
    madam.

OLIVIA.
For him, I think not on him: for his
    thoughts,
Would they were blanks rather than fill'd
    with me!

VIOLA.
Madam, I come to whet your gentle
    thoughts
On his behalf:—

OLIVIA.
        O, by your leave, I pray you:
I bade you never speak again of him:
But, would you undertake another suit,
I had rather hear you to solicit that
Than music from the spheres.

VIOLA.
        Dear lady,—

OLIVIA.
Give me leave, beseech you: I did send,
After the last enchantment you did here,
A ring in chase of you; so did I abuse

Myself, my servant, and, I fear me, you:
Under your hard construction must I sit;
To force that on you, in a shameful
     cunning,
Which you knew none of yours. What
     might you think?
Have you not set mine honour at the stake,
And baited it with all the unmuzzl'd
     thoughts
That tyrannous heart can think? To one of
     your receiving
Enough is shown: a cypress, not a bosom,
Hides my heart: so let me hear you speak.

Viola.
I pity you.

Olivia.
               That's a degree to love.

Viola.
No, not a grise; for 'tis a vulgar proof
That very oft we pity enemies.

Olivia.
Why, then, methinks 'tis time to smile
     again:
O world, how apt the poor are to be proud!
If one should be a prey, how much the
     better
To fall before the lion than the wolf!
                                   [*Clock strikes.*]
The clock upbraids me with the waste of
     time.—
Be not afraid, good youth, I will not have
     you:
And yet, when wit and youth is come to
     harvest,
Your wife is like to reap a proper man.
There lies your way, due west.

Viola.
                    Then westward-ho!—
Grace and good disposition 'tend your
     ladyship!
You'll nothing, madam, to my lord by me?

Olivia.
Stay:
I pr'ythee tell me what thou think'st of me.

Viola.
That you do think you are not what you are.

Olivia.
If I think so, I think the same of you.

Viola.
Then think you right; I am not what I am.

Olivia.
I would you were as I would have you be!

Viola.
Would it be better, madam, than I am,
I wish it might; for now I am your fool.

Olivia.
O what a deal of scorn looks beautiful
In the contempt and anger of his lip!
A murd'rous guilt shows not itself more
     soon
Than love that would seem hid: love's
     night is noon.
Cesario, by the roses of the spring,
By maidhood, honour, truth, and
     everything,
I love thee so that, maugre all thy pride,
Nor wit, nor reason, can my passion hide.
Do not extort thy reasons from this clause,
For, that I woo, thou therefore hast no
     cause:
But rather reason thus with reason fetter:
Love sought is good, but given unsought
     is better.

Viola.
By innocence I swear, and by my youth,
I have one heart, one bosom, and one
     truth,
And that no woman has; nor never none
Shall mistress be of it, save I alone.
And so adieu, good madam; never more
Will I my master's tears to you deplore.

Olivia.
Yet come again: for thou, perhaps, mayst
     move
That heart, which now abhors, to like his
     love.
                                        [*Exeunt.*]

SCENE II
A room in Olivia's house.
[*Enter* Sir Toby Belch, Sir Andrew
     Aguecheek, *and* Fabian.]

Sir Andrew.
No, faith, I'll not stay a jot longer.

Sir Toby.
Thy reason, dear venom: give thy reason.

FABIAN.
You must needs yield your reason, Sir Andrew.

SIR ANDREW.
Marry, I saw your niece do more favours to the count's servingman than ever she bestowed upon me; I saw't i' the orchard.

SIR TOBY.
Did she see thee the while, old boy? tell me that.

SIR ANDREW.
As plain as I see you now.

FABIAN.
This was a great argument of love in her toward you.

SIR ANDREW.
'Slight! will you make an ass o' me?

FABIAN.
I will prove it legitimate, sir, upon the oaths of judgment and reason.

SIR TOBY.
And they have been grand jurymen since before Noah was a sailor.

FABIAN.
She did show favour to the youth in your sight only to exasperate you, to awake your dormouse valour, to put fire in your heart and brimstone in your liver. You should then have accosted her; and with some excellent jests, fire-new from the mint, you should have banged the youth into dumbness. This was looked for at your hand, and this was baulked: the double gilt of this opportunity you let time wash off, and you are now sailed into the north of my lady's opinion; where you will hang like an icicle on Dutchman's beard, unless you do redeem it by some laudable attempt either of valour or policy.

SIR ANDREW.
And't be any way, it must be with valour: for policy I hate; I had as lief be a Brownist as a politician.

SIR TOBY.
Why, then, build me thy fortunes upon the basis of valour. Challenge me the count's youth to fight with him; hurt him in eleven places; my niece shall take note of it: and assure thyself there is no love-broker in the world can more prevail in man's commendation with woman than report of valour.

FABIAN.
There is no way but this, Sir Andrew.

SIR ANDREW.
Will either of you bear me a challenge to him?

SIR TOBY.
Go, write it in a martial hand; be curst and brief; it is no matter how witty, so it be eloquent and full of invention; taunt him with the licence of ink; if thou "thou'st" him some thrice, it shall not be amiss; and as many lies as will lie in thy sheet of paper, although the sheet were big enough for the bed of Ware in England, set 'em down; go about it. Let there be gall enough in thy ink; though thou write with a goose-pen, no matter. About it.

SIR ANDREW.
Where shall I find you?

SIR TOBY.
We'll call thee at the *cubiculo*. Go.
                    [*Exit* SIR ANDREW.]

FABIAN.
This is a dear manakin to you, Sir Toby.

SIR TOBY.
I have been dear to him, lad; some two thousand strong, or so.

FABIAN.
We shall have a rare letter from him: but you'll not deliver it.

SIR TOBY.
Never trust me then; and by all means stir on the youth to an answer. I think oxen and wainropes cannot hale them together. For Andrew, if he were opened and you find so much blood in his liver as will clog the foot of a flea, I'll eat the rest of the anatomy.

FABIAN.
And his opposite, the youth, bears in his visage no great presage of cruelty.
                    [*Enter* MARIA.]

SIR TOBY.
Look where the youngest wren of nine comes.

MARIA.
If you desire the spleen, and will laugh
yourselves into stitches, follow me: yond
gull Malvolio is turned heathen, a very
renegado; for there is no Christian, that
means to be saved by believing rightly, can
ever believe such impossible passages of
grossness. He's in yellow stockings.

SIR TOBY.
And cross-gartered?

MARIA.
Most villainously; like a pedant that keeps
a school i' the church.—I have dogged him
like his murderer. He does obey every point
of the letter that I dropped to betray him.
He does smile his face into more lines than
is in the new map, with the augmentation of
the Indies: you have not seen such a thing
as 'tis; I can hardly forbear hurling things at
him. I know my lady will strike him; if she
do, he'll smile and take't for a great favour.

SIR TOBY.
Come, bring us, bring us where he is.

[*Exeunt.*]

SCENE III

A street.

[*Enter* ANTONIO *and* SEBASTIAN.]

SEBASTIAN.
I would not by my will have troubled you;
But since you make your pleasure of your
    pains,
I will no further chide you.

ANTONIO.
I could not stay behind you: my desire,
More sharp than filed steel, did spur me
    forth;
And not all love to see you,—though so
    much,
As might have drawn one to a longer
    voyage,—
But jealousy what might befall your travel,
Being skilless in these parts; which to a
    stranger,
Unguided and unfriended, often prove
Rough and unhospitable. My willing love,
The rather by these arguments of fear,
Set forth in your pursuit.

SEBASTIAN.
              My kind Antonio,
I can no other answer make but thanks,
And thanks, and ever thanks. Often good
    turns
Are shuffled off with such uncurrent pay;
But were my worth, as is my conscience,
    firm,
You should find better dealing. What's
    to do?
Shall we go see the reliques of this town?

ANTONIO.
To-morrow, sir; best, first, go see your
    lodging.

SEBASTIAN.
I am not weary, and 'tis long to night;
I pray you, let us satisfy our eyes
With the memorials and the things of
    fame
That do renown this city.

ANTONIO.
              Would you'd pardon me;
I do not without danger walk these streets:
Once in a sea-fight, 'gainst the count, his
    galleys,
I did some service; of such note, indeed,
That, were I ta'en here, it would scarce be
    answered.

SEBASTIAN.
Belike you slew great number of his
    people?

ANTONIO.
The offence is not of such a bloody nature;
Albeit the quality of the time and quarrel
Might well have given us bloody
    argument.
It might have since been answered in
    repaying
What we took from them; which, for
    traffic's sake,
Most of our city did: only myself stood out;
For which, if I be lapsed in this place,
I shall pay dear.

SEBASTIAN.
             Do not then walk too open.

ANTONIO.
It doth not fit me. Hold, sir, here's my
    purse;

In the south suburbs, at the Elephant,
Is best to lodge: I will bespeak our diet
Whiles you beguile the time and feed your
    knowledge
With viewing of the town; there shall you
    have me.

SEBASTIAN.

Why I your purse?

ANTONIO.

Haply your eye shall light upon some toy
You have desire to purchase; and your store,
I think, is not for idle markets, sir.

SEBASTIAN.

I'll be your purse-bearer, and leave you for
An hour.

ANTONIO.

       To the Elephant.—

SEBASTIAN.

             I do remember.

[Exeunt.]

SCENE IV

Olivia's garden.

[Enter OLIVIA *and* MARIA.*]*

OLIVIA.

I have sent after him. He says he'll come;
How shall I feast him? what bestow on
    him?
For youth is bought more oft than begg'd
    or borrow'd.
I speak too loud.—
Where is Malvolio?—He is sad and civil,
And suits well for a servant with my
    fortunes;—
Where is Malvolio?

MARIA.

He's coming, madam; but in very strange
manner. He is sure possessed.

OLIVIA.

Why, what's the matter? does he rave?

MARIA.

No, madam, he does nothing but smile:
your ladyship were best to have some guard
about you if he come; for, sure, the man is
tainted in his wits.

OLIVIA.

Go call him hither.—I'm as mad as he,
If sad and merry madness equal be.—

[Enter MALVOLIO.*]*

How now, Malvolio?

MALVOLIO.

Sweet lady, ho, ho. *[Smiles fantastically.]*

OLIVIA.

Smil'st thou?
I sent for thee upon a sad occasion.

MALVOLIO.

Sad, lady? I could be sad: this does make
some obstruction in the blood, this cross-
gartering. But what of that? If it please the
eye of one, it is with me as the very true
sonnet is: "Please one and please all."

OLIVIA.

Why, how dost thou, man? what is the
    matter with thee?

MALVOLIO.

Not black in my mind, though yellow in
    my legs.
It did come to his hands, and commands
    shall be executed.
I think we do know the sweet Roman
    hand.

OLIVIA.

Wilt thou go to bed, Malvolio?

MALVOLIO.

To bed? ay, sweetheart; and I'll come to
    thee.

OLIVIA.

God comfort thee! Why dost thou smile so,
and kiss thy hand so oft?

MARIA.

How do you, Malvolio?

MALVOLIO.

At your request? Yes; nightingales answer
    daws.

MARIA.

Why appear you with this ridiculous
boldness before my lady?

MALVOLIO.

"Be not afraid of greatness":—'twas well
    writ.

OLIVIA.

What meanest thou by that, Malvolio?

MALVOLIO.

"Some are born great,"—

OLIVIA.

Ha?

Malvolio.

"Some achieve greatness,"—

Olivia.

What say'st thou?

Malvolio.

"And some have greatness thrust upon them."

Olivia.

Heaven restore thee!

Malvolio.

"Remember who commended thy yellow stockings."

Olivia.

Thy yellow stockings?

Malvolio.

"And wished to see thee cross-gartered."

Olivia.

Cross-gartered?

Malvolio.

"Go to: thou art made, if thou desirest to be so":—

Olivia.

Am I made?

Malvolio.

"If not, let me see thee a servant still."

Olivia.

Why, this is very midsummer madness.

[Enter Servant.]

Servant.

Madam, the young gentleman of the Count Orsino's is returned; I could hardly entreat him back; he attends your ladyship's pleasure.

Olivia.

I'll come to him. [*Exit* Servant.] Good Maria, let this fellow be looked to. Where's my cousin Toby? Let some of my people have a special care of him; I would not have him miscarry for the half of my dowry.

[Exeunt Olivia *and* Maria.]

Malvolio.

O, ho! do you come near me now? No worse man than Sir Toby to look to me? This concurs directly with the letter: she sends him on purpose, that I may appear stubborn to him; for she incites me to that in the letter. "Cast thy humble slough," says she;—"be opposite with a kinsman, surly with servants,—let thy tongue tang with arguments of state,—put thyself into the trick of singularity";—and consequently, sets down the manner how; as, a sad face, a reverend carriage, a slow tongue, in the habit of some sir of note, and so forth. I have limed her; but it is Jove's doing, and Jove make me thankful! And, when she went away now, "Let this fellow be looked to"; Fellow! not Malvolio, nor after my degree, but fellow. Why, everything adheres together; that no dram of a scruple, no scruple of a scruple, no obstacle, no incredulous or unsafe circumstance,—What can be said? Nothing, that can be, can come between me and the full prospect of my hopes. Well, Jove, not I, is the doer of this, and he is to be thanked.

[Re-enter Maria, *with* Sir Toby Belch *and* Fabian.]

Sir Toby.

Which way is he, in the name of sanctity? If all the devils of hell be drawn in little, and Legion himself possessed him, yet I'll speak to him.

Fabian.

Here he is, here he is:—How is't with you, sir? how is't with you, man?

Malvolio.

Go off; I discard you; let me enjoy my private; go off.

Maria.

Lo, how hollow the fiend speaks within him! did not I tell you?—Sir Toby, my lady prays you to have a care of him.

Malvolio.

Ah, ha! does she so?

Sir Toby.

Go to, go to; peace, peace, we must deal gently with him; let me alone. How do you, Malvolio? how is't with you? What, man! defy the devil: consider, he's an enemy to mankind.

Malvolio.

Do you know what you say?

Maria.

La you, an you speak ill of the devil, how he takes it at heart! Pray God he be not bewitched.

FABIAN.

Carry his water to the wise woman.

MARIA.

Marry, and it shall be done to-morrow morning, if I live. My lady would not lose him for more than I'll say.

MALVOLIO.

How now, mistress!

MARIA.

O lord!

SIR TOBY.

Pr'ythee hold thy peace; this is not the way. Do you not see you move him? let me alone with him.

FABIAN.

No way but gentleness; gently, gently: the fiend is rough, and will not be roughly used.

SIR TOBY.

Why, how now, my bawcock? how dost thou, chuck?

MALVOLIO.

Sir?

SIR TOBY.

Ay, Biddy, come with me. What, man! 'tis not for gravity to play at cherry-pit with Satan. Hang him, foul collier!

MARIA.

Get him to say his prayers; good Sir Toby, get him to pray.

MALVOLIO.

My prayers, minx?

MARIA.

No, I warrant you, he will not hear of godliness.

MALVOLIO.

Go, hang yourselves all! you are idle shallow things; I am not of your element; you shall know more hereafter.

[Exit.]

SIR TOBY.

Is't possible?

FABIAN.

If this were played upon a stage now, I could condemn it as an improbable fiction.

SIR TOBY.

His very genius hath taken the infection of the device, man.

MARIA.

Nay, pursue him now; lest the device take air and taint.

FABIAN.

Why, we shall make him mad indeed.

MARIA.

The house will be the quieter.

SIR TOBY.

Come, we'll have him in a dark room and bound. My niece is already in the belief that he's mad; we may carry it thus, for our pleasure and his penance, till our very pastime, tired out of breath, prompt us to have mercy on him: at which time we will bring the device to the bar, and crown thee for a finder of madmen. But see, but see.

[Enter SIR ANDREW AGUECHEEK.]

FABIAN.

More matter for a May morning.

SIR ANDREW.

Here's the challenge, read it; I warrant there's vinegar and pepper in't.

FABIAN.

Is't so saucy?

SIR ANDREW.

Ay, is't, I warrant him; do but read.

SIR TOBY.

Give me. *[Reads.]* "Youth, whatsoever thou art, thou art but a scurvy fellow."

FABIAN.

Good and valiant.

SIR TOBY.

"Wonder not, nor admire not in thy mind, why I do call thee so, for I will show thee no reason for't."

FABIAN.

A good note: that keeps you from the blow of the law.

SIR TOBY.

"Thou comest to the Lady Olivia, and in my sight she uses thee kindly: but thou liest in thy throat; that is not the matter I challenge thee for."

FABIAN.

Very brief, and to exceeding good senseless.

SIR TOBY.

"I will waylay thee going home; where if it be thy chance to kill me,"—

FABIAN.
Good.
SIR TOBY.
"Thou kill'st me like a rogue and a villain."
FABIAN.
Still you keep o' the windy side of the law.
Good.
SIR TOBY.
"Fare thee well; and God have mercy upon
one of our souls! He may have mercy upon
mine; but my hope is better, and so look to
thyself. Thy friend, as thou usest him, and
thy sworn enemy, Andrew Aguecheek." If
this letter move him not, his legs cannot:
I'll give't him.
MARIA.
You may have very fit occasion for't; he is
now in some commerce with my lady, and
will by and by depart.
SIR TOBY.
Go, Sir Andrew; scout me for him at the
corner of the orchard, like a bum-bailiff;
so soon as ever thou seest him, draw; and
as thou drawest, swear horrible; for it
comes to pass oft that a terrible oath, with
a swaggering accent sharply twanged off,
gives manhood more approbation than ever
proof itself would have earned him. Away.
SIR ANDREW.
Nay, let me alone for swearing.
                    [*Exit.*]
SIR TOBY.
Now will not I deliver his letter; for
the behaviour of the young gentleman
gives him out to be of good capacity and
breeding; his employment between his lord
and my niece confirms no less; therefore
this letter, being so excellently ignorant,
will breed no terror in the youth: he will
find it comes from a clodpole. But, sir, I will
deliver his challenge by word of mouth, set
upon Aguecheek notable report of valour,
and drive the gentleman,—as I know his
youth will aptly receive it,—into a most
hideous opinion of his rage, skill, fury, and
impetuosity. This will so fright them both
that they will kill one another by the look,
like cockatrices.

                    [*Enter* OLIVIA *and* VIOLA.]
FABIAN.
Here he comes with your niece; give them
way till he take leave, and presently after
him.
SIR TOBY.
I will meditate the while upon some horrid
message for a challenge.
          [*Exeunt* SIR TOBY, FABIAN, *and* MARIA.]
OLIVIA.
I have said too much unto a heart of stone,
And laid mine honour too unchary on it:
There's something in me that reproves my
     fault;
But such a headstrong potent fault it is
That it but mocks reproof.
VIOLA.
With the same 'haviour that your passion
     bears
Goes on my master's griefs.
OLIVIA.
Here, wear this jewel for me; 'tis my
     picture;
Refuse it not; it hath no tongue to vex you:
And, I beseech you, come again to-morrow.
What shall you ask of me that I'll deny,
That, honour saved, may upon asking give?
VIOLA.
Nothing but this, your true love for my
     master.
OLIVIA.
How with mine honour may I give him
     that
Which I have given to you?
VIOLA.
                              I will acquit you.
OLIVIA.
Well, come again to-morrow. Fare thee
     well;
A fiend like thee might bear my soul to
     hell.
                    [*Exit.*]
          [*Re-enter* SIR TOBY BELCH *and*
                    FABIAN.]
SIR TOBY.
Gentleman, God save thee.
VIOLA.
And you, sir.

SIR TOBY.

That defence thou hast, betake thee to't. Of what nature the wrongs are thou hast done him, I know not; but thy intercepter, full of despite, bloody as the hunter, attends thee at the orchard end: dismount thy tuck, be yare in thy preparation, for thy assailant is quick, skilful, and deadly.

VIOLA.

You mistake, sir; I am sure no man hath any quarrel to me; my remembrance is very free and clear from any image of offence done to any man.

SIR TOBY.

You'll find it otherwise, I assure you: therefore, if you hold your life at any price, betake you to your guard; for your opposite hath in him what youth, strength, skill, and wrath, can furnish man withal.

VIOLA.

I pray you, sir, what is he?

SIR TOBY.

He is knight, dubbed with unhacked rapier and on carpet consideration; but he is a devil in private brawl; souls and bodies hath he divorced three; and his incensement at this moment is so implacable that satisfaction can be none but by pangs of death and sepulchre: hob-nob is his word; give't or take't.

VIOLA.

I will return again into the house and desire some conduct of the lady. I am no fighter. I have heard of some kind of men that put quarrels purposely on others to taste their valour: belike this is a man of that quirk.

SIR TOBY.

Sir, no; his indignation derives itself out of a very competent injury; therefore, get you on and give him his desire. Back you shall not to the house, unless you undertake that with me which with as much safety you might answer him: therefore on, or strip your sword stark naked; for meddle you must, that's certain, or forswear to wear iron about you.

VIOLA.

This is as uncivil as strange. I beseech you,

do me this courteous office as to know of the knight what my offence to him is; it is something of my negligence, nothing of my purpose.

SIR TOBY.

I will do so. Signior Fabian, stay you by this gentleman till my return.

[Exit SIR TOBY.]

VIOLA.

Pray you, sir, do you know of this matter?

FABIAN.

I know the knight is incensed against you, even to a mortal arbitrement; but nothing of the circumstance more.

VIOLA.

I beseech you, what manner of man is he?

FABIAN.

Nothing of that wonderful promise, to read him by his form, as you are like to find him in the proof of his valour. He is indeed, sir, the most skilful, bloody, and fatal opposite that you could possibly have found in any part of Illyria. Will you walk towards him? I will make your peace with him if I can.

VIOLA.

I shall be much bound to you for't. I am one that would rather go with sir priest than sir knight: I care not who knows so much of my mettle.

[Exeunt.]

[Re-enter SIR TOBY with SIR ANDREW.]

SIR TOBY.

Why, man, he's a very devil; I have not seen such a virago. I had a pass with him, rapier, scabbard, and all, and he gives me the stuck-in with such a mortal motion that it is inevitable; and on the answer, he pays you as surely as your feet hit the ground they step on. They say he has been fencer to the Sophy.

SIR ANDREW.

Pox on't, I'll not meddle with him.

SIR TOBY.

Ay, but he will not now be pacified: Fabian can scarce hold him yonder.

SIR ANDREW.

Plague on't; an I thought he had been valiant, and so cunning in fence, I'd have

571

seen him damned ere I'd have challenged him. Let him let the matter slip and I'll give him my horse, grey Capilet.

Sir Toby.

I'll make the motion. Stand here, make a good show on't; this shall end without the perdition of souls. [*Aside.*] Marry, I'll ride your horse as well as I ride you.

[*Re-enter* Fabian *and* Viola.]

[*To* Fabian.] I have his horse to take up the quarrel; I have persuaded him the youth's a devil.

Fabian.

He is as horribly conceited of him; and pants and looks pale, as if a bear were at his heels.

Sir Toby.

There's no remedy, sir: he will fight with you for's oath sake: marry, he hath better bethought him of his quarrel, and he finds that now scarce to be worth talking of: therefore, draw for the supportance of his vow; he protests he will not hurt you.

Viola. [*Aside.*]

Pray God defend me! A little thing would make me tell them how much I lack of a man.

Fabian.

Give ground if you see him furious.

Sir Toby.

Come, Sir Andrew, there's no remedy; the gentleman will, for his honour's sake, have one bout with you: he cannot by the duello avoid it; but he has promised me, as he is a gentleman and a soldier, he will not hurt you. Come on: to't.

Sir Andrew.

Pray God he keep his oath!

[*Draws.*]

[*Enter* Antonio.]

Viola.

I do assure you 'tis against my will.

[*Draws.*]

Antonio.

Put up your sword:—if this young gentleman
Have done offence, I take the fault on me;
If you offend him, I for him defy you.

[*Drawing.*]

Sir Toby.

You, sir! why, what are you?

Antonio.

One, sir, that for his love dares yet do more
Than you have heard him brag to you he
   will.

Sir Toby.

Nay, if you be an undertaker, I am for you.

[*Draws.*]

[*Enter two* Officers.]

Fabian.

O good Sir Toby, hold; here come the officers.

Sir Toby. [*To* Antonio.]

I'll be with you anon.

Viola. [*To* Sir Andrew.]

Pray, sir, put your sword up, if you please.

Sir Andrew.

Marry, will I, sir; and for that I promised you, I'll be as good as my word. He will bear you easily and reins well.

First Officer.

This is the man; do thy office.

Second Officer.

Antonio, I arrest thee at the suit of Count Orsino.

Antonio.

You do mistake me, sir.

First Officer.

No, sir, no jot; I know your favour well,
Though now you have no sea-cap on your
   head.—
Take him away; he knows I know him
   well.

Antonio.

I must obey. [*To* Viola.] This comes with
   seeking you;
But there's no remedy; I shall answer it.
What will you do? Now my necessity
Makes me to ask you for my purse. It
   grieves me
Much more for what I cannot do for you
Than what befalls myself. You stand
   amazed;
But be of comfort.

Second Officer.

           Come, sir, away.

TWELFTH NIGHT   ACT III, SCENE IV

ANTONIO.
I must entreat of you some of that money.
VIOLA.
What money, sir?
For the fair kindness you have showed
   me here,
And part being prompted by your present
   trouble,
Out of my lean and low ability
I'll lend you something; my having is not
   much;
I'll make division of my present with you:
Hold, there is half my coffer.
ANTONIO.
             Will you deny me now?
Is't possible that my deserts to you
Can lack persuasion? Do not tempt my
   misery,
Lest that it make me so unsound a man
As to upbraid you with those kindnesses
That I have done for you.
VIOLA.
             I know of none,
Nor know I you by voice or any feature:
I hate ingratitude more in a man
Than lying, vainness, babbling,
   drunkenness,
Or any taint of vice whose strong
   corruption
Inhabits our frail blood.
ANTONIO.
            O heavens themselves!
SECOND OFFICER.
Come, sir, I pray you go.
ANTONIO.
Let me speak a little. This youth that you
   see here
I snatched one half out of the jaws of death,
Relieved him with such sanctity of love,—
And to his image, which methought did
   promise
Most venerable worth, did I devotion.
FIRST OFFICER.
What's that to us? The time goes by; away.
ANTONIO.
But O how vile an idol proves this god!
Thou hast, Sebastian, done good feature
   shame.

In nature there's no blemish but the mind;
None can be call'd deform'd but the
   unkind:
Virtue is beauty; but the beauteous-evil
Are empty trunks, o'erflourished by the
   devil.
FIRST OFFICER.
The man grows mad; away with him.
   Come, come, sir.
ANTONIO.
Lead me on.
   [*Exeunt* OFFICERS *with* ANTONIO.]
VIOLA.
Methinks his words do from such passion
   fly
That he believes himself; so do not I.
Prove true, imagination; O prove true,
That I, dear brother, be now ta'en for you!
SIR TOBY.
Come hither, knight; come hither, Fabian;
we'll whisper o'er a couplet or two of most
sage saws.
VIOLA.
He named Sebastian; I my brother know
Yet living in my glass; even such and so
In favour was my brother; and he went
Still in this fashion, colour, ornament,
For him I imitate. O, if it prove,
Tempests are kind, and salt waves fresh
   in love!
                [*Exit.*]
SIR TOBY.
A very dishonest paltry boy, and more a
coward than a hare: his dishonesty appears
in leaving his friend here in necessity, and
denying him; and for his cowardship, ask
Fabian.
FABIAN.
A coward, a most devout coward, religious
   in it.
SIR ANDREW.
'Slid, I'll after him again and beat him.
SIR TOBY.
Do, cuff him soundly, but never draw thy
   sword.
SIR ANDREW.
And I do not,—
                [*Exit.*]

573

Fabian.

Come, let's see the event.

Sir Toby.

I dare lay any money 'twill be nothing yet.

[*Exeunt.*]

ACT IV
SCENE I

The street before Olivia's house.

[*Enter* Sebastian *and* Clown.]

Clown.

Will you make me believe that I am not sent for you?

Sebastian.

Go to, go to, thou art a foolish fellow;
Let me be clear of thee.

Clown.

Well held out, i' faith! No, I do not know you; nor I am not sent to you by my lady, to bid you come speak with her; nor your name is not Master Cesario; nor this is not my nose neither.—Nothing that is so is so.

Sebastian.

I pr'ythee vent thy folly somewhere else.
Thou know'st not me.

Clown.

Vent my folly! he has heard that word of some great man, and now applies it to a fool. Vent my folly! I am afraid this great lubber, the world, will prove a cockney.—I pr'ythee now, ungird thy strangeness, and tell me what I shall vent to my lady. Shall I vent to her that thou art coming?

Sebastian.

I pr'ythee, foolish Greek, depart from me;
There's money for thee; if you tarry longer
I shall give worse payment.

Clown.

By my troth, thou hast an open hand:—
These wise men that give fools money get themselves a good report after fourteen years' purchase.

[*Enter* Sir Andrew, Sir Toby, *and* Fabian.]

Sir Andrew.

Now, sir, have I met you again? there's for you.

[*Striking* Sebastian.]

Sebastian.

Why, there's for thee, and there, and there.
Are all the people mad?

[*Beating* Sir Andrew.]

Sir Toby.

Hold, sir, or I'll throw your dagger o'er the house.

Clown.

This will I tell my lady straight. I would not be in some of your coats for twopence.

[*Exit* Clown.]

Sir Toby.

Come on, sir; hold.

[*Holding* Sebastian.]

Sir Andrew.

Nay, let him alone; I'll go another way to work with him; I'll have an action of battery against him, if there be any law in Illyria: though I struck him first, yet it's no matter for that.

Sebastian.

Let go thy hand.

Sir Toby.

Come, sir, I will not let you go. Come, my young soldier, put up your iron: you are well fleshed; come on.

Sebastian.

I will be free from thee. What wouldst thou now? If thou dar'st tempt me further, draw thy sword.

[*Draws.*]

Sir Toby.

What, what? Nay, then I must have an ounce or two of this malapert blood from you.

[*Draws.*]

[*Enter* Olivia.]

Olivia.

Hold, Toby; on thy life, I charge thee hold.

Sir Toby.

Madam?

Olivia.

Will it be ever thus? Ungracious wretch,
Fit for the mountains and the barbarous caves,
Where manners ne'er were preach'd! Out of my sight!
Be not offended, dear Cesario!—

Rudesby, be gone!
[*Exeunt* Sir Toby, Sir Andrew, *and*
    Fabian.]
                        I pr'ythee, gentle friend,
Let thy fair wisdom, not thy passion, sway
In this uncivil and unjust extent
Against thy peace. Go with me to my
    house,
And hear thou there how many fruitless
    pranks
This ruffian hath botch'd up, that thou
    thereby
Mayst smile at this: thou shalt not choose
    but go;
Do not deny. Beshrew his soul for me,
He started one poor heart of mine in thee.

Sebastian.
What relish is in this? how runs the
    stream?
Or I am mad, or else this is a dream:—
Let fancy still my sense in Lethe steep;
If it be thus to dream, still let me sleep!

Olivia.
Nay, come, I pr'ythee. Would thou'dst be
    ruled by me!

Sebastian.
Madam, I will.

Olivia.
                O, say so, and so be!
                [*Exeunt.*]

SCENE II

A room in Olivia's house.
[*Enter* Maria *and* Clown.]

Maria.
Nay, I pr'ythee, put on this gown and this
beard; make him believe thou art Sir Topas
the curate; do it quickly: I'll call Sir Toby
the whilst.
                [*Exit* Maria.]

Clown.
Well, I'll put it on, and I will dissemble
myself in't; and I would I were the first that
ever dissembled in such a gown. I am not
tall enough to become the function well:
nor lean enough to be thought a good
student: but to be said, an honest man and
a good housekeeper, goes as fairly as to

say, a careful man and a great scholar. The
competitors enter.
                [*Enter* Sir Toby Belch *and* Maria.]

Sir Toby.
Jove bless thee, Master Parson.

Clown.
Bonos dies, Sir Toby: for as the old hermit
of Prague, that never saw pen and ink, very
wittily said to a niece of King Gorboduc,
"That that is, is"; so I, being master parson,
am master parson: for what is that but that?
and is but is?

Sir Toby.
To him, Sir Topas.

Clown.
What, hoa, I say,—Peace in this prison!

Sir Toby.
The knave counterfeits well; a good knave.

Malvolio. [*In an inner chamber.*]
Who calls there?

Clown.
Sir Topas the curate, who comes to visit
Malvolio the lunatic.

Malvolio.
Sir Topas, Sir Topas, good Sir Topas, go to
my lady.

Clown.
Out, hyperbolical fiend! how vexest thou
this man? talkest thou nothing but of ladies?

Sir Toby.
Well said, master parson.

Malvolio.
Sir Topas, never was man thus wronged:
good Sir Topas, do not think I am mad;
they have laid me here in hideous darkness.

Clown.
Fie, thou dishonest Sathan! I call thee by
the most modest terms; for I am one of
those gentle ones that will use the devil
himself with courtesy. Say'st thou that
house is dark?

Malvolio.
As hell, Sir Topas.

Clown.
Why, it hath bay windows transparent as
barricadoes, and the clear storeys toward
the south-north are as lustrous as ebony;
and yet complainest thou of obstruction?

MALVOLIO.
I am not mad, Sir Topas; I say to you this house is dark.

CLOWN.
Madman, thou errest. I say there is no darkness but ignorance; in which thou art more puzzled than the Egyptians in their fog.

MALVOLIO.
I say this house is as dark as ignorance, though ignorance were as dark as hell; and I say there was never man thus abused. I am no more mad than you are; make the trial of it in any constant question.

CLOWN.
What is the opinion of Pythagoras concerning wild-fowl?

MALVOLIO.
That the soul of our grandam might haply inhabit a bird.

CLOWN.
What thinkest thou of his opinion?

MALVOLIO.
I think nobly of the soul, and no way approve his opinion.

CLOWN.
Fare thee well. Remain thou still in darkness: thou shalt hold the opinion of Pythagoras ere I will allow of thy wits; and fear to kill a woodcock, lest thou dispossess the soul of thy grandam. Fare thee well.

MALVOLIO.
Sir Topas, Sir Topas!

SIR TOBY.
My most exquisite Sir Topas!

CLOWN.
Nay, I am for all waters.

MARIA.
Thou mightst have done this without thy beard and gown: he sees thee not.

SIR TOBY.
To him in thine own voice, and bring me word how thou findest him; I would we were well rid of this knavery. If he may be conveniently delivered, I would he were; for I am now so far in offence with my niece that I cannot pursue with any safety this

sport to the upshot. Come by and by to my chamber.

[*Exeunt* SIR TOBY *and* MARIA.]

CLOWN. [*Sings.*]
    Hey, Robin, jolly Robin,
      Tell me how thy lady does.

MALVOLIO.
Fool,—

CLOWN.
"My lady is unkind, perdy."

MALVOLIO.
Fool,—

CLOWN.
"Alas, why is she so?"

MALVOLIO.
Fool, I say;—

CLOWN.
"She loves another"—Who calls, ha?

MALVOLIO.
Good fool, as ever thou wilt deserve well at my hand, help me to a candle, and pen, ink, and paper; as I am a gentleman, I will live to be thankful to thee for't.

CLOWN.
Master Malvolio!

MALVOLIO.
Ay, good fool.

CLOWN.
Alas, sir, how fell you besides your five wits?

MALVOLIO.
Fool, there was never man so notoriously abused; I am as well in my wits, fool, as thou art.

CLOWN.
But as well? then you are mad indeed, if you be no better in your wits than a fool.

MALVOLIO.
They have here propertied me; keep me in darkness, send ministers to me, asses, and do all they can to face me out of my wits.

CLOWN.
Advise you what you say: the minister is here.—Malvolio, thy wits the heavens restore! endeavour thyself to sleep, and leave thy vain bibble-babble.

MALVOLIO.
Sir Topas,—

Clown.

Maintain no words with him, good fellow.
Who, I, sir? Not I, sir. God b'wi' you, good
Sir Topas.—Marry, amen.—I will sir, I
will.

Malvolio.

Fool, fool, fool, I say,—

Clown.

Alas, sir, be patient. What say you, sir? I am
shent for speaking to you.

Malvolio.

Good fool, help me to some light and some
paper; I tell thee I am as well in my wits as
any man in Illyria.

Clown.

Well-a-day,—that you were, sir!

Malvolio.

By this hand, I am: Good fool, some ink,
paper, and light, and convey what I will set
down to my lady; it shall advantage thee
more than ever the bearing of letter did.

Clown.

I will help you to't. But tell me true, are you
not mad indeed? or do you but counterfeit?

Malvolio.

Believe me, I am not; I tell thee true.

Clown.

Nay, I'll ne'er believe a madman till I see
his brains.
I will fetch you light, and paper, and ink.

Malvolio.

Fool, I'll requite it in the highest degree: I
pr'ythee be gone.

Clown. [*Sings.*]

> I am gone, sir,
>   And anon, sir,
> I'll be with you again,
>   In a trice,
>   Like to the old vice,
> Your need to sustain;
> Who with dagger of lath,
> In his rage and his wrath,
>   Cries ah, ha! to the devil:
> Like a mad lad,
> Pare thy nails, dad.
>   Adieu, goodman devil.
>   [*Exit.*]

SCENE III

Olivia's garden.
[*Enter* Sebastian.]

Sebastian.

This is the air; that is the glorious sun;
This pearl she gave me, I do feel't and see't:
And though 'tis wonder that enwraps me
   thus,
Yet 'tis not madness. Where's Antonio,
   then?
I could not find him at the Elephant;
Yet there he was; and there I found this
   credit,
That he did range the town to seek me out.
His counsel now might do me golden
   service;
For though my soul disputes well with my
   sense,
That this may be some error, but no
   madness,
Yet doth this accident and flood of fortune
So far exceed all instance, all discourse,
That I am ready to distrust mine eyes
And wrangle with my reason, that
   persuades me
To any other trust but that I am mad,
Or else the lady's mad; yet if 'twere so,
She could not sway her house, command
   her followers,
Take and give back affairs and their
   despatch
With such a smooth, discreet, and stable
   bearing,
As I perceive she does: there's something
   in't
That is deceivable. But here comes the
   lady.
     [*Enter* Olivia *and a* Priest.]

Olivia.

Blame not this haste of mine. If you mean
   well,
Now go with me and with this holy man
Into the chantry by: there, before him
And underneath that consecrated roof,
Plight me the full assurance of your faith,
That my most jealous and too doubtful
   soul
May live at peace. He shall conceal it

Whiles you are willing it shall come to
    note;
What time we will our celebration keep
According to my birth.—What do you
    say?

SEBASTIAN.

I'll follow this good man, and go with you;
And, having sworn truth, ever will be true.

OLIVIA.

Then lead the way, good father;—and
    heavens so shine
That they may fairly note this act of
    mine!

                    [*Exeunt.*]

ACT V
SCENE I

The street before Olivia's house.
[*Enter* CLOWN *and* FABIAN.]

FABIAN.

Now, as thou lovest me, let me see his letter.

CLOWN.

Good Master Fabian, grant me another
request.

FABIAN.

Anything.

CLOWN.

Do not desire to see this letter.

FABIAN.

This is to give a dog; and in recompense
desire my dog again.

[*Enter* DUKE, VIOLA, *and* ATTENDANTS.]

DUKE.

Belong you to the Lady Olivia, friends?

CLOWN.

Ay, sir; we are some of her trappings.

DUKE.

I know thee well. How dost thou, my good
fellow?

CLOWN.

Truly, sir, the better for my foes and the
worse for my friends.

DUKE.

Just the contrary; the better for thy friends.

CLOWN.

No, sir, the worse.

DUKE.

How can that be?

CLOWN.

Marry, sir, they praise me and make an ass
of me; now my foes tell me plainly I am
an ass: so that by my foes, sir, I profit in
the knowledge of myself, and by my friends
I am abused: so that, conclusions to be as
kisses, if your four negatives make your two
affirmatives, why then, the worse for my
friends and the better for my foes.

DUKE.

Why, this is excellent.

CLOWN.

By my troth, sir, no; though it please you to
be one of my friends.

DUKE.

Thou shalt not be the worse for me; there's
gold.

CLOWN.

But that it would be double-dealing, sir, I
would you could make it another.

DUKE.

O, you give me ill counsel.

CLOWN.

Put your grace in your pocket, sir, for this
once, and let your flesh and blood obey it.

DUKE.

Well, I will be so much a sinner to be a
double-dealer: there's another.

CLOWN.

Primo, secundo, tertio, is a good play; and
the old saying is, the third pays for all; the
triplex, sir, is a good tripping measure; or
the bells of Saint Bennet, sir, may put you
in mind; one, two, three.

DUKE.

You can fool no more money out of me at
this throw: if you will let your lady know I
am here to speak with her, and bring her
along with you, it may awake my bounty
further.

CLOWN.

Marry, sir, lullaby to your bounty till I come
again. I go, sir; but I would not have you
to think that my desire of having is the sin
of covetousness: but, as you say, sir, let your
bounty take a nap; I will awake it anon.

                    [*Exit* CLOWN.]
            [*Enter* ANTONIO *and* OFFICERS.]

VIOLA.

Here comes the man, sir, that did rescue
me.

DUKE.

That face of his I do remember well:
Yet when I saw it last it was besmeared
As black as Vulcan in the smoke of war:
A bawbling vessel was he captain of,
For shallow draught and bulk unprizable;
With which such scathful grapple did he
make
With the most noble bottom of our fleet
That very envy and the tongue of loss
Cried fame and honour on him.—What's
the matter?

FIRST OFFICER.

Orsino, this is that Antonio
That took the Phoenix and her fraught
from Candy:
And this is he that did the Tiger board
When your young nephew Titus lost his
leg:
Here in the streets, desperate of shame
and state,
In private brabble did we apprehend him.

VIOLA.

He did me kindness, sir; drew on my side;
But, in conclusion, put strange speech
upon me.
I know not what 'twas, but distraction.

DUKE.

Notable pirate! thou salt-water thief!
What foolish boldness brought thee to
their mercies,
Whom thou, in terms so bloody and so
dear,
Hast made thine enemies?

ANTONIO.

                                       Orsino, noble sir,
Be pleased that I shake off these names
you give me:
Antonio never yet was thief or pirate,
Though, I confess, on base and ground
enough,
Orsino's enemy. A witchcraft drew me
hither:
That most ingrateful boy there, by your
side

From the rude sea's enraged and foamy
mouth
Did I redeem; a wreck past hope he was:
His life I gave him, and did thereto add
My love, without retention or restraint,
All his in dedication: for his sake,
Did I expose myself, pure for his love,
Into the danger of this adverse town;
Drew to defend him when he was beset:
Where being apprehended, his false
cunning,—
Not meaning to partake with me in
danger,—
Taught him to face me out of his
acquaintance,
And grew a twenty-years-removed thing
While one would wink; denied me mine
own purse,
Which I had recommended to his use
Not half an hour before.

VIOLA.

                                       How can this be?

DUKE.

When came he to this town?

ANTONIO.

To-day, my lord; and for three months
before,—
No interim, not a minute's vacancy,—
Both day and night did we keep company.
[*Enter* OLIVIA *and* ATTENDANTS.]

DUKE.

Here comes the countess; now heaven
walks on earth.—
But for thee, fellow, fellow, thy words are
madness:
Three months this youth hath tended
upon me;
But more of that anon.—Take him aside.

OLIVIA.

What would my lord, but that he may not
have,
Wherein Olivia may seem serviceable!—
Cesario, you do not keep promise with
me.

VIOLA.

Madam?

DUKE.

Gracious Olivia,—

OLIVIA.
What do you say, Cesario?—Good my
    lord,—
VIOLA.
My lord would speak, my duty hushes me.
OLIVIA.
If it be aught to the old tune, my lord,
It is as fat and fulsome to mine ear
As howling after music.
DUKE.
                                    Still so cruel?
OLIVIA.
Still so constant, lord.
DUKE.
What! to perverseness? you uncivil lady,
To whose ingrate and unauspicious altars
My soul the faithfull'st offerings hath
    breathed out
That e'er devotion tender'd! What shall
    I do?
OLIVIA.
Even what it please my lord, that shall
    become him.
DUKE.
Why should I not, had I the heart to do it.
Like to the Egyptian thief, at point of
    death,
Kill what I love; a savage jealousy
That sometime savours nobly.—But hear
    me this:
Since you to non-regardance cast my
    faith,
And that I partly know the instrument
That screws me from my true place in your
    favour,
Live you the marble-breasted tyrant still;
But this your minion, whom I know you
    love,
And whom, by heaven I swear, I tender
    dearly,
Him will I tear out of that cruel eye
Where he sits crowned in his master's
    sprite.—
Come, boy, with me; my thoughts are ripe
    in mischief:
I'll sacrifice the lamb that I do love,
To spite a raven's heart within a dove.
                                    [Going.]

VIOLA.
And I, most jocund, apt, and willingly,
To do you rest, a thousand deaths would
    die.
OLIVIA.
Where goes Cesario?
VIOLA.
                        After him I love
More than I love these eyes, more than
    my life,
More, by all mores, than e'er I shall love
    wife;
If I do feign, you witnesses above
Punish my life for tainting of my love!
OLIVIA.
Ah me, detested! how am I beguil'd!
VIOLA.
Who does beguile you? who does do you
    wrong?
OLIVIA.
Hast thou forgot thyself? Is it so long?—
Call forth the holy father.
                    [Exit an ATTENDANT.]
DUKE. [To VIOLA.]
                                    Come, away!
OLIVIA.
Whither, my lord? Cesario, husband,
    stay.
DUKE.
Husband?
OLIVIA.
                Ay, husband, can he that deny?
DUKE.
Her husband, sirrah?
VIOLA.
                        No, my lord, not I.
OLIVIA.
Alas, it is the baseness of thy fear
That makes thee strangle thy propriety:
Fear not, Cesario, take thy fortunes up;
Be that thou know'st thou art, and then
    thou art
As great as that thou fear'st—O, welcome,
    father!
            [Re-enter ATTENDANT and PRIEST.]
Father, I charge thee, by thy reverence,
Here to unfold,—though lately we
    intended

To keep in darkness what occasion now
Reveals before 'tis ripe,—what thou dost
    know
Hath newly passed between this youth
    and me.

PRIEST.
A contract of eternal bond of love,
Confirmed by mutual joinder of your
    hands,
Attested by the holy close of lips,
Strengthen'd by interchangement of your
    rings;
And all the ceremony of this compact
Sealed in my function, by my testimony:
Since when, my watch hath told me,
    toward my grave,
I have travelled but two hours.

DUKE.
O thou dissembling cub! What wilt thou
    be,
When time hath sowed a grizzle on thy
    case?
Or will not else thy craft so quickly grow
That thine own trip shall be thine
    overthrow?
Farewell, and take her; but direct thy feet
Where thou and I henceforth may never
    meet.

VIOLA.
My lord, I do protest,—

OLIVIA.
              O, do not swear;
Hold little faith, though thou has too
    much fear.

    [*Enter* SIR ANDREW AGUECHEEK,
        with his head broke.]

SIR ANDREW.
For the love of God, a surgeon; send one
presently to Sir Toby.

OLIVIA.
What's the matter?

SIR ANDREW.
He has broke my head across, and has given
Sir Toby a bloody coxcomb too: for the love
of God, your help: I had rather than forty
pound I were at home.

OLIVIA.
Who has done this, Sir Andrew?

SIR ANDREW.
The count's gentleman, one Cesario: we
took him for a coward, but he's the very
devil incardinate.

DUKE.
My gentleman, Cesario?

SIR ANDREW.
Od's lifelings, here he is:—You broke my
head for nothing; and that that I did, I was
set on to do't by Sir Toby.

VIOLA.
Why do you speak to me? I never hurt
    you:
You drew your sword upon me without
    cause;
But I bespake you fair and hurt you not.

SIR ANDREW.
If a bloody coxcomb be a hurt, you have
hurt me; I think you set nothing by a
bloody coxcomb. [*Enter* SIR TOBY BELCH,
drunk, led by the CLOWN.] Here comes Sir
Toby halting; you shall hear more: but if
he had not been in drink he would have
tickled you othergates than he did.

DUKE.
How now, gentleman? how is't with you?

SIR TOBY.
That's all one; he has hurt me, and there's
the end on't.—Sot, didst see Dick Surgeon,
sot?

CLOWN.
O, he's drunk, Sir Toby, an hour agone; his
eyes were set at eight i' the morning.

SIR TOBY.
Then he's a rogue. After a passy-measure, or
a pavin, I hate a drunken rogue.

OLIVIA.
Away with him. Who hath made this
havoc with them?

SIR ANDREW.
I'll help you, Sir Toby, because we'll be
dressed together.

SIR TOBY.
Will you help an ass-head, and a coxcomb,
and a knave? a thin-faced knave, a gull?

OLIVIA.
Get him to bed, and let his hurt be looked
    to.

[Exeunt Clown, Sir Toby, *and* Sir Andrew.]
[Enter Sebastian.]

Sebastian.
I am sorry, madam, I have hurt your kinsman;
But, had it been the brother of my blood,
I must have done no less, with wit and safety.
You throw a strange regard upon me, and by that
I do perceive it hath offended you;
Pardon me, sweet one, even for the vows
We made each other but so late ago.

Duke.
One face, one voice, one habit, and two persons;
A natural perspective, that is, and is not.

Sebastian.
Antonio, O my dear Antonio!
How have the hours rack'd and tortur'd me
Since I have lost thee.

Antonio.
Sebastian are you?

Sebastian.
                    Fear'st thou that, Antonio?

Antonio.
How have you made division of yourself?—
An apple, cleft in two, is not more twin
Than these two creatures. Which is Sebastian?

Olivia.
Most wonderful!

Sebastian.
Do I stand there? I never had a brother:
Nor can there be that deity in my nature
Of here and everywhere. I had a sister
Whom the blind waves and surges have devoured:—
[To Viola.] Of charity, what kin are you to me?
What countryman, what name, what parentage?

Viola.
Of Messaline: Sebastian was my father;
Such a Sebastian was my brother too:
So went he suited to his watery tomb:

If spirits can assume both form and suit,
You come to fright us.

Sebastian.
                    A spirit I am indeed:
But am in that dimension grossly clad,
Which from the womb I did participate.
Were you a woman, as the rest goes even,
I should my tears let fall upon your cheek,
And say—Thrice welcome, drowned Viola!

Viola.
My father had a mole upon his brow.

Sebastian.
And so had mine.

Viola.
And died that day when Viola from her birth
Had numbered thirteen years.

Sebastian.
O, that record is lively in my soul!
He finished, indeed, his mortal act
That day that made my sister thirteen years.

Viola.
If nothing lets to make us happy both
But this my masculine usurp'd attire,
Do not embrace me till each circumstance
Of place, time, fortune, do cohere, and jump
That I am Viola: which to confirm,
I'll bring you to a captain in this town,
Where lie my maiden weeds; by whose gentle help
I was preserv'd to serve this noble count;
All the occurrence of my fortune since
Hath been between this lady and this lord.

Sebastian. *[To* Olivia.]
So comes it, lady, you have been mistook:
But nature to her bias drew in that.
You would have been contracted to a maid;
Nor are you therein, by my life, deceived;
You are betroth'd both to a maid and man.

Duke.
Be not amazed; right noble is his blood.—
If this be so, as yet the glass seems true,
I shall have share in this most happy wreck:
[To Viola.] Boy, thou hast said to me a thousand times,

Thou never shouldst love woman like to
me.

Viola.
And all those sayings will I over-swear;
And all those swearings keep as true in
soul
As doth that orbed continent the fire
That severs day from night.

Duke.
                            Give me thy hand;
And let me see thee in thy woman's weeds.

Viola.
The captain that did bring me first on
shore
Hath my maid's garments: he, upon some
action,
Is now in durance, at Malvolio's suit;
A gentleman and follower of my lady's.

Olivia.
He shall enlarge him:—Fetch Malvolio
hither:—
And yet, alas, now I remember me,
They say, poor gentleman, he's much
distract.
            [*Re-enter* Clown, *with a letter.*]
A most extracting frenzy of mine own
From my remembrance clearly banished
his.—
How does he, sirrah?

Clown.
Truly, madam, he holds Belzebub at the
stave's end as well as a man in his case may
do: he has here writ a letter to you; I should
have given it you to-day morning, but as a
madman's epistles are no gospels, so it skills
not much when they are delivered.

Olivia.
Open it, and read it.

Clown.
Look then to be well edified when the
fool delivers the madman: [*Reads.*] "By the
Lord, madam,—"

Olivia.
How now! art thou mad?

Clown.
No, madam, I do but read madness: an your
ladyship will have it as it ought to be, you
must allow vox.

Olivia.
Pr'ythee, read i' thy right wits.

Clown.
So I do, madonna; but to read his right
wits is to read thus; therefore perpend, my
princess, and give ear.

Olivia. [*To* Fabian.]
Read it you, sirrah.

Fabian. [*Reads.*]
"By the Lord, madam, you wrong me,
and the world shall know it: though you
have put me into darkness and given your
drunken cousin rule over me, yet have I the
benefit of my senses as well as your ladyship.
I have your own letter that induced me to
the semblance I put on; with the which
I doubt not but to do myself much right
or you much shame. Think of me as you
please. I leave my duty a little unthought
of, and speak out of my injury.
                  The madly-used Malvolio."

Olivia.
Did he write this?

Clown.
Ay, madam.

Duke.
This savours not much of distraction.

Olivia.
See him delivered, Fabian: bring him
hither.
            [*Exit* Fabian.]
My lord, so please you, these things
further thought on,
To think me as well a sister as a wife,
One day shall crown the alliance on't, so
please you,
Here at my house, and at my proper
cost.

Duke.
Madam, I am most apt to embrace your
offer.—
[*To* Viola.] Your master quits you; and,
for your service done him,
So much against the mettle of your sex,
So far beneath your soft and tender
breeding,
And since you called me master for so
long,

Here is my hand; you shall from this time be
Your master's mistress.

OLIVIA.
       A sister?—you are she.
[*Re-enter* FABIAN *with* MALVOLIO.]

DUKE.
Is this the madman?

OLIVIA.
       Ay, my lord, this same;
How now, Malvolio?

MALVOLIO.
    Madam, you have done me wrong,
Notorious wrong.

OLIVIA.
       Have I, Malvolio? no.

MALVOLIO.
Lady, you have. Pray you peruse that letter.
You must not now deny it is your hand,
Write from it, if you can, in hand or phrase;
Or say 'tis not your seal, not your invention:
You can say none of this. Well, grant it then,
And tell me, in the modesty of honour,
Why you have given me such clear lights of favour;
Bade me come smiling and cross-garter'd to you;
To put on yellow stockings, and to frown
Upon Sir Toby and the lighter people:
And, acting this in an obedient hope,
Why have you suffer'd me to be imprison'd,
Kept in a dark house, visited by the priest,
And made the most notorious geck and gull
That e'er invention played on? tell me why.

OLIVIA.
Alas, Malvolio, this is not my writing,
Though, I confess, much like the character:
But out of question, 'tis Maria's hand.
And now I do bethink me, it was she
First told me thou wast mad; then cam'st in smiling,

And in such forms which here were presuppos'd
Upon thee in the letter. Pr'ythee, be content:
This practice hath most shrewdly pass'd upon thee:
But, when we know the grounds and authors of it,
Thou shalt be both the plaintiff and the judge
Of thine own cause.

FABIAN.
     Good madam, hear me speak;
And let no quarrel, nor no brawl to come,
Taint the condition of this present hour,
Which I have wonder'd at. In hope it shall not,
Most freely I confess, myself and Toby
Set this device against Malvolio here,
Upon some stubborn and uncourteous parts
We had conceiv'd against him. Maria writ
The letter, at Sir Toby's great importance;
In recompense whereof he hath married her.
How with a sportful malice it was follow'd
May rather pluck on laughter than revenge,
If that the injuries be justly weigh'd
That have on both sides past.

OLIVIA.
Alas, poor fool! how have they baffled thee!

CLOWN.
Why, "some are born great, some achieve greatness, and some have greatness thrown upon them." I was one, sir, in this interlude;—one Sir Topas, sir; but that's all one:—"By the Lord, fool, I am not mad";—But do you remember? "Madam, why laugh you at such a barren rascal? An you smile not, he's gagged"? And thus the whirligig of time brings in his revenges.

MALVOLIO.
I'll be revenged on the whole pack of you.
       [*Exit.*]

OLIVIA.
He hath been most notoriously abus'd.

DUKE.
Pursue him, and entreat him to a peace:—
He hath not told us of the captain yet;
When that is known, and golden time
    convents,
A solemn combination shall be made
Of our dear souls.—Meantime, sweet
    sister,
We will not part from hence.—Cesario,
    come:
For so you shall be while you are a man;
But, when in other habits you are seen,
Orsino's mistress, and his fancy's queen.
                [*Exeunt.*]
CLOWN. [*Sings.*]
  When that I was and a little tiny boy,
    With hey, ho, the wind and the rain,
  A foolish thing was but a toy,
    For the rain it raineth every day.

But when I came to man's estate,
  With hey, ho, the wind and the rain,
'Gainst knave and thief men shut their
    gate,
  For the rain it raineth every day.
But when I came, alas! to wive,
  With hey, ho, the wind and the rain,
By swaggering could I never thrive,
  For the rain it raineth every day.
But when I came unto my bed,
  With hey, ho, the wind and the rain,
With toss-pots still had drunken head,
  For the rain it raineth every day.
A great while ago the world begun,
  With hey, ho, the wind and the rain,
But that's all one, our play is done,
  And we'll strive to please you every day.
                [*Exit.*]

The Winter's Tale

Dramatis Personae

LEONTES, *King of Sicilia*
MAMILLIUS, *his son*
CAMILLO, *a Sicilian lord*
ANTIGONUS, *a Sicilian lord*
CLEOMENES, *a Sicilian lord*
DION, *a Sicilian lord*
POLIXENES, *King of Bohemia*
FLORIZEL, *his son*
ARCHIDAMUS, *a Bohemian lord*
An old SHEPHERD, *reputed father of*
Perdita
CLOWN, *his son*
AUTOLYCUS, *a rogue*
MARINER
GAOLER
SERVANT *to the old shepherd*
Other SICILIAN LORDS
SICILIAN GENTLEMEN

OFFICERS *of a court of judicature*
HERMIONE, *queen to Leontes*
PERDITA, *daughter to Leontes and*
Hermione
PAULINA, *wife to Antigonus*
EMILIA, *a lady attending on the queen*
MOPSA, *shepherdess*
DORCAS, *shepherdess*
Other LADIES, *attending on the queen*
LORDS, LADIES, *and*
ATTENDANTS; SATYRS
for a dance; SHEPHERDS,
SHEPHERDESSES, GUARDS, &C.
TIME, *as Chorus*

SCENE: *Sometimes in Sicilia; sometimes in*
Bohemia.

ACT I
SCENE I

Sicilia. An ante-chamber in Leontes's palace.
[*Enter* CAMILLO *and* ARCHIDAMUS.]

ARCHIDAMUS.
If you shall chance, Camillo, to visit Bohemia, on the like occasion whereon my services are now on foot, you shall see, as I have said, great difference betwixt our Bohemia and your Sicilia.

CAMILLO.
I think this coming summer the King of Sicilia means to pay Bohemia the visitation which he justly owes him.

ARCHIDAMUS.
Wherein our entertainment shall shame us we will be justified in our loves; for indeed,—

CAMILLO.
Beseech you,—

ARCHIDAMUS.
Verily, I speak it in the freedom of

my knowledge: we cannot with such magnificence—in so rare—I know not what to say.—We will give you sleepy drinks, that your senses, unintelligent of our insufficience, may, though they cannot praise us, as little accuse us.

CAMILLO.
You pay a great deal too dear for what's given freely.

ARCHIDAMUS.
Believe me, I speak as my understanding instructs me and as mine honesty puts it to utterance.

CAMILLO.
Sicilia cannot show himself overkind to Bohemia. They were trained together in their childhoods; and there rooted betwixt them then such an affection which cannot choose but branch now. Since their more mature dignities and royal necessities made separation of their society, their encounters, though not personal, have been royally

attorneyed with interchange of gifts, letters, loving embassies; that they have seemed to be together, though absent; shook hands, as over a vast; and embraced as it were from the ends of opposed winds. The heavens continue their loves!

ARCHIDAMUS.
I think there is not in the world either malice or matter to alter it. You have an unspeakable comfort of your young Prince Mamillius: it is a gentleman of the greatest promise that ever came into my note.

CAMILLO.
I very well agree with you in the hopes of him. It is a gallant child; one that indeed physics the subject, makes old hearts fresh: they that went on crutches ere he was born desire yet their life to see him a man.

ARCHIDAMUS.
Would they else be content to die?

CAMILLO.
Yes, if there were no other excuse why they should desire to live.

ARCHIDAMUS.
If the king had no son, they would desire to live on crutches till he had one.

[*Exeunt.*]

SCENE II

The same. A room of state in the palace.
[*Enter* LEONTES, POLIXENES, HERMIONE,
MAMILLIUS, CAMILLO,
and ATTENDANTS.]

POLIXENES.
Nine changes of the watery star hath been
The shepherd's note since we have left our throne
Without a burden: time as long again
Would be fill'd up, my brother, with our thanks;
And yet we should, for perpetuity,
Go hence in debt: and therefore, like a cipher,
Yet standing in rich place, I multiply
With one we-thank-you many thousands more
That go before it.

LEONTES.
                    Stay your thanks a while,
And pay them when you part.

POLIXENES.
                    Sir, that's to-morrow.
I am question'd by my fears, of what may chance
Or breed upon our absence; that may blow
No sneaping winds at home, to make us say,
"This is put forth too truly." Besides, I have stay'd
To tire your royalty.

LEONTES.
                    We are tougher, brother,
Than you can put us to't.

POLIXENES.
                    No longer stay.

LEONTES.
One seven-night longer.

POLIXENES.
                    Very sooth, to-morrow.

LEONTES.
We'll part the time between 's then: and in that
I'll no gainsaying.

POLIXENES.
                    Press me not, beseech you, so,
There is no tongue that moves, none, none i' the world,
So soon as yours, could win me: so it should now,
Were there necessity in your request, although
'Twere needful I denied it. My affairs
Do even drag me homeward: which to hinder,
Were, in your love a whip to me; my stay
To you a charge and trouble: to save both,
Farewell, our brother.

LEONTES.
                    Tongue-tied, our queen? Speak you.

HERMIONE.
I had thought, sir, to have held my peace until
You had drawn oaths from him not to stay. You, sir,
Charge him too coldly. Tell him you are sure

All in Bohemia's well: this satisfaction
The by-gone day proclaimed: say this to
    him,
He's beat from his best ward.
LEONTES.
                Well said, Hermione.
HERMIONE.
To tell he longs to see his son were strong:
But let him say so then, and let him go;
But let him swear so, and he shall not stay,
We'll thwack him hence with distaffs.—
      [*To* POLIXENES.]
Yet of your royal presence I'll adventure
The borrow of a week. When at Bohemia
You take my lord, I'll give him my
    commission
To let him there a month behind the gest
Prefix'd for's parting:—yet, good deed,
    Leontes,
I love thee not a jar of the clock behind
What lady she her lord.—You'll stay?
POLIXENES.
                  No, madam.
HERMIONE.
Nay, but you will?
POLIXENES.
            I may not, verily.
HERMIONE.
Verily!
You put me off with limber vows; but I,
Though you would seek to unsphere the
    stars with oaths,
Should yet say, "Sir, no going." Verily,
You shall not go; a lady's verily is
As potent as a lord's. Will go yet?
Force me to keep you as a prisoner,
Not like a guest: so you shall pay your fees
When you depart, and save your thanks.
How say you?
My prisoner or my guest? by your dread
    "verily,"
One of them you shall be.
POLIXENES.
          Your guest, then, madam:
To be your prisoner should import
    offending;
Which is for me less easy to commit
Than you to punish.

HERMIONE.
              Not your gaoler then,
But your kind hostess. Come, I'll question
    you
Of my lord's tricks and yours when you
    were boys.
You were pretty lordings then.
POLIXENES.
             We were, fair queen,
Two lads that thought there was no more
    behind
But such a day to-morrow as to-day,
And to be boy eternal.
HERMIONE.
Was not my lord the verier wag o' the two?
POLIXENES.
We were as twinn'd lambs that did frisk i'
    the sun
And bleat the one at th' other. What we
    chang'd
Was innocence for innocence; we knew
    not
The doctrine of ill-doing, nor dream'd
That any did. Had we pursu'd that life,
And our weak spirits ne'er been higher
    rear'd
With stronger blood, we should have
    answer'd heaven
Boldly, "Not guilty," the imposition clear'd
Hereditary ours.
HERMIONE.
             By this we gather
You have tripp'd since.
POLIXENES.
          O my most sacred lady,
Temptations have since then been born
    to 's! for
In those unfledg'd days was my wife a girl;
Your precious self had then not cross'd
    the eyes
Of my young play-fellow.
HERMIONE.
              Grace to boot!
Of this make no conclusion, lest you say
Your queen and I are devils: yet, go on;
The offences we have made you do we'll
    answer;
If you first sinn'd with us, and that with us

You did continue fault, and that you slipp'd
   not
With any but with us.
LEONTES.
               Is he won yet?
HERMIONE.
He'll stay, my lord.
LEONTES.
          At my request he would not.
Hermione, my dearest, thou never spok'st
To better purpose.
HERMIONE.
         Never?
LEONTES.
            Never, but once.
HERMIONE.
What! have I twice said well? when was't
   before?
I pr'ythee tell me; cram 's with praise, and
   make 's
As fat as tame things: one good deed
   dying tongueless
Slaughters a thousand waiting upon that.
Our praises are our wages; you may ride 's
With one soft kiss a thousand furlongs ere
With spur we heat an acre. But to the
   goal:—
My last good deed was to entreat his stay;
What was my first? it has an elder sister,
Or I mistake you: O, would her name were
   Grace!
But once before I spoke to the purpose—
   when?
Nay, let me have't; I long.
LEONTES.
           Why, that was when
Three crabbed months had sour'd
   themselves to death,
Ere I could make thee open thy white
   hand
And clap thyself my love; then didst thou
   utter
"I am yours for ever."
HERMIONE.
          It is Grace indeed.
Why, lo you now, I have spoke to the
   purpose twice;
The one for ever earn'd a royal husband;

Th' other for some while a friend.
     [*Giving her hand to* POLIXENES.]
LEONTES. [*Aside.*]
            Too hot, too hot!
To mingle friendship far is mingling
   bloods.
I have tremor cordis on me;—my heart
   dances;
But not for joy,—not joy.—This
   entertainment
May a free face put on; derive a liberty
From heartiness, from bounty, fertile
   bosom,
And well become the agent: 't may, I grant:
But to be paddling palms and pinching
   fingers,
As now they are; and making practis'd
   smiles
As in a looking-glass; and then to sigh, as
   'twere
The mort o' the deer: O, that is
   entertainment
My bosom likes not, nor my brows,—
   Mamillius,
Art thou my boy?
MAMILLIUS.
          Ay, my good lord.
LEONTES.
                I' fecks!
Why, that's my bawcock. What! hast
   smutch'd thy nose?—
They say it is a copy out of mine. Come,
   captain,
We must be neat;—not neat, but cleanly,
   captain:
And yet the steer, the heifer, and the calf,
Are all call'd neat.—Still virginalling
Upon his palm?—How now, you wanton
   calf!
Art thou my calf?
MAMILLIUS.
         Yes, if you will, my lord.
LEONTES.
Thou want'st a rough pash, and the shoots
   that I have,
To be full like me:—yet they say we are
Almost as like as eggs; women say so,
That will say anything: but were they false

As o'er-dy'd blacks, as wind, as waters,—
false
As dice are to be wish'd by one that fixes
No bourn 'twixt his and mine; yet were
it true
To say this boy were like me.—Come, sir
page,
Look on me with your welkin eye: sweet
villain!
Most dear'st! my collop! Can thy dam?
may't be?
Affection! thy intention stabs the centre:
Thou dost make possible things not so
held,
Communicat'st with dreams;—how can
this be?—
With what's unreal thou co-active art,
And fellow'st nothing: then 'tis very
credent
Thou mayst co-join with something; and
thou dost,
And that beyond commission; and I find
it,—
And that to the infection of my brains
And hardening of my brows.
POLIXENES.
                 What means Sicilia?
HERMIONE.
He something seems unsettled.
POLIXENES.
                   How! my lord!
What cheer? How is't with you, best
brother?
HERMIONE.
                      You look
As if you held a brow of much distraction:
Are you mov'd, my lord?
LEONTES.
               No, in good earnest.—
How sometimes nature will betray its folly,
Its tenderness, and make itself a pastime
To harder bosoms! Looking on the lines
Of my boy's face, methoughts I did recoil
Twenty-three years; and saw myself
unbreech'd,
In my green velvet coat; my dagger
muzzled,
Lest it should bite its master, and so prove,

As ornaments oft do, too dangerous.
How like, methought, I then was to this
kernel,
This squash, this gentleman.—Mine
honest friend,
Will you take eggs for money?
MAMILLIUS.
No, my lord, I'll fight.
LEONTES.
You will? Why, happy man be 's dole! My
brother,
Are you so fond of your young prince as
we
Do seem to be of ours?
POLIXENES.
                     If at home, sir,
He's all my exercise, my mirth, my matter:
Now my sworn friend, and then mine
enemy;
My parasite, my soldier, statesman, all:
He makes a July's day short as December;
And with his varying childness cures in
me
Thoughts that would thick my blood.
LEONTES.
                  So stands this squire
Offic'd with me. We two will walk, my
lord,
And leave you to your graver steps.—
Hermione,
How thou lov'st us show in our brother's
welcome;
Let what is dear in Sicily be cheap:
Next to thyself and my young rover, he's
Apparent to my heart.
HERMIONE.
                If you would seek us,
We are yours i' the garden. Shall 's attend
you there?
LEONTES.
To your own bents dispose you: you'll be
found,
Be you beneath the sky. [*Aside.*] I am
angling now.
Though you perceive me not how I give
line.
Go to, go to!
     [*Observing* POLIXENES *and* HERMIONE.]

How she holds up the neb, the bill to him!
And arms her with the boldness of a wife
To her allowing husband!
    [*Exeunt* POLIXENES, HERMIONE, *and*
        ATTENDANTS.*]*
                  Gone already!
Inch-thick, knee-deep, o'er head and ears a
    fork'd one!—
Go, play, boy, play:—thy mother plays,
    and I
Play too; but so disgrac'd a part, whose
    issue
Will hiss me to my grave: contempt and
    clamour
Will be my knell.—Go, play, boy, play.—
    There have been,
Or I am much deceiv'd, cuckolds ere now;
And many a man there is, even at this
    present,
Now while I speak this, holds his wife by
    the arm
That little thinks she has been sluic'd in
    his absence,
And his pond fish'd by his next neighbour,
    by
Sir Smile, his neighbour; nay, there's
    comfort in't,
Whiles other men have gates, and those
    gates open'd,
As mine, against their will: should all
    despair
That hath revolted wives, the tenth of
    mankind
Would hang themselves. Physic for't
    there's none;
It is a bawdy planet, that will strike
Where 'tis predominant; and 'tis powerful,
    think it,
From east, west, north, and south: be it
    concluded,
No barricado for a belly; know't;
It will let in and out the enemy
With bag and baggage. Many thousand
    of us
Have the disease, and feel't not.—How
    now, boy!

MAMILLIUS.
I am like you, they say.

LEONTES.
          Why, that's some comfort.—
What! Camillo there?

CAMILLO.
             Ay, my good lord.

LEONTES.
Go play, Mamillius; thou'rt an honest
    man.—
          [*Exit* MAMILLIUS.]
Camillo, this great sir will yet stay longer.

CAMILLO.
You had much ado to make his anchor
    hold:
When you cast out, it still came home.

LEONTES.
             Didst note it?

CAMILLO.
He would not stay at your petitions; made
His business more material.

LEONTES.
           Didst perceive it?—
[*Aside.*] They're here with me already;
    whispering, rounding,
"Sicilia is a so-forth." 'Tis far gone
When I shall gust it last.—How came't,
    Camillo,
That he did stay?

CAMILLO.
         At the good queen's entreaty.

LEONTES.
At the queen's be't: "good" should be
    pertinent;
But so it is, it is not. Was this taken
By any understanding pate but thine?
For thy conceit is soaking, will draw in
More than the common blocks:—not
    noted, is't,
But of the finer natures? by some severals
Of head-piece extraordinary? lower messes
Perchance are to this business purblind?
    say.

CAMILLO.
Business, my lord! I think most understand
Bohemia stays here longer.

LEONTES.
           Ha!

CAMILLO.
           Stays here longer.

Leontes.
Ay, but why?

Camillo.
To satisfy your highness, and the entreaties
Of our most gracious mistress.

Leontes.
         Satisfy
Th' entreaties of your mistress!—satisfy!—
Let that suffice. I have trusted thee,
     Camillo,
With all the nearest things to my heart,
     as well
My chamber-councils, wherein, priest-like,
     thou
Hast cleans'd my bosom; I from thee
     departed
Thy penitent reform'd: but we have been
Deceiv'd in thy integrity, deceiv'd
In that which seems so.

Camillo.
         Be it forbid, my lord!

Leontes.
To bide upon't,—thou art not honest; or,
If thou inclin'st that way, thou art a
     coward,
Which hoxes honesty behind, restraining
From course requir'd; or else thou must be
     counted
A servant grafted in my serious trust,
And therein negligent; or else a fool
That seest a game play'd home, the rich
     stake drawn,
And tak'st it all for jest.

Camillo.
         My gracious lord,
I may be negligent, foolish, and fearful;
In every one of these no man is free,
But that his negligence, his folly, fear,
Among the infinite doings of the world,
Sometime puts forth: in your affairs, my
     lord,
If ever I were wilful-negligent,
It was my folly; if industriously
I play'd the fool, it was my negligence,
Not weighing well the end; if ever fearful
To do a thing, where I the issue doubted,
Whereof the execution did cry out
Against the non-performance, 'twas a fear

Which oft affects the wisest: these, my
     lord,
Are such allow'd infirmities that honesty
Is never free of. But, beseech your grace,
Be plainer with me; let me know my
     trespass
By its own visage: if I then deny it,
'Tis none of mine.

Leontes.
         Have not you seen, Camillo,—
But that's past doubt: you have, or your
     eye-glass
Is thicker than a cuckold's horn,—or
     heard,—
For, to a vision so apparent, rumour
Cannot be mute,—or thought,—for
     cogitation
Resides not in that man that does not
     think it,—
My wife is slippery? If thou wilt
     confess,—
Or else be impudently negative,
To have nor eyes nor ears nor thought,—
     then say
My wife's a hobby-horse; deserves a name
As rank as any flax-wench that puts to
Before her troth-plight: say't and justify't.

Camillo.
I would not be a stander-by to hear
My sovereign mistress clouded so, without
My present vengeance taken: 'shrew my
     heart,
You never spoke what did become you less
Than this; which to reiterate were sin
As deep as that, though true.

Leontes.
         Is whispering nothing?
Is leaning cheek to cheek? is meeting
     noses?
Kissing with inside lip? Stopping the
     career
Of laughter with a sigh?—a note infallible
Of breaking honesty;—horsing foot on
     foot?
Skulking in corners? wishing clocks more
     swift;
Hours, minutes; noon, midnight? and all
     eyes

Blind with the pin and web but theirs,
    theirs only,
That would unseen be wicked?—is this
    nothing?
Why, then the world and all that's in't is
    nothing;
The covering sky is nothing; Bohemia
    nothing;
My wife is nothing; nor nothing have
    these nothings,
If this be nothing.

CAMILLO.
              Good my lord, be cur'd
Of this diseas'd opinion, and betimes;
For 'tis most dangerous.

LEONTES.
              Say it be, 'tis true.

CAMILLO.
No, no, my lord.

LEONTES.
              It is; you lie, you lie:
I say thou liest, Camillo, and I hate thee;
Pronounce thee a gross lout, a mindless
    slave;
Or else a hovering temporizer, that
Canst with thine eyes at once see good
    and evil,
Inclining to them both.—Were my wife's
    liver
Infected as her life, she would not live
The running of one glass.

CAMILLO.
              Who does infect her?

LEONTES.
Why, he that wears her like her medal,
    hanging
About his neck, Bohemia: who—if I
Had servants true about me, that bare
    eyes
To see alike mine honour as their profits,
Their own particular thrifts,—they would
    do that
Which should undo more doing: ay, and
    thou,
His cupbearer,—whom I from meaner
    form
Have bench'd and rear'd to worship; who
    mayst see,

Plainly as heaven sees earth and earth sees
    heaven,
How I am galled,—mightst bespice a cup,
To give mine enemy a lasting wink;
Which draught to me were cordial.

CAMILLO.
              Sir, my lord,
I could do this; and that with no rash
    potion,
But with a ling'ring dram, that should not
    work
Maliciously like poison: but I cannot
Believe this crack to be in my dread
    mistress,
So sovereignly being honourable.
I have lov'd thee,—

LEONTES.
           Make that thy question, and go rot!
Dost think I am so muddy, so unsettled,
To appoint myself in this vexation; sully
The purity and whiteness of my sheets,—
Which to preserve is sleep; which being
    spotted
Is goads, thorns, nettles, tails of wasps;
Give scandal to the blood o' the prince,
    my son,—
Who I do think is mine, and love as
    mine,—
Without ripe moving to't?—Would I do
    this?
Could man so blench?

CAMILLO.
           I must believe you, sir:
I do; and will fetch off Bohemia for't;
Provided that, when he's remov'd, your
    highness
Will take again your queen as yours at
    first,
Even for your son's sake; and thereby for
    sealing
The injury of tongues in courts and
    kingdoms
Known and allied to yours.

LEONTES.
             Thou dost advise me
Even so as I mine own course have set
    down:
I'll give no blemish to her honour, none.

CAMILLO.
My lord,
Go then; and with a countenance as clear
As friendship wears at feasts, keep with
   Bohemia
And with your queen: I am his cupbearer.
If from me he have wholesome beverage,
Account me not your servant.
LEONTES.
                This is all:
Do't, and thou hast the one-half of my
   heart;
Do't not, thou splitt'st thine own.
CAMILLO.
             I'll do't, my lord.
LEONTES.
I will seem friendly, as thou hast advis'd
   me.
                [*Exit.*]
CAMILLO.
O miserable lady!—But, for me,
What case stand I in? I must be the
   poisoner
Of good Polixenes: and my ground to do't
Is the obedience to a master; one
Who, in rebellion with himself, will have
All that are his so too.—To do this deed,
Promotion follows: if I could find example
Of thousands that had struck anointed
   kings
And flourish'd after, I'd not do't; but since
Nor brass, nor stone, nor parchment, bears
   not one,
Let villainy itself forswear't. I must
Forsake the court: to do't, or no, is certain
To me a break-neck. Happy star reign
   now!
Here comes Bohemia.
          [*Enter* POLIXENES.]
POLIXENES.
           This is strange! methinks
My favour here begins to warp. Not
   speak?—
Good-day, Camillo.
CAMILLO.
            Hail, most royal sir!
POLIXENES.
What is the news i' the court?

CAMILLO.
            None rare, my lord.
POLIXENES.
The king hath on him such a countenance
As he had lost some province, and a region
Lov'd as he loves himself; even now I met
   him
With customary compliment; when he,
Wafting his eyes to the contrary, and
   falling
A lip of much contempt, speeds from me;
So leaves me to consider what is breeding
That changes thus his manners.
CAMILLO.
I dare not know, my lord.
POLIXENES.
How! dare not! do not. Do you know, and
   dare not
Be intelligent to me? 'Tis thereabouts;
For, to yourself, what you do know, you
   must,
And cannot say, you dare not. Good
   Camillo,
Your chang'd complexions are to me a
   mirror
Which shows me mine chang'd too; for I
   must be
A party in this alteration, finding
Myself thus alter'd with't.
CAMILLO.
              There is a sickness
Which puts some of us in distemper; but
I cannot name the disease; and it is caught
Of you that yet are well.
POLIXENES.
            How! caught of me!
Make me not sighted like the basilisk:
I have look'd on thousands who have sped
   the better
By my regard, but kill'd none so. Camillo,—
As you are certainly a gentleman, thereto
Clerk-like, experienc'd, which no less
   adorns
Our gentry than our parents' noble names,
In whose success we are gentle,—I
   beseech you,
If you know aught which does behove my
   knowledge

Thereof to be inform'd, imprison't not
In ignorant concealment.

CAMILLO.
                                        I may not answer.

POLIXENES.
A sickness caught of me, and yet I well!
I must be answer'd.—Dost thou hear,
    Camillo,
I conjure thee, by all the parts of man
Which honour does acknowledge, whereof
    the least
Is not this suit of mine,—that thou declare
What incidency thou dost guess of harm
Is creeping toward me; how far off, how
    near;
Which way to be prevented, if to be;
If not, how best to bear it.

CAMILLO.
                            Sir, I will tell you;
Since I am charg'd in honour, and by him
That I think honourable: therefore mark my
    counsel,
Which must be ev'n as swiftly follow'd as
I mean to utter it, or both yourself and me
Cry lost, and so goodnight!

POLIXENES.
                            On, good Camillo.

CAMILLO.
I am appointed him to murder you.

POLIXENES.
By whom, Camillo?

CAMILLO.
                        By the king.

POLIXENES.
                                    For what?

CAMILLO.
He thinks, nay, with all confidence he
    swears,
As he had seen't or been an instrument
To vice you to't, that you have touch'd his
    queen
Forbiddenly.

POLIXENES.
                    O, then my best blood turn
To an infected jelly, and my name
Be yok'd with his that did betray the best!
Turn then my freshest reputation to
A savour that may strike the dullest nostril

Where I arrive, and my approach be
    shunn'd,
Nay, hated too, worse than the great'st
    infection
That e'er was heard or read!

CAMILLO.
                            Swear his thought over
By each particular star in heaven and
By all their influences, you may as well
Forbid the sea for to obey the moon
As, or by oath remove, or counsel shake
The fabric of his folly, whose foundation
Is pil'd upon his faith, and will continue
The standing of his body.

POLIXENES.
                            How should this grow?

CAMILLO.
I know not: but I am sure 'tis safer to
Avoid what's grown than question how
    'tis born.
If, therefore you dare trust my honesty,—
That lies enclosed in this trunk, which you
Shall bear along impawn'd,—away to-
    night.
Your followers I will whisper to the
    business;
And will, by twos and threes, at several
    posterns,
Clear them o' the city: for myself, I'll put
My fortunes to your service, which are
    here
By this discovery lost. Be not uncertain;
For, by the honour of my parents, I
Have utter'd truth: which if you seek to
    prove,
I dare not stand by; nor shall you be safer
Than one condemn'd by the king's own
    mouth, thereon
His execution sworn.

POLIXENES.
                            I do believe thee;
I saw his heart in his face. Give me thy
    hand;
Be pilot to me, and thy places shall
Still neighbour mine. My ships are ready,
    and
My people did expect my hence departure
Two days ago.—This jealousy

Is for a precious creature: as she's rare,
Must it be great; and, as his person's
     mighty,
Must it be violent; and as he does conceive
He is dishonour'd by a man which ever
Profess'd to him, why, his revenges must
In that be made more bitter. Fear
     o'ershades me;
Good expedition be my friend, and comfort
The gracious queen, part of this theme, but
     nothing
Of his ill-ta'en suspicion! Come, Camillo;
I will respect thee as a father, if
Thou bear'st my life off hence: let us avoid.

CAMILLO.
It is in mine authority to command
The keys of all the posterns: please your
     highness
To take the urgent hour: come, sir, away.
                                   [*Exeunt.*]

ACT II
SCENE I

Sicilia. A room in the palace.
[*Enter* HERMIONE, MAMILLIUS, *and*
     LADIES.]

HERMIONE.
Take the boy to you: he so troubles me,
'Tis past enduring.

FIRST LADY.
                     Come, my gracious lord,
Shall I be your playfellow?

MAMILLIUS.
                              No, I'll none of you.

FIRST LADY.
Why, my sweet lord?

MAMILLIUS.
You'll kiss me hard, and speak to me as if
I were a baby still. [*To* SECOND LADY.] I
     love you better.

SECOND LADY.
And why so, my lord?

MAMILLIUS.
                       Not for because
Your brows are blacker; yet black brows,
     they say,
Become some women best; so that there
     be not

Too much hair there, but in a semicircle
Or a half-moon made with a pen.

SECOND LADY.
                         Who taught you this?

MAMILLIUS.
I learn'd it out of women's faces.—Pray
     now,
What colour are your eyebrows?

FIRST LADY.
                              Blue, my lord.

MAMILLIUS.
Nay, that's a mock: I have seen a lady's
     nose
That has been blue, but not her eyebrows.

FIRST LADY.
                                    Hark ye:
The queen your mother rounds apace. We
     shall
Present our services to a fine new prince
One of these days; and then you'd wanton
     with us,
If we would have you.

SECOND LADY.
                      She is spread of late
Into a goodly bulk: good time encounter
     her!

HERMIONE.
What wisdom stirs amongst you? Come,
     sir, now
I am for you again: pray you sit by us,
And tell 's a tale.

MAMILLIUS.
                   Merry or sad shall't be?

HERMIONE.
As merry as you will.

MAMILLIUS.
A sad tale's best for winter. I have one
Of sprites and goblins.

HERMIONE.
                        Let's have that, good sir.
Come on, sit down;—come on, and do
     your best
To fright me with your sprites: you're
     powerful at it.

MAMILLIUS.
There was a man,—

HERMIONE.
                    Nay, come, sit down: then on.

MAMILLIUS.
Dwelt by a churchyard:—I will tell it
 softly;
Yond crickets shall not hear it.
HERMIONE.
                              Come on, then,
And give't me in mine ear.
  [*Enter* LEONTES, ANTIGONUS, LORDS,
                and GUARDS.]
LEONTES.
Was he met there? his train? Camillo with
 him?
FIRST LORD.
Behind the tuft of pines I met them; never
Saw I men scour so on their way: I ey'd
 them
Even to their ships.
LEONTES.
                    How bles'd am I
In my just censure, in my true opinion!—
Alack, for lesser knowledge!—How
 accurs'd
In being so blest!—There may be in the
 cup
A spider steep'd, and one may drink,
 depart,
And yet partake no venom; for his
 knowledge
Is not infected; but if one present
The abhorr'd ingredient to his eye, make
 known
How he hath drunk, he cracks his gorge,
 his sides,
With violent hefts; I have drunk, and seen
 the spider.
Camillo was his help in this, his pander:—
There is a plot against my life, my crown;
All's true that is mistrusted:—that false
 villain
Whom I employ'd, was pre-employ'd by
 him:
He has discover'd my design, and I
Remain a pinch'd thing; yea, a very trick
For them to play at will.—How came the
 posterns
So easily open?
FIRST LORD.
              By his great authority;

Which often hath no less prevail'd than so,
On your command.
LEONTES.
                    I know't too well.—
Give me the boy; I am glad you did not
 nurse him:
Though he does bear some signs of me,
 yet you
Have too much blood in him.
HERMIONE.
                    What is this? sport?
LEONTES.
Bear the boy hence; he shall not come
 about her;
Away with him!—and let her sport herself
With that she's big with;—for 'tis
 Polixenes
Has made thee swell thus.
  [*Exit* MAMILLIUS, *with some of the*
                GUARDS.]
HERMIONE.
                    But I'd say he had not,
And I'll be sworn you would believe my
 saying,
Howe'er you learn the nayward.
LEONTES.
                    You, my lords,
Look on her, mark her well; be but about
To say, "she is a goodly lady" and
The justice of your hearts will thereto add,
"'Tis pity she's not honest, honourable":
Praise her but for this her without-door
 form,—
Which, on my faith, deserves high
 speech,—and straight
The shrug, the hum or ha,—these petty
 brands
That calumny doth use:—O, I am out,
That mercy does; for calumny will sear
Virtue itself:—these shrugs, these hum's,
 and ha's,
When you have said "she's goodly," come
 between,
Ere you can say "she's honest": but be it
 known,
From him that has most cause to grieve it
 should be,
She's an adultress!

HERMIONE.
                Should a villain say so,
The most replenish'd villain in the world,
He were as much more villain: you, my
    lord,
Do but mistake.
LEONTES.
                You have mistook, my lady,
Polixenes for Leontes: O thou thing,
Which I'll not call a creature of thy place,
Lest barbarism, making me the precedent,
Should a like language use to all degrees,
And mannerly distinguishment leave out
Betwixt the prince and beggar!—I have
    said,
She's an adultress; I have said with whom:
More, she's a traitor; and Camillo is
A federary with her; and one that knows
What she should shame to know herself
But with her most vile principal, that she's
A bed-swerver, even as bad as those
That vulgars give boldest titles; ay, and
    privy
To this their late escape.
HERMIONE.
                No, by my life,
Privy to none of this. How will this grieve
    you,
When you shall come to clearer
    knowledge, that
You thus have publish'd me! Gentle my
    lord,
You scarce can right me throughly then,
    to say
You did mistake.
LEONTES.
                No; if I mistake
In those foundations which I build upon,
The centre is not big enough to bear
A school-boy's top.—Away with her to
    prison!
He who shall speak for her is afar off guilty
But that he speaks.
HERMIONE.
                There's some ill planet reigns:
I must be patient till the heavens look
With an aspect more favourable.—Good
    my lords,

I am not prone to weeping, as our sex
Commonly are; the want of which vain
    dew
Perchance shall dry your pities; but I have
That honourable grief lodg'd here, which
    burns
Worse than tears drown: beseech you all,
    my lords,
With thoughts so qualified as your
    charities
Shall best instruct you, measure me;—and
    so
The king's will be perform'd!
LEONTES. [*To the* GUARD.]
                Shall I be heard?
HERMIONE.
Who is't that goes with me? Beseech your
    highness
My women may be with me; for, you see,
My plight requires it.—Do not weep,
    good fools;
There is no cause: when you shall know your
    mistress
Has deserv'd prison, then abound in tears
As I come out: this action I now go on
Is for my better grace.—Adieu, my lord:
I never wish'd to see you sorry; now
I trust I shall.—My women, come; you
    have leave.
LEONTES.
Go, do our bidding; hence!
                [*Exeunt* QUEEN *and* LADIES, *with*
                                GUARDS.]
FIRST LORD.
Beseech your highness, call the queen
    again.
ANTIGONUS.
Be certain what you do, sir, lest your justice
Prove violence, in the which three great
    ones suffer,
Yourself, your queen, your son.
FIRST LORD.
                For her, my lord,—
I dare my life lay down,—and will do't, sir,
Please you to accept it,—that the queen
    is spotless
I' the eyes of heaven and to you; I mean
In this which you accuse her.

ANTIGONUS.

                If it prove
She's otherwise, I'll keep my stables where
I lodge my wife; I'll go in couples with
  her;
Than when I feel and see her no further
  trust her;
For every inch of woman in the world,
Ay, every dram of woman's flesh, is false,
If she be.
LEONTES.

      Hold your peaces.
FIRST LORD.

             Good my lord,—
ANTIGONUS.
It is for you we speak, not for ourselves:
You are abus'd, and by some putter-on
That will be damn'd for't: would I knew
  the villain,
I would land-damn him. Be she honour-
  flaw'd,—
I have three daughters; the eldest is eleven;
The second and the third, nine and some
  five;
If this prove true, they'll pay for't. By mine
  honour,
I'll geld 'em all: fourteen they shall not see,
To bring false generations: they are co-
  heirs;
And I had rather glib myself than they
Should not produce fair issue.
LEONTES.

            Cease; no more.
You smell this business with a sense as
  cold
As is a dead man's nose: but I do see't and
  feel't
As you feel doing thus; and see withal
The instruments that feel.
ANTIGONUS.

            If it be so,
We need no grave to bury honesty;
There's not a grain of it the face to sweeten
Of the whole dungy earth.
LEONTES.

        What! Lack I credit?
FIRST LORD.
I had rather you did lack than I, my lord,

Upon this ground: and more it would
  content me
To have her honour true than your
  suspicion;
Be blam'd for't how you might.
LEONTES.

          Why, what need we
Commune with you of this, but rather
  follow
Our forceful instigation? Our prerogative
Calls not your counsels; but our natural
  goodness
Imparts this; which, if you,—or stupified
Or seeming so in skill,—cannot or will not
Relish a truth, like us, inform yourselves
We need no more of your advice: the
  matter,
The loss, the gain, the ord'ring on't, is all
Properly ours.
ANTIGONUS.

        And I wish, my liege,
You had only in your silent judgment
  tried it,
Without more overture.
LEONTES.

         How could that be?
Either thou art most ignorant by age,
Or thou wert born a fool. Camillo's flight,
Added to their familiarity,—
Which was as gross as ever touch'd
  conjecture,
That lack'd sight only, nought for
  approbation,
But only seeing, all other circumstances
Made up to th' deed,—doth push on this
  proceeding.
Yet, for a greater confirmation,—
For, in an act of this importance, 'twere
Most piteous to be wild, I have despatch'd
  in post
To sacred Delphos, to Apollo's temple,
Cleomenes and Dion, whom you know
Of stuff'd sufficiency: now, from the oracle
They will bring all, whose spiritual counsel
  had,
Shall stop or spur me. Have I done well?
FIRST LORD.
Well done, my lord,—

LEONTES.
Though I am satisfied, and need no more
Than what I know, yet shall the oracle
Give rest to the minds of others such as he
Whose ignorant credulity will not
Come up to th' truth: so have we thought
   it good
From our free person she should be
   confin'd;
Lest that the treachery of the two fled
   hence
Be left her to perform. Come, follow us;
We are to speak in public; for this
   business
Will raise us all.
ANTIGONUS. [*Aside.*]
            To laughter, as I take it,
If the good truth were known.
         [*Exeunt.*]

SCENE II

The same. The outer room of a prison.
[*Enter* PAULINA *and* ATTENDANTS.]
PAULINA.
The keeper of the prison,—call to him;
Let him have knowledge who I am.
       [*Exit an* ATTENDANT.]
                    Good lady!
No court in Europe is too good for thee;
What dost thou then in prison?
[*Re-enter* ATTENDANT, *with the* KEEPER.]
                 Now, good sir,
You know me, do you not?
KEEPER.
              For a worthy lady,
And one who much I honour.
PAULINA.
               Pray you, then,
Conduct me to the queen.
KEEPER.
I may not, madam; to the contrary
I have express commandment.
PAULINA.
                 Here's ado,
To lock up honesty and honour from
The access of gentle visitors!—Is't lawful,
   pray you,
To see her women? any of them? Emilia?

KEEPER.
So please you, madam, to put
Apart these your attendants, I
Shall bring Emilia forth.
PAULINA.
             I pray now, call her.
Withdraw yourselves.
       [*Exeunt* ATTENDANTS.]
KEEPER.
               And, madam,
I must be present at your conference.
PAULINA.
Well, be't so, pr'ythee. [*Exit* KEEPER.]
Here's such ado to make no stain a stain
As passes colouring. [*Re-enter* KEEPER,
   with EMILIA.] Dear gentlewoman,
How fares our gracious lady?
EMILIA.
As well as one so great and so forlorn
May hold together: on her frights and
   griefs,—
Which never tender lady hath borne
   greater,—
She is, something before her time, deliver'd.
PAULINA.
A boy?
EMILIA.
       A daughter; and a goodly babe,
Lusty, and like to live: the queen receives
Much comfort in't; says, "My poor
   prisoner,
I am as innocent as you."
PAULINA.
             I dare be sworn;—
These dangerous unsafe lunes i' the king,
   beshrew them!
He must be told on't, and he shall: the
   office
Becomes a woman best; I'll take't upon
   me;
If I prove honey-mouth'd, let my tongue
   blister;
And never to my red-look'd anger be
The trumpet any more.—Pray you, Emilia,
Commend my best obedience to the
   queen;
If she dares trust me with her little babe,
I'll show't the king, and undertake to be

Her advocate to th' loud'st. We do not know
How he may soften at the sight o' the child:
The silence often of pure innocence
Persuades, when speaking fails.

EMILIA.

Most worthy madam,
Your honour and your goodness is so
    evident,
That your free undertaking cannot miss
A thriving issue: there is no lady living
So meet for this great errand. Please your
    ladyship
To visit the next room, I'll presently
Acquaint the queen of your most noble
    offer;
Who but to-day hammer'd of this design,
But durst not tempt a minister of honour,
Lest she should be denied.

PAULINA.

Tell her, Emilia,
I'll use that tongue I have: if wit flow
    from it
As boldness from my bosom, let't not be
    doubted
I shall do good.

EMILIA.

Now be you bless'd for it!
I'll to the queen: please you come
    something nearer.

KEEPER.

Madam, if 't please the queen to send the
    babe,
I know not what I shall incur to pass it,
Having no warrant.

PAULINA.

You need not fear it, sir:
This child was prisoner to the womb, and
    is,
By law and process of great nature thence
Freed and enfranchis'd: not a party to
The anger of the king, nor guilty of,
If any be, the trespass of the queen.

KEEPER.

I do believe it.

PAULINA.

Do not you fear: upon mine honour, I
Will stand betwixt you and danger.
            [*Exeunt.*]

SCENE III

The same. A room in the palace.
[*Enter* LEONTES, ANTIGONUS, LORDS,
    and other ATTENDANTS.]

LEONTES.

Nor night nor day no rest: it is but
    weakness
To bear the matter thus,—mere weakness. If
The cause were not in being,—part o' the
    cause,
She the adultress; for the harlot king
Is quite beyond mine arm, out of the blank
And level of my brain, plot-proof; but she
I can hook to me:—say that she were gone,
Given to the fire, a moiety of my rest
Might come to me again.—Who's there?

FIRST ATTENDANT.

My lord?

LEONTES.

How does the boy?

FIRST ATTENDANT.

He took good rest to-night;
'Tis hop'd his sickness is discharg'd.

LEONTES.

To see his nobleness!
Conceiving the dishonour of his mother,
He straight declin'd, droop'd, took it
    deeply,
Fasten'd and fix'd the shame on't in himself,
Threw off his spirit, his appetite, his sleep,
And downright languish'd. Leave me
    solely:—go,
See how he fares. [*Exit* FIRST
    ATTENDANT.] Fie, fie! no thought of
    him;
The very thought of my revenges that way
Recoil upon me: in himself too mighty,
And in his parties, his alliance,—let him
    be,
Until a time may serve: for present
    vengeance,
Take it on her. Camillo and Polixenes
Laugh at me; make their pastime at my
    sorrow:
They should not laugh if I could reach
    them; nor
Shall she within my power.
            [*Enter* PAULINA, *with a* CHILD.]

First Lord.
                          You must not enter.
Paulina.
Nay, rather, good my lords, be second to
      me:
Fear you his tyrannous passion more, alas,
Than the queen's life? a gracious innocent
      soul,
More free than he is jealous.
Antigonus.
                          That's enough.
Second Attendant.
Madam, he hath not slept to-night; commanded
None should come at him.
Paulina.
                          Not so hot, good sir;
I come to bring him sleep. 'Tis such as
      you,—
That creep like shadows by him, and do
      sigh
At each his needless heavings,—such as
      you
Nourish the cause of his awaking: I
Do come, with words as med'cinal as true,
Honest as either, to purge him of that
      humour
That presses him from sleep.
Leontes.
                          What noise there, ho?
Paulina.
No noise, my lord; but needful conference
About some gossips for your highness.
Leontes.
                          How!—
Away with that audacious lady!—
      Antigonus,
I charg'd thee that she should not come
      about me:
I knew she would.
Antigonus.
                    I told her so, my lord,
On your displeasure's peril, and on mine,
She should not visit you.
Leontes.
                    What, canst not rule her?
Paulina.
From all dishonesty he can: in this,—

Unless he take the course that you have
      done,
Commit me for committing honour,—
      trust it,
He shall not rule me.
Antigonus.
                          La you now, you hear
When she will take the rein, I let her run;
But she'll not stumble.
Paulina.
                          Good my liege, I come,—
And, I beseech you, hear me, who
      professes
Myself your loyal servant, your physician,
Your most obedient counsellor: yet that
      dares
Less appear so, in comforting your evils,
Than such as most seem yours:—I say I
      come
From your good queen.
Leontes.
                          Good queen!
Paulina.
Good queen, my lord, good queen: I say,
      good queen;
And would by combat make her good, so
      were I
A man, the worst about you.
Leontes.
                          Force her hence!
Paulina.
Let him that makes but trifles of his eyes
First hand me: on mine own accord I'll
      off;
But first I'll do my errand.—The good
      queen,
For she is good, hath brought you forth a
      daughter;
Here 'tis; commends it to your blessing.
                    [*Laying down the* Child.]
Leontes.
                                        Out!
A mankind witch! Hence with her, out o'
      door:
A most intelligencing bawd!
Paulina.
                          Not so:
I am as ignorant in that as you

In so entitling me; and no less honest
Than you are mad; which is enough, I'll
   warrant,
As this world goes, to pass for honest.

LEONTES.

                        Traitors!
Will you not push her out? Give her the
   bastard:
Thou dotard! [*To* ANTIGONUS.] Thou art
   woman-tir'd, unroosted
By thy Dame Partlet here:—take up the
   bastard;
Take't up, I say; give't to thy crone.

PAULINA.

                       For ever
Unvenerable be thy hands, if thou
Tak'st up the princess by that forced
   baseness
Which he has put upon't!

LEONTES.

               He dreads his wife.

PAULINA.

So I would you did; then 'twere past all
   doubt
You'd call your children yours.

LEONTES.

               A nest of traitors?

ANTIGONUS.

I am none, by this good light.

PAULINA.

                 Nor I; nor any,
But one that's here; and that's himself:
   for he
The sacred honour of himself, his queen's,
His hopeful son's, his babe's, betrays to
   slander,
Whose sting is sharper than the sword's;
   and will not,—
For, as the case now stands, it is a curse
He cannot be compell'd to't,—once remove
The root of his opinion, which is rotten
As ever oak or stone was sound.

LEONTES.

                   A callet
Of boundless tongue, who late hath beat
   her husband,
And now baits me!—This brat is none of
   mine;

It is the issue of Polixenes:
Hence with it! and together with the dam,
Commit them to the fire.

PAULINA.

                  It is yours!
And, might we lay the old proverb to your
   charge,
So like you 'tis the worse.—Behold, my
   lords,
Although the print be little, the whole
   matter
And copy of the father,—eye, nose, lip,
The trick of his frown, his forehead; nay,
   the valley,
The pretty dimples of his chin and cheek;
   his smiles;
The very mould and frame of hand, nail,
   finger:—
And thou, good goddess Nature, which
   hast made it
So like to him that got it, if thou hast
The ordering of the mind too, 'mongst all
   colours
No yellow in't, lest she suspect, as he does,
Her children not her husband's!

LEONTES.

                 A gross hag!
And, losel, thou art worthy to be hang'd
That wilt not stay her tongue.

ANTIGONUS.

            Hang all the husbands
That cannot do that feat, you'll leave
   yourself
Hardly one subject.

LEONTES.

           Once more, take her hence.

PAULINA.

A most unworthy and unnatural lord
Can do no more.

LEONTES.

             I'll have thee burn'd.

PAULINA.

                 I care not.
It is an heretic that makes the fire,
Not she which burns in't. I'll not call you
   tyrant
But this most cruel usage of your queen,—
Not able to produce more accusation

Than your own weak-hing'd fancy, something savours
Of tyranny, and will ignoble make you,
Yea, scandalous to the world.

LEONTES.

                On your allegiance,
Out of the chamber with her! Were I a tyrant,
Where were her life? She durst not call me so,
If she did know me one. Away with her!

PAULINA.

I pray you, do not push me; I'll be gone.—
Look to your babe, my lord; 'tis yours: Jove send her
A better guiding spirit!—What needs these hands?
You that are thus so tender o'er his follies,
Will never do him good, not one of you.
So, so:—farewell; we are gone.

                [Exit.]

LEONTES.

Thou, traitor, hast set on thy wife to this.
My child?—away with't.—Even thou, that hast
A heart so tender o'er it, take it hence,
And see it instantly consum'd with fire;
Even thou, and none but thou. Take it up straight:
Within this hour bring me word 'tis done,—
And by good testimony,—or I'll seize thy life,
With that thou else call'st thine. If thou refuse,
And wilt encounter with my wrath, say so;
The bastard-brains with these my proper hands
Shall I dash out. Go, take it to the fire;
For thou set'st on thy wife.

ANTIGONUS.

                I did not, sir:
These lords, my noble fellows, if they please,
Can clear me in't.

LORDS.

             We can:—my royal liege,
He is not guilty of her coming hither.

LEONTES.

You're liars all.

FIRST LORD.

Beseech your highness, give us better credit:
We have always truly serv'd you; and beseech
So to esteem of us: and on our knees we beg,—
As recompense of our dear services,
Past and to come, that you do change this purpose,
Which, being so horrible, so bloody, must
Lead on to some foul issue: we all kneel.

LEONTES.

I am a feather for each wind that blows:—
Shall I live on, to see this bastard kneel
And call me father? better burn it now,
Than curse it then. But, be it; let it live:—
It shall not neither. [*To* ANTIGONUS.] You, sir, come you hither:
You that have been so tenderly officious
With Lady Margery, your midwife, there,
To save this bastard's life,—for 'tis a bastard,
So sure as this beard's grey,—what will you adventure
To save this brat's life?

ANTIGONUS.

              Anything, my lord,
That my ability may undergo,
And nobleness impose: at least, thus much;
I'll pawn the little blood which I have left
To save the innocent:—anything possible.

LEONTES.

It shall be possible. Swear by this sword
Thou wilt perform my bidding.

ANTIGONUS.

              I will, my lord.

LEONTES.

Mark, and perform it,—seest thou? for the fail
Of any point in't shall not only be
Death to thyself, but to thy lewd-tongu'd wife,
Whom for this time we pardon. We enjoin thee,

As thou art liegeman to us, that thou carry
This female bastard hence; and that thou
    bear it
To some remote and desert place, quite
    out
Of our dominions; and that there thou
    leave it,
Without more mercy, to it own protection
And favour of the climate. As by strange
    fortune
It came to us, I do in justice charge thee,
On thy soul's peril and thy body's torture,
That thou commend it strangely to some
    place
Where chance may nurse or end it. Take
    it up.
ANTIGONUS.
I swear to do this, though a present death
Had been more merciful.—Come on, poor
    babe:
Some powerful spirit instruct the kites
    and ravens
To be thy nurses! Wolves and bears, they
    say,
Casting their savageness aside, have done
Like offices of pity.—Sir, be prosperous
In more than this deed does require!—and
    blessing,
Against this cruelty, fight on thy side,
Poor thing, condemn'd to loss!
          [*Exit with the* CHILD.]
LEONTES.
                    No, I'll not rear
Another's issue.
SECOND ATTENDANT.
               Please your highness, posts
From those you sent to the oracle are come
An hour since: Cleomenes and Dion,
Being well arriv'd from Delphos, are both
    landed,
Hasting to the court.
FIRST LORD.
          So please you, sir, their speed
Hath been beyond account.
LEONTES.
               Twenty-three days
They have been absent: 'tis good speed;
    foretells

The great Apollo suddenly will have
The truth of this appear. Prepare you,
    lords;
Summon a session, that we may arraign
Our most disloyal lady; for, as she hath
Been publicly accus'd, so shall she have
A just and open trial. While she lives,
My heart will be a burden to me. Leave
    me;
And think upon my bidding.
               [*Exeunt.*]

ACT III
SCENE I
Sicilia. A street in some town.
[*Enter* CLEOMENES *and* DION.]
CLEOMENES.
The climate's delicate; the air most sweet;
Fertile the isle; the temple much
    surpassing
The common praise it bears.
DION.
               I shall report,
For most it caught me, the celestial
    habits,—
Methinks I so should term them,—and
    the reverence
Of the grave wearers. O, the sacrifice!
How ceremonious, solemn, and unearthly,
It was i' the offering!
CLEOMENES.
               But of all, the burst
And the ear-deaf'ning voice o' the oracle,
Kin to Jove's thunder, so surprised my
    sense
That I was nothing.
DION.
               If the event o' the journey
Prove as successful to the queen,—O, be't
    so!—
As it hath been to us rare, pleasant,
    speedy,
The time is worth the use on't.
CLEOMENES.
               Great Apollo
Turn all to th' best! These proclamations,
So forcing faults upon Hermione,
I little like.

DION.

          The violent carriage of it
Will clear or end the business: when the
    oracle,—
Thus by Apollo's great divine seal'd up,—
Shall the contents discover, something
    rare
Even then will rush to knowledge. Go,
    fresh horses!
And gracious be the issue!
               [*Exeunt.*]

SCENE II

The same. A court of justice.
[*Enter* LEONTES, LORDS, *and* OFFICERS
appear, properly seated.]

LEONTES.

This sessions,—to our great grief we
    pronounce,—
Even pushes 'gainst our heart;—the party
    tried,
The daughter of a king, our wife; and one
Of us too much belov'd. Let us be clear'd
Of being tyrannous, since we so openly
Proceed in justice; which shall have due
    course,
Even to the guilt or the purgation.—
Produce the prisoner.

OFFICER.

It is his highness' pleasure that the queen
Appear in person here in court.—

CRIER.

                 Silence!
[HERMIONE *is brought in guarded;* PAULINA
    and LADIES *attending.*]

LEONTES.

Read the indictment.

OFFICER. [*Reads.*]

"Hermione, queen to the worthy Leontes,
King of Sicilia, thou art here accused and
arraigned of high treason, in committing
adultery with Polixenes, King of Bohemia;
and conspiring with Camillo to take away
the life of our sovereign lord the king,
thy royal husband: the pretence whereof
being by circumstances partly laid open,
thou, Hermione, contrary to the faith and
allegiance of true subject, didst counsel and

aid them, for their better safety, to fly away
by night."

HERMIONE.

Since what I am to say must be but that
Which contradicts my accusation, and
The testimony on my part no other
But what comes from myself, it shall scarce
    boot me
To say "Not guilty": mine integrity,
Being counted falsehood, shall, as I express
    it,
Be so receiv'd. But thus,—if powers divine
Behold our human actions,—as they do,—
I doubt not, then, but innocence shall make
False accusation blush, and tyranny
Tremble at patience.—You, my lord, best
    know,—
Who least will seem to do so,—my past
    life
Hath been as continent, as chaste, as true,
As I am now unhappy: which is more
Than history can pattern, though devis'd
And play'd to take spectators; for behold
    me,—
A fellow of the royal bed, which owe
A moiety of the throne, a great king's
    daughter,
The mother to a hopeful prince,—here
    standing
To prate and talk for life and honour 'fore
Who please to come and hear. For life, I
    prize it
As I weigh grief, which I would spare: for
    honour,
'Tis a derivative from me to mine,
And only that I stand for. I appeal
To your own conscience, sir, before
    Polixenes
Came to your court, how I was in your
    grace,
How merited to be so; since he came,
With what encounter so uncurrent I
Have strain'd t' appear thus: if one jot
    beyond
The bound of honour, or in act or will
That way inclining, harden'd be the hearts
Of all that hear me, and my near'st of kin
Cry fie upon my grave!

Leontes.

                I ne'er heard yet
That any of these bolder vices wanted
Less impudence to gainsay what they did
Than to perform it first.

Hermione.

              That's true enough;
Though 'tis a saying, sir, not due to me.

Leontes.

You will not own it.

Hermione.

            More than mistress of
Which comes to me in name of fault, I
    must not
At all acknowledge. For Polixenes,—
With whom I am accus'd,—I do confess
I lov'd him, as in honour he requir'd;
With such a kind of love as might become
A lady like me; with a love even such,
So and no other, as yourself commanded:
Which not to have done, I think had been
    in me
Both disobedience and ingratitude
To you and toward your friend; whose love
    had spoke,
Ever since it could speak, from an infant,
    freely,
That it was yours. Now for conspiracy,
I know not how it tastes; though it be
    dish'd
For me to try how: all I know of it
Is that Camillo was an honest man;
And why he left your court, the gods
    themselves,
Wotting no more than I, are ignorant.

Leontes.

You knew of his departure, as you know
What you have underta'en to do in 's
    absence.

Hermione.

Sir,
You speak a language that I understand
    not:
My life stands in the level of your dreams,
Which I'll lay down.

Leontes.

          Your actions are my dreams;
You had a bastard by Polixenes,

And I but dream'd it: as you were past all
    shame,—
Those of your fact are so,—so past all
    truth:
Which to deny concerns more than avails;
    for as
Thy brat hath been cast out, like to itself,
No father owning it,—which is, indeed,
More criminal in thee than it,—so thou
Shalt feel our justice; in whose easiest
    passage
Look for no less than death.

Hermione.

           Sir, spare your threats:
The bug which you would fright me with,
    I seek.
To me can life be no commodity:
The crown and comfort of my life, your
    favour,
I do give lost; for I do feel it gone,
But know not how it went: my second joy,
And first-fruits of my body, from his
    presence
I am barr'd, like one infectious: my third
    comfort,
Starr'd most unluckily, is from my
    breast,—
The innocent milk in its most innocent
    mouth,—
Hal'd out to murder: myself on every post
Proclaim'd a strumpet; with immodest
    hatred
The child-bed privilege denied, which
    'longs
To women of all fashion; lastly, hurried
Here to this place, i' the open air, before
I have got strength of limit. Now, my liege,
Tell me what blessings I have here alive,
That I should fear to die. Therefore
    proceed.
But yet hear this; mistake me not;—no
    life,—
I prize it not a straw,—but for mine
    honour,
Which I would free, if I shall be
    condemn'd
Upon surmises—all proofs sleeping else,
But what your jealousies awake—I tell you

'Tis rigour, and not law.—Your honours all,
I do refer me to the oracle:
Apollo be my judge!

FIRST LORD.
                       This your request
Is altogether just: therefore, bring forth,
And in Apollo's name, his oracle.
    [*Exeunt certain* OFFICERS.]

HERMIONE.
The Emperor of Russia was my father;
O that he were alive, and here beholding
His daughter's trial! that he did but see
The flatness of my misery; yet with eyes
Of pity, not revenge!
    [*Re-enter* OFFICERS, *with* CLEOMENES
            and DION.]

OFFICER.
You here shall swear upon this sword of
    justice,
That you, Cleomenes and Dion, have
Been both at Delphos, and from thence have
    brought
This seal'd-up oracle, by the hand deliver'd
Of great Apollo's priest; and that since
    then,
You have not dar'd to break the holy seal,
Nor read the secrets in't.

CLEOMENES AND DION.
                  All this we swear.

LEONTES.
Break up the seals and read.

OFFICER. [*Reads.*]
"Hermione is chaste; Polixenes blameless;
Camillo a true subject; Leontes a jealous
tyrant; his innocent babe truly begotten;
and the king shall live without an heir, if
that which is lost be not found."

LORDS.
Now blessed be the great Apollo!

HERMIONE.
                     Praised!

LEONTES.
Hast thou read truth?

OFFICER.
              Ay, my lord; even so
As it is here set down.

LEONTES.
There is no truth at all i' the oracle:

The sessions shall proceed: this is mere
    falsehood!
        [*Enter a* SERVANT *hastily.*]

SERVANT.
My lord the king, the king!

LEONTES.
               What is the business?

SERVANT.
O sir, I shall be hated to report it:
The prince your son, with mere conceit
    and fear
Of the queen's speed, is gone.

LEONTES.
                  How! gone?

SERVANT.
                    Is dead.

LEONTES.
Apollo's angry; and the heavens themselves
Do strike at my injustice. [HERMIONE
    faints.] How now, there!

PAULINA.
This news is mortal to the queen:—Look
    down
And see what death is doing.

LEONTES.
                Take her hence:
Her heart is but o'ercharg'd; she will
    recover.—
I have too much believ'd mine own
    suspicion:—
Beseech you tenderly apply to her
Some remedies for life. [*Exeunt* PAULINA
    and LADIES *with* HERMIONE.] Apollo,
    pardon
My great profaneness 'gainst thine
    oracle!—
I'll reconcile me to Polixenes;
New woo my queen; recall the good
    Camillo—
Whom I proclaim a man of truth, of
    mercy;
For, being transported by my jealousies
To bloody thoughts and to revenge, I
    chose
Camillo for the minister to poison
My friend Polixenes: which had been
    done,
But that the good mind of Camillo tardied

My swift command, though I with death
     and with
Reward did threaten and encourage him,
Not doing it and being done: he, most
     humane,
And fill'd with honour, to my kingly guest
Unclasp'd my practice; quit his fortunes
     here,
Which you knew great; and to the certain
     hazard
Of all incertainties himself commended,
No richer than his honour:—how he
     glisters
Thorough my rust! And how his piety
Does my deeds make the blacker!

          [*Re-enter* PAULINA.]

PAULINA.
                              Woe the while!
O, cut my lace, lest my heart, cracking it,
Break too!

FIRST LORD.
          What fit is this, good lady?

PAULINA.
What studied torments, tyrant, hast for
     me?
What wheels? racks? fires? what flaying?
     boiling
In leads or oils? what old or newer torture
Must I receive, whose every word deserves
To taste of thy most worst? Thy tyranny
Together working with thy jealousies,—
Fancies too weak for boys, too green and
     idle
For girls of nine,—O, think what they
     have done,
And then run mad indeed,—stark mad!
     for all
Thy by-gone fooleries were but spices of it.
That thou betray'dst Polixenes, 'twas
     nothing;
That did but show thee, of a fool,
     inconstant,
And damnable ingrateful; nor was't much
Thou wouldst have poison'd good
     Camillo's honour,
To have him kill a king; poor trespasses,—
More monstrous standing by: whereof I
     reckon

The casting forth to crows thy baby
     daughter,
To be or none or little, though a devil
Would have shed water out of fire ere
     done't;
Nor is't directly laid to thee, the death
Of the young prince, whose honourable
     thoughts,
Thoughts high for one so tender,—cleft
     the heart
That could conceive a gross and foolish
     sire
Blemish'd his gracious dam: this is not,—
     no,
Laid to thy answer: but the last,—O lords,
When I have said, cry, "Woe!"—the queen,
     the queen,
The sweetest, dearest creature's dead; and
     vengeance for't
Not dropp'd down yet.

FIRST LORD.
                    The higher powers forbid!

PAULINA.
I say she's dead: I'll swear't. If word nor
     oath
Prevail not, go and see: if you can bring
Tincture, or lustre, in her lip, her eye,
Heat outwardly or breath within, I'll serve
     you
As I would do the gods.—But, O thou
     tyrant!
Do not repent these things; for they are
     heavier
Than all thy woes can stir; therefore
     betake thee
To nothing but despair. A thousand
     knees
Ten thousand years together, naked,
     fasting,
Upon a barren mountain, and still winter
In storm perpetual, could not move the
     gods
To look that way thou wert.

LEONTES.
                         Go on, go on:
Thou canst not speak too much; I have
     deserv'd
All tongues to talk their bitterest!

First Lord.

Say no more:
Howe'er the business goes, you have made
fault
I' the boldness of your speech.

Paulina.

I am sorry for't:
All faults I make, when I shall come to
know them,
I do repent. Alas, I have show'd too much
The rashness of a woman: he is touch'd
To th' noble heart. What's gone and what's
past help,
Should be past grief: do not receive
affliction
At my petition; I beseech you, rather
Let me be punish'd, that have minded
you
Of what you should forget. Now, good
my liege,
Sir, royal sir, forgive a foolish woman:
The love I bore your queen,—lo, fool
again!—
I'll speak of her no more, nor of your
children;
I'll not remember you of my own lord,
Who is lost too: take your patience to
you,
And I'll say nothing.

Leontes.

Thou didst speak but well,
When most the truth; which I receive
much better
Than to be pitied of thee. Pr'ythee, bring
me
To the dead bodies of my queen and son:
One grave shall be for both; upon them
shall
The causes of their death appear, unto
Our shame perpetual. Once a day I'll
visit
The chapel where they lie; and tears shed
there
Shall be my recreation: so long as nature
Will bear up with this exercise, so long
I daily vow to use it. Come, and lead me
To these sorrows.

[Exeunt.]

SCENE III

Bohemia. A desert country near the sea.
[*Enter* Antigonus *with the* Child,
and a Mariner.]

Antigonus.

Thou art perfect, then, our ship hath
touch'd upon
The deserts of Bohemia?

Mariner.

Ay, my lord; and fear
We have landed in ill time: the skies look
grimly,
And threaten present blusters. In my
conscience,
The heavens with that we have in hand
are angry,
And frown upon 's.

Antigonus.

Their sacred wills be done!—Go, get
aboard;
Look to thy bark: I'll not be long
before
I call upon thee.

Mariner.

Make your best haste; and go not
Too far i' the land: 'tis like to be loud
weather;
Besides, this place is famous for the
creatures
Of prey that keep upon't.

Antigonus.

Go thou away:
I'll follow instantly.

Mariner.

I am glad at heart
To be so rid o' th' business.
[*Exit.*]

Antigonus.

Come, poor babe:—
I have heard—but not believ'd—the spirits
of the dead
May walk again: if such thing be, thy
mother
Appear'd to me last night; for ne'er was
dream
So like a waking. To me comes a creature,
Sometimes her head on one side, some
another:

I never saw a vessel of like sorrow,
So fill'd and so becoming: in pure white
   robes,
Like very sanctity, she did approach
My cabin where I lay: thrice bow'd before
   me;
And, gasping to begin some speech, her
   eyes
Became two spouts: the fury spent, anon
Did this break from her: "Good
   Antigonus,
Since fate, against thy better disposition,
Hath made thy person for the thrower-out
Of my poor babe, according to thine
   oath,—
Places remote enough are in Bohemia,
There weep, and leave it crying; and, for
   the babe
Is counted lost for ever, Perdita,
I pr'ythee call't. For this ungentle
   business,
Put on thee by my lord, thou ne'er shalt
   see
Thy wife Paulina more": so, with shrieks,
She melted into air. Affrighted much,
I did in time collect myself; and thought
This was so, and no slumber. Dreams are
   toys;
Yet, for this once, yea, superstitiously,
I will be squar'd by this. I do believe
Hermione hath suffer'd death, and that
Apollo would, this being indeed the
   issue
Of King Polixenes, it should here be
   laid,
Either for life or death, upon the earth
Of its right father. Blossom, speed thee
   well!
       [Laying down the CHILD.]
There lie; and there thy character: there
   these;
       [Laying down a bundle.]
Which may if fortune please, both breed
   thee, pretty,
And still rest thine. The storm begins:—
   poor wretch,
That for thy mother's fault art thus
   expos'd

To loss and what may follow! Weep I
   cannot,
But my heart bleeds: and most accurs'd
   am I
To be by oath enjoin'd to this. Farewell!
The day frowns more and more: thou'rt like
   to have
A lullaby too rough: I never saw
The heavens so dim by day. A savage
   clamour!
Well may I get aboard! This is the chase:
I am gone for ever.
       [Exit, pursued by a bear.]
       [Enter an old SHEPHERD.]

SHEPHERD.

I would there were no age between ten
and three-and-twenty, or that youth would
sleep out the rest; for there is nothing in
the between but getting wenches with
child, wronging the ancientry, stealing,
fighting.—Hark you now! Would any but
these boiled brains of nineteen and two-
and-twenty hunt this weather? They have
scared away two of my best sheep, which
I fear the wolf will sooner find than the
master: if anywhere I have them, 'tis by the
sea-side, browsing of ivy.—Good luck, an't
be thy will! what have we here? [*Taking
up the* CHILD.] Mercy on's, a bairn: A
very pretty bairn! A boy or a child, I wonder?
A pretty one; a very pretty one: sure, some
scape: though I am not bookish, yet I can
read waiting-gentlewoman in the scape.
This has been some stair-work, some
trunk-work, some behind-door-work; they
were warmer that got this than the poor
thing is here. I'll take it up for pity: yet I'll
tarry till my son comes; he hallaed but even
now.—Whoa, ho hoa!

CLOWN. [*Within.*]

Hilloa, loa!

SHEPHERD.

What, art so near? If thou'lt see a thing
to talk on when thou art dead and rotten,
come hither. [*Enter* CLOWN.] What ail'st
thou, man?

CLOWN.

I have seen two such sights, by sea and by

land!— but I am not to say it is a sea, for it is now the sky: betwixt the firmament and it, you cannot thrust a bodkin's point.

SHEPHERD.

Why, boy, how is it?

CLOWN.

I would you did but see how it chafes, how it rages, how it takes up the shore! But that's not to the point. O, the most piteous cry of the poor souls! sometimes to see 'em, and not to see 'em; now the ship boring the moon with her mainmast, and anon swallowed with yest and froth, as you'd thrust a cork into a hogshead. And then for the land service,—to see how the bear tore out his shoulder-bone; how he cried to me for help, and said his name was Antigonus, a nobleman.—But to make an end of the ship,—to see how the sea flap-dragon'd it:—but first, how the poor souls roared, and the sea mocked them;—and how the poor gentleman roared, and the bear mocked him,—both roaring louder than the sea or weather.

SHEPHERD.

Name of mercy! when was this, boy?

CLOWN.

Now, now; I have not winked since I saw these sights: the men are not yet cold under water, nor the bear half dined on the gentleman; he's at it now.

SHEPHERD.

Would I had been by to have helped the old man!

CLOWN.

I would you had been by the ship-side, to have helped her: there your charity would have lacked footing.

SHEPHERD. [*Aside.*]

Heavy matters, heavy matters! But look thee here, boy. Now bless thyself: thou mettest with things dying, I with things new-born. Here's a sight for thee; look thee, a bearing-cloth for a squire's child! look thee here; take up, take up, boy; open't. So, let's see:—it was told me I should be rich by the fairies: this is some changeling:— open't. What's within, boy?

CLOWN.

You're a made old man; if the sins of your youth are forgiven you, you're well to live. Gold! all gold!

SHEPHERD.

This is fairy-gold, boy, and 'twill prove so: up with it, keep it close: home, home, the next way! We are lucky, boy: and to be so still requires nothing but secrecy—Let my sheep go:—come, good boy, the next way home.

CLOWN.

Go you the next way with your findings. I'll go see if the bear be gone from the gentleman, and how much he hath eaten: they are never curst but when they are hungry: if there be any of him left, I'll bury it.

SHEPHERD.

That's a good deed. If thou mayest discern by that which is left of him what he is, fetch me to the sight of him.

CLOWN.

Marry, will I; and you shall help to put him i' the ground.

SHEPHERD.

'Tis a lucky day, boy; and we'll do good deeds on't.

[*Exeunt.*]

ACT IV

[*Enter* TIME, *as Chorus.*]

TIME.

I,—that please some, try all; both joy and terror

Of good and bad; that make and unfold error,—

Now take upon me, in the name of Time,

To use my wings. Impute it not a crime

To me or my swift passage, that I slide

O'er sixteen years, and leave the growth untried

Of that wide gap, since it is in my power

To o'erthrow law, and in one self-born hour

To plant and o'erwhelm custom. Let me pass

The same I am, ere ancient'st order was

Or what is now received: I witness to
The times that brought them in; so shall
    I do
To the freshest things now reigning, and
    make stale
The glistering of this present, as my tale
Now seems to it. Your patience this
    allowing,
I turn my glass, and give my scene such
    growing
As you had slept between. Leontes leaving
The effects of his fond jealousies, so
    grieving
That he shuts up himself; imagine me,
Gentle spectators, that I now may be
In fair Bohemia; and remember well,
I mention'd a son o' the king's, which
    Florizel
I now name to you; and with speed so pace
To speak of Perdita, now grown in grace
Equal with wondering: what of her ensues,
I list not prophesy; but let Time's news
Be known when 'tis brought forth:—a
    shepherd's daughter,
And what to her adheres, which follows
    after,
Is the argument of Time. Of this allow,
If ever you have spent time worse ere now;
If never, yet that Time himself doth say
He wishes earnestly you never may.
            [*Exit.*]

SCENE I

Bohemia. A room in the palace of Polixenes.
    [*Enter* POLIXENES *and* CAMILLO.]

POLIXENES.
I pray thee, good Camillo, be no more
importunate: 'tis a sickness denying thee
anything; a death to grant this.

CAMILLO.
It is fifteen years since I saw my country;
though I have for the most part been aired
abroad, I desire to lay my bones there.
Besides, the penitent king, my master,
hath sent for me; to whose feeling sorrows
I might be some allay, or I o'erween to
think so,—which is another spur to my
departure.

POLIXENES.
As thou lovest me, Camillo, wipe not out
the rest of thy services by leaving me now:
the need I have of thee, thine own goodness
hath made; better not to have had thee
than thus to want thee; thou, having made
me businesses which none without thee
can sufficiently manage, must either stay to
execute them thyself, or take away with thee
the very services thou hast done; which if I
have not enough considered,—as too much
I cannot,—to be more thankful to thee
shall be my study; and my profit therein the
heaping friendships. Of that fatal country
Sicilia, pr'ythee, speak no more; whose very
naming punishes me with the remembrance
of that penitent, as thou call'st him, and
reconciled king, my brother; whose loss of
his most precious queen and children are
even now to be afresh lamented. Say to me,
when sawest thou the Prince Florizel, my
son? Kings are no less unhappy, their issue
not being gracious, than they are in losing
them when they have approved their virtues.

CAMILLO.
Sir, it is three days since I saw the prince.
What his happier affairs may be, are to me
unknown; but I have missingly noted he
is of late much retired from court, and is
less frequent to his princely exercises than
formerly he hath appeared.

POLIXENES.
I have considered so much, Camillo, and
with some care; so far that I have eyes
under my service which look upon his
removedness; from whom I have this
intelligence,—that he is seldom from the
house of a most homely shepherd,—a
man, they say, that from very nothing, and
beyond the imagination of his neighbours,
is grown into an unspeakable estate.

CAMILLO.
I have heard, sir, of such a man, who hath
a daughter of most rare note: the report of
her is extended more than can be thought
to begin from such a cottage.

POLIXENES.
That's likewise part of my intelligence: but,

I fear, the angle that plucks our son thither.
Thou shalt accompany us to the place;
where we will, not appearing what we are,
have some question with the shepherd; from
whose simplicity I think it not uneasy to get
the cause of my son's resort thither. Pr'ythee,
be my present partner in this business, and
lay aside the thoughts of Sicilia.

CAMILLO.

I willingly obey your command.

POLIXENES.

My best Camillo!—We must disguise
ourselves.

[Exeunt.]

SCENE II

The same. A road near the shepherd's cottage.
[Enter AUTOLYCUS.]

AUTOLYCUS. *[Sings.]*

When daffodils begin to peer,—
  With, hey! the doxy over the dale,—
Why, then comes in the sweet o' the
    year:
  For the red blood reigns in the
    winter's pale.
The white sheet bleaching on the
    hedge,—
  With, hey! the sweet birds, O, how
    they sing!
Doth set my pugging tooth on edge;
  For a quart of ale is a dish for a king.
The lark, that tirra-lirra chants,—
  With, hey! with, hey! the thrush and
    the jay,
Are summer songs for me and my aunts,
  While we lie tumbling in the hay.

I have serv'd Prince Florizel, and in my
time wore three-pile; but now I am out of
service.

[Sings.]

But shall I go mourn for that, my dear?
  The pale moon shines by night:
And when I wander here and there,
  I then do most go right.
If tinkers may have leave to live,
  And bear the sow-skin budget,
Then my account I well may give
  And in the stocks avouch it.

My traffic is sheets; when the kite builds,
look to lesser linen. My father named me
Autolycus; who being, I as am, littered
under Mercury, was likewise a snapper-up
of unconsidered trifles. With die and drab
I purchased this caparison; and my revenue
is the silly-cheat: gallows and knock are
too powerful on the highway; beating and
hanging are terrors to me; for the life to
come, I sleep out the thought of it.—A
prize! a prize!

[Enter CLOWN.]

CLOWN.

Let me see:—every 'leven wether tods;
every tod yields pound and odd shilling;
fifteen hundred shorn, what comes the
wool to?

AUTOLYCUS. *[Aside.]*

If the springe hold, the cock's mine.

CLOWN.

I cannot do't without counters.—Let
me see; what am I to buy for our sheep-
shearing feast? "Three pound of sugar; five
pound of currants; rice"—what will this
sister of mine do with rice? But my father
hath made her mistress of the feast, and
she lays it on. She hath made me four and
twenty nosegays for the shearers,—three-
man song-men all, and very good ones; but
they are most of them means and bases; but
one puritan amongst them, and he sings
psalms to hornpipes. I must have saffron to
colour the warden pies; "mace—dates,"—
none, that's out of my note; "nutmegs,
seven; a race or two of ginger,"—but that
I may beg; "four pound of prunes, and as
many of raisins o' the sun."

AUTOLYCUS. *[Grovelling on the ground.]*

O that ever I was born!

CLOWN.

I' the name of me,—

AUTOLYCUS.

O, help me, help me! Pluck but off these
rags; and then, death, death!

CLOWN.

Alack, poor soul! thou hast need of more
rags to lay on thee, rather than have these
off.

AUTOLYCUS.

O sir, the loathsomeness of them offend me more than the stripes I have received, which are mighty ones and millions.

CLOWN.

Alas, poor man! a million of beating may come to a great matter.

AUTOLYCUS.

I am robb'd, sir, and beaten; my money and apparel ta'en from me, and these detestable things put upon me.

CLOWN.

What, by a horseman or a footman?

AUTOLYCUS.

A footman, sweet sir, a footman.

CLOWN.

Indeed, he should be a footman, by the garments he has left with thee: if this be a horseman's coat, it hath seen very hot service. Lend me thy hand, I'll help thee: come, lend me thy hand.

[*Helping him up.*]

AUTOLYCUS.

O, good sir, tenderly, O!

CLOWN.

Alas, poor soul!

AUTOLYCUS.

O, good sir, softly, good sir: I fear, sir, my shoulder blade is out.

CLOWN.

How now! canst stand?

AUTOLYCUS.

Softly, dear sir! [*Picks his pocket.*] good sir, softly; you ha' done me a charitable office.

CLOWN.

Dost lack any money? I have a little money for thee.

AUTOLYCUS.

No, good sweet sir; no, I beseech you, sir: I have a kinsman not past three quarters of a mile hence, unto whom I was going; I shall there have money or anything I want: offer me no money, I pray you; that kills my heart.

CLOWN.

What manner of fellow was he that robbed you?

AUTOLYCUS.

A fellow, sir, that I have known to go about with troll-my-dames; I knew him once a servant of the prince; I cannot tell, good sir, for which of his virtues it was, but he was certainly whipped out of the court.

CLOWN.

His vices, you would say; there's no virtue whipped out of the court: they cherish it, to make it stay there; and yet it will no more but abide.

AUTOLYCUS.

Vices, I would say, sir. I know this man well: he hath been since an ape-bearer; then a process-server, a bailiff; then he compassed a motion of the Prodigal Son, and married a tinker's wife within a mile where my land and living lies; and, having flown over many knavish professions, he settled only in rogue: some call him Autolycus.

CLOWN.

Out upon him! prig, for my life, prig: he haunts wakes, fairs, and bear-baitings.

AUTOLYCUS.

Very true, sir; he, sir, he; that's the rogue that put me into this apparel.

CLOWN.

Not a more cowardly rogue in all Bohemia; if you had but looked big and spit at him, he'd have run.

AUTOLYCUS.

I must confess to you, sir, I am no fighter: I am false of heart that way; and that he knew, I warrant him.

CLOWN.

How do you now?

AUTOLYCUS.

Sweet sir, much better than I was; I can stand and walk: I will even take my leave of you and pace softly towards my kinsman's.

CLOWN.

Shall I bring thee on the way?

AUTOLYCUS.

No, good-faced sir; no, sweet sir.

CLOWN.

Then fare thee well: I must go buy spices for our sheep-shearing.

AUTOLYCUS.

Prosper you, sweet sir! [*Exit* CLOWN.] Your purse is not hot enough to purchase

your spice. I'll be with you at your sheep-
shearing too. If I make not this cheat bring
out another, and the shearers prove sheep,
let me be unrolled, and my name put in the
book of virtue!

[*Sings.*]

Jog on, jog on, the footpath way,
    And merrily hent the stile-a:
A merry heart goes all the day,
    Your sad tires in a mile-a.
[*Exit.*]

SCENE III

The same. A shepherd's cottage.
[*Enter* Florizel *and* Perdita.]

Florizel.

These your unusual weeds to each part
    of you
Do give a life,—no shepherdess, but Flora
Peering in April's front. This your sheep-
    shearing
Is as a meeting of the petty gods,
And you the queen on't.

Perdita.

               Sir, my gracious lord,
To chide at your extremes it not becomes
    me,—
O, pardon that I name them!—your high
    self,
The gracious mark o' the land, you have
    obscur'd
With a swain's wearing; and me, poor
    lowly maid,
Most goddess-like prank'd up. But that
    our feasts
In every mess have folly, and the feeders
Digest it with a custom, I should blush
To see you so attir'd; swoon, I think,
To show myself a glass.

Florizel.

              I bless the time
When my good falcon made her flight
    across
Thy father's ground.

Perdita.

          Now Jove afford you cause!
To me the difference forges dread: your
    greatness

Hath not been us'd to fear. Even now I
    tremble
To think your father, by some accident,
Should pass this way, as you did. O, the
    fates!
How would he look to see his work, so
    noble,
Vilely bound up? What would he say? Or
    how
Should I, in these my borrow'd flaunts,
    behold
The sternness of his presence?

Florizel.

                   Apprehend
Nothing but jollity. The gods themselves,
Humbling their deities to love, have
    taken
The shapes of beasts upon them: Jupiter
Became a bull and bellow'd; the green
    Neptune
A ram and bleated; and the fire-rob'd god,
Golden Apollo, a poor humble swain,
As I seem now:—their transformations
Were never for a piece of beauty rarer,—
Nor in a way so chaste, since my desires
Run not before mine honour, nor my lusts
Burn hotter than my faith.

Perdita.

                 O, but, sir,
Your resolution cannot hold when 'tis
Oppos'd, as it must be, by the power of
    the king:
One of these two must be necessities,
Which then will speak, that you must
    change this purpose,
Or I my life.

Florizel.

           Thou dearest Perdita,
With these forc'd thoughts, I pr'ythee,
    darken not
The mirth o' the feast: or I'll be thine, my
    fair,
Or not my father's; for I cannot be
Mine own, nor anything to any, if
I be not thine: to this I am most constant,
Though destiny say no. Be merry, gentle;
Strangle such thoughts as these with any
    thing

That you behold the while. Your guests are
  coming:
Lift up your countenance, as it were the
  day
Of celebration of that nuptial which
We two have sworn shall come.
PERDITA.
                              O lady Fortune,
Stand you auspicious!
FLORIZEL.
                      See, your guests approach:
Address yourself to entertain them
  sprightly,
And let's be red with mirth.
    [*Enter* SHEPHERD, *with* POLIXENES *and*
      CAMILLO, *disguised;* CLOWN, MOPSA,
      DORCAS, *with* OTHERS.]
SHEPHERD.
Fie, daughter! When my old wife liv'd,
  upon
This day she was both pantler, butler,
  cook;
Both dame and servant; welcom'd all;
  serv'd all;
Would sing her song and dance her turn;
  now here
At upper end o' the table, now i' the
  middle;
On his shoulder, and his; her face o' fire
With labour, and the thing she took to
  quench it
She would to each one sip. You are retir'd,
As if you were a feasted one, and not
The hostess of the meeting: pray you, bid
These unknown friends to us welcome,
  for it is
A way to make us better friends, more
  known.
Come, quench your blushes, and present
  yourself
That which you are, mistress o' the feast:
  come on,
And bid us welcome to your sheep-
  shearing,
As your good flock shall prosper.
PERDITA. [*To* POLIXENES.]
                              Sir, welcome!
It is my father's will I should take on me

The hostess-ship o' the day:—
  [*To* CAMILLO.] You're welcome, sir!
Give me those flowers there, Dorcas.—
  Reverend sirs,
For you there's rosemary and rue; these
  keep
Seeming and savour all the winter long:
Grace and remembrance be to you both!
And welcome to our shearing!
POLIXENES.
                              Shepherdess—
A fair one are you!—well you fit our ages
With flowers of winter.
PERDITA.
              Sir, the year growing ancient,—
Not yet on summer's death nor on the
  birth
Of trembling winter,—the fairest flowers
  o' the season
Are our carnations and streak'd gillyvors,
Which some call nature's bastards: of that
  kind
Our rustic garden's barren; and I care not
To get slips of them.
POLIXENES.
                  Wherefore, gentle maiden,
Do you neglect them?
PERDITA.
                      For I have heard it said
There is an art which, in their piedness,
  shares
With great creating nature.
POLIXENES.
                          Say there be;
Yet nature is made better by no mean
But nature makes that mean; so, o'er that
  art
Which you say adds to nature, is an art
That nature makes. You see, sweet maid,
  we marry
A gentler scion to the wildest stock,
And make conceive a bark of baser kind
By bud of nobler race. This is an art
Which does mend nature,—change it
  rather; but
The art itself is nature.
PERDITA.
                          So it is.

POLIXENES.
Then make your garden rich in gillyvors,
And do not call them bastards.
PERDITA.
                              I'll not put
The dibble in earth to set one slip of them;
No more than were I painted, I would wish
This youth should say, 'twere well, and only
    therefore
Desire to breed by me.—Here's flowers
    for you;
Hot lavender, mints, savory, marjoram;
The marigold, that goes to bed with the
    sun,
And with him rises weeping; these are
    flowers
Of middle summer, and I think they are
    given
To men of middle age. You're very
    welcome!
CAMILLO.
I should leave grazing, were I of your flock,
And only live by gazing.
PERDITA.
                              Out, alas!
You'd be so lean that blasts of January
Would blow you through and through.—
    Now, my fairest friend,
I would I had some flowers o' the spring
    that might
Become your time of day;—and yours,
    and yours,
That wear upon your virgin branches yet
Your maidenheads growing.—O
    Proserpina,
From the flowers now, that, frighted, thou
    lett'st fall
From Dis's waggon!—daffodils,
That come before the swallow dares, and
    take
The winds of March with beauty; violets
    dim
But sweeter than the lids of Juno's eyes
Or Cytherea's breath; pale primroses,
That die unmarried ere they can behold
Bright Phoebus in his strength,—a malady
Most incident to maids; bold oxlips, and
The crown-imperial; lilies of all kinds,

The flower-de-luce being one.—O, these
    I lack,
To make you garlands of; and, my sweet
    friend,
To strew him o'er and o'er!
FLORIZEL.
                              What, like a corse?
PERDITA.
No; like a bank for love to lie and play on;
Not like a corse; or if,—not to be buried,
But quick, and in mine arms. Come, take
    your flowers;
Methinks I play as I have seen them do
In Whitsun pastorals: sure, this robe of
    mine
Does change my disposition.
FLORIZEL.
                              What you do
Still betters what is done. When you
    speak, sweet,
I'd have you do it ever; when you sing,
I'd have you buy and sell so; so give alms;
Pray so; and, for the ordering your affairs,
To sing them too: when you do dance, I
    wish you
A wave o' the sea, that you might ever do
Nothing but that; move still, still so, and
    own
No other function: each your doing,
So singular in each particular,
Crowns what you are doing in the present
    deeds,
That all your acts are queens.
PERDITA.
                              O Doricles,
Your praises are too large: but that your
    youth,
And the true blood which peeps fairly
    through it,
Do plainly give you out an unstained
    shepherd,
With wisdom I might fear, my Doricles,
You woo'd me the false way.
FLORIZEL.
                              I think you have
As little skill to fear as I have purpose
To put you to't. But, come; our dance, I
    pray:

Your hand, my Perdita; so turtles pair
That never mean to part.
PERDITA.

I'll swear for 'em.
POLIXENES.
This is the prettiest low-born lass that ever
Ran on the green-sward: nothing she does
    or seems
But smacks of something greater than
    herself,
Too noble for this place.
CAMILLO.

He tells her something
That makes her blood look out: good
    sooth, she is
The queen of curds and cream.
CLOWN.

Come on, strike up!
DORCAS.
Mopsa must be your mistress; marry, garlic,
To mend her kissing with!
MOPSA

Now, in good time!
CLOWN.
Not a word, a word; we stand upon our
    manners.—
Come, strike up!
    [*Music. Here a dance of* SHEPHERDS *and*
        SHEPHERDESSES.]
POLIXENES.
Pray, good shepherd, what fair swain is this
Which dances with your daughter?
SHEPHERD.
They call him Doricles; and boasts himself
To have a worthy feeding; but I have it
Upon his own report, and I believe it:
He looks like sooth. He says he loves my
    daughter:
I think so too; for never gaz'd the moon
Upon the water as he'll stand, and read,
As 'twere, my daughter's eyes: and, to be
    plain,
I think there is not half a kiss to choose
Who loves another best.
POLIXENES.

She dances featly.
SHEPHERD.
So she does anything; though I report it,

That should be silent; if young Doricles
Do light upon her, she shall bring him
    that
Which he not dreams of.
        [*Enter a* SERVANT.]
SERVANT.
O master, if you did but hear the pedlar at
the door, you would never dance again after
a tabor and pipe; no, the bagpipe could not
move you: he sings several tunes faster than
you'll tell money: he utters them as he had
eaten ballads, and all men's ears grew to his
tunes.
CLOWN.
He could never come better: he shall come
in. I love a ballad but even too well, if it be
doleful matter merrily set down, or a very
pleasant thing indeed and sung lamentably.
SERVANT.
He hath songs for man or woman of all
sizes; no milliner can so fit his customers
with gloves: he has the prettiest love-
songs for maids; so without bawdry, which
is strange; with such delicate burdens
of "dildos" and "fadings," "jump her and
thump her"; and where some stretch-
mouth'd rascal would, as it were, mean
mischief, and break a foul gap into the
matter, he makes the maid to answer,
"Whoop, do me no harm, good man"—
puts him off, slights him, with "Whoop, do
me no harm, good man."
POLIXENES.
This is a brave fellow.
CLOWN.
Believe me, thou talkest of an admirable
conceited fellow. Has he any unbraided
wares?
SERVANT.
He hath ribbons of all the colours i' the
rainbow; points, more than all the lawyers in
Bohemia can learnedly handle, though they
come to him by the gross; inkles, caddisses,
cambrics, lawns; why he sings 'em over as
they were gods or goddesses; you would
think a smock were a she-angel, he so chants
to the sleeve-hand and the work about the
square on't.

CLOWN.

Pr'ythee bring him in; and let him approach singing.

PERDITA.

Forewarn him that he use no scurrilous words in his tunes.

[*Exit* SERVANT.]

CLOWN.

You have of these pedlars that have more in them than you'd think, sister.

PERDITA.

Ay, good brother, or go about to think.

[*Enter* AUTOLYCUS, *singing.*]

AUTOLYCUS.

    Lawn as white as driven snow;
    Cypress black as e'er was crow;
    Gloves as sweet as damask-roses;
    Masks for faces and for noses;
    Bugle-bracelet, necklace amber,
    Perfume for a lady's chamber;
    Golden quoifs and stomachers,
    For my lads to give their dears;
    Pins and poking-sticks of steel,
    What maids lack from head to heel.
    Come, buy of me, come; come buy,
        come buy;
    Buy, lads, or else your lasses cry:
        Come, buy.

CLOWN.

If I were not in love with Mopsa, thou shouldst take no money of me; but being enthralled as I am, it will also be the bondage of certain ribbons and gloves.

MOPSA.

I was promis'd them against the feast; but they come not too late now.

DORCAS.

He hath promised you more than that, or there be liars.

MOPSA.

He hath paid you all he promised you: may be he has paid you more,—which will shame you to give him again.

CLOWN.

Is there no manners left among maids? will they wear their plackets where they should bear their faces? Is there not milking-time, when you are going to bed, or kiln-hole,

to whistle off these secrets, but you must be tittle-tattling before all our guests? 'tis well they are whispering. Clamour your tongues, and not a word more.

MOPSA.

I have done. Come, you promised me a tawdry lace, and a pair of sweet gloves.

CLOWN.

Have I not told thee how I was cozened by the way, and lost all my money?

AUTOLYCUS.

And indeed, sir, there are cozeners abroad; therefore it behoves men to be wary.

CLOWN.

Fear not thou, man; thou shalt lose nothing here.

AUTOLYCUS.

I hope so, sir; for I have about me many parcels of charge.

CLOWN.

What hast here? ballads?

MOPSA.

Pray now, buy some: I love a ballad in print a-life; for then we are sure they are true.

AUTOLYCUS.

Here's one to a very doleful tune. How a usurer's wife was brought to bed of twenty money-bags at a burden, and how she long'd to eat adders' heads and toads carbonadoed.

MOPSA.

Is it true, think you?

AUTOLYCUS.

Very true; and but a month old.

DORCAS.

Bless me from marrying a usurer!

AUTOLYCUS.

Here's the midwife's name to't, one Mistress Taleporter, and five or six honest wives that were present. Why should I carry lies abroad?

MOPSA.

Pray you now, buy it.

CLOWN.

Come on, lay it by; and let's first see more ballads; we'll buy the other things anon.

AUTOLYCUS.

Here's another ballad, of a fish that

appeared upon the coast on Wednesday the fourscore of April, forty thousand fathom above water, and sung this ballad against the hard hearts of maids: it was thought she was a woman, and was turned into a cold fish for she would not exchange flesh with one that loved her. The ballad is very pitiful, and as true.

DORCAS.

Is it true too, think you?

AUTOLYCUS.

Five justices' hands at it; and witnesses more than my pack will hold.

CLOWN.

Lay it by too: another.

AUTOLYCUS.

This is a merry ballad; but a very pretty one.

MOPSA.

Let's have some merry ones.

AUTOLYCUS.

Why, this is a passing merry one, and goes to the tune of "Two maids wooing a man." There's scarce a maid westward but she sings it: 'tis in request, I can tell you.

MOPSA.

We can both sing it: if thou'lt bear a part, thou shalt hear; 'tis in three parts.

DORCAS.

We had the tune on't a month ago.

AUTOLYCUS.

I can bear my part; you must know 'tis my occupation: have at it with you.

                    [*Song.*]

AUTOLYCUS.

   Get you hence, for I must go
   Where it fits not you to know.

DORCAS.

   Whither?

MOPSA.

       O, whither?

DORCAS.

           Whither?

MOPSA.

   It becomes thy oath full well
   Thou to me thy secrets tell.

DORCAS.

   Me too! Let me go thither.

MOPSA.

   Or thou goest to the grange or mill:

DORCAS.

   If to either, thou dost ill.

AUTOLYCUS.

   Neither.

DORCAS.

       What, neither?

AUTOLYCUS.

            Neither.

DORCAS.

   Thou hast sworn my love to be;

MOPSA.

   Thou hast sworn it more to me;
   Then whither goest?—say, whither?

CLOWN.

We'll have this song out anon by ourselves; my father and the gentlemen are in sad talk, and we'll not trouble them.—Come, bring away thy pack after me.—Wenches, I'll buy for you both:—Pedlar, let's have the first choice.—Follow me, girls.

   [*Exit with* DORCAS *and* MOPSA.]

AUTOLYCUS. [*Aside.*]

And you shall pay well for 'em. [*Sings.*]

   Will you buy any tape,
   Or lace for your cape,
  My dainty duck, my dear-a?
   Any silk, any thread,
   Any toys for your head,
 Of the new'st and fin'st, fin'st wear-a?
   Come to the pedlar;
   Money's a meddler
 That doth utter all men's ware-a.

       [*Exit.*]

    [*Re-enter* SERVANT.]

SERVANT.

Master, there is three carters, three shepherds, three neat-herds, three swine-herds, that have made themselves all men of hair; they call themselves saltiers: and they have dance which the wenches say is a gallimaufry of gambols, because they are not in't; but they themselves are o' the mind—if it be not too rough for some that know little but bowling—it will please plentifully.

SHEPHERD.

Away! we'll none on't; here has been too

much homely foolery already.—I know, sir,
we weary you.

POLIXENES.

You weary those that refresh us: pray, let's
see these four threes of herdsmen.

SERVANT.

One three of them, by their own report, sir,
hath danced before the king; and not the
worst of the three but jumps twelve foot
and a half by the squire.

SHEPHERD.

Leave your prating: since these good men
are pleased, let them come in; but quickly
now.

SERVANT.

Why, they stay at door, sir.

　　　　　　　　[*Exit.*]

　　[*Enter* TWELVE RUSTICS, *habited like*
　　Satyrs. They dance, and then exeunt.]

POLIXENES.

O, father, you'll know more of that
　　hereafter.—

[*To* CAMILLO.] Is it not too far gone?—
　　'Tis time to part them.—

He's simple and tells much. [*To*
　　FLORIZEL.] How now, fair shepherd!
Your heart is full of something that does
　　take
Your mind from feasting. Sooth, when I
　　was young
And handed love as you do, I was wont
To load my she with knacks: I would have
　　ransack'd
The pedlar's silken treasury and have
　　pour'd it
To her acceptance; you have let him go,
And nothing marted with him. If your
　　lass
Interpretation should abuse, and call this
Your lack of love or bounty, you were
　　straited
For a reply, at least if you make a care
Of happy holding her.

FLORIZEL.

　　　　　　　　　Old sir, I know
She prizes not such trifles as these are:
The gifts she looks from me are pack'd
　　and lock'd

Up in my heart; which I have given
　　already,
But not deliver'd.—O, hear me breathe
　　my life
Before this ancient sir, who, it should seem,
Hath sometime lov'd,—I take thy hand!
　　this hand,
As soft as dove's down, and as white as it,
Or Ethiopian's tooth, or the fann'd snow
　　that's bolted
By the northern blasts twice o'er.

POLIXENES.

　　　　　　　　　What follows this?—
How prettily the young swain seems to
　　wash
The hand was fair before!—I have put
　　you out:
But to your protestation; let me hear
What you profess.

FLORIZEL.

　　　　　　　Do, and be witness to't.

POLIXENES.

And this my neighbour, too?

FLORIZEL.

　　　　　　　　　And he, and more
Than he, and men, the earth, the heavens,
　　and all:
That, were I crown'd the most imperial
　　monarch,
Thereof most worthy; were I the fairest
　　youth
That ever made eye swerve; had force and
　　knowledge
More than was ever man's, I would not
　　prize them
Without her love: for her employ them all;
Commend them, and condemn them to
　　her service,
Or to their own perdition.

POLIXENES.

　　　　　　　　　Fairly offer'd.

CAMILLO.

This shows a sound affection.

SHEPHERD.

　　　　　　　　　But, my daughter,
Say you the like to him?

PERDITA.

　　　　　　　　　I cannot speak

So well, nothing so well; no, nor mean
    better:
By the pattern of mine own thoughts I
    cut out
The purity of his.
SHEPHERD.
              Take hands, a bargain!—
And, friends unknown, you shall bear
    witness to't:
I give my daughter to him, and will make
Her portion equal his.
FLORIZEL.
              O, that must be
I' the virtue of your daughter: one being
    dead,
I shall have more than you can dream of
    yet;
Enough then for your wonder: but come
    on,
Contract us 'fore these witnesses.
SHEPHERD.
           Come, your hand;—
And, daughter, yours.
POLIXENES.
        Soft, swain, awhile, beseech you;
Have you a father?
FLORIZEL.
          I have; but what of him?
POLIXENES.
Knows he of this?
FLORIZEL.
         He neither does nor shall.
POLIXENES.
Methinks a father
Is, at the nuptial of his son, a guest
That best becomes the table. Pray you,
    once more;
Is not your father grown incapable
Of reasonable affairs? is he not stupid
With age and altering rheums? can he
    speak? hear?
Know man from man? dispute his own
    estate?
Lies he not bed-rid? and again does
    nothing
But what he did being childish?
FLORIZEL.
             No, good sir;

He has his health, and ampler strength
    indeed
Than most have of his age.
POLIXENES.
            By my white beard,
You offer him, if this be so, a wrong
Something unfilial: reason my son
Should choose himself a wife; but as good
    reason
The father,—all whose joy is nothing else
But fair posterity,—should hold some
    counsel
In such a business.
FLORIZEL.
             I yield all this;
But, for some other reasons, my grave sir,
Which 'tis not fit you know, I not acquaint
My father of this business.
POLIXENES.
            Let him know't.
FLORIZEL.
He shall not.
POLIXENES.
        Pr'ythee, let him.
FLORIZEL.
           No, he must not.
SHEPHERD.
Let him, my son: he shall not need to
    grieve
At knowing of thy choice.
FLORIZEL.
        Come, come, he must not.—
Mark our contract.
POLIXENES. [*Discovering himself.*]
        Mark your divorce, young sir,
Whom son I dare not call; thou art too
    base
To be acknowledged: thou a sceptre's heir,
That thus affects a sheep-hook!—Thou,
    old traitor,
I am sorry that, by hanging thee, I can but
Shorten thy life one week.—And thou,
    fresh piece
Of excellent witchcraft, who of force must
    know
The royal fool thou cop'st with,—
SHEPHERD.
           O, my heart!

POLIXENES.

I'll have thy beauty scratch'd with briers, and made
More homely than thy state. For thee, fond boy,—
If I may ever know thou dost but sigh
That thou no more shalt see this knack,—as never
I mean thou shalt,—we'll bar thee from succession;
Not hold thee of our blood, no, not our kin,
Far than Deucalion off:—mark thou my words:
Follow us to the court.—Thou churl, for this time,
Though full of our displeasure, yet we free thee
From the dead blow of it. And you, enchantment,
Worthy enough a herdsman; yea, him too
That makes himself, but for our honour therein,
Unworthy thee,—if ever henceforth thou
These rural latches to his entrance open,
Or hoop his body more with thy embraces,
I will devise a death as cruel for thee
As thou art tender to't.

                [Exit.]

PERDITA.

                Even here undone!
I was not much afeard: for once or twice
I was about to speak, and tell him plainly
The self-same sun that shines upon his court
Hides not his visage from our cottage, but
Looks on alike. *[To FLORIZEL.]* Will't please you, sir, be gone?
I told you what would come of this! Beseech you,
Of your own state take care: this dream of mine,
Being now awake, I'll queen it no inch further,
But milk my ewes, and weep.

CAMILLO.

                Why, how now, father!
Speak ere thou diest.

SHEPHERD.

                I cannot speak, nor think,
Nor dare to know that which I know. *[To FLORIZEL.]* O, sir,
You have undone a man of fourscore-three,
That thought to fill his grave in quiet; yea,
To die upon the bed my father died,
To lie close by his honest bones! but now
Some hangman must put on my shroud, and lay me
Where no priest shovels in dust. *[To PERDITA.]* O cursed wretch,
That knew'st this was the prince, and wouldst adventure
To mingle faith with him!—Undone, undone!
If I might die within this hour, I have liv'd
To die when I desire.

                [Exit.]

FLORIZEL.

              Why look you so upon me?
I am but sorry, not afeard; delay'd,
But nothing alt'red: what I was, I am:
More straining on for plucking back; not following
My leash unwillingly.

CAMILLO.

              Gracious, my lord,
You know your father's temper: at this time
He will allow no speech,—which I do guess
You do not purpose to him,—and as hardly
Will he endure your sight as yet, I fear:
Then, till the fury of his highness settle,
Come not before him.

FLORIZEL.

              I not purpose it.
I think Camillo?

CAMILLO.

              Even he, my lord.

PERDITA.

How often have I told you 'twould be thus!
How often said my dignity would last
But till 'twere known!

FLORIZEL.

                              It cannot fail but by
The violation of my faith; and then
Let nature crush the sides o' the earth
    together
And mar the seeds within!—Lift up thy
    looks.—
From my succession wipe me, father; I
Am heir to my affection.

CAMILLO.

                              Be advis'd.

FLORIZEL.

I am,—and by my fancy; if my reason
Will thereto be obedient, I have reason;
If not, my senses, better pleas'd with
    madness,
Do bid it welcome.

CAMILLO.

                              This is desperate, sir.

FLORIZEL.

So call it: but it does fulfil my vow:
I needs must think it honesty. Camillo,
Not for Bohemia, nor the pomp that may
Be thereat glean'd; for all the sun sees or
The close earth wombs, or the profound
    seas hide
In unknown fathoms, will I break my oath
To this my fair belov'd: therefore, I pray
    you,
As you have ever been my father's
    honour'd friend
When he shall miss me,—as, in faith, I
    mean not
To see him any more,—cast your good
    counsels
Upon his passion: let myself and fortune
Tug for the time to come. This you may
    know,
And so deliver,—I am put to sea
With her, whom here I cannot hold on
    shore;
And, most opportune to her need, I have
A vessel rides fast by, but not prepar'd
For this design. What course I mean to
    hold
Shall nothing benefit your knowledge,
    nor
Concern me the reporting.

CAMILLO.

                              O, my lord,
I would your spirit were easier for advice,
Or stronger for your need.

FLORIZEL.

Hark, Perdita. [*Takes her aside.*]
[*To* CAMILLO.] I'll hear you by and by.

CAMILLO.

                              He's irremovable,
Resolv'd for flight. Now were I happy if
His going I could frame to serve my turn;
Save him from danger, do him love and
    honour;
Purchase the sight again of dear Sicilia
And that unhappy king, my master, whom
I so much thirst to see.

FLORIZEL.

                              Now, good Camillo,
I am so fraught with curious business that
I leave out ceremony.

CAMILLO.

                              Sir, I think
You have heard of my poor services, i' the
    love
That I have borne your father?

FLORIZEL.

                              Very nobly
Have you deserv'd: it is my father's music
To speak your deeds; not little of his care
To have them recompens'd as thought on.

CAMILLO.

                              Well, my lord,
If you may please to think I love the king,
And, through him, what's nearest to him,
    which is
Your gracious self, embrace but my
    direction,—
If your more ponderous and settled project
May suffer alteration,—on mine honour,
I'll point you where you shall have such
    receiving
As shall become your highness; where
    you may
Enjoy your mistress,—from the whom,
    I see,
There's no disjunction to be made, but by,
As heavens forfend! your ruin,—marry
    her;

And,—with my best endeavours in your
    absence—
Your discontenting father strive to qualify,
And bring him up to liking.

FLORIZEL.
                     How, Camillo,
May this, almost a miracle, be done?
That I may call thee something more than
    man,
And, after that, trust to thee.

CAMILLO.
                Have you thought on
A place whereto you'll go?

FLORIZEL.
                  Not any yet;
But as the unthought-on accident is guilty
To what we wildly do; so we profess
Ourselves to be the slaves of chance, and
    flies
Of every wind that blows.

CAMILLO.
                 Then list to me:
This follows,—if you will not change your
    purpose,
But undergo this flight,—make for Sicilia;
And there present yourself and your fair
    princess,
For so, I see, she must be,—'fore Leontes:
She shall be habited as it becomes
The partner of your bed. Methinks I see
Leontes opening his free arms, and
    weeping
His welcomes forth; asks thee, the son,
    forgiveness,
As 'twere i' the father's person; kisses the
    hands
Of your fresh princess; o'er and o'er divides
    him
'Twixt his unkindness and his kindness,—
    the one
He chides to hell, and bids the other grow
Faster than thought or time.

FLORIZEL.
                Worthy Camillo,
What colour for my visitation shall I
Hold up before him?

CAMILLO.
            Sent by the king your father

To greet him and to give him comforts.
    Sir,
The manner of your bearing towards him,
    with
What you as from your father, shall deliver,
Things known betwixt us three, I'll write
    you down;
The which shall point you forth at every
    sitting,
What you must say; that he shall not
    perceive
But that you have your father's bosom
    there,
And speak his very heart.

FLORIZEL.
               I am bound to you:
There is some sap in this.

CAMILLO.
            A course more promising
Than a wild dedication of yourselves
To unpath'd waters, undream'd shores,
    most certain
To miseries enough: no hope to help you;
But as you shake off one to take another:
Nothing so certain as your anchors; who
Do their best office if they can but stay
    you
Where you'll be loath to be: besides, you
    know
Prosperity's the very bond of love,
Whose fresh complexion and whose heart
    together
Affliction alters.

PERDITA.
             One of these is true:
I think affliction may subdue the cheek,
But not take in the mind.

CAMILLO.
               Yea, say you so?
There shall not at your father's house,
    these seven years
Be born another such.

FLORIZEL.
             My good Camillo,
She is as forward of her breeding as
She is i' the rear our birth.

CAMILLO.
             I cannot say 'tis pity

She lacks instruction; for she seems a
   mistress
To most that teach.

PERDITA.

          Your pardon, sir; for this:
I'll blush you thanks.

FLORIZEL.

          My prettiest Perdita!—
But, O, the thorns we stand upon!—
   Camillo,—
Preserver of my father, now of me;
The medicine of our house!—how shall
   we do?
We are not furnish'd like Bohemia's son;
Nor shall appear in Sicilia.

CAMILLO.

          My lord,
Fear none of this: I think you know my
   fortunes
Do all lie there: it shall be so my care
To have you royally appointed as if
The scene you play were mine. For
   instance, sir,
That you may know you shall not want,—
   one word.

          [*They talk aside.*]
       [*Re-enter* AUTOLYCUS.]

AUTOLYCUS.

Ha, ha! what a fool Honesty is! and
Trust, his sworn brother, a very simple
gentleman! I have sold all my trumpery;
not a counterfeit stone, not a riband, glass,
pomander, brooch, table-book, ballad,
knife, tape, glove, shoe-tie, bracelet, horn-
ring, to keep my pack from fasting;—they
throng who should buy first, as if my
trinkets had been hallowed, and brought
a benediction to the buyer: by which
means I saw whose purse was best in
picture; and what I saw, to my good use I
remembered. My clown—who wants but
something to be a reasonable man—grew
so in love with the wenches' song that he
would not stir his pettitoes till he had both
tune and words; which so drew the rest of
the herd to me that all their other senses
stuck in ears: you might have pinched a
placket,—it was senseless; 'twas nothing

to geld a codpiece of a purse; I would
have filed keys off that hung in chains: no
hearing, no feeling, but my sir's song, and
admiring the nothing of it. So that, in this
time of lethargy, I picked and cut most of
their festival purses; and had not the old
man come in with whoobub against his
daughter and the king's son, and scared
my choughs from the chaff, I had not left a
purse alive in the whole army.

    [CAMILLO, FLORIZEL, *and* PERDITA
           come forward.]

CAMILLO.

Nay, but my letters, by this means being
   there
So soon as you arrive, shall clear that
   doubt.

FLORIZEL.

And those that you'll procure from king
   Leontes,—

CAMILLO.

Shall satisfy your father.

PERDITA.

          Happy be you!
All that you speak shows fair.

CAMILLO. [*Seeing* AUTOLYCUS.]
          Who have we here?
We'll make an instrument of this; omit
Nothing may give us aid.

AUTOLYCUS. [*Aside.*]
If they have overheard me now,—why,
   hanging.

CAMILLO.

How now, good fellow! why shakest thou
so? Fear not, man; here's no harm intended
to thee.

AUTOLYCUS.

I am a poor fellow, sir.

CAMILLO.

Why, be so still; here's nobody will steal that
from thee: yet, for the outside of thy poverty
we must make an exchange; therefore disease
thee instantly,—thou must think there's a
necessity in't,—and change garments with
this gentleman: though the pennyworth on
his side be the worst, yet hold thee, there's
some boot.

          [*Giving money.*]

Autolycus.

I am a poor fellow, sir: [*Aside.*] I know ye
well enough.

Camillo.

Nay, pr'ythee dispatch: the gentleman is
half flay'd already.

Autolycus.

Are you in earnest, sir? [*Aside.*] I smell the
trick on't.

Florizel.

Dispatch, I pr'ythee.

Autolycus.

Indeed, I have had earnest; but I cannot
with conscience take it.

Camillo.

Unbuckle, unbuckle.—

[*Florizel and Autolycus exchange
garments.*]

Fortunate mistress,—let my prophecy
Come home to you!—you must retire
        yourself
Into some covert; take your sweetheart's hat
And pluck it o'er your brows, muffle your
        face,
Dismantle you; and, as you can, disliken
The truth of your own seeming; that you
        may,—
For I do fear eyes over,—to shipboard
Get undescried.

Perdita.

                I see the play so lies
That I must bear a part.

Camillo.

                        No remedy.—

Have you done there?

Florizel.

                Should I now meet my father,
He would not call me son.

Camillo.

Nay, you shall have no hat. [*Giving it to
        Perdita.*]
Come, lady, come.—Farewell, my friend.

Autolycus.

                                Adieu, sir.

Florizel.

O Perdita, what have we twain forgot!
Pray you, a word.

        [*They converse apart.*]

Camillo. [*Aside.*]

What I do next, shall be to tell the king
Of this escape, and whither they are
        bound;
Wherein, my hope is, I shall so prevail
To force him after: in whose company
I shall re-view Sicilia; for whose sight
I have a woman's longing.

Florizel.

                        Fortune speed us!—
Thus we set on, Camillo, to the sea-side.

Camillo.

The swifter speed the better.

        [*Exeunt* Florizel, Perdita, *and*
                Camillo.]

Autolycus.

I understand the business, I hear it:—to
have an open ear, a quick eye, and a nimble
hand, is necessary for a cut-purse; a good
nose is requisite also, to smell out work
for the other senses. I see this is the time
that the unjust man doth thrive. What an
exchange had this been without boot? what
a boot is here with this exchange? Sure, the
gods do this year connive at us, and we
may do anything extempore. The prince
himself is about a piece of iniquity,—
stealing away from his father with his clog
at his heels: if I thought it were a piece
of honesty to acquaint the king withal, I
would not do't: I hold it the more knavery
to conceal it; and therein am I constant
to my profession. [*Re-enter* Clown *and*
Shepherd.] Aside, aside;—here is more
matter for a hot brain: every lane's end,
every shop, church, session, hanging, yields
a careful man work.

Clown.

See, see; what a man you are now! There
is no other way but to tell the king she's
a changeling, and none of your flesh and
blood.

Shepherd.

Nay, but hear me.

Clown.

Nay, but hear me.

Shepherd.

Go to, then.

Clown.

She being none of your flesh and blood, your flesh and blood has not offended the king; and so your flesh and blood is not to be punished by him. Show those things you found about her; those secret things,—all but what she has with her: this being done, let the law go whistle; I warrant you.

Shepherd.

I will tell the king all, every word,—yea, and his son's pranks too; who, I may say, is no honest man neither to his father nor to me, to go about to make me the king's brother-in-law.

Clown.

Indeed, brother-in-law was the farthest off you could have been to him; and then your blood had been the dearer by I know how much an ounce.

Autolycus. [*Aside.*]

Very wisely, puppies!

Shepherd.

Well, let us to the king: there is that in this fardel will make him scratch his beard!

Autolycus. [*Aside.*]

I know not what impediment this complaint may be to the flight of my master.

Clown.

Pray heartily he be at palace.

Autolycus. [*Aside.*]

Though I am not naturally honest, I am so sometimes by chance. Let me pocket up my pedlar's excrement. [*Takes off his false beard.*] How now, rustics! whither are you bound?

Shepherd.

To the palace, an it like your worship.

Autolycus.

Your affairs there, what, with whom, the condition of that fardel, the place of your dwelling, your names, your ages, of what having, breeding, and anything that is fitting to be known? discover.

Clown.

We are but plain fellows, sir.

Autolycus.

A lie: you are rough and hairy. Let me have no lying; it becomes none but tradesmen, and they often give us soldiers the lie: but we pay them for it with stamped coin, not stabbing steel; therefore they do not give us the lie.

Clown.

Your worship had like to have given us one, if you had not taken yourself with the manner.

Shepherd.

Are you a courtier, an't like you, sir?

Autolycus.

Whether it like me or no, I am a courtier. Seest thou not the air of the court in these enfoldings? hath not my gait in it the measure of the court? receives not thy nose court-odour from me? reflect I not on thy baseness court-contempt? Think'st thou, for that I insinuate, or toaze from thee thy business, I am therefore no courtier? I am courtier cap-à-pie, and one that will either push on or pluck back thy business there: whereupon I command thee to open thy affair.

Shepherd.

My business, sir, is to the king.

Autolycus.

What advocate hast thou to him?

Shepherd.

I know not, an't like you.

Clown.

Advocate's the court-word for a pheasant; say you have none.

Shepherd.

None, sir; I have no pheasant, cock nor hen.

Autolycus.

How bless'd are we that are not simple men!

Yet nature might have made me as these are,

Therefore I will not disdain.

Clown.

This cannot be but a great courtier.

Shepherd.

His garments are rich, but he wears them not handsomely.

Clown.

He seems to be the more noble in being

fantastical: a great man, I'll warrant; I know by the picking on's teeth.

Autolycus.

The fardel there? what's i' the fardel? Wherefore that box?

Shepherd.

Sir, there lies such secrets in this fardel and box which none must know but the king; and which he shall know within this hour, if I may come to the speech of him.

Autolycus.

Age, thou hast lost thy labour.

Shepherd.

Why, sir?

Autolycus.

The king is not at the palace; he is gone aboard a new ship to purge melancholy and air himself: for, if thou beest capable of things serious, thou must know the king is full of grief.

Shepherd.

So 'tis said, sir,—about his son, that should have married a shepherd's daughter.

Autolycus.

If that shepherd be not in hand-fast, let him fly: the curses he shall have, the tortures he shall feel, will break the back of man, the heart of monster.

Clown.

Think you so, sir?

Autolycus.

Not he alone shall suffer what wit can make heavy and vengeance bitter; but those that are germane to him, though removed fifty times, shall all come under the hangman: which, though it be great pity, yet it is necessary. An old sheep-whistling rogue, a ram-tender, to offer to have his daughter come into grace! Some say he shall be stoned; but that death is too soft for him, say I. Draw our throne into a sheep-cote!—all deaths are too few, the sharpest too easy.

Clown.

Has the old man e'er a son, sir, do you hear, an't like you, sir?

Autolycus.

He has a son,—who shall be flayed alive; then 'nointed over with honey, set on the head of a wasp's nest; then stand till he be three quarters and a dram dead; then recovered again with aqua-vitae or some other hot infusion; then, raw as he is, and in the hottest day prognostication proclaims, shall he be set against a brick wall, the sun looking with a southward eye upon him,—where he is to behold him with flies blown to death. But what talk we of these traitorly rascals, whose miseries are to be smiled at, their offences being so capital? Tell me,—for you seem to be honest plain men,—what you have to the king: being something gently considered, I'll bring you where he is aboard, tender your persons to his presence, whisper him in your behalfs; and if it be in man besides the king to effect your suits, here is man shall do it.

Clown.

He seems to be of great authority: close with him, give him gold; and though authority be a stubborn bear, yet he is oft led by the nose with gold: show the inside of your purse to the outside of his hand, and no more ado. Remember,—ston'd and flayed alive.

Shepherd.

An't please you, sir, to undertake the business for us, here is that gold I have: I'll make it as much more, and leave this young man in pawn till I bring it you.

Autolycus.

After I have done what I promised?

Shepherd.

Ay, sir.

Autolycus.

Well, give me the moiety. Are you a party in this business?

Clown.

In some sort, sir: but though my case be a pitiful one, I hope I shall not be flayed out of it.

Autolycus.

O, that's the case of the shepherd's son. Hang him, he'll be made an example.

Clown.

Comfort, good comfort! We must to the king and show our strange sights. He must know 'tis none of your daughter nor my sister; we are gone else. Sir, I will give you as much as this old man does, when the business is performed; and remain, as he says, your pawn till it be brought you.

AUTOLYCUS.

I will trust you. Walk before toward the sea-side; go on the right-hand; I will but look upon the hedge, and follow you.

CLOWN.

We are blessed in this man, as I may say, even blessed.

SHEPHERD.

Let's before, as he bids us: he was provided to do us good.

[*Exeunt* SHEPHERD *and* CLOWN.]

AUTOLYCUS.

If I had a mind to be honest, I see Fortune would not suffer me: she drops booties in my mouth. I am courted now with a double occasion,—gold, and a means to do the prince my master good; which who knows how that may turn back to my advancement? I will bring these two moles, these blind ones, aboard him: if he think it fit to shore them again, and that the complaint they have to the king concerns him nothing, let him call me rogue for being so far officious; for I am proof against that title, and what shame else belongs to't. To him will I present them: there may be matter in it.

[*Exit.*]

ACT V
SCENE I

Sicilia. A room in the palace of Leontes.
[*Enter* LEONTES, CLEOMENES, DION, PAULINA, *and* OTHERS.]

CLEOMENES.

Sir, you have done enough, and have perform'd
A saint-like sorrow: no fault could you make
Which you have not redeem'd; indeed, paid down
More penitence than done trespass: at the last,

Do as the heavens have done, forget your evil;
With them, forgive yourself.

LEONTES.
        Whilst I remember
Her and her virtues, I cannot forget
My blemishes in them; and so still think of
The wrong I did myself: which was so much
That heirless it hath made my kingdom, and
Destroy'd the sweet'st companion that e'er man
Bred his hopes out of.

PAULINA.
        True, too true, my lord;
If, one by one, you wedded all the world,
Or from the all that are took something good,
To make a perfect woman, she you kill'd
Would be unparallel'd.

LEONTES.
        I think so.—Kill'd!
She I kill'd! I did so: but thou strik'st me
Sorely, to say I did: it is as bitter
Upon thy tongue as in my thought: now, good now,
Say so but seldom.

CLEOMENES.
        Not at all, good lady;
You might have spoken a thousand things that would
Have done the time more benefit, and grac'd
Your kindness better.

PAULINA.
        You are one of those
Would have him wed again.

DION.
        If you would not so,
You pity not the state, nor the remembrance
Of his most sovereign name; consider little
What dangers, by his highness' fail of issue,
May drop upon his kingdom, and devour
Incertain lookers-on. What were more holy

Than to rejoice the former queen is well?
What holier than,—for royalty's repair,
For present comfort, and for future
    good,—
To bless the bed of majesty again
With a sweet fellow to't?
Paulina.
                              There is none worthy,
Respecting her that's gone. Besides, the
    gods
Will have fulfill'd their secret purposes;
For has not the divine Apollo said,
Is't not the tenour of his oracle,
That King Leontes shall not have an heir
Till his lost child be found? which that
    it shall,
Is all as monstrous to our human reason
As my Antigonus to break his grave
And come again to me; who, on my life,
Did perish with the infant. 'Tis your
    counsel
My lord should to the heavens be contrary,
Oppose against their wills. [*To* Leontes.]
    Care not for issue;
The crown will find an heir: great
    Alexander
Left his to the worthiest; so his successor
Was like to be the best.
Leontes.
                              Good Paulina,—
Who hast the memory of Hermione,
I know, in honour,—O that ever I
Had squar'd me to thy counsel!—then,
    even now,
I might have look'd upon my queen's full
    eyes,
Have taken treasure from her lips,—
Paulina.
                              And left them
More rich for what they yielded.
Leontes.
                              Thou speak'st truth.
No more such wives; therefore, no wife:
    one worse,
And better us'd, would make her sainted
    spirit
Again possess her corpse; and on this
    stage,—

Where we offend her now,—appear soul-
    vexed,
And begin, "Why to me?"
Paulina.
                              Had she such power,
She had just cause.
Leontes.
                              She had; and would incense me
To murder her I married.
Paulina.
                              I should so.
Were I the ghost that walk'd, I'd bid you
    mark
Her eye, and tell me for what dull part in't
You chose her: then I'd shriek, that even
    your ears
Should rift to hear me; and the words that
    follow'd
Should be "Remember mine!"
Leontes.
                              Stars, stars,
And all eyes else dead coals!—fear thou
    no wife;
I'll have no wife, Paulina.
Paulina.
                              Will you swear
Never to marry but by my free leave?
Leontes.
Never, Paulina; so be bless'd my spirit!
Paulina.
Then, good my lords, bear witness to his
    oath.
Cleomenes.
You tempt him over-much.
Paulina.
                              Unless another,
As like Hermione as is her picture,
Affront his eye.
Cleomenes.
                              Good madam,—
Paulina.
                              I have done.
Yet, if my lord will marry,—if you will, sir,
No remedy but you will,—give me the
    office
To choose you a queen: she shall not be
    so young
As was your former; but she shall be such

As, walk'd your first queen's ghost, it should
    take joy
To see her in your arms.

LEONTES.
                          My true Paulina,
We shall not marry till thou bidd'st us.

PAULINA.
                                    That
Shall be when your first queen's again in
    breath;
Never till then.

[*Enter a* GENTLEMAN.]

GENTLEMAN.
One that gives out himself Prince Florizel,
Son of Polixenes, with his princess,—she
The fairest I have yet beheld,—desires
    access
To your high presence.

LEONTES.
                  What with him? he comes not
Like to his father's greatness: his approach,
So out of circumstance and sudden, tells us
'Tis not a visitation fram'd, but forc'd
By need and accident. What train?

GENTLEMAN.
                                    But few,
And those but mean.

LEONTES.
              His princess, say you, with him?

GENTLEMAN.
Ay; the most peerless piece of earth, I
    think,
That e'er the sun shone bright on.

PAULINA.
                                O Hermione,
As every present time doth boast itself
Above a better gone, so must thy grave
Give way to what's seen now! Sir, you
    yourself
Have said and writ so,—but your writing
    now
Is colder than that theme,—"She had not
    been,
Nor was not to be equall'd"; thus your
    verse
Flow'd with her beauty once; 'tis shrewdly
    ebb'd,
To say you have seen a better.

GENTLEMAN.
                            Pardon, madam:
The one I have almost forgot,—your
    pardon;—
The other, when she has obtain'd your eye,
Will have your tongue too. This is a
    creature,
Would she begin a sect, might quench
    the zeal
Of all professors else; make proselytes
Of who she but bid follow.

PAULINA.
                              How! not women?

GENTLEMAN.
Women will love her that she is a woman
More worth than any man; men, that
    she is
The rarest of all women.

LEONTES.
                          Go, Cleomenes;
Yourself, assisted with your honour'd
    friends,
Bring them to our embracement.—

[*Exeunt* CLEOMENES, LORDS, *and*
                          GENTLEMAN.]
                            Still, 'tis strange
He thus should steal upon us.

PAULINA.
                        Had our prince,—
Jewel of children,—seen this hour, he had
    pair'd
Well with this lord: there was not full a
    month
Between their births.

LEONTES.
          Pr'ythee, no more; cease; thou know'st
He dies to me again when talk'd of: sure,
When I shall see this gentleman, thy
    speeches
Will bring me to consider that which may
Unfurnish me of reason.—They are
    come.—

[*Re-enter* CLEOMENES, *with* FLORIZEL,
        PERDITA, *and* ATTENDANTS.]

Your mother was most true to wedlock,
    prince;
For she did print your royal father off,
Conceiving you: were I but twenty-one,

Your father's image is so hit in you,
His very air, that I should call you brother,
As I did him, and speak of something
    wildly
By us perform'd before. Most dearly
    welcome!
And your fair princess,—goddess! O, alas!
I lost a couple that 'twixt heaven and earth
Might thus have stood, begetting wonder,
    as
You, gracious couple, do! And then I
    lost,—
All mine own folly,—the society,
Amity too, of your brave father, whom,
Though bearing misery, I desire my life
Once more to look on him.

FLORIZEL.
                            By his command
Have I here touch'd Sicilia, and from him
Give you all greetings that a king, at
    friend,
Can send his brother: and, but infirmity,—
Which waits upon worn times, hath
    something seiz'd
His wish'd ability, he had himself
The lands and waters 'twixt your throne
    and his
Measur'd, to look upon you; whom he
    loves,
He bade me say so,—more than all the
    sceptres
And those that bear them, living.

LEONTES.
                            O my brother,—
Good gentleman, the wrongs I have done
    thee stir
Afresh within me; and these thy offices,
So rarely kind, are as interpreters
Of my behind-hand slackness!—Welcome
    hither,
As is the spring to the earth. And hath
    he too
Expos'd this paragon to the fearful usage,—
At least ungentle,—of the dreadful
    Neptune,
To greet a man not worth her pains, much
    less
The adventure of her person?

FLORIZEL.
                            Good, my lord,
She came from Libya.

LEONTES.
                            Where the warlike Smalus,
That noble honour'd lord, is fear'd and
    lov'd?

FLORIZEL.
Most royal sir, from thence; from him
    whose daughter
His tears proclaim'd his, parting with her:
    thence,
A prosperous south-wind friendly, we have
    cross'd,
To execute the charge my father gave me,
For visiting your highness: my best train
I have from your Sicilian shores dismiss'd;
Who for Bohemia bend, to signify
Not only my success in Libya, sir,
But my arrival, and my wife's, in safety
Here, where we are.

LEONTES.
                            The blessed gods
Purge all infection from our air whilst you
Do climate here! You have a holy father,
A graceful gentleman; against whose
    person,
So sacred as it is, I have done sin:
For which the heavens, taking angry
    note,
Have left me issueless; and your father's
    bless'd,—
As he from heaven merits it,—with you
Worthy his goodness. What might I have
    been,
Might I a son and daughter now have
    look'd on,
Such goodly things as you!
                    [Enter a LORD.]

LORD.
                            Most noble sir,
That which I shall report will bear no
    credit,
Were not the proof so nigh. Please you,
    great sir,
Bohemia greets you from himself by me;
Desires you to attach his son, who has,—
His dignity and duty both cast off,—

Fled from his father, from his hopes, and
    with
A shepherd's daughter.

LEONTES.
                        Where's Bohemia? speak.

LORD.
Here in your city; I now came from him:
I speak amazedly; and it becomes
My marvel and my message. To your court
Whiles he was hast'ning,—in the chase,
    it seems,
Of this fair couple,—meets he on the way
The father of this seeming lady and
Her brother, having both their country
    quitted
With this young prince.

FLORIZEL.
                        Camillo has betray'd me;
Whose honour and whose honesty, till
    now,
Endur'd all weathers.

LORD.
                        Lay't so to his charge;
He's with the king your father.

LEONTES.
                        Who? Camillo?

LORD.
Camillo, sir; I spake with him; who now
Has these poor men in question. Never
    saw I
Wretches so quake: they kneel, they kiss
    the earth;
Forswear themselves as often as they
    speak:
Bohemia stops his ears, and threatens
    them
With divers deaths in death.

PERDITA.
                        O my poor father!—
The heaven sets spies upon us, will not
    have
Our contract celebrated.

LEONTES.
                        You are married?

FLORIZEL.
We are not, sir, nor are we like to be;
The stars, I see, will kiss the valleys first:—
The odds for high and low's alike.

LEONTES.
                        My lord,
Is this the daughter of a king?

FLORIZEL.
                        She is,
When once she is my wife.

LEONTES.
That once, I see by your good father's
    speed,
Will come on very slowly. I am sorry,
Most sorry, you have broken from his
    liking,
Where you were tied in duty; and as sorry
Your choice is not so rich in worth as
    beauty,
That you might well enjoy her.

FLORIZEL.
                        Dear, look up:
Though Fortune, visible an enemy,
Should chase us with my father, power
    no jot
Hath she to change our loves.—Beseech
    you, sir,
Remember since you ow'd no more to
    time
Than I do now: with thought of such
    affections,
Step forth mine advocate; at your request
My father will grant precious things as
    trifles.

LEONTES.
Would he do so, I'd beg your precious
    mistress,
Which he counts but a trifle.

PAULINA.
                        Sir, my liege,
Your eye hath too much youth in't: not a
    month
'Fore your queen died, she was more worth
    such gazes
Than what you look on now.

LEONTES.
                        I thought of her
Even in these looks I made. [*To*
    FLORIZEL.] But your petition
Is yet unanswer'd. I will to your father.
Your honour not o'erthrown by your
    desires,

635

I am friend to them and you: upon which errand
I now go toward him; therefore, follow me,
And mark what way I make. Come, good my lord.

[Exeunt.]

SCENE II

The same. Before the palace.

[Enter AUTOLYCUS *and a* GENTLEMAN.*]*

AUTOLYCUS.

Beseech you, sir, were you present at this relation?

FIRST GENTLEMAN.

I was by at the opening of the fardel, heard the old shepherd deliver the manner how he found it: whereupon, after a little amazedness, we were all commanded out of the chamber; only this, methought I heard the shepherd say he found the child.

AUTOLYCUS.

I would most gladly know the issue of it.

FIRST GENTLEMAN.

I make a broken delivery of the business; but the changes I perceived in the king and Camillo were very notes of admiration. They seem'd almost, with staring on one another, to tear the cases of their eyes; there was speech in their dumbness, language in their very gesture; they looked as they had heard of a world ransomed, or one destroyed: a notable passion of wonder appeared in them; but the wisest beholder, that knew no more but seeing could not say if the importance were joy or sorrow;— but in the extremity of the one, it must needs be. Here comes a gentleman that happily knows more. [*Enter a* SECOND GENTLEMAN.] The news, Rogero?

SECOND GENTLEMAN.

Nothing but bonfires: the oracle is fulfilled: the king's daughter is found: such a deal of wonder is broken out within this hour that ballad-makers cannot be able to express it. Here comes the Lady Paulina's steward: he can deliver you more. [*Enter a* THIRD GENTLEMAN.] How goes it now, sir? This news, which is called true, is so like an old tale that the verity of it is in strong suspicion. Has the king found his heir?

THIRD GENTLEMAN.

Most true, if ever truth were pregnant by circumstance. That which you hear you'll swear you see, there is such unity in the proofs. The mantle of Queen Hermione; her jewel about the neck of it; the letters of Antigonus, found with it, which they know to be his character; the majesty of the creature in resemblance of the mother; the affection of nobleness, which nature shows above her breeding; and many other evidences,—proclaim her with all certainty to be the king's daughter. Did you see the meeting of the two kings?

SECOND GENTLEMAN.

No.

THIRD GENTLEMAN.

Then you have lost a sight which was to be seen, cannot be spoken of. There might you have beheld one joy crown another, so and in such manner that it seemed sorrow wept to take leave of them; for their joy waded in tears. There was casting up of eyes, holding up of hands, with countenance of such distraction that they were to be known by garment, not by favour. Our king, being ready to leap out of himself for joy of his found daughter, as if that joy were now become a loss, cries, "O, thy mother, thy mother!" then asks Bohemia forgiveness; then embraces his son-in-law; then again worries he his daughter with clipping her; now he thanks the old shepherd, which stands by like a weather-bitten conduit of many kings' reigns. I never heard of such another encounter, which lames report to follow it, and undoes description to do it.

SECOND GENTLEMAN.

What, pray you, became of Antigonus, that carried hence the child?

THIRD GENTLEMAN.

Like an old tale still, which will have matter to rehearse, though credit be asleep and not an ear open. He was torn to pieces with a bear: this avouches the shepherd's son, who has not only his innocence,—which seems much,—to justify him, but a handkerchief and rings of his, that Paulina knows.

FIRST GENTLEMAN.

What became of his bark and his followers?

THIRD GENTLEMAN.

Wrecked the same instant of their master's death, and in the view of the shepherd: so that all the instruments which aided to expose the child were even then lost when it was found. But, O, the noble combat that 'twixt joy and sorrow was fought in Paulina! She had one eye declined for the loss of her husband, another elevated that the oracle was fulfilled: she lifted the princess from the earth, and so locks her in embracing, as if she would pin her to her heart, that she might no more be in danger of losing.

FIRST GENTLEMAN.

The dignity of this act was worth the audience of kings and princes; for by such was it acted.

THIRD GENTLEMAN.

One of the prettiest touches of all, and that which angled for mine eyes,—caught the water, though not the fish,—was, when at the relation of the queen's death, with the manner how she came to it,—bravely confessed and lamented by the king,—how attentivenes wounded his daughter; till, from one sign of dolour to another, she did with an "Alas!"—I would fain say, bleed tears; for I am sure my heart wept blood. Who was most marble there changed colour; some swooned, all sorrowed: if all the world could have seen it, the woe had been universal.

FIRST GENTLEMAN.

Are they returned to the court?

THIRD GENTLEMAN.

No: the princess hearing of her mother's statue, which is in the keeping of Paulina,—a piece many years in doing and now newly performed by that rare Italian master, Julio Romano, who, had he himself eternity, and could put breath into his work, would beguile nature of her custom, so perfectly he is her ape: he so near to Hermione hath

done Hermione that they say one would speak to her and stand in hope of answer:— thither with all greediness of affection are they gone; and there they intend to sup.

SECOND GENTLEMAN.

I thought she had some great matter there in hand; for she hath privately twice or thrice a day, ever since the death of Hermione, visited that removed house. Shall we thither, and with our company piece the rejoicing?

FIRST GENTLEMAN.

Who would be thence that has the benefit of access? every wink of an eye some new grace will be born: our absence makes us unthrifty to our knowledge. Let's along.

[*Exeunt* GENTLEMEN.]

AUTOLYCUS.

Now, had I not the dash of my former life in me, would preferment drop on my head. I brought the old man and his son aboard the prince; told him I heard them talk of a fardel and I know not what; but he at that time over-fond of the shepherd's daughter,—so he then took her to be,—who began to be much sea-sick, and himself little better, extremity of weather continuing, this mystery remained undiscover'd. But 'tis all one to me; for had I been the finder-out of this secret, it would not have relish'd among my other discredits. Here come those I have done good to against my will, and already appearing in the blossoms of their fortune.

[*Enter* SHEPHERD *and* CLOWN.]

SHEPHERD.

Come, boy; I am past more children, but thy sons and daughters will be all gentlemen born.

CLOWN.

You are well met, sir: you denied to fight with me this other day, because I was no gentleman born. See you these clothes? say you see them not and think me still no gentleman born: you were best say these robes are not gentlemen born. Give me the lie, do; and try whether I am not now a gentleman born.

Autolycus.

I know you are now, sir, a gentleman born.

Clown.

Ay, and have been so any time these four hours.

Shepherd.

And so have I, boy!

Clown.

So you have:—but I was a gentleman born before my father; for the king's son took me by the hand and called me brother; and then the two kings called my father brother; and then the prince, my brother, and the princess, my sister, called my father father; and so we wept; and there was the first gentleman-like tears that ever we shed.

Shepherd.

We may live, son, to shed many more.

Clown.

Ay; or else 'twere hard luck, being in so preposterous estate as we are.

Autolycus.

I humbly beseech you, sir, to pardon me all the faults I have committed to your worship, and to give me your good report to the prince my master.

Shepherd.

Pr'ythee, son, do; for we must be gentle, now we are gentlemen.

Clown.

Thou wilt amend thy life?

Autolycus.

Ay, an it like your good worship.

Clown.

Give me thy hand: I will swear to the prince thou art as honest a true fellow as any is in Bohemia.

Shepherd.

You may say it, but not swear it.

Clown.

Not swear it, now I am a gentleman? Let boors and franklins say it, I'll swear it.

Shepherd.

How if it be false, son?

Clown.

If it be ne'er so false, a true gentleman may swear it in the behalf of his friend.—And I'll swear to the prince thou art a tall fellow of thy hands and that thou wilt not be drunk; but I know thou art no tall fellow of thy hands and that thou wilt be drunk: but I'll swear it; and I would thou wouldst be a tall fellow of thy hands.

Autolycus.

I will prove so, sir, to my power.

Clown.

Ay, by any means, prove a tall fellow: if I do not wonder how thou darest venture to be drunk, not being a tall fellow, trust me not. Hark! the kings and the princes, our kindred, are going to see the queen's picture. Come, follow us: we'll be thy good masters.

[*Exeunt.*]

SCENE III

The same. A room in Paulina's house.

[*Enter* Leontes, Polixenes, Florizel, Perdita, Camillo, Paulina, Lords, *and* Attendants.]

Leontes.

O grave and good Paulina, the great comfort
That I have had of thee!

Paulina.

What, sovereign sir,
I did not well, I meant well. All my services
You have paid home: but that you have vouchsaf'd,
With your crown'd brother and these your contracted
Heirs of your kingdoms, my poor house to visit,
It is a surplus of your grace which never
My life may last to answer.

Leontes.

O Paulina,
We honour you with trouble:—but we came
To see the statue of our queen: your gallery
Have we pass'd through, not without much content
In many singularities; but we saw not
That which my daughter came to look upon,
The statue of her mother.

Paulina.

          As she liv'd peerless,
So her dead likeness, I do well believe,
Excels whatever yet you look'd upon
Or hand of man hath done; therefore I
    keep it
Lonely, apart. But here it is: prepare
To see the life as lively mock'd as ever
Still sleep mock'd death: behold; and say
    'tis well.

[Paulina *undraws a curtain, and discovers*
    Hermione, *standing as a statue.*]

I like your silence,—it the more shows off
Your wonder: but yet speak;—first, you,
    my liege.
Comes it not something near?

Leontes.

          Her natural posture!—
Chide me, dear stone, that I may say
    indeed
Thou art Hermione; or rather, thou art she
In thy not chiding; for she was as tender
As infancy and grace.—But yet, Paulina,
Hermione was not so much wrinkled;
    nothing
So aged, as this seems.

Polixenes.

          O, not by much!

Paulina.

So much the more our carver's excellence;
Which lets go by some sixteen years, and
    makes her
As she liv'd now.

Leontes.

        As now she might have done,
So much to my good comfort, as it is
Now piercing to my soul. O, thus she
    stood,
Even with such life of majesty,—warm
    life,
As now it coldly stands,—when first I
    woo'd her!
I am asham'd: does not the stone rebuke
    me
For being more stone than it?—O royal
    piece,
There's magic in thy majesty; which has
My evils conjur'd to remembrance; and

From thy admiring daughter took the
    spirits,
Standing like stone with thee!

Perdita.

          And give me leave;
And do not say 'tis superstition, that
I kneel, and then implore her blessing.—
    Lady,
Dear queen, that ended when I but began,
Give me that hand of yours to kiss.

Paulina.

          O, patience!
The statue is but newly fix'd, the colour's
Not dry.

Camillo.

My lord, your sorrow was too sore laid on,
Which sixteen winters cannot blow away,
So many summers dry; scarce any joy
Did ever so long live; no sorrow
But kill'd itself much sooner.

Polixenes.

          Dear my brother,
Let him that was the cause of this have
    power
To take off so much grief from you as he
Will piece up in himself.

Paulina.

          Indeed, my lord,
If I had thought the sight of my poor
    image
Would thus have wrought you, for the
    stone is mine,
I'd not have show'd it.

Leontes.

        Do not draw the curtain.

Paulina.

No longer shall you gaze on't; lest your
    fancy
May think anon it moves.

Leontes.

          Let be, let be.—
Would I were dead, but that, methinks,
    already—
What was he that did make it? See, my
    lord,
Would you not deem it breath'd, and that
    those veins
Did verily bear blood?

POLIXENES.

                        Masterly done:
The very life seems warm upon her lip.

LEONTES.

The fixture of her eye has motion in't,
As we are mock'd with art.

PAULINA.

                      I'll draw the curtain:
My lord's almost so far transported that
He'll think anon it lives.

LEONTES.

                    O sweet Paulina,
Make me to think so twenty years
   together!
No settled senses of the world can match
The pleasure of that madness. Let't alone.

PAULINA.

I am sorry, sir, I have thus far stirr'd you: but
I could afflict you further.

LEONTES.

                 Do, Paulina;
For this affliction has a taste as sweet
As any cordial comfort.—Still, methinks,
There is an air comes from her: what fine
   chisel
Could ever yet cut breath? Let no man
   mock me,
For I will kiss her!

PAULINA.

               Good my lord, forbear:
The ruddiness upon her lip is wet;
You'll mar it if you kiss it; stain your own
With oily painting. Shall I draw the
   curtain?

LEONTES.

No, not these twenty years.

PERDITA.

               So long could I
Stand by, a looker-on.

PAULINA.

             Either forbear,
Quit presently the chapel, or resolve you
For more amazement. If you can behold it,
I'll make the statue move indeed, descend,
And take you by the hand, but then you'll
   think,—
Which I protest against,—I am assisted
By wicked powers.

LEONTES.

             What you can make her do
I am content to look on: what to speak,
I am content to hear; for 'tis as easy
To make her speak as move.

PAULINA.

               It is requir'd
You do awake your faith. Then all stand
   still;
Or those that think it is unlawful business
I am about, let them depart.

LEONTES.

              Proceed:
No foot shall stir.

PAULINA.

       Music, awake her: strike! [*Music.*]
'Tis time; descend; be stone no more;
   approach;
Strike all that look upon with marvel.
   Come;
I'll fill your grave up: stir; nay, come away;
Bequeath to death your numbness, for
   from him
Dear life redeems you.—You perceive she
   stirs.

[*HERMIONE comes down from the pedestal.*]

Start not; her actions shall be holy as
You hear my spell is lawful: do not shun
   her
Until you see her die again; for then
You kill her double. Nay, present your
   hand:
When she was young you woo'd her; now
   in age
Is she become the suitor?

LEONTES. [*Embracing her.*]

              O, she's warm!
If this be magic, let it be an art
Lawful as eating.

POLIXENES.

            She embraces him.

CAMILLO.

She hangs about his neck:
If she pertain to life, let her speak too.

POLIXENES.

Ay, and make it manifest where she has
   liv'd,
Or how stol'n from the dead.

PAULINA.

That she is living,
Were it but told you, should be hooted at
Like an old tale; but it appears she lives,
Though yet she speak not. Mark a little
while.—
Please you to interpose, fair madam: kneel,
And pray your mother's blessing. Turn,
good lady;
Our Perdita is found.
[*Presenting* PERDITA, *who kneels to*
HERMIONE.]

HERMIONE.

You gods, look down,
And from your sacred vials pour your
graces
Upon my daughter's head!—Tell me, mine
own,
Where hast thou been preserv'd? where
liv'd? how found
Thy father's court? for thou shalt hear that
I,—
Knowing by Paulina that the oracle
Gave hope thou wast in being,—have
preserv'd
Myself to see the issue.

PAULINA.

There's time enough for that;
Lest they desire upon this push to trouble
Your joys with like relation.—Go together,
You precious winners all; your exultation
Partake to every one. I, an old turtle,
Will wing me to some wither'd bough,
and there
My mate, that's never to be found again,
Lament till I am lost.

LEONTES.

O peace, Paulina!
Thou shouldst a husband take by my
consent,
As I by thine a wife: this is a match,
And made between's by vows. Thou hast
found mine;
But how, is to be question'd: for I saw her,
As I thought, dead; and have, in vain, said
many
A prayer upon her grave. I'll not seek
far,—
For him, I partly know his mind,—to find
thee
An honourable husband.—Come,
Camillo,
And take her by the hand, whose worth and
honesty
Is richly noted, and here justified
By us, a pair of kings.—Let's from this
place.—
What! look upon my brother:—both your
pardons,
That e'er I put between your holy looks
My ill suspicion.—This your son-in-law,
And son unto the king, whom heavens
directing,
Is troth-plight to your daughter.—Good
Paulina,
Lead us from hence; where we may
leisurely
Each one demand, and answer to his part
Perform'd in this wide gap of time, since
first
We were dissever'd: hastily lead away!
[*Exeunt.*]

Word Cloud Classics

Adventures of Huckleberry Finn

The Adventures of Sherlock Holmes

Aesop's Fables

Alice's Adventures in Wonderland
and Through the Looking-Glass

Anna Karenina

Anne of Green Gables

The Art of War

The Awakening and Other Stories

The Beautiful and Damned
and Other Stories

The Brothers Grimm 101 Fairy Tales

The Brothers Grimm Volume II:
110 Grimmer Fairy Tales

Classic Horror Tales

Classic Westerns: Zane Grey

The Count of Monte Cristo

Crime and Punishment

Frankenstein

Hans Christian Andersen Tales

H. P. Lovecraft Cthulhu
Mythos Tales

The Inventions, Researches, and
Writings of Nikola Tesla

The Jungle Book

Leaves of Grass

Les Misérables

My Ántonia

Narrative of the Life of Frederick
Douglass and Other Works

Odyssey

Peter Pan

The Phantom of the Opera

The Picture of Dorian Gray

Pride and Prejudice

The Romantic Poets

Selected Works of
Alexander Hamilton

Sense and Sensibility

Shakespeare's Sonnets and
Other Poems

Treasure Island

Uncle Tom's Cabin, or Life
Among the Lowly

The Wind in the Willows
and Other Stories

The Wizard of Oz

Wuthering Heights

For more titles, please visit our website:
www.canterburyclassicsbooks.com